T4-ALC-079

The quintessential volume for every library, school or music-industry professional! And a treasury of information for the home of every music lover!

Over 12,000 selections from every category of music! The "standards" of Berlin, Gershwin, Rodgers and Hart and/or Hammerstein, Porter, Ellington, etc. . . . the film scores of Max Steiner, Jerry Goldsmith, John Williams, etc. . . . the early works of Septimus Winner, Henry Clay Work, Daniel Emmett, Thomas A. Dorsey, etc. . . . the modern output of Bob Dylan, Neil Diamond, Paul Simon, Paul Williams, Paul McCartney, Bacharach & David, etc. . . . and the newer wave: Jackson Browne, Don Henley, Glenn Frey, Billy Joel, Elvis Costello, Chrissie Hynde, Georgio Moroder, and many more.

America's renowned "country" music is represented by the "evergreens" of Hank Williams, Fred Rose, John Loudermilk, Boudleaux Bryant, etc., as well as the current compositions of Billy Sherrill, Sonny Throckmorton, Jerry Chesnut, Larry Gatlin, Willie Nelson, Merle Haggard, Tom T. Hall, Dolly Parton, and many more. The jazz of Miles Davis, Charlie Parker; the blues of Muddy Waters, John Lee Hooker, etc. . . . the rock n' roll of Chuck Berry, Bo Diddley, Buddy Holly, etc.! Over 2,000 composers and lyricists (and their best known songs) in alphabetical order!

Classical music . . . the complete spectrum is painted in copious detail! In one section, the great classical composers (1500 to 1900) and their principal works . . . in another section, the 20th century's best-known modernists . . . Ravel, Schoenberg, Stravinsky, Satie, Britten, Copland, Cage, Reich, etc. Over 1,200 composers and many thousands of their principal works are presented.

This one volume eliminates searching through hundreds of music books to find salient data! A pronouncing, illustrated dictionary clarifies over 4,000 musical terms, describes all instruments and their ranges, and discusses the latest developments and language of serious and popular music. And a concise "Elements of Music" encyclopedia unravels the mysteries of musical notation, shows all keys and scales, and explains chords, intervals, harmonic analysis as well as the directions and marks of performance.

Finally, this book contains a complete list of the Academy Award (OSCAR) nominations and winners for song and score from 1934–1980, and recapitulates all of the song awards (from inception) by the American Theatre Wing (TONY) and the National Academy Of Recorded Arts and Sciences (GRAMMY)!

CARLTON'S
COMPLETE
REFERENCE BOOK
OF
MUSIC

BY

JOSEPH R. CARLTON

CARNEGIE LIBRARY
LIVINGSTONE COLLEGE
SALISBURY, N. C. 28144

COPYRIGHT © 1980 BY JOSEPH R. CARLTON

All Rights Reserved. No portion of this book may be reproduced for use in any media without written permission of the publisher.

The publisher and the author are confident of the accuracy of the information herein but no liability is assumed for the application or use of same.

Library Of Congress # TXV 41-181

ISBN 0-937348-00-7

PRINTED IN THE UNITED STATES OF AMERICA

CARLTON PUBLICATIONS, INC.

STUDIO CITY, CALIFORNIA

TO EILEEN, my special lady.

INTRODUCTION . . . I have spent forty years in the music business, beginning as music editor for The Billboard and proceéding as vice president of artists and repertoire for major recording companies (RCA Victor, Mercury Records, ABC Command Records and manager, CBS Records), president of my own recording company (Carlton Records) and in recent years as the head of publication companies.

I have been fortunate, therefore, to have spent most of my life in daily business and social contacts with many of the finest composers and artists in every area of the music profession. In fact, I am a "professional" and I have always felt the need for a "professional" compilation of the songs and language of the craft without self-serving hyperbole nor with "snobbish" hauteur for categories or labels in music. The magnitude of this collection speaks for itself. An exhaustive amount of research and time has been devoted to its completion, and every impersonal means of evaluation — performance, publication, printed literature, sales, "trade" charts, "awards" listings — has been employed to cull the contents in this ambitious attempt to sum up 200 years of music reference. Obviously, however, some subjective values must come into play in making judgments of "best known" music and musical terms. I apologize for any omissions the reader may find objectionable and promise to correct these in future editions. Please note that the emphasis of this book is placed on the composer, the songwriter, the song or composition, and the fundamentals of music education . . . formal and vernacular, popular and serious. Categories are used simply to make reference easier! The author shares the view of many of our greatest composers that there is only good music and bad music. All other labels or tags are invalid.

I am grateful to many people for their assistance but particularly I convey my warmest thanks to Professor Pamela J. Carlton, William D. Carlton, (loving and learned children) Linda Chelgren, Ronny Schiff, Judy Porter Goldmark and to the various librarians (at the Library of Congress in Washington, D.C. and Silver Spring, Md., the Los Angeles Public Library including the main library as well as the Studio City and Beverly Hills branches, the New York Public Library and the University of California at Los Angeles) whose cooperation was enormous.

J.R.C.

Cover and Logo Design: Rancho Deluxe Design, Santa Monica, Ca.
Typography: Phyllis MacFadden, Palos Verdes Estates, Ca.
and
Alexander Typesetting, Inc., Indianapolis, Ind.
Illustrations: Mrs. Margaret Oliver, Santa Monica, Ca.

CONTENTS

BEST-KNOWN SONGS AND INSTRUMENTAL MUSIC HEARD IN THE U.S.A. FROM 1780 TO 1980 including POPULAR, ROCK, COUNTRY, SOUL, BLUES, JAZZ, GOSPEL, INSPIRATIONAL, THEATER AND FILM MUSIC with COMPOSER AND LYRICIST CREDITS

Songs are alphabetically arranged in accordance with the first word of each title, NOT including the English articles "A", "An" and "The". Such articles appear at the end of each title.

With foreign-language titles, however, first-word "articles" may or may not be excluded in terms of the alphabetical order. The inconsistency is deliberate to provide easier reference. To locate foreign-language titles, therefore, please consult alphabetical listings under the first or second word of a given title.

(Instr.) — abbreviation for instrumental!
Designates a selection that has no known
lyric or is best-known for its non-vocal
performance.

w/ = words by   w&m/ = words and music by
m/ = music by

1980 SUPPLEMENT

AND THE BEAT GOES ON (1980)
w&m/Leon Sylvers, William Shelby, Stephen Shockley

ANOTHER ONE BITES THE DUST (1980)
w&m/John Deacon

CADILLAC RANCH (1980)
w&m/Bruce Springsteen

CLOUDS (1980)
w&m/Nicholas Ashford, Valerie Simpson

COULD I HAVE THIS DANCE (1980)
w&m/W. Holyfield, B. House

CRUSH ON YOU (1980)
w&m/Bruce Springsteen

DARKNESS ON THE EDGE OF TOWN (1980)
w&m/Bruce Springsteen

DAY IN THE LIFE, A
w&m/John Lennon

DREAM IS OVER, THE
w&m/John Lennon

DREAMER (1980)
w&m/Rick Davies

DREAMING (1980)
w&m/Leo Sayer, Alan Tarney

GOING UP THE COUNTRY
w&m/Robert Hite, Harry Vestine, Alan Wilson

HARD TIMES ARE OVER (1980)
w&m/Yoko Ono

HEROES (1980)
w&m/Lionel Richie

HE STOPPED LOVING HER TODAY (1980)
w&m/George Jones

HE'S SO SHY (1980)
w&m/Tom Snow, Cynthia Weill

HE'S THE GREATEST DANCER (1980)
w&m/Nile Rodgers, Bernard Edwards

HIGH SOCIETY (1980)
w&m/Nile Rodgers, Bernard Edwards

HIT ME WITH YOUR BEST SHOT (1980)
w&m/E. Schwartz

HOW DO I SURVIVE (1980)
w&m/Michael McDonald, Patrick Henderson

HUNGRY HEART (1980)
w&m/Bruce Springsteen

I BELIEVE IN YOU (1980)
w&m/R. Cook, S. Hogin

I'M NOT READY YET (1980)
w&m/Tom T. Hall

I AM BUT A SMALL VOICE (1980)
w&m/Odina Batnag

INDEPENDENCE DAY (1980)
w&m/Bruce Springsteen

IT'S MY TURN (1980)
w&m/Michael Masser, Carole Bayer Sager

IT'S NOT WHAT YOU GOT (1980)
w&m/Leon Sylvers, William Shelby, Stephen Shockley

JACKSON CAGE (1980)
w&m/Bruce Springsteen

JESUS IS LOVE (1980)
w&m/Lionel Richie

KISS, KISS, KISS (1980)
w&m/Yoko Ono

LADY (1980)
w&m/Lionel Richie Jr.

LANDLORD (1980)
w&m/Nicholas Ashford, Valerie Simpson

LIFE IS JUST WHAT YOU MAKE IT
w&m/Alan Osmond

LITTLE IS ENOUGH, A (1980)
w&m/Pete Townshend

LOOK WHAT YOU'VE DONE TO ME (1980)
w&m/David Foster, Boz Scaggs

LOSING YOU (1980)
w&m/John Lennon

LOVELY ONE (1980)
w&m/Michael Jackson, R. Jackson

LOVING UP A STORM (1980)
w&m/Danny Morrison, Johnny Slate

MASTER BLASTER (1980)
w&m/Stevie Wonder

MIDDLE AGE CRAZY (1980)
w&m/Sonny Throckmorton

MIGHTY SPIRIT (1980)
w&m/Lionel Richie

MY HEART (1980)
w&m/Don Pfrimmer, Charles Quillen

NEVER BE THE SAME (1980)
w&m/Christopher Cross

OLD HABITS (1980)
w&m/Hank Williams Jr.

ON THE ROAD AGAIN (1980)
w&m/Willie Nelson

ONE STEP CLOSER (1980)
w&m/Michael McDonald, Patrick Henderson

OUT HERE ON MY OWN (1980)
w&m/Michael Gore, Lesley Gore

OUT ON THE STREET (1980
w&m/Bruce Springsteen

POINT BLANK (1980)
w&m/Bruce Springsteen

PRICE YOU PAY, THE (1980)
w&m/Bruce Springsteen

REAL LOVE (1980)
w&m/Michael McDonald, Patrick Henderson

SHE BELIEVES IN ME (1980)
w&m/Steve Gibb

SHERRY DARLING (1980)
w&m/Bruce Springsteen

SHE'S SO COLD (1980)
w&m/Nick Jagger, Keith Richard

SILENT NIGHT (After The Fight) (1980)
w&m/John Schweers

SOMETIMES A FANTASY (1980)
w&m/Billy Joel

STARTING OVER (1980)
w&m/John Lennon

STOLEN CAR (1980)
w&m/Bruce Springsteen

SUDDENLY (1980)
w&m/John Farrar

TIES THAT BIND, THE (1980)
w&m/Bruce Springsteen

THAT GIRL COULD SING (1980)
w&m/Jackson Browne

THEME FROM THE DUKES OF HAZZARD (1980)
w&m/Waylon Jennings

TWO HEARTS (1980)
w&m/Bruce Springsteen

WATCHING THE WHEELS (1980)
w&m/John Lennon

WOMAN IN LOVE (1980)
w&m/Barry Gibb, Robin Gibb

WRECK ON THE HIGHWAY (1980)
w&m/Bruce Springsteen

YOU CAN LOOK (But You Better Not Touch) (1980)
w&m/Bruce Springsteen

 **SONGS**

A

"A" YOU'RE ADORABLE
w & m/Buddy Kaye, Sydney
Lippman, Fred Wise

AARON SLICK FROM PUNKIN'
CREEK (film score)
m/Robert Emmett Dolan

ABA DABA HONEYMOON
w&m/Walter Donovan, Arthur Fields

ABC
w&m/Frederick Perren, Berry
Gordy, Jr., Deke Richards,
Alphonzo Mizell

ABIDE WITH ME (Fast Falls
The Eventide)
m/William H. Monk (from the song
"Evening")
w/Henry Francis Lyte

ABILENE
w&m/John D. Loudermilk, Lester
Brown, Bob Gibson, Albert Stanton

ABOUT A QUARTER TO NINE
m/Harry Warren
w/Al Dubin

ABOUT GROWN
w&m/Chuck Berry

ABOVE AND BEYOND (The Call
of Love)
w&m/Harlan Howard

ABRAHAM, MARTIN and JOHN
w&m/Dick Holler

ABSENCE MAKES THE HEART
GROW FONDER
m/Herbert Dillea
w/Arthur Gillespie

ACCENT ON YOUTH
m/Vee Lawnhurst
w/Tot Seymour

AC-CEN-TCHU-ATE THE
POSITIVE
m/Harold Arlen
w/Johnny Mercer

ACE IN THE HOLE
w&m/Cole Porter

ACID QUEEN, THE
w&m/Peter Townshend

ACROSS THE ALLEY FROM
THE ALAMO
w&m/Joe Greene

ACROSS THE GREAT DIVIDE
w&m/J. Robbie Robertson

ACROSS THE WIDE MISSOURI
w&m/Jimmy Shirl (based on the
traditional song "Shenandoah")

ADDRESS UNKNOWN
(film score)
m/Morris Stoloff

ADELAIDE'S LAMENT
w&m/Frank Loesser

ADIOS
m/Enric Madriguera
w/E. Woods

ADVENTURES OF ROBIN
HOOD (film score)
m/Erich Wolfgang Korngold

ADVISE AND CONSENT
(film score)
m/Jerry Fielding

AFFAIR TO REMEMBER, AN
m/Harry Warren
w&m/Harold Adamson, Leo McCarey

AFFAIR TO REMEMBER, AN
(film score)
m/Hugo Friedhofer

AFRAID
w&m/Fred Rose

AFRICAN QUEEN, THE
(film score)
m/Allan Gray

AFRICAN VILLAGE (instr.)
m/McCoy Tyner

AFRICAN WALTZ (instr.)
m/Galt MacDermot

AFRIKAAN BEAT
m/Bert Kaempfert
w/June Tansey

AFRO-BLUE
w&m/Mongo Santamaria

AFRO ROOTS
w&m/Mongo Santamaria

AFTER GRADUATION DAY
m/Sidney Lippman
w/Sylvia Dee

AFTER I SAY I'M SORRY
m/Walter Donaldson
w/Abe Lyman

AFTER SUNDOWN
m/Nacio Herb Brown
w/Arthur Freed

AFTER THE BALL
w&m/Charles K. Harris

AFTER THE FIRE IS GONE
w&m/Willie Nelson

AFTER THE LOVE HAS GONE
w&m/David Foster, Jay Graydon,
Bill Champlin

AFTER THE LOVIN'
w&m/Richie Adams, Alan Bernstein

AFTER THE THRILL IS GONE
w&m/Don Henley, Glenn Frey

AFTER YOU GET WHAT YOU
WANT
w&m/Irving Berlin

AFTER YOU'VE GONE
m/J. Turner Layton
w/Henry Creamer

AFTERNOON DELIGHT
w&m/Bill Danoff, Kathy "Taffy"
Nivert Danoff

AFTERNOON IN PARIS (instr.)
m/John Lewis

AGAIN
m/Lionel Newman
w/Dorcas Cochran

AGONY AND THE ECSTASY,
THE (film score)
m/Alex North

AH, LEAVE ME NOT TO PINE
m/Sir Arthur Sullivan
w/Sir William Schwenk Gilbert

AH PAREE
m/Jule Styne
w/Stephen Sondheim

AH SWEET MYSTERY OF LIFE
m/Victor Herbert
w/Rida Johnson Young

AHAB THE ARAB
w&m/Ray Stevens

AIN'T GONNA BE TREATED
THIS WAY
w&m/Woody Guthrie

AIN'T GONNA CHANGE MY
MUSIC
w&m/James Messina,
Kenneth Loggins

AIN'T GONNA GRIEVE
w&m/Robert Dylan

AIN'T HAD NO LOVIN'
w&m/Dallas Frazier

AIN'T IT A BAD THING
w&m/R. Dean Taylor

AIN'T IT A SHAME
w&m/Al W. Brown

AIN'T IT A SHAME
w&m/Antoine "Fats" Domino, Dave
Bartholomew

AIN'T IT A SHAME ABOUT
MAME
m/James V. Monaco
m/Johnny Burke

AIN'T LOVE A GOOD THING
w&m/Dallas Frazier

AIN'T MISBEHAVIN'
m/Thomas "Fats" Waller
m/Andy Razaf

AIN'T NO MOUNTAIN HIGH
ENOUGH
w&m/Valerie Simpson, Nicholas
Ashford

AIN'T NO STOPPIN' US NOW
w&m/Gene McFadden, John
Whitehead, Jerry Cohen

AIN'T NO SUNSHINE
w&m/Bill Withers

**AIN'T NO WAY TO MAKE A BAD
LOVE GROW**
w&m/Sonny Throckmorton

**AIN'T NO WOMAN LIKE THE
ONE I GOT**
w&m/Dennis Lambert, Brian Potter

**AIN'T NOTHING LIKE THE
REAL THING**
w&m/Valerie Simpson, Nicholas
Ashford

AIN'T SHE SWEET
m/Milton Ager
w/Jack Yellen

AIN'T THAT A GROOVE
w&m/James Brown

AIN'T THAT A LOT OF LOVE
w&m/Homer Banks, William D.
Parker

AIN'T THAT COLD BABY
w&m/T-Bone Walker

**AIN'T THAT LOVING YOU (For
More Reasons Than One)**
w&m/Homer Banks, Allen Jones

AIN'T THAT PECULIAR
w&m/Eddie Holland, Norman
Whitfield

AIN'T TOO PROUD TO BEG
w&m/Eddie Holland, Norman
Whitfield

AIN'T WE GOT FUN
m/Richard A. Whiting
w/Raymond B. Egan, Gus Kahn

AIREGIN (instr.)
m/Sonny Rollins

AIRGUN (instr.)
m/Wes Montgomery

AIRMAIL SPECIAL (instr.)
m/Benny Goodman

**"AIRPORT" LOVE THEME
(instr.)**
m/Alfred Newman

AJA
w&m/Donald Fagen, Walter Becker

AL DI LA
m/Carlo Donida
w/Ervin M. Drake

ALABAMA JUBILEE
m/Jack Yellen
w/George L. Cobb

ALABAMY BOUND
m/Ray Henderson, Bud Green
w/Buddy DeSylva

ALABAMA WILD MAN
w&m/Jerry Reed

ALAMO, THE (film score)
m/Dimitri Tiomkin

ALBATROSS
w&m/Judy Collins

ALBATROSS
w&m/Peter Green

**ALEXANDER DON'T YOU
LOVE YOUR BABY NO MORE**
m/Harry Von Tilzer
w/Andrew B. Sterling

**ALEXANDER'S RAGTIME
BAND**
w&m/Irving Berlin

**ALEXANDER'S RAGTIME
BAND (film score)**
m/Alfred Newman

ALFIE
m/Burt Bacharach
w/Hal David

ALICE BLUE (instr.)
m/Ferde Grofe

ALICE'S RESTAURANT
w&m/Arlo Guthrie

**ALICE BLUE GOWN (In My
Sweet Little)**
w&m/Harry Austin Tierney, Joseph
McCarthy

ALIEN (film score)
m/Jerry Goldsmith

ALIVE
w&m/Barry, Maurice, and
Robin Gibb (Bee Gees)

**ALL ABOARD FOR BLANKET
BAY**
m/Harry Von Tilzer
w/Andrew B. Sterling

ALL ALONE
w&m/Irving Berlin

ALL ALONE
m/Harry Von Tilzer
w/William Dillon

**ALL ALONG THE
WATCHTOWER**
w&m/Robert Dylan

**ALL AROUND THE
CHRISTMAS TREE**
w&m/Raymond Scott

ALL AT ONCE YOU LOVE HER
m/Richard Rodgers
w/Oscar Hammerstein II

ALL BY MYSELF
w&m/Irving Berlin

ALL BY MYSELF
w&m/"Big Bill" Broonzy

ALL BY MYSELF
w&m/Eric Carmen

ALL BY MYSELF
w&m/Antoine "Fats" Domino, Dave
Bartholomew

**ALL DAY AND ALL OF THE
NIGHT**
w&m/Raymond Douglas Davies

ALL DAY MUSIC
w&m/Lee Oskar, Howard E. Scott,
Charles W. Miller, Lonnie L. Jordan,
Morris DeWayne Dickerson, Thomas
S. Allen, Harold R. Brown

**ALL DRESSED UP WITH A
BROKEN HEART**
w&m/Fred Fisher, Stella Unger,
Harold Stern

ALL FOR YOU
m/Victor Herbert
w/Henry Blossom

ALL HIS CHILDREN
m/Henry Mancini
w/Alan and Marilyn Bergman

ALL I CAN DO
w&m/Dolly Parton

ALL I DO IS DREAM OF YOU
m/Nacio Herb Brown
w/Arthur Freed

ALL I EVER NEED IS YOU
w&m/Sonny Bono, Cher (Cherilyn
S. La Pierre)

ALL I HAVE TO DO IS DREAM
w&m/Boudleaux Bryant

**ALL I HAVE TO OFFER YOU
IS ME**
w&m/Dallas Frazier, A.L. (Doodle)
Owens

ALL I KNOW
w&m/Jimmy Webb

ALL I NEED
w&m/Eddie Holland, Frank Wilson,
R. Dean Taylor

ALL I NEED
w&m/John Kander, Fred Ebb

ALL I NEED IS THE GIRL
m/Jule Styne
w/Stephen Sondheim

ALL I REALLY WANT TO DO
w&m/Robert Dylan

ALL I WANT
w&m/Joni Mitchell

**ALL I WANT FOR CHRISTMAS
IS MY TWO FRONT TEETH**
w&m/Donald Yetter Gardner

ALL I'LL EVER NEED IS YOU
w&m/Johnny Nash

ALL IN LOVE IS FAIR
w&m/Stevie Wonder

ALL MY LOVE
m/Paul Durand
w/Mitchell Parish

**ALL MY LOVE BELONGS
TO YOU**
w&m/Henry Glover, Sally Nix

ALL NIGHT BLUES
w&m/Richard M. Jones

ALL NIGHT LONG BABY
w&m/T-Bone Walker

**ALL OF A SUDDEN MY HEART
SINGS**
w&m/Harold Rome (adapted from
the French song "Ma Mie" by
Jamblan and Herpin)

ALL OF ME
m/Gerald Marks
w/Seymour Simons

ALL OF YOU
w&m/Cole Porter

ALL OR NOTHING AT ALL
m/Arthur Altman
w/Jack Lawrence

ALL OVER AGAIN
w&m/John R. (Johnny) Cash

ALL OVER THE WORLD
m/Albert Frisch
w/Charles Tobias

ALL OVER YOU
w&m/Robert Dylan

**ALL QUIET ALONG THE
POTOMAC**
w&m/John Hill Hewitt,
Lamar Fontaine

ALL RIGHT
w&m/Faron Young

ALL RIGHT NOW
w&m/Sinon F. St. George Kirke,
Paul Rodgers

ALL SHOOK UP
w&m/Otis Blackwell, Elvis Presley

**ALL THAT MONEY CAN BUY
(film score)**
m/Bernard Herrman

**ALL THE GIRLS LOVE A
SAILOR MAN**
m/Victor Jacobi
w/Adrian Ross, Arthur Anderson

**ALL THE GOLD IN
CALIFORNIA**
w&m/Larry Gatlin

**ALL THE LONEY WOMEN IN
THE WORLD**
w&m/Bill Anderson

ALL THE THINGS YOU ARE
m/Jerome Kern
w/Oscar Hammerstein II

ALL THE TIME
w&m/Mel Tillis, Wayne Walker

ALL THE YOUNG DUDES
w&m/David Bowie

ALL THE WAY
m/James Van Heusen
w/Sammy Cahn

ALL THESE THINGS
w&m/Allen Toussaint

ALL THINGS MUST PASS
w&m/George Harrison

ALL THIS AND HEAVEN TOO
m/James Van Heusen
w/Edgar DeLange

ALL THROUGH THE NIGHT
w&m/Cole Porter

ALL YOU NEED IS LOVE
w&m/Paul McCartney, John Lennon

**ALL YOU WANT TO DO IS
DANCE**
m/Arthur Johnston
w/Johnny Burke

**ALLA EN EL RANCHO GRANDE
(My Ranch)**
m/Emilio D. Uranga
w/Bartley Costello

ALLAH'S HOLIDAY
m/Rudolf Friml
w/Otto Harbach

ALLEGHENY MOON
w&m/Al Hoffman, Dick Manning

ALLEY ALLY OXEN FREE
w&m/Rod McKuen, Tom Drake,
Steven Yates

ALLEY CAT
w&m/Frank Bjorn

ALLEY OOP
w&m/Dallas Frazier

ALLEZ-VOUS-EN GO AWAY
w&m/Cole Porter

ALMOST
w&m/Vic McAlpin, Jack Tombs

ALMOST CUT MY HAIR
w&m/David Crosby

ALMOST IN YOUR ARMS
w&m/Ray Evans, Jay H. Livingston

ALMOST LIKE BEING IN LOVE
m/Frederick Loewe
w/Alan Jay Lerner

ALMOST LUCY
w&m/Al Stewart

**ALMOST PERFECT AFFAIR,
AN (film score)**
m/Georges Delerue

ALMOST PERSUADED
w&m/Glenn Sutton, Billy Sherrill

ALONE
m/Nacio Herb Brown
w/Arthur Freed

ALONE AGAIN NATURALLY
w&m/Gilbert O'Sullivan

ALONE TOGETHER
m/Arthur Schwartz
w/Howard Dietz

ALONE TOO LONG
m/Mark James
w/Cynthia Weil

ALONG CAME JONES
w&m/Ray Stevens

ALONG CAME MARY
w&m/Terry Kirkman

ALONG THE NAVAJO TRAIL
w&m/Dick Charles, Larry Markes,
Edgar DeLange

**ALONG THE ROCKY ROAD TO
DUBLIN**
m/Bert Grant
w/Joseph Young

ALONG THE SANTA FE TRAIL
m/Will Grosz
w/Al Dubin, Edwina Coolidge

ALONG WITH ME
w&m/Harold Rome

ALT WIEN (instr.)
m/Leopold Godowsky

ALVIN'S HARMONICA
w&m/Ross Bagdasarian

ALWAYS
w&m/Irving Berlin

ALWAYS AND FOREVER
w&m/Rod Temperton

ALWAYS IN MY HEART
m/Ernesto Lecuona
w/Kim Gannon

ALWAYS IN THE WAY
w&m/Charles K. Harris

ALWAYS SOMETHING THERE TO REMIND ME (THERE'S)
m/Burt Bacharach
w/Hal David

ALWAYS TRUE TO YOU IN MY FASHION
w&m/Cole Porter

AM I BLUE
m/Harry Akst
w/Harry Akst, Grant Clarke

AM I LOSING YOU
w&m/L. Russell Brown, Irwin Levine

AM I LOSING YOU
w&m/Jim Reeves

AMANDA
w&m/Bob McDill

AMAPOLA (Pretty Little Poppy)
m/Joseph M. LaCalle
w/Albert Gamse

AMARILLO
w&m/Rodney Crowell

AMAZING GRACE
m/Composer unknown; believed 18th century southern U.S. regional source
w/John Newton

AMELIA
w&m/Joni Mitchell

AMERICA
m/Leonard Bernstein
w/Stephen Sondheim

AMERICA
w&m/Paul Simon

AMERICA I LOVE YOU
m/Archie Gottler
w/Edgar Leslie

AMERICA THE BEAUTIFUL
m/Samuel A. Ward (from the melody "Materna", based on the hymn "O Mother Dear Jerusalem")
w/Katherine Lee Bates

AMERICAN BEAUTY RAG
w&m/Joseph Francis Lamb

AMERICAN BEAUTY ROSE
m/Redd Evans, Arthur Altman
w/Hal David

AMERICAN DREAM, AN
w&m/Rodney Crowell

AMERICAN GIGOLO (film score)
m/Georgia Maroder

AMERICAN GIRL
w&m/Tom Petty

AMERICAN GIRLS
w&m/Rick Springfield

AMERICAN PIE
w&m/Don McClean

AMERICAN TANGO (instr.)
m/Joe Zawinul

AMERICAN TRILOGY, AN
w&m/Mickey Newbury (music based on American Civil War folk songs)

AMERICAN WALTZ, THE
m/Peter DeRose
w/Mitchell Parish

AMERICAN WOMAN
w&m/Randy Bachman, Burton Cummings, Kate Peterson

AMERICANIZATION OF EMILY, THE (film score)
m/Johnny Mandel

AMERICANS, THE
w&m/Gordon Sinclair (musical setting from "The Battle Hymn Of The Republic")

AMIGO'S GUITAR
w&m/Muriel D. Wright (Kitty Wells), Roy Botkin, John D. Loudermilk

AMITYVILLE HORROR, THE (film score)
m/Lalo Schifrin

AMONG MY SOUVENIRS
w&m/Horatio Nicholls, Edgar Leslie

AMOR
m/Gabriel Ruiz
w/Sunny Skylar

AMOS MOSES
w&m/Jerry Reed

ANASTASIA
m/Alfred Newman
w/Paul Francis Webster

ANATOLE OF PARIS
w&m/Sylvia Fine

ANATOMY OF A MURDER (film score)
m/Duke Ellington

ANCHORS AWEIGH
m/Charles A. Zimmerman
w/Alfred H. Miles

AND HER TEARS FLOWED LIKE WINE
w&m/Joe Greene, Stan Kenton

AND I LOVE HER
w&m/Paul McCartney, John Lennon

AND I LOVE YOU SO
w&m/Don McClean

AND KEEP ON-A TRUCKIN'
w&m/C. W. McCall

AND MIMI
m/Nat Simon
w/Jimmy Kennedy

AND SO DO I
w&m/Stephen Weiss, Paul Mann

AND SHE'S MINE
w&m/Kenneth Hodges

AND SO TO SLEEP AGAIN
m/Joe Marsala
w/Sunny Skylar

AND THAT REMINDS YOU (MY HEART REMINDS ME)
m/Carmello Bargoni (instrumental version known as "Autumn Concerto")
w/Al Stillman

AND THE ANGELS SING
m/Harry (Ziggy) Elman
w/Johnny Mercer

AND THE BEAT GOES ON
w&m/Shelby Shockley, L. Sylvers

AND THE GREEN GRASS GREW ALL AROUND
m/Harry Von Tilzer
w/William Jerome

AND THIS IS MY BELOVED
w&m/George (Chet) Forrest, Robert Wright (adapted from classical composition by Alexander Borodin)

AND WHEN I DIE
w&m/Laura Nyro

ANDERSON TAPES, THE (film score)
m/Quincy Jones

ANGEL FACE
m/Victor Herbert
w/Robert B. Smith

ANGEL FROM MONTGOMERY
w&m/John Prine

ANGELA MIA
m/Erno Rapee
w/Lew Pollack

ANGELICA
w&m/Barry Mann, Cynthia Weil

ANGELINA
m/Allan Roberts
w/Doris Fisher

ANGELINA BAKER
w&m/Stephens Collins Foster

ANGELUS, THE
m/Victor Herbert
w/Robert B. Smith

ANGELS IN THE OUTFIELD (film score)
m/Daniele Amfitheatrof

ANGELUS, THE
m/Victor Herbert
w/Robert B. Smith

ANGIE
w&m/Mick Jagger, Keith Richards

ANGIE BABY
w&m/Alan O'Day

ANGRY YOUNG MAN
w&m/Billy Joel

ANIMA E CORE
m/Salve d'Esposito
w/Harry Akst, Mann Curtis

ANIMAL CRACKERS IN MY SOUP
m/Ray Henderson
w/Irving Caesar, Ted Koehler

ANITA YOU'RE DREAMING
w&m/Waylon Jennings,
Don Bowman

ANNA MARIE
w&m/Cindy Walker

ANNE OF A THOUSAND DAYS (film score)
m/Georges Delerue

ANNIE DOESN'T LIVE HERE ANY MORE
m/Harold Spina
w/Johnny Burke, Joseph Young

ANNIE HAD A BABY
w&m/Henry Glover, Lois Mann

ANNIE LAURIE
m/Lady John Montague-
Douglas Scott
w/William Douglas, (attributed but not verified)

ANNIE LISLE
w&m/H.S. Thompson

ANNIE MAE
w&m/Natalie Cole

ANNIE'S SONG
w&m/John Denver

ANNIVERSARY SONG, THE
w&m/Al Jolson, Saul Chaplin (music based on Ivanovici's "Danube Waves")

ANNIVERSARY WALTZ
w&m/Dave Franklin, Al Dubin

ANOTHER BRICK IN THE WALL
w&m/Roger Waters

ANOTHER COUNTRY
w&m/Rod McKuen, Barry McGuire

ANOTHER LONELY SONG
w&m/Billy Sherrill, Tammy Wynette

ANOTHER NIGHT LIKE THIS
m/Ernesto Lecuona
w/Harry Ruby

ANOTHER PARK, ANOTHER SUNDAY
w&m/Thomas Johnston

ANOTHER SATURDAY NIGHT
w&m/Cat Stevens

ANOTHER SATURDAY NIGHT
w&m/Sam Cooke

(Hey Won't You Play)
ANOTHER SOMEBODY DONE SOMEBODY WRONG SONG
w&m/Chips Moman, Larry Butler

ANOTHER TIME, ANOTHER PLACE
m/Jerry Ross
m/Richard Adler

ANOTHER OP'NING, ANOTHER SHOW
w&m/Cole Porter

ANOTHER PLACE, ANOTHER TIME
w&m/Jerry Chesnut

ANSWER, THE
w&m/Natalie Cole

ANSWER ME, MY LOVE
m/Gerhard Winkler
w/Carl Sigman

ANSWERING MACHINE
w&m/Rupert Holmes

ANTHONY ADVERSE (film score)
m/Erich Wolfgang Korngold,
Leo F. Forbstein

ANTHROPOLOGY (instr.)
m/Dizzy Gillespie

ANTICIPATION
w&m/Carly Simon

ANTIQUES (instr.)
m/Ornett Coleman

ANY OLD PORT IN A STORM
w&m/Frederick Allen (Kerry) Mills,
Arthur J. Lamb

ANY OLD TIME
w&m/Jimmy Rodgers

ANY WEDNESDAY (film score)
m/George Duning

ANYDAY
w&m/Eric Clapton, Bobby Whitlock

ANYMORE
w&m/Vic McAlpin, Roy F. Drusky,
Marie Wilson

ANYONE CAN MOVE A MOUNTAIN
w&m/John D. Marks

ANYONE CAN WHISTLE
w&m/Stephen Sondheim

ANYONE WHO HAD A HEART
m/Burt Bacharach
w/Hal David

ANYONE WOULD LOVE YOU
w&m/Harold Rome

ANYPLACE I HANG MY HAT IS HOME
m/Harold Arlen
w/Johnny Mercer

ANYTHING GOES
w&m/Cole Porter

ANYTHING THAT'S ROCK 'N 'ROLL
w&m/Tom Petty

ANYTHING YOU CAN DO
w&m/Irving Berlin

ANYTIME
w&m/Herbert Happy Lawson

ANYWAY YOU WANT ME
w&m/Aaron Schroeder, Cliff Owens

ANYWHERE
w&m/Valerie Simpson, Nicholas (Nick) Ashford

ANYWHERE
m/Jule Styne
w/Sammy Cahn

ANYWHERE I WANDER
w&m/Frank Loesser

APARTMENT, THE (film score)
m/Adolph Deutsch

APARTMENT NO. 9
w&m/Johnny Paycheck

APOLOGIZE
w&m/John Lee Hooker

APPLE BLOSSOM WEDDING
m/Nat Simon
w/Jimmy Kennedy

APPLE FOR THE TEACHER, AN
m/James V. Monaco
w/Johnny Burke

APPLE GREEN
w&m/Charles Singleton

APPLE HONEY
w&m/Woody Herman

APPLE SCRUFFS
w&m/George Harrison

APRIL FOOLS, THE (film score)
m/Marvin Hamlisch

APRIL IN PARIS
m/Vernon Duke
w/E.Y. Harburg

APRIL IN PORTUGAL (Coimbra)
m/Raul Ferrao
w/Jimmy Kennedy

APRIL LOVE
m/Sammy Fain
w/Paul Francis Webster

APRIL SHOWERS
m/Louis Silvers
w/Buddy DeSylva

AQUALUNG
w&m/Ian Anderson

AQUARIUS
m/Galt MacDermot
w/James Rado, Gerome Ragni

ARABESQUE (film score)
m/Henry Mancini

ARBOUR ZENA (instr.)
m/Keith Jarrett

ARE YOU EVERYTHING
w&m/Thomas Bell, Linda Creed

ARE YOU EXPERIENCED
w&m/Jimi Hendrix

ARE YOU FROM DIXIE
w&m/George L. Cobb, Jack Yellen

ARE YOU FROM HEAVEN
m/Anatole Friedland
w/L. Wolfe Gilbert

ARE YOU HAVING ANY FUN
m/Sammy Fain
w/Jack Yellen

ARE YOU IN THERE
m/John Barry
w/David Pomeranz

**ARE YOU LONESOME
TONIGHT**
m/Lou Handman
w/Roy Turk

**ARE YOU ON THE ROAD TO
LOVIN' ME AGAIN**
w&m/Robert Morrison,
Debbie Hupp

**ARE YOU SURE HANK DONE IT
THIS WAY**
w&m/Waylon Jennings

ARE YOU TEASING ME
w&m/Ira Louvin, Charles Louvin

**ARE YOU THERE WITH
ANOTHER GIRL**
m/Burt Bacharach
w/Hal David

**AREN'T YOU GLAD YOU'RE
YOU**
m/James Van Heusen
w/Johnny Burke

**AREN'T YOU KIND OF GLAD
WE DID**
m/George Gershwin
w/Ira Gershwin

ARIZONA
w&m/Mark Lindsay

ARM IN ARM
w&m/Meredith Willson

**ARMY AIR CORPS, THE (Off
We Go Into The Wild Blue
Yonder) - Official song of the U.S.
Air Force**
w&m/Robert M. Crawford

AROUND AND AROUND
w&m/Chuck Berry

AROUND THE CORNER
w&m/Art Kassel

AROUND THE WORLD
m/Victor Young
w/Harold Adamson

**ARRAH GO ON, I'M GONNA GO
BACK TO OREGON**
m/Bert Grant
w/Joseph Young, Samuel L. Lewis

ARRIVEDERCI ROMA
m/R. Rascel
w/Carl Sigman

ART FOR ART'S SAKE
w&m/Eric Stewart, Lol Creme,
Graham Gouldman

ART OF DYING, THE
w&m/George Harrison

ARTHUR
w&m/Raymond Douglas Davies

**ARTHUR MURRAY TAUGHT
ME DANCING IN A HURRY**
m/Victor Schertzinger
w/Johnny Mercer

ARTISTRY IN RHYTHM (instr.)
m/Stan Kenton

ARTISTRY JUMPS
m/Stan Kenton

AS LONG AS HE NEEDS ME
w&m/Lionel Bart

AS LONG AS I LIVE
w&m/Roy Claxton Acuff

AS LONG AS I LIVE
m/Harold Arlen
w/Ted Koehler

AS LONG AS THERE'S MUSIC
m/Jule Styne
w/Sammy Cahn

**AS ON THROUGH THE
SEASONS WE SAIL**
w&m/Cole Porter

**AS SOON AS I HANG UP THE
PHONE**
w&m/Conway Twitty

AS TIME GOES BY
w&m/Herman Hupfeld

AS YOU DESIRE ME
w&m/Allie Wrubel

ASIA MINOR (instr.)
m/Walter Melrose

ASK ANYONE WHO KNOWS
w&m/Alvin S. Kaufman, Edward
Seiler, Sol Marcus

ASK ME NO QUESTIONS
w&m/Robert Wells, David Saxon

ASLEEP IN THE DEEP
m/Henry W. Petrie
w/Arthur J. Lamb

A'SOALIN'
w&m/Paul Stookey, Tracy Batteast,
Elena Mezzetti

ASPEN/THESE DAYS
w&m/Dan Fogelberg

**AT A GEORGIA CAMP
MEETING**
w&m/Frederick Allen (Kerry Mills)

AT A PERFUME COUNTER
m/Joseph A. Burke
w/Edgar Leslie

AT AN OLD TRYSTING PLACE
w&m/Edward Alexander MacDowell

AT DAWNING
m/Charles Wakefield Cadman
w/Nelle Richmond Eberhart

AT LAST
m/Harry Warren
w/Mack Gordon

AT LONG LAST LOVE
w&m/Cole Porter

AT SEVENTEEN
w&m/Janis Ian

AT SUNDOWN
w&m/Walter Donaldson

AT THE BALALAIKA
w&m/George (Chet) Forrest,
Robert Wright

AT THE CODFISH BALL
w&m/Lew Pollack, Jack Yellen,
Sidney D. Mitchell

AT THE HOP
w&m/David White Tricker,
J. Medora

AT THE JAZZ LAND BALL
w&m/Original Dixieland Jazz Band
(see composer listing)

**AT THE WOODCHOPPER'S
BALL**
w&m/Woody Herman, Joe Bishop

AT THE ZOO
w&m/Paul Simon

AT YOUR COMMAND
w&m/Harry Tobias, Harry Barris,
Bing Crosby

A-TISKET, A-TASKET
w&m/Van Alexander, Ella Fitzgerald

ATLANTIS
w&m/Donovan

ATLANTIS (instr.)
m/Sun Ra

ATTICA BLUES
w&m/Archie Shepp

ATTITUDE DANCING
w&m/Carly Simon

AU REVOIR BUT NOT GOODBYE
w&m/Albert Von Tilzer, Lew Brown

AU REVOIR PLEASANT DREAMS
m/Jean Schwartz
w/Jack Meskill

AUF WIEDERSEHN
m/Sigmund Romberg
w/Herbert Reynolds

AUF WIEDERSEHN, MY DEAR
w&m/E.G. Nelson, Al Hoffman, Al Goodhart, Milton Ager

AULD LANG SYNE
m/Old Scottish air (questionably attributed to William Shield)
w/Robert Burns

AURA LEE
m/George R. Poulton
w/W.W.Fisdick

AUNT HAGAR'S BLUES
m/W.C.Handy
w/J.Tim Brymn

AUNTIE MAME (film score)
m/Brenislau Kaper

AUTUMN IN NEW YORK
w&m/Vernon Duke

AUTUMN LEAVES
m/Joseph Kosma
w/Johnny Mercer

AUTUMN NOCTURNE
m/Josef Myrow
w/Kim Gannon

AUTUMN OF MY LIFE
w&m/Bobby Goldsboro

AUTUMN SERENADE
m/Peter DeRose
w/Sammy Gallop

AVALON
m/Vincent Rose
w/Al Jolson, Buddy DeSylva

AVE MARIA (Hail Mary; Ave Gratia Plena Dominus Tecum)
m/Charles Francois Gounod (adapted from J.S. Bach's "1st Prelude In C Major of "The Well Tempered Clavier' ")
w/Alphonse De Lamartine

AVE MARIA
m/Franz Peter Schubert
(Opus 52, No. 6)
w/based on Sir Walter Scott's "Lady Of The Lake"

AWAITING ON YOU ALL
w&m/George Harrison

Addenda:

AFTER MR. TENG (instr.)
m/Toshiko Akiyoshi

AGAINST THE WIND
w&m/Bob Seger

AIN'T NO BIGGER FOOL
w&m/Frederick Perren, Dino Fekaris

ALL NIGHT LONG
w&m/Joseph Walsh

ALL I SEE IS YOUR FACE
w&m/Dan Hill

ALL THINGS ARE POSSIBLE
w&m/Dan Peek

ASHES BY NOW
w&m/Rodney Crowell

ATOMIC
w&m/Deborah Harry, J. Destri

 SONGS

B

BABALU
w&m/Miguelito Valdes

BABBITT AND THE BROMIDE, THE
m/George Gershwin
w/Ira Gershwin

BABE
w&m/Dennis De Young

BABE I'M GONNA LEAVE YOU
w&m/James Page

BABES IN ARMS
m/Richard Rodgers
w/Lorenz (Larry) Hart

BABIES ON OUR BLOCK, THE
m/David Braham
w/Ed Harrigan

BABIK (instr.)
m/Django Reinhardt

BABY (You've Got What It Takes)
w&m/Clyde Otis, Murray Stein

BABY BABY ALL THE TIME
w&m/Bobby Troup

BABY BABY DON'T CRY
w&m/William (Smokey) Robinson Jr.,
Al Cleveland, Terry Johnson

BABY BLUE
w&m/Peter Ham, Thomas Evans

BABY BLUE EYES
m/Jesse Greer
w/Walter Hirsch, George Jessel

BABY COME BACK
w&m/Peter Beckett, John Charles
"J.C." Crowley

BABY DOLL (film score)
m/Kenyon Hopkins

BABY DON'T GET HOOKED ON ME
w&m/Mac Davis

BABY DON'T GO
w&m/Sonny Bono

BABY DON'T GO
w&m/Karla Bonoff, Kenny Edwards

BABY DON'T TAKE YOUR LOVE
w&m/Van McCoy

BABY DON'T TELL ON ME
w&m/James Andrew Rushing

BABY DRIVE
w&m/Peter Criss, Stan Penridge

BABY ELEPHANT WALK
w&m/Hal David, Henry Mancini

BABY FACE
m/Harry Akst
w/Benny Davis

BABY HOLD ON
w&m/Eddie Money, Jimmy Lyon

BABY I LOVE YOU
w&m/Jeff Barry, Ellie Greenwich

BABY I LOVE YOU
w&m/Ronnie Shannon

BABY I LOVE YOU
w&m/John Lee Hooker

BABY I LOVE YOUR WAY
w&m/Peter Frampton

BABY I NEED YOUR LOVING
w&m/Eddie Holland, Brian
Holland, Lamont Dozier

BABY I'LL GIVE IT TO YOU
w&m/Dash Crofts, James Seals

BABY I'M-A WANT YOU
w&m/David Gates

BABY I'M YOURS
w&m/Van McCoy

BABY IT'S COLD OUTSIDE
w&m/Frank Loesser

BABY IT'S YOU
m/Burt Bacharach
w/Hal David

BABY LET ME HOLD YOUR HAND
w&m/Ray Charles

BABY LOVE
w&m/Eddie Holland, Brian Holland,
Lamont Dozier

BABY MAKER, THE (film score)
m/Fred Karlin
w/Tylwyth Kymry

BABY MINE
m/Archibald Johnston
w/Charles MacKay

BABY SHOES
m/Al Piantadosi
w/Joe Goodwin, Ed Rose

BABY STOP CRYING
w&m/Robert Dylan

BABY TAKE A BOW
m/Jay Gorney
w/Lew Brown

BABY TALKS DIRTY
w&m/Doug Fieger, Berton Averre

BABY THE RAIN MUST FALL
m/Elmer Bernstein
w/Ernie Sheldon

BABY THE RAIN MUST FALL (film score)
m/Elmer Bernstein

BABY WHAT A BIG SURPRISE
w&m/James Pankow

BABY WON'T YOU LET ME ROCK AND ROLL YOU
w&m/Alvin Lee

BABY WON'T YOU PLEASE COME HOME
w&m/Clarence Williams,
Charles Warfield

BABY WORKOUT
w&m/Jackie Wilson, Alonzo Tucker

BABY YOU'RE RIGHT
w&m/James Brown, Joe Tex

BABY YOU'RE TOO MUCH
m/Duke Ellington
w/Don George

BABYLON IS FALLEN
w&m/Henry Clay Work

BABY'S BIRTHDAY PARTY
w&m/Ann Ronell

BABY'S GONE
w&m/Conway Twitty, Billy Parks

BACHELOR IN PARADISE (film score)
m/Henry Mancini

BACCHANAL RAG, THE
w&m/Louis A. Hirsch

BACK, BACK, BACK TO BALTIMORE
m/Egbert Anson Van Alstyne
w/Harry H. Williams

BACK BAY SHUFFLE (instr.)
m/Artie Shaw, Teddie McCrae

BACK COUNTRY SUITE, THE
w&m/Mose Allison

BACK DOOR MAN
w&m/Willie Dixon

BACK DOWN TO EARTH
w&m/Carly Simon

BACK HOME AGAIN
w&m/Chuck Berry

BACK HOME AGAIN
w&m/John Denver

BACK HOME AGAIN IN INDIANA
m/James F. Hanley
w/Ballard MacDonald

BACK HOME IN TENNESSEE
m/Walter Donaldson
w/William Jerome

BACK IN MY ARMS AGAIN
w&m/Eddie Holland, Brian Holland,
Lamont Dozier

BACK IN THE SADDLE
w&m/Joe Perry, Steve Tyler

BACK IN THE SADDLE AGAIN
w&m/Gene Autry

BACK IN YOUR OWN BACKYARD
m/Dave Dreyer, Al Jolson
w/Billy Rose

BACK TO DONEGAL
w&m/Steve Graham

BACK TO DREAMIN' AGAIN
w&m/Kenny Nolan

BACK TO THE ISLAND
w&m/Leon Russell

BACK TOGETHER AGAIN
w&m/Daryl Hall, John Oates

BACK UP, BUDDY
w&m/Boudleaux Bryant

BACK UP TRAIN
w&m/Al Green

BACK WHERE YOU BELONG
w&m/Mick Jones

BACKLASH
w&m/Freddie Hubbard

BACKTRACK
w&m/Faron Young, Alex Zanetis

BAD AND THE BEAUTIFUL, THE (film score)
m/David Raksin

BAD BAD LEROY BROWN
w&m/Jim Croce

BAD BLOOD
w&m/Neil Sedaka, Phillip Cody

BAD BREAKS
w&m/Cat Stevens

BAD CASE OF LOVING YOU
w&m/John Moon Martin

BAD DREAM BLUES
w&m/David Van Ronk

BAD GIRLS
w&m/Donna Summer, Bruce Sudano,
Joe Esposito, Eddie Hokenson

BAD LUCK
w&m/Jules Taub, Saul Ling

BAD MOON RISING
w&m/John C. Fogerty

BAD NEWS
w&m/John D. Loudermilk

BAD NEWS BEARS, THE (film score)
m/Jerry Fielding

BADLANDS
w&m/Bruce Springsteen

BAGS GROOVE (instr.)
m/Miles Dewey Davis

BAIA
m/Ary Barroso
w/Ray Gilbert

BAKER STREET
w&m/Gerry Rafferty

BALI HAI
m/Richard Rodgers
w/Oscar Hammerstein II

BALL AND CHAIN BLUES
w&m/Joshua Daniel White

BALL O'FIRE
w&m/Richard M. Jones

BALL OF FIRE
w&m/Tommy James, Bob King

BALLAD FOR A FRIEND
w&m/Robert Dylan

BALLAD FOR AMERICANS
m/Earl Robinson
w/John Latouche

BALLAD IN PLAIN D
w&m/Robert Dylan

BALLAD OF DAVY CROCKETT, THE
m/George Burns
w/Tom Blackburn

BALLAD OF EASY RIDER
w&m/Roger McGuinn

BALLAD OF JOHN AND YOKO, THE
w&m/John Lennon, Yoko Ono

BALLAD OF RODGER YOUNG, THE
w&m/Frank Loesser

BALLAD OF SIR FRANKIE CRISP
w&m/George Harrison

BALLAD OF THE ALAMO, THE
m/Dimitri Tiomkin
w/Paul Francis Webster

BALLAD OF THE GREEN BERETS
w&m/Barry Sadler

BALLAD OF TWO BROTHERS
w&m/Curly Putnam, Buddy Killen,
Bobby Braddock

BALLERINA
w&m/Carl Sigman, Bob Russell

BALLIN' THE JACK
w&m/Chris Smith, James Burris

BALTIMORE
w&m/Boudleaux Bryant,
Felice Bryant

BALTIMORE
w&m/Randy Newman

BAM, BAM, BAMY SHORE
m/Ray Henderson
w/Mort Dixon

BAMBALINA
m/Herbert Stothart,
Vincent Youmans
w/Otto Harbach, Oscar
Hammerstein II

BAMBOO
w&m/David Van Ronk

BANAPPLE GAS
w&m/Cat Stevens

BAND OF GOLD
w&m/Ronald Dunbar,
Edythe Wayne

BAND OF GOLD
w&m/Jack Taylor, Bob Musel

BAND ON THE RUN
w&m/Paul and Linda McCartne

BAND PLAYED ON, THE
m/Charles B. Ward
w/John E. Palmer

BANDANA DAYS
m/Eubie Blake
w/Noble Sissle

BANDS OF GOLD
w&m/Webb Pierce, Hal Eddy,
Cliff Parman

BANGLA DESH
w&m/George Harrison

BANK DICK, THE (film score)
m/Charles Previn

BANNED IN BOSTON
w&m/Fred Tobias

BAPTISM OF JESSE TAYLOR, THE
w&m/Dallas Frazier, Whitey Shafer

BARBARELLA (film score)
m/Charles Fox, Bob Crewe

BARCELONA
w&m/Stephen Sondheim

BARK FOR BARKSDALE (instr.)
m/Gerry Mulligan

BARNABY JONES (TV theme)
m/Jerry Goldsmith

BARNACLE BILL THE SAILOR
w&m/Carson J. Robison

BARNEY GOOGLE
m/Con Conrad
w/Billy Rose

BAROQUE A NOVA (instr.)
m/Mason Williams

BARRACUDA
w&m/Ann Wilson, Nancy Wilson,
Rodger Fisher, Derosier

**BARRELHOUSE BREAKDOWN
(instr.)**
m/Pete K.H. Johnson

**BARRETTS OF WIMPOLE
STREET (film score)**
m/Bronislau Kaper

BASIE BOOGIE
m/William (Count) Basie
w/Milt Ebins

BASS ON TOP (instr.)
m/Meade "Lux" Lewis

BATAAN (film score)
m/Bronislau Kaper

BATMAN (TV Theme)
m/Neal Hefti

BATTLE CRY (film score)
m/Max Steiner

**BATTLE CRY OF FREEDOM,
THE**
w&m/George Frederick Root

**BATTLE HYMN OF THE
REPUBLIC, THE**
m/from the melody of "John Brown's
Body" which was based on "Glory
Hallelujah", believed composed by
William Steffe
w/Julia Ward Howe

BATTLE OF NEW ORLEANS
m/from the folk melody "The 8th
of January"
w/Jimmy Driftwood

**BATTLE OF PRAGUE, THE
(instr.)**
m/Franz Kotzwara

BATTLEGROUND (film score)
m/Lennie Hayton

**BAUBLES, BANGLES
AND BEADS**
w&m/George (Chet) Forrest, Robert
Wright (music adapted from
composition by Alexander Borodin)

BE
w&m/Neil Diamond

BE A CLOWN
w&m/Cole Porter

BE ANYTHING (But Be Mine)
w&m/Irving Gordon

BE BETTER TO YOUR BABY
w&m/Justin Tubb

BE BOP A LULA
w&m/Gene Vincent, Don Graves

BE CAREFUL IT'S MY HEART
w&m/Irving Berlin

BE HONEST WITH ME
w&m/Fred Rose, Gene Autry

BE KIND TO YOUR PARENTS
w&m/Harold Rome

BE MINE
m/Harold Spina
w/John M. Elliott

BE MINE TONIGHT
w&m/Sunny Skylar

BE MY BABY
w&m/Phil Spector, Jeff Barry,
Ellie Greenwich

BE MY GUEST
w&m/Antoine "Fats" Domino,
Dave Bartholomew

BE MY LIFE'S COMPANION
m/Milton DeLugg
w/Bob Hilliard

BE MY LITTLE BUMBLE BEE
m/Henry I. Marshall
w/Stanley Murphy

BE MY LOVE
m/Nicholas Brodsky
w/Sammy Cahn

BE MY LOVER
w&m/Michael Bruce

BE NICE TO ME
w&m/Todd Rundgren

BE STILL MY HEART
w&m/John C. Egan, Allan Flynn

BE TRUE TO YOUR SCHOOL
w&m/Brian Wilson

BEALE STREET BLUES
w&m/W.C.Handy

BEANS AND CORNBREAD
w&m/Fleecie Moore, Freddie Clark

BEANS, BEANS, BEANS
w&m/Chris Smith, Elmer Bowman

BEAR CAT CRAWL (instr.)
m/Meade "Lux" Lewis

BEARCAT SHUFFLE (instr.)
m/Mary Lou Williams

BEAST OF BURDEN
w&m/Mick Jagger, Keith Richards

BEAT GOES ON, THE
w&m/Sonny Bono

**BEAT ME DADDY EIGHT TO
THE BAR**
w&m/Hugh Denham Prince,
Don Raye

Beatrice Fairfax
m/James V. Monaco
w/Joseph McCarthy, Grant Clarke

BEAUTIFUL
w&m/Carole King

BEAUTIFUL ANNABELLE LEE
m/George W. Meyer
w/Alfred Brvan

**BEAUTIFUL BROTHER OF
MINE**
w&m/Curtis Mayfield

BEAUTIFUL DREAMER
w&m/Stephen Collins Foster

BEAUTIFUL DREAMER
w&m/Natalie Cole

BEATIFUL GIRL
m/Nacio Herb Brown
w/Arthur Freed

**BEAUTIFUL ISLE OF
SOMEWHERE**
m/John S. Fearis
w/Jessie B. Pounds

BEAUTIFUL LADY IN BLUE, A
m/Samuel M. Lewis
w/J. Fred Coots

BEAUTIFUL MORNING, A
w&m/Eddie Brigati, Felix Cavaliere

BEAUTIFUL OHIO
m/Robert King
w/Ballard MacDonald

BEAUTIFUL PEOPLE
w&m/Kenny O'Dell

BEAUTIFUL PEOPLE
w&m/Melanie

BEAUTIFUL STRANGER, THE
w&m/Rod McKuen

BEAUTIFUL SUNDAY
w&m/Daniel Boone

**BEAUTY IS A RARE THING
(instr.)**
m/Ornette Coleman

BEAUTY IS ONLY SKIN DEEP
w&m/Eddie Holland, Norman
Whitfield

BE-BOP BABY
w&m/Pearl Lendhurst

BECAUSE
m/Guy D'Hardelot (French words
and music)
w/Edward Teschemacher
(English words)

BECAUSE I LOVE YOU
w&m/Georgie Fame

BECAUSE OF YOU
m/Dudley Wilkinson
w/Arthur Hammerstein

BECAUSE THE NIGHT
w&m/Patti Smith, Bruce
Springsteen

BECAUSE THEY'RE YOUNG
w&m/Aaron Schroeder, Wally Gold

BECAUSE YOU'RE MINE
m/Nicholas Brodsky
w/Sammy Cahn

BED OF ROSES
w&m/Harold W. Reid

BEDELIA
m/Jean Schwartz
w/William Jerome

**BEDKNOBS AND
BROOMSTICKS**
w&m/Richard M. Sherman,
Robert B. Sherman

BEDTIME STORY
w&m/Billy Sherrill, Glenn Sutton

BEECHWOOD 4-5789
w&m/Marvin Gaye, William
Stevenson, George Gordy

BEEN TO CANAAN
w&m/Carole King

**BEEN TOO LONG ON
THE ROAD**
w&m/David Gates

BEER BARREL POLKA
m/Jaromir Vejvoda
w/Lew Brown

BEFORE I'M OVER YOU
w&m/Betty Sue Perry

**BEFORE MY HEART
FINDS OUT**
w&m/Randy Goodrum

BEFORE MY TIME
w&m/Ben Peters

**BEFORE THE NEXT
TEARDROP FALLS**
m/Ben Peters
w/Vivian Keith

**BEFORE THE PARADE
PASSES BY**
w&m/Jerry Herman

BEFORE THIS DAY ENDS
w&m/Vic McAlpin, Roy F. Drusky,
Marie Wilson

BEFORE YOU CALL
w&m/Fred Rose

BEFORE YOU GO
w&m/Buck Owens

BEG YOUR PARDON
w&m/Beasley Smith,
Francis Craig

BEGAT, THE
m/Burton Lane
w/E.Y. Harburg

BEGGARS OPERA, THE (opera)
m/traditional English folk airs
w/John Gay

BEGGING TO YOU
w&m/Marty Robbins

BEGIN THE BEGUINE
w&m/Cole Porter

**BEGINNING TO FEEL THE
PAIN**
w&m/Mac Davis

BEGINNINGS
w&m/Robert Lamm

BEHIND BLUE EYES
w&m/Peter Townshend

BEHIND CLOSED DOORS
w&m/Kenny O'Dell

BEHIND THAT LOCKED DOOR
w&m/George Harrison

BEHIND THE RAIN
w&m/Herb Alpert

**BEHOLD A PALE HORSE
(film score)**
m/Maurice Jarre

**BEHOLD THE LORD HIGH
EXECUTIONER**
m/Sir Arthur Sullivan
w/Sir William Schwenk
    Gilbert

BEI MIR BIST DU SCHÖN
m/Saul Chaplin, Sholom Secunda
w/Jacob Jacobs, Sammy Cahn

BEING ALIVE
w&m/Stephen Sondheim

BELIEVE IN HUMANITY
w&m/Carole King

**BELIEVE ME IF ALL THOSE
ENDEARING YOUNG CHARMS**
m/from the traditional Irish melody
"My Lodging Is On The Cold
Ground"

BELIEVE WHAT YOU SAY
w&m/Dorsey Burnette,
Johnny Burnette

**BELL BOOK AND CANDLE
(film score)**
m/George Duning

BELL BOTTOM BLUES
w&m/Eric Clapton

BELL BOTTOM TROUSERS
m/from a sea chantey of unknown
origin
w/Moe Jaffee

BELLAVIA (instr.)
m/Chuck Mangione

BELLE
w&m/Al Green

BELLE, BELLE (My Liberty Belle)
w&m/Bob Merrill

BELLE OF THE BALL
m/Leroy Anderson
w/Mitchell Parish

BELLES OF SOUTHERN BELL
w&m/Don Wayne

BELLS OF RHYMNEY, THE
m/Pete Seeger
w/Idris Davies

**BELLS OF ST. MARY'S, THE
(film score)**
m/Robert Emmett Dolan

BELLS OF ST. MARY'S, THE
m/A. Emmett Adams
w/Douglas Furber

BELLY UP TO THE BAR BOYS
w&m/Meredith Willson

BELOW THE SURFACE
w&m/Dan Fogelberg

BEN
m/Walter Scharf
w/Don Black

**BEN BOLT (Oh! Don't You
Remember)**
m/Nelson Kneass
w/Thomas Dunn English

BEN HUR (film score)
m/Miklos Rozsa

BEND DOWN SISTER
m/Con Conrad
w/Ballard MacDonald,
Dave Silverstein

BENEATH STILL WATERS
w&m/Dallas Frazier

**BENNY GOODMAN STORY, The
(film score)**
m/Henry Mancini

BEOUF RIVER ROAD
w&m/Tony Joe White

BERMUDA BUGGY RIDE
m/Sanford Green
w/Mack David

BERNADETTE
w&m/Eddie Holland, Brian Holland,
Lamont Dozier

**BERT WILLIAMS (Pacific Rag)
(instr.)**
m/Ferdinand " Jelly Roll" Morton

BERTHA BUTT BOOGIE
w&m/Jimmy Castor

BESAME MUCHO
m/Consuelo Velazquez
w/Sunny Skylar

BESIDE A BABBLING BROOK
m/Walter Donaldson
w/Gus Kahn

BESS YOU IS MY WOMAN NOW
m/George Gershwin
w/Ira Gershwin, DuBose Heyward

BEST FRIEND
w&m/Harry Edward Nilsson

BEST IS YET TO COME, THE
m/Cy Coleman
w/Carolyn Leigh

BEST OF ALL POSSIBLE WORLDS, THE
w&m/Kris Kristofferson

BEST OF MY LOVE
w&m/Maurice White, Albert McKay
Wanda Hutchinson

BEST OF MY LOVE, THE
w&m/J.D. Souther, Glenn Frey,
Donald Henley

BEST THING
w&m/Dennis De Young,
James Young

BEST THING FOR YOU, THE
w&m/Irving Berlin

BEST THINGS IN LIFE ARE FREE, THE
m/Ray Henderson
w/Lew Brown Buddy DeSylva

BEST YEARS OF OUR LIVES, THE (film score)
m/Hugo Friedhofer

BET YOUR LIFE I DO
w&m/Errol Brown, Tony Wilson

BETCHA BY GOLLY WOW
w&m/Thomas Bell, Linda Creed

BETH
w&m/Peter Criss, Stan Penridge,
Bob Ezrin

BETHENA (instr.)
m/Scott Joplin

BETTER LOVE NEXT TIME
w&m/Steve Pippin, Larry Keith,
Johnny Slate

BETTER LUCK NEXT TIME
w&m/Irving Berlin

BETTER PLACE TO BE, A
w&m/Harry Chapin

BETTER THAN EVER
m/Marvin Hamlisch
w/Carole Bayer Sager

BETTY (instr.)
m/David Rose

BETTY CO-ED
w&m/Rudy Vallee, J. Paul Fogarty

BETWEEN THE DEVIL AND THE DEEP BLUE SEA
m/Harold Arlen
w/Ted Koehler

BETWEEN YOU AND ME
w&m/Cole Porter

BEULAH'S BOOGIE
w&m/Lionel Hampton

BEVERLY HILLBILLIES (TV theme)
m/D. Curtis Massey

BEWARE BROTHER BEWARE
w&m/Fleecie Moore, Morry Lasco,
Dick Adams

BEWARE OF DARKNESS
w&m/George Harrison

BEWITCHED, BOTHERED AND BEWILDERED
m/Richard Rodgers
w/Lorenz (Larry) Hart

BEYOND THE BLUE HORIZON
m/Richard Whiting,
W. Franke Harling
w/Leo Robin

BEYOND THE RAINBOW
w&m/Leon Pober, Webley Edwards

BEYOND THE SEA (La Mer)
m/Charles Trenet
w/Jack Lawrence

BEYOND THE SUNSET
m/Blanche Kerr Brock
w/Virgil P. Brock

BIBBIDI BOBBIDI BOO
m/Jerry Livingston, Al Hoffman
w/Mack David

BIBLE TELLS ME SO, THE
w&m/Dale Evans

BIDIN' MY TIME
m/George Gershwin
w/Ira Gershwin

BIG BAD JOHN
w&m/Jimmy Dean

BIG BILL BLUES
w&m/"Big Bill" Broonzy

BIG D
w&m/Frank Loesser

BIG IN VEGAS
w&m/Buck Owens, Terry Stafford

BIG MABEL MURPHY
w&m/Dallas Frazier

BIG BIG WORLD
w&m/Dorsey Burnette,
Johnny Burnette

BIG BRASS BAND FROM BRAZIL
w&m/Carl Sigman, Bob Hilliard

BIG FOUR POSTER BED
w&m/Shel Silverstein

BIG GIRLS DON'T CRY
w&m/Bob Gaudio, Bob Crewe

BIG HUNK O'LOVE, A
w&m/Aaron Schroeder, Sid Wyche

BIG IRON
w&m/Marty Robbins

BIG MOVIE SHOW IN THE SKY, THE
m/Robert Emmett Dolan
w/Johnny Mercer

BIG NOISE FROM WINNETKA
m/Robert (Bob) Haggart
w/Ray Bauduc

BIG RIVER
w&m/John R. (Johnny) Cash

BIG SHOT
w&m/Billy Joel

BIG SPENDER
m/Cy Coleman
w/Dorothy Fields

BIG YELLOW TAXI
w&m/Joni Mitchell

BIGGEST PARAKEETS IN TOWN, THE
w&m/Jud Strunk

BIJOU (instr.)
m/Bill Harris

BILBAO SONG, THE
m/Kurt Weill
w/Johnny Mercer

BILL
m/Jerome Kern
w/P.G. Wodehouse

BILL BAILEY, WON'T YOU PLEASE COME HOME
w&m/Hughie Cannon

BILLBOARD, THE (March)
m/John N. Klohr

BILLIE'S BLUES
w&m/Billie Holiday

BILLION DOLLAR BABIES
w&m/Vincent Furnier

BILLY BAYOU
w&m/Roger Miller

BIRD DOG
w&m/Boudleaux Bryant

BIRD IN A GILDED CAGE, A
m/Harry Von Tilzer
w/Arthur J. Lamb

BIRD MAN OF ALCATRAZ (film score)
m/Elmer Bernstein

BIRD ON NELLIE'S HAT, THE
m/Alfred Solman
w/Arthur J. Lamb

BIRDS OF BRITAIN, THE (instr.)
m/Bob Crewe

BIRDS OF A FEATHER
m/James Van Heusen
w/Johnny Burke

BIRDS ON THE WIRE
w&m/Leonard Cohen

BIRMINGHAM BLUES
w&m/John Lee Hooker

BIRMINGHAM BLUES
w&m/Don Wayne

**BIRMINGHAM BREAKDOWN
(instr.)**
m/Duke Ellington

BIRTH OF THE BLUES
m/Ray Henderson
w/Lew Brown, Buddy DeSylva

BIRTH OF THE COOL (instr.)
m/Miles Dewey Davis

BITCH IS BACK, THE
m/Elton John
w/Bernie Taupin

BITCHES BREW (instr.)
m/Miles Dewey Davis

BITE THE BULLET (film score)
m/Alex North

BITTER BAD
w&m/Melanie

BITTER WITH THE SWEET
w&m/Carole King

BLACK AND BLUE
m/Thomas "Fats" Waller,
Harry Brooks
w/Andy Razaf

**BLACK AND TAN FANTASY
(instr.)**
m/Duke Ellington

BLACK BEAUTY (instr.)
m/Duke Ellington

BLACK BOTTOM
m/Ray Henderson
w/Lew Brown, Buddy DeSylva

BLACK BOTTOM STOMP (instr.)
m/Ferdinand "Jelly Roll" Morton

BLACK COFFEE
m/Sonny Burke
w/Paul Francis Webster

BLACK COW
w&m/Donald Fagan, Walter Becker

BLACK CROW BLUES
w&m/Robert Dylan

BLACK FRIDAY
w&m/Donald Fagan, Walter Becker

BLACK GYPSY (instr.)
m/Archie Shepp

BLACK HOLE, THE (film score)
m/John Barry

BLACK HORSE TROOP (march)
m/John Philip Sousa

BLACK MAGIC WOMAN
w&m/Peter Green

BLACK MARIA
w&m/Todd Rundgren

BLACK NIGHT
w&m/Jessie Mae Robinson

BLACK ORCHID
w&m/Stevie Wonder

BLACK ORPHEUS (film score)
m/Luis Bonfa, Antonio Carlos Jobim

**BLACK PRIEST OF THE
ANDES (cantata)**
w&m/Mary Lou Williams

BLACK REQUIEM
w&m/Quincy Jones, Ray Charles

**BLACK SAINT AND THE
SINNER LADY, THE (instr.)**
m/Charles Mingus

BLACK SWAN, THE (film score)
m/Alfred Newman

BLACK THORN ROSE (instr.)
m/Joe Zawinul

BLACK WATER
w&m/Paul Simmon

BLACK WOMAN, A (instr.)
m/Archie Shepp

BLACKBERRY WAY
w&m/Ray Wood

BLAH-BLAH-BLAH
m/George Gershwin
w/Ira Gershwin

**BLAME IT ON MY LAST
AFFAIR**
w&m/Henry Nemo

BLAME IT ON MY YOUTH
m/Oscar Levant
w/Edward Heyman

BLAME IT ON THE BLUES
w&m/Thomas Andrew Dorsey

**BLAME IT ON THE BOSSA
NOVA**
w&m/Barry Mann,
Cynthia We

BLESS 'EM ALL
w&m/original: Jimmie Huhes, Frank
Lee, revised American words:
Al Stillman

BLESS THIS HOUSE
m/May H. Brahe
w/Helen Taylor

BLESS YOU
w&m/Barry Mann, Cynthia Weil

BLESS YOUR HEART
w&m/Freddie Hart, Jack Lebsock

BLESSED ASSURANCE
m/Mrs. Joseph F. Knapp
w/Fanny Crosby Van Alstyne

**BLEST BE THE TIE THAT
BINDS**
m/Hans Georg Naegeli (from the
German song "Dennis")
w/John Fawcett

BLIND LEMON
w&m/Huddie (Leadbelly) Ledbetter

BLIND MAN'S BLUFF (instr.)
m/Duke Ellington

BLINDED BY THE LIGHT
w&m/Bruce Springsteen

BLIZZARD, THE
w&m/Harlan Howard

BLONDES (Have More Fun)
w&m/Rod Stewart

**BLOOD RED AND GOING
DOWN**
w&m/Curly Putnam

BLOODY MARY MORNING
w&m/Willie Nelson

BLOODY WELL RIGHT
w&m/Roger Hodgson, Rick Davies

BLOW AWAY
w&m/George Harrison

BLOW GABRIEL BLOW
w&m/Cole Porter

BLOW YOUR WHISTLE
w&m/Harry Wayne Casey,
Richard Finch

BLOWIN' AWAY
w&m/Laura Nyro

BLOWIN' IN THE WIND
w&m/Robert Dylan

BLUE AGAIN
m/Jimmy McHugh
w/Dorothy Fields

**BLUE AND THE GRAY, THE
(A Mother's Gift To Her Country)**
w&m/Paul Dresser

BLUE AND SENTIMENTAL
m/William (Count) Basie,
Jerry Livingston
w/Mack David

BLUE BAYOU
w&m/Roy Orbison, Joe Melson

BLUE BELL
m/Edward Madden
w/Theodore F. Morse,
Theodora (Dolly) Morse

BLUE BIRD
w&m/Stephen Stills

BLUE BIRD OF HAPPINESS
m/Sandor Harmati
w/Edward Heyman

BLUE BLUE DAY
w&m/Don Gibson

BLUE BOY
w&m/Boudleaux Bryant

BLUE CHAMPAGNE
m/H. Grady Watts
w/Jimmy Eaton

BLUE CHRISTMAS
m/Billy Hayes
w/Jay W. Johnson

BLUE COLLAR MAN
(Long Nights)
w&m/Tommy Shaw

BLUE EYES CRYING IN THE RAIN
w&m/Fred Rose

BLUE FLAME
w&m/Joe Bishop, Leo Corday,
Jimmy Noble

BLUE GRASS BREAKDOWN
(instr.)
m/William Smith Monroe

BLUE HAWAII
m/Ralph Rainger
w/Leo Robin

BLUE IS THE NIGHT
w&m/Fred Fisher

BLUE KENTUCKY GIRL
w&m/Johnny Mullins

BLUE LIGHT (instr.)
m/Duke Ellington

BLUE LIGHT BOOGIE
w&m/Jessie Mae Robinson,
Louis Jordan

BLUE LOU (instr.)
m/Edgar Melvin Sampson

BLUE MAX, THE (film score)
m/Jerry Goldsmith

BLUE MINOR (instr.)
m/Edgar Melvin Sampson

BLUE MODE (instr.)
m/Jay Jay Johnson

BLUE MONDAY
w&m/Antoine "Fats" Domino,
Dave Bartholomew

BLUE MONEY
w&m/Van Morrison

BLUE MONK (instr.)
m/Thelonious Sphere Monk

BLUE MOON
m/Richard Rodgers
w/Lorenz (Larry) Hart

BLUE MOON OF KENTUCKY
(instr.)
m/William Smith Monroe

BLUE ROOM
m/Richard Rodgers
w/Lorenz (Larry) Hart

BLUE ORCHIDS
w&m/Hoagy Carmichael

BLUE 'N 'BOOGIE (instr.)
m/Miles Dewey Davis

BLUE ON BLUE
m/Burt Bacharach
w/Hal David

BLUE PRELUDE
w&m/Gordon Jenkins, Joe Bishop

BLUE REVERIE (instr.)
m/Duke Ellington

BLUE SEPTEMBER
m/Peter DeRose
w/Mitchell Parish

BLUE SERGE (instr.)
m/Duke Ellington,
Mercer Ellington

BLUE 7 (instr.)
m/Sonny Rollins

BLUE SHADOWS
w&m/Joe Thomas, George Rhodes

BLUE SIDE OF LONESOME
w&m/Leon Payne

BLUE SKIES
w&m/Irving Berlin

BLUE SKIRT WALTZ
m/Vaclava Blacha
w/Mitchell Parish

BLUE SKY
w&m/Richard Betts

BLUE SPOON
w&m/Jimmy Witherspoon

BLUE STAR
m/Victor Young
w/Edward Heyman

BLUE STEEL BLUES
w&m/Ted Daffan

BLUE SUEDE SHOES
w&m/Carl Lee Perkins

BLUE TAIL FLY
(Jimmy, Crack Corn)
m/Daniel Decatur Emmett

BLUE TANGO
m/Leroy Anderson
w/Mitchell Parish

BLUE TRAIN (Of The Heartbreak Line)
w&m/John D. Loudermilk

BLUE TURNING GRAY OVER YOU
m/Thomas "Fats" Waller
w/Andy Razaf

BLUE VELVET
w&m/Lee Morris, Bernie Wayne

BLUE YODELS
w&m/Jimmy Rodgers

BLUEBERRY HILL
w&m/Larry Stock, Al Lewis,
Vincent Rose

BLUEBIRD
w&m/Leon Russell

BLUER THAN BLUE
w&m/Randy Goodrum

BLUES, THE (instr.)
m/Duke Ellington

BLUES AFTER HOURS
w&m/Jack Teagarden

BLUES BEFORE SUNRISE
w&m/Leroy Carr

BLUES CITY SHAKEDOWN
w&m/John Mayall

BLUES FOR JOHN (instr.)
m/Mary Lou Williams

BLUES HAD A BABY AND THEY NAMED IT ROCK AND ROLL
w&m/Muddy Waters,
Brownie McGhee

BLUES I LOVE TO SING, THE
m/Duke Ellington
w/Bob Miley

BLUES IN C SHARP MINOR
(instr.)
m/Theodore (Teddy) Wilson

BLUES IN THE DARK
w&m/James Andrew Rushing

BLUES IN THE NIGHT
m/Harold Arlen
w/Johnny Mercer

BLUES MINOR (instr.)
m/John Coltrane

BLUES MY NAUGHTY SWEETIE GIVES TO ME
w&m/Carey Morgan,
Charles McCarron

BLUES ON PARADE
w&m/Woody Herman, Toby Tyler

BLUES ON THE CEILING
w&m/Fred Neil

BLUES PETITE (instr.)
m/Charlie Shavers

BLUESETTE
m/Jean Thielemans
w/Norman Gimbel

BOB AND CAROL AND TED AND ALICE (film score)
m/Quincy Jones

BOB WHITE (Whatcha Gonna Swing Tonight)
w&m/Bernard D. Hanighen,
Johnny Mercer

BOB WILLS IS STILL THE KING
w&m/Waylon Jennings

BOBBY SOX BLUES
w&m/Dootsie Williams

BOBO, THE (film score)
m/Frances Lai

BODY AND SOUL
m/John Green
w/Edward Heyman, Robert Sour,
Frank Eyton

BOHEMIAN RHAPSODY
w&m/Brian May

BOLD AND THE BRAVE (film score)
m/Herschel Burke Gilbert

BOLD AS LOVE
w&m/Jimi Hendrix

BOLERO (instr.)
m/Maurice Ravel

BOLL WEEVIL
w&m/Antoine "Fats" Domino,
Dave Bartholomew

BOLL WEEVIL, THE
w&m/Huddie (Leadbelly) Ledbetter

BOLL WEEVIL SONG, THE
w&m/Brook Benton, Clyde Otis

BOMBER, THE
w&m/Joseph F. Walsh

BONANZA (TV theme)
w&m/Ray Evans,
Jay Harold Livingston

BONAPARTE'S RETREAT
w&m/Pee Wee King, Redd Stewart

BONEY FINGERS
w&m/Hoyt Axton, Renee Armand

BONJOUR TRISTESSE (film score)
m/Georges Auric

BONY MARONE
w&m/Larry Williams

BOO HOO
w&m/Edward Heyman, John Jacob
Loeb, Carmen Lombardo

BOOGIE CHILD
w&m/Barry, Maurice and Robin Gibb

BOOGIE CHILLEN'

w&m/John Lee Hooker

BOOGIE DOWN
w&m/Anita Poree, Jerry Eugene
Peters

BOOGIE FEVER
w&m/Frederick Perren,
Keni St. Lewis

BOOGIE NIGHTS
w&m/Rod Temperton

BOOGIE ON REGGAE WOMAN
w&m/Stevie Wonder

BOOGIE OOGIE OOGIE
w&m/Percy Kibble, Janice Johnson

BOOGIE SHOES
w&m/Harry Wayne Casey,
Richard Finch

BOOGIE WOOGIE BUGLE BOY
w&m/Hugh Denham Prince,
Don Raye

BOOGIE WOOGIE PRAYER (Cafe Society Swing & The Boogie Woogie)
w&m/Joe Turner, Albert C.
Ammons, Pete K.H. Johnson

BOOGIE WOOGIE STOMP (instr.)
m/Albert C. Ammons

BOOK OF LOVE
w&m/Warren Davis, George Malone,
Charles Patrick

BOOTBLACK, THE
w&m/David Braham

BOOTS OF SPANISH LEATHER
w&m/Robert Dylan

BOPLICITY (instr.)
m/Miles Dewey Davis

BOPPIN' THE BLUES
w&m/Carl Lee Perkins

BORDER SONG
m/Elton John
w/Bernie Taupin

BORN FREE
m/John Barry
w/Don Black

BORN ON THE BAYOU
w&m/John C. Fogerty

BORN TO BE BLUE
w&m/Mel Torme, Robert Wells

BORN TO BE TOGETHER
w&m/Barry Mann, Cynthia Weil,
Phil Spector

BORN TO BE WILD
w&m/John Kay, Michael Monarch,
Goldy McJohn

BORN TO RUN
w&m/Bruce Springsteen

BORN TOO LATE
w&m/Fred Tobias, Charles Strouse

BORROWED TIME
w&m/Dennis De Young, Tommy Sha

BOSS OF THE BLUES
w&m/Joe Turner, Pete K.H. Johnson

BOTH SIDES NOW
w&m/Joni Mitchell

BOTTLE OF WINE
w&m/Thomas R. Paxton

BOTTLE LET ME DOWN, THE
w&m/Merle Haggard

BOULDER TO BIRMINGHAM
w&m/Rodney Crowell,
Emmylou Harris

BOULEVARD OF BROKEN DREAMS
m/Harry Warren
w/Al Dubin

BOUND FOR GLORY
w&m/Woody Guthrie

BOUQUET OF ROSES
m/Steve Nelson
m/Bob Hilliard

BOWERY, THE
w&m/Percy Gaunt,
Charles H. Hoyt

BOXER, THE
w&m/Paul Simon

BOY FROM . . . THE
w&m/Stephen Sondheim

BOY MEETS HORN
m/Duke Ellington
w/Irving Mills

BOY NAMED SUE, A
w&m/Shel Silverstein

BOY NEXT DOOR, THE
w&m/Ralph Blane, Hugh Martin

BOY SCOUTS OF AMERICA (march)
m/Edwin Franko Goldman

BOY SCOUTS OF AMERCIA (march)
m/John Philip Sousa

BOYS ARE COMING HOME TODAY, THE
w&m/Paul Dresser

BOYS IN THE TREES
w&m/Carly Simon

BRAID THE RAVEN HAIR
m/Sir Arthur Sullivan
w/Sir William Schwenk
Gilbert

BRAND NEW KEY
w&m/Melanie

BRAND NEW ME
w&m/Jerry Butler, Kenneth Gamble,
Theresa Bell

BRAVE NEW WORLD
w&m/Steve Miller

BRAZIL
w&m/Bob Russell, Ary Barroso

BRAZIL (film score)
m/Walter Scharf

**BRAZILIAN SLEIGH BELLS
(instr.)**
m/Percy Faith

BRANDED MAN
w&m/Merle Haggard

BRASS IN POCKET
w&m/Chrissie Hyde, Pete Farndon

BREAK DOWN
w&m/Tom Petty

BREAK MY MIND
w&m/John D. Loudermilk

**BREAK THE NEWS TO
MOTHER**
w&m/Charles K. Harris

BREAK UP TO MAKE UP
w&m/Thomas Bell, Linda Creed,
Kenneth Gamble

BREAKDOWN DAYS
w&m/Alan Parsons, Eric Woolfson

**BREAKFAST AT TIFFANY'S
(film score)**
m/Henry Mancini

BREAKING AWAY (film score)
m/Pat Williams

**BREAKING IN A BRAND
NEW   BROKEN HEART**
w&m/Howard Greenfield,
Jack Keller

BREAKING UP IS HARD TO DO
w&m/Neil Sedaka,
Howard Greenfield

BREATHLESS
w&m/Otis Blackwell

**BREEZE (Blow My Baby Back
To Me)**
m/James F. Hanley
w/Ballad MacDonald

BREEZE AND I, THE
m/Ernesto Lecuona (based on
"Andalucia")
w/Al Stillman

**BREEZE FROM ALABAMA, A
(instr.)**
m/Scott Joplin

**BREEZIN' ALONG WITH THE
BREEZE**
m/Richard Whiting,
Seymour Simons
w/Haven Gillespie

BRIAN'S SONG (instr.)
m/Michel Legrand

BRIDGE OF SIGHS, THE
w&m/James Thornton

**BRIDGE OVER TROUBLED
WATER**
w&m/Paul Simon

**BRIGHTEN THE CORNER
WHERE YOU ARE**
m/Charles H. Gabriel Sr.
w/Ina Duley Ogdon

**BRIGHTLY DAWNS OUR
WEDDING DAY**
m/Sir Arthur Sullivan
w/Sir William Schwenk Gilbert

**BRING A LITTLE SUNSHINE
TO MY HEART**
w&m/Ben Raleigh, Mark Barkan

**BRING BACK THOSE
MINSTREL DAYS**
m/Martin Broones
w/Ballard MacDonald

**BRING BACK YOUR LOVE
TO ME**
w&m/Don Gibson

BRING IT ON HOME TO ME
w&m/Sam Cooke

BRINGING IT ALL BACK HOME
w&m/Robert Dylan

BROADWAY HOTEL
w&m/Al Stewart

BROADWAY MELODY
m/Nacio Herb Brown
w/Arthur Freed

BROKEN ARROW
w&m/Neil Young

BROKEN-HEARTED ME
w&m/Randy Goodrum

BROKEN HEARTED MELODY
m/Sherman Edwards
w/Hal David

BROKEN LADY
w&m/Larry Gatlin

BROKEN LANCE (film score)
w&m/Leigh Harline

BROKENHEARTED
w&m/William (Smokey)
Robinson, Jr.

BRONTOSAURUS
w&m/Roy Wood

BROOKLYN ROADS
w&m/Neil Diamond

BROTHER, BROTHER
w&m/Carole King

**BROTHER CAN YOU SPARE A
DIME**
w&m/Jay Gorney, E.Y. Harburg

BROTHER LOUIE
w&m/Errol Brown, Tony Wilson

**BROTHER LOVE'S TRAVELIN'
SALVATION SHOW**
w&m/Neil Diamond

BROTHER SUN, SISTER MOON
w&m/Donovan

BROTHER MAN
w&m/George Johnson, Dave Grusin,
Louis Johnson

BROTHERHOOD OF MAN
w&m/Frank Loesser

**BROTHERS AND OTHER
MOTHERS (instr.)**
m/Al Cohn

**BROTHERS KARAMAZOV
(film score)**
m/Bronislau Kaper

BROWN BIRD SINGING, A
m/Haydn Wood
w/Rayden Barrie

BROWN-EYED GIRL
w&m/Van Morrison

BROWN EYED WOMAN
w&m/Barry Mann, Cynthia Weil

**BROWN EYES WHY ARE YOU
BLUE**
m/George W. Meyer
w/Alfred Bryan

BROWN OCTOBER ALE
m/Reginald DeKoven
w/Harry B. Smith

BROWN SUGAR
w&m/Mick Jagger, Keith Richard

**BRUSH UP YOUR
SHAKESPEARE**
w&m/Cole Porter

BUCK PRIVATES (film score)
m/Charles Previn

BUCKLE DOWN WINSOCKI
w&m/Ralph Blane, Hugh Martin

BUDS WON'T BUD
m/Harold Arlen
w/E.Y. Harburg

BUENA SERA
w&m/Carl Sigman, Peter DeRose

BUENOS AIRES
m/Andrew Lloyd Webber
w/Tim Rice

BUENOS DIAS ARGENTINA
w&m/Ben Raleigh, V. Jurgens

BUFFALO GALS (Lubly Fan)
w&m/Cool White

BUGLE CALL RAG
w&m/Billy Meyers

BUHAINA'S DELIGHT
w&m/Freddie Hubbard

BUNNY HUG RAG (instr.)
m/George L. Cobb

BURN DOWN THE MISSION
m/Elton John
w/Bernie Taupin

BURNING MEMORIES
w&m/Mel Tillis, Wayne Walker

BURST IN WITH THE DAWN
w&m/Al Jarreau

BUS DRIVER
w&m/Muddy Waters,
Terry Abramson

BUSHEL AND A PECK, A
w&m/Frank Loesser

BUSTED
w&m/Harlan Howard

BUT BEAUTIFUL
m/James Van Heusen
w/Johnny Burke

BUT IN THE MORNING, NO
w&m/Cole Porter

BUT NOT FOR ME
m/George Gershwin
w/Ira Gershwin

BUTTERFIELD 8 (film score)
m/Bronislau Kaper

BUTTON UP YOUR OVERCOAT
m/Ray Henderson
w/Lew Brown, Buddy DeSylva

BUTTONS AND BOWS
w&m/Ray Evans,
Jay Harold Livingston

BUZZ ME
w&m/Fleecie Moore, Dick Adams

BY A MEADOW BROOK
w&m/Edward Alexander MacDowell

BY A WATERFALL
m/Sammy Fain
w/Irving Kahal

BY MYSELF
m/Arthur Schwartz
w/Howard Dietz

BY STRAUSS
m/George Gershwin
w/Ira Gershwin

BY THE BEAUTIFUL SEA
m/Harry Carroll
w/Harold Atteridge

BY THE BEND OF THE RIVER
w&m/Clara Edwards (pseud.
Bernard Haig)

BY THE FIRESIDE
w&m/Ray Noble

**BY THE LIGHT OF THE
SILVERY MOON**
m/Gus Edwards
w/Edward Madden

BY THE RIVER SAINTE MARIE
m/Harry Warren
w/Edgar Leslie

**BY THE TIME I GET TO
PHOENIX**
w&m/Jimmy Webb

BYE BYE BABY
m/Jule Styne
w/Leo Robin

BYE BYE BLACKBIRD
m/Ray Henderson
w/Mort Dixon

BYE BYE BLUES
w&m/Chauncey Gray, Fred Hamm,
Dave Bennett

BYE BYE BABY
m/Lou Handman
w/Walter Hirsch

BYE BYE LOVE
w&m/Boudleaux Bryant,
Felice Bryant

Addenda:

BACK SIDE OF THIRTY
w&m/John Conlee

BLUE COLLAR (film score)
m/Jack Nitzsche

**BLUES FOR BOUFFEMONT
(instr.)**
m/Bud Powell

BOSS WRITER, THE
w&m/Nicholas Ashford,
Valerie Simpson

BOULEVARD
w&m/Jackson Browne

BOUNCING WITH BUD (instr.)
m/Bud Powell

BRANNIGAN (film score)
m/Dominic Frontiere

BUD'S BUBBLE (instr.)
m/Bud Powell

BUSTIN' OUT
w&m/Rick James

BYRDLIKE (instr.)
m/Freddie Hubbard

 SONGS

C

C & D (instr.)
m/Ornette Coleman

C JAM BLUES (instr.)
m/Duke Ellington, Barney Bigard

CA, C'EST L'AMOUR
w&m/Cole Porter

CAB DRIVER
w&m/C. Carson Parks

CABALLA NEGRO (Black Horse)
w&m/Perez Prado

CABARET
m/John Kander
w/Fred Ebb

CABIN IN THE SKY
m/Vernon Duke
w/John Latouche

CACTUS FLOWER (film score)
m/Quincy Jones

CADILLAC WALK
w&m/John Moon Martin

CAFE
w&m/C.W. McCall

CAFE SOCIETY RAG
w&m/Joe Turner, Albert C.
Ammons, Pete K.H. Johnson

CAISSONS GO ROLLING
ALONG, THE (The Caisson Song)
w&m/Edmund L. Gruber

CAJUN BABY
w&m/Hank Williams Sr.,
Hank Williams Jr.,

CAKEWALK IN THE SKY, THE
w&m/Benjamin R. Harney

CALCUTTA
m/Lee Pockriss, Heino Gaze
w/Paul J. Vance

CALCUTTA CUTIE (instr.)
m/Morace Silver

CALDONIA
w&m/Fleecie Moore

CALENDAR GIRL
w&m/Neil Sedaka,
Howard Greenfield

CALIFORNIA
w&m/Robert Dylan

CALIFORNIA'S COTTON
FIELDS
w&m/Dallas Frazier

CALIFORNIA DREAMIN'
w&m/John Phillips, Michelle G.
Phillips

CALIFORNIA DAY
w&m/Bill Danoff, Kathy "Taffy"
Nivert Danoff

CALIFORNIA GIRLS
w&m/Brian Wilson

CALIFORNIA HERE I COME
w&m/Joseph Meyer, Buddy
DeSylva, Al Jolson

CALIFORNIA SOUL
w&m/Valerie Simpson, Nicholas
Ashford

CALL, THE
w&m/Gene MacClellan

CALL ME
w&m/Tony Hatch

CALL ME
w&m/Deborah Harry, Georgio
Moroder

CALL ME (Come Back Home)
w&m/Al Green, Al Jackson Jr.

CALL ME DARLING
m/German words and music: Bert
Reisfeld, Mort Fryberg, Rolf Marbet
w/English words: Dorothy Dick

CALL ME IRRESPONSIBLE
m/James Van Heusen
w/Sammy Cahn

CALL ME MADAM (film score)
m/Alfred Newman

CALL ME UP SOME RAINY
AFTERNOON
w&m/Irving Berlin

CALL OF THE CANYON
w&m/William J. (Billy) Hill

CALLING DR. LOVE
w&m/Gene Simmons

CALLING TO HER BOY JUST
ONCE AGAIN
w&m/Paul Dresser

CALYPSO
w&m/John Denver

CALYPSO MELODY
w&m/Larry Clinton

CAMEL HOP (instr.)
m/Mary Lou Williams

CAMELIA
w&m/Marty Robbins

CAMELOT
m/Frederick Loewe
w/Alan Jay Lerner

CAMELOT (film score)
m/Alfred Newman, Ken Darby

CAMPTOWN RACES
w&m/Stephen C. Foster

CAN ANYONE EXPLAIN
m/Bennie Benjamin
w/George Weiss

CAN BROADWAY DO
WITHOUT ME
w&m/Jimmy Durante

CAN I GET A WITNESS
w&m/Eddie Holland, Brian Holland,
Lamont Dozier

CAN I HELP IT
w&m/Brook Benton

CAN WE STILL BE FRIENDS
w&m/Todd Rundgren

CAN YOU FEEL IT
w&m/Bobby Goldsboro

CAN YOU FIND IT IN YOUR
HEART
m/Robert Allen
w/Al Stillman

CAN YOU PLEASE CRAWL OUT
YOUR WINDOW
w&m/Robert Dylan

CANADIAN BOAT SONG
m/from the French-Canadian
folk song "Dans Mon Chemin"
w/Thomas Moore

CANADIAN CAPERS
w&m/Gus Chandler, Bert White,
Henry Cohen

CANADIAN SUNSET
m/Eddie Heywood
w/Norman Gimbel

CANCEL THE FLOWERS
w&m/Sol Marcus, Edward Seiler,
Bennie Benjamin

CANDIDA
w&m/Irwin Levine, Toni Wine

CANDLE IN THE WIND
m/Elton John
w/Bernie Taupin

CANDLE ON THE WATER
w&m/Al Kasha, Joel Hirshhorn

CANDY
w&m/Joan Whitney, Alex Kramer,
Mack Davis

CANDY AND CAKE
w&m/Bob Merrill

CANDY KID, THE
w&m/Tony Romeo

CANDY KISSES
w&m/George Morgan

CANDY MAN
w&m/Leslie Bricusse,
Anthony Newley

CANNONBALL
w&m/Duane Eddy

CAN'T BUY A THRILL
w&m/Donald Fagen, Walter Becker

CAN'T BUY ME LOVE
w&m/Paul McCartney, John Lennon

CAN'T FIND MY WAY HOME
w&m/Stevie Winwood

CAN'T GET ENOUGH OF YOUR LOVE
w&m/Paul Rodgers, Simon F. Kirke

CAN'T GET ENOUGH OF YOUR LOVE, BABE
w&m/Barry White

CAN'T GET INDIANA OFF MY MIND
m/Hoagy Carmichael
w/Robert DeLeon

CAN'T GET IT OUT OF MY HEAD
w&m/Jeff Lynne

CAN'T GET OUT OF THIS MOOD
m/Jimmy McHugh
w/Frank Loesser

CAN'T GET USED TO LOSING YOU
w&m/Mort Shuman, Doc (Jerome) Pomus

CAN'T HELP BUT CRYING SOMETIMES
w&m/Joshua D. White

CAN'T HELP FALLING IN LOVE
w&m/Hugo Peretti, Luigi Creatore, George Weiss

CAN'T HELP LOVIN' DAT MAN OF MINE
m/Jerome Kern
w/Oscar Hammerstein II

CAN'T LET HER GO
w&m/Freddie Hubbard

CAN'T PUT A PRICE ON LOVE
w&m/Doug Fieger, Berton Averre

CAN'T STOP DANCING
w&m/Ray Stevens, John

CAN'T TAKE MY EYES OFF OF YOU
w&m/Bob Crewe, Bob Gaudio

CAN'T WAIT NO LONGER
w&m/Michael Bloomfield

CAN'T WE BE FRIENDS
m/Kay Swift
w/Paul James (James P. Warburg)

CAN'T WE GET TOGETHER
m/Thomas "Fats" Waller, Harry Brooks
w/Andy Razaf

CAN'T WE TALK IT OVER
m/Victor Young
w/Ned Washington

CAN'T YO' HEAH ME CALLIN' CAROLINE
m/Caro Roma
w/William H. Gardner

CANTELOUPE ISLAND
w&m/Herbie Hancock

CANTERBURY TALE, A (film score)
m/Allan Gray

CANTINA BLUE
w&m/Sol Lake

CAPE VERDEAN BLUES (instr.)
m/Horace Silver

CAPRICE RAG (instr.)
m/James P. Johnson

CAPRICE VIENNOIS (instr.)
m/Fritz Kreisler

CAPRICORN ONE (film score)
m/Jerry Goldsmith

CAPTAIN BLOOD (film score)
m/Erich Wolfgang Korngold

CAPTAIN FROM CASTILE (film score)
m/Alfred Newman

CAPTAIN JACK
w&m/Billy Joel

CAPTURED ANGEL
w&m/Dan Fogelberg

CARAVAN
w&m/Irving Mills, Duke Ellington Juan Tizol

CAREFULLY ON TIPTOE STEALING
m/Sir Arthur Sullivan
w/Sir William Schwenk Gilbert

CAREFULLY TAUGHT (You Have To Be)
m/Richard Rodgers
w/Oscar Hammerstein II

CARELESS
w&m/Dick Jurgens, Eddy Howard, Lew Quadling

CARELESS HANDS
w&m/Carl Sigman, Bob Hilliard

CARELESS KISSES
w&m/Tim Spencer

CAREY
w&m/Joni Mitchell

CARIBOU
m/Elton John
w/Bernie Taupin

CARIOCA, THE
m/Vincent Youmans
w/Edward Eliscu, Gus Kahn

CARISSIMA
w&m/Arthur A. Penn

CARMELITA
w&m/Warren Zevon

CARNIVAL PARADE (La Comparsa)
m/Ernesto Lecuona
w/Albert Gamse

CAROL OF THE BELLS
m/M. Leontovich
w/Peter J. Wilhousky

CAROL OF THE BIRDS
w&m/John Jacob Niles

CAROL
w&m/Al Stewart

CAROLINA IN MY MIND
w&m/James Taylor

CAROLINA IN THE MORNING
m/Walter Donaldson
w/Gus Kahn

CAROLINA MOON
m/Joseph Burke
w/Benny Davis

CAROLINA SHOUT (instr.)
w&m/James P. Johnson

CAROLINE
w&m/Brian Wilson

CARPET MAN
w&m/Jimmy Webb

CARRIAGE TRADE (instr.)
m/Richard Hayman

CARRIE
w&m/Albert Von Tilzer, Junie McCree

CARRY ME BACK TO OLD VIRGINNY (There's Where)
w&m/James A. Bland

CARRY ME BACK TO OLD VIRGINNY (De Floating Scow)
w&m/Charles T. White

CARRY ME BACK TO THE LONE PRAIRIE
w&m/Carson J. Robison

CARRY ME BACK TO THE SWEET SUNNY SOUTH
w&m/John Hill Hewitt

CARRY ON
w&m/Stephen Stills

CARRY ON WAYWARD SON
w&m/Steve Walsh, Kerry Livgren, Phillip Ehart, Robert Steinhardt, David Hope, Richard Williams

CASA MANANA
w&m/Cindy Walker

CASABLANCA(film score)
m/Max Steiner

CASCADES, THE (instr.)
m/Scott Joplin

CASEY JONES
m/Eddie Newton
w/T. Laurence Siebert

CASPER THE FRIENDLY GHOST
m/Jerry Livingston
w/Mack David

CAST A GIANT SHADOW (film score)
m/Elmer Bernstein

CAST YOUR FATE TO THE WIND
w&m/Vince Guaraldi, Carel Werber

CASTLE IN THE SAND
m/Alfred Newman
w/Ralph Blane

CASTLE OF DREAMS
m/Harry A. Tierney (adapted from Chopin's "Minute Waltz")
w/Joseph McCarthy

CASTLE ROCK
w&m/Ervin M. Drake, Jimmy Shirl

CASTLE WALLS
w&m/Dennis De Young

CAT, THE (instr.)
m/Lalo Schifrin

CAT BALLOU
m/Jerry Livingston
w/Mack David

CAT BALLOU (film score)
m/Frank De Vol

CATCH A FALLING STAR
m/Lee Pockriss
w/Paul J. Vance

CATCH THE WIND
w&m/Donovan

CATHEDRAL
w&m/Graham Nash

CATHY'S CLOWN
w&m/Don Everly, Phil Everly

CAT'S IN THE CRADLE, THE
w&m/Harry Chapin

CATTLE CALL
w&m/D.H. (Tex) Owens

CAUGHT IN A DREAM
w&m/Michael Bruce

C. C. RIDER
w&m/Chuck Willis
(Adapted from early American folk music, source unknown)

CECELIA
m/Dave Dreyer
w/Herman Ruby

CECILIA
w&m/Paul Simon

CECIL'S BOOGIE
w&m/Cecil Gant

CELEBRATE ME HOME
w&m/Kenneth Loggins

CENTURY CITY
w&m/Tom Petty

CERTAIN SMILE, A
m/Sammy Fain
w/Paul Francis Webster

CERVEZA (instr.)
m/Shorty Rogers

C'EST LA VIE
w&m/Gregory Lake

C'EST MAGNIFIQUE
w&m/Cole Porter

C'EST SI BON
m/Henri Betti
w/Jerry Seelen

CHAIN
w&m/Stephanie (Stevie) Nicks, Lindsay Buckingham, Christine P. McVie

CHAIN GANG
w&m/Sam Cooke

CHAIN GANG BLUES
w&m/Thomas Andrew Dorsey

CHAIN OF FOOLS
w&m/Don Covay

CHAINS
w&m/Carole King, Gerry Goffin

CHAINS OF LOVE
w&m/Ahmet Ertegun, Van Wells

CHAIR, THE
w&m/Marty Robbins

CHAMELEON
w&m/Herbie Hancock

CHAMPAGNE WALTZ, THE
m/Con Conrad, Ben Oakland
w/Milton Drake

CHANCES ARE
m/Robert Allen
w/Al Stillman

CHANGE OF HEART
w&m/Eric Carmen

CHANGE OF HEART
m/Jule Styne
w/Harold Adamson

CHANGE PARTNERS
w&m/Irving Berlin

CHANGES
w&m/David Bowie

CHANGES IN LATITUDES, CHANGES IN ATTITUDES
w&m/Jimmy Buffett

CHANGING PARTNERS
m/Larry Coleman
w/Joseph Darion

CHANGING TIMES
w&m/Rev. James Cleveland

CHANSON D'AMOUR
w&m/Wayne Shanklin

CHANT, THE (instr.)
m/Ferdinand "Jelly Roll" Morton

CHANTEZ, CHANTEZ
m/Irving Fields
w/Albert Gamse

CHANTICLEER RAG, THE
m/Albert Gumble
w/Edward Madden

CHANTILLY LACE
w&m/J.P. Richardson (Big Bopper)

CHAPEL IN THE MOONLIGHT
w&m/Jeff Barry, Ellie Greenwich

CHAPEL OF THE ROSES
w&m/Abel Baer

CHAPTER TWO (film score)
m/Marvin Hamlisch

CHARADE
m/Henry Mancini
w/Johnny Mercer

CHARADE (film score)
m/Henry Mancini

CHARGE OF THE LIGHT BRIGADE, THE (film score)
m/John Addison

CHARLESTON
w&m/James P. Johnson, Cecil Mack (a/k/a Richard C. McPherson)

CHARLEY MY BOY
m/Ted Fiorito
w/Gus Kahn

CHARLIE
w&m/Tompall Glaser

CHARMAINE
w&m/Lew Pollack, Erno Rapee

CHASE, THE (instr.)
m/Dexter Gordon, Wardell Gray

CHASE, THE (instr.)
m/Tadd Dameron

CHASING THE SUN
w&m/Rod McKuen

CHATTANOOGA CHOO CHOO
m/Harry Warren
w/Mack Gordon

CHATTERBOX
w&m/Jerome Brainin, Allan Roberts

CHATTERBOX (instr.)
m/Duke Ellington

CHATTANOOGIE SHOE SHINE
BOY
w&m/Jack Stapp, Harry Stone

CHEATER'S KIT
w&m/Rory Bourke

CHEATIN' ON ME
w&m/Lew Pollack, Jack Yellen

CHEEK TO CHEEK
w&m/Irving Berlin

CHEERFUL LITTLE EARFUL
m/Harry Warren
w/Ira Gershwin, Billy Rose

CHEESEBURGER IN
PARADISE
w&m/Jimmy Buffett

CHELSEA BRIDGE
w&m/Billy Strayhorn

CHELSEA MORNING
w&m/Joni Mitchell

CHERIE, I LOVE YOU
w&m/Lillian Rosedale Goodman

CHERISH
w&m/Terry Kirkman

CHEROKEE
w&m/Ray Noble

CHERRY
w&m/Don Redman, Ray Gilbert

CHERRY CHERRY
w&m/Neil Diamond

CHERRY PINK AND APPLE
BLOSSOM WHITE
m/Louiguy
w/Mack David

CHEST FEVER
w&m/J. Robbie Robertson

CHESTNUT VALLEY RAG
(instr.)
w&m/Trevor Jay Tichenor

CHESTER (Let Tyrants Shake
Their Iron Rod)
w&m/William Billings

CHEYENNE
m/Egbert Anson Van Alstyne
w/Harry H. Williams

CHIAPENECAS (Hand Clapping
Song, THE
m/M. V. De Campo
w/Albert Gamse (best known
English version)

CHI BABA, CHI BABA
m/Jerry Livingston, Al Hoffman
w/Mack David

CHICA CHICA BOOM CHIC
m/Harry Warren
w/Mack Gordon

CHICAGO
w&m/Graham Nash

CHICAGO (That Toddling Town)
w&m/Fred Fisher

CHICAGO BREAKDOWN
(instr.)
m/Ferdinand "Jerry Roll" Morton

CHICK-A-BOOM
w&m/Richard Monda

CHICKEN REEL
m/Leroy Anderson

CHICKERY CHICK
m/Sidney Lippman
w/Sylvia Dee

CHICO AND THE MAN
(TV Theme)
m/Jose Feliciano

CHILD OF MINE
w&m/Carole King, Gerry Goffin

CHILD OF OUR TIMES
w&m/P. F. Sloan

CHILDREN OF THE NIGHT
(instr.)
m/Wayne Shorter

CHILDREN OF SANCHEZ
(instr.)
m/Chuck Mangione

CHILI BEAN
w&m/Albert Von Tilzer, Lew Brown

CHIM CHIM CHEREE
w&m/Richard M. Sherman, Robert
B. Sherman

CHIME BELLS
w&m/Elton Britt

CHIMES BLUES
w&m/Charles Edward Davenport

CHINA DOLL (instr.)
m/Leroy Anderson

CHINA GROVE
w&m/Thomas Johnston

CHINATOWN MY CHINATOWN
m/Jean Schwartz
w/William Jerome

CHIN-CHIN
m/Ivan Caryll
w/Harry Morton

CHINESE LULLABY
w&m/Robert Hood Bowers

CHIPMUNK SONG, THE
w&m/Ross Bagdasarian

CHIQUITA
m/Benny Andersson, Bjorn Ulvaeus
w/Stig Anderson

CHIQUITA BANANA
w&m/Leonard MacKenzie Jr.,
William Wirges, Garth Montgomery

CHITTY CHITTY BANG BANG
w&m/Richard M. Sherman, Robert
B. Sherman

CHLO-E
w&m/Charles Neil Daniels,
Richard Whiting

CHLOE (I've Got To Go Where
You Are)
m/Neil Moret
w/Gus Kahn

CHOKIN' KING, THE
w&m/Harlan Howard

CHOO CHOO CH'BOOGIE
w&m/Milton Gabler, Vaughn
Horton, Denver Darling

CHOO CHOO MAMA
w&m/Alvin Lee

CHOPIN'S WILLOWS (instr.)
w/Adam Makowicz

CHRIST THE REDEEMER
w&m/James (Reverend) Cleveland

CHRISTINE SIXTEEN
w&m/Gene Simmons

CHRISTMAS IN KILLARNEY
m/John Redmond, Frank Weldon
w/James Cavanaugh

CHRISTMAS SONG, THE
w&m/Robert Wells, Mel Torme

CHRYSANTHEMUM, THE
(instr.)
m/Scott Joplin

CHUCK E'S IN LOVE
w&m/Rickie Lee Jones

CHUG-A-LUG
w&m/Roger Miller

CIELITO LINDO (Ay,Ay,Ay,Ay
Cantay No Llores)
w&m/Carlos Fernandez

CIAO CIAO BAMBINO
m/M. Modugno
w/Mitchell Parish

CIGARETTES, WHISKEY AND
WILD, WILD WOMEN
w&m/Tim Spencer

CIMARRON
w&m/Johnny Bond

CINCINNATI LOU
w&m/Merle Travis, Shug Fisher

CINCINNATI OHIO
w&m/Bill Anderson

CINDERELLA LIBERTY
(film score)
m/John Williams

CINDERELLA ROCKEFELLA
m/Mason Williams
w/Nancy Ames

CINNAMON
w&m/Johnny Cymbal

CINNAMON GIRL
w&m/Neil Young

CIRCLE GAME, THE
w&m/Joni Mitchell

CIRCLES
w&m/Alvin Lee

CIRIBIRIBIN
m/A. Pestalozza
w/Rudolf Thaler

CISCO KID, THE
w&m/see composer listing under
Lee Oskar

CITIZEN KANE (film score)
m/Bernard Herrman

CITY CALLED HEAVEN
w&m/Bob Warren

CITY GIRL
w&m/Michael Bloomfield

CITY LIGHTS
w&m/Bill Anderson

**CIVILIZATION
(Bongo, Bongo,Bongo)**
m/Carl Sigman
w/Bob Hilliard

CLAIR
m/Sir Arthur Sullivan
w/Sir William Schwenk Gilbert

**CLANCY LOWERED
THE BOOM**
w&m/Johnny Lange, Walter H.
(Hy) Heath

**CLAP HANDS HERE COMES
CHARLEY**
m/Joseph Meyer,
Ballard MacDonald
w/Billy Rose

CLAP YO' HANDS
m/George Gershwin
w/Ira Gershwin

CLARINET LAMENT
m/Duke Ellington

**CLARINET MARMALADE
(instr.)**
m/Ferdinand "Jelly Roll" Morton,
Leon Rappolo, Paul Mares,
Nick LaRocca, Larry Shields

CLASS OF '57
w&m/Harold W. Reid, Don Reid

CLASSICAL GAS
m/Mason Williams

CLAUDETTE
w&m/Roy Orbison, Joe Melson

CLEAN UP WOMAN
w&m/Clarence Reid,
Willis Clarke

CLEAR OUT OF THIS WORLD
m/Jimmy McHugh
w/Al Dubin

CLIMAX RAG (instr.)
m/James S. Scott

CLIMB EV'RY MOUNTAIN
m/Richard Rodgers
w/Oscar Hammerstein II

**CLIMBING OVER ROCK
MOUNTAIN**
m/Sir Arthur Sullivan
w/Sir William Schwenk Gilbert

CLOG DANCE(instr.)
m/Percy Aldridge Grainger

CLOSE AS PAGES IN A BOOK
m/Sigmund Romberg
w/Dorothy Fields

CLOSE DEM WINDOWS
w&m/James A. Bland

**CLOSE ENCOUNTERS OF
THE THIRD KIND (film score)**
m/John Williams

**CLOSE ENCOUNTERS OF
THE THIRD KIND (Theme)**
m/John Williams

CLOSE SHAVE (instr.)
m/Charlie Shavers, John Kirby

CLOSE TO YOU
m/Jerry Livingston
w/Al Hoffman

**(They Long To Be) CLOSE TO
YOU**
m/Burt Bacharach
w/Hal David

CLOUDY (instr.)
m/Mary Lou Williams

C'MON EVERYBODY
m/Jerry Capehart,
Eddie Cochran

CO CO
m/Mike Chapman, Nicky Chinn

COAL MINER'S DAUGHTER
w&m/Loretta Lynn

COAL TATOO
w&m/Billy Edd Wheeler

COAT OF MANY COLORS
w&m/Dolly Parton

COAX ME A LITTLE BIT
w&m/Nat Simon, Charles Tobias

**(Stay Away From) COCAINE
TRAIN, THE**
w&m/Johnny Paycheck

COCKEYED OPTIMIST, A
m/Richard Rodgers
w/Oscar Hammerstein II

COCKTAILS FOR TWO
m/Arthur Johnston
w/Sam Coslow

**COCKEYED MAYOR OF
KAUNAKAUKAI, THE**
w&m/Alex R. Anderson

**COCKLESHELL HEROES,
THE (film score)**
m/John Addison

COCONUT
w&m/Harry Edward Nilsson

COFFEE SONG, THE
m/Richard Miles
w/Bob Hilliard

COLD AS ICE
w&m/Mike Jones, Ian Richard
McDonald

COLD HIGHWAY
m/Elton John
w/Bernie Taupin

COLD MORNING LIGHT
w&m/Todd Rundgren

COLD RAIN
w&m/Graham Nash

COLD SWEAT
w&m/James Brown, Alfred Ellis

COLD TURKEY
w&m/John Lennon, Yoko Ono

COLLECTOR, THE (film score)
m/Maurice Jarre

COLLEGE RHYTHM
m/Harry Revel
w/Mack Gordon

COLLEGIATE
w&m/Lew Brown,
Nathan J. Bonx,
Moe Jaffe

**COLLINS' BODY LIES IN
SOUND CAVE**
w&m/Joshua D. White

COLOMBIA
w&m/William Billings

COLOR HIM FATHER
w&m/Richard Spencer

**COLARADO (Have You Ever
Been Down To)**
w&m/Merle Haggard

COLORADO BLUES
w&m/Euday Louis Bowman

COLORS
w&m/Donovan

COLOUR MY WORLD
w&m/James Pankow

COLUMBIA, THE GEM OF THE OCEAN
w&m/Thomas a Becket

COMA (film score)
m/Jerry Goldsmith

COMANCHE (film score)
m/Herschel Burke Gilbert

COME A LITTLE BIT CLOSER
w&m/Tommy Boyce, Bobby Hart, Wes Farrell

COME ALONG MY MANDY
w&m/Jack Norworth, Nora Bayes,Tom Mellor, Alfred J. Lawrence, Harry Gilford

COME ALONG WITH ME
w&m/Cole Porter

COME AND DREAM ALONG
w&m/Natalie Cole

COME AND GET IT
w&m/Peter Ham, Thomas Evans

COME BACK, BABY
w&m/Ray Charles

COME BACK HOME
w&m/Bobby Goldsboro

COME BACK TO ME
m/Burton Lane
w/Alan Jay Lerner

COME BACK TO US BARBARA LEWIS HARE KRISHNA BEAUREGARD
w&m/John Prine

COME BLOW YOUR HORN
m/James Van Heusen
w/Sammy Cahn

COME BACK MY HONEY BOY
m/John Stromberg
w/Edgar Smith

COME CLOSER TO ME
w&m/Al Stewart, Osvaldo Farres

COME DOWN, MA EVENIN' STAR
m/John Stromberg
w/Robert B. Smith

COME FLY WITH ME
m/James Van Heusen
w/Sammy Cahn

COME FOLLOW-FOLLOW ME
m/Fred Karlin
w/Tylwyth Kymry

COME GONE (instr.)
m/Sonny Rollins

COME HOME DEWEY WE WON'T DO A THING TO YOU
w&m/Paul Dresser

COME HOME FATHER
w&m/Henry Clay Work

COME IN OUT OF THE RAIN
w&m/Melissa Manchester, Carole Bayer Sager

COME INTO MY HEART
w&m/Lloyd Price, Harold Logan

COME INTO MY LIFE
w&m/Jimmy Cliff
(James Chambers)

COME INTO THE GARDEN MAUDE
m/Sir Michael W. Balfe
w/Alfred Lord Tennyson

COME JOSEPHINE IN MY FLYING MACHINE
m/Fred Fisher
w/Alfred Bryan

COME LIVE WITH ME
w&m/Boudleaux Bryant, Felice Bryant

COME LIVE YOUR LIFE WITH ME
w&m/Wilbur(Billy) Meshel, Nino Rota, Larry Kusik

COME MONDAY
w&m/Jimmy Buffett

COME NESTLE IN MY ARMS
m/Victor Jacobi
w/Adrian Ross, Arthur Anderson

COME ON, BABY
w&m/Ellas McDaniel
(Bo Diddley)

COME ON DOWN TO MY BOAT
w&m/Lary Larden, Dennis Larden

COME ON, LET'S GO
w&m/Richie Valens

COME PRIMA (For The Last Time)
w&m/Buck Ram, M. Panzeri

COME RAIN OR COME SHINE
m/Harold Arlen
w/Johnny Mercer

COME RUNNING
w&m/Van Morrison

COME SATURDAY MORNING
m/Fred Karlin
w/Dory Langdon Previn

COME SEE ABOUT ME
w&m/Eddie Holland, Brian Holland. Lamont Dozier

COME SILVER MOON
w&m/Charles A. White

COME SOFTLY TO ME
w&m/Gary R. Troxel, Barbara L. Ellis, Gretchen D. Christopher

COME STAY WITH ME
w&m/Jackie De Shannon

COME SUNDAY (instr.)
m/Duke Ellington

COME SUNDOWN
w&m/Kris Kristofferson

COME TELL ME WHAT'S YOUR ANSWER, YET OR NO
w&m/ Paul Dresser

COME ON UP
w&m/Felix Cavaliere

COME TO ME
m/Henry Mancini
w/Don Black

COME TO THE MARDI GRAS
w&m/Ervin M. Drake, Jimmy Shirl, Max Bulhões, Milton de Oliveira

COME TOGETHER, OH DARLING
w&m/Paul McCartney, John Lennon

COME UNTO ME, YE WEARY
m/Lowell Mason
w/Catherine H. Watterman

COME WITH ME
w&m/Waylon Jennings, C. Howard

COME ON-A MY HOUSE
w&m/Ross Bagdasarian, William Saroyan

COME ON OVER
w&m/Barry, Maurice, Robin Gibb

COME TO ME, BEND TO ME
m/Frederick Loewe
w/Alan Jay Lerner

COME UP AND SEE ME SOMETIME
m/Louis Alter
w/Arthur Swanstrom

COME WHERE MY LOVE LIES DREAMING
w&m/Stephen C. Foster

COMEDY TONIGHT
w&m/Stephen Sondheim

COMES ONCE IN A LIFETIME
m/Betty Comden, Adolph Green
w/Jule Styne

COMIC, THE (film score)
m/John M. Elliott

COMIN' HOME BABY (instr.)
m/Herbie Mann

COMIN' IN ON A WING AND A PRAYER
m/Jimmy McHugh
w/Harold Adamson

COMIN' INTO LOS ANGELES
w&m/Arlo Guthrie

COMIN' THRO' THE RYE
m/from an old Scottish air,
source unknown
w/Robert Burns

COMING OF THE ROADS
w&m/Billy Edd Wheeler

COMME SI, COMME SA
w&m/Alex Kramer, Joan Whitney

COMMOTION
w&m/John C. Fogerty

COMPANY
w&m/Stephen Sondheim

CONCENTRATE
m/Alfred Newman
w/Otto Harbach

CONCENTRATIN' ON YOU
m/Thomas "Fats" Waller
w/Andy Razaf

CONCERTO FOR COOTIE (instr.)
m/Duke Ellington

CONCERTO GROSSO (instr.)
m/Herbie Mann

CONCORDE (instr.)
m/John Lewis

CONCRETE JUNGLE, THE (film score)
m/John Dankworth

CONDEMNED WITHOUT TRIAL
w&m/Hal Blair, Don Robertson

CONFESS
m/Bennie Benjamin
w/George D. Weiss

CONFIRMATION (instr.)
m/Charlie Parker

CONFUSION
w&m/Jeff Lynne

CONGENIALITY (instr.)
m/Ornette Coleman

CONGO
w&m/Ellas McDaniel
(Bo Diddley)

CONNECTICUT
w&m/Ralph Blane, Hugh Martin

CONSIDER YOURSELF
w&m/Lionel Bart

CONSOLATION
m/Theodore F. Morse
w/Edward Madden

CONSTANT RAIN
w&m/Sergio Mendes

CONSTANTINOPLE
w&m/Harry Carlton

CONSTANTLY
m/Bert Williams
w/Chris Smith, James Henry Burris

CONSTELLATION (instr.)
m/Charlie Parker

CONTENTED
m/Don Bestor
w/Roy Turk

CONTINENTAL, THE
m/Herbert Magidson
w/Con Conrad

CONVICT AND THE BIRD, THE
w&m/Paul Dresser

COOL
m/Leonard Bernstein
w/Stephen Sondheim

COOL CHANGE
w&m/Glen Shorrock

COOL HAND LUKE (film score)
m/Lalo Schifrin

COOL WATER
w&m/Bob Nolan

COOP DE GRAAS (instr.)
m/Shorty Rogers

COPACABANA
w&m/Barry Manilow, Bruce Springsteen, Jack Feldman, Hector Garredo

COPENHAGEN
w&m/Walter Melrose, Charlie Davis

COPPER BROWN
w&m/Muddy Waters, Marva Brooks

COPPER COLORED GAL
m/J. Fred Coots
w/Benny Davis

COQUETTE
w&m/Carmen Lombardo, John Green, Gus Kahn

CORAL REEF(instr.)
m/Neal Hefti

CORAZON
w&m/Carole King

CORNER OF MY LIFE, THE
w&m/Bill Anderson

CORPS, THE (West Point Hymn)
w&m/W. Franke Harling

CORRINA, CORRINA
w&m/Robert Dylan

CORTEZ THE KILLER
w&m/Neil Young

COSI COSA
m/Bronislau Kaper
w/Ned Washington, Walter Jurmann

COSMIC CHAOS (instr.)
m/Sun Ra

COSMIC WHEEL
w&m/Donovan

COSSACK LOVE SONG, THE
m/Herbert Stothart
w/Oscar Hammerstein II, Otto Harbach

COST OF LOVE
w&m/Mark Goldenberg

COTTON CANDY
w&m/Frederick Perren, Keni St. Lewis

COTTON COMES TO HARLEM (film score)
m/Galt MacDermot

COTTON FIELDS
w&m/Huddie (Leadbelly) Ledbetter

COTTON TAIL RAG
w&m/Joseph Francis Lamb

COTTONTAIL (instr.)
m/Duke Ellington

COULD IT BE MAGIC
w&m/Barry Manilow, Adrienne Anderson (music adapted from Chopin's "Prelude in C Minor")

COULD IT BE YOU
w&m/Cole Porter

COULDN'T I JUST TELL YOU
w&m/Todd Rundgren

COUNT EVERY STAR
m/Bruno Coquatrix
w/Sammy Gallop

COUNT YOUR BLESSINGS
w&m/Irving Berlin

COUNTIN' THE BLUES
w&m/Gertrude "Ma" Rainey

COUNTRY BOY
w&m/Boudleaux Bryant, Felice Bryant

COUNTRY BOY BLUES
w&m/"Big Bill" Broonzy

COUNTRY BOY, YOU GOT
YOUR FEET IN L.A.
w&m/Dennis Lambert,
Brian Potter

COUNTRY BUMPKIN
w&m/Don Wayne

COUNTRY CLUB (instr.)
m/Scott Joplin

COUNTRY COMFORT
m/Elton John
w/Bernie Taupin

COUNTRY GARDENS (instr.)
m/Percy Aldridge Grainger

COUNTRY GIRL
w&m/Neil Young

COUNTRY GIRL-CITY MAN
w&m/Billy Vera, Judy Clay

COUNTRY IS
w&m/Tom T. Hall

COUPLE MORE YEARS
w&m/Shel Silverstein

COUNTRY MUSIC IS HERE TO
STAY
w&m/Ferlin Husky

COUNTRY PIE
w&m/Robert Dylan

COUNTRY ROAD
w&m/James Taylor

COUNTRY SUNSHINE
w&m/Dottie West, Bill Davis

COUNTY FAIR
w&m/Robert Wells, Mel Torme

COUPLE OF SWELLS, A
w&m/Irving Berlin

COURT AND SPARK
w&m/Joni Mitchell

COUSIN KEVIN
w&m/John Entwhistle

COVER OF THE ROLLING
STONE
w&m/Shel Silverstein

COWARD OF THE COUNTY
w&m/Roger Bowling, Billy Edd
Wheeler

COWBOY AND THE LADY,
THE (film score)
m/Alfred Newman

COW COW BLUES
w&m/Charles Edward Davenport

COW COW BOOGIE
w&m/Charles Edward Davenport

COW COW BOOGIE
w&m/Don Raye, Gene De Paul,
Benny Carter

COWBOY HAS TO SING, A
w&m/Bob Dolan

COWOY IN THE
CONTINENTAL SUIT, THE
w&m/Marty Robbins

COWBOYS TO GIRLS
w&m/Kenneth Gamble,
Leon Huff

COWBOY'S WORK IS NEVER
DONE, A
w&m/Sonny Bono, Cher
Cherilyn S. LaPierre)

COWGIRL IN THE SAND
w&m/Neil Young

COYOTE
w&m/Joni Mitchell

CRACKERBOX PALACE
w&m/George Harrison

CRACKIN' UP
w&m/Ellas McDaniel
(Bo Diddley)

CRACKLIN' ROSIE
w&m/Neil Diamond

CRAWFISH
w&m/Sol Lake

CRAWLIN'
w&m/Rudolph Toombs

CRAWLIN' KING SNAKE
w&m/John Lee Hooker

CRAZY
w&m/Willie Nelson

CRAZY
w&m/Cat Stevens

CRAZY ARMS
w&m/Ralph Mooney,
Charles Seals

CRAZY BLUES
w&m/Perry Bradford

CRAZY CRAZY BABY
w&m/Freddy Fender

CRAZY HE CALLS ME
w&m/Bob Russell, Carl Sigman

CRAZY FEELING
w&m/Carl Douglas

CRAZY HEART
w&m/Fred Rose,
Maurice Murray

CRAZY JANE
m/John Dary, G. Gilbert
w/Matthew G. Lewis

CRAZY LEGS
w&m/Jerry Reed

CRAZY LITTLE THING
CALLED LOVE
w&m/Freddie Mercury

CRAZY ON YOU
w&m/Ann Wilson, Nancy Wilson,
Roger Fisher

CRAZY RHYTHM
m/Roger Wolfe Kahn,
Joseph Meyer
w/Irving Caesar

CRAZY WATER
m/Elton John
w/Bernie Taupin

CRAZY WILD DESIRE
w&m/Webb Pierce, Mel Tillis

CREEQUE ALLEY
w&m/John Phillips, Michelle G.
Phillips

CREPUSCULE (instr.)
m/Django Reinhardt

CRIME AND PUNISHMENT
(film score)
m/Herschel Burke Gilbert

CRIMSON AND CLOVER
w&m/Tommy James, Bob King

CRIMINAL CHILD, THE
m/Sir Arthur Sullivan
w/Sir William Schwenk Gilbert

CRINOLINE DAYS
w&m/Irving Berlin

CRISS CROSS (instr.)
m/Thelonious Sphere Monk

CROCODILE ROCK
m/Elton John
w/Bernie Taupin

CROSS BREEDING (instr.)
m/Ornette Coleman

CROSS EYED CAT
w&m/Muddy Waters

CROSS EYED MARY
w&m/Ian Anderson

CROSS OVER THE BRIDGE
m/Benny Benjamin
w/George D. Weiss

CROSS YOUR FINGERS
m/J. Fred Coots
w/Benny Davis,
Arthur Swanstrom

CROSSTOWN
w&m/Nat Simon, John Redmond

CRUISIN'
w&m/William (Smokey)Robinson Jr
in co w/Marvin Tarplin

CRUISING DOWN THE RIVER
m/Neil Tollerton
w/Eily Beadell

CRY
w&m/Churchill Kohlman

CRY BABY
w&m/Johnny Otis,
Marco De La Garde

CRY CRY CRY
w&m/Sylvia V. Robinson

CRY ME A RIVER
w&m/Arthur Hamilton

CRY OF THE WILD GOOSE
w&m/Terry Gilkyson

CRY TERROR (film score)
w&m/Howard Manucy Jackson

CRY THE BELOVED COUNTRY
m/Kurt Weill
w/Maxwell Anderson

CRYIN' FOR THE CAROLINES
m/Harry Warren
w/Samuel M. Lewis,
Joseph Young

CRYING
w&m/Roy Orbison, Joe Melson

CRYING IN MY SLEEP
w&m/Jimmy Webb

CRYING IN THE CHAPEL
w&m/Artie Glenn

CRYING IN THE RAIN
w&m/Carole King, Howard
Greenfield

CRYSTAL
w&m/Stephanie (Stevie) Nicks

CRYSTAL BALL
w&m/Tommy Shaw

CRYSTAL BLUE PERSUASION
w&m/Tommy James, Bob King

CUBAN LOVE SONG, THE
m/Herbert Stothart,
Jimmy McHugh
w/Dorothy Fields

CUBANOLA GLIDE
m/Harry Von Tilzer
w/Vincent P. Bryan

**CUDDLE UP A LITTLE
CLOSER, LOVEY MINE**
m/Karl Hoschna
w/Otto A. Harbach

CUDDLY TOY
w&m/Harry Edward Nilsson

CUANTO LE GUSTO
m/Ary Barroso
w/Ray Gilbert

CUMANA
w&m/Harold Spina,
Barclay Allen

**CUMPARSITA, LA
(The Masked One)**
m/G.H. Matos Rodriguez

**CUP OF COFFEE, A
SANDWICH AND YOU, A**
m/Joseph Meyer
w/Billy Rose, Al Dubin

CUPID
w&m/Sam Cooke

CUPID'S BOOGIE
w&m/Johnny Otis

**CURSE OF AN ACHING
HEART, THE (You Made Me
What I Am Today)**
m/Al Piantadosi
w/Henry Fink

**CURSE OF THE DREAMER,
THE**
w&m/Paul Dresser

CYNTHIA
m/Gustave A. Kerker
w/Harry B. Smith

Addenda:

CHILD IS BORN, A
w&m/Thad Jones

**CHILDREN IN THE TEMPLE
GROUND**
m/Toshiko Akiyoshi

COLORS OF MY LIFE, THE
m/Cy Coleman
w/Michael Stewart

COMING UP
w&m/Paul McCartney

**COMMANDOS STRIKE AT
DAWN (film score)**
m/Morris Stoloff
w&m/Louis Gruenberg

COVER GIRL (film score)
m/Morris Stoloff
w&m/Carmen Dragon

SONGS

D

DA DOO RON RON (When He Walked Me Home)
w&m/Jeff Barry, Ellie Greenwich, Phil Spector

DADDY
w&m/Bobby Troup

DADDY AND HOME
w&m/Jimmy Rodgers

DADDY, DADDY
w&m/Rudolph Toombs

DADDY DON'T YOU WALK SO FAST
w&m/Daniel Boone

DADDY FRANK (The Guitar Man)
w&m/Merle Haggard

DADDY HAS A SWEETHEART AND MOTHER IS HER NAME
m/David Stamper
w/Gene Buck

DADDY LONG LEGS (film score)
m/Hugo Friedhofer

DADDY, ROLL 'EM
w&m/Will Holt

DADDY SANG BASS
w&m/Carl Lee Perkins

DADDY WAS AN OLD TIME PREACHER MAN
w&m/Dolly Parton, Dorothy Jo Hope

DADDY WHAT IF
w&m/Shel Silverstein

DADDY YOUR MAMA IS LONESOME FOR YOU
w&m/Jimmy Durante

DADDY YOU'VE BEEN A MOTHER TO ME
m/Fred Fisher
w/Alfred Bryan

DADDY'S LITTLE BOY
w&m/Will Collins

DADDY'S LITTLE GIRL
m/Theodore F. Morse
w/Edward Madden

DADDY'S LITTLE GIRL
w&m/Horace Gerlach, Bobby Burke

DADDY'S LITTLE MAN
w&m/Mac Davis

DAISY A DAY, A
w&m/Jed Strunk

DAISY BELL (Daisy, Daisy Give Your Answer Do)
w&m/Harry Dacre

DAISY KENYON (film score)
m/David Raksin

DAISY MAE
w&m/Floyd Tillman

DAMAGE IS DONE, THE
w&m/Mick Jones

DAMERONIA (instr.)
m/Tadd Dameron

DAMN IF IF KNOW
w&m/Archie Shepp

DAMNED IF I DO
w&m/Alan Parsons, Eric Woolfson

DANCE A CACHUCA
m/Sir Arthur Sullivan
w/Sir William Schwenk Gilbert

DANCE, DANCE, DANCE (Yowsah, Yowsah, Yowsah)
w&m/Nile Rodgers, Bernard Edwards, Kenny Lehman

DANCE OF THE SPANISH ONION (instr.)
m/David Rose

DANCE TO THE MUSIC
w&m/Sly Stone

DANCE WITH A DOLLY WITH A HOLE IN HER STOCKING
w&m/Terry Shand, Jimmy Eaton, Mickey Leader

DANCE WITH ME
w&m/Peter Brown, Robert Rans

DANCE WITH ME
w&m/John Hall, Johanna Hall

DANCE WITH ME HENRY (revised version of "Work With Me Annie")
w&m/Hank Ballard, Johnny Otis, Etta James

DANCING DAYS
w&m/James Page, Robert Plant

DANCING FOOL
w&m/Frank Zappa

DANCING IN THE DARK
m/Arthur Schwartz
Howard Dietz

DANCING IN THE STREET
w&m/William Stevenson, Ivy Hunter, Marvin Gaye

DANCING IN THE STREET
w&m/John Phillips

DANCING ON THE CEILING
m/Richard Rodgers
w/Lorenz (Larry) Hart

DANCING QUEEN
m/Benny Andersson, Bjorn Ulvaeus
w/Stig Anderson

DANCING TAMBOURINE (instr.)
m/W. C. Polla

DANCING WITH TEARS IN MY EYES
m/Joseph Burke
w/Al Dubin

DANG ME
w&m/Roger Miller

DANGER OF A STRANGER
w&m/Shel Silverstein, Even Stevens

DANGLING CONVERSATION
w&m/Paul Simon

DANIEL
m/Elton John
w/Bernie Taupin

DANIEL AND THE SACRED HARP
w&m/J. Robbie Robertson

DANKE SCHOEN
m/Bert Kaempfert
w/Kurt Schwabach, Milt Gabler

DANNY BOY
m/Music adapted from Irish traditional air "Farewell to Cuchulain", also known as "The Londonderry Air"
w&m/Frederick Edward Weatherly

DANNY BY MY SIDE
m/David Braham
m/Ed Harrigan

DANNY DEEVER
m/Walter Damrosch
w/Rudyard Kipling

DANNY'S SONG
w&m/Kenneth Loggins

DANSERO (instr.)
m/Richard Hayman

DAPPER DAN
w&m/Albert Von Tilzer, Lew Brown

DARDANELLA
w&m/Johnny S. Black, Fred Fisher, Felix BErnard

DARK AS A DUNGEON
w&m/Merle Travis

DARK AT THE TOP OF THE STAIRS (film score)
m/Max Steiner

DARK AT THE TOP OF THE STAIRS (Theme from)
m/Max Steiner

DARK END OF THE STREET
w&m/Chips Moman, Dan Penn

DARK HORSE
w&m/George Harrison

DARKTOWN POKER CLUB
w&m/Jean Havez

DARLIN'
w&m/Brian Wilson, Mike Love

DARLING, JE VOUS AIME BEAUCOUP
w&m/Anna Sosenko

DARLING NELLIE GRAY
w&m/Benjamin Russell Hanby

DARN THAT DREAM
m/James Van Heusen
w/Edgar DeLange

DAUGHTER OF ROSIE O'GRADY, THE
m/Walter Donaldson
w/Monty C. Brice

DAVE'S RAG (instr.)
m/David Alan Jasen

DAVY JONES' LOCKER
w&m/Henry W. Petrie

DAWN ON THE DESERT (instr.)
m/Charlie Shavers

DAWNING IS THE DAY
w&m/Justin Hayward

DAY AFTER
w&m/Alan Parsons, Eric Woolfson

DAY AFTER DAY
m/Arthur Schwartz
w/Howard Dietz

DAY AT THE RACES, A (film score)
m/Bronislau Kaper

DAY BY DAY
w&m/Stephen Schwartz

DAY BY DAY
m/Axel Stordahl, Paul Weston
w/Sammy Cahn

DAY DREAMS
m/Robert Hood Bowers
w/Robert B. Smith

DAY IN, DAY OUT
m/Rube Bloom
m/Johnny Mercer

DAY IN THE LIFE OF A FOOL, A
m/Luiz Bonfa
w/Carl Sigman

DAY IN THE LIFE OF A TREE, A
m/Elton John
w/Bernie Taupin

DAY IS DONE
w&m/Peter Yarrow

DAY O
w&m/Irving Burgess (adapted from traditional Jamaican folk music)

DAY OF THE DOLPHIN (film score)
m/Georges Delerue

DAY OF THE LOCUSTS
w&m/Robert Dylan

DAY THAT CLAYTON DELANEY DIED, THE
w&m/Tom T. Hall

DAY THAT YOU GREW OLDER, THE
w&m/Paul Dresser

DAY THE RAINS CAME, THE
m/Gilbert Becaud
w/Carl Sigman

DAY TRIPPER
w&m/John Lennon, Paul McCartney

DAY YOU CAME ALONG, THE
m/Arthur Johnson
w/Sam Coslow

DAYBREAK (from "Grand Canyon Suite")
m/Ferde Grofe
w/Harold Adamson

DAYBREAK
m/Barry Manilow
w/Adrienne Anderson

DAYBREAK EXPRESS (instr.)
m/Duke Ellington

DAYDREAM
w&m/John B. Sebastian

DAYDREAM BELIEVER
w&m/John Stewart

DAYDREAMING
m/Harry Warren
w/Al Dubin, Gus Kahn

DAY'S GONE DOWN (Still Got The Light In Your Eyes)
w&m/Gerry Rafferty

DAYS OF WINE AND ROSES (film score)
m/Henry Mancini
w/Johnny Mercer

DAYTIME FRIENDS
w&m/Ben Peters

DAZED AND CONFUSED
w&m/James Page, Robert Plant

DE DE DINAH
w&m/Peter DeAngelis

DE GOLDEN WEDDING
w&m/James A. Bland

DEACON BLUES
w&m/Donald Fagen, Walter Becker

DEACON'S HOP
w&m/Big Jay McNeally

DEAD DRUNK BLUES
w&m/Gertrude "Ma" Rainey

DEAD END STREET
w&m/Ben Raleigh, Dave Axelrod

DEAD MAN'S CURVE
w&m/Brian Wilson, Jan Berry, Roger Christian, Artie Kornfeld

DEAD SKUNK
w&m/Loudon Wainwright III

DEADEND STREET
w&m/Raymond Douglas Davies

DEAR BRIGITTE (film score)
m/George Duning

DEAR DIARY
w&m/Ray Thomas

DEAR HEART (film score)
m/Henry Mancini

DEAR HEART
m/Henry Mancini
w/Jay Livingston, Ray Evans

DEAR HEARTS AND GENTLE PEOPLE
m/Sammy Fain
w/Bob Hilliard

DEAR LANDLORD
w&m/Robert Dylan

DEAR LITTLE BOY OF MINE
m/Ernest R. Ball
w/J. Keirn Brennan

DEAR LITTLE GIRL
m/George Gershwin
w/Ira Gershwin

DEAR MAMA
w&m/Merle Kilgore

DEAR MARY
w&m/Steve Miller

DEAR MR. FANTASY
w&m/Steve Winwood, Jim Capaldi, Chris Wood

DEAR MRS. APPLEBY
w&m/Wilbur (Billy) Meshel, Phil Barr

DEARIE
m/David Mann
w/Bob Hilliard

DEATH OF A SALESMAN (film score)
m/Alex North

DEAR OLD GIRL
m/Theodore F. Morse
w/Richard Buck

DEAR OLD SOUTHLAND
w&m/Henry Creamer, J. Turner Layton

DEAR UNCLE SAM
w&m/Loretta Lynn

DEAR WORLD
w&m/Jerry Herman

DEAREST DARLING
w&m/Ellas McDaniel (Bo Diddley)

DEARIE
w&m/Clare Kummer

DEARIE
m/David Mann
w/Bob Hilliard

DEARLY BELOVED
m/Jerome Kern
w/Johnny Mercer

DEATH CELL ROUNDER BLUES
w&m/Michael Bloomfield

DEATH IN MY FAMILY
w&m/Michael Bloomfield

DEATH OF EMMETT TILL, THE
w&m/Robert Dylan

DECEMBER, 1963 (Oh, What a NIGHT)
w&m/Bob Gaudio

DEDICATED FOLLOWER OF FASHION
w&m/Raymond Douglas Davies

DEDICATED TO YOU
m/Saul Chaplin
w/Sammy Cahn, Hy Zaret

DEDICATION TO POETS AND WRITERS (instr.)
m/Ornette Coleman

DEE DEE (instr.)
m/Ornette Coleman

DEED I DO
m/Fred Rose
w/Walter Hirsch

DEEP BLUE
w&m/George Harrison

DEEP DOWN IN FLORIDA
w&m/Muddy Waters

DEEP FOREST (instr.)
m/Earl (Fatha)Hines

DEEP IN A DREAM
m/James Van Heusen
w/Eddie DeLange

DEEP IN MY HEART DEAR
m/Sigmund Romberg
w/Dorothy Donnelly

DEEP IN THE HEART OF TEXAS
m/Don Swander
w/June Hershey

DEEP IN YOUR EYES
m/Victor Jacobi
w/William LeBaron

DEEP MOANIN' BLUES
w&m/Gertrude "Ma" Rainey

DEEP NIGHT
w&m/Rudy Vallee,
Charles Henderson

DEEP PURPLE
m/Peter DeRose
w/Mitchell Parish

DEEPER AND DEEPER
w&m/Ronald Dunbar, Edythe
Wayne, Norma Toney

DEJA VU
m/Isaac Hayes
w/Adrienne Anderson

DEJA VU
w&m/David Crosby

DELIA
w&m/Joshua D. White

DELICADO
w&m/Jack Lawrence, Waldyr
Azevedo

DELISHIOUS
m/George Gershwin
w/Ira Gershwin

DELTA DAWN
w&m/Larry Collins, Alex Harvey

DELTA DAY
w&m/Kris Kristofferson,
Marijohn Wilkin

DELTA DIRT
w&m/Larry Gatlin

DELTA LADY
w&m/Leon Russell

DELTA SERENADE (instr.)
w&m/Duke Ellington

DEPORTEE
w&m/Woody Guthrie, Martin
Hoffman

DER FUEHRER'S FACE
w&m/Oliver G. Wallace

DESAFINADO (Slightly Out of Tune)
m/Antonio Carlos Jobim
w/Jessie Cavanaugh (Spanish words
by Newton Mendonca)

DESERT FOX, THE (film score)
m/Daniele Amfitheatrof

DESERT RATS (film score)
m/Leigh Harline

DESERT SANDS
w&m/Stuff Smith

DESERT SONG, THE (Blue Heaven)
m/Sigmund Romberg
w/Otto Harbach, Oscar
Hammerstein II

DESERTED FARM, A
w&m/Edward Alexander MacDowell

DESIRE
w&m/Barry, Robin and Maurice
Gibb

DESIREE (film score)
m/Alex North

DESIREE
w&m/Neil Diamond

DESOLATION ROW
w&m/Robert Dylan

DESPAIR TO HOPE (instr.)
m/Don Ellis

DESPERADO
w&m/Jackson Browne

DESTINY (instr.)
m/Sydney Bayne

DESTRUCTION BLUES
w&m/Jimmy Witherspoon

DETOUR
w&m/Paul Westmoreland

DETROIT CITY
w&m/Mel Tillis, Danny Dill

DETROIT ROCK CITY
w&m/Paul Stanley, Bob Ezrin

DEVIL'S BITE
w&m/Todd Rundgren

DEVOTED TO YOU
w&m/Bryant Boudleaux

DEVOTED TO YOU
w&m/Carly Simon, James Taylor

DEVOTION
w&m/Maurice White, Phillip Bailey

DEVIL WENT DOWN TO GEORGIA, THE
w&m/Charlie Daniels

DEVIL WOMAN
w&m/Marty Robbins

DEVIL YOU
w&m/Rich Dodson

DEWEY SQUARE (instr.)
m/Charlie Parker

DEXTER'S MINOR MAD (instr.)
m/Dexter Gordon

DEXTER RIDES AGAIN (instr.)
m/Dexter Gordon

DIAMOND GIRL
w&m/Dash Crofts, James Seals

DIAMONDS ARE A GIRL'S
BEST FRIEND
m/Jule Styne
w/Leo Robin

DIAMONDS ARE FOREVER
m/John Barry
w/Don Black

DIANA
w&m/Paul Anka

DIANE
w&m/Lew Pollack, Erno Rapee

DIARY
w&m/David Gates

DIARY, THE
w&m/Neil Sedaka,
Howard Greenfield

DIARY OF ANNE FRANK, THE
(film score)
m/Alfred Newman

DID I REMEMBER
m/Walter Donaldson
w/Harold Adamson

DID YOU EVER GET THAT
FEELING IN THE MOONLIGHT
w&m/Larry Stock, Ira Schuster

DID YOU EVER HAVE TO
MAKE UP YOUR MIND
w&m/John B. Sebastian

DID YOU EVER SEE A DREAM
WALKING
m/Harry Revel
w/Mack Gordon

DIDN'T I (Blow Your Mind This
Time)
w&m/Thomas Bell, William Hart

DIDN'T WE
w&m/Jimmy Webb

DIFFERENT DRUM
w&m/Mike Nesmith

DIG (instr.)
m/Miles Dewey Davis

DIGA DIGA DOO
m/Jimmy McHugh
w/Dorothy Fields

DILL PICKLES RAG (instr.)
m/Charles Leslie Johnson

DIM ALL THE LIGHTS
w&m/Donna Summer

DIMINUENDO IN BLUE (instr.)
m/Duke Ellington

DINAH
m/Harry Akst
w/Samuel M. Lewis, Joseph Young

DINAH (Kiss Me Honey Do)
m/John Stromberg
w/Edgar Smith

DINAH FLO
w&m/Boz Scaggs

DING-DONG, DING-DONG
w&m/George Harrison

DING DONG THE WITCH IS
DEAD
m/Harold Arlen
w/E. Y. Harburg

DINNER AT EIGHT
m/Jimmy McHugh
w/Dorothy Fields

DINNER AT EIGHT (film score)
m/William Axt

DINNER MUSIC FOR A PACK
OF HUNGRY CANNIBALS
(instr.)
m/Raymond Scott

DIPSY DOODLE, THE
w&m/Larry Clinton

DIRTY DOZEN (film score)
m/Frank DeVol

DIRTY WORK
w&m/Donald Fagen, Walter Becker

DISCO DUCK
w&m/Rick Dees

DISCO QUEEN
w&m/Errol Brown, Tony Wilson

DIS-SATISFIED
w&m/Bill Anderson, Jan Howard,
Carter Howard

DISTANT DRUMS
w&m/Cindy Walker

DIVE BOMBER (instr.)
m/Pete Johnson

DIVORCE AMERICAN STYLE
(film score)
m/Dave Grusin

DIVORCE ME C.O.D.
w&m/Merle Travis, Cliffie Stone

DIXIE
w&m/Daniel Decatur Emmett

DIZZY
w&m/Tommy Roe, F. Wheeler

DIZZY FINGERS (instr.)
m/Edward E. (Zev) Confrey

DIZZY MISS LIZZY
w&m/Larry Williams

DJ FOR A DAY
w&m/Tom T. Hall

DJANGO (instr.)
m/John Lewis

D'NATURAL BLUES
w&m/Henry Glover, Lucky Millinder

DO DO DO
m/George Gershin
Ira Gershwin

DO I WORRY
w&m/Bobby Worth

DO I HEAR A WALTZ
m/Richard Rodgers
w/Stephen Sondheim

DO I LOVE YOU
w&m/Paul Anka, Alain Le Govic,
Yves Dessca, Michel Pelay

DO I LOVE YOU
w&m/Cole Porter

DO I REALLY LOVE YOU
w&m/Jay Richards (Arthur Pine)

DO IT
w&m/Neil Diamond

DO IT AGAIN
m/George Gershwin
w/Buddy DeSylva

DO IT AGAIN
w&m/Donald Fagen, Walter Becker

DO IT AGAIN
w&m/Brian Wilson, Mike Love

DO IT AGAIN TONIGHT
w&m/Larry Gatlin

DO IT ANY WAY YOU WANNA
w&m/Leon Huff

DO NOTHIN' TILL YOU HEAR
FROM ME
m/Duke Ellington
w/Bob Russell

DO-RE-MI
m/Richard Rodgers
w/Oscar Hammerstein II

DO RIGHT
w&m/Paul Davis

DO RIGHT WOMAN, DO RIGHT
MAN
w&m/Chips Moman, Dan Penn

DO SOMETHING FOR ME
w&m/William (Billy) Ward

DO THAT TO ME ONE MORE
TIME
w&m/Toni Tennille

DO WAH DIDDY
w&m/Jeff Barry, Ellie Greenwich

DO YA
w&m/Jeff Lynne

DO YOU BELIVE IN MAGIC
w&m/John B. Sebastian

DO YOU CARE
w&m/Lew Quadling, Jack Elliott

DO YOU EVER THINK OF ME
w&m/Wilbur (Billy) Meshel

DO YOU FEEL LIKE WE DO
w&m/Peter Frampton

DO YOU KNOW THE WAY TO SAN JOSE
m/Burt Bacharach
w/Hal David

DO YOU KNOW WHAT I MEAN
w&m/Lee Michaels

DO YOU KNOW WHAT IT MEANS TO MISS NEW ORLEANS
m/Louis Alter
w/Edgar Leslie

DO YOU KNOW WHERE YOU'RE GOING TO (Theme from "Mahogany)
m/Michael Masser
w/Gerry Goffin

DO YOU KNOW YOU ARE MY SUNSHINE
w&m/Don Reid, Harold Reid

DO YOU LOVE ME
w&m/Berry Gordy, Jr.

DO YOU REALLY HAVE A HEART
w&m/Paul Williams, Roger Nichols

DO YOU REMEMBER LOVE
m/Reginald DeKoven
w/Harry B. Smith

DO YOU REMEMBER THESE
w&m/Harry W. Reid, Don Reid, Larry Lee

DO YOU THINK I'M SEXY
w&m/Rod Stewart, Carmine Appice

DO YOU WANNA DANCE
w&m/Bobby Freeman

DO WHAT YOU WANT, BE WHAT YOU ARE
w&m/John Oates, Daryl Hall

(Sitting On The) DOCK OF THE BAY
w&m/Otis Redding, Steve Cropper

DOCTOR, LAWYER, INDIAN CHIEF
m/Hoagy Carmichael
w/Paul Francis Webster

DOCTOR MY EYES
w&m/Jackson Browne

DOCTOR ZHIVAGO (film score)
m/Maurice Jarre

DOCTOR'S ORDERS
w&m/Roger Greenaway, Roger Cook

DODGING A DIVORCEE
w&m/Reginald Foresythe

DOES ANYBODY REALLY KNOW WHAT TIME IT IS
w&m/Robert Lamm

DOES THE SPEARMINT LOSE ITS FLAVOR ON THE BEDPOST OVERNIGHT
m/Ernest Breuer
w/Billy Rose

DOES YOUR HEART BEAT FOR ME
m/Howard Johnson, Russ Morgan
w/Mitchell Parish

DOESN'T ANYBODY KNOW MY NAME
w&m/Rod McKuen

DOIN' ALLRIGHT (instr.)
m/Dexter Gordon

DOIN' WHAT COMES NATURALLY
w&m/Irving Berlin

DOING THE NEW LOW-DOWN
m/Jimmy McHugh
w/Dorothy Fields

DOLCE FAR NIENTE
w&m/Meredith Willson

DOLORES
m/Louis Alter
w/Frank Loesser

DOLORES (instr.)
m/Wayne Shorter

DOMINIQUE
m/Soeur Sourre (Sister Luc-Gabrielle)
w/Noel Regney

DOMINO
w&m/Don Raye, Louis Ferrar

DOMINO
w&m/Van Morrison

DONKEY SERENADE, THE
m/Herbert Stothart, Rudolf Friml
w/Robert Wright, George "Chet" Forrest

DONNA
w&m/Richie Valens

DONNA THE PRIMA DONNA
w&m/Dion Di Mucci, Ernest Maresca

DON'T ASK ME QUESTIONS
w&m/Graham Parker

DON'T BE A DROP OUT
w&m/James Brown

DON'T BE ANGRY
w&m/Donna Fargo

DON'T BE ANGRY
w&m/Rosemarie McCoy, Nappy Brown, Fred Mendelsohn

DON'T BE CRUEL
w&m/Otis Blackwell, Elvis Presley

DON'T BE SO MEAN TO BABY
w&m/Peggy Lee, Dave Barbour

DON'T BE THAT WAY
m/Benny Goodman, Edgar Sampson, Chick Webb
w/Mitchell Parish

DON'T BLAME IT ON ME
w&m/Antoine "Fats" Domino, Dave Bartholomew

DON'T BLAME ME
m/Jimmy McHugh
w/Dorothy Fields

DON'T BLAME IT ALL ON BROADWAY
m/Bert Grant
w/Joseph Young, Harry Williams

DON'T BREAK THE HEART THAT LOVES YOU
m/Murray Mencher
w/Benny Davis

DON'T BRING LULU
m/Ray Henderson
w/Billy Rose, Lew Brown

DON'T BRING ME POSIES
w&m/Fred Rose

DON'T BURN THE CANDLE AT BOTH ENDS
w&m/Louis Jordan, Benny Carter, Irving Gordon

DON'T CALL ME FROM A HONKY TONK
w&m/Harlan Howard

DON'T COST YOU NOTHIN'
w&m/Nicholas (Nick) Ashford, Valerie Simpson

DON'T COME HOME A-DRINKIN' WITH LOVIN' ON YOUR MIND
w&m/Loretta Lynn

DON'T CRY BABY
m/James P. Johnson
w/Stella Unger

DON'T CRY DADDY
w&m/Mac Davis

DON'T CRY FOR ME ARGENTINA
m/Andrew Lloyd Webber
w/Tim Rice

DON'T CRY JOE
w&m/Joe Marsala

DON'T CRY OUT LOUD
m/Peter Allen
w/Carole Bayer Sager

DON'T DECEIVE ME
w&m/Chuck Willis

DON'T DO IT
w&m/J. Robbie Robertson

DON'T DO ME LIKE THAT
w&m/Tom Petty

**DON'T DRINK THE WATER
(film score)**
m/Pat Williams

DON'T EVER LEAVE ME
m/Jerome Kern
w/Oscar Hammerstein II

DON'T EXPLAIN
w&m/Billy Holiday

**DON'T FALL IN LOVE WITH A
DREAMER**
w&m/Kim Carnes, David Ellingson

DON'T FENCE ME IN
w&m/Cole Porter

DON'T FIGHT IT
w&m/Wilson Pickett, Steve Cropper

DON'T FORBID ME
w&m/Charles Singleton

**DON'T GET AROUND MUCH
ANYMORE**
m/Duke Ellington
w/Bob Russell

DON'T GIVE UP ON ME
w&m/Ben Peters

DON'T GIVE UP ON US
w&m/Tony MacCaulay

**DON'T GIVE UP THE OLD
LOVE FOR THE NEW**
w&m/James Thanton

DON'T GIVE UP THE SHIP
m/Harry Warren
w/Al Dubin

**DON'T GO BREAKING MY
HEART**
m/Elton John
w/Bernie Taupin

DON'T GO TO STRANGERS
w&m/Redd Evans, Dave Mann

**DON'T IT MAKE MY BROWN
EYES BLUE**
w&m/Richard Leigh

DON'T JUST STAND THERE
w&m/Ernest Tubb, Cherokee
Jack Henley

**DON'T KEEP MY LONELY TOO
LONG**
w&m/Melba Montgomery

DON'T KNOCK MY LOVE
w&m/Wilson Pickett, Brad Shapiro

DON'T LEAVE ME THIS WAY
w&m/Kenneth Gamble, Leon Huff,
Cary Gilbert

DON'T LET IT SHOW
w&m/Alan Parsons, Eric Woolfson

DON'T LET JULIA FOOL YA
w&m/Jerome Brainin, Art Kassel

**DON'T LET LOVE HANG YOU
UP**
w&m/Jerry Butler, Kenneth Gamble,
Leon Huff

**DON'T LET ME BE LONELY
TONIGHT**
w&m/James Taylor

DON'T LET ME TOUCH YOU
w&m/Marty Robbins, Billy Sherrill

**DON'T LET THE STARS GET IN
YOUR EYES**
w&m/Slim Willet

DON'T LET THE SUN GO DOWN
m/Elton John
w/Bernie Taupin

DON'T LOOK BACK
w&m/Tom Scholz

DON'T LOOK NOW
w&m/John C. Fogerty

DON'T MAKE ME OVER
m/Burt Bacharach
w/Hal David

DON'T MESS WITH BILL
w&m/William (Smokey) Robinson, Jr.

**DON'T PLAY THAT SONG (You
Lied)**
w&m/Ahmet Ertegun, Betty Nelson

**DON'T PUT YOUR DAUGHTER
ON THE STAGE MRS.
WORTHINGTON**
w&m/Noel Coward

DON'T PULL YOUR LOVE
w&m/Dennis Lambert, Brian Potter

DON'T RAIN ON MY PARADE
m/Jule Styne
w/Bob Merrill

**DON'T ROB ANOTHER MAN'S
CASTLE**
w&m/Jenny Lou Carson

DON'T SAY GOODNIGHT
w&m/Audolph Isley, O'Kelly Isley,
Ronald Isley, E. Isley, M. Isley, C.
Jasher.

**DON'T SAY NOTHING BAD
ABOUT MY BABY**
w&m/Carole King, Gerry Goffin

DON'T SHE LOOK GOOD
w&m/Jerry Chesnut

**DON'T SHOOT ME, I'M ONLY
THE PIANO PLAYER**
m/Elton John
w/Bernie Taupin

**DON'T SIT UNDER THE APPLE
TRE WITH ANYONE ELSE BUT
ME**
m/Sam H. Stept
w/Lew Brown, Charles Tobias

DON'T SLEEP IN THE SUBWAY
w&m/Tony Hatch, Jackie Trent

DON'T STOP
w&m/Christine P. McVie

DON'T STOP IT NOW
w&m/Errol Brown, Tony Wilson

**DON'T STOP 'TIL YOU GET
ENOUGH**
w&m/Michael Joe Jackson

DON'T SWEETHEART ME
m/Cliff Friend
w/Charles Tobias

**DON'T TAKE AWAY THE
MUSIC**
w&m/Frederick Perren, Keni St.
Lewis, Christine Yarion

DON'T TAKE ME HOME
m/Harry Von Tilzer
w/Vincent P. Bryan

**DON'T TAKE YOUR GUNS TO
TOWN**
w&m/John R. Cash

**DON'T TAKE YOUR LOVE
FROM ME**
w&m/Henry Nemo

**DON'T TELL HER THAT YOU
LOVE HER**
w&m/Paul Dresser

**DON'T TELL ME YOUR
TROUBLES**
w&m/Don Gibson

**DON'T THINK TWICE IT'S ALL
RIGHT**
w&m/Robert Dylan

DON'T TOUCH ME
w&m/Hank Cochran

**DON'T WANT TO LIVE
WITHOUT IT**
w&m/Cory Lerios, David Jenkins

DON'T WASTE MY TIME
w&m/John Mayall

DON'T WORRY ABOUT ME
m/Rube Bloom
w/Ted Koehler

DON'T WORRY BABY
w&m/Brian Wilson, Roger Christian,
H. Jamiph

DON'T WORRY 'BOUT ME
w&m/Rube Bloom, Ted Koehler

DON'T YOU KNOW
w&m/Bobby Worth (music adapted
from Puccini's "Musetta's Waltz")

DON'T YOU MISS YOUR BABY
m/William (Count) Basie,
Eddie Durham
w/James A. Rushing

DON'T YA TELL HENRY
w&m/Robert Dylan

**DO YOU WANT A PAPER
DEARIE**
m/Ludwig Englander
w/Harry B. Smith

**DON'T YOU WORRY 'BOUT A
THING**
w&m/Stevie Wonder

DOODLIN' SONG, A
m/Cy Coleman
w/Carolyn Leigh

DOOLIN' PATTON
w&m/J.D. Souther, Glenn Frey,
Donald Henley, Jackson Browne

**DOOR IS STILL OPEN TO MY
HEART, THE**
w&m/Chuck Willis

DOOR TO DOOR
w&m/John C. Fogerty

DOOR'S ALWAYS OPEN, THE
w&m/Bob McDill, Dickey Lee

DORAVILLE
w&m/Buddy Buie, Robert Nix,
Barry Bailey

DOUBLE CROSSING BLUES
w&m/Johnny Otis

**DOUBLE INDEMNITY
(film score)**
m/Miklos Rozsa

DOUBLE LIFE, A (film score)
m/Miklos Rozsa

DOUBLE VISION
w&m/Mick Jones, Lou Gramm

DOVE, THE
m/Jacques Brel
w/English words: Alisdair Clayre
French words: Jacques Brel

DO-WACKA-DO
w&m/Roger Miller

DOWN ALONG THE COVE
w&m/Robert Dylan

**DOWN AMONG THE
SHELTERING PALMS**
m/Abe Olman
w/James Brockman

**DOWN AMONG THE SUGAR
CANE**
m/Chris Smith (Avery & Hart)
w/Cecil Mack

DOWN ARGENTINE WAY
m/Harry Warren
w/Mack Gordon

DOWN BY THE O-HI-O
m/Abe Olman
w/Jack Yellen

**DOWN BY THE OLD MILL
STREAM**
w&m/Tell Taylor

**DOWN BY THE WINEGAR
WOIKS**
w&m/Don Bestor, Roger Lewis,
Walter Donovan

DOWN IN JUNGLE TOWN
m/Theodore F. Morse
w/Edward Madden

DOWN IN BOM-BOMBAY
m/Harry Carroll
w/Ballard MacDonald

DOWN IN THE BOONDOCKS
w&m/Joe South

**DOWN IN THE DEPTHS (ON
THE NINETIETH FLOOR)**
w&m/Cole Porter

DOWN ON ME
w&m/Janis Joplin

DOWN ON THE CORNER
w&m/John C. Fogerty

DOWN ON THE FARM
m/Harry Von Tilzer
w/Raymond A. Browne

DOWN SOUTH (instr.)
m/W. H. Myddleton

DOWN THE FIELD
m/Stanleigh P. Freedman
w/C.W. O'Connor

DOWN THE HIGHWAY
w&m/Robert Dylan

DOWN THE OLD OX ROAD
m/Arthur Johnston
w/Sam Coslow

DOWN WENT McGINTY
w&m/Joseph Flynn

**DOWN WHERE THE COTTON
BLOSSOMS GREW**
m/Harry Von Tilzer
w/Andrew B. Sterling

**DOWN WHERE THE SWANEE
RIVER FLOWS**
w&m/Albert Von Tilzer, Charles S.
Alberte, Charles McCarron

**DOWN WHERE THE
WURZBURGER FLOWS**
m/Harry Von Tilzer
w/Vincent P. Bryan

DOWN WITH LOVE
m/Harold Arlen
w/E. Y. Harburg

DOWN YONDER
w&m/L. Wolfe Gilbert

DOWNHILL RACER (film score)
m/Kenyon Hopkins

DOWN IN THE FLOOD
w&m/Robert Dylan

DOWNTOWN
w&m/Tony Hatch

DRAG CITY
w&m/Brian Wilson, Jan Berry,
Roger Christian

DRAGGIN' THE LINE
w&m/Tommy James, Bob King

DRAGNET (Theme)
w&m/Walter Schumann

DRAW THE LINE
w&m/Joe Perry, Steve Tyler

DREAM
w&m/Johnny Mercer

**DREAM A LITTLE DREAM OF
ME**
m/Fabian Andre, Wilbur Schwandt
w/Gus Kahn

DREAM ALONG WITH ME
w&m/Carl Sigman

DREAM BABY
w&m/Sonny Bono, Cher (Cherilyn S.
LaPierre)

**DREAM BABY (How Long Must
I Dream)**
m/Cindy Walker

DREAM, DREAM, DREAM
w&m/John Redman, Louis Ricca

DREAM, DREAM, DREAM
m/Jimmy McHugh
w/Mitchell Parish

DREAM GIRL
w&m/Jesse Belvin, Marvin Phillips

DREAM GOES ON FOREVER, A
w&m/Todd Rundgren

**DREAM IS A WISH YOUR
HEART MAKES, A**
m/Jerry Livingston, Al Hoffman
w/Mack David

DRINK TO ME ONLY WITH THINE EYES
m/traditional English air, sometimes attributed to a "Colonel R. Mellish"
w/Ben Jonson

DRINKIN' MY BABY OFF MY MIND
w&m/Eddie Rabbitt, Even Stevens

DRINKING SONG
m/Sigmund Romberg
w/Dorothy Donnelly

DROP KICK ME JESUS
w&m/Paul Craft

DROP ME OFF IN HARLEM (instr.)
m/Duke Ellington

DROWNING IN THE SEA OF LOVE
w&m/Kenneth Gamble, Leon Huff

DRUMMER BOY OF SHILOH
w&m/William S. Hays

DRUMS IN MY HEART
m/Vincent Youmans
w/Edward Heyman

DRY CLEANER FROM DES MOINES, THE
w&m/Joni Mitchell

DRY SPELL BLUES
w&m/Son House

DUELING BANJOS (Feuding Banjos) (instr.)
m/Arthur Smith

DUKE OF EARL
w&m/Gene Chandler, Earl Edwards, Bernie Williams

DUKE'S CHOICE (instr.)
m/Charles Mingus

DUKE STEPS OUT, THE (instr.)
m/Duke Ellington

DREAM LOVER
w&m/Bobby Darin

DREAM LOVER
m/Victor Schertzinger
w/Clifford Grey

DREAM OF MY BOYHOOD DAYS w&m/Paul Dresser

DREAM ON
w&m/Joe Perry, Steve Tyler

DREAM PAINTER
w&m/Dallas Frazier, Whitey Shafer

DREAM WEAVER
m/Keith Jarrett

DREAM WEAVER
w&m/Gary Wright

DREAMBOAT ANNIE
w&m/Ann Wilson, Nancy Wilson

DREAMER WITH A PENNY, A
w&m/Lester Lee, Allan Roberts

(He's My) DREAMBOAT
w&m/John D. Loudermilk

DREAMER'S HOLIDAY, A
w&m/Mabel Wayne, Kim Gannon

DREAMIN'
w&m/Dorsey Burnette, Johnny Burnette

DREAMING
w&m/Deborah Harry, Chris Stein

DREAMS
w&m/Stephanie (Stevie) Nicks

DREAMS GO BY
w&m/Harry Chapin

DREAMS OF THE EVERYDAY HOUSEWIFE
w&m/Chris Gantry

DR. HONORIS CAUSA (instr.)
m/Joe Zawinul

DRIFT AWAY
w&m/Mentor Williams

DRIFTER, THE
w&m/Jerry Goldstein, Bob Feldman, Richard Gottehrel

DRIFTER'S ESCAPE
w&m/Robert Dylan

DRIFTING AND DREAMING
m/Egbert Anson Van Alstyne
w/Haven Gillespie

DRIFTING FROM TOWN TO TOWN
w&m/Robert Calvin Bland

DULCINEA
m/Mitch Leigh
w/Joe Darion

DUM DUM
w&m/Jackie DeShannon, Shari Sheeley

DUMB BLONDE
w&m/Dolly Parton

DUNGAREE DOLL
m/Sherman Edwards
w/Ben Raleigh

DUSK IN UPPER SANDUSKY (instr.)
m/Jimmy Dorsey

DUST IN THE WIND
w&m/Steve Walsh, Kerry Livgren, Phillip Ehart, Robert Steinhardt, David Hope, Richard Williams

DUST ON THE MOON (Canto INDIO)
m/Ernesto Lecuona
w/Stanley Adams

D'YE KEN JOHN PEEl (John Peel)
m/traditional English folk air; composer unknown
w/John Woodcock Graves

Addenda:

DISCO APOCALYPSE
w&m/Jackson Browne

DRIFTWOOD
w&m/Justin Hayward

DRIVIN' MY LIFE AWAY
w&m/Eddie Rabbitt, Even Steves, D. Malloy

 **SONGS**

E

E STREET SHUFFLE, THE
w&m/Bruce Springsteen

EACH NIGHT AT NINE
w&m/Floyd Tillman

EADIE WAS A LADY
m/Nacio Herb Brown
w/Richard A. Whiting,
Buddy DeSylva

EAGLE, THE
m/David Braham
w/C. L. Stout

EAGLE AND ME, THE
m/Harold Arlen
w/E.Y. Harburg

EARL, THE (instr.)
m/Earl (Fatha) Hines

EARL'S BREAKDOWN (instr.)
m/Earl Scruggs, Lester Flatt

EARLY AUTUMN
m/Woody Herman, Ralph Burns
w/Johnny Mercer

EARLY IN THE MORNING
w&m/Louis Jordan, Leo Hickman,
Dallas Bartley

EARLY IN THE MORNING
w&m/Buddy Holly

EARLY MORNING LOVE
w&m/Kenneth Gamble, Leon Huff

EARLY IN DE MORNIN'
w&m/William S. Hays

EARTH ANGEL
w&m/Jesse Belvin

EARTH'S CREATION
w&m/Stevie Wonder

EASE ON DOWN THE ROAD
w&m/Charles Smalls

EASY COME, EASY GO
m/John Green
w/Martin Charnin

EASY LOOK
w&m/Curly Putnam

EASY PART'S OVER, THE
w&m/Bill Rice, Jerry Foster

EAST OF ST. LOUIS BLUES
w&m/W. C. Handy

EAST OF THE SUN AND WEST OF THE MOON
w&m/Brooks Bowman

EASTER PARADE
w&m/Irving Berlin

EASY LOVING
w&m/Freddie Hart

EASY TO LOVE
w&m/Cole Porter

EASY TO REMEMBER, IT'S
m/Richard Rodgers
w/Lorenz (Larry) Hart

EASY WINNERS (instr.)
m/Scott Joplin

EAT THAT CHICKEN (instr.)
m/Charles Mingus

EASY TO LOVE
m/Ralph Rainger
w/Leo Robin

EBB TIDE
m/Robert Maxwell
w/Carl Sigman

EBONY EYES
w&m/John D. Loudermilk

EBONY EYES
w&m/Bob Welch

ECHO OF SPRING (instr.)
m/Willie The Lion Smith

ECHOES OF HARLEM (instr.)
m/Duke Ellington

EDELWEISS
m/Richard Rodgers
w/Oscar Hammerstein II

EDGE OF THE UNIVERSE
w&m/Barry, Maurice and
Robin Gibb

EGO
m/Elton John

EIGHT BY TEN
w&m/Bill Anderson, Walter Haynes

EIGHT MILED HIGH
w&m/Roger McGuinn

EIGHT MILES HIGHER
w&m/David Crosby, Gene Clark,
James McGuinn

EIGHTEEN
w&m/Michael Bruce, Vincent
Furnier, Neal A. Smith, Dennis
Dunnaway, Glen Buxton

EIGHTEEN YELLOW ROSES
w&m/Bobby Darin

EILY MACHREE
m/David Braham
w/C. L. Stout

EL CAMINO REAL (instr.)
m/Jay Jay Johnson

EL CAPITAN (instr.)
m/John Philip Sousa

EL CHOCLO (The Owl)
w&m/Spanish words and music:
A. G. Villoldo

EL CONDOR PASA
m/Jorge Milchberg, Daniel Robles
w/Paul Simon

EL PASO
w&m/Marty Robbins

ELEANOR RIGBY
w&m/Paul McCartney, John Lennon

ELDERBERRY WINE
m/Elton John
w/Bernie Taupin

ELEPHANT MAN
w&m/Ellas McDaniel (Bo Diddley)

ELI'S COMING
w&m/Laura Nyro

ELITE SYNCOPATION (instr.)
m/Scott Joplin

ELLEN BAYNE
w&m/Stephen C. Foster

ELLIE RHEE (Carry Me Back To Tennessee)
w&m/Septimus Winner

ELMER GANTRY (film score)
m/Andre Previn

ELMER'S TUNE
w&m/Dick Jurgens, Sammy Gallop,
Elmer Albrecht

ELORA (instr.)
m/Jay Jay Johnson

EMALINE
m/Frank Perkins
w/Mitchell Parish

EMBRACEABLE YOU
m/George Gershwin
w/Ira Gershwin

EMANCIPATION DAY
m/David Braham
w/C. L. Stout

EMMA
w&m/Errol Brown, Tony Wilson

EMPIRE STRIKES BACK, THE (film score)
m/John Williams

EMPTY ARMS
w&m/Ivory Joe Hunter

EMPTY HANDED HEART
w&m/Warren Zevon

EMPTY PAGES
w&m/Steve Winwood, Jim Capaldi

EMPTY POCKETS FILLED WITH LOVE
w&m/Irving Berlin

EMPTY SADDLES
w&m/Billy Hill

ENCHANTED
w&m/Buck Ram

ENCHANTED ISLAND
m/Robert Allen
w/Al Stillman

ENDLESSLY
w&m/Brook Benton, Clyde Otis

ENDLESSLY
m/Walter Kent
w/Kim Gannon

ENGINE, ENGINE
NUMBER NINE
w&m/Roger Miller

ENGLAND SWING
w&m/Roger Miller

ENJOY YOURSELF
w&m/Kenneth Gamble, Leon Huff

ENJOY YOURSELF (It's Later
Than You Think)
m/Herbert Magidson
w/Carl Sigman

ENOUGH IS ENOUGH
w&m/Paul Jabara

ENTERTAINER, THE
w&m/Billy Joel

ENTERTAINER, THE (instr.)
m/Scott Joplin

ENTERTAINER, THE
(film score)
m/John Addison

EPHRAHAM
w&m/Irving Berlin

EPISTROPHY (instr.)
m/Thelonious Sphere Monk

ERES TU
w&m/Juan Calderon

ERONEL (instr.)
m/Thelonious Sphere Monk

ESCALATOR OVER THE HILL
m/Carla Bley
w/Paul Haines

ESCAPE (The Pina Colada Song)
w&m/Rupert Holmes

ESPECIALLY FOR YOU
w&m/Orrin Tucker, Phil Grogan

ESPECIALLY FOR YOU
w&m/Orrin Tucker, Phil Grogan

ESTRELLITA (Little Star)
m/Manuel M. Ponce
w/Frank La Forge

ETERNALLY ("Terry" theme)
m/Charles Spencer Chaplin
w/Geoffrey Parsons

ETHEL MAE
w&m/Arthur Crudup

EUGENIA (instr.)
m/Scott Joplin

EUPHORIC SOUNDS (instr.)
m/Scott Joplin

EVANGELINE
w&m/William S. Hays

EVE OF DESTRUCTION
w&m/P. F. Sloan

EVELINA
m/Harold Arlen
w/E. Y. Harburg

EVEN IT UP
w&m/Ann Wilson, Nancy Wilson,
S. Ennis

EVEN NOW
w&m/Barry Manilow, Marty Panzer

EVEN THE LOSERS
w&m/Tom Petty

EVENIN' BOOGIE
w&m/Jeremy Spencer

EVENTUALLY
w&m/Carole King, Gerry Goffin

EVERGREEN (Love Theme From
"A Star is Born")
w&m/Barbra Streisand,
Paul Williams

EVERLASTING LOVE
w&m/Bobby Russell, Buzz Cason

EVERY BEAT OF MY HEART
w&m/Johnny Otis

EVERY BREATH I TAKE
w&m/Carole King, Gerry Goffin

EVERY DAY BLUES
w&m/Eddie Durham

EVERY FACE TELLS A STORY
m/Michael Allison, Peter Sills
w/Don Black

EVERY KINDA PEOPLE
w&m/Robert Palmer

EVERY LITTLE BIT HELPS
w&m/Fred Fisher, George Whiting

EVERY LITTLE MOVEMENT
HAS A MEANING ALL ITS OWN
m/Karl Hoschna
w/Otto A. Harbach

EVERY MOTHER'S SON
w&m/Steve Winwood, Jim Capaldi

EVERY NIGHT ABOUT THIS
TIME
m/James V. Monaco
w/Ted Koehler

EVERY NIGHT THERE'S A
LIGHT
w&m/Paul Dresser

EVERY PICTURE TELLS A
STORY
w&m/Rod Stewart, Ron Wood

EVERY STREET'S A
BOULEVARD IN OLD
NEW YORK
m/Jule Styne
w/Bob Hilliard

EVERY TIME I TURN THE
RADIO ON
w&m/Bill Anderson

EVERY TUB
w&m/William (Count) Basie, Eddie
Durham, Harry Edison

EVERY WHICH WAY BUT
LOOSE
w&m/Stephen Dorff, Milton
L. Brown, Thomas (Snuff) Garrett

EVERYBODY DANCE
w&m/Nile Rodgers,
Bernard Edwards

EVERYBODY GOTTA PAY
SOME DUES
w&m/William (Smokey) Robinson Jr.

EVERYBODY IS A STAR
w&m/Sly Stone

EVERYBODY LOVES A LOVE
SONG
w&m/Mac Davis

EVERYBODY LOVES A LOVER
m/Robert Allen
w/Richard Adler

EVERYBODY LOVES A RAIN
SONG
w&m/Chips Moman, Mark James

EVERYBODY LOVES MY BABY
w&m/Spencer Williams, Jack Palmer

EVERYBODY LOVES
SOMEBODY
m/Kermit (Ken) Lane
Irving Taylor

EVERYBODY NEEDS A
RAINBOW
w&m/Layng Martine

EVERYBODY NEEDS LOVE
w&m/Stephen Bishop

EVERYBODY OUGHT TO HAVE
A MAID
w&m/Stephen Sondheim

EVERYBODY STEP
w&m/Irving Berlin

EVERYBODY WORKS BUT
FATHER
w&m/Jean Havez

EVERYBODY'S DOIN' IT
w&m/Irving Berlin

EVERYBODY'S GOT A HOME
BUT ME
m/Richard Rodgers
w/Oscar Hammerstein II

EVERYBODY'S GOT A LAUGHING PLACE
m/Ray Gilbert
w/Allie Wrubel

EVERYBODY'S GOT THE RIGHT TO LOVE
w&m/Lou Stallman

EVERYBODY'S HAD THE BLUES
w&m/Merle Haggard

EVERYBODY'S OUT OF TOWN
m/Burt Bacharach
w/Hal David

EVERYBODY'S SOMEBODY'S FOOL
w&m/Jack Keller,
Howard Greenfield

EVERYBODY'S SOMEBODY'S FOOL
w&m/Gladys Hampton, Regina Adams, Ace Adams

EVERYBODY'S TALKIN'
(Echoes)
w&m/Fred Neil

EVERYBODY'S TRYING TO BE MY BABY
w&m/Carl Perkins

EVERYDAY I HAVE THE BLUES
w&m/Peter Chatman

EVERYDAY OF MY LIFE
w&m/Natalie Cole

EVERYDAY PEOPLE
w&m/Sly Stone

EVERYONE'S AGREED
w&m/Gerry Rafferty, Joe Egan

EVERYONE'S GONE TO THE MOON
w&m/Jonathan King

EVERYTHING A MAN COULD EVER NEED
w&m/Mac Davis

EVERYTHING DEPENDS ON YOU (instr.)
m/Earl (Fatha) Hines

EVERYTHING HAPPENS TO ME
m/Matt Dennis
w/Thomas M. Adair

EVERYTHING I HAVE IS YOURS
m/Burton Lane
w/Harold Adamson

EVERYTHING I OWN
w&m/David Gates

EVERYTHING IS BEAUTIFUL
w&m/Ray Stevens

EVERYTHING IS PEACHES DOWN IN GEORGIA
m/Milton Ager, George W. Meyer
w/Grant Clarke

EVERYTHING I'VE GOT
m/Richard Rodgers
w/Lorenz (Larry) Hart

EVERYTHING OLD IS NEW AGAIN
m/Peter Allen
w/Carole Bayer Sager

EVERYTHING STOPS FOR TEA
m/Al Hoffman, Al Goodhart
w/Maurice Sigler

EVERYTHING'S ALRIGHT
w&m/John D. Loudermilk

EVERYTHING'S BEEN DONE BEFORE
m/Edwin H. Knopf
w/Harold Adamson

EVERYTHING'S COMING UP ROSES
m/Jule Styne
w/Stephen Sondheim

EVERYWHERE (instr.)
m/Bill Harris

EVERYWHERE YOU GO
m/Mark Fisher, Larry Shay
w/Joe Goodwin

EVIDENCE (instr.)
m/Thelonious Sphere Monk

EVIL BLUES
w&m/James Andrew Rushing

EVIL GAL BLUES
w&m/Leonard Feather,
Lionel Hampton

EVIL ON YOUR MIND
w&m/Harlan Howard

EVIL WOMAN
w&m/Jeff Lynne

EV'RYTHING I LOVE
w&m/Cole Porter

EV'RY TIME WE SAY GOODBYE
w&m/Cole Porter

EXACTLY LIKE YOU
m/Jimmy McHugh
w/Dorothy Fields

EXCUSE ME (I Think I've Got A Heartache)
w&m/Buck Owens, Harlan Howard

EXODUS (film score)
m/Ernest Gold

EXODUS
m/Ernest Gold
w/Pat Boone

EXPRESSWAY TO YOUR HEART
w&m/Kenneth Gamble, Leon Huff

EYES OF A CHILD
w&m/John Lodge

EYES OF A NEW YORK WOMAN
w&m/Mark James

EYES OF LOVE, THE
m/Quincy Jones
w/Bob Russell

EYES OF SILVER
w&m/Thomas Johnston

EYES OF TEXAS, THE
w&m/J.L. Sinclair

EXORCIST, THE (film score)
m/Jack Nitzsche

EXPRESSIVE GLANCES
m/Sir Arthur Sullivan
w/Sir William Schwenk Gilbert

Addenda:

EBONY MOONBEAMS (instr.)
m/George Cables

EMOTIONAL RESCUE
w&m/Mick Jagger, Keith Richard

EMPTY LIVES
w&m/Graham Parker

ENDLESS NIGHT
w&m/Graham Parker

EVERYONE'S A WINNER
w&m/Errol Brown

 SONGS

F

FACE ON THE DIME, THE
w&m/Harold Rome

FACE THE FIRE
w&m/Dan Fogelberg

FACE TO FACE
w&m/Raymond Douglas Davies

FACE TO THE WALL
w&m/Bill Anderson, Faron Young

FACES AND PLACES (instr.)
m/Ornette Coleman

FACING YOU (instr.)
m/Keith Jarrett

FACTS OF LIFE, THE
w&m/Johnny Mercer

FADED LOVE
w&m/Bob Wills, John Wills

FAHRENHEIT 451 (film score)
m/Bernard Herrmann

FAINT HEART NEVER WON FAIR LADY
m/Sir Arthur Sullivan
w/Sir William Schwenk Gilbert

FAIREST OF THE FAIR (instr.)
m/John Philip Sousa

FAIRYTALE
w&m/Bonnie Pointer, Anita Pointer

FAITHFUL FOREVER
m/Ralph Rainger
w/Leo Robin

FAITHLESS LOVE
w&m/J.D. Souther

FAKIN' IT
w&m/Paul Simon

FALLEN ANGEL
w&m/Marijohn Wilkin, Wayne P. Walker, Webb Pierce

FALLIN'
w&m/Neil Sedaka, Howard Greenfield

FALLING IN LOVE AGAIN
w&m/Samuel M. Lerner, Frederick Hollander

FALLING IN LOVE WITH LOVE
m/Richard Rodgers
w/Lorenz (Larry) Hart

FAME
w&m/David Bowie

FAMILY AFFAIR
w&m/Sly Stone

FAMILY TRADITION
w&m/Hank Williams Jr.

FAMILY BIBLE
w&m/Willie Nelson

FANCY COLOURS
w&m/Robert Lamm

FANNY (film score)
m/Morris Stoloff

FANCY FREE
m/Harold Arlen
w/Johnny Mercer

FANNY, BE TENDER
w&m/Barry, Maurice and Robin Gibb

FANTASY
w&m/Maurice White, Verdin White, E. Del Bamo

FANTASY OF SORROW
w&m/Jackson Browne

FAR AWAY
w&m/Cole Porter

FAR AWAY PLACES
w&m/Alex Kramer, Joan Whitney

FAR, FAR AWAY
w&m/Don Gibson

FARAWAY PART OF TOWN
m/Andre Previn
w/Dory L. Previn

FARE THEE WELL, ANNABELLE
m/Mort Dixon
w/Allie Wrubel

FAREWELL
w&m/Robert Dylan

FAREWELL AMANDA
w&m/Cole Porter

FAREWELL MY OWN
m/Sir Arthur Sullivan
w/Sir William Schwenk Gilbert

FAREWELL TO ARMS
w&m/Abner Silver, Allie Wrubel

FARMER'S DAUGHTER, THE (film score)
m/Leigh Harline

FARMING
w&m/Cole Porter

FARTHER ON
w&m/Jackson Browne

FASCINATING RHYTHM
m/George Gershwin
w/Ira Gershwin

FASCINATION
w&m/Dick Manning (music adapted from F.D. Marchetti's "Valse Tzigane"

FASTER HORSES
w&m/Tom T. Hall

FAT CITY (film score)
m/Marvin Hamlisch

FAT MAN
w&m/Antoine "Fats" Domino, Dave Bartholomew

FATHER AND SON
w&m/Robert Dylan

FATHER OF THE BRIDE (film score)
m/Adolph Deutsch

FAVORITE, THE (instr.)
m/Scott Joplin

FEEL LIKE MAKIN' LOVE
w&m/Eugene McDaniels

FEELIN' STRONGER EVERY DAY
w&m/James Pankow, Peter Cetera

FEELING GOOD
w&m/Leslie Bricusse, Anthony Newley

FEELINGS (¿Dime?)
w&m/Morris Albert

FEELS LIKE THE FIRST TIME
w&m/Mick Jones, Ian Richard McDonald

FEELS SO GOOD (instr.)
m/Chuck Mangione

FELIZ NAVIDAD
w&m/Jose Feliciano

FELLA WITH AN UMBRELLA, A
w&m/Irving Berlin

FELLOW NEEDS A GIRL, A
m/Richard Rodgers
w/Oscar Hammerstein II

FERDINAND THE BULL
w&m/Albert Hay Malotte, Larry Morey

FERNANDO
m/Benny Andersson, Bjorn Ulvaeus
w/Stig Anderson

FESTIVAL RAG (instr.)
m/David Alan Jasen

FEUDIN' AND FIGHTIN'
m/Burton Lane
w/Al Dubin

FEVER
w&m/John Davenport, Eddie Cooley

FEZ, THE
w&m/Donald Fagen, Walter Booker

FIDDLE ABOUT
w&m/John Entwhistle

FIDDLE FADDLE
m/Leroy Anderson
w/Mitchell Parish

FIDDLER ON THE ROOF
m/Jerry Bock
w/Sheldon Harnick

FIELD ARTILLERY (march)
m/John Philip Sousa (based on
Edmund L. Gruber's "The Caissons
Go Rolling Along")

FIFTH STREET BLUES
w&m/Charles Edward Davenport

FIFTY MILLION FRENCHMEN
CAN'T BE WRONG
m/Fred Fisher
w/Billy Rose

52ND STREET
w&m/Billy Joel

52ND STREET THEME (instr.)
m/Dizzy Gillespie

59TH STREET BRIDGE SONG,
THE (Feelin' Groovy)
w&m/Paul Simon

50 WAYS TO LEAVE YOUR
LOVER
w&m/Paul Simon

FIG LEAF RAG (instr.)
m/Scott Joplin

FIGHTING SEABEES, THE
(film score)
m/Walter Scharf, Roy Webb

FIGHTING SIDE OF ME, THE
w&m/Merle Haggard

FILL MY EYES
w&m/Cat Stevens

FILTHY McNASTY (instr.)
m/Horace Silver

FINE AND DANDY
m/Kay Swift
w/Paul James (James P. Warburg)

FIND 'EM, FOOL 'EM,
FORGET 'EM
w&m/Goerge H. Jackson, Roe Hall

FIND ME A PRIMITIVE MAN
w&m/Cole Porter

FIND OUT
w&m/John D. Loudermilk

FIND OUT WHAT THEY LIKE
m/Thomas "Fats" Waller
w/Andy Razaf

FINE AND MELLOW
w&m/Billie Holiday

FINE ROMANCE, A
m/Jerome Kern
w/Dorothy Fields

FINGER BREAKER, THE (instr.)
m/Ferdinand "Jelly Roll" Morton

FINGER PICKIN' (instr.)
m/Wes Montgomery

FINGER POPPIN' TIME
w&m/Hank Ballard

FINGER TIPS
w&m/Stevie Wonder

FINIAN'S RAINBOW (film score)
m/Ray J. Heindorf

FINS
w&m/Jimmy Buffett, D. McColl,
B. Chance

FIRE
w&m/Jimi Hendrix

FIRE AND RAIN
w&m/James Taylor

FIRE BRIGADE
w&m/Roy Wood

FIRE LAKE
w&m/Bob Seger

FIREBALL MAIL
w&m/Roy Claxton Acuff

FIREFLY
m/Cy Coleman
w/Carolyn Leigh

FIRST CUT IS THE DEEPEST,
THE
w&m/Cat Stevens

FIRST EPISODE
m/Elton John
w/Bernie Taupin

FIRST GUN IS FIRED, THE
w&m/George Frederick Root

FIRST LIGHT
w&m/Freddie Hubbard

FIRST LOVE (film score)
m/Andre Previn
w&m/Charles Previn

FIRST OF MAY
w&m/Barry, Maurice and Robin
Gibb

FIRST THING EVERY
MORNING, THE
w&m/Jimmy Dean, Ruth Roberts

FIRST TIME EVER I SAW YOUR
FACE, THE
w&m/Ewan MacColl

FISH CHEER
w&m/Joseph (Country Joe)
McDonald, Barry "The Fish" Melton

FIST CITY
w&m/Loretta Lynn

FIT AS A FIDDLE
m/Al Hoffman, Arthur Freed
w/Al Goodhart

5D (Fifth Dimension)
w&m/Roger McGuinn

FIVE FOOT HIGH AND RISING
w&m/John R. Cash

FIVE FOOT TWO, EYES OF
BLUE
m/Ray Henderson
w/Samuel M. Lewis, Joseph Young

FIVE LITTLE FINGERS
w&m/Bill Anderson

500 MILES HIGH (instr.)
m/Chick Corea

FIVE FOOT HIGH AND RISING
w&m/John R. Cash

FIVE MINUTES MORE
m/Jule Styne
w/Sammy Cahn

FIVE O'CLOCK WHISTLE
m/Josef Myrow
w/Kim Gannon

FIVE PENNIES, THE
w&m/Sylvia Fine

FLAMINGO
m/Theodore J. (Ted) Grouya
w/Edmund Anderson

FLAMING YOUTH (instr.)
m/Duke Ellington

FLAMING YOUTH
w&m/Paul "Ace" Frehley, Paul
Stanley, Gene Simmons, Bob Ezrin

FLAPPERETTE (instr.)
m/Jesse Greer

FLAT FOOT FLOOGIE
m/Bulee (Slim) Gaillard
w/Bud Green

FLEE AS A BIRD
w&m/Mary S. B. Danna (music
arranged by George F. Root)

FLEET'S IN, THE
m/Victor Schertzinger
w/Johnny Mercer

FLESH AND BLOOD
w&m/John R. Cash

FLIP FLOP AND FLY
w&m/Joe Turner, Charles Calhoun

FLIRTATION WALK
m/Mort Dixon
w/Allie Wrubel

FLOW GENTLY SWEET AFTON
(Afton Water)
m/James E. Spilman (familiar U.S.
version which is not the original
musical setting)
w/Robert Burns

FLOWERS IN THE RAIN
w&m/Roy Wood

CARNEGIE LIBRARY
LIVINGSTONE COLLEGE
SALISBURY, N. C. 28144

FLOWERS ON THE WALL
w&m/Lew De Witt

FLOWERS THAT BLOOM IN THE SPRING, THE
m/Sir Arthur Sullivan
w/Sir William Schwenk Gilbert

FLUTTER LITTLE BIRD
m/Gustav Luders
w/George Ade

FLY LIKE AN EAGLE
w&m/Steve Miller

FLY ME TO THE MOON (In Other Words)
w&m/Bart Howard

FLY ROBIN FLY
w&m/Silvester Levay

FLY WITH THE WIND (instr.)
m/McCoy Tyner

FLYIN' HOME
w&m/Lionel Hampton, Benny Goodman

FLYING DOWN TO RIO
m/Vincent Youmans
w/Edward Eliscu

FLYING HOME
w&m/Benny Goodman, Lionel Hampton

FM (No Static At All)
w&m/Donald Fagen, Walter Becker

FOGGY BOTTOM (instr.)
m/Mary Lou Williams

FOGGY DAY, A
m/George Gershwin
w/Ira Gershwin

FOGGY DAY (instr.)
m/Charles Mingus

FOGGY MOUNTAIN BREAKDOWN (instr.)
m/Earl Scruggs, Lester Flatt

FOGGY RIVER
w&m/Fred Rose

FOLKS WHO LIVE ON THE HILL, THE
m/Jerome Kern
w/Oscar Hammerstein II

FOLLOW ME
w&m/John Denver

FOLLOW ME
m/Frederick Loewe
w/Alan Jay Lerner

FOLLOW ME (Love Theme from Mutiny On The Bounty)
m/Bronislau Kaper
w/Paul Francis Webster

FOLSOM PRISON
w&m/John R. Cash

FOOL ON THE HILL, THE
w&m/John Lennon, Paul McCartney

FOOLED AROUND AND FELL IN LOVE
w&m/Elvin Bishop

FOOLIN' AROUND
w&m/Buck Owens, Harlan Howard

FOOLISH LITTLE GIRL
w&m/Helen Miller, Howard Greenfield

FOOLS RUSH IN
w&m/Rube Bloom, Johnny Mercer

FOOTSTEPS
w&m/Barry Mann, Hank Hunter

FOR A MINUTE THERE
w&m/Bill Rice, Jerry Foster

FOR ALL WE KNOW
m/Fred Karlin
w/Robb Wilson, Arthur James

FOR ALL WE KNOW
m/J. Fred Coots
w/Samuel M. Lewis

FOR DANCERS ONLY (Pigeon Walk) (instr.)
m/James V. Monaco

FONTAINBLEAU (instr.)
m/Tadd Dameron

FONTESSA (instr.)
m/John Lewis

FOOL IN LOVE
w&m/Ike Turner

FOOL SUCH AS I
w&m/Robert Dylan

FOOL SUCH AS I, A
w&m/Bill Trader

FOOLED AGAIN (I Don't Like It)
w&m/Tom Petty

FOOLING YOURSELF (The Angry Young Man)
w&m/Tommy Shaw

FOOLISH HEART
m/Kurt Weill
w/Ogden Nash

FOOLS RUSH IN
m/Rube Bloom
w/Johnny Mercer

FOOL, FOOL, FOOL
w&m/Ahmet Ertegun

FOOL FOR YOU
w&m/Ray Charles

FOOL IN LOVE
w&m/Joe Jackson

FOOL IN THE RAIN
w&m/James Page, Robert Plant, John Paul Jones

FOR EVERY MAN THERE'S A WOMAN
m/Harold Arlen
w/Leo Robin

FOR EVERYMAN
w&m/Jackson Browne

FOR HE'S GOING TO MARRY YUM YUM
m/Sir Arthur Sullivan
w/Sir William Schwenk Gilbert

FOR LOVE OF IVY
m/Quincy Jones
w/Bob Russell

FOR LOVE OF IVY (film score)
m/Quincy Jones

FOR ME AND MY GAL
m/George W. Meyer
w/Edgar Leslie, E. Ray Goetz

FOR MY BABY
w&m/Brook Benton,Clyde Otis

FOR MY LADY
w&m/Ray Thomas

FOR OLD TIMES SAKE
w&m/Charles K. Harris

FOR ONCE IN MY LIFE
m/Orlando Murden
w/Ronald Miller

FOR RENT
w&m/Sonny James, Jack Morrow

FOR THE GOOD TIMES
w&m/Kris Kristofferson

FOR THE LOVE OF MONEY
w&m/Kenneth Gamble, Leon Huff, Anthony Jackson

FOR WHAT IT'S WORTH
w&m/Stephen Stills

FOR YOU
m/Joseph A. Burke
w/Al Dubin

FOR YOU FOR ME FOR EVERMORE
m/George Gershwin
w/Ira Gershwin

FOR YOUR LOVE
w&m/Ed Townsend

FOR YOUR PERCIOUS LOE
w&m/Jerry Butler, Arthur Brooks, Richard Brooks

FOREVER AMBER (film score)
m/David Raksin

w&m/Robert Dylan

FORGET DOMANI
m/Riz Ortolani
w/Norman Newell

FORT APACHE (film score)
m/Richard Hageman

FORT WORTH AND DALLAS BLUES
w&m/Huddie (Leadbelly) Ledbelly

FORT WORTH BLUES
w&m/Euday Louis Bowman

FORTUNATE SON
w&m/John C. Fogerty

FORTY-FIVE MINUTES FROM BROADWAY
w&m/George M. Cohan

FORTY MILES OF BAD ROAD
w&m/Duane Eddy

FORTY SECOND STREET
m/Harry Warren
w/Al Dubin

FOUND A CURE
w&m/Valerie Simpson, Nicholas (Nick) Ashford

FOUNTAIN IN THE PARK, THE (While Strolling In The Park One Day)
w&m/Ed Haley

FOUR (instr.)
m/Miles Dewey Davis

FOUR FEATHERS, THE (film score)
m/Miklos Rozsa

FOUR ON SIX (instr.)
m/Wes Montgomery

FOUR WALLS
w&m/George Campbell, Marvin Moore

FOUR WALLS
m/Dave Dreyer
w/Billy Rose

FOUR WINDS AND THE SEVEN SEAS, THE
m/Don Rodney
w/Hal David

1432 FRANKLIN PIKE CIRCLE HERO
w&m/Bobby Russell

FOURTH TIME AROUND
w&m/Robert Dylan

FOX, THE (film score)
m/Lalo Schifrin

FOX ON THE RUN
w&m/Tony Hazzard

FOXES (film score)
m/Georgio Moroder

FOXY LADY
w&m/Jimi Hendrix

FRANCENE
w&m/William Gibbons, Frank Beard, Dusty Hill

FRANCES (instr.)
m/Ferdinand "Jelly Roll" Morton

FRANK MILLS
m/Galt MacDermot
w/James Rado, Gerome Ragni

FRANKENSTEIN
w&m/Edgar Winter, Ronnie Montrose

FRANKIE
w&m/Neil Sedaka, Howard Greenfield

FRANKIE'S BLUES
w&m/David Van Ronk

FRANKLIN D. ROOSEVELT JONES
w&m/Harold Rome

FRASQUITA SERENADE (My Little Nest of Heavenly Blue)
m/Franz Lehar
w/Sigmund Spaeth

FREAK, LE
w&m/Nile Rodgers, Bernard Edwards

FREAKISH (instr.)
m/Ferdinand "Jelly Roll" Morton

FREDDIE FREELOADER (instr.)
m/Miles Dewey Davis

FREDDY'S DEAD
w&m/Curtis Mayfield

FREE
w&m/Deniece Williams

FREE BIRD
w&m/Ronald Wayne Van Zant, Garry Rossington, Larken Allen Collins

FREE FOR ALL
w&m/Freddie Hubbard

FREE FOR ALL (instr.)
m/Wayne Shorter

FREE LANCE, THE (march)
m/John Philip Sousa

FREE MAN IN PARIS
w&m/Joni Mitchell

FREE YOURSELF, BE YOURSELF
w&m/George Johnson, Louis Johnson

FREEDOM
w&m/Jimi Hendrix

FREEDOM RIDER
w&m/Steve Winwood, Jim Capaldi

FREEDOM SUITE, THE (instr.)
m/Sonny Rollins

FRENCH CONNECTION, THE (film score)
m/Don Ellis

FRENCH LESSON, THE
w&m/Roger Edens, Betty Comden, Adolph Green

FRENESI
w&m/Bob Russell, Albert Dominguez

FRIDAY ON MY MIND
w&m/Harry Vanda, George Young

FRIEND, LOVER, WOMAN, WIFE
w&m/Mac Davis

FRIENDLY PERSUASION (film score)
m/Dimitri Tiomkin

FRIENDLY PERSUASION
m/Dimitri Tiomkin
w/Paul Francis Webster

FRIENDS
m/Elton John
w/Bernie Taupin

FRIENDSHIP
w&m/Cole Porter

FRIM FRAM SAUCE, THE
w&m/Redd Evans

FRISCO MABLE JOY
w&m/Mickey Newbury

FRISKY
w&m/Sly Stone

FROG-I-MORE RAG (instr.)
m/Ferdinand "Jelly Roll" Morton

FROG LEGS RAG (instr.)
m/James S. Scott

FROM A BUICK 6
w&m/Robert Dylan

FROM ALPHA TO OMEGA
w&m/Cole Porter

FROM AN INDIAN LODGE
w&m/Edward Alexander MacDowell

FROM EVERY KIND OF MAN
m/Sir Arthur Sullivan
w/Sir William Schwenk Gilbert

FROM HERE TO ETERNITY (film score)
m/Morris Stoloff in co w/George Duning

FROM HERE TO ETERNITY
w&m/Robert Wells, Fred Karger

FROM ME TO YOU
w&m/John Lennon, Paul McCartner

54

FROM THE BEGINNING
w&m/Keith Emerson, Gregory Lake,
Carl Palmer

**FROM THE BOTTOM OF MY
HEART**
w&m/Denny Laine, Michael Pinder

**FROM THE LAND OF THE SKY
BLUE WATER**
m/Charles Wakefield Cadman
w/Nelle Richmond Eberhart

**FROM THE VINE CAME THE
GRAPE**
w&m/Paul Cunningham, Leonard
Whitcup

FROM THIS MOMENT ON
w&m/Cole Porter

FROM UNCLE REMUS
w&m/Edward Alexander MacDowell

FROSTY THE SNOW MAN
m/Jack Rollins
w/Steve Nelson

FUGITIVE, THE (film score)
m/Richard Hageman

FUGUE FOR TIN HORNS
w&m/Frank Loesser

**FULL MOON AND EMPTY
ARMS**
w&m/Buddy Kaye, Ted Mossman
(music adapted from Rachmaninoff's
"Second Piano Concerto")

FULL OF FIRE
w&m/Al Green

FUN TO BE FOOLED
m/Harold Arlen
w/E.Y. Harburg, Ira Gershwin

FUN, FUN, FUN
w&m/Brian Wilson, Mike Love

FUNGUS AMUNGUS, A (instr.)
m/Mary Lou Williams

FUNICULI-FUNICULA
m/Luigi Denza
w/Various English word versions

FUNK #49
w&m/Joseph F. Walsh

FUNNY (How Time Slips Away)
w&m/Willie Nelson

FUNNY FACE
w&m/Donna Fargo

FUNNY FACE
m/George Gershwin

**FUNNY FAMILIAR
 FORGOTTEN FEELINGS**
w&m/Mickey Newbury

FUNNY FUNNY
w&m/Mike Chapman, Nicky Chinn

FUNNY GIRL
m/Jule Styne
w/Bob Merrill

FUNNY WAY OF LAUGHIN'
w&m/Hank Cochran

FUTURE, THE
w&m/Gordon Jenkins

FUZZY WUZZY
m/Jerry Livingston
w/Al Hoffman, Milton Drake

Addenda:

FAME
w&m/Michael Gore, D. Pritchard

FIRE
w&m/BRUCE SPRINGSTEEN

FIRECRACKER
w&m/Ricardo Williams

14 OR FIGHT
w&m/Barry Mann, Cynthia Weil

FUNKYTOWN
w&m/Steven Greenberg

SONGS

G

GABY GLIDE, THE
w&m/Louis A Hirsch

GAL IN CALICO, A
m/Arthur Schwartz
w/Leo Robin

GALLANT MEN
m/American Traditional
w/Senator Everett McKinley
Dirksen

GALVESTON
w&m/Jimmy Webb

GAMBLER, THE
w&m/Donald Alan Schlitz

GAMES PEOPLE PLAY
w&m/Joe South

**GANG THAT SANG HEART OF
MY HEART, THE**
w&m/Ben Ryan

GARDEN IN THE RAIN, A
m/Carroll Gibbons
w/James Dyrenforth

GARDEN OF MY DREAMS
m/David Stamper
w/Gene Buck, Louis A Hirsch

GARDEN OF ROMANCE, THE
m/Emmerich Kalman
w/Guy Bolton

GARDEN OF ROSES
m/Johann C. Schmid
w/James Dempsey

GARDEN PARTY
w&m/Rick Nelson

GASOLINE ALLEY
w&m/Rod Stewart, Ron Wood

GATES OF EDEN
w&m/Robert Dylan

GAUCHO SERENADE
m/John Redmond, Nat Simon
w/James Cavanaugh

GAUDEAMUS IGITUR
m/13th Century Psalm also used by
Brahms in his "Academic
Festival Overture"
w/C.W. Kindleben

**GAY RANCHERO, A
(Las Altenitas)**
m/J.J. Espinosa
w/Abe Tuvim, Francis Luban

GAY WHITE WAY, THE
m/Ludwig Englander
w/J. Clarence Harvey

GEE
w&m/William E. Davis, Morris Levy

**GEE BABY AIN'T I GOOD TO
YOU**
w&m/Don Redman

**GEE BUT IT'S GREAT TO MEET
A FRIEND FROM YOUR HOME
TOWN**
w&m/Fred Fisher, William Tracey,
James McGavisk

GEE BUT IT'S HARD
w&m/Thomas Andrew Dorsey

GEE, BUT IT'S LONELY
w&m/Phil Everly

GEE DAD IT'S A WURLITZER
w&m/Howard Fenton

GEE OFFICER KRUPKE
m/Leonard Bernstein
w/Stephen Sondheim

GEE WHIZ
w&m/Carla Thomas

GEECHY JOE
w&m/Albert Andrew Gibson

GENTLE ANNIE
w&m/Stephen C. Foster

GENTLE ON MY MIND
w&m/John Hartford

GENTLEMAN IS A DOPE, THE
m/Richard Rodgers
w/Oscar Hammerstein II

**GENUINE TONG FUNERAL, A
(instr.)**
m/Carla Bley

GEORGIA
m/Walter Donaldson
w/Howard E. Johnson

GEORGIA ON MY MIND
m/Hoagy Carmichael
w/Stuart Gorrell

GEORGIA PINES
w&m/Tony Joe White

GEORGIA SUNSHINE
w&m/Jerry Reed

GEORGY GIRL
w&m/Tom Springfield, Jim Dale

GERTIE FROM BIZERTE
m/Walter Kent
w/James Cavanaugh, Bob Cutter

GESÙ BAMBINO
m/Pietro A. Yon
w/English words: Frederick H.
Martens. Italian words:
Pietro A. Yon

**GET A LITTLE DIRT ON YOUR
HANDS**
w&m/Bill Anderson

GET A MOVE ON
w&m/Eddie Money, Paul Collins,
Lloyd Chiate

GET AWAY
w&m/Georgie Fame

GET BACK
w&m/Paul McCartney, John Lennon

GET CLOSER
w&m/Dash Crofts, James Seals

GET DANCIN'
w&m/Kenny Nolan, Bob Crewe

GET DOWN
w&m/Curtis Mayfield

GET DOWN
m/Sir Arthur Sullivan
w/Sir William Schwenk Gilbert

GET DOWN TONIGHT
w&m/Henry Wayne Casey, Richard
Finch

GET HAPPY
m/Harold Arlen
w/Ted Koehler

GET IT
w&m/Hank Ballard, Alonzo Tucker

GET IT RIGHT NEXT TIME
w&m/Gerry Rafferty

**GET ME TO THE CHURCH ON
TIME**
m/Frederick Loewe
w/Alan Jay Lerner

GET OFF
w&m/Ish Ledesma, Richie Puente

GET OFF MY CLOUD
w&m/Mick Jagger, Keith Richard

**GET OUT AND GET UNDER
THE MOON**
w&m/Larry Shay, Charles Tobias,
William Jerome

GET OUT OF TOWN
w&m/Cole Porter

GET READY
w&m/William (Smokey) Robinson, Jr.

GET RHYTHM
w&m/John R. Cash

**GET TOGETHER (C'mon People
Now Smile On Your Brother)**
w&m/Chet Powers

GET UP AND BOOGIE
w&m/Silvester Levay

GET UP, STAND
w&m/Bob Marley

GET YOUR ROCKS OFF
w&m/Robert Dylan

**GETTIN' OLD BEFORE MY
TIME**
w&m/Merle Kilgore

GETTING IN TUNE
w&m/Peter Townshend

GETTING TO KNOW YOU
m/Richard Rodgers
w/Oscar Hammerstein II

GHETTO CHILD
w&m/Thomas Bell, Linda Creed

GHOST AND MRS. MUIR, THE (film score)
m/Dimitri Tiomkin

G.I. JIVE
w&m/Johnny Mercer

GIANNINA MIA
m/Rudolf Friml
w/Otto Harbach

GIANT (film score)
m/Dimitri Tiomkin

GIBRALTAR (instr.)
m/Joe Zawinul

GIDDYUP GO
w&m/Red Sovine, Tommy Hill

GIFT OF LOVE, THE
m/Sammy Fain
w/Paul Francis Webster

GIGI
m/Frederick Loewe
w/Alan Jay Lerner

GOLDA (film score)
m/Hugo Friedhofer

GIMME A LITTLE KISS WILL YA HUH
m/Maceo Pinkard
w/Roy Turk

GIMME DAT DING
w&m/Albert L. Hammond, Mike Hazelwood

GIMME, GIMME, GIMME
w&m/Benny Anderson

GIMME LITTLE SIGN
w&m/Brenton Wood

GIMME SHELTER
w&m/Mick Jagger, Keith Richard

GIMME SOME LOVIN
w&m/Steve Winwood, Muff Winwood, Spencer Davis

GIMME SOME TIME
w&m/Natalie Cole

GIN AND COCOANUT WATER
w&m/Frederick Wilmoth Hendricks

GIRL DON'T COME
w&m/Chris Andrews

GIRL FRIEND, THE
m/Richard Rodgers
w/Lorenz (Larry) Hart

GIRL FRIEND OF THE WHIRLING DERVISH, THE
m/Harry Warren
w/Al Dubin, Johnny Mercer

GIRL FROM IPANEMA, THE
m/Antonio Carlos Jobim
English w/Norman Gimbel
Spanish w/Vinicius de Moraes

GIRL IN SATIN, THE
m/Leroy Anderson

GIRL OF MY DREAMS
w&m/Charles (Sunny) Clapp

GIRL OF THE NORTH COUNTRY
w&m/Robert Dylan

GIRL ON THE MAGAZINE COVER, THE
w&m/Irving Berlin

GIRL TALK
w&m/Bobby Troup

GIRL TALK (instr.)
m/Neal Hefti

GIRL THAT I MARRY, THE
w&m/Irving Berlin

GIRL WATCHER
w&m/Wayne Pittman

GIRL WITH THE LIGHT BLUE HAIR (instr.)
m/Raymond Scott

GIRL, YOU'll BE A WOMAN NOW
w&m/Neil Diamond

GIRL OF MY DREAMS
w&m/Irving Berlin

GIRL'S SCHOOL
w&m/Paul and Linda McCartney

GITANERIAS (instr.)
m/Ernesto Lecuona

GITARZAN
w&m/Ray Stevens, Bill Everett

GIVE A LITTLE BIT
w&m/Roger Hodgson, Rick Davies

GIVE A LITTLE WHISTLE
m/Leigh Harline
w/Ned Washington

GIVE A MAN A HORSE HE CAN RIDE
m/Geoffrey O'Hara
w/James Thomson

GIVE IT ALL YOU GOT
w&m/Chuck Mangione

GIVE IT UP
w&m/Bonnie Lynn Raitt

GIVE IT UP OR TURN IT LOOSE
w&m/James Brown

GIVE ME A SWEETHEART
w&m/John D. Loudermilk

GIVE ME LOVE (Give Me Peace)
w&m/George Harrison

GIVE ME THE MOONLIGHT, GIVE ME THE GIRL
w&m/Albert Von Tilzer, Lew Brown

GIVE ME THE SIMPLE LIFE
m/Harry Ruby
w/Rube Bloom

GIVE ME YOUR TIRED, YOUR POOR
w&m/Irving Berlin (based on Statue of Liberty's inscription poem by Emma Lazar)

GIVE MY REGARDS TO BROADWAY
w&m/George M. Cohan

GIVE MYSELF A PARTY
w&m/Don Gibson

GIVE PEACE A CHANCE/ REMEMBER LOVE
w&m/John Lennon, Yoko Ono

GIVE US BACK OUR OLD COMMANDER (Little Mac, The People's Pride)
w&m/Septimus Winner

GIVING IT ALL AWAY
w&m/Leo Sayer, David Courtney

GIVING UP ON LOVE
w&m/Jerry Goldstein, Bob Feldman, Richard Gottehrer

GLAD
w&m/Steve Winwood

GLADIOLUS (instr.)
m/Scott Joplin

GLENDALE FIRE (instr.)
m/Meade 'Lux" Lewis

GLENN MILLER STORY, THE (film score)
m/Henry Mancini

GLOOMY SUNDAY
m/Rezio Seress
w/Samuel M. Lewis

GLORIA
w&m/Van Morrison, George Ivan Morrison

GLORY OF LOVE, THE
w&m/Billy Hill

GLORY ROAD, DE
m/Jacques Wolfe
w/Clement Wood

GLOW-WORM, THE
m/Paul Lincke
w/Original words: Lilla Cayley Robinson.
Revised words: Johnny Mercer

GO AWAY LITTLE GIRL
w&m/Carol King, Gerry Goffin

GO DOWN GAMBLING
w&m/David Clayton-Thomas

GO INTO YOUR DANCE
m/Harry Warren
w/Al Dubin

GO ON AND COAX ME
m/Harry Von Tilzer
w/Andrew B. Sterling

GO TO THE MARDI GRAS
w&m/Henry R. Byrd

GO 'WAY FROM MY WINDOW
w&m/John Jacob Niles

GO WHERE YOU WANNA GO
w&m/John Phillips

GO YOUR OWN WAY
w&m/Lindsay Buckingham

GOD BLESS AMERICA
w&m/Irving Berlin

GOD BLESS OUR BOYS
w&m/George Bennard

GOD BLESS THE CHILD
w&m/Billie Holiday

GOD, COUNTRY AND MY BABY
w&m/Dorsey Burnette,
Johnny Burnette

GOD IS AMAZING
w&m/Deniece Williams

GOD OF THUNDER
w&m/Paul Stanley

GOD ONLY KNOWS
w&m/Brian Wilson, Tony Asher

GOD'S COLORING BOOK
w&m/Dolly Parton

GOD'S COUNTRY
w&m/Beasley Smith, Haven
Gillespie

GOIN' BACK
w&m/Carole King, Gerry Goffin

GOIN' HOME
w&m/Antoine "Fats" Domino,
Dave Bartholomew

GOIN' HOME
w&m/William Arms Fisher (adapted
from Anton Dvorak's "New World
Symphony, Op. 95)

GOIN' MOBILE
w&m/Peter Townshend

GOIN' OUT OF MY HEAD
w&m/Teddy Randazzo,
Bobby Weinstein

GOIN' STEADY
w&m/Faron Young

GOIN' TO CHICAGO
w&m/James Andrew Rushing

GOIN' TO THE RIVER
w&m/Antoine "Fats" Domino,
Dave Bartholomew

GOING HOME
w&m/Mick Jagger, Keith Richard

GOING IN CIRCLES
w&m/Anita Poree, Jerry
Eugene Peters

GOING IN WITH MY EYES OPEN
w&m/Tony MacCaulay

GOING MY WAY
m/James Van Heusen
w/Johnny Burke

GOING MY WAY (film score)
m/Robert Emmett Dolan

GOING TO A GO-GO
w&m/William (Smokey) Robinson,
Jr., Marvin Moore, Bobby Rogers,
Marvin Tarplin

GOING TO CALIFORNIA
w&m/James Page, Robert Plant

GOLD DUST WOMAN
w&m/Stephanie (Stevie) Nicks

GOLD RUSH IS OVER, THE
w&m/Cindy Walker

GOLDEN AND SILVER (waltz)
m/Franz Lehar
w/Adrian Ross

GOLDEN DAY OF LOVE, THE
m/Victor Jacobi
w/Adrian Ross, Arthur Anderson

GOLDEN DAYS
m/Sigmund Romberg
w/Dorothy Donnelly

GOLDEN EARRINGS
m/Victor Young
w/Jay Linvingstone, Ray Evans

GOLDEN GATE
w&m/Joseph Meyer, Billy Rose,
Dave Dreyer, Al Jolson

GOLDEN LADY
w&m/Stevie Wonder

GOLDEN ROCKET, THE
w&m/Hank Snow

GOLDEN STRIKER, THE (instr.)
m/John Lewis

GOLDEN YEARS
w&m/David Bowie

GOLDFINGER
m/John Barry
w/Anthony Newley, Leslie Bricusse

GOLLY CHARLIE
m/Gustave A. Kerker
w/Hugh Morton

GONE AND LEFT ME BLUES
w&m/Johnny Bond

GONE FISHIN'
w&m/Nick Kenny, Charles Kenny

GONE TOO FAR
w&m/John Ford Coley

GONE WITH THE WIND (film score)
m/Max Steiner

GONE WITH THE WIND (instr.)
m/William (Count) Basie

GONE WITH THE WIND
m/Herbert Magidson
w/Allie Wrubel

GONNA BUILD A MOUNTAIN
w&m/Leslie Bricusse,
Anthony Newley

GONNA FLY NOW (Theme from "Rocky")
m/Bill Conti
w/Carol Connors, Ayn Robbins

GONNA GET A GIRL
w&m/Haward Simon, Al Lewis

GOOD BAIT (instr.)
m/John Coltrane

GOOD EARTH, THE (instr.)
m/Neil Hefti

GOOD EVENING CAROLINE
w&m/Albert Von Tilzer,
Jack Norworth

GOOD FEELIN'
w&m/T-Bone Walker

GOOD FOR NOTHIN' JOE
w&m/Rube Bloom, Ted Koehler

GOOD GIRLS DON'T
w&m/Doug Fieger

GOOD HEARTED WOMAN, A
w&m/Willie Nelson,
Waylon Jennings

GOOD LOVIN'
w&m/Felix Cavaliere, Eddie Brigati

GOOD LOVIN'
w&m/Ahmet Ertegun, Leroy
Kirkland, Denny Taylor, Jesse Stone

GOOD LOVIN'
w&m/Billy Sherrill

GOOD LOVIN' (Love You, Yes I Do)
w&m/Robert Calvin Bland

GOOD LUCK CHARM
w&m/Aaron Schroeder, Wally Gold

GOOD MAN IS HARD TO FIND, A
w&m/Eddie Green

GOOD MORNING FREEDOM
(Blue Mink)
w&m/Albert L. Hammond, Mike Hazelwood

GOOD MORNING JUDGE
w&m/Eric Stewart, Lol Creme, Graham Goulding

GOOD MORNING MR. ZIP-ZIP-ZIP
w&m/Robert Lloyd

GOOD MORROW,
GOOD LOVER
m/Sir Arthur Sullivan
w/Sir William Schwenk Gilbert

GOOD MORNING STARSHINE
m/Galt MacDermot
w/James Rado, Gerome Ragni

GOOD NEWS
m/Ray Henderson
w/Lew Brown, Buddy DeSylva

GOOD NEWS
w&m/Sam Cooke

GOOD NEWS
w&m/George Richey, Billy Sherrill, Norro Wilson

GOOD NIGHT LADIES
m/Egbert Anson Van Alstyne
w/Harry H. Williams

GOOD NIGHT SWEETHEART
w&m/Ray Noble, Jimmy Campbell, Reg Connelly

GOOD OLD DAYS, THE
m/Gustave A. Kerker
w/Hugh Morton

GOOD THINGS
w&m/Billy Sherrill, Norro Wilson, Carmol Taylor

GOOD TIMES (TV theme)
m/Dave Grusin

GOOD TIMES, BAD TIMES
w&m/James Page, Robert Plant, John Paul Jones, John "Bonzo" Bonham

GOOD VIBRATIONS
w&m/Brian Wilson, Mike Love

GOOD YEAR FOR ROSES, A
w&m/Jerry Chesnut

GOODBYE AGAIN
w&m/John Denver

GOODBYE BECKY COHEN
w&m/Irving Berlin

GOODBYE BROADWAY,
HELLO FRANCE
m/C. Francis Reisner
w/Renny Davis, Billy Baskette

GOODBYE COLUMBUS
(film score)
m/Charles Fox

GOODBYE CRUEL WORL
w&m/Gloria Shayne

GOODBYE EVES OF BLUE
m/Harry Armstrong
w/James J. Walker

GOODBYE GIRL, THE
(film score)
m/Dave Grusin

GOODBYE GIRLS I'M
THROUGH
m/Ivan Caryll
w/John Golden

GOODBYE, GOOD LUCK GOD
BLESS YOU
m/Ernest R. Ball
w/J. Keirn Brennan

GOODBYE MY LADY LOVE
w&m/Charles K. Harris, Joseph E. Howard

GOODBYE PORK PIE HAT
(instr.)
m/Charles Mingus

GOODBYE STRANGER
w&m/Roger Hodgson, Rick Davies

GOODBYE YELLOW BRICK
ROAD
m/Elton John
w/Bernie Taupin

GOODBYE IRENE
w&m/Huddie (Leadbelly) Ledbetter

GOODNIGHT MY LOVE
m/Harry Revel
w/Mack Gordon

GOODNIGHT MY SOMEONE
w&m/Meredith Willson

GOODNIGHT MY LOVE
w&m/Jesse Belvin

GOODY, GOODY
m/Matt Malneck
w/Johnny Mercer

GOODY, GOODY GUMDROPS
w&m/Jerry Kasenetz, Jeff Katz

GOOF AND I, THE (instr.)
m/Al Cohn

GOOFUS
m/Wayne King, Burke Bivens
w/Gus Kahn

GOSPEL SINGER, THE
w&m/Tony Joe White

GOT A FEELING
w&m/John Phillips, Dennis Doherty

GOT A JOB
w&m/Berry Gordy Jr., Tyrone Carlo, William "Smokey" Robinson Jr.

GOT MY MOJO WORKING
w&m/Muddy Waters

GOT THE ALL OVERS FOR YOU
w&m/Freddie Hart

GOT TO GET YOU INTO MY
LIFE
w&m/Paul McCartney, John Lennon

GOT TO LOVE SOMEBODY
w&m/Nile Rodgers, Bernard Edwards

GOT YOU ON MY MIND
w&m/Joe Thomas, Howard Biggs

GOTTA GET UP WITHOUT HER
w&m/Harry Edward Nilsson

GOTTA GET YOU OFF MY
MIND
w&m/Solomon Burke, Delores Burke

GOTTA SAVE SOMEBODY
w&m/Robert Dylan

GOTTA SEE JANE
w&m/R. Dean Taylor

GOTTA TRAVEL ON
w&m/Pete Seeger, Paul Clayton, Lee Hays, David Lazar, Fred Hellerman, Ronnie Gilbert, Larry Ehrlich

GOVINDA
w&m/George Harrison

GRADUATE, THE (film score)
m/Dave Grusin

GRADUATION DAY
m/Joe Sherman
w/Noel Sherman

GRANADA
w&m/Augustin Lara

GRAND HOTEL (film score)
m/William Axt

GRAND ILLUSION, THE
w&m/Dennis De Young

GRANDFATHER'S CLOCK
w&m/Henry Clay Work

GRANDMA HARP
w&m/Merle Haggard

GRANDMA'S HANDS
w&m/Bill Withers

GRANDPA'S SPELLS (instr.)
m/Ferdinand "Jelly Roll" Morton

GRASS IS GETTING GREENER,
THE
w&m/W.S.Stevenson, Cecil Gant

GRAVY WALTZ
w&m/Steve Allen, Ray Brown

GRAZING IN THE GRASS
w&m/Harry James Elston,
Philemon Hou

GREAT BIRD (instr.)
m/Keith Jarrett

GREAT DAY
m/Vincent Youmans
w&m/Edward Eliscu, Billy Rose

GREAT GATSBY, THE
(film score)
m/Robert Emmett Dolan (1949
film version) Nelson Riddle (1974
film version)

GREAT IMPOSTER, THE
w&m/Jackie De Shannon,
Shari Sheeley

GREAT IMPOSTER, THE (film
score)
m/Henry Mancini

GREAT LIE, THE
w&m/Albert Andrew Gibson

GREAT PRETENDER, THE
w&m/Buck Ram

GREAT RACE, THE (film score)
m/Henry Mancini

GREAT SPECKLE BIRD
w&m/Roy Claxton Acuff

GREEN (Bein' Green)
w&m/Joseph Raposo

GREEN DOLPHIN STREET
(film score)
m/Bronislau Kaper

GREEN DOOR, THE
m/Bob Davie
w/Marvin Moore

GREEN EYED LADY
w&m/Jerry Corbetta, Robert
Webber, Robert Raymond

GREEN EYES
m/Nilo Menendez
w/English words: E. Rivera,
E. Woods Spanish words: Adolfo
Utrera

GREEN FIELDS
w&m/Terry Gilkyson, Frank Miller,
Richard Dehr

GREEN GREEN
w&m/Randy Sparks, Barry McGuire

GREEN GREEN GRASS OF
HOME
w&m/Curly Putnam

GREEN LEAVES OF SUMMER
m/Dimitri Tiomkin
w/Paul F. Webster

GREEN MANSIONS (film score)
m/Bronislau Kaper

GREEN PASTURES, THE
(film score)
m/Erich Wolfgang Korngold

GREEN RIVER
w&m/John C. Fogerty

GREEN TAMBOURINE
w&m/Paul Leka, Shelby Pina

GREENBACK DOLLAR
w&m/Hoyt Axton

GRIEVING
w&m/Billy Strayhorn,
Duke Ellington

GRIN AND BEAR IT
w&m/John D. Loudermilk, Marijohn
Wilkin

GRINNIN' IN YOUR FACE
w&m/Son House

GRIZZLY BEAR, THE
w&m/Irving Berlin

GROOVE LINE, THE
w&m/Rod Temperton

GROOVY KIND OF LOVE, A
m/Toni Wine
w/Carole Bayer Sager

GROOVIN'
w&m/Felix Cavaliere, Eddie Brigati

GROVIN' HIGH (instr.)
m/Dizzy Gillespie

GROOVIN' TIME
w&m/Otis Redding, Steve Cropper

GROWING UP
w&m/Bruce Springsteen

GUANTANAMERA (Lady of
Guantanamo)
w&m/Jose Marti

GUESS I'M DOIN' FINE
w&m/Robert Dylan

GUESS WHO
w&m/Jesse Belvin, Jo Ann Belvin

GUESS WHO'S COMING TO
DINNER (film score)
w&m/Frank De Vol

GUILTY
w&m/Alex Zanetis

GUILTY
m/Harry Akst, Richard A. Whiting
w/Gus Kahn, Harry Akst

GUINNEVERE
w&m/David Crosby

GUITAR AND PEN
w&m/Peter Townshend

GUITAR BOOGIE (instr.)
m/Arthur Smith

GUITAR MAN
w&m/Duane Eddy, Lee Hazlewood

GUITAR MAN
w&m/Jerry Reed

GUITAR MAN, THE
w&m/David Gates

GUITAR POLKA
w&m/Al Dexter

GULF COAST BLUES (instr.)
m/Clarence Williams

GUNS OF NAVARONE, THE
(film score)
m/Dimitri Tiomkin

GUNS OF NAVORONE, THE
m/Dimitri Tiomkin
w/Paul Francis Webster

GUNSLINGER
w&m/Ellas McDaniel (Bo Diddley)

GUY IS A GUY, A
w&m/Oscar Brand

GUY NAMED JOE, A
w&m/Harlan Howard

GUYS AND DOLLS
w&m/Frank Loesser

GYPSIES, TRAMPS AND
THIEVES
w&m/Sonny Bono, Cher (Cherilyn S.
La Pierre)

GYPSY BLUES
m/Eubie Blake
w/Noble Sissle

GYPSY IN MY SOUL, THE
w&m/Moe Jaffe, Clay A. Boland

GYPSY LOU
w&m/Robert Dylan

GYPSY LOVE SONG (Slumber
On My Little Gypsy Sweetheart)
m/Victor Herbert
w/Harry B. Smith

GYPSY MAN
w&m/See listing of composers under
name Lee Oskar

GYPSY, THE
w&m/Billy Reid

GYPSY WOMAN
w&m/Curtis Mayfield

GYPSY WIND
w&m/Dan Fogelberg

Addenda:

GAMES WITHOUT FRONTIERS
w&m/Peter Gabriel

GETTING MARRIED TODAY
w&m/Stephen Sondheim

GIDGET (film score)
m/Morris Stoloff

GIRL'S SCHOOL (film score)
m/Morris Stoloff

GIVE ME THE NIGHT
w&m/Rod Temperton

GLASS ENCLOSURE (instr.)
m/Bud Powell

GLIDE
w&m/Nathaniel Phillips,
Bruce Smith

GOOD LORD LOVES YOU, THE
w&m/Richard Fagan

GOOD OLD BOYS LIKE ME
w&m/Bob McDill

GOOD ROCKING TONIGHT
w&m/Roy Brown

GOODNIGHT TONIGHT
w&m/Paul McCartney

GOT TO BE REAL
w&m/David Paich

GREAT LIE, THE
w&m/Albert Andrew Gibson

 **SONGS**

H

HAD TO FALL IN LOVE
w&m/Justin Hayward

HAIL COLUMBIA
m/Phillip Phile
w/Joseph Hopkinson

HAIL! HAIL! ROCK AND ROLL
w&m/Bill Danoff, Kathy "Taffy"
Nivert Danoff

**HAIL HAIL THE GANG'S ALL
HERE**
m/Sir Arthur Sullivan (adapted by
Theodore Morse from "With
Catlike Tread")
w/Theodora (Dolly) Morse

HAIL TO THE CHIEF
m/James Anderson
w/Sir Walter Scott

HAIR
m/Galt MacDermot
w/James Rado, Gerome Ragni

HAIR OF GOLD, EYES OF BLUE
w&m/Sunny Skylar

HAITIAN DIVORCE
w&m/Donald Fagen, Walter Becker

HAITIAN FIGHT SONG (instr.)
m/Charles Mingus

HALF A MILE AWAY
w&m/Billy Joel

HALF BREED
w&m/Sonny Bono, Cher (Cherilyn S.
LaPierre)

HALFWAY TO PARADISE
w&m/Carole King, Gerry Goffin

HALLELUJAH
m/Vincent Youmans
w/Leo Robin, Clifford Grey

**HALLS OF MONTEZUMA (film
score)**
m/Sol Kaplan

HAMBONE
w&m/Archie Shepp

**HAND ME DOWN MY WALKING
STICK**
w&m/James A. Bland

**HAND THAT ROCKS THE
CRADLE, THE**
m/William H. Holmes
w/Charles W. Berkeley

**HANDS ACROSS THE SEA
(march)**
m/John Philip Sousa

HANDS ACROSS THE TABLE
m/Jean Delettre
w/Mitchell Parish

HANDY MAN
w&m/Otis Blackwell, Jimmy Jones,
Charles Merenstein

HANG IN THERE GIRL
w&m/Freddie Hart

HANG ON SLOOPY
w&m/Rick Derringer

HANG UP YOUR HANG UPS
w&m/Herbie Hancock

HANG YOUR HEAD IN SHAME
w&m/Fred Rose, Ed G. Nelson
Steve Nelson

**HANG YOUR HEART ON A
HICKORY LIMB**
m/James V. Monaco
w/Johnny Burke

HANGING TREE, THE
m/Jerry Livingston
w/Mack David

HANGOVER TAVERN
w&m/Hank Thompson

**HANK WILLIAMS YOU WROTE
MY LIFE**
w&m/Paul Craft

HANKY PANKY
w&m/Tommy James, Bob King

**HANNAH WON'T YOU OPEN
THAT DOOR**
m/Harry Von Tilzer
w/Andrew B. Sterling

**HANS CHRISTIAN ANDERSEN
(film score)**
m/Walter Scharf

HAPLESS CHILD, THE
m/Michael Mantler (based on
Edward Gorey poem)

HAPPENING, THE
w&m/Eddie Holland, Brian Holland,
Lamont Dozier

HAPPENING, THE (film score)
m/Frank DeVol

**HAPPIEST GIRL IN THE
WHOLE U.S.A., THE**
w&m/Donna Fargo

HAPPINESS IS
w&m/Paul Evans, Paul Parnes

**HAPPINESS IS A THING
CALLED JOE**
m/Harold Arlen
w/E.Y. Harburg

HAPPY
w&m/Mick Jagger, Keith Richard

HAPPY ANNIVERSARY
w&m/Glenn Shorrock

HAPPY BIRTHDAY DARLIN'
w&m/Conway Twitty, C. Howard

HAPPY BIRTHDAY TO ME
w&m/Bill Anderson

**HAPPY BIRTHDAY SWEET
SIXTEEN**
w&m/Neil Sedaka,
Howard Greenfield

**HAPPY BIRTHDAY TO YOU
(originally Good Morning To All)**
m/Mildred J. Hill
w/Patty Smith Hill

HAPPY DAYS
m/Charles Fox
w/Norman Gimbel

**HAPPY DAYS ARE HERE
AGAIN**
m/Milton Ager
w/Jack Yellen

HAPPY FEET
m/Milton Ager
w/Jack Yellen

HAPPY GO LUCKY LOCAL
m/Duke Ellington

HAPPY-GO-LUCKY-ME
w&m/Paul Evans, Al Byron

HAPPY HOLIDAY
w&m/Irving Berlin

HAPPY IN LOVE
m/Sammy Fain
w/Jack Yellen

HAPPY MAN
w&m/B.J. Thomas

HAPPY SHADES OF BLUE
w&m/Freddie Cannon, Bob Crewe,
Frank C. Slay Jr.

HAPPY STATE OF MIND
w&m/Bill Anderson

HAPPY TALK
m/Richard Rodgers
w/Oscar Hammerstein II

HAPPY TIME, THE
m/Dimitri Tiomkin
w/Ned Washington

HAPPY TRAILS
w&m/Dale Evans

**HAPPY WANDERER, THE
(Val-De Ri Val-De Rah)**
m/Friedrich W. Moeller
w/Antonia Ridge

HARBOR LIGHTS
m/Will Grosz (Hugh Williams)
w/Jimmy Kennedy

HARD AIN'T IT HARD
w&m/Woody Guthrie

HARD DAY'S NIGHT, A
w&m/Paul McCartney, John Lennon

HARD-HEADED WOMAN
w&m/Cat Stevens

HARD HEARTED HANNAH
m/Milton Ager
w/Jack Yellen, Bob Bigelow
Charles Bates

HARD LOVING LOSER
w&m/Richard Fariña

HARD LUCK WOMAN
w&m/Paul Stanley

HARD MONKEYS
w&m/Alvin Lee

HARD RAIN'S GONNA FALL, A
w&m/Robert Dylan

HARD TIME
w&m/David Paich, Boz Scaggs

HARD TIME BLUES
w&m/Joshua D. White

HARD TIMES COME AGAIN NO MORE
w&m/Stephen C. Foster

HARD TO GET
w&m/Jack Segal

HARDCORE (1979) (film score)
m/Jack Nitzsche

HARLEM AIRSHAFT (instr.)
m/Duke Ellington

HARLEM JAZZ SCENE, THE (instr.)
m/Charlie Christian

HARLEM ON MY MIND
w&m/Irving Berlin

HARLEM STRUT (instr.)
m/James P. Johnson

HARMONICA PLAYER, THE
w&m/David W. De Frentresse Guion

HARMONIQUE (instr.)
m/John Coltrane

HARMONY
m/Elton John
w/Bernie Taupin

HARMONY IN HARLEM
w&m/Duke Ellington,
Johnny Hodges

HARP THAT ONCE THRO' TARA'S HALLS, THE
m/from the Irish folk melody "Gramachree"
w/Thomas Moore

HARPER (film score)
m/Johnny Mandel

HARPER VALLEY P.T.A.
w&m/Tom T. Hall

HARRIGAN
w&m/George M. Cohan

HARRY AND TONTO (film theme)
m/Bill Conti

HARVEY GIRLS, THE (film score)
m/Lennie Hayton

HAS ANYONE HERE SEEN KELLY
w&m/C.W. Murphy, Will Letters
(American revision: William C. McKenna)

HATARI (film score)
m/Henry Mancini

HATFUL OF RAIN, A (film score)
m/Bernard Herrmann

HATS OFF TO LARRY
w&m/Del Shannon

HAVE A HEART
m/Jerome Kern
w/Gene Buck, P.G. Wodehouse

HAVE A LITTLE FAITH
w&m/Glenn Sutton, Billy Sherrill

HAVE A LITTLE FAITH IN ME
m/Harry Warren
w/Samuel M. Lewis, Joseph Young

HAVE I TOLD YOU LATELY
w&m/Harold Rome

HAVE I TOLD YOU LATELY THAT I LOVE YOU
w&m/Scott Wiseman

HAVE MERCY BABY
w&m/William (Billy) Ward

HAVE MERCY ON THE CRIMINAL
m/Elton John
w/Bernie Taupin

HAVE YOU EVER BEEN LONELY
m/Peter DeRose
w/George Brown

HAVE YOU EVER SEEN THE RAIN
w&m/John C. Fogerty

HAVE YOU FORGOTTEN SO SOON
w&m/Abner Silver

HAVE YOU HEARD
w&m/Michael Pinder

HAVE YOU MET MISS JONES
m/Richard Rodgers
w/Lorenz (Larry) Hart

HAVE YOU NEVER BEEN MELLOW
w&m/John Farrar

HAVE YOU SEEN HER FACE
w&m/Roger McGuinn

HAVE YOURSELF A MERRY LITTLE CHRISTMAS
w&m/Ralph Blane, Hugh Martin

HAVEN'T GOT TIME FOR THE RAIN
w&m/Candy Simon

(YOU'RE) HAVING MY BABY
w&m/Paul Anka

HAWAIIAN EYE
m/Jerry Livingston
w/Mack David

HAWAIIAN PARADISE
w&m/Harry Owens

HAWAIIAN WEDDING SONG (Ke Kali Nei Ao)
w&m/Dick Manning, Al Hoffman,
Charles E. King

HAZEL DELL, THE
w&m/George Frederick Root

HE
m/Jack Richards
w/Richard Mullan

HE AIN'T HEAVY . . . HE'S MY BROTHER
m/Robert W. Scott
w/Bob Russell

HE BELIEVES IN ME
w&m/Bernie Wayne, Ervin Drake

HE BROUGHT HOME ANOTHER
w&m/Paul Dresser

HE DON'T LOVE YOU LIKE I DO
w&m/Jerry Butler, Curtis Mayfield

HE FOUGHT FOR A CAUSE HE THOUGHT WAS RIGHT
w&m/Paul Dresser

HE IS AN ENGLISHMAN
m/Sir Arthur Sullivan
w/Sir William Schwenk Gilbert

HE LOVES AND SHE LOVES
m/George Gershwin
w/Ira Gershwin

HE PLAYED REAL GOOD FOR FREE
w&m/Joni Mitchell

HE TOUCHED ME
m/William J. Gaither
w/William J. Gaither, Gloria Gaither

HE TOUCHED ME
w&m/Ira Levin, Milton Schafer

HE WILL BREAK YOUR HEART
w&m/Curtis Mayfield, Jerry Butler,
Calvin Carter

HE WAS A MARRIED MAN
m/Ludwig Englander
w/Harry B. Smith

HEADING DOWN THE WRONG HIGHWAY
w&m/Ted Daffan

HEAR ME LORD
w&m/George Harrison

HEAR ME TALKING TO YOU
w&m/Gertrude "Ma" Rainey

HEART BEAT (film score)
m/Jack Nitzsche

HEART
m/Jerry Ross
w/Richard Adler

HEART AND SOUL
m/Hoagy Carmichael
w/Frank Loesser

HEART AND SOUL
w&m/Reverend James Cleveland

HEART FULL OF LOVE, A
w&m/Eddy Arnold, Roy Soehnel,
Steve Nelson

HEART HOTELS
w&m/Dan Fogelberg

HEART IN HAND
w&m/Jackie DeShannon, Shari
Sheeley

HEART IS A LONELY HUNTER, THE (film score)
m/Dave Grusin

HEART OF GLASS
w&m/Deborah Harry, Chris Stein

HEART OF GOLD
w&m/Neil Young

HEART OVER MIND
w&m/Mel Tillis

HEARTACHE
w&m/Jim Reeves

HEARTACHE TONIGHT
w&m/J.D. Souther, Glenn Frey,
Donald Henley, Bob Seger

HEARTACHES
m/Al Hoffman
w/John Klenner

HEARTACHES BY THE NUMBER
w&m/Harlan Howard

HEARTBREAK HOTEL
w&m/Mae Boren Axton, Elvis
Presley, Tommy Durden

HEARTBREAK, U.S.A.
w&m/Harlan Howard

HEARTBREAKER
w&m/Dolly Parton

HEARTLESS
w&m/Ann Wilson, Nancy Wilson

HEARTS AND FLOWERS (Coeurs et Fleures)
m/Theodore Moses-Tobani
w/Mary D. Prine

HEARTS IN DIXIE (Film score)
m/Howard Manucy Jackson

HEARTS ON FIRE
w&m/Walter Egan

HEARTS ON FIRE
w&m/Eddie Rabbitt, Even Stevens,
Don Tyler

HEAT WAVE
w&m/Irving Berlin

(Love Is Like A) HEAT WAVE
w&m/Eddie Holland, Brian Holland,
Lamont Dozier

HEATHER HONEY
w&m/Tommy Roe

HEATHER ON THE HILL, THE
m/Frederick Loewe
w/Alan Jay Lerner

HEAVEN AND HELL
w&m/John Entwhistle

HEAVEN CAN WAIT
m/James Van Heusen
w/Edgar DeLange

HEAVEN CAN WAIT (film score)
m/Dave Grusin

HEAVEN DROPS HER CURTAIN DOWN
m/Sammy Mysels
w/George Mysels

HEAVEN KNOWS
w&m/Donna Summer, Georgio
Moroder, Pete Bellotte

HEAVEN KNOWS MR. ALLISON (film score)
m/Georges Auric

HEAVEN MAKES YOU HAPPY
w&m/Bobby Bloom

HEAVEN MUST BE MISSING AN ANGEL
w&m/Frederick Perren,
Keni St. Lewis

HEAVEN MUST HAVE SENT YOU
w&m/Eddie Holland, Brian Holland,
Lamont Dozier

HEAVEN SAYS HELLO
w&m/Cindy Walker

HEAVEN WAS A DRINK OF WINE
w&m/Merle Haggard, R. Lane

HEAVEN WILL PROTECT THE WORKING GIRL
m/A. Baldwin Sloane
w/Edgar Smith

HEAVY MUSIC
w&m/Bob Seger

HE'D HAVE TO GET UNDER
w&m/Maurice Abrahams,
Grant Clarke

HEIDELBERG STEIN SONG, THE
m/Gustav Luders
w/Frank Pixley

HEIGH-HO, HEIGH-HO
w&m/Frank E. Churchill,
Larry Morey

HEIRESS, THE (film score)
m/Aaron Copland

HEJIRA
w&m/Joni Mitchell

HELEN WHEELS
w&m/Paul and Linda McCartney

HELIOTROPE (instr.)
m/Ferde Grofe

HE'LL HAVE TO GET UNDER, GET OUT AND GET UNDER
m/Maurice Abrahams
w/Edgar Leslie, Grant Clarke

HE'LL HAVE TO GO
w&m/Joe Allison, Audrey Allison

HELLO BLUEBIRD
w&m/Cliff Friend

HELLO CENTRAL GIVE ME HEAVEN
w&m/Charles K. Harris

HELLO CENTRAL GIVE ME NO MAN'S LAND
m/Jean Schwartz
w/Samuel M. Lewis, Joseph Young

HELLO DARLIN'
w&m/Conway Twitty

HELLO DOLLY
w&m/Jerry Herman

HELLO FOOL
w&m/Willie Nelson, James Coleman

HELLO FRISCO HELLO
w&m/Gene Buck, Louis A. Hirsch

HELLO, IT'S ME
w&m/Todd Rundgren

HELLO MARY LOU
w&m/Gene Pitney

HELLO MUDDAH, HELLO FADDAH
w&m/Alan Sherman (music adapted
from Amilcare Poincelli's "Dance Of
The Hours")

HELLO MY BABY
m/Joseph (Joe) Howard
w/Ida Emerson

HELLO OUT THERE
w&m/John Prine

HELLO STRANGER
w&m/Barbara Lewis

HELLO VIET NAM
w&m/Tom T. Hall

HELLO WALLS
w&m/Willie Nelson

HELLO YOUNG LOVERS
m/Richard Rodgers
w/Oscar Hammerstein II

HELP IS ON ITS WAY
w&m/Glenn Shorrock

HELP ME
w&m/Larry Gatlin

HELP ME
w&m/Joni Mitchell

**HELP ME MAKE IT THROUGH
THE NIGHT**
w&m/Kris Kristofferson

HELP ME RONDA
w&m/Brian Wilson

HELPLESS
w&m/Neil Young

HELTER SKELTER
w&m/Charle Luckeyth Roberts

**HER BATHING SUIT NEVER
GOT WET**
w&m/Charles Tobias, Nat Simon

HER NAME IS
w&m/Bobby Braddock

HER ROYAL MAJESTY
w&m/Carole King, Gerry Goffin

**HERE COME THOSE TEARS
AGAIN**
w&m/Jackson Browne, Nancy
Farnsworth

HERE COMES MY BABY
w&m/Cat Stevens

HERE COMES MY GIRL
w&m/Tom Petty

**HERE COMES MY BABY BACK
AGAIN**
w&m/Dottie West, Bill West

HERE COMES SANTA CLAUS
w&m/Gene Autry

**HERE COMES THAT RAINY
DAY FEELING AGAIN**
w&m/Roger Greenaway, Roger Cook

HERE COMES THE RAIN BABY
w&m/Mickey Newbury

**HERE COMES THE SHOW
BOAT**
m/Maceo Pinkard
w/Billy Rose

HERE COMES THE SUN
w&m/Geroge Harrison

HERE I AM (Come and Take Me)
w&m/Al Green

HERE I AM AGAIN
w&m/Shel Silverstein

HERE I'LL STAY
m/Kurt Weill
Alan Jay Lerner

HERE IN MY ARMS
m/Richard Rodgers
w/Lorenz (Larry) Hart

HERE IT COMES AGAIN
w&m/Roger Greenaway, Roger Cook

**HERE, THERE AND
EVERYWHERE**
w&m/Paul McCartney, John Lennon

HERE THEY COME
w&m/Alvin Lee

HERE YOU COME AGAIN
w&m/Barry Mann, Cynthia Weil

HERNANDO'S HIDEAWAY
m/Jerry Ross
w/Richard Adler

HERO BLUES
w&m/Robert Dylan

HERE'S A HOW-DE-DO
m/Sir Arthur Sullivan
w/Sir William Schwenk Gilbert

HERE'S LOVE
w&m/Meredith Willson

HERE'S THAT RAINY DAY
m/James Van Heusen
w/Johnny Burke

HERE'S TO MY LADY
w&m/Rube Bloom, Johnny Mercer

HERE'S TO THE LOSERS
w&m/Robert Wells, Jack Segal

HEROES
w&m/David Bowie

HE'S A COUSIN OF MINE
w&m/Chris Smith, Cecil Mack,
Silvio Hein

**HE'S A DEVIL IN HIS OWN
HOME TOWN**
m/Irving Berlin
w/Irving Berlin, Grant Clarke

HE'S A REBEL
w&m/Phil Spector

HE'S A TRAMP
w&m/Peggy Lee, Sonny Burke

HE'S ALIVE
w&m/Don Francisco

HE'S ME PAL
m/Gus Edwards
w/Vincent P. Bryan

HE'S MISTA KNOW IT ALL
w&m/Stevie Wonder

HE'S MY FRIEND
w&m/Meredith Willson

HE'S 1A IN THE ARMY
w&m/Redd Evans

HE'S ONLY A PRAYER AWAY
w&m/Johnny Lange

HE'S SO FINE
w&m/Ronnie Mack

HE'S SO HEAVENLY
w&m/Jackie DeShannon,
Shari Sheeley

HE'S SURE THE BOY I LOVE
w&m/Barry Mann, Cynthia Weil

HE'S THAT KIND OF FRIEND
w&m/Walter Hawkins, Tremayne
Hawkins

HEY BO DIDDLEY
w&m/Ellas McDaniel (Bo Diddley)

HEY BOBBY
w&m/Joseph "Country Joe"
McDonald

HEY FOREMAN
w&m/Michael Bloomfield

HEY GIRL
w&m/John Phillips, Michelle Gilliam
Phillips

HEY GIRL
w&m/Carole King, Gerry Goffin

HEY GOOD LOOKING
m/Matt Malneck
w/Frank Loesser

HEY JEALOUS LOVER
w&m/Kay Twomey, Sammy Cahn,
Bee Walker

HEY JOE
w&m/Boudleaux Bryant

HEY JOE
w&m/Jimi Hendrix

HEY JOE
w&m/James Pons, William Rinehart

HEY JUDE
w&m/Paul McCartney, John Lennon

HEY LITTLE GIRL
w&m/Otis Blackwell, Bobby
Stevenson

HEY LITTLE ONE
w&m/Barry De Vorzon, Dorsey
Burnette

HEY LOLLY LOLLY
w&m/Woody Guthrie

HEY LOOK ME OVER
m/Cy Coleman
w/Carolyn Leigh

HEY LORETTA
w&m/Shel Silverstein

HEY MISS FANNIE
w&m/Ahmet Ertegun

HEY MR. BANJO
w&m/Norman Malkin, Freddy
Morgan

HEY MR. BLUEBIRD
w&m/Cindy Walker

HEY, PAULA
w&m/Ray Hildebrand

HEY THERE
m/Jerry Ross
w/Richard Adler

HEY TONIGHT
w&m/John C. Fogerty

HI DIDDLE DEE DEE
m/Leigh Harline
w/Ned Washington

HI-DIDDLE-DEE-DEE
m/Leigh Harline
w/Ned Washington

HICKORY WIND
w&m/Gram Parson

HI LILI HI LO
m/Bronislau Kaper
w/Helen Deutsch

HI NEIGHBOR
w&m/Jack Owens

HIAWATHA
w&m/Charles Neil Daniels, James
O'Dea

HI-DO-HO
w&m/Carole King, Gerry Goffin

HICKORY WIND
w&m/Gram Parson

HIGH AND THE MIGHTY, THE
(film score)
m/Dimitri Tiomkin

HIGH AND THE MIGHTY
THE
m/Dimitri Tiomkin
w/Ned Washington

HIGH FLYING BIRD
m/Elton John
w/Bernie Taupin

HIGH HOPES
m/James Van Heusen
w/Sammy Cahn

HIGH NOON (film score)
m/Dimitri Tiomkin

HIGH NOON (Do Not Forsake
Me)
m/Dimitri Tiomkin
w/Ned Washington

HIGH ON A WINDY HILL
w&m/Alex C. Kramer, Joan Whitney
Kramer

HIGH OUT OF TIME
w&m/Carole King, Gerry Goffin

HIGH SCHOOL CADETS
(march)
m/John Philip Sousa

HIGH SIERRA (film score)
m/Adolph Deutsch

HIGH SOCIETY
w&m/Clarence Williams, Walter
Melrose

HIGHER AND HIGHER
w&m/Joel Hirschhorn, Al Kasha

HIGHER AND HIGHER (Your
Love Has Lifted Me)
w&m/Carl Smith

HIGHER GROUND
w&m/Stevie Wonder

HIGHWAY 61 REVISITED
w&m/Robert Dylan

HIJACK (instr.)
m/Herbie Mann

HILO HATTIE
w&m/John Avery Noble,
Don McDiarmid

HILLS OF HOME, THE
m/Oscar J. Fox
w/Florida Calhoun

HIM
w&m/Rupert Holmes

HINDUSTAN
w&m/Oliver G. Wallace, Harold T.
Weeks

HIPPY HIPPY SHAKE, THE
w&m/Chan Romero

HIS EYES IS ON THE
SPARROW
m/Charles H. Gabriel Sr.
w/Mrs. C.D. Martin

HIS FEET'S TOO BIG FOR
DE BED
m/Sammy Mysels
w/Dick Sanford

HIS LAST THOUGHTS WERE
OF YOU
m/Joseph W. Stern
w/Edward B. Marks

HIS LATEST FLAME
w&m/Doc (Jerome) Pomus, Mort
Shuman

HIS NAME IS WONDERFUL
w&m/Audrey Mieir

HISSING OF SUMMER LAWNS,
THE
w&m/Joni Mitchell

HIT PARADE OF 1943
(film score)
m/Walter Scharf

HIT THE ROAD JACK
w&m/Percy Mayfield

HIT THE ROAD TO
DREAMLAND
m/Harold Arlen
w/Johnny Mercer

HITCH HIKE
w&m/William Stevenson, Clarence
Paul, Marvin Gaye

HITCHCOCK RAILWAY
w&m/José Feliciano

HITCHY KOO
m/Lewis F. Muir, Maurice Abrahams
w/L. Wolfe Gilbert

HOBO
w&m/Son House

HOBO BLUES
w&m/John Lee Hooker

HOEDOWN (instr.)
m/Oliver Nelson

HO-HO SONG, THE
w&m/Red Buttons, Allan Walker

HOLD 'EM JOE
w&m/Harry Thomas

HOLD ME
w&m/Ben Black, Art Hickman

HOLD ME, THRILL ME, KISS
ME
w&m/Harry Noble

HOLD ME TIGHT
w&m/Johnny Nash

HOLD MY HAND
w&m/Jack Lawrence, Richard Myers

HOLD ON I'M COMING
w&m/Isaac Hayes, David Porter

HOLD ON TO MY LOVE
w&m/Robin Gibb, Blue Weaver

HOLD THE FORT
w&m/Philip P. Bliss

HOLD THE LINE
w&m/David Paich

HOLD TIGHT-HOLD TIGHT
w&m/Leonard Ware

HOLD YOUR HEAD UP
w&m/Rodney Argent

HOLDING ON TO NOTHING
w&m/Jerry Chesnut

HOLDIN' ON TO YESTERDAY
w&m/David Pack, Joe Puerta,
Burleigh G.A. Drummond

HOLE IN MY SHOE
w&m/Steve Winwood, Jim Capaldi

HOLIDAY
w&m/Barry, Maurice and
Robin Gibb

HOLIDAY FOR LOVE
w&m/Mel Tillis, Webb Pierce,
Wayne Walker

HOLIDAY FOR STRINGS
m/David Rose
m/Sammy Gallop

**HOLIDAY FOR TROMBONES
(instr.)**
m/David Rose

HOLLY HOLY
w&m/Neil Diamond

HOLLY, JOLLY CHRISTMAS A
w&m/John D. Marks

**HOLLYWOOD CANTEEN (film
score)**
m/Ray Heindorf

HOLLYWOOD NIGHTS
w&m/Bob Seger

HOLY CITY, THE
m/Michael Maybrick
w/Frederick E. Weatherly

HOLY, HOLY, HOLY
m/John Bacchus Dykes (from the
song "Nicaea")
w/Reginald Heber

HOLY ONE
w&m/Freddy Fender

HOME
w&m/Karla Bonoff

HOME
w&m/Roger Miller

HOME (When Shadows Fall)
w&m/Peter Van Steeden, Jr., Harry
Clarkson, Jeff Clarkson

HOME AGAIN
w&m/Carole King

HOME AND DRY
w&m/Gerry Rafferty

HOME AT LAST
w&m/Donald Fagen, Walter Becker

HOME CALL
w&m/Jimmy Rodgers

HOME COOKIN' (instr.)
m/Horace Silver

HOME FOR THE HOLIDAYS
m/Robert Allen
w/Al Stillman

**HOME IS WHERE THE HEART
IS**
w&m/Manuel Klein

HOME OF THE BLUES
w&m/John R. Cash, Glenn Douglas,
Vic McAlpin

**HOME ON THE RANGE (Oh Give
Me A Home Where The Buffalo
Roam)**
m/Daniel E. Kelly
w/Brewster (Bruce) Higley
(authorship attributed with no
official verification)

HOME SWEET HOME
m/Sir Henry Rowley Bishop (from his
opera "Clari", or "The Maid of
Milan")
w/John Howard Payne

w&m/Joe Perry, Steve Tyler

HOME WHERE I BELONG
w&m/B.J. Thomas

**HOME YOU'RE TEARING
DOWN, THE**
w&m/Betty Sue Perry

HOMECOMING
w&m/Tom T. Hall

HOMEWARD BOUND
w&m/Paul Simon

HONDO (film score)
m/Hugo Friedhofer

HONEST AND TRULY
w&m/Fred Rose

HONESTY
w&m/Billy Joel

HONEY
w&m/Bobby Russell

HONEY
m/Richard A. Whiting, Seymour
Simons
w/Haven Gillespie

HONEY BABE
m/Max Steiner
w/Paul Francis Webster

HONEY BOY
w&m/Jack Norworth, Albert Von
Tilzer

HONEY BUN
m/Richard Rodgers
w/Oscar Hammerstein II

HONEY DON'T
w&m/Carl Lee Perkins

HONEY HONEY
m/Benny Andersson, Bjorn Ulvaeus
w/Stig Anderson

HONEY HUSH
w&m/Joe Turner

HONEY IN THE HONEYCOMB
m/Vernon Duke
w/John Latouche

HONEY LOVE
w&m/Clyde McPhatter, Jerry Wexler

HONEY SONG, THE
w&m/D. Curtis Massey

HONEYCOMB
w&m/Bob Merrill

HONEYSUCKLE ROSE
m/Thomas "Fats" Waller
w/Andy Razaf

HONG KONG BLUES
w&m/Hoagy Carmichael

HONKY CAT
m/Elton John
w/Bernie Taupin

HONKY TONK
w&m/Henry Glover, Bill Doggett,
Shep Shephard, Billy Butler, Clifford
Scott

HONKY TONK BLUES
w&m/Al Dexter

HONKY TONK MAN
w&m/Johnny Horton, Tillman
Franks, Howard Hausey

HONKY TONK SONG
w&m/Mel Tillis, A.R. Peddy

HONKY TONKY TOWN
m/Harry Austin Tierney
w/Joseph McCarthy

HONKY-TONK TRAIN (instr.)
m/Meade "Lux" Lewis

HONKY TONK WOMAN
w&m/Mick Jagger, Keith Richard

HONOLULU LULU
w&m/Jan Berry, Roger Christian,
Lou Adler

HOOCHIE KOOCHEY MAN
w&m/Muddy Waters

HOOKED ON A FEELING
w&m/Mark James

HOOKED ON YOU
w&m/David Gates

HOOP DEE DOO
m/Milton DeLugg
w/Frank Loesser

**HOORAY FOR CAPTAIN
Spaulding**
m/Harry Ruby
w/Bert Kalmar

HOORAY FOR HAZEL
w&m/Tommy Roe

HOORAY FOR HOLLYWOOD
m/Richard Whiting
w/Johnny Mercer

HOORAY FOR LOVE
m/Harold Arlen
w/Leo Robin

HOP SCOTCH POLKA
m/William Whitlock, Gene Rayburn
w/Carl Sigman

HOPELESSLY DEVOTED TO YOU
w&m/John Farrar

HORSE WITH NO NAME, A
w&m/Dewey Bunnell

HORSESHOE FROM THE DOOR, THE
m/David Braham
w/Ed Harrrigan

HOSTESS WITH THE MOSTES' ON THE Ball, THE
w&m/Irving Berlin

HOT BLOODED
w&m/Mick Jones, Lou Gramm

HOT CANARY, THE
m/Paul Nero (adapted from music by F. Poliakin)
w/Ray Gilbert

HOT CHILD IN THE CITY
w&m/Nick Gilder

HOT DIGGETY
w&m/Al Hoffman, Dick Manning

HOT FUN IN THE SUMMERTIME
w&m/Sly Stone

HOT LEGS
w&m/Rod Stewart, Gary Grainger

HOT LINE
w&m/Frederick Perren,
Keni St. Lewi

HOT LIPS
w&m/Henry Busse, Lou Davis,
Henry W. Lange

HOT PANTS
w&m/James Brown

HOT STUFF
w&m/Mick Jagger, Keith Richard

HOTEL CALIFORNIA
w&m/Glenn Frey, Don Henley, Don Felder

HOTTER THAN HELL
w&m/Paul Stanley

HOUSE AT POOH CORNER
w&m/Kenneth Loggins

HOUSE BY THE SIDE OF THE ROAD, THE
m/Grace W. Gulesian
w/Sam Walter Foss

HOUSE I LIVE IN, THE
m/Earl Robinson
w/John Latouche

HOUSE IS NOT A HOME, A
m/Burt Bacharach
w/Hal David

HOUSE OF BLUE LIGHTS, THE
w&m/Don Raye, Freddie Slack

HOUSE WITH LOVE IN IT, A
m/Sidney Lippman
w/Sylvia Dee

HOUSEBOAT (film score)
m/George Duning

HOUSEBOAT (Theme)
m/George Duning
w/Steve Allen

HOUSTON
w&m/Lee Hazelwood

HOW ABOUT YOU
m/Burton Lane
w/Ralph Freed

HOW I AM TO KNOW
w&m/Dorothy Parker, Jack King

HOW ARE THINGS IN GLOCCA MORRA
m/Burton Lane
w/E.Y. Harburg

HOW BLUE THE NIGHT
m/Jimmy McHugh
w/Harold Adamson

HOW CAN I BE SURE
w&m/Felix Cavaliere, Eddie Brigati

HOW CAN I UNLOVE YOU
w&m/Joe South

HOW CAN YOU MEND A BROKEN HEART
w&m/Barry, Maurice and Robin Gibb

HOW COME YOU DO ME LIKE YOU DO
w&m/Gene Austin, Roy Bergere

HOW COULD YOU BELIEVE ME WHEN I SAID I LOVED YOU
m/Burton Lane
w/Alan Jay Lerner

HOW DEEP IS THE OCEAN
w&m/Irving Berlin

HOW DEEP IS YOUR LOVE
w&m/Barry, Maurice and Robin Gibb

HOW DID HE LOOK
w&m/Abner Silver

HOW DO I MAKE YOU
w&m/Billy Steinberg

HOW DO YOU SPEAK TO AN ANGEL
m/Jule Styne
w/Bob Hilliard

HOW DO YOU DO IT
w&m/Mitch Murray

HOW DO YOU SLEEP
w&m/John Lennon

HOW DO YOU TALK TO A BABY
w&m/Webb Pierce, Wayne P. Walker

HOW GREAT THOU ART
m/attributed to Carl Bober (some authorities contend melody adapted from Franz Shubert's "The Almighty")
w/Stuart K. Hine

HOW GREEN WAS MY VALLEY (film score)
m/Alfred Newman

HOW HIGH THE MOON
m/Morgan Lewis
w/Nancy Hamilton

HOW IMPORTANT CAN IT BE
m/Bennie Benjamin
w/George D. Weiss

HOW INSENSITIVE (Insensatez)
m/Antonio Carlos Jobim

HOW IT IS
m/Michael Mantler (based on Samuel Becket poem)

HOW LITTLE WE KNOW
m/Hoagy Carmichael
w/Johnny Mercer

HOW LONG
w&m/Antoine "Fats" Domino, Dave Bartholomew

HOW LONG HAS IT BEEN
w&m/Sonny Throckmorton

HOW LONG HAS THIS BEEN GOING ON
m/George Gershwin
w/Ira Gershwin

HOW LONG, HOW LONG
w&m/Leroy Carr

HOW LONG WILL MY BABY BE GONE
w&m/Buck Owens

HOW LUCKY CAN YOU GET
m/John Kander
w/Fred Ebb

HOW MANY HEARTS HAVE YOU BROKEN
m/Alvin S. Kaufman
w/Marty Symes

HOW MANY TIMES HAVE I SAID I LOVE YOU
w&m/Irving Berlin

HOW MUCH I FEEL
w&m/David Pack, Joe Puerta,
Burleigh G.A. Drummond

**HOW MUCH IS THAT DOGGIE
IN THE WINDOW**
w&m/Bob Merrill

HOW MUCH LOVE
w&m/Leo Sayer, Barry Mann

**HOW SWEET IT IS
(To Be Loved By You)**
w&m/Eddie Holland, Brian Holland,
Lamont Dozier

HOW TO HANDLE A WOMAN
m/Frederick Loewe
w/Alan Jay Lerner

**HOW YA GONNA KEEP 'EM
DOWN ON THE FARM**
m/Walter Donaldson
w/Samuel M. Lewis, Joseph Young

**HOW'S THE WORLD
TREATING YOU**
w&m/Boudleaux Bryant, Chet Atkins

HUBBA, HUBBA, HUBBA, A
m/Jimmy McHugh
w/Harold Adamson

HUCKLEBERRY DUCK (instr.)
m/Raymond Scott

HUCKLEBUCK, THE
w&m/Roy Alfred, Albert Andrew
Gibson

HUCKSTERS, THE (film score)
m/Lennie Hayton

HUD (film score)
m/Elmer Bernstein

HUGGIN' AND CHALKIN'
w&m/Kermit Goell

HUMMINGBIRD
w&m/Dash Crofts, James Seals

HUMPTY DUMPTY HEART
w&m/Hank Thompson

**HUNCHBACK OF NOTRE
DAME (film score) 1957**
m/Georges Auric

**HUNDRED POUNDS OF CLAY,
A**
w&m/Luther Dixon, Bob Elgin, Kay
Rogers

**HUNDRED YEARS FROM
TODAY, A**
m/Victor Young
w/Ned Washington, Joseph Young

HUNGARIAN RAG (instr.)
m/Julius Lenzberg (adapted from
Franz Liszt's "Hungarian
Rhapsody")

HUNGRY
w&m/Barry Mann, Cynthia Weil

HUNGRY EYES
w&m/Merle Haggard

HUNKY DORY
w&m/David Bowie

HURRICANE
w&m/Robert Dylan

HURT, THE
w&m/Cat Stevens

HURT SO BAD
w&m/Teddy Randazzo, Bobby
Weinstein, Bobby Hart

HURTIN'S ALL OVER, THE
w&m/Harlan Howard

HURTS ME TO MY HEART
w&m/Charles Singleton,
Rosemarie McCoy

HUSBANDS AND WIVES
w&m/Roger Miller

HUSH
w&m/Joe South

**HUSH HUSH SWEET
CHARLOTTE (film score)**
m/Frank De Vol

HUSTLE, THE
w&m/Van McCoy

HUT SUT SONG, THE
w&m/Jack Owens, Leo V. Killian,
Ted McMichael

**HYMN THE 7TH GALAXY
(instr.)**
m/Chick Corea

Addenda:

HALF THE WAY
w&m/Ralph Murphy

HAVEN'T YOU HEARD
w&m/Patrice Rushen

HEART OF THE NIGHT
w&m/Paul Cotton

HOLD ON HOLD OUT
w&m/Jackson Browne

 **SONGS**

I

I AIN'T DOWN YET
w&m/Meredith Willson

I AIN'T GONNA EAT MY HEART OUT ANYMORE
w&m/Felix Cavaliere, Eddie Brigati

I AIN'T GOT NOBODY
m/Spencer Williams, Dave Peyton
w/Roger Graham

I AIN'T LIVING LONG LIKE THIS
w&m/Rodney Crowell

I AIN'T NEVER
w&m/Mel Tillis, Webb Pierce

I ALMOST CALLED YOUR NAME
w&m/Margaret Lewis,
Mira Smith

I ALMOST LOST MY MIND
w&m/Ivory Joe Hunter

I AM A CHILD
w&m/Neil Young

I AM A COURTIER GRAVE AND SERIOUS
m/Sir Arthur Sullivan
w/Sir William Schwenk Gilbert

I AM A LONESOME HOBO
w&m/Robert Dylan

I AM A ROCK
w&m/Paul Simon

I AM AN AMERICAN
w&m/Paul Cunningham, Leonard Whitcup, Ira Schuster

I AM, I SAID
w&m/Neil Diamond

I AM LOVED
w&m/Cole Porter

I AM THE CAPTAIN OF THE PINAFORE
m/Sir Arthur Sullivan
w/Sir William Schwenk Gilbert

I AM THE MONARCH OF THE SEA
m/Sir Arthur Sullivan
w/Sir William Schwenk Gilbert

I AM WOMAN
m/Ray Burton
w/Helen Reddy

I AM YOURS TRULY
m/Gustav Luders
w/George Ade

I APOLOGIZE
m/Al Hoffman, Ed Nelson
w/Al Goodhart

I ASKED THE LORD
w&m/Johnny Lange, Jimmy Duncan

I BELIEVE
w&m/Ervin M. Drake, Jimmy Shirl, Al Stillman, Irvin Graham

I BELIEVE (When I Fall In Love It Will Be Forever)
w&m/Stevie Wonder, Yvonne Wright

I BELIEVE IN EVERYTHING
w&m/John Entwhistle

I BELIEVE IN JESUS
w&m/Mac Davis

I BELIEVE IN LOVE
w&m/Kenneth Loggins

I BELIEVE IN MUSIC
w&m/Mac Davis

I BELIEVE IN SUNSHINE
w&m/Roger Miller

I BELIEVE IN YOU
w&m/Frank Loesser

I BELIEVE YOU
w&m/Donald J. Adrissi, Richard P. Adrissi

I BELONG TO YOU AND ONLY YOU
w&m/Barry White

I CAINT SAY NO
m/Richard Rodgers
w/Oscar Hammerstein II

I CAME HERE TO TALK FOR JOE
m/Sam H. Stept
w/Lew Brown

m/Sammy Fain
w/Irving Kahal

I CAN GET IT FOR YOU WHOLESALE
m/Sol Kaplan

I CAN HELP
w&m/Billy Swan

I CAN MEND YOUR BROKEN HEART
w&m/Don Gibson

I CAN SEE CLEARLY NOW
w&m/Johnny Nash

I CANNOT TELL WHAT THIS LOVE MAY BE
m/Sir Arthur Sullivan
w/Sir William Schwenk Gilbert

I CAN'T BE MYSELF
w&m/Merle Haggard

I CAN'T BE SATISFIED
w&m/Muddy Waters

I CAN'T BEGIN TO TELL YOU
m/James V. Monaco
w/Mack Gordon

I CAN'T BELIEVE THAT IT'S ALL OVER
w&m/Ben Peters

I CAN'T BELIEVE THAT YOU'RE IN LOVE WITH ME
m/Jimmy McHugh
w/Clarence Gaskill

I CAN'T BELIEVE THAT YOU'VE STOPPED LOVING ME
w&m/Dallas Frazier, A.L. (Doodle) Owens

I CAN'T GET STARTED
m/Vernon Duke
w/Ira Gershwin

I CAN'T GIVE YOU ANYTHING BUT LOVE BABY
m/Jimmy McHugh
w/Dorothy Fields

I CAN'T GO ON
w&m/Antoine "Fats" Domino, Dave Bartholomew

I CAN'T GO ON WITHOUT YOU
w&m/Henry Glover, Sally Nix

I CAN'T HEAR YOU
w&m/Carole King, Gerry Goffin

I CAN'T HELP BUT WONDER (Where I'm Bound)
w&m/Thomas R. Paxton

I CAN'T HELP IT
w&m/Robin Gibb, Barry Gibb, Maurice Gibb

I CAN'T HELP MYSELF
w&m/Eddie Holland, Brian Holland, Lamont Dozie

I CAN'T HELP MYSELF
w&m/Eddie Rabbitt, Even Stevens

I CAN'T REMEMBER
w&m/Bill Anderson, Bette Anderson

I CAN'T SEE ME WITHOUT YOU
w&m/Conway Twitty

I CAN'T SEE NOBODY
w&m/Barry, Maurice and Robin Gibb

I CAN'T STAND UP ALONE
w&m/Martha Carson

I CAN'T STAY MAD AT YOU
w&m/Carole King, Gerry Goffin

I CAN'T STOP LOVING YOU
w&m/Don Gibson

I CAN'T TELL WHY I LOVE YOU BUT I DO
m/Gus Edwards
w/Will D. Cobb

I CAN'T TELL YOU WHY
w&m/Don Henley, Glenn Frey,
T. Schmit

I CAN'T TURN YOU LOOSE
w&m/Otis Redding

I CAN'T WAIT
w&m/Mark Goldenberg, Andrew
Gold

I CAN'T WAIT ANY LONGER
w&m/Bill Anderson, Buddy Killen

I CONCENTRATE ON YOU
w&m/Cole Porter

I COULD GO ON SINGING
m/Harold Arlen
w/E.Y. Harburg

**I COULD HAVE BEEN A
SAILOR**
w&m/Peter Allen

**I COULD HAVE DANCED ALL
NIGHT**
m/Frederick Loewe
w/Alan Jay Lerner

I COULD HAVE TOLD YOU
m/James Van Heusen
w/Carl Sigman

I COULD WRITE A BOOK
m/Richard Rodgers
w/Lorenz (Larry) Hart

**I COULDN'T SLEEP A WINK
LAST NIGHT**
m/Jimmy McHugh
w/Harold Adamson

I COVER THE WATERFRONT
m/John Green
w/Edward Heyman

I CRIED A TEAR
w&m/Al Julia, Fred Jacobson

I CRIED FOR YOU
m/Abe Lyman, Gus Arnheim
w/Arthur Freed

**I CRIED THE BLUE OUT OF
MY EYES**
w&m/Loretta Lynn

I CRY ALONE
m/Burt Bacharach
w/Hal David

**I DIDN'T COME TO NEW YORK
TO MEET A GUY FROM MY
HOME TOWN**
w&m/Wilbur (Billy) Meshel,
Fred Anisfield

I DIDN'T KNOW ABOUT YOU
m/Duke Ellington

**I DIDN'T KNOW WHAT TIME
IT WAS**
m/Richard Rodgers
w/Lorenz (Larry) Hart

**I DIDN'T RAISE MY BOY TO BE
A SOLDIER**
m/Al Piantadosi
w/Alfred Bryan

**I DIDN'T SLIP, I WASN'T
PUSHED, I FELL**
w&m/Edward Pola, George Wyle

I DIG ROCK AND ROLL MUSIC
w&m/Paul Stookey, James Mason,
Dave Dixon

I DO, I DO, I DO, I DO
m/Benny Andersson, Bjorn Ulvaeus
w/Stig Anderson

I DO MY SWINGING AT HOME
w&m/Billy Sherrill

**I DON'T BELIEVE I'LL FALL
IN LOVE TODAY**
w&m/Harlan Howard

I DON'T BELIEVE YOU
w&m/Robert Dylan

I DON'T CARE
w&m/Webb Pierce, Cindy Walker

I DON'T CARE
m/Harry O. Sutton
w/Jean Lenox

**I DON'T CARE (Just As Long
As You Love Me)**
w&m/Buck Owens

I DON'T CARE ANYMORE
w&m/George Harrison

**I DON'T CARE IF THE SUN
DON'T SHINE**
w&m/Mack David

I DON'T HURT ANYMORE
m/Jack Rollins
w/Don Robertson

I DON'T KNOW
w&m/Joe Thomas, Willie Mabon

**I DON'T KNOW ENOUGH
ABOUT YOU**
w&m/Peggy Lee, Dave Barbour

**I DON'T KNOW HOW TO LOVE
HIM**
m/Andrew Lloyd Webber
w/Tim Rice

I DON'T KNOW WHY
m/Fred E. Ahlert
w/Roy Turk

**I DON'T LIKE TO SLEEP
ALONE**
w&m/Paul Anka

**I DON'T LOVE YOU ANY
MORE**
w&m/Bill Anderson

I DON'T MIND
w&m/James Brown

**I DON'T SEE ME IN YOUR
EYES ANYMORE**
m/Bennie Benjamin
w/Geroge D. Weiss

**I DON'T STAND THE GHOST
OF A CHANCE WITH YOU**
m/Victor Young
w/Big Crosby, Ned Washington

I DON'T WANNA PLAY HOUSE
w&m/Billy Sherrill, Glen Sutton

I DON'T WANT TO CRY
w&m/Larry Gatlin

**I DON'T WANT TO CRY
ANYMORE**
w&m/James Monaco, Johnny Burke

**I DON'T WANT TO GET
DRAFTED**
w&m/Frank Zappa

I DON'T WANT TO KNOW
w&m/Stephanie (Stevie) Nicks

I DON'T WANT TO LOSE YOU
w&m/Billy Sherrill, Norro Wilson,
Steve Davis

**I DON'T WANT TO PLAY IN
YOUR YARD**
m/Henry W. Petrie
w/Philip Wingate

**I DON'T WANT TO SET THE
WORLD ON FIRE**
m/Bennie Benjamin
w/Edward Seiler, Sol Marcus, Eddie
Durham

**I DON'T WANT TO WALK
WITHOUT YOU**
m/Jule Styne
w/Frank Loesser

I DON'T WANT YOUR KISSES
w&m/Fred Fisher, M.M. Broones

I DOUBLE DARE YOU
m/Jimmy Eaton
w/Terry Shand

**I DREAM OF JEANIE WITH
THE LIGHT BROWN HAIR**
w&m/Stephen C. Foster

I DREAM OF YOU
w&m/Marjorie Goetschius, Edna
Osser

I DREAM TOO MUCH
m/Jerome Kern
w/Dorothy Fields

**I DREAMT I DWELT IN
MARBLE HALLS (The Bohemian
Girl)**
m/Michael William Balfe
w/Alfred Bunn

I ENJOY BEING A GIRL
m/Richard Rodgers
w/Oscar Hammerstein II

I FELL IN LOVE TOO EASILY
m/Jule Styne
w/Sammy Cahn

I FALL IN LOVE WITH YOU EVERY DAY
m/Arthur Altman
w/Jack Lawrence

I FALL IN LOVE WITH YOU EVERY DAY
m/Manning Sherwin
w/Frank Loesser

I FALL TO PIECES
w&m/Hank Cochran, Harlan Howard

I FAW GO DOWN AN' GO BOOM
w&m/James Brockman, Leonard Stevens, B.B.B. Donaldson

I FEEL A SONG COMIN' ON
m/Jimmy McHugh
w/Dorothy Fields

I FEEL FINE
w&m/Paul McCartney, John Lennon

I FEEL LIKE A FEATHER IN THE BREEZE
m/Harry Revel
w/Mack Gordon

I FEEL LIKE GOING HOME
w&m/Muddy Waters

I FEEL LIKE I'M FIXIN' TO DIE RAG
w&m/Joseph "Country Joe" McDonald

I FEEL LOVE
w&m/Donna Summer, Georgio Moroder, Pete Bellotte

I FEEL PRETTY
m/Leonard Bernstein
w/Stephen Sondheim

I FEEL THE EARTH MOVE
w&m/Carole King

I FOUGHT THE LAW
w&m/Sonny Curtis

I FOUND A MILLION DOLLAR BABY In A Five and Ten Cent Store
m/Harry Warren
w/Billy Rose, Mort Dixon

I FOUND A NEW BABY
w&m/Jack Palmer, Spencer Williams

I GET A KICK OUT OF YOU
w&m/Cole Porter

I GET ALONG WITHOUT YOU VERY WELL
w&m/Hoagy Carmichael

I GET AROUND
w&m/Brian Wilson

I GET CARRIED AWAY
m/Leonard Bernstein
w/Betty Comden, Adolph Green

I GET IDEAS
m/adapted from the Argentine tango "Adios Muchachos" by Sanders
w/Dorcas Cochran

I GET THE BLUES WHEN IT RAINS
w&m/Marcy Klauber

I GET THE FEVER
w&m/Bill Anderson

I GO CRAZY
w&m/Paul Davis

I GO TO RIO
m/Peter Allen
w/Adrienne Anderson

I GOT A LINE ON YOU
w&m/Jay Ferguson, Mark Andes

I GOT A NAME
w&m/Jim Croce, Norman Gimbel

I GOT IT BAD AND THAT AIN'T GOOD
m/Duke Ellington
w/Paul Francis Webster

I GOT LIFE
m/Galt MacDermot
w/James Rado, Gerome Ragni

I GOT PLENTY O' NUTHIN'
m/George Gershwin
w/Dubose Heyward, Ira Gershwin

I GOT RHYTHM
m/Geroge Gershwin
w/Ira Gershwin

I GOT STONED AND I MISSED IT
w&m/Jim Stafford

I GOT STRIPES
w&m/John R. Cash, Charlie Williams

I GOT STUNG
w&m/Aaron Schroeder, David Hill

I GOT THE FEELIN'
w&m/James Brown

I GOT THE FEELIN'
w&m/Neil Diamond

I GOT THE NEWS
w&m/Donald Fagen, Walter Becker

I GOT THE SUN IN THE MORNING
w&m/Irving Berlin

I GOT YOU
w&m/James Brown

I GOT YOU BABE
w&m/Sonny Bono, Cher (Cherilyn S. LaPierre)

I GOTCHA
w&m/Joe Tex

I GOTTA RIGHT TO SING THE BLUES
m/Harold Arlen
w/Ted Koehler

I GUESS I'LL HAVE TO CHANGE MY PLAN
m/Arthur Schwartz
w/Howard Dietz

I GUESS I'll HAVE TO DREAM THE REST
w&m/Michael S. Stoner, Harold Green

I GUESS I'LL HAVE TO TELEGRAPH MY BABY
w&m/George M. Cohan

I HAD A DREAM
w&m/John B. Sebastian

I HAD A HAT WHEN I CAME IN
w&m/James A. Mooney

I HAD A WOMAN
w&m/Joshua Daniel White

I HAD THE CRAZIEST DREAM
m/Harry Warren
w/Mack Gordon

I HADN'T ANYONE 'TIL YOU
w&m/Ray Noble

I HATE GOODBYES
w&m/Bill Rice, Jerry Foster

I HATE YOU, DARLING
w&m/Cole Porter

I HAVE A SONG TO SING, O
m/Sir Arthur Sullivan
w/Sir William Schwenk Gilbert

I HAVE BUT ONE HEART
w&m/Johnny Farrow

I HAVE DREAMED
m/Richard Rodgers
w/Oscar Hammerstein II

I HEAR A RHAPSODY
w&m/George Fragos, Jack Baker

I HEAR A SYMPHONY
w&m/Eddie Holland, Brian Holland, Lamont Dozier

I HEAR A THRUSH AT EVE
m/Charles Wakefield Cadman
w/Nelle Richmond Eberhart

I HEAR AMERICA CALLING
w&m/Richard Hageman

I HEAR AMERICA SINGING
m/Peter De Rose
w/Samuel L. Lewis

I HEAR MUSIC
m/Burton Lane
w/Frank Loesser

I HEARD A FOREST PRAYING
m/Peter De Rose
w/Samuel M. Lewis

I HEARD THE BELLS ON CHRISTMAS DAY
w&m/John D. Marks

I HONESTLY LOVE YOU
w&m/Jeff Barry, Peter Allen

I HOPE GABRIEL LIKES MY MUSIC
w&m/Stuff Smith

I JUST CAN'T HELP BELIEVING
w&m/Barry Mann, Cynthia Weil

I JUST CAN'T STAY MARRIED TO YOU
w&m/Rory Bourke, Charlie Black, Jerry Gillespie

I JUST ROLL ALONG
m/Peter De Rose
w/Jo Trent

I JUST WANNA STOP
w&m/Ross Vannelli

I JUST WANT TO GO BACK AND START THE WHOLE THING OVER
w&m/Paul Dresser

I JUST WANT TO BE YOUR EVERYTHING
w&m/Barry Gibb

I JUST WANT TO FEEL THE MAGIC
w&m/Rory Bourke, Mel McDaniel

I JUST WANT TO LOVE
w&m/Eddie Rabbitt, Even Stevens, David Malloy

(In Dreams) I KISS YOUR HAND MADAME
m/Ralph Erwin
w/Fritz Rotter, Samuel M. Lewis, Joseph Young

I KNOW A PLACE
w&m/Tony Hatch

I KNOW A HEARTACHE WHEN I SEE ONE
w&m/Rory Bourke, Charlie Black, Kerry Chater

I KNOW A YOUTH
m/Sir Arthur Sullivan
w/Sir William Schwenk Gilbert

I KNOW I'M LOSING YOU
w&m/Eddie Holland, Norman Whitfield, Cornelius Grant

I KNOW MOONLIGHT
w&m/Joshua D. White

I KNOW NOW
m/Victor Jacobi
w/Harry B. Smith

I KNOW THAT YOU KNOW
m/Vincent Youmans
w/Anne Caldwell

I LAUGHED AT LOVE
w&m/Abner Silver

I LEFT MY BABY
w&m/Albert Andrew Gibson

I LEFT MY HEART AT THE STAGE DOOR CANTEEN
w&m/Irving Berlin

I LEFT MY HEART IN SAN FRANCISCO
m/George Cory
w/Douglass Cross

I LET A SONG GO OUT OF MY HEART
m/Duke Ellington
w/Henry Nemo, Irving Mills

I LIKE BEER
w&m/Tom T. Hall

I LIKE DREAMIN'
w&m/Kenny Nolan

I LIKE IT LIKE THAT
w&m/William (Smokey) Robinson Jr.
Marvin Tarplin

I LIKE IT LIKE THAT
w&m/Chris Kenner, Allen Toussaint

I LIKE MOUNTAIN MUSIC
m/Frank Weldon
w/James Cavanaugh

I LIKE THE LIKES OF YOU
m/Vernon Duke
w/E.Y. Harburg

I LIKE TO DO IT
w&m/Harry Wayne Casey, Richard Finch

I LIVED MY LIFE
w&m/Antoine "Fats" Domino, Dave Bartholomew

I LOOKED AWAY
w&m/Eric Clapton, Bobby Whitlock

I LOST MY SUGAR IN SALT LAKE CITY
w&m/Johnny Lange, Leon T. Rene

I LOVE
w&m/Tom T. Hall

I LOVE A LASSIE (Ma Scotch Bluebell)
w&m/Sir Harry Lauder, Gerald Grafton

I LOVE A PARADE
m/Harold Arlen
w/Ted Koehler

I LOVE A PIANO
w&m/Irving Berlin

I LOVE AMERICA
w&m/Noe Coward

I LOVE COFFEE, I LOVE TEA
m/Henry Russell
w/Vick Knight

I LOVE HOW YOU LOVE ME
w&m/Barry Mann, Larry Kolber

I LOVE LOUISA
m/Arthur Schwartz
Howard Dietz

I LOVE MY DOG
w&m/Cat Stevens

I LOVE MUSIC
w&m/Kenneth Gamble, Leon Huff

I LOVE MY FRIEND
w&m/Billy Sherrill, Norro Wilson

I LOVE MY LITTLE HONEY
w&m/Benjamin R. Harney

I LOVE MY WIFE BUT OH YOU KID
m/Harry Armstrong
w/Billy Clark

I LOVE NEW YORK
w&m/Steve Karmen

I LOVE PARIS
w&m/Cole Porter

I LOVE THE NAME OF MARY
m/Ernest R. Ball, Chauncey Olcott
w/George Graff Jr.

I LOVE TO TELL THE STORY
m/William G. Fischer
w/Katherine Hankey

I LOVE THE NIGHT LIFE
w&m/Alicia Bridges, Susan Hutcheson

I LOVE TO DANCE WITH ANNIE
w&m/Boudleaux Bryant, Felice Bryant

I LOVE YOU
w&m/George M. Cohan

I LOVE YOU
w&m/Cole Porter

I LOVE YOU
w&m/Donna Summer, Georgio Moroder, Pete Bellotte

I LOVE YOU
w&m/Tommy Tucker

I LOVE YOU (For Sentimental Reasons)
w&m/Deke Watson, William Best

I LOVE YOU A 1,000 TIMES
w&m/Inez Foxx, Luther Dixon

I LOVE YOU BECAUSE
w&m/Leon Payne

I LOVE YOU DROPS
w&m/Bill Anderson

I LOVE YOU PORGY
m/George Gershwin
w/Dubose Heyward, Ira Gershwin

I LOVE YOU SO MUCH
m/Harry Ruby
w/Bert Kalmar

I LOVE YOU SO MUCH IT HURTS
w&m/Floyd Tillman

I LOVE YOU, THAT'S THE ONE THING I KNOW
m/Anatole Friedland
w/L. Wolfe Gilbert

I LOVE YOU TRULY
w&m/Carrie Jacobs Bond

I LOVES YOU PORGY
m/George Gershwin
w/Dubose Heyward, Ira Gershwin

I LOVE YOU YES I DO
w&m/Sally Nix, Henry Glover,

I LOVE YOU, YOU LOVE ME
w&m/Phil Spector

I MARRIED AN ANGEL
m/Richard Rodgers
w/Lorenz (Larry) Hart

I MAY BE GONE FOR A LONG, LONG TIME
w&m/Albert Von Tilzer, Lew Brown

I MAY BE WRONG BUT I THINK YOU'RE WONDERFUL
m/Henry Sullivan
w/Harry Ruskin

I MAY NEVER PASS THIS WAY AGAIN
m/Irving Melsher
w/Murray Wizell

I MEAN YOU (instr.)
m/Thelonious Sphere Monk

I MET A FRIEND OF YOURS TODAY
w&m/Bob McDill,
Wayland Holyfield

I MET HER ON MONDAY
m/Charles Newman
w/Allie Wrubel

I MIGHT BE YOUR ONCE IN A WHILE
m/Victor Herbert
w/Robert B. Smith

I MISS YOU
w&m/Hank Cochran, Cliff Cochran

I MISS YOU ALREADY
w&m/Faron Young, Marvin Rainwater

I MISS YOU MOST OF ALL
m/James V. Monaco
w/Joseph McCarthy

I MISSED YOU
w&m/Bill Anderson

I MUST SEE ANNIE TONIGHT
m/Cliff Friend
w/Dave Franklin

I NEED A LOVER
w&m/Johnny Cougar

I NEED THEE EV'RY HOUR
m/Reverend Robert Lowry
Annie Sherwood Hawks

I NEED YOU NOW
w&m/Al Jacobs, Jimmy Crane

I NEED YOU SO
w&m/Ivory Joe Hunter

I NEVER CRY
w&m/Alice Cooper, Richard Wagner

I NEVER DRANK BEHIND THE BAR
m/David Braham
w/Ed Harrigan

I NEVER KNEW
m/Ted Fiorito
w/Gus Kahn

I NEVER KNEW I COULD LOVE ANYBODY
w&m/Raymond B. Egan, Gus Kahn

I NEVER LOVED A MAN THE WAY I LOVE YOU
w&m/Ronnie Shannon

I NEVER ONCE STOPPED LOVING YOU
w&m/Bill Anderson, Jan Howard

I NEVER SAID I LOVE YOU
m/Archie Jordan
w/Hal David

I NEVER SANG FOR MY FATHER (film score)
m/Barry Mann

I ONLY HAVE EYES FOR YOU
m/Harry Warren
w/Al Dubin

I ONLY KNOW
w&m/Dinah Washington, Richard Johnson

I REALLY DON'T WANT TO KNOW
w&m/Don Robertson, Howard Barnes

I REMEMBER IT WELL
m/Frederick Loewe
w/Alan Jay Lerner

I REMEMBER YESTERDAY
w&m/Georgio Moroder, Pete Bellotte, Donna Summer

I REMEMBER YOU
m/Victor Schertzinger
w/Johnny Mercer

I ROBOT
w&m/Alan Parsons, Eric Woolfson

I SAID MY PAJAMAS AND PUT ON MY PRAYERS
w&m/Edward Pola, George Wyle

I SAW HER AGAIN
w&m/John Phillips, Dennis Doherty

I SAW MOMMY KISSING SANTA CLAUS
w&m/Tommie Connor

I SAW STARS
m/Al Hoffman, Al Goodhart
w/Maurice Sigler

I SAW THE LIGHT
w&m/Todd Rundgren

I SAY A LITTLE PRAYER
m/Burt Bacharach
w/Hal David

I SCREAM, YOU SCREAM, WE ALL SCREAM FOR ICE CREAM
m/Robert King
w/Howard Johnson

I SECOND THAT EMOTION
w&m/William (Smokey) Robinson Jr., Alfred Cleveland

I SEE A MILLION PEOPLE
m/Una Mae Carlisle
w/Robert Sour

I SEE YOUR FACE BEFORE ME
m/Arthur Schwartz
w/Howard Dietz

I SENT A LETTER TO SANTA
w&m/Vincent Rose, Larry Stock, Jack Meskill

I SHALL BE FREE
w&m/Robert Dylan

I SHALL BE RELEASED
w&m/Robert Dylan

I SHOT THE SHERIFF
w&m/Bob Marley

I SHOULD CARE
m/Axel Stordahl, Paul Weston
w/Sammy Cahn

I SOLD MY HEART TO THE JUNKMAN
w&m/Leon T. Rene, Otis J. Rene, Jr.

I STAND ACCUSED
w&m/Jerry Butler, William E. Butler

I STARTED A JOKE
w&m/Barry, Robin and Maurice Gibb

(TODAY) I STARTED LOVING YOU AGAIN
w&m/Merle Haggard, Bonnie Owens

I STILL CAN'T BELIEVE YOU'RE GONE
w&m/Willie Nelson

I STILL GET JEALOUS
m/Jule Styne
w/Sammy Cahn

I STILL GET A THRILL
m/J. Fred Coots
w/Benny Davis

I STILL LOVE TO KISS YOU GOODNIGHT
m/Harold Spina
w/Walter Bullock

I STILL SEE ELISA
m/Frederick Loewe
Alan Jay Lerner

I STOLE THE PRINCE
m/Sir Arthur Sullivan
w/Sir William Schwenk Gilbert

I SURRENDER DEAR
m/Harry Barris
w/Gordon Clifford

I QUIT MY PRETTY MAMA
w&m/Ivory Joe Hunter

I PLAN TO STAY A BELIEVER
w&m/Curtis Mayfield

I PLAYED FIDDLE FOR THE CZAR
m/Harry Revel
w/Mack Gordon

I PLEDGE MY LOVE
w&m/Frederick Perren, Dino Fekaris

I POURED MY HEART INTO A SONG
w&m/Irving Berlin

I PROMISE TO REMEMBER
w&m/Jimmy Castor

I PUT A SPELL ON YOU
w&m/Screamin' Jay Hawkins

I PUT A SPELL ON YOU
w&m/Leon Russell

I TAKE A LOT OF PRIDE IN WHAT I AM
w&m/Merle Haggard

I TAKE IT ON HOME
w&m/Kenny O'Dell

I TAKE THE CHANCE
w&m/Ira Louvin, Charles Louvin

I TALK TO THE TREES
m/Frederick Loewe
w/Alan Jay Lerner

I THANK THE LORD FOR THE NIGHT TIME
w&m/Neil Diamond

I THANK YOU
w&m/Isaac Hayes, David Porter

I THINK I LOVE YOU
w&m/Tony Romeo

I THINK I'M GONNA KILL MYSELF
m/Elton John
w/Bernie Taupin

I THINK IT'S GOING TO RAIN TODAY
w&m/Randy Newman

I THINK WE'RE ALONE NOW
w&m/Tommy James, Bob King

I THOUGHT ABOUT YOU
m/James Van Heusen
w/Johnny Mercer

I THOUGHT IT WAS YOU
w&m/Herbie Hancock

I THOUGHT OF YOU TODAY
w&m/Homer Banks, Chuck Brooks

I THREW A KISS IN THE OCEAN
w&m/Irving Berlin

I THREW IT ALL AWAY
w&m/Robert Dylan

I UNDERSTAND
m/Mabel Wayne
w/Kim Gannon

I UPS TO HIM
w&m/Jimmy Durante

I USED TO LOVE YOU BUT IT'S ALL OVER NOW
w&m/Albert Von Tilzer, Lew Brown

I WAITED TOO LONG
w&m/Neil Sedaka,
Howard Greenfield

I WALK A LITTLE FASTER
m/Cy Coleman
w/Carolyn Leigh

I WALK ALONE
m/Walter Schumann
w/Vick Knight

I WALK THE LINE
w&m/John R. Cash

I WANNA BE AROUND
m/Sadie Vimmerstedt
w/Johnny Mercer

I WANNA BE FREE
w&m/Tommy Boyce, Bobby Hart

I WANNA BE FREE
w&m/Loretta Lynn

I WANNA BE LOVED
m/Johnny Green
w/Billy Rose, Edward Heyman

I WANNA BE LOVED BY YOU
m/Herbert Stothart, Harry Ruby
w/Bert Kalmar

I WANNA BE YOUR LOVER
w&m/Robert Dylan

I WANNA BE YOUR LOVER
w&m/Prince

I WANNA LEARN A LOVE SONG
w&m/Harry Chapin

I WANNA LIVE
w&m/John D. Loudermilk

I WANNA LOVE HIM SO BAD
w&m/Jeff Barry, Ellie Greenwich

I WANNA LOVE MY LIFE AWAY
w&m/Gene Pitney

I WANT A GIRL JUST LIKE THE GIRL THAT MARRIED DEAR OLD DAD
m/Harry Von Tilzer
w/William Dillon

I WANT A LITTLE GIRL
w&m/T-Bone Walker

I WANT TO BE HAPPY
m/Vincent Youmans
w/Irving Caesar

I WANT TO GO BACK TO MICHIGAN
w&m/Irving Berlin

I WANT TO TAKE YOU HIGHER
w&m/Sly Stone

I WANT TO THANK YOU
w&m/Otis Redding

I WANT TO THANK YOU
w&m/Rory Bourke

I WANT TO THANK YOUR FOLKS
w&m/Rory Bourke

I WANT TO THANK YOUR FOLKS
m/Bennie Benjamin
w/George D. Weiss

I WENT TO A MARVELOUS PARTY
w&m/Noel Coward

I WANT TO GO WITH YOU
w&m/Hank Cochran

I WANT TO HOLD YOUR HAND
w&m/Paul McCartney, John Lennon

I WANT TO WALK YOU HOME
w&m/Antoine "Fats" Domino, Dave Bartholomew

I WANT YOU TO WANT ME
w&m/Harry Tobias, Jack Stern

I WANT WHAT I WANT WHEN I WANT IT
m/Victor Herbert
w/Henry Blossom

I WANT YOU
w&m/Robert Dylan

I WANT YOU TO WANT ME TO WANT YOU
m/Fred Fisher
w/Alfred Bryan

I WANT YOU TONIGHT
w&m/Cory Lerios, David Jenkins, Allee Willis

I WAS BORN A COUNTRY GIRL
w&m/Dottie West, Bill West

I WAS BORN IN VIRGINIA
w&m/George M. Cohan

I WAS LUCKY
w&m/Jack Meskill, Jack Stern

I WAS MADE FOR LOVING YOU
w&m/Vincent Poncia, Paul Stanley, Desmond Child

I WAS MADE TO LOVE HER
w&m/Stevie Wonder, Henry Cosby, Sylvia Moy, Lulu Hardaway

I WAS ONLY JOKING
w&m/Rod Stewart, Gary Grainger

I WAS THERE
w&m/Don Reid

I WASHED MY FACE IN THE MORNING DEW
w&m/Tom T. Hall

I WENT TO YOUR WEDDING
w&m/Jessie Mae Robinson

I WHISTLE A HAPPY TUNE
m/Richard Rodgers
w/Oscar Hammerstein II

I WILL ALWAYS LOVE YOU
w&m/Dolly Parton

I WILL NEVER PASS THIS WAY AGAIN
w&m/Ronnie Gaylord

I WILL SURVIVE
w&m/Frederick Perren, Dino Fekaris

I WILL WAIT FOR YOU
m/Michel Legrand, Jacques Demy
w/Norman Gimbel

I WISH I COULD SHIMMY LIKE MY SISTER KATE
w&m/Armand J. Piron

I WISH I DIDN'T LOVE YOU SO
w&m/Frank Loesser

I WISH I HAD A GIRL
m/Grace Leroy Kahn
w/Gus Kahn

I WISH I WAS CRAZY AGAIN
w&m/Bob McDill

I WISH I WAS 18 AGAIN
w&m/Sonny Throckmorton

I WISH I WERE IN LOVE AGAIN
m/Richard Rodgers
w/Lorenz (Larry) Hart

I WISH I WERE TWINS
w&m/Joseph Meyer, Frank Loesser, Eddie DeLange

I WISH THAT YOU WERE HERE TONIGHT
w&m/Paul Dresser

I WISH YOU LOVE (Que reste-t'il de nos amours)
m/Charles Trenet
w/English words: Albert A. Beach (Lee Wilson) French words: Charles Trenet

I WISHED ON THE MOON
w&m/Dorothy Parker, Ralph Rainger

I WONDER AS I WANDER
w&m/John Jacob Niles

I WONDER IF I CARE AS MUCH
w&m/Don Everly, Phil Everly

I WONDER IF I EVER SAID GOODBYE
w&m/Mickey Newbury

I WONDER IF SHE'LL EVER COME BACK TO ME
w&m/Paul Dresser

I WONDER IF YOU STILL CARE FOR ME
m/Ted Snyder
w/Harry B. Smith, Francis Wheeler

I WONDER IF THEY EVER THINK OF ME
w&m/Merle Haggard

I WONDER WHAT SHE'S DOING TONIGHT
w&m/Tommy Boyce, Bobby Hart

I WONDER WHAT'S BECOME OF SALLY
m/Milton Ager
w/Jack Yellen

I WONDER WHEN WE'LL EVER KNOW (The Wonder of It All)
w&m/Fred Rose

I WONDER WHERE SHE IS TONIGHT
w&m/Paul Dresser

I WONDER WHY
m/J. Fred Coots
w/Raymond W. Klages

I WONDER WHERE YOU ARE TONIGHT
w&m/Johnny Bond

I WONDER WHO'S KISSING HER NOW
m/Joseph (Joe) Howard, Harold Orlob, Will M. Hough, Frank R. Adams

I WON'T CRY ANYMORE
m/Albert Frisch
w&m/Fred Wise

I WON'T DANCE
m/Jerome Kern
w/Dorothy Fields, Oscar Hammerstein II, Otto Harbach

I WON'T FORGET YOU
w&m/Harlan Howard

I WON'T LAST A DAY WITHOUT YOU
w&m/Paul Williams, Roger Nichols

I WOULDN'T EVER CHANGE A THING
w&m/Rod Stewart

I WOULDN'T WANT TO BE LIKE YOU
w&m/Alan Parsons, Eric Woolfson

I WRITE THE SONGS
w&m/Bruce Johnston

I YI YI YI YI LIKE YOU VERY MUCH
m/Harry Warren
w/Mack Gordon

ICE STATION ZEBRA (film score)
m/Michel Legrand

I'D BE A LEGEND IN MY TIME
w&m/Don Gibson

I'D BE SATISFIED
w&m/William (Billy) Ward

I'D CLIMB THE HIGHEST MOUNTAIN
m/Sidney Clare
w/Lew Brown

I'D DO ANYTHING
w&m/Lionel Bart

I'D FIGHT THE WORLD
w&m/Hank Cochran, Joe Allison

I'D HAVE YOU ANYTIME
w&m/Robert Dylan, George Harrison

I'D KNOW YOU ANYWHERE
m/Jimmy McHugh
w/Johnny Mercer

I'D LIKE TO TEACH THE WORLD TO SING IN PERFECT HARMONY
w&m/Roger Greenaway, Billy Davis, Bill Backner, Roger Cook

I'D LOVE TO CHANGE THE WORLD
w&m/Alvin Lee

I'D LOVE TO LIVE IN LOVELAND (With a Girl Like You)
w&m/W.R. Williams

I'D RATHER LEAVE WHILE I'M IN LOVE
m/Peter Allen
w/Carole Bayer Sager

I'D RATHER BE AN OLD MAN'S SWEETHEART
w&m/Candi Staton, Calvin Carter

I'D STILL BELIEVE YOU TRUE
w&m/Paul Dresser

IDA, SWEET AS APPLE CIDER
m/Eddie Leonard
w/Eddie Munson

IDA WAS A TWELVEMONTH OLD
m/Sir Arthur Sullivan
w/Sir William Schwenk Gilbert

IDAHO
w&m/Jesse Stone

IF
m/Tolchard Evans
w/Robert Hargreaves, Stanley J. Damerell

IF
w&m/David Gates

IF A GIRL LIKE YOU LOVED A BOY LIKE ME
m/Gus Edwards
w/Will D. Cobb

IF A MAN ANSWERS
w&m/Bobby Darin

IF A WOMAN ANSWERS
w&m/Barrry Mann, Cynthia Weil

IF DREAMS COME TRUE
w&m/Edgar Melvin Sampson

IF DREAMS COME TRUE
m/Robert Allen
w/Al Stillman

IF EVER I SHOULD LEAVE YOU
m/Frederick Loewe
w/Alan Jay Lerner

IF HE COMES IN I'M GOING OUT
m/Chris Smith
w/Cecil Mack

IF HE WALKED INTO MY LIFE
w&m/Jerry Herman

IF I CAN HELP SOMEBODY
w&m/Alma Bazel Androzzo

IF I CAN'T HAVE YOU
w&m/Barry, Maurice and Robin Gibb

IF I COULD BE WITH YOU ONE HOUR TONIGHT
m/James P. Johnson
w/Henry Creamer

IF I COULD ONLY WIN YOUR LOVE
w&m/Ira Louvin, Charles Louvin

IF I DIDN'T CARE
w&m/Jack Lawrence

IF I EVER FALL IN LOVE WITH A HONKY TONK GIRL
w&m/Tom T. Hall

IF I EVER SEE YOU AGAIN
w&m/Joseph Brooks

IF I GET LUCKY
w&m/Arthur Crudup

IF I GIVE MY HEART TO YOU
w&m/Milton Gabler, Jimmie Crane, Al Jacobs, Jimmy Brewster

IF I HAD A HAMMER
w&m/Pete Seeger, Lee Hays

IF I HAD A TALKING PICTURE OF YOU
m/Ray Henderson
w/Lew Brown, Buddy DeSylva

IF I HAD MY DRUTHERS
m/Gene DePaul
w/Johnny Mercer

IF I HAD MY LIFE TO LIVE OVER
w&m/Henry Tobias, Moe Jaffe, Larry Vincent

IF I HAD MY WAY
m/James Kendis
w/Lou Klein

IF I HAD YOU
w&m/Reg Connelly, Jimmy Campbell, Ted Shapiro

IF I KISS YOU (Will You Go Away)
w&m/Liz Anderson

IF I KNEW YOU WERE COMIN' I'D HAVE BAKED A CAKE
w&m/Albert J. Trace, Al Hoffman, Bob Merrill

IF I KNOCK THE "L" OUT OF KELLY
m/Bert Grant
w/Samuel M. Lewis

IF I LOVE AGAIN
m/John Murray
w/Ben Oakland

IF I LOVED YOU
m/Richard Rodgers
w/Oscar Hammerstein II

IF I NEEDED SOMEONE
w&m/George Harrison

IF I ONLY HAD A BRAIN
m/Harold Arlen
w/E.Y. Harburg

IF I RULED THE WORLD
w&m/Leslie Bricusse, Cyril Ornandel

IF I SAID YOU HAVE A BEAUTIFUL BODY, WOULD YOU HOLD IT AGAINST ME
w&m/David Bellamy

IF I SHOULD LOSE YOU
m/Ralph Rainger
w/Leo Robin

IF I WERE A BELL
w&m/Frank Loesser

IF I WERE A CARPENTER
w&m/Tim Hardin

IF I WAS A MILLIONAIRE
m/Gus Edwards
w/Will D. Cobb

IF I WERE A RICH MAN
m/Jerry Bock
w/Sheldon Harnick

IF I WERE KING (film score)
m/Richard Hageman

IF IT AIN'T LOVE (Let's Leave It Alone)
w&m/Dallas Frazier

IF IT'S ALL THE SAME TO YOU
w&m/Bill Anderson

IF IT'S THE LAST THING I DO
m/Saul Chaplin
w/Sammy Cahn

IF LOVE MUST GO
w&m/Will Jennings

IF LOVING YOU IS WRONG (I Don't Want To Be Right)
w&m/Homer Banks, Raymond Jackson, Carl M. Hampton

IF LOVING YOU IS WRONG
w&m/Rod Stewart

IF MY FRIENDS COULD SEE ME NOW
m/Cy Coleman
w/Dorothy Fields

IF MY HEART HAD WINDOWS
w&m/Dallas Frazier

IF NOT FOR YOU
w&m/Robert Dylan

IF 6 WAS 9
w&m/Jimi Hendrix

IF SOMEBODY THERE CHANCED TO BE
m/Sir Arthur Sullivan
w/Sir William Schwenk Gilbert

IF THE BACK DOOR COULD TALK
w&m/Alex Zanetis, Grady Martin

IF THERE'S A HELL DOWN BELOW, WE'RE ALL GONNA GO
w&m/Curtis Mayfield

IF THERE IS SOMEONE LOVELIER THAN YOU
m/Arthur Schwartz
w/Howard Dietz

IF THIS ISN'T LOVE
m/Burton Lane
w/E.Y. Harburg

IF WE MAKE IT THROUGH DECEMBER
w&m/Merle Haggard

IF WE ONLY HAVE LOVE
m/Jacques Brel
w/English words: Mort Shuman, Eric Blau.
French words: Jacques Brel

IF WE'RE NOT BACK IN LOVE BY MONDAY
w&m/Sonny Throckmorton, Glenn Martin

IF WE'RE WEAK ENOUGH TO TARRY
m/Sir Arthur Sullivan
w/Sir William Schwenk Gilbert

IF YOU ARE BUT A DREAM
w&m/Jack Fulton, Nathan J. Bonx, Moe Jaffe

IF YOU BUILD A BETTER MOUSETRAP
m/Victor Schertzinger
w/Johnny Mercer

IF YOU CAN LIVE WITH IT (I Can Live Without It)
w&m/Bill Anderson

IF YOU CAN'T FEEL IT
w&m/Freddie Hart

IF YOU CAN'T GET A DRUM WITH A BOOM-BOOM-BOOM, GET A TUBA WITH AN OOM-PAH-PAH
m/Arthur Altman
w/Hal David

IF YOU DON'T WANT ME BLUES
w&m/Perry Bradford

IF YOU DON'T WANT MY LOVE
w&m/Phil Spector, John Prine

IF YOU GIVE ME YOUR ATTENTION
m/Sir Arthur Sullivan
w/Sir William Schwenk Gilbert

IF YOU GO AWAY (Ne Me Quitte Pas)
m/Jacques Brel
w/English words: Rod McKuen
French words: Jacques Brel

IF YOU GOTTA GO, GO NOW
w&m/Robert Dylan

IF YOU JUST BELIEVE
w&m/Reverend James Cleveland

IF YOU KNEW SUSIE
m/Joseph Meyer
w/Buddy DeSylva

IF YOU KNOW WHAT I MEAN
w&m/Neil Diamond

IF YOU LEAVE ME
w&m/David Van Ronk

IF YOU LEAVE ME NOW
w&m/James Pankow

IF YOU LIKE ME LIKE I LIKE YOU
w&m/Clarence Williams, Thomas "Fats" Waller, Spencer Williams

IF YOU LOVE ME (Let Me Know)
w&m/John Rostill

IF YOU LOVE THESE BLUES
w&m/Michael Bloomfield

IF YOU NEED ME
w&m/Wilson Pickett, Robert Bateman, Sonny Sanders

IF YOU REMEMBER ME
m/Marvin Hamlisch
w/Carole Bayer Sager

IF YOU SEE HER, SAY HELLO
w&m/Robert Dylan

IF YOU SEE MY SWEETHEART
w&m/Paul Dresser

IF YOU THINK I LOVE YOU NOW (I've Just Started)
w&m/Curly Putnam, Billy Sherrill

IF YOU WANT A RECEIPT
m/Sir ARthur Sullivan
w/Sir William Schwenk Gilbert

IF YOU WANT ME TO STAY
w&m/Sly Stone

IF YOU WANT TO KNOW WHO WE ARE
m/Sir Arthur Sullivan
w/Sir William Schwenk Gilbert

IF YOU'RE READY COME GO WITH ME
w&m/Homer Banks, Carl M. Hampton, Raymond Jackson

IF YOU'RE ANXIOUS FOR TO SHINE
m/Sir Arthur Sullivan
w/Sir William Schwenk Gilbert

I'LL ALWAYS BE IN LOVE WITH YOU
m/Sam H. Stept
w/Bud Green

I'LL ALWAYS CALL YOUR NAME
w&m/Glenn Shorrock

I'LL ALWAYS LOVE YOU
w&m/Ray Evans, Jay Livingston

I'LL BE AROUND
w&m/Alec Wilder

I'LL BE AROUND (Whenever You Want Me)
w&m/Thomas Bell, Phillip Hurtt

I'LL BE COMING BACK FOR MORE
w&m/Curly Putnam, S. Whipple

I'LL BE DOGGONE
w&m/William (Smokey) Robinson, Jr., Warren Moore, Bobby Rogers

I'LL BE GLAD WHEN YOU'RE DEAD YOU RASCAL YOU
w&m/Sam Theard, Charles Davenport (claimed authorship)

I'LL BE HOME FOR CHRISTMAS
m/Walter Kent
w/Kim Gannon, Buck Ram

I'LL BE READY WHEN THE GREAT DAY COMES
w&m/Perry Bradford

I'LL BE SEEING YOU
m/Sammy Fain
w/Irving Kahal

I'LL BE THE OTHER WOMAN
w&m/Homer Banks, Carl M. Hampton

I'LL BE THERE
w&m/Berry Gordy Jr., Hal Davis, Willie Hutch, Bob West

I'LL BE THINKING OF YOU
w&m/Andrae Crouch

I'LL BE WITH YOU IN APPLE BLOSSOM TIME
w&m/Neville Fleeson, Albert Von Tilzer

I'LL BE YOUR BABY TONIGHT
w&m/Robert Dylan

I'LL BE YOUR SHELTER (In Time Of Storm)
w&m/Homer Banks, Carl M. Hampton, Raymond Jackson

I'LL BUILD A STAIRWAY TO PARADISE
m/George Gershwin
w/Buddy DeSylva, Ira Gershwin

I'LL BUY THAT DREAM
m/Herb Magidson
w/Allie Wrubel

I'LL CLOSE MY EYES
w&m/Buddy Kaye, Billy Reid

I'LL CRY TOMORROW (film score)
m/Alex North

I'LL DANCE AT YOUR WEDDING
m/Ben Oakland
w/Herb Magidson

I'LL DANCE AT YOUR WEDDING
m/Hoagy Carmichael
w/Frank Loesser

I'LL DO ANYTHING YOU WANT ME TO
w&m/Barry White

I'LL DO IT ALL OVER AGAIN
w&m/Wayland Holyfield, Bob McDill

I'LL FOLLOW MY SECRET HEART
w&m/Noel Coward

I'LL GET BY
m/Fred E. Ahlert
w/Roy Turk

I'LL GO HOME WITH BONNIE JEAN
m/Frederick Loewe
w/Alan Jay Lerner

I'LL GO ON ALONE
w&m/Marty Robbins

I'LL GO TO MY GRAVE LOVING YOU
w&m/Don Reid

I'LL HAVE TO SAY I LOVE YOU IN A SONG
w&m/Jim Croce

I'LL HOLD YOU IN MY HEART (Till I Can Hold You In My Arms)
w&m/Eddy Arnold, Thomas Dilbeck, Hal Horton

I'LL KEEP ON LOVIN' YOU
w&m/Floyd Tillman

I'LL KNOW
w&m/Frank Loesser

I'LL LIVE FOR YOU
m/Gustav Luders
w/George Ade

I'LL MEET YOU HALFWAY
w&m/Gerry Goffin, Wes Farrell

I'LL NEVER BE ALONE
w&m/Rod McKuen

I'LL NEVER BE FREE
m/Bennie Benjamin
w/George D. Weiss

I'LL NEVER BE THE SAME
m/Frank Signorelli, Matt Malneck
w/Gus Kahn

I'LL NEVER FALL IN LOVE AGAIN
m/Burt Bacharach
w/Hal David

I'LL NEVER FIND ANOTHER YOU
w&m/Tom Springfield

I'LL NEVER GET OVER YOU
w&m/Don Everly, Phil Everly

I'LL NEVER GIVE YOU UP
w&m/Jerry Butler, Kenneth Gamble, Leon Huff

I'LL NEVER LET A DAY PASS BY
m/Victor Schertzinger
w/Frank Loesser

I'LL NEVER LET YOU GO LITTLE DARLING
w&m/Jimmy Wakely

I'LL NEVER LOVE THIS WAY AGAIN
w&m/Richard Kerr, Will Jennings

I'LL NEVER SAY GOODBYE
w&m/David Shire, Richard Maltby, Jr.

I'LL NEVER SAY NEVER AGAIN AGAIN
w&m/Harry M. Woods

I'LL NEVER SAY NO
w&m/Meredith Willson

I'LL NEVER SLIP AROUND AGAIN
w&m/Floyd Tillman

I'LL NEVER SMILE AGAIN
w&m/Ruth Lowe

I'LL NEVER STAND IN YOUR WAY
w&m/Fred Rose, Hy Heath

I'LL NEVER STOP LOVING YOU
m/Nicholas Brodsky
w/Sammy Cahn

I'LL PAINT YOU A SONG
w&m/Mac Davis

I'LL PLAY FOR YOU
w&m/Dash Crofts, James Seals

I'LL REMEMBER APRIL
w&m/Don Raye, Gene DePaul

I'LL SAY IT'S TRUE
w&m/John R. Cash

I'LL SEE YOU AGAIN
w&m/Noel Coward

I'LL SEE YOU IN MY DREAMS
m/Isham Jones
w/Gus Kahn

I'LL SING YOU A THOUSAND LOVE SONGS
m/Harry Warren
w/Al Dubin

I'LL STRING ALONG WITH YOU
m/Harry Warren
w/Al Dubin

I'LL SUPPLY THE LOVE
w&m/David Paich

I'LL TAKE CARE OF YOU
w&m/Brook Benton

I'LL TAKE ROMANCE
m/Ben Oakland
w/Oscar Hammerstein II

I'LL TAKE YOU HOME AGAIN, KATHLEEN
w&m/Thomas P. Westendorf

I'LL TAKE YOU THERE
w&m/Roebuck "Pop" Staples

I'LL TRY A LITTLE BIT HARDER
w&m/Donna Fargo

I'LL TRY SOMETHING NEW
w&m/William (Smokey) Robinson Jr

I'LL WALK ALONE
m/Jule Styne
w/Sammy Cahn

I'M A BELIEVER
w&m/Neil Diamond

I'M A DING DONG DADDY FROM DUMAS
w&m/Phil Baxter

I'M A DREAMER, AREN'T WE ALL
m/Ray Henderson
w/Lew Brown, Buddy DeSylva

I'M A DRIFTER
w&m/Bobby Goldsboro

I'M A FOOL TO CARE
w&m/Ted Daffan

I'M A FOOL TO WANT YOU
w&m/Joel Herron

I'M A LONELY LITTLE PETUNIA IN AN ONION PATCH
m/John N. Kamano
w/William E. Faber

I'M A LONESOME FUGITIVE
w&m/Liz Anderson, Casey Anderson

I'M A MAN
w&m/Ellas McDaniel (Bo Diddley)

I'M A RAMBLIN' MAN
w&m/Waylon Jennings

I'M A VAMP FROM EAST BROADWAY
w&m/Irving Berlin

I'M A YANKEE DOODLE DANDY
w&m/George M. Cohan

I'M AFRAID TO GO HOME IN THE DARK
m/Egbert Anson Van Alstyne
w/Harry H. Williams

I'M ALL DRESSED UP WITH A BROKEN HEART
m/Fred Fisher
w/Stella Unger

I'M ALWAYS CHASING RAINBOWS
m/Harry Carroll (adapted from Chopin's "Fantasie Impromptu in C-Sharp Minor")
w/Joseph McCarthy

I'M AN ACROBAT'S WIFE
w&m/Noel Coward

I'M AN OLD COWHAND
w&m/Johnny Mercer

I'M BEGINNING TO SEE THE LIGHT
m/Duke Ellington, Harry James Johnny Hodges
w/Don George

I'M BUILDING UP TO AN AWFUL LET-DOWN
m/Fred Astaire, Hal Borne
w/Johnny Mercer

I'M CALLED LITTLE BUTTERCUP
m/Sir Arthur Sullivan
w/Sir William Schwenk Gilbert

I'M CHECKING OUT, GOOM BYE (instr.)
m/Duke Ellington

I'M COMIN' HOME
w&m/Thomas Bell, Linda Creed

I'M COMING HOME
w&m/Tommy James, Bob King

I'M CONFESSIN' (That I Love You)
w&m/Doc Dougherty, Ellis Reynolds

I'M DOING FINE NOW
w&m/Thomas Bell, Marshall Sherman

I'M DOWN TO MY LAST I LOVE
w&m/Glenn Sutton, Billy Sherrill

I'M EASY
w&m/Keith Carradine

I'M FALLING IN LOVE WITH SOMEONE
m/Victor Herbert
w/Rida Johnson Young

I'M FLYING
m/Mark (Moose) Charlap
w/Carolyn Leigh

I'M FOREVER BLOWING BUBBLES
m/James Kendis, John Williams Kellette
w/James Brockman, Nat Vincent

I'M FREE
w&m/Peter Townshend

I'M GETTING BETTER
w&m/Jim Reeves

I'M GETTING SENTIMENTAL OVER YOU
m/George Bassman
w/Ned Washington

I'M GLAD I'M NOT YOUNG ANYMORE
m/Frederick Loewe
w/Alan Jay Lerner

I'M GLAD THERE IS YOU
m/Jimmy Dorsey
w/Paul Madeira Mertz

I'M GOING BACK TO LIVING IN THE CITY
w&m/Carole King, Charles Larkey

I'M GOING BACK TO WHUR I CAME FROM
w&m/Carson J. Robison

I'M GOING HOME
w&m/Alvin Lee

I'M GONNA BE STRONG
w&m/Barry Mann, Cynthia Weil

I'M GONNA CHANGE EVERYTHING
w&m/Alex Zanetis

I'M GONNA FIGHT FOR YOU JB
w&m/John Mayall

I'M GONNA GET MARRIED
w&m/Lloyd Price, Harold Logan

I'M GONNA GO FISHIN' (instr.)
m/Duke Ellington

I'M GONNA HAVE TO TELL HER
w&m/Homer Banks, Carl M. Hampton, Raymond Jackson, Percy Mayfield

I'M GONNA LAUGH YOU RIGHT OUT OF MY LIFE
m/Cy Coleman
w/Joseph Allan McCarthy

I'M GONNA LIVE 'TIL I DIE
w&m/Walter Kent, Mann Curtis, Al Hoffman

I'M GONNA LOVE YOU
w&m/Barry Mann, Cynthia Weil

I'M GONNA LOVE YOU JUST A LITTLE MORE
w&m/Barry White

I'M GONNA MAKE YOU LOVE ME
w&m/Paul Leka

I'M GONNA MOVE TO THE OUTSKIRTS OF TOWN
m/William Weldon
w/Andy Razaf

I'M GONNA SIT RIGHT DOWN AND WRITE MYSELF A LETTER
m/Fred E. Ahlert
w/Joseph Young

I'M GONNA WALK AND TALK WITH MY LORD
w&m/Martha Carson

I'M GONNA WASH THAT MAN RIGHT OUTA MY HAIR
m/Richard Rodgers
w/Oscar Hammerstein II

I'M GONNA WRITE A SONG
w&m/Glenn Sutton

I'M HANGING UP MY HEART FOR YOU
w&m/Don Covay, John Berry

I'M HENRY THE VIII
w&m/Fred Murray, R.P. Weston

I'M HER FOOL
w&m/Billy Swan

I'M IN A DANCING MOOD
m/Al Hoffman, Maurice Sigler
w/Al Goodhart

I'M IN YOU
w&m/Peter Frampton

I'M IN LOVE
w&m/Bobby Womack

I'M IN LOVE AGAIN
w&m/Antoine "Fats" Domino,
Dave Bartholomew

I'M IN LOVE AGAIN
w&m/Cole Porter

I'M IN LOVE AGAIN
w&m/Vic McAlpin, George Morgan

**I'M IN LOVE WITH A
WONDERFUL GUY**
m/Richard Rodgers
w/Oscar Hammerstein II

I'M IN THE MOOD
w&m/John Lee Hooker, Jules Taub

I'M IN THE MOOD FOR LOVE
m/Jimmy McHugh
w/Dorothy Fields

I'M INTO SOMETHING GOOD
w&m/Carole King, Gerry Goffin

I'M JUST A LONELY BOY
w&m/Paul Anka

I'M JUST A LUCKY SO AND SO
m/Duke Ellington
w/Mack David

**I'M JUST A SINGER IN A ROCK
& ROLL BAND**
w&m/John Lodge

I'M JUST A VAGABOND LOVER
w&m/Rudy Vallee,
Leon Zimmerman

I'M JUST WILD ABOUT HARRY
m/Eubie Blake
w/Noble Sissle

I'M LATE
m/Sammy Fain
w/Bob Hilliard

**I'M LIKE A FISH OUT OF
WATER**
m/Richard Whiting
w/Johnny Mercer

I'M LONESOME TOO
w&m/Jimmy Rodgers

I'M LOOKING (For A World)
w&m/John D. Loudermilk

**I'M LOOKING OVER A FOUR
LEAF CLOVER**
m/Harry Woods
w/Mort Dixon

I'M LOSING YOU
w&m/Rod Stewart

I'M MANDY, FLY ME
w&m/Eric Stewart, Lol Creme,
Graham Gouldman

I'M MOVING ON
w&m/Hank Snow

I'M MY OWN GRANDPAW
w&m/Moe Jaffe, Dwight B. Latham

I'M NOBODY'S BABY
m/Milton Ager, Lester Santly
w/Benny Davis

I'M NOT LISA
w&m/Jessi Colter

I'M NOT AT ALL IN LOVE
m/Jerry Ross
w/Richard Adler

I'M NOT IN LOVE
w&m/Eric Stewart, Lol Creme,
Graham Gouldman

I'M O.K.
w&m/Dennis De Young, James
Young

I'M OLD FASHIONED
m/Jerome Kern
w/Johnny Mercer

I'M ON FIRE
w&m/Dwight Twilley

**I'M ON MY WAY TO
MANDALAY**
w&m/Fred Fisher, Alfred Bryan

I'M POPEYE THE SAILOR MAN
w&m/Samuel M. Lerner

**I'M PUTTING ALL MY EGGS IN
ONE BASKET**
w&m/Irving Berlin

I'M READY
w&m/Willie Dixon

I'M READY
w&m/Antoine "Fats" Domino,
Dave Bartholomew

I'M READY FOR LOVE
w&m/Eddie Holland, Brian Holland,
Lamont Dozier

I'M SAVING MY LOVE
w&m/Alex Zanetis

I'M SCARED
w&m/Burton Cummings

I'M SHOOTING HIGH
m/Jimmy McHugh
w/Ted Koehler

**I'M SITTING ON TOP OF THE
WORLD**
m/Ray Henderson
w/Samuel M. Lewis, Joseph Young

**I'M SO AFRAID OF LOSING
YOU AGAIN**
w&m/Dallas Frazier, A.L. (Doodle)
Owens

I'M SO WEARY OF IT ALL
w&m/Noel Coward

**I'M STEPPING OUT WITH A
MEMORY TONIGHT**
m/Herb Magidson
w/Allie Wrubel

I'M STILL IN LOVE WITH YOU
w&m/Al Green

I'M STILL LOVING YOU
w&m/Glenn Sutton, George Richey

I'M STONE IN LOVE WITH YOU
w&m/Thomas Bell, Anthony Bell,
Linda Creed

I'M THE BELLE OF NEW YORK
m/Gustave A. Kerker
w/Hugh Morton

**I'M THE LONESOMEST GAL
IN TOWN**
w&m/Albert Von Tilzer, Lew Brown

I'M THROUGH WITH LOVE
m/MAtt Malneck
w/Joseph A. Livingston

**I'M THROWING RICE AT THE
GIRL I LOVE**
w&m/Eddy Arnold

I'M TIRED
w&m/Mel Tillis, Ray Price,
A.R. Peddy

I'M WALKING BEHIND YOU
w&m/Billy Reid

**I'M WAITING FOR SHIPS THAT
NEVER COME IN**
w&m/Abe Olman, Jack Yellen,
William Raskin

I'M WAITING JUST FOR YOU
w&m/Henry Glover, Lucky Millinder

I'M WALKIN'
w&m/Antoine "Fats" Domino,
Dave Bartholomew

**I'M WORKING ON A BUILDING
(instr.)**
m/William Smith Monroe

I'M YOUR BOOGIE MAN
w&m/Harry Wayne Casey, Richard
Finch

**I'M YOUR HOOCHIE KOOCHIE
MAN**
w&m/Willie Dixon

I'M YOURS
w&m/Robert Mellin

I'M YOURS
w&m/Don Robertson, Hal Blair

IMAGES (instr.)
m/Michel Legrand

IMAGINARY LOVER
w&m/Buddy Buie, Robert Nix,
Dean Daughtry

IMAGINATION
m/James Van Heusen
w/Johnny Burke

IMAGINE
w&m/John Lennon

IMMIGRANT, THE
w&m/Neil Sedaka, Phillip Cody

IMMIGRATION MAN
w&m/Graham Nash

IMPOSSIBLE
w&m/Steve Allen

IMPOSSIBLE DREAM, THE
m/Mitch Leigh
w/Joe Darion

IN A KINGDOM OF OUR OWN
w&m/George M. Cohan

IN A LITTLE GYPSY TEA ROOM
m/Joseph A. Burke
w/Edgar Leslie

IN A LITTLE SPANISH TOWN
m/Mabel Wayne
w/Samuel M. Lewis, Joseph Young

IN A MELLOTONE (instr.)
m/Duke Ellington

IN A MISSION BY THE SEA
m/Peter De Rose
w/Billy Hill

IN A MIST (instr.)
m/Bix Beiderbecke

**IN A MONASTERY GARDEN
(instr.)**
m/William Aston

IN A NUTSHELL (instr.)
m/Percy Aldridge Grainger

IN A PERSIAN GARDEN
m/Liza Lehman
w/Edward Fitzgerald (adapted from
"The Rubaiyat" by Omar Khayyam)

IN A SENTIMENTAL MOOD
w&m/Duke Ellington, Irving Mills

**IN A SHADY NOOK BY A
BABBLING BROOK**
w&m/Ed. G. Nelson, Harry Pease

**IN A SHANTY IN OLD SHANTY
TOWN**
m/Ira Schuster, Little Jack Little
w/Joseph Young

IN A SILENT WAY (instr.)
m/Joe Zawinul

**IN AN EIGHTEENTH
CENTURY DRAWING ROOM
(instr.)**
m/Raymond Scott
w/Jack Lawrence

IN AUTUMN
w&m/Edward Alexander MacDowell

IN CHI CHI CASTENANGO
m/Jay Gorney
w/Henry Myers

IN COLD BLOOD (film score)
m/Quincy Jones

IN DEAR OLD ILLINOIS
w&m/Paul Dresser

**IN ENTERPRISE OF MARTIAL
KIND**
m/Sir Arthur Sullivan
w/Sir William Schwenk Gilbert

**IN FRANCE THEY KISS ON
MAIN STREET**
w&m/Joni Mitchell

**IN GOOD OLD NEW YORK
TOWN**
w&m/Paul Dresser

IN LOVE IN VAIN
m/Jerome Kern
w/Leo Robin

**IN MEMORY OF ELIZAETH
REED**
w&m/Richard Betts

IN MY ARMS
m/Theodore J. (Ted) Grouya
w/Frank Loesser

IN MY HEART
w&m/Reverend James Cleveland

IN MY LITTLE RED BOOK
m/Nat Simon, Raymond A. Bloch
w/Al Stillman

IN MY MERRY OLDSMOBILE
m/Gus Edwards
w/Vincent P. Bryan

IN MY ROOM
w&m/Brian Wilson, Gary Usher

IN MY ROOM
m/Lee J. Pockriss
w/Paul Vance

IN OLD CHICAGO (film score)
m/Louis Silvers

IN OLD OKLAHOMA (film score)
m/Walter Scharf

IN SIAM
w&m/Manuel Klein

IN THE BLUE OF EVENING
w&m/Hoagy Carmichael

IN THE BLUE OF EVENING
w/Alfonso D'Artega
w/Tom Adair

**IN THE BLUE RIDGE
MOUNTAINS OF VIRGINIA (My
Blue Ridge Mountain Home)**
w&m/Carson J. Robison

**IN THE CHAPEL IN THE
MOONLIGHT**
w&m/Billy Hill

**IN THE COOL, COOL, COOL OF
THE EVENING**
m/Hoagy Carmichael
w/Johnny Mercer

**IN THE EVENING BY THE
MOONLIGHT**
w&m/James A. Bland

IN THE GARDEN
w&m/C. Austin Miles

**IN THE GARDEN OF
TOMORROW**
m/Jessie L. Deppen
w/George Graff Jr.

IN THE GHETTO
w&m/Mac Davis

**IN THE GOOD OLD
SUMMERTIME**
w&m/Ren Shields, George Evans

IN THE GREAT SOMEWHERE
w&m/Paul Dresser

**IN THE HEAT OF THE NIGHT
(film score)**
m/Quincy Jones

IN THE HEAT OF THE NIGHT
w&m/Mike Chapman, Nicky Chinn

IN THE JAILHOUSE NOW
w&m/Jimmy Rodgers

**IN THE LAND OF OO-BLA-DEE
(instr.)**
m/Mary Lou Williams

IN THE LIGHT (instr.)
m/Keith Jarrett

**IN THE LITTLE RED SCHOOL
HOUSE**
w&m/James Alexander Brennan,
Al Wilson

**IN THE LUXEMBOURG
GARDENS**
w&m/Kathleen Lockhart Manning

**IN THE MERRY MONTH OF
MAY**
w&m/Ren Shields, George Evans

**IN THE MIDDLE OF AN
ISLAND**
m/Nicholas Acquaviva
w/Ted Varnick

**IN THE MIDDLE OF THE
NIGHT**
w&m/Jessie Mae Robinson

IN THE MIDNIGHT HOUR
w&m/Steve Cropper, Wilson Pickett

IN THE MISTY MOONLIGHT
w&m/Cindy Walker

IN THE MOOD
m/Joseph C. Garland
w/Andy Razaf

IN THE MORNING BY THE BRIGHT LIGHT
w&m/James A. Bland

IN THE SHADE OF THE OLD APPLE TREE
m/Egbert Anson Van Alstyne
w/Harry H. Williams

IN THE SHADOWS
m/Herman Finck
w/E. Ray Goetz

IN THE STILL OF THE NIGHT
w&m/Cole Porter

IN THE STONE
w&m/Allee Willis, David Foster,
Maurice White

IN THE SWEET BYE AND BYE
m/Harry Von Tilzer
w/Vincent P. Bryan

IN THE WEE SMALL HOURS OF THE MORNING
m/David Mann
w/Bob Hilliard

IN THE YEAR 2525
w&m/Rick Evans

IN YOUR OWN QUIET WAY
m/Harold Arlen
w/E.Y. Harburg

IN YOUR OWN SWEET WAY (instr.)
m/Dave Brubeck

INCHWORM
w&m/Frank Loesser

INDEPENDENCE
w&m/William Billings

INDIAN GIVER
w&m/Jerry Kasenetz, Jeff Katz

INDIAN HUNTER, THE
w&m/Henry Russell

INDIAN LAKE
w&m/Tony Romeo

INDIAN LOVE CALL
m/Rudolf Friml
w/Otto Harbach,
Oscar Hammerstein II

INDIAN RESERVATION
w&m/John D. Loudermilk

INDIAN SUMMER
m/Victor Herbert
w/Al Dubin

(BACK HOME AGAIN IN) INDIANA
m/James F. Hanley
w/Ballard MacDonald

INDIANA MOON
m/Isham Jones
w/Benny Davis

INDIANA WANTS ME
w&m/R. Dean Taylor

INDIGO (instr.)
m/Ferde Grofe

INFINITY PROMENADE (instr.)
w/Shorty Rogers

INFORMER, THE (film score)
w&m/Max Steiner

INHERIT THE WIND (film score)
m/Ernest Gold

INITIATION
w&m/Todd Rundgren

INKA DINKA DOO
m/Jimmy Durante
w/Ben Ryan

INNER CITY BLUES (Make Me Wanna Holler)
w&m/Marvin Gaye, James Nyx, Jr.

INSEPARABLE
w&m/Marvin Yancy, Chuck Jackson

INTERMEZZO (A Love Story)
m/Heinz Provost
w/Robert Henning

INTERNATIONAL RAG
w&m/Irving Berlin

INTERNATIONALE, THE (L'Internationale)
m/Pierre De Geyter
w/Eugene Pottier

INTERSTATE FORTY
w&m/John D. Loudermilk

INTO EACH LIFE SOME RAIN MUST FALL
m/Allan Roberts
w/Doris Fisher

INTO THE MYSTIC
w&m/Van Morrison

INVINCIBLE EAGLE (march)
m/John Philip Sousa

INVITATION (instr.)
m/Bronislau Kaper

INVITATION TO THE BLUES
m/Allan Roberts, Arthur Gershwin
w/Doris Fisher

INVITATION TO THE BLUES
w&m/Roger Miller

INVITATION TO THE DANCE (Aufforderung Zum Tanze) (instr.)
m/Carl Maria Von Weber)

IOLA (instr.)
m/Charles Leslie Johnson

IRELAND MUST BE HEAVEN
m/Fred Fisher
w/Howard E. Johnson,
Joseph McCarthy

IRENE
m/Harry Austin Tierney
w/Joseph McCarthy

IRISH JUBILEE, THE
m/Charles Lawlor
w/James Thornton

IRMA LA DOUCE (film score)
m/Andre Previn

IRONSIDE (TV theme)
m/Quincy Jones

IS HE THE ONLY MAN IN THE WORLD
w&m/Irving Berlin

IS IT A DREAM
m/Gustave A. Kerker
w/Charles A. Byrne

IS IT REALLY OVER
w&m/Jim Reeves

IS IT TRUE WHAT THEY SAY ABOUT DIXIE
m/Gerald Marks
w/Sammy Lerner, Irving Caesar

IS LIFE A BOON
m/Sir Arthur Sullivan
w/Sir William Schwenk Gilbert

IS PARIS BURNING (film score)
m/Maurice Jarre

IS THAT THE WAY
w&m/Steve Kipner, Fred Goodman

IS THIS LOVE
w&m/Bob Harley

IS THIS ME
w&m/Dottie West, Bill West

IS YOU OR IS YOU AIN'T MY BABY
w&m/Louis Jordan, Billy Austin

I'SE A-MUGGIN'
w&m/Stuff Smith

ISLAND GIRL
m/Elton John
w/Bernie Taupin

ISLAND IN THE SUN
w&m/Irving Burgess (adapted from traditional Jamaican folk music)

IT'S A CUTE LITTLE WAY OF
MY OWN
m/Harry A. Tierney
w/Alfred Bryan

IT'S A FUNKY THING (instr.)
m/Herbie Mann

IT'S A GOOD DAY
w&m/Peggy Lee, Dave Barbour

IT'S A GREAT DAY FOR THE
IRISH
w&m/Roger Edens

IT'S A GREAT LIFE
w&m/Joe Allison, Audrey Allison

IT'S A HAP HAP HAPPY DAY
w&m/Sammy Timberg

IT'S A HEARTACHE
w&m/Ronnie Scott

IT'S A LAUGH
w&m/John Oates, Daryl Hall

IT'S A LONG, LONG, LONELY
HIGHWAY
w&m/Doc (Jerome) Pomus, Mort
Shuman

IT'S A LONG, LONG WAY TO
TIPPERARY
w&m/Jack Judge, Harry Williams

IT'S A LONG WAY THERE
w&m/Glenn Shorrock

IT'S A LOVELY DAY TODAY
w&m/Irving Berlin

IT'S A MAD MAD MAD MAD
WORLD (film score)
m/Ernest Gold

IT'S A MAD MAD MAD MAD
WORLD
m/Ernest Gold
w/Mack David

IT'S A MAN'S MAN'S MAN'S
WORLD
w&m/James Brown, Betty Jean
Newsome

IT'S A MIRACLE
w&m/Barry Manilow, Marty Panzer

IT'S A MOST UNUSUAL DAY
m/Jimmy McHugh
w/Harold Adamson

IT'S A SIN
w&m/Fred Rose, Zeb Turner

IT'S A SIN TO TELL A LIE
w&m/William Mayhew

IT'S A SMALL WORLD
w&m/Richard M. Sherman, Robert
B. Sherman

IT'S ALL IN THE GAME
m/Charles Gates Dawes
w/Carl Sigman

IT'S ALL IN THE MOVIES
w&m/Merle Haggard

IT'S ALL OVER
w&m/Don Everly

IT'S ALL OVER
w&m/Harlan Howard, Jan Howard

IT'S ALL OVER NOW
w&m/Robert Dylan

IT'S ALL RIGHT WITH ME
w&m/Cole Porter

IT'S ALL WRONG BUT IT'S ALL
RIGHT
w&m/Dolly Parton

IT'S ALWAYS YOU
m/James Van Heusen
w/Johnny Burke

IT'S AN OLD SOUTHERN
CUSTOM
w&m/Joseph Meyer, Jack Yellen

IT'S BEEN A LONG, LONG,
TIME
m/Jule Styne
w/Sammy Cahn

IT'S DELIGHTFUL TO BE
MARRIED
m/Vincent Scotto, (from the French
song "La petite Tonkinoise")
w/Anna Held

IT'S DE-LOVELY
w&m/Cole Porter

IT'S EASIER SAID THAN DONE
w&m/John Jacob Loeb, Carmen
Lombardo

IT'S EASY TO REMEMBER
m/Richard Rodgers
w/Lorenz (Larry) Hart

IT'S EASY TO SAY (Song from
'10')
m/Henry Mancini
w/Robert Nells

IT'S ECTASY (When You Lay
Down Next To Me)
w&m/Barry White

IT'S FORTY MILES FROM
SCHENECTADY TO TROY
m/Gustave A. Kerker
w/Hugh Morton

IT'S FOUR IN THE MORNING
w&m/Jerry Chesnut

IT'S GETTING BETTER
w&m/Barry Mann, Cynthia Weil

IT'S GOING TO TAKE SOME
TIME
w&m/Carole King, Toni Stern

IT'S GONNA COME DOWN
(On You)
w&m/Dash Crofts, James Seals

IT'S GONNA WORK OUT FINE
w&m/Rodemarie McCoy,
Sylvia McKinney

IT'S IMPOSSIBLE (Somios
Novios)
m/Armando Manzanero
w/Sid Wayne

IT'S JUST A MATTER OF TIME
w&m/Brook Benton, Clyde Otis,
Belford Hendricks

IT'S LATE
w&m/Brian May

IT'S LIKE WE NEVER SAID
GOODBYE
w&m/Roger Greenaway, Geoffrey
Stephens

IT'S LOVE
m/Leonard Bernstein
w/Betty Comden, Adolph Green

IT'S MAGIC
m/Jule Styne
w/Sammy Cahn

IT'S MIDNIGHT
w&m/Jerry Chesnut

IT'S MORNING
w&m/Jessi Colter

IT'S MY LIFE
w&m/Roger Atkins, Carl D'Errico

IT'S NICE TO HAVE A
SWEETHEART
m/Gustav A. Kerker
w/R.H. Burnside

IT'S ANYBODY'S SPRING
m/James Van Heusen
w/Johnny Burke

IT'S NOT FOR ME TO SAY
m/Robert Allen
w/Al Stillman

IT'S NOT KILLING ME
w&m/Michael Bloomfield

IT'S NOT LOVE (But It's Not
Bad)
w&m/Hank Cochran, Glenn Martin

IT'S NOT THE SPOTLIGHT
w&m/Gerry Goffin, Barry Goldberg

IT'S NOT UNUSUAL
w&m/Gordon Mills, Les Reed

IT'S NOTHIN' TO ME
w&m/Jim Reeves

IT'S NOW OR NEVER
w&m/Aaron Schroeder, Wally Gold
(adapted from Eduardo di Capua's
"O Sole Mio")

IT'S ONE OF THOSE NIGHTS
w&m/Tony Romeo

ISLE OF CAPRI
m/Will Grosz (Hugh Williams)
w/Jimmy Kennedy

ISLE OF OUR DREAMS, THE
m/Victor Herbert
w/Henry Blossom

ISN'T IT A PITY
w&m/George Harrison

ISN'T IT ROMANTIC
m/Richard Rodgers
w/Lorenz (Larry) Hart

ISN'T LIFE STRANGE
w&m/John Lodge

ISN'T SHE LOVELY
w&m/Stevie Wonder

ISN'T THAT JUST LIKE LOVE
m/James Van Heusen
w/Johnny Burke

ISN'T THIS A LOVELY DAY TO BE CAUGHT IN THE RAIN
w&m/Irving Berlin

ISRAELITES, THE
w&m/Desmond Dekker

ISTANBUL (Not Constantinople)
m/Nat Simon
w/Jimmy Kennedy

IT AIN'T GONNA RAIN NO MO'
w&m/Wendell Woods Hall

IT AIN'T ME BABE
w&m/Robert Dylan

IT AIN'T NECESSARILY SO
m/Geroge Gershwin
w/Ira Gershwin

IT ALL COMES BACK TO ME NOW
w&m/Alex Kramer, Joan Whitney Kramer

IT ALL DEPENDS ON YOU
m/Ray Henderson
w/Lew Brown, Buddy DeSylva

IT CAME UPON THE MIDNIGHT CLEAR
m/Richard Storrs Wills
w/Rev. Edmund Hamilton Sears

IT CAN'T BE TRUE (Theme from "Now Voyager")
m/Max Steiner
w/Kim Gannon

IT COULD HAPEN TO YOU
m/James Van Heusen
w/Johnny Burke

IT DO FEEL GOOD
w&m/Donna Fargo

IT DOESN'T MATTER ANYMORE
w&m/Buddy Holly

IT DON'T MATTER TO ME
w&m/David Gates

IT DON'T MEAN A THING IF IT AIN'T GOT THAT SWING
m/Duke Elligton
w/Irving Mills

IT FEELS SO GOOD (instr.)
m/Charlie Shavers

IT GOES LIKE IT GOES
m/David Shire
w/Norman Gimbel

IT HAD BETTER BE TONIGHT
m/Henry Mancini
w/Johnny Mercer

IT HAD TO BE YOU
m/Isham Jones
w&m/Gus Kahn

IT HAPPENED IN MONTEREY
m/Mabel Wayne
w/Billy Rose

IT HAPPENED IN SUN VALLEY
m/Harry Warren
w/Mack Gordon

IT HURTS TO BE IN LOVE
w&m/Helen Miller,
Howard Greenfield

IT IS NO SECRET (What God Can Do)
m/Stuart Hamblen

IT ISN'T FAIR
w&m/Richard Himber

IT ISN'T YOUR HEART THAT BREAKS
w&m/Fred Tobias, Stan Lebowsky

IT JUST TORE ME UP
w&m/Floyd Tillman

IT LOOKS LIKE RAIN IN CHERRY BLOSSOM LANE
m/Joseph A. Burke
w/Edgar Leslie

IT MAKES NO DIFFERENCE NOW
w&m/Jimmy Davis

IT MAKES NO DIFFERENCE NOW
w&m/Floyd Tillman

IT MIGHT AS WELL BE SPRING
m/Richard Rodgers
w&m/Oscar Hammerstein II

IT MIGHT AS WELL RAIN UNTIL SEPTEMBER
w&m/Carole King, Gerry Goffin

IT MUST BE JELLY ('Cause Jam Don't Shake Like That)
w&m/J. Chalmers MacGregor

IT NEVER ENTERED MY MIND
m/Richard Rodgers
w/Lorenz (Larry) Hart

IT NEVER RAINS IN SOUTHERN CALIFORNIA
w&m/Albert L. Hammond, Mike Hazelwood

IT ONLY HAPPENS WHEN I DANCE WITH YOU
w&m/Irving Berlin

IT ONLY HURTS FOR A LITTLE WHILE
w&m/Fred Spielman, Mack David

IT ONLY TAKES A MOMENT
w&m/Jerry Herman

IT TAKES A LITTLE RAIN WITH THE SUNSHINE
m/Harry Carroll
w/Ballard MacDonald

IT TAKES A LOT TO LAUGH, IT TAKES A TRAIN TO CRY
w&m/Robert Dylan

IT TAKES PEOPLE LIKE YOU
w&m/Buck Owens

IT WAS A VERY GOOD YEAR
w&m/Ervin M. Drake

IT WAS ALMOST LIKE A SONG
m/Archie Jordan
w/Hal David

IT WAS SO BEAUTIFUL
m/Harry Barris
w/Arthur Freed

IT WAS WRITTEN IN THE STARS
m/Harold Arlen
w/Leo Robin

IT WASN'T GOD WHO MADE HONKY TONK ANGELS
w&m/J.D. Miller

IT WON'T BE WRONG
w&m/Roger McGuinn

IT WOULDN'T HAVE MADE ANY DIFFERENCE
w&m/Todd Rundgren

ITALIAN STREET SONG
m/Victor Herbert
w/Rida Johnson Young

IT'S A BIG WIDE WONDERFUL WORLD
w&m/John Rox

IT'S A BLUE WORLD
w&m/George (Chet) Forrest,
Robert Wright

IT'S A CHEATIN' SITUATION
w&m/Curly Putnam, Sonny Throckmorton

IT'S ONLY A PAPER MOON
m/Harold Arlen
w/Billy Rose, E.Y. Harburg

IT'S ONLY LOVE
w&m/Mark James

IT'S ONLY LOVE
w&m/William Gibbons, Frank Beard,
Dusty Hill

IT'S ONLY MAKE BELIEVE
w&m/Conway Twitty, Jack Nance

IT'S OVER
w&m/Boz Scaggs, David Paich

IT'S RIGHT HERE WITH ME
w&m/Perry Bradford

IT'S SAD TO BELONG
w&m/John Ford Coley, Danny Seals

IT'S SO EASY
w&m/Buddy Holly, Norman Petty

**IT'S SO NICE TO HAVE A MAN
AROUND THE HOUSE**
w&m/Harold Spina, Jack Elliott

IT'S THE ARMY
w&m/Philip Egner

IT'S THE DREAMER IN ME
w&m/Jimmy Dorsey, James Van
Heusen

**IT'S SO HARD TO SAY
GOODBYE TO YESTERDAY**
w&m/Frederick Perren, Christine
Yarion

IT'S THE SAME OLD SONG
w&m/Eddie Holland, Brian Holland,
Lamont Dozier

IT'S THE SAME OLD SONG
w&m/Harry Wayne Casey, Richard
Finch

IT'S THE TALK OF THE TOWN
m/Jerry Livingston
w/Al J. Neiburg, Marty Symes

IT'S TOO LATE
w&m/Chuck Willis

IT'S TOO LATE
w&m/Carole King, Toni Stern

IT'S UP TO YOU
w&m/Justin Hayward

IT'S YOU I LOVE
w&m/Antoine "Fats" Domino,
Dave Bartholomew

IT'S YOUR THING
w&m/O'Kelly Isley, Rudolph Isley,
Ronald Isley

IT'S YOUR WORLD
w&m/Marty Robbins

**ITSY BITSY TEENIE WEENIE
YELLOW POLKA DOT BIKINI**
m/Lee J. Pockriss
w/Paul Vance

IVANHOE (film score)
m/Miklos Rozsa

**I'VE A LONGING IN MY HEART
FOR YOU, LOUISE**
w&m/Charles K. Harris

**I'VE A SHOOTING BOX IN
SCOTLAND**
w&m/Cole Porter

**I'VE ALREADY LOVED YOU
IN MY MIND**
w&m/Conway Twitty

I'VE BEEN KISSED BEFORE
w&m/Bob Russell, Lester Lee

**I'VE BEEN LOVING YOU TOO
LONG**
w&m/Otis Redding, Jerry Butler

I'VE BEEN THINKING
w&m/Boudleaux Bryant

I'VE BEEN THIS WAY BEFORE
w&m/Neil Diamond

I'VE COME AWFUL CLOSE
w&m/Hank Thompson

**I'VE DONE ENOUGH DYIN'
TODAY**
w&m/Larry Gatlin

**I'VE ENJOYED AS MUCH OF
THIS AS I CAN STAND**
w&m/Bill Anderson

I'VE GOT A CRUSH ON YOU
m/George Gershwin
w/Ira Gershwin

I'VE GOT A FEELING
w&m/Ellas McDaniel (Bo Diddley)

**I'VE GOT A FEELING I'M
FALLING**
m/Thomas "Fats" Waller
w/Billy Rose

**I'VE GOT A FEELING (We'll Be
Seeing Each Other Again)**
w&m/Homer Banks, Carl M.
Hampton

**I'VE GOT A FEELIN' YOU'RE
FOOLING**
m/Nacio Herb Brown
w/Arthur Freed

I'VE GOT A LITTLE LIST
m/Sir Arthur Sullivan
w/Sir William Schwenk Gilbert

**I'VE GOT A LOVELY BUNCH OF
COCOANUTS**
w&m/Fred Heatherton

**I'VE GOT A GAL IN
KALAMAZOO**
m/Harry Warren
w/Mack Gordon

I'VE GOT A NAME
w&m/Jim Croce

**I'VE GOT A POCKETFUL OF
DREAMS**
m/James Monaco
w/Johnny Burke

**I'VE GOT A THING ABOUT
YOU BABY**
w&m/Tony Joe White

**I'VE GOT A TIGER BY THE
TAIL**
w&m/Harlan Howard, Buck Owens

I'VE GOT A WOMAN
w&m/Ray Charles

**I'VE GOT AN INVITATION TO A
DANCE**
m/Jerry Livingston
w/Al J. Neiburg, Marty Symes

**I'VE GOT FIVE DOLLARS AND
IT'S SATURDAY NIGHT**
w&m/Ted Daffan

I'VE GOT LOVE ON MY MIND
w&m/Marvin Yaney, Chuck Jackson

I'VE GOT MY EYES ON YOU
w&m/Cole Porter

**I'VE GOT MY LOVE TO KEEP
ME WARM**
w&m/Irving Berlin

**I'VE GOT RINGS ON MY
FINGERS (Mumbo, Jumbo,
Jijiboo O'Shea)**
m/Maurice Scott
w/Weston & Barnes

I'VE GOT SO MUCH TO GIVE
w&m/Barry White

I'VE GOT THE BLUES (instr.)
m/James Moody

**I'VE GOT THE WORLD ON A
STRING**
m/Harold Arlen
w/Ted Koehler

I'VE GOT TO HAVE YOU
w&m/Kris Kristofferson

**I'VE GOT TO USE MY
IMAGINATION**
w&m/Gerry Goffin, Barry Goldberg

**I'VE GOT YOU UNDER MY
SKIN**
w&m/Cole Porter

I'VE GOT YOUR NUMBER
m/Cy Coleman
w/Carolyn Leigh

I'VE GOTTA CROW
m/Mark (Moose) Charlap
w/Carolyn Leigh

I'VE GOTTA GET A MESSAGE TO YOU
w&m/Barry, Maurice and Robin Gibb

I'VE GROWN ACCUSTOMED TO HER FACE
m/Frederick Loewe
w/Alan Jay Lerner

I'VE HEARD THAT SONG BEFORE
m/Jule Styne
w/Sammy Cahn

I'VE JUST COME BACK TO SAY GOODBYE
w&m/Charles K. Harris

I'VE LOST MY BABY
w&m/Jeremy Spencer

I'VE NEVER BEEN IN LOVE BEFORE
w&m/Frank Loesser

I'VE NEVER LOVED ANYONE MORE
w&m/Mike Nesmith, Linda Hargrove

I'VE SEEN THAT MOVIE TOO
m/Elton John
w/Bernie Taupin

I'VE STILL GOT MY HEALTH
w&m/Cole Porter

I'VE TOLD EVERY LITTLE STAR
m/Jerome Kern
w/Oscar Hammerstein II

IVORY TOWER
w&m/Jack Fulton, Lois Steele

IVY
w&m/Hoagy Carmichael

IVY (film score)
m/Daniele Amfitheatrof

Addenda:

I JUST FALL IN LOVE AGAIN
w&m/Larry Herbstritt

I JUST WANT TO BE
w&m/Larry Blackman

I WANT TO LIVE
w&m/John Denver

I WAS MADE FOR DANCIN'
w&m/Joe Brooks

IF YOU'RE BLACK, GET BACK
w&m/William "Big Bill" Broonzy

I'LL COME RUNNING
w&m/Livingston Taylor, Morgan Creek

I'M ALIVE
w&m/Jeff Lynn

I'M EVERY WOMAN
w&m/Nicholas Ashford, Valerie Simpson

I'M STILL HERE
w&m/Stephen Sondheim

IN AMERICA
w&m/Charlie Daniels, C. Hayward, J. DiGregorio, T. Crain, F. Edwards, J. Marshall

IS THIS LOVE
w&m/Bob Marley

IMPERIAL MARCH, THE (Darth Vader's Theme) (instr.)
m/John Williams

INDIA (instr.)
m/John Coltrane

IT SEEMS TO HANG ON
w&m/Nicholas Ashford, Valerie Simpson

IT'S STILL ROCK 'N' ROLL TO ME
w&m/Billy Joel

**SONGS**

J, K

JA DA
w&m/Robert Louis (Bob) Carleton

JACK IN THE BOX (instr.)
m/Edward E. (Zev) Confrey

JACK THE BEAR (instr.)
m/Duke Ellington

JACKIE ROBINSON STORY, THE (film score)
m/Herschel Burke Gilbert

JACKIE WILSON SAID
w&m/Van Morrison

JACKSON
w&m/John R. Cash, June Carter Cash

JACKSON
w&m/Billy Edd Wheeler

JADE VISIONS (instr.)
m/Bill Evans

JAHBERO (instr.)
m/Tadd Dameron

JALOUSIE (JEALOUSY) (instr.)
m/Jacob Gade (adapted by Walter Paul)

JAM UP, JELLY TIGHT
w&m/Tommy Roe

JAMBOREE JONES
w&m/Johnny Mercer

JAMAICA FAREWELL
w&m/Irving Burgess
(adapted from traditional Jamaican folk music)

JAMAICAN RHUMBA
w&m/Michael S. Stoner

JAMES (HOLD THE LADDER STEADY)
w&m/John D. Loudermilk

JAMES DEAN
w&m/J. D. Souther, Glenn Frey, Donald Henley, Jackson Browne

JAMIE
w&m/William Stevenson, Barrett Strong

JANE
w&m/Paul Kantner, David Frieberg, Craig Chaquico, J. McPherson

JANE EYRE (film score)
m/Bernard Herrmann

JAPANESE SANDMAN, THE
m/Richard A. Whiting
w/Raymond B. Egan

JANUARY 23-30, 1978
w&m/Steve Forest

JASPER
w&m/Jim Stafford

J'ATTENDRAI (I'LL BE YOURS)
m/Dino Olivieri
French w/Louis Poterat
English w/Anna Sosenko

JAVA
w&m/Allen Toussaint, Freddy Friday, Alvin Tyler, Marilyn Shack

JAWS (film score)
m/John Williams

JAWS 2 (film score)
m/John Williams

JAWS, THEME FROM (instr.)
m/John Williams

JAZZ CONVULSIONS (instr.)
m/Duke Ellington

JAZZ LEGATO (instr.)
m/Leroy Anderson

JAZZ MAN
w&m/Carole King, Toni Stern

JAZZ NOCTURNE (instr.)
m/Dana Suesse

JAZZ PIZZICATO (instr.)
m/Leroy Anderson

JAZZ SINGER, THE (film score)
m/Ray John Heindorf

JAZZ SINGER, THE (film score-1927)
m/Louis Silvers

JAZZ SUITE ON THE MASS TEXTS (instr.)
m/Lalo Schifrin

JAZZ WALTZ (instr.)
m/Shorty Rogers

JEALOUS HEART
w&m/Jenny Lou Carson

JEALOUS HEARTED MAN
w&m/Muddy Waters

JEAN
w&m/Rod McKuen

JEAN
w&m/Paul Dresser

JEAN GENIE, THE
w&m/David Bowie

JEANNINE, I DREAM OF LILAC TIME
m/Nathaniel Shilkret
w/L. Wolfe Gilbert

JEANS ON
w&m/Roger Greenaway, David Dundas

JEEPERS CREEPERS
m/Harry Warren
w/Johnny Mercer

JELINDA'S THEME
w&m/Barry DeVorzon

JELLY BEAN BLUES
w&m/Gertrude "Ma" Rainey

JELLY, JELLY (instr.)
m/Earl (Fatha) Hines

JELLY ROLL BLUES (DOCTOR JAZZ (instr.)
m/Ferdinand "Jelly Roll" Morton

JENNIE LEE
m/Harry Von Tilzer
w/Arthur J. Lamb

JENNIE LEE
w&m/Jan Berry, Arnie Ginsberg

JENNY
w&m/John Mayall

JENNY KISSED ME
w&m/Roy C. Bennett, Sid Tepper

JENNY JENNY
w&m/Little Richard, Enotris Johnson

JEREMIAH PEABODY'S POLY-UNSATURATED QUICK DIS-SOLVING FAST ACTING, PLEASANT TASTING GREEN AND PURPLE PILLS
w&m/Ray Stevens

JERICHO
w&m/Richard Myers, Leo Robin

JERSEY BOUNCE
w&m/Buddy Feyne, Bobby Plater, Tiny Bradshaw, Edward Johnson, Robert B. Wright

JERU (instr.)
m/Gerry Mulligan

JERUSALEM
w&m/Herb Alpert

JESSICA
w&m/Richard Betts

JESUS IS JUST ALRIGHT
w&m/Roger McGuinn

JESUS IS LORD
w&m/Andrae Crouch

JESUS, LOVER OF MY SOUL
m/Simeon Buckley
w/Charles Wesley

JESUS LOVES THE LITTLE CHILDREN
m/George Frederick Root (based on his song "Tramp, Tramp, Tramp")
w/C. H. Woolston

JESUS TAKES A HOLD
w&m/Merle Haggard

JESUS WAS A CAPRICORN
w&m/Kris Kristofferson

JEZEBEL
w&m/Wayne Shanklin

JIG SAW PUZZLE (instr.)
m/Adam Makowicz

JIM
w&m/Nelson H. Shawn, Caesar
Petrillo, Edward Ross

JIM CROW TRAIN
w&m/Joshua D. White

JIM DANDY
w&m/Lincoln Chase

JIM FISK
w&m/William J. Scanlan (unverified,
but considered probable author)

**JIM JUDSON - FROM THE
TOWN OF HACKENSACK**
w&m/Paul Dresser

JIMINY CRICKET
m/Leigh Harline
w/Ned Washington

JIMMY MACK
w&m/Eddie Holland, Brian Holland,
Lamont Dozier

JIMMY THE KID
w&m/Jimmy Rodgers, Bob Neville

**JIMMY THE WELL-DRESSED
MAN**
m/Jimmy Durante

JIMMY VALENTINE
m/Gus Edwards
w/Edward Madden

JIMMY'S BLUES
w&m/James A. Rushing

**JINGLE BELLS (ONE HORSE
OPEN SLEIGH)**
w&m/Rev. John S. Pierpont

JINGLE JANGLE JINGLE
m/Joseph J. Lilley
w/Frank Loesser

JINGLE JINGLE JINGLE
w&m/John D. Marks

JIVE TALKIN'
w&m/Barry, Maurice and Robin Gibb

JOANNA
w&m/Stephen Sondheim

JOANNE
w&m/Mike Nesmith

JOANNA (film score)
m/Rod McKuen

JOANNA (instr.)
m/Henry Mancini

JOE TURNER BLUES
w&m/W. C. Handy

JOEY, JOEY, JOEY
w&m/Frank Loesser

JOHN AND MARY (film score)
m/Quincy Jones

JOHN BROWN
w&m/Robert Dylan

JOHN HENRY BLUES
w&m/W. C. Handy

JOHN WESLEY HARDING
w&m/Robert Dylan

JOHNNY ANGEL
m/Lee J. Pockriss
w/Lyn Duddy

JOHNNY ANGEL (film score)
m/Leigh Harline

JOHNNY B. GOODE
w&m/Chuck Berry

**JOHNNY DOUGHBOY (film
score)**
m/Walter Scharf

**JOHNNY DOUGHBOY FOUND
A ROSE IN IRELAND**
m/Kay Twomey, Allan Roberts
w/Al Goodhart

JOHNNY GET ANGRY
m/Sherman Edwards
w/Hal David

JOHNNY ONE NOTE
m/Richard Rodgers
w/Lorenz (Larry) Hart

JOHNNY ONE TIME
w&m/Dallas Frazier, A.L. (Doodle)
Owens

JOHNNY REB
w&m/Merle Kilgore

JOHN'S IDEA (instr.)
m/William (Count) Basie, Eddie
Durham

JOHNSON & TURNER BLUES
w&m/Joe Turner Pete K.H. Johnson

JOHNSON RAG
w&m/Jack Lawrence, Guy Hall,
Henry Kleinauf

JOINT IS JUMPIN', THE
m/Thomas "Fats" Waller
w/Andy Razaf

JOKER, THE
w&m/Leslie Bricusse, Anthony
Newley

JOLENE
w&m/Dolly Parton

JOLLY ROGERS (instr.)
m/Shorty Rogers

JONES BOY, THE
w&m/Vic Mizzy, Mann Curtis

**JORDAN IS A HARD ROAD TO
TRAVEL**
w&m/Daniel Decatur Emmett

JOSEPH, JOSEPH
m/Saul Chaplin
w/Sammy Cahn

JOSEPHINE
w&m/Val Burton, Will Jason

JOSEPHINE
m/Wayne King, Burke Bivens
w/Gus Kahn

**JOSEPHINE PLEASE NO LEAN
ON THE BELL**
w&m/Ed. G. Nelson, Harry Pease

JOSHUA
w&m/Dolly Parton

JOSIE w&m/Donald Fagen, Walter
Becker

**JOURNEY TO THE CENTER OF
THE EARTH (film score)**
m/Bernard Herrmann

JOY
w&m/Harry Edward Nilsson

JOY TO THE WORLD
w&m/Hoyt Axton

JUBA DANCE (instr.)
m/Robert Nathaniel Dett

JUBILATION
w&m/Paul Anka

JUBILATION T. CORNPONE
m/Gene DePaul
w/Johnny Mercer

**JUDGMENT AT NUREMBURG
(film score)**
m/Ernest Gold

JUKE BOX BABY
w&m/Alan Parsons, Eric Woolfson

JUKE BOX SATURDAY NIGHT
m/Paul J. McGrane
w/Al Stillman

JULIA (film score)
m/George Delerue

JULIUS CAESAR (film score)
m/Miklos Rozsa

JUMP FOR JOY
m/Duke Ellington
w/Paul Francis Webster

JUMP INTO THE FIRE
w&m/Harry Edward Nilsson

JUMP OVER
w&m/Frank C. Slay Jr., Bob Crewe,
Freddie Cannon

**JUMPIN' AT THE WOODSIDE
(instr.)**
m/William (Count) Basie

**JUMPIN' IN THE PUMP ROOM
(instr.)**
m/Charlie Shavers

JUMPIN' JACK FLASH
w&m/Mick Jagger, Keith Richard

JUMPIN' WITH SYMPHONY SID (instr.)
m/Lester Young

JUNE COMES AROUND EVERY YEAR
m/Harold Arlen
w/Johnny Mercer

JUNE IN JANUARY
m/Ralph Rainger
w/Leo Robin

JUNE IS BUSTIN' OUT ALL OVER
m/Richard Rodgers
w/Oscar Hammerstein II

JUNE NIGHT
m/Cliff Friend
w/Abel Baer

JUNGLE BOOK (instr.)
m/Joe Zawinul

JUNGLE BOOK, THE (film score)
m/Miklos Rozsa

JUNGOSO (instr.)
m/Sonny Rollins

JUNIOR'S FARM
w&m/Paul and Linda McCartney

JUNK MAN RAG
w&m/Charles L. Roberts

JURAME (PROMISE LOVE)
m/Maria Grever
w/Frederick Herman Martens

JUST A CLOSER WALK WITH THEE
m/Kenneth Morris
w/various English word versions

JUST A COTTAGE SMALL BY A WATERFALL
m/James Frederick Hanley
w/Buddy DeSylva

JUST A DREAM
w&m/"Big Bill" Broonzy

JUST A GIGOLO
m/Leonello Casucci
w/Irving Caesar

JUST A LITTLE BIT OF LOVE
m/Victor Jacobi
w/Harry B. Smith

JUST A LITTLE BIT SOUTH OF NORTH CAROLINA
m/Bette Cannon, Arthur Shaftel
w/Sunny Skylar

JUST A LITTLE LOVIN' (EARLY IN THE MORNING)
w&m/Barry Mann, Cynthia Weil

JUST AN ECHO IN THE VALLEY
w&m/Harry M. Woods

JUST AN OLD LOVE OF MINE
w&m/Peggy Lee, Dave Barbour

JUST AROUND THE CORNER
m/Harry Von Tilzer
w/Dolf Singer

JUST AS THE SUN WENT DOWN
w&m/Lyn Udall

JUST BECAUSE
w&m/Sydney Robin

JUST BECAUSE
w&m/Lloyd Price

JUST BECAUSE SHE MADE DEM GOO-GOO EYES
w&m/Hughie Cannon, John Queen

JUST BEFORE THE BATTLE, MOTHER
w&m/George Frederick Root

JUST DROPPED IN
w&m/Mickey Newbury

JUST FOR OLD TIME'S SAKE
w&m/Nat (King) Cole

JUST FOR WHAT I AM
w&m/Dallas Frazier, A.L. (Doodle) Owens

JUST IN LOVE
m/David Rose
w/Leo Robin

JUST IN TIME
m/Jule Styne
w/Betty Comden, Adolph Green

JUST LIKE A GYPSY
w&m/Seymour Simons, Nora Bayes

JUST LIKE A WOMAN
w&m/Robert Dylan

JUST LIKE ME
w&m/Fred Rose

JUST LIKE TOM THUMB'S BLUES
w&m/Robert Dylan

JUST A LITTLE LOVIN' (WILL GO A LONG WAY)
w&m/Eddy Arnold, Zeke Clements

JUST A LITTLE TOO MUCH
w&m/Dorsey Burnette, Johnny Burnette

JUST A MEMORY
m/Ray Henderson
w/Lew Brown, Buddy DeSylva

JUST A SONG BEFORE I GO
w&m/Graham Nash

JUST A-WEARYIN' FOR YOU
m/Carrie Jacobs Bond
w/Frank Stanton

JUST ONCE IN MY LIFE
w&m/Phil Spector, Carole King, Gerry Goffin

JUST ONE GIRL
m/Lyn Udall
w/Karl Kennett

JUST ONE OF THOSE THINGS
w&m/Cole Porter

JUST ONE SMILE
w&m/Randy Newman

JUST ONE TIME
w&m/Don Gibson

JUST SITTIN' AND A-ROCKIN'
m/Duke Ellington
w/Lee Gaines

JUST SQUEEZE ME
m/Duke Ellington
w/Lee Gaines

JUST TELL THEM THAT YOU SAW ME
w&m/Paul Dresser

JUST THE WAY YOU ARE
w&m/Billy Joel

JUST TOO MANY PEOPLE
w&m/Vincent Poncia, Melissa Manchester

JUST YOU 'N' ME
w&m/James Pankow

JUST LONG ENOUGH TO SAY GOODBYE
w&m/Bill Rice, Jerry Foster

JUST LONESOME
m/Carrie Jacobs Bond
w/Harriet Axtell Johnstone

JUST MAKE LOVE TO ME
w&m/Willie Dixon

JUST MARRIED
w&m/Barry DeVorzon, Al Allen

JUST ONE MORE CHANCE
m/Arthur Johnston
w/Sam Coslow

KALEIDOSCOPE (instr.)
m/Ornette Coleman

KANSAS CITY BLUES
w&m/Euday Louis Bowman

KANSAS CITY BOMBER (film score)
m/Don Ellis

KANSAS CITY RAG (instr.)
m/James S. Scott

KANSAS CITY SONG
w&m/Buck Owens, Red Simpson

KANSAS CITY STOMP (instr.)
m/Ferdinand "Jelly Roll" Morton

Kashmiri Song (Pale Hands I
Loved)
m/Amy Woodford-Finden
w/Lawrence Hope

KATE
w&m/Marty Robbins

KATHLEEN MAVOURNEEN
m/Frederick W. N. Crouch
w/Annie B. Crawford

KATIE LIED
w&m/Donald Fagen, Walter Becker

KATIE WENT TO HAITI
w&m/Cole Porter

KATMANDU
w&m/Cat Stevens

KATMANDU
w&m/Bob Seger

KAW-LIGA
w&m/Fred Rose, Hank Williams

KEEP IT A SECRET
w&m/Jessie Mae Robinson

KEEP IT COMIN' LOVE
w&m/Harry Wayne Casey, Richard
Finch

KEEP ON DANCING
w&m/ Andrew F. Love, Allen Jones,
Richard Shann

KEEP ON DOIN' WHAT YOU'RE
DOIN'
m/Harry Ruby
w/Bert Kalmar

KEEP ON GROWING
w&m/Eric Clapton, Bobby Whitlock

KEEP ON THE SUNNY SIDE
m/Theodore F. Morse
w/Jack Drislane

KEEP ON TRUCKIN'
w&m/Anita Poree, Frank G. Wilson,
Leonard Caston

KEEP SEARCHIN'
w&m/Del Shannon

KEEP SMILING AT TROUBLE
w&m/Al Jolson, Buddy DeSylva,
Lewis Gensler

KEEP THE HOME FIRES
BURNING
m/Ivor Novello
w/Lena Guilbert Ford

KEEP YOUNG AND BEAUTIFUL
m/Harry Warren
w/Al Dubin

KEEP YOUR ARMS AROUND
ME
w&m/Arthur Crudup

KEEP YOUR HANDS OFF MY
BABY
w&m/Carole King, Gerry Goffin

KEEP YOUR HANDS ON YOUR
HEART
w&m/"Big Bill" Broonzy

KEEPIN' OUT OF MISCHIEF
NOW
m/Thomas "Fats" Waller
w/Andy Razaf

KEEPING UP WITH THE JONES
w&m/Justin Tubb

KENTUCKY BABE
m/Adam Geibel
w/Richard Buck

KENTUCKY GAMBLER
w&m/Dolly Parton

KENTUCKY RAIN
w&m/Eddie Rabbitt, Dick Heard

KENTUCKY SUE
w&m/Albert Von Tilzer, Lew Brown

KENTUCKY WOMAN
w&m/Neil Diamond

KERRY DANCE, THE
w&m/James Lyman Molloy

KEYS OF THE KINGDOM (film
score)
m/Alfred Newman

KICK IT OUT
w&m/Ann Wilson

KICKIN' THE GONG AROUND
m/Harold Arlen
w/Ted Koehler

KICKS
w&m/Barry Mann, Cynthia Weil

KID
w&m/Chrissie Hynde, Pete Farndon

KID CHARLEMAGNE
w&m/Donald Fagen, Walter Becker

KIDDIO
w&m/Brook Benton, Clyde Otis

KIDS
m/Charles Strouse
w/Lee Adams

KIDS ARE ALRIGHT, THE
w&m/Peter Townshend

KIDS SAY THE DARNDEST
THINGS
w&m/Billy Sherrill, Glenn Sutton

KILL ME IF YOU CAN (TV
theme)
m/Bill Conti

KILLARNEY
m/Michael W. Balfe
w/Edmund Falconer

KISS IN THE DARK, A
m/Victor Herbert
w/Buddy DeSylva

KISS IT AND MAKE IT BETTER
w&m/Mac Davis

KISS ME AGAIN
m/Victor Herbert
w/Henry Blossom

KISS ME HONEY KISS ME
m/Ted Snyder
w/Irving Berlin

KISS OF FIRE
w&m/Robert Hill, Lester Allen
(adapted from A. G. Villoldo's "El
Choclo"

KISS THE BOYS GOODBYE
m/Victor Schertzinger
w/Frank Loesser

KISS TO BUILD A DREAM ON,
A
m/Harry Ruby
w/Bert Kalmar, Oscar
Hammerstein II

KISS WALTZ, THE (IL BACIO)
m/Luigi Arditi
w/M. Aldighieri

KISS WALTZ, THE
m/Joseph A. Burke
w/Al Dubin

KISS WALTZ, THE
m/Ivan Caryll
w/Harry Morton

KISS YOU ALL OVER
w&m/Mike Chapman, Nicky Chinn

KISS YOUR MAN GOODBYE
w&m/Don Everly, Phil Everly

KISSES SWEETER THAN WINE
w&m/Pete Seeger, Joel Newman,
Ronnie Gilbert, Lee Hays, Fred
Hellerman

KISSING MY LOVE
w&m/Bill Withers

KISSING OF GEORGIE, THE
w&m/Rod Stewart

KITTEN ON THE KEYS (instr.)
m/Edward E. (Zev) Confrey

K-K-K-KATY
w&m/Geoffrey O'Hara

KNACK, THE
m/John Barry
w/Leslie Bricusse

KNEE DEEP IN LOVING YOU
w&m/Sonny Throckmorton

KNEE DEEP IN THE BLUES
w&m/Melvin Endsley

KILLER QUEEN
w&m/Brian May

KILLERS, THE (film score)
m/Miklos Rozsa

KILLING ME SOFTLY WITH HIS SONG
m/Charles Fox
w/Norman Gimbel

KIND CAPTAIN I'VE IMPORTANT INFORMATION
m/Sir Arthur Sullivan
w/Sir William Schwenk Gilbert

KIND OF BLUE (instr.)
m/Miles Dewey Davis

"KING" (film score)
m/Billy Goldenberg

KING AND I, THE (film score)
m/Alfred Newman

KING COTTON (march)
m/John Philip Sousa

KING FOR A DAY
m/Ted Fiorito
w/Samuel M. Lewis, Joseph Young

KING IS COMING, THE
m/William J. Gaither
w/William J. Gaither, Gloria Gaither

KING KONG (PT. 1)
w&m/Jimmy Castor

KING OF ALL KINGS, THE
w&m/Stuart Hamblen

KING OF NOTHING
w&m/James Seals

KING OF THE NIGHT TIME WORLD
w&m/Paul Stanley, Kim Fowley, Mark Anthony, Bob Ezrin

KING OF THE ROAD
w&m/Roger Miller

KING PORTER STOMP (instr.)
m/Ferdinand "Jelly Roll" Morton

KINGDOM COMING (THE YEAR OF JUBILO)
w&m/Henry Clay Work

KINGS AND QUEENS
w&m/Steve Tyler, Joe Perry

KINGS ROW (film score)
m/Erich Wolfgang Korngold

KINKAJOU, THE
m/Harry Austin Tierney
w/Joseph McCarthy

KIPLING "JUNGLE BOOK" (instr.)
m/Percy Aldridge Grainger

KISS AN ANGEL GOOD MORNING
w&m/Ben Peters

KNICE AND KNIFTY (instr.)
m/Roy Frederick Bargy

KNOCK ON WOOD
w&m/Homer Banks, Carl M. Hampton

KNOCK ON WOOD
w&m/Eddie Floyd, Steve Cropper

KNOCK ON WOOD
w&m/Sylvia Fine

KNOCK THREE TIMES
w&m/Irwin Levine, L. Russell Brown

KNOCKIN' ON HEAVEN'S DOOR
w&m/Robert Dylan

KNOWING ME, KNOWING YOU
m/Benny Andersson, Bjorn Ulvaeus
w/Stig Anderson

KNOWING WHEN TO LEAVE
m/Burt Bacharach
w/Hal David

KO-KO JOE
w&m/Jerry Reed

KODACHROME
w&m/Paul Simon

KOTCH (film score)
m/Marvin Hamlisch

KOKO JOE
w&m/Sonny Bono

KUNG FU FIGHTING
w&m/Carl Douglas

KUUM (BACKHAND) (instr.)
m/Keith Jarrett

KOOKIE, KOOKIE (LEND ME YOUR COMB)
w&m/Irving Taylor

KO KO MO (I LOVE YOU SO)
w&m/Eunice Levy, Forest Wilson, Jake Porter

Addenda:

JESSE
w&m/Carly Simon, M. Manieri

JUSTINE
w&m/Mark Goldenberg

KOGUN (instr.)
m/Toshiko Akiyoshi

SONGS

L

L. A. FREEWAY
w&m/Jerry Jeff Walker

LA BAMBA
m/Ralph Rainger
w/Leo Robin

LA COMPARSA (CARNIVAL PARADE)
m/Ernesto Lecuona
w/Albert Gamse

LA DEE DAH
w&m/Bob Crewe, Frank C. Slay Jr.

LA FIESTA (instr.)
m/Chick Corea

LA GOLONDRINA (THE SWALLOW)
m/Narciso Serrandell
Spanish
w/B. Niceto de Zamacois

LA GRANGE
w&m/William Gibbons, Frank Beard, Dusty Hill

LA PALOMA (THE DOVE)
w&m/Sebastian Yradier

LA VIE EN ROSE
m/Louiguy
w/Mack David

LADDIE BOY
m/Gus Edwards
w/Will D. Cobb

LADIES OF THE CANYON
w&m/Joni Mitchell

LADY
w&m/Dennis De Young

LADY
m/Bert Kaempfert, Herbert Rehbein
w/Charles Singleton, Larry Kusik

LADY BIRD (instr.)
m/Tadd Dameron

LADY BLUE
w&m/Leon Russell

LADY CAME FROM BALTIMORE, THE
w&m/Tim Hardin

LADY D'ARBAVILLE
w&m/Cat Stevens

LADY FRIEND
w&m/Roger McGuinn

LADY IN RED, THE
m/Mort Dixon
w/Allie Wrubel

LADY IS A TRAMP, THE
m/Richard Rodgers
w/Lorenz (Larry) Hart

LADY JANE
w&m/Mick Jagger

LADY MARMALADE
w&m/Bob Crewe, Kenny Nolan

LADY OF SPAIN
m/Tolchard Evans
w/Erell Reaves

LADY OF THE EVENING
w&m/Irving Berlin

LADY OF THE ISLAND
w&m/Graham Nash

LADY PLAY YOUR MANDOLIN
m/Oscar Levant
w/Irving Caesar

LADY SINGS THE BLUES (film score)
m/Michel Legrand

LADY'S IN LOVE WITH YOU, THE
m/Burton Lane
w/Frank Loesser

LA-LA MEANS I LOVE YOU
w&m/Thomas Bell, William A. Hart

LAMBETH WALK
w&m/Noel Gay

LAMENT OF THE CHEROKEE RESERVATION
w&m/John D. Loudermilk

LAMENTATION OVER BOSTON
w&m/William Billings (new words to melody of "By the Waters of Babylon", a psalm by Billings)

LAMENTO BORINCANO
w&m/Rafael Hernandez

LAMENTO GITANO (instr.)
m/Maria Grever

L'AMOUR, TOUJOURS L'AMOUR
m/Rudolf Friml
w/Catherine Chisholm Cushing

LAMP IS LOW, THE
m/Peter DeRose, Mitchell Parish
w/Mitchell Parish

LAMPLIGHT
w&m/David Essex, Jeff Wayne

LAMPLIGHTER'S SERENADE, THE
m/Hoagy Carmichael
w/Paul Francis Webster

LAND OF GOLDEN DREAMS, THE
m/E. F. Dusenberry
w/C. M. Denison

LAND OF MAKE BELIEVE (instr.)
m/Chuck Mangione

LAND OF 1,000 DANCES
w&m/Chris Kenner

LANGUAGE OF LOVE, THE
w&m/John D. Loudermilk

LARA'S THEME FROM DOCTOR ZHIVAGO (instr.)
m/Maurice Jarre
w/(see "Somewhere My Love" for lyric version)

LASS WITH THE DELICATE AIR, THE (a/k/a YOUNG MOLLY WHO LIVES AT THE FOOT OF THE HILL)
m/Michael Arne
w/source unknown

LASS WITH THE DELICATE AIR
m/Lou Singer
w/Hy Zaret

LASSIE COME HOME (film score)
m/Daniele Amfitheatrof

LAST BLUES SONG, THE
w&m/Barry Mann, Cynthia Weil

LAST CHANGE TEXACO, THE
w&m/Rickie Lee Jones

LAST CHEATER'S WALTZ
w&m/Sonny Throckmorton

LAST DANCE
w&m/Paul Jabara

LAST DATE
w&m/Floyd Cramer

LAST FAREWELL THE
w&m/Roger Whittaker

LAST LOVE SONG, THE
w&m/Hank Williams Jr.

LAST NIGHT ON THE BACK PORCH
m/Carl Schraubstader
w/Lew Brown

LAST ONE TO TOUCH ME, THE
w&m/Dolly Parton

LAST THING ON MY MIND, THE
w&m/Neil Diamond

LAST THING ON MY MIND
w&m/Thomas R. Paxton

LAST TIME I SAW PARIS, THE
m/Jerome Kern
w/Oscar Hammerstein II

LAST TRAIN TO CLARKSVILLE
w&m/Tommy Boyce, Bobby Hart

LAST TIME I FELT LIKE THIS THE
m/Marvin Hamlisch
w/Alan and Marilyn Bergman

LAST WORD IN LONESOME IS ME, THE
w&m/Roger Miller

LAST NIGHT WHEN WE WERE YOUNG
m/Harold Arlen
w/E. Y. Harburg

LAST ROUNDUP, THE
w&m/Billy Hill

LAST TANGO IN PARIS (instr.)
m/Gato Barbieri

LAST WALTZ, THE
w&m/Webb Pierce, Myrna Freeman

LATE FOR THE SKY
w&m/Jackson Browne

LAUGH AND THE WORLD LAUGHS WITH YOU
m/Louis F. Gottschalk
w/Ella Wheeler Wilcox

LAUGH CLOWN LAUGH
m/Ted Fiorito
w/Samuel M. Lewis, Joseph Young

LAUGHING
w&m/Burton Cummings, Randy Bachman

LAUGHING ON THE OUTSIDE, CRYING ON THE INSIDE
w&m/Bernie Wayne, Ben Raleigh

LAUGHTER IN THE RAIN
w&m/Neil Sedaka, Phillip Cody

LAURA
m/David Raksin
w/Johnny Mercer

LAURA (WHAT'S HE GOT THAT I AIN'T GOT)
w&m/Margie Singleton, Leon Ashley

LAVENDER BLUE (Dilly Dilly)
w&m/Larry Morey, Eliot Daniel
(music adapted from an old English folk melody)

LAVENDER HILL MOB, THE (film score)
m/Georges Auric

LAVERNE AND SHIRLEY (TV theme/instr.)
m/Charles Fox

LAW IS THE TRUE EMBODIMENT, THE
m/Sir Arthur Sullivan
w/Sir William Schwenk Gilbert

LAWD YOU MADE THE NIGHT TOO LONG
m/Victor Young
w/Samuel M. Lewis

LAWDY MISS CLAWDY
w&m/Lloyd Price

LAWMAN (film score)
m/Jerry Fielding

LAWRENCE OF ARABIA (THEME FROM, instr.)
m/Maurice Jarre

LAWRENCE OF ARABIA (film score)
m/Maurice Jarre

LAWS MUST CHANGE, THE
w&m/John Mayall

LAY BACK IN THE ARMS OF SOMEONE
w&m/Mike Chapman, Nicky Chinn

LAY DOWN (CANDLES IN THE RAIN)
w&m/Melanie

LAY DOWN BESIDE ME
w&m/Tompall Glaser

LAY DOWN YOUR WEARY TUNE
w&m/Robert Dylan

LAY LADY LAY
w&m/Robert Dylan

LAY SOME HAPPINESS ON ME
w&m/Jean Chapel, Bob Jennings

LAYLA
w&m/Eric Clapton, Jim Gordon

LAZY
w&m/Irving Berlin

LAZY AFTERNOON
m/Jerome Moross
w/John Latouche

LAZY DAY
w&m/Ray Thomas

LAZY RHAPSODY
m/Howard Manucy Jackson

LAZY RIVER
m/Hoagy Carmichael
w/Sidney Arodin

LAZYBONES
m/Hoagy Carmichael
w/Johnny Mercer

L. DAVID SLOANE
w&m/Billy Meshel

LEAD KINDLY LIGHT
m/John Bacchus Dykes (from the song "Lux Benigna")
w/John Henry Newman

LEAD ME ON
w&m/Allee Willis

LEAD ON
w&m/Glenn Frey, Donald Henley

LEADER OF THE PACK
w&m/Jeff Barry, Ellie Greenwich, George Morton

LEAN ON ME
w&m/Bill Withers

LEAP, THE (instr.)
m/Miles Dewey Davis

LEARN TO CROON
m/Arthur Johnston
w/Sam Coslow

LEARNIN' THE BLUES
w&m/Dolores Silvers

LEARNING TO LEAN
w&m/John Stallings

LEAVING ON A JET PLANE
w&m/John Denver

LEAVIN' ON YOUR MIND
w&m/Webb Pierce, Wayne P. Walker

LEAVIN' THIS MORNING
w&m/Gertrude "Ma" Rainey

LEFT ALONE
w&m/Billie Holiday

LEFT MY GAL IN THE MOUNTAINS
w&m/Carson J. Robison

LEGEND IN YOUR OWN TIME
w&m/Carly Simon

LEGEND OF BONNIE AND CLYDE
w&m/Merle Haggard, Bonnie Owens

LEMON TREE
w&m/Will Holt

LEOLA (instr.)
m/Scott Joplin

LEROY
w&m/Jack Scott

LESS THAN ZERO
w&m/Elvis Costello

LESSON IN LEAVIN', A
w&m/Randy Goodrum, B. Maher

LESSON OF LOVE, THE
w&m/Fred Rose, Nat Vincent

LESTER LEAPS IN (instr.)
m/Lester Young

LESTER LEFT TOWN (instr.)
m/Wayne Shorter

LET A SMILE BE YOUR UMBRELLA
w&m/Irving Kahal, Sammy Fain, Francis Wheeler

LET 'EM IN
w&m/Paul and Linda McCartney

LET ERIN REMEMBER THE DAYS OF OLD
m/from the traditional Irish song "The Red Fox"
w/Thomas Moore

LET HER
w&m/Gary Benson

LET IT ALONE
m/Bert Williams
w/Alex Rogers

LET IT BE
w&m/Paul McCartney, John Lennon

LET IT BE ME
w&m/Curtis Mayfield, Jerry Butler

LET IT GROW
w&m/Eric Clapton

LET IT RIDE
w&m/Randy Bachman, C.F. Turner

LET IT SNOW, LET IT SNOW, LET IT SNOW
m/Jule Styne
w/Sammy Cahn

LET ME BE THE CLOCK
w&m/William (Smokey) Robinson Jr.

LET ME BE THE ONE
w&m/Barry Mann, Larry Kolber

LET ME BE THE ONE
w&m/Paul Williams, Roger Nichols

LET ME BE THE ONE
w&m/W. S. Stevenson, Paul Blevins, Joe Holson

LET ME BE THERE
w&m/John Rostill

LET ME CALL YOU SWEETHEART
m/Leo Friedman
w/Beth Slater Whitson

LET ME CRY
w&m/Johnny Nash

LET ME ENTERTAIN YOU
m/Jule Styne
w/Stephen Sondheim

LET ME GO LOVE
w&m/Michael McDonald, B. J. Foster

LET ME GO LOVER
w&m/Jenny Lou Carson, Al Hill (new words)

LET ME KNOW (I HAVE A RIGHT)
w&m/Frederick Perren, Dino Fekaris

LET ME LOVE YOU TONIGHT
m/Rene Touzet
w/Mitchell Parish

LET ME OFF UPTOWN
w&m/Redd Evans

LET ME SING AND I'M HAPPY
w&m/Irving Berlin

LET THE GOOD TIMES ROLL
w&m/Fleecie Moore, Sam Theard

LET THE GOOD TIMES ROLL
w&m/Leonard Lee

LET THE MUSIC PLAY
w&m/Barry White

LET THE REST OF THE WORLD GO BY
m/Ernest R. Ball
w/J. Keirn Brennan

LET THE SUNSHINE IN
m/Galt MacDermot
w/James Rado, Gerome Ragni

LET THE WORLD KEEP ON A-TURNING
w&m/Buck Owens

LET THERE BE PEACE ON EARTH (LET IT BEGIN WITH ME)
w&m/Jill Jackson, Seymour (Sy) Miller

LET YOUR LOVE FLOW
w&m/Lawrence Williams

LET YOURSELF GO
w&m/Irving Berlin

LET'S ALL SING LIKE THE BIRDIES SING
m/Tolchard Evans
w/Robert Hargreaves, Stanley J. Damerell

LET'S BE BUDDIES
w&m/Cole Porter

LET'S CALL IT A DAY
w&m/Henry Glover

LET'S CALL THE WHOLE THING OFF
m/George Gershwin
w/Ira Gershwin

LET'S DO IT (LET'S FALL IN LOVE)
w&m/Cole Porter

LET'S DO IT AGAIN
w&m/Curtis Mayfield

LET'S FACE THE MUSIC AND DANCE
w&m/Irving Berlin

LET'S FALL IN LOVE
m/Harold Arlen
w/Ted Koehler

LET'S FLY AWAY
w&m/Cole Porter

LET'S GET AWAY FROM IT ALL
m/Matt Dennis
w/Thomas A. Adair

LET'S GET IT ON
w&m/Ed Townsend, Marvin Gaye

LET'S GET TO THE NITTY GRITTY (instr.)
m/Horace Silver

LET'S GET TOGETHER (ONE LAST TIME)
w&m/George Richey, Billy Sherrill

LET'S GET SERIOUS
w&m/Stevie Wonder, L. Garrett

LET'S GO GET STONED
w&m/Valerie Simpson, Nicholas Ashford

LET'S GO, LET'S GO, LET'S GO
w&m/Hank Ballard

LET'S GO ROCK AND ROLL
w&m/Harry Wayne Casey, Richard Finch

LET'S HAVE A LITTLE
w&m/Vic McAlpin, Ruth E. Coletharp

LET'S HAVE ANOTHER CUP OF COFFEE
w&m/Irving Berlin

LET'S KISS AND MAKE UP
m/George Gershwin
w/Ira Gershwin

LET'S LOVE
w&m/Paul and Linda McCartney

LET'S MISBEHAVE
w&m/Cole Porter

LET'S NOT TALK ABOUT LOVE
w&m/Cole Porter

LET'S PUT OUT THE LIGHTS AND GO TO SLEEP
w&m/Herman Hupfeld

LET'S SPEND THE NIGHT TOGETHER
w&m/Mick Jagger, Keith Richard

LET'S STAY TOGETHER
w&m/Al Green, Willie Mitchell, Al Jackson Jr.

LET'S TAKE A WALK AROUND THE BLOCK
m/Harold Arlen
w/E. Y. Harburg, Ira Gershwin

LET'S TAKE AN OLD FASHIONED WALK
w&m/Irving Berlin

LET'S TAKE THE LONG WAY HOME
m/Harold Arlen
w/Johnny Mercer

LET'S TWIST AGAIN
w&m/Kal Mann, Dave Appell

LET'S WORK TOGETHER
w&m/Wilbert Harrison

LETTER, THE
w&m/Wayne Carson Thompson

LETTER, THE
w&m/Karla Bonoff

LETTER PERFECT
w&m/Al Jarreau

LETTER SONG
m/Fritz Kreisler
w/William Le Baron

LETTER SONG, THE
m/Oscar Straus
w/Stanislaus Stange

LETTER THAT NEVER CAME, THE
w&m/Paul Dresser

LETTERS HAVE NO ARMS
w&m/Ernest Tubb, Artie Gibson

LEVON
m/Elton John
w/Bernie Taupin

LIBERTY BELL (march)
m/John Philip Sousa

LIEBESFREUD (instr.)
m/Fritz Kreisler

LIDA ROSE
w&m/Meredith Willson

LIDO SHUFFLE
w&m/Boz Scaggs, David Paich

LIE TO ME
w&m/Brook Benton, Margie Singleton

LIFE AND TIMES OF JUDGE ROY BEAN, THE (filmscore)
m/Maurice Jarre

LIFE GETS TEEJUS DON'T IT
w&m/Carson J. Robison

LIFE GOES ON
w&m/Paul Williams, Craig Doerge

LIFE IN THE FAST LANE
w&m/Donald Henley, Glenn Frey, Joseph F. Walsh

LIFE IS A CARNIVAL
w&m/J. Robbie Robertson

LIFE IS WHAT YOU MAKE IT
m/Marvin Hamlisch
w/Johnny Mercer

LIFE ON THE OCEAN WAVE, A
w&m/Henry Russell

LIFE IS JUST A BOWL OF CHERRIES
m/Ray Henderson
w/Lew Brown, Buddy DeSylva

LIFE IS A SONG
m/Fred E. Ahlert
w/Joseph Young

LIFE LET US CHERISH
m/Hans Georg Naegeli (from the German song "Freut Euch Des Lebebs")
w/Unknown source

LIFE UPON THE WICKED STAGE
m/Jerome Kern
w/Oscar Hammerstein II

LIFE WITH FATHER (film score)
m/Max Steiner

LIFEBOAT (film score)
m/Hugo Friedhofer

LIFE'S BEEN GOOD TO ME
w&m/Joseph F. Walsh

LIFT EVERY VOICE AND SING
w&m/James W. Johnson, J. Rosamond Johnson

LIGHT A CANDLE IN THE CHAPEL
w&m/Ed. G. Nelson, Harry Pease

LIGHT AND SWEET (instr.)
m/Edgar Melvin Sampson

LIGHT AS A FEATHER (instr.)
m/Chick Corea

LIGHT IN THE CITY
w&m/Jeff Lynne

LIGHT MY FIRE
w&m/Jose Feliciano

LIGHT OF A CLEAR BLUE MORNING
w&m/Dolly Parton

LIGHTS OUT
w&m/Billy Hill

LIKE A HURRICANE
w&m/Neil Young

LIKE A ROLLING STONE
w&m/Robert Dylan

LI'L LIZA JANE (LITTLE LIZA JANE)
w&m/Countess Ada DeLachau

LILACS IN THE RAIN
m/Peter DeRose
w/Mitchell Parish

LILI (film score)
m/Bronislau Kaper

LILIES OF THE FIELD (film score)
m/Jerry Goldsmith

LILITH (film score)
m/Kenyon Hopkins

LILLI MARLENE
w&m/Hans Leip, Norbert Schultze, Tommie Connor

LILY OF THE VALLEY
m/Anatol Friedland
w/L. Wolfe Gilbert

LILY WHITE
w&m/Cat Stevens

LIMEHOUSE BLUES
m/Philip Braham
w/Douglas Furber

LIMELIGHT (film score)
m/Charles S. Chaplin, Raymond Rasch, Larry Russell

LINCOLN, GRANT OR LEE
w&m/Paul Dresser

LINDA
w&m/Ann Ronell, Jack Lawrence

LINDA ON MY MIND
w&m/Conway Twitty

LINE FOR LYONS (instr.)
m/Gerry Mulligan

LINGER AWHILE
w&m/Vincent Rose, Harry Owens

LION IN WINTER, THE (film score)
m/John Barry

LION SLEEPS TONIGHT, THE (Wimoweh)
m/Music based on a Zulu folk song
w&m/Hugo Peretti, Luigi Creatore, George Weiss, Albert Stanton, Paul Campbell, Solomon Linda

LISA LISTEN TO ME
w&m/David Clayton-Thomas

LISBON ANTIGUA (LISBOA ANTIGUA)
m/Raul Portela
w/Harry Dupree

LIST OF ADRIAN MESSENGER, THE (film score)
m/Jerry Goldsmith

LISTEN TO A COUNTRY SONG
w&m/James Messina

LISTEN TO HER HEART
w/mTom Petty

LISTEN TO THE GERMAN BAND
m/Harry Revel
w/Mack Gordon

LISTEN TO THE MOCKING BIRD
w&m/Septimus Winner

LISTEN TO THE MUSIC
w&m/Thomas Johnston

LISTEN TO THE WARM
w&m/Rod McKuen

LITTLE ANNIE ROONEY
w&m/Michael Nolan

LITTLE ARK, THE (film score)
m/Fred Karlin, Tylwyth Kymry

LITTLE ARROWS
w&m/Albert L. Hammond, Mike Hazelwood

LITTLE BIRD, THE
w&m/John D. Loudermilk

LITTLE BIRD TOLD ME, A
w&m/Harvey Oliver Brooks

LITTLE BIT IN LOVE, A
m/Leonard Bernstein
w/Betty Comden, Adolph Green

LITTLE BIT INDEPENDENT, A
m/Joseph A. Burke
w/Edgar Leslie

LITTLE BIT ME, LITTLE BIT YOU, A
w&m/Neil Diamond

LITTLE BIT OF HEAVEN, A
m/Ernest R. Ball
w/J. Keirn Brennan

LITTLE BIT OF LOVE, A
w&m/Ken Ascher

LITTLE BIT OF ME
w&m/Melanie

LITTLE BIT OF RAIN
w&m/Fred Neil

LITTLE BITTY TEAR, A
w&m/Hank Cochran

LITTLE BOY SAD
w&m/Dorsey Burnette, Johnny Burnette

LITTLE BRAINS, A LITTLE TALENT, A
m/Jerry Ross
w/Richard Adler

**LITTLE BROWN CHURCH IN THE VALE, THE
(COME TO THE CHURCH IN THE WILDWOOD)**
w&m/Dr. William S. Pitts

LITTLE BROWN JUG, THE
w&m/J. E. Winner (R.A. Eastburn)

LITTLE BY LITTLE
m/Robert Emmett Dolan
w/Walter O'Keefe

LITTLE CRIMINALS
w&m/Randy Newman

LITTLE DARLING
w&m/Maurice Williams

LITTLE DEUCE COUPE
w&m/Brian Wilson

LITTLE DEVIL
w&m/Neil Sedaka, Howard Greenfield

LITTLE DIANNE
w&m/Dion Di Mucci

LITTLE DID I KNOW
w&m/Phil Spector

LITTLE DRUMMER BOY, THE
w&m/Harry Simeone, Henry Onorati

LITTLE DUTCH MILL
m/Harry Barris
w/Ralph Freed

LITTLE GIRL
m/Francis Henry
w/Madeline Hyde

LITTLE GIRL
w&m/Muddy Waters

LITTLE GIRL BLUE
m/Richard Rodgers
w/Lorenz (Larry) Hart

LITTLE GIRL FROM LITTLE ROCK, A
m/Jule Styne
w/Leo Robin

LITTLE GIRL GONE
w&m/Donna Fargo

LITTLE GIRL GOODBYE
m/Victor Jacobi
w/William LeBaron

LITTLE GRAY HOME IN THE WEST
m/Herman Lohr
w/D. Eardley-Wilmot

LITTLE GREEN APPLES
w&m/Bobby Russell

LITTLE GREEN VALLEY
w&m/Carson J. Robison

LITTLE HIDEAWAY
w&m/Leon Russell

LITTLE HONDA
w&m/Brian Wilson

LITTLE JAZZ BIRD
m/George Gershwin
w/Ira Gershwin

LITTLE JEANNIE
m/Elton John
w/Gary Osborne

**LITTLE JOE FROM CHICAGO
(instr.)**
m/Mary Lou Williams

LITTLE JOHNNY JONES
w&m/George M. Cohan

LITTLE KISS EACH MORNING, A
w&m/Harry M. Woods

LITTLE LESS CONVERSATION, A
w&m/Mac Davis

LITTLE LOST CHILD, THE
m/Joseph W. Stern
w/Edward B. Marks

LITTLE MAN SITTIN' ON A FENCE
w&m/Joshua D. White

LITTLE MAN YOU'VE HAD A BUSY DAY
w&m/Al Hoffman, Maurice Sigler, Mabel Wayne

LITTLE OLD LADY
m/Hoagy Carmichael
w/Stanley Adams

LITTLE OLD LOG CABIN IN THE LANE
w&m/William S. Harp

LITTLE ORPHAN ANNIE
w&m/Joe L. Sanders

LITTLE QUEEN
w&m/Ann Wilson, Nancy Wilson, Roger Fisher

LITTLE RED RIDING HOOD
w&m/J. P. Richardson (Big Bopper)

**LITTLE ROOTIE TOOTIE
(instr.)**
m/Thelonious Sphere Monk

LITTLE ROSA
w&m/Webb Pierce, Red Sovine

LITTLE SIR ECHO
w&m/Joe Marsala, Beatrice Marsala, J. S. Fearis, L. K. Smith

LITTLE SISTER
w&m/Doc (Jerome) Pomus, Mort Shuman

LITTLE STAR
w&m/Vito Picone

LITTLE STREET WHERE OLD FRIENDS MEET, A
w&m/Harry M. Woods, Gus Kahn

LITTLE TALK WITH JESUS, A
w&m/Thomas Andrew Dorsey

LITTLE THINGS YOU DO TOGETHER, THE
w&m/Stephen Sondheim

LITTLE TIN BOX
m/Jerry Bock
w/Sheldon Harnick

LITTLE TOWN FLIRT
w&m/Del Shannon, M. McKenzie

LITTLE WHITE CLOUD THAT CRIED, THE
w&m/Johnnie Ray

LITTLE WHITE DONKEY, THE
w&m/Harry Noble

LITTLE WHITE DONKEY, THE (Le petit ane blanc) (instr.)
m/Jacques Ibert

LITTLE WHITE DUCK, THE
w&m/Bernard Zaritsky

LITTLE WHITE LIES
w&m/Walter Donaldson

LITTLE WILLIE
w&m/Mike Chapman, Nicky Chinn

LITTLE WILLIE LEAPS (instr.)
m/Miles Dewey Davis

LIVE AND LET DIE
w&m/Paul and Linda McCartney

LIVE AND LET LIVE
w&m/Cole Porter

LIVE FAST, LOVE HARD, DIE YOUNG
w&m/Joe Allison

LIVE FOR LIFE
m/Francis Lai
w/Norman Gimbel

LIVERY STABLE BLUES
w&m/Original Dixieland Jazz Band (see composer listing under same)

LIVIN' FOR THE CITY
w&m/Stevie Wonder

LIVIN' THING
w&m/Jeff Lynne

LIVIN' WITH THE SHADES PULLED DOWN
w&m/Merle Haggard

LIVING AND DYING IN 3/4 TIME
w&m/Jimmy Buffett

LIVING FREE (film score)
m/Sol Kaplan

LIVING IN A HOUSE FULL OF LOVE
w&m/Billy Sherrill, Glenn Sutton

LIVING IN THE CITY
w&m/Stevie Wonder

LIVING IN THE MATERIAL WORLD
w&m/George Harrison

LIVING IN THE PAST
w&m/Ian Anderson

LIVING IN THE U. S. A.
w&m/Steve Miller

LIVING NEXT DOOR TO ALICE
w&m/Mike Chapman, Nicky Chinn

LIZA
m/George Gershwin
w/Ira Gershwin, Gus Kahn

LLOYDS OF LONDON (film score)
m/Louis Silvers

LOCH LOMOND
m/Lady John Montague-Douglas Scott
w/William Douglas (attributed to Douglas but not verified)

LOCO-MOTION (THE)
w&m/Carole King, Gerry Goffin

LOCOMOTIVE BREATH
w&m/Ian Anderson

LODI
w&m/John C. Fogerty

LOGICAL SONG, THE
w&m/Roger Hodgson, Rick Davies

LOLA
w&m/Raymond Douglas Davies

LOLLIPOP
w&m/Beverly Ross, Julius Dixon

LOLLIPOPS AND ROSES
w&m/Anthony Velona

LONDON BLUES (instr.)
m/Ferdinand "Jelly Roll" Morton, Leon Rappolo, Paul Mares

LONDON PRIDE
w&m/Noel Coward

LONDONDERRY AIR
m/Irish traditional air "Farewell to Cuchulain" (see Danny Boy)

LONELY AGAIN
w&m/Jean Chapel

LONELY AT THE TOP
w&m/Randy Newman

LONELY BLUE BOY
m/Ben Weisman
w/Fred Wise

LONELY BOY
w&m/Andrew Gold

LONELY BULL, THE
w&m/Sol Lake

LONELY HEART KNOWS, A
w&m/Hank Thompson

LONELY ONE, THE
w&m/Duane Eddy

LONELY STREET
w&m/Carl Belew, Kenny Sowder, W. S. Stevenson

LONELY TEARDROP
w&m/Berry Gordy Jr., Gwen Gordy, Tyrone Carolo

LONELY WORLD
w&m/Dion Di Mucci, Ernest Maresca

LONE STAR TRAIL
w&m/Cindy Walker

LONELINESS OF THE LONG DISTANCE RUNNER, THE (film score)
m/John Addison

LONELY DAYS
w&m/Barry, Maurice and Robin Gibb

LONELY GIRL
w&m/Ray Evans, Jay Livingston

LONELY ONES, THE (instr.)
m/Duke Ellington

LONELY TOO LONG
w&m/Felix Cavaliere

LONELY TOWN
m/Leonard Bernstein
w/Betty Comden, Adolph Green

LONELY WOMAN (instr.)
m/Ornette Coleman

LONER, THE
w&m/Rod McKuen

LONESOME
m/George W. Meyer
w/Edgar Leslie

LONESOME AND BLUE
m/George D. Weiss
w/Bennie Benjamin

LONESOME AND SORRY
m/Con Conrad
w/Benny Davis

LONESOME BLUES
w&m/Perry Bradford

LONESOME COWBOY
w&m/Roy C. Bennett, Sid Tepper

LONESOME, LOVESICK PUPPY DOG
w&m/Billy Edd Wheeler

LONESOME NUMBER ONE
w&m/Don Gibson

LONESOME 7-7203
w&m/Justin Tubb

LONESOME WOMAN BLUES
w&m/T-Bone Walker

LONESOME ROAD, THE
w&m/Gene Austin, Nathanie Shilkret

LONESOME ROMEO
w&m/Johnny Nash

LONESOME TOWN
w&m/Baker Knight

LONESOMEST, LONESOME, THE
w&m/Mac Davis

LONG AGO (AND FAR AWAY)
m/Jerome Kern
w/Ira Gershwin

LONG AGO AND FAR AWAY
w&m/James Taylor

LONG AGO, FAR AWAY
w&m/Robert Dylan

LONG AND WINDING ROAD, THE
w&m/Paul McCartney, John Lennon

LONG AS I CAN SEE THE LIGHT
w&m/John C. Fogerty

LONG BEFORE I KNEW YOU
m/Jule Styne
w/Betty Comden, Adolph Green

LONG BLACK VEIL, THE
w&m/Marijohn Wilkin, Danny Dill

LONG DISTANCE
w&m/Muddy Waters

LONG FELLOW SERENADE
w&m/Neil Diamond

LONG FLOWING ROBE
w&m/Todd Rundgren

LONG HOT SUMMER, THE
m/Alex North
w/Sammy Cahn

LONG HOT SUMMER, THE (film score)
m/Alex North

LONG, LONG WAY FROM HOME
w&m/Mick Jones, Lou Gramm, Jan Richard McDonald

LONG RUN, THE
w&m/Donald Henley, Glenn Frey

LONG TALL GLASSES
w&m/Leo Sayer, David Courtney

LONG TALL MAMA
w&m/"Big Bill" Broonzy

LONG TALL SALLY
w&m/Little Richard, Robert A. Blackwell, Enotris Johnson

LONG TIME
w&m/Tom Scholz

LONG TIME COMING
w&m/David Crosby

LONG TIME GONE
w&m/Robert Dylan

LONG TRAIN RUNNING
w&m/Thomas Johnston

LONG VOYAGE HOME, THE (film score)
m/Richard Hageman

LONG WAY HOME, THE
w&m/Neil Diamond

LONG WAY TO GO, A
w&m/Barry Mann, Cynthia Weil

LONGER
w&m/Dan Fogelberg

LONGER BOATS
w&m/Cat Stevens

LONGEST DAY, THE
w&m/Paul Anka

LONGEST WALK, THE
w&m/Fred Spielman, Eddie Pola

LONGING FOR YOU
m/Theodore F. Morse
w/Jack Drislane

LOOK AT MINE
w&m/Tony Hatch

LOOK FOR THE SILVER LINING
m/Jerome Kern
w/Buddy DeSylva

LOOK FOR THE SILVER LINING (film score)
m/Ray John Heindorf

LOOK IN MY EYES PRETTY WOMAN
w&m/Dennis Lambert, Brian Potter

LOOK LITTLE GIRL
w&m/Meredith Willson

LOOK NO FURTHER
w&m/Richard Rodgers

LOOK OF LOVE, THE
m/Burt Bacharach
w/Hal David

LOOK OUT FOR JIMMY VALENTINE
m/Gus Edwards
w/Edward Madden

LOOK OUT FOR MY LOVE
w&m/Neil Young

LOOK THROUGH MY WINDOW
w&m/John Phillips

LOOK TO THE RAINBOW
m/Burton Lane
w/E. Y. Harburg

LOOK WHAT YOU DONE FOR ME
w&m/Al Green, Willie Mitchell, Al Jackson Jr.

LOOK WHO'S BLUE
w&m/Don Gibson

LOOK WHO'S DANCIN'
m/Arthur Schwartz
w/Dorothy Fields

LOOKIE LOOKIE LOOKIE HERE COMES COOKIE
w&m/Mack Gordon

LOOKIN' OUT MY BACK DOOR
w&m/John C. Fogerty

LOOKING AT THE WORLD THRU ROSE COLORED GLASES
w&m/Tommy Malie, Jimmy Steiger

LOOKING BACK
w&m/Bob Seger

LOOKING BACK
w&m/Brook Benton, Clyde Otis, Belford Hendricks

LOOKING FOR A BOY
m/George Gershwin
w/Ira Gershwin

LOOKING THROUGH THE EYES OF LOVE
w&m/Barry Mann, Cynthia Weil

LOOKS LIKE WE MADE IT
w&m/Richard Kerr, Will Jennings

LOOP DE LOO
m/Vic Mizzy
w/Mann Curtis

LORD JIM (film score)
m/Bronislau Kaper

LORD KNOWS I'M DRINKING, THE
w&m/Bill Anderson

(I GUESS) LORD MUST BE IN NEW YORK CITY, THE
w&m/Harry Edward Nilsson

LORD'S PRAYER, THE
m/musical setting to Biblical text by Albert Hay Malotte

LORELEI
w&m/Dennis De Young, James Young

LORELEI, DIE (1837)
m/Friedrich Silcher
w/Poem by Heinrich Heine

LORELEI, THE
m/George Gershwin
w/Ira Gershwin

LORENA
m/Joseph P. Webster
w/Rev. H. D. L. Webster

LORRAINE, MY BEAUTIFUL LORRAINE
w&m/Fred Fisher, Alfred Bryan

LOS OLVIDADOS
w&m/Archie Shepp

LOSER'S CATHEDRAL
w&m/Glenn Sutton, Billy Sherrill

LOSING YOUR LOVE
w&mBill Anderson, Buddy Killen

**LOSING YOU
(WAS WORTH THIS BROKEN
HEART)**
w&m/Helen Carter

LOST
m/Phil Ohman, Macy O. Teetor
w/Johnny Mercer

LOST CHORD, THE
m/Sir Arthur Sullivan
w/Adelaide Proctor

**LOST HER LOVE ON OUR LAST
DATE**
w&m/Conway Twitty, Floyd Cramer

LOST HIGHWAY
w&m/Leon Payne

LOST IN A FOG
m/Jimmy McHugh
w/Dorothy Fields

LOST IN LOVE
w&m/Robie Porter, Rick Chertoff,
Charles Fisher

LOST IN LOVE
w&m/Graham Russell

LOST IN LOVELINESS
m/Sigmund Romberg
w/Leo Robin

LOST IN MEDITATION (instr.)
m/Duke Ellington

LOST IN THE STARS
m/Kurt Weill
w/Maxwell Anderson

LOST HER IN THE SUN
w&m/John Stewart

LOST SOMEONE
w&m/James Brown, Lloyd
Stallworth, Bobby Byrd

**LOST WEEKEND, THE (film
score)**
m/Miklos Rozsa

LOT OF LIVIN' TO DO, A
m/Charles Strouse
w/Lee Adams

LOTTA LOVE
w&m/Nicolette Larson

LOTTA LOVE
w&m/Neil Young

**LOUD LET THE BUGLES
SOUND**
m/Gustave A. Kerker
w/Frederick Ranken

**LOUDLY LET THE TRUMPET
BRAY**
m/Sir Arthur Sullivan
w/Sir William Schwenk Gilbert

LOUIE LOUIE
w&m/Richard Berry

LOUISE
m/Richard A. Whiting
w/Leo Robin

LOUISIANA HAYRIDE
m/Arthur Schwartz
w/Howard Eitz

LOUISIANA RAIN
w&m/Tom Petty

LOU'SIANA BELLE
w&m/Stephen C. Foster

L-O-V-E
m/Bert Kaempfert
w/Milt Gabler

LOVE
w&m/Ralph Blane, Hugh Martin

LOVE AIN'T FOR KEEPING
w&m/Peter Townshend

LOVE ALIVE
w&m/Ann Wilson, Roger Fisher,
Nancy Wilson

**LOVE AMERICAN STYLE (TV
theme-instr.)**
m/Charles Fox

LOVE AND MARRIAGE
m/James Van Heusen
w/Sammy Cahn

LOVE BOAT (TV theme-instr.)
m/Charles Fox

LOVE BOAT, THE
m/Victor Herbert
w/Gene Buck

LOVE BUG ITCH
w&m/Jenny Lou Carson, Roy Botkin

**LOVE BUG WILL BITE YOU IF
YOU DON'T WATCH OUT, THE**
w&m/Pinky Tomlin

LOVE CAME TO ME
w&m/Dion Di Mucci, J. Falbo

LOVE CHANT (instr.)
m/Charles Mingus

LOVE CHILD
w&m/Rod McKuen

LOVE CHILD
w&m/R. Dean Taylor

**LOVE DIVINE, ALL LOVES
EXCELLING**
m/John Zundel
w/Charles Wesley

LOVE FOR SALE
w&m/Cole Porter

**LOVE GROWS (WHERE MY
ROSEMARY GOES)**
w&m/Roger Greenway, Roger Cook

LOVE GUN
w&m/Paul Stanley

LOVE HAS COME MY WAY
w&m/Don Gibson

**LOVE HAS MADE YOU
BEAUTIFUL**
w&m/Merle Kilgore

LOVE HAS WINGS
m/Emmerich Kalman
w/C. C. S. Cushing, E. P. Heath

LOVE HURTS
w&m/Boudleaux Bryant

LOVE I LOST
w&m/Kenneth Gamble, Leon Huff

LOVE IN BLOOM
m/Ralph Rainger
w/Leo Robin

LOVE IS
w&m/George Johnson, Louis
Johnson, Quincy Jones, Peggy Jones

LOVE IS A HURTIN' THING
w&m/Ben Raleigh, Dave Linden

**LOVE IS A MANY-
SPLENDORED THING**
m/Sammy Fain
w/Paul Francis Webster

**LOVE IS A MANY-
SPLENDORED THING (film
score)**
m/Alfred Newman

LOVE IS A PLAINTIVE SONG
m/Sir Arthur Sullivan
w/Sir William Schwenk Gilbert

LOVE IS A ROSE
w&m/Neil Young

LOVE IS A SECRET
w&m/Ellas McDaniel (Bo Diddley)

LOVE IS A SOMETIMES THING
w&m/Jan Howard, Bill Anderson

**LOVE IS BLUE (L'Amour Est
Bleu)**
m/Andre Popp
w/English words: Bryan Blackburn

LOVE IS COMING DOWN
w&m/Peter Townshend

LOVE IS HERE TO STAY
m/George Gershwin
w/Ira Gershwin

LOVE IS IN THE AIR
w&m/John Paul Young

LOVE IS JUST A FOUR-LETTER WORD
w&m/Robert Dylan

LOVE IS JUST ANOTHER WORD
w&m/Harry Chapin

LOVE IS JUST AROUND THE CORNER
m/Lewis E. Gensler
w/Leo Robin

LOVE IS LIKE A BUTTERFLY
w&m/Dolly Parton

LOVE IS LIKE A RAINBOW
w&m/Manuel Klein

LOVE IS NO EXCUSE
w&m/Justin Tubb

LOVE IS STRANGE
w&m/Sylvia V. Robinson, Mickey Baker, Ellas McDaniel

LOVE IS SWEEPING THE COUNTRY
m/George Gershwin
w/Ira Gershwin

LOVE IS THE ANSWER
w&m/Todd Rundgren

LOVE IS THE MESSAGE
w&m/Kenneth Gamble, Leon Huff

LOVE IS THE REASON
m/Arthur Schwartz
w/Dorothy Fields

LOVE IS THE SWEETEST THING
w&m/Ray Noble

LOVE IS THE THING
m/Victor Young
w/Ned Washington

LOVE IS WHERE YOU FIND IT
m/Harry Warren
w/Al Dubin, Johnny Mercer

LOVE IS WHERE YOU FIND IT
m/Nacio Herb Brown
w/Earl K. Brent

LOVE LETTERS
m/Victor Young
w/Edward Heyman

LOVE LETTERS IN THE SAND
m/J. Fred Coots
w/Nick Kenny, Charles Kenny

LOVE LIKE A MAN
w&m/Alvin Lee

LOVE LOCKED OUT
w&m/Ray Noble, Max Kester

LOVE LOOK AWAY
m/Richard Rodgers
w/Oscar Hammerstein II

LOVE MACHINE
w&m/Pete Moore, Billy Griffin

LOVE MAKES THE WORLD GO AROUND
m/William Furst
w/Clyde Fitch

LOVE MAKES THE WORLD GO 'ROUND
w&m/Bob Merrill

LOVE MAY BE A MYSTERY
m/Victor Jacobi
w/Harry B. Smith, Harry Graham

LOVE ME
w&m/Antoine "Fats" Domino, Dave Bartholomew

LOVE ME AGAIN
w&m/Allee Willis, David Lasley

LOVE ME AND THE WORLD IS MINE
m/Ernest R. Ball
w/David Reed Jr.

LOVE ME LITTLE, LOVE ME LONG
w&m/Percy Gaunt

LOVE ME OR LEAVE ME
m/Walter Donaldson
w/Gus Kahn

LOVE ME TENDER
w&m/Elvis Presley, Vera Matson
(music adapted from the traditional folk song "Aura Lee")

LOVE ME TONIGHT
m/Richard Rodgers
w/Lorenz (Larry) Hart

LOVE ME TONIGHT
m/Rudolf Friml
w/Brian Hooker

LOVE ME WITH ALL YOUR HEART
m/Carlos Rigual, Mario Rigual, Carlos A. Martinoli, w&m/Sunny Skylar

LOVE MOON
m/Ivan Caryll
w/Anne Caldwell

LOVE MY BABY
w&m/Robert Calvin Bland

LOVE NEST, THE
m/Louis A. Hirsch
w/Otto Harbach

LOVE OF MINE
m/Victor Jacobi
w/Adrian Ross, Arthur Anderson

LOVE OF MY LIFE
m/Artie Shaw
w/Johnny Mercer

LOVE OF MY MAN, THE
w&m/Ed Townshend

LOVE OR LET ME BE LONELY
w&m/Anita Poree, Jerry Eugene Peters, Clarence A. Scarbourough

LOVE OR SOMETHING LIKE IT
w&m/Kenny Rogers, Steve Glassmeyer

LOVE SENDS A LITTLE GIFT OF ROSES
m/John Openshaw
w/Leslie Cooke

LOVE SHE CAN COUNT ON, A
w&m/William (Smokey) Robinson Jr.

LOVE SO RIGHT
w&m/Barry, Maurice and Robin Gibb

LOVE SONG (instr.)
m/George Cables

LOVE SOMEBODY
w&m/Alex C. Kramer, Joan Whitney Kramer

LOVE SONG
w&m/Kenneth Loggins

LOVE SONG FOR JEFFREY
m/Peter Allen
w/Helen Reddy

LOVE STORY (film score)
m/Frances Lai

LOVE STORY (WHERE DO I BEGIN)
m/Frances Lai
w/Carl Sigman

LOVE SUPREME, A (instr.)
m/John Coltrane

LOVE SURVIVED
w&m/Bill Rice, Jerry Foster

LOVE TAKES A LONG TIME GROWIN'
w&m/Roger Atkins, Helen Miller

LOVE THE ONE YOU'RE WITH
w&m/Stephen Stills

LOVE THY NEIGHBOR
m/Harry Revel
w/Mack Gordon

LOVE WALKED IN
m/George Gershwin
w/Ira Gershwin

LOVE WILL FIND A WAY
w&m/Cory Lerios, David Jenkins

LOVE WILL FIND A WAY
m/Eubie Blake
w/Noble Sissle

LOVE WILL KEEP US
TOGETHER
w&m/Neil Sedaka, Howard
Greenfield

LOVE WITH THE PROPER
STRANGER
m/Elmer Bernstein
w/Johnny Mercer

LOVE YOU FUNNY THING
m/Fred E. Ahlert
w/Roy Turk

LOVE YOUR MAGIC SPELL IS
EVERYWHERE
m/Edmund Goulding
w/Elsie Janis

LOVELIEST NIGHT OF THE
YEAR, THE
m/Irving Aaronson (adapted from
Juventino Rosa's "Sobre las olas")
w/Paul Francis Webster

LOVELINESS OF YOU, THE
m/Harry Revel
w/Mack Gordon

LOVELY
w&m/Stephen Sondheim

LOVELY DAY
w&m/Bill Withers

LOVELY HULA HANDS
w&m/Alex R. Anderson

LOVELY LADY
m/Jimmy McHugh
w/Ted Koehler

LOVELY LADY (AIN'T LOVE
GRAND)
m/Dave Stamper, Harold Levy
w/Cyrus D. Wood

LOVELY TO LOOK AT
m/Jerome Kern, Jimmy McHugh
w/Dorothy Fields

LOVELY TO SEE YOU
w&m/Justin Hayward

LOVELY WAY TO SPEND AN
EVENING, A
m/Jimmy McHugh
w/Harold Adamson

LOVER
m/Richard Rodgers
w/Lorenz (Larry) Hart

LOVER AND FRIEND
w&m/Minnie Riperton, Keni St.
Lewis, Dick Rudolph, Gene Dozier

LOVER AND HIS LASS, A
(instr.)
m/John Dankworth

LOVER COME BACK TO ME
m/Sigmund Romberg
w/Oscar Hammerstein II

LOWDOWN
w&m/Boz Scaggs, David Paich

LOWDOWN BLUES
m/Eubie Blake
w/Noble Sissle

LUCILLE
w&m/Roger Bowling, Hal Bynum

LOVER MAN (OH WHERE CAN
YOU BE)
w&m/Roger J. (Ram) Ramirez,
Jimmy Davis, Jimmy Sherman

LOVER'S QUESTION, A
w&m/Brook Benton, Jimmy
Williams

LOVERS AND OTHER
STRANGERS (film score)
m/Fred Karlin

LOVER'S PRAYER, A
w&m/Ernest Maresca

LOVERS WHO WANDER
w&m/Ernest Maresca, Dion Di
Mucci

LOVEY DOVEY
w&m/Memphis Curtis

LOVE'S BEEN GOOD TO ME
w&m/Rod McKuen

LOVE'S GONNA LIVE HERE
w&m/Buck Owens

LOVE'S GROWN DEEP
w&m/Kenny Nolan

LOVES ME LIKE A ROCK
w&m/Paul Simon

LOVE'S OWN SWEET SONG
m/Emmerich Kalman
w/C. C. S. Cushing, E. P. Heath

LOVE'S OLD SWEET SONG
m/James Lyman Molloy
w/G. C. Bingham

LOVE'S THEME
w&m/Barry White

LOVIN' MACHINE
w&m/Larry Kingston

LOVIN' YOU
w&m/John B. Sebastian

LOVING HER WAS EASIER
w&m/Kris Kristofferson

LOVING PLACE
w&m/Gale Garnett

LOVING YOU
w&m/Al Jarreau

LUCILLE
w&m/Little Richard, Albert Collins

LUCK BE A LADY
w&m/Frank Loesser

LUCKENBACK, TEXAS
w&m/Chips Moman, Bobby
Emmons

LUCKY MAN
w&m/Keith Emerson, Gregory Lake,
Carl Palmer

LUCRETIA McEVIL
w&m/David Clayton-Thomas

LUCY IN THE SKY WITH
DIAMONDS
w&m/Paul McCartney, John Lennon

LUCKY DAY
m/Ray Henderson
 w/Lew Brown, Buddy DeSylva

LUCKY IN LOVE
m/Ray Henderson
 w/Lew Brown, Buddy DeSylva

LUCKY ME
w&m/Rory Bourke, Charlie Black

LUCKY SEVEN (instr.)
m/Bob James

LULLABY IN RHYTHM
w&m/Edgar Melvin Sampson,
Benny Goodman

LULLABY OF BIRDLAND
m/George Shearing
w/George Weiss

LULLABY OF BROADWAY
m/Harry Warren
w/Al Dubin

LULLABY OF THE LEAVES
m/Bernice Petkere
w/Joseph Young

LULLABY YODEL
w&m/Jimmy Rodgers

LULU'S BACK IN TOWN
m/Harry Warren
w/Al Dubin

LUMINESCENCE (instr.)
m/Keith Jarrett

LUSH LIFE
w&m/Billy Strayhorn

LUX BOOGIE (instr.)
m/Meade "Lux" Lewis

LYDIA THE TATOOED LADY
m/Harold Arlen
w/E. Y. Harburg

LYDIA (film score)
m/Miklos Rozsa

LYIN' EYES
w&m/Donald Henley, Glenn Frey

110

Addenda:

LATE IN THE EVENING
w&m/Paul Simon

**LET THE MUSIC DO THE
TALKING**
w&m/Joe Perry

LET THE MUSIC TAKE ME
w&m/Patrice Rushen

LET'S MISBEHAVE
w&m/Cole Porter

SONGS

M

MA BLUSHIN' ROSIE (MA POSIE SWEET)
m/John Stromberg
w/Edgar Smith

MA, HE'S MAKING EYES AT ME
m/Sidney Clare
w/Con Conrad

MA MA BELLE
w&m/Jeff Lynne

MacARTHUR PARK
w&m/Jimmy Webb

MACHO MAN
w&m/Jacques Morali

MACK THE KNIFE
m/Kurt Weill
w/Marc Blitzstein

MACUSHLA
m/Dermot MacMurrough
w/Josephine V. Rowe

MACUSHLA
w&m/Dan J. Sullivan

MAD
w&m/Tom T. Hall

MAD ABOUT HIM, SAD ABOUT HIM, HOW CAN I BE GLAD WITHOUT HIM BLUES
w&m/Dick Charles, Larry Markes

MAD ABOUT MUSIC (film score)
m/Charles Previn

MAD ABOUT THE BOY
w&m/Noel Coward

MAD ABOUT YOU
m/Victor Young
w/Ned Washington

MAD DOGS AND ENGLISHMEN
w&m/Noel Coward

MAD HOUSE (instr.)
m/Earl (Fatha) Hines

MAD LOVE
w&m/Mark Goldenberg

MADE FOR EACH OTHER
w&m/Ervin M. Drake, Jimmy Shirl

MADE FOR EACH OTHER
w&m/Trade Martin

MADEMOISELLE
w&m/Dennis De Young, Thomas Shaw

MADEMOISELLE FROM ARMENTIERES
w&m/From the World War I era; authorship claimed by one Alfred J. Walden (pen name, Harry Wincott) but claim has not been recognized! Various lyric versions have been published.

MADE TO LOVE
w&m/Phil Everly

MADLY IN LOVE
m/Vernon Duke
w/Ogden Nash

MAGGIE MAY
w&m/Rod Stewart, M. Quittendon

MAGGIE MURPHY'S HOME
m/David Braham
w/Ed Harrigan

MAGGIE'S FARM
w&m/Robert Dylan

MAGIC BUS
w&m/Peter Townshend

MAGIC CARPET RIDE
w&m/John Kay, Michael Monarch, Goldy McJohn

MAGIC CITY, THE (instr.)
m/Sun Ra

MAGIC IS THE MOONLIGHT
m/Maria Grever
w/Charles Pasquale

MAGIC ISLAND, THE
w&m/Bernie Wayne, Johnny Mercer

MAGIC MAN
w&m/Ann Wilson, Nancy Wilson

MAGIC MIRROR
w&m/Leon Russell

MAGIC MOMENT
m/Arthur Schwartz
w/Howard Dietz

MAGIC MOMENTS
m/Burt Bacharach
w/Hal David

MAGIC OF JU-JU, THE
w&m/Archie Shepp

MAGIC TOUCH, THE
w&m/Bernie Wayne

MAGIC TOWN
w&m/Barry Mann, Cynthia Weil

MAGICAL MYSTERY TOUR
w&m/David Pack, Joe Puerta Burleigh, G. A. Drummond

MAGNET AND STEEL
w&m/Walter Egan

MAGNET AND THE CHURN, THE
m/Sir Arthur Sullivan
w/Sir William Schwenk Gilbert

MAGNETIC RAG (instr.)
m/Scott Joplin

MAGNIFICENT AMBERSONS, THE (film score)
m/Bernard Herrmann

MAGNIFICENT SANCTUARY BAND, THE
w&m/Dorsey Burnette

MAGNIFICENT YANKEE, THE (film score)
m/David Raksin

MAGUS, THE (film score)
m/John Dankworth

MAHOGANY (film score)
m/Walter Scharf

MAIDEN FAIR TO SEE, A
m/Sir Arthur Sullivan
w/Sir William Schwenk Gilbert

MAIDEN VOYAGE
w&m/Herbie Hancock

MAIDEN WITH THE DREAMY EYES
w&m/James W. Johnson, Bob Cole

MAINSTREET
w&m/Bob Seger

MAINE
w&m/Richard Rodgers

MAIRZY DOATS
m/Jerry Livingston
w/Al Hoffman, Milton Drake

MAJOR AND THE MINOR, THE (film score)
m/Robert Emmett Dolan

MAJOR DUNDEE (film score)
m/Daniele Amfitheatrof

MAJOR DUNDEE MARCH
m/Daniele Amfitheatrof
w/Ned Washington

MAKE BELIEVE
m/Jerome Kern
w/Oscar Hammerstein II

MAKE BELIEVE
m/Jack Shilkret
w/Benny Davis

MAKE BELIEVE
w&m/Bo Gentry

MAKE BELIEVE BALLROOM
m/Paul Denniker
w/Andy Razaf

MAKE IT ANOTHER OLD FASHIONED PLEASE
w&m/Cole Porter

MAKE IT EASY ON YOURSELF
m/Burt Bacharach
w/Hal David

MAKE IT WITH YOU
w&m/David Gates

MAKE LOVE TO ME
m/melody of "Tin Roof Blues"
by:Ben Pollack, Walter
Melrose, Leon Rappolo, Paul Wares,
George Brunes, Mel Stitzler
w/Bill Norvas, Allan Copeland

MAKE ME AN ISLAND
w&m/Albert L. Hammond, Mike
Hazelwood

MAKE ME BELONG TO YOU
w&m/Billy Vera

MAKE ME SMILE
w&m/James Pankow

MAKE ME YOUR BABY
w&m/Helen Miller, Roger Atkins

MAKE SOMEONE HAPPY
m/Jule Styne
w/Betty Comden, Adolph Green

MAKE THE MAN LOVE ME
m/Arthur Schwartz
w/Dorothy Fields

MAKE THE MAN LOVE ME
w&m/Barry Mann, Cynthia Weil

MAKE THE WORLD GO AWAY
w&m/Hank Cochran

**MAKE YOUR OWN KIND OF
MUSIC**
w&m/Barry Mann, Cynthia Weil

**MAKE YOURSELF
COMFORTABLE**
w&m/Bob Merrill

MAKIN' WHOOPEE
m/Walter Donaldson
w/Gus Kahn

MAKING IT (film score)
m/Charles Fox

MAKING IT
w&m/Frederick Perren, Dino Fekaris

**MAKING OUR DREAMS COME
TRUE**
m/Charles Fox
w/Norman Gimbel

MALA FEMINNA
w&m/Toto (female lyric by Ray
Allen)

MALAGUENA (instr.)
m/Ernesto Lecuona

**MALCOLM, MALCOLM-
SEMPRE MALCOLM (instr.)**
m/Archie Shepp

**MALTESE FALCON, THE (film
score)**
m/Adolph Deutsch

MAMA
w&m/Phil Brito

MAMA DON'T ALLOW
w&m/Charles E. Davenport (claimed
authorship)

**MAMA DON'T WANT NO PEAS
AND RICE AND COCOANUT
OIL**
m/Charlie Lofthouse
w/L. Wolfe Gilbert

**MAMA GOES WHERE PAPA
GOES**
m/Milton Ager
w/Jack Yellen

MAMA INEZ
m/Elisco Grenet
w/L. Wolfe Gilbert

MAMA LOVES PAPA
w&m/Abel Baer, Cliff Friend

MAMA SANG A SONG
w&m/Bill Anderson

**MAMA TOLD ME NOT TO
COME**
w&m/Randy Newman

MAMA TOO TIGHT (instr.)
m/Archie Shepp

MAMA TRIED
w&m/Merle Haggard

MAMA YOU BEEN ON MY MIND
w&m/Robert Dylan

MAMACITA
w&m/Barry Mann, Cynthia Weil

MAMBO BABY
w&m/Rosemarie McCoy, Charles
Singleton

MAMBO ITALIANO
w&m/Bob Merrill

**MAMBO NO. 5, MAMBO NO. 8,
MAMBO NO. 10**
w&m/Perez Prado

MAME
w&m/Jerry Herman

MAMIE
w&m/Muddy Waters, Jimmy Rogers

**MAMMAS, DON'T LET YOUR
BABIES GROW UP TO BE
COWBOYS**
w&m/Ed Bruce, Patsy Bruce

MAM'SELLE
m/Edmund Goulding
w/Mack Gordon

**MAN AND A WOMAN, A (film
score)**
m/Frances Lai

MAN CHASES A GIRL, A
w&m/Irving Berlin

MAN I LOVE, THE
m/George Gershwin
w/Ira Gershwin

**MAN IN THE GRAY FLANNEL
SUIT, THE (film score)**
m/Bernard Herrmann

MAN IN THE MIRROR
w&m/Dan Fogelberg

MAN IN THE WILDERNESS
w&m/Tommy Shaw

MAN OF LA MANCHA
m/Mitch Leigh
w/Joseph Darion

**MAN OF LA MANCHA (film
score)**
m/Lawrence Rosenthal

**MAN THAT BROKE THE BANK
AT MONTE CARLO, THE**
w&m/Fred Gilbert

MAN THAT GOT AWAY, THE
m/Harold Arlen
w/Ira Gershwin

MAN UPSTAIRS, THE
w&m/Harold Stanley, Gerry
Manners, Dorinda Morgan

**MAN WHO COMES AROUND,
THE**
w&m/Tommy Tucker

**MAN WHO FOUND THE LOST
CHORD, THE**
w&m/Jimmy Durante

**MAN WHO SHOT LIBERTY
VALANCE, THE**
m/Burt Bacharach
w/Hal David

**MAN WHO WOULD WOO A
FAIR MAID, A**
m/Sir Arthur Sullivan
w/Sir William Schwenk Gilbert

MAN WITH A DREAM, A
m/Victor Young
w/Stella Unger

**MAN WITH THE GOLDEN GUN,
THE**
m/John Barry
w/Don Black

MAN WITHOUT A DREAM, A
w&m/Carole King, Gerry Goffin

MANAGUA, NICARAGUA
m/Irving Fields
w/Albert Gamse

MANANA
w&m/Peggy Lee, Dave Barbour

MANDOLIN WIND
w&m/Rod Stewart

MANDOLINS IN THE MOONLIGHT
w&m/Aaron Schroeder, George D. Weiss

MANDY
w&m/Irving Berlin

MANDY (formerly "BRANDY")
w&m/Richard Kerr, Scott English

MANDY LEE
w&m/Thurland Chattaway

MANHA DE CARNAVAL
w&m/Luis Bonfa

MANHATTAN
m/Richard Rodgers
w/Lorenz (Larry) Hart

MANHATTAN BEACH (march)
m/John Philip Sousa

MANHATTAN SERENADE
m/Louis Alter
w/Harold Adamson

MANHATTAN SKYLINE
w&m/Richard Maltby Jr., David Shire

MANHATTAN TOWER (suite)
w&m/Gordon Jenkins

MANIC Depression
w&m/Jimi Hendrix

MANNISH BOY
w&m/Muddy Waters, Ellas McDaniel, Melvin London

MANSION OF ACHING HEARTS, THE
m/Harry Von Tilzer
w/Arthur J. Lamb

MANSION ON THE HILL, A
w&m/Fred Rose, Hank Williams

MANSION OVER THE HILLTOP
w&m/Rev. Ira Stamphill

MANTECA (instr.)
m/Dizzy Gillespie

MANY TEARS AGO
w&m/Winfield Scott

MAPLE LEAF RAG (instr.)
m/Scott Joplin

MARCH ECCENTRIQUE (instr.)
m/Adolph Deutsch

MARCH OF THE MUSKETEERS
m/Rudolf Friml
w/P. G. Wodehouse, Clifford Grey

MARCH OF THE SIAMESE CHILDREN (from "THE KING AND I") (instr.)
m/Richard Rodgers

MARCH OF THE UNITED NATIONS (instr.)
m/Adolph Deutsch

MARCHETA
w&m/Victor Scherztzinger

MARCHING ALONG TOGETHER
w&m/Mort Dixon, Edward Pola, Franz K. W. Steininger

MARCHING THROUGH GEORGIA
w&m/Henry Clay Work

MARGARITAVILLE
w&m/Jimmy Buffett

MARGERY (instr.)
m/Charles Neil Daniels

MARGIE
m/Con Conrad, J. Russell Robinson
w/Benny Davis

MARGIE'S AT THE LINCOLN PARK INN
w&m/Tom T. Hall

MARGOT (instr.)
m/Adolph Deutsch

MARGUERITE
w&m/Charles A. White

MARIA
m/Leonard Bernstein
w/Stephen Sondheim

MARIA
m/Richard Rodgers
w/Oscar Hammerstein II

MARIA ELENA
m/Lorenzo Barcelata
w/Bob Russell

MARIA LA O (instr.)
m/Ernesto Lecuona

MARIANNE
w&m/Frank Miller, Richard Dehr, Terry Gilkyson (music adapted from a Bahamian folk song)

MARIE
w&m/Irving Berlin

MARIE FROM SUNNY ITALY
w&m/Irving Berlin

MARLENA
w&m/Bob Gaudio

MARMALADE, MOLASSES AND HONEY
m/Maurice Jarre
w/Marilyn and Alan Bergman

MARRAKESH EXPRESS
w&m/Graham Nash

MARRIAGE OF A YOUNG STOCKBROKER (film score)
m/Fred Karlin

MARRIAGE VOWS
w&m/Hank Snow

MARRIED I CAN ALWAYS GET
w&m/Gordon Jenkins

MARSELLAISE LA
w&m/Claude Joseph Rouget De L'Isle

MARTA
m/Moises Simon
w/L. Wolfe Gilbert

MARSHMALLOW MOON
w&m/Ray Evans, Jay H. Livingston

MARVELOUS TOY, THE
w&m/Thomas R. Paxton

MARY LOU
w&m/Abe Lyman, George Waggner, J. Russell Robinson

MARYLAND, MY MARYLAND
m/adapted from the German folk song "O Tannenbaum"
w/James Ryder Randall

MARY'S A GRAND OLD NAME
w&m/George M. Cohan

MAS QUE NADA
w&m/Sergio Mendes

M*A*S*H* (film score)
m/Johnny Mandel

MASQUERADE IS OVER, THE
m/Herb Magidson
w/Allie Wrubel

MASSACHUSETTS
w&m/Barry, Maurice and Robin Gibb

MASSACHUSETTS
w&m/Charles L. Roberts

MASSA'S IN THE COLD, COLD GROUND
w&m/Stephen C. Foster

MASTERS OF WAR
w&m/Robert Dylan

MATADOR, THE
w&m/John R. Cash, June Carter Cash

MATCH BOX BLUES
w&m/Carl Lee Perkins

MATCHMAKER, THE (film score)
m/Adolph Deutsch

MATCHMAKER, MATCHMAKER
m/Jerry Bock
w/Sheldon Harnick

MATILDA, MATILDA
w&m/Harry Thomas

MATTINATA
m/Ruggiero Leoncavallo
w/English words: two versions (1)
"Tis The Day" by Edward
Teschemacher (2) "You're Breaking
My Heart" by Sunny Skylar, Pat
Genaro
Italian words by Leoncavallo

MAXIM'S (film score)
m/Franz Lehar
w/Adrian Ross

MAY I
m/Harry Revel
w/Mack Gordon

MAY I SING TO YOU
w&m/Eddie Fisher, Charles Tobias,
Harry Akst

MAY I TAKE A GIANT STEP
w&m/Jerry Kasanetz, Jeff Katz

**MAY THE BIRD OF PARADISE
FLY UP YOUR NOSE**
w&m/"Little" Jimmy Dickens

**MAY THE GOOD LORD BLESS
AND KEEP YOU**
w&m/Meredith Willson

MAY YOU ALWAYS
w&m/Dick Charles, Larry Markes

MAYBE
m/George Gershwin
w/Ira Gershwin

**MAYBE (YOU'LL THINK OF
ME)**
w&m/Allan Flynn, Frank Madden

MAYBE I'M A FOOL
w&m/Eddie Money, Lloyd Chiate,
Lee Garrett, Robert
Taylor

MAYBE I'M AMAZED
w&m/Paul and Linda McCartney

MAYBE IT'S BECAUSE
m/Harry Ruby
w/Johnnie Scott

MAYBE THIS TIME
m/John Kander
w/Fred Ebb

MAYBE TOMORROW
w&m/Don Everly, Phil Everly

MAYBE YOU'LL BE THERE
m/Rube Bloom
w/Sammy Gallop

MAYBE YOUR BABY
w&m/Stevie Wonder

MAYBELLENE
w&m/Chuck Berry, Russ Fratto,
Alan Freed

MAYA LOVE
w&m/George Harrison

MAYERLING (film score)
m/Frances Lai

ME AND BABY
w&m/Leon Russell

ME AND BABY BROTHER
w&m/See composer listing under
Lee Oskar

ME AND BOBBY McGEE
w&m/Kris Kristofferson, Fred
Foster

ME AND JESUS
w&m/Tom T. Hall

**ME AND JULIO DOWN BY THE
SCHOOLYARD**
w&m/Paul Simon

ME AND LITTLE ANDY
w&m/Dolly Parton

ME AND MILLIE
w&m/Bobby Goldsboro

ME AND MY ARROW
w&m/Harry Edward Nilsson

ME AND MY SHADOW
m/Dave Dreyer, Billy Rose
w/Billy Rose

ME AND MY TEDDY BEAR
m/J. Fred Coots
w/Leo Talent

**MEADOWLAND (S) (CAVALRY
OF THE STEPPES)**
m/Lev Knipper
w/Russian words: Victor Gussev
English words - two versions: (1)
Olga Paul (2) Harold J. Rome

MEADOWS
w&m/Joseph F. Walsh

MEAN BONE BOOGIE (Blues)
w&m/T-Bone Walker

MEAN OLD FRISCO BLUES
w&m/Arthur Crudup

MEAN OLD WORLD
w&m/Billy Vera

MEAN TO ME
m/Fred E. Ahlert
w/Roy Turk

MEAT AND POTATOES
w&m/Irving Berlin

MEDITATION
m/Antonio Carlos Jobim
w/Norman Gimbel
w/Spanish: Newton Mendonca

MEET ME IN BUBBLE LAND
m/Isham Jones
w/Casper Nathan, Joe Manne

MEET ME IN ST. LOUIS, LOUIS
m/Frederick Allen Mills
w/Andrew B. Sterling

**MEET ME TONIGHT IN
DREAMLAND**
m/Leo Friedman
w/Beth Slater Whitson

**MEET ME WHEN THE
LANTERNS GLOW**
w&m/Manuel Klein

**MEET NERO WOLFE (film
score)**
m/Hoard Manucy Jackson

MEET THE METS
w&m/Ruth Roberts, William Katz

MELANCHOLY MAN
w&m/Michael Pinder

**MELBA WALTZ (SE SERAN
ROSE)**
m/Luigi Arditi
w/Pietro Mazzini

MELINDA
m/Burton Lane
w/Alan Jay Lerner

MELINDA
w&m/Jerry Butler, Jerry Peters

MELISSA
w&m/Gregg L. Allman, Duane
Allman

MELLOW YELLOW
w&m/Donovan

MELODIE D'AMOUR
m/Henri Salvador
w/Leo Johns

MELODY FROM THE SKY, A
m/Louis Alter
w/Sidney D. Mitchell

MELODY IN 4F
w&m/Sylvia Fine, Max Liebman

MELODY OF LOVE
m/H. Engelmann
w/Tom Glazer

**MEMBER OF THE WEDDING
(film score)**
m/Alex North

MEMORIES
w&m/Mac Davis

MEMORIES
m/Egbert A. Van Alstyne
w/Gus Kahn

MEMORIES ARE MADE OF THIS
w&m/Terry Gilkyson, Frank Miller, Richard Dehr

MEMORIES OF YOU
m/Eubie Blake
w/Andy Razaf

MEMORY LANE
w&m/Larry Spier, Con Conrad, Buddy DeSylva

MEMPHIS
w&m/Chuck Berry

MEMPHIS BLUES, THE
m/W. C. Handy
w/George A. Norton

MEMPHIS UNDERGROUND instr.)
m/Herbie Mann

MEN IN WHITE (film score)
m/William Axt

MENDOCINO
w&m/Doug Sahm

MENE, MENE TEKEL
w&m/Harold Rome

MENTAL JOURNEY
w&m/Margie Singleton

MENTION MY NAME IN SHEBOYGAN
m/Sammy Mysel
w/Dick Sanford

MERCY ISLAND (film score)
m/Walter Scharf, Cy Feuer

MERCY, MERCY
w&m/Don Covay, Ronald Miller

MERCY, MERCY ME (THE ECOLOGY)
w&m/Marvin Gaye

MERCY, MERCY, MERCY (instr.)
m/Joe Zawinul

MERRILL'S MARAUDERS (film score)
m/Howard Manucy Jackson

MERRY-GO-ROUND BROKE DOWN, THE
w&m/Dave Franklin, Cliff Friend

MERRY WIDOW WALTZ, THE
m/Franz Lehar
w/Adrian Ross

MESS OF BLUES
w&m/Doc (Jerome) Pomus, Mort Mort Shuman

MESSAGE FROM THE NILE (instr.)
m/McCoy Tyner

MESSAGE OF THE RED RED ROSE
m/Gustav Luders
w/Frank Pixley

MESSAGE OF THE VIOLET
m/Gustav Luders
w/Frank Pixley

MESSAGE TO GARCIA, A (film score)
m/Louis Silvers

MESSAGE TO MICHAEL
m/Burt Bacharach
w/Hal David

METEOR (film score)
m/Laurence Rosenthal

MEXICALI ROSE
m/Jack B. Tenney
w/Helen Stone

MEXICAN HAT DANCE (JARABE TAPATIO)
w&m/F. Patrichala

MEXICO
w&m/James Taylor

MIAMI BEACH RHUMBA
m/Irving Fields
w/Albert Gamse

MICHELLE
w&m/Paul McCartney, John Lennon

MICKEY'S MONKEY
w&m/Eddie Holland, Brian Holland, Lamont Dozier

MIDDLE AGE CRAZY
w&m/Sonny Throckmorton

MIDDLE OF THE NIGHT
w&m/Ahmet Ertegun

MIDNIGHT
w&m/Barry De Vorzon, Ward Chandler

MIDNIGHT
w&m/Boudleaux Bryant, Chet Atkins

MIDNIGHT ANGEL
w&m/Robert Morrison, Bill Anthony

MIDNIGHT BLUE
w&m/Melissa Manchester, Carole Bayer Sager

MIDNIGHT COWBOY (Theme)
m/John Barry

MIDNIGHT EXPRESS (film score)
m/Georgio Moroder

MIDNIGHT FLYER
w&m/Fred Rose, Hy Heath

MIDNIGHT FLYER
w&m/Mayme Watts, Robert Mosley

MIDNIGHT HOUR BLUES
w&m/Leroy Carr

MIDNIGHT IN MOSCOW (MOSCOW NIGHTS) (instr.)
m/Vasily Solovyev-Sedoy

MIDNIGHT IN PARIS
w&m/Con Conrad, Herb Magidson

MIDNIGHT MASQUERADE
w&m/Jack Manus, Bernard Bierman, Arthur Bierman

MIDNIGHT MOVER
w&m/Bobby Womack

MIDNIGHT RAMBLER
w&m/Mick Jagger, Keith Richard

MIDNIGHT RIDER
w&m/Gregg L. Allman, K. Payne

MIDNIGHT SPECIAL, THE
w&m/Huddie (Leadbelly) Ledbetter

MIDNIGHT TROT (instr.)
m/George L. Cobb

MIDSUMMER NIGHT'S DREAM, A (film score)
m/Erich Wolfgang Korngold

MIGHTY GOOD LOVIN'
w&m/William (Smokey) Robinson Jr.

MIGHTY LAK' A ROSE
m/Ethelbert W. Nevin
w/Frank L. Stanton

MIGHTY, MIGHTY
w&m/Maurice White, Verdine White

MIGHTY, MIGHTY
w&m/Curtis Mayfield

MIGRANT, THE
w&m/Tony Joe White

MILANO (instr.)
m/John Lewis

MILENBERG JOYS (instr.)
m/Ferdinand "Jelly Roll" Morton, Leon Rappolo, Paul Mares

MILESTONES (instr.)
m/Miles Dewey Davis

MILK AND HONEY
w&m/Jerry Herman

MILKMAN, KEEP THOSE BOTTLES QUIET
w&m/Don Raye, Gene DePaul

MILKMAN'S MATINEE
m/Paul Denniker
w/Andy Razaf

MILLION DOLLAR BASH
w&m/Robert Dylan

MILLION DOLLAR MYSTERY RAG
w&m/David W. DeFentresse Guion

MILLION TO ONE, A
w&m/Phil Medley

MILO'S THEME (instr.)
m/Don Ellis

MIMI
m/Richard Rodgers
w/Lorenz (Larry) Hart

MIND EXCURSION
w&m/Vincent Poncia, Pete Anders

MIND GAMES
w&m/John Lennon

MINE
m/George Gershwin
w/Ira Gershwin

MINE FOR ME
w&m/Paul and Linda McCartney

MINGUS
w&m/Joni Mitchell

MINNIE THE MOOCHER
w&m/Cab Calloway, Clarence Gaskill, Irving Mills

MINSTREL BOY, THE
m/from the traditional Irish melody "The Moreen"
w/Thomas Moore

MINSTREL'S RETURN FROM THE WAR, THE
w&m/John Hill Hewitt

MINUET IN JAZZ (instr.)
m/Raymond Scott

MINUTE BY MINUTE
w&m/Michael McDonald, Lester Abrams

MIRACLE MAN
w&m/Elvis Costello

MIRACLE WORKER, THE (film score)
m/Laurence Rosenthal

MIRAME ASI
m/Eduardo Sanchez De Fuentes
w/English word versions by:
(1) Frederick Herman Martens "Grant Those Glances" (2) Carol Raven "Look At Me"

MISERY LOVES COMPANY
w&m/Jerry Reed

MISFITS, THE (film score)
m/Alex North

MISS ANNABELLE LEE
w&m/Lew Pollack, Sidney Clare, Harry Richman

MISS OTIS REGRETS
w&m/Cole Porter

MISS YOU
w&m/Harry Tobias, Charles Tobias, Henry Tobias

MISS YOU
w&m/Mick Jagger, Keith Richards

MISSING YOU
w&m/Red Sovine, Dale Noe

MISSION: IMPOSSIBLE (Theme)
m/Lalo Schifrin

M-I-S-S-I-S-S-I-P-P-I
m/Harry A. Tierney
w/Joseph McCarthy

MISSISSIPPI
w&m/Charlie Daniels

MISSISSIPPI COUNTY FARM BLUES
w&m/Son House

MISSISSIPPI MOON
w&m/Jimmy Rodgers

MISSISSIPPI MUD
m/Harry Barris
w/James Cavanaugh

MISSISSIPPI RIVER BLUES
w&m/"Big Bill" Broonzy

MISSOURI WALTZ, THE
w&m/James Royce Shannon
(original music by John Valentine Eppel adapted by Frederick Knight Logan)

MIST OVER THE MOON, A
m/Ben Oakland
w/Oscar Hammerstein II

MISTER AND MISSISSIPPI
w&m/Irving Gordon

MISTER BLUE
w&m/Dewayne Blackwell

MISTER FIVE BY FIVE
w&m/Don Raye, Gene De Paul

MISTER GALLAGHER AND MISTER SHEAN
w&m/Ed Gallagher, Al Shean

MISTER JOHNSON, TURN ME LOOSE
w&m/Benjamin R. Harney

MISTER LONELY
m/Gene Allan
w/Bobby Vinton

MISTER LOVEMAKER
w&m/Johnny Paycheck

MISTO CHRISTOFO COLUMBO
w&m/Ray Evans, Jay Livingston

MISTRUSTIN' BLUES
w&m/Johnny Otis

MISTY
m/Erroll Garner
w/Johnny Burke

MISTY BLUE
w&m/Bob Montgomery

MIXED EMOTIONS
w&m/Stuart Loucheim

MIXED UP CONFUSION
w&m/Robert Dylan

McHALE'S NAVY (film score)
m/Jerry Fielding

McKENNA'S GOLD (film score)
m/Quincy Jones

MOANIN' LOW
m/Ralph Rainger
w/Howard Dietz

MOBILE
w&m/Robert Wells, David J. Holt

MOCKING BIRD HILL
w&m/Vaughn Horton

MOCKINGBIRD
w&m/Inez Foxx, Charles Foxx

MOCKINGBIRD
w&m/Carly Simon, James Taylor

MODEL OF A MODERN MAJOR GENERAL
m/Sir Arthur Sullivan
w/Sir William Schwenk Gilbert

MOJO MAN
w&m/Sly Stone

MOLE, THE (instr.)
w&m/Harry James, Leroy Holmes

MOLLIE DARLING
w&m/William S. Hays

MOLLY MALONE
w&m/George M. Cohan

MOLLY O
w&m/William J. Scanlan

MOLLY ON THE SHORE (instr.)
m/Percy Aldridge Grainger

MOMENT I SAW YOU, THE
w&m/Manning Sherwin

MOMENT TO MOMENT
m/Henry Mancini
w/Johnny Mercer

MOMENT TO MOMENT (film score)
m/Henry Mancini

MOMENTS LIKE THIS
m/Burton Lane
w/Frank Loesser

MOMENTS TO REMEMBER
m/Robert Allen
w/Al Stillman

118

MOMMY FOR A DAY
w&m/Buck Owens, Harlan Howard

MONA
w&m/Ellas McDaniel (Bo Diddley)

MONA BONE JAKON
w&m/Cat Stevens

MONA LISA
w&m/Ray Evans, Jay H. Livingston

MONDAY, MONDAY
w&m/John Phillips

MONDAY MORNING
w&m/Lindsay Buckingham

MONEY
w&m/Dwight Twilley

MONEY
w&m/Roger Walters

MONEY SONG, THE
w&m/Harold Rome

MONEY'S GETTING CHEAPER
w&m/Jimmy Witherspoon

MONKEY TIME, THE
w&m/Curtis Mayfield

MONK'S DREAM (instr.)
m/Thelonious Sphere Monk

MONK'S MOOD (instr.)
m/Thelonious Sphere Monk

MONTEGO BAY
w&m/Jeff Barry, Bobby Bloom

MONY, MONY
w&m/Tommy James, Bob King

MOOCHE, THE
w&m/Duke Ellington, Irving Mills

MOOD INDIGO
w&m/Duke Ellington, Leon (Barney)
Bigard, Irving Mills

MOODY BLUE
w&m/Mark James

MOODY WOMAN
w&m/Jerry Butler, Kenneth Gamble,
Leon Huff, Theresa Bell

MOODY'S MOOD (instr.)
m/James Moody

MOODY'S WORKSHOP (instr.)
m/James Moody

MOON AND I, THE
m/Sir Arthur Sullivan
w/Sir William Schwenk Gilbert

MOON AND SIXPENCE, THE
(film score)
m/Dimitri Tiomkin

MOON DEAR
w&m/Manuel Klein

MOON GOT IN MY EYES, THE
m/Arthur Johnston
w/Johnny Burke

MOON IS BLUE, THE (film score)
m/Herschel Burke Gilbert

MOON IS BLUE, THE
m/Herschel Burke Gilbert
w/Sylvia Fine

MOON IS LOW, THE
m/Nacio Herb Brown
w/Arthur Freed

MOON LOVE
m/Andre Kostelanetz, Mack David,
(adapted from Tchaikovsky's
Symphony No. 5)
w/Mack David

MOON OF MANIKOORA, THE
m/Alfred Newman
w/Frank Loesser

MOON OVER MIAMI
m/Joseph A. Burke
w/Edgar Leslie

MOON RIVER
m/Henry Mancini
w/Johnny Mercer

MOON SHADOW
w&m/Cat Stevens

MOON SONG
m/Arthur Johnston
w/Sam Coslow

MOON WAS YELLOW, THE
m/Fred E. Ahlert
w/Edgar Leslie

MOONDANCE
w&m/Van Morrison

MOONGLOW
m/Will Hudson
w/Eddie DeLange, Irving Mills

MOONLIGHT AT KILLARNEY
w&m/William J. Scanlan

MOONLIGHT BAY
m/Percy Wenrich
w/Edward Madden

MOONLIGHT BECOMES YOU
m/James Van Heusen
w/Johnny Burke

MOONLIGHT COCKTAIL
w&m/Charles Luckeyth Robert, Kim
Gannon

MOONLIGHT GAMBLER
m/Philip Springer
w/Bob Hilliard

MOONLIGHT AND ROSES
w&m/Ben Black, Neil Moret
(adapted from Edwin H.
Lemare's "Andantino")

MOONLIGHT IN VERMONT
w&m/John M. Blackburn, Karl
Suessdorf

MOONLIGHT MOOD
m/Peter De Rose
w/Harold Adamson

MOONLIGHT ON THE GANGES
m/Sherman Myers
w/Chester Wallace

MOONLIGHT SERENADE
m/Glenn Miller
w/Mitchell Parish

MOONLIGHT SONG
m/Reginald DeKoven
w/Harry B. Smith

MOONSHINE LULLABY
w&m/Irving Berlin

MOONSHINE WHISKEY
w&m/Van Morrison

MOPPIN' THE BRIDE (instr.)
m/Django Reinhardt

**MORE (THEME FROM MONDO
CANE)**
m/Riz Ortolani
w/Nino Oliviero, Norman Newell, M.
Ciorciolini

MORE AND MORE
m/Jerome Kern
w/E. Y. Harburg

MORE AND MORE
w&m/Merle Kilgore, Webb Pierce

MORE I CANNOT WISH YOU
w&m/Frank Loesser

MORE I SEE YOU, THE
m/Harry Warren
w/Mack Gordon

MORE, MORE, MORE (Part 1)
w&m/Gregg Diamond

MORE THAN A FEELING
w&m/Tom Scholz

MORE THAN A WOMAN
w&m/Barry, Maurice & Robin Gibb

**MORE THAN ANYTHING ELSE
IN THE WORLD**
w&m/Leon Payne

MORE THAN YOU KNOW
m/Vincent Youmans
w/Edward Eliscu, Billy Rose

MORNING
w&m/Oley Speaks, Frank L. Stanton

MORNING AIR (instr.)
m/Willie the Lion Smith

MORNING AFTER, THE
w&m/Joel Hirschhorn, Al Kasha

MORNING AFTER, THE
m/Harold Arlen
w/Dory Langdon Previn

MORNING DEW
w&m/Tim Hardin

MORNING GLORY (instr.)
m/Mary Lou Williams

MORNING HAS BROKEN
w&m/Cat Stevens, Eleanor Farjeon

MORNINGSIDE OF THE MOUNTAIN, THE
w&m/Larry Stock, Dick Manning

MOSAIC
w&m/Freddie Hubbard

MOST BEAUTIFUL GIRL, THE
w&m/Billy Sherrill, Norro Wilson, Rory Bourke

MOST BEAUTIFUL GIRL IN THE WORLD, THE
m/Richard Rodgers
w/Lorenz (Larry) Hart

MOST HAPPY FELLA, THE
w&m/Frank Loesser

MOST WONDERFUL DAY OF THE YEAR, THE
w&m/JOhn D. Marks

MOTH AND THE FLAME, THE
m/Max S. Witt
w/George Taggert

MOTHER
w&m/John Lennon, Yoko Ono

M-O-T-H-E-R (A WORD THAT MEANS THE WORLD TO ME)
m/Theodore F. Morse
w/Howard E. Johnson

MOTHER AND CHILD REUNION
w&m/Paul Simon

MOTHER MACHREE
m/Chauncey Olcott, Ernest R. Ball
w/Rida Johnson Young

MOTHER NATURE'S WINE
w&m/Jerry Corbetta, Robert Webber, Robert Raymond

MOTHER PIN A ROSE ON ME (MOTHER, MOTHER, MOTHER PIN A ROSE ON ME)
w&m/Dave Lewis, Paul Schindler, Bob Adams

MOTHER, THE QUEEN OF MY HEART
w&m/Jimmy Rodgers, Hoyt Bryant

MOTHER WAS A LADY (IF JACK WERE ONLY HERE)
m/Joseph W. Stern
w/Edward B. Marks

MOTHER WORE TIGHTS (film score)
m/Alfred Newman

MOTORCYCLE SONG, THE
w&m/Arlo Guthrie

MOTORING ALONG (instr.)
m/Al Cohn, Zoot Sims

MOULIN ROUGE (film score)
m/Georges Auric

MOUNTAIN BUGLE, THE
w&m/John Hill Hewitt

MOUNTAIN GREENERY
m/Richard Rodgers
w/Lorenz (Larry) Hart

MOUNTAIN HIGH, VALLEY LOW
w&m/Bernard D. Hanighen

MOUNTAIN JACK BLUES
w&m/Gertrude "Ma" Rainey

MOUNTAINS DON'T SEEM HIGH, THE
w&m/Craig Morris

MOUNTIES, THE
m/Rudolf Friml
w/Otto Harbach, Oscar Hammerstein II

MOUSE THAT ROARED, THE (film score)
m/Edwin Astley

MOVE 'EM OUT
w&m/Delaney Bramlett, Bonnie Lynn Bramlett

MOVE ON UP
w&m/Curtis Mayfield

MOVIN' ON
w&m/Hank Thompson

MOVIN' OUT (ANTHONY'S SONG)
w&m/Billy Joel

MOZAMBIQUE
w&m/Robert Dylan

MR. AND MRS. IS THE NAME
m/Mort Dixon
w/Allie Wrubel

MR. BASS MAN
w&m/Johnny Cymbal

MR. BLANDINGS BUILDS HIS DREAM HOME (film score)
m/Leigh Harline

MR. BLUE
w&m/Dewayne Blackwell

MR. BLUE SKY
w&m/Jeff Lynne

MR. BOJANGLES
w&m/Jerry Jeff Walker

MR. BUDWING (film score)
m/Kenyon Hopkins

MR. BUSINESSMAN
w&m/Ray Stevens

MR. DEEDS GOES TO TOWN (film score)
m/Howard Manucy Johnson

MR. DOOLEY
m/Jean Schwartz
w/William Jerome

MR. HOBBS TAKES A VACATION (film score)
m/Henry Mancini

MR. KRUSCHEV
w&m/Ellas McDaniel (Bo Diddley)

MR. LUCKY
w&m/Ray Evans, Jay H. Livingston

MR. LUCKY (instr.)
m/Henry Mancini

MR. MEADOWLARK
m/Walter Donaldson
w/Johnny Mercer

MR. NIGHT
w&m/Kenneth Loggins

MR. PAGANINI
m/Arthur Johnston
w/Sam Coslow

MR. SANDMAN
w&m/Francis Drake Ballard

MR. SMITH GOES TO WASHINGTON (film score)
m/Dimitri Tiomkin

MR. SPACEMAN
w&m/Roger McGuinn

MR. SOUL
w&m/Neil Young

MR. TAMBOURINE MAN
w&m/Robert Dylan

MR. TOUCHDOWN, U. S. A.
w&m/Ruth Roberts, William Katz

MR. VOLUNTEER
w&m/Paul Dresser

MR. WONDERFUL
m/Jerry Bock
w/George D. Weiss, Larry Holofcener

MRS. BROWN YOU'VE GOT A LOVELY DAUGHTER
w&m/Trevor Peacock

MRS. PARKINGTON (film score)
m/Bronislau Kaper

MRS. ROBINSON
w&m/Paul Simon

MUDDY MISSISSIPPI LINE
w&m/Bobby Goldsboro

MUDDY WATER
m/Peter DeRose, Harry Richman
w/Jo Trent

MUDDY WATER BLUES
w&m/Thomas Andrew Dorsey

MUDSLIDE SLIM
w&m/James Taylor

MULESKINNER BLUES
w&m/Jimmy Rodgers, George Vaughn

MULE TRAIN
w&m/Johnny Lange, Fred Glickman, Walter Henry (Hy) Heath

MULLIGAN GUARD, THE
m/David Braham
w/Ed Harrigan

MUSIC BOX DANCER
w&m/Frank Mills

MUSIC BOX RAG
w&m/Charles L. Roberts

MUSIC FOR PEARL (instr.)
m/Mary Lou Williams

MUSIC GOES ROUND AND ROUND, THE
w&m/Mike Riley, Edward Farley

MUSIC MAESTRO PLEASE
m/Herb Magidson
w/Allie Wrubel

MUSIC MAN, (film score)
m/Ray John Heindorf

MUSIC MUSIC MUSIC (PUT ANOTHER NICKEL IN)
w&m/Stephan Weiss, Bernie Baum

MUSIC MUST CHANGE, THE
w&m/Peter Townshend

MUSIC TO WATCH GIRLS BY (instr.)
m/Bob Crewe

MUST YOU THROW DUST IN MY FACE
w&m/Ira Louvin, Charles Louvin

MUTINY ON THE BOUNTY (film score)
m/Bronislau Kaper

MY ADOBE HACIENDA
w&m/Louise Massey

MY BABE
w&m/Willie Dixon

MY BABY JUST CARES FOR ME
m/Walter Donaldson
w/Gus Kahn

MY BABY LOVES ME
w&m/Sylvia Moy, William Stevenson, Ivy Hunter

MY BABY PACKED UP MY MIND AND LEFT ME
w&m/Dallas Frazier

MY BACK PAGES
w&m/Robert Dylan

MY BACK PAGES
w&m/Roger McGuinn

MY BELOVED
w&m/Ray Evans, Jay H. Livingston

MY BEAUTIFUL LADY
m/Ivan Caryll
w/Harry Morton

MY BEST FRIEND'S WIFE
w&m/Paul Anka

MY BEST GIRL'S A CORKER
w&m/John Stromberg

MY BEST TO YOU
m/Isham Jones
w/Gene Willadsen

MY BLACK MAMA
w&m/Son House

MY BLUE HEAVEN
m/Walter Donaldson
w/George Whiting

MY BOLERO
m/Nat Simon
w/Jimmy Kennedy

MY BONNIE LASSIE
w&m/Roy C. Bennett, Sid Tepper

MY BOY, YOU MAKE TAKE IT FROM ME
m/Sir Arthur Sullivan
w/Sir William Schwenk Gilbert

MY BOYFRIEND'S BACK
w&m/Jerry Goldtein, Bob Feldman, Richard Gottehrer

MY BUDDY
m/Walter Donaldson
w/Gus Kahn

MY CASTLE ON THE NILE
w&m/James W. Johnson, J. Rosamond Johnson, Bob Cole

MY CATHEDRAL
m/Mabel Wayne
w/Hal Eddy

MY CHERIE AMOR
w&m/Sylvia Moy, Stevie Wonder, Henry Cosby

MY COUNTRY
w&m/Jud Strunk

MY COUNTRY LOVE SONG
w&m/David W. De Fentresse Guion

MY CUP RUNNETH OVER
w&m/Tom Jones, Harvey Schmidt

MY DAD
w&m/Barry Mann, Cynthia Weil

MY DARLING, MY DARLING
w&m/Frank Loesser

MY DEVOTION
w&m/Roc Hillman, Johnny Napton

MY DING A LING
w&m/Chuck Berry

MY DREAM IS YOURS
w&m/Ralph Blane, Harry Warren

MY DREAMS ARE GETTING BETTER ALL THE TIME
w&m/Vic Mizzy, Mann Curtis

MY EARS SHOULD BURN
w&m/Roger Miller

MY ELUSIVE DREAMS
w&m/Curly Putnam, Billy Sherrill

MY EYES ADORED YOU
w&m/Bob Crewe, Kenny Nolan

MY FAIR LADY (film score)
m/Andre Previn

MY FAIR SHARE
w&m/Dash Crofts, James Seals

MY FAITH LOOKS UP TO THEE
m/Lowell Mason
w/Ray Palmer

MY FAITHFUL STRADIVARI
m/Emmerich Kalman
w/E. P. Heath

MY FATE IS IN YOUR HANDS
m/Thomas "Fats" Waller
w/Andy Razaf

MY FATHER
w&m/Judy Collins

MY FAVORITE THINGS
m/Richard Rodgers
w/Oscar Hammerstein II

MY FOOLISH HEART
m/Victor Young
w/Ned Washington

MY FRIEND
w&m/Boz Scaggs, James Davis

MY FRIEND ON THE RIGHT
w&m/Faron Young, Red Lane

MY FRIENDS ARE GONNA BE STRANGERS
w&m/Liz Anderson, Casey Anderson

MY FUNNY VALENTINE
m/Richard Rodgers
w/Lorenz (Larry) Hart

MY FUTURE JUST PASSED
m/Richard A. Whiting
w/George Marion Jr.

MY GAL SAL (film score)
m/Alfred Newman

MY GAL SAL (THEY CALLED HER FRIVOLOUS SAL)
w&m/Paul Dresser

MY GENERATION
w&m/Peter Townshend

MY GIRL
w&m/Jerry Goldstein, Bob Feldman,
Richard Gottehrer

MY GIRL
w&m/William (Smokey)
Robinson Jr.

MY GIRL BILL
w&m/Jim Stafford

MY GUY
w&m/William (Smokey)
Robinson Jr.

MY HANDY MAN
m/Eubie Blake
w/Andy Razaf

MY HANG UP IS YOU
w&m/Freddie Hart

MY HAPPINESS
m/Borney Bergantine
w/Betty Peterson

MY HEART CRIES FOR YOU
m/Percy Faith (adapted from the
French folk song "Chanson de
Marie Antoinette")
w/Carl Sigman

**MY HEART BELONGS TO
DADDY**
w&m/Cole Porter

**MY HEART HAS A MIND OF
ITS OWN**
w&m/Jack Keller, Howard
Greenfield

MY HEART IS AN OPEN BOOK
m/Lee J. Pockriss
w/Hal David

MY HEART IS SO FULL OF YOU
w&m/Frank Loesser

**MY HEART IS TAKING
LESSONS**
m/James V. Monaco
w/Johnny Burke

MY HEART SKIPS A BEAT
w&m/Buck Owens

**MY HEART STILL CLINGS TO
THE OLD FIRST LOVE**
w&m/Paul Dresser

MY HEART STOOD STILL
m/Richard Rodgers
w/Lorenz (Larry) Hart

MY HERO
m/Oscar Straus
w/Stanislaus Stange

**MY HEROES HAVE ALWAYS
BEEN COWBOYS**
w&m/Sharon Vaughan

MY HONEY'S LOVIN' ARMS
w&m/Joseph Meyer, Jack Yellen

MY HORSE AIN'T HUNGRY
w&m/John Jacob Niles

MY IDEAL
m/Richard A. Whiting, Newell Chase
w/Leo Robin

MY ISLE OF GOLDEN DREAMS
m/Walter Blaufus
w/Gus Kahn

MY KIND OF GIRL
w&m/Leslie Bricusse

MY KIND OF TOWN
m/James Van Heusen
w/Sammy Cahn

MY KINDA LOVE
m/Louis Alter
w/Jo Trent

MY LADY LOVES TO DANCE
m/Milton DeLugg
w/Sammy Gallop

MY LANDLADY
m/Bert Williams
w/F. E. Mierich, James T. Bryan

MY LAST DATE WITH YOU
w&m/Boudleaux Bryant, Floyd
Cramer, Skeeter Davis

MY LIFE
w&m/Bill Anderson

MY LIFE
w&m/Billy Joel

**MY LIFE IN A STOLEN
MOMENT**
w&m/Robert Dylan

MY LIPS ARE SEALED
w&m/Hal Blair, Ben Weisman, Bill
Peppers

MY LITTLE BUCKAROO
w&m/M. K. Jerome, Jack Scholl

**MY LITTLE CORNER OF THE
WORLD**
m/Lee Pockriss
w/Bob Hilliard

MY LITTLE DREAM GIRL
m/Anatole Friedland
w/L. Wolfe Gilbert

**MY LITTLE GEORGIA ROSE
(instr.)**
m/William Smith Monroe

MY LITTLE GIRL
w&m/Albert Von Tilzer, Samuel M.
Lewis, William Dillon

**MY LITTLE GRASS SHACK IN
KEALAKEKUA,
HAWAII**
w&m/John Avery Noble

**MY LITTLE NEST OF
HEAVENLY BLUE**
m/Franz Lehar (adapted from
"Frasquita Serenade")
w/Sigmund Spaeth

**MY LITTLE OL' HOME DOWN
IN NEW ORLEANS**
w&m/Jimmy Rodgers

MY LITTLE TOWN
w&m/Paul Simon

MY LOVE
w&m/Tony Hatch

MY LOVE
w&m/Paul Anka

MY LOVE
m/Victor Young
w/New Washington

MY LOVE
w&m/Paul and Linda McCartney

MY LOVE, MY LOVE
m/Nicholas Acquaviva
w/Bob Haymes

MY LOVE GOES WITH YOU
m/Marvin Hamlisch
w/Carole Bayer Sager

MY LOVE IS A WANDERER
w&m/Bart Howard

MY LOVE'S A ROSE
w&m/Charles A. White

MY LUCKY STAR
m/Nacio Herb Brown
w/Arthur Freed

MY MAGGIE
w&m/William J. Scanlan

MY MAMMY
m/Walter Donaldson
w/Samuel M. Lewis, Joseph Young

MY MAN
w&m/Billy Sherrill, Norro Wilson,
Rory Bourke

MY MAN (MON HOMME)
m/Maurice Yvain
w/Channing Pollock

MY MAN'S GONE NOW
m/George Gershwin
w/DuBose Heyward

MY MARIA
w&m/B.W. Stevenson

MY MARY
w&m/Stuart Hamblen

MY MELANCHOLY BABY
m/Ernie Burnett
w/George A. Morton

MY MELLOW MAN
w&m/"Big Bill" Broonzy

MY MELODY OF LOVE
m/Henry Mayer
w/English words: Bobby Vinton
w/German words: George Buscher

MY MERRY GO ROUND
w&m/Johnny Nash

MY MAN'S GONE NOW
m/George Gershwin
w/DuBose Heyward

MY MOTHER WAS A LADY
m/Joseph W. Stern
w/Edward B. Marks

MY MOTHER'S EYES
m/Abel Baer
w/L. Wolfe Gilbert

MY MOTHER'S ROSARY
m/George W. Meyer
w/Samuel M. Lewis

MY, MY, HEY, HEY
w&m/Neil Young

**MY NAME IS JOHN
WELLINGTON WELLS**
m/Sir Arthur Sullivan
w/Sir William Schwenk Gilbert

MY NELLIE'S BLUE EYES
w&m/William J. Scanlan

MY OBJECT ALL SUBLIME
m/Sir Arthur Sullivan
w/Sir William Schwenk Gilbert

MY OLD AUNT SALLY
w&m/Daniel Decatur Emmett

MY OLD FLAME
m/Arthur Johnston
w/Sam Coslow

MY OLD LADY
w&m/Michael Bloomfield

MY OLD MAN
w&m/Joni Mitchell

MY OLD PAL
w&m/Jimmy Rodgers

MY OLD SCHOOL
w&m/Donald Fagen, Walter Becker

MY ONE AND ONLY
m/George Gershwin
w/Ira Gershwin

MY ONE AND ONLY HEART
m/Robert Allen
w/Al Stillman

**MY ONE AND ONLY
HIGHLAND FLING**
m/Harry Warren
w/Ira Gershwin

**MY ONE AND ONLY
JIMMY BOY**
w&m/David Gates

MY ONE AND ONLY LOVE
w&m/Jack Lawrence

MY OWN
m/Jimmy McHugh
w/Harold Adamson

MY OWN IONA
m/Anatole Friedland
w/L. Wolfe Gilbert

MY OWN KIND OF HAT
w&m/Merle Haggard, R. Lane

MY OWN TRUE LOVE
m/Max Steiner
w/Mack David

MY PRAYER
m/Georges Boulanger
w/Jimmy Kennedy

MY RAMBLER ROSE
m/David Stamper
w/Gene Buck, Louis A. Hirsch

MY RAMBLIN' BOY
w&m/Thomas R. Paxton

MY RESISTANCE IS LOW
m/Hoagy Carmichael
w/Harold Adamson

MY REVERIE
w&m/Larry Clinton

MY ROMANCE
m/Richard Rodgers
w/Lorenz (Larry) Hart

MY SHARONA
w&m/Doug Fieger, Berton Averre

MY SHAWL
m/Xavier Cugat
w/Stanley Adams

MY SHINING HOUR
m/Harold Arlen
w/Johnny Mercer

MY SHIP
m/Kurt Weill
w/Ira Gershwin

MY SILENT LOVE
m/melody of "Jazz Nocturne" by
Dana Suesse
w/Edward Heyman

MY SIN
m/Ray Henderson
w/Lew Brown, Buddy DeSylva

MY SISTER AND I
m/Joan Whitney Kramer, Alex
Kramer
w/Hy Zaret

MY SON
w&m/Jan Howard

MY SONG
w&m/Michael Pinder

MY SOUTHERN ROSE
w&m/Earl Taylor

MY SPECIAL ANGEL
w&m/Jimmy Duncan

MY STORY
w&m/Chuck Willis

MY SUGAR IS SO REFINED
m/Sidney Lippman
w/Sylvia Dee

MY SWEET ADAIR
m/Anatole Friedland
w/L. Wolfe Gilbert

MY SWEET LADY
w&m/John Denver

MY SWEET LORD
w&m/George Harrison

**MY SWEETHEART'S THE MAN
IN THE MOON**
w&m/James Thornton

MY TANE
w&m/John Avery Noble

MY TIME IS YOUR TIME
w&m/H. M. Tennant, R. H. Hooper

MY TOREADOR
m/Jose Padilla
w/William Cary Duncan

MY TRIBUTE
w&m/Andrae Crouch

MY TRUE LOVE
w&m/Jack Scott

MY TRULY TRULY FAIR
w&m/Bob Merrill

MY WAY
w&m/Paul Anka, Jacques Revaux,
Claude Francois

MY WAY OF LIFE
m/Bert Kaempfert
w/Carl Sigman

MY WHOLE WORLD ENDED
w&m/Harvey Fuqua, Johnny Bristol,
Pam Sawyer, Jimmy Roach

MY WIFE
w&m/John Entwhistle

**MY WIFE'S GONE TO THE
COUNTRY**
m/Ted Snyder
w/Irving Berlin, George Whiting

MY WILD IRISH ROSE
w&m/Chauncey Olcott

MY WISH
w&m/Meredith Willson

**MY WOMAN, MY WOMAN, MY
WIFE**
w&m/Marty Robbins

MY WOMAN'S GONE WRONG
w&m/Leroy Carr

MY WOMAN'S GOOD TO ME
w&m/Glenn Sutton, Billy Sherrill

MY WORLD
w&m/Barry, Maurice and Robin Gibb

MY WORLD BEGINS AND ENDS WITH YOU
w&m/Steve Pippin, Larry Keith

MY WORLD IS EMPTY WITHOUT YOU
w&m/Eddie Holland, Brian Holland, Lamont Dozier

MYSTERIOSO (instr.)
m/Thelonious Sphere Monk

Addenda:

MAGIC
w&m/John Farrar

MAIN EVENT, THE
w&m/Bruce Roberts, Paul Jabara

MANEUVERS
w&m/Graham Parker

MINAMATA (instr. suite)
m/Toshiko Akiyoshi

MIDNIGHT SUN
w&m/Joseph Francis (Sonny) Burke, Lionel Hampton

MORE LOVE
w&m/William (Smokey) Robinson Jr.

MORNING SONG (instr.)
m/George Cables

SONGS

N

NA NA HEY HEY KISS HIM GOODBYE
w&m/Paul Leka

NADIA'S THEME (earlier versions of same melody entitled (1) COTTON'S DREAM (2) BLESS THE BEASTS AND CHILDREN
w&m/Barry De Vorzon, Perry Botkin Jr.

NADINE
w&m/Alan Freed

NAGASAKI
m/Harry Warren
w/Mort Dixon

NAIMA (instr.)
m/John Coltrane

NAKED DANCE, THE (instr.)
m/Ferdinand "Jelly Roll" Morton

NAKED JUNGLE, THE (film score)
m/Daniele Amfitheatrof

NAME OF THE GAME, THE
m/Benny Andersson, Bjorn Ulvaeus
w/Stig Anderson

NANCY (WITH THE LAUGHING FACE)
m/James Van Heusen
w/Phil Silvers

NASHVILLE
m/Ray Stevens

NATIONAL EMBLEM (march)
m/E. E. Bagley

NATURAL THING
w&m/Thomas Johnston

NATURAL WOMAN, A
w&m/Jerry Wexler, Gerry Goffin, Carole King

NATURE BOY
w&m/Eden Ahbez

NAUGHTY GIRL
w&m/Mac Davis

NAUGHTY HULA EYES
w&m/John Avery Noble, Andy Iona

NAUGHTY LADY OF SHADY LANE, THE
w&m/Roy C. Bennett, Sid Tepper

NEAPOLITAN LOVE SONG
m/Victor Herbert
w/Henry Blossom

NEAPOLITAN NIGHTS
m/J. C. Zamecnick
w/Harry D. Kerr

NEAR YOU
w&m/Francis Craig, Kermit Goell

NEARER MY GOD, TO THEE
m/Lowell Mason (from the song "Bethany")
w/Sarah Flower Adams

NEARNESS OF YOU, THE
m/Hoagy Carmichael
w/Ned Washington

'NEATH THE SOUTH SEA MOON
m/David Stamper
w/Gene Buck, Louis A. Hirsch

'NEATH THE SOUTHERN MOON
m/Victor Herbert
w/Rida Johnson Young

NEED TO BELONG
w&m/Curtis Mayfield

NEEDLES AND PINS
w&m/Sonny Bono

NEFERTITI (instr.)
m/Wayne Shorter

NELLY BLY
w&m/Stephen C. Foster

NELLY KELLY, I LOVE YOU
w&m/George M. Cohan

NELLY WAS A LADY
w&m/Stephen C. Foster

NEON ROSE
w&m/Rory Bourke, Gayle Barnhill

N-E-R-V-O-U-S
w&m/Ian Whitcomb

NEVER BE ANYONE ELSE BUT YOU
w&m/Baker Knight

NEVER BEEN TO SPAIN
w&m/Hoyt Axton

NEVER CAN SAY GOODBYE
w&m/Clifton D. Davis

NEVER COMES THE DAY
w&m/Justin Hayward

NEVER ENDING SONG OF LOVE
w&m/Delaney Bramlett, Bonnie Lynn Bramlett

NEVER FORGET
w&m/Christine Perfect McVie

NEVER GOING BACK AGAIN
w&m/Lindsay Buckingham

NEVER GONNA FALL IN LOVE AGAIN
w&m/Eric Carmen

NEVER HAD A LOVE
w&m/Cory Lerios, David Jenkins

NEVER IN A MILLION YEARS
m/Harry Revel
w/Mack Gordon

NEVER LEAVE YOU LONELY
w&m/George Johnson, Louis Johnson, Peggy Jones

NEVER LET ME GO
w&m/Ray Evans, Jay H. Livingston

NEVER MAKE ME CRY
w&m/Christine Perfect McVie

NEVER MIND THE WHY AND WHEREFORE
m/Sir Arthur Sullivan
w/Sir William Schwenk Gilbert

NEVER MY LOVE
w&m/Donald J. Adrissi, Richard P. Adrissi

NEVER MY LOVE
w&m/Terry Kirkman

NEVER, NEVER GONNA GIVE YA UP
w&m/Barry White

NEVER NEVER LAND
m/Jule Stein
w/Betty Comden, Adolph Green

NEVER NO MO' BLUES
w&m/Jimmy Rodgers

NEVER ON SUNDAY (film score)
m/Manos Hadjidakis

NEVER ON SUNDAY
m/Manos Hadjidakis
w/Billy Towne

NEVER TOO LATE
w&m/Ray Evans, Jay H. Livingston

NEVER TRUST A WOMAN
w&m/Jenny Lou Carson

NEVERTHELESS
m/Harry Ruby
w/Bert Kalmar

NEVERTHELESS
w&m/Gregg L. Allman, Duane Allman

NEW ASHMOLEAN MARCHING SOCIETY, THE
w&m/Frank Loesser

NEW CENTURIONS, THE (film score)
m/Quincy Jones

NEW KID IN TOWN
w&m/J. D. Souther, Glenn Frey, Donald Henley

NEW MOTHER NATURE
w&m/Burton Cummings

NEW ORLEANS
w&m/Neil Diamond

NEW WORLD COMNG
w&m/Barry Mann, Cynthia Weil

NEW WORLD IN THE MORNING
w&m/Roger Whittaker

NEW YORK
m/Ludwig Englander
w/Harry B. Smith

NEW YORK HIPPODROME MARCH
m/John Philip Sousa

NEW YORK MINING DISASTER
w&m/Barry, Maurice and Robin Gibb

NEW YORK, NEW YORK
m/Leonard Bernstein
w/Betty Comden, Adolph Green

NEW YORK STATE OF MIND
w&m/Billy Joel

NEW YORK'S A LONELY TOWN
w&m/Vincent Poncia, Pete Anders

NEXT DOOR TO AN ANGEL
w&m/Neil Sedaka, Howard Greenfield

NEXT IN LINE
w&m/John R. Cash

NEXT PLANE TO LONDON
w&m/Kenny O'Dell

NICE 'N' EASY
w&m/Marilyn and Alan Bergman

NICE TO BE AROUND
w&m/Paul Williams, John Williams

NICE TO BE HERE
w&m/Ray Thomas

NICE WORK IF YOU CAN GET IT
m/George Gershwin
w/Ira Gershwin

NICKEL SONG, THE
w&m/Melanie

NIGHT AND DAY
w&m/Cole Porter

NIGHT FEVER
w&m/Barry, Maurice and Robin Gibbs

NIGHT HAS A THOUSAND EYES, THE
m/Jerome Brainin
w/Buddy Bernier

NIGHT IN TUNISIA, A (instr.)
m/Dizzy Gillespie, Frank Paparelli

NIGHT IS FILLED WITH MUSIC, THE
w&m/Irving Berlin

NIGHT IS YOUNG AND YOU'RE SO BEAUTIFUL, THE
w&m/Irving Kahal, Dana Suesse, Billy Rose

NIGHT LIFE
w&m/Willie Nelson

NIGHT MOVES
w&m/Bob Seger

NIGHT OF FEAR
w&m/Roy Wood

NIGHT OF THE GENERALS, THE (film score)
m/Maurice Jarre

NIGHT THE LIGHTS WENT OUT IN GEORGIA, THE
w&m/Bobby Russell

NIGHT THEY DROVE OLD DIXIE DOWN, THE
w&m/J. Robbie Robertson

NIGHT THEY INVENTED CHAMPAGNE, THE
m/Frederick Loewe
w/Alan Jay Lerner

NIGHT TIME MAGIC
w&m/Larry Gatlin

NIGHT TRAIN TO MEMPHIS
w&m/Beasley Smith

NIGHT TRAIN TO MEMPHIS
w&m/Roy C. Acuff

NIGHT WE CALLED IT A DAY, THE
m/Matt Dennis
w/Thomas M. Adair

NIGHTINGALE
w&m/Carole King, David Palmer

NIGHTINGALE SANG IN BERKELEY SQUARE, A
w&m/Manning Sherwin

NIGHTS ARE FOREVER WITHOUT YOU
w&m/John Ford Coley, Danny Seals

NIGHTS IN WHITE SATIN
w&m/Justin Hayward

NIGHTS ON BROADWAY
w&m/Barry, Maurice and Robin Gibb

NINA NEVER KNEW
m/Louis Alter
w/Milton Drake

1980
w&m/Herb Alpert

1941 (film score)
m/John Williams

NINETY MILES AN HOUR
w&m/Hal Blair, Don Robertson

99
w&m/David Paich

NINETY NINE MILES FROM L.A.
m/Albert Hammond
w/Hal David

NINETY NINE OUT OF A HUNDRED WANNA BE LOVED
w&m/Al Sherman, Al Lewis

NINOTCHKA (film score)
m/Werner Heyman

NO ANSWER
m/Michael Mantler (based on Samuel Becket poem)

NO BED OF ROSES
w&m/Dale Evans

NO CHARGE
w&m/Harlan Howard

NO EASY WAY DOWN
w&m/Carole King, Gerry Goffin

NO LOVE HAVE I
w&m/Mel Tillis

NO MAN IS AN ISLAND
w&m/Alex Kramer, Joan Whitney

NO MAN'S LAND
w&m/Bob Seger

NO MONEY DOWN
w&m/Chuck Berry

NO MOON AT ALL
m/David Mann
w/Redd Evans

NO MORE TEARS
w&m/Paul Jabara, Bruce Roberts

NO MYSTERY (instr.)
m/Chick Corea

NO NO A THOUSAND TIMES NO
w&m/Al Sherman, Al Lewis, Abner Silver

NO NO JOE
w&m/Silvester Levay

NO NO NANETTE
w&m/Otto Harbach

NO, NO, NO
w&m/Tommy Tucker

NO NO NORA
m/Ted Fiorito
w/Gus Kahn, Ernie Erdman

NO NO SONG, THE
w&m/Hoyt Axton

NO NOT MUCH
m/Robert Allen
w/Al Stillman

NO ONE EVER LOVED MORE THAN I
m/Joseph W. Stern
w/Edward B. Marks

NO ONE KNOWS
w&m/Ken Hecht, Ernest Maresca

NO ONE WILL EVER KNOW
w&m/Fred Rose, Mel Foree

NO OTHER LOVE
m/Richard Rodgers
w/Oscar Hammerstein II

**NO PARTICULAR PLACE
TO GO**
w&m/Chuck Berry

NO ROLLIN' BLUES
w&m/Jimmy Witherspoon

NO SAD SONG
w&m/Carole King, Toni Stern

NO SALT ON HER TAIL
w&m/John Phillips

NO STRINGS
w&m/Richard Rodgers

**NO STRINGS ATTACHED
(instr.**
m/Richard Hayman

NO TIME
w&m/Burton Cummings, Randy
Bachman

NO TWO PEOPLE
w&m/Frank Loesser

NO VACANCY
w&m/Merle Travis, Cliffie Stone

NO WOMAN, NO CRY
w&m/Bob Marley

**NOBLES OF THE MYSTIC
SHRINE (march)**
m/John Philip Sousa

NOBODY
w&m/Thomas Johnston

NOBODY
m/Bert Williams
w/Alex Rogers

NOBODY BUT A FOOL
w&m/Bill Anderson

NOBODY BUT YOU
w&m/Barry Mann, Cynthia Weil

NOBODY DOES IT BETTER
m/Marvin Hamlisch
w/Carole Bayer Sager

NOBODY KNOWS (instr.)
m/Lester Young

**NOBODY KNOWS, NOBODY
CARES**
w&m/Charles K. Harris

**NOBODY KNOWS AND
NOBODY SEEMS TO CARE**
w&m/Irving Berlin

NOBODY WINS
w&m/Kris Kristofferson

**NOBODY'S DARLIN' BUT
MINE**
w&m/Jimmy Davis

NOBODY'S FOOL BUT YOURS
w&m/Buck Owens

NOBODY'S RAG (instr.)
m/David Alan Jasen

NOBODY'S SWEETHEART
m/Billy Meyers, Ernie Erdman
w/Gus Kahn

NOCHE CARIBE (instr.)
m/Percy Faith

NOLA
m/Felix Arndt
w/Sunny Skylar

**NON DIMENTICAR (DON'T
FORGET)**
m/P. G. Redi
w/English words: Shelley Dobbins
w/Italian words: Michele Galdieri

**NONE BUT THE LONELY
HEART**
m/Peter Illich Tchaikovsky
w/Johann Wolfgang Von Goethe

NONE SHALL PART US
m/Sir Arthur Sullivan
w/Sir William Schwenk Gilbert

NONPAREIL (instr.)
m/Scott Joplin

NORMAN
w&m/John D. Loudermilk

**NORTH BY NORTHWEST (film
score)**
m/Bernard Herrmann

NORTH COUNTRY BLUES
w&m/Robert Dylan

NORTH STAR, THE (film score)
m/Aaron Copland

NORTH TO ALASKA
w&m/Mike Phillips

NORTHWEST PASSAGE (instr.)
m/Ralph Burns, Woody Herman,
m/Greig (Chubby) Jackson

NORWEIGAN WOOD
w&m/Paul McCartney, John Lennon

NOSTALGIA (instr.)
m/David Rose

NOTHING BUT HEARTACHES
w&m/Eddie Holland, Brian Holland,
Lamont Dozier

NOT FADE AWAY
w&m/Mick Jagger, Keith Richard

**NOT FOR ALL THE RICE IN
CHINA**
w&m/Irving Berlin

NOT LIKE MINE
w&m/Natalie Cole, Marvin Yancy,
Chuck Jackson

NOT MINE
m/Victor Schertzinger
w/Johnny Mercer

NOT ONE MINUTE MORE
w&m/Don Robertson, Hal Blair

**NOT SO SWEET MARTHA
LORRAINE**
w&m/Joseph "Country Joe"
McDonald

**NOTHING AS ORIGINAL
AS YOU**
w&m/Don Reid

**NOTHING CAN CHANGE THIS
LOVE**
w&m/Sam Cooke

NOTHING CAN STOP ME
w&m/Curtis Mayfield

NOTHING FROM NOTHING
m/Billy Preston
w/Bruce Fisher

NOTHING GOOD COMES EASY
w&m/Barry Mann, Cynthia Weil

**NOTHING'S TOO GOOD FOR
MY BABY**
w&m/William Stevenson, Henry
Cosby, Sylvia Moy

**NOW IS THE HOUR (MAORI
FAREWELL SONG)**
m/Clement Scott
w/English words: Dorothy Stewart
w/Maori words: Maewae Kaihau

NOW IT CAN BE TOLD
w&m/Irving Berlin

NOW THE DAY IS OVER
m/Joseph Barnby
w/Sabine Baring-Gould

NOW THE DAY IS OVER
w&m/Oley Speaks

**NOW TO THE BANQUET WE
PRESS**m/Sir Arthur Sullivan
w/Sir William Schwenk Gilbert

NOW VOYAGER
m/Max Steiner

NOWHERE TO RUN
w&m/Eddie Holland, Brian Holland,
Lamont Dozier

NOW'S THE TIME (instr.)
m/Charlie Parker

**NOW'S THE TIME TO FALL IN
LOVE (POTATOES ARE
CHEAPER, TOMATOES
ARE CHEAPER)**
m/Al Lewis
w/Al Sherman

NUAGES (instr.)
m/Django Reinhardt

NUBIAN SUNDANCE (instr.)
m/Joe Zawinul

NUMBER 9 DREAM
w&m/John Lennon

NUMBER 12 TRAIN
w&m/Joshua D. White

NUMBER TWENTY NINE
w&m/William S. Hays

NUTBUSH CITY LIMITS
w&m/Bob Seger

NUTROCKER
w&m/Keith Emerson, Gregory Lake,
Carl Palmer

Addenda:

NIRVANA (instr.)
m/Herbie Mann

NEW YORK, NEW YORK
m/John Kander, w/Fred Ebb

NO NIGHT SO LONG
w&m/Richard Kerr, Will Jennings

O

O CUBA
m/Eduardo Sanchez De Fuentes
w/Frederick Herman Martens

O DUE LIEBER AUGUSTIN
(a/k/a Ach Du Lieber Augustin)
w&m/Marx Augustin

O LITTLE TOWN OF
BETHLEHEM
m/Lewis H. Redner
(from the song "St. Louis")
w/Phillips Brooks

O MY DARLING O MY PET
m/Sir Arthur Sullivan
w/Sir William Schwenk Gilbert

O SOLE MIO
m/Eduardo Di Capua
w/Giovanni Capurro

OBJECT OF MY AFFECTION,
THE
m/James W. Grier
w/Pinky Tomlin, Coy Poe

OB-LA-DI, OB-LA-DA
w&m/Paul McCartney, John Lennon

OCEANA ROLL
m/Lucien Denni
w/Roger Lewis

ODDS AND ENDS
w&m/Robert Dylan

ODDS AND ENDS (BITS AND
PIECES)
w&m/Harlan Howard

ODE TO BILLY JOE
w&m/Bobbie Gentry

ODE TO THE LITTLE BROWN
SHACK OUT BACK
w&m/Billy Edd Wheeler

OF ALL THE YOUNG LADIES
I KNOW
m/Sir Arthur Sullivan
w/Sir William Schwenk Gilbert

OF HUMAN BONDAGE (film
score)
m/Erich Wolfgang Korngold

OF MICE AND MEN (film score)
m/Aaron Copland

OF THEE I SING
m/George Gershwin
w/Ira Gershwin

OF THEE I SING
w&m/Leon Russell

OFF MINOR (instr.)
m/Thelonious Sphere Monk

OFF SHORE
m/Leo Diamond
w/Steve Graham

OFF THE WALL
w&m/Rod Temperton

OGNI VOLTA
w&m/Paul Anka

OH, A PRIVATE BUFFOON
m/Sir Arthur Sullivan
w/Sir William Schwenk Gilbert

OH BABE WHAT WOULD YOU
SAY
w&m/Norman Smith

OH BABY DOLL
w&m/Chuck Berry

OH BETTER FAR TO LIVE
AND DIE
m/Sir Arthur Sullivan
w/Sir William Schwenk Gilbert

OH BOYS CARRY ME 'LONG
w&m/Stephen C. Foster

OH BUT I DO
m/Arthur Schwartz
w/Leo Robin

OH BY JINGO
m/Albert Von Tilzer
w/Lew Brown

OH CAROL
w&m/Neil Sedaka, Howard
Greenfield

OH, DEM GOLDEN SLIPPERS
w&m/James A. Bland

OH DADDY
w&m/Christine Perfect McVie

OH DEM GOLDEN SLIPPERS
w&m/James A. Bland

OH DIDN'T HE RAMBLE
w&m/James Weldon Johnson, J.
Rosamond Johnson. Bob Cole

OH FOOLISH DAY
m/Sir Arthur Sullivan
w/Sir William Schwenk Gilbert

OH GENTLEMEN LISTEN
m/Sir Arthur Sullivan
w/Sir William Schwenk Gilbert

OH HAPPY DAY
m/E. F. Rimbault (American
arrangement: Edwin Hawkins)
w/Philip Doddridge

OH HOW I HATE TO GET UP
IN THE MORNING
w&m/Irving Berlin

OH HOW I MISS YOU TONIGHT
m/Joseph A. Burke, Mark Fisher
w/Benny Davis

OH HOW SHE COULD YACKI
HACKI WICKI WACKI WOO
w&m/Albert Von Tilzer, Charles
McCarron, Stanley Murphy

OH, IS THERE NOT ONE
MAIDEN BREAST
m/Sir Arthur Sullivan
w/Sir William Schwenk Gilbert

OH JENNY
w&m/Bob Welch

OH JOHNNY, OH JOHNNY, OH
m/Abe Olman
w/Ed Rose

OH, LADY BE GOOD
m/George Gershwin
w/Ira Gershwin

OH, LONESOME ME
w&m/Don Gibson

OH LOOK AT ME NOW
w&m/Joseph Bushkin

OH ME, OH MY
w&m/Al Green

OH MISS HANNAH!
m/Jessie L. Deppen
w/Thekla Hollingsworth

OH NO, NOT MY BABY
w&m/Carole King, Gerry Goffin

OH PRETTY WOMAN
w&m/Roy Orbison, Joe Melson

OH PROMISE ME
w&m/Reginald DeKoven
w/Harry B. Smith

OH SINGER
w&m/Margaret Lewis, Mira Smith

OH SISTER
w&m/Robert Dylan

OH, SUCH A STRANGER
w&m/Don Gibson

OH! SUSANNA
w&m/Stephen C. Foster

OH, WHAT A BEAUTIFUL
MORNING
m/Richard Rodgers
w/Oscar Hammerstein II

OH, WHAT A NIGHT
w&m/Bob Gaudio, Judy Parker

OH WHAT A NIGHT FOR
DANCING
w&m/Barry White, Vance Wilson

OH WHAT A PAL WAS MARY
m/Pete Wendling
w/Bert Kalmar, Edgar Leslie

OH WHAT IT SEEMED TO BE
m/Bennie Benjamin
w/George D. Weiss, Frankie Carle

OH, YOKO
w&m/John Lennon

OH YOU BEAUTIFUL DOLL
m/Nat D. Ayer
w/A. Seymour Brown

OH YOU CRAZY MOON
m/James Van Heusen
w/Johnny Burke

OH YOU NASTY MAN
m/Ray Henderson
w/Irving Caesar, Jack Yellen

OHIO
w&m/Neil Young

OHIO
m/Leonard Bernstein
w/Betty Comden, Adolph Green

OKIE FROM MUSKOGEE
w&m/Roy Edward Burris, Merle
Haggard

OKLAHOMA
m/Richard Rodgers
w/Oscar Hammerstein II

OKLAHOMA HILLS
w&m/Hank Thompson

**OKLAHOMA SUNDAY
MORNING**
w&m/Tony MacCaulay, Albert L.
Hammond, Michael Hazlewood

O-KO-LE MA-LU-NA
w&m/Harry Owens

OL' MAN REBOP (instr.)
m/Dizzy Gillespie

OL' MAN RIVER
m/Jerome Kern
w/Oscar Hammerstein II

OLD ARM CHAIR, THE
w&m/Henry Russell

OLD BLACK JOE
w&m/Stephen C. Foster

OLE BUTTERMILK SKY
m/Hoagy Carmichael
w/Jack Brooks

OLD CAPE COD
w&m/Claire Rothrock, Milt Takus,
Allan Jeffrey

OLD DAN TUCKER
w&m/Daniel Decatur Emmett

OLD DOG TRAY
w&m/Stephen C. Foster

**OLD DOGS, CHILDREN AND
WATERMELON WINE**
w&m/Tom T. Hall

OLD FASHIONED GARDEN
w&m/Cole Porter

**OLD FASHIONED LOVE SONG,
AN**
w&m/Paul Williams

**OLD FLAME FLICKERS AND I
WONDER WHY, THE**
w&m/Paul Dresser

**OLD FOLKS AT HOME
(SWANEE RIVER)**
w&m/Stephen C. Foster

OLD GREY MARE, THE
m/Frank Panella (adapted from
"Down In Alabam," by J. Warner)
w/Source unknown

OLD HOMER FILLER-UP
w&m/C. W. McCall

OLD KENTUCKY HOME, THE
w&m/Stephen C. Foster

OLD LAMPLIGHTER, THE
w&m/Nat Simon, Charles B. Tobias

OLD MAN AND HIS HORN
w&m/Dallas Harms

**OLD MAN AND THE SEA, THE
(film score)**
m/Dimitri Tiomkin

OLD MAN BLUES (instr.)
m/Duke Ellington

**OLD MAN FROM THE
MOUNTAIN, THE**
w&m/Merle Haggard

OLD MAN MANHATTAN
m/Gustave A. Kerker
w/Joseph Herbert

OLD MASTER PAINTER, THE
w&m/Beasley Smith, Haven
Gillespie

OLD OLD WOODSTOCK
w&m/Van Morrison

OLD PIANO ROLL BLUES, THE
w&m/Cy Coben

OLD RECORDS
w&m/Merle Kilgore, Arthur Thomas

OLD RUGGED CROSS, THE
w&m/Reverend George Bennard

**(REMEMBER THE DAYS OF
THE) OLD SCHOOLYARD**
w&m/Cat Stevens

OLD SHEP
w&m/Red Foley

OLD SOFT SHOE, THE
m/Morgan Lewis
w/Nancy Hamilton

OLD SPINNING WHEEL, THE
w&m/Billy Hill

OLD TIME LOVE
w&m/Kenny O'Dell

OLD UNCLE NED
w&m/Stephen C. Foster

OLEO (instr.)
m/Sonny Rollins

OMEN (film score)
m/Jerry Goldsmith

OMEN II: DAMIEN (film score)
m/Jerry Goldsmith

OMEOMY (instr.)
m/Roy Frederick Bargy

ON A CLEAR DAY
m/Burton Lane
w/Alan Jay Lerner

**ON A LITTLE STREET IN
SINGAPORE**
m/Peter De Rose
w/Billy Hill

ON A SLOW BOAT TO CHINA
w&m/Frank Loesser

ON A SUNDAY AFTERNOON
m/Harry Von Tilzer
w&m/Andrew B. Sterling

ON A SUNDAY BY THE SEA
m/Jule Styne
w/Sammy Cahn

ON AND ON
w&m/Stephen Bishop

ON ATLANTIC BEACH
m/Harry A. Tierney
w/Joseph McCarthy

**ON BEHALF OF THE VISITING
FIREMEN**
m/Walter Donaldson
w/Johnny Mercer

ON BRAVE OLD ARMY TEAM
w&m/Philip Egner

ON BROADWAY
w&m/Barry Mann, Cynthia Weil,
Jerry Lieber, Mike Stoller

ON PARADE (march)
m/John Philip Sousa

ON THE ALAMO
m/Isham Jones
w/Gus Kahn

**ON THE ATCHISON, TOPEKA
AND THE SANTA FE**
m/Harry Warren
w/Johnny Mercer

**ON THE BANKS OF THE
WABASH FAR AWAY**
w&m/Paul Dresser

ON THE BEACH (film score)
m/Ernest Gold

ON THE BEACH, THEME FROM
m/Ernest Gold
w/Steve Allen

ON THE BEACH AT BALI BALI
w&m/Jack Meskill, Al Sherman,
Abner Silver

ON THE BEACH AT WAIKIKI
m/Henry Kailimai
w/G. H. Stover

ON THE BENCHES IN THE PARK
w&m/James Thornton

ON THE BOARDWALK AT ATLANTIC CITY
m/Josef Myrow
w/Mack Gordon

ON THE BORDER
w&m/Glenn Frey, Don Henley, J. D. Souther

ON THE BORDER
w&m/Al Stewart

ON THE COVER OF THE MUSIC CITY NEWS
w&m/Buck Owens, Shel Silverstein, James B. Shaw

ON THE GOOD SHIP LOLLIPOP
m/Sidney Clare
w/Richard A. Whiting

ON THE ISLE OF MAY
m/Andre Kostelanetz (adapted from Tchaikovsky's "String Quartet In D Major")
w/Mack David

ON THE MALL (March)
m/Edwin Franko Goldman

ON THE MISSISSIPPI
m/Harry Carroll, Arthur Fields
w/Ballard MacDonald

ON THE OLD FALL RIVER LINE
m/Harry Von Tilzer
w/Andrew B. Sterling

ON THE PIKE (instr.)
m/James S. Scott

ON THE RADIO
w&m/Donna Summer, Georgio Moroder

ON THE REBOUND
w&m/Floyd Cramer

ON THE ROAD AGAIN
w&m/Robert Dylan

ON THE ROAD TO FIND OUT
w&m/Cat Stevene
w/mCat Stevens
w&m/Cat Stevens

ON THE ROAD TO MANDALAY
w&m/Oley Speaks, Rudyard Kipling

ON THE SENTIMENTAL SIDE
m/James V. Monaco
w/Johnny Burke

ON THE STREET WHERE YOU LIVE
m/Frederick Loewe
w/Alan Jay Lerner

ON THE SUNNY SIDE OF THE STREET
m/Jimmy McHugh
w/Dorothy Fields

ON THE TOWN (film score)
m/Lenny Hayton

ON TOP OF SPAGHETTI
m/Adapted from traditional folk song "On Top of Old Smokey"
w/Tom Glazer

ON WISCONSIN
m/W. T. Purdy
w/Carl Beck

ON YOUR TOES
m/Richard Rodgers
w/Lorenz (Larry) Hart

ONCE A DAY
w&m/Bill Anderson

ONCE IN A LIFE TIME
w&m/Anthony Newley, Leslie Bricusse

ONCE IN A WHILE
m/Michael Edwards
w/Bud Green

ONCE IN LOVE WITH AMY
w&m/Frank Loesser

ONCE MORE WITH FEELING
w&m/Kris Kristofferson, Shel Silverstein

ONCE THERE WAS A TIME
w&m/Alvin Lee

ONCE UPON A TIME
m/Charles Strouse
w/Lee Adams

ONCE UPON A TIME
w&m/William Stevenson, Clarence Paul, Dave Hamilton, Barney Ales

ONCE YOU'VE HAD THE BEST
w&m/Johnny Paycheck

ONE
m/Marvin Hamlisch
w/Edward Kleban

ONE
w&m/Harry Edward Nilsson

ONE ALONE
m/Sigmund Romberg
w&m/Otto Harbach, Oscar Hammerstein II

ONE DAY AT A TIME
m/Elton John
w/Bernie Taupin

ONE DAY AT A TIME
w&m/Jeff Barry, Ellie Greenwich

ONE DAY AT A TIME
w&m/Marijohn Wilkin, Kris Kristofferson

ONE DAY I WILL
w&m/John Stallings, Walt Mills

ONE DAY IN MY LIFE
w&m/Neil Sedaka, Howard Greenfield

ONE DOZEN ROSES
m/Dick Jurgens, Walter Donavan
w/Roger Lewis, Country Washburn

ONE EYED JACKS (film score)
m/Hugo Friedhofer

ONE FINE DAY
w&m/Carole King, Gerry Goffin

ONE FLEW OVER THE CUCKOO'S NEST (1975) (film score)
m/Jack Nitzsche

ONE GOOD TURN
w&m/Al Jarreau

ONE HAS MY NAME, THE OTHER HAS MY HEART
w&m/Hal Blair, Eddie Dean, Dearest Dean

ONE HELL OF A WOMAN
w&m/Mac Davis, Mark James

ONE HOUR WITH YOU
m/Richard A. Whiting
w/Leo Robin

ONE FOR MY BABY
m/Harold Arlen
w/Johnny Mercer

ONE HUNDRED MEN AND A GIRL (film score)
m/Charles Previn

ONE I LOVE BELONGS TO SOMEBODY ELSE, THE
m/Isham Jones
w/Gus Kahn

ONE KISS
m/Sigmund Romberg
w/Oscar Hammerstein II

ONE LESS BELL TO ANSWER
m/Burt Bacharach
w/Hal David

ONE LESS SET OF FOOTSTEPS
w&m/Jim Croce

ONE LIFE TO LIVE
m/Kurt Weill
w/Ira Gershwin

ONE LITTLE CANDLE
w&m/George Mysels, J. Malory Roach

ONE MAN BAND
w&m/Thomas Bell, Linda Creed

ONE MAN PARADE
w&m/James Taylor

ONE MAN WOMAN, ONE WOMAN MAN
w&m/Paul Anka

ONE MEAT BALL
m/Lou Singer
w/Hy Zaret

ONE MILLION B.C. (film score)
m/Werner Heyman

ONE MINT JULEP
w&m/Rudolph Toombs

ONE MINUTE TO ONE
m/J. Fred Coots
w/Samuel M. Lewis

ONE MORE MILE
w&m/Tom T. Hall

ONE MORE RIDE
w&m/Bob Nolan

ONE MORE TIME
w&m/Mel Tillis

ONE MORE TIME TO LIVE
w&m/John Lodge

ONE NIGHT IN JUNE
w&m/Charles K. Harris

ONE NIGHT OF LOVE
m/Victor Schertzinger
w/Gus Kahn

ONE NIGHT OF LOVE (film score)
m/Louis Silvers

ONE NOTE SAMBA (SAMBA DE UNA NOTA SO)
m/Antonio Carlos Jobim

ONE O'CLOCK JUMP
m/William (Count) Basie
w/Lee Gaines

ONE OF A KIND
w&m/Billy Sherrill, Steve Davis

ONE OF THESE DAYS
w&m/Alvin Lee

ONE OF THESE NIGHTS
w&m/Glenn Frey, Don Henley

ONE OF THOSE SONGS
w&m/Will Holt

ONE PADDLE, TWO PADDLE
w&m/Kui Lee

ONE ROOM COUNTRY SHACK
w&m/Mose Allison

ONE ROSE, THE (THAT'S LEFT IN MY HEART)
w&m/Lani McIntire, Del Lyon

ONE SCOTCH, ONE BOURBON, ONE BEER
w&m/Rudolph Toombs

ONE SONG
w&m/Larry Morey, Frank E. Churchill

ONE SUNNY DAY
w&m/Danny Kirwen

ONE TIN SOLDIER (THE LEGEND OF BILLY JACK)
w&m/Dennis Lambert, Brian Potter

ONE TO ONE
w&m/Bill Rice, Jerry Foster

ONE TOKE OVER THE LINE
w&m/ Michael Brewer, Thomas Shipley

ONE TOUCH OF VENUS
m/Kurt Weill
w/Ogden Nash

ONE TWO BUTTON YOUR SHOE
m/Arthur Johnston
w/Johnny Burke

1, 2, 3 RED LIGHT
w&m/Jerry Kasanetz, Jeff Katz

10538 OVERTURE
w&m/Jeff Lynne

ONE WAY OR ANOTHER
w&m/Deborah Harry, Nigel Harrison

ONE WAY OUT
w&m/Gregg Allman, Duane Allman

ONE WHO REALLY LOVES YOU
w&m/William (Smokey) Robinson Jr.

ONEY
w&m/Jerry Chesnut

ONE'S ON THE WAY
w&m/Shel Silverstein

ONLY A HOBO
w&m/Robert Dylan

ONLY A LONELY HEART SEES
w&m/Felix Cavaliere

ONLY A PAWN IN THEIR GAME
w&m/Robert Dylan

ONLY A ROSE
m/Rudolf Friml
w/Brian Hooker

ONLY IN AMERICA
w&m/Barry Mann, Cynthia Weil, Jerry Lieber, Mike Stoller

ONLY FOREVER
m/James V. Monaco
w/Johnny Burke

ONLY LOVE
w&m/Rod McKuen

ONLY LOVE CAN BREAK A HEART
m/Burt Bacharach
w/Hal David

ONLY LOVE IS REAL
w&m/Carole King

ONLY THE GOOD DIE YOUNG
w&m/Billy Joel

ONLY THE LONELY
w&m/Roy Orbison, Joe Melson

ONLY THE STRONG SURVIVE
w&m/Jerry Butler, Kenneth Gamble, Leon Huff

ONLY YESTERDAY
m/Richard Carpenter
w/John Bettis

ONLY YOU
w&m/Buck Ram, Ande Rand

ONWARD CHRISTIAN SOLDIERS
m/Sir Arthur Sullivan
w/Sabine Baring-Gould

ONYX CLUB SPREE
w&m/Stuff Smith

OOBIE DOOBIE
w&m/Roy Orbison, Joe Melson

OOGUM, BOOGUM SONG, THE
w&m/Brenton Wood

OOH BABY
w&m/Gilbert O'Sullivan

OOH LAS VEGAS
w&m/Gram Parsons

OOH, OOH, OOH
w&m/Lloyd Price

OOOH LOOK-A-THERE AIN'T SHE PRETTY
w&m/Clarence E. Todd

OOOH MY HEAD (Boogie With Stu)
w&m/Richie Valens

OOH WHAT A FEELING
w&m/Johnny Nash

OPEN A NEW WINDOW
w&m/Jerry Herman

OPEN THE DOOR, RICHARD
m/Jack McVea, Dan Howell
w/"Dusty" Fletcher, John Mason

OPEN UP THEM PEARLY GATES
w&m/Carson J. Robison

OPEN UP YOUR HEART
w&m/Buck Owens

OPERA RAG
w&m/Irving Berlin

OPERATIC RAG
m/Julius Lenzberg (adapted from classic operatic themes)

OPERATOR (THAT'S NOT THE WAY IT FEELS)
w&m/Jim Croce

OPHELIA
w&m/J. Robbie Robertson

OPUS IN PASTELS
m/Stan Kenton

OPUS ONE
w&m/Sy Oliver

ORANGE BLOSSOM SPECIAL
w&m/Ervin T. Rouse

ORANGE COLORED SKY
m/Milton Delugg
w/William Stein

ORANGE GROVE IN CALIFORNIA
w&m/Irving Berlin

ORANGE LADY (instr.)
m/Joe Zawinul

ORBITS (instr.)
m/Wayne Shorter

ORCHIDS IN THE MONLIGHT
m/Vincent Youmans
w/Edward Eliscu

ORGAN GRINDER'S SONG, THE
w&m/Will Hudson, Mitchell Parish, Irving Mills

ORIGINAL DIXIELAND ONE STEP
(Original Dixieland Jazz Band) (see composer listing under same)

ORIGINAL RAGS (instr.)
m/Scott Joplin

ORNITHOLOGY (instr.)
m/Charlie Parker

ORPHEUS (film score)
m/Georges Auric

OSTRICH WALK
w&m/Original Dixieland Jazz Band (see composer listing under same)

OTHER CHEEK, THE
w&m/Wayne Walker

OTHER SIDE OF RAIN, THE
w&m/Fred Neil

OTHER WOMAN, THE
w&m/Betty Sue Perry

OUI OUI MARIE
w&m/Fred Fisher, Alfred Bryan, Joseph McCarthy

OUR COUNTRY MAY SHE ALWAYS BE RIGHT
w&m/Paul Dresser

OUR DANCING DAUGHTERS (film score)
m/William Axt

OUR DAY WILL COME
m/Mort Garson
w/Bob Hilliard

OUR DIRECTOR (march)
m/F. E. Bigelow

OUR HEARTS WERE YOUNG AND GAY (film score)
m/Werner Heyman

OUR HOME
w&m/Graham Nash

OUR LADY OF FATIMA
w&m/Gladys Gollahon

OUR LOVE
m/Larry Clinton, Bob Emmerich (adapted from Theme from Tchaikovsky's "Romeo and Juliet")
w/Buddy Bernier

OUR LOVE
w&m/Donna Summer, Georgio Moroder

OUR LOVE AFFAIR
w&m/Roger Edens, Georgie Stoll

OUR LOVE IS HERE TO STAY
m/George Gershwin
w/Ira Gershwin

OUR MAN FLINT (film score)
m/Jerry Goldsmith

OUR NATIVE LAND
w&m/John Hill Hewitt

OUR TOWN (film score)
m/Aaron Copland

OUR VINES HAVE TENDER GRAPES (film score)
m/Bronislau Kaper

OUR WALTZ (instr.)
m/David Rose

OURS
w&m/Cole Porter

OUT AND ABOUT
w&m/Tommy Boyce, Bobby Hart

OUT BEHIND THE BARN
w&m/"Little" Jimmy Dickens

OUT IN THE COLD AGAIN
w&m/Rube Bloom, Ted Koehler

OUT IN THE COUNTRY
w&m/Paul Williams, Roger Nichols

OUT OF HAND
w&m/Jeff Barry

OUT OF NOWHERE
m/John Green
w/Edward Heyman

OUT OF SPACE
w&m/Joe Bishop, H. Eugene Gifford

OUT OF THE CLEAR BLUE SKY
m/Vernon Duke
w/Ogden Nash

OUT OF THIS WORLD
m/Harold Arlen
w/Johnny Mercer

OUT OF THIS WORLD (instr.)
m/John Coltrane

OUT THE BLUE
w&m/John Lennon

OUTLAW BLUES
w&m/Robert Dylan

OUTLAW BLUES
w&m/John Oates

OUTLAW JESSIE WALES, THE (film score)
m/Jerry Fielding

OUTSIDE IN (film score)
m/Randy Edelman

OUTSIDE MY WINDOW
w&m/Stevie Wonder

OVER AND OVER
w&m/Christine Perfect McVie

OVER AND OVER
m/Bert Kaempfert
w/Carl Sigman

OVER AND OVER AGAIN
m/Richard Rodgers
w/Lorenz (Larry) Hart

OVER MY HEAD
w&m/Christine Perfect McVie

OVER THE HILL TO THE POORHOUSE
w&m/David Braham

OVER THE HILLS AND FAR AWAY
w&m/James Page, Robert Plant

OVER SOMEBODY ELSE'S SHOULDER
w&m/Al Sherman, Al Lewis

OVER THE RAINBOW
m/Harold Arlen
w/E. Y. Harburg

OVER THERE
w&m/George M. Cohan

OVERDRIVE
w&m/Boz Scaggs

Addenda:

ONE IN A MILLION YOU
w&m/Sam Dees

 **SONGS**

P, Q

P.S. I LOVE YOU
m/Gordon Jenkins
w/Johnny Mercer

PACK UP YOUR SINS
w&m/Irving Berlin

PACK UP YOUR SORROWS
w&m/Richard Fariña

PACK UP YOUR TROUBLES IN YOUR OLD KITBAG AND SMILE SMILE SMILE
m/Felix Powell
w/George Asaf

PADDLIN' MADELIN' HOME
w&m/Harry M. Woods

PADDY DUFFY'S CART
m/David Braham
w/Ed Harrigan

PAGAN LOVE SONG, THE
m/Nacio Herb Brown
w/Arthur Freed

PAINT IT BLACK
w&m/Mick Jagger, Keith Richard

PAINT YOUR WAGON (film score)
m/Nelson Riddle

PAINTING THE CLOUDS WITH SUNSHINE
m/Joseph A. Burke
w/Al Dubin

PALISADES PARK
w&m/Chuck Barris

PALM LEAF RAG (instr.)
m/Scott Joplin

PANASSIE STOMP (instr.)
m/William (Count) Basie

PANDORA'S GOLDEN HEEBIE JEEBIES
w&m/Terry Kirkman

PAPA LOVES MAMBO
w&m/Dick Manning, Al Hoffman, Bix Reichner

PAPA WON'T YOU DANCE WITH ME
m/Jule Styne
w/Sammy Cahn

PAPA'S GOT A BRAND NEW BAG
w&m/James Brown

PAPER CHASE (film score)
m/John Williams

PAPER CHASE (TV theme)
m/Charles Fox
w/Norman Gimbel

PAPER CUP
w&m/Jimmy Webb

PAPER DOLL
w&m/Johnny S. Black

PAPER MACHÉ
m/Burt Bacharach
w/Hal David

PAPER ROSES
w&m/Fred Spielman, Janice Torre

PAPER ROSIE
w&m/Dallas Harms

PAPER SUN
w&m/Steve Winwood, Jim Capaldi

PAPER TIGER
w&m/John D. Loudermilk

PAPERBACK WRITER
w&m/John Lennon, Paul McCartney

PAPPILON (film score)
m/Jerry Goldsmith

PARA VIGO ME VOY (instr.)
m/Ernesto Lecuona

PARADISE
m/Nacio Herb Brown
w/Gordon Clifford

PARAGON RAG (instr.)
m/Scott Joplin

PARDON ME, MY DEAR ALPHONSE, AFTER YOU MY DEAR GASTON
m/Harry Von Tilzer
w/Vincent P. Bryan

PARDON ME PRETTY BABY
w&m/Jack Meskill, Al Sherman, Abner Silver

PARDON MY SOUTHERN ACCENT
m/Matt Malneck
w/Johnny Mercer

PARADE OF THE WOODEN SOLDIERS
m/Leon Jessel
w/Ballard MacDonald

PAREE!
m/Jose Padilla
w/Leo Robin

PARIS AFTER DARK (film score)
m/Hugo Friedhofer

PARIS IN THE SPRING
m/Harry Revel
w/Mack Gordon

PARIS WAKES UP AND SMILES
w&m/Irving Berlin

PARLEZ MOI D'AMOUR
m/Jean Lenoir
w/Bruce Siever

PARNELL (film score)
m/William Axt

PART OF THE PLAN
w&m/Dan Fogelberg

PARTY GIRL
w&m/Louis J. Zerato, Ernest Maresca

PARTY GIRL
w&m/Elvis Costello

PARTY'S OVER, THE
m/Jule Styne
w/Betty Comden, Adolph Green

PARTY'S OVER, THE
w&m/Willie Nelson

PASS ME BY
m/Cy Coleman
w/Carolyn Leigh

PASS THAT PEACE PIPE
w&m/Roger Edens, Hugh Martin, Ralph Blane

PASTEL BLUE
m/Charlie Shavers
w/Artie Shaw

PASTURES GREEN
w&m/Rod McKuen

PATCHES
w&m/Barry Mann, Larry Kilber

PATCHES (I'M DEPENDING ON YOU)
w&m/Ronald Dunbar, General Johnson

PATH THAT LEADS THE OTHER WAY, THE
w&m/Paul Dresser

PATRICIA
w&m/Perez Prado

PATRICK'S DAY PARADE
m/David Braham
w/Ed Harrigan

PATTON (film score)
m/Jerry Goldsmith

PAVANNE
m/Morton Gould
w/Gladys Shelley

PAVLOVA
w&m/Sylvia Fine

PAWNBROKER, THE (film score)
m/Quincy Jones

PAY TO THE PIPER
w&m/Ronald Dunbar, General Johnson, Greg S. Perry, Angelo Bond

PEACE (THE SHAPE OF JAZZ TO COME) (instr.)
m/Ornette Coleman

PEACE IN THE VALLEY
w&m/Thomas Andrew Dorsey

PEACE PIECE (instr.)
m/Bill Evans

PEACE TRAIN
w&m/Cat Stevens

PEACE WILL COME
w&m/Melanie

PEACEFUL HENRY (instr.)
m/Edward Harry Kelly

PEACHERINE RAG (instr.)
m/Scott Joplin

PEACHES 'N' CREAM
w&m/Tommy Boyce, Steve Venet

PEANUT VENDOR, THE
m/Moises Simon (adapted from
"El Mancinero")
w/L. Wolfe Gilbert, Marion Sunshine

PEANUTS AND DIAMONDS
w&m/Bobby Braddock

PEACH, THE (instr.)
m/Ferdinand (Jelly Roll) Morton

PEARLY SHELLS
w&m/Leon Pober, Webley Edwards

PEEK-A-BOO
w&m/William J. Scanlan

PEEL ME A NANNER
w&m/Bill Anderson

PEG
w&m/Walter Becker, Donald Fagen
PEG O' MY HEART
m/Fred Fisher
w/Alfred Bryan

PEGGY O'MOORE
w&m/William J. Scanlan

PEGGY O'NEILL
w&m/Ed. G. Nelson, Harry Pease,
Gilbert Dodge

PEGGY SUE
w&m/Buddy Holly

PENNIES FROM HEAVEN
m/Arthur Johnston
w/Johnny Burke

PENTHOUSE SERENADE
w&m/Val Burton, Will Jason

PENNSYLVANIA POLKA
w&m/Lester Lee, Zeke Manners

PENNSYLVANIA 6-5000
m/Jerry Gray
w/Carl Sigman

PENNY ANNIE
w&m/Larry Gatlin

PENNY LANE
w&m/Paul McCartney, John Lennon

**PENNYWHISTLE SONG, THE
(instr.)**
m/Leroy Anderson

PEOPLE
m/Jule Styne
w/Bob Merrill

PEOPLE ARE CHANGING
w&m/Timmy Thomas

PEOPLE CHANGE
w&m/Rod McKuen

PEOPLE GET READY
w&m/Curtis Mayfield

PEOPLE GOT TO BE FREE
w&m/Felix Cavaliere, Eddie Brigati

PEOPLE GOTTA MOVE
w&m/Ross Vannelli, Gino Vannelli

PEOPLE IN LOVE
w&m/Eric Stewart, Lol Creme,
Graham Gouldman

PEOPLE IN LOVE
w&m/Johnny Nash

**PEOPLE THAT YOU NEVER
GET TO LOVE, THE**
w&m/Rupert Holmes

**PEOPLE WILL SAY WE'RE IN
LOVE**
m/Richard Rodgers
w/Oscar Hammerstein II

PEP (instr.)
m/Ferdinand "Jelly Roll" Morton

PEPPERMINT TWIST, THE
w&m/Henry Glover, Joey Dee

PERCEPTIONS (instr.)
m/Jay Jay Johnson

PERDIDO
w&m/Ervin M. Drake, Hans J.
Lengsfelder, Juan Tizol

PERFECT DAY, A
w&m/Carrie Jacobs Bond

PERFECT MATCH, A
w&m/Ben Peters, Glenn Sutton

PERFECT RAG, THE (instr.)
m/Ferdinand "Jelly Roll" Morton

PERFECT SONG, THE
m/James Carl Briel
w/Clarence Lucas

PERFIDIA
m/Alberto Dominguez
w/Milton Leeds

PERFORMANCE (film score)
m/Jack Nitzsche

PERSONALITY
m/James Van Heusen
w/Johnny Burke

(You've Got) PERSONALITY
w&m/Lloyd Price, Harold Logan

PETE KELLY'S BLUES (instr.)
m/Ray John Heindorf

PETER COTTONTAIL
m/Jack Rollins
w/Steve Nelson

PETER GUNN (instr.)
m/Henry Mancini

PETER PIPER
w&m/Frank Mills

**PETTICOAT JUNCTION
(TV theme)**
w&m/D. Curtis Massey

PETTIN' IN THE PARK
m/Harry Warren
w/Al Dubin

PHILADELPHIA FREEDOM
m/Elton John
w/Bernie Taupin

PHOENIX
w&m/Dan Fogelberg

PIANO ECHOES (instr.)
m/Vincent Lopez, Adolph Deutsch

PIANO MAN
w&m/Billy Joel

PIANOFLAGE (instr.)
m/Roy Frederick Bargy

PICADOR, THE (march)
m/John Philip Sousa

PICCOLINO, THE
w&m/Irving Berlin

PICCOLO PETE
w&m/Phil Baxter

**PICK ME UP ON YOUR WAY
DOWN**
w&m/Harlan Howard

PICK OF THE WEEK
w&m/Liz Anderson

**PICKING UP THE PIECES OF
MY LIFE**
w&m/Mac Davis

"PICNIC" THEME
m/George Duning
w/Steve Allen

PICNIC (film score)
m/George Duning

PIECES OF APRIL
w&m/Dave Loggins

PIECES OF DREAMS
m/Michel Legrand
w/Alan and Marilyn Bergman

PILLOW TALK (film score)
m/Frank DeVol

PILLOW TALK
w&m/Sylvia V. Robinson, Michael Burton

PILLOW TALK
w&m/Inez James, Buddy Pepper

PINBALL WIZARD
w&m/Peter Townshend

PINE CONES AND HOLLY BERRIES
w&m/Meredith Willson

PINEAPPLE RAG (instr.)
m/Scott Joplin

PINETOP'S BOOGIE (instr.)
m/Pinetop Smith

PINEY WOOD HILLS
w&m/Buffy Sainte-Marie

PINK COCKTAIL FOR A BLUE LADY, A
m/Herb Magidson
w/Ben Oakland

PINK PANTHER, THE (film score)
m/Henry Mancini

PINK PANTHER THEME (instr.)
m/Henry Mancini

PINOCCHIO (film score)
m/Leigh Harline

PINS AND NEEDLES
w&m/Roy Claxton Acuff

PISTOL PACKIN' MAMA
w&m/Al Dexter

PITCHER OF BEER, THE
m/David Braham
w/Ed Harrigan

PITHECANTHROPUS ERECTUS (instr.)
m/Charles Mingus

PITTSBURGH, PENNSYLVANIA
w&m/Bob Merrill

PITY THE POOR IMMIGRANTS
w&m/Robert Dylan

PLACE IN THE SUN, A
m/Bryan Wells
w/Ronald Miller

PLACE IN THE SUN, A
w&m/Cory Lerios, Bud Cockrell

PLANET OF THE APES (film score)
m/Jerry Goldsmith

PLAY A SIMPLE MELODY
w&m/Irving Berlin

PLAY A SONG FOR DANCING
w&m/Alan and Marilyn Bergman

PLAY FIDDLE PLAY
m/Emery Deutsch, Arthur Altman
w/Jack Lawrence

PLAY GUITAR PLAY
w&m/Conway Twitty

PLAY GYPSIES, DANCE GYPSIES
m/Emmerich Kalman
w/Harry B. Smith, Alfred Gruenwald

PLAY IT AGAIN, SAM (film score)
m/Billy Goldenberg

PLAY ME
w/mNeil Diamond

PLAY THAT BARBER SHOP CHORD
m/Lewis F. Muir
w/William G. Tracey

PLAY THAT FUNKY MUSIC
w&m/Bob Parissi

PLAYGROUND IN MY MIND
w&m/Paul J. Vance

PLAZA SUITE (film score)
m/Maurice Jarre

PLEASANT MOMENTS (instr.)
m/Scott Joplin

PLEASANT VALLEY SUNDAY
w&m/Carole King, Gerry Goffin

PLEASE
m/Ralph Rainger
w/Leo Robin

PLEASE COME TO BOSTON
w&m/Dave Loggins

PLEASE DADDY (DON'T GET DRUNK THIS CHRISTMAS)
w&m/Bill Danoff, Kathy "Taffy" Nivert Danoff

PLEASE DON'T GO
w&m/Harry Wayne Casey, Richard Finch

PLEASE DON'T LEAVE
w&m/Lauren Wood

PLEASE DON'T LEAVE ME
w&m/Antoine "Fats" Domino, Dave Bartholomew

PLEASE DON'T SAY NO, SAY MAYBE
m/Sammy Fain
w/Ralph Freed

PLEASE DON'T STOP LOVING ME
w&m/Dolly Parton

PLEASE DON'T TALK ABOUT WHEN I'M GONE
m/Sidney Clare
w/Sam H. Stept

PLEASE FORGIVE ME (instr.)
m/Duke Ellington

PLEASE GO WAY AND LET ME SLEEP
w&m/Harry Von Tilzer

PLEASE HELP ME, I'M FALLING
w&m/Hank Locklin

PLEASE HELP ME, I'M FALLING
w&m/Don Robertson, Hal Blair

PLEASE LOVE ME
w&m/B. B. King, Jules Taub

PLEASE MR. PLEASE
w&m/John Rostill

PLEASE MR. POSTMAN
w&m/Brian Holland, Robert Bateman, Freddie Gorman, Georgia Dobbins, William Garret

PLEASE, PLEASE ME
w&m/Paul McCartney, John Lennon

PLEASE, PLEASE, PLEASE
w&m/James Brown, John Terry

PLEASE TAKE A LETTER MISS BROWN
w&m/Paul Cunningham, Ernie Burnett

PLEASURE DOME OF KUBLA KHAN (instr.)
m/Charles Tomlinson Griffes

PLEDGING MY LOVE
w&m/Don Robey, Ferdinand Washington

PLEDGING MY TIME
w&m/Robert Dylan

PLINK, PLANK, PLUNK (instr.)
m/Leroy Anderson

PO' FOLKS
w&m/Bill Anderson

POCKET FULL OF MIRACLES (film score)
m/Walter Scharf

POEM FOR BRASS (instr.)
m/Jay Jay Johnson

POETRY MAN
w&m/Phoebe Snow

POINCIANA
w&m/Nat Simon, Buddy Bernier

POINT OF KNOW RETURN
w&m/Steve Walsh, Kenny Livgren, Phillip Ehart, Robert Steinhardt, David Hope, Richard Williams

POLICE STORY (film score)
m/Jerry Goldsmith

POLICEMAN'S LOT IS NOT A HAPPY ONE, A
m/Sir Arthur Sullivan
w/Sir William Schwenk Gilbert

POLK SALAD ANNIE
w&m/Tony Joe White

POLKA DOTS AND MOONBEAMS
m/James Van Heusen
w/Johnny Burke

PONY BOY
w&m/Richard Betts

PONY TIME
w&m/Don Covay, John Berry

POOR BABY
w&m/Tony Romeo

POOR BOY
w&m/Woody Guthrie

POOR BOY BLUES
w&m/Robert Dylan

POOR BUTTERFLY
m/Raymond Hubbell
w/John Golden

POOR FOOL
w&m/Ike Turner

POOR LITTLE FOOL
w&m/Shari Sheeley

POOR LITTLE JIMMY
w&m/Don Wayne

POOR LITTLE RHODE ISLAND
m/Jule Styne
w/Sammy Cahn

POOR ME
w&m/Antoine "Fats" Domino, Dave Bartholomew

POOR OLD HEARTSICK ME
w&m/Helen Carter

POOR PEOPLE OF PARIS
w&m/Jack Lawrence, Marguerite Monnot

POOR, POOR PITIFUL ME
w&m/Warren Zevon

POOR WANDERING ONE
m/Sir Arthur Sullivan
w/Sir William Schwenk Gilbert

POP MUZIK
w&m/Robin Scott

POPSICLES AND ICICLES
w&m/David Gates

PORCUPINE RAG (instr.)
m/Charles Leslie Johnson

PORGY
m/Jimmy McHugh
w/Dorothy Fields

PORGY AND BESS (film score)
m/Andre Previn, Ken Darby

PORK AND BEANS
w&m/Charles L. Roberts

PORT AU PRINCE
w&m/Bernie Wayne

PORT OF RICO
w&m/Illinois Jacquet

PORTNOY'S COMPLAINT (film score)
m/Michel Legrand

PORTRAIT OF A GUINEA FARM (instr.)
m/Claude Thornhill

PORTRAIT OF BERT WILLIAMS (instr.)
m/Duke Ellington

PORTRAIT OF MY LOVE
m/Cyril Ornandel
w/Norman Newell

POSEIDON ADVENTURE (film score)
m/John Williams

POSITIVELY FOURTH STREET
w&m/Robert Dylan

POT LIKKER
w&m/Henry Glover

POUR ME ANOTHER TEQUILA
w&m/Eddie Rabbitt, Dave Malloy, Even Stevens

POWER OF GOLD
w&m/Dan Fogelberg

POWER HOUSE
w&m/Ellas McDaniel (Bo Diddley)

POWER OF LOVE
w&m/Billy Edd Wheeler

POWDER RAG (instr.)
m/Charles Leslie Johnson

POWDER YOUR FACE WITH SUNSHINE
w&m/Carmen Lombardo, Stanley Rochinski

POWER TO THE PEOPLE
w&m/John Lennon, Yoko Ono

POWERHOUSE (instr.)
m/Raymond Scott

PRAISE GOD FROM WHOM ALL BLESSINGS FLOW
m/From a 1551 Psalter, published in Geneva, composer unknown
w/Bishop Thomas Ken

PRAISE THE LORD AND PASS THE AMMUNITION
w&m/Frank Loesser

PRAYER (DEATH & THE FLOWER)
m/Keith Jarrett

PREACHER, THE (instr.)
m/Horace Silver

PREACHIN' THE BLUES
w&m/Son House

PRECIOUS AND FEW
w&m/Walt Nims

PRECIOUS LOVE
w&m/Bob Welch

PRECIOUS MEMORIES
w&m/J.B.F. Wright

PRELUDE TO A KISS (instr.)
m/Duke Ellington

PRESIDENT CLEVELAND MARCH, THE
m/Charles A. White

PRETEND
w&m/Cliff Parman, Lew Douglas, Frank Lavere

PRETEND I NEVER HAPPENED
w&m/Willie Nelson

PRETEND YOU DON't SEE HER
w&m/Steve Allen

PRETENDER, THE
w&m/Jackson Browne

PRETTY BABY
m/Egbert Van Alstyne, Tony Jackson
w/Gus Kahn

PRETTY BALLERINA
w&m/Michael Brown

PRETTY GIRL IS LIKE A MELODY, A
w&m/Irving Berlin

PRETTY LITTLE ANGEL EYES
w&m/Tommy Boyce, Bobby Hart

PRETTY MAMA
w&m/David Van Ronk

PRETTY PAPER
w&m/Willie Nelson

PRETTY, PRETTY
m/Peter Allen
w/Hal Hackady

PRETTY-EYED BABY (instr.)
m/Mary Lou Williams

PRETZEL LOGIC
w&m/Donald Fagen, Walter Becker

PRICE FOR LOVING YOU, THE
w&m/Marie Wilson, Ray Price

PRIESTS
w&m/Leonard Cohen

PRIME OF MISS JEAN BRODIE (film score)
m/Rod McKuen

PRIMROSE LANE
w&m/Wayne Shanklin, George (Red) Callender

PRINCE AND THE PAUPER, THE (film score)
m/Erich Wolfgang Korngold

PRINCESITA (LITTLE PRINCESS)
m/Jose Padilla
w/Frederic Herman Martens

PRINCESS POO-POO-LY
w&m/Harry Owens

PRISONER IN DISGUISE
w&m/J. D. Souther

PRISONER OF LOVE
m/Russ Columbo, Clarence Gaskill
w/Leo Robin

PRISONER OF SHARK ISLAND (film score)
m/Hugo Friedhofer

PRISONER OF YOUR LOVE
w&m/Peter Beckett, John Charles "J.C." Crowley

PRISONER'S SONG, THE
w&m/Guy Massey (music adapted from a traditional folk air)

PRITHEE, PRETTY MAIDEN
m/Sir Arthur Sullivan
w/Sir William Schwenk Gilbert

PROMENADE
m/Leroy Anderson
w/Mitchell Parish

PROMISE, THE
w&m/Alan and Marilyn Bergman

PROMISED LAND, THE
w&m/Chuck Berry

PROMISED LAND, THE
w&m/Bruce Springsteen

PRICE OF LOVE, THE
w&m/Don Everly, Phil Everly

PRIDE AND JOY
w&m/Marvin Gaye, Norman Whitfield, William Stevenson

PRICE OF THE WOLVERINES (march)
m/John Philip Sousa

PRIDE OF THE YANKEES (film score)
m/Leigh Harline

PROMISES, PROMISES
m/Burt Bacharach
w/Hal David

PROUD
w&m/Barry Mann, Cynthia Weil

PROUD MARY
w&m/John C. Fogerty

PROVE IT ALL NIGHT
w&m/Bruce Springsteen

P.S. I LOVE YOU
m/Gordon Jenkins
w/Johnny Mercer

PSYCHO (film score)
m/Bernard Herrmann

PT 109
w&m/Marijohn Wilkin, Fred Burch

PUDDIN' HEAD JONES
m/Lou Handman
w/Alfred Bryan

PUFF (THE MAGIC DRAGON)
w&m/Peter Yarrow, Leonard Lipton

PUPPET MAN
w&m/Neil Sedaka, Howard Greenfield

PUPPY LOVE
w&m/Paul Anka

PURE AND EASY
w&m/Peter Townshend

PURE LOVE
w&m/Eddie Rabbitt

PURPLE HAZE
w&m/Jimi Hendrix

PUSH DEM CLOUDS AWAY
w&m/Percy Gaunt

PUSHER, THE
w&m/Hoyt Axton

PUT A LITTLE LOVE IN YOUR HEART
w&m/Jackie De Shannon, Jimmy Holiday, Randy Myers

PUT 'EM IN A BOX
m/Jule Styne
w/Bob Hilliard

PUT IT OFF UNTIL TOMORROW
w&m/Dolly Parton, B.E. Owens

PUT ON A HAPPY FACE
m/Charles Strouse
w/Lee Adams

PUT ON YOUR OLD GRAY BONNETT
m/Percy Wenrich
w/Stanley Murphy

PUT ON YOUR SUNDAY CLOTHES
w&m/Jerry Herman

PUT THE BLAME ON MAME
m/Allan Roberts
w/Doris Fisher

PUT YOUR ARMS AROUND ME HONEY
w&m/Albert Von Tilzer, Junie McCree

PUT YOUR CLOTHES BACK ON
w&m/Billy Sherrill, Steve Davis

PUT YOUR DREAMS AWAY
w&m/Ruth Lowe, Paul Mann

PUT YOUR HAND IN THE HAND
w&m/Gene MacClellan

PUT YOUR HEAD ON MY SHOULDER
w&m/Paul Anka

PUTTING ON THE RITZ
w&m/Irving Berlin

PUZZLEMENT, A
m/Richard Rodgers
w/Oscar Hammerstein II

PYRAMID (instr.)
m/Duke Ellington

Q
w&m/George Johnson, Louis Johnson

QUANDO, QUANDO, QUANDO
w&m/Ervin M. Drake

QUARTER TO THREE
w&m/Gary U.S. Bonds

QUE SERA SERA (WHATEVER WILL BE, WILL BE)
w&m/Ray Evans, Jay H. Livingston

QUEEN OF CLUBS
w&m/Harry Wayne Casey, Richard Finch

QUEEN OF SPADES
w&m/Dennis De Young, James Young

QUEEN OF THE SILVER DOLLAR
w&m/Shel Silverstein

QUEEN OF THE STARDUST BALLROOM (film score)
m/Billy Goldenberg

QUEER NOTIONS (instr.)
m/Coleman Hawkins

QUEL RICO EL MAMBO
w&m/Perez Prado

QUESTION
w&m/Justin Hayward

QUICK JOEY SMALL
w&m/Jerry Kasenetz, Jeff Katz

QUICKSILVER GIRL
w&m/Steve Miller

QUIET GIRL, A
m/Leonard Bernstein
w/Betty Comden, Adolph Green

**QUIET NIGHTS OF QUIET
STARS (CORCAVADO)**
m/Antonio Carlos Jobim
w/Astrud Gilberto

**QUIET PLEASE, THERE'S A
LADY ON STAGE**
m/Peter Allen
w/Carole Bayer Sager

QUIET TEAR, A
w&m/Herb Alpert, Johnny Flamingo

QUIET VILLAGE
w&m/Les Baxter

QUITS
w&m/Bill Anderson

QUO VADIS (film score)
m/Miklos Rozsa

Addenda:

POPI (film score)
m/Dominic Frontiere

SONGS

R

R. M. BLUES
w&m/Roy Milton

RACING WITH THE MOON
w&m/Vaughn Monroe

RADIO RADIO
w&m/Elvis Costello

RAG DOLL
w&m/Bob Crewe, Bob Gaudio

RAG, MAMA, RAG
w&m/J. Robbie Robertson

RAG MOP
w&m/Johnnie Lee Wills, Deacon
Anderson

RAGGING THE SCALE (instr.)
m/Edward B. Claypoole

RAGS TO RICHES
m/Jerry Ross
w/Richard Adler

RAGTIME COWBOY JOE
m/Lewis F. Muir, Maurice Abrahams
w/Grant Clarke

RAGTIME DANCE, THE (instr.)
m/Scott Joplin

RAGTIME JOCKEY MAN
w&m/Irving Berlin

RAGTIME NIGHTINGALE
w&m/Joseph Frances Lamb

RAGTIME ORIOLE (instr.)
m/James S. Scott

RAGTIME VIOLIN
w&m/Irving Berlin

RAILROAD BLUES
w&m/Charles L. Roberts

RAIN FOREST
w&m/Archie Shepp

RAIN IN SPAIN, THE
m/Frederick Loewe
w/Alan Jay Lerner

RAIN ON THE ROOF
w&m/Ann Ronell

**RAIN, THE PARK AND OTHER
THINGS, THE**
w&m/Arthur Kornfeld, Al Duboff

RAINBOW CONNECTION
w&m/Paul Williams, Ken Ascher

RAINBOW IN YOUR EYES
w&m/Leon Russell

RAINBOW ON THE RIVER
m/Louis Alter
w&m/Paul Francis Webster

**RAINBOWS ALL OVER YOUR
BLUES**
w&m/John B. Sebastian

**RAINDROPS KEEP FALLIN' ON
MY HEAD**
m/Burt Bacharach
w/Hal David

RAINING IN MY HEART
w&m/Boudleaux Bryant, Felice
Bryant

RAINING IN MY HEART
w&m/Buddy Holly

RAINMAKER, THE (film score)
m/Alex North

RAINS CAME, THE
w&m/Doug Sahm

**RAINY DAY WOMAN NO. 12
& 35**
w&m/Robert Dylan

RAINY DAYS AND MONDAYS
w&m/Paul Williams, Roger Nichols

RAINY JANE
w&m/Neil Sedaka, Howard
Greenfield

RAINY NIGHT IN GEORGIA, A
w&m/Tony Joe White

RAINY NIGHT IN RIO, A
m/Arthur Schwartz
w/Leo Robin

RAISED ON ROBBERY
w&m/Joni Mitchell

RAISED ON ROCK
w&m/Mark James

**RAISIN IN THE SUN, A (film
score)**
m/Laurence Rosenthal

RAMBLIN' GAMBLIN' MAN
w&m/Bob Seger

RAMBLIN' MAN
w&m/Richard Betts

RAMBLIN' ROSE
m/Joe Sherman
w/Noel Sherman

RAMONA
m/Mabel Wayne
w/L. Wolfe Gilbert

RAMROD
w&m/Duane Eddy

RANGERS SONG, THE
m/Harry A. Tierney
w/Joseph McCarthy

**RAPSODIE ESPAGNOLE
(SPANISH RHAPSODY) (instr.)**
m/Maurice Ravel

RASHOMON (film score)
m/Laurence Rosenthal

RATED X
w&m/Loretta Lynn

RAUNCHY
w&m/William E. Justis Jr., Sidney
Manker

RAVE ON
w&m/Buddy Holly

RAVISHING RUBY
w&m/Tom T. Hall

RAY OF HOPE, A
w&m/Felix Cavaliere, Eddie Brigati

REACH OUT AND TOUCH
w&m/Valerie Simpson, Nicholas
Ashford

REACH OUT FOR ME
m/Burt Bacharach
w/Hal David

**REACH OUT YOUR HAND AND
TOUCH SOMEBODY**
w&m/Billy Sherrill, Tammy Wynette

REACHING FOR THE MOON
w&m/Irving Berlin

READY FOR THE 80'S
w&m/Jacques Morali

READY OR NOT
w&m/Jackson Browne

READY OR NOT
w&m/Herbie Hancock

REACH OUT I'LL BE THERE
w&m/Eddie Holland, Brian Holland,
Lamont Dozier

**READY TO TAKE A CHANCE
AGAIN**
m/Charles Fox
w/Norman Gimbel

REAL LIVE GIRL
m/Cy Coleman
w/Carolyn Leigh

REASON FOR WAITING
w&m/Ian Anderson

REASON TO BELIEVE
w&m/Tim Hardin

REASON TO BELIEVE
w&m/Rod Stewart

REASONS
w&m/Maurice White, Phillip Bailey,
Larry Dunn

**REBECCA OF SUNNYBROOK
FARM (film score)**
m/Hugo Friedhofer

**REBECCA OF SUNNYBROOK
FARM**
m/Albert Gumble /A. Seymour
Brown

REBEL ROUSER
w&m/Duane Eddy, Lee Hazlewood

REBIRTH (instr.)
m/McCoy Tyner

RECONSIDER ME
w&m/Margaret Lewis, Mira Smith

RED BADGE OF COURAGE, THE (film score)
m/Bronislau Kaper

RED CLAY
w&m/Freddie Hubbard

RED, HOT AND BLUE
w&m/Cole Porter

RED HOT MAMA
w&m/Fred Rose

RED NECK FRIEND
w&m/Jackson Browne

RED NECKS, WHITE SOCKS AND BLUE RIBBON BEER
w&m/Bob McDill, Wayland Holyfield, Chuck Neese

RED PONY, THE (film score)
m/Aaron Copland

RED RED WINE
w&m/Neil Diamond

RED ROSE RAG (instr.)
m/Percy Wenrich

RED ROSES FOR A BLUE LADY
w&m/Roy C. Bennett, Sid Tepper

RED SAILS IN THE SUNSET
m/Will Grosz (Hugh Williams)
w/Jimmy Kennedy

RED SILK STOCKINGS AND GREEN PERFUME
m/Sammy Mysels
w/Bob Hilliard

RED TOP
w&m/Lionel Hampton, Ben Kynard

RED WAGON
w&m/Richard M. Jones

RED WING
w&m/Frederick Allen (Kerry) Mills, Thurland Chattaway

REDWOOD TREE
w&m/Van Morrison

REELIN' AND ROCKIN'
w&m/Chuck Berry

REELIN' IN THE YEARS
w&m/Donald Fagen, Walter Becker

REFLECTION RAG (instr.)
m/Scott Joplin

REFLECTIONS
w&m/Eddie Holland, Brian Holland, Lamont Dozier

REFRAIN AUDACIOUS TAR
m/Sir Arthur Sullivan
w/Sir William Schwenk Gilbert

REFUGEE
w&m/Tom Petty, M. Campbell

REISENWEBER RAG
w&m/Original Dixieland Jazz Band
(see comoser listing under same)

REIVERS, THE (film score)
m/John Williams

RELAXING AT TOURO (instr.)
m/Muggsy Spanier

RELEASE ME
w&m/William E. Justis Jr., Sidney Manker

RELEASE ME
w&m/Eddie Miller, Dub Williams, Robert Yount

REMARK YOU MADE, A (instr.)
m/Joe Zawinul

REMEMBER
w&m/Irving Berlin

REMEMBER (WALKIN' IN THE SAND)
w&m/George "Shadow" Morton

REMEMBER BOY YOU'RE IRISH
w&m/William J. Scanlan

REMEMBER ME
m/Harry Warren
w/Al Dubin

REMEMBER PEARL HARBOR
m/Sammy Kaye
w/Don Reid

REMEMBERING
w&m/Jerry Reed

REMINISCING
w&m/Glenn Shorrock

RENEGADE
w&m/Tommy Shaw

REQUIEM FOR A HEAVYWEIGHT (film score)
m/Laurence Rosenthal

RESPECT
w&m/Otis Redding

RESTLESS FAREWELL
w&m/Robert Dylan

RETROSPECT
w&m/William Billings

RETURN OF SWEET LORRAINE, The
w&m/Joseph "Country Joe" McDonald

RETURN OF THE PRODIGAL SON, THE
w&m/Freddie Hubbard

RETURN TO SENDER
w&m/Otis Blackwell, Weinfield Scott

REUBEN, REUBEN I'VE BEEN THINKING
w&m/Percy Gaunt

REUNION IN VIENNA (film score)
m/William Axt

REUNITED
w&m/Frederick Perren, Dino Fekaris

REVEREND MR. BLACK
w&m/Billy Edd Wheeler

RHAPSODY IN BLUE (film score)
m/Ray John Heindorf

RHAPSODY IN WHITE
w&m/Barry White

RHAPSODY NEGRA (instr.)
m/Ernesto Lecuona

RHIANNON
w&m/Stephanie (Stevie) Nicks

RHINESTONE COWBOY
w&m/Larry Weiss

RHUMBA BOOGIE, THE
w&m/Hank Snow

RHUMBOOGIE
w&m/Don Raye, Hugh D. Prince

RHYTHM IS OUR BUSINESS
m/Saul Chaplin
w/Sammy Cahn

RHYTHM OF THE RAIN
w&m/John Gummoe

RHYTHM OF THE RAIN
w&m/Jack Meskill, Jack Stein

RICH AND RARE WERE THE GEMS SHE WORE
m/From the traditional Irish melody "The Summer is Coming"
w/Thomas Moore

RICH GIRL
w&m/Daryl Hall

RICHARD'S WINDOW (THEME FROM "THE OTHER SIDE OF THE MOUNTAIN")
w&m/Charles Fox, Norman Gimbel

RICHEST MAN IN THE WORLD, THE
w&m/Boudleaux Bryant

RICH YOUNG AND PRETTY (film score)
m/Nicholas Brodzsky

RIDE A WHITE SWAN
w&m/Marc Bolan

RIDE 'EM COWBOY
w&m/Paul Davis

RIDE MY SEE SAW
w&m/John Lodge

RIDE THE WILD SURF
w&m/Jan Berry, Roger Christian,
Brian Wilson

RIDERS IN THE SKY
w&m/Stan Jones

RIDIN' DOWN THE CANYON
m/Smiley Burnett
w/Gene Autry

RIDIN' HIGH
w&m/Cole Porter

RIDIN' THUMB
w&m/Dash Crofts, James Seals

RIFFIN' THE SCOTCH
w&m/Billie Holiday

RIFIFI (film score)
m/Georges Auric

RIFF SONG
m/Sigmund Romberg
w/Otto Harbach, Oscar
Hammerstein II

RIFFTIDE (instr.)
m/Coleman Hawkins

RIGHT AS THE RAIN
m/Harold Arlen
w/E. Y. Harburg

RIGHT BETWEEN THE EYES
w&m/Graham Nash

RIGHT DOWN THE LINE
w&m/Gerry Rafferty

RIGHT NOW (instr.)
m/Herbie Mann

**RIGHT ON THE TIP OF MY
TONGUE**
w&m/Van McCoy

RIGHT ON TIME
w&m/George Johnson, Louis
Johnson, Quincy Jones

RIGHT THING TO DO, THE
w&m/Carly Simon

**RIKKI DON'T LOSE THAT
NUMBER**
w&m/Donald Fagen, Walter Becker

RING DEM BELLS (instr.)
m/Duke Ellington

RING OF FIRE (film score)
m/Duane Eddy

RING OF FIRE
w&m/Merle Kilgore, June Carter
Cash

RING RING
m/Benny Andersson, Bjorn Ulvaeus
w/Stig Anderson

RING, RING THE BANJO
w&m/Stephen C. Foster

RING THE LIVING BELL
w&m/Melanie

RINGO
w&m/Don Robertson, Hal Blaine

RIO LOBO (film score)
m/Jerry Goldsmith

RIO RITA
m/Harry Tierney
w/Joseph McCarthy

**RIOT IN CELL BLOCK 11 (film
score)**
m/Herschel Burke Gilbert

RIP VAN WINKLE
w&m/Frank Pardo, Joseph Pardo
Robert Hovorka

RIPPLES OF THE NILE
w&m/Charles L. Roberts

RIPPLING WATERS (instr.)
m/Willie The Lion Smith

RISE
w&m/Randy Badazz, Andrew Armer

RISE AND SHINE
w&m/Carl Lee Perkins

RISE 'N' SHINE
m/Vincent Youmans
w/Buddy De Sylva

RISING ABOVE IT ALL
w&m/Bill Rice, Jerry Foster

**RISING EARLY IN THE
MORNING**
m/Sir Arthur Sullivan
w/Sir William Schwenk Gilbert

**RITUAL FIRE DANCE (From
"EL AMOR BRUJO") (instr.)**
m/Manuel De Falla

**RIVER STAY 'WAY FROM MY
DOOR**
m/Harry Woods
w/Mort Dixon

RIVER BOAT
w&m/Bill Anderson

RIVERBOAT SHUFFLE
m/Hoagy Carmichael
w/Michell Parish, Dick Voynow,
Irving Mills

**RIVER DEEP, MOUNTAIN
HIGH**
w&m/Phil Spector, Jeff Barry, Ellie
Greenwich

RIVERSIDE
w&m/Dewey Bunnell

RIVERSIDE BLUES
w&m/Thomas Andrew Dorsey

RIVERSIDE BLUES
w&m/Richard M. Jones

ROADRUNNER
w&m/Ellas McDaniel (Bo Diddley)

ROAD RUNNER (I'M A)
w&m/Eddie Holland, Brian Holland
Lamont Dozier

ROAD TO GLORY (film score)
m/Louis Silvers

ROAD TO MOROCCO
m/James Van Heusen
w/Johnny Burke

ROAD TO RIO, THE (film score
m/Robert Emmett Dolan

ROAMIN' IN THE GLOAMIN'
w&m/Sir Harry Lauder, Frank Folley

ROANOKE (instr.)
m/William Smith Monroe

ROBE, THE (film score)
m/Alfred Newman

ROBIN ADAIR
m/From traditional Irish song
"Eileen Aroon"
w/Lady Caroline Keppel

ROBIN HOOD
w&m/Carl Sigman

ROBIN'S SONG
w&m/Chuck Barris

ROCK AND ROLL ALL NITE
w&m/Paul Stanley, Gene Simmons

ROCK & ROLL BOOGIE (instr.)
m/Pete Johnson

ROCK & ROLL HOOCHIE KOO
w&m/Rick Derringer

ROCK AND ROLL LULLABY
w&m/Barry Mann, Cynthia Weil

ROCK AND ROLL MADONNA
m/Elton John
w/Bernie Taupin

**ROCK AND ROLL MUSIC TO
THE WORLD**
w&m/Alvin Lee

ROCK AND ROLL WALTZ, THE
w&m/Dick Ware, Shorty Allan

ROCK AND ROLL WOMAN
w&m/Stephen Stills

ROCK AROUND THE CLOCK
m/Jimmy De Knight (James E.
Meyers)
w/Max C. Freedman

ROCK CITY BOOGIE
w&m/Joe Allison

ROCK IT BOOGIE (instr.)
m/Pete Johnson

ROCK ME
w&m/Thomas Andrew Dorsey

ROCK ME
w&m/Muddy Waters

ROCK ME ALL NIGHT LONG
w&m/Jimmy Ricks, Billy Sandford

ROCK ME GENTLY
w&m/Andy Kim

ROCK ME MAMA
w&m/Arthur Crudup

ROCK ME ON THE WATER
w&m/Jackson Browne

ROCK OF AGES
m/Thomas Hastings
w/Augustus Montague Toplady

ROCK OF THE WESTIES
m/Elton John
w/Bernie Taupin

ROCK STEADY
w&m/Aretha Franklin

ROCKABYE YOUR BABY WITH A DIXIE MELODY
m/Jean Schwartz
w/Samuel M. Lewis, Joseph Young

ROCKET RIDE
w&m/Paul "Ace" Frehley, Sean Delaney

ROCK 'N' ROLL HEAVEN
w&m/Alan O' Day

ROCK ON
w&m/David Essex, Jeff Wayne

ROCK WITH YOU
w&m/Rod Temperton

ROCK-A-BYE BABY (ON THE TREE TOP)
w&m/Effie I. Canning

ROCK-A-BYE YOUR BABY BLUES
m/Billy Hill
w/Larry Yoell

ROCKABYE YOUR BABY WITH A DIXIE MELODY
m/Jean Schwartz
w/Samuel M. Lewis, Joseph Young

ROCKER (instr.)
m/Gerry Mulligan

ROCKET MAN
m/Elton John
w/Bernie Taupin

ROCKFORD FILES
m/Mike Post

ROCKIN' AND ROLLIN'
w&m/Chuck Berry

ROCKIN' AROUND THE CHRISTMAS TREE
w&m/John D. Marks

ROCKIN' BLUES
w&m/Johnny Otis

ROCKIN' CHAIR
w&m/Hoagy Carmichael

ROCKIN' GOOD WAY, A
w&m/Brook Benton, Clyde Otis, Gladyces De Jesus

ROCKIN' IN RHYTHM (instr.)
m/Duke Ellington

ROCKIN' ROBIN
w&m/Jimmie Thomas

ROCKIN' ROLL BABY
w&m/Thomas Bell, Linda Creed

ROCKIN' THE CLOCK (instr.)
m/Meade "Lux" Lewis

ROCK'n ME
w&m/Steve Miller

ROCK 'N' ROLL MUSIC
w&m/Chuck Berry

ROCK 'N' ROLL NIGGER
w&m/Patti Smith

ROCK 'N' SUICIDE
w&m/David Bowie

ROCKS IN MY BED (instr.)
m/Duke Ellington

ROCKY MOUNTAIN HIGH
w&m/John Denver

ROCKY MOUNTAIN MUSIC
w&m/Eddie Rabbitt

ROCKY MOUNTAIN WAY
w&m/Joseph F. Walsh, Joe Vitale, Ken Passerelli, Rocke Groce

ROCKY TOP
w&m/Boudleaux Bryant, Felice Bryant

ROGUE SONG, THE
m/Herbert Stothart
w/Clifford Grey

ROLL ALONG COVERED WAGON
w&m/Jimmy Kennedy

ROLL ALONG PRAIRIE MOON
w&m/Albert Von Tilzer, Cecil Mack (Richard C. McPherson) Ted Fiorito

ROLL ANOTHER NUMBER
w&m/Neil Young

ROLL AWAY THE STONE
w&m/Leon Russell, G. Dempsey

ROLL MUDDY RIVER
w&m/Betty Sue Perry

ROLL OUT, HEAVE THAT COTTON
w&m/William Shakespeare Hays

ROLL OVER BEETHOVEN
w&m/Chuck Berry

ROLL 'EM (instr.)
m/Mary Lou Williams

ROLLER SKATIN' MATE
w&m/Frederick Perren, Dino Fekaris

ROLLIN' IN MY SWEET BABY'S ARMS
w&m/Buck Owens

ROLLER COASTER
w&m/Mark James

ROLLER COASTER
w&m/Natalie Cole

ROLLIN' STONE
w&m/Muddy Waters

ROLLIN' WITH THE FLOW
w&m/Jerry Hayes

ROLY POLY
w&m/Fred Rose

ROMAN HOLIDAY (film score)
m/Georges Auric

ROMANCE
m/Sigmund Romberg
w/Otto Harbach, Oscar Hammerstein II

ROMANCE IN THE DARK
w&m/Lil Green

ROMANCE RUNS IN THE FAMILY
w&m/Al Hoffman, Al Goodhart, Mann Curtis

ROMANTIC GUY, I, A
w&m/Francis H. Stanton, Del Sharbutt

ROMANTIC WARRIOR (instr.)
m/Chick Corea

ROMEO'S TUNE
w&m/Steve Forbert

ROOM FULL OF ROSES
w&m/Tim Spencer

ROOM WITHOUT WINDOWS, A
w&m/Ervin M. Drake

ROOMIN' HOUSE BOOGIE
w&m/Jessie Mae Robinson

ROOSEVELT AND IRA LEE
w&m/Tony Joe White

ROOTS (Theme From) (TV instr.)
m/Gerald Fried

ROOTS (TV score)
m/Quincy Jones (main theme by Gerald Fried, as above)

ROOTS, ROCK, REGGAE
w&m/Bob Marley

ROSALIE
w&m/Cole Porter

ROSALIE THE PRAIRIE FLOWER
w&m/George Frederick Root

ROSALINDA'S EYES
w&m/Billy Joel

ROSALITA
w&m/Al Dexter

ROSALITA (COME OUT TONIGHT)
w&m/Bruce Springsteen

ROSARY, THE
m/Ethelbert W. Nevin
w/Robert C. Rogers

ROSE AND A BABY RUTH, A
w&m/John D. Loudermilk

ROSE, THE
w&m/Amanda McBroom

(I NEVER PROMISED YOU A) ROSE GARDEN
w&m/Joe South

ROSE LEAF RAG (instr.)
m/Scott Joplin

ROSE-MARIE
m/Rudolf Friml
w/Otto Harbach, Oscar Hammerstein II

ROSEMARY
w&m/Antoine "Fats" Domino, Dave Bartholomew

ROSE O'DAY (THE FILLA-GA-DUSHA SONG)
w&m/Charles Tobias, Al Lewis

ROSE OF NO MAN'S LAND
m/James Alexander Brennan
w/Jack Caddingan

ROSE OF WASHINGTON SQUARE
m/James F. Hanley
w/Ballard MacDonald

ROSE TATOO, THE (film score)
m/Alex North

ROSES ARE RED
w&m/Paul Evans, Al Bryon

ROSES IN THE RAIN
m/Neil Moret
w/Richard A. Whiting

ROSES IN THE RAIN
m/Irving Melsher
w/Remus Harris

ROSES IN THE RAIN
m/Albert Frisch
w/Fred Wise

ROSES OF PICARDY
m/Haydn Wood
w/Frederick E. Weatherly

ROSETIME AND YOU
m/Charles L. Roberts
w/Alex Rogers

ROSETTA (instr.)
m/Earl (Fatha) Hines

ROSIE THE RIVETER
w&m/Redd Evans, John J. Loeb

ROTATION
w&m/Randy Badazz, Andrew Armer

ROUND AND ROUND
w&m/Lou Stallman, Joseph Shapiro

ROUND MIDNIGHT (instr.)
m/John Coltrane

ROUNDABOUT
m/Vernon Duke
w/Ogden Nash

ROUTE 66
w&m/Bobby Troup

ROVING KIND, THE
w&m/Jessie Cavanaugh, Arnold Stanton (music adapted from old English folk song known as "The Rakish Kind" or "The Pirate Ship")

ROW ROW ROW
m/James V. Monaco
w/William Jerome

ROXY ROLLER
w&m/Nick Gilder, James McCulloch

ROYAL GARDEN BLUES (instr.)
w&m/Clarence Williams

ROYAL SCAM
w&m/Donald Fagen, Walter Becker

RUB IT IN
w&m/Layng Martine

RUBBER BULLETS
w&m/Lol Creme, Graham Gouldman

RUBBER DUCKIE
w&m/Joseph Raposo

RUBY
m/M. Roamheld
w/Mitchell Parish

RUBY AND THE PEARL, THE
w&m/Ray Evans, Jay H. Livingston

RUBY, DON'T TAKE YOUR LOVE TO TOWN
w&m/Mel Tillis

RUBY TUESDAY
w&m/Mick Jagger, Keith Richard

RUDOLPH THE RED NOSED REINDEER
w&m/John D. Marks

RUFENREDDY (instr.)
m/Roy Frederick Bargy

RUM AND COCA-COLA
w&m/Morey Amsterdam

RUMOR, THE
w&m/J. Robbie Robertson

RUMORS
w&m/Helen Miller, Roger Atkins

RUMORS ARE FLYING
m/Bennie Benjamin
w/George D. Weiss

RUMORS
w&m/Neil Sedaka, Howard Greenfield

RUMOURHAS IT
w&m/Donna Summer, Georgio Moroder, Pete Bellotte

RUMPUS IN RICHMOND (instr.)
m/Duke Ellington

RUN LIKE HELL
w&m/Roger Waters, David Gilmour

RUN RUN RUN
w&m/Jay Ferguson, Mark Andes

RUN THROUGH THE JUNGLE
w&m/John C. Fogerty

RUN TO HIM
w&m/Gerry Goffin, Jack Keller

RUN TO ME
w&m/Barry, Maurice and Robin Gibb

RUNAROUND SUE
w&m/Dion Di Mucci, Robert Schwartz, Ernest Maresca

RUNAWAY
w&m/Del Shannon, Max T. Crook

RUNAWAY BLUES
w&m/Gertrude "Ma" Rainey

RUNNIN' AWAY
w&m/Sly Stone

RUNNIN' FOR YOUR LOVIN'
w&m/George Johnson, Louis Johnson

RUNNIN' WILD
m/A. Harrington Gibbs, James P. Johnson
w/Joseph W. Grey, Leo Wood

RUNNING BEAR
w&m/J. P. Richardson (Big Bopper)

RUNNING ON EMPTY
w&m/Jackson Browne

RUNNING SCARED
w&m/Roy Orbison, Joe Melson

RUSSIAN LULLABY
w&m/Irving Berlin

RUSSIAN RAG
m/George L. Cobb (instr.)
(music adapted from Rachmaninoff Prelude, Po. 3, No. 2)

**RUSSIANS ARE COMING, THE,
THE RUSSIANS ARE COMING**

(film score)

m/Johnny Mandel

**RUSTLE OF SPRING (instr.)
(FRUHLINGSTRAUSCHEN)**
m/Christian Sinding

RYAN'S DAUGHTER (film score)
m/Maurice Jarre

Addenda:

ROYAL MILE, THE
w&m/Gerry Rafferty

 **SONGS**

S

SABRE AND SPURS (march)
m/John Philip Sousa

SABRE DANCE (instr.)
m/Aram Ilyich Khachaturian (from the "Gayne Ballet")

SACK OF WOE (instr.)
m/Julian (Cannonball) Adderly

SAD CAFE
w&m/Glenn Frey, Don Henley

SAD EYES
w&m/Robert John

SAD MOVIES (MAKE ME CRY)
w&m/John D. Loudermilk

SADIE SALOME, GO HOME
m/Irving Berlin
w/Edgar Leslie

SAFE IN THE ARMS OF JESUS
m/W. H. Doane
w/Fanny Crosby Van Alstyne

SAGA OF JENNY, THE
m/Kurt Weill
w/Ira Gershwin

SAGINAW, MICHIGAN
w&m/Bill Anderson

SAIL ALONG SILV'RY MOON
m/Percy Wenrich
w/Harry Tobias

SAIL AWAY
w&m/Noel Coward

SAIL AWAY
w&m/Randy Newman

SAIL ON
w&m/Lionel Richie

SAILBOAT IN THE MOONLIGHT. A
w&m/John Jacob Loeb, Carmen Lombardo

SAILIN' AWAY ON THE HENRY CLAY
m/Egbert Van Alstyne
w/Gus Kahn

SAILING ON THE LAKE
w&m/David Braham

ST. CHARLES
w&m/Paul Kantner, Craig Chaquico, Jesse Barish Thunderhawk

ST. DOMINIE'S PREVIEW
w&m/Van Morrison

ST. JAMES INFIRMARY
w&m/Joe Primrose

ST. LOUIS
w&m/Harry Vanda, George Young

ST. LOUIS BLUES
w&m/W. C. Handy

ST. THOMAS (instr.)
m/Sonny Rollins

SALLY
m/Jerome Kern
w/Clifford Grey

SALLY G
w&m/Paul and Linda McCartney

SALLY IN OUR ALLEY
w&m/Henry Carey

SALLY IN OUR ALLEY
m/Ludwig Englander
w/George V. Hobart

SALLY WON'T COME BACK
m/David Stamper
w/Gene Buck

SAL'S GOT A SUGAR LIP
w&m/Jimmy Driftwood

SALTY PAPA BLUES
w&m/Leonard Feather, Lionel Hampton

SALUD DINERO Y AMOR
m/Rodolfo Sciammarella
w/Al Stillman

SAM HILL
w&m/Merle Haggard

SÁMA LAYUCA (instr.)
m/McCoy Tyner

SAME OLD STORY, THE
m/Ludwig Englander
w/Harry B. Smith

SAM'S PLACE
w&m/Buck Owens

SAM'S SONG
w&m/Lew Quadling, Jack Elliott

SAN ANTONIO
m/Egbert Van Alstyne
w/Harry Williams

SAN ANTONIO ROSE
w&m/Bob Wills

SAN FERNANDO VALLEY
w&m/Gordon Jenkins

SAN FRANCISCO (film score)
m/Bronislau Kaper

SAN FRANCISCO
m/Bronislau Kaper, Walter Jurmann
w/Gus Kahn

SAN FRANCISCO (BE SURE TO WEAR FLOWERS IN YOUR HAIR)
w&m/John Phillips

SAN FRANCISCO DUES
w&m/Chuck Berry

SAND IN MY SHOES
m/Victor Schertizinger
w/Frank Loesser

SAND PEBBLES, THE (film score)
m/Jerry Goldsmith

SANDMAN
w&m/Dewey Bunnell

SANDPIPER, THE (film score)
m/Johnny Mandel

SANDS OF THE KALAMARI (film score)
m/John Dankworth

SANDY
w&m/Dion Di Mucci, Steve Brandt

SANFORD AND SON (TV theme)
m/Quincy Jones

SANTA BABY
m/Philip Springer
w/Joan Javits, Tony Springer

SANTA CLAUS IS COMING TO TOWN
m/J. Fred Coots
w/Haven Gillespie

SANTA CLAUS IS RIDING THE TRAIL
w&m/Jack Meskill, Archie Gottler

SANTA LUCIA
m/Teodoro Cottrau
w/Earliest English words: Thomas Oliphant/Teodoro Cottrau, Italian words)

SARA
w&m/Stephanie (Stevie) Nicks

SARA SMILE
w&m/John Oates, Daryl Hall

SARABAND (instr.)
m/Leroy Anderson

SATAN TAKES A HOLIDAY
w&m/Larry Clinton

SATCHEL MOUTH SWING (instr.)
m/Louis Armstrong

SATIN DOLL
m/Duke Ellington, Billy Strayhorn
w/Johnny Mercer

(CAN'T GET NO) SATISFACTION
w&m/Mick Jagger, Keith Richard

SATISFIED
w&m/Martha Carson

SATISFIED MAN, A
w&m/J. H. (Red) Hayes, Jack Rhodes

SATISFIED MAN, A
w&m/Bill Rice, Jerry Foster

SATURDAY IN THE PARK
w&m/Robert Lamm

**SATURDAY MORNING
CONFUSION**
w&m/Bobby Russell

**SATURDAY NIGHT AT THE
MOVIES**
w&m/Barry Mann, Cynthia Weil

**SATURDAY NIGHT AT THE
WORLD (instr.)**
m/Mason Williams

SATURDAY NIGHT FISH FRY
w&m/Louis Jordan, Ellis Walsh

**SATURDAY NIGHT FUNCTION
(instr.)**
m/Duke Ellington

**SATURDAY NIGHT IN THE
SUMMERTIME**
w&m/Joel Hirschhorn, Al Kasha

**SATURDAY NIGHT IS THE
LONELIEST NIGHT IN THE
WEEK**
m/Jule Styne
w&m/Sammy Cahn

SATURDAY NIGHT SPECIAL
w&m/Ronald Wayne Van Zant,
Garry Rossington, Larken Allen
Collins

SATURDAY NIGHT'S ALRIGHT
m/Elton John
w/Bernie Taupin

SATURDAY NITE
w&m/Maurice White, Phillip Bailey,
Al McKay

SAVE IT FOR A RAINY DAY
w&m/Stephen Bishop

SAVE IT PRETTY MAMA
w&m/Don Redman

SAVE ME A PLACE
w&m/Lindsay Buckingham

SAVE THE COUNTRY
w&m/Laura Nyro

**SAVE THE LAST DANCE FOR
ME**
w&m/Doc (Jerome) Pomus, Mort
Shuman

SAVE YOUR SUGAR FOR ME
w&m/Tony Joe White

SAWMILL
w&m/Mel Tillis, Horace Whatley

**SAY HAS ANYBODY SEEN MY
SWEET GYPSY ROSE**
w&m/Irwin Levine, L. Russell Brown

SAY I AM
w&m/Tommy Jones, Bob King

SAY IT AGAIN
w&m/Bob McDill

**SAY IT LOUD, I'M BLACK AND
I'M PROUD**
w&m/James Brown

SAY IT ISN'T SO
w&m/Irving Berlin

SAY IT WITH FLOWERS
w&m/Albert Von Tilzer, Neville
Fleeson

SAY IT WITH MUSIC
w&m/Irving Berlin

SAY MAN
w&m/Ellas McDaniel (Bo Diddley)

**SAY, ONE (IS A LONELY
NUMBER)**
w&m/Jerry Goldstein, Louis Peceres

SAY SI SI
m/Ernesto Lecuona
w/Al Stillman, Frances Luban

SAY YOU LOVE ME
w&m/Christine Perfect McVie

**SAY YOU'LL STAY UNTIL
TOMORROW**
w&m/Roger Greenaway, Roger Cook

SAYONARA
w&m/Irving Berlin

SAYS MY HEART
m/Burton Lane
w/Frank Loesser

**SCARBOROUGH FAIR/
CANTICLE**
w&m/Paul Simon

SCARLET RIBBONS
m/Evelyn Danzig (Mrs. Manuel W.
Levine)
w/Jack Segal

SCATTER BRAIN
m/Frankie Masters, Keene-Bear
w/Johnny Burke

SCAVENGER HUNT (film score)
m/Billy Goldenberg

SCHÖN ROSMARIN (instr.)
m/Fritz Kreisler

SCHOOL DAYS
m/Gus Edwards
w/Will D. Cobb

SCHOOL'S OUT
w&m/Michael Bruce, Vincent
Furnier

SCOTLAND (instr.)
m/William S. Monroe

SCOTTSBORO BLUES
w&m/Huddie (leadbelly) Ledbetter

**SCRATCHIN' IN THE GRAVEL
(instr.)**
m/Mary Lou Williams

SCREAMIN' AND CRYIN'
w&m/Muddy Waters

SEA HAWK, THE (film score)
m/Erich Wolfgang Korngold

SEA OF HEARTBREAK
w&m/Don Gibson

SEARCHLIGHT RAG (instr.)
m/Scott Joplin

**(I'VE BEEN) SEARCHIN' SO
LONG**
w&m/James Pankow

SEASONS
w&m/Steve Miller, Ben Sidran

**SEASONS IN THE SUN (LE
MORIBOND)**
m/Jacques Brel
w/Rod McKuen (English words)
Jacques Brel (French Words)

SECRET AGENT MAN
w&m/P. F. Sloan, Steve Barri

SECRET LOVE
m/Sammy Fain
w/Paul Francis Webster

SECOND CHORUS
m/Andre Previn
w/Dory Langdon Previn

SECOND HAND EMOTION
w&m/Rory Bourke, Charlie Black

SECOND HAND NEWS
w&m/Lindsay Buckingham

SECOND HAND ROSE
m/James F. Hanley
w/Grant Clarke

**SECOND HAND ROSE
(SECOND HAND HEART)**
w&m/Harlan Howard

SECOND TIME AROUND, THE
m/James Van Heusen
w/Sammy Cahn

**SECRET LIFE OF WALTER
MITTY, THE (film score)**
m/David Raksin

SEESAW
w&m/Steve Cropper, Don Covay

SEE SEE RIDER BLUES
w&m/Gertrude "Ma" Rainey

**SEE WHAT THE BOYS IN THE
BACK ROOM WILL HAVE**
m/Frederick Hollander
w/Frank Loesser

SEE YOU IN SEPTEMBER
m/Sherman Edwards
w/Sid Wayne

SEE YOU LATER ALLIGATOR
w&m/Robert Guidry

SEE YOU WHEN I GET THERE
w&m/Kenneth Gamble, Leon Huff

SEEKER, THE
w&m/Dolly Parton

SEEMS LIKE OLD TIMES
w&m/John Jacob Loeb, Carmen Lombardo

SEMPER FIDELIS (march)
m/John Philip Sousa

SEMPER PARATUS (official U.S. Coast Guard song)
w&m/Francis Saltus Van Boskerck

SEND IN THE CLOWNS
w&m/Stephen Sondheim

SEND ME AWAY WITH A SMILE
m/Al Piantadosi
w/Louis Weslyn

SEND ME NO WINE
w&m/John Lodge

SEND ME THE PILLOW YOU DREAM ON
w&m/Hank Locklin

SEND ONE YOUR LOVE
w&m/Stevie Wonder

SENSATION
w&m/Original Dixie Land Jazz Band (see composer listing under same)

SENT FOR YOU YESTERDAY, AND HERE YOU COME TODAY
w&m/Eddie Durham, James A. Rushing

SENTIMENTAL JOURNEY
m/Les Brown, Ben Homer
w/Bud Green

SENTIMENTAL ME
w&m/James T. Morehead, Jimmy Cassin

SENTIMENTAL RHAPSODY
m/Alfred Newman
w/Harold Adamson

SENTIMENTAL LADY
w&m/Bob Welch

SEPTEMBER
w&m/Maurice White, Allee Willis, Alan McKay

SEPTEMBER IN THE RAIN
m/Harry Warren
w/Al Dubin

SEPTEMBER MORN'
w&m/Neil Diamond, Gilbert Becaud

SEPTEMBER OF MY YEARS
m/James Van Heusen
w/Sammy Cahn

SEPTEMBER SONG
m/Kurt Weill
w/Maxwell Anderson

SERENADE
m/Sigmund Romberg
w/Dorothy Donnelly

SERENADE (from "Les Millions d'Arlequin")
m/Riccardo Drigo

SERENADE (SERENATA, OP. 6, NO. 1)
m/Enrico Toselli
w/Sigmund Spaeth

SERENADE FOR A WEALTHY WIDOW
w&m/Stuff Smith

SERENADE IN BLUE
m/Harry Warren
w/Mack Gordon

SERENADE OF THE BELLS
w&m/Kay Twomey, Al Goodhart

SERENATA
m/Leroy Anderson
w/Mitchell Parish

SERPENTINE FIRE
w&m/Maurice White, Verdine White, Sonny Burke

SET HIM FREE
w&m/Marie Wilson, Mary DePew, Helen Moyers

SET ME FREE
w&m/Raymond Douglas Davies

SETTING THE WOODS ON FIRE
w&m/Ed. G. Nelson, Fred Rose

SEVEN BRIDES FOR SEVEN BROTHERS (film score)
m/Adolph Deutsch

SEVEN COME ELEVEN (instr.)
m/Charlie Christian

SEVEN DAYS IN MAY (film score)
m/Jerry Goldsmith

SEVEN DAYS TO NOON
m/John Addison

SEVEN LITTLE GIRLS (SITTING IN THE BACK SEAT)
m/Lee J. Pockriss, Bob Hilliard

SEVEN LONG DAYS
w&m/Jessie Mae Robinson

SEVEN ROOMS OF GLOOM
w&m/Eddie Holland, Brian Holland, Lamont Dozier

SEVEN STEPS TO HEAVEN (instr.)
m/Miles Dewey Davis

720 IN THE BOOKS
m/Jan Savitt
w/Harold Adamson

SEVENTH HEAVEN (film score)
m/Louis Silvers

77 SUNSET STRIP
m/Jerry Livingston
w/Mack David

SEVENTY SIX TROMBONES
w&m/Meredith Willson

SEXY WAYS
w&m/Hank Ballard

SEXY DANCER
w&m/Prince

SHADOWS OF A DOUBT (A COMPLEX KID)
w&m/Tom Petty

SHADOW OF YOUR SMILE, THE
m/Johnny Mandel
w/Paul Francis Webster

SHADOW WALTZ
m/Harry Warren
w/Al Dubin

SHADOW WALTZ, THE (instr.)
w&m/Sonny Rollins

SHADOWLAND (instr.)
m/Lawrence B. Gilbert

SHADOWS (film score)
m/Charles Mingus

SHADOWS
w&m/Barry De Vorzon

SHADOWS IN THE MOONLIGHT
w&m/Rory Bourke, Charlie Black

"SHAFT," THEME FROM
w&m/Isaac Hayes

SHAKE
w&m/Sam Cooke

SHAKE ME, WAKE ME (WHEN IT'S OVER)
w&m/Eddie Holland, Brian Holland, Lamont Dozier

SHAKE RATTLE AND ROLL
w&m/Charles Calhoun

(SHAKE, SHAKE, SHAKE) SHAKE YOUR BOOTY
w&m/Harry Wayne Casey, Richard Finch

SHAKE YOUR GROOVE THING
w&m/Frederick Perren, Dino Fekaris

SHAKIN' ALL OVER
w&m/Peter Townshend

SHAKING THE BLUES AWAY
w&m/Irving Berlin

SHAKY GROUND
w&m/Phoebe Snow

SHA-LA-LA MAKE ME HAPPY
w&m/Al Green

SHALL WE DANCE
m/George Gershwin
w/Ira Gershwin

SHALL WE DANCE
m/Richard Rodgers
w/Oscar Hammerstein II

SHALOM
w&m/Jerry Herman

SHAMBALA
w&m/Danny Moore

SHAME, SHAME
w&m/Albert L. Hammond, Mike
Hazelwood

SHAME, SHAME, SHAME
w&m/Sylvia V. Robinson

SHANGRI LA
m/Matt Malneck, Robert Maxwell
w/Carl Sigman

SHANNON
w&m/Henry Gross

**SHANTY IN OLD SHANTY
TOWN, A**
w&m/Ira Schuster, Joseph Young,
Little Jack Little

SHAPE I'M IN, THE
w&m/J. Robbie Robertson

**SHAPE OF THINGS TO
COME, THE**
w&m/Barry Mann, Cynthia Weil

SHARE THE LAND
w&m/Burton Cummings
SHARING
w&m/Steve Pippin, Larry Keith,
Johnny Slate
SHARKS (film score)
m/Alex North

SHAVE 'EM DRY BLUES
w&m/Gertrude "Ma" Rainey

SHAW NUFF(instr.)
m/Dizzy Gillespie

SHAZAM
w&m/Duane Eddy

**SH-BOOM, LIFE COULD BE A
DREAM**
w&m/Carl Feaster, James Kerp,
Floyd McCrae, William Edwards

SHE AIN'T GOT NO HAIR
w&m/Henry R. Byrd

SHE BELIEVES IN ME
w&m/Steve Gibb

SHE BELONGS TO ME
w&m/Robert Dylan

SHE CALLED ME BABY
w&m/Harlan Howard

SHE DID IT
w&m/Eric Carmen

SHE DIDN'T SAY YES
m/Jerome Kern
w/Otto Harbach

**SHE EVEN WOKE ME UP TO
SAY GOODBYE**
w&m/Mickey Newbury

SHE IS MA DAISY
w&m/Sir Harry Lauder, Frank Folley

**SHE IS MORE TO BE PITIED
THAN CENSURED**
w&m/William B. Gray

**SHE IS THE SUNSHINE OF
VIRGINIA**
m/Harry Carroll
w/Ballard MacDonald

SHE LOVES ME
m/Jerry Bock
w/Sheldon Harnick

**SHE MAY HAVE SEEN BETTER
DAYS**
w&m/James Thornton

SHE NEVER KNEW ME
w&m/Bob McDill, Wayland
Holyfield

SHE REMINDS ME OF YOU
m/Harry Revel
w/Mack Gordon

SHE SAY OOM DOOBY DOOM
w&m/Barry Mann

**SHE SELLS SEA SHELLS (THE
BEAUTY SHOP)**
m/Harry M. Gifford
w/Terry Sullivan

SHE THINKS I STILL CARE
w&m/Dickey Lee

SHE WENT TO THE CITY
w&m/Paul Dresser

**SHE WORE A YELLOW RIBBON
(film score)**m/Richard Hageman

SHEIK OF ARABY, THE
m/Ted Snyder
w/Harry B. Smith, Francis Wheeler

SHEILA
w&m/Tommy Roe

SHERRY
w&m/Bob Gaudio

SHE'S A LADY
w&m/John B. Sebastian

**SHE'S A LATIN FROM
MANHATTAN**
m/Harry Warren
w/Al Dubin

SHE'S A LITTLE BIT COUNTRY
w&m/Harlan Howard

SHE'S ABOUT A MOVER
w&m/Doug Sahm

SHE'S ALL WOMAN
w&m/Thomas Bell, Linda Creed

SHE'S ALWAYS A WOMAN
w&m/Billy Joel

SHE'S ALL I GOT
w&m/Gary U.S. Bonds, Jerry
Williams, Jr.

SHE'S FUNNY THAT WAY
w&m/Charles Neil Daniels (Neil
Moret), Richard Whiting

SHE'S GONE
w&m/Daryl Hall, John Oates

SHE'S GOT YOU
w&m/Hank Cochran

SHE'S IN LOVE WITH YOU
w&m/Mike Chapman, Nicky Chinn

SHE'S LEAVING HOME
w&m/Paul McCartney, John Lennon

**SHE'S NOT JUST ANOTHER
WOMAN**
w&m/Ronald Dunbar, Clyde D.
Wilson

SHE'S NOT THERE
w&m/Rodney Argent

SHIEK OF ARABY, THE
m/Ted Snyder
w/Harry B. Smith

SHILO
w&m/Neil Diamond

S-H-I-N-E
m/Ford Dabney
w/Cecil Mack

SHINE ON HARVEST MOON
w&m/Jack Norworth, Nora Bayes

SHINE ON YOUR SHOES, A
m/Arthur Schwartz
w/Howard Dietz

SHINE THE LIVING LIGHT
w&m/Melanie

SHINING STAR
w&m/Maurice White, Phillip Bailey,
Larry Dunn

SHIP OF FOOLS (film score)
m/Ernest Gold

SHIP WITHOUT A SAIL, A
m/Richard Rodgers
w/Lorenz (Larry) Hart

SHIPS
w&m/Ian Hunter

SHOE SHINE BOY
m/Saul Chaplin
w/Sammy Cahn

SHOE STRING RAG (instr.)
m/David Alan Jasen

**SHOES OF THE FISHERMAN,
THE (film score)**
m/Alex North

**SHOO FLY, (SHEW! FLY) DON'T
BOTHER ME**
m/Frank Campbell
w/Billy Reeves

SHOO SHOO BABY
w&m/Phil Moore

**SHOOFLY PIE AND APPLE PAN
DOWDY**
m/Guy Wood
w/Sammy Gallop

**SHOOP SHOOP SONG (IT'S IN
HIS KISS)**
w&m/Rudy Clark

SHOP AROUND
w&m/Berry Gordy Jr., William
"Smokey" Robinson Jr.

**SHOP AROUND THE CORNER,
THE (film score)**
m/Werner Heyman

SHORT FAT FANNIE
w&m/Larry Williams

SHORT ON LOVE
w&m/John D. Loudermilk

SHORT PEOPLE
w&m/Randy Newman

SHORT SHORTS
w&m/Bob Gaudio, Thomas Austin,
Bill Crandall, Bill Dalton

SHORT STOP (instr.)
m/Shorty Rogers

SHORT'NIN' BREAD
w&m/Jacques Wolfe

SHORTY GEORGE (instr.)
m/William (Count) Basie, Albert
(Andy) Gibson, Harry Edison

**SHOT IN THE DARK, A
(film score)**
m/Henry Mancini

SHOTGUN
w&m/Autry De Walt

SHOULD I REVEAL
m/Nacio Herb Brown
w/Arthur Freed

**SHOULD'VE NEVER HAVE
LET HIM GO**
w&m/Neil Sedaka, Phillip Cody

SHOULD WE TELL HIM
w&m/Don Everly, Phil Everly

SHOULDER TO CRY ON, A
w&m/Merle Haggard

SHOOT
w&m/O'Kelly Isley, Rudolph Isley,
Ronald Isley

SHOUT SISTER SHOUT
w&m/Clarence Williams

SHOUT SISTER SHOUT
w&m/Arthur Crudup

SHOWDOWN
w&m/Jeff Lynne

SHOW ME
w&m/Joe Tex

SHOW-ME RAG, THE (instr.)
m/Trebor Jay Tichenor

SHOW ME THE WAY
w&m/Peter Frampton

**SHOW ME THE WAY TO GO
HOME**
w&m/Irving King

SHOW MUST GO ON, THE
w&m/Leo Sayer, David Courtney

SHOWER THE PEOPLE
w&m/James Taylor

SHRINE OF ST. CECELIA, THE
w&m/Carroll Loveday

SHUFFLE ALONG
m/Eubie Blake
w/Noble Sissle

SHUFFLE OFF TO BUFFALO
m/Harry Warren
w/Al Dubin

SHY AND SLY
w&m/Charles L. Robert

SI, PERO NO
w&m/Moncada and Paco Cepero

SIAM
m/Fred Fisher
w/Howard E. Johnson

SIBONEY
m/Ernesto Lecuona
w/Theodora (Dolly) Morse

SIBYL
m/Victor Jacobi
w/Harry B. Smith, Harry Graham

SICK CITY
m/Elton John
w/Bernie Taupin

SIDE BY SIDE
m/Harry Woods
w/Gus Kahn

SIDE BY SIDE
w&m/Stephen Sondheim

SIDEWALK BLUES (instr.)
m/Ferdinand (Jelly Roll) Morton

SIDEWALK HOBO
w&m/Tony Joe White

**SIDEWALKS OF NEW YORK,
THE**
w&m/Charles B. Lawlor, James W.
Blake

SIDEWINDER, THE (instr.)
m/Lee Morgan

SIGH, CRY, ALMOST DIE
w&m/Don Everly, Phil Everly

**SIGNED SEALED AND
DELIVERED**
w&m/Cowboy Copas, Lois Mann

**SIGNED, SEALED,
DELIVERED I'M YOURS**
w&m/Stevie Wonder, Lee Garrett,
Sireeta Wright, Lulu Mae Hardaway

SILENCE
m/Michael Mantler (based on Harold
Pinter poem)

SILENT NIGHT! HOLY NIGHT!
m/Franz Xavier Gruber
w/Joseph Mohr

SILHOUETTES
w&m/Frank C. Slay Jr., Bob Crewe

SILICOSIS BLUES
w&m/Joshua D. White
SILLY LOVE SONGS
w&m/Paul and Linda McCartney

SILVER AND GOLD
w&m/John D Marks

SILVER BELL
m/Percy Wenrich
w/Edward Madden

SILVER BELLS
w&m/Ray Evans, Jay H. Livingston

SILVER BLUE
w&m/J.D. Souther

SILVER DOLLAR
w&m/Jack Palmer, Clarke Van Ness

SILVER MOON
m/Sigmund Romberg
w/Dorothy Donnelly

SILVER MOON
w&m/Mike Nesmith

**SILVER SHADOWS AND
GOLDEN DREAMS**
w&m/Lew Pollack, Charles Newman

SILVER SWAY RAG (instr.)
m/Scott Joplin

**SILVER THREADS AMONG
THE GOLD**
m/Hart Pease Danks
w/Eben E. Rexford

SILVER THREADS AND GOLDEN NEEDLES
w&m/Tom Springfield

SILVER TONGUED DEVIL AND I, THE
m/Sir Arthur Sullivan
w/Sir William Schwenk Gilbert

SIMON SAYS
w&m/Jerry Kasenetz, Jeff Katz

SIMPEL, GIMPEL (instr.)
m/Horst Jankowski

SIN CITY
w&m/Gram Parsons

SINCE I KISSED MY BABY GOODBYE
w&m/Cole Porter

SINCE I LOST MY BABY
w&m/William (Smokey) Robinson Jr., Warren Moore

SINCE I MET YOU BABY
w&m/Ivory Joe Hunter

SINCE JESUS CAME INTO MY HEART
m/Charles H. Gabriel Sr.

SINCE YOU WENT AWAY (film score)
m/Max Steiner

SINCE YOU WENT AWAY
w&m/James Weldon Johnson, J. Rosamond Johnson

SINCE YOU'VE ASKED
w&m/Judy Collins

SINCE YOU'VE BEEN GONE (SWEET, SWEET BABY)
w&m/Aretha Franklin, Ted White

SINCERELY
w&m/Alan Freed, Harvey Fuqua

SING
w&m/Joseph Raposo

SING A BAD SONG
w&m/Merle Haggard

SING A SONG
w&m/Maurice White, Alan McKay

SING A SONG OF SUNBEAMS
m/James Monaco
w/Johnny Burke

SING BABY SING
m/Lew Pollack
w/Jack Yellen

SING FOR THE DAY
w&m/Tommy Shaw

SING FOR YOUR SUPPER
m/Richard Rodgers
w/Lorenz (Larry) Hart

SING ME A SONG OF THE ISLANDS
w&m/Harry Owens

SING SOMETHING SIMPLE
w&m/Herman Hupfeld

SING YOU SINNERS
m/W. Franke Harling
w/Sam Coslow

SINGIN' IN THE RAIN
m/Nacio Herb Brown
w/Arthur Freed

SINGIN' IN THE RAIN (film score)
m/Lennie Hayton

SINGIN' MY SONG
w&m/Dallas Frazier

SINGING A VAGABOND SONG
w&m/Harry Richman, Sam Messenheimer, Val Burton

SINGING HILLS, THE
m/Sammy Mysels
w/Dick Sanford

SINGING MY SONG
w&m/Glenn Sutton, Tammy Wynette, Billy Sherrill

SINGIN' THE BLUES
m/Jimmy McHugh
w/Dorothy Fields

SINGING THE BLUES
w&m/Melvin Endsley

SINK THE Bismarck
w&m/Johnny Horton, Tillman Franks

SINNER KISSED AN ANGEL, A
w&m/Larry Shayne, Mack David

SINNERMAN
w&m/Will Holt

SIOUX CITY SUE
m/Dick Thomas
w/Max C. Freedman

SIPPI
w&m/James P. Johnson, Henry Creamer, Clarence Todd

SIPPIN' CIDER THRU A STRAW
w&m/Carey Morgan, Lee David

SIT DOWN YOU'RE ROCKIN' THE BOAT
w&m/Frank Loesser

SITTIN' IN THE BALCONY
w&m/John D. Loudermilk

SITTING
w&m/Cat Stevens

SITTING BY THE WINDOW
w&m/Paul Peter Insetta

SITTING IN THE RAIN
w&m/John Mayall

SITTING ON THE EDGE OF THE OCEAN
w&m/Ronnie Scott, Steve Wolfe

SIR DUKE
w&m/Stevie Wonder

SISTER DISCO
w&m/Peter Townshend

SISTERS OF MERCY
w&m/Leonard Cohen

SIX LESSONS FROM MADAM LAZONGA
m/James V. Monaco
w/Charles Newman

634-5789
w&m/Eddie Floyd, Steve Cropper

627 STOMP (instr.)
m/Pete Johnson

SIXTEEN CANDLES
w&m/Luther Dixon, Allyson R. Khent

SIXTEEN TONS
w&m/Merle Travis

SKIDMORE FANCY BALL
m/David Braham
w/Ed Harrigan

SKIDROW BLUES
w&m/Jimmy Witherspoon

SKINNY LEGS AND ALL
w&m/Joe Tex

SKY DIVE
w&m/Freddie Hubbard

SKYBIRD
w&m/Neil Diamond

SKYLARK
m/Hoagy Carmichael
w/Johnny Mercer

SKYLINE PIGEON
m/Elton John
w/Bernie Taupin

SKYRIDE (instr.)
m/Adolph Deutsch, Vincent Lopez

SLAP THAT BASS
m/George Gershwin
w/Ira Gershwin

SLAUGHTER ON TENTH AVENUE (instr.)
Richard Rodgers

SLAVE DEALER'S SONG
m/Ludwig Englander
w/Harry B. Smith

SLEEP WARM
m/Lew Spence
w/Marilyn and Alan Bergman

SLEEPING SINGLE IN A DOUBLE BED
w&m/Kye Fleming, Dennis Morgan

SLEEPY HEAD
m/Jesse Greer
w/Benny Davis

SLEEPY LAGOON
w&m/Jack Lawrence, Eric Coates

SLEEPY TIME GAL
m/Richard A. Whiting, Ange Lorenzo
w/Raymond B. Egan, Joseph R. Alden

SLEIGH RIDE
m/Leroy Anderson
w/Mitchell Parish

SLICK
w&m/Herb Alpert, John Pisano

SLIP SLIDING AWAY
w&m/Paul Simon

SLIPOVA (instr.)
m/Roy Frederick Bargy

SLIPPIN' AND SLIDIN'
w&m/Little Richard, Albert Collins, James Smith

SLIPPIN' AWAY
w&m/Bill Anderson

SLIPPIN' INTO DARKNESS
w&m/see composer listing under Lee Oskar

SLIPPING AROUND
w&m/Floyd Tillman

SLOW DANCER
w&m/Boz Scaggs

SLOW DANCING DON'T TURN ME ON
w&m/Donald J. Adrissi, Richard P. Adrissi

SLOW POKE
w&m/Pee Wee King, Redd Stewart, Chilton Price

SLOW TRAIN COMING
w&m/Robert Dylan

SLOWLY
w&m/Webb Pierce, Tommy Hill

SLUMMING ON PARK AVENUE
w&m/Irving Berlin

SMACKWATER JACK
w&m/Carole King, Gerry Goffin

SMALL FRY
m/Hoagy Carmichael
w/Frank Loesser

SMALL TALK
m/Jerry Ross
w/Richard Adler

SMALL WORLD
m/Jule Styne
w/Stephen Sondheim

SMARTY
w&m/Jack Norworth, Albert Von Tilzer

SMILE
m/Charles Spencer Chaplin
w/John Turner, Geoffrey Parsons

SMILE A LITTLE SMILE FOR ME
w&m/Tony MacCaulay, Geoff Stephens

SMILE, DARN YA, SMILE
w&m/Jack Meskill, Charles O'Flynn, Max Rich

SMILE WILL GO A LONG LONG WAY, A
m/Harry Akst
w/Benny Davis

SMILES
m/Lee S. Roberts
w/J. Will Callahan

SMILIN'
w&m/Sly Stone

SMILIN' THROUGH (film score)
m/William Axt

SMILIN' THROUGH
w&m/Arthur A. Penn

SMOKE DREAMS
m/Nacio Herb Brown
w/Arthur Freed

SMOKE GETS IN YOUR EYES
m/Jerome Kern
w/Otto Harbach

SMOKE RINGS
m/H. Eugene Gifford
w/Ned Washington

SMOKE, SMOKE, SMOKE (THAT CIGARETTE)
w&m/Tex Williams, Merle Travis

SMOKEY THE BEAR
m/Jack Rollins
w/Steve Nelson

SMO-O-O-OTH ONE, A (instr.)
m/Charlie Christian

SNEAKAWAY (instr.)
m/Willie the Lion Smith

SNEAKIN' AROUND
w&m/Jessie Mae Robinson

SNEEKY PETE (instr.)
m/Charles Leslie Johnson

SNOOKUMS (instr.)
m/Charles Leslie Johnson

SNOOKY OOKUMS
w&m/Irving Berlin

SNOOTIE LITTLE CUTIE
w&m/Bobby Troup

SNOW QUEEN
w&m/Carole King, Gerry Goffin

SNOW WHITE AND THE SEVEN DWARFS (film score)
m/Leigh Harline

SNOWBIRD
w&m/Gene MacClellan

SNOWFALL (instr.)
m/Claude Thornhill

SNOWS OF KILIMANJARO (film score)
m/Bernard Herrmann

SNUGGLED ON YOUR SHOULDER
m/Carmen Lombardo
w/Joseph Young

SO BLUE
m/Ray Henderson
w/Lew Brown, Buddy DeSylva

SO DEAR TO MY HEART
w&m/Irving Taylor

SO DEEP
w&m/Shari Sheeley, Jackie DeShannon

SO DEEP WITHIN YOU
w&m/Michael Pinder

SO DO I
m/Arthur Johnston
w/Johnny Burke

SO FAR AWAY
w&m/Carole King

SO FINE
w&m/Jeff Lynne

SO GLAD YOU'RE MINE
w&m/Arthur Crudup

SO HELP ME
m/James Van Heusen
w/Edgar DeLange

SO IN LOVE
w&m/Cole Porter

SO IN LOVE
m/David Rose
w/Leo Robin

SO INTO YOU
w&m/Buddy Buie, Robert Nix, Dean Daughtry

SO LITTLE TIME
m/Dimitri Tiomkin
w/Paul Francis Webster

SO LONG
m/Irving Melsher
w/Remus Harris, Russ Morgan

SO LONG DEARIE
w&m/Jerry Herman

SO LONG DIXIE
w&m/Barry Mann, Cynthia Weil

SO LONG GIRL
w&m/Al Jarreau

SO LONG IT'S BEEN GOOD TO KNOW YUH
w&m/Woody Guthrie

SO LONG MARIANNE
/&m/Leonard Cohen

SO LONG, MARY
w&m/George M. Cohan

SO LONG, OO-LONG
m/Harry Ruby
w/Bert Kalmer

SO LONG PAL
w&m/Al Dexter

SO MUCH LOVE
w&m/Van McCoy

SO NEAR AND YET SO FAR
w&m/Cole Porter

SO RARE
m/Jerry Herbst
w/John Rufus (Jack) Sharpe III

SO ROUND, SO FIRM, SO FULLY PACKED
w&m/Merle Travis, Cliffie Stone, Eddie Kirk

SO SAD (TO WATCH GOOD LOVE GO BAD)
w&m/Don Everly

SO SAD THE SONG
w&m/Gerry Goffin, Michael Masser

SO THIS IS LOVE
m/Jerry Livingston
w/Mack David

SO THIS IS LOVE
w&m/Lew DeWitt, Don Reid

SO TIRED
w&m/Russ Morgan, Jack Stuart

SO TRUE
w&m/Russ Morgan, Jack Stuart

SO WHAT (instr.)
m/Miles Dewey Davis

SO WHAT
w&m/Joseph F. Walsh

SO WHAT'S NEW
w&m/Peggy Lee, John Pisano

SO YOU THINK YOU'RE A COWBOY
w&m/Willie Nelson, Hank Cochran

SO YOU WIN AGAIN
w&m/Errol Brown, Tony Wilson

SOCIETY'S CHILD
w&m/Janis Ian

SOFT LIGHTS AND SWEET MUSIC
w&m/Irving Berlin

SOFTLY AS IN A MORNING SUNRISE
m/Sigmund Romberg
w/Oscar Hammerstein II

SOFTLY THRO' THE SUMMER NIGHT
m/Emmerich Kalman
w/C. C. S. Cushing, E. P. Heath

SOFTLY WHISPERING I LOVE YOU
w&m/Roger Greenaway, Roger Cook

SOLACE (instr.)
m/Scott Joplin

SOLDIER BOY
w&m/Albert Von Tilzer, Lew Brown

SOLDIER'S JOY
w&m/Jimmy Driftwood

SOLDIER'S LAST LETTER
w&m/Redd Stewart, Ernest Tubb

SOLID GOLD CADILLAC, THE (film score)
m/Bronislau Kaper

SOLID MEN TO THE FRONT (instr.)
m/John Philip Sousa

SOLILOQUY
m/Richard Rodgers
w/Oscar Hammerstein II

SOLILOQUY (instr.)
m/Rube Bloom

SOLITIARE
w&m/Neil Sedaka, Howard Greenfield

SOLITARY MAN
w&m/Neil Diamond

SOLITUDE
m/Duke Ellington
w/Eddie DeLange, Irving Mills

SOLO FLIGHT (instr.)
m/Charlie Christian

SOME BROKEN HEARTS NEVER MEND
w&m/Wayland Holyfield

SOME DAY
m/Rudolf Friml
w/Brian Hooker

SOME DAY MY PRINCE WILL COME
w&m/Larry Morey, Frank E. Churchill

SOME ENCHANTED EVENING
m/Richard Rodgers
w/Oscar Hammerstein II

SOME FOLKS
w&m/Stephen Foster

SOME FOLKS NEVER LEARN
w&m/Kenneth Gamble, Leon Huff

SOME KIND OF WONDERFUL
w&m/Carole King, Gerry Goffin

SOME LIKE IT HOT (film score)
m/Adolph Deutsch

SOME OF MY BEST FRIENDS ARE THE BLUES
w&m/Jimmy Witherspoon

SOME OTHER TIME
w&m/Alan Parsons, Eric Woolfson

SOME PEOPLE
m/Jule Styne
w/Stephen Sondheim

SOME SUNDAY MORNING
m/Ray John Heindorf, M. K. Jerome
w/Ted Koehler

SOME SUNDAY MORNING
m/Richard A. Whiting
w/Gus Kahn, Raymond B. Egan

SOME SUNNY DAY
w&m/Irving Berlin

SOME SWEET DAY
m/David Stamper
w/Gene Buck, Louis A. Hirsch

SOME TIME IN NEW YORK CITY
w&m/John Lennon, Yoko Ono

SOMEBODY BAD STOLE DE WEDDING BELL
m/David Mann
w/Bob Hilliard

SOMEBODY BIGGER THAN YOU AND I
w&m/Johnny Lange, Walter H. (Hy) Heath, Sonny Burke

SOMEBODY ELSE IS TAKING MY PLACE
w&m/Russ Morgan, Dick Howard, Bob Ellsworth

SOMEBODY LIED
m/Bert Williams
w/Jeff T. Brainen, Evan Lloyd

SOMEBODY LIKE ME
w&m/Wayne Carson

SOMEBODY LOVES ME
m/George Gershwin, Ballard MacDonald
w/Buddy DeSylva

SOMEBODY LOVES YOU
w&m/Peter DeRose, Charles Tobias,
Harry Tobias

**SOMEBODY SOMEWHERE
DON'T KNOW WHAT HE'S
MISSING TONIGHT**
w&m/Lola Jean Dillon

SOMEBODY STOLE MY GAL
w&m/Leo Wood

SOMEBODY TO LOVE
w&m/Darby Slick, Grace Slick

**SOMEBODY UP THERE LIKES
ME (film score)**
m/Bronislau Kaper

SOMEBODY'S BACK IN TOWN
w&m/Teddy Wilburn, Doyle
Wilburn, Don Helms

**SOMEBODY'S COMING TO MY
HOUSE**
w&m/Irving Berlin

**SOMEBODY'S WATCHING
YOU**
w&m/Sly Stone

**SOMEDAY (YOU'LL WANT ME
TO WANT YOU)**
w&m/James S. Hodges

SOMEDAY, I'LL BE A FARMER
w&m/Melanie

SOMEDAY I'LL FIND YOU
w&m/Noel Coward

SOMEDAY MAN
w&m/Paul Williams, Roger Nichols

SOMEDAY
w&m/Dave Loggins

SOMEDAY NEVER COMES
w&m/John C. Fogerty

SOMEDAY SOMEWHERE
w&m/Thomas Andrew Dorsey

SOMEDAY SOON
w&m/Ian Tyson

**SOMEDAY WE'LL BE
TOGETHER**
w&m/Harvey Fuqua, Johnny Bristol,
Jackey Beavers

SOMEDAY WE'LL LOOK BACK
w&m/Merle Haggard

SOMEDAY YOU'LL BE OLD
w&m/Kenneth Gamble, Leon Huff

**SOMEDAY YOU'LL FIND YOUR
BLUEBIRD**
m/Alfred Newman
w/Mack Gordon

**SOMEONE IS SENDING ME
FLOWERS**
m/David Baker
w/Sheldon Harnick

**SOMEONE'S ROCKING MY
DREAMBOAT**
w&m/Leon T. Rene, Otis Rene Jr.

**SOMEONE'S WAITING FOR
YOU**
m/Sammy Fain
w/Carol Connors, Ayn Robbins

**SOMEONE SAVED MY LIFE
TONIGHT**
m/Elton John
w/Bernie Taupin

**SOMEONE TO GIVE MY LOVE
TO**
w&m/Bill Rice, Jerry Foster

**SOMEONE TO LAY DOWN
BESIDE ME**
w&m/Karla Bonoff

**SOMEONE TO WATCH OVER
ME**
m/George Gershwin
w/Ira Gershwin

SOMETHIN' STUPID
w&m/C. Carson Parks

SOMETHING
w&m/George Harrison

SOMETHING ABOUT YOU
w&m/Brian Holland, Eddie Holland,
Lamont Dozier

SOMETHING BEAUTIFUL
m/William J. Gaither
w/William J. Gaither, Gloria Gaither

SOMETHING ELSE (instr.)
m/Ornette Coleman

SOMETHING ELSE
w&m/Jerry Capehart, Eddie
Cochran

SOMETHING FISHY
w&m/Dolly Parton

SOMETHING FOR THE BOYS
w&m/Cole Porter

SOMETHING INSIDE OF ME
w&m/Danny Kirwen

SOMETHING SENTIMENTAL
w&m/Irving Taylor

SOMETHING SO RIGHT
w&m/Paul Simon

**SOMETHING TO REMEMBER
YOU BY**
m/Arthur Schwartz
w/Howard Dietz

SOMETHING WONDERFUL
m/Richard Rodgers
w/Oscar Hammerstein II

SOMETHING YOU GOT
w&m/Chris Kenner

SOMETHING'S BURNING
w&m/Mac Davis

SOMETHING'S COMING
m/Leonard Bernstein
w/Stephen Sondheim

SOMETHING'S GOTTA GIVE
w&m/Johnny Mercer

SOMETHING'S WRONG
w&m/Antoine "Fats" Domino, Dave
Bartholomew

SOMETIMES
w&m/Bill Anderson

SOMETIMES I'M HAPPY
m/Irving Caesar
w/Vincent Youmans

**SOMETIMES WHEN WE
TOUCH**
w&m/Barry Mann, Dan Hill

SOMEWHERE
m/Leonard Bernstein
w/Stephen Sondheim

**SOMEWHERE ALONG THE
WAY**
m/Kurt Adams
w/Sammy Gallop

SOMEWHERE IN THE NIGHT
w&m/Will Jennings, Richard Kerr

**SOMEWHERE MY LOVE (based
on "LARA'S THEME" from
"DOCTOR ZHIVAGO")**
m/Maurice Jarre
w/Paul Frances Webster

**SONG OF BERNADETTE, THE
(film score)**
m/Alfred Newman

**SON OF HICKORY HOLLER'S
TRAMP, THE**
w&m/Dallas Frazier

SON OF SHAFT
w&m/Homer Banks, Allen Jones,
William Brown

SONG OF THE BANDIT
w&m/Bob Nolan

SONG FOR YOU, A
w&m/Leon Russell

**SONG FROM MOULIN ROUGE,
THE**
m/Georges Auric
w/Bill Engvick

SONG I LIKE TO SING, THE
w&m/Kris Kristofferson

SONG IS ENDED, THE
w&m/Irving Berlin

SONG IS YOU, THE
m/Jerome Kern
w/Oscar Hammerstein II

SONG OF HAPPINESS (instr.)
m/McCoy Tyner

SONG OF JOY, A
m/Orbe-Waldo De Los Rio (based on finale from Beethoven's Ninth Symphony)
w/Spanish:Orbe-Waldo De Los Rios
w/English: Ross Parker

SONG OF LOVE
m/Sigmund Romberg
w/Dorothy Donnelly

SONG OF LOVE (film score)
m/Bronislau Kaper

SONG OF SONGS, THE
m/Harold Vicars
w/English: Clarence Lucas
w/French: Maurice Vancaire

SONG OF THE BAYOU (instr.)
m/Rube Bloom

SONG OF THE FLAME
m/Herbert Stothart, George Gershwin
w/Otto Harbach, Oscar Hammerstein II

SONG OF THE ISLANDS (NA LEI O HAWAII)
w&m/Charles E. King

SONG OF THE NAIROBI TRIO (instr.)
m/Robert Maxwell

SONG OF THE NEW WORLD (instr.)
m/McCoy Tyner

SONG OF THE OPEN ROAD
w&m/Albert Hay Malotte

SONG OF THE VAGABONDS
m/Rudolf Friml
w/Brian Hooker

SONG ON THE RADIO
w&m/Al Stewart

SONG SUNG BLUE
w&m/Neil Diamond

SONG TO REMEMBER, A (film score)
m/Miklos Rozsa, Morris Stoloff

SONG TO WOODY
w&m/Robert Dylan

SONG WITHOUT END (film score)
m/George Duning

SONGS
w&m/Barry Mann, Cynthia Weil

SONGS OF THE GAMBLING MAN
w&m/John Jacob Niles

SONGS WE MADE LOVE TO, THE
w&m/Bill Rice, Jerry Foster

SONNEYMOON FOR TWO (instr.)
m/Sonny Rollins

SONNY BOY
w&m/Al Jolson, Buddy DeSylva, Lew Brown, Ray Henderson

SON'S BLUES
w&m/Son House

SONS OF KATIE ELDER, THE
m/Elmer Bernstein
w/Ernie Sheldon

SOOLAIMON
w&m/Neil Diamond

SOON
m/George Gershwin
w/Ira Gershwin

SOON AND VERY SOON
w&m/Andrae Crouch

SOPHISTICATED LADY
m/Duke Ellington
w/Mitchell Parish, Irving Mills

SOPHISTICATED LADY
w&m/Natalie Cole, Marvin Yancy, Chuck Jackson

SOPHISTICATED SWING
m/Will Hudson
w/Mitchell Parish

SORRY
m/Richard A. Whiting
w/Buddy Pepper

SORRY HER LOT
m/Sir Arthur Sullivan
w/Sir William Schwenk Gilbert

SORRY SEEMS TO BE THE HARDEST WORD
m/Elton John
w/Bernie Taupin

(YOU'RE MY) SOUL AND INSPIRATION
w&m/Barry Mann, Cynthia Weil

SOUL DEEP
w&m/Wayne Carson Thompson

SOUL FRANCISCO
w&m/Tony Joe White

SOUL LIMBO
w&m/Steve Cropper, Al Jackson Booker T. Jones, Donald Dunn

SOULFUL STRUT
w&m/William Sanders, Eugene Record

SOUL MAN
w&m/Homer Banks, Carl M. Hampton

SOUL MAN
w&m/Isaac Hayes, David Porter

SOUL SHAKE
w&m/Delaney Bramlett, Bonnie Lynn Bramlett

SOUL SONG
w&m/George Richey, Norro Wilson, Billy Sherrill

SOUL TRAIN
w&m/James R. Cobb Jr., Buddy Buie

SOULFUL STRUT
w&m/Eugene Record, William Sanders

SOUND AND THE FURY, THE (film score)
m/Alex North

SOUND AND VISION
w&m/David Bowie

SOUND OF JOY (instr.)
m/Sun Ra

SOUND OF MUSIC, THE
m/Richard Rodgers
w/Oscar Hammerstein II

SOUND OF PHILIADELPHIA
w&m/Leon Huff, Kenneth Gamble

SOUND OFF
w&m/Philip Egner

SOUND YOUR FUNKY HORN
w&m/Harry Wayne Casey, Richard Finch

SOUNDS OF SILENCE
w&m/Paul Simon

SOUTH AMERICA , TAKE IT AWAY
w&m/Harold Rome

SOUTH BOUND
w&m/Richard Betts

SOUTH OF THE BORDER
m/Michael Carr
w/Jimmy Kennedy

SOUTHBOUND BLUES
w&m/Leroy Carr

SOUTHBOUND TRAIN
w&m/Graham Nash

SOUTH IS GONNA DO IT, THE
w&m/Charlie Daniels

SOUT

SOUTHERN CALIFORNIA
w&m/George Richey, Billy Sherrill, Roger Bowling

SOUTHERN FLOOD BLUES
w&m/"Big Bill" Broonzy

SOUTHERN MAN
w&m/Neil Young

SOUTHERN NIGHTS
w&m/Allen Toussaint

SOUVENIRS
w&m/Dan Fogelberg

SPACE COWBOY
w&m/Steve Miller, Ben Sidram

SPACE ODDITY
w&m/David Bowie

SPACEMAN
w&m/Harry E. Nilsson

ŚPAIN
m/Isham Jones
w/Gus Kahn

SPAIN (instr.)
m/Chick Corea

SPANIARD THAT BLIGHTED MY LIFE, THE
w&m/Billy Merson

SPANISH EYES
m/Bert Kaempfert
w/Charles Singleton, Eddie Snyder

SPANISH FLEA
w&m/Julius Wechter, Cissy Wechter

SPANISH GUITAR
w&m/Ellas McDaniel (Bo Diddley)

SPANISH HARLEM
w&m/Phil Spector, Jerry Lieber

SPARROW IN THE TREE TOP
w&m/Bob Merrill

SPARTACUS (film score)
m/Alex North

SPEAK LOW
m/Kurt Weill
w/Ogden Nash

SPEAK SOFTLY LOVE (LOVE THEME FROM "THE GODFATHER")
m/Nino Rota
w/Larry Kusik

SPEAK TO THE SKY
w&m/Rick Springfield

SPECIAL DELIVERY
w&m/Jerry Kasanetz, Jeff Katz

SPECIAL LADY
w&m/Harry Ray, Al Goodman

SPEEDY GONZALES
w&m/Buddy Kaye, David Hill, Ethel Lee

SPELLBINDER
w&m/Mick Jones, Lou Gramm

SPELLBOUND (film score)
m/Miklos Rozsa

SPELLBOUND
m/Miklos Rozsa
w/Mack David

SPIDERS AND SNAKES
w&m/David Bellamy

SPINNING WHEEL
w&m/David Clayton-Thomas

SPIRIT IN THE NIGHT
w&m/Bruce Springsteen

SPIRIT OF AMERICA
w&m/Brian Wilson, Roger Christian

SPLISH SPLASH
w&m/Bobby Darin

SPOOKY
w&m/Dennis Yost, Wally Eaton

S'POSIN'
m/Paul Denniker
w/Andy Razaf

SPOON CALLS HOOTIE
w&m/Jimmy Witherspoon

SPOON RIVER (instr.)
m/Percy Aldridge Grainger

SPOONFUL OF SUGAR, A
w&m/Richard M. Sherman, Robert B. Sherman

SPRING AFFAIR
w&m/Donna Summer, Georgio Moroder, Pete Bellotte

SPRING AGAIN
w&m/Kenneth Gamble, Leon Huff

SPRING AGAIN
m/Vernon Duke
w/Ira Gershwin

SPRING FEVER (instr.)
m/Rube Bloom

SPRING HAS SPRUNG
m/Arthur Schwartz
w/Dorothy Fields

SPRING IS HERE
m/Richard Rodgers
w/Lorenz (Larry) Hart

SPRING WILL BE A LITTLE LATE THIS YEAR
w&m/Frank Loesser

SPRINGFIELD PLANE
w&m/Kenny O'Dell

SPUR NOT THE NOBLY BORN
m/Sir Arthur Sullivan
w/Sir William Schwenk Gilbert

SPY WHO CAME IN FROM THE COLD (film score)
m/Sol Kaplan

SQUARE DANCE FOR EIGHT EGYPTIAN MUMMIES (instr.)
m/Raymond Scott

SQUEEZE BOX
w&m/Peter Townshend

SQUEEZE ME
m/Thomas "Fats" Waller
w/Clarence Williams

STAGE FRIGHT
w&m/J. Robbie Robertson

STAGECOACH (film score)
m/Jerry Goldsmith

STAGECOACH (film score, 1939)
m/Richard Hageman

STAGGER LEE
w&m/Lloyd Price, Harold Logan (adapted from folk song "Stack-O-Lee")

STAIRWAY TO HEAVEN
w&m/Neil Sedaka, Howard Greenfield

STAIRWAY TO HEAVEN
w&m/James Page

STAIRWAY TO HEAVEN (film score)
m/Allan Gray

STAIRWAY TO THE STARS
m/Matt Malneck, Frank Signorelli
w/Mitchell Parish

STAMP OUT LONELINESS
w&m/Carl Belew, Van Givens

STAND
w&m/Sly Stone

STAND BACK
w&m/Gregg Allman, Duane Allman

STAND BY ME
w&m/Ben E. King, Jerry Lieber, Mike Stoller

STAND BY YOUR MAN
w&m/Tammy Wynette

STAND TALL
w&m/Burton Cumnmings

STAND UP AND CHEER
m/Harry Akst
w/Harry Akst, Lew Brown

STAND UP, STAND UP FOR JESUS
m/George James Webb
w/Reverend George Duffield

STANDING AT THE STATION
w&m/Alvin Lee

STANDING IN THE SHADOWS
w&m/Hank Williams Jr.

STANDING IN THE SHADOWS OF LOVE
w&m/Brian Holland, Eddie Holland, Lamont Dozier

STANDING ON THE CORNER
w&m/Frank Loesser

STANLEY STEAMER, THE
w&m/Ralph Blane, Harry Warren

STAR
w&m/Allee Willis, Maurice White, E. Del Bamo

STAR CHILDREN (instr.)
m/Don Ellis

STAR EYES
m/Gene DePaul
w/Don Raye

STAR IS BORN, A (film score)
m/Ray John Heindorf

STAR SPANGLED BANNER, THE
m/adapted from an old English song ("To Anacreon In Heaven")
w/Francis Scott Key

STAR TREK (TV theme)
m/Alexander Courage
w/Gene Roddenberry

STAR TREK (film score)
m/Jerry Goldsmith

STAR WARS (theme from and film score)
m/John Williams

STARDUST
m/Hoagy Carmichael
w/Mitchell Parish

STARE AND STARE
w&m/Curtis Mayfield

STARLIGHT
m/Lee J. Pockriss
w/Paul Vance

STARLIT HOUR, THE
m/Peter De Rose
w/Mitchell Parish

STARS AND STRIPES FOREVER, THE (march)
m/John Philip Sousa

STARS FELL ON ALABAMA
m/Frank Perkins
w/Mitchell Parish

START OFF EACH DAY WITH A SONG
w&m/Jimmy Durante

STARTING HERE, STARTING NOW
w&m/David Shire, Richard Maltby Jr.

STARVATION BLUES
w&m/"Big Bill" Broonzy

STATE STREET JIVE
w&m/Charles Edward Davenport

STATELY HOMES OF ENGLAND, THE
w&m/Noel Coward

STATUES WITHOUT HEARTS
w&m/Larry Gatlin

STAY
m/Richard Rodgers
w/Stephen Sondheim

STAY
w&m/Maurice Williams

STAY AS SWEET AS YOU ARE
m/Harry Revel
w/Mack Gordon

STAY ON THE RIGHT SIDE SISTER
w&m/Rube Bloom, Ted Koehler

STAY/THE LOAD OUT
w&m/Jackson Browne

STAY WELL
m/Kurt Weill
w/Maxwell Anderson

STAY WITH THE HAPPY PEOPLE
m/Jule Styne
w/Bob Hilliard

STAYIN' ALIVE
w&m/Barry, Maurice and Robin Gibb

STAYIN' IN
w&m/John D. Loudermilk

STEALIN' BLUES
w&m/Charles Edward Davenport

STEALIN' TIME
w&m/Gerry Rafferty

STEAM HEAT
m/Jerry Ross
w/Richard Adler

STEAMBOAT BILL
w&m/Ren Shields, The Leighton Brothers

STEAMBOAT STOMP (instr.)
m/Ferdinand "Jelly Roll" Morton

STEIN SONG, THE
w&m/Rudy Vallee, adaptor/original music: E. A. Fenstad
original words: Lincoln Colcord

STELLA BY STARLIGHT
m/Victor Young
w/Ned Washington

STEPPIN' IN A SLIDE ZONE
w&m/John Lodge

STEPPIN' OUT
w&m/Neil Sedaka, Phillip Cody

STEPPIN' OUT, I'M GONNA BOOGIE TONIGHT
w&m/Irwin Levine, L. Russell Brown

STEPPIN' OUT WITH MY BABY
w&m/Irving Berlin

STEPPIN' PRETTY (instr.)
m/Mary Lou Williams

STEREOPHONIC SOUND
w&m/Cole Porter

STERILE CUCKOO, THE (film score)
m/Fred Karlin

STILETTO
w&m/Billy Joel

(I LOVE YOU) STILL
w&m/Bill Anderson

STILL
w&m/Lionel Richie

STILL CRAZY AFTER ALL THESE YEARS
w&m/Paul Simon

STILL THE ONE
w&m/John Hall, Joanna Hall

STILL THE SAME
w&m/Bob Seger

STIR IT UP
w&m/Johnny Nash

STOLEN MOMENTS (instr.)
m/Oliver Nelson

STOMP
w&m/Rod Temperton, George Johnson, Louis Johnson, U. Johnson

STOMPIN' AT THE SAVOY
m/Benny Goodman, Chick Webb, Edgar Sampson
w/Andy Razaf

STONE COLD DEAD IN THE MARKET
w&m/Frederick Wilmoth Hendricks

STONED SOUL PICNIC
w&m/Laura Nyro

STONES
w&m/Neil Diamond

STONEY END
w&m/Laura Nyro

STOOD UP
w&m/Dub Dickerson, Erma Herrold

STOP AND SMELL THE ROSES
w&m/Mac Davis, Doc Severinsen

STOP! IN THE NAME OF LOVE
w&m/Eddie Holland, Brian Holland, Lamont Dozier

STOP THE RAG
w&m/Irving Berlin

STOP THE WORLD (AND LET ME OFF)
w&m/W. S. Stevenson, Carl Belew

STOP YER TICKLING, JOCK
w&m/Sir Harry Lauder, J. D. Harper

STOP YOUR SOBBING
w&m/Raymond Douglas Davies

STOPTIME RAG (instr.)
m/Scott Joplin

STORMS
w&m/Stephanie (Stevie) Nicks

STORMY MONDAY BLUES (instr.)
m/Earl (Fatha) Hines

STORMY WEATHER
m/Harold Arlen
w/Ted Koehler

STORY IN YOUR EYES, THE
w&m/Justin Hayward

STORY OF A STARRY NIGHT
m/Jerry Livingston
w/Al Hoffman

STORY OF ISAAC, THE
w&m/Leonard Cohen

STORY OF LOUIS PASTEUR (film score)
m/Erich Wolfgang Korngold

STORY OF THE ROSE, THE (HEART OF MY HEART I LOVE YOU)
m/Andrew Mack
w/"Alice"

STORYBOOK CHILDREN
w&m/Billy Vera, Judy Clay

STOUTHEARTED MEN
m/Sigmund Romberg
w/Oscar Hammerstein II

STOVE PIPE STOMP
w&m/"Big Bill" Broonzy

STRAIGHT LIFE, THE
w&m/Sonny Curtis

STRAIGHT NO CHASER (instr.)
m/Thelonious Sphere Monk

STRAIGHT ON
w&m/Ann Wilson, Nancy Wilson

STRAIGHT SHOOTER
w&m/John Phillips

STRAIGHTEN UP AND FLY RIGHT
w&m/Nat (King) Cole

STRANGE ADVENTURE
m/Sir Arthur Sullivan
w/Sir William Schwenk Gilbert

STRANGE ARE THE WAYS OF LOVE
m/Sammy Fain
w/Paul Francis Webster

STRANGE FRUIT
m/Billie Holiday
w/Lewis Allan

STRANGE INTERLUDE
m/Phil Baker, Ben Bernie
w/Walter Hirsch

STRANGE MAGIC
w&m/Jeff Lynne

STRANGE MUSIC
w&m/George (Chet) Forrest, Robert Wright (music adapted from composition by Edvard Grieg)

STRANGE THINGS ARE HAPPENING
w&m/Red Buttons, Allan Walker

STRANGE THINGS HAPPENING EVERY DAY
w&m/Rosetta Tharpe

STRANGER
w&m/Kris Kristofferson

STRANGER CALLED THE BLUES
w&m/Robert Wells, Mel Torme

STRANGER IN A STRANGE LAND
w&m/Leon Russell

STRANGER IN PARADISE
w&m/George (Chet) Forrest, Robert Wright (music adapted from composition by Alexander Borodin)

STRANGER IN TOWN
w&m/Del Shannon

STRANGER IN TOWN
w&m/Mel Torme

STRANGER ON THE SHORE
w&m/Robert Mellin, Acker Bilk

STRANGER, THE
w&m/Billy Joel

STRANGER TO HIMSELF
w&m/Steve Winwood, Jim Capaldi

STRANGER TO ME, A
w&m/Don Gibson

STRANGERS IN THE NIGHT
m/Bert Kaempfert
w/Charles Singleton, Eddie Snyder

STRANGERS WHEN WE MEET (film score)
m/George Duning

STRAW DOGS (film score)
m/Jerry Fielding

STRAWBERRY FIELDS FOREVER
w&m/John Lennon, Paul McCartney

STRAWBERRY LETTER 23
w&m/Shuggie Otis

STRAWBERRY ROAN
w&m/Nathaniel Hawthorne Vincent, Fred Howard

STREAK, THE
w&m/Rav Stevens

STREET FIGHTING MAN
w&m/Mick Jagger, Keith Richard

STREET NAMED HELL (instr.)
m/Sun Ra

STREET OF DREAMS
m/Victor Young
w/Sam M. Lewis

STREET TALK
w&m/Bob Crewe

STREETCAR NAMED DESIRE, A (film score)
m/Alex North

STREETLIFE SERENADE
w&m/Billy Joel

STREETS OF BALTIMORE
w&m/Harlan Howard, Tompall Glaser

STREETS OF CAIRO, THE (POOR LITTLE COUNTRY MAID)
w&m/James Thornton

STREETS OF NEW YORK, THE
m/Victor Herbert
w/Henry Blossom

STRENUOUS LIFE, THE (instr.)
m/Scott Joplin

STRICTLY INSTRUMENTAL
m/Bennie Benjamin, Edgar Battle
w/Sol Marcus, Edward Seiler

STRIKE UP THE BAND
m/George Gershwin
w/Ira Gershwin

STRIKE UP THE BAND, HERE COMES A SAILOR
m/Charles B. Ward
w/Andrew B. Sterling

STRING OF PEARLS, A
m/Jerry Grey
w/Edgar DeLange

STROLL, THE
w&m/Clyde Otis, Nancy Lee

STRUTTIN' WITH SOME BARBECUE (instr.)
m/Louis Armstrong

STUCK IN THE MIDDLE WITH YOU
w&m/Gerry Rafferty, Joe Egan

STUCK ON YOU
w&m/Aaron Schroeder, J. Leslie
McFarland

STUFF LIKE THAT (instr.)
m/Quincy Jones

STUMBLING (instr.)
m/Edward E. (Zev) Confrey

STUPID CUPID
w&m/Howard Greenfield, Neil
Sedaka

**SUBTERRANEAN HOMESICK
BLUES**
w&m/Robert Dylan

SUCCESS STORY
w&m/John Entwhistle

SUCH A NIGHT
w&m/Lincoln Chase

SUDDENLY
m/Vernon Duke
w/E. Y. Harburg, Billy Rose

SUDDENLY IT'S SPRING
m/James Van Heusen
w/Johnny Burke

**SUDDENLY THERE'S A
VALLEY**
w&m/Chuck Meyer, Biff Jones

SUFFRAGETTE CITY
w&m/David Bowie

SUGAR BLUES
w&m/Clarence Williams, Lucy
Fletcher

SUGAR CANE (instr.)
m/Scott Joplin

SUGAR DADDY
w&m/Christine Perfect McVie

SUGAR DADDY
w&m/David Bellamy

SUGAR FOOT RAY
w&m/Vaughn Horton, Hank Garland

SUGAR FOOT STOMP
w&m/Walter Melrose, Louis
Armstrong, Joe "King" Oliver

SUGAR LOAF (instr.)
m/Shorty Rogers

SUGAR MOUNTAIN
w&m/Neil Young

SUGAR SUGAR
w&m/Jeff Barry, Andy Kim

SUGAR THE ROAD
w&m/Alvin Lee

SUGARFOOT (instr.)
m/Ray John Heindorf

SUITE: JUDY BLUE EYES
w&m/Stephen Stills

SUITE MADAME BLUE
w&m/Dennis De Young

SUMMER
w&m/see composer listing under Lee
Oskar

SUMMER BREEZE
w&m/Dash Crofts, James Seals

SUMMER IS A-COMIN' IN
m/Vernon Duke
w/John Latouche

**SUMMER KNOWS, THE (theme
from "SUMMER OF '42")**
w&m/Michel Legrand, Alan and
Marilyn Bergman

SUMMER OF '42 (film score)
m/Michel Legrand

SUMMER PLACE, A (theme)
m/Max Steiner

SUMMER PLACE, A (film score)
m/Max Steiner

SUMMIT RIDGE DRIVE (instr.)
m/Artie Shaw

SUMMER SAMBA
m/Marcus Valle, Sergio Paulo Valle
w/Norman Gimbel

SUMMER WIND
w&m/Robert Dylan

SUMMER WINE
w&m/Lee Hazlewood

SUMMERTIME
m/George Gershwin
w/Dubose Heyward

SUMMERTIME BLUES
w&m/Eddie Cochran, Jerry
Capehart

SUN DANCE (instr.)
m/John Lewis

SUN MYTH, THE (instr.)
m/Sun Ra

SUN SONG (instr.)
m/Sun Ra

SUNBONNET SUE
m/Gus Edwards
w/Will D. Cobb

SUNDAY IN THE PARK
w&m/Harold Rome

SUNDAY KIND OF LOVE, A
w&m/Barbara Belle, Anita Leonard

**SUNDAY, MONDAY OR
ALWAYS**
m/James Van Heusen
w/Johnny Burke

**SUNDAY MORNING COMIN'
DOWN**
w&m/Kris Kristofferson

**SUNDAY MORNING
SUNSHINE**
w&m/Harry Chapin

SUNDAY PAPERS
w&m/Joe Jackson

SUNDAY STREET
w&m/David Van Ronk

SUNDAY SUN
w&m/Neil Diamond

SUNDAY SUNRISE
w&m/Mark James

SUNDOWN BLUES
w&m/Tony Joe White

SUNFLOWER
w&m/Mack David

SUNFLOWER RAG (instr.)
m/Scott Joplin

SUNGLASSES
w&m/John D. Loudermilk

SUNNY
m/Jerome Kern
w/Otto Harbach, Oscar
Hammerstein II

SUNNY
w&m/Bobby Hebb

SUNNY SIDE UP
m/Ray Henderson
w/Lew Brown, Buddy DeSylva

SUNRISE
w&m/Eric Carmen

SUNRISE SERENADE
w&m/Frankie Carle, Jack Lawrence

SUNRISE SUNSET
m/Jerry Bock
w/Sheldon Harnick

SUNSHINE
w&m/Jonathan Edwards

**SUNSHINE, LILLIPOPS AND
RAINBOWS**
m/Marvin Hamlisch
w/Howard Liebling

SUNSHINE OF YOUR EYES
m/Jack Bruce, Peter Brown
w/Eric Clapton

**SUNSHINE OF YOUR SMILE,
THE**
m/Lillian Ray
w/Leonard Cooke

**SUNSHINE ON MY
SHOULDERS**
w&m/John Denver, Taylor Kris

SUNSHINE SUPERMAN
w&m/Donovan

SUPER BAD
w&m/James Brown

SUPER MANN
m/Herbie Mann

**SUPERCALIFRAGILISTIC-
EXPIALIDOCIOUS**
w&m/Richard M. Sherman, Robert
B. Sherman

SUPERFLY
w&m/Curtis Mayfield

SUPERMAN
w&m/Donna Fargo

SUPERMAN, THEME FROM
(film theme)
w&m/John Williams

SUPERSTAR
w&m/Leon Russell, Bonnie Bramlett

SUPERSTITION
w&m/Stevie Wonder

SUPPERTIME
w&m/Irving Berlin

SURF CITY
w&m/Jan Berry, Brian Wilson

SURFER GIRL
w&m/Brian Wilson, Mike Love

SURFIN'
w&m/Brian Wilson, Mike Love

SURFIN' SAFARI
w&m/Brian Wilson, Mike Love

SURFIN' U. S. A.
w&m/Brian Wilson, Mike Love

SURRENDER
w&m/Doc (Jerome)Pomus, Mort
Shuman

**SURREY WITH THE FRINGE
ON TOP, THE**
m/Richard Rodgers
w/Oscar Hammerstein II

SUSAN JANE
w&m/William S. Hayes

SUSAN WHEN SHE TRIED
w&m/Don Reid

SUSANNE
w&m/Leonard Cohen

SUSAN'S RAG (instr.)
m/David Alan Jasen

SUSPICIOUS
w&m/Eddie Rabbitt, Randy
McCormick, David Malloy

SUSPICIOUS MINDS
w&m/Mark James

SUSPICIOUS MINDS
w&m/Waylon Jennings

SUZIE
m/Elton John
w/Bernie Taupin

SWAMP WITCH
w&m/Jim Stafford

SWANEE
m/George Gershwin
w/Irving Caesar

S.W.A.T., THEME FROM
m/Barry De Vorzon

**SWAY THE COT GENTLY FOR
THE BABY'S ASLEEP**
m/David Braham
w/Hartley Neville

SWEDISH RHAPSODY
m/Percy Faith, Hugo Alfven
w/Carl Sigman

**SWEET ADELINE (YOU'RE
THE FLOWER OF MY HEART,
SWEET ADELINE)**
m/Harry Armstrong
w/Richard Gerard Husch

SWEET AND HOT
m/Harold Arlen
w/Jack Yellen

SWEET AND LOW-DOWN
m/George Gershwin
w/Ira Gershwin

SWEET AND LOVELY
w&m/Charles Neil Daniels, Gus
Arnheim, Jules Lemare, Harry
Tobias

SWEET BABY JAMES
w&m/James Taylor

SWEET BLINDNESS
w&m/Laura Nyro

SWEET BY AND BY
m/Joseph P. Webster
w/S. Fillmore

SWEET CAROLINE
w&m/Neil Diamond

SWEET CHERRY WINE
w&m/Tommy James, Bob King

SWEET CITY WOMAN
w&m/Rich Dodson

SWEET DREAM
w&m/Ian Anderson

SWEET DREAMS
w&m/Don Gibson

**SWEET DREAMS,
SWEETHEART**
m/M. K. Jerome
w/Ted Koehler

SWEET EMILY
w&m/Leon Russell

SWEET EMOTION
w&m/Steve Tyler, Joe Perry

SWEET FANTASY
w&m/Rory Bourke

SWEET GENEVIEVE
m/Henry Tucker
w/George Cooper

SWEET GEORGIA BROWN
m/Maceo Pinkard
w/Ben Bernie, Kenneth Casey

SWEET HEARTACHES
m/Nat Simon
w/Jimmy Kennedy

SWEET HITCHHIKER
w&m/John C. Fogerty

SWEET HOME ALABAMA
w&m/Ronald Wayne Van Zant, Gary
Rossington, Larken Allen Collins

SWEET HOUR OF PRAYER
m/William Batchelder Bradbury
w/William N. Walford

SWEET LADY
m/Frank Crumit, Dave Zoob
w/Howard E. Johnson

SWEET LEILANI
w&m/Harry Owens

SWEET LIFE
w&m/Paul Davis

SWEET LITTLE ANGEL
w&m/Jules Taub, B. B. King

SWEET LITTLE SIXTEEN
w&m/Chuck Berry

SWEET LORRAINE
m/Clifford R. Burwell
w/Mitchell Parish

SWEET MADNESS
m/Victor Young
w/Ned Washington

SWEET MAGNOLIA BLOSSOM
w&m/Rory Bourke, Gayle Barnhill

SWEET MARY ANN
m/David Braham
w/Ed Harrigan

SWEET MUSIC MAN
w&m/Kenny Rogers

SWEET PAINTED LADIES
m/Elton John
w/Bernie Taupin

SWEET PEA
w&m/Tommy Roe

SWEET ROSIE O'GRADY
w&m/Maude Nugent Jerome, (Mrs.
William Jerome)

SWEET ROUGH MAN
w&m/Gertrude "Ma" Rainey

BOOK ORDER

SUBSCRIBER NUMBER	HOLD CODE	ALPHA PREFIX
545798	0	—

L. C. CARD NUMBER

CLASS NO.

ORD. NO.

DATE 10-30-81

ORDER DATE

REC'D DLR: ALLEN

AUTHOR: CARLTON, J. R.

TITLE: CARLTON'S COMPLETE REFERENCE BOOK OF MUSIC

SBN

PUBL: CARLTON PUB.   PLACE: CA

LIST PRICE: 40.00   YEAR: 1980   VOLS:

EDITION: SERIES:

ACC. NO.

REC. BY:

VAR. IN ED   0

COST:

FUND: MUSIC/COB

NO. OF BOOKS: ONE

LIVINGSTONE COLLEGE LIB.

SUBSCRIBER NAME

7/71

SWEET SAVANNAH
w&m/Paul Dresser

SWEET SEASONS
w&m/Carole King, Toni Stern

SWEET SIXTEEN
w&m/Ahmet Ertegun

SWEET SIXTEEN
m/David Stamper
w/Gene Buck

SWEET SOUL MUSIC
w&m/Otis Redding, Arthur Conley,
Sam Cooke

SWEET SUE (JUST YOU)
m/Victor Young
w/Will J. Harris

SWEET SURRENDER
w&m/David Gates

SWEET SWEETHEART
w&m/Carole King, Gerry Goffin

SWEET SWEETIE DEE (instr.)
m/Horace Silver

SWEET TALKIN' WOMAN
w&m/Jeff Lynne

SWEET VIOLETS
m/Cy Coben (based on traditional
folk song)

SWEET WOMAN LIKE YOU
w&m/Joe Tex

SWEETEST SOUNDS, THE
w&m/Richard Rodgers

**SWEETEST STORY EVER
TOLD, The (TELL ME DO YOU
LOVE ME)**
w&m/R. M. Stults

**SWEETHEART OF SIGMA CHI,
THE**
m/F. Dudleigh Vernor
w/Bryon D. Stokes

**SWEETHEART OF SIGMUND
FREUD (instr.)**
m/Shorty Rogers

SWEETHEART TREE, THE
m/Henry Mancini
w/Johnny Mercer

SWEETHEARTS
m/Victor Herbert
w/Robert B. Smith

SWEETHEARTS
m/Victor Herbert
w/Robert B. Smith

**SWEETHEARTS OF
STRANGERS**
w&m/Jimmy Davis

SWIM
w&m/Sly Stone

SWIMMER, THE (film score)
m/Marvin Hamlisch

SWING BROTHER SWING
w&m/Clarence Williams

SWING HIGH, SWING LOW
m/Burton Lane
w/Ralph Freed

**SWING LOW SWEET
CADILLAC (instr.)**
m/Dizzy Gillespie

SWING TO BOP (instr.)
m/Charlie Christian

**SWING WIDE YOUR GATE OF
LOVE**
w&m/Hank Thompson

SWINGIN' DOWN THE LANE
m/Gus Kahn
w/Isham Jones

SWINGING ON A STAR
m/James Van Heusen
w/Johnny Burke

SWINGIN' ON C
w&m/Eddie Durham

SWINGIN' THE BLUES
m/William (Count) Basie, Eddie
Durham

SWINGING DOORS
w&m/Merle Haggard

SWISS SUITE (instr.)
m/Oliver Nelson

S'WONDERFUL
m/George Gershwin
w/Ira Gershwin

SYLVIA
w&m/Oley Speaks, Clinton Scollard

SYLVIA'S MOTHER
w&m/Shel Silverstein

SYMPATHY
m/Rudolf Friml
w/Otto Harbach

SYMPATHY FOR THE DEVIL
w&m/Mick Jagger, Keith Richard

SYMPHONETTE (instr.)
m/Tadd Dameron

SYMPHONY
w&m/Jack Lawrence

SYNCOPATED CLOCK, THE
m/Leroy Anderson

SYNCOPATED WALK
w&m/Irving Berlin

Addenda:

SCHOOL DAYS
w&m/Loudon Wainwright III

STAND BESIDE ME
w&m/Tompall Glaser

STRAIGHT NO CHASER (instr.)
m/Bud Powell

STUPEFACTION
w&m/Graham Parker

SULTANS OF SWING
w&m/Mark Knopfler

 **SONGS**

T

T BONE BLUES
w&m/T-Bone Walker

T BONE SHUFFLE
w&m/T-Bone Walker

T FOR TEXAS
w&m/Jimmy Rodgers

"T" 99 BLUES
w&m/Jules Taub, Jimmy Nelson

TADD WALK (instr.)
m/Tadd Dameron

TAKE A CHANCE ON ME
m/Benny Andersson, Bjorn Ulvaeus
w/Stig Anderson

TAKE A GIANT STEP
w&m/Carole King, Gerry Goffin

TAKE A LETTER MARIA
w&m/R. B. Greaves

TAKE A MESSAGE TO MARY
w&m/Boudleaux Bryant, Felice
Bryant

**TAKE A NUMBER FROM ONE
TO TEN**
m/Harry Revel
w/Mack Gordon

**TAKE A PAIR OF SPARKLING
EYES**
m/Sir Arthur Sullivan
w/Sir William Schwenk Gilbert

TAKE A WHIFF ON ME
w&m/Huddie (Leadbelly) Ledbetter

TAKE BACK YOUR GOLD
m/Monroe H. Rosenfeld
w/Louis W. Pritzkow

TAKE BACK YOUR MINK
w&m/Frank Loesser

**TAKE CARE OF YOUR
HOMEWORK**
w&m/Homer Banks, Raymond
Jackson, Don Davis, Tom Kelly

TAKE FIVE (instr.)
m/Paul Desmond

**TAKE GOOD CARE OF MY
BABY**
w&m/Carole King, Gerry Goffin

TAKE HER TO JAMAICA
m/Irving Fields
w/Albert Gamse

TAKE HIM
m/Richard Rodgers
w/Lorenz (Larry) Hart

TAKE IT EASY
w&m/Jackson Browne, Glenn Frey

TAKE IT SLOW JOE
m/Harold Arlen
w/E. Y. Harburg

TAKE LOVE EASY (instr.)
m/Duke Ellington

TAKE LOVE EASY (instr.)
m/Duke Ellington

TAKE ME
w&m/Rube Bloom, Ted Koehler

TAKE ME
w&m/Leon Payne, George Jones

TAKE ME ALONG
w&m/Bob Merrill

TAKE ME BACK BABY
w&m/James Andrew Rushing

**TAKE ME BACK TO MY BOOTS
AND SADDLE**
w&m/Leonard Whitcup

**TAKE ME BACK TO NEW YORK
TOWN**
m/Harry Von Tilzer
w/Andrew B. Sterling

**TAKE ME HOME COUNTRY
ROADS**
m/John Denver
w/Bill Danoff, Taffy Nivert Danoff

**TAKE ME HOME WHERE THE
SWEET MAGNOLIA BLOOMS**
w&m/John Hill Hewitt

**TAKE ME I'M YOURS (film
score)**
m/Michael Henderson

TAKE ME IN YOUR ARMS
w&m/Fritz Rotter

**TAKE ME IN YOUR ARMS AND
HOLD ME**
w&m/Cindy Walker

**TAKE ME OUT TO THE BALL
GAME**
w&m/Albert Von Tilzer, Jack
Norworth

**TAKE ME TO THAT SWANEE
SHORE**
m/Lewis F. Muir
w/L. Wolfe Gilbert

TAKE ME TO THE PILOT
m/Elton John
w/Bernie Taupin

TAKE ME WITH YOU, DEARIE
w&m/Albert Von Tilzer, Junie
McCree

**TAKE MY HAND PRECIOUS
LORD**
w&m/Thomas Andrew Dorsey

TAKE MY HEART
m/Fred E. Ahlert
w/Joseph Young

TAKE-OFF (instr.)
m/Miles Dewey Davis

TAKE OFF A LITTLE BIT
w&m/Irving Berlin

TAKE OFF THE COAT
w&m/Harold Rome

**TAKE THAT LOOK OFF YOUR
FACE**
m/Andrew Lloyd Webber
w/Don Black

TAKE THE "A" TRAIN
w&m/Billy Strayhorn, Lee Gaines

TAKE THE LONG WAY HOME
w&m/Roger Hodgson, Rick Davies

TAKE THE MOMENT
m/Richard Rodgers
w/Stephen Sondheim

**TAKE THE MONEY AND RUN
(film score)**
m/Marvin Hamlisch

**TAKE THESE CHAINS FROM
MY HEART**
m/Walter Henry (Hy) Heath
w/Fred Rose

**TAKE THIS JOB AND SHOVE
IT**
w&m/David Allen Coe

TAKE TIME TO KNOW HER
w&m/Steve Davis

**TAKE YOUR GIRLIE TO THE
MOVIES**
m/Pete Wendling
w/Edgar Leslie, Bert Kalmar

TAKES TWO TO TANGO
w&m/Dick Manning, Al Hoffman

TAKIN' CARE OF BUSINESS
w&m/Randy Bachman

TAKIN' IT TO THE STREETS
w&m/Michael McDonald

TAKING A CHANCE ON LOVE
m/Vernon Duke
w/John Latouche

TAKING IN THE TOWN
m/David Braham
w/Ed Harrigan

**TALE OF THE BUMBLEBEE,
THE**
m/Gustav Luders
w/Frank Pixley

**TALE OF THE KANGAROO,
THE**
m/Gustav Landers
w/Frank Pixley

TALE OF THE SEA SHELL, THE
m/Gustav Luders
w/Frank Pixley

TALK ABOUT THE GOOD
TIMES
w&m/Jerry Reed

TALK BACK TREMBLING LIPS
w&m/John D. Loudermilk

TALK THAT TALK
w&m/Sid Wyche

TALK TO THE ANIMALS
w&m/Leslie Bricusse

TALKING OLD SOLDIERS
m/Elton John
w/Bernie Taupin

TALL DARK STRANGER
w&m/Buck Owens

TALL OAK TREE
w&m/Dorsey Burnette, Johnny
Burnette

TALLAHASSEE LASSIE
w&m/Freddie Cannon, Bob Crewe,
Frank C. Slay Jr.

TAMBOURINE CHINOIS (instr.)
m/Fritz Kreisler

TAMMANY
m/Gus Edwards
w/Vincent P. Bryan

TAMMY
w&m/Ray Evans, Jay H. Livingston

TAMPICO
m/Allan Roberts
w/Doris Fisher

TANGERINE
m/Victor Schertzinger
w/Johnny Mercer

TANGLED MIND, A
w&m/Ted Daffan

TANGLED UP IN BLUE
w&m/Robert Dylan

TANGO OF ROSES (TANGO
DELLE ROSE)
m/Schreier-Bottero
w/Albert Gamse

TAOS, NEW MEXICO
w&m/R. Dean Taylor

TAPESTRY
w&m/Carole King

TAPIOCA
w&m/James A. Bland

TA-RA-RA-BOOM-DE-RE
w&m/Henry J. Sayers

TARA'S THEME (from "GONE
WITH THE WIND")
m/Max Steiner

TASTE OF HONEY, A
m/Robert W. Scott
w/Ric Marlow

TASTE OF HONEY, A (film score)
m/John Addison

TASTY PUDDING (instr.)
m/Al Cohn

TATOOED LOVE BOYS
w&m/Chrissie Hynde, Pete Farndon

TAXI
w&m/Harry Chapin

TAXI, THEME FROM (ANGELA)
(instr.)
m/Bob James

TAXI WAR DANCE (instr.)
m/Lester Young

TEA AND SYMPATHY (film
score)
m/Adolph Deutsch

TEA FOR THE TILLERMAN
w&m/Cat Stevens

TEA FOR TWO
m/ Vincent Youmans
w/Irving Caesar

TEACH ME HOW TO KISS
m/Gustave A. Kerker
w/Hugh Morton

TEACH ME TONIGHT
m/Gene De Paul
w/Sammy Cahn

TEACH YOUR CHILDREN
w&m/Graham Nash

TEACHER
w&m/Ian Anderson

TEACHER I NEED YOU
m/Elton John
w/Bernie Taupin

TEACHER, TEACHER
m/Robert Allen
w/Al Stillman

TEAPOT (instr.)
m/Jay Jay Johnson

TEAR DOWN THE WALLS
w&m/Fred Neil

TEARDROPS FROM MY EYES
w&m/Rudolph Toombs

TEARS
m/Louis Armstrong
w/Lillian Hardin

TEARS BROKE OUT ON ME
w&m/Hank Cochran

TEARS OF A CLOWN, THE
w&m/Stevie Wonder, William
"Smokey" Robinson Jr., Henry
Cosby

TEARS OF RAGE
m/Richard Manuel
w/Robert Dylan

TEARS ON MY PILLOW
m/Fred Rose
w/Gene Autry

TEARS ON MY PILLOW
w&m/Al Lewis, Sylvester Bradford

TEASIN'
m/Philip Springer
w/Richard Adler

TEASING
w&m/Albert Von Tilzer, Cecil Mack
(Richard C. McPherson)

TEDDY
w&m/Paul Anka

TEDDY BEAR
w&m/Kal Mann, Bernie Lowe

TEDDY BEAR
w&m/Red Sovine, Tommy Hill, Billy
Joe Burnette, Dale Royal

TEEN AGER IN LOVE, A
w&m/Doc (Jerome) Pomus, Mort
Shuman

TEEN ANGEL
w&m/Dion Di Mucci, Fred Patrick,
Murray Singer

TEENAGE CRUSH
w&m/Joe Allison, Audrey Allison

TEENAGE IDOL
m/Elton John
w/Bernie Taupin

TELEPHONE LINE
w&m/Jeff Lynne

TELL EVERYBODY
w&m/Herbie Hancock

TELL IT TO MY FACE
w&m/Dan Fogelberg

TELL LAURA I LOVE HER
w&m/Ben Raleigh, Jeff Barry

TELL ME A BEDTIME STORY
w&m/Irving Berlin

TELL ME LITTLE GYPSY
w&m/Irving Berlin

TELL ME MOMMA
w&m/Robert Dylan

TELL ME MORE AND MORE
AND THEN SOME
w&m/Billie Holiday

TELL ME PRETTY MAIDEN
(ARE THERE ANY MORE AT
HOME LIKE YOU)
w&m/Leslie Stuart

TELL ME PRETTY MAIDEN
m/Thomas A. Barrett
w/Owen Hall

TELL ME SOMETHING GOOD
w&m/Stevie Wonder

TELL ME WHAT IT'S LIKE
w&m/Ben Peters

TELL ME WHY
w&m/Al Alberts, Marty Gold

TELL MOTHER I'LL BE THERE
w&m/Charles M. Fillmore

TELL THE TRUTH
w&m/Brook Benton, Clyde Otis,
Jimmy Williams

TEMPTATION
m/Nacio Herb Brown
w/Arthur Freed

"10" (film score)
m/Henry Mancini

TEN CENTS A DANCE
m/Richard Rodgers
w/Lorenz (Larry) Hart

**TEN COMMANDMENTS, THE
(film score)**
m/Elmer Bernstein

TEN LITTLE BOTTLES
w&m/Johnny Bond

**TEN LITTLE FINGERS AND
TEN LITTLE TOES**
w&m/Ira Schuster, Ed G. Nelson,
Harry Pease

TEN LITTLE INDIANS
w&m/Harry Edward Nilsson

**TEN NORTH FREDERICK (film
score)**
m/Leigh Harline

**TENDER IS THE NIGHT (film
score)**
m/Bernard Herrman

TENDER IS THE NIGHT
m/Sammy Fain
w/Paul Francis Webster

TENDER TRAP, THE
m/James Van Heusen
w/Sammy Cahn

TENDERLY
m/Walter Gross
w/Jack Lawrence

TENNESSEE STUD
w&m/Jimmy Driftwood

TENNESSEE WALTZ, THE
w&m/Pee Wee King, Redd Stewart

TENOR MADNESS (instr.)
w&m/Sonny Rollins

TENTERFIELD SADDLER
w&m/Peter Allen

TENTH AVENUE FREEZE OUT
w&m/Bruce Springsteen

**TENTING ON THE OLD CAMP
GROUND**
w&m/Walter Kittredge

TEQUILA
w&m/Chuck Rio

TEXARKANA BABY
w&m/Fred Rose, Cottonseed Clark

TEXAS FOX TROT
w&m/David W. DeFentresse Guion

TEXAS HOP
w&m/Jules Taub, Pee Wee Crayton

TEXAS PLAINS
w&m/Stuart Hamblen

TEXAS WHEN I DIE
w&m/Ed Bruce, Patsy Bruce, Bobby
Borcher

**THANK GOD I'M A COUNTRY
BOY**
w&m/John Martin Sommers

**THANK HEAVEN FOR LITTLE
GIRLS**
m/Frederick Loewe
w/Alan Jay Lerner

**THANK THE LORD FOR THE
NIGHT TIME**
w&m/Neil Diamond

THANK YOU
w&m/Sly Stone

**THANK YOU FOR A LOVELY
EVENING**
m/Jimmy McHugh
w/Dorothy Fields

**THANK YOU FOR BEING A
FRIEND**
w&m/Andrew Gold

THANK YOU FOR CALLING
w&m/Cindy Walker

THANK YOU PRETTY BABY
w&m/Brook Benton, Clyde Otis

THANK YOUR FATHER
m/Ray Henderson
w/Lew Brown, Buddy DeSylva

THANKS
m/Arthur Johnston
w/Sam Coslow

THANKS A MILLION
m/Arthur Johnston, Ted Fiorito
w/Gus Kahn

THANKS FOR THE MEMORY
m/Ralph Rainger
w/Leo Robin

THAT CERTAIN FEELING
m/George Gershwin
w/Ira Gershwin

THAT CERTAIN PARTY
m/Walter Donaldson
w/Gus Kahn

THAT DO MAKE IT NICE
w&m/Eddy Arnold, Fred Ebb, Paul
Klein

THAT FACE
w&m/Alan Bergman, Marilyn
Bergman, Lew Spence

THAT FUNNY FEELING
w&m/Bobby Darin

**THAT HEART BELONGS
TO ME**
w&m/Webb Pierce

THAT LUCKY OLD SUN
m/Beasley Smith
w/Haven Gillespie

**THAT MESMERIZING
MENDELSSOHN TUNE**
w&m/Irving Berlin

THAT OLD BLACK MAGIC
m/Harold Arlen
w/Johnny Mercer

THAT OLD DEVIL MOON
m/Burton Lane
w/E. Y. Harburg

THAT OLD FEELING
m/Sammy Fain
w/Lew Brown

THAT OLD GIRL OF MINE
m/Egbert Anson Van Alstyne
w/Earle C. Jones

THAT OLD GANG OF MINE
m/Ray Henderson
w/Mort Dixon, Billy Rose

**THAT SILVER HAIRED DADDY
OF MINE**
m/m/Jimmy Long
w/Gene Autry

THAT SLY OLD GENTLEMAN
m/James Monaco
w/Johnny Burke

**THAT SONG IS DRIVING ME
CRAZY**
w&m/Tom T. Hall

THAT THING CALLED LOVE
w&m/Perry Bradford

THAT'LL BE THE DAY
w&m/Buddy Holly, Norman Petty,
Jerry Allison

THAT'S A NO NO
w&m/Ben Peters

THAT'S A PLENTY
w&m/Henry Creamer, Bert A.
Williams

THAT'S A-PLENTY
w&m/Lew Pollack, Ray Gilbert

THAT'S ALL
w&m/Bob Haymes, Alan Brandt

THAT'S ALL I NEED
w&m/Lincoln Chase, Howard Biggs,
LaVern Baker

**THAT'S ALL I WANT
FROM YOU**
w&m/Fritz Rotter

THAT'S ALL RIGHT
w&m/Arthur Crudup

THAT'S AMORE
m/Harry Warren
w/Jack Brooks

THAT'S ENTERTAINMENT
m/Arthur Schwartz
w/Howard Dietz

THAT'S FOR ME
m/James Monaco
w/Johnny Burke

THAT'S FOR ME
m/Richard Rodgers
w/Oscar Hammerstein II

THAT'S HIM
m/Kurt Weill
w/Ogden Nash

**THAT'S HOW I GOT TO
MEMPHIS**
w&m/Tom T. Hall

**THAT'S HOW MUCH I LOVE
YOU**
w&m/Eddy Arnold, Wallace Fowler

THAT'S MY DESIRE
m/Helmy Kresa
w/Carroll Loveday

THAT'S MY WEAKNESS NOW
m/Sam H. Stept
w/Bud Green

THAT'S RIGHT (instr.)
m/Shorty Rogers

THAT'S ROCK 'N' ROLL
w&m/Eric Carmen

**THAT'S THE CHANCE I'LL
HAVE TO TAKE**
w&m/Waylon Jennings

**THAT'S THE NOO I WEAR A
KILT**
w&m/Sir Harry Lauder, A. B. Kendal

THAT'S THE WAY (I LIKE IT)
w&m/Harry Wayne Casey, Richard
Finch

**THAT'S THE WAY I'VE
ALWAYS HEARD IT SHOULD
BE**
w&m/Carly Simon, Jacob Brackman

**THAT'S THE WAY OF THE
WORLD**
w&m/Maurice White, Verdine White,
Charles Stepney

**THAT'S WHAT I LIKE ABOUT
THE SOUTH**
w&m/Andy Razaf

**THAT'S WHAT I WANT FOR
CHRISTMAS**
m/Gerald Marks
w/Irving Caesar

**THAT'S WHAT IT'S LIKE TO BE
LONESOME**
w&m/Bill Anderson

THAT'S WHAT YOU THINK
w&m/Pinky Tomlin

**THAT'S WHEN I SEE THE
BLUES**
w&m/Carl Belew, W. S. Stevenson

**THAT'S WHEN THE MUSIC
TAKES ME**
w&m/Neil Sedaka

**THAT'S WHERE MY HEART IS
TONIGHT**
w&m/Paul Dresser

THAT'S WHY
w&m/Berry Gordy Jr., Tyrone Carlo,
Gwen Gordy

THAT'S WHY I LOVE YOU
w&m/Andrew Gold

THEM THERE EYES
w&m/Wiliiam G. Tracey, Maceo
Pinkard, Doris Tauber

**THEME OF THE REPEAT
(instr.)**
m/Tadd Dameron

THEN AND ONLY THEN
w&m/Bill Anderson

THEN HE KISSED ME
w&m/Phil Spector, Jeff Barry, Ellie
Greenwich

THEN I'LL BE HAPPY
m/Sidney Clare, Clifford Friend
w/Lew Brown

**THEN YOU CAN TELL ME
GOODBYE**
w&m/John D. Loudermilk

**THEN YOU'VE NEVER BEEN
BLUE**
w&m/Samuel M. Lewis, Joseph
Young

THERE ARE SUCH THINGS
m/Abel Baer, George Meyer
w/Stanley Adams

THERE BUT FOR YOU GO I
m/Frederick Loewe
w/Alan Jay Lerner

**THERE GOES MY
EVERYTHING**
w&m/Dallas Frazier

THERE GOES MY HEART
m/Abner Silver
w/Benny Davis

**THERE GOES THAT SONG
AGAIN**
m/Jule Styne
w/Sammy Cahn

**THERE GREW A LITTLE
FLOWER**
m/Sir Arthur Sullivan
w/Sir William Schwenk Gilbert

THERE IS NO GREATER LOVE
m/Isham Jones
w/Marty Symes

THERE I'VE SAID IT AGAIN
m/David Mann
w/Redd Evans

**THERE IS NOTHING LIKE A
DAME**
m/Richard Rodgers
w/Oscar Hammerstein II

THERE LIVED A KING
m/Sir Arthur Sullivan
w/Sir William Schwenk Gilbert

THERE MUST BE A WAY
m/David Saxon
w/Sammy Gallop

**THERE NEVER WAS A GIRL
LIKE YOU**
m/Egbert Anson Van Alstyne
w/Harry H. Williams

THERE NEVER WAS A TIME
w&m/Margaret Lewis, Mira Smith

**THERE OUGHTA BE A
MOONLIGHT SAVING TIME**
w&m/Harry Richman, Irving Kahal

**THERE SHE IS, MISS
AMERICA**
w&m/Bernie Wayne

THERE WAS A TIME
m/Sir Arthur Sullivan
w/Sir William Schwenk Gilbert

**THERE WILL NEVER BE
ANOTHER YOU**
m/Harry Warren
w/Mack Gordon

THERE WON'T BE ANYMORE
w&m/Charlie Rich

**THERE WON'T BE NO
COUNTRY MUSIC**
w&m/C. W. McCall

THERE YOU GO
w&m/John R. Cash

THERE'LL BE A HOT TIME IN THE OLD TOWN TONIGHT
m/Theodore A. Metz
w/Joe Hayden

THERE'LL BE SOME CHANGES MADE
m/W. Benton Overstreet
w/Billy Higgins

THERE'S A BIG WHEEL
w&m/Don Gibson

THERE'S A BOAT DAT'S LEAVIN' SOON FOR NEW YORK
m/George Gershwin
w/Ira Gershwin

THERE'S A BROKEN HEART FOR EVERY LIGHT ON BROADWAY
m/Fred Fisher
w/Howard E. Johnson

THERE'S A CABIN IN THE PINE
w&m/Billy Hill

THERE'S A GIRL IN THE HEART OF MARYLAND
m/Harry Carroll
w/Ballard MacDonald

THERE'S A GOLD MINE IN THE SKY
w&m/Nick Kenny, Charles Kenny

THERE'S A GREAT DAY COMING MANANA
m/Burton Lane
w/E. Y. Harburg

THERE'S A HOME IN WYOMING
w&m/Billy Hill

THERE'S A LITTLE BIT OF BAD IN EVERY GOOD GIRL
w&m/Fred Fisher, Grant Clarke

THERE'S A LITTLE STAR SHINING FOR YOU
w&m/James Thornton

THERE'S LIFE IN THE OLD DOG YET
m/Ivan Caryll
w/P. G. Wodehouse

THERE'S A LONG LONG TRAIL (A'WINDING)
m/Elliott (Zo) Alonzo
w/Stoddard King

THERE'S A LULL IN MY LIFE
m/Harry Revel
w/Mack Gordon

THERE'S A MAN IN MY LIFE
m/Thomas "Fats" Waller
w/George Marion Jr.

THERE'S A NEW MOON OVER MY SHOULDER
w&m/Jimmy Davis, Ekko Whelan, Lee Blastic

THERE'S A PARTY GOIN' ON
w&m/Glenn Sutton, Billy Sherrill

THERE'S A RAINBOW 'ROUND MY SHOULDER
m/Dave Dreyer, Al Jolson
w/Billy Rose

THERE'S A SMALL HOTEL
m/Richard Rodgers
w/Lorenz (Larry) Hart

THERE'S A STAR-SPANGLED BANNER WAVING SOMEWHERE (THE BALLAD OF FRANCIS POWERS)
w&m/Paul Roberts, Red River Dave, Shelly Darnell

THERE'S ALWAYS A SEAT IN THE PARLOR FOR YOU
w&m/William J. Scanlan

THERE'S DANGER IN YOUR EYES, CHERIE
w&m/Harry Richman, Jack Meskill, Pete Wendling

THERE'S GOTTA BE SOMETHING BETTER THAN THIS
m/Cy Coleman
w/Dorothy Fields

THERE'S MUSIC IN THE AIR
m/George Frederick Root
w/Frances J. Crosby

THERE'S NO BUSINESS LIKE SHOWBUSINESS
w&m/Irving Berlin

THERE'S NO NORTH OR SOUTH TODAY
w&m/Paul Dresser

THERE'S NO NORTH OR SOUTH TODAY
w&m/Paul Dresser

THERE'S NO OTHER LIKE MY BABY
w&m/Phil Spector

THERE'S NO TOMORROW
m/adapted from Eduardo De Capio's "O Sole Mio"
w&m/Al Hoffman, Leo Corday, Leon Carr

THERE'S ONLY ONE OF YOU
m/Robert Allen
w/Al Stillman

THERE'S YES YES IN YOUR EYES
m/Joseph H. Santly
w/Cliff Friend

THERMO
w&m/Freddie Hubbard

THESE ARE NOT MY PEOPLE
w&m/Joe South

THESE BOOTS ARE MADE FOR WALKIN'
w&m/Lee Hazelwood

THESE DAYS
w&m/Jackson Browne

THESE EYES
w&m/Randy Bachman, Burton Cummings

THESE HANDS
w&m/Eddie Noack

THESE THINGS SHALL PASS
w&m/Stuart Hamblen

THEY ALL FOLLOW ME
m/Gustave A. Kerker
w/Hugh Morton

THEY ALL LAUGHED
m/George Gershwin
w/Ira Gershwin

THEY CALL THE WIND MARIA
m/Frederick Loewe
w/Alan Jay Lerner

THEY CALLED IT DIXIELAND
m/Richard A. Whiting
w/Raymond B. Egan

THEY CAN'T TAKE THAT AWAY FROM ME
m/George Gershwin
w/Ira Gershwin

THEY CUT DOWN THE OLD PINE TREE
w&m/William Raskin, Billy Hill

THEY DIDN'T BELIEVE ME
m/Jerome Kern
w/Herbert Reynolds (M. E. Rourke)

THEY DON'T MAKE 'EM LIKE MY DADDY
w&m/Jerry Chesnut

THEY GO WILD SIMPLY WILD OVER ME
m/Fred Fisher
w/Joseph McCarthy

THEY LIKE IKE
w&m/Irving Berlin

THEY LOVED ME
w&m/Irving Berlin

THEY SAY IT'S WONDERFUL
w&m/Irving Berlin

THEY SAY
m/Paul Mann, Stephen Weiss
w/Edward Heyman

THEY WERE DOING THE MAMBO
w&m/Don Raye, Sonny Burke

THEY'LL NEVER TAKE HER LOVE FROM ME
w&m/Leon Payne

THEY'RE EITHER TOO YOUNG OR TOO OLD
m/Arthur Schwartz
w/Frank Loesser

THEY'RE PLAYING OUR SONG
m/Marvin Hamlisch
w/Carole Bayer Sager

THICK AS A BRICK
w&m/Ian Anderson, Gerald Bastock

THIEF OF BAGDAD, THE (film score)
m/Miklos Rozsa

THIN MAN, THE (film score)
m/William Axt

THINE ALONE
m/Victor Herbert
w/Henry Blossom

THING, THE
w&m/Charles Green

THING CALLED LOVE
w&m/Jerry Reed

THINGS
w&m/Bobby Darin

THINGS ARE SELDOM WHAT THEY SEEM
m/Sir Arthur Sullivan
w/Sir William Schwenk Gilbert

THINGS HAVE GOT TO CHANGE
w&m/Archie Shepp

THINGS WE DID LAST SUMMER, THE
m/Jule Styne
w/Sammy Cahn

THINGS WE DO IN LOVE, THE
w&m/Eric Stewart, Lol Creme, Graham Gouldman

THINK
w&m/Aretha Franklin, Ted White

THINKING OF YOU
m/Walter Donaldson
w/Paul Ash

THINKING OF YOU
m/Harry Ruby
w/Bert Kalmar

THINKING OF YOU
w&m/Kenneth Loggins, James Messina

THIRD MAN THEME (instr.)
m/Anton Karas

THIRTY THREE YEARS
w&m/Muddy Waters, Charles E. Williams

THIS BITTER EARTH
w&m/Clyde Otis

THIS CAN'T BE LOVE
m/Richard Rodgers
w/Lorenz (Larry) Hart

THIS COULD BE THE START OF SOMETHING BIG
w&m/Steve Allen

THIS DIAMOND RING
w&m/Gary Lewis, Al Kooper

THIS EMPTY PLACE
m/Burt Bacharach
w/Hal David

THIS FLIGHT TONIGHT
w&m/Joni Mitchell

THIS GUITAR
w&m/George Harrison

THIS GUY'S IN LOVE WITH YOU
m/Burt Bacharach
w/Hal David

THIS HEART OF MINE
m/Harry Warren
w/Arthur Freed

THIS HERE
w&m/Bobby Timmons

THIS IS A GREAT COUNTRY
w&m/Irving Berlin

THIS IS ALL I ASK
w&m/Gordon Jenkins

THIS IS FOR ALBERT (instr.)
m/Wayne Shorter

THIS IS IT
w&m/Kenneth Loggins, Michael McDonald

THIS IS IT
w&m/Cindy Walker

THIS IS MY COUNTRY
w&m/Don Raye, Al Jacobs

THIS IS MY NIGHT TO DREAM
m/James Monaco
w/Johnny Burke

THIS IS MY PRAYER
w&m/Buddy Kaye, Philip Springer

THIS IS NO LAUGHING MATTER
m/Albert Frisch
w/Buddy Kaye

THIS IS THE ARMY, MR. JONES
w&m/Irving Berlin

THIS IS THE ARMY (film score)
m/Ray John Heindorf

THIS IS THE LIFE
w&m/Irving Berlin

THIS IS THE MISSUS
m/Ray Henderson
w/Lew Brown

THIS IS THE NIGHT
w&m/Redd Evans

THIS IS THE THANKS I GET
w&m/Eddy Arnold, Tommy Dilbeck

THIS IS WHERE I CAME IN
w&m/Harold Spina, Walter Bullock

THIS IS WORTH FIGHTING FOR
m/Sam H. Stept
w/Edgar DeLange

THIS LAND IS YOUR LAND
w&m/Woody Guthrie

THIS LITTLE GIRL OF MINE
w&m/Ray Charles (adapted from an early spiritual of unknown authorship)

THIS LOVE OF MINE
w&m/Frank Sinatra, Sol Parker, Hank Sanicola

THIS MASQUERADE
w&m/Leon Russell

THIS NEARLY WAS MINE
m/Richard Rodgers
w/Oscar Hammerstein II

THIS OLE HOUSE
w&m/Sturart Hamblen

THIS ONE'S FOR YOU
w&m/Barry Manilow, Marty Panzer

THIS SPORTING LIFE
w&m/Ian Whitcomb

THIS TIME
w&m/Waylon Jennings

THIS TIME I'M IN IT FOR LOVE
w&m/Steve Pippin, Larry Keith, J. Slate

THIS TIME THE DREAM'S ON ME
m/Harold Arlen
w/Johnny Mercer

THIS WILL BE
w&m/Marvin Yancy, Chuck Jackson

THIS WORLD
w&m/Roebuck "Pop" Staples

THIS YEAR'S KISSES
w&m/Irving Berlin

THOMAS CROWN AFFAIR, THE (film score)
m/Michel Legrand

THOROUGHLY MODERN MILLIE
m/James Van Heusen
w/Sammy Cahn

THOSE LAZY, HAZY, CRAZY DAYS OF SUMMER
w&m/Charles Tobias, Hans Carste

THOSE WEDDING BELLS SHALL NOT RING OUT
w&m/Monroe Rosenfeld

THOSE WERE THE DAYS
w&m/Gene Raskin

THOSE WONDERFUL YEARS
w&m/Webb Pierce, Don Schroeder

THOU SHALT NOT STEAL
w&m/John D. Loudermilk

THOU SWELL
m/Richard Rodgers
w/Lorenz (Larry) Hart

THOUSAND ISLAND SONG, THE (FLORENCE)
m/Carl Sigman
w/Bob Hilliard

THOUSAND MILES AGO, A
w&m/Webb Pierce, Mel Tillis

THOUSAND VIOLINS, A
w&m/Ray Evans, Jay H. Livingston

THREE BELLS, THE (WHILE THE ANGELUS WAS RINGING)
m/Jean Villard (from the French song "Les Trois Cloches")
w/Dick Manning

THREE COINS IN THE FOUNTAIN
m/Jule Styne
w/Sammy Cahn

THREE DAYS
w&m/Willie Nelson, Faron Young

THREE FACES OF EVE, THE (film score)
m/Robert Emmett Dolan

THREE LITTLE FISHIES
w&m/Horace Kirby Dowell

THREE LITTLE MAIDS FROM SCHOOL
m/Sir Arthur Sullivan
w/Sir WIlliam Schwenk Gilbert

THREE LITTLE SISTERS
w&m/Irving Taylor

THREE LITTLE WORDS
m/Harry Ruby
w/Bert Kalmar

THREE NIGHTS A WEEK
w&m/Antoine "Fats" Domino, Dave Bartholomew

THREE O'CLOCK BLUES
w&m/Jules Taub, B. B. King

THREE O'CLOCK IN THE MORNING
m/Julian Robledo
w/Theodora (Dolly) Morse

THREE ROSES
w&m/Dewey Bunnell

THREE STEPS TO THE PHONE
w&m/Harlan Howard

3:10 TO YUMA (film score)
m/George Duning

THREE TIMES A LADY
w&m/Lionel Richie

THREE WINDOW COUPE
w&m/Jan Berry, Roger Christian

THREE WINDOWS (instr.)
m/John Lewis

THRILL IS GONE, THE
m/Ray Henderson
w/Lew Brown, Buddy DeSylva

THROUGH A LONG AND SLEEPLESS NIGHT
m/Alfred Newman
w/Mack Gordon

THROUGH THE EYES OF LOVE
m/Marvin Hamlisch
w/Carole Bayer Sager

THROUGH THE YEARS
m/Vincent Youmans
w/Edward Heyman

THROW ANOTHER LOG ON THE FIRE
w&m/Charles Tobias, Jack Scholl, Murray Mencher

THROW HIM DOWN, McCLOSKEY
w&m/J. W. Kelly

THROW ME A ROSE
m/Emmerich Kalman
w/P. G. Wodehouse, Herbert Reynolds

THUMBALINA
w&m/Frank Loesser

THUNDER AND LIGHTING
w&m/Chi Coltrane

THUNDER IN MY HEART
w&m/Leo Sayer, Thomas Snow

THUNDER ISLAND
w&m/Jay Ferguson, Mark Andes

THUNDERBALL
m/John Barry
w/Leslie Bricusse

THUNDERER, THE (march)
m/John Philip Sousa

THURSDAY BLUES
w&m/James Andrew Rushing

TICKET TO RIDE
w&m/Paul McCartney, John Lennon

TICKLETOE (instr.)
m/Lester Young

TICO TICO
m/Zequinha Abreu, Aloysio Oliveira
w/Ervin M. Drake

TIE A YELLOW RIBBON ROUND THE OLE OAK TREE
w&m/L. Russell Brown, Irwin Levine

TIE ME KANGAROO DOWN SPORT
w&m/Rolf Harris

TIE YOUR MOTHER DOWN
w&m/Brian May

TIGER RAG
w&m/Original Dixieland Jazz Band (see composer listing under same)

TIGER WOMAN
w&m/Claude King, Merle Kilgore

TIGHT ROPE
w&m/Leon Russell

TIGHTEN UP
w&m/Archie Bell, Billy H. Buttier

TIJUANA GIFT SHOP (instr.)
m/Charles Mingus

TIJUANA TAXI
w&m/Johnny Flamingo, Bud Coleman

'TIL I CAN MAKE IT ON MY OWN
w&m/George Richey, Tammy Wynette, Billy Sherrill

TIL I KISSED
w&m/Don Everly

TILL
m/Charles Danvers
w/Carl Sigman

TILL I GAIN CONTROL AGAIN
w&m/Rodney Crowell

TILL THE CLOUDS ROLL BY
m/Jerome Kern
w/P. G. Wodehouse

TILL THE END OF TIME
w&m/Ted Mossman, Buddy Kaye (adapted from Chopin's "Polonaise In A-Flat Major, Op. 53)

TILL THE RIVERS ALL RUN DRY
w&m/Wayland Holyfield, Don Williams

TILL THE SANDS OF THE DESERT GROW COLD
m/Ernest R. Ball
w/George Graff

TILL THEN
w&m/Sol Marcus, Edward Seiler

TILL THERE WAS YOU
w&m/Meredith Willson

TILL WE MEET AGAIN
m/Richard A. Whiting
w/Raymond B. Egan

TIMBER
w&m/Joshua D. White

TIMBER I'M FALLING
w&m/Dallas Frazier, Ferlin Husky

TIME AFTER TIME
m/Jule Styne
w/Sammy Cahn

TIME AFTER TIME (film score)
m/Miklos Rozsa

TIME AND AGAIN
w&m/Stuff Smith

TIME AND LOVE
w&m/Laura Nyro

TIME FOR EVERYTHING, A
w&m/Ian Anderson

TIME FOR US, A
m/Nino Rota
w/Larry Kusik, Eddy Snyder

TIME IN A BOTTLE
w&m/Jim Croce

TIME IS RIGHT
w&m/Steve Cropper, Booker T. Jones, Al Jackson, Donald Dunn

TIME OF THE SEASON
w&m/Rodney Argent

TIME ON MY HANDS
m/Vincent Youmans
w/Mack Gordon, Harold Adamson

TIME OUT
w&m/Eddie Durham

TIME PASSAGES
w&m/Al Stewart, Peter White

TIME PASSES SLOWLY
w&m/Robert Dylan

TIME TO GET DOWN
w&m/Kenneth Gamble, Leon Huff

TIME TO KILL
w&m/J. Robbie Robertson

TIME WAITS FOR NO ONE
m/Cliff Friend
w/Charles Tobias

TIME WAS WHEN LOVE AND I
m/Sir Arthur Sullivan
w/Sir William Schwenk Gilbert

TIME'S A-WASTING
m/Duke Ellington, Mercer Ellington
w/Don George

TIMES THEY ARE A' CHANGIN', THE
w&m/Robert Dylan

TIN PAN ALLEY (film score)
m/Alfred Newman

TIN ROOF BLUES(instr.)
m/Ben Pollack, Walter Melrose, Leon Rappolo, Paul Wares, Georges Brunes, Mel Stitzler (see "Make Love To Me" for lyric version)

TINA MARIE
w&m/Bob Merrill

TING-A-LING
w&m/Ahmet Ertegun

TINY BUBBLES (HUA LI'I)
w&m/Leon Porter

TINY DANCER
m/Elton John
w/Bernie Taupin

TI-PI-TIN
m/Maria Grever
w/Raymond Leveen

TIP OF MY FINGERS, THE
w&m/Bill Anderson

TIP TOE THROUGH THE TULIPS
m/Joseph A. Burke
w/Al Dubin

TIPPERARY BLUES
w&m/Euday Louis Bowman

(I'M SO) TIRED OF BEING ALONE
w&m/Al Green

TIRED OF WAITING FOR YOU
w&m/Raymond Douglas Davies

'TIS AUTUMN
w&m/Henry Nemo

'TIS THE LAST ROSE OF SUMMER
m/from the traditional Irish melody "Groves Of Blarney"
w/Thomas Moore

TITANIC (film score)
m/Bronislau Kaper

TIT-WILLOW
m/Sir Arthur Sullivan
w/Sir William Schwenk Gilbert

TO A WATER LILY
w&m/Edward Alexander MacDowell

TO A WILD ROSE
w&m/Edward Alexander MacDowell

TO BE LOVED
w&m/Berry Gordy Jr., Tyrone Carlo, Gwen Gordy

TO CRY YOU A SONG
w&m/Ian Anderson

TO DADDY
w&m/Dolly Parton

TO DIE IN THE SUMMERTIME
w&m/Rod McKuen

TO EACH HIS OWN
w&m/Ray Evans, Jay H. Livingston

TO GET TO YOU
w&m/Jean Chapel

TO HAVE SOMEBODY
w&m/Barry, Maurice and Robin Gibb

TO KILL A MOCKINGBIRD
m/Elmer Bernstein
w/Mack David

TO KNOW HIM IS TO LOVE HIM
w&m/Phil Spector

TO LIFE
m/Jerry Bock
w/Sheldon Harnick

TO LOVE
w&m/Carole King, Gerry Goffin

TO MAKE A MAN
w&m/Loretta Lynn

TO MY WIFE
w&m/Harold Rome

TO PARIS WITH LOVE (film score)
m/Edwin Astley

TO REST LET HIM GENTLY BE LAID
m/David Braham
w/George Cooper

TO SEE AN ANGEL CRY
w&m/Conway Twitty

TO SIR WITH LOVE
m/Mark London
w/Don Black

TO SUSAN ON THE WEST COAST WAITING
w&m/Donovan

TO THE ENDS OF THE EARTH
m/Joe Sherman
w/Noel Sherman

TO THE LAND OF MY OWN ROMANCE
m/Victor Herbert
w/Harry B. Smith

TO YOU SWEETHEART, ALOHA
w&m/Harry Owens

TOAST AND MARMALADE FOR TEA
w&m/Steve Kipner, Fred Goodman

TOAST OF NEW ORLEANS, THE (film score)
m/Nicholas Brodzsky

TODAY
w&m/Hank Thompson

TOGETHER
m/Ray Henderson
w/Lew Brown, Buddy DeSylva

TOGETHER AGAIN
w&m/Buck Owens

TOGETHER ALONE
w&m/Melanie

TOGETHER WHEREVER WE GO
m/Jule Styne
w/Stephen Sondheim

TOLD AT SUNSET
w&m/Edward Alexander MacDowell

TOM CAT BLUES (instr.)
m/Ferdinand "Jelly Roll" Morton

TOM JOAD
w&m/Woody Guthrie

TOM JONES (film score)
m/John Addison

TOMBSTONE BLUES
w&m/Robert Dylan

TOMMY CAN YOU HEAR ME
w&m/Peter Townshend

TOMORROW
m/Charles Strouse
w/Martin Charnin

TOMORROW IS THE QUESTION (instr.)
m/Ornette Coleman

TOMORROW NEVER COMES
w&m/Johnny Bond, Ernest Tubb

TONGUE IN CHEEK
w&m/Jerry Corbetta, Robert Webber, Robert Raymond

TONGUE TIED BLUES
w&m/Alan Freed

TONIGHT
m/Leonard Bernstein
w/Stephen Sondheim

TONIGHT
m/Elton John
w/Bernie Taupin

TONIGHT MY BABY'S COMING DOWN
w&m/Billy Sherrill, Glenn Sutton

TONIGHT WE LOVE
m/Freddy Martin, Ray Austin (adapted from Tchaikovsky's "First Piano Concerto") w/Bobby Worth

TONIGHT YOU BELONG TO ME
w&m/Billy Rose

TONIGHT'S THE NIGHT
w&m/Don Covay, Solomon Burke

TONIGHT'S THE NIGHT
w&m/Rod Stewart

TONIGHT'S THE NIGHT
w&m/Neil Young

TOO BLUE TO CRY
w&m/Al Dexter

TOO CLOSE FOR COMFORT
w&m/George D. Weiss, Jerry Bock, Larry Holofcener

TOO DARN HOT
w&m/Cole Porter

TOO FAT POLKA
w&m/Ross MacLean, Arthur Richardson

TOO LATE
w&m/Jimmy Wakely

TOO LATE TO WORRY
w&m/Al Dexter

TOO MANY MONDAYS
w&m/Barry Mann, Cynthia Weil

TOO MARVELOUS FOR WORDS
m/Richard Whiting
w/Johnny Mercer

TOO MUCH IN LOVE
m/Walter Kent
w/Kim Gannon

TOO MANY FISH IN THE SEA
w&m/Eddie Holland, Brian Holland, Lamont Dozier

TOO MUCH HEAVE
w&m/Barry, Maurice and Robin Gibb

TOO MUCH MONKEY BUSINESS
w&m/Chuck Berry

TOO MUCH TOO LITTLE TOO LATE
w&m/Steve Kipner, John Vallins

TOO YOUNG
m/Sidney Lippman
w/Sylvia Dee

TOO-RA-LOO-RA-LOO-RAL (THAT'S AN IRISH LULLABY)
w&m/James Royce Shannon

TOO YOUNG TO GO STEADY
m/Jimmy McHugh
w/Harold Adamson

TOOT TOOT TOOTSIE, GOODBYE
m/Ted Fiorito
w/Gus Kahn, Ernie Erdman, Dan Russo, Robert King

TOOTIN' THROUGH THE ROOF (instr.)
m/Duke Ellington

TOP HAT, WHITE TIE AND TAILS
w&m/Irving Berlin

TOP LINER RAG
w&m/Joseph Francis Lamb

TOP OF THE WORLD
m/Richard Carpenter
w/John Bettis

TOPKAPI (film score)
m/Manos Hadjidakis

TOPPER RETURNS (film score)
m/Werner Heyman

TOPSY
w&m/Eddie Durham

TORN BETWEEN TWO LOVERS
w&m/Peter Yarrow, Phillip Jarrell

TORTURE
w&m/John D. Loudermilk

TOTEM TOM TOM
m/Herbert Stothart, Rudolf Friml
w/Otto Harbach, Oscar Hammerstein II

TOUCH A HAND, MAKE A FRIEND
w&m/Homer Banks, Carl M. Hampton, Raymond Jackson

TOUCH OF EVIL (film score)
m/Henry Mancini

TOUCH OF YOUR HAND, THE
m/Jerome Kern
w/Otto Harbach

TOUCH OF YOUR LIPS, THE
w&m/Ray Noble

TOUCH ME IN THE MORNING
m/Michael Masser
w/Ronald Miller

TOUCHING HOME
w&m/Dallas Frazier, A. L. (Doodle) Owens

TOUCHING JESUS
w&m/John Stallings

TOUGH LUCK BLUES
w&m/Gertrude "Ma" Rainey

TOURIST, THE
w&m/Gerry Rafferty

TOWERING INFERNO (film score)
m/John Williams

TOWN WITHOUT PITY
m/Burt Bacharach
w/Hal David

TOY TRUMPET, THE (instr.)
m/Raymond Scott

TOYLAND
m/Victor Herbert
w/Glen MacDonough

TOYS IN THE ATTIC (film score)
m/George Duning

TRA LA LA LA
w&m/Ike Turner

TRACES
w&m/Buddy Buie, James R. Cobb Jr., Emory Gordy Jr.

TRACES
w&m/Dennis Yost, Wally Eaton

TRACKS OF MY TEARS, THE
w&m/William (Smokey) Robinson Jr., Marvin Tarplin, Warren Moore

TRAFFIC JAM (instr.)
m/Artie Shaw, Teddy McCrae

TRAGEDY
w&m/Barry, Maurice and Robin Gibb

TRAIL HERDING COWBOY
w&m/Bob Nolan

TRAIL OF THE LONESOME PINE, THE
m/Harry Carroll
w/Ballard MacDonald

TRAIN, THE
w&m/Jerry Kasenetz, Jeff Katz

TRAIN, THE (COLORS OF LOVE)
w&m/Albert L. Hammond, Mike Hazelwood

TRAIN IS GONE, THE
w&m/Michael Bloomfield

TRAINS AND BOATS AND PLANES
m/Burt Bacharach
w/Hal David

TRAMP! TRAMP! TRAMP!
m/Victor Herbert
w/Rida Johnson Young

TRAMP, TRAMP, TRAMP (THE PRISONER'S HOPE)
w&m/George Frederick Root

TRANEING IN (instr.)
m/John Coltrane

TRANQUILLO
w&m/James Taylor, Carly Simon, Arif Mardin

TRANQUILLO (MEET MY HEART)
w&m/Carly Simon, James Taylor, Arif Mardin

TRANSITION (instr.)
m/John Coltrane

TRANSISTOR SISTER
w&m/Freddie Cannon, Bob Crewe, Frank C. Slay Jr.

TRAVELIN' BLUES
w&m/Jimmy Rodgers, Shelley Lee Alley

TRAVELIN' MAN
w&m/Rick Nelson

TRAVELLIN' BAND
w&m/John C. Fogerty

TRAVELLING MAN
w&m/Dolly Parton

TREASURE OF LOVE
w&m/Joe Shapiro, Lou Stallman

TREASURE OF LOVE
w&m/J. P. Richardson (Big Bopper)

TREASURE OF SIERRA MADRE (film score)
m/Max Steiner

TREASURE OF THE GOLDEN CONDOR (film score)
m/Bronislau Kaper

TREASURES UNTOLD
w&m/Jimmy Rodgers, Elsworth T. Cozzens

TREAT HER LIKE A LADY
w&m/Edward Lee Cornelius, Jr.

TREE IN THE MEADOW, A
w&m/Billy Reid

TREE IN THE PARK, A
m/Richard Rodgers
w/Lorenz (Larry) Hart

TREES
m/Oscar Rasbach
w/Joyce Kilmer

TREMONISHA (opera)
w&m/Scott Joplin

TRIANGLE
w&m/Jean Chapel, Robert Taubert

TRICK OF THE LIGHT
w&m/John Entwhistle

TRIFLIN' GAL
w&m/Cindy Walker

TRIP TO HEAVEN
w&m/Freddie Hart

TROLLEY SONG, THE
w&m/Ralph Blane, Hugh Martin

TROPIC APPETITES
m/Carla Bley
w/Paul Haines

TROUBLE
w&m/Meredith Willson

TROUBLE BLUES
w&m/Son House

TROUBLE IN MIND
w&m/Richard M. Jones

TROUBLE NO MORE
w&m/Muddy Waters

TRUCK DRIVERS' BLUES
w&m/Ted Daffan

TRUCKIN'
w&m/Rube Bloom, Ted Koehler

TRUE GRIT (film score)
m/Elmer Bernstein

TRUE GRIT
m/Elmer Berstein
w/Don Black

TRUE LOVE
w&m/Cole Porter

TRUE LOVE IS GREATER THAN FRIENDSHIP
w&m/Carl Lee Perkins

TRUE, TRUE LOVE, A
w&m/Bobby Darin

TRUMPETER'S LULLABY, A
m/Leroy Anderson

TRUST
w&m/Paul Williams, Roger Nichols

TRUST NO MAN
w&m/Gertrude "Ma" Rainey

TRY A LITTLE KINDNESS
w&m/Bobby Austin, Thomas Sapaugh

TRY A LITTLE TENDERNESS
w&m/Harry M. Wood, Jimmy Campbell, Reg Connelly

TRY IT BABY
w&m/Berry Gordy Jr.

TRY ME
w&m/James Brown

TRY ME I KNOW WE CAN MAKE IT
w&m/Donna Summer, Georgio Moroder, Pete Bellotte

TRY ME ONE MORE TIME
w&m/Ernest Tubb

TRY TO REMEMBER
w&m/Tom Jones, Harvey Schmidt
TRYING
w&m/Billy Vaughn
TUBBY THE TUBA
m/George Kleinsinger
w/Paul Tripp
TUBULAR BELLS (instr.)
m/Mike Oldfield
TUESDAY HEARTBREAK
w&m/Stevie Wonder
TULARE DUST
w&m/Merle Haggard
TULIP TIME
m/David Stamper
w/Gene Buck
TUMBLEWEED CONNECTION
m/Elton John
w/Bernie Taupin
TUMBLING DICE
w&m/Mick Jagger, Keith Richard
TUMBLING TUMBLEWEEDS
w&m/Bob Nolan
TUNE UP (instr.)
m/Miles Dewey Davis
TUNNEL OF LOVE
w&m/Walter Egan
TUPELO HONEY
w&m/Van Morrison
TURN AROUND, LOOK AT ME
w&m/Jerry Capehart
TURN BACK THE HANDS OF TIME
w&m/Jimmy Eaton, Larry Wagner

TUTTI FRUTTI
w&m/Little Richard, Joe Lubin, Dorothy LaBostrie
TUXEDO JUNCTION
w&m/Buddy Feyne, Erskine Hawkins, William Johnson, Julian Dash
TWEEDLE DEE
w&m/Winfield Scott
TWELFTH OF NEVER, THE
m/Jerry Livingston
w/Paul Francis Webster
TWELFTH STREET RAG
m/Euday L. Bowman
w/original words: James S. Sumner
w/revised words: Andy Razaf
TWELVE ANGRY MEN (film score)
m/Kenyon Hopkins

TWENTY FIVE MILES
w&m/Harvey Fuqua, Johnny Bristol, Edwin Starr, Jerry Wexler, Bert Berns
25 or 6 TO 4
w&m/Robert Lamm
TWENTY FOUR HOURS FROM TULSA
m/Burt Bacharach
w/Hal David
TWENTY FOUR HOURS OF SUNSHINE
m/Peter De Rose
w/Carl Sigman
TWENTY LOVE-SICK MAIDENS, WE
m/Sir Arthur Sullivan
w/Sir William Schwenk Gilbert
TURN THE WORLD AROUND THE OTHER WAY
w&m/Ben Peters
TURN TO STONE
w&m/Jeff Lynne
TURN TO STONE
w&m/Joseph F. Walsh
TURN! TURN! TURN!
w&m/Pete Seeger (words from "The Book of Ecclesiastes")
TURN YOUR RADIO ON
w&m/Ray Stevens
TURNSTILE (instr.)
m/Gerry Mulligan
TUSH
w&m/William Gibbons, Frank Beard, Dusty Hill
TUSK
w&m/Lindsay Buckingham
TWENTY THIRD PSALM
w&m/musical setting to Biblical text by Albert Hay Malotte
TWILIGHT IN TURKEY (instr.)
m/Raymond Scott
TWILIGHT ON THE TRAIL
m/Louis Alter
w/Sidney D. Mitchell
TWILIGHT TIME
w&m/Morty Nevins, Al Nevins, Artie Dunn, Buck Ram
TWIST, THE
w&m/Hank Ballard
TWIST AND SHOUT
w&m/Phil Medley, Bert Russell
TWISTIN' THE NIGHT AWAY
w&m/Sam Cooke

TWO BIT MANCHILD
w&m/Neil Diamond
TWO BY TWO
m/Richard Rodgers
w/Stephen Sondheim
TWO CIGARETTES IN THE DARK
w&m/Lew Pollack, Paul Francis Webster
TWO DIFFERENT WORLDS
m/Al Frisch
w/Sid Wayne
TWO DOORS DOWN
w&m/Dolly Parton
TWO FINE PEOPLE
w&m/Cat Stevens
TWO FOR THE SEESAW (film score)
m/Andre Previn
TWO HEARTS IN THREE QUARTER TIME
m/Robert Stolz
w/Joseph Young
TWO HEARTS THAT PASS IN THE NIGHT (DAME DE TUS ROSAS)
m/Ernest Lecuona
w/Forman Brown
200 MOTELS (film score)
m/Frank Zappa
TWO LADIES IN DE SHADE OF DE BANANA TREE
m/Harold Arlen
w/Truman Capote
TWO LOST SOULS
m/Jerry Ross
w/Richard Adler
TWO LOVERS
w&m/William (Smokey) Robinson Jr.
TWO LOVES HAVE I
w&m/John Murray

TWO LOVES HAVE I
m/Barry Trivers
w/Ben Oakland
TWO O'CLOCK JUMP (instr.)
m/Harry James, William (Count) Basie, Benny Goodman

TWO ROSES
m/Ludwig Englander
w/Stanislau Stange
TWO SLEEPY PEOPLE
m/Hoagy Carmichael
w/Frank Loesser

TWO TICKETS TO GEORGIA
m/J. Fred Coots
w/Charles Tobias, Joseph Young

TWO TICKETS TO PARADISE
w&m/Eddie Money

TYPEWRITER, THE
m/Leroy Anderson

TZENA, TZENA, TZENA
m/Issachar Miron (adapted by Julius Grossman)
w/Mitchell Parish

Addenda:

**TAKE YOUR TIME
(DO IT RIGHT)**
w&m/Harold Clayton, Sigidi

THEY WERE DOING THE MAMBO
m/Sonny Burke
w/Don Raye

THINK ON ME (instr.)
m/George Cables

THIS MOMENT IN TIME
w&m/Alan Bernstein, Richard Adams

**TRAIN ROBBERS, THE
(film score)**
m/Dominic Frontiere

TREASURE
w&m/Rod Temperton

 **SONGS**

U, V

UGLY DUCKLING, THE
w&m/Albert Hay Malotte

UKULELE LADY
m/Richard Whiting
w/Gus Kahn

UMBRELLAS OF CHERBOURG
(Film Score)
m/Michel Legrand

UMBRIAGO
m/Jimmy Durante
w/Irving Caesar

UNBIRTHDAY SONG
m/Jerry Livingston
w/Mack David

UNBORN CHILD
w&m/James Seals, Lana Bogan

UNCHAINED MELODY
m/Alex North
w/Hy Zaret

UNCHAINED MELODY (film
score)
m/Alex North

UNCLE ALBERT/ADMIRAL
HALSEY
w&m/Paul and Linda McCartney

UNCEL PEN (instr.)
m/William Smith Monroe

UNCLE SAM SAYS
w&m/Joshua D. White

UNDECIDED
m/Charlie Shavers
w/Sid Robin

UNDECIDED BLUES
w&m/James Andrew Rushing

UNDER A BLANKET OF BLUE
m/Isham Jones
w/Al J. Neiburg, Jerry Livingston,
Marty Symes

UNDER MOONSHINE
w&m/Ray Thomas

UNDER MY THUMB
w&m/Mick Jagger, Keith Richard

UNDER MY WHEELS
w&m/Michael Bruce

UNDER PARIS SKIES
w&m/Hubert Giraud, Kim Gannon

UNDER THE ANHEUSER
BUSCH
m/Harry Von Tilzer
w/Andrew B. Sterling

UNDER THE BAMBOO TREE
w&m/J. Rosamond Johnson, Bob
Cole

UNDER THE INFLUENCE OF
LOVE
w&m/Harlan Howard, Buck Owens

UNDER THE YUM YUM TREE
m/Harry Von Tilzer
w/Andrew B. Sterling

UNDER TWO FLAGS (film score)
m/Louis Silvers

UNDERCOVER ANGEL
w&m/Alan O'Day

UNDERNEATH THE ARCHES
w&m/Bud Flanagan, Joseph
McCarthy

UNDERNEATH THE HARLEM
MOON
m/Harry Revel
w/Mack Gordon

UNEASY RIDER
w&m/Charlie Daniels, Don Rubin

UNFORGETTABLE
w&m/Irving Gordon

UNICORN, THE
w&m/Shel Silverstein

UNION MAID
w&m/Woody Guthrie

UNIVERSAL SOLDIER, THE
w&m/Buffy Sainte-Marie

UNTIL IT'S TIME FOR YOU TO
GO
w&m/Buffy Sainte-Marie

UNTIL THE NEXT TEARDROP
FALLS
w&m/Freddy Fender, Huey P.
Meaux

UNTIL THE REAL THING
COMES ALONG
m/Saul Chaplin
w/Sammy Cahn

UNTIL THE REAL THING
COMES ALONG
w&m/Mann Holiner, Alberta Nichols
Holiner

UNTIL THEN
w&m/Stuart Hamblen

UP ABOVE MY HEAD, I HEAR
MUSIC IN THE AIR
w&m/Rosetta Tharpe

UP AROUND THE BEND
w&m/John C. Fogerty

UP FROM THE SKIES
w&m/Jimi Hendrix

UP IN A BALLOON
m/Percy Wenrich
w/Ren Shields

UP IN ARMS (film score)
m/Ray John Heindorf

UP 'N ADAM (instr.)
m/Lester Young

UP ON CRIPPLE CREEK
w&m/J. Robbie Robertson

UP ON THE ROOF
w&m/Carole King, Gerry Goffin

UP THE DOWN STAIRCASE
(film score)
m/Fred Karlin

UP THE NECK
w&m/Chrissie Hyde, Pete Farndon

UP THE SANDBOX (film score)
m/Billy Goldenberg

UPTIGHT (EVERYTHING'S
ALRIGHT)
w&m/Stevie Wonder, Sylvia Moy,
Henry Cosby

UP, UP AND AWAY
w&m/Jimmy Webb

UP, UP IN MY AEROPLANE
m/Gus Edwards
w/Edward Madden

UPTOWN
w&m/Barry Mann, Cynthia Weil

U. S. MALE
w&m/Jerry Reed

U. S. OF A.
w&m/Donna Fargo

USE ME
w&m/Bill Withers

USE YOUR IMAGINATION
w&m/Cole Porter

VACANT CHAIR, THE (WE
SHALL MEET BUT WE SHALL
MISS HIM)
m/George Frederick Root
w/H. S. Washburn

VAHEVALA
w&m/Kenneth Loggins, James
Messina

VALENCIA
m/Jose Padilla
w/Clifford Grey

VALENTINA WAY
w&m/Al Stewart

VALENTINE LOVE
w&m/Michael Henderson

VALLERI
w&m/Tommy Boyce, Bobby Hart

VALLEY OF LIFE (instr.)
m/McCoy Tyner

VALSE BLUETTE (instr.)
m/Riccardo Drigo

VALSE HOT (instr.)
m/Sonny Rollins

VANESSA
w&m/Bernie Wayne

VARSITY DRAG
m/Ray Henderson
w/Lew Brown, Buddy DeSylva

VAYA CON DIOS
w&m/Inez James, Buddy Pepper,
Larry Russell

VAYA CON DIOS (MAY GOD BE WITH YOU)
w&m/Larry Russell, Inez James

VENDOME (instr.)
m/John Lewis

VENDREDI 13 (instr.)
m/Django Reinhardt

VENTURA HIGHWAY
w&m/Dewey Bunnell

VENUS
w&m/Ed Marshall

VENUS DE MILO (instr.)
m/Gerry Mulligan

VENUS IN BLUE JEANS
w&m/Howard Greenfield, Jack
Keller

VERY PRECIOUS LOVE, A
m/Sammy Fain
w/Paul Francis Webster

VERY SPECIAL LOVE SONG, A
w&m/Billy Sherrill, Norro Wilson

VERY THOUGHT OF YOU, THE
w&m/Ray Noble

VICTIM OF LOVE
w&m/Don Henley, Glenn Frey, J. D.
Souther, Don Felder

VICTIM OF LOVE
w&m/Pete Belotte, S. Levay

VICTORIA
w&m/Raymond Douglas Davies

VICTORY AT SEA (TV score)
m/Richard Rodgers

VIENNA DREAMS
m/Rudolf Sieczynski
w/Irving Caesar

VIGILANTE MAN
w&m/Woody Guthrie

VILIA
m/Franz Lehar
w/Adrian Ross

VILLAGE OF ST. BERNADETTE, THE
w&m/Eula Parker

VINCENT
w&m/Don McClean

VIOLET
m/Ivan Caryll
w/James O'Dea

VIOLETS FOR YOUR FURS
m/Matt Dennis
w/Thomas M. Adair

VIRGINIAN, THE (TV theme) (instr.)
m/Percy Faith

VISION (instr.)
m/McCoy Tyner

VISIONS OF JOHANNA
w&m/Robert Dylan

VIVA LAS VEGAS
w&m/Doc (Jerome) Pomus, Mort
Shuman

VIVA ZAPATA (film score)
m/Alex North

VOICE OF FREEDOM
w&m/James Kirk

VOICE OF THE HUDSON, THE
w&m/Paul Dresser

VOICE OF THE HUDSON, THE
w&m/Paul Dresser

VOLARE (NEL BLU, DIPINTO BLU)
m/Domenico Modugno
w/Mitchell Parish

VON RYAN'S EXPRESS (film score)
m/Jerry Goldsmith

VOODOO MAN
m/Alfred Newman
w/Otto Harbach

VOYAGE OF THE DAMNED (film score)
m/Lalo Schifrin

Addenda:

UN POCO LOCO (instr.)
m/Bud Powell

UPSIDE DOWN
w&m/Nile Rodgers, Bernard Edwards

VOODOO LADY (instr.)
m/George Cables

SONGS

W

WABASH BLUES
m/Fred Meinken
w/Dave Ringle

WABASH CANNONBALL
w&m/Roy Claxton Acuff

WAGON WHEELS
m/Peter De Rose
w&m/Billy Hill

WAIT, THE
w&m/Chrissie Hynde, Peter Farndon

WAIT FOR ME
w&m/Daryl Hall

WAIT FOR ME MARY
w&m/Nat Simon, Charles Tobias,
Harry Tobias

WAIT FOR THE WAGON
m/George P. Knauff
w/source unknown

**WAIT 'TIL THE SUN SHINES
NELLIE**
m/Harry Von Tilzer
w/Andrew B. Sterling

**WAIT TILL THE COWS COME
HOME**
m/Ivan Caryll
w/Anne Caldwell

WAIT TILL YOU SEE HER
m/Richard Rodgers
w/Lorenz (Larry) Hart

**WAITIN' AT THE GATE FOR
KATY**
m/Richard Whiting
w/Gus Kahn

WAITIN' IN SCHOOL
w&m/Dorsey Burnette, Johnny
Burnette

**WAITIN' IN YOUR WELFARE
LINE**
w&m/Buck Owens, Nathan Stuckey,
Don Rich

WAITING
w&m/Harry Edward Nilsson

WAITING AT THE CHURCH
w&m/Henry E. Pether

WAITING FOR A TRAIN
w&m/Jimmy Rodgers

**WAITING FOR THE ROBERT E.
LEE**
m/Lewis F. Muir
w/L. Wolfe Gilbert

**WAITING FOR THE TRAIN TO
COME IN**
w&m/Martin Block, Sunny Skylar

WAKE NICODEMUS
w&m/Henry Clay Work

**WAKE THE TOWN AND TELL
THE PEOPLE**
m/Jerry Livingston
w/Sammy Gallop

WAKE UP AND LIVE
m/Harry Revel
w/Mack Gordon

WAKE UP LITTLE SUSIE
w&m/Boudleaux Bryant, Felice
Bryant

WAKING UP ALONE
w&m/Paul Williams

WALK A MILE IN MY SHOES
w&m/Joe South

WALK AWAY
w&m/Joseph F. Walsh

WALK AWAY RENEE
w&m/Michael Brown

**WALK IN DE MIDDLE OF THE
ROAD**
w&m/William S. Hays

**WALK IN THE BLACK FOREST,
A (instr.)**
m/Horst Jankowski

WALK LIKE A MAN
w&m/Bob Gaudio, Bob Crewe

WALK ME TO THE DOOR
w&m/Conway Twitty

WALK ON BY
m/Burt Bacharach
w/Hal David

WALK ON THE WILD SIDE
m/Elmer Bernstein
w/Mack David

WALK ON WATER
w&m/Neil Diamond

WALK OUT BACKWARDS
w&m/Bill Anderson

WALK RIGHT BACK
w&m/Sonny Curtis

WALK RIGHT IN
w&m/Erik Darling, Willard Svanoe,
Hosie Woods, Gus Cannon

WALK TALL, WALK STRAIGHT
w&m/Don Wayne

WALK THIS WAY
w&m/Steve Tyler, Joe Perry

WALKIN' (instr.)
m/Miles Dewey Davis

WALKIN' BY THE RIVER
m/Una Mae Carlisle
w/Robert Sour

WALKIN' DOWN THE LINE
w&m/Robert Dylan

WALKIN' IN THE SUNSHINE
w&m/Roger Miller

**WALKIN' MY BABY BACK
HOME**
w&m/Harry Richman, Roy Turk,
Fred E. Ahlert

**WALKIN' THE FLOOR OVER
YOU**
w&m/Ernest Tubb

WALKIN' TO MISSOURI
w&m/Bob Merrill

WALKIN' TO NEW ORLEANS
w&m/Antoine "Fats" Domino, Dave
Bartholomew

**WALKING AND SWINGING
(instr.)**
m/Mary Lou Williams

**WALKING DOWN TO
WASHINGTON**
m/Sammy Mysels
w/Dick Sanford, Redd Evans

**WALKING IN JERUSALEM
(instr.)**
m/William Smith Monroe

WALKING IN RHYTHM
w&m/Barney Perry

WALKING IN THE RAIN
w&m/Barry Mann, Cynthia Weil, Phil
Spector

WALL STREET RAG (instr.)
m/Scott Joplin

WALL TO WALL LOVE
w&m/Helen Carter, June Carter

WALL, THE
w&m/Freddie Hart

**WALLFLOWER (DANCE WITH
ME HENRY)**
w&m/Johnny Otis, Hank Ballard,
Etta James

WALTONS, THE (TV theme)
m/Jerry Goldsmith

WALTZ FOR DEBBY (instr.)
m/Bill Evans

**WALTZ ME AROUND AGAIN
WILLIE**
m/Ren Shields
w/Will D. Cobb

**WALTZ YOU SAVED FOR ME,
THE**
m/Wayne King, Emil Flindt
w/Gus Kahn

WALTZING MATILDA
m/Marie Cowan
w/A. B. Paterson

WAND'RING MINSTREL, A
m/Sir Arthur Sullivan
w/Sir William Schwenk Gilbert

WANG WANG BLUES
w&m/Henry Busse, Gus Mueller,
Buster Johnson

WANG WANG DOODLE
w&m/Willie Dixon

WANTED
w&m/Lois Steele, Jack Fulton

WANTING YOU
m/Sigmund Romberg
w/Oscar Hammerstein II

WAR DANCE FOR WOODEN
INDIANS (instr.)
m/Raymond Scott

WARM ALL OVER
w&m/Frank Loesser

WARM AND WILLING
w&m/Ray Evans, Jay H. Livingston

WARM VALLEY (instr.)
m/Duke Ellington

WARM WAYS
w&m/Christine Perfect McVie

WARSAW CONCERTO (instr.)
m/Richard Addinsell

WAS IT RAIN
m/Lou Handman
w/Walter Hirsch

WAS THAT THE HUMAN
THING TO DO
m/Sammy Fain
w/Joseph Young

WASHBOARD BLUES
m/Hoagy Carmichael
w/Mitchell Parish

WASHINGTON AND LEE
SWING
m/Thornton W. Allen
w/C. A. Robbins

WASHINGTON POST MARCH
m/John Philip Sousa

WASN'T BORN TO FOLLOW
w&m/Carole King, Gerry Goffin

WASTED DAYS AND WASTED
NIGHTS
w&m/Freddy Fender, Wayne
Duncan

WASTED WORDS
w&m/Gregg L. Allman, Duane
Allman

WASTED WORDS
w&m/Don Gibson

WATCH WHAT HAPPENS
m/Michel Legrand
w/Norman Gimbel

WATCHIN' SCOTT GROW
w&m/Mac Davis

WATCHING THE DETECTIVES
w&m/Elvis Costello

WATCHING THE TRAINS GO
BY
w&m/Tony Joe White

WATER BOY
w&m/Avery Robinson

WATERFRONT
w&m/John Lee Hooker

WATERLOO
w&m/John D. Loudermilk, Marijohn
Wilkin

WATERLOO
m/Benny Anersson, Bjorn Ulvaeus
w/Stig Anderson

WATERMARK
w&m/Jimmy Webb

WATERMELON MAN
w&m/Herbie Hancock

WAVE (instr.)
m/Antonio Carlos Jobim

WAVE TO ME MY LADY
w&m/William Stein, Frank Loesser

WAVELENGTH
w&m/Van Morrison

WAY DOWN
w&m/Layng Martine

WAY DOWN IN OLD INDIANA
w&m/Paul Dresser

WAY DOWN SOUTH
w&m/Stephen C. Foster

WAY DOWN YONDER IN NEW
ORLEANS
m/J. Turner Layton
w/Henry Creamer

WAY DOWN YONDER IN THE
CORN FIELD
m/Gus Edwards
w/Will D. Cobb

WAY I WANT TO TOUCH YOU,
THE
w&m/Toni Tennille

WAY OUT THERE
w&m/Bob Nolan

WAY OVER YONDER
w&m/Carole King

WAY OUT YONDER IN THE
GOLDEN WEST
w&m/Percy Wenrich

WAY WE WERE, THE
m/Marvin Hamlisch
w/Marilyn and Alan Bergman

WAY YOU DO THE THINGS
YOU DO, THE
w&m/Robert Rogers

WAY YOU LOOK TONIGHT,
THEm/Jerome Kern
w/Dorothy Fields

WAYWARD WIND, THE
w&m/Herbert Newman, Stan
Lebowsky

WAYS OF A WOMAN IN LOVE
w&m/William E. Justis Jr., Charlie
Rich

WAYS TO LOVE A MAN, THE
w&m/Glenn Sutton, Tammy
Wynette, Billy Sherrill

WE ARE COMING, FATHER
ABRAHAM
w&m/Stephen C. Foster

WE ARE DAINTY LITTLE
FAIRIES
m/Sir Arthur Sullivan
w/Sir William Schwenk Gilbert

WE ARE FAMILY
w&m/Nile Rodgers, Bernard
Edwards

WE ARE THE CHAMPIONS
w&m/Brian May

WE CAN'T GO LIVIN' LIKE
THIS
w&m/Eddie Rabbitt, Even Stevens

WE DID IT BEFORE AND WE
CAN DO IT AGAIN
m/Cliff Friend
w/Charles Tobias

WE FIGHT TOMORROW
MOTHER
w&m/Paul Dresser

WE GOT BY
w&m/Al Jarreau

WE GOT TO GET YOU A
WOMAN
w&m/Todd Rundgren

WE GOT TO HAVE PEACE
w&m/Curtis Mayfield

WE KISS IN A SHADOW
m/Richard Rodgers
w/Oscar Hammerstein II

WE LIVE IN TWO DIFFERENT
WORLDS
w&m/Fred Rose

WE MAY NEVER LOVE LIKE
THIS AGAIN
w&m/Joel Hirschhorn, Al Kasha

WE MAY NEVER PASS THIS
WAY AGAIN
w&m/Dash Crofts, James Seals

WE MISSED YOU
w&m/Bill Anderson

WE MUST BE VIGILANT (AMERICAN PATROL)
m/Joseph A. Burke
w/Edgar Leslie

WE MUST HAVE BEEN OUT OF OUR MINDS
w&m/Melba Montgomery

WE NEED A LITTLE CHRISTMAS
w&m/Jerry Herman

WE PARTED BY THE RIVER
w&m/William S. Hays

WE SAIL THE OCEAN BLUE
m/Sir Arthur Sullivan
w/Sir William Schwenk Gilbert

WE SHALL BE FREE
w&m/Huddie (Leadbelly) Ledbetter

WE SHALL OVERCOME
w&m/Pete Seeger, Zilphia Horton, Frank Hamilton, Guy Carawan

WE THREE KINGS OF ORIENT ARE
w&m/John Henry Hopkins

WE TWO SHALL MEET AGAIN
m/Emmerich Kalman
w/Harry B. Smith

WE UNDERSTAND EACH OTHER
w&m/Kenneth Gamble, Leon Huff

WE USED TO
w&m/Dolly Parton

WEE BABY BLUES (instr.)
m/Pete Johnson

WEE DEOCH-AN-DORIS, A
w&m/Sir Harry Lauder, Gerald Grafton

WEE WEE HOURS
m/Chuck Berry
w/Chuck Berry, Alan Freed, Russ Fratto

WEEK IN A COUNTY JAIL, A
w&m/Tom T. Hall

WEEKEND IN NEW ENGLAND
w&m/Randy Edelman

WEEP NO MORE MY MAMMY
w&m/Lew Pollack, Sidney D. Mitchell, Sidney Clare

WEEPING WILLOW (instr.)
m/Scott Joplin

WEDDING BELL BLUES
w&m/Laura Nyro

WEDDING BELLS ARE BREAKING UP THAT OLD GANG OF MINE
w&m/Irving Kahal, Sammy Fain Willie Raskin

WEDDING CAKE, THE
w&m/Margaret Lewis, Mira Smith

WEDDING MARCH (instr.)
m/Felix Mendellsohn

WEDDING OF THE PAINTED DOLL, THE
m/Nacio Herb Brown
w/Arthur Freed

WEDNESDAY NIGHT PRAYER MEETING (instr.)
m/Charles Mingus

WEIGHT, THE
w&m/J. Robbie Robertson

WELCOME BACK
w&m/John B. Sebastian

WELCOME TO MY DREAM
m/James Van Heusen
w/Johnny Burke

WELCOME TO MY WORLD
w&m/Ray Winkler, John Hathcock

WELCOME TO THE CLUB
w&m/Mae Boren Axton

WELCOME TO THE CLUB
w&m/Mel Torme

WELFARE BLUES
w&m/Joshua D. White

WE'LL BE TOGETHER AGAIN
w&m/Frankie Laine, Carl Fischer

WE'LL MAKE HAY WHILE THE SUN SHINES
m/Nacio Herb Brown
w/Arthur Freed

WE'LL NEVER HAVE TO SAY GOODBYE AGAIN
w&m/John Ford Coley, Danny Seals

WELL RESPECTED MAN, A
w&m/Raymond Douglas Davies

WE'LL SING IN THE SUNSHINE

w&m/Gale Garnett

WENDY
w&m/Brian Wilson

WE'RE A WINNER
w&m/Curtis Mayfield

WE'RE CALLED GONDOLIERI
m/Sir Arthur Sullivan
w/Sir William Schwenk Gilbert

WE'RE GONNA GET TOGETHER
w&m/Buck Owens

WERE I THY BRIDE
m/Sir Arthur Sullivan
w/Sir William Schwenk Gilbert

WE'RE IN THE MONEY
m/Harry Warren
w/Al Dubin

WE'RE NOT GONNA TAKE IT
w&m/Peter Townshend

WE'RE NOT THE JET SET
w&m/Bobby Braddock

WE'RE OFF TO SEE THE WIZARD
m/Harold Arlen
w/E. Y. Harburg

WE'RE OVER
w&m/Barry Mann, Cynthia Weil

WERE THINE THAT SPECIAL FACE
w&m/Cole Porter

WE'RE WORKING OUR WAY THROUGH COLLEGE
m/Richard Whiting
w/Johnny Mercer

WERE YOU NOT TO KO-KO PLIGHTED
m/Sir Arthur Sullivan
w/Sir William Schwenk Gilbert

WERE YOU SINCERE
w&m/Jack Meskill, Vincent Rose

WEREWOLVES OF LONDON
w&m/Warren Zevon, Leroy P. Marinell, Robert Wachte

WEST END BLUES (instr.)
w&m/Clarence Williams

WEST POINT MARCH
w&m/Philip Egner

WEST POINT STORY, THE (film score)
m/Ray John Heindorf

WEST WIND
m/Kurt Weill
w/Ogden Nash

WE'VE GOT LOVE
w&m/Frederick Perren, Dino Fekaris

WE'VE GOT TO GET OUT OF THIS PLACE
w&m/Barry Mann, Cynthia Weil

WE'VE GOT TONIGHT
w&m/Bob Seger

WE'VE ONLY JUST BEGUN
w&m/Paul Williams, Roger Nichols

WHAM (RE BOB BOOM BAM)
w&m/Eddie Durham

WHAT A DIFFERNCE A DAY MADE
m/Maria Grever
w/Stanley Adams

WHAT A DREAM
w&m/Chuck Willis

WHAT A FOOL BELIEVES
w&m/Kenneth Loggins, Michael McDonald

WHAT A FRIEND WE HAVE IN JESUS
m/Charles C. Converse (from the song "Erie")
w/Joseph Scriven

WHAT A MAN MY MAN IS
w&m/Glenn Sutton

WHAT A PARTY
w&m/Antoine "Fats" Domino, Dave Bartholomew

WHAT A PIECE OF WORK IS MAN
m/Galt MacDermot
w/James Rado, Gerome Ragni

WHAT A PRICE
w&m/Antoine "Fats" Domino, Dave Bartholomew

WHAT A WONDERFUL WORLD
m/George Douglas
w/George D. Weiss

WHAT AM I GONNA DO
w&m/Carole King, Toni Stern

WHAT AM I GONNA DO WITH YOU
w&m/Barry White

WHAT AM I LIVING FOR
w&m/Art Harris, Fred Jay

WHAT ARE THE WILD WAVES SAYING
m/Stephen Glover
w/Joseph Edwards Carpenter

WHAT ARE YOU DOING NEW YEAR'S EVE
w&m/Frank Loesser

WHAT ARE YOU DOING THE REST OF YOUR LIFE
m/Michel Legrand
w/Alan Bergman, Marilyn Bergman

WHAT CAN I DO WITH THIS BROKEN HEART
w&m/John Ford Coley, Danny Seals, B. Gundry

WHAT CAN I SAY
w&m/Boz Scaggs, David Paich

WHAT CAN I SAY AFTER I SAY I'M SORRY
m/Walter Donaldson
w/Abe Lyman

WHAT DID I HAVE THAT I DON'T HAVE
m/Burton Lane
w/Alan Jay Lerner

WHAT DO WE GET FROM BOSTON? BEANS, BEANS, BEANS
w&m/Frank Silver, Irving Cohn

WHAT DO YOU DO IN THE "INFANTRY"
w&m/Frank Loesser

WHAT DO YOU WANT
w&m/Eddie Rabbitt, Even Stevens

WHAT DO YOU WANT THE GIRL TO DO
w&m/Allen Toussaint

WHAT DO YOU WANT TO MAKE THOSE EYES AT ME FOR
m/James V. Monaco
w/Joseph McCarthy, Howard E. Johnson

WHAT DOES IT TAKE (TO WIN YOUR LOVE)
w&m/Harvey Fuqua, Vernon Bullock, Johnny Bristol

WHAT GOES UP, MUST COME DOWN
w&m/Rube Bloom, Ted Koehler

WHAT HAPPENED TO BLUE EYES
w&m/Jessi Colter

WHAT HAVE THEY DONE TO MY SONG, MA (LOOK WHAT THEY'VE DONE TO MY SONG)
w&m/Melanie

WHAT I DID FOR LOVE
m/Marvin Hamlisch
w/Edward Kleban

WHAT IN THE WORLD
w&m/Jack Scott

WHAT IN THE WORLD WOULD COMPARE TO THIS
m/Gustave A. Kerker
w/Charles A. Byrne

WHAT IS HOME WITHOUT A MOTHER
w&m/Septimus Winner

WHAT IS LIFE
w&m/George Harrison

WHAT IS LIFE WITHOUT LOVE
w&m/Vic McAlpin, Eddy Arnold, Owen Bradley

WHAT IS LOVE
m/Lee J. Pockriss
w/Paul Vance

WHAT IS THERE TO SAY
m/Vernon Duke
w/E. Y. Harburg

WHAT IS THIS THING CALLED LOVE
w&m/Cole Porter

WHAT I'VE GOT IN MIND
w&m/Kenny O'Dell

WHAT KIND O' MAN IS YOU
w&m/Hoagy Carmichael

WHAT KIND OF FOOL AM I
w&m/Leslie Bricusse, Anthony Newley

WHAT KIND OF LOVE IS THIS
w&m/Johnny Nash

WHAT LOCKS THE DOOR
w&m/Vic McAlpin

WHAT LOVE (instr.)
m/Charles Mingus

WHAT MADE MILWAUKEE FAMOUS
w&m/Glenn Sutton

WHAT MAKES YOU THINK YOU ARE THE ONE
w&m/Lindsay Buckingham

WHAT NOW MY LOVE
m/Gilbert Becaud
w/Carl Sigman

WHAT THE DICKENS (instr.)
m/John Dankworth

WHAT THE WORLD NEEDS NOW IS LOVE
m/Burt Bacharach
w/Hal David

WHAT WE'RE FIGHTING FOR
w&m/Tom T. Hall

WHAT WOULD THE CHILDREN THINK
w&m/Rick Springfield

WHAT WOULD WE DO WITHOUT YOU
w&m/Stephen Sondheim

WHAT YOU GOIN' TO DO
WHEN THE RENT COMES
'ROUND (RUFUS RASTUS
JOHNSON BROWN)
m/Harry Von Tilzer
w/Andrew B. Sterling

WHAT'CHA GONNA DO
w&m/Ahmet Ertegun

WHATCHA GONNA DO
w&m/Cory Lerios, David Jenkins

WHAT'D I SAY
w&m/Ray Charles

WHATEVER GETS YOU
THROUGH THE NIGHT
w&m/John Lennon

WHATEVER HAPPENED TO
BABY JANE (film score)
m/Frank DeVol

WHATEVER HAPPENED TO
RANDOLPH SCOTT
w&m/Don Reid, Harold Reid

WHATEVER LOLA WANTS
m/Jerry Ross
w/Richard Adler

WHAT'LL I DO
w&m/Irving Berlin

WHAT'S GOING ON
w&m/Renaldo Benson, Marvin Gaye

WHAT'S GOOD ABOUT
GOODBYE
m/Harold Arlen
w/Leo Robin

WHAT'S HAPPENED TO THE
TOTS
w&m/Noel Coward

WHAT'S NEW
m/Robert (Bob) Haggart
w/Johnny Burke

WHAT'S NEW PUSSYCAT
m/Burt Bacharach
w/Hal David

WHAT'S SO GOOD ABOUT
GOODBYE
w&m/William (Smokey) Robinson Jr.

WHAT'S THE GOOD WORD MR.
BLUEBIRD
m/Jerry Livingston
w/Al Hoffman, Allan Roberts

WHAT'S THE MATTER WITH
YOU BABY
w&m/Clarence Paul, Barney Ales

WHAT'S THE REASON
m/James W. Grier
w/Pinky Tomlin

WHAT'S THE USE OF
ANYTHING
m/Ludwig Englander
w/Harry B. Smith

WHAT'S THE USE OF
WOND'RIN
m/Richard Rodgers
w/Oscar Hammerstein II

WHAT'S YOUR MAMA'S NAME
CHILD
w&m/Dallas Frazier, Earl
Montgomery

WHAT'S YOUR NAME
w&m/Ronald W. Van Zant, Garry
Rossington, Larken A. Collins

**WHAT'S YOUR STORY
MORNING GLORY (instr.)**
m/Mary Lou Williams

WHEEL OF FORTUNE
m/Bennie Benjamin
w/George D. Weiss

WHEEL OF HURT
w&m/Charles Singleton, Eddie
Snyder

WHEELS
w&m/Johnny Flamingo, Norman
Petty

WHEELS
w&m/Gram Parsons

WHEN
w&m/Paul Evans, Jack Reardon

WHEN A GYPSY MAKES HIS
VIOLIN CRY
m/Emery Deutsch
w/Jimmy Rogan, Richard B. Smith

WHEN A MAN LOVES A
WOMAN
w&m/Andrew Wright, Calvin H.
Lewis

WHEN A MERRY MAIDEN
MARRIES
m/Sir Arthur Sullivan
w/Sir William Schwenk Gilbert

WHEN A WOOER GOES
A-WOOING
m/Sir Arthur Sullivan
w/Sir William Schwenk Gilbert

WHEN ALL NIGHT LONG
m/Sir Arthur Sullivan
w/Sir William Schwenk Gilbert

WHEN BRITAIN REALLY
RULED THE WAVES
m/Sir Arthur Sullivan
w/Sir William Schwenk Gilbert

WHEN CHLOE SINGS A SONG
m/John Stromberg
w/Edgar Smith

WHEN CUPID CALLS
m/Victor Jacobi
w/Harry B. Smith, Harry Graham

WHEN DAY IS DONE
m/Robert Katscher (melody from
original Viennese song "Madonna")
w/Buddy DeSylva

WHEN DID YOU LEAVE
HEAVEN
m/Richard Whiting
w/Walter Bullock

WHERE DO THE CHILDREN
PLAY
w&m/Cat Stevens

WHEN FIRST MY OLD, OLD
LOVE I KNEW
m/Sir Arthur Sullivan
w/Sir William Schwenk Gilbert

WHEN FRANCIS DANCES
WITH ME
m/Sol Violinsky
w/Ben Ryan

WHEN FREDERIC WAS A
LITTLE LAD
m/Sir Arthur Sullivan
w/Sir William Schwenk Gilbert

WHEN I BEEN DRINKING
w&m/"Big Bill" Broonzy

WHEN I FALL IN LOVE
m/Victor Young
w/Edward Heyman

WHEN I FIRST PUT THIS
UNIFORM ON
m/Sir Arthur Sullivan
w/Sir William Schwenk Gilbert

WHEN I GET YOU ALONE
TONIGHT
m/Fred Fisher
w/Joe Goodwin

WHEN I GO OUT OF DOOR
m/Sir Arthur Sullivan
w/Sir William Schwenk Gilbert

WHEN I GOOD FRIENDS WAS
CALL'D TO THE BAR
m/Sir Arthur Sullivan
w/Sir William Schwenk Gilbert

WHEN I GROW TOO OLD TO
DREAM
m/Sigmund Romberg
w/Oscar Hammerstein II

WHEN I HAVE SUNG MY SONGS
w&m/Ernest Charles

WHEN I LEAVE THE WORLD BEHIND
w&m/Irving Berlin

WHEN I LOST YOU
w&m/Irving Berlin

WHEN I NEED YOU
m/Albert Hammond
w/Carole Bayer Sager

WHEN I SEE AN ELEPHANT FLY
w&m/Frank E. Churchill, Ned Washington, Oliver G. Wallace

WHEN I STOP DREAMING
w&m/Ira Louvin, Charles Louvin

WHEN I TAKE MY SUGAR TO TEA
m/Sammy Fain
w/Irving Kahal, Rev. Norman Connor

WHEN I WANTED YOU
w&m/Gino Cunico

WHEN I WAS A LAD
m/Sir Arthur Sullivan
w/Sir William Schwenk Gilbert

WHEN I WENT TO THE BAR
m/Sir Arthur Sullivan
w/Sir William Schwenk Gilbert

WHEN I'M AWAY FROM YOU DEAR
w&m/Paul Dresser

WHEN I'M NOT NEAR THE GIRL I LOVE
m/Burton Lane
w/E. Y. Harburg

WHEN IRISH EYES ARE SMILING
m/Ernest R. Ball, Chauncey Olcott
w/George Graff Jr.

WHEN IT'S DARKNESS ON THE DELTA
m/Al J. Neiburg, Jerry Livingston
w/Marty Symes

WHEN IT'S ROUND-UP TIME IN HEAVEN
w&m/Jimmy Davis

WHEN IT'S SLEEPYTIME DOWN SOUTH
w&m/Leon T. Rene, Clarence Muse, Otis J. Rene Jr.

WHEN IT'S SPRINGTIME IN ALASKA
w&m/Johnny Horton

WHEN IT'S SPRINGTIME IN KILLARNEY
w&m/Dan J. Sullivan

WHEN IT'S SPRINGTIME IN THE ROCKIES
m/Robert Sauer
w/Mary Hale Woolsey, Milton Taggart

WHEN JOANNA LOVED ME
m/Bob Wells
w/Jack Segal

WHEN JOHNNY COMES MARCHING HOME
w&m/Patrick S. Gilmore

WHEN MAIDEN LOVES
m/Sir Arthur Sullivan
w/Sir William Schwenk Gilbert

WHEN MY BABY SMILES AT ME
w&m/Ted Lewis, Andrew B. Sterling, Bill Munroe, Harry Von Tilzer

WHEN MY DREAMS COME TRUE
w&m/Irving Berlin

WHEN MY DREAMBOAT COMES HOME
m/Cliff Friend
w/Dave Franklin

WHEN MY LITTLE GIRL IS SMILING
w&m/Carole King, Gerry Goffin

WHEN MY SUGAR WALKS DOWN THE STREET
m/Jimmy McHugh
w/Gene Austin, Irving Mills

WHEN OUR GALLANT NORMAN FOES
m/Sir Arthur Sullivan
w/Sir William Schwenk Gilbert

WHEN POVERTY'S TEARS EBB AND FLOW
m/David Braham
w/Ed Harrigan

WHEN SHADOWS FALL
w&m/Charles (Sunny) Clapp

WHEN SHALL I FIND HIM
m/Ludwin Englander
w/Harry B. Smith

WHEN SUNNY GETS BLUE
m/Marvin Fisher
w/Jack Segal

WHEN THE ANGELUS IS RINGING
m/Bert Grant
w/Joseph Young

WHEN THE BIRDS HAVE SUNG THEMSELVES TO SLEEP
w&m/Paul Dresser

WHEN THE BLOOM IS ON THE SAGE
w&m/Nathaniel Hawthorne Vincent, Fred Howard

WHEN THE BOYS COME HOME
w&m/Oley Speaks

WHEN THE LEAVES BEGIN TO TURN
w&m/Charles A. White

WHEN THE LEAVES COME TUMBLING DOWN
w&m/Richard Howard

WHEN THE LIGHTS GO ON AGAIN ALL OVER THE WORLD
w&m/Edward Seiler, Sol Marcus, Bennie Benjamin

WHEN THE LOVELIGHT STARTS SHINING THROUGH HIS EYES
w&m/Eddie Holland, Brian Holland, Lamont Dozier

WHEN THE MIDNIGHT CHOO-CHOO LEAVES FOR ALABAM'
w&m/Irving Berlin

WHEN THE MIGHTY ORGAN PLAYED "O PROMISE ME"
w&m/Abner Silver

WHEN THE MOON COMES OVER THE MOUNTAIN
m/Kate Smith, Harry Woods
w/Howard E. Johnson

WHEN THE MORNING COMES
w&m/Hoyt Axton

WHEN THE NIGHT WIND HOWLS
m/Sir Arthur Sullivan
w/Sir William Schwenk Gilbert

WHEN THE ONE YOU LOVE LOVES YOU
w&m/Abel Baer

WHEN THE ORGAN PLAYED 'O PROMISE ME'
w&m/Jack Meskill

WHEN THE RED RED ROBIN COMES BOB-BOB-BOBBIN' ALONG
w&m/Harry M. Wood

WHEN THE SAINTS GO MARCHING IN
Famous New Orleans jazz classic dating from early 20th Century! Source unknown; some scholars believe music either is of Bahamian origin or derives from Gospel song "When The Saints Come In For Crowning."

WHEN THE SUN COMES OUT
m/Harold Arlen
w/Ted Koehler

WHEN THE SUN GOES DOWN
w&m/Arthur A. Penn

WHEN THE SWALLOWS COME BACK TO CAPISTRANO
w&m/Leon T. Rene

WHEN THE TINGLE BECOMES A CHILL
w&m/Lola Jean Dillon

WHEN THE WORLD WAS YOUNG
m/M. Philippe-Gerard
w/Johnny Mercer

WHEN 'TIS MOONLIGHT
w&m/Charles A. White

WHEN TWO WORLDS COLLIDE
w&m/Bill Anderson, Roger Miller

WHEN WE MEET IN THE SWEET BYE AND BYE
w&m/Harry Von Tilzer
Stanley Murphy

WHEN WE'RE DANCING CLOSE AND SLOW
w&m/Prince

WHEN WILL I BE LOVED
w&m/Phil Asher

WHEN WILL I BE LOVED
w&m/Phil Everly

WHEN WILL I SEE YOU AGAIN
w&m/Kenneth Gamble, Leon Huff

WHEN YOU AND I WERE YOUNG MAGGIE
m/J. A. Butterfield
w/George W. Johnson

WHEN YOU GET RIGHT DOWN TO IT
w&m/Barry Mann

WHEN YOU LEAVE, DON'T SLAM THE DOOR
w&m/Joe Allison

WHEN YOU LOOK INTO THE HEART OF A ROSE
m/Florence Methven
w/Marian Gillespie

WHEN YOU WALK IN THE ROOM
w&m/Jackie De Shannon

WHEN YOU WERE SWEET SIXTEEN
w&m/James Thornton

WHEN YOU WISH UPON A STAR
m/Leigh Harline
w/Ned Washington

WHEN YOU WORE A TULIP AND I WORE A BIG RED ROSE
m/Percy Wenrich
w/Jack Francis Mahoney

WHEN YOUR HAIR HAS TURNED TO SILVER
m/Peter De Rose
w/Charles Tobias

WHEN YOU'RE A LONG LONG WAY FROM HOME
w&m/Samuel M. Lewis, George W. Meyer

WHEN YOU'RE AWAY
m/Bert Grant
w/A. Seymour Brown, Joseph Young

WHEN YOU'RE AWAY
m/Victor Herbert
w/Henry Blossom

WHEN YOU'RE HOT YOU'RE HOT
w&m/Jerry Reed

WHEN YOU'RE IN LOVE
m/Arthur Schwartz
w/Maxwell Anderson

WHEN YOU'RE IN LOVE
m/Gene De Paul
w/Johnny Mercer

WHEN YOU'RE LYING AWARE
m/Sir Arthur Sullivan
w/Sir William Schwenk Gilbert

WHEN YOU'RE SMILING
m/Mark Fisher, Larry Shay
w/Joe Goodwin

WHEN YOU'RE YOUNG AND IN LOVE
w&m/Van McCoy

WHEN YUBA PLAYS THE RHUMBA ON THE TUBA
w&m/Herman Hupfeld

WHENEVER I CALL YOU FRIEND
w&m/Kenneth Loggins, Melissa Manchester

WHERE AM I GOING
m/Cy Coleman
w/Dorothy Fields

WHERE ARE THE FRIENDS OF OTHER DAYS
w&m/Paul Dresser

WHERE DID OUR LOVE GO
w&m/Eddie Holland, Brian Holland, Lamont Dozier

WHERE DID ROBINSON CRUSOE GO WITH FRIDAY ON SATURDAY NIGHT
m/George W. Meyer
w/Samuel M. Lewis, Joseph Young

WHERE DID THE NIGHT GO
w&m/Harold Rome

WHERE DID THEY GO LORD
w&m/Dallas Frazier, A.L. (Doodle) Owens

WHERE DID YOU GET THAT HAT
w&m/Joseph J. Sullivan

WHERE DO I BEGIN (THEME FROM "LOVE STORY")
m/Frances Lai
w/Carl Sigman

WHERE DO WE GO FROM HERE BOYS
m/Percy Wenrich
w/Howard E. Johnson

WHERE DOES THE GOOD TIMES GO
w&m/Buck Owens

WHERE HAVE ALL THE FLOWERS GONE
w&m/Pete Seeger, Joe Hickerson

WHERE HAVE I KNOWN YOU BEFORE (Instr.)
m/Chick Corea

WHERE IS LOVE
w&m/Lionel Bart

WHERE IS MY CASTLE
w&m/Dallas Frazier

WHERE IS MY WAND'RING BOY TONIGHT
w&m/Rev. Robert Lowry

WHERE IS THE LIFE THAT LATE I LED
w&m/Cole Porter

WHERE IS THE LOVE
w&m/Harry Wayne Casey, Richard Finch, Willie Clarke, Betty Wright

WHERE OH WHERE
w&m/Cole Porter

WHERE O WHERE HAS MY LITTLE DOG GONE
w&m/Septimus Winner (music adapted from a German folk song)

WHERE OR WHEN
m/Richard Rodgers
w/Lorenz (Larry) Hart

WHERE THE BLUE OF THE NIGHT MEETS THE GOLD OF THE DAY
m/Fred E. Ahlert
w/Roy Turk, Bing Crosby

WHERE THE BOYS ARE
w&m/Neil Sedaka, Howard Greenfield

WHERE THE MORNING GLORIES GROW
m/Richard A. Whiting
w/Raymond E. Egan, Gus Kahn

WHERE THE MORNING GLORIES TWINE AROUND THE DOOR
m/Harry Von Tilzer
w/Andrew B. Sterling

WHERE THE RIVER SHANNON FLOWS
w&m/James J. Russell

WHERE THE SUN HAS NEVER SHONE
w&m/Jonathan King

WHERE WAS MOSES WHEN THE LIGHTS WENT OUT
m/Al Piantadosi
w/Edgar Leslie

WHERE WERE YOU (ON OUR WEDDING DAY)
w&m/Lloyd Price, Harold Logan

WHERE WERE YOU WHEN I NEEDED YOU
w&m/Bernie Wayne, Marvin Moore

WHERE YOU LEAD
w&m/Carole King, Toni Stern

WHERE'S POPPA (film score)
m/John M. Elliott

WHERE'S THAT RAINBOW
m/RIchard Rodgers
w/Lorenz (Larry) Hart

WHERE'S THE BOY
m/George Gershwin
w/Ira Gershwin

WHERE'S THE PLAYGROUND SUSIE
w&m/Jimmy Webb

WHIFFENPOOF SONG, THE
w&m/Rudy Vallee, adaptor/original music: Guy Scull, original words: Meade Minnigerode, George S. Pomeroy

WHILE MY GUITAR GENTLY WEEPS
w&m/George Harrison

WHILE STROLLING THROUGH THE PARK ONE DAY (THE FOUNTAIN IN THE PARK)
w&m/Robert King

WHILE THE CITY SLEEPS
m/Charles Strouse
w/Lee Adams

WHILE THE CITY SLEEPS (film score)
m/Herschel Burke Gilbert

WHILE WE'RE YOUNG
m/Alec Wilder, Morty Palitz
w/William Engvick

WHILE YOU DANCED DANCED DANCED
w&m/Stephen Weiss

WHISPERING
w&m/Vincent Rose, John Schonberger, Richard Schonberger

WHISTLER AND HIS DOG, THE (instr.)
m/Arthur Pryor

WHISKEY BENT AND HELL BOUND
w&m/Hank Williams Jr.

WHISKEY MAN
w&m/John Entwhistle

WHISPERING GRASS
m/Fred Fisher
w/Doris Fisher

WHISPERING HOPE
w&m/Septimus Winner

WHISPERS IN THE DARK
m/Frederick Hollander
w/Leo Robin

WHISTLE WHILE YOU WORK
w&m/Larry Morey, Frank E. Churchill

WHISTLING AWAY IN THE DARK
m/Henry Mancini
w/Johnny Mercer

WHITE CLIFFS OF DOVER, THE
m/Walter Kent
w/Nat Burton

WHITE CHRISTMAS
w&m/Irving Berlin

WHITE LIGHTNING
w&m/J. P. Richardson (Big Bopper)

WHITE PEACOCK, THE (from "ROMAN SKETCHES"; instr.)
m/Charles Tomlinson Griffes

WHITE RABBIT
w&m/Grace Slick

WHITE RHYTHM AND BLUES
w&m/J. D. Souther

WHITE SILVER SANDS
w&m/Gladys Reinhardt, Charles "Red" Matthews

WHITE SPORT COAT (AND A PINK CARNATION), A
w&m/Marty Robbins

WHITER SHADE OF PALE, A
m/Gary Brooker
w/Keith Reid

WHITHER THOU GOEST
w&m/Guy Singer

WHO
m/Jerome Kern
w/Otto Harbach, Oscar Hammerstein II

WHO AM I
m/Jule Styne
w/Walter Bullock

WHO ARE YOU
w&m/Peter Townshend

WHO ARE YOU NOW
m/Jule Styne
w/Bob Merrill

WHO CAN I TURN TO
w&m/Leslie Bricusse, Anthony Newley

WHO CARES
m/George Gershwin
w/Ira Gershwin

WHO CARES FOR ME
w&m/Don Gibson

WHO DONE IT? (WHODUNIT)
w&m/Frederick Perren, Keni St. Lewis

WHO DO YOU KNOW IN HEAVEN
m/Peter De Rose
w/Al Stillman

WHO DO YOU LOVE
w&m/Ellas McDaniel (Bo Diddley)

WHO DO YOU LOVE I HOPE
w&m/Irving Berlin

WHO DO YOU TRUST
w&m/Muddy Waters

WHO LOVES YOU
w&m/Bob Gaudio, Judy Parker

WHO NEEDS YOU
m/Robert Allen
w/Al Stillman

WHO PAID THE RENT FOR MRS. RIP VAN WINKLE
w&m/Fred Fisher, Alfred Bryan

WHO PUT THE BOMP (IN THE BOMP BA BOMP BA BOMP)
w&m/Gerry Goffin, Barry Mann

WHO SHOT SAM
w&m/George Jones, Darrell Edwards, Ray Jackson

WHO TAKES CARE OF THE CARETAKER'S DAUGHTER, WHILE THE CARETAKER'S BUSY TAKING CARE
m/Edward Ward
w/Chick Endor

WHO THREW THE OVERALLS IN MISTRESS MURPHY'S CHOWDER
w&m/George L. Geifer

WHO THREW THE WHISKEY IN THE WELL
m/John Benson Brooks
w/Edgar De Lange

WHO WALKS IN WHEN I WALK OUT
m/Al Hoffman
w/Al Goodhart

WHO WAS IT
w&m/Norman Smith

WHO WILL BE WITH YOU WHEN I'M FAR AWAY
w&m/Jimmy Durante

WHO WILL BUY
w&m/Lionel Bart

WHOA SAILOR
w&m/Hank Thompson

WHOEVER FINDS THIS -- I LOVE YOU
w&m/Mac Davis

WHOEVER YOU ARE I LOVE YOU
m/1Burt Bacharach
w/Hal David

WHOLE LOT OF LOVIN'
w&m/Antoine "Fats" Domino, Dave Bartholomew

WHOLE LOTTA LOVE
w&m/James Page, Robert Plant, John Paul Jones, John "Bonzo" Bonham

WHOLE LOTTA SHAKIN' GOIN' ON
w&m/Sunny David, David Williams

WHO'LL BE THE NEXT IN LINE
w&m/Raymond Douglas Davies

WHO'LL BUY MY VIOLETS
m/Jose Padilla
w/Ray Goetz

WHO'LL STOP THE RAIN
w&m/John C. Fogerty

WHO'S AFRAID OF THE BIG BAD WOLF
w&m/Frank E. Churchill, Ann Ronnell

WHO'S AFRAID OF VIRGINIA WOOLF (film score)
m/Alex North

WHO'S GONNA MOW YOUR GRASS
w&m/Buck Owens

WHO'S GOT THE PAIN
m/Jerry Ross
w/Richard Adler

WHO'S IN THE STRAWBERRY PATCH WITH SALLY
w&m/Irwin Levine, L. Russell Brown

WHO'S MAKING LOVE
w&m/Homer Banks, Raymond Jackson, Donald Davis

WHO'S SORRY NOW
m/Ted Snyder, Harry Ruby
w/Bert Kalmar

WHO'S YOUR LITTLE WHOO-ZIS
m/Ben Bernie, Al Goering
w/Walter Hirsch

WHOSE SHOULDER WILL YOU CRY ON
w&m/Kitty Wells, Billy Wallace

WHY
m/Peter DeAngelis
w/Bob Marcucci

WHY BABY WHY
w&m/George Jones, Darrell Edwards

WHY CAN'T I
m/Richard Rodgers
w/Lorenz (Larry) Hart

WHY CAN'T WE BE FRIENDS
w&m/see composer listing under Lee Oskar

WHY CAN'T WE LIVE TOGETHER
w&m/Timmy Thomas

WHY CAN'T YOU BEHAVE
w&m/Cole Porter

WHY DO FOOLS FALL IN LOVE
w&m/Frankie Lymon, George Goldner

WHY DO I LOVE YOU
m/Jerome Kern
w/Oscar Hammerstein II

WHY DO THEY ALWAYS SAY NO
w&m/Ed. G. Nelson, Harry Pease

WHY DON'T WE DO THIS MORE OFTEN
m/Allie Wrubel
w/Charles Newman

WHY DON'T YOU BELIEVE ME
w&m/Lew Douglas, King Laney, Roy Rodde

WHY DON'T YOU HAUL OFF AND LOVE ME
w&m/Wayne Raney, Lonnie Glosson

WHY DON'T YOU **LIVE** SO GOD CAN USE YOU
w&m/Muddy Waters

WHY DON'T YOU SPEND THE NIGHT
w&m/Bob McDill

WHY ME (LORD)
w&m/Kris Kristofferson

WHY SHOULD I BE LONELY
w&m/Jimmy Rodgers

WHY SHOULD'NT I
w&m/Cole Porter

WHY TRY TO CHANGE ME NOW
m/Cy Coleman
w/Joseph Allan McCarthy

WHY WAS I BORN
m/Jerome Kern
w/Oscar Hammerstein II

WICHITA LINEMAN
w&m/Jimmy Webb

WIFE OF THE PARTY
w&m/Liz Anderson

WILD AGE
w&m/Warren Zevon

WILD BUNCH, THE (film score)
m/Jerry Fielding

WILD CHERRIES RAG
w&m/Ted Snyder

WILD HONEY
w&m/Harry Tobias, Neil Moret

WILD HORSES
w&m/Mick Jagger, Keith Richard

WILD MAN BLUES (instr.)
m/Louis Armstrong

WILD NIGHT
w&m/Van Morrison

WILD THING
w&m/Larry Page

WILD WEEKEND
w&m/Bill Anderson

WILD WORLD
w&m/Cat Stevens

WILDCAT BLUES
w&m/Clarence Williams, Thomas "Fats" Waller

WILDFLOWER
m/Herbert Stothart, Vincent Youmans
w/Otto Harbach, Oscar Hammerstein II

WILDFLOWER RAG (instr.)
m/Clarence Williams

WILDROOT (instr.)
m/Neal Hefti, Woody Herman

WILDWOOD WEED
w&m/Jim Stafford

WILHEMINA
m/Josef Myrow
w/Mack Gordon

WILL O' THE WISP
w&m/Edward Alexander MacDowell

WILL THE CIRCLE BE
UNBROKEN
w&m/A. P. Carter

WILL YOU BE STAYING AFTER
SUNDAY
w&m/Joel Hirschhorn, Al Kasha

WILL YOU LOVE ME IN
DECEMBER AS YOU DO IN
MAY
m/Ernest R. Ball
w/James J. Walker

WILL YOU LOVE ME
TOMORROW
w&m/Melanie

WILL YOU LOVE ME
TOMORROW
w&m/Carole King, Gerry Goffin

WILL YOU REMEMBER
m/Sigmund Romberg
w/Rida Johnson Young

WILL YOU STILL BE MINE
m/Matt Dennis
w&m/Thomas M. Adair

WILLIE
w&m/Joni Mitchell

WILLIE AND LAURA MAE
JONES
w&m/Tony Joe White

WILLIE WONKA AND THE
CHOCOLATE FACTORY (film
score)
m/Walter Scharf, Leslie Bricusse,
Anthony Newley

WILLKOMMEN
m/John Kander
w/Fred Ebb

WILLOW WEEP FOR ME
w&m/Ann Ronell

WINCHESTER CATHEDRAL
w&m/Geoff Stephens

WIND CRIES MARY, THE
w&m/Jimi Hendrix

WINDJAMMER
w&m/Freddie Hubbard

WINDMILLS OF YOUR MIND,
THE
m/Michel Legrand
w/Alan and Marilyn Bergman

WINDOW UP ABOVE
w&m/George Jones

WINDOWS OF THE WORLD
m/Burt Bacharach
w/Hal David

WINDY
w&m/Ruthann Friedman

WINDY AND WARM
w&m/John D. Loudermilk

WINE WOMEN AND SONG
w&m/Betty Sue Perry

WING AND A PRAYER, A (film
score)
m/Hugo Friedhofer

WINGED VICTORY (film score)
m/David Rose

WINGS OVER JORDAN
w&m/Thomas Andrew Dorsey

WINNER, THE
w&m/Shel Silverstein

WINSTON CHURCHILL: THE
VALIANT YEARS (TV score)
m/Richard Rodgers

WINTER MELODY
w&m/Donna Summer, Georgio
Moroder, Pete Bellotte

WINTER SONG
w&m/Barry DeVorzon, Mitch Bottler

WINTER WONDERLAND
m/Felix Bernard
w/Richard B. Smith

WINTERGREEN FOR
PRESIDENT
m/George Gershwin
w/Ira Gershwin

WISHIN' AND HOPIN'
m/Burt Bacharach
w/Hal David

WISHING
w&m/Buddy DeSylva

WISHING I HAD LISTENED TO
YOUR SONG
w&m/Jerry Chesnut

WITCH DOCTOR
w&m/Ross Bagdasarian

WITCHCRAFT
m/Cy Coleman
w/Carolyn Leigh

WITH A LITTLE BIT OF LUCK
m/Frederick Loewe
w/Alan Jay Lerner

WITH A LITTLE LUCK
w&m/Paul and Linda McCartney

WITH A SENSE OF DEEP
EMOTION
m/Sir Arthur Sullivan
w/Sir William Schwenk Gilbert

WITH A SONG IN MY HEART
(film score)
m/Alfred Newman

WITH A SONG IN MY HEART
m/Richard Rodgers
w/Lorenz (Larry) Hart

WITH ALL HER FAULTS I LOVE
HER STILL
w&m/Monroe H. Rosenfeld

WITH CATLIKE TREAD
m/Sir Arthur Sullivan
w/Sir William Schwenk Gilbert

WITH EVERY BREATH I TAKE
m/Ralph Rainger
w/Leo Robin

WITH MY EYES WIDE OPEN
I'M DREAMING
m/Harry Revel
w/Mack Gordon

WITH MY LOVE
w&m/Barry, Maurice and Robin
Gibb

WITH PEN IN HAND
w&m/Bobby Goldsboro

WITH PEN IN HAND
w&m/Billy Vera

WITH SO LITTLE TO BE SURE
OF
w&m/Stephen Sondheim

WITH THE RAIN AND THE
RAIN IN YOUR HAIR
w&m/Clara Edwards (pseud:
Bernard Haig), Jack Lawrence

WITH THESE HANDS
m/Abner Silver
w/Benny Davis

WITH YOU
w&m/Prince

WITH YOU I'M BORN AGAIN
m/David Shire
w/Carol Connors

WITHIN MY MEMORY
w&m/Mac Davis

WITHOUT A SONG
m/Vincent Youmans
w/Billy Rose, Edward Eliscu

WITHOUT YOU
w&m/Harry Edward Nilsson

WITH PLENTY OF MONEY AND YOU
m/Harry Warren
w/Al Dubin

WITHOUT A WORD OF WARNING
m/Harry Revel
w/Mack Gordon

WITNESS FOR THE PROSECUTION (film score)
m/Ernest Gold

WIVES AND LOVERS
m/Burt Bacharach
w/Hal David

WIZ, THE (film score)
m/Quincy Jones

WOKE UP THIS MORNING
w&m/B. B. King, Jules Taub

WOLFCREEK PASS
w&m/C. W. McCall

WOLVERTON MOUNTAIN
w&m/Merle Kilgore, Claude King

WOMAN (SENSUOUS WOMAN)
w&m/Gary S. Paxton

WOMAN, A LOVER, A FRIEND
w&m/Sid Wyche

WOMAN ALWAYS KNOWS, A
w&m/Billy Sherrill

WOMAN IS A SOMETIME THING, A
m/George Gershwin
w/Dubose Heyward

WOMAN IN LOVE, A
w&m/Frank Loesser

WOMAN IS THE NIGGER OF THE WORLD
w&m/John Lennon, Yoko Ono

WOMAN TO WOMAN
w&m/Billy Sherrill

WOMEN I'VE NEVER HAD
w&m/Hank Williams Jr.

WONDER COULD I LIVE THERE ANYMORE
w&m/Bill Rice

WONDER WOMAN (TV theme) (instr.)
m/Charles Fox

WONDERFUL COPENHAGEN
w&m/Frank Loesser

WONDERFUL DAY LIKE TODAY, A
w&m/Leslie Briscusse, Anthony Newley

WONDERFUL GUY, A
m/Richard Rodgers
m/Oscar Hammerstein Ii
w/Oscar Hammerstein II

WONDERFUL ONE
m/Ferde Grofe, Paul Whiteman
(adapted from a melody by Marshall Nielan)
w/Dorothy Terris

WONDERFUL, WONDERFUL
m/Sherman Edwards
w/Ben Raleigh

WONDERFUL WORLD, BEAUTIFUL PEOPLE
w&m/Jimmy Cliff (James Chambers)

WONDERFUL WORLD OF THE BROTHERS GRIMM, THE (film score)
m/Leigh Harline

WONDERLAND BY NIGHT
w&m/Lincoln Chase, Klauss Gunter Newman

WONDERS YOU PERFORM, THE
w&m/Jerry Chestnut

WON'T GET FOOLED AGAIN
w&m/Peter Townshend

WON'T YOU COME TO MY HOUSE
m/Egbert Anson Van Alstyne
w/Harry H. Williams

WOODCHUCK SONG
w&m/Roy C. Bennett, Sid Tepper

WOODEN SHIPS
w&m/David Crosby, Stephen Stills, Paul Kanter

WOODMAN! SPARE THAT TREE
m/Henry Russell
w/George Pope Morris

WOODMAN, WOODMAN SPARE THAT TREE
w&m/Irving Berlin

WOODSTOCK
w&m/Joni Mitchell

WOODY WOODPECKER SONG, THE
w&m/Ramez Idriss, George Tibbles

WOODYN' YOU (instr.)
m/Dizzy Gillespie

WORDS
w&m/Barry, Maurice and Robin Gibb

WORDS OF LOVE
w&m/John Phillips

WORK WITH ME ANNIE
w&m/Hank Ballard

WORKIN' AT THE CARWASH BLUES
w&m/Jim Croce

WORKIN' MAN BLUES
w&m/Merle Haggard

WORKING MAN
w&m/Michael Bloomfield

WORKING MY BACK BACK TO YOU
w&m/Sandy Linzer, Denny Randell

WORKING ON A GROOVY THING
w&m/Neil Sedaka, Roger Atkins

WORLD I USED TO KNOW, THE
w&m/Rod McKuen

WORLD IS A GHETTO, THE
w&m/see composer listing under Lee Oskar

WORLD IS A TOY SHOP, THE
m/Ludwig Englander
w/Harry B. Smith

WORLD IS WAITING FOR THE SUNRISE, THE
m/Ernest Seitz

w/Eugene Lockhart

WORLD OF STONE
w&m/George Harrison

WORLD OF SUZY WONG (film score)
m/George Duning

WORLD THAT NEVER WAS, A
m/Sammy Fain
w/Paul Francis Webster

WORLD TURNING
w&m/Christine Perfect McVie, Lindsay Buckingham

WORLD WE KNEW, THE (OVER AND OVER)
m/Bert Kaempfert, Herbert Rehbein
w/Carl Sigman

WORRIED MAN BLUES
w&m/Woody Guthrie

WORRIED MIND
w&m/Ted Daffan

WORRIED OVER YOU
w&m/Fred Rose, Ed. G. Nelson
Steve Nelson

WORST THAT COULD HAPPEN, THE
w&m/Jimmy Webb

WOULD YOU
m/Nacio Herb Brown
w/Arthur Freed

WOULD YOU CARE
w&m/Charles K. Harris

**WOULD YOU HOLD IT
AGAINST ME**
w&m/Dottie West, Bill West

**WOULD YOU KNOW THE KIND
OF MAID**
m/Sir Arthur Sullivan
w/Sir William Schwenk Gilbert

**WOULD YOU LIKE TO TAKE A
WALK**
m/Mort Dixon, Billy Rose
w/Harry Warren

WOULDN'T IT BE FUN
w&m/Cole Porter

WOULDN'T IT BE LOVERLY
m/Frederick Loewe
w/Alan Jay Lerner

WOULDN'T IT BE NICE
w&m/Brian Wilson, Tony Asher

**WRAP YOUR TROUBLES IN
DREAMS**
m/Harry Barris
w/Ted Koehler, Billy Moll

WRECK OF THE OLD '97
w&m/Henry Whittier, Charles W.
Noell, Fred J. Lewey (music based on
Henry C. Work's "The Ship That
Never Returned")

WRECK ON THE HIGHWAY
w&m/Roy Claxton Acuff

WRITE ME A LETTER
w&m/William S. Hays

WRITTEN ON THE WIND
m/Victor Young
w/Sammy Cahn

WRONG NOTE RAG
m/Leonard Bernstein
w/Betty Comden, Adolph Green

WUNDERBAR
w&m/Cole Porter

WURLITZER PRIZE, THE
w&m/Chips Moman, Bobby
Emmons

**WUTHERING HEIGHTS (film
score)**
m/Alfred Newman

Addenda:

**WHAT EVER HAPPENED TO
US**
w&m/Loudon Wainwright III

**WHERE WERE YOU WHEN I
WAS FALLING IN LOVE**
w&m/Sam Lorber, Jeff Silbar,
Steve Lucas

XANADU
w&m/Jeff Lynne

 **SONGS**

Y, Z

YAKETY SAX
w&m/Boots Randolph

YALE BULLDOG SONG
w&m/Cole Porter

YAM, THE
w&m/Irving Berlin

YAMA, YAMA MAN, THE
m/Karl Hoschna
w/George Collin Davis

YANCE SPECIAL (instr.)
m/Meade "Lux" Lewis

YANK AT ETON, A (film score)
m/Bronislau Kaper

YANK ON THE BURMA ROAD, A (film score)
m/Lennie Hayton

YANKEE DOODLE BOY, THE
w&m/George M. Cohan

YANKEE DOODLE DANDY (film score)
m/Ray John Heindorf

YARDBIRD SUITE (instr.)
m/Charlie Parker

YASMINA
w&m/Archie Shepp

YEAR OF THE CAT
w&m/Al Stewart, Peter Wood

YEAR 3000 BLUES
w&m/Alvin Lee

YEARNING
m/Joseph Burke
w/Benny Davis

YEH YEH
w&m/Mongo Santamaria

YELLOW BIRD
w&m/Alan and Marilyn Bergman, Norman Luboff

YELLOW ROSE OF TEXAS
w&m/Don George (based on an 1853 march attributed to one "J. K."The march later was used as the basis for "The Song Of The Texas Rangers".)

YES I CAN
m/Charles Strouse
w/Lee Adams

YES I'M READY
w&m/Barbara Mason

YES INDEED
w&m/Sy Oliver

YES SIR THAT'S MY BABY
m/Walter Donaldson
w/Gus Kahn

YES WE CAN CAN
w&m/Allen Toussaint

YES, WE HAVE NO BANANAS
w&m/Frank Silver, Irving Cohn

YESTERDAY
w&m/John Lennon, Paul McCartney

YESTERDAY I HEARD THE RAIN (ESTA TARDE VI LLOVER)
m/Armando Manzanero
w/Gene Lees

YESTERDAY MAN
w&m/Chris Andrews

YESTERDAYS
m/Jerome Kern
w&m/Otto Harbach, Oscar Hammerstein II

YIDDISHE MOMME, A
m/Jack Yellen, Lew Pollack
m/Jack Yellen

Y. M. C. A.
w&m/Jacques Morali

YODELING COWBOY
w&m/Jimmy Rodgers

YONDER COMES A SUCKER
w&m/Jim Reeves

YOU
w&m/George Harrison

YOU AIN'T GOIN' NOWHERE
w&m/Robert Dylan

YOU AIN'T HEARD NOTHIN' YET
m/Gus Kahn
w/Buddy DeSylva, Al Jolson

YOU AIN'T WOMAN ENOUGH
w&m/Loretta Lynn

YOU ALONE
m/Robert Allen
w/Al Stillman

YOU ALONE
w&m/Val Burton, Will Jason

YOU ALWAYS HURT THE ONE YOU LOVE
m/Allan Roberts
w/Doris Fisher

YOU AND I
w&m/Meredith Willson

YOU AND I
w&m/Stevie Wonder

YOU AND ME
w&m/Alice Cooper, Richard Wagner

YOU AND ME
w&m/George Richey

YOU AND ME AGAINST THE WORLD
w&m/Paul Williams, Ken Ascher

YOU AMD MY OLD GUITAR
w&m/Jimmy Rodgers

YOU AND THE NIGHT AND THE MUSIC
m/Arthur Schwartz
w/Howard Dietz

YOU AND YOUR SWEET LOVE
w&m/Bill Anderson

YOU ARE BEAUTIFUL
m/Richard Rodgers
w/Oscar Hammerstein II

YOU ARE FOR LOVING
w&m/Ralph Blane, Hugh Martin

YOU ARE FREE
m/Victor Jacobi
w/William Le Baron

YOU ARE LOVE
m/Jerome Kern
w/Oscar Hammerstein II

YOU ARE MINE EVERMORE
m/Emmerich Kalman
w/Harry B. Smith

YOU ARE MY DESTINY
w&m/Paul Anka

YOU ARE MY HEAVEN
w&m/Stevie Wonder, Eric Mercury

YOU ARE MY LUCKY STAR
m/Nacio Herb Brown
w/Arthur Freed, Buddy DeSylva

YOU ARE MY MIRACLE
w&m/Roger Whittaker

YOU ARE MY STARSHIP
w&m/Michael Henderson

YOU ARE MY SUNSHINE
w&m/Jimmy Davis, Charlie Mitchell

YOU ARE NEVER AWAY
m/Richard Rodgers
w/Oscar Hammerstein II

YOU ARE ON MY MIND
w&m/James Pankow

YOU ARE SIXTEEN
m/Richard Rodgers
w/Oscar Hammerstein II

YOU ARE SO BEAUTIFUL
m/Billy Preston
w/Bruce Fisher

YOU ARE THE SUNSHINE OF MY LIFE
w&m/Stevie Wonder

YOU ARE THE WOMAN
w&m/Rick Roberts

YOU ARE WOMAN (I AM MAN)
m/Jule Styne
w/Bob Merrill

YOU BABY (NOBODY BUT YOU)
w&m/P. F. Sloan, Steve Barri

YOU BEAT ME TO THE PUNCH
w&m/William (Smokey) Robinson
Jr., Ronald White

YOU BELONG TO ME
w&m/Carly Simon, Mike McDonald

YOU BELONG TO ME
w&m/Pee Wee King, Redd Stewart,
Chilton Price

YOU BELONG TO MY HEART
m/Augustin Lara
w/Ray Gilbert

YOU BETTA KNOW IT
w&m/Jackie Wilson, Norm Henry

YOU BETTER RUN
w&m/Felix Cavaliere, Eddie Brigati

YOU BO DIDDLEY
w&m/Ellas McDaniel (Bo Diddley)

**YOU BROUGHT A NEW KIND
OF LOVE TO ME**
w&m/Irving Kahal, Sammy Fain,
Rev. Norman Connor

**YOU CALL EVERYBODY
DARLIN'**
w&m/Albert J. Trace, Ben L. Trace,
Sam Martin

**YOU CALL IT MADNESS BUT I
CALL IT LOVE**
m/Con Conrad, Russ Colombo
w/Gladys Du Bois, Paul Gregory

**YOU CAME A LONG WAY FROM
ST. LOUIS**
w&m/Bob Russell, John Benson
Brooks

YOU CAN NEVER GO HOME
w&m/Justin Hayward

**YOU CAN'T ALWAYS GET
WHAT YOU WANT**
w&m/Mick Jagger, Keith Richard

**YOU CAN'T ARGUE WITH A
SICK MIND**
w&m/Joseph F. Walsh

YOU CAN'T BE A BEACON
w&m/Donna Fargo

YOU CAN'T BE TRUE DEAR
m/Hans Otten (from the German
song "Du Kannst Nicht TreuSein")
music adapted by Ken Griffin
w/English: Hal Cotton
w/German: Gerhard Ebeler

YOU CAN'T BE TRUE DEAR
m/Dave Dreyer
w/Jack Edwards

**YOU CAN'T BREAK THE
CHAINS OF LOVE**
w&m/Jimmy Wakely

**YOU CAN'T GET A MAN WITH A
GUN**
w&m/Irving Berlin

**YOU CAN'T HAVE
EVERYTHING**
m/Harry Revel
w/Mack Gordon

YOU CAN'T HURRY LOVE
w&m/Eddie Holland, Brian Holland,
Lamont Dozier

**YOU CAN'T JUDGE A BOOK BY
THE COVER**
w&m/Willie Dixon

**YOU CAN'T KEEP A GOOD MAN
DOWN**
w&m/Perry Bradford

**YOU CAN'T PICK A ROSE IN
DECEMBER**
w&m/Leon Payne

**YOU CAN'T PULL THE WOOL
OVER MY EYES**
m/Milton Ager, Murray Mencher
w/Charles Newman

**YOU CAN'T STOP ME FROM
DREAMING**
m/Cliff Friend
w/Dave Franklin

YOU COMB HER HAIR
w&m/Hank Cochran Harlan Howard

YOU CRIED WOLF
w&m/Todd Rundgren

YOU COULDN'T BE CUTER
m/Jerome Kern
w/Dorothy Fields

YOU DECORATED MY LIFE
w&m/Robert Morrison, Debbie
Hupp

YOU DO SOMETHING TO ME
w&m/Cole Porter

YOU DONE ME WRONG
w&m/Antoine "Fats" Domino, Dave
Bartholomew

**YOU DON'T BRING ME
FLOWERS**
w&m/Neil Diamond, Alan and
Marilyn Bergman

**YOU DON'T HAVE TO BE A
STAR (TO BE IN MY SHOW)**
w&m/James Dean

YOU DON'T HAVE TO CRY
w&m/Stephen Stills

YOU DON'T KNOW ME
w&m/Eddy Arnold, Cindy Walker

**YOU DON'T KNOW WHAT
LONESOME IS**
w&m/Joe Washburne

YOU DON'T LOVE ME
w&m/T-Bone Walker

**YOU DON'T MESS AROUND
WITH JIM**
w&m/Jim Croce

YOU DON'T SEE ME
w&m/Al Jarreau

YOU FASCINATE ME SO
m/Cy Coleman
w/Carolyn Leigh

YOU GIVE ME LOVING
w&m/Alvin Lee

**YOU GAVE ME THE GATE AND
I'M SWINGING (instr.)**
m/Duke Ellington

YOU GO TO MY HEAD
m/J. Fred Coots
w/Haven Gillespie

YOU GOT A NERVE
w&m/Rod Stewart

YOU GOT ME FLOATIN'
w&m/Jimi Hendrix

YOU GOT THAT RIGHT
w&m/Ronald W. Van Zant, Garry
Rossington, Larken Allen Collins

YOU GOT TO ME
w&m/Neil Diamond

**YOU GOTTA BE A FOOTBALL
HERO**
w&m/Al Lewis, Al Sherman

**YOU GROW SWEETER AS THE
YEARS GO BY**
w&m/Johnny Mercer

YOU HAD TO BE THERE
w&m/Jimmy Buffett

YOU HAVEN'T DONE NOTHIN'
w&m/Stevie Wonder

YOU HIT THE SPOT
m/Harry Revel
w/Mack Gordon

**YOU KEEP COMING BACK
LIKE A SONG**
w&m/Irving Berlin

YOU KEEP ME HANGING ON
w&m/Eddie Holland, Brian Holland,
Lamont Dozier

**YOU KNOW HOW TALK GETS
AROUND**
w&m/Fred Rose

YOU KNOW I LOVE YOU
w&m/B. B. King, Jules Taub

YOU KNOW ME
w&m/Paul Williams, Ken Ascher

YOU LIGHT UP MY LIFE
w&m/Joseph Brooks

YOU LOVE THE THUNDER
w&m/Jackson Browne

YOU MAKE ME FEEL LIKE DANCING
w&m/Leo Sayer, Vincent Poncia

YOU MAKE ME FEEL SO YOUNG
m/Josef Myrow
w/Mack Gordon

YOU MADE ME HAPPY
w&m/Eddie Durham

YOU MADE ME LOVE YOU
m/James V. Monaco
w/Joseph McCarthy

YOU MAKE LOVING FUN
w&m/Christine Perfect McVie

YOU MAKE ME FEEL BRAND NEW
w&m/Thomas Bell, Linda Creed

YOU MAKE ME FEEL SO YOUNG
 m/Josef Myrow
w/Mack Gordon

YOU MAY BE RIGHT
w&m/Billy Joel

YOU MEAN THE WORLD TO ME
w&m/Glenn Sutton, Billy Sherrill

YOU MUST HAVE BEEN A BEAUTIFUL BABY
m/Harry Warren
w/Johnny Mercer

YOU NEED LOVE
w&m/Dennis De Young

YOU NEEDED ME
w&m/Randy Goodman

YOU NEVER CAN TELL (C'EST LA VIE)
w&m/Chuck Berry

YOU NEVER CRY LIKE A LOVER
w&m/J. D. Souther, Donald Henley

YOU NEVER MISS A REAL GOOD THING
w&m/Bob McDill

YOU NEVER MISS THE WATER TIL THE WELL RUNS DRY
w&m/Rollin Howard

YOU NEVER SAY YES, YOU NEVER SAY NO
w&m/Art Kassel

YOU ONLY LIVE TWICE
m/John Barry
w/Leslie Bricusse

YOU OUGHTA BE IN PICTURES
m/Dan Suesse
w/Edward Heyman

YOU OUGHT TO BE WITH ME
w&m/Al Green

YOU PICK ME UP (AND PUT ME DOWN)
w&m/Randy Goodrum, B. Maher

YOU REALLY GOT ME
w&m/Raymond Douglas Davies

YOU REMIND ME OF MY MOTHER
w&m/George M. Cohan

YOU SAY THE NICEST THINGS BABY
m/Jimmy McHugh, Mack Gordon
w/Harold Adamson

YOU SAY THE SWEETEST THINGS BABY
m/Harry Warren
w/Mack Gordon

YOU SHOULD BE DANCING
w&m/Barry, Maurice and Robin Gibb

YOU SHOW ME YOUR HEART
w&m/Tom T. Hall

YOU STEPPED OUT OF A DREAM
m/Nacio Herb Brown
w/Gus Kahn

YOU TELL HER I STUTTER
m/Cliff Friend
w/Billy Rose

YOU TELL ME YOUR DREAMS, I'LL TELL YOU MINE
w&m/Charles Neil Daniels, Seymour Rice, Albert H. Brown

YOU TOOK ADVANTAGE OF ME
m/Richard Rodgers
w/Lorenz (Larry) Hart

YOU TOOK ALL THE RAMBLIN' OUT OF ME
w&m/Jerry Reed

YOU TOOK HER OFF MY HANDS
w&m/Harlan Howard, Wynn Stewart, Skeets McDonald

YOU TURN ME AROUND
w&m/Barry Mann, Cynthia Weil

YOU TURN ME ON
w&m/Ian Whitcomb

YOU TURN ME ON I'M A RADIO
w&m/Joni Mitchell

YOU TURNED THE TABLES ON ME
m/Louis Alter
w/Sidney D. Mitchell

YOU UPSET ME BABY
w&m/B. B. King, Joe Josea

YOU WALK BY
w&m/Bernie Wayne, Ben Raleigh

YOU WEAR IT WELL
w&m/Rod Stewart, M. Quittendon

YOU WERE ALWAYS THERE
w&m/Donna Fargo

YOU WERE MEANT FOR ME
m/Nacio Herb Brown
w/Arthur Freed

YOU WERE MEANT FOR ME
m/Eubie Blake
w/Noble Sissle

YOU WERE NEVER LOVELIER
m/Jerome Kern
w/Johnny Mercer

YOU WERE THERE
w&m/Noel Coward

YOU WON'T BE SATISFIED
w&m/Larry Stock, Freddy James

YOU, YOU, YOU
m/Peter DeAngelis
w/Jean Sawyer

YOU'D BE SO NICE TO COME HOME TO
w&m/Cole Porter

YOU'D BE SURPRISED
w&m/Irving Berlin

YOU'LL ACCOMPANY ME
w&m/Bob Seger

YOU'LL ALWAYS BE THE SAME SWEET GIRL
m/Harry Von Tilzer
w/Andrew B. Sterling

YOU'LL LOSE A GOOD THING
w&m/Barbara Linda Ozen

YOU'LL NEVER FIND ANOTHER LOVE LIKE MINE
w&m/Kenneth Gamble, Leon Huff

YOU'LL NEVER GET TO HEAVEN
m/Burt Bacharach
w/Hal David

YOU'LL NEVER KNOW
m/Harry Warren
w/Mack Gordon

YOU'LL NEVER WALK ALONE
m/Richard Rodgers
w/Oscar Hammerstein II

YOUNG AMERICANS, THE
w&m/David Bowie

YOUNG AND BEAUTIFUL
w&m/Abner Silver

YOUNG AND FOOLISH
m/Albert Hague
w/Arnold B. Horwitt

YOUNG AT HEART
m/Johnny Richards
w/Carolyn Leigh

YOUNG BLOOD
w&m/Doc (Jerome) Pomus, Mort
Shuman

YOUNG LAND, THE (film score)
m/Dimitri Tiomkin

YOUNG LIONS, THE (film score)
m/Hugo Friedhofer

YOUNG LOVE
w&m/Carole Joyner, Ric Cartey

YOUNG MAN BLUES
w&m/Peter Townshend

YOUNG MAN WITH A HORN,
THE
m/George Stoll
w/Ralph Freed

YOUNG MAN WITH A HORN
(film score)
m/Ray John Heindorf

YOUNG MAN'S BLUES
m/Elton John
w/Bernie Taupin

YOUNG STREPHRON IS THE
KIND OF LOUT
m/Sir Arthur Sullivan
m/Sir William Schwenk Gilbert

YOUNGER GIRL
w&m/John B. Sebastian

YOUNGER THAN SPRINGTIME
m/Richard Rodgers
w/Oscar Hammerstein II

YOUR BULLDOG DRINKS
CHAMPAGNE
w&m/Jim Stafford

YOUR CASH AIN'T NOTHING
BUT TRASH
w&m/Charles Calhoun

YOUR EYES HAVE TOLD ME
SO
m/Egbert Anson Van Alstyne
w/Gus Kahn, Walter Blaufus

YOUR FATHER'S
MOUSTACHE
w&m/Woody Herman, Chubby
Jackson, Bill Harris

YOUR FEET'S TOO BIG
w&m/Fred Fisher, Ada Benson, John
Hancock

YOUR GOD COMES FIRST,
YOUR COUNTRY NEXT, THEN
MOTHER DEAR
w&m/Paul Dresser

YOUR GOOD GIRL'S GONNA
GO BAD
w&m/Glenn Sutton, Billy Sherrill

YOUR HEART TURNED LEFT
w&m/Harlan Howard

YOUR KISS
m/Alfred Newman
w/Frank Loesser

YOUR MAMA DON'T DANCE
w&m/James Messina, Kenneth
Loggins

YOUR MOTHER'S SON-IN-LAW
w&m/Billie Holiday

YOUR OLD COLD SHOULDER
w&m/Richard Leigh

YOUR OLD LOVE LETTER
w&m/Johnny Bond

YOUR OLD USED TO BE
w&m/Faron Young, Hilda M. Young

YOUR PRETTY ROSES CAME
TOO LATE
w&m/Bill Rice, Jerry Foster

YOUR RED WAGON
w&m/Don Raye, Gene De Paul

YOUR SIDE OF THE BED
w&m/Mac Davis

YOUR SMILING FACE
w&m/James Taylor

YOUR SONG
m/Elton John
w/Bernie Taupin

YOUR TENDER LOVING CARE
w&m/Buck Owens

YOU'RE A BIG BOY NOW
w&m/John B. Sebastian

YOU'RE A BUILDER UPPER
m/Harold Arlen
w/Ira Gershwin, E. Y. Harburg

YOU'RE A GRAND OLD FLAG
w&m/George M. Cohan

YOU'RE A PART OF ME
w&m/Kim Carnes

YOU'RE A SWEETHEART
m/Jimmy McHugh
w/Harold Adamson

YOU'RE A WONDERFUL ONE
w&m/Eddie Holland, Brian Holland,
Lamont Dozier

YOU'RE ALL I NEED TO GET
BY
w&m/Valerie Simpson, Nicholas
Ashford

YOU'RE ALL I WANT FOR
CHRISTMAS
w&m/Seger Ellis

YOU'RE ALL INVITED TO MY
MANSION
w&m/John Stallings

YOU'RE AN OLD SMOOTHIE
m/Nacio Herb Brown
w/Richard A. Whiting, Buddy
DeSylva

YOU'RE AS WELCOME AS THE
FLOWERS
w&m/Dan J. Sullivan

YOU'RE BREAKING MY
HEART
m/Pat Genaro (adapted from
Leoncavallo's "Mattinata")
w/Sunny Skylar

YOU'RE BREAKING MY
HEART
w&m/Harry Edward Nilsson

YOU'RE DRIVING ME CRAZY
m/Walter Donaldson
w/Gus Kahn

YOU'RE FROM TEXAS
w&m/Cindy Walker

YOU'RE GETTING TO BE A
HABIT WITH ME
m/Harry Warren
w/Al Dubin

YOU'RE GONNA HEAR FROM
ME
m/Andre Previn
w/Dory Langdon Previn

YOU'RE GONNA LOSE YOUR
GAL
m/James V. Monaco
w/Joseph Young

YOU'RE GONNA MISS ME
WHEN I'M DEAD
w&m/Muddy Waters

YOU'RE GOOD FOR ME
w&m/Mac Davis

YOU'RE GOOD FOR ME
w&m/Don Covay, Horace Ott

YOU'RE HAVING MY BABY
w&m/Paul Anka

YOU'RE IN MY HEART
w&m/Rod Stewart

YOU'RE IN THE RIGHT
CHURCH BUT THE WRONG
PEW
w&m/Chris Smith, Cecil Mack

YOU'RE JUST IN LOVE
w&m/Irving Berlin

YOU'RE KILLING MY LOVE
w&m/Michael Bloomfield

YOU'RE LOOKIN' AT COUNTRY
w&m/Loretta Lynn

YOU'RE LUCKY TO ME
m/Eubie Blake
w/Andy Razaf

YOU'RE MAKING A FOOL OUT OF ME
w&m/Tompall Glaser

YOU'RE MY BABY
m/Nat D. Ayer
w/A. Seymour Brown

YOU'RE MY EVERYTHING
m/Harry Warren
w/Mort Dixon, Joseph Young

YOU'RE MY GIRL
m/Jule Styne
w/Sammy Cahn

YOU'RE MY MAN
w&m/Glenn Sutton

YOU'RE MY THRILL
m/Jay Gorney
w/Sidney Clare

YOU'RE A SWEET LITTLE HEADACHE
m/Ralph Rainger
w/Leo Robin

YOU'RE NEARER
m/Richard Rodgers
w/Lorenz (Larry) Hart

YOU'RE NO GOOD
w&m/Clint Ballard Jr.

YOU'RE NOBODY 'TIL SOMEBODY LOVES YOU
w&m/Russ Morgan, Larry Stock, James Cavanaugh

YOU'RE NOT MINE ANYMORE
w&m/Webb Pierce, Doyle Wilburn, Teddy Wilburn

YOU'RE ONLY LONELY
w&m/J. D. Souther

YOU'RE SENSATIONAL
w&m/Cole Porter

YOU'RE SIXTEEN
w&m/Richard M. Sherman, Robert B. Sherman

YOU'RE SO FINE
w&m/Walter Jacobs

YOU'RE SO FINE
w&m/Lance Finnie, Willis Schoefield

YOU'RE SO UNDERSTANDING
w&m/Bernie Wayne, Ben Raleigh

YOU'RE STILL MINE
w&m/Faron Young, Eddie Thorne

YOU'RE STILL MY BABY
w&m/Chuck Willis

YOU'RE THE CREAM IN MY COFFEE
m/Ray Henderson
w/Lew Brown, Buddy DeSylva

YOU'RE THE FIRST, THE LAST, MY EVERYTHING
w&m/Barry White

YOU'RE THE GIRL I'M LOOKING FOR
m/Gustave A. Kerker
w/Joseph Herbert

YOU'RE THE LOVE
w&m/Dash Crofts, James Seals

YOU'RE THE LOVE
w&m/David Batteau, Louis Shelton

YOU'RE THE ONE
w&m/Sly Stone

YOU'RE THE ONLY STAR IN MY BLUE HEAVEN
w&m/Gene Autry

YOU'RE THE ONLY WORLD I KNOW
w&m/Sonny James, Robert F. Tubert

YOU'RE THE REASON I'M LIVING
w&m/Bobby Darin

YOU'RE THE TOP
w&m/Cole Porter

YOURS (QUIEREME MUCHO)
m/Gonzalo Roig
w/Albert Gamse, Jack Sherr

YOURS IS MY HEART ALONE
m/Franz Lehar
w/Harry B. Smith: English words
Alfred Gruenwald and Fritz Loehner-Beda: German words from "Dein Ist Mein Ganzes Herz"

YOURS LOVE
w&m/Harlan Howard

YOURS UNTIL TOMORROW
w&m/Carole King, Gerry Goffin

YOU'VE BEEN A GOOD WAGON BUT YOU DONE BROKE DOWN
w&m/Benjamin R. Harney

YOU'VE GOT A FRIEND
w&m/Carole King

YOU'VE GOT ME CRYING AGAIN m/Isham Jones
w/Charles Newman

YOU'VE GOT ME IN THE PALM OF YOUR HAND
m/James V. Monaco
w/Edgar Leslie

YOU'VE GOT THAT THING
w&m/Cole Porter

YOU'VE GOT TO SEE MOMMA EVERY NIGHT
m/Con Conrad
w/Billy Rose

YOU'VE GOT WHAT IT TAKES
w&m/Tyrone Carlo, Gwen Gordy

YOU'VE GOT YOUR TROUBLES
w&m/Roger Greenaway, Roger Cook

YOU'VE LOST THAT LOVIN' FEELING
w&m/Phil Spector, Barry Mann, Cynthia Weil

YOU'VE MADE ME SO VERY HAPPY
w&m/Berry Gordy Jr., Frank Wilson, Brenda Holloway, Patrice Holloway

YOU'VE NEVER BEEN THIS FAR BEFORE
w&m/Conway Twitty

YOU'VE REALLY GOT A HOLD ON ME
w&m/William (Smokey) Robinson Jr.

YSABEL'S TABLE DANCE (instr.)
m/Charles Mingus

YUK-A-PUK
w&m/Morey Amsterdam

YUMMY, YUMMY, YUMMY
w&m/Jerry Kasenetz, Jeff Katz

ZERO HOUR (instr.)
m/Pete Johnson

ZIGEUNER
w&m/Noel Coward

ZIGGY STARDUST
w&m/David Bowie

ZING WENT THE STRINGS OF MY HEART
w&m/James Frederick Hanley

ZIP
m/Richard Rodgers
w/Lorenz (Larry) Hart

ZIP A DEE DOO DAH
m/Allie Wrubel
w/Ray Gilbert

ZODIAC SUITE (instr.)
m/Mary Lou Williams

ZODIAC VARIATIONS (instr.)
m/John Dankworth

ZOOTCASE (instr.)
m/Al Cohn, Zoot Sims

BEST-KNOWN COMPOSERS AND LYRICISTS
OF
POPULAR, ROCK, COUNTRY, SOUL, BLUES, JAZZ, GOSPEL INSPIRATIONAL, THEATER and FILM MUSIC HEARD IN THE U.S.A. FROM 1780 TO 1980

Alphabetically listed, along with "Best-known songs or instrumentals"
of each composer or lyricist, as well as
nationality, date of birth and/or death (or date of copyright)
and individual or group collaborators.

.

ABBREVIATIONS:
w/ = words by
m/ = music by
in co. w/ = in collaboration with

POPULAR COMPOSERS
& LYRICISTS

A

AARONSON, IRVING
1895-1963, American
m/Irving Aaronson
Loveliest Night Of The Year, The
(melody adapted from Juventino
Rosa's "Sobre las elas")
    w/Paul Francis Webster

ABRAHAMS, MAURICE
(Maurie Abrams)
1883-1931, American
He'd Have To Get Under
    w&m in co w/Grant Clarke

ACQUAVIVA, NICHOLAS (Nick)
1927, American
m/Nicholas Acquaviva
In The Middle Of An Island
    w/Ted Varnick
My Love, My Love
    w/Bob Haymes

ACUFF, ROY CLAXTON
1903, American
w&m/Roy Claxton Acuff
As Long As I Live
Fireball Mail
Great Speckle Bird
Night Train To Memphis
Pins And Needles
Wabash Cannonball
Wreck On The Highway

ADAIR, THOMAS M. (Tom)
1913, American
w/Thomas Adair
m/Matt Dennis
Everything Happens To Me
Let's Get Away From It All
Night We Called It A Day, The
Violets For Your Furs
Will You Still Be Mine

ADAMS, A. EMMETT
English
m/A. Emmett Adams
w/Douglas Furber
Bells Of St. Mary's, The (1917)

ADAMS, LEE
1924, American
w/Lee Adams
m/Charles Strouse
A Lot Of Livin' To Do
Kids
Once Upon A Time
Put On A Happy Face
While The City Sleeps
Yes I Can

ADAMS, RICHIE
American
After The Lovin' (1976)
    w&m in co w/Alan Bernstein

ADAMS, STANLEY
1907, American
w/Stanley Adams

Little Old Lady
    m/Hoagy Carmichael
My Shawl
    m/Xavier Cugat
There Are Such Things
    m/Abel Baer, George Meyer
What A Diff'rence A Day Made
    m/Maria Grever

ADAMSON, HAROLD
1906-1980 American
w/Harold Adamson
Affair To Remember, An
    m/Harry Warren, Leo McCarey
Around The World
    m/Victor Young
**Comin' In On A Wing And A
Prayer**
    m/Jimmy McHugh
Daybreak
    m/Ferde Grofe
Did I Remember
    m/Walter Donaldson
Everything I Have Is Yours
    m/Burton Lane
Everything's Been Done Before
    m/Edwin H. Knopf
**I Couldn't Sleep A Wink Last
Night**
    m/Jimmy McHugh
It's A Most Unusual Day
    m/Jimmy McHugh
How Blue The Night
    m/Jimmy McHugh
Hubba, Hubba, Hubba, A
    m/Jimmy McHugh
Manhattan Serenade
    m/Louis Alter
Moonlight Mood
    m/Peter De Rose
My Resistance Is Low
    m/Hoagy Carmichael
My Own
    m/Jimmy McHugh
**Lovely Way To Spend An
Evening, A**
    m/Jimmy McHugh
Sentimental Rhapsody
    m/Alfred Newman
720 In The Books
    m/Jan Savitt
Time On My Hands
    m/Mack Gordon, Vincent
    Youmans
Too Young To Go Steady
    m/Jimmy McHugh
You Say The Nicest Things Baby
    m/Jimmy McHugh, Mack Gordon
You're A Sweetheart
    m/Jimmy McHugh

ADDERLY, JULIAN (Cannonball)
1928-1975, American
m/Cannonball Adderly (instr.)
Sack Of Woe

ADDINSELL, RICHARD
1904, English
m/Richard Addinsell
Warsaw Concerto (1942) instr.
Film scores
Beau Brummel (1954)
Black Rose, The (1950)
Gaslight (1940)
Goodbye Mr. Chips (1939)
MacBeth (1961)
Tom Brown's Schooldays (1951)

ADDISON, JOHN
English
m/John Addison
Film scores
Charge Of The Light Brigade,
The (1968)
Cockleshell Heroes, The (1956)
Entertainer, The (1960)
Loneliness Of The Long Distance
Runner (1962)
Seven Days To Noon (1950)
Taste Of Honey, A (1962)
Tom Jones (1963)

ADLER, RICHARD
1921, American
w/Richard Adler
m/Jerry Ross
(except for Everybody Loves A
Lover – m/Robert Allen)
A Little Brains, A Little Talent
Another Time, Another Place
Everybody Loves A Lover
Heart
Hernando's Hideaway
Hey There
I'm Not At All In Love
Rags To Riches
Small Talk
Steam Heat
Two Lost Souls
Whatever Lola Wants
Who's Got The Pain

ADRISSI, DONALD J.
American
w&m/Donald J. Adrissi
in co w/Richard P. Adrissi
I Believe You (1977)
Never My Love (1967)
Slow Dancing Don't Turn Me On

AGER, MILTON
1893-1971, American
m/Milton Ager
Ain't She Sweet
    w/Jack Yellen
Auf Wiedersehn, My Dear
    w/Al Hoffman, Ed Nelson, Al
    Goodhart
Happy Days Are Here Again
    w/Jack Yellen

Happy Feet
    w/Jack Yellen

Hard-Hearted Hannah
w/Jack Yellen, Bob Begelow,
Charles Bates
I Wonder What's Become Of Sally
w/Jack Yellen
I'm Nobody's Baby
w/Benny Davis, Lester Santly
Everything Is Peaches Down In Georgia
co composer – George W. Meyer
w/Grant Clarke
Mama Goes Where Papa Goes
w/Jack Yellen
You Can't Pull The Wool Over My Eyes
w/Charles Newman, Murray
Mencher (Ted Murray)

AHBEZ, EDEN
1908, American
w&m/Eden Ahbez
Nature Boy

AHLERT, FRED E.
1892-1953, American
m/Fred E. Ahlert
I Don't Know Why
w/Roy Turk
I'll Get By
w/Roy Turk
I'm Gonna Sit Right Down And Write Myself A Letter
w/Joseph Young
Life Is A Song
w/Joseph Young
Love You Funny Thing
w/Roy Turk
Mean To Me
w/Roy Turk
Moon Was Yellow, The
w/Edgar Leslie
Take My Heart
w/Joseph Young
Walkin' My Baby Back Home
w/Roy Turk, Harry Richman
Where The Blue Of The Night (Meets The Gold Of The Day)
w/Roy Turk, Bing Crosby

AKST, HARRY
1894-1963, American
m/Harry Akst
Am I Blue
w/Grant Clarke
Anima E Core
m/Salve D'Esposito
w/Harry Akst, Mann Curtis
Baby Face
w/Benny Davis
Dinah
w/Samuel M. Lewis, Joseph
Young
Guilty
co-composer – Richard A. Whiting
w/Gus Kahn

Smile Will Go A Long, Long Way, A
w/Benny Davis
Stand Up And Cheer
w/Lew Brown

ALBERT, MORRIS
1951, American
w&m/Morris Albert
Feelings (i Dime?)

ALBERTS, AL
1922, American
w&m/Al Alberts in co w/Marty Gold
Tell Me Why

ALBRECHT, ELMER
1901-1959, American
w&m/Elmer Albrecht in co w/Sammy
Gallop, Dick Jurgens
Elmer's Tune

ALEXANDER, VAN
1915-1941, American
w&m/Van Alexander
A-Tisket, A-Tasket
in co w/Ella Fitzgerald (adapation
of traditional nursery rhyme)
Where Oh Where Has My Little Dog Gone
(adaptation of traditional nursery
rhyme)

ALFRED, ROY
1916, American
w&m/Roy Alfred
Hucklebuck, The

ALLAN, LEWIS
American
w&m/Lewis Allan
Strange Fruit

ALLEN, PETER
1940, Australian/American
m/Peter Allen
Don't Cry Out Loud
w/Carole Bayer Sager
Everything Old Is New Again
w/Carle Bayer Sager
I Could Have Been A Sailor
w&m/Peter Allen
I Honestly Love You
w/Jeff Barry
Quiet Please, There's A Lady On Stage
w/Carole Bayer Sager
I Go To Rio
w/Adrienne Anderson
I'd Rather Leave While I'm In Love
w/Carole Bayer Sager
Love Song For Jeffrey
w/Helen Reddy
Pretty, Pretty
w/Hal Hackady
Tenterfield Saddler
w&m/Peter Allen

ALLEN, ROBERT
1928, American
m/Robert Allen
w/Al Stillman (except for
"Everybody Loves A Lover" - w/
Richard Adler)
Can You Find It In Your Heart
Chances Are
Enchanted Island
Everybody Loves A Lover
w/Richard Adler
Home For The Holidays
If Dreams Come True
It's Not For Me To Say
My One And Only Heart
Moments To Remember
No Not Much
Teacher, Teacher
There's Only One Of You
Who Needs You
You Alone

ALLEN, STEVE
1921, American
Gravy Waltz
w&m in co w/Ray Brown
"Houseboat" Theme
m/George Duning
w/Steve Allen
Impossible
w&m/Steve Allen
"On The Beach" Theme
m/Ernest Gold
w/Steve Allen
"Picnic" Theme
m/George Duning
w/Steve Allen
Pretend You Don't See Her
w&m/Steve Allen
This Could Be The Start Of Something Big
w&m/Steve Allen

ALLEN, THOMAS SYLVESTER "Papa Dee"
1931, American
See list of selections under Lee Oskar

ALLEN, THORNTON W.
American
m/Thornton W. Allen
w/C.A. Robbins
Washington And Lee Swing (1910)

ALLISON, JOE
American
w&m/Joe Allison
He'll Have To Go
in co w/Audrey Allison
It's A Great Life
in co w/Audrey Allison
Live Fast, Love Hard, Die Young
w&m/Joe Allison
Rock City Boogie
w&m/Joe Allison

214

Teenage Crush
  in co w/Audrey Allison
When You Leave, Don't Slam
The Door
  w&m/Joe Allison

ALLISON, MOSE JOHN JR.
1927, American
w&m/Mose Allison
Back Country Suite, The
One Room Country Shack

ALLMAN, GREGG L.
1947, American
w&m/in co w/Duane Allman (brother,
1946-1971) except for Midnight
Rider
Melissa
Midnight Rider
  in co w/K. Payne
Nevertheless
One Way Out
Stand Back
Wasted Words

ALONZO, ELLIOTT (Zo)
1891-1964, American
m/Elliott (Zo) Alonzo
w/Stoddard King
There's A Long Long Trail
A'Winding

ALPERT, HERB
1935, American
w&m/Herb Alpert
Behind The Rain
Jerusalem
1980
Quiet Tear, A
  in co w/Johnny Flamingo
Slick
  in co w/John Pisano

ALTER, LOUIS
1902, American
m/Louis Alter
Come Up And See Me Sometime
  w/Arthur Swanstrom
Do You Know What It Means To
Miss New Orleans
  w/Edgar Leslie
Dolores
  w/Frank Loesser
Manhattan Serenade
  w/Harold Adamson
Melody From The Sky, A
  w/Sidney D. Mitchell
My Kinda Love
  w/Jo Trent
Nina Never Knew
  w/Milton Drake
Rainbow On The River
  w/Paul Francis Webster
Twilight On The Trail
  w/Sidney D. Mitchell
You Turned The Tables On Me
  w/Sidney D. Mitchell

ALTMAN, ARTHUR
1934, American
m/Arthur Altman
Play Fiddle Play
  co-composer – Emery Deutsch
  w/Jack Lawrence
I Fall In Love With You Every Day
  w/Jack Lawrence
All Or Nothing At All
  w/Jack Lawrence
American Beauty Rose
  w/Hal David

AMFITHEATROF, DANIELE
1901, American
m/Daniele Amfitheatrof
Major Dundee March (instr.)
Film scores
Angels In The Outfield (1951)
Desert Fox, The (1951)
Ivy (1951)
Lassie Come Home (1943)
Major Dundee (1965)
Naked Jungle, The (1954)

AMMONS, ALBERT C.
1907-1949, American
m/Albert C. Ammons
Boogie Woogie Prayer (Cafe
Society Rag & The Boogie
Woogie)
  in co w/Pete K.H. Johnson, Joe
  Turner
Boogie Woogie Stomp
Cafe Society Rag
  in co w/Pete K.H. Johnson, Joe
  Turner

AMSTERDAM, MOREY
1912, American
w&m/Morey Amsterdam
Rum And Coca-Cola
(adapted from Caribbean folk song)
Yuk-A-Puk

ANDERSON, ADRIENNE
American
w/Adrienne Anderson
Could It Be Magic (1977)
  m/Barry Manilow (based on
  Chopin's Prelude In C Minor)
Daybreak
  m/Barry Manilow
Deja Vu
  m/Isaac Hayes

ANDERSON, BILL
1937, American
w&m/Bill Anderson
All The Lonely Women In The
World
Cincinnati Ohio
City Lights
Corner Of My Life, The
Dis-Satisfied
  in co w/Jan Howard, Carter
  Howard

Eight By Ten
  in co w/Walter Haynes
Every Time I Turn The Radio On
Face To The Wall
  in co w/Faron Young
Five Little Fingers
Get A Little Dirt On Your Hands
Happy Birthday To Me
Happy State Of Mind
I Can't Remember
  in co w/Bette Anderson
I Can't Wait Any Longer
  in co w/Buddy Killen
I Don't Love You Any More
I Get The Fever
I Love You Drops
I Missed Me
I Never Once Stopped Loving You
  in co w/Jan Howard
If It's All The Same To You
If You Can Live With It (I Can Live
Without It)
I've Enjoyed As Much Of This As
  I Can Stand
Lord Knows I'm Drinking, The
Losing Your Love
  in co w/Buddy Killen
Mama Sang A Song
My Life
Nobody But A Fool
Once A Day
Peel Me A Nanner
Po' Folks
Quits
River Boat
Saginaw Michigan
Slippin' Away
Sometimes
(I Love You) Still
That's What It's Like To Be
  Lonesome
Then & Only Then
Tip Of My Fingers, The
Walk Out Backwards
We Missed You
When Two Worlds Collide
  in co w/Roger Miller
Wild Weekend
You & Your Sweet Love

ANDERSON, IAN
1947, English
w&m/Ian Anderson
Aqualung
Cross Eyed Mary
Living In The Past
Locomotive Breath
Reason For Waiting
Sweet Dream
Teacher
Thick As A Brick
  in co w/Gerald Bastock
Time For Everything, A
To Cry You A Song

ANDERSON, LEROY
1908-1975, American
m/Leroy Anderson
(where no lyricist credits are shown,
selection is best known as an instru-
mental)
Belle Of The Ball
    w/Mitchell Parish
Blue Tango
    w/Mitchell Parish
Chicken Reel
China Doll
Fiddle Faddle
    w/Mitchell Parish
Girl In Satin, The
Jazz Legato
Jazz Pizzicato
Pennywhistle Song, The
Plink, Plank, Plunk
Promenade
    w/Mitchell Parish
Saraband
Serenata
    w/Mitchell Parish
Sleigh Ride
    w/Mitchell Parish
Syncopated Clock, The
Trumpeter's Lullaby, A
Typewriter, The

ANDERSON, LIZ
1930, American
w&m/Liz Anderson
If I Kiss You Will You Go Away
I'm A Lonesome Fugitive
    in co w/Casey Anderson
My Friends Are Gonna Be
    Strangers
    in co w/Casey Anderson
Pick Of The Week
Wife Of The Party

ANDERSON, MAXWELL
1888-1959, American
w/Maxwell Anderson
m/Kurt Weill (except When You're In
Love, m/Arthur Schwartz)
Cry The Beloved Country
Lost In The Stars
September Song
Stay Well
When You're In Love

ANDERSON, R. ALEX
1894-1978, American
w&m/Alex R. Anderson
Cockeyed Mayor Of
    Kaunakaukai, The
Lovely Hula Hands

ANDERSON, STIG
Swedish
w/Stig Anderson
m/Benny Andersson, Bjorn Ulvaeus
See listing of selections under
Benny Andersson

ANDERSSON, BENNY
(Goran Bror Benny Andersson)
1946, Swedish
m/Benny Andersson in co w/Bjorn
Ulvaeus
w/Stig Anderson
Chiquita
Dancing Queen
Fernando
Gimme, Gimme, Gimme
Honey, Honey
I Do, I Do, I Do
Knowing Me, Knowing You
Name Of The Game, The
Ring Ring
Take A Chance On Me
Waterloo

ANDRE, FABIAN
1910, 1960, American
m/Fabian Andre
Dream A Little Dream Of Me
    co-composer/Wilbur Schwandt
    w/Gus Kahn

ANDREWS, CHRIS
English
w&m/Chris Andrews
Girl Don't Come (1965)
Yesterday Man (1966)

ANDROZZO, ALMA BAZEL
1912, American
w&m/Alma Bazel Androzzo
If I Can Help Somebody (1945)

ANKA, PAUL
1941, Canadian/American
w&m/Paul Anka
Diana
Do I Love You
    in co w/Alain Le Govic, Yves
    Dessca, Michel Pelay
I Don't Like To Sleep Alone
I'm Just A Lonely Boy
Jubilation
Longest Day, The
My Best Friend's Wife
My Love
My Way
    in co w/Jacques Revaux,
    Claude Francois
Ogni Volta
One Man Woman/One
    Woman Man
Puppy Love
Put Your Head On My Shoulder
Teddy
You Are My Destiny
You're Having My Baby

ANTHEIL, GEORGE
1900-1959, American (see classical
composers)
m/George Antheil
Film scores

Ballet Mechanique (1924) (ballet)
Plainsman, The (1936)
Specter Of The Roses (1946)
Knock On Any Door (1949)
Not As A Stranger (1955)
Pride And The Passion, The (1957)

ARDITI, LUIGI
1822-1903, Italian
m/Luigi Arditi
Kiss Waltz, The (Il Bacio)
    w/S. Aldighieri
Melba Waltz (Se Seran Rose)
    w/Pietro Mazzini

ARGENT, RODNEY TERRENCE
1945, English
w&m/Rodney Argent
Hold Your Head Up
She's Not There
Time Of The Season

ARLEN, HAROLD
21905, American
m/Harold Arlen
Ac-Cen-Tchu-Ate The Positive
    w/Johnny Mercer
Anyplace I Hang My Hat Is Home
    w/Johnny Mercer
As Long As I Live
    w/Ted Koehler
Between The Devil And The Deep
    Blue Sea
    w/Ted Koehler
Blues In The Night
    w/Johnny Mercer
Buds Won't Bud
    w/E. Y. Harburg
Come Rain Or Come Shine
    w/Johnny Mercer
Ding Dong The Witch Is Dead
    w/E.Y. Harburg
Down With Love
    w/E.Y. Harburg

Eagle And Me, The
    w/E.Y. Harburg
Evelina
    w/E.Y. Harburg
Fancy Free
    w/Johnny Mercer
For Every Man There's A Woman
    w/Leo Robin
Fun To Be Fooled
    w/E.Y. Harburg, Ira Gershwin
Get Happy
    w/Ted Koehler
Happiness Is A Thing Called Joe
    w/E.Y. Harburg
Happy As The Day Is Long
    w/Ted Koehler
Hit The Road To Dreamland
    w/Johnny Mercer
Hooray For Love
    w/Leo Robin

I Could Go On Singing
    w/E.Y. Harburg
I Don't Think I'll End It All Today
    w/E.Y. Harburg
I Got A Song
    w/E.Y. Harburg
I Gotta Right To Sing The Blues
    w/Ted Koehler
I Love A Parade
    w/Ted Koehler
If I Only Had A Brain
    w/E.Y. Harburg
In Your Own Quiet Way
    w/E.Y. Harburg
It Was Written In The Stars
    w/Leo Robin
It's Only A Paper Moon
    w/E.Y. Harburg, Billy Rose
I've Got The World On A String
    w/Ted Koehler
June Comes Around Every Year
    w/Johnny Mercer
Kickin' The Gong Around
    w/Koehler
Last Night When We Were Young
    w/Ted Koehler
Let's Fall In Love
    w/Ted Koehler
Let's Take A Walk Around The Block
    w/E.Y. Harburg, Ira Gershwin
Let's Take The Long Way Home
    w/Johnny Mercer
Lydia The Tatooed Lady
    w/E.Y. Harburg
Man That Got Away, The
    w/Ira Gershwin
My Shining Hour
    w/Johnny Mercer
One For My Baby
    w/Johnny Mercer
Out Of This World
    w/Johnny Mercer
Over The Rainbow
    w/E.Y. Harburg
Right As The Rain
    w/E.Y. Harburg
Stormy Weather
    w/Ted Koehler
Sweet And Hot
    w/Jack Yellen
Take It Slow Joe
    w/E.Y. Harburg
That Old Black Magic
    w/Johnny Mercer
This Time The Dream's On Me
    w/Johnny Mercer
Two Ladies In De Shade Of De Banana Tree
    w/Truman Capote
We're Off To See The Wizard
    w/E.Y. Harburg
What's Good About Goodbye
    w/Leo Robin

When The Sun Comes Out
    w/Ted Koehler
You're A Builder Upper
    w/Ira Gershwin, E.Y. Harburg

ARMSTRONG, HARRY
1879-1951, American
m/Harry Armstrong
Goodbye Eyes Of Blue
    w/James J. Walker
I Love My Wife But Oh You Kid
    w/Billy Clark
Sweet Adeline (You're The Flower Of My Heart, Sweet Adeline)
    w/Richard Gerard Husch

ARMSTRONG, LOUIS (Satchmo, Pops)
1900-1971, American
    m/Louis Armstrong (instr.)
Satchel Mouth Swing
Sugar Foot Stomp
Struttin' With Some Barbecue
Tears – co-composer Lillian Hardin
Wild Man Blues

ARNDT, FELIX
1889-1918, American
m/Felix Arndt
Nola
    w/Sunny Skylar

ARNE, MICHAEL
17th century, English
m/Michael Arne
w/traditional, source unknown
Lass With The Delicate Air
(also known as "Young Molly Who Lives At The Foot Of The Hill")

ARNE, THOMAS
1710-1788, English
w&m/Thomas Arne
Rule Britannia

ARNHEIM, GUS
1897-1955, American
w&m/Gus Arnheim
I Cried For You
    in co w/Abe Lyman, Arthur Freed
Sweet And Lovely
    in co w/Harry Tobias, Jules Lemare

ARNOLD, EDDY
(Richard Edward Arnold)
1918, American
w&m/Eddy Arnold
Heart Full Of Love, A
    in co w/Roy Soehnel, Steve Nelson
I'll Hold You In My Heart (Till I Can Hold You In My Arms)
    in co w/Thomas Dilbeck, Hal Harton
I'm Throwing Rice At the Girl I Love
    w&m/Eddy Arnold

Just A Little Lovin' (Will Go A Long Way)
    in co w/Zeke Clements
That Do Make It Nice
    in co w/Fred Ebb, Paul Klein
This Is The Thanks I Get
    in co w/Tommy Dilbeck
That's How Much I Love You
    in co w/Wallace Fowler
What Is Life Without Love
    in co w/Vic McAlpin, Owen Bradley
You Don't Know Me
    in co w/Cindy Walker

ARNOLD, MALCOLM
English
m/Malcolm Arnold
Film scores
Belles Of St. Trinian's, The (1955)
Breaking The Sound Barrier (1952)
Bridge On The River Kwai, The (1957)
David Copperfield (1970)
Captain's Paradise, The (1953)
Chalk Garden, The (1964)
Dunkirk (1958)
Hobson's Choice (1954)
Inn Of The Sixth Happiness, The (1958)
Island In The Sun (1957)
Trapeze (1956)
Tunes Of Glory (1960)

ASHER, PHIL
American
w&m/Phil Asher
When Will I Be Loved (1975)

ASHFORD, NICHOLAS (Nick)
1943, American
w&m in co w/Valerie Simpson
See list of selections under Valerie Simpson

ASTLEY, EDWIN
English
m/Edwin Astley
Film scores
Mouse That Roared, The (1959)
To Paris With Love (1955)
ASTON, WILLIAM
(Albert William Ketelbey)
1880-1959, English
m/William Aston (instr.)
In A Monastery Garden (1915)

ATKINS, ROGER
American
w&m/Roger Atkins
It's My Life (1965)
    in co w/Carl D'Errico
Love Takes A Long Time Growin' (1966)
    in co w/Helen Miller
Make Me Your Baby (1965)
    in co w/Helen Miller

ATTERIDGE, (Richard) HAROLD
1886-1938, American
w/Harold Atteridge
m/Harry Carroll
By The Beautiful Sea

AUGUSTIN, MARX
d. 1705, Austrian
German w&m/Marx Augustin (unverified) w/various anonymous
English versions
O Du Lieber Augustin (also known as **Ach Du Lieber Augustin**)

AURIC, GEORGES
1899, French
m/Georges Auric
Song From Moulin Rouge, The
    w/Bill Engvick
Film scores:
Bonjour Tristesse (1958)
Heaven Knows Mr. Allison (1957)
Hunchback Of Notre Dame,
The (1957)
Lavender Hill Mob, The (1951)
Moulin Rouge (1952)
Orpheus (1949)
Rififi (1956)
Roman Holiday (1953)

AUSTIN, GENE
1900, American
w&m/Gene Austin

How Come You Do Me Like You Do
    in co w/Roy Bergere
Lonesome Road, The
    in co w/Nathaniel Shilkret
When My Sugar Walks Down The Street
    in co w/Jimmy McHugh, Irving Mills

AUTRY, GENE
1907, American
Back In The Saddle Again
    w&m/Gene Autry
Be Honest With Me
    m/Fred Rose
Here Comes Santa Claus
    w&m/Gene Autry
Ridin' Down The Canyon
    m/Smiley Burnett
Tears On My Pillow
    m/Fred Rose
That Silver Haired Daddy Of Mine
    m/Jimmy Long
You're The Only Star In My Blue Heaven
    w&m/Gene Autry

AXT, WILLIAM
1888-1959, American
m/William Axt

Film scores:
Dinner At Eight (1933)
Grand Hotel
Men In White (1934)
Our Dancing Daughters (1928)
Parnell (1937)
Reunion In Vienna (1933)
Smilin' Through (1932)
Thin Man, The (1934)

AXTON, HOYT
1938, American
w&m/Hoyt Axton
Boney Fingers
    in co w/Renee Armand
Greenback Dollar
Joy To The World
Never Been To Spain
No No Song, The
Pusher, The
When The Morning Comes

AXTON, MAE BOREN
1913, American
w&m/Mae Boren Axton
Heartbreak Hotel
    in co w/Elvis Presley, Tommy Durden
Welcome To The Club
    w&m/Mae Boren Axton

POPULAR COMPOSERS & LYRICISTS

B

BACHARACH, BURT F.
1928, American
m/Burt Bacharach
w/Hal David
Alfie
Always Something There To Remind Me (There's)
Anyone Who Had A Heart
Are You There With Another Girl
Baby It's You
Blue On Blue
(They Long To Be) Close To You
Do You Know The Way To San Jose
Don't Make Me Over
Everybody's Out Of Town
House Is Not A Home, A
I Cry Alone
I Say A Little Prayer
I'll Never Fall In Love Again
Knowing When To Leave
Look Of Love, The
Magic Moments
Make It Easy On Yourself
Man Who Shot Liberty Valance, The
Message To Michael
One Less Bell To Answer
Only Love Can Break A Heart
Paper Maché
Promises, Promises
Raindrops Keep Fallin' On My Head
Reach Out For Me
This Empty Place
This Guy's In Love With You
Town Without Pity
Trains And Boats And Planes
Twenty Four Hours From Tulsa
Walk On By
What The World Needs Now Is Love
What's New Pussycat
Whoever You Are I Love You
Windows Of The World
Wishin' and Hopin'
Wives And Lovers
You'll Never Get To Heaven
Film scores
Butch Cassidy And The Sundance Kid (1969)
Casino Royale (1967)
What's New Pussycat (1965)

BACHMAN, RANDY
(Randy Charles Bachman)
1943, Canadian
w&m/Randy Bachman
American Woman
in co w/Burton Cummings, Kate Peterson
Laughing
in co w/Burton Cummings

No Time
in co w/Burton Cummings
Let It Ride
in co w/C.F. Turner
Takin' Care Of Business
w&m/Randy Bachman
These Eyes
in co w/Burton Cummings
You Ain't Seen Nothing Yet
in co w/Burton Cummings

BADAZZ, RANDY
1955, American
w&m in co w/Andrew Armer
Rise (1979)
Rotation (1979)

BAER, ABEL
1893, American
w&m/Abel Baer
Chapel Of The Roses
June Night
in co w/Cliff Friend
Mama Loves Papa
in co w/Cliff Friend
My Mother's Eyes
in co w/L. Wolfe Gilbert
There Are Such Things
in co w/Stanley Adams, George W. Meyer
When The One You Love Loves You

BAGDASARIAN, ROSS
(David Seville)
1919-1972, American
w&m/Ross Bagdasarian
Alvin's Harmonica
Chipmunk Song, The
Come On-A My House
in co w/William Saroyan
Witch Doctor

BAGLEY, E.E.
American
m/E.E. Bagley
National Emblem (march) (1906)

BAKER, LAVERN
1928, American
w&m in co w/Lincoln Chase, Howard Biggs
That's All I Need

BAKER, PHIL
1896-1963, American
m/Phil Baker
w/Ben Bernie, Walter Hirsch
Strange Interlude

BALFE, MICHAEL WILLIAM (SIR)
1808-1870, Irish
m/Sir Michael William Balfe
Come Into The Garden Maude
w/Alfred Lord Tennyson

I Dreamt I Dwelt In Marble Halls (1843)
w/Alfred Bunn
Killarney (1862)
w/Edmund Falconer

BALL, ERNEST R.
1878-1927, American
m/Ernest R. Ball
A Little Bit Of Heaven
w/J. Keirn Brennan
Dear Little Boy Of Mine
w/J. Keirn Brennan
Goodbye, Good Luck, God Bless You
w/J. Keirn Brennan
I Love The Name Of Mary
co-composer Chauncey Olcott
w/George Graff Jr.
Let The Rest Of The World Go By
w/J. Keirn Brennan
Love Me And The World Is Mine
w/David Reed Jr.
Mother Machree
co-composer Chauncey Olcott
w/Rida Johnson Young
Till The Sands Of The Desert Grow Cold
w/George Graff Jr.
When Irish Eyes Are Smiling
co-composer Chauncey Olcott
w/George Graff Jr.
Will You Love Me In December As You Do In May
w/James J. Walker

BALLARD, CLINT JR.
American
w&m/Clint Ballard Jr.
You're No Good (1963)

BALLARD, FRANCIS DRAKE
(Pat)
1899-1960, American
w&m/Francis Drake Ballard
Mr. Sandman

BALLARD, HANK
1932, American
w&m/Hank Ballard
Dance With Me Henry
revised version of "Work With Me Annie;" the revision in co w/Johnny Otis and Etta James
Finger Poppin' Time
Get It
in co w/Alonzo Tucker
Let's Go, Let's Go, Let's Go
Twist, The
Sexy Ways
Work With Me Annie

BANKS, HOMER
1941, American
w&m/Homer Banks

Ain't That A Lot Of Love
in co w/William D. Parker
Ain't That Loving You (For More Reasons Than One)
in co w/Allen Jones
I Thought Of You Today
in co w/Chuck Brooks
If Loving You Is Wrong (I Don't Want To Be Right)
in co w/Raymond Jackson, Carl M. Hampton
If You're Ready Come Go With Me
in co w/Carl Hampton, Raymond Jackson
I'll Be The Other Woman
in co w/Carl M. Hampton
I'll Be Your Shelter (In Time Of Storm)
in co w/Carl M. Hampton, Raymond Jackson
I'm Gonna Have To Tell Her
in co w/Carl M. Hampton, Raymond Jackson, Percy Mayfield
I've Got A Feeling (We'll Be Seeing Each Other Again)
in co w/Carl M. Hampton
Knock On Wood
in co w/Carl M. Hampton
Son Of Shaft
in co w/Allen Jones, William Brown
Soul Man
in co w/Carl M. Hampton
Take Care Of Your Homework
in co w/Raymond Jackson, Don Davis, Tom Kelly
Touch A Hand Make A Friend
in co w/Carl M. Hampton, Raymond Jackson
Who's Making Love
in co w/Raymond Jackson, Donald Davis

BARBIERI, GATO
Brazilian
m/Gato Barbieri
Last Tango In Paris (instr.) (1973)

BARBOUR, DAVID (Dave)
1912-1965, American
m/David Barbour
w/Peggy Lee
See list of selections under Peggy Lee

BARGY, ROY FREDERICK
1894-1974, American
m/Roy Frederick Bargy (instr.)
Knice And Knifty
Omeomy
Pianoflage
Rufenreddy
Slipova

BARING-GOULD, SABINE
English
w/Sabine Barine-Gould
Now The Day Is Over (1869)
m/Joseph Barnby
Onward Christian Soldiers (1871)
m/Sir Arthur Sullivan

BARRETT, THOMAS A. (Leslie Stuart)
English
m/Thomas A. Barrett
w/Owen Hall
Tell Me Pretty Maiden (1900)

BARRIS, CHUCK
1930, American
w&m/Chuck Barris
Palisades Park (1962)
Robin's Song (1980)

BARRIS, HARRY
1905-1962, American
m/Harry Barris
At Your Command
w/Bing Crosby, Harry Tobias
I Surrender Dear
w/Gordon Clifford
It Was So Beautiful
w/Arthur Freed
Little Dutch Mill
w/Ralph Freed
Mississippi Mud
w/James Cavanaugh
Wrap Your Troubles In Dreams
w/Ted Koehler, Billy Moll

BARRY, JEFF
1940, American
w&m/Jeff Barry
Baby I Love You
in co w/Ellie Greenwich
Be My Baby
in co w/Ellie Greenwich, Phil Spector
Chapel In The Moonlight
in co w/Ellie Greenwich
Da Doo Ron Ron (When He Walked Me Home)
in co w/Ellie Greenwich, Phil Spector
Do Wah Diddy
in co w/Ellie Greenwich
I Honestly Love You
in co w/Peter Allen
I Wanna Love Him So Bad
in co w/Ellie Greenwich
Leader Of The Pack
in co w/Ellie Greenwich, George Morton
Montego Bay
in co w/Bobby Bloom
One Day At A Time
in co w/Ellie Greenwich

Out Of Hand
w&m/Jeff Barry
River Deep Mountain High
in co w/Ellie Greenwich, Phil Spector
Sugar Sugar
in co w/Andy Kim
Then He Kissed Me
in co w/Ellie Greenwich, Phil Spector

BARRY, JOHN
English
m/John Barry
Are You In There
w/David Pomeranz
Born Free (1966)
w/Don Black
Diamonds Are Forever
w/Don Black
Goldfinger
w/Leslie Bricusse, Anthony Newley
Knack, The
w/Leslie Bricusse
Man With The Golden Gun, The
w/Don Black
Midnight Cowboy (theme)
Thunderball
w/Leslie Bricusse
You Only Live Twice
w/Leslie Bricusse
Film scores
Born Free (1966)
Black Hole (1979)
Diamonds Are Forever
From Russia With Love
Goldfinger
Ipcress File, The
King Rat
Lion In Winter, The (1968)
Midnight Cowboy
On Her Majesty's Secret Service
Petulia
Thunderball
You Only Live Twice
Zulu

BART, LIONEL
1936, English
w&m/Lionel Bart
As Long As He Needs Me
Consider Yourself
I'd Do Anything
Where Is Love
Who Will Buy
Film score
Black Beauty

BARTHOLOMEW, DAVE
American
All w&m/written in collaboration with Antoine "Fats" Domino. See listing of selections under Antoine "Fats" Domino

BASIE, WILLIAM (Count)
1906, American
m/William (Count) Basie
Basie Boogie
    w/Milt Ebbins
Blue And Sentimental
    co-composer Jerry Livingston
    w/Mack David
Don't You Miss Your Baby
    co-composer Eddie Durham
    w/James A. Rushing
Gone With The Wind (instr.)
Good Morning Blues
    co-composer Eddie Durham
    w/James A. Rushing
John's Idea
    co-composer Eddie Durham
Jumpin At The Woodside (instr.)
One O'Clock Jump
    w/Lee Gaines
Panassie Stomp (instr.)
Shorty George (instr.)
    co-composers Albert (Andy)
    Gibson, Harry Edison
Swingin' The Blues (instr.)
    co-composer Eddie Durham
Two O'Clock Jump (instr.)
    co-composers Benny Goodman,
    Harry James

BATES, KATHERINE LEE
1859-1929, American
w/Katherine Lee Bates
m/Samuel A. Ward
America The Beautiful
(from the melody "Materna" based
on the hymn "O Mother Dear
Jerusaleum")

BATTEAU, DAVID
American
w&m in co w/Louis Shelton
You're The Love (1978)

BAXTER, LES
1922, American
w&m/Les Baxter
Quiet Village

BAXTER, PHIL
1896-1931, American
w&m/Phil Baxter
**I'm A Ding Dong Daddy From
   Dumas**
Piccolo Pete

BAYNE, SYDNEY
English
m/Sydney Bayne (instrumental)
Destiny (1912)

BECKER, WALTER
1950, American
w&m in co w/Donald Fagen
See list of selections under Donald
Fagen

BECKET, THOMAS A.
born early 19th century, not to be
confused with the 12th century
Archbishop of Canterbury
American
w&m/Thomas A. Becket
**Columbia, The Gem Of The Ocean
(1843)**

BECKETT, PETER
English
w&m in co w/John Charles "J.C."
Crowley
Baby Come Back (1977)
Prisoner Of Your Love (1978)

BEIDERBECKE, BIX
1903-1931, American
m/Bix Beiderbecke
In A Mist (1928) (instr.)

BELEW, CARL
w&m/Carl Belew
Lonely Street (1956)
    in co w/Kenny Sowder, W.S.
    Stevenson
Stamp Out Loneliness
    in co w/Van Givens
Stop The World (And Let Me Off)
    in co w/W. S. Stevenson
That's When I See The Blues
    in co w/W.S. Stevenson

BELL, ARCHIE
1944, American
w&m in co w/Billy H. Buttier
Tighten Up
BELL, THOMAS
American
w&m/Thomas Bell
Betcha By Golly Wow
    in co w/Linda Creed
Break Up To Make Up
    in co w/Linda Creed, Kenneth
    Gamble
**Didn't I (Blow Your Mind This
    Time)**
    in co w/William Hart
Ghetto Child
    in co w/Linda Creed
**I'll Be Around (Whenever You
    Want Me)**
    in co w/Phillip Hurtt
I'm Comin' Home
    in co w/Linda Creed
I'm Doing Fine Now
    in co w/Marshall Sherman
I'm Stone In Love With You
    in co w/Anthony Bell, Linda Creed
La-La Means I Love You
    in co w/William A. Hart
One Man Band
    in co w/Linda Creed
People Make The World Go 'Round
    in co w/Linda Creed

Rockin' Roll Baby
    in co w/Linda Creed
She's All Woman
    in co w/Linda Creed
You Are Everything
    in co w/Linda Creed
You Make Me Feel Brand New
    in co w/Linda Creed

BELLAMY, DAVID
1941, American
w&m/David Bellamy
**If I Said You Have A Beautiful
Body, Would You Hold It Against
    Me (1979)**
Spiders And Snakes
Sugar Daddy

BELLE, BARBARA
1922, American
w&m in co w/Anita Leonard
A Sunday Kind Of Love

BELVIN, JESSE
American
w&m/Jessie Belvin
Dream Girl
    in co w/Marvin Phillips (1953)
Earth Angel (1954)
Goodnight My Love (1955)
Guess Who (1970)
    in co w/Jo Ann Belvin

BENJAMIN, BENNIE
1907, American
m/Bennie Benjamin
Can Anyone Explain
    w& m/George D. Weiss
Cancel The Flowers
    w& m/Edward Seiler, Sol
    Marcus
Confess
    w& m/George D. Weiss
Cross Over The Bridge
    w& m/George D. Weiss
How Important Can It Be
    w& m/George D. Weiss
**I Don't See Me In Your Eyes
    Anymore**
    w& m/George D. Weiss
**I Don't Want To Set The World
    On Fire**
    w& m/Edward Seiler, Sol
    Marcus, Eddie Durham
I Want To Thank Your Folks
    w& m/George D. Weiss
I'll Never Be Free
    w& m/George D. Weiss
Lonesome And Blue
    w& m/George D. Weiss
Oh What It Seemed To Be
    w& m/George D. Weiss, Frankie
    Carle
Rumors Are Flying
    w& m/George D. Weiss

Strictly Instrumental
w& m/Edward Seiler, Sol
Marcus, Edgar Battle
Wheel Of Fortune
w& m/George D. Weiss
**When The Lights Go On Again All
Over The World**
w& m/Edward Seiler, Sol
Marcus

BENNARD, GEORGE (Reverend)
1873-1958, American
w&m/George Bennard
God Bless Our Boys
Old Rugged Cross, The

BENNETT, ROY C.
11918, American
w&m in co w/Sid Tepper
Jenny Kissed Me
Lonesome Cowboy
My Bonnie Lassie
**Naughty Lady Of Shady Lane,
The**
Red Roses For A Blue Lady
Woodchuck Song

BENSON, GARY
American
w&m/Gary Benson
Let Her In (1976)

BENTON, BROOK
1931, American
w&m/Brook Benton
Boll Weevil Song, The
in co w/Clyde Otis
Can I Help It
Endlessly
in co w/Clyde Otis
For My Baby
in co w/Clyde Otis
I'll Take Care Of You
It's Just A Matter Of Time
in co w/Clyde Otis,Belford
Hendricks
Kiddio
in co w/Clyde Otis
Lie To Me
in co w/Margie Singleton
Looking Back
in co w/Clyde Otis, Belford
Hendricks
Lover's Question, A
in co w/Jimmy Williams
Rockin' Good Way, A
in co w/Clyde Otis, Gladyces De
Jesus
Tell The Truth
in co w/Clyde Otis, Jimmy
Williams
Thank You Pretty Baby
in co w/Clyde Otis

BERGANTINE, BORNEY
1909-1954, American

m/Borney Bergantine
w/Betty Peterson
My Happiness (1948)

BERGMAN, ALAN
1925, American
BERGMAN, MARILYN
1929, American
w&m in co w/ Alan
Bergman
All His Children
in co w/Henry Mancini
Last Time I Felt Like This, The
in co w/Marvin Hamlisch
Marmalade, Molasses And Honey
in co w/Maurice Jarre
Nice 'n' Easy
Pieces Of Dreams
in co w/Michel Legrand
Play A Song For Dancing
Promise, The
That Face
in co w/Lew Spence
**Summer Knows, The (Theme
from Summer Of '42)**
in co w/Michel Legrand
Way We Were, The
in co w/Marvin Hamlisch
**What Are You Doing The Rest Of
Your Life**
in co w/Michel Legrand
Windmills Of Your Mind, The
in co w/Michel Legrand
Yellow Bird
in co w/Norman Luboff
You Don't Bring Me Flowers
in co w/Neil Diamond

BERLIN, IRVING
1888, American
After You Get What You Want
Alexander's Ragtime Band
All Alone
All By Myself
Always
Anything You Can Do
Be Careful It's My Heart
Best Thing For You, The
Better Luck Next Time
Blue Skies
Call Me Up Some Rainy Afternoon
Change Partners
Cheek To Cheek
Count Your Blessings
Couple Of Swells, A
Crinoline Days
Doin' What Comes Naturally
Empty Pockets Filled With Love
Ephraham
Easter Parade
Everybody's Doin' It
Everybody Step
Fella With An Umbrella, A

Girl On The Magazine Cover, The
Girl That I Marry
Girls of My Dreams
Give Me Your Tired, Your Poor
(based on Statue of Liberty in-
scription from the poem 'The New
Colossus" by Emma Lazarus
God Bless America
Goodbye Becky Cohen
Grizzly Bear, The
Happy Holiday
Harlem On My Mind
Heat Wave
**He's A Devil In His Own
Home Town**
co-lyricist Grant Clarke
**Hostess With The Mostes' On The
Ball, The**
How Deep Is The Ocean
**How Many Times Have I Said I
Love You**
I Got The Sun In The Morning
**I Left My Heart At The Stage
Door Canteen**
I Love A Piano
**I'm Putting All My Eggs In
One Basket**
I Poured My Heart Into A Song
I Threw A Kiss In The Ocean
I Want To Go Back To Michigan
International Rag
Is He The Only Man In The World
**Isn't This A Lovely Day To Be
Caught In The Rain**
**It Only Happens When I Dance
With You**
It's A Lovely Day Today
**I've Got My Love To Keep Me
Warm**
Kiss Me My Honey Kiss Me
m/Ted Snyder
Lady Of The Evening
Lazy
Let Me Sing And I'm Happy
Let Yourself Go
Let's Face The Music And Dance
Let's Have Another Cup Of Coffee
**Let's Take An Old Fashioned
Walk**
Man Chases A Girl, A
Mandy
Marie
Marie From Sunny Italy
Meat And Potatoes
Moonshine Lullaby
My Wife's Gone To The Country
co-lyricist George Whiting
m/Ted Snyder
Night Is Filled With Music, The
**Nobody Knows And Nobody
Seems To Care**
Not For All The Rice In China
Now It Can Be Told

Oh How I Hate To Get Up In The
    Morning
Opera Rag
Orange Grove In California
Pack Up Your Sins
Paris Wakes Up And Smiles
Piccolino, The
Play A Simple Melody
Pretty Girl Is Like A Melody, A
Putting On The Ritz
Ragtime Jockey Man
Ragtime Violin
Reaching For The Moon
Remember
Russian Lullaby
Say It Isn't So
Say It With Music
Sayonara
Shaking The Blues Away
Slumming On Park Avenue
Snooky Ookums
Soft Lights And Sweet Music
Somebody's Coming To My
    House
Some Sunny Day
Song Is Ended, The
Steppin' Out With My Baby
Stop The Rag
Suppertime
Syncopated Walk
Take Off A Little Bit
Tell Me A Bedtime Story
Tell Me Little Gypsy
That Mesmerizing Mendelssohn
    Tune
They Like Ike
They Loved Me
There's No Business Like
    Showbusiness
They Say It's Wonderful
This Is A Great Country
This Is The Army Mr. Jones
This Is The Life
This Year's Kisses
Top Hat, White Tie And Tails
What'll I Do
When I Leave The World Behind
When I Lost You
When My Dreams Come True
When The Midnight Choo-Choo
    Leaves For Alabam'
White Christmas
Who Do You Love I Hope
Woodman, Woodman Spare That
    Tree
Yam, The
You Can't Get A Man With A Gun
You Keep Coming Back Like A
    Song
You'd Be Surprised

You're Just In Love

BERNSTEIN, ELMER
1922, American
m/Elmer Bernstein
Baby The Rain Must Fall
    w/Ernie Sheldon
Love With The Proper Stranger
    w/Johnny Mercer
Sons Of Katie Elder, The
    w/Ernie Sheldon
To Kill A Mocking Bird
    w/Mack David
True Grit
    w/Don Black
Walk On The Wild Side
    w/Mack David
Film scores
Baby The Rain Must Fall
Bird Man Of Alcatraz
Cast A Giant Shadow
Hud
Love With The Proper Stranger
Sons Of Katie Elder, The
Ten Commandments, The
Thoroughly Modern Millie
To Kill A Mockingbird
True Grit
Walk On The Wild Side

BERNSTEIN, LEONARD
1918, American
(also see listing under "Classical
Music Composers of the 20th
Century)
m/Leonard Bernstein
America
    w/Stephen Sondheim
BERNARD, FELIX
1897-1944, American
m/Felix Bernard
Dardanella
    in co w/Fred Fisher, Johnny
    S. Black
Winter Wonderland
    in co w/Dick Smith

BERNIE, BEN
1891-1943, American
w&m/Ben Bernie
Sweet Georgia Brown
    in co w/Maceo Pinkard, Kenneth
    Casey
Who's Your Little Whoosis
    in co w/Walter Hirsch, Al Goering

BERNIER, BUDDY
1910, American
w/Buddy Bernier
Night Has A Thousand Eyes, The
    m/Jerome Brainin

Our Love
    m/Larry Clinton, Bob Emmerich
    (adaptation Tchaikovsky theme
    from "Romeo And Juliet")

Cool
    w/Stephen Sondheim
Gee, Officer Krupke
    w/Stephen Sondheim
I Feel Pretty
    w/Stephen Sondheim
I Get Carried Away
    w/Betty Comden, Adolph Green
It's Love
    w/Betty Comden, Adolph Green
Little Bit In Love, A
    w/Betty Comden, Adolph Green
Lonely Town
    w/Betty Comden, Adolph Green
Maria
    w/Stephen Sondheim
New York, New York
    w/Betty Comden, Adolph Green
Ohio
    w/Betty Comden, Adolph Green
Quiet Girl, A
    Betty Comden, Adolph Green
Something's Coming
    w/Stephen Sondheim
Tonight
    w/Stephen Sondheim
Wrong Note Rag
    w/Betty Comden, Adolph Green
Film score
On The Waterfront

BERRY, CHUCK
1926, American
w&m/Chuck Berry
About Grown
Around And Around
Back Home Again
Johnny B. Goode
Maybellene
    in co w/Alan Freed, Russ Fratto
Memphis
My Ding A Ling
No Money Down
No Particular Place To Go
Oh Baby Doll
Reelin' And Rockin'
Rockin' And Rollin'
Rock 'n' Roll Music
Roll Over Beethoven
San Francisco Dues
Sweet Little Sixteen
Too Much Monkey Business
Wee Wee Hours
    in co w/Alan Freed, Russ Fratto
You Never Can Tell (C'est La Vie)
Promised Land, The

BERRY, JAN
1941, American
w&m/Jan Berry
Dead Man's Curve
    in co w/Roger Christian, Brian
    Wilson, Artie Kornfeld

Drag City
in co w/Roger Christian, Brian
Wilson
Honolulu Lulu
in co w/Roger Christian, Lou Adler
Jennie Lee
in co w/Arnie Ginsberg
Ride The Wild Surf
in co w/Roger Christian, Brian
Wilson
Surf City
in co w/Brian Wilson
Three Window Coupe
in co w/Roger Christian

BERRY, RICHARD
American
w&m/Richard Berry
Louie Louie (1963)

BETTS, RICHARD
1943, American
w&m/Richard Betts
Blue Sky
In Memory Of Elizabeth Reed
Jessica
Pony Boy
Ramblin' Man
Southbound

BIGELOW, F.E.
American
m/F.E. Bigelow
Our Director (march) (1926)

BILLINGS, WILLIAM
1748-1800, American
w&m/William Billings
**Chester (Let Tyrants Shake Their
Iron Rod)**
Columbia
Independence
Lamentation Over Boston
(new words to melody of psalm
"By The Waters Of Babylon" by
Billings)
Retrospect
BISHOP, ELVIN
1942, American
w&m/Elvin Bishop
**Fooled Around And Fell In Love
(1976)**
Sure Feels Good (1975)
Travelin' Shoes (1974)

BISHOP, JOE
1907, American
m/Joe Bishop
At The Woodchopper's Ball
in co w/Wood Herman
Blue Flame
in co w/Leo Corday, Jimmy Noble
Blue Prelude
in co w/Gordon Jenkins
Out Of Space
in co w/H. Eugene Gifford

BISHOP, STEPHEN
1951, American
w&m/Stephen Bishop
Everybody Needs Love
On And On
Save It For A Rainy Day

BJORN, FRANK
Danish
w&m/Frank Bjorn
Alley Cat (1962)

BLACK, BEN
1889-1950, American
w&m/Ben Black
Hold Me
in co w/Art Hickman
Moonlight And Roses
in co w/Neil Moret, adapted from
Edwin H. Lemare's "Andantino"

BLACK, DON
English
w/Don Black
Ben (1971)
m/Walter Scharf
Born Free (1966)
m/John Barry
Come To Me (1976)
m/Henry Mancini
Diamonds Are Forever (1972)
m/John Barry
Every Face Tells A Story
m/Michael Allison, Peter Sills
Man With The Golden Gun, The
m/John Barry
To Sir With Love (1967)
m/Mark London
True Grit (1969)
m/Elmer Bernstein
**Take That Look Off Your Face
(1980)**
m/Andrew Lloyd Webber

BLACK, JOHNNY S.
c. 1896, American
w&m/Johnny S. Black
Dardanella
in co w/Fred Fisher, Felix
Bernard
Paper Doll

BLACKBURN, JOHN M.
1914, American
w&m in co w/Karl Suessdorf
Moonlight In Vermont

BLACKWELL, DEWAYNE
American
w&m/Dewayne Blackwell
Mister Blue (1959)

BLACKWELL, OTIS
1918, American
w&m/Otis Blackwell
All Shook Up
in co w/Elvis Presley

Breathless
Don't Be Cruel
in co w/Elvin Presley
Handy Man
in co w/Jimmy Jones, Charles
Merenstein
Hey Little Girl
in co w/Bobby Stevenson
Return To Sender
in co w/Weinfield Scott

BLAIR, HAL
1915, American
w&m/Hal Blair
Condemned Without Trial
in co w/Don Robertson
**One Has My Name, The Other
Has My Heart**
in co w/Eddie Dean, Dearest
Dean
My Lips Are Sealed
in co w/Ben Weisman, Bill
Peppers
Ninety Miles An Hour
in co w/Don Robertson

BLAKE, JAMES HUBERT
(Eubie)
m/Eubie Blake
Bandana Days
w/Noble Sissle
Charleston Rag (instr.)
I'm Just Wild About Harry
w/Noble Sissle
Love Will Find A Way
w/Noble Sissle
Lowdown Blues
w/Noble Sissle
Memories Of You
w/Andy Razaf
My Handy Man
w/Andy Razaf
You're Lucky To Me
w/Andy Razaf

BLAKE, JAMES W.
1862-1935, American
w&m in co w/Charles B. Lawlor
Sidewalks Of New York, The

BLAND, JAMES A.
1854-1911, American
w&m/James A. Bland
**Carry Me Back To Old Virginny
(1878)**
Close Dem Windows
**Hand Me Down My Walking Stick
(1880)**
**In The Evening By The
Moonlight (1879)**
Oh Dem Golden Slippers (1879)
Tapioca
BLAND, ROBERT CALVIN
(Bobby)
1930, American
w&m/Robert Calvin Bland

Drifting From Town To Town
Good Lovin' (Love You, Yes I Do)
Love My Baby

BLANE, RALPH
1914, American
w&m/Ralph Blane
Boy Next Door, The
in co w/Hugh Martin
Buckle Down Winsocki
in co w/Hugh Martin
Connecticut
in co w/Hugh Martin
**Have Yourself A Merry Little
  Christmas**
in co w/Hugh Martin
Love
w&m in co w/Hugh Martin
My Dream Is Yours
in co w/Harry Warren
Pas That Peacepipe
in co w/Hugh Martin, Roger
Edens
Stanley Steamer, The
in co w/Harry Warren
Trolley Song, The
in co w/Hugh Martin
You Are For Loving
in co w/Hugh Martin

BLEY, CARLA
1941, American
m/Carla Bley
w/Paul Haines
Escalator Over The Hill
Genuine Tong Funeral, A (instr.)
Tropic Appetites

BLISS, PHILIP P.
American
w&m/Philip P. Bliss
Hold The Fort

BLOOM, BOBBY
1944-1976, American
w&m/Bobby Bloom
Heavy Makes You Happy
Montego Bay
in co w/Jeff Barry

BLOOM, RUBE
1902-1976, American
w&m/Rube Bloom
Day In Day Out
in co w/Johnny Mercer
Don't Worry 'Bout Me
in co w/Ted Koehler
Fools Rush In
in co w/Johnny Mercer
Give Me The Simple Life
in co w/Harry Ruby
Good For Nothin' Joe
in co w/Ted Koehler
Here's To My Lady
in co w/Johnny Mercer
Maybe You'll Be There
in co w/Sammy Gallop

Out In The Cold Again
in co w/Ted Koehler
Penthouse Serenade
in co w/Ted Koehler
Soliloquy (instr.) (rag)
Song Of The Bayou (instr.)
Spring Fever (Instr.) (rag)
Stay On The Right Side Sister
in co w/Ted Koehler
Take Me
in co w/Ted Koehler
Truckin'
in co w/Ted Koehler
What Goes Up, Must Come Down
in co w/Ted Koehler

BLOOMFIELD, MICHAEL (Mike)
1943, American
w&m/Michael Bloomfield
Can't Wait No Longer
City Girl
Death Cell Rounder Blues
Death In My Family
Hey Foreman
If You Love These Blues
It's Not Killing Me
My Old Lady
Train Is Gone, The
Working Man
You're Killing My Love

BLOSSOM, HENRY
1866-1919, American
w/Henry Blossom
m/Victor Herbert
All For You
**I Want What I Want When I
  Want It**
Isle Of Our Dreams, The
Kiss Me Again
Neopolitan Love Song
Streets Of New York, The
Thine Alone
When You're Away

BOCK, JERRY
1928, American
m/Jerry Bock w/Sheldon Harnick
except as indicated
Fiddler On The Roof
If I Were A Rich Man
Little Tin Box
Matchmaker, Matchmaker
Mr. Wonderful
in co w/George D. Weiss,
Larry Holofcener
She Loves Me
Sunrise Sunset
To Life
Too Close For Comfort
in co w/George D. Weiss, Larry
Holofcener

BOLAN, MARC (Marc Feld)
1948, English
w&m/Marc Bolan
Ride A White Swan (1971)

BOND, CARRIE JACOBS
1862-1946, American
m& w/Carrie Jacobs Bond
I Love You Truly (w&m)
Just A-Wearyin' For You
w/Frank Stanton
Just Lonesome
w/Harriet Axtell Johnstone
Perfect Day, A

BOND, JOHNNY
1915, American
w&m/Johnny Bond
Cimarron
Gone And Left Me Blues
I Wonder Where You Are Tonight
Ten Little Bottles
Tomorrow Never Comes
in co w/Ernest Tubb
Your Old Love Letters

BONDS, GARY U.S.
1939, American
w&m/Gary U.S. Bonds
Quarter To Three
She's All I Got
in co w/Jerry Williams Jr.

BONFA, LUIS
Brazilian
m/Luis Bonfa
Black Orpheus
(score in co w/Antonio Carlos Jobim)
Manha De Carnaval
w&m/Luis Bonfa

BONO, SONNY
(Salvatore Philip Bono)
1935, American
w&m/Sonny Bono
All I Ever Need Is You
in co w/Cher (Cherilyn S.
LaPierre)
Baby Don't Go
Beat Goes On, The
Cowboy's Work Is Never Done, A
in co w/Cher (Cherilyn S.
LaPierre)
Dream Baby
in co w/Cher (Cherilyn S.
LaPierre)
Gypsies, Tramps And Thieves
in co w/Cher (Cherilyn S.
LaPierre)
I Got You Babe
in co w/Cher (Cherilyn S.
LaPierre)
Koko Joe
Needles And Pins
Half Breed
in co w/Cher (Cherilyn S.
LaPierre)

BONOFF, KARLA
1952, American
w&m/Karla Bonoff

Baby Don't Go
in co w/Kenny Edwards
Home
Someone To Lay Down Beside Me
Letter, The

BONX, NATHAN J.
1900-1950, American
w&m/Nathan J. Bonx
Collegiate
in co w/Moe Jaffe, Lew Brown
If You Are But A Dream
in co w/Jack Fulton, Moe Jaffe

BOONE, DANIEL (Peter Lee Stirling)
English
w&m/Daniel Boone
Beautiful Sunday (1972)
Daddy Don't You Walk So Fast (1972)

BOONE, PAT (Charles Eugene Boone)
1934, American
w/Pat Boone
m/Ernest Gold
Exodus

BOURKE, RORY
1942, American
w&m/Rory Bourke
Cheater's Kit
I Just Can't Stay Married To You
in co w/Charlie Black, Jerry Gillespie
I Just Want To Feel The Magic
in co w/Mel McDaniel
I Know A Heartache When I See One
in co w/Charlie Black, Kerry Chater
I Want To Thank You
Lucky Me
in co w/Charlie Black
Most Beautiful Girl In The World, The
in co w/Norro Wilson, Billy Sherrill
Neon Rose
in co w/Gayle Barnhill
Second Hand Emotion
in co w/Charlie Black
Shadows In The Moonlight
in co w/Charlie Black
Sweet Fantasy
Sweet Magnolia Blossom
in co w/Gayle Barnhill

BOWERS, ROBERT HOOD
1877-1941, American
w&m/Robert Hood Bowers
Chinese Lullaby (1919)

BOWIE, DAVID
1947, English
w&m/David Bowie

All The Young Dudes
Changes
Fame
Golden Years
Heroes
Hunky Dory
Jean Genie, The
Rock'N' Suicide
Sound And Vision
Space Oddity
Suffragette City
Young Americans, The
Ziggy Stardust

BOWLING, ROGER
American
w&m/Roger Bowling
Coward Of The County
in co w/B.E. Wheeler
Lucille (1977)
in co w/Hal Bynum
Southern California
in co w/Billy Sherrill, George Richey

BOWMAN, EUDAY LOUIS
1887-1949, American
w&m/Euday Louis Bowman
Colorado Blues
Fort Worth Blues
Kansas City Blues
12th Street Rag
Tipperary Blues

BOWMAN, BROOKS
1913-1937, American
w&m/Brooks Bowman
East Of The Sun And West Of The Moon

BOYCE, TOMMY
1944, American
w&m/Tommy Boyce
Come A Little Bit Closer
in co w/Bobby Hart, Wes Farrell
in co w/Bobby Hart
I Wanna Be Free
I Wonder What She's Doing Tonight
Last Train To Clarksville
Out And About
Peaches "N" Cream
in co w/Steve Venet
Pretty Little Angel Eyes
in co w/Bobby Hart
Valleri

BRADDOCK, BOBBY
American
w&m/Bobby Braddock
Her Name Is
Peanuts And Diamonds
We're Not The Jet Set (1975)

BRADFORD, PERRY
1893, American
w&m/Perry Bradford

Crazy Blues
If You Don't Want Me Blues
It's Right Here With Me
I'll Be Ready When The Great Day Comes
Lonesome Blues
That Thing Called Love
You Can't Keep A Good Man Down

BRAHAM, DAVID
1838-1905, American
m/David Braham
w/Ed Harrigan (except as indicated)
Babies On Our Block, The
Bootblack, The-w&m
Danny By My Side
Eagle, The
w/C.L. Stout
Eily Machree
w/C.L. Stout
Emancipation Day
w/C.L. Stout
Horseshoe From The Door, The
I Never Drank Behind The Bar
Maggie Murphy's Home
Mulligan Guard, The
Paddy Duffy's Cart
Patrick's Day Parade
Pitcher Of Beer, The
Over The Hill To The Poorhouse - w&m
Sailing On The Lake w&m
Skidmore Fancy Ball
Sweet Mary Ann
Sway The Cot Gently For The Baby's Asleep
w/Hartley Neville
Taking In The Town
To Rest Let Him Gently Be Laid
w/George Cooper
When Poverty's Tears Ebb And Flow

BRAHAM, PHILIP
English
m/Philip Braham
w/Douglas Furber
Limehouse Blues (1922)

BRAHE, MAY H.
English
m/May H. Brahe
w/Helen Taylor
Bless This House (1927)

BRAININ, JEROME
1916, American
w&m/Jerome Brainin
Chatterbox
in co w/Allan Roberts
Don't Let Julia Fool Ya
in co w/Art Kassel

Night Has A Thousand Eyes, The
    in co w/Buddy Bernier

BRAMLETT, DELANEY
1939, American
w&m/Delaney Bramlett
in co w/Bonnie Lynn Bramlett
Move 'Em Out
Never Ending Song Of Love
Soul Shake

BRAND, OSCAR
American
w&m/Oscar Brand
Guy Is A Guy, A (1952)

BREIL, JAMES CARL
American
m/James Carl Breil
w/Clarence Lucas
Perfect Song, The (1915)

BREL, JACQUES
French
m&French w/Jacques Brel
Dove, The
    wEng./Alisdair Clayre
If We Only Have Love
    w Eng./Mort Shuman, Eric Blau
If You Go Away (Ne Me Quitte
    Pas) (1959)
    w Eng./Rod McKuen
Seasons In The Sun
    (Le Moribond) (1961)
    w Eng./Rod McKuen

BRENNAN, JAMES
ALEXANDER
1885-1956, American
w&m/James Alexander Brennan
In The Little Red School House
    in co w/Al Wilson
Rose Of No Man's Land
    w/Jack Caddingan

BRENNAN, J. KEIRN
1873-1948, American
w/J. Keirn Brennan
m/Ernest Ball
A Little Bit Of Heaven
Dear Little Boy Of Mine
Goodbye, Good Luck, God Bless
    You
Let The Rest Of The World Go By

BREWER, MICHAEL
1944, American
w&m/Michael Brewer
in co w/Thomas Shipley
One Toke Over The Line

BRICUSSE, LESLIE
English
w&m/Leslie Bricusse
Candy Man, The
    in co w/Anthony Newley
Feeling Good
    in co w/Anthony Newley

Goldfinger
    in co w/Anthony Newley, John
Barry
Gonna Build A Mountain
    in co w/Anthony Newley
If I Ruled The World
    in co w/Cyril Ornandel
Joker, The
    in co w/Anthony Newley
Knack, The
    in co w/John Barry
My Kind Of Girl
Once In A Life Time
    in co w/Anthony Newley
Talk To The Animals
Thunderball
    in co w/John Barry
What Kind Of Fool Am I
    in co w/Anthony Newley
Who Can I Turn To
    in co w/Anthony Newley
Wonderful Day Like Today, A
    in co w/Anthony Newley
You Only Live Twice
    in co w/John Barry

BRIDGES, ALICIA
1953, American
w&m in co w/Susan Hutcheson
I Love The Night Life

BRIGATI, EDDIE
1946, American
w&m in co w/Felix Cavaliere
See list of selections under Felix
Cavaliere

BRITO, PHIL (Philip Colombrito)
1915
w&m/Phil Brito
Mama

BRITT, ELTON (James Britt
Baker)
1913-1972, American
w&m/Elton Britt
Chime Bells

BROCK, BLANCHE KERR
1888-1958, American
m/Blanche Kerr Brock
w/Virgil P. Brock
Beyond The Sunset

BROCKMAN, JAMES
1886-1972, American
w&m/James Brockman
Down Among The Sheltering
    Palms
    in co w/Abe Olman
I Faw Down An' Go Boom
    in co w/Leonard Stevens, B.B.B.
Donaldson

I'm Forever Blowing Bubbles
    in co w/James Kendis, Nat
Vincent

BRODSZKY, NICHOLAS
American
m/Nicholas Brodszky
w/Sammy Cahn
Be My Love (1949)
Because You're Mine (1951)
I'll Never Stop Loving You (1955)
Film Scores:
Because You're Mine
Rich Young And Pretty
Toast of New Orleans, The

BROOKER, GARY
1949, English
m/Gary Brooker
w/Keith Reid
Whiter Shade Of Pale, A

BROOKS, HARVEY OLIVER
1889, American
w&m/Harvey Oliver Brooks
Little Bird Told Me, A (1948)

BROOKS, JACK
1912, American
w&m/Jack Brooks
Ole Buttermilk Sky
    in co w/Hoagy Carmichael
That's Amore
    in co w/Harry Warren

BROOKS, JOSEPH (Joe)
American
w&m/Joseph Brooks
If I Ever See You Again
You Light Up My Life

BROONZY, WILLIAM LEE
CONLEY ("Big Bill")
1892-1958, American
w&m/"Big Bill" Broonzy
All By Myself
Big Bill Blues
Country Boy Blues
If You're Black, Get Back
Just A Dream
Keep Your Hands On Your Heart
Long Tall Mama
Mississippi River Blues
My Mellow Man
Southern Flood Blues
Starvation Blues
Stove Pipe Stomp
When I Been Drinking

BROWN, A. SEYMOUR
1885-1947, American
w/A. Seymour Brown
Oh You Beautiful Doll (1911)
    m/Nat D. Ayer
Rebecca Of Sunny-brook Farm
(1914)
    m/Albert Gumble
When You're Away
    co-lyricist Joseph Young
    m/Bert Grant

You're My Baby (1912)
    m/Nat D. Ayer

BROWN, AL W.
1884-1924, American
w&m/Al W. Brown
Ain't It A Shame (1922)

BROWN, ERROL
Jamaican
    w&m in co w/Tony Wilson
Bet Your Life I Do
Brother Louie (1973)
Emma (1975)
Disco Queen (1975)
Don't Stop It Now (1976)
So You Win Again (1977)

BROWN, HAROLD RAY
1946, American
See list of selections and
collaborators under Lee Oskar

BROWN, JAMES
1928, American
w&m/James Brown
Ain't That A Groove
Baby You're Right
    in co w/Joe Tex
Cold Sweat
    in co w/Alfred Ellis
Don't Be A Drop Out
Give It Up Or Turn It Loose
Hot Pants
I Don't Mind
I Got The Feelin'
I Got You
It's A Man's Man's Man's World
    in co w/Betty Jean Newsome
Lost Someone
    in co w/Lloyd Stallworth, Bobby
    Byrd
Papa's Got A Brand New Bag
Please Please Please
    in co w/John Terry
Say It Loud, I'm Black And
       I'm Proud
Super Bad
Try Me

BROWN, LEW
1893-1958, American
w/Lew Brown
Baby Take A Bow
    m/Jay Gorney
Beer Barrel Polka
    m/Jaromir Vejvoda
Best Things In Life Are Free, The
    co-lyricist Buddy DeSylva
    m/Ray Henderson
Birth Of The Blues
    co-lyricist Buddy DeSylva
    m/Ray Henderson
Black Bottom
    co-lyricist Buddy DeSylva
    m/Ray Henderson

Button Up Your Overcoat
    co-lyricist Buddy DeSylva
    m/Ray Henderson
Collegiate
    co-lyricist Moe Jaffe
    m/Nathan J. Bonx
Don't Bring Lulu
    co-lyricist Billy Rose
    m/Ray Henderson
Don't Sit Under The Apple Tree
    With Anyone Else But Me
    co-lyricist Charles Tobias
    m/Sam H. Stapt
Give Me The Moonlight, Give Me
    The Girl
    m/Albert Von Tilzer
Good News
    co-lyricist Buddy DeSylva
    m/Ray Henderson
I Came Here To Talk For Joe
    m/Sam H. Stept
I Used To Love You But It's All
    Over Now
    m/Albert Von Tilzer
I'd Climb The Highest Mountain
    m/Sidney Clare
I'm A Dreamer, Aren't We All
    co-lyricist Buddy DeSylva
    m/Ray Henderson
If I Had A Talking Picture Of You
    co-lyricist Buddy DeSylva
    m/Ray Henderson
It All Depends On You
    co-lyricist Buddy DeSylva
    m/Ray Henderson
Just A Memory
    co-lyricist Buddy DeSylva
    m/Ray Henderson
Last Night On The Back Porch
    m/Carl Schraubstader
Life Is Just A Bowl Of Cherries
    co-lyricist Buddy DeSylva
    m/Ray Henderson
Lucky Day
    co-lyricist Buddy DeSylva
    m/Ray Henderson
Lucky In Love
    co-lyricist Buddy DeSylva
    m/Ray Henderson
My Sin
    co-lyricist Buddy DeSylva
    m/Ray Henderson
Oh By Jingo
    m/Albert Von Tilzer
Shine
So Blue
    co-lyricist Buddy DeSylva
    m/Ray Henderson
Sonny Boy
    co-lyricist Buddy DeSylva,
    Al Jolson
    m/Ray Henderson
Stand Up And Cheer
    m/Harry Akst

Sunny Side Up
    co-lyricist Buddy DeSylva
    m/Ray Henderson
Thank Your Father
    co-lyricist Buddy DeSylva
    m/Ray Henderson
That Old Feeling
    m/Sammy Fain
Then I'll Be Happy
    m/Sidney Clare, Clifford Friend
This Is The Missus
    m/Ray Henderson
Thrill Is Gone, The
    co-lyricist Buddy DeSylva
    m/Ray Henderson
Together
    co-lyricist Buddy DeSylva
    m/Ray Henderson
Varsity Drag
    co-lyricist Buddy DeSylva
    m/Ray Henderson
You're The Cream In My Coffee
    co-lyricist Buddy DeSylva
    m/Ray Henderson

BROWN, L. RUSSELL
(Lawrence Russell Brown)
American
w&m in co w/Irwin Levine
See list of selections under Irwin
Levine

BROWN, MICHAEL
American
w&m/Michael Brown
Walk Away Renee (1966)
Pretty Ballerina (1967)

BROWN, NACIO HERB
1896-1964, American
m/Nacio Herb Brown
w/Arthur Freed(except as indicated)
After Sundown
Alone
All I Do Is Dream Of You
Beautiful Girl
Broadway Melody
Broadway Rhythm
Eadie Was A Lady
    w/Richard A. Whiting,
    Buddy DeSylva
I've Got A Feelin' You're Foolin'
Love Is Where You Find It
Moon Is Low, The
My Lucky Star
Pagan Love Song, The
Paradise
    w/Gordon Clifford
Should I Reveal
Singin' In The Rain
Smoke Dreams
Temptation
Wedding Of The Painted Doll,
    The
We'll Make Hay While The Sun
    Shines

Would You
You Are My Lucky Star
　w/Arthur Freed, Buddy DeSylva
You Stepped Out Of A Dream
　w/Gus Kahn
You Were Meant For Me
You're An Old Smoothie
　w/Richard A. Whiting,
　Buddy DeSylva

BROWN, PETER
1953, American
w&m in co w/Robert Rans
Dance With Me
Do You Wanna Get Funky With
　Me

BROWNE, JACKSON
1948, American
w&m/Jackson Browne
Desperado
Doctor My Eyes
Fantasy Of Sorrow
Farther On
For Everyman
Here Come Those Tears Again
　in co w/Nancy Farnsworth
Hold On Hold Out
James Dean
　in co w/Don Henley, Glenn Frey,
　J.D. Souther
Late For The Sky
Pretender, The
Ready Or Not
Red Neck Friend
Rock Me On The Water
Running On Empty
Stay/The Load Out
Take It Easy
　in co w/Glenn Frey
These Days
You Love The Thunder

BRUBECK, DAVE
1920, American
m/Dave Brubeck (instr.)
Blue Rondo A La Turk
In Your Own Sweet Way

BRUCE, ED
American
w&m/Ed Bruce
Mammas, Don't Let Your Babies
Grow Up To Be Cowboys (1978)
　in co w/Patsy Bruce
Texas When I Die (1979)
　in co w/Patsy Bruce,
　Bobby Borchers

BRUCE, MICHAEL
1947, American
w&m/Michael Bruce
Caught In A Dream
Be My Lover
Billion Dollar Babies
　in co w/Vincent Furnier
Eighteen
　in co w/Vincent Furnier (Alice
　Cooper), Neal A. Smith, Dennis
　Dunaway, Glen Boxton
School's Out
　in co w/Vincent Furnier
Under My Wheels

BRYAN, ALFRED
1871-1958, American
w/Alfred Bryan
Beautiful Annabelle Lee
　m/George W. Meyer
Brown Eyes Why Are You Blue
　m/George W. Meyer
Come Josephine In My Flying
　Machine
　m/Fred Fisher
Daddy You've Been A Mother To
　Me
　m/Fred Fisher
I Didn't Raise My Boy To Be
　A Soldier
　m/Al Piantadosi
I Want You To Want Me To
　Want You
　m/Fred Fisher
Peg O' My Heart
　m/Fred Fisher
Puddin' Head Jones
　m/Lou Handman

BRYANT, BOUDLEAUX
1920, American
w&m/Boudleaux Bryant
All I Have To Do Is Dream
Back Up, Buddy
Baltimore
　in co w/Felice Bryant
Bird Dog
Blue Boy
Bye Bye Love
　in co w/Felice Bryant
Come Live With Me
　in co w/Felice Bryant
Country Boy
　in co w/Felice Bryant
Devoted To You
Hey Joe
How's The World Treating You?
　in co w/Chet Atkins
I Love To Dance With Annie
　in co w/Felice Bryant
I've Been Thinking
Love Hurts
Midnight
　in co w/Chet Atkins

My Last Date With You
　in co w/Floyd Cramer, Skeeter
　Davis
Raining In My Heart
　in co w/Felice Bryant
Richest Man In The World, The
Rocky Top, in co w/Felice Bryant
Take A Message To Mary
　in co w/Felice Bryant
Wake Up Little Susie
　in co w/Felice Bryant

BUCK, GENE
(Edward Eugene Buck)
1885-1957, American
w/Gene Buck
Daddy Has A Sweetheart And
　Mother Is Her Name
　m/David Stamper
Garden Of My Dreams
　co-lyricist Louis A. Hirsch
　m/David Stamper
Have A Heart
　co-lyricist: P.G. Wodehouse
　m/Jerome Kern
Hello Frisco
　m/Louis A Hirsch
Love Boat, The
　m/Victor Herbert
My Rambler Rose
　co-lyricist: Louis A. Hirsch
　m/David Stamper
'Neath The South Sea Moon
　co-lyricist: Louis A Hirsch
　m/David Stamper
Sally Won't You Come Back
　m/David Stamper
Some Sweet Day
　co-lyricist: Louis A. Hirsch
　m/David Stamper
Sweet Sixteen
　m/David Stamper
Tulip Time
　m/David Stamper

BUCK, RICHARD
1870-1956, American
w/Richard Buck
Dear Old Girl
　m/Theodore F. Morse
Kentucky Babe
　m/Adam Geibel

BUCKINGHAM, LINDSAY
1949, American
w&m/Lindsay Buckingham
Chain
　in co w/Christine McVie,
　Stephanie Nicks
Go Your Own Way
Monday Morning
Never Going Back Again
Save Me A Place
Second Hand News
Tusk

What Makes You Think You Are
   The One
World Turning
   in co w/Christine McVie

BUFFETT, JIMMY
1946, American
w&m/Jimmy Buffett
**Changes In Latitudes, Changes
   In Attitudes**
Cheeseburger In Paradise
Come Monday
Living And Dying In 3/4 Time
Margaritaville
You Had To Be There

BUIE, BUDDY
American
w&m/Buddy Buie
Doraville (1974)
   in co w/Robert Nix, Barry Bailey
Imaginary Lover (1978)
   in co w/Robert Nix,
   Dean Daughtry
So Into You (1977)
   in co w/Robert Nix,
   Dean Daughtry
Soul Train
   in co w/James R. Cobb Jr.
Traces
   in co w/James R. Cobb Jr.,
   Emory Gordy Jr.

BULLOCK, WALTER
1907-1953, American
w/Walter Bullock
**I Still Love To Kiss
   You Goodnight**
   m/Harold Spina
This Is Where I Came In
   m/Harold Spina
When Did You Leave Heaven
   m/Richard Whiting

BUNNELL, DEWEY
1951, American
w&m/Dewey Bunnell
in co w/Dan Peck, Gerry Beckley
Horse With No Name, A
Riverside
Sandman
Three Roses
Ventura Highway

BURGIE, IRVING
(Lord Burgess)
1924, American
w&m/Irving Burgess
Music adapted from traditional
Jamaican calypso melodies.
**Day O (version recorded by
   Harry Belafonte)**
Island In The Sun
Jamaica Farewell

BURKE, JOSEPH FRANCIS (Sonny)
1914-1980, American
m/Joseph F. (Sonny) Burke
Black Coffee
   w/Paul Francis Webster
**How It Lies, How It Lies,
   How It Lies**
Midnight Sun
   in co w/Lionel Hampton
Somebody Bigger Than You And I
   in co w/Johnny Lange,
   Walter (Hy) Heath

BURKE, JOHNNY
1908-1964, American
w/Johnny Burke
Ain't It A Shame About Mame
   m/James Monaco
All You Want To Do Is Dance
   m/Arthur Johnston
An Apple For The Teacher
   m/James Monaco
**Annie Doesn't Live
      Here Anymore**
   co-lyricist: Joseph Young
   m/Harold Spina
Aren't You Glad You're You
   m/James Van Heusen
Birds Of A Feather
   m/James Van Heusen
But Beautiful
   m/James Van Heusen
Going My Way
   m/James Van Heusen
**Hang Your Heart On A
      Hickory Limb**
   m/James Monaco
Here's That Rainy Day
   m/James Van Heusen
I Don't Want To Cry Anymore
   m/James Monaco
Imagination
   m/James Van Heusen
Isn't That Just Like Love
   m/James Van Heusen
It Could Happen To You
   m/James Van Heusen
It's Always You
   m/James Van Heusen
It's Anybody's Spring
   m/James Van Heusen
I've Got A Pocketful Of Dreams
   m/James Monaco
Misty
   m/Erroll Garner
Moon got In My Eyes, The
   m/Arthur Johnston
Moonlight Becomes You
   James Van Heusen
My Heart Is Taking Lessons
   m/James Monaco
On The Sentimental Side
   m/James Monaco

One Two Button Your Shoe
   m/Arthur Johnston
Only Forever
   m/James Monaco
Oh You Crazy Moon
   m/James Van Heusen
Pennies From Heaven
   m/Arthur Johnston
Personality
   m/James Van Heusen
Polka Dots And Moonbeams
   m/James Van Heusen
Road To Morocco
   James Van Heusen
Scatter Brain
   m/Frankie Masters, Keene Bear
Sing A Song Of Sunbeams
   m/James Monaco
So Do I
   m/Arthur Johnston
Suddenly It's Spring
   m/James Van Heusen
Sunday, Monday Or Always
   m/James Van Heusen
Swinging On A Star
   m/James Van Heusen
That's For Me
   m/James Monaco
That Sly Old Gentleman
   m/James Monaco
This Is My Night To Dream
   m/James Monaco
Welcome To My Dream
   m/James Van Heusen
What's New
   m/Bob Haggart

BURKE, JOSEPH A.
1884-1950, American
m/Joseph A. Burke
At A Perfume Counter
   w/Edgar Leslie
Carolina Moon
   w/Benny Davis
Dancing With Tears In My Eyes
   w/Al Dubin
For You
   w/Al Dubin
In A Little Gypsy Tearoom
   w/Edgar Leslie
**It Looks Like Rain In Cherry
      Blossom Lane**
   w/Edgar Leslie
Kiss Waltz, The
   w/Al Dubin
Little Bit Independent, A
   w/Edgar Leslie
Moon Over Miami
   w/Edgar Leslie
Oh How I Miss You Tonight
   co-composer: Mark Fisher
   w/Benny Davis

**Painting The Clouds
    With Sunshine**
    w/Al Dubin
Tip Toe Through The Tulips
    w/Al Dubin
**We Must Be Vigilant (American
    Patrol)**
    w/Edgar Leslie
Yearning
    w/Benny Davis
BURKE, SOLOMON
American
w&m/Solomon Burke
in co w/Delores Burke
Gotta Get You Off My Mind (1965)

BURNETTE, DORSEY
1922-1979, American
w&m/Dorsey Burnette
in co w/Johnny Burnette except
where indicated
Believe What You Say
Big Big World
Dreamin'
God, Country And My Baby
Here I Go Again
    w&m/Dorsey Burnette
Hey Little One
    in co w/Barry De Vorzon
Just A Little Too Much
Little Boy Sad
**Magnificent Sanctuary
Band, The**
    w&m/Dorsey Burnette
Tall Oak Tree
Waitin' In School

BURNETTE, JOHNNY
1934-1964, American
Many songs by Johnny Burnette
written in collaboration with
Dorsey Burnette. See list of
selections under Dorsey Burnette.

BURNS, GEORGE
American
m/George Burns
w/Tom Blackburn
Ballad Of Davy Crockett, The

BURNS, RALPH
1922, American
m/Ralph Burns
Early Autumn
    co-composer: Woody Herman
    w/Johnny Mercer
Northwest Passage
    co-composer: Woody Herman,
    Greig (Chubby) Jackson
Film Score:
All That Jazz (1979)

BURNS, ROBERT
1759-1796, Scottish
w/Robert Burns
Auld Lang Syne
    m/old Scottish air, questionably
    attributed to William Shield
Comin' Thro' The Rye
    m/old Scottish air,
    source unknown
**Flow Gently, Sweet Afton
(Afton Water)**
    m/James E. Spilman (1838),
    American composer of familiar
    U.S. version; not the original
    musical setting

BURTON, VAL
1899, English/American
w&m/Val Burton
Josephine
    in co w/Will Jason
Penthouse Serenade
    in co w/Will Jason
Singing A Vagabond Song
    in co w/Harry Richman
You Alone
    in co w/Will Jason

BUSHKIN, JOSEPH (Joe)
1916
w&m/Joseph Bushkin
Oh Look At Me Now

BUSSE, HENRY
1894-1955, German/American
m/Henry Busse
Hot Lips
    in co w/Lou Davis,
    Henry W. Lange

Wang Wang Blues
    in co w/Gus Mueller,
    Buster Johnson

BUTLER, JERRY
1939, American
w&m/Jerry Butler
Brand New Me
    in co w/Kenneth Gamble,
    Theresa Bell
Don't Let Love Hang You Up
    in co w/Kenneth Gamble,
    Leon Huff
For Your Precious Love
    in co w/Arthur Brooks,
    Richard Brooks
He Don't Love You Like I Do
    Curtis Mayfield
He Will Break Your Heart
    in co w/Curtis Mayfield,
    Calvin Carter
I Stand Accused
    in co w/William E. Butler
I'll Never Give You Up
    in co w/Kenneth Gamble,
    Leon Huff
I've Been Loving You Too Long
    in co w/Otis Redding
Let It Be Me
Melinda
    in co w/Jerry Peters
Moody Woman
    in co w/Kenneth Gamble,
    Leon Huff, Theresa Bell
Only The Strong Survive
    in co w/Kenneth Gamble
    Leon Huff

BUTTONS, RED
1919, American
w&m in co w/Allan Walker
Ho-Ho Song, The
Strange Things Are Happening

BYRD, HENRY R.
1919-1980, American
w&m/Henry R. Byrd
Go To The Mardi Gras (1959)
She Ain't Got No Hair (1950)

Addenda:

BOFILL, ANGELA
1955, American
w&m/Angela Bofil
Feelin's Love, The

BROWN, ROY
1936, American
w&m/Roy Brown
Good Rocking Tonight

POPULAR COMPOSERS & LYRICISTS

C

234

CADMAN, CHARLES WAKEFIELD
1881-1946, American
m/Charles Wakefield Cadman
w/Nelle Richmond Eberhart
At Dawning
From The Land Of The Sky Blue Water
I Hear A Thrush At Eve

CAESAR, IRVING
1895, American
w/Irving Caesar
Animal Crackers In My Soup
  co-lyricist: Ted Koehler
  m/Ray Henderson
Crazy Rhythm
  m/Roger Wolfe Kahn,
  Joseph Meyer
I Want To Be Happy
  co-lyricist: Sammy Lerner
  m/Gerald Marks
Just A Gigolo
  m/Leonello Casucci
Lady Play Your Mandolin
  m/Oscar Levant
Oh You Nasty Man
  co-lyricist: Jack Yellen
  m/Ray Henderson
Sometimes I'm Happy
  m/Vincent Youmans
Swanee
  m/George Gershwin
Tea For Two
  m/Vincent Youmans
That's What I Want For Christmas
  m/Gerald Marks
Umbriago
  m/Jimmy Durante

CAHN, SAMMY
1913, American
w/Sammy Cahn
All The Way
  m/James Van Heusen
Anywhere
  m/Jule Styne
Be My Love
  m/Nicholas Brodzsky
Because You're Mine
  m/Nicholas Brodzsky
Bei Mir Bist Du Schön
  original w/Jacob Jacobs
  m/Saul Chaplin, Sholom Secunda
Call Me Irresponsible
  m/James Van Heusen
Come Blow Your Horn
  m/James Van Heusen
Come Fly With Me
  m/James Van Heusen
Day By Day
  m/Axel Stordahl, Paul Weston

Dedicated To You
  co-lyricist: Hy Zaret
  m/Saul Chaplin
Five Minutes More
  m/Jule Styne
Hey, Jealous Lover
  m/Kay Twomey, Bea Walker
High Hopes
  m/James Van Heusen
I Fall In Love Too Easily
  m/Jule Styne
I Should Care
  m/Axel Stordahl, Paul Weston
I Still Get Jealous
  m/Jule Styne
If It's The Last Thing I Do
  m/Saul Chaplin
I'll Never Stop Loving You
  m/Nicholas Brodzsky
I'll Walk Alone
  m/Jule Styne
It's Been A Long Long Time
  m/Jule Styne
It's Magic
  m/Jule Styne
(It Seems) I've Heard That Song Before
  m/Jule Styne
Joseph, Joseph
  m/Saul Chaplin
Let It Snow, Let It Snow, Let It Snow
  m/Jule Styne
Love And Marriage
  m/James Van Heusen
My Kind Of Town
  m/James Van Heusen
Papa Won't You Dance With Me
  m/Jule Styne
Please Be Kind
  m/Saul Chaplin
Poor Little Rhode Island
  m/Jule Styne
Rhythm Is Our Business
  m/Saul Chaplin
Saturday Night Is The Loneliest Night In The Week
  m/Jule Styne
Second Time Around, The
  m/James Van Heusen
September Of My Years
  m/James Van Heusen
Shoeshine Boy
  m/Saul Chaplin
Teach Me Tonight
  m/Gene De Paul

Tender Trap, The
  m/James Van Heusen
Things We Did Last Summer, The
  m/Jule Styne
Thoroughly Modern Millie
  m/James Van Heusen

Three Coins In The Fountain
  m/Jule Styne
Time After Time
  m/Jule Styne
Touch Of Class, A
  m/George Barrie
Until The Real Thing Comes Along
  m/Saul Chaplin
Written On The Wind
  m/Victor Young
You're My Girl
  m/Jule Styne

CALDERON, JUAN
Spanish
w&m/Juan Calderon
Eres Tu (1973)

CALHOUN, CHARLES
American
w&m/Charles Calhoun
Flip Flop And Fly
  in co w/Joe Turner
Shake Rattle And Roll (1954)
Your Cash Ain't Nothing But Trash

CALLOWAY, CAB
1907, American
w&m in co w/Clarence Gaskill and Irving Mills
Minnie The Moocher

CAMPBELL, FRANK
American
m/Frank Campbell
w/Billy Reeves
Shoo Fly, (Shew! Fly) Don't Bother Me (1869)

CAMPBELL, GEORGE
American
w&m/George Campbell
in co w/Marvin Moore
Four Walls (1957)

CAMPO, M.V.
Cuban
Chiapanecas
  w/Albert Gamse (1938)

CANNING, EFFIE I.
American
w&m/Effie I. Canning
Rock-A-Bye Baby (On The Tree Top)

CANNON, FREDDIE
(Fred Pocariello)
1940, American
w&m/Freddie Cannon in co w/Bob Crewe, Frank C. Slay Jr.
Happy Shades Of Blue
Jump Over
Tallahassee Lassie
Transistor Sister

CANNON, HUGHIE
American
w&m/Hughie Cannon
Bill Bailey Won't You Please
    Come Home (1902)
Just Because She Made Dem
    Goo-Goo Eyes (1900)
    in co w/John Queen

CAPALDI, JIM
1944, English
w&m/Jim Capaldi
in co w/Steve Winwood
See list of selections under
Steve Winwood.

CAPEHART, JERRY
1938, American
w&m/Jerry Capehart in co w/Eddie
Cochran
C'mon Everybody
Something Else
Summertime Blues
Turn Around, Look At Me

CAREY, HENRY
1690-1743, English
w&m/Henry Carey
Sally in Our Alley (1715)

CARLE, FRANKIE
1903, American
m/Frankie Carle
Oh, What It Seemed To Be
    in co w/Bennie Benjamin
    George D. Weiss
Sunrise Serenade
    in co w/Jack Lawrence

CARMICHAEL, HOAGY
(Hoagland Howard Carmichael)
1899, American
m& w/Hoagy Carmichael
Blue Orchids
Can't Get Indiana Off My Mind
    w/Robert De Leon
Doctor, Lawyer, Indian Chief
    w/Paul Francis Webster
Georgia On My Mind
    w/Stuart Gorrell
Heart And Soul
    w/Frank Loesser
Hong Kong Blues
How Little We Know
    w/Johnny Mercer
I Get Along Without You
    Very Well
I'll Dance At Your Wedding
    w/Frank Loesser
In The Blue Of Evening
In The Cool, Cool, Cool
    Of The Evening
    w/Johnny Mercer
Ivy
Lamplighter's Serenade, The
    w/Paul Francis Webster

Lazybones
    w/Johnny Mercer
Lazy River
    w/Sidney Arodin
Little Old Lady
    w/Stanley Adams
My Resistance Is Low
    w/Harold Adams
Nearness Of You, The
    w/Ned Washington
Ole Buttermilk Sky
    w/Jack Brooks
Riverboat Shuffle
    w/Mitchell Parish, Dick Voynow,
    Irving Mills
Rockin' Chair
Skylark
    w/Johnny Mercer
Small Fry
    w/Frank Loesser
Stardust
    w/Mitchell Parish
Two Sleepy People
    w/Frank Loesser
Washboard Blues
What Kind O' Man Is You

CARNES, KIM
1949, American
w&m/Kim Carnes
Don't Fall In Love With
    A Dreamer (1980)
    in co w/David Ellingson
You're A Part Of Me

CARPENTER, RICHARD
1945, American
m/Richard Carpenter
w/John Bettis
Top Of The World
Only Yesterday

CARR, LEON
1910, American
w&m in co w/Al Hoffman
and Leo Corday
There's No tomorrow
music adapted from the Italian
folk song "O Sole Mio"

CARR, LEROY
1905-1935, American
w&m/Leroy Carr
Blues Before Sunrise
How Long, How Long
Midnight Hour Blues
My Woman's Gone Wrong
Southbound Blues

CARRADINE, KEITH
1950, American
w&m/Keith Carradine
I'm Easy

CARLISLE, UNA MAE
1918-1956, American
m/Una Mae Carlisle
w/Robert Sour
I See A Million People
Walkin' By The River

CARLTON, HARRY
English
w&m/Harry Carlton
Constantinople (1928)

CARLETON, ROBERT LOUIS
(Bob)
1896-1956, American
w&m/Robert Louis Carleton
Ja Da (1918)

CARMEN, ERIC
1949, American
w&m/Eric Carmen
All By Myself
Change Of Heart
Never Gonna Fall In Love Again
She Did It
Sunrise
That's Rock 'N' Roll

CARROLL, HARRY
1892-1962, American
m/Harry Carroll
By The Beautiful Sea
    w/Harold Atteridge
Down In Bom-Bombay
    w/Ballard MacDonald
I'm Always Chasing Rainbows
    w/Joseph McCarthy (music
adapted from Chopin's "Fantasie
Impromptu In C-Sharp Minor")
It Takes A Little Rain With
    The Sunshine
    w/Ballard MacDonald
On The Mississippi
    co-composer: Arthur Fields
    w/Ballard MacDonald
She Is The Sunshine Of Virginia
    w/Ballard MacDonald
There's A Girl In The Heart
    Of Maryland
    w/Ballard MacDonald
Trail Of The Lonesome Pine, The
    w/Ballard MacDonald

CARSON, JENNY LOU
1927, American
w&m/Jenny Lou Carson
Don't Rob Another Man's Castle
Let Me Go Lover
    in co w/Al Hill (new lyric)
Love Bug Itch
    in co w/Roy Botkin
Never Trust A Woman
Jealous Heart (1949)

CARSON, MARTHA
(Martha Ambergay)
1921, American
w&m/Martha Carson
I Can't Stand Up Alone
I'm Gonna Walk And Talk With
    My Lord
Satisfied

CARSON, WAYNE
American
w&m/Wayne Carson
Somebody Like Me (1967)

CARTER, ALVIN PLEASANT
(A.P.) DELANEY
1891-1960, American
w&m/A.P. Carter
Will The Circle Be Unbroken
    (a/k/a Can The Circle
    Be Unbroken)
The best-known current version
of this song is a 1935 copyright
with original words and music by
A.P. Carter. It is thought to be
based on a 19th century gospel
folk song emanating from the
Southern U.S. Ozark mountains
region.

CARTER, HELEN
1933, American
w&m/Helen Carter
Losing You (Was Worth This
    Broken Heart)
Poor Old Heartsick Me
Wall To Wall Love
    in co w/June Carter

CARTER, JUNE
(June Carter Cash)
American
w&m/June Carter
Matador, the
    in co w/Johnny Cash
Ring Of Fire (1963)
    in co w/Merle Kilgore
Wall To Wall Love
    in co w/Helen Carter

CARTEY, RIC
1940, American
w&m in co w/Carole Joyner
Young Love

CARYLL, IVAN
1861-1921, American
m/Ivan Caryll
Chin-Chin
    w/Harry Morton
Goodbye, Girls I'm Through
    w/John Golden
Kiss Waltz, The
    w/Harry Morton
Love Moon
    w/Anne Caldwell

My Beautiful Lady
    w/Harry Morton
There's Life In The Old Dog Yet
    w/P.G. Wodehouse
Violet
    w/James O'Dea
Wait Till The Cows Come Home
    w/Anne Caldwell

CASEY, HARRY WAYNE ('K.C.')
1951, American
w&m/Harry Wayne Casey
in co w/Richard Finch
Blow Your Whistle
Boogie Shoes
Get Down Tonight
I Like To Do It
I'm Your Boogie Man
It's The Same Old Song
Keep It Comin' Love
Let's Go Rock And Roll
Please Don't Go
Queen Of Clubs
(Shake, Shake, Shake)
    Shake Your Booty
Sound Your Funky Horn
That's The Way (I Like It)
Where Is The Love
    in co w/Betty Wright,
    Willie Clarke, Richard Finch

CASH, JOHN R. (Johnny)
1932, American
w&m/John R. Cash
All Over Again
Big River
Don't Take Your Guns To Town
Five Foot High And Rising
Flesh And Blood
Folsom Prison
Get Rhythm
Home Of The Blues
    in co w/Glenn Douglas,
    Vic McAlpin
I Got Stripes
    in co w/Charlie Williams
I Walk The Line
Jackson
    in co w/June Carter
Matador, The
    in co w/June Carter
Next In Line

CASTOR, JIMMY
1938, American
w&m/Jimmy Castor
Bertha Butt Boogie, The
I Promise To Remember
King Kong (Pt. 1)

CAVALIERE, FELIX
1944, American
w&m in co w/Eddie Brigati, except
where indicated.

Beautiful Morning, A
Come On Up
    w&m/Felix Cavaliere
Girl Like You, A
Good Lovin'
Groovin'
How Can I Be Sure
I Ain't Gonna Eat My Heart
    Out Anymore
Lonely Too Long
    w&m/Felix Cavaliere
Only A Lonely Heart Sees
    w&m/Felix Cavaliere
People Got To Be Free
Ray Of Hope, A
You Better Run

CAVANAUGH, JAMES
1905, American
w/James Cavanaugh
Christmas In Killarney
    m/John Redmond, Frank Weldon
Gaucho Serenade, The
    m/John Redmond, Nat Simon
Gertie From Bizerte
    m/Walter Kent, Bob Cutter
I Like Mountain Music
    m/Frank Weldon
Mississippi Mud
    m/Harry Barris
You're Nobody 'Til Somebody
    Loves You
    m/Larry Stock

CAVANAUGH, JESSIE
American
w&m/Jessie Cavanaugh
w&m/Arnold Stanton
Roving Kind, The (1950) - music
adapted from an old English folk
song known as "The Rakish
Kind" or "The Pirate Ship"

CHANDLER, GENE
1937, American
w&m/Gene Chandler
in co w/Earl Edwards,
Bernie Williams
Duke Of Earl, The

CHANDLER, GUS
w&m in co w/Bert White,
Henry Cohen
Canadian Capers

CHAMPLIN, BILL
American
w&m/Bill Champlin
After The Love Has Gone (1979)
    in co w/David Foster,
    Jay Graydon

CHAPEL, JEAN
1928, American
w&m/Jean Chapel

Lay Some Happiness On Me
    in co w/Bob Jennings
Lonely Again
To Get To You
Triangle
    in co w/Robert Taubert

CHAPIN, HARRY
1942, American
w&m/Harry Chapin
Better Place To Be, A
Cat's In The Cradle, The
Dreams Go By
I Wanna Learn A Love Song
Love Is Just Another Word
Taxi
Sunday Morning Sunshine

**CHAPLIN, CHARLES
SPENCER (Charlie Chaplin)**
1889-1977, English
m/Charles Spencer Chaplin
Eternally ("Terry" theme)
    w/Geoffrey Parsons
Smile
    w/John Turner, Geoffrey Parsons
Film Scores:
City Lights (1931)
Countess From Hong
Kong, The (1966)
Great Dictator, The (1940)
Kid, The (1921)
Modern Times (1936)
Monsieur Verdoux (1947)
Limelight (1952)
    in co w/Raymond Rasch,
    Larry Russell

CHAPLIN, SAUL
1912
m/Saul Chaplin
**Anniversary Song (after
    Ivanovici's "Danube Waves")**
    w/Al Jolson
Bei Mir Bist Du Schön
    co-composer: Sholom Secunda
    w/Sammy Cahn
    (original w/Jacob Jacobs)
Dedicated To You
    w/Sammy Cahn
If It's The Last Thing I Do
    w/Sammy Cahn
Joseph, Joseph
    w/Sammy Cahn
Please Be Kind
    w/Sammy Cahn
Rhythm Is Our Business
    w/Sammy Cahn
Shoe Shine Boy
    w/Sammy Cahn
**Until The Real Thing
    Comes Along**
    w/Sammy Cahn

CHAPMAN, MIKE
English
w&m/Mike Chapman
in co w/Nicky Chinn
Co Co (1971)
Funny Funny (1970)
In The Heat Of The Night
Kiss You All Over
**Lay Back In The Arms
    Of Someone**
Little Willie (1973)
Living Next Door To Alice
She's In Love With You

CHARLES, DICK
1919, American
w&m/Dick Charles
in co w/Larry Markes
Along The Navajo Trail
    in co w/Edgar DeLange
**Mad About Him, Sad About Him,
How Can I Be Glad Without Him
    Blues**
May You Always

CHARLES, ERNEST
1895, American
w&m/Ernest Charles
**When I Have Sung My Songs
(1934)**

CHARLES, RAY
1930, American
w&m/Ray Charles
Baby Let Me Hold Your Hand
Come Back, Baby
Fool For You
I've Got A Woman
**This Little Girl Of Mine - adapted
    from an early spiritual of
    unknown authorship**
What'd I Say

CHASE, LINCOLN
American
w&m/Lincoln Chase
Jim Dandy (1957)
Such A Night (1954)
That's All I Need (1955)
    in co w/Howard Biggs,
    LaVern Baker
Wonderland By Night (1961)
    in co w/Klauss Gunter Neuman

CHATMAN, PETER
American
w&m/Peter Chatman
**Everyday I Have The
    Blues (1950)**

CHATTAWAY, THURLAND
1872-1947, American
w&m/Thurland Chattaway
Mandy Lee (1899)
Red Wing
    in co w/Frederick Allen
    (Kerry) Mills

CHESNUT, JERRY
American
w&m/Jerry Chestnut
Another Place, Another Time
Don't She Look Good
Good Year For Roses, A
Holding On To Nothing
It's Four In The Morning
It's Midnight
Oney
**They Don't Make Em Like My
    Daddy**
Wonders You Perform, The
**Wishing I Had Listened
    To Your Song**

CHINN, NICKY
English
w&m/Nicky Chinn
in co w/Mike Chapman
In The Heat Of The Night
**Lay Back In The Arms
    Of Someone**
Living Next Door To Alice
She's In Love With You

CHRISTIAN, CHARLIE
1919-1942, American
m/Charlie Christian (instrumental)
Harlem Jazz Scene, The
Seven Come Eleven
Smo-o-o-o-oth One, A
Solo Flight
Swing To Bop

CHURCHILL, FRANK E.
1901-1942, American
m/Frank E. Churchill
Heigh-Ho, Heigh-Ho
    in co w/Larry Morey
One Song
    in co w/Larry Morey
Some Day My Prince Will Come
    in co w/Larry Morey
Who's Afraid Of The Big Bad Wolf
    in co w/Ann Ronnell
When I See An Elephant Fly
    in co w/Ned Washington,
    Oliver G. Wallace

CLAPP, CHARLES (Sunny)
1899-1962, American
w&m/Charles (Sunny) Clapp
Girl Of My Dreams
When Shadows Fall

CLAPTON, ERIC
1945, English
w&m/Eric Clapton
Anyday
    in co w/Bobby Whitlock
Bell Bottom Blues
I Looked Away
    in co w/Bobby Whitlock
Keep On Growing
    in co w/Bobby Whitlock

Layla
   in co w/Jim Gordon
Let It Grow
Sunshine Of Your Love
   in co w/Jack Bruce, Peter Brown

CLARE, SIDNEY
1892, American
m/Sidney Clare
I'd Climb The Highest Mountain
   w/Lew Brown
Ma, He's Making Eyes At Me
   w/Con Conrad
Miss Annabelle Lee
   w/Lew Pollack, Harry Richman
On The Good Ship Lollipop
   w/Richard A Whiting
Please Don't Talk About Me
     When I'm Gone
   w/Sam H. Stept
Then I'll Be Happy
   co-composer Cliff Friend
   w/Lew Brown
You're My Thrill
   w/Jay Gorney

CLARK, RUDY
American
w&m/Rudy Clark
Shoop Shoop Song (It's In His
     Kiss) (1964)

CLARKE, GRANT
1891-1931, American
w/Grant Clarke
Am I Blue
   m/Harry Akst
Beatrice Fairfax
   co-lyricist Joseph McCarthy
   mJames V. Monaco
Everything Is Peaches Down In
     Georgia
   m/Milton Ager, Edgar Leslie
He's Have To Get Under, Get Out
     And Get Under
   m/Edgar Leslie
Ragtime Cowboy Joe
   m/Lewis F. Muir,
   Maurice Abrahams
Second Hand Rose
   m/James F. Hanley

CLAYPOOLE, EDWARD B.
1883-1952, American
m/Edward B. Claypoole
Ragging The Scale (1915) (instr.)

CLAYTON-THOMAS, DAVID
1941, English
w&m/David Clayton-Thomas
Go Down Gambling
Lisa Listen To Me
Lucretia McEvil
Spinning Wheel

CLIFF, JIMMY
(James Chambers)
1948, Jamaican
w&m/Jimmy Cliff
Come Into My Life
Wonderful World,
Beautiful People

CLEVELAND, JAMES
(Reverend)
American
w&m/James Cleveland
Changing Times
Christ The Redeemer
Heart And Soul
If You Just Believe
In My Heart
Jesus Is The Best Thing That
     Ever Happened To Me

CLINTON, LARRY
1909, American
w&m/Larry Clinton (except for
"Our Love")
Calypso Melody
Dipsy Doodle, The
My Reverie
Our Love
   in co w/Buddy Bernier,
   Bob Emmerich (after theme from
   Tchaikovsky's "Romeo
   and Juliet')
Satan Takes A Holiday

COBB, GEORGE L.
1886-1942, American
w&m/George L. Cobb
Alabama Jubilee
   in co w/Jack Yellen
Are You From Dixie
   in co w/Jack Yellen
Bunny Hug Rag (instr.)
Midnight Trot (instr.)
Russian Rag (adapted from
Rachmaninoff "Prelude, Op.3,
     No.2") (instr.)

COBB, JAMES R. JR.
1944, American
w&m/James R. Cobb Jr.
Soul Train
   in co w/Buddy Buie
Traces
   in co w/Buddy Buie,
   Emory Gordy Jr.

COBB, WILL D.
1876-1930, American
w/Will D. Cobb
m/Gus Edwards
I Can't Tell Why I Love You
     But I Do
If A Girl Like You Loves A Boy Like
     Me
Laddie Boy
School Days

Sunbonnet Sue
Waltz Me Around Again Willie
Way Down Yonder
     In The Cornfield

COBEN, CY
1919, American
w&m/Cy Coben
Old Piano Roll Blues, The
Sweet Violets (based on
     traditional folk song)

COCHRAN, DORCAS
American
w/Dorcas Cochran
Again (1948)
   m/Lionel Newman
I Get Ideas (1951)
   adapted from the Argentine tango
   "Adios Muchachas" by Sanders

COCHRAN, EDDIE
1938-1960, American
w&m/Eddie Cochran
in co w/Jerry Capehart
C'Mon Everybody
Something Else
Summertime Blues

COCHRAN, HANK (Henry)
1935, American
w&m/Hank Cochran
Don't Touch Me
Funny Way Of Laughin'
I Fall To Pieces
   in co w/Harlan Howard
I Miss You
   in co w/Cliff Cochran
I Want To Go With You
I'd Fight The World
   in co w/Joe Allison
It's Not Love (But It's Not Bad)
   in co w/Glenn Martin
Little Bitty Tear, A
Make The World Go Away
She's Got You
So You Think You're A Cowboy
   in co w/Willie Nelson
Tears Broke Out On Me
You Comb Her Hair
   in co w/Harlan Howard

COE, DAVID ALLEN
American
w&m/David Allen Coe
Take This Job And
     Shove It (1978)

COHAN, GEORGE M.
1878-1942, American
w&m/George M. Cohan
Forty-Five Minutes
     From Broadway
Give My Regards To Broadway
Harrigan
I Guess I'll Have to Telegraph My
     Baby

I Love You
I Was Born In Virginia
I'm A Yankee Doodle Dandy
In A Kingdom Of Our Own
Little Johnny Jones
Mary's A Grand Old Name
Molly Malone
Nelly Kelly, I Love You
Over There
So Long, Mary
Yankee Doodle Boy, The
You Remind Me Of My Mother
You're A Grand Old Flag

COHEN, HENRY
American
m/Henry Cohen
w/Gus Chandler, Bert White
Canadian Capers (1915)

COHEN, LEONARD
1935, Canadian
w&m/Leonard Cohen
Bird On The Wire
Priests
Sisters Of Mercy
So Long Marianne
Story Of Isaac, The
Susanne

COHN, AL
1925, American
m/Al Cohn (instr.)
Brothers And Other Mothers
Goof And I, The
Motoring Along
     in co w/Zoot Sims
Tasty Pudding
Zootcase
     in co w/Zoot Sims

COHN, IRVING
1898-1961, American
w&m in co w/Frank Silver
Yes We Have No Bananas

COLE, BOB
American
w&m in co w/J. Rosamond Johnson
Under The Bamboo Tree (1902)

COLE, NAT (KING)
(Nathaniel Adams Cole)
1919-1965, American
w&m/Nat (King) Cole
Straighten Up And Fly Right
Just For Old Time's Sake

COLE, NATALIE MARIA
(Mrs. Marvin Yancy)
1950, American
w&m/Natalie Cole
Annie Mae
Answer, The
Beautiful Dreamer
Come And Dream Along

Everyday Of My Life
Gimme Some Time
Not Like Mine
     in co w/Marvin Yancy,
     Chuck Jackson
Roller Coaster
Sophisticated Lady
     in co w/Marvin Yancy
     Chuck Jackson

COLEMAN, CY
1929, American
m/Cy Coleman
Best Is Yet To Come, The
     w/Carolyn Leigh
Big Spender
     w/Dorothy Fields
Doodling Song, A
     w/Carolyn Leigh
Firefly
     w/Carolyn Leigh
Hey Look Me Over
     w/Carolyn Leigh
If My Friends Could See Me Now
     w/Dorothy Fields
I'm Gonna Laugh You Right Out
     Of My Life
     w/Joseph Allan McCarthy
I've Got Your Number
     w/Carolyn Leigh
I Walk A Little Faster
     w/Carolyn Leigh
Pass Me By
     w/Carolyn Leigh
Real Live Girl
     w/Carolyn Leigh
There's Gotta Be Something
     Better Than This
     w/Dorothy Fields
Where Am I Going
     w/Dorothy Fields
Why Try To Change Me Now
     w/Joseph Allan McCarthy
Witchcraft
     w/Carolyn Leigh

COLEMAN, ORNETT
1930, American
m/Ornett Coleman (instr.)
Antiques
Beauty Is A Rare Thing
C & D
Cross Breeding
Congeniality
Dee Dee
Dedication to Poets And Writers
Faces And Places
Kaleidoscope
Lonely Woman
Peace (The Shape Of Jazz To
     Come)
Something Else
Tomorrow Is The Question

COLEY, JOHN FORD
(John Edward Colley)
1948, American
w&m/John Ford Coley
Gone Too Far
It's Sad To Belong
     in co w/Danny Seals
Nights Are Forever Without You
     in co w/Danny Seals
We'll Never Have To Say
     Goodbye Again
     in co w/Danny Seals
What Can I Do With
     This Broken Heart
     in co w/Danny Seals, B. Gundry

COLLINS, JUDY
1939, American
w&m/Judy Collins
Albatross
My Father
Since You've Asked

COLLINS, LARRY
American
w&m/Larry Collins
in co w/Alex Harvey
Delta Dawn (1972)

COLLINS, WILL
1893, American
w&m/Will Collins
Daddy's Little Boy

COLTER, JESSI
1946, American
w&m/Jessi Colter
I'm Not Lisa
It's Morning
What Happened To Blue Eyes

COLTRANE, CHI
1948, American
w&m/Chi Coltrane
Thunder And Lighting

COLTRANE, JOHN
1926-1967, American
m/John Coltrane (instr.)
Blues Minor
Good Bait
Harmonique
Love Supreme, A
Naima
Out Of This World
Round Midnight
Traneing In
Transition

COMDEN, BETTY
1915, American
w/Betty Comden
in co w/Adolph Green
Be A Santa
     m/Jule Styne

Comes Once In A Lifetime
    m/Jule Styne
French Lesson, The
    m/Rogher Edens
I Get Carried Away
    m/Leonard Bernstein
It's Love
    m/Leonard Bernstein
Just In Time
    m/Jule Styne
Little Bit In Love, A
    m/Leonard Bernstein
Lonely Town
    m/Leonard Bernstein
Long Before I Knew You
    m/Jule Styne
Make Someone Happy
    m/Jule Styne
New York, New York
    m/Leonard Bernstein
Ohio
    m/Leonard Bernstein
Party's Over, The
    m/Jule Styne
Quiet Girl, A
    m/Leonard Bernstein
Wrong Note Rag
    m/Leonard Bernstein

CONFREY, EDWARD ELZEAR
(Zev)
1895-1971, American
m/Edward E. (Zev) Confrey (instr.)
Dizzy Fingers (1923)
Jack In The Box (1927)
Kitten On The Keys (1921)
Stumbling (1922)

CONNELLY, REGINALD
English
w&m/Reginald Connelly
    in co w/Jimmy Campbell,
    Ted Shapiro
If I Had You (1928)

CONNOR, TOMMIE
American
w&m/Tommie Connor
I Saw Mommy Kissing
        Santa Claus (1952)

CONNORS, CAROL
American
w/Carol Conners
Gonna Fly, Now (Theme
       from Rocky) (1978)
    co-lyricist Ayn Robbins
    m/Bill Conti
Someone's Waiting For You
    co-lyricist Ayn Robbins
    m/Sammy Fain
With You I'm Born Again (1979)
    m/David Shire

CONRAD, CON
(Conrad K. Dober)
1891-1938, American
m/Con Conrad
Barney Google
    w/Billy Rose
Bend Down Sister
    w/Ballard MacDonald,
    Dave Silverstein
Champagne Waltz, The
    co-composer Ben Oakland
    w/Milton Drake
Continental, The
    w/Herb Magidson
Lonesome And Sorry
    w/Benny Davis
Ma, He's Making Eyes At Me
    w/Sidney Clare
Margie
    co-composer J. Russell Robinson
    wBenny Davis
Midnight In Paris
    w/Herb Magidson
You Call It Madness But I Call
    It Love
    co-composer Russ Colombo
    w/Gladys DuBois, Paul Gregory
You've Got to See Mamma Ev'ry
    Night
    w/Billy Rose

CONTI, BILL
1940, American
m/Bill Conti
Gonna Fly Now
(Theme from "Rocky")
    w/Carol Connors, Ayn Robbins
Kill Me If You Can (TV Theme)
Harry And Tonto (Film Theme)

CONVERSE, CHARLES C.
American
m/Charles C. Converse
w/Joseph Scriven
What a Friend We Have In Jesus

COOK, ROGER
1940, English
Words and music to many songs
written in collaboration with Roger
Greenaway. See list of selections
under Roger Greenaway.

COOKE SAM
1935-1964, American
w&m/Sam Cooke
Another Saturday Night
Bring It On Home To Me
Chain Gang
Cupid
Good News
Nothing Can Change This Love
Shake
Twistin' The Night Away

COOPER, ALICE
(Vincent Furnier)
1948, American
Words and music by Alice Cooper in
collaboration with Michael Bruce.
See selections under Michael Bruce.
Additional songs in collaboration
with Richard Wagner:
I Never Cry
You And Me

COOTS, J. FRED
1897, American
m/J. Fred Coots
Beautiful Lady In Blue, A
    w/Samuel M. Lewis
Copper Colored Gal
    w/Benny Davis
Cross Your Fingers
    w/Benny Davis,
    Arthur Swanstrom
For All We Know
    w/Samuel M. Lewis
I Still Get A Thrill
    w/Benny Davis
I Wonder Why
    w/Raymond W. Klages
Love Letters In The Sand
    w/Nick Kenny, Charles Kenny
Me And My Teddy Bear
    w/J. Winters
One Minute To One
    w/Samuel M. Lewis
Santa Claus Is Coming To Town
    w/Haven Gillespie
Two Tickets To Georgia
    w/Charles Tobias, Joseph Young
You Go To My Head
    w/Haven Gillespie

COPAS, COWBOY
1913-1963, American
w&m/Cowboy Copas
    in co w/Lois Mann
Signed Sealed And Delivered

COPELAND, ALLAN
1926, American
w&m/Allan Copeland
    in co w/Bill Norvas
m/Leon Rappolo, Paul Wares,
Ben Pollack, George Brunes
Mel Stitzel, Walter Melrose
Make Love To Me (music based on
    "Tin Roof Blues")

COPLAND AARON
1900, American
m/Aaron Copland
(see listing under classical
composers)
Theme from El Salon Mexico
Film Scores:
Heiress, The (1949)
North Star, The (1943)

Of Mice And Men (1940)
Our Town (1940)
Red Pony, The (1949)

CORBETTA, JERRY
1947, American
w&m/Jerry Corbetta
in co w/Robert Webber,
Robert Raymond
Green Eyed Lady
Tongue In Cheek
Mother Nature's Wine

COREA, CHICK
1941, American
m/Chick Corea (instr.)
500 Miles High
Hymn the 7th Galaxy
La Fiesta
Light As A Feather
No Mystery
Romantic Warrior
Spain
Where Have I Known You Before

CORNELIUS, EDWARD LEE JR.
1943, American
w&m/Edward Lee Cornelius Jr.
Treat Her Like A Lady (1970)

CORY, GEORGE
1920, American
m/George Cory
w/Douglass Cross
I Left My Heart In San Francisco

COSLOW, SAM
1902, American
w/Sam Coslow
m/Arthur Johnston (except for "Sing
You Sinners" m/W. Franke Harling)
Cocktails For Two
Day You Came Along, The
Down The Old Ox Road
Just One More Chance
Learn To Croon
Moon Song
Mr. Paganini
My Old Flame
Sing You Sinners
Thanks

COSTELLO, ELVIS
English
w&m/Elvis Costello
Girls Talk (1980)
Less Than Zero
Miracle Man
Party Girl (1978)
Radio, Radio (1978)
Talking In The Dark (1980)
Watching The Detectives

COTTRAU, TEODORO
1827-1879, Italian
Italian w&m/Teodoro Cottrau
Earliest English translation by

Thomas Oliphant (1849)
Santa Lucia

COUGAR, JOHNNY
American
w&m/Johnny Cougar
I Need A Lover (1979)

COWAN, MARIE
Australian
m/Marie Cowan
w/A.B. Paterson
Waltzing Matilda (1936)

COWARD, NOEL
1899-1973, English
w&m/Noel Coward
I Love America
I Went To A Marvelous Party
I'll Follow My Secret Heart
I'll See You Again
I'm An Acrobat's Wife
I'm So Weary Of It All
Don't Put Your Daughter On The
        Stage Mrs. Worthington
London Pride
Mad About The Boy
Mad Dogs And Englishmen
Parisian Pierrot
Sail Away
Someday I'll Find You
Stately Homes Of England, The
There's Life In The Old Girl Yet
What's Happened To The Tots
You Were There
Zigeuner

COVAY, DON
American
w&m/Don Covay
Chain Of Fools (1967)
I'm Hanging Up My Heart For
        You (1962)
    in co w/John Berry
Mercy, Mercy (1964)
    in co w/Ronald Miller
Pony Time (1961)
    in co w/John Berry
See Saw (1969)
    in co w/Steve Cropper
Tonight's The Night (1965)
    in co w/Solomon Burke
You're Good For Me (1964)
    in co w/Horace Ott

CRAFT, PAUL
American
w&m/Paul Craft
Drop Kick Me Jesus
Hank Williams You Wrote
        My Life

CRAMER, FLOYD
1933, American
w&m/Floyd Cramer
Last Date
On The Rebound

CRANE, JIMMIE
1910, American
w&m/Jimmie Crane in co w/Al Jacobs
If I Give My Heart To You
I Need You Now

CRAWFORD, ROBERT M.
1899-1961, American
w&m/Robert M. Crawford
Army Air Corps, The (Off We Go
Into The Wild Blue Yonder)
        (official song of the
        U.S. Air Force)

CREAMER, HENRY
1879-1930, American
w&m/Henry Creamer
After You've Gone
    in co w/J. Turner Layton
Dear Old Southland
    in co w/J. Turner Layton
If I Could Be With You
        One Hour Tonight
    in co w/James P. Johnson
Sippi
    in co w/James P. Johnson,
    Clarence Todd
That's A Plenty
    in co w/Bert A. Williams
Way Down Yonder In
        New Orleans
    in co w/J. Turner Layton

CREED, LINDA
American
Words and music by Linda Creed in
collaboration with Thomas Bell. See
list of selections under Thomas Bell.

CREWE, BOB
1930, American
w&m/Bob Crewe
Big Girls Don't Cry
    in co w/Bob Gaudio
Birds Of Britain, The (instr.)
Can't Take My Eyes Off Of You
    in co w/Bob Gaudio
Happy Shades Of Blue
    in co w/Frank C. Slay Jr.,
    Freddie Cannon
Jump Over
    in co w/Frank C. Slay Jr.,
    Freddie Cannon
La Dee Dah
    in co w/Frank C. Slay Jr.
Lady Marmalade
    in co w/Kenny Nolan
Music To Watch Girls By (instr.)
My Eyes Adored You
    in co w/Kenny Nolan
Rag Doll
    in co w/Bob Gaudio
Silhouettes
    in co w/Frank C. Slay Jr.

Street Talk
Tallahassee Lassie
   in co w/Frank C. Slay Jr.,
   Freddie Cannon
Transistor Sister
   in co w/Frank C. Slay Jr.,
   Freddie Cannon
Walk Like A Man
   in co w/Bob Gaudio
Film Score:
Barbarella (1968)

CRISS, PETER
1945, American
w&m/Peter Criss
Baby Driver
   in co w/Stan Penridge
Beth
   in co w/Stan Penridge, Bob Ezrin

CROCE, JIM
1942-1973, American
w&m/Jim Croce
Bad Bad Leroy Brown
I'll Have To Say I Love You In
   A Song
I've Got A Name
   in co w/Norman Gimbel
One Less Set Of Footsteps
Operator (That's Not The Way
   It Feels)
Time In A Bottle
Workin' At The Carwash Blues
You Don't Mess Around With Jim
CROFTS, DASH
1940, American
Words and music in collaboration
with James (Jimmy) Seals. See list of
selections under James Seals.

CROPPER, STEVE
American
w&m/Steve Cropper
(Sittin' On) Dock Of The
   Bay, The (1967)
   in co w/Otis Redding
Don't Fight It (1965)
   in co w/Wilson Pickett
In The Midnight Hour (1965)
   in co w/Wilson Pickett
Knock On Wood (1966)
   in co w/Eddie Floyd

See Saw (1969)
   in co w/Don Covay

634-5789 (1966)
   in co w/Eddie Floyd
Soul Limbo (1969)
   in co w/Al Jackson, Booker T.
Jones, Donald Dunn

Time Is Right (1969)
   in co w/Booker T. Jones,
Al Jackson, Donald Dunn

CROSBY, BING
(Harry Lillis Crosby)
1904-1976, American
w&m/Bing Crosby
At Your Command
   in co w/Harry Barris,
   Harry Tobias
I Don't Stand The Ghost Of A
   Chance With You
   in co w/Ned Washington,
   Victor Young
Where The Blue Of The Night
   Meets The Gold Of The Day
   in co w/Roy Turk, Fred E. Ahlert

CROSBY, DAVID
1941, American
w&m/David Crosby
Almost Cut My Hair
Deja Vu
Eight Miles Higher
   in co w/Gene Clark,
   James McGuinn
Guinnevere
Long Time Coming
Wooden Ships
   in co w/Stephen Stills,
   Paul Kanter
CROSS, CHRISTOPHER
American
w&m/Christopher Cross
Ride Like The Wind (1980)
Sailing (1980)
CROSS, DOUGLASS
1920, American
w/Douglass Cross
m/George Cory
I Left My Heart In San Francisco

CROUCH, ANDRAE
American
w&m/Andrae Crouch
I'll Be Thinking Of You
Jesus Is Lord (1979)
My Tribute
Soon And Very Soon

CROUCH, FREDERICK
WILLIAM NICHOLS
Irish
m/Frederick William Nichols Crouch
w/Annie Barry Crawford
Kathleen Mavourneen (1840)

CROWELL, RODNEY
American
w&m/Rodney Crowell
Amarillo
American Dream, An (1980)
Ashes By Now
Boulder To Birmingham
   in co w/Emmylou Harris
I Ain't Living Long
   Like This (1980)
Till I Gain Control Again

CRUDUP, ARTHUR (Big Boy)
1905, American
w&m/Arthur Crudup
Ethel Mae
If I Get Lucky
Keep Your Arms Around Me
Mean Old Frisco Blues
Rock Me Mama
Shout Sister Shout
So Glad You're Mine
That's All Right

CUMMINGS, BURTON
1947, Canadian
w&m/Burton Cummings
American Woman
   in co w/Randy Bachman
   Kate Peterson
I'm Scared
New Mother Nature
Laughing
   in co w/Randy Bachman
No Time
   in co w/Randy Bachman
Share The Land
Stand Tall
These Eyes
   in co w/Randy Bachman

CUNICO, GINO
American
w&m/Gino Cunico
When I Wanted You (1979)

CUNNINGHAM, PAUL
1890-1960, American
w&m/Paul Cunningham
From The Vine Came The Grape
   in co w/Leonard Whitcup

I Am An American
   in co w/Leonard Whitcup,
   Ira Schuster
Please Take A Letter Miss Brown
   in co w/Ernie Burnett

CURTIS, MANN
1911, American
w/Mann Curtis
Anima e Core
   co-lyricist Harry Akst
   m/Salve d'Esposito
I'm Gonna Live Till I Die
   m/Al Hoffman, Walter Kent
Jones Boy, The
   m/Vic Mizzy
My Dreams Are Getting
   Better All The Time
   m/Vic Mizzy
Loop de Loo
   m/Vic Mizzy
Romance Runs In The Family
   m/Al Livingston

CURTIS, SONNY
American
w&m/Sonny Curtis
I Fought The Law (1966)
Love Is All Around
Straight Life, The (1969)
Walk Right Back

CYMBAL, JOHNNY
American

w&m/Johnny Cymbal
Cinnamon (1968)
Mr. Bass Man (1963)

Addenda:
CLAYTON, HAROLD
American
w&m/Harold Clayton
Take Your Time (Do It Right)
(1980)
in co w/Sigidi

POPULAR COMPOSERS
& LYRICISTS

D

DACRE, HARRY
American
w&m/Harry Dacre
**Daisy Bell (Daisy, Daisy Give Me
Your Answer Do)**

DAFFAN, TED
(Theron Eugene Daffan)
1912, American
w&m/Ted Daffan
Blue Steel Blues
**Heading Down The
Wrong Highway**
I'm A Fool To Care
**I've Got Five Dollars And It's
Saturday Night**
Tangled Mind, A
Truck Drivers' Blues
Worried Mind

DAMERON, TADD
1917-1965, American
m/Tadd Dameron (instr.)
Chase, The
Dameronia
Fontainbleau
Jahbero
Lady Bird
Symphonette
Tadd Walk
Theme Of The Repeat

DAMROSCH, WALTER
1862-1950, American
m/Walter Damrosch
w/Rudyard Kipling
Danny Deever (1897)

DANA, MARY S. B.
American
w&m/Mary S. B. Dana
m/arr. George F. Root
Flee As A Bird (1857)

DANIELS, Charles Neil
Pseudonyms:
**(Neil Moret, Lamonte C. Jones,
Jules Lemare, Charlie Hill,
Sidney Carter, L'Albert)**
1878-1943, American
w&m/Charles Neil Daniels
Chlo-E
in co w/Richard Whiting
Hiawatha
in co w/James O'Dea
Margery (instr.)
Moonlight And Roses
in co w/Ben Black
She's Funny That Way
in co w/Richard Whiting
Sweet And Lovely
in co w/Harry Tobias
**You Tell Me Your Dream,
I'll Tell You Mine**
in co w/Seymour Rice,
Albert H. Brown

DANIELS, CHARLIE
1936, American
w&m/Charlie Daniels
Devil Went Down to Georgia, The
Mississippi
South Is Gonna Do It, The
Uneasy Rider
in co w/Don Rubin

DANKS, HART PEASE
American
m/Hart Pease Danks
w/Eben E. Rexford
**Silver Threads
Among The Gold (1873)**

DANKWORTH, JOHNNY
1927, English
m/Johnny Dankworth (instr.)
Lover And His Lass, A
What The Dickens
Zodiac Variations
Film scores:
Concrete Jungle, The (1962)
Magus, The (1968)
Sands Of The Kalahari (1965)

DANOFF, BILL
1946, American
w&m/Bill Danoff
in co w/Kathy "Taffy" Nivert Danoff
Afternoon Delight
California Day
Hail! Hail! Rock And Roll
**Please Daddy (Don't Get Drunk
This Christmas)**
Take Me Home Country Roads
in co w/John Denver,
Kathy "Taffy" Danoff

DANZIG, EVELYN
(Mrs. Manuel W. Levine)
1902, American
m/Evelyn Danzig
w/Jack Segal
Scarlet Ribbons

DARIN, BOBBY
1936-1973, American
w&m/Bobby Darin
Dream Lover
Eighteen Yellow Roses
If A Man Answers
Splish Splash
That Funny Feeling
Things
True, True Love, A
You're The Reason I'm Living

DARION, JOSEPH (Joe)
1917, American
w/Joseph Darion
Changing Partners
m/Larry Coleman
Dulcinea
m/Mitch Leigh

Impossible Dream, The
m/Mitch Leigh
Man Of La Mancha
m/Mitch Leigh

DARLING, ERIK
American
w&m/Erik Darling
in co w/Willard Svanoe,
Hosie Woods, Gus Cannon
Walk Right In (1963)

D'ARTEGA, ALFONSO
1907, American
m/Alfonso D'Artega
w/Tom Adair
In The Blue Of Evening (1942)

**DAVENPORT, CHARLES
EDWARD (Cow Cow)**
1894-1955, American
w&m/Charles Edward Davenport
Chimes Blues
Cow Cow Blues
Cow Cow Boogie
Fifth Street Blues
**I'll Be Glad When You're Dead
You Rascal You**
(claimed authorship)
Mama Don't Allow
(claimed authorship)
State Street Jive
Stealin' Blues

DAVENPORT, JOHN
American
w&m/John Davenport
in co w/Eddie Cooley
Fever (1956)

DAVID, HAL
1921, American
Words to many songs in co with music
of Burt Bacharach. See selections
under Burt Bacharach.

Add'l. songs; w/Hal David
American Beauty Rose
m/Redd Evans, Arthur Altman
**Four Winds And The
Seven Seas, The**
m/Don Rodney
I Never Said I Love You
m/Archie Jordan
**If You Can't Get A Drum With A
Boom-Boom-Boom, Get A Tuba
With An Oom-Pah-Pah**
m/Arthur Altman
It Was Almost Like A Song
m/Archie Jordan
Ninety Nine Miles From L. A.
m/Albert Hammond

DAVID, LEE
1891, American
w&m/Lee David

Tonight You Belong To Me
in co w/Billy Rose
Sipping Cider Thru A Straw
in co w/Carey Morgan

DAVID, MACK
1912, American
w&m/Mack David
Bermuda Buggy Ride
m/Sanford Green
Bibbidi Bobbidi Boo
m/Jerry Livingston, Al Hoffman
Blue And Sentimental
m/Jerry Livingston,
William (Count) Basie
Candy
m/Joan Whitney, Alex Kramer
Casper The Friendly Ghost
m/Jerry Livingston
Cat Ballou
m/Jerry Livingston
Chi Baba, Chi Baba
m/Jerry Livingston, Al Hoffman
**Cherry Pink and Apple Blossom
White**
m/Louiguy
**Dream Is A Wish Your
Heart Makes, A**
m/Jerry Livingston, Al Hoffman
Hanging Tree, The
m/Jerry Livingston
Hawaiian Eye
m/Jerry Livingston
**I Don't Care If The
Sun Don't Shine**
I'm Just A Lucky So And So
It Only Hurts For A Little While
m/Fred Spielman
La Vie En Rose
m/Louiguy
Moon Love
m/Andre Kostelanetz,
Mack Davis
(adapted from Tchaikovsky's
Symphony No. 5)
My Own True Love
m/Max Steiner
On The Isle Of May
m/Andre Kostelanetz (adapted
from Tchaikovsky's String
Quartet In D Major)
Sinner Kissed An Angel, A
m/Larry Shayne
Spellbound
m/Miklos Rozsa
Sunflower
To Kill A Mockingbird
m/Elmer Bernstein
Unbirthday Song, The
m/Jerry Livingston
Walk On The Wild Side
m/Elmer Bernstein

DAVID, SUNNY
American
w&m/Sunny David
in co w/David Williams
**Whole Lotta Shakin' Goin' On
(1958)**

**DAVIES, RAYMOND DOUGLAS
(Ray)**
1944, English
w&m/Raymond Douglas Davies
All Day And All Of The Night
Arthur
Deadend Street
Dedicated Follower Of Fashion
Face To Face
Lola
Set Me Free
Stop Your Sobbing
Tired Of Waiting For You
Victoria
Well Respected Man, A
Who'll Be The Next In Line
You Really Got Me

DAVIS, CHARLIE
American
w&m/Charlie Davis
Copenhagen (1924)
in co w/Walter Melrose

DAVIS, BENNY
1895-1979, American
w/Benny Davis
Baby Face
m/Harry Akst
Carolina Moon
m/Joseph Burke
Copper Colored Gal
m/J. Fred Coots
Cross Your Fingers
co-lyricist Arthur Swanstrom
m/J. Fred Coots
**Goodbye Broadway,
Hello France**
co-lyricist Billy Baskette
m/C. Francis Reisner
I'm Nobody's Baby
m/Milton Ager, Lester Santly
I Still Get A Thrill
m/J. Fred Coots
Lonesome And Sorry
m/Con Conrad
Make Believe
m/Jack Shilkret
Margie
m/Con Conrad, J.
Russell Robinson

With These Hands
m/Abner Silver
Yearning
m/Joseph Burke

**Smile Will Go A Long
Long Way, A**
m/Harry Akst
There Goes My Heart
m/Abner Silver
DAVIS, CLIFTON D.
American
w&m/Clifton D. Davis
Never Can Say Goodbye (1970)

DAVIS JIMMY
(James Houston Davis)
1902, American
w&m/Jimmy Davis
It Makes No Difference Now
Nobody's Darlin' But Mine
Sweethearts Or Strangers
**There's A New Moon Over
My Shoulder**
in co w/Ekko Whelan, Lee Blastic
**When It's Round-Up
Time In Heaven**
You Are My Sunshine
in co w/Charlie Mitchell

DAVIS, MAC
1941, American
w&m/Mac Davis
Baby Don't Get Hooked On Me
Beginning To Feel The Pain
Daddy's Little Man
Don't Cry Daddy
Everybody Loves A Love Song
**Everything A Man
Could Ever Need**
Friend, Lover, Woman, Wife
I Believe In Jesus
I Believe In Music
I'll Paint You A Song
In The Ghetto
Kiss It And Make It Better
Little Less Conversation, A
Lonesomest, Lonesome, The
Memories
Naughty Girl
One Hell Of A Woman
in co w/Mark James
Picking Up The Pieces Of My Life
Something's Burning
Stop And Smell The Roses
in co w/Doc Severinsen
Watchin' Scott Grow
Whoever Finds This -- I Love You
Within My Memory
Your Side Of The Bed
You're Good For Me

DAVIS, MILES DEWEY
1926, American
m/Miles Dewey Davis
Bags Groove
Birth Of The Cool
Bitches Brew
Blue 'n' Boogie

Boplicity
Dig
Four
Freddie Freeloader
In A Silent Way
Kind Of Blue
Leap, The
Little Willie Leaps
Milestones
Seven Steps To Heaven
So What
Take-Off
Tune Up
Walkin'

DAVIS, PAUL
1948, American
w&m/Paul Davis
Do Right
I Go Crazy
Ride 'Em Cowboy
Sweet Life

DAVIS, STEVE
American
w&m/Steve Davis
Take Time To Know Her (1967)

DAVIS, WARREN
American
w&m/Warren Davis
in co w/George Malone,
Charles Patrick
Book Of Love (1958)

DAVIS, WILLIAM E.
American
w&m/William E. Davis
in co w/Morris Levy
Gee (1954)

DEAN, JIMMY
1928, American
w&m/Jimmy Dean
Big Bad John
First Thing Every Morning, The
in co w/Ruth Roberts

DEANGELIS, PETER
1929, American
m/Peter DeAngelis
De De Dinah (w&m)
Why
w/Bob Marcucci
You, You, You
w/Jean Sawyer

DE CAMPO, M.V.
Mexican
m/M.V. De Campo
Mexican folk song with various
English lyrics extant. Best known of
the latter are those written by Albert
Gamse.
Chiapanecas
(The Hand Clapping Song)

DEE, SYLVIA
(Josephine Moore Proffitt)
1914, American
w/Sylvia Dee
m/Sidney Lippman
After Graduation Day
Chickery Chick
House With Love In It, A
My Sugar Is So Refined
Too Young

DEES, RICK
(Rigdon Osmond Dees III)
1950, American
w&m/Rick Dees
Disco Duck

DE GEYTER, PIERRE
French
m/Pierre De Geyter
w/Eugene Pottier
Internationale, The
(L'Internationale)

DEKKER, DESMOND
1942, Jamaican
w&m/Desmond Dekker
Israelites, The

DeKOVEN, REGINALD
(Henry Louis)
1859-1920, American
m/Reginald DeKoven
w/Harry B. Smith
Armorer's Song (1891)
Brown October Ale (1891)
Do You Remember Love?
I Am The Sheriff
Of Nottingham (1891)
Moonlight Song
Oh Promise Me (1889)
Tinker's Song (1891)

DE LACHAU, COUNTESS ADA
American
w&m/Countess Ada De Lachau
Li'l Liza Jane (Little Liza
Jane) (1916)

DELANGE, EDGAR (Eddie)
1904-1949, American
w/Edgar DeLange
All This And Heaven Too
m/James Van Heusen
Along The Navajo Trail
m/Dick Charles, Larry Markes
Darn That Dream
m/James Van Heusen
Heaven Can Wait
m/James Van Heusen
Moonglow
m/Will Hudson, Irving Mills
So Help Me
m/James Van Heusen
Solitude
co-lyricist Irving Mills
m/Duke Ellington

String Of Pearls, A
m/Jerry Gray
This Is Worth Fighting For
m/Sam H. Stept
Who Threw The Whiskey
In The Well
m/John Benson Brooks

DE L'ISLE, CLAUDE
JOSEPH ROUGET
1760-1836, French
w&m/Claude Joseph
Rouget De L'Isle
La Marseillaise

DE LOS RIOS, ORBE-WALDO
Spanish w&m/Orbe-Waldo
De Los Rios
Song Of Joy, A (1970)
English w/Ross Parker
(based on the theme of
the finale from Beethoven's Ninth
Symphony, which was based on the
poem "An Die Freude",Ode To Joy,
authored by Friedrich Von Schiller)

DELUGG, MILTON
1918, American
m/Milton Delugg
Be My Life's Companion
w/Bob Hilliard
Hoop Dee Doo
w/Frank Loesser
My Lady Loves To Dance
w/Sammy Gallop
Orange Colored Sky
w/William Stein

DEMPSEY, JAMES
(Powell I. Ford, Paul Grayson)
1876-1918, American
w/James Dempsey
m/Johann C. Schmid (1890-1951)
Garden Of Roses, The (1909)

DENNIS, MATT
1914, American
m/Matt Dennis
w/Thomas M. Adair, except as noted
Everything Happens To Me
Let's Get Away From It All
Little Man With A Candy Cigar
w/Brigham Townsend
Night We Called It A Day, The
Violets For Your Furs
Will You Still Be Mine

DENVER, JOHN
1943, American
w&m/John Denver, except as noted
Annie's Song
Back Home Again
Calypso
Follow Me
Goodbye Again
Leaving On A Jet Plane

My Sweet Lady
Rocky Mountain High
Sunshine On My Shoulders
   in co w/Taylor Kriss
Take Me Home Country Roads
   in co w/Bill Danoff, Taffy Nivert

DENZA, LUIGI
Italian
m/Luigi Denza
Various English word versions
Funiculi-Funicula (1880)

DePAUL, GENE
1919, American
m/Gene DePaul
Cow Cow Boogie
   w/Don Raye
If I Had My Druthers
   w/Johnny Mercer
I'll Remember April
   w/Don Raye
Jubilation T. Cornpone
   w/Johnny Mercer
Milkman Keep Those
    Bottles Quiet
   w/Don Raye
Mister Five By Five
   w/Don Raye
Star Eyes
   w/Don Raye
Teach Me Tonight
   w/Sammy Cahn
When You're In Love
   w/Johnny Mercer

DEPPEN, JESSIE L.
1881-1956, American
m/Jessie L. Deppen
In The Garden
    Of Tomorrow (1924)
   w/George Graff Jr.
Oh Miss Hannah! (1924)
   w/Thekla Hollingsworth

DE ROSE, PETER
1900-1953, American
m/Peter De Rose
Autumn Serenade
   w/Sammy Gallop
Buena Sera
   w/Carl Sigman
Deep Purple
   w/Mitchell Parish
Have You Ever Been Lonely
   w/George Brown
I Hear America Singing
   w/Samuel M. Lewis
I Heard A Forest Praying
   w/Samuel M. Lewis
Lamp Is Low, The
   w/Mitchell Parish, Bert Shefter
Lilacs In The Rain
   w/Mitchell Parish

Muddy Water
   w/Jo Trent, Harry Richman
Somebody Loves You
   w/Charles Tobias, Harry Tobias
Wagon Wheels
   w/Billy Hill
When Your Hair Has
    Turned To Silver
   w/Charles Tobias
Who Do You Know In Heaven
   w/Al Stillman

DERRINGER, RICK
(Richard Zehringer)
1947, American
w&m/Rick Derringer
Hang On Sloopy
Rock & Roll Hoochie Koo

DE SHANNON, JACKIE
1944, American
w&m/Jackie De Shannon
in co w/Shari Sheeley except as noted
Come Stay With Me (w&m)
Dum Dum
Great Imposter, The
Heart In Hand
He's So Heavenly
Put A Little Love In Your Heart
   in co w/Jimmy Holiday,
   Randy Myers
So Deep
When You Walk In
    The Room (w&m)

DESMOND, PAUL
d.1977, American
m/Paul Desmond
Take Five (instr.)

DESYLVA, B. G. (Buddy)
1895-1950, American
w/B.G. (Buddy) DeSylva
Alabamy Bound
   m/Ray Henderson, Bud Green
April Showers
   m/Louis Silvers
Avalon
   co-lyricist Al Jolson
   m/Vincent Rose
Best Things In Life Are Free, The
   co-lyricist Lew Brown
   m/Ray Henderson
Birth Of The Blues, The
   co-lyricist Lew Brown
   m/Ray Henderson
Black Bottom
   co-lyricist Lew Brown
   m/Ray Henderson
Button Up Your Overcoat
   co-lyricist Lew Brown
   m/Ray Henderson
California Here I Come
   co-lyricist Al Jolson
   m/Joseph Meyer

Do It Again
   m/George Gershwin
Eadie Was A Lady
   m/Nacio Herb Brown,
   Richard A. Whiting
Good News
   co-lyricist Lew Brown
   m/Ray Henderson
If I Had A Talking
    Picture Of You
   co-lyricist Lew Brown
   m/Ray Henderson
If You Knew Susie
   m/Joseph Meyer
I'll Build A Stairway
    To Paradise
   co-lyricist Ira Gershwin
   m/George Gershwin
It All Depends On You
   co-lyricist Lew Brown
   m/Ray Henderson
Just A Memory
   co-lyricist Lew Brown
   m/Ray Henderson
Kiss In The Dark, A
   m/Victor Herbert
Life Is Just A Bowl Of Cherries
   co-lyricist Lew Brown
   m/Ray Henderson
Look For The Silver Lining
   m/Jerome Kern
Lucky Day
   co-lyricist Lew Brown
   m/Ray Henderson
Lucky In Love
   co-lyricist Lew Brown
   m/Ray Henderson
My Sin
   co-lyricist Lew Brown
   m/Ray Henderson
Rise 'n' Shine
   mVincent Youmans
So Blue
   co-lyricist Lew Brown
   m/Ray Henderson
Somebody Loves Me
   m/George Gershwin,
   Ballard MacDonald
Sonny Boy
   co-lyricist Lew Brown, Al Jolson
   m/Ray Henderson
Sunny Side Up
   co-lyricist Lew Brown
   m/Ray Henderson
Thank Your Father
   co-lyricist Lew Brown
   m/Ray Henderson
Thrill Is Gone, The
   co-lyricist Lew Brown
   m/Ray Henderson
Together
   co-lyricist Lew Brown
   m/Ray Henderson

Varsity Drag, The
  co-lyricist Lew Brown
  m/Ray Henderson
When Day Is Done
  m/Robert Katscher
Why Do I Love You
  co-lyricist Oscar Hammerstrin II
  m/Jerome Kern
Wishing (w&m)
You're An Old Smoothie
  m/Nacio Herb Brown,
  Richard A. Whiting
You Ain't Heard Nothing Yet
  co-lyricist Al Jolson
  m/Gus Kahn
You Are My Lucky Star
  co-lyricist Arthur Freed
  m/Nacio Herb Brown
You're The Cream In My Coffee
  co-lyricist Lew Brown
  m/Ray Henderson

DETT, ROBERT NATHANIEL
1882-1943, American
m/Robert Nathaniel Dett
Juba Dance (from the suite "In The Bottoms") (1913, instr.)

DEUTSCH, ADOLPH
1897-1980, American
m/Adolph Deutsch (instr.)
March Eccentrique
March Of The United Nations
Margot
Piano Echoes
  in co w/Vincent Lopez
Skyride
  in co w/Vincent Lopez
Film scores:
Apartment, The
Father Of The Bride
High Sierra
Maltese Falcon, The
Matchmaker, The
Seven Brides For Seven Brothers
Some Like It Hot
Tea And Sympathy

DEUTSCH, EMERY
1907, American
m/Emery Deutsch
Play Fiddle Play
  co-composer Arthur Altman
  w/Jack Lawrence
When A Gypsy
     Makes His Violin Cry
  w/Jimmy Rogan,
  Richard B. Smith

DEUTSCH, HELEN
American
w/Helen Deutsch
m/Bronislaw Kaper
Hi Lili Hi Lo (1952)

DE VOL, FRANK
1911, American
m/Frank De Vol
Film Scores:
Cat Ballou
Dirty Dozen
Guess Who's Coming To Dinner
Happening, The
Hush Hush Sweet Charlotte
Pillow Talk
Whatever Happened To Baby Jane

DE VORZON, BARRY
American
w&m/Barry De Vorzon
Jelinda's Theme
Just Married
  in co w/Al Allen
Hey Little One
  in co w/Dorsey Burnette
Midnight (1978)
  in co w/Ward Chandler
Nadia's Theme (1978)
(earlier versions of same melody entitled: "Cotton's Dream", "Bless The Beasts And Children")
  in co w/Perry Botkin Jr.
Shadows (1978)
S.W.A.T., Theme From
    (1978 instr.)
Winter Song (1978)
  in co w/Mitch Bottler

DEWALT, AUTRY
(Junior Walker Jr.)
1942, American
w&m/Autry DeWalt
Shotgun (1965)

DE WITT, LEW
1938, American
w&m/Lew De Witt
Flowers On The Wall
So This Is Love
  in co w/Don Reid

DEXTER, AL
(Albert Poindexter)
1905, American
w&m/Al Dexter
Guitar Polka
Honky Tonk Blues
Pistol Packin' Mama
Rosalita
So Long Pal
Too Blue To Cry
Too Late To Worry

DE YOUNG, DENNIS
1945, American
w&m/Dennis De Young
Babe
Best Thing
  in co w/James Young

Borrowed Time
  in co w/Tommy Shaw
Castle Walls
Come Sail Away
Grand Illusion, The
I'm O.K.
  in co w/James Young
Lady
Light Up
Lorelei
  in co w/James Young
Mademoiselle
  in co w/Thomas Shaw
Queen Of Spades
  in co w/James Young
Suite Madame Blue
You Need Love

D'HARDELOT, GUY
French
m&French lyric/Guy D'Hardelot
English w/Edward Teschemacher
Because

DI CAPUA, EDUARDO
Italian
m/Eduardo DiCapua
w/Giovanni Capurro
O Sole Mio (1901)

DIAMOND, GREGG
American
w&m/Gregg Diamond
More, More, More (Part 1) (1976)

DIAMOND, LEO
1910, American
m/Leo Diamond
w/Steve Graham
Off Shore

DIAMOND, NEIL
1941, American
w&m/Neil Diamond
Be
Brooklyn Roads
Brother Love's Travelin'
    Salvation Show
Cherry, Cherry
Cracklin' Rosie
Desiree
Do It
Girl You'll Be A Woman Soon
Holly Holy
I Am, I Said
I Got The Feelin'
I Thank The Lord For
  The Night Time
If You Know What I Mean
I'm A Believer
I've Been This Way Before
Kentucky Woman
Last Thing On My Mind, The
Little Bit Me, Little
    Bit You, A

Long Way Home, The
Longfellow Serenade
New Orleans
Play Me
Red Red Wine
September Morn'
    in co w/Gilbert Becaud
Shilo
Skybird
Solitary Man
Song Sung Blue
Soolaimon
Stones
Sunday Sun
Sweet Caroline
Thank The Lord
    For The Night Time
Two Bit Manchild
Walk On Water
You Don't Bring Me Flowers
    in co w/Alan & Marilyn Bergman
You Got To Me

DICKENS, "LITTLE" JIMMY
1925, American
w&m/"Little" Jimmy Dickens
May The Bird Of Paradise
    Fly Up Your Nose
Out Behind The Barn
Where Were You When The
    Ship Hit The Sand

DICKERSON, DUB
American
w&m/Dub Dickerson
in co w/Erma Herrold
Stood Up (1957)

**DICKERSON, MORRIS
DeWAYNE "B.B."**
1949, American
See list of selections and
collaborators under
Lee Oskar

DIDDLEY, BO
(Ellas McDaniel)
1929, American
w&m/Ellas McDaniel (Bo Diddley)
Come On, Baby
Congo
Crackin' Up
Dearest Darling
Elephant Man
Gunslinger
Hey Bo Diddley
I'm A Man
I've Got A Feeling
Love Is A Secret
Mona
Mr. Kruschev
Power House
Roadrunner
Say Man
Spanish Guitar
Who Do You Love

You Bo Diddley

DIETZ, HOWARD
1896, American
w/Howard Dietz
m/Arthur Schwartz, except for
"Moanin' Low", composed by Ralph
Rainger)
Alone Together
By Myself
Dancing In The Dark
Day After Day
I Guess I'll Have To Change
    My Plan
I Love Louisa
I See Your Face Before Me
If There Is Someone
    Lovelier Than You
Louisiana Hayride
Magic Moment
Moanin' Low
Shine On Your Shoes, A
Something To Remember You By
That's Entertainment
You And The Night
    And The Music

DILLEA, HERBERT
American
m/Herbert Dillea
w/Arthur Gillespie
Absence Makes The Heart
    Grow Fonder (1900)

DILLON, LOLA JEAN
American
w&m/Lola Jean Dillon
Somebody Somewhere Don't
  Know What He's Missing Tonight
When The Tingle
    Becomes A Chill

DI MUCCI, DION (a/k/a DION)
1939, American, w&m/Dion Di Mucci
Donna The Prima Donna
    in co w/Ernest Maresca
Little Dianne
Lonely World
    in co w/Ernest Maresca
Love Came To Me
    in co w/J. Falbo
Lovers Who Wander
    in co w/Ernest Maresca
Runaround Sue
    in co w/Ernest Maresca, Robert
    Schwartz
Sandy
    in co w/Steve Brandt
Teen Angel
    in co w/Fred Patrick,
    Murray Singer

**DIRKSEN, EVERETT
McKINLEY (Senator)**
d.1969, American
w/Everett McKinley Dirksen
(recitative)

Music-American traditional
Gallant Men (1966)

DIXON, LUTHER
American
w&m/Luther Dixon
Hundred Pounds Of
    Clay, A (1961)
    in co w/Bob Elgin, Kay Rogers
Sixteen Candles (1959)
    in co w/Allyson R. Khent

DIXON, MORT
1892-1956, American
w/Mort Dixon
Bam, Bam, Bamy Shore
    m/Ray Henderson
Bye Bye Blackbird
    m/Ray Henderson
Flirtation Walk
    m/Allie Wrubel
I Found A Million Dollar Baby In
    A Five And Ten Cent Store
    co-lyricist Billy Rose
    m/Harry Warren
I'm Looking Over A
    Four Leaf Clover
    m/Harry Woods
Lady In Red, The
    m/Allie Wrubel
Marching Along Together
    m/Edward Pola,
    Franz K.N. Steiniger
Mr. And Mrs. Is The Name
    m/Allie Wrubel
Nagasaki
    m/Harry Warren
River Stay 'Way From My Door
    m/Harry Woods
That Old Gang Of Mine
    co-lyricist Billy Rose
    m/Ray Henderson
Would You Like To Take A Walk
    co-lyricist Billy Rose
    m/Harry Warren
You're My Everything
    co-lyricist Joseph Young
    m/Harry Warren

DIXON, WILLIE JAMES
1915, American
w&m/Willie Dixon
Back Door Man
I'm Ready (1954)
I'm Your Hoochie
    Koochie Man (1951)
Just Make Love To Me (1954)
My Babe (1955)
Wang Dang Doodle (1966)
You Can't Judge A Book
    By The Cover

DOBBINS, SHELLEY
American
w/Shelley Dobbins
m/P.G. Redi
Italian w/Michele Galdieri

Non Dimenticar
(Don't Forget) (1953)

DODDRIGE, PHILIP (Reverend)
English
w/Philip Doddridge (1755)
m/E.F. Rimbault
American arrangement by
Edwin Hawkins (1969)
Oh Happy Day

DODSON, RICH
1948, Canadian
w&m/Rich Dodson
Devil You
Sweet City Woman

DOLAN, ROBERT EMMETT
1906, American
m/Robert Emmett Dolan
Big Movie Show In The Sky, The
w/John H. Mercer
Little By Little
w/Walter O'Keefe
Film scores:
Aaron Slick From Punkin' Creek
Bells Of St. Mary's, The
Going My Way
Great Gatsby, The (1949)
Major And The Minor, The
Road To Rio, The
Three Faces Of Eve, The

DOMINO, ANTOINE "FATS"
1928, American
w&m in co w/Dave Bartholomew
Ain't It A Shame
All By Myself
Be My Guest
Blue Monday
Boll Weevil
Don't Blame It On Me
Fat Man
Goin' Home
Goin' To The River
How Long
I Can't Go On
I Lived My Life
I Want To Walk You Home
I'm In Love Again
I'm Ready
I'm Walkin'
It's You I Love
Love Me
Poor Me
Please Don't Leave Me
Rosemary
Something's Wrong
Three Nights A Week
Walkin' To New Orleans
What A Party
What A Price
Whole Lot Of Lovin'
You Done Me Wrong

DONALDSON, WALTER
1893-1947, American
m/Walter Donaldson
After I Say I'm Sorry
w/Abe Lyman
At Sundown (w&m)
Back Home In Tennessee
w/William Jerome
Beside A Babbling Brook
w/Gus Kahn
Carolina In The Morning
w/Gus kahn
Daughter Of Rosie O'Grady, The
w/Monry C. Brice
Did I Remember
w/Harold Adamson
How Ya Gonna Keep 'Em Down
On The Farm
w/Samuel M. Lewis,
Joseph Young
Little White Lies (w&m)
Love Me Or Leave Me
w/Gus Kahn
Mr. Meadowlark
w/Johnny Mercer
Makin' Whoopee
w/Gus Kahn
My Baby Just Cares For Me
w/Gus Kahn
My Blue Heaven
w/George Whiting
My Buddy
w/Gus Kahn
My Mammy
w/Samuel M. Lewis,
Joseph Young
On Behalf Of The
Visiting Firemen
w/Johnny Mercer
That Certain Party
w/Gus Kahn
Thinking Of You
w/Paul Ash
What Can I Say After
I Say I'm Sorry
w/Abe Lyman
Yes Sir That's My Baby
w/Gus Kahn
You're Driving Me Crazy
w/Gus Kahn

DONNELLY, DOROTHY
1880-1928, American
w/Dorothy Donnelly
m/Sigmund Romberg
Deep In My Heart Dear
Drinking Song
Golden Days
Serenade
Silver Moon

DONOVAN
(Donovan Phillip Leitch)
1946, Scottish/English
w&m/Donovan

Atlantis
Brother Sun, Sister Moon
Catch The Wind
Colors
Cosmic Wheel
Mellow Yellow
Music Maker, The
Sunshine Superman
To Susan On The
West Coast Waiting

DONOVAN, WALTER
1888-1964, American
w&m/Walter Donovan
Aba Daba Honeymoon
in co w/Arthur Fields
Down By The Winegar Woiks
in co w/Don Bester, Roger Lewis
One Dozen Roses
in co w/Roger Lewis

DORFF, STEPHEN
American
w&m/Stephen Dorff
Every Which Way
But Loose (1979)
in co w/Milton L. Brown,
Thomas (Snuff) Garrett
Fire In The Morning
in co w/G. Harju, L. Herbstritt

DORSEY, JIMMY
1904-1957, American
m/Jimmy Dorsey
Dusk In Upper Sandusky (instr.)
I'm Glad There Is You
in co w/Paul Madeira Mertz
It's The Dreamer In Me
in co w/James Van Heusen

DORSEY, THOMAS ANDREW
1899, American
w&m/Thomas Andrew Dorsey
Blame It On The Blues
Chain Gang Blues
Gee But It's Hard
Little Talk With Jesus, A
Muddy Water Blues
Peace In The Valley
Riverside Blues
Rock Me
Someday Somewhere
Take My Hand Precious Lord
When The Last Mile Is Finished
Wings Over Jordan

DOUGHERTY, DOC
American
w&m/Doc Dougherty
in co w/Ellis Reynolds
I'm Confessin'
(That I Love You) (1930)

DOUGLAS, CARL
Jamaican
w&m/Carl Douglas
Crazy Feeling (1964)
Kung Fu Fighting (1974)

DOUGLAS, LEW
American
w&m/Lew Douglas
Pretend
    in co w/Cliff Parman,
                Frank Lavere
Why Don't You Believe Me
    in co w/King Laney, Roy Rodde

DOWELL, HORACE KIRBY
(Saxie)
1904, American
w&m/Horace Kirby Dowell
Three Little Fishies

DOZIER, LAMONT
American
Many songs written
in co w/Eddie Holland. See list of
selections under Eddie Holland.

DRAKE, ERVIN M.
1934, American
w&m/Ervin M. Drake
Al Di La
    Eng. w/Ervin M. Drake
    m/Carlo Donida
Castle Rock
    in co w/Jimmy Shirl
Come To The Mardi Gras
    in co w/Jimmy Shirl, Max Bulhões,
    Milton De Oliveira
I Believe
    in co w/Jimmy Shirl, Al Stillman,
    Irvin Graham
It Was A Very Good Year
Made For Each Other
    in co w/Jimmy Shirl
Perdido
    in co w/Hans J. Lengsfelder,
    Juan Tizol
Room Without Windows, A
Tico Tico
    in co w/Zequinha Abreu,
    Aloysio Oliveira

DRAKE, MILTON
1916, American
w&m/Milton Drake
Mairzy Doats
    in co w/Al Hoffman,
    Jerry Livingston
Nina Never Knew
    in co w/Louis Alter

DRESSER, PAUL
1857-1906, American
w&m/Paul Dresser
Blue And The Gray, The
    (A Mother's Gift To Her Country)
Boys Are Coming Home Today,
    The
Calling To Her Boy
    Just Once Again

Come Home Dewey We Won't Do
    A Thing To You
Come Tell Me What's Your
    Answer Yes Or No
Curse Of The Dreamer, The
Day That You Grew Older, The
Don't Tell Her That You Love Her
Dream Of My Boyhood Days
He Brought Home Another
He Fought For A Cause He
    Thought Was Right
I Just Want To Go Back And
    Start The Whole Thing Over
I Wish that You Were
    Here Tonight
I Wonder If She'll Ever Come
    Back To Me
I Wonder Where She Is Tonight
I'd Still Believe You True
If You See My Sweetheart
In Dear Old Illinois
In Good Old New York Town
In The Great Somewhere
Jean (1895)
Jim Judson - From The Town
    Of Hackensack
Just Tell Them That You Saw Me
Lincoln, Grant Or Lee
Mr. Volunteer
My Gal Sal (They Called Her
    Frivolous Sal)
My Heart Still Clings To
    The Old First Love
Old Flame Flickers And I
    Wonder Why, The
On The Banks Of The
    Wabash Far Away
Our Country, May She
    Always Be Right
Path That Leads
    The Other Way, The
She Went To The City
Sweet Savannah
That's Where My Heart
    Is Tonight
There's No North Or
    South Today
Voice Of The Hudson, The
Way Down In Old Indiana
We Fight Tomorrow Mother
When I'm Away From You Dear
When The Birds Have
    Sung Themselves To Sleep
Where Are The
    Friends Of Other Days
Your God Comes First,
    Your Country Next,
    Then Mother Dear

DREYER, DAVE
1894, American
m/Dave Dreyer
Back In Your Own Backyard
    w/Al Jolson, Billy Rose

DRIFTWOOD, JIMMY
(James Morris)
1917, American
w&m/Jimmy Driftwood
Battle Of New Orleans (music
based on traditional melody
"The 8th of January")
Sal's Got A Sugar Lip
Soldier's Joy
Tennessee Stud

DRIGO, RICCARDO
1846-1930, Italian
m/Riccardo Drigo
Serenade (from "Les Millions
d'Arlequin")
Valse Bluette

DUBIN, AL
1891-1945, American
w/Al Dubin
About A Quarter To Nine
    m/Harry Warren
Along The Santa Fe Trail
    co-lyricist Edwina Coolidge
    m/Will Grosz
Boulevard Of Broken Dreams
    m/Harry Warren
Clear Out Of This World
    m/Jimmy McHugh
Cup Of Coffee, A Sandwich
    And You, A
    co-lyricist Billy Rose
    m/Joseph Meyer
Dancing With Tears In
    My Eyes
    m/Joseph Burke
Daydreaming
    co-lyricist Gus Kahn
    m/Harry Warren
Don't Give Up The Ship
    m/Harry Warren
Feudin' And Fightin'
    m/Burton Lane
For You
    m/Joseph Burke
Forty Second Street
    m/Harry Warren
Cecelia
    w/Herman Ruby
Four Walls
    w/Billy Rose
Me And My Shadow
    w/Al Jolson, Billy Rose
There's A Rainbow 'Round
    My Shoulder
    w/Al Jolson, Billy Rose
You Can't Be True Dear
    w/Jack Edwards
Girl Friend Of The Whirling
    Dervish, The
    co-lyricist Johnny Mercer
    m/Harry Warren
Go Into Your Dance
    m/Harry Warren

I Only Have Eyes For You
m/Harry Warren
**I'll Sing You A Thousand
Love Songs**
m/Harry Warren
I'll String Along With You
m/Harry Warren
Indian Summer
m/Victor Herbert
Keep Young And Beautiful
m/Harry Warren
Kiss Waltz, The
m/Joseph Burke
Love Is Where You Find It
co-lyricist Johnny Mercer
m/Harry Warren
Lullaby Of Broadway
m/Harry Warren
Lulu's Back In Town
m/Harry Warren
**Painting The Clouds
With Sunshine**
m/Joseph Burke
Pettin' In The Park
m/Harry Warren
Remember Me
m/Harry Warren
September In The Rain
m/Harry Warren
Shadow Waltz
m/Harry Warren
**She's A Latin
From Manhattan**
m/Harry Warren
Shuffle Off To Buffalo
m/Harry Warren
**Tip-Toe Thru' The
Tulips With Me**
m/Joseph Burke
We're In The Money
m/Harry Warren
With Plenty Of Money And You
m/Harry Warren
**You're Getting To Be A
Habit With Me**
m/Harry Warren

**DUFFIELD, GEORGE
(Reverend)**
American
w/Rev. George Duffield
m/George James Webb
**Stand Up, Stand
Up For Jesus (1858)**

**DUKE, VERNON
(Vladimir Dukelsy)**
1903-1969, American
m/Vernon Duke
April In Paris
w/E.Y. Harburg
Autumn In New York (w&m)
Cabin In The Sky
w/John Latouche

Honey In The Honeycomb
w/John Latouche
I Can't Get Started
w/Ira Gershwin
I Like The Likes Of You
w/E.Y. Harburg
Madly In Love
w/Ogden Nash
Spring Again
w/Ira Gershwin
Suddenly
w/E.Y. Harburg, Billy Rose
Taking A Chance On Love
w/John Latouche, Ted Fetter
What Is There To Say
w/E.Y. Harburg

DUNBAR, RONALD
American
w&m/Ronald Dunbar
Band Of Gold (1970)
in co w/Edythe Wayne
**Patches (I'm Depending On
You) (1970)**
in co w/General Johnson
Deeper And Deeper
in co w/Edythe Wayne,
Norma Toney
Pay To The Piper (1970)
in co w/General Johnson, Greg S.
Perry, Angelo Bond
**She's Not Just
Another Woman (1970)**
in co w/Clyde D. Wilson

DUNCAN, JIMMY
American
w&m/Jimmy Duncan
My Special Angel (1958)

DUNING, GEORGE
1908, American
m/George Duning
Picnic
w/Steve Allen
Film scores:
Any Wednesday
Bell Book And Candle
Dear Brigitte
From Here To Eternity
Houseboat
Picnic
Song Without End
Strangers When We Meet
3:10 To Yuma
Toys In The Attic
World Of Suzy Wong

DUPREE, HARRY
1911, American
w/Harry Dupree
m/Raul Portela
Lisbon Antigua (Lisboa Antigua)

DURANTE, JIMMY
1895-1980, American
Music (and/or words)
Can Broadway Do Without Me
**Daddy Your Mamma Is
Lonesome For You**
I Ups To Him
Inka Dinka Doo
w/Ben Ryan
Jimmy The Well Dressed Man
**Man Who Found The
Lost Chord, The**
Start Off Each Day With A Song
Umbriago
w/Irving Caesar
**Who Will Be With You When
I'm Far Away**

DURHAM, EDDIE
1909, American
w&m/Eddie Durham
Don't You Miss Your Baby
in co w/James A. Rushing,
William (Count) Basie
Every Day Blues
Every Tub
in co w/William (Count) Basie
Good Morning Blues
in co w/James A. Rushing,
William (Count) Basie
John's Idea
**Sent For You Yesterday And Here
You Come Today**
in co w/James A. Rushing
Swingin' On C
Swinging The Blues
in co w/William (Count) Basie
Time Out
Topsy
Wham (Re Bob Boom Bam)
You Made Me Happy

DUSENBERRY, E.F.
American
m/E.F. Dusenberry
w/C.M. Denison
**Land Of Golden
Dreams, The (1912)**

DYKES, JOHN BACCHUS
English
m/John Bacchus Dykes
**Holy, Holy, Holy
(from the song "Nicaea")**
w/Reginald Heber
**Lead, Kindly Light (from the
song "Lux Benigna") (1868)**
w/John Henry Newman

DYLAN, ROBERT (Bob)
1941, American
w&m/Robert Dylan
Ain't Gonna Grieve
All Along The Watchtower
All I Really Want To Do

All Over You
Baby Stop Crying
Ballad For A Friend
Ballad In Plain D
Black Crow Blues
Blowin' In The Wind
Boots Of Spanish Leather
Bringing It All Back Home
California
Can You Please Crawl
        Out Your Window
Corrina, Corrina
Country Pie
Day Of The Locusts
Dear Landlord
Death Of Emmett Till, The
Desolation Row
Don't Think Twice It's All Right
Don't Ya Tell Henry
Down Along The Cove
Down In The Flood
Down The Highway
Drifter's Escape
Farewell
Father Of Night
Fool Such As I
Forever Young
Fourth Time Around
From A Buick 6
Gates Of Eden
Get Your Rocks Off
Girl Of The North Country
Gotta Serve Somebody
Guess I'm Doin' Fine
Gypsy Lou

Hard Rain's Gonna Fall, A
Hero Blues
Highway 61 Revisited
Hurricane
I Am A Lonesome Hobo
I Don't Believe You
I Pity The Poor Immigrants
I Shall Be Free
I Shall Be Released
I Threw It All Away
I Wanna Be Your Lover
I Want You
I'll Be Your Baby Tonight
I'd Have You Anytime
    in co w/George Harrison
If Not For You
If You Gotta Go, Go Now
If You See Her, Say Hello
It Ain't Me Babe
It's All Over Now
It Takes A Lot To Laugh,
        It Takes A Train To Cry
John Brown
John Wesley Harding
Just Like A Woman
Just Like Tom Thumb's Blues
Knockin' On Heaven's Door
Lay Lady Lay
Lay Down Your Weary Tune
Like A Rolling Stone
Long Ago, Far Away
Long Time Gone
Love Is Just A Four-Letter Word
Maggie's Farm
Mama You Been On My Mind

Masters Of War
Million Dollar Bash
Mixed Up Confusion
Mozambique
Mr. Tambourine Man
My Back Pages
My Life In A Stolen Moment
North Country Blues
Odds And Ends
Oh Sister
Only A Hobo
On The Road Again
Only A Pawn In Their Game
Outlaw Blues
Pledging My Time
Poor Boy Blues
Positively Fourth Street
Rainy Day Woman No. 12 & 35
Restless Farewell
She Belongs To Me
Slow Train Coming
Song To Woody
Suberranean Homesick Blues
Summer Wind
Tangled Up In Blue
Tears Of Rage
    m/Richard Manuel

Tell Me Momma
Time Passes Slowly
Times They Are A'Changin', The
Tombstone Blues
Visions Of Johanna
Walkin' Down The Line
You Ain't Goin' Nowhere

Addenda:

DEACON, JOHN
English, 1951
w&m/John Deacon
Another One Bites The Dust

DOWNES, PATRICK
American
w&m/Patrick Downes
Waimea Lullaby (1979)

POPULAR COMPOSERS
& LYRICISTS

E , F

EATON, JIMMY
1906, American
w&m/Jimmy Eaton
Blue Champagne
in co w/H. Grady Watts
**Dance With A Dolly With A
        Hole In Her Stocking**
in co w/Terry Shand,
Mickey Leader
I Double Dare You
in co w/Terry Shand
Turn Back The Hands Of Time
in co w/Larry Wagner

EBB, FRED
American
w/Fred Ebb
m/John Kander
All I Need
Cabaret
How Lucky Can You Get
Maybe This Time
New York, New York
Willkommen
**EBERHART, NELLE
RICHMOND**
1871-1944, American
w/Nelle Richmond Eberhart
m/Charles Wakefield Cadman
At Dawning
**From The Land Of
        The Sky Blue Water**
I Hear A Thrush At Eve

EDDY, DUANE
1938, American
w&m/Duane Eddy
Cannonball
Forty Miles Of Bad Road
Guitar Man
in co w/Lee Hazlewood
Lonely, One, The
Ramrod
Rebel Rouser
in co w/Lee Hazlewood
Shazam
Film score:
Ring Of Fire

EDELMAN, RANDY
American
w&m/Randy Edelman
Weekend In New England (1976)
Film score:
Outside In

EDENS, ROGER
1905, American
w&m/Roger Edens
French Lesson, The
in co w/Betty Comden,
Adolph Green
It's A Great Day For The Irish
Our Love Affair
in co w/Georgie Stoll

Pass That Peace Pipe
in co w/Hugh Martin,
Ralph Blane
Film Scores:
Annie Get Your Gun
in co w/Adolph Deutsch
On The Town
in co w/Lennie Hayton

EDISON, HARRY "SWEETS"
1915, American
m/Harry "Sweets" Edison
Shorty George (instr.)
Every Tub (instr.)

EDWARDS, BERNARD
American
Many songs written in co w/Nile
Rodgers. See list of selections under
Nile Rodgers.

EDWARDS, CLARA
(Bernard Haig)
American
w&m/Clara Edwards
By The Bend Of The River (1927)
**With The Wind And The Rain
        In Your Hair**
in co w/Jack Lawrence

EDWARDS, EDWIN B. (Eddie)
1891-1963
w&m/Edwin B. Edwards
Tiger Rag

EDWARDS, GUS
1879-1945, American
m/Gus Edwards
By The Light Of The Silvery Moon
w/Edward Madden
He's Me Pal
w/Vincent P. Bryan
**I Can't Tell Why I Love
        You But I Do**
w/Will D. Cobb
**If A Girl Like You Loved A
        Boy Like Me**
w/Will D. Cobb
If I Was A Millionaire
w/Will D. Cobb
In My Merry Oldsmobile
w/Vincent P. Bryan
Jimmy Valentine
w/Edward Madden
Laddie Boy
w/Will D. Cobb
School Days
w/Will D. Cobb
Sunbonnet Sue
w/Will D. Cobb
Tammany
w/Vincent P. Bryan
**Way Down Yonder In The Corn
        Field**
w/Will D. Cobb

EDWARDS, JONATHAN
1946, American
w&m/Jonathan Edwards
Sunshine

EDWARDS, SHERMAN
1919, American
m/Sherman Edwards
Broken Hearted Melody
w/Hal David
Dungaree Doll
w/Ben Raleigh
Johnny Get Angry
w/Hal David
See You In September
w/Sid Wayne
Wonderful, Wonderful
w/Ben Raleigh

EGAN, JOHN C. (Jack)
1892-1940, American
w&m/John C. Egan
in co w/Allan Flynn
Be Still My Heart

EGAN, RAYMOND B.
1890-1952, American
w/Raymond B. Egan
Ain't We Got Fun
co-lyricist Gus Kahn
m/Richard A. Whiting
**I Never Knew I Could
        Love Anybody**
m/Gus Kahn
Japanese Sandman, The
m/Richard A. Whiting
Sleepy Time Gal
co-lyricist Joseph R. Alden
m/Richard A. Whiting,
Ange Lorenzo
Some Sunday Morning
m/Richard A. Whiting, Gus Kahn
They Called It Dixieland
m/Richard A. Whiting
Till We Meet Again
m/Richard A. Whiting
**Where The Morning
        Glories Grow**
m/Richard A. Whiting, Gus Kahn

EGAN, WALTER
1948, American
w&m/Walter Egan
Hearts On Fire
Magnet And Steel
Tunnel Of Love

EGNER, PHILIP
1870-1956, American
w&m/Philip Egner
It's The Army
On Brave Old Army Team
Sound Off
West Point March

ELISCU, EDWARD
1902, American
w/Edward Eliscu
Carioca, The
   co-lyricist Gus Kahn
   m/Vincent Youmans
Flying Down To Rio
   m/Vincent Youmans
Great Day
   co-lyricist Billy Rose
   m/Vincent Youmans
More Than You Know
   co-lyricist Billy Rose
   m/Vincent Youmans
Orchids In The Moonlight
   m/Vincent Youmans
Without A Song
   co-lyricist Billy Rose
   m/Vincent Youmans

ELLINGTON, DUKE
(Edward Kennedy Ellington)
1899-1974, American
m/Duke Ellington
Baby You're Too Much
   w/Don George
Birminham Breakdown
Black And Tan Fantasy
Black Beauty
Blind Man's Bluff
Blues I Love To Sing, The
   w/Bob Miley
Blue Light
Blues, The
Blue Reverie
Boy Meets Horn
   w/Irving Mills

Blue Serge
   co-composer Mercer Ellington
C Jam Blues
   co-composer Barney Bigard
Caravan
   co-composer Juan Tizol
   w/Irving Mills
C'est Comme Ca
   w/Marshall Barer

Chatterbox
Clarinet Lament
Come Sunday
Concerto For Cootie
Cottontail
Daybreak Express
Delta Serenade
Diminuendo In Blue
Do Nothin' Till You
            Hear From Me
   w/Bob Russell
Don't Get Around Much Anymore
   w/Bob Russell
Drop Me Off In Harlem
Duke Steps Out, The
Echoes Of Harlem

Esquire Swank
   w/Johnny Hodges
Everything But You
   w/Harry James, Don George
Flaming Youth
Grieving
   co-composer Billy Strayhorn
Happy Go Lucky Local
Harlem Airshaft
Harmony In Harlem
   co-composer Johnny Hodges
I Didn't Know About You
I Got It Bad And That Ain't Good
   w/Paul Francis Webster
I Let A Song Go Out Of My Heart
   w/Henry Nemo, Irving Mills
I'm Beginning To See The Light
   co-composers Harry James,
   Johnny Hodges
   w/Don George
In A Mellotone
In A Sentimental Mood
It Don't Mean A Thing If
         It Ain't Got That Swing
   w/Irving Mills
I'm Checking Out, Goom Bye
I'm Gonna Go Fishin'
I'm Just A Lucky So And So
Jack The Bear
Jazz Convulsions
Jump For Joy
   w/Paul Francis Webster
Just Sittin' And A-Rockin'
   w/Lee Gaines
Just Squeeze Me
   w/Lee Gaines
Lost In Meditation
Lonely Ones, The
Mood Indigo
   co-composer Barney Bigard
   w/Irving Mills
Old Man Blues
Please Forgive Me
Poco Mucho
   w/Don George
Portrait Of Bert Williams
Prelude To A Kiss
Primping At The Prom
Pyramid
Ready Go!
   co-composer Billy Strayhorn

Rhummbop
   co-composer Billy Strayhorn

Ring Dem Bells
Rockin' In Rhythm
Rocks In My Bed
Rumpus In Richmond
Satin Doll
   co-composer Billy Strayhorn
   w/Johnny Mercer

Saturday Night Function
Serious Serenade
Soda Fountain Rag

Solitude
   w/Eddie De Lange,
   Irving Mills
Sophisticated Lady
   w/Mitchell Parish, Irving Mills
Strange Feeling
   co-composer Billy Strayhorn
Suddenly It Jumped
Suburban Beauty
Stomp Look And Listen
Take Love Easy
Tell Me The Truth
Three Cent Stomp
Time's A-Wasting
   co-composer Mercer Ellington
   w/Don George
Total Jazz
   co-composer Billy Strayhorn
Warm Valley
You Dirty Dog
You Gave Me The Gate
            And I'm Swinging
Film scores:
Anatomy Of A Murder (1959)
Paris Blues

ELLIOTT, JOHN M. (Jack)
1914, American
w&m/John M. (Jack) Elliott
Be Mine
   in co w/Harold Spina
Do You Care
   in co w/Lew Quadling
It's So Nice To Have A
            Man Around The House
   in co w/Harold Spina
Sam's Song
   in co w/Lew Quadling
Film Scores:
Comic, The
Where's Poppa

ELLIOTT, ZO
American
m/Zo Elliott
w/Stoddard King
There's A Long, Long Trail (1913)

ELLIS, DON
1934-1978, American
m/Don Ellis (instr.)
Despair To Hope
Milo's Theme
Star Children
Film scores:
French Connection, The
Kansas City Bomber

ELLIS, SEGER
1904, American
w&m/Seger Ellis
You're All I Want For Christmas

ELSTON, HARRY JAMES
1938, American
w&m/Harry James Elston
in co w/Philemon Hou
Grazing In The Grass (1969)

EMERSON, KEITH
1944, English
w&m/Keith Emerson
in co w/Gregory Lake, Carl Palmer
Lucky Man
Nutrocker
From The Beginning

EMMETT, DANIEL
DECATUR (Dan)
1815-1904, American
w&m/Dan Emmett
Blue Tail Fly
⠀⠀⠀⠀**(Jimmy, Crack Corn)**
Dixie
Jordan Is A Hard Road To Travel
My Old Aunt Sally
Old Dan Tucker

ENDOR, CHICK
American
w&m/Chick Endor
Who Takes Care Of The
⠀⠀⠀⠀**Caretaker's Daughter**
⠀⠀⠀⠀**While The Caretaker's**
⠀⠀⠀⠀**Busy Taking Care (1925)**

ENDSLEY, MELVIN
American
w&m/Melvin Endsley
Knee Deep In The Blues (1957)
Singing The Blues (1957)

ENGLANDER, LUDWIG
1859-1914, American
m/Ludwig Englander
w/Harry B. Smith, except as noted.
Don't You Want A Paper Dearie
Gay White Way, The
⠀⠀⠀⠀w/J. Clarence Harvey
He Was A Married Man
New York
Sally In Our Alley
⠀⠀⠀⠀w/George V. Hobart
Same Old Story, The
Slave Dealer's Song
Two Roses
⠀⠀⠀⠀w/Stanislau Stange
What's The Use Of Anything
When Shall I Find Him
World Is A Toy Shop, The

ENGVICK, WILLIAM
American
w/William Engvick
Anna (El N. Zumbon) (1952)
⠀⠀⠀⠀m/R. Vatro
While We're Young
⠀⠀⠀⠀m/Alec Wilder, Morty Palitz
April Age, The
⠀⠀⠀⠀m/Alec Wilder

ENTWISTLE, JOHN
1946, English
w&m/John Entwistle
Cousin Kevin
Fiddle About

Heaven And Hell
I Believe In Everything
Success Story
My Wife
Trick Of The Light
Whiskey Man

ERDMAN, ERNIE
1879-1946, American
m/Ernie Erdman
No No Nora
⠀⠀⠀⠀in co w/Ted Fiorito, Gus Kahn
Nobody's Sweetheart
⠀⠀⠀⠀in co w/Gus Kahn, Billy Meyers,
⠀⠀⠀⠀Elmer Schoebel
Toot Toot Tootsie, Goodbye
⠀⠀⠀⠀in co w/Gus Kahn, Dan Russo,
⠀⠀⠀⠀Ted Fiorito, Robert King

ERTEGUN, AHMET
1923, American
w&m/Ahmet Ertegun
Chains Of Love
⠀⠀⠀⠀in co w/Van Wells
Don't Play That Song (You Lied)
⠀⠀⠀⠀in co w/Betty Nelson
Fool, Fool, Fool
Good Lovin'
⠀⠀⠀⠀in co w/Leroy Kirkland, Denny
⠀⠀⠀⠀Taylor, Jesse Stone
Hey Miss Fannie
Lovey Dovey
⠀⠀⠀⠀in co w/Memphis Curtis
Middle Of The Night
Sweet Sixteen
Ting-A-Ling
What 'Cha Gonna Do

ESSEX, DAVID (David Cook)
1947, English
w&m/David Essex
in co w/Jeff Wayne
Lamplight
Rock On

EVANS, BILL
1929-1980, American
m/Bill Evans (instr.)
Jade Visions
Peace Piece
Waltz For Debby

EVANS, DALE
(Mrs. Roy Rogers)
1912, American
w&m/Dale Evans
Bible Tells Me So, The
Happy Trails
No Bed Of Roses

EVANS, PAUL
1938, American
w&m/Paul Evans
Happy-Go-Lucky Me
⠀⠀⠀⠀in co w/Al Byron
Happiness Is
⠀⠀⠀⠀in co w/Paul Parnes

Roses Are Red
⠀⠀⠀⠀in co w/Al Byron
When
⠀⠀⠀⠀in co w/Jack Reardon

EVANS, RAYMOND B. (Ray)
1915, American
All w&m written
in co w/Jay Harold Livingston
Almost In Your Arms
Bonanza (theme)
Buttons And Bows
Dear Heart
⠀⠀⠀⠀m/Henry Mancini
Golden Earrings
⠀⠀⠀⠀m/Victor Young
I'll Always Love
⠀⠀⠀⠀**You (Querida Mia)**
Lonely Girl
Marshmallow Moon
Misto Christofo Columbo
Mona Lisa
Mr. Lucky
My Beloved
Never Let Me Go
Never Too Late
Que Sera Sera (Whatever
⠀⠀⠀⠀**Will Be, Will Be)**
Ruby And The Pearl, The
Silver Bells
Tammy
To Each His Own
Thousand Violins, A
Warm And Willing

EVANS, REDD (Louis)
1912-1972, American
w&m/Redd Evans
American Beauty Rose
⠀⠀⠀⠀in co w/Arthur Altman,
⠀⠀⠀⠀Hal David
Don't Go To Strangers
⠀⠀⠀⠀in co w/David Mann
Frim Fram Sauce, The
He's 1A In The Army
Let Me Off Uptown
No Moon At All
⠀⠀⠀⠀in co w/David Mann
Rosie The Riveter
⠀⠀⠀⠀in co w/John J. Loeb
There I've Said It Again
⠀⠀⠀⠀in co w/David Mann
This Is The Night

EVANS, RICK
American
w&m/Rick Evans
In The Year 2525 (1969)

EVANS, TOLCHARD
English
m/Tolchard Evans
If (1950, U.S.A.)
⠀⠀⠀⠀w/Robert Hargreaves,
⠀⠀⠀⠀Stanley J. Damerell**

Lady Of Spain (1931)
    w/Erell Reaves
Let's All Sing Like
        The Birdies Sing (1932)
    w/Robert Hargreaves,
    Stanley J. Damerell

EVERLY, DON
1937, American
w&m/Don Everly
Cathy's Clown
    in co w/Phil Everly
I Wonder If I Care As Much
    in co w/Phil Everly
I'll Never Get Over You
    in co w/Phil Everly
It's All Over
Kiss Your Man Goodbye
    in co w/Phil Everly
Maybe Tomorrow
    in co w/Phil Everly
Price Of Love, The
    in co w/Phil Everly
Should We Tell Him
    in co w/Phil Everly

Sigh, Cry, Almost Die
    in co w/Phil Everly
So Sad (To Watch Good
        Love Go Bad)
Til I Kissed You

EVERLY, PHIL
1939, American
Cathy's Clown
    in co w/Don Everly
Gee, But It's Lonely
I Wonder If I Care As Much
    in co w/Don Everly
I'll Never Get Over You
    in co w/Don Everly
Kiss Your Man Goodbye
    in co w/Don Everly
Made To Love
Maybe Tomorrow
    in co w/Don Everly
Price Of Love, The
    in co w/Don Everly
Should We Tell Him
    in co w/Don Everly

Sigh, Cry, Almost Die
    in co w/Don Everly
When Will I Be Loved

EZRIN, BOB
American
w&m/Bob Ezrin
Beth (1976)
    in co w/Peter Criss, Stan Penridge
Detroit Rock City (1976)
    in co w/Paul Stanley
Flaming Youth (1976)
    in co w/Paul "Ace" Frehley,
    Paul Stanley, Gene Simmons
King Of The Night
        Time World (1976)
    in co w/Kim Fowley,
    Mark Anthony, Paul Stanley

FABER, WILLIAM E.
1902, American
w/William E. Faber
m/John N. Kamano
I'm A Lonely Little Petunia
       In An Onion Patch

FAGEN, DONALD
1948, American
w&m/in co w/Walter Becker
AJA
Black Cow
Black Friday
Can't Buy A Thrill
Deacon Blues
Dirty Work
Do It Again
Fez, The
FM (No Static At All)
Haitian Divorce
Home At Last
I Got The News
Josie
Katie Lied
Kid Charlemagne
My Old School
Peg
Pretzel Logic
Reelin' In The Years
Rikki Don't Lose That Number

FAITH, PERCY
1908-1976, American
m/Percy Faith
Brazilian Sleigh Bells (instr.)
My Heart Cries For You (adapted
    from French folk song "Chanson
    deMarie Antoinette"
    w/Carl Sigman
Noche Caribe (instr.)
Virginian Theme, The (instr.)

FAIN, SAMMY
1902, American
m/Sammy Fain
April Love
    w/Paul Francis Webster
Are You Having Any Fun
    w/Jack Yellen
By A Waterfall
    w/Irving Kahal
Certain Smile, A
    w/Paul Francis Webster
Dear Hearts And Gentle People
    w/Bob Hilliard
Gift Of Love, The
    w/Paul Francis Webster
Happy In Love
    w/Jack Yellen
I Can Dream, Can't I
    w/Irving Kahal
I'll Be Seeing You
    w/Irving Kahal

I'm Late
    w/Bob Hilliard
Let A Smile Be Your Umbrella
    w/Irving Kahal
Love Is A Many
        Splendored Thing
    w/Paul Francis Webster
Please Don't Say No, Say Maybe
    w/Ralph Freed
Secret Love
    w/Paul Francis Webster
Someone's Waiting For You
    w/Carol Connors, Ayn Robbins
Strange Are The Ways Of Love
    w/Paul Francis Webster
Tender Is The Night
    w/Paul Francis Webster
That Old Feeling
    w/Lew Brown
Very Precious Love, A
    w/Paul Francis Webster
Was That the Human Thing To Do
    w/Joseph Young
Wedding Bells Are Breaking Up
        That Old Gang Of Mine
    w/Irving Kahal
When I Take My Sugar To Tea
    w/Irving Kahal,
    Rev. Norman Connor
World That Never Was, A
    w/Paul Francis Webster
You Brought A New Kind
        Of Love To Me
    w/Irving Kahal,
    Rev. Norman Connor

FALLA, MANUEL DE
1876-1946, Spanish
m/Manuel De Falla (instr.)
Ritual Fire Dance (from "El Amor
        Brujo") (1924)

FAME, GEORGIE (Clive Powell)
1943, English
w&m/Georgie Fame
Because I Love You
Get Away

FARGO, DONNA
(Yvonee Vaughn Silver)
1949, American
w&m/Donna Fargo
Don't Be Angry
Funny Face
Happiest Girl In The
        Whole U.S.A., The
I'll Try A Little Bit Harder
It Do Feel Good
Little Girl Gone
Superman
U.S. of A.
You Can't Be A Beacon
You Were Always There

FARIÑA, RICHARD
American
w&m/Richard Farina
Hard Loving Loser (1966)
Pack Up Your Sorrows (1964)
FARRAR, JOHN
English
w&m/John Farrar
Have You Never
        Been Mellow (1975)
Hopelessly Devoted
        To You (1976)
Magic
You're The One
        That I Want (1978)
FARROW, JOHNNY
1912, American
w&m/Johnny Farrow
I Have But One Heart

FAWCETT, JOHN
English
w/John Fawcett
m/Hans Georg Nageli
Blest Be The Tie That Binds

FEARIS, JOHN S.
American
m/John S. Fearis
w/Jessie B. Pounds
Beautiful Isle Of Somewhere

FEASTER, CLAUDE
American
w&m/Claude Feaster
in co w/Carl Feaster, James Keys,
Floyd McCrae, William Edwards
Sh-Boom, Life Could Be
        A Dream (1954)

FEATHER, LEONARD G.
1914, American
w&m/Leonard G. Feather
in co w/Lionel Hampton
Evil Gal Blues
Salty Papa Blues

FEKARIS, DINO
American
Many songs by Dino Fekaris in co
w/Frederick Perren. See list of
selections under Frederick Perren.

FELICIANO, JOSE
1945, American
w&m/Jose Feliciano
Chico And The Man, (theme)
Feliz Navidad
Hitchcock Railway
Light My Fire

FENDER, FREDDY
(Baldemar Huerta)
1937, American
w&m/Freddy Fender
Crazy Crazy Baby
Holy One

Wasted Days And Wasted Nights
in co w/Wayne Duncan
When The Next Teardrop Falls
in co w/Huey P. Meaux

FENTON, HOWARD
American
w&m/Howard Fenton
Gee Dad It's A Wurlitzer

FERGUSON, JAY
1947, American
w&m/Jay Ferguson
in co w/Mark Andes
I Got A Line On You
Run Run Run
Thunder Island (w&m)

FERNANDEZ, CARLOS
Mexican
Spanish w&m/Carlos Fernandez
Cielito Lindo (Ay, Ay, Ay, Ay
    Cantay No Llores)
    (Dear Little Heaven)

FEYNE, BUDDY
1912, American
w/Buddy Feyne
Jersey Bounce
in co w/Bobby Plater,
Tiny Bradshaw, Edward Johnson,
Robert B. Wright
Tuxedo Junction
in co w/Erskine Hawkins,
William Johnson, Julian Dash

FIEGER, DOUG
American
w&m/Doug Fieger
Baby Talks Dirty (1980)
in co w/Berton Averre
Can't Put A Price On Love (1980)
in co w/Berton Averre
Good Girls Don't (1979)
My Sharona (1979)
in co w/Berton Averre

FIELDING, JERRY
1923-1980, American
m/Jerry Fielding
Film scores:
Advise And Consent (1961)
Bad News Bears, The
Lawman
McHale's Navy
Outlaw Jessie Wales, The
Straw Dogs
Wild Bunch, The
FIELDS, ARTHUR
1888-1953, American
w&m/Arthur Fields
Aba Daba Honeymoon
in co w/Walter Donovan
On The Mississippi
in co w/Ballard MacDonald
Harry Carroll

FIELDS, DOROTHY
1905-1977, American
w/Dorothy Fields
Big Spender
m/Cy Coleman
Blue Again
m/Jimmy McHugh
Close As Pages In A Book
m/Sigmund Romberg
Cuban Love Song
m/Jimmy McHugh
Diga Diga Doo
m/Jimmy McHugh
Dinner At Eight
m/Jimmy McHugh
Doing The New Low-Down
m/Jimmy McHugh
Don't Blame Me
m/Jimmy McHugh
Exactly Like You
m/Jimmy McHugh
Fine Romance, A
m/Jerome Kern
I Can't Give You Anything
    But Love Baby
    m/Jimmy McHugh
I Dream Too Much
m/Jerome Kern
I Feel A Song Comin' On
m/Jimmy McHugh
I Won't Dance
co-lyricists Otto Harbach
Oscar Hammerstein II
m/Jerome Kern
If My Friends Could See Me Now
m/Cy Coleman
Look Who's Dancin'
m/Arthur Schwartz
Lost In A Fog
m/Jimmy McHugh
I'm In The Mood For Love
m/Jimmy McHugh
Love Is The Reason
m/Arthur Schwartz
Lovely To Look At
m/Jerome Kern, Jimmy McHugh
Make The Man Love Me
m/Arthur Schwartz
On The Sunny Side Of The Street
m/Jimmy McHugh
Porgy
m/Jimmy McHugh
Singin' The Blues
m/Jimmy McHugh
Spring Has Sprung
m/Arthur Schwartz
Thank You For A Lovely Evening
m/Jimmy McHugh
Way You Look Tonight, The
m/Jerome Kern
You Couldn't Be Cuter
m/Jerome Kern

FIELDS, IRVING
1915, American
m/Irving Fields
w/Albert Gamse
Chantez, Chantez
Managua, Nicaragua
Miami Beach Rhumba
Take Her To Jamaica

FILLMORE, CHARLES M.
American
w&m/Charles M. Fillmore
Tell Mother I'll Be There (1890)

FINCH, RICHARD
1954, American
w&m/in co w/Harry Wayne ('K.C.')
Casey. See list of selections under
Harry Wayne ('K.C.') Casey.

FINCK, HERMAN
English
m/Herman Finck
w/E. Ray Goetz
In The Shadows (1911)

FINNIE, LANCE
American
w&m/Lance Finnie
in co w/Willis Schoefield
You're So Fine (1959)

FINE, SYLVIA
1916, American
w&m/Sylvia Fine
Anatole Of Paris
Five Pennies, The
Knock On Wood
Moon Is Blue, The
m/Herschel Burke Gilbert
Melody In 4F
in co w/Max Liebman
Pavlova

FIORITO, TED
1900
m/Ted Fiorito
Charley My Boy
w/Gus Kahn
I Never Knew
w/Gus Kahn
King For A Day
w/Samuel M. Lewis,
Joseph Young
Laugh, Clown Laugh
w/Samuel M. Lewis,
Joseph Young
No No Nora
w/Gus Kahn, Ernie Erdman
Then You've Never Been Blue
w/Samuel M. Lewis,
Joseph Young
Roll Along Prairie Moon
w/Cecil Mack,
Albert Von Tilzer

Thanks A Million
   co-lyricist Arthur Johnston
   w/Gus Kahn
Toot Toot Tootsie, Goodbye
   w/Gus Kahn, Ernie Erdman,
   Dan Russo, Robert King

FISHER, DORIS
1915
w/Doris Fisher
Angelina
   m/Allan Roberts
Into Each Life Some
      Rain Must Fall
   m/Allan Roberts
Invitation To The Blues
   m/Allan Roberts,
   Arthur Gershwin
Put The Blame On Mame
   m/Allan Roberts
Tampico
   m/Allan Roberts
Whispering Grass
   m/Fred Fisher
You Always Hurt The
      One You Love
   m/Allan Roberts

FISHER, EDDIE
1932, American
w&m/Eddie Fisher
in co w/Charles Tobias, Harry Akst
May I Sing To You (1954)

FISHER, FRED
1875-1942, American
w&m/Fred Fisher
All Dressed Up
      With A Broken Heart
   in co w/Stella Unger,
   Harold Stern
Blue Is The Night
Chicago (That Toddling Town)
Come Josephine In
      My Flying Machine
   in co w/Alfred Bryan
Daddy You've Been A
      Mother To Me
   in co w/Alfred Bryan
Dardanella
   in co w/Felix Bernard,
   Johnny S. Black
Every Little Bit Helps
   in co w/George Whiting
Gee But It's Great To Meet A
   Friend From Your Home Town
   in co w/William Tracey,
   James McGavisk
I Don't Want Your Kisses
   in co w/M.M. Broones
I Want You To Want Me
   To Want You
   in co w/Alfred Bryan

I'm On My Way To Mandalay
   in co w/Alfred Bryan
Ireland Must Be Heaven
   in co w/Joseph McCarthy,
   Howard Johnson
Lorraine, My
      Beautiful Lorraine
   in co w/Alfred Bryan
Oui, Oui Marie
   in co w/Alfred Bryan,
   Joseph McCarthy
Peg O' My Heart
   in co w/Alfred Bryan
Siam
   in co w/Howard Johnson
There's A Broken Heart For
      Every Light On Broadway
   in co w/Howard Johnson
There's A Little Bit Of Bad
      In Every Good Girl
   in co w/Grant Clarke
They Go Wild Simply
      Wild Over Me
   in co w/Joseph McCarthy
When I Get You Alone Tonight
   in co w/Joe Goodwin
Whispering Grass
   in co w/Doris Fisher
Who Paid The Rent For
      Mrs. Rip Van Winkle
   in co w/Alfred Bryan
Your Feet's Too Big
   in co w/Ada Benson,
   John Hancock

FISHER, MARVIN
1916, American
m/Marvin Fisher
w/Jack Segal
When Sunny Gets Blue

FISHER, WILLIAM ARMS
1861-1948, American
w&m/William Arms Fisher
**Goin' Home (1922) (Music
adapted from Anton Dvorak's
"New World Symphony", Op. 95)**

FITZGERALD, ELLA
1918, American
w&m/Ella Fitzgerald
in co w/Van Alexander
A-Tisket, A-Tasket

FLAMINGO, JOHNNY
American
w&m/Johnny Flamingo
Tijuana Taxi (1965)
   in co w/Bud Coleman
Wheels (1960)
   in co w/Norman Petty

FLANAGAN, BUD
English
w&m/Bud Flanagan
Add't'l Amer. w/Joseph McCarthy
Underneath The Arches

FLATT, LESTER RAYMOND
1914, American
m/Lester Flatt
in co w/Earl Scruggs
Earl's Breakdown (instr.)
Foggy Mountain
      Breakdown (instr.)

FLEESON, NEVILLE
1887-1945, American
w&m/Neville Fleeson
in co w/Albert Von Tilzer
I'll Be With You In
      Apple Blossom Time

FLEMING, KYE
American
w&m/Kye Fleming
in co w/Dennis Morgan
Sleeping Single In
      A Double Bed (1979)

FLETCHER, "DUSTY"
American
w/"Dusty" Fletcher
in co w/John Mason
m/Jack McVea, Dan Howell
Open The Door, Richard (1947)

FLOYD, EDDIE
1935, American
w&m/Eddie Floyd
in co w/Steve Cropper
Knock On Wood
634-5789

FLYNN, ALLAN
1894-1965, American
w&m/Allan Flynn
in co w/Frank Madden
Maybe (You'll Think Of Me)

FLYNN, JOSEPH
Irish
w&m/Joseph Flynn
Down Went McGinty (1889)

FOGELBERG, DAN
1951, American
w&m/Dan Fogelberg
Aspen/These Days
Below the Surface
Captured Angel
Face The Fire
Gypsy Wind
Heart Hotels
Longer
Man In The Mirror
Part Of The Plan
Phoenix
Power Of Gold
Souvenirs
Tell It To My Face

FOGERTY, JOHN C.
1945, American
w&m/John C. Fogerty

Bad Moon Rising
Born On The Bayou
Commotion
Don't Look Now
Door To Door
Down On The Corner
Effigy
Fortunate Son
Green River
Have You Ever Seen The Rain
Hey Tonight
Lodi
Long As I Can See The Light
Lookin' Out My Back Door
Proud Mary
Run Through The Jungle
Someday Never Comes
Sweet Hitchhiker
Travellin' Band
Up Around The Bend
Who'll Stop The Rain

FOLEY, RED
(Clyde Julian Foley)
1910, American
w&m/Red Foley
Old Shep

FORBERT, STEVE
1955, American
w&m/Steve Forbert
January 23-30, 1978
Romeo's Tune (1979)
Sweet Love That You Give, The

FORBSTEIN, LEO F.
American
m/Leo F. Forbstein
Film score:
Anthony Adverse (1936)

FORESYTHE, REGINALD
English
m/Reginald Foresythe
Dodging A
        Divorcee (1935) (instr.)

FORREST, GEORGE (Chet)
1915, American
w&m/George (Chet) Forrest
in co w/Robert Wright
And This Is My Beloved (adapted
    from Alexander Borodin's
    "Prince Igor", opera containing
    the Polovtsian Dances")
At The Balalaika
Baubles, Bangles And Beads
    (adapted from Alexander
    Borodin's "Prince
    Igor" as above)
Donkey Serenade (adapted from
    music of Rudolf Friml's
    "Chansonette")
        orig. w/Sigmund Spaeth
It's A Blue World

Stranger, In Paradise (adapted
    from Alexander Borodin's
    "Prince Igor", as above)
Strange Music (adapted from
    Edvard Grieg's "Wedding Day At
    Trold Haugen" and "Nocturne")

FOSTER, DAVID
American
w&m/David Foster
After The Love Has Gone (1979)
    in co w/Jay Graydon,
    Bill Champlin
Breakdown Dead Ahead (1980)
    in co w/Boz Scaggs

FOSTER, JERRY
American
w&m/in co w/Bill Rice
See list of selections under Bill Rice

FOSTER, STEPHEN COLLINS
1826-1864, American
w&m/Stephen Collins Foster
Angelina Baker
Beautiful Dreamer
Camptown Races, De
Come Where My Love
        Lies Dreaming
Ellen Bayne
Gentle Annie
Hard Times Come Again No More
Jeanie With The Light
        Brown Hair
Lou'siana Belle
Massa's In de Cold Ground
My Old Kentucky Home, Good
        Night
Nelly Bly
Nelly Was A Lady
Oh Boys Carry Me 'Long
Oh! Susanna
Old Black Joe
Old Dog Tray
Old Folks At Home
        (Swanee River)
Old Uncle Ned
Ring, Ring The, Banjo
Some Folks
Way Down South
We Are Coming, Father Abraham
Willie, We Have Missed You

FOX, CHARLES
1939, American
m/Charles Fox
Happy Days
    w/Norman Gimbel
Killing Me Softly With His Song
    w/Norman Gimbel
Laverne And Shirley (TV theme)
    w/Norman Gimbel
Love American Style (TV theme)
Love Boat (TV theme)
Making Our Dreams Come True
    w/Norman Gimbel

Paper Chase (TV theme)
Ready To Take A Chance Again
    w/Norman Gimbel
Richard's Window (theme from
    "The Other Side Of
    The Mountain")
    w/Norman Gimbel
Wonder Woman (TV theme)
Film scores:
Barbarella
Goodbye Columbus
Making It

FOX, OSCAR J.
1879-1961, American
m/Oscar J. Fox
w/Floride Calhoun
Hills Of Home, The (1925)

FRAGOS, GEORGE
American
w&m/George Fragos
in co w/Jack Baker
I Hear A Rhapsody (1940)

FRAMPTON, PETER
1950, English
w&m/Peter Frampton
Baby I Love Your Way
Do You Feel Like We Do
I'm In You
Show Me The Way

FRANCISCO, DON
American
w&m/Don Francisco
He's Alive (1979)

FRANKLIN, ARETHA
1942, American
w&m/Aretha Franklin
Rock Steady
Since You've Been Gone
        (Sweet, Sweet Baby)
    in co w/Ted White
Think
    in co w/Ted White

FRANKLIN, DAVE
1909-1970, American
w&m/Dave Franklin
Anniversary Waltz
    in co w/Al Dubin
I Must See Annie Tonight
    in co w/Cliff Friend
Merry-Go-Round
        Broke Down, The
    in co w/Cliff Friend
When My Dream
        Boat Comes Home
    in co w/Cliff Friend
You Can't Stop Me
        From Dreaming
    in co w/Cliff Friend

FOXX, INEZ
American
w&m/Inez Foxx

I Love You A 1,000 Times (1966)
in co w/Luther Dixon
Mockingbird (1963)
in co w/Charles Foxx

FRAZIER, DALLAS
1939, American
w&m/Dallas Frazier
Ain't Had No Lovin'
Alley Oop
Ain't Love A Good Thing
All I Have To Offer You Is Me
in co w/A.L. (Doodle) Owens
Baptism Of Jesse Taylor, The
in co w/Whitey Shafer
Beneath Still Waters
Big Mabel Murphy
California Cotton Fields
Dream Painter
in co w/Whitey Shafer
I Can't Believe That You've
Stopped Loving Me
in co w/A.L. (Doodle) Owens
If It Ain't Love (Let's Leave
It Alone)
If My Heart Had Windows
I'm So Afraid Of
Losing You Again
in co w/A.L. (Doodle) Owens
Johnny One Time
in co w/A.L. (Doodle) Owens
Just For What I Am
in co w/A.L. (Doodle) Owens
My Baby Packed Up My Mind
And Left Me
Singin' My Song
Son Of Hickory Holler's
Tramp, The
There Goes My Everything
Timber I'm Falling
in co w/Ferlin Husky
Touching Home
in co w/A.L. (Doodle) Owens
What's Your Mama's Name Child
in co w/Earl Montgomery
Where Did They Go Lord
in co w/A.L. (Doodle) Owens
Where Is My Castle

FREED, ALAN
1922-1965, American
w&m/Alan Freed
Maybellene
in co w/Chuck Berry, Russ Fratto
Nadine
Sincerely
in co w/Harvey Fuqua
Tongue Tied Blues

FREED, ARTHUR
1894, American
w/Arthur Freed
After Sundown
m/Nacio Herb Brown

All I Do Is Dream Of You
m/Nacio Herb Brown
Alone
m/Nacio Herb Brown
Beautiful Girl
m/Nacio Herb Brown
Broadway Melody
m/Nacio Herb Brown
Broadway Rhythm
m/Nacio Herb Brown
Fit As A Fiddle
m/Al Hoffman, Al Goodhart
I Cried For You
m/Gus Arnheim, Abe Lyman
It Was So Beautiful
m/Harry Barris
I've Got A Feelin' You're Foolin'
m/Nacio Herb Brown
Moon Is Low, The
m/Nacio Herb Brown
My Lucky Star
m/Nacio Herb Brown
Pagan Love Song
m/Nacio Herb Brown
Should I Reveal
m/Nacio Herb Brown
Singin' In the Rain
m/Nacio Herb Brown
Smoke Dreams
m/Nacio Herb Brown
Temptation
m/Nacio Herb Brown
This Heart Of Mine
m/Harry Warren
Wedding Of The Painted
Doll, The
m/Nacio Herb Brown
We'll Make Hay While
The Sun Shines
m/Nacio Herb Brown
Would You
m/Nacio Herb Brown
You Are My Lucky Star
co-lyricist Buddy DeSylva
m/Nacio Herb Brown
You Were Meant For Me
m/Nacio Herb Brown

FREED, RALPH
1907-1973, American
w/Ralph Freed
How About You
m/Burton Lane
Little Dutch Mill
m/Harry Barris
Please Don't Say No Say Maybe
m/Sammy Fain
Swing High, Swing Low
m/Burton Lane
Young Man With A Horn, The
m/George Stoll

FREEDMAN, MAX C.
1893-1962, American
w/Max C. Freedman

Rock Around The Clock
m/Jimmy DeKnight
(James E. Myers)
Sioux City Sue
m/Dick Thomas

FREEDMAN, STANLEIGH P.
American
m/Stanleigh P. Freedman
w/C.W. O'Connor
Down The Field (march) (1911)

FREEMAN, BOBBY
American
w&m/Bobby Freeman
Do You Wanna Dance

FREHLEY, PAUL "ACE"
1950, American
w&m/Paul "Ace" Frehley
Flaming Youth
in co w/Paul Stanley, Bob Ezrin
Gene Simmons
Rocket Ride
in co w/Sean Delaney

FREY, GLENN
1948, American
w&m/in co w/Don Henley, except for
the selection "Take It Easy", in co
only w/Jackson Browne. See list of
selections under Don Henley.

FRIED, GERALD
American
m/Gerald Fried
Theme From "Roots"
(instr.) (1977)

FRIEDHOFER, HUGO
American
m/Hugo Friedhofer
Film scores:
Affair To Remember, An (1957)
Best Years Of Our Lives, The (1946)
Daddy Long Legs (1931)
Gilda (1946)
Hondo (1953)
Lifeboat (1943)
One Eyed Jacks (1961)
Paris After Dark (1943)
Prisoner Of Shark Island, The (1936)
Rebecca Of Sunnybrook Farm (1932)
Wing And A Prayer, A (1944)
Young Lions, The (1958)

FRIEDLAND, ANATOLE
1888-1938, American
m/Anatole Friedland
w/L. Wolfe Gilbert
Are You From Heaven
I Love You, That's The One
Thing I Know
Lily Of The Valley
My Little Dream Girl
My Own Iona
My Sweet Adair

FRIEDMAN, LEO
1869-1927, American
m/Leo Friedman
Let Me Call You Sweetheart
　w/Beth Slater Whitson
Meet Me Tonight In Dreamland
　w/Beth Slater Whitson

FRIEDMAN, RUTHANN
American
w&m/Ruthann Friedman
Windy (1967)

FRIEND, CLIFF
1893-1974, American
m/Cliff Friend
Don't Sweetheart Me
　w/Charles Tobias
Hello Bluebird
I Must See Annie Tonight
　w/Dave Franklin
June Night
　w/Abel Baer
**Merry Go Round
　　　Broke Down,The**
　w/Dave Franklin
Then I'll Be Happy
　w/Lew Brown, Sidney Clare
There's Yes Yes In Your Eyes
　w/Joseph H. Santly
Time Waits For No One
　w/Charles Tobias
**We Did It Before And We Can
　　　Do It Again**
　w/Charles Tobias
**When My Dreamboat
　　　Comes Home**
　w/Dave Franklin
**You Can't Stop Me
　　　From Dreaming**
　w/Dave Franklin
You tell Her I Stutter
　w/Billy Rose

FRIML, RUDOLF
1879-1978, American
m/Rudolf Friml
Allah's Holiday
　w/Otto Harbach
**Donkey Serenade, The (adapted
　from "Chanson"; lyric version
　"Chansonette"; words by
　Sigmund Spaeth**
　w/Robert Wright, George Forrest
Giannina Mia
　w/Otto Harbach
Indian Love Call
　w/Otto Harbach,
　　Oscar Hammerstein II

L'Amour, Toujours L'Amour
　w/Catherine Chisholm Cushing
Love Me Tonight
　w/Brian Hooker
March Of The Musketeers
　w/P.G. Wodehouse, Clifford Grey
Mounties, The
　w/Otto Harbach,
　　Oscar Hammerstein II
Only A Rose
　w/Brian Hooker
Rose-Marie
　w/Otto Harbach,
　　Oscar Hammerstein II
Some Day
　w/Brian Hooker
Song Of The Vagabonds
　w/Brian Hooker
Sympathy
　w/Otto Harbach

FRISCH, ALBERT
1916, American
m/Albert Frisch
All Over The World
　w/Charles Tobias
I Won't Cry Anymore
　w/Fred Wise
Roses In The Rain
　w/Fred Wise
This Is No Laughing Matter
　w/Buddy Kaye
Two Different Worlds
　w/Sid Wayne

FRIZZELL, LEFTY
1928-1975, American
w&m/Lefty Frizzell
Always Late (With Your Kisses)
　in co w/Blackie Crawford
**(Honey, Baby, Hurry) Bring Your
　　　Sweet Self Back To Me**
Don't Stay Away
　in co w/Loys Southerland
**Forever (And Always)
　　　Give Me More, More, More
　　　(Of Your Kisses)**
　in co w/Ray Price
**How Long Will It Take
　　　(To Stop Loving You)**
I Love You A Thousand Ways
　in co w/Jim Beck
I Want To Be With You Always
　in co w/Jim Beck
**I'm An Old Old Man (Tryin'
　　　To Live While I Can)**
**If You've Got The Money (I've
　　　Got The Time)**
　in co w/Jim Beck

Mom And Dad's Waltz
That's The Way Love Goes
　in co w/Whitey Shafer
Time Changes Things
　in co w/Lessie Lyle

FRONTIERE, DOMINIC
1932, American
m/ Dominic Frontiere
Film Scores: *Brannigan, Popi, Train
Robbers, The;* TV Scores: *Breaking
Away, Vegas*

**FUENTES, EDUARDO
SANCHEZ DE**
Cuban
Spanish w&m/Eduardo
Sanchez De Fuentes
Mirame Asi (1928)
　Eng. w/Frederick Herman
　Martens (title "Grant Those
　Glances") Carol Raven (title,
　"Look At Me")
O Cuba (1928)
　Eng. w/Frederick
　Herman Martens

FULTON, JACK
1903, American
w&m/Jack Fulton
If You Are But A Dream
　in co w/Nathan J. Bonx, Moe Jaffe
Ivory Tower
　in co w/Lois Steele
Wanted
　in co w/Lois Steele

FUQUA, HARVEY
1932, American
w&m/Harvey Fuqua
My Whole World Ended
　in co w/Johnny Bristol,
　Pam Sawyer, Jimmy Roach
Sincerely
　in co w/Alan Freed
Someday We'll Be Together
　in co w/Johnny Bristol, Jackey
　Beavers
**What Does It Take
　　　(To Win Your Love)**
　in co w/Vernon Bullock, Johnny
　Bristol
Twenty Five Miles
　in co w/Johnny Bristol, Edwin
　Starr, Jerry Wexler, Bert Berns

FURST, WILLIAM
English
m/William Furst
w/Clyde Fitch

**Love Makes The World
　　　Go 'Round (1896)**

POPULAR COMPOSERS
& LYRICISTS

G

GABLER, MILTON
1911, American
w&m/Milton Gabler
Choo Choo Ch' Boogie
 in co w/Vaughn Horton,
 Denver Darling
If I Give My Heart To You
 in co w/Jimmie Crane, Al Jacobs
 Jimmy Brewster
L-O-V-E
 in co w/Bert Kaempfert
Tell Me Why
 in co w/Al Alberts, Marty Gold

GABRIEL, CHARLES H. SR.
1856-1932, American
m/Charles H. Gabriel, Sr.
Brighten The Corner
 Where You Are
 w/Ina Duley Ogdon
His Eye Is On The Sparrow
 w/Mrs. C. D. Martin
Since Jesus Came Into My Heart

GADE, JACOB
French
m/Jacob Gade
Jalousie (Jealousy) (1926) (instr.)
 music adapted/Walter Paul

GAITHER, WILLIAM J.
American
m/William J. Gaither
w/William J. Gaither, Gloria Gaither
King Is Coming, The (1970)
He Touched Me (1963)
Something Beautiful (1971)

GALLAGHER, ED
American
w&m/in co w/Al Shean
Mister Gallagher And
 Mister Shean

GALLOP, SAMMY
1915-1971, American
w/Sammy Gallop
Autumn Serenade
 m/Peter De Rose
Count Every Star
 m/Bruno Coquatrix
Elmer's Tune
 m/Elmer Albrecht, Dick Jurgens
Holiday For Strings
 m/David Rose
Maybe You'll Be There
 m/Rube Bloom
My Lady Loves To Dance
 m/Milton Delugg
Shoofly Pie And Apple
 Pan Dowdy
 m/Guy Wood
Somewhere Along The Way
 m/Kurt Adams
There Must Be A Way
 m/David Saxon

Wake The Town And
 Tell The People
 m/Jerry Livingston

GAMBLE, KENNETH
American
w&m/Kenneth Gamble
Brand New Me
 in co w/Jerry Butler, Theresa Bell
Break Up To Make Up
 in co w/Thomas Bell, Linda Creed
Cowboys To Girls
 in co w/Leon Huff
Don't Leave Me This Way
 in co w/Leon Huff, Cary Gilbert
Don't Let Love Hang You Up
 in co w/Jerry Butler, Leon Huff
Drowning In The Sea Of Love
 in co w/Leon Huff
Early Morning Love
 in co w/Leon Huff
Enjoy Yourself
 in co w/Leon Huff
Expressway To Your Heart
 in co w/Leon Huff
For The Love Of Money
 in co w/Leon Huff,
 Anthony Jackson
I Love Music
 in co w/Leon Huff
I'll Never Give You Up
 in co w/Leon Huff, Jerry Butler
Love I Lost
 in co w/Leon Huff
Love Is The Message
 in co w/Leon Huff
Moody Woman
 in co w/Jerry Butler, Theresa Bell
Only The Strong Survive
 in co w/Jerry Butler, Leon Huff
See You When I Get There
 in co w/Leon Huff
Some Folks Never Learn
 in co w/Leon Huff
Someday You'll Be Old
 in co w/Leon Huff
Sound Of Philadelphia
 in co w/Leon Huff
Spring Again
 in co w/Leon Huff
Time To Get Down
 in co w/Leon Huff
We Understand Each Other
 in co w/Leon Huff
When Will I See You Again
 in co w/Leon Huff
You'll Never Find Another
 Love Like Mine
 in co w/Leon Huff

GAMSE, ALBERT
1910, American
w/Albert Gamse
Amapola (Pretty Little Poppy)
 m/Joseph M. LaCalle

Chantez, Chantez
 m/Irving Fields
La Comparsa (Carnival Parade)
 m/Ernesto Lecuona
Managua, Nicaragua
 m/Irving Fields
Miami Beach Rhumba
 m/Irving Fields
Take Her To Jamaica
 m/Irving Fields
Yours (Quiereme Mucho)
 co-lyricist Jack Sherr
 m/Gonzalo Roig
Tango Of Roses
 (Tango Delle Rose)
 m/Schreier-Bottero

GANNON, KIM
(James Kimball Gannon)
1900, American
w&m/Kim Gannon
Always In My Heart
 in co w/Ernesto Lecuona
Autumn Nocturne
 in co w/Josef Myrow
Dreamer's Holiday, A
 in co w/Mabel Wayne
Five O'Clock Whistle
 in co w/Josef Myrow
I Understand
 in co w/Mabel Wayne
I'll Be Home For Christmas
 in co w/Walter Kent, Buck Ram
Moonlight Cocktail
 in co w/C. Luckeyth Roberts
Under Paris Skies
 in co w/Hubert Giraud (from the
 French melody
 "Soul le ciel de Paris")

GANT, CECIL
American
w&m/Cecil Gant
Cecil's Boogie (1945)
Grass Is Getting
 Greener, The (1945)
 in co w/W. S. Stevenson

GANTRY, CHRIS
American
w&m/Chris Gantry
Dreams Of The
 Everyday Housewife (1969)

GARDNER, DONALD
YETTER (Don)
1912, American
w&m/Donald Yetter Gardner
All I Want For Christmas Is My
 Two Front Teeth

GARDNER, WILLIAM HENRY
1865-1932, American
w/William Henry Gardner
m/Carol Roma
Can't Yo' Heah Me
 Callin' Caroline

GARLAND, JOSEPH C. (Joe)
1903, American
m/Joseph C. Garland
w/Andy Razaf
In The Mood

GARNER, ERROLL
1923-1976, American
m/Erroll Garner
w/Johnny Burke
Misty

GARNETT, GALE
American
w&m/Gale Garnett
Loving Place (1964)
We'll Sing In The Sunshine (1964)

GATES, DAVID
1940, American
w&m/David Gates
Baby I'm-A Want You
Been Too Long On The Road
Diary
Everything I Own
If
Guitar Man, The
Hooked On You
It Don't Matter To Me
Make It With You
My One And Only Jimmy Boy
Popsicles And Icicles
Sweet Surrender

GATLIN, LARRY
1949, American
w&m/Larry Gatlin
All The Gold In California
Broken Lady
Delta Dirt
Do It Again Tonight
Help Me
I Don't Want To Cry
I've Done Enough Dyin' Today
Night Time Magic
Penny Annie
Statues Without Hearts

GAUDIO, BOB
1942, American
w&m/Bob Gaudio
Big Girls Don't Cry
   in co w/Bob Crewe
Can't Take My Eyes Off Of You
   in co w/Bob Crewe
**December, 1963 (Oh,
   What A Night)**
   in co w/Judy Parker
Marlena
Rag Doll
   in co w/Bob Crewe
Sherry
Short Shorts
   in co w/Thomas Austin,
   Bill Crandall, Bill Dalton

Walk Like A Man
   in co w/Bob Crewe
Who Loves You
   in co w/Judy Parker

GAUNT, PERCY
1852-1896, American
w&m/Percy Gaunt
Bowery, The (1893)
   in co w/Charles H. Hoyt
**Love Me Little, Love
   Me Long (1893)**
Push Dem Clouds Away (1893)
**Reuben, Beuben I've
   Been Thinking (1893)**

GAY, JOHN
1685-1732, English
w/John Gay
Music from traditional English airs of
18th century or earlier, composers
unknown.
Beggars Opera, The

GAY, NOEL
English
w&m/Noel Gay
in co w/Douglas Furber
Lambeth Walk (1937)

GAYE, MARVIN
1939, American
w&m/Marvin Gaye
Beechwood 4-5789
   in co w/William Stevenson,
   George Gordy
Dancing In The Street
   in co w/Ivy Hunter,
   William Stevenson
Hitch Hike
   in co w/William Stevenson,
   Clarence Paul
**Inner City Blues (Make Me
   Wanna Holler)**
   in co w/James Nyx Jr.
Let's Get It On
   in co w/Ed Townsend
Mercy, Mercy Me (The Ecology)
Pride And Joy
   in co w/Norman Whitfield,
   William Stevenson
What's Going On
   in co w/Renaldo Benson

GAYLORD, RONNIE
American
w&m/Ronnie Gaylord
I Will Never Pass This Way Again

GEIFER, GEORGE L.
American
w&m/George L. Geifer
**Who Threw The Overalls In
   Mistress Murphy's Chowder**

GENTRY, Bo
American
w&m/Bo Gentry
Make Believe (1969)

GENTRY, BOBBIE
1944, American
w&m/Bobbie Gentry
Ode To Billy Joe

GEORGE, DON
1909, American
w&m/Don George
I'm Beginning To See The Light
   in co w/Duke Ellington,
   Harry James, Johnny Hodges
Yellow Rose Of Texas (1955)
   music based on an 1853 march
   attributed to one "J.K."; later
   used as "The Song Of The
   Texas Rangers"

GERLACH, HORACE
American
w&m/Horace Gerlach
in co w/Bobby Burke
Daddy's Little Girl (1949)

GERSHWIN, GEORGE
1898-1937, American
Also see listing under "Classical
Music composers of
the 20th Century".
m/George Gershwin
Aren't You Kind Of Glad We Did
   w/Ira Gershwin
Babbitt And The Bromide, The
   w/Ira Gershwin
Bess, You Is My Woman Now
   w/DuBose Heyward,
   Ira Gershwin
Bidin' My Time
   w/Ira Gershwin
Blah-Blah-Blah
   w/Ira Gershwin
But Not For Me
   w/Ira Gershwin
By Strauss
   w/Ira Gershwin
Clap Yo' Hands
   w/Ira Gershwin
Dear Little Girl
   w/Ira Gershwin
Delishious
   w/Ira Gershwin
Do Do Do
   w/Ira Gershwin
Do It Again
   w/B.G. (Buddy) DeSylva
Embraceable You
   w/Ira Gershwin
Fascinating Rhythm
   w/Ira Gershwin
Foggy Day, A
   w/Ira Gershwin

For You, For Me, For Evermore
  w/Ira Gershwin
Funny Face
  w/Ira Gershwin
He Loves And She Loves
  w/Ira Gershwin
**How Long Has This
Been Going On**
  w/Ira Gershwin
I Got Plenty O'Nuthin'
  w/DuBose Heyward,
  Ira Gershwin
I Got Rhythm
  w/Ira Gershwin
I Loves You, Porgy
  w/DuBose Heyward,
  Ira Gershwin
I'll Build A Stairway To Paradise
  w/Ira Gershwin,
  B.G. (Buddy) DeSylva
It Ain't Necessarily So
  w/Ira Gershwin
I've Got A Crush On You
  w/Ira Gershwin
Just Another Rhumba
  w/Ira Gershwin
Let's Call The Whole Thing Off
  w/Ira Gershwin
Let's Kiss And Make Up
  w/Ira Gershwin
Little Jazz Bird
  w/Ira Gershwin
Liza
  w/Ira Gershwin, Gus Kahn
Looking For A Boy
  w/Ira Gershwin
Lorelei, The
  w/Ira Gershwin
Love Is Here To Stay
  w/Ira Gershwin
Love Is Sweeping The Country
  w/Ira Gershwin
Love Walked In
  w/Ira Gershwin
Man I Love, The
  w/Ira Gershwin
Maybe
  w/Ira Gershwin
Mine
  w/Ira Gershwin

My Man's Gone Now
  w/DuBose Heyward
My One And Only
  w/Ira Gershwin
Nice Work If You Can Get It
  w/Ira Gershwin
Of Thee I Sing
  w/Ira Gershwin

Our Love Is Here To Stay
  w/Ira Gershwin
Shall We Dance
  w/Ira Gershwin

Slap That Bass
  w/Ira Gershwin
Somebody Loves Me
  w/B.G. (Buddy) DeSylva,
  Ballard MacDonald
Someone To Watch Over Me
  w/Ira Gershwin
Soon
  w/Ira Gershwin
Strike Up The Band
  w/Ira Gershwin
Summertime
  w/DuBose Heyward
Swanee
  w/Irving Caesar
Sweet And Low-Down
  w/Ira Gershwin
S'Wonderful
  w/Ira Gershwin
**Tchaikovsky (And
Other Russians)**
  w/Ira Gershwin
That Certain Feeling
  w/Ira Gershwin
**There's A Boat Dat's Leavin'
Soon For New York**
  w/Ira Gershwin
They All Laughed
  w/Ira Gershwin
**They Can't Take That
Away From Me**
  w/Ira Gershwin
Where's The Boy
  w/Ira Gershwin
Who Cares
  w/Ira Gershwin
Wintergreen For President
  w/Ira Gershwin
Woman Is A Sometime Thing, A
  w/DuBose Heyward

GERSHWIN, IRA
1896, American
w&m/in co with music of George
Gershwin (brother). See list of
selections under George Gershwin.
Add'tl.songs:
w/Ira Gershwin
Cheerful Little Earful
  co-lyricist Billy Rose
  m/Harry Warren
I Can't Get Started
  m/Vernon Duke
Long Ago (And Far Away)
  m/Jerome Kern
Man That Got Away, The
  m/Harold Arlen
My One And Only Highland Fling
  m/Harry Warren
My Ship
  m/Kurt Weill
One Life To Live
  m/Kurt Weill

Saga Of Jenny, the
  m/Kurt Weill
Spring Again
  m/Vernon Duke
Sunny Disposish (Americana)
  m/Philip Charig
You're A Builder Upper
  co-lyricist E.Y. Harburg
  m/Harold Arlen

GIBB, BARRY
1947
GIBB, MAURICE
1949
GIBB, ROBIN
1949
(known as THE BEE GEES)
English/Australian
w&m/Barry, Maurice & Robin Gibb
Alive
Boogie Child
Come On Over
Desire
Edge Of The Universe
Fanny Be Tender (With My Love)
First Of May
Hold On To My Love
  w&m/Robin Gibb, Blue Weaver
Holiday
**How Can You Mend
A Broken Heart**
How Deep Is Your Love
I Can't Help It
I Can't See Nobody
**I Just Want To Be
Your Everything**
  w&m/Barry Gibb
I Started A Joke
If I Can't Have You
**I've Gotta Get A Message
To You**
Jive Talkin'
Lonely Days
Love So Right
**Massachusetts (The Lights
Went Out In)**
More Than A Woman
My World
New York Mining Disaster 1941
Night Fever
Nights On Broadway
Run To Me
Stayin' Alive
To Love Somebody
Too Much Heaven
Tragedy
With My Love
Words
You Should Be Dancing

GIBB, STEVE
American
w&m/Steve Gibb
She Believes In Me (1979)

GIBBONS, CARROLL
English
m/Carroll Gibbons
w/James Dyrenforth
Garden In The Rain, A (1928)

GIBBONS, WILLIAM
1949, American
w&m/William Gibbons
in co w/Frank Beard, Dusty Hill
Francene
It's Only Love
La Grange
Tush

GIBSON, Albert Andrew (Andy)
1913-1961, American
w&m/Albert Andrew Gibson
Geechy Joe
Great Lie, The
Hucklebuck, The
   in co w/Roy Alfred
I Left My Baby
Shorty George
   in co w/William (Count) Basie,
   Harry Edison

GIBSON, DON
1928, American
w&m/Don Gibson
Blue, Blue Day
Bring Back Your Love To Me
Don't Tell Me Your Troubles
Far, Far Away
Give Myself A Party
I Can Mend Your Broken Heart
I Can't Stop Loving You
I'd Be A Legend In My Time
Just One Time
Lonesome Number One
Look Who's Blue
Love Has Come My Way
Oh, Lonesome Me
Oh, Such A Stranger
Sea Of Heartbreak
Stranger To Me, A
Sweet Dreams
There's A Big Wheel
Wasted Words
Who Cares For Me

GIFFORD, HARRY M.
English
m/Harry M. Gifford
w/Terry Sullivan
She Sells Sea Shells (The
Beauty Shop) (1908)

GILBERT, FRED
English
w&m/Fred Gilbert
Man That Broke The Bank At
Monte Carlo, The (1892)

GILBERT, HERSCHEL BURKE
American
m/Herschel Burke Gilbert

Film scores:
Bold And The Brave, The (1956)
Comanche (1956)
Crime And Punishment (1959)
Jackie Robinson Story, The (1950)
Moon Is Blue, The (1953)
Riot In Cell Block 11 (1954)
While The City Sleeps (1956)

GILBERT, LAWRENCE B.
American
m/Lawrence B. Gilbert
Shadowland (1914) (instr.)

GILBERT, L. WOLFE
1886-1970, American
w/L. Wolfe Gilbert
Down Yonder
Hitchy Koo
   m/Lewis F. Muir,
   Maurice Abrahams
Jeannine, I Dream Of Lilac Time
   m/Nathaniel Shilkret
Lily Of The Valley
   m/Anatol Friedland
Mama Don't Want No Peas And
Rice And Cocoanut Oil
   m/Charlie Lofthouse
Mama Inez
   m/Eliseo Grenet
Marta
   m/Moises Simon
My Mother's Eyes
   m/Abel Baer
Peanut Vendor, The
   co-lyricist Marion Sunshine
   m/Moises Simon (adaptation of
   El Manicero)
Ramona
   m/Mabel Wayne
Waiting For The Robert E. Lee
   m/Lewis F. Muir

GILBERT, RAY
1912, American
w/Ray Gilbert
Baia
   m/Ary Barroso
Cherry
   m/Don Redman
Cuanto Le Gusto
   m/Ary Barroso
Hot Canary, The
   m/Paul Nero (adapted from music
   by F. Poliakin)
That's A Plenty
You Belong To My Heart
   m/Augustin Lara
Zip A Dee Doo Dah
   m/Allie Wrubel

GILDER, NICK
1951, Canadian
w&m/Nick Gilder

Hot Child In The City (1978)
Roxy Roller (1976)
   in co w/James McCulloch

GILKYSON, TERRY
American
w&m/Terry Gilkyson
Bare Necessities, The (1967)
Cry Of The Wild
Goose, The (1950)
Green Fields (1960)
   in co w/Frank Miller,
   Richard Dehr
Marianne (1955)
   in co w/Frank Miller,
   Richard Dehr (music adapted
   from a folk song of the Bahamas)
Memories Are Made
Of This (1955)
   in co w/Frank Miller,
   Richard Dehr

GILLESPIE, DIZZY
(John Birks Gillespie)
1917, American
m/Dizzy Gillespie (instrs.)
Anthropology
52nd Street Theme
Groovin' High
Manteca
Night In Tunisia, A
   in co w/Frank Paparelli
Ol' Man Rebop
Shaw Nuff
Swing Low Sweet Cadillac
Woodyn' You

GILLESPIE, HAVEN
1888-1975, American
w/Haven Gillespie
Breezin' Along With The Breeze
   m/Richard A. Whiting,
   Seymour Simons
Drifting And Dreaming
   m/Egbert Van Alstyne
Santa Claus Is Coming To Town
   m/J. Fred Coots
That Lucky Old Sun
   m/Beasley Smith
You Go To My Head
   m/J. Fred Coots

GILLESPIE, MARIAN
1889-1946, American
w/Marian Gillespie
m/Florence Methven
When You Look Into The Heart
Of A Rose (1918)

GILMORE, PATRICK
SARSFIELD (Louis Lambert)
American
w&m/Patrick Sarsfield Gilmore
When Johnny Comes Marching
Home (1863)

GIMBEL, NORMAN
American
w/Norman Gimbel
Bluesette
    m/Jean Thielemans
Canadian Sunset
    m/Eddie Heywood
Girl From Ipanema, The
    m/Antonio Carlos Jobim
Happy Days
    m/Charles Fox
I Got A Name
    m/Jim Croce
I Will Wait For You
    m/Michel Legrand
It Goes Like It Goes
    m/David Shire
Killing Me Softly With His Song
    m/Charles Fox
Live For Life
    m/Francis Lai
Making Our Dreams Come True
    m/Charles Fox
Meditation
    m/Antonio Carlos Jobim
Ready To Take A Chance Again
    m/Charles Fox
**Richard's Window (theme from
    "The Other Side Of
    The Mountain")**
    m/Charles Fox
Summer Samba
    m/Marcus Valle,
    Sergio Paulo Valle
Watch What Happens
    m/Michel Legrand
TV Themes:
See list of selections
under Charles Fox.

GLASER, TOMPALL
1935, American
w&m/Tompall Glaser
Charlie
Lay Down Beside Me
Stand Beside Me
You're Making A Fool Out Of Me

GLAZER, TOM
1914, American
w/Tom Glazer
Melody Of Love
    m/H. Engelmann
On Top Of Spaghetti
    music based on traditional folk
    song "On Top Of Old Smokey"

GLENN, ARTIE
American
w&m/Artie Glenn
Crying In The Chapel

GLICKMAN, FRED
1903, American
w&m/Fred Glickman
in co w/Johnny Lange,
Walter Henry (Hy) Heath
Mule Train

GLOVER, HENRY
1921, American
w&m/Henry Glover
All My Love Belongs To You
    in co w/Sally Nix
Annie Had A Baby
    in co w/Lois Mann
D' Natural Blues
    in co w/Lucky Millinder
Drown In My Tears
Honky Tonk
    in co w/Bill Doggett,
    Shep Shephard, Billy Butler
    Clifford Scott
I Can't Go On Without You
    in co w/Sally Nix
I Love You Yes I Do
    in co w/Sally Nix
I'm Waiting Just For You
    in co w/Lucky Millinder
Let's Call It A Day
Peppermint Twist, The
    in co w/Joey Dee
Pot Likker
**You Don't Have To Be A Star
    (To Be In My Show)**
    in co w/James Dean

GLOVER, STEPHEN
English
m/Stephen Glover
w/Joseph Edwards Carpenter
**What Are The Wild
    Waves Saying (1850)**

GODOWSKY, LEOPOLD
1870-1938, Russian/American
m/Leopold Godowsky (instr.)
Alt Wien (1920)

GOELL, KERMIT
1915, American
w&m/Kermit Goell
Huggin And Chalkin'
Near You
    in co w/Francis Craig

**GOETHE VON,
JOHANN WOLFGANG**
1749-1832, German
German w/Johann
Wolfgang von Goethe.
Music by Petr Ilich Tchaikovsky.
None But The Lonely Heart

GOETSCHIUS, MARJORIE
1915, American
w&m/Marjorie Goetschius
in co w/Edna Osser
I Dream Of You

GOETZ, E. RAY
1886-1954, American
w/E. Ray Goetz
For Me And My Gal
    co-lyricist Edgar Leslie
    m/George W. Meyer
Who'll Buy My Violets
    m/Jose Padilla

GOFFIN, GERRY
1939, American
Many songs by Gerry Goffin
in co w/Carole King. See list of
selections under Carole King.
Add't. songs/Gerry Goffin
**Do You Know Where You're
    Going To (Theme from
    "Mahogany")**
    in co w/Michael Masser
I'll Meet You Halfway
    in co w/Wes Farrell
It's Not The Spotlight
    in co w/Barry Goldberg
I've Got To Use My Imagination
    in co w/Barry Goldberg
Run To Him
    in co w/Jack Keller
So Sad The Song
    in co w/Michael Masser
**Who Put The Bomp (In The Bomp
    Ba Bomp Ba Bomp)**
    in co w/Barry Mann

GOLD, ANDREW
1951, American
w&m/Andrew Gold
I Can't Wait
    in co w/Mark Goldenberg
Lonely Boy
Thank You For Being A Friend
That's Why I Love You

GOLD, ERNEST
1921, American
m/Ernest Gold
Exodus
    m/Pat Boone
It's A Mad Mad Mad Mad World
    m/Mack David
On The Beach
    m/Steve Allen
Film scores:
Exodus (1960)
Inherit The Wind (1960)
It's A Mad Mad Mad
    Mad World (1963)
Judgment At Nurenburg (1961)
On The Beach (1959)
Picnic (1948)
Ship Of Fools (1965)
Witness For The Prosecution (1957)

GOLD, WALLY
1928, American
w&m/Wally Gold
in co w/Aaron Schroeder

See list of selections
under Aaron Schroeder

GOLDEN, JOHN
1874-1955, American
w/John Golden
Poor Butterfly
    m/Raymond Hubbell

GOLDENBERG, MARK
American
w&m/Mark Goldenberg
I Can't Wait (1980)
    in co w/Andrew Gold
Mad Love (1980)
Cost Of Love (1980)

**GOLDENBERG, WILLIAM
LEON (Billy)**
Film scores:
"King"
Play It Again, Sam (1972)
Queen Of The Stardust Ballroom
Scavenger Hunt (1979)
Up The Sandbox (1972)

GOLDMAN, EDWIN FRANKO
1878-1956, American
m/Edwin Franko Goldman
Boy Scouts Of America (march)
On The Mall (march) (1923)

GOLDSBORO, BOBBY
1941, American
w&m/Bobby Goldsboro
Autumn Of My Life
Can You Feel It
Come Back Home
I'm A Drifter
Me And Millie
Muddy Mississippi Line
With Pen In Hand

GOLDSMITH, JERRY
American
m/Jerry Goldsmith
Film scores:
Alien (1979)
Blue Max, The (1966)
Capricorn One (1978)
Coma (1978)
Lilies Of The Field (1963)
List Of Adrian
  Messenger, The (1963)
Omen (1977)
Omen II (1978)
Our Man Flint (1966)
Pappilon (1973)
Patton (1974)
Planet Of The Apes (1968)
Police Story
Rio Lobo (1970)
Sand Pebbles, The (1966)
Seven Days In May (1964)
Star Trek (1979)
Von Ryan's Express (1965)

TV themes:
Barnaby Jones
Waltons, The

GOLDSTEIN, JERRY
American
w&m in co w/Lee Oskar. See list of
selections under Lee Oskar.
Songs in co w/Bob Feldman,
Richard Gottehrer.
Drifter, The
Giving Up On Love (1963)
My Boyfriend's Back (1963)
My Girl (1965)
Say, One (Is A Lonely Number)
    in co w/Louis Peceres

GOLLAHON, GLADYS
1908, American
w&m/Gladys Gollahon
Our Lady Of Fatima (1950)

GOODHART, AL
1905-1955, American
w/Al Goodhart
Auf Wiedersehen My Dear
    m/Ed Nelson, Al Hoffman,
    Milton Ager
Fit As A Fiddle
    m/Al Hoffman, Arthur Freed
I Apologize
    m/Al Hoffman, Ed Nelson
I'm In A Dancing Mood
    m/Al Hoffman, Maurice Sigler
**Johnny Doughboy Found A Rose
In Ireland**
    m/Kay Twomey, Allan Roberts
Who Walks In When I Walk Out
    m/Al Hoffman

GOODMAN, BENNY
1909, American
m/Benny Goodman
Airmail Special (instr.)
    in co w/James R. Mundy
Don't Be That Way
    in co w/Edgar Sampson,
    Mitchell Parish, Chick Webb
Flying Home
    in co w/Lionel Hampton
Lullaby In Rhythm
    in co w/Edgar M. Sampson
Stompin' At The Savoy
    in co w/Edgar Sampson, Andy
    Razaf
Two O'Clock Jump
    in co w/William (Count) Basie,
    Harry James

**GOODMAN, LILLIAN
ROSEDALE**
1887, American
w&m/Lillian Rosedale Goodman
Cherie, I Love You (1926)

GOODRUM, RANDY
1947, American
w&m/Randy Goodrum
Before My Heart Finds Out
Bluer Than Blue
Broken-Hearted Me
Lesson In Leavin'
    in co w/B. Maher
You Needed Me
**You Pick Me Up
(And Put Me Down)**
    in co w/B. Maher

GOODWIN, JOE
1889-1943, American
w/Joe Goodwin
Everywhere You Go
    m/Mark Fisher, Larry Shay
When I Get You Alone Tonight
    m/Fred Fisher
When You're Smiling
    m/Mark Fisher, Larry Shay

GORDON, DEXTER
1923, American/Danish
m/Dexter Gordon (instrs.)
Chase, The
    in co w/Wardell Gray
Dexter's Minor Mad
Dexter Rides Again
Doin' Allright
Swingin' Affair, A

GORDON, IRVING
1915, American
w&m/Irving Gordon
Be Anything (But Be Mine)
Mister And Mississippi
Unforgettable

GORDON, MACK
1904-1959, American
w/Mack Gordon
At Last
    m/Harry Warren
Chattanooga Choo Choo
    m/Harry Warren
Chica Chica Boom Chic
    m/Harry Warren
College Rhythm
    m/Harry Revel
**Did You Ever See
A Dream Walking**
    m/Harry Revel
Down Argentine Way
    m/Harry Warren
Goodnight My Love
    m/Harry Revel
I Can't Begin To Tell You
    m/James V. Monaco
**I Feel Like A Feather
In The Breeze**
    m/Harry Revel
I Had The Craziest Dream
    m/Harry Warren

I Played Fiddle For The Czar
  m/Harry Revel
I Yi Yi Yi Yi Like You Very Much
  m/Harry Warren
It Happened In Sun Valley
  m/Harry Warren
Kalamazoo
  m/Harry Warren
Listen To The German Band
  m/Harry Revel
Lookie Lookie Lookie
  Here Comes Cookie
  w&m/Mack Gordon
Love Thy Neighbor
  m/Harry Revel
Loveliness Of You, The
  m/Harry Revel
Mam'selle
  m/Edmund Goulding
May I
  m/Harry Revel
More I See You, The
  m/Harry Warren
Never In A Million Years
  m/Harry Revel
On The Boardwalk At
  Atlantic City
  m/Josef Myrow
Paris In The Spring
  m/Harry Revel
Serenade In Blue
  m/Harry Warren
She Reminds Me Of You
  m/Harry Revel
Stay As Sweet As You Are
  m/Harry Revel
Take A Number From One To Ten
  m/Harry Revel
There Will Never Be Another You
  m/Harry Warren
There's A Lull In My Life
  m/Harry Revel
This Is The Beginning Of The End
  w&m/Mack Gordon
Through A Long And
  Sleepless Night
  m/Alfred Newman
Time On My Hands
  co-lyricist Harold Adamson
  m/Vincent Youmans
Underneath The Harlem Moon
  m/Harry Revel
Wake Up And Live
  m/Harry Revel
Wilhemina
  m/Josef Myrow
With My Eyes Wide
  Open I'm Dreaming
  m/Harry Revel
Without A Word Of Warning
  m/Harry Revel
You Can't Have Everything
  m/Harry Revel

You Hit The Spot
  m/Harry Revel
You Make Me Feel So Young
  m/Josef Myrow
You Say The Sweetest
  Things Baby
  m/Harry Warren
You'll Never Know
  m/Harry Warren

GORDY, BERRY JR.
1929, American
w&m/Berry Gordy Jr.
ABC
  in co w/Deke Richards,
  Frederick Perren,
  Alphonso Migell
Do You Love Me
Got A Job
  in co w/Tyrone Carlo,
  William "Smokey" Robinson
I'll Be There
  in co w/Hal Davis,
  Willie Hutch, Bob West
Lonely Teardrop
  in co w/Gwen Gordy,
  Tyrone Carlo
Shop Around
  in co w/William
  "Smokey" Robinson
That's Why
  in co w/Tyrone Carlo,
  Gwen Gordy
To Be Loved
  in co w/Tyrone Carlo,
  Gwen Gordy
Try It Baby
You've Got What It Takes
  in co w/Tyrone Carlo,
  Gwen Gordy
You've Made Me So Very Happy
  in co w/Frank Wilson,
  Brenda Holloway,
  Patrice Holloway

GORNEY, JAY
1896, American
m/Jay Gorney
Baby Take A Bow
  w/Lew Brown
Brother Can You Spare A Dime
  w/E.Y. Harburg
In Chi Chi Castenango
  w/Henry Myers
You're My Thrill
  w/Sidney Clare

GOULD, MORTON
1913, American
See listing under "Best Known
Classical Composers of
the 20th Century")
m/Morton Gould
Pavanne
  w/Gladys Shelley

GOULDING, EDMUND
1891-1959, American
m/Edmund Goulding
Love Your Magic Spell
  Is Everywhere
  w/Elsie Janis
Mam'selle
  w/Mack Gordon

GOUNOD,
CHARLES FRANCOIS
1818-1893, French
m/Charles Francois Gounod
(adapted from J.S. Bach's "1st
Prelude In C Major Of The Well
Tempered Clavier")
  w/Alphone De Lamartine
Ave Maria (Hail Mary) (Ave Maria
  Plena Dominus Tecum)

GRAFF, GEORGE
1886, American
w/George Graff
I Love The Name Of Mary
  m/Chauncey Olcott
Till The Sands Of The Desert
  Grow Cold
  m/Ernest R. Ball
When Irish Eyes Are Smiling
  m/Ernest R. Ball

GRAHAM, ROGER
1885-1938, American
w/Roger Graham
m/Spencer Williams, Dave Peyton
I Ain't Got Nobody (1916)

GRAHAM, STEVE
American
w&m/Steve Graham
Back To Donegal (1942)

GRAINGER,
PERCY ALDRIDGE
1882-1961, American
m/Percy Aldridge Grainger (instr.)
Clog Dance
Country Gardens
In A Nutshell
Kipling "Jungle Book"
Molly On The Shore
Spoon River

GRANT, BERT
1878-1951, American
m/Bert Grant
Along The Rocky Road To
  Dublin (1915)
  w/Joseph Young
Arrah Go On I'm Gonna Go
  Back To Oregon (1916)
  w/Joseph Young,
  Samuel M. Lewis
Don't Blame It All On
  Broadway (1913)
  wJoseph Young,
  Harry Williams

**If I Knock The "L" Out Of
 Kelly (1916)**
   w/Joseph Young,
   Samuel M. Lewis
**When The Angelus
 Is Ringing (1914)**
   w/Joseph Young

GRAVES, JOHN WOODCOCK
18th Century, English
w/John Woodcock Graves
Music from traditional English folk
sources; composer unknown.
**D'ye Ken John Peel (also known
 as "John Peel") (1820)**

GRAY, ALLAN
English
m/Allan Gray
Film scores:
African Queen, The (1951)
Canterbury Tale, A
Stairway To Heaven

GRAY, CHAUNCEY
1904, American
w&m/Chauncey Gray
in co w/Fredd Hamm, Dave Bennett
Bye Bye Blues

GRAY, JERRY
1915, American
m/Jerry Gray
Pennsylvania 6-5000
   w/Carl Sigman
String Of Pearls, A
   w/Eddie De Lange

GRAY, WILLIAM B.
American
w&m/William B. Gray
**She Is More to Be Pitied
 Than Censured**

GREAN, CHARLES
American
w&m/Charles Grean
Thing, The

GREAVES, R. B.
American
w&m/R.B. Greaves
Take A Letter Maria (1970)

GREEN, ADOLPH
1915, American
All words/Betty Comden and
Adolph Green
Be A Santa
   m/Jule Styne
Comes Once In A Lifetime
   m/Jule Styne
I Get Carried Away
   m/Leonard Bernstein
It's Love
   m/Leonard Berstein
French Lesson, The
   m/Betty Comden, Adolph Green

Just In Time
   m/Jule Styne
Little Bit In Love, A
   m/Leonard Bernstein
Lonely Town
   m/Leonard Bernstein
Long Before I Knew You
   m/Jule Styne
Make Someone Happy
   m/Jule Styne
New York, New York
   m/Leonard Bernstein
Ohio
   m/Leonard Bernstein
Party's Over, The
   m/Jule Styne
Quiet Girl, A
   m/Leonard Bernstein
Wrong Note Rag
   m/Leonard Bernstein

GREEN, AL
1946, American
w&m/Al Green
Back Up Train
Belle
Call Me (Come Back Home)
   in co w/Al Jackson Jr.
Full Of Fire
Here I Am (Come And Take Me)
I'm Still In Love With You
Let's Stay Together
   in co w/Willie Mitchell,
   Al Jackson Jr.
Look What You Done For Me
   in co w/Willie Mitchell,
   Al Jackson Jr.
(I'm So) Tired Of Being Alone
Oh Me Oh My
Sha-La-La Make Me Happy
You Ought To Be With Me

GREEN, BUD
1897, American
w/Bud Green
Alabamy Bound
   co-lyricist Buddy DeSylva
   m/Ray Henderson
Flat Foot Floogie
   m/Bulee (Slim) Gaillard
I'll Always Be In Love With You
   m/Sam H. Stept
Once In A While
   m/Michael Edwards
Sentimental Journey
   m/Les Brown, Ben Homer
That's My Weakness Now
   m/Sam H. Stept

GREEN, EDDIE
American
w&m/Eddie Green
**Good Man Is Hard To Find, A
 (1918)**

GREEN, JOHN
1908, American
m/John Green
Body And Soul
   w/Edward Heyman, Robert Sour,
   Frank Eyton
Coquette
   co-lyricist Carmen Lombardo
   w/Gus Kahn
Easy Come, Easy Go
   w/Martin Charnin
I Cover The Waterfront
   w/Edward Heyman
I Wanna Be Loved
   w/Edward Heyman, Billy Rose
Out Of Nowhere
   w/Edward Heyman
Film scores:
An American In Paris (1954)
   in co w/Saul Chaplin
Great Caruso, The (1951)
It Happened In Brooklyn (1947)
Pepe (1960)
Raintree County (1957)
They Shoot Horses, Don't
 They (1969)
Weekend At The Waldorf (1945)
Easter Parade (1948)
Oliver (1968)

GREEN, LIL
1922-1954, American
w&m/Lil Green
Romance In The Dark

GREEN, PETER
1948, English
w&m/Peter Green
Albatross
Black Magic Woman

GREENE, JOE
1915
w&m/Joe Greene
**Across The Alley From
 The Alamo**
And Her Tears Flowed Like Wine
   in co w/Stan Kenton

GREENAWAY, ROGER
1942, English
w&m/Roger Greenaway
in co w/Roger Cook, except as noted
Doctor's Orders
Here It Comes Again
**Here Comes That Rainy Day
 Feeling Again**
**I'd Like To Teach The World To
 Sing (In Perfect Harmony)**
   in co w/Billy Davis,
   Bill Backer, Roger Cook
It's Like We Never Said Goodbye
   in co w/Geoffrey Stephens
**Love Grows (Where My Rosemary
 Goes)**

Jeans On
in co w/David Dundas
Say You'll Stay Until Tomorrow
Softly Whispering I Love You
You've Got Your Troubles

GREENFIELD, HOWARD
1939, American
w&m/Howard Greenfield
Breaking In A Brand New
 Broken Heart
in co w/Jack Keller
Breaking Up Is Hard To Do
in co w/Neil Sedaka
Calendar Girl
in co w/Neil Sedaka

Crying In the Rain

in co w/Carole King
Diary, The
in co w/Neil Sedaka
Everybody's Somebody's Fool
in co w/Jack Keller
Fallin'
in co w/Neil Sedaka
Foolish Little Girl
in co w/Helen Miller
Frankie
in co w/Neil Sedaka
Happy Birthday Sweet Sixteen
in co w/Neil Sedaka
I Waited Too Long
in co w/Neil Sedaka
It Hurts To Be In Love
in co w/Helen Miller
Little Devil
in co w/Neil Sedaka
Love Will Keep Us Togehter
in co w/Neil Sedaka
My Heart Has A Mind Of Its Own
in co w/Jack Keller
Next Door To An Angel
in co w/Neil Sedaka
Oh Carol
in co w/Neil Sedaka
One Day Of Your Life
in co w/Neil Sedaka
Puppet Man
in co w/Neil Sedaka
Rainy Jane
in co w/Neil Sedaka
Rumors
in co w/Helen Miller
Solitaire
in co w/Neil Sedaka
Stairway To Heaven
in co w/Neil Sedaka
Stupid Cupid
in co w/Neil Sedaka
Venus In Blue Jeans
in co w/Jack Keller
Where The Boys Are
in co w/Neil Sedaka

GREENWICH, ELLIE
1941, American
w&m/Ellie Greenwich
in co w/Jeff Barry
See list of selections under
Jeff Barry.

GREER, JESSE
1896, American
m/Jesse Greer
Baby Blue Eyes (1922)
in co w/Walter Hirsch,
George Jessel
Flapperette (instr.) (1926)
Sleepy Head (1926)
w/Benny Davis

GREVER MARIA
1894-1951, Mexican/American
m/Maria Grever (and Spanish words)
Jurame (Promise Love)
Eng. w/Frederick
Herman Martens
Lamento Gitano (instr.)
Magic Is The Moonlight
Eng. w/Charles Pasquale
Ti-Pi-Tin
Eng. w/Raymond Leveen
What A Diff'rence A Day Made
(Cuando Vuelva A Tu Lado)
Eng. w/Stanley Adams

GREY, CLIFFFORD
1887-1941, English
w/Clifford Grey
Got A Date With An Angel
co-lyricist Sonnie Miller
m/Joseph Towbridge,
Jack Waller
Hallelujah
co-lyricist Leo Robin
m/Vincent Youmans
If You Were The Only Girl In
 The World
m/Nat D. Ayer
Rogue Song, The
m/Herbert Stothart
Sally
m/Jerome Kern
Valencia
m/Jose Padilla
Wild Rose
m/Jerome Kern

GREY, JOSEPH W.
1879-1956, American
w/Joseph W. Grey
Runnin' Wild
co-lyricist Leo Wood
m/A. Harrington Gibbs

GRIER, JAMES W. (Jimmie)
19902-1959
m/James W. Grier

Object Of My Affection, The
in co w/Pinky Tomlin, Coy Poe
What's The Reason
in co w/Pinky Tomlin

GRIFFES, CHARLES
TOMLINSON
1884-1920, American
m/Charles Tomlinson Griffes (instr.)
Pleasure Dome Of Kubla Khan
White Peacock, The (from
 "Roman Sketches") (1917)

GRIFFIN, KEN
American
m/Ken Griffen
Eng. w/Hal Cotton
You Can't Be True Dear (1948)
Music adapted from the German
song "Du Kannst Nicht Treu
Sein" (1935)
m/Hans Otten
German w/Gerhard Ebeler

GROFE, FERDE
1892-1972, American
m/Ferde Grofe
Alice Blue (instr.)
Daybreak (from the Grand
 Canyon Suite)
w/Harold Adamson
Heliotrope (instr.)
Indigo (instr.)
Wonderful One
co-composer Paul Whiteman
(adapted from a melody by
Marshall Nielan)
w/Dorothy Terris

GROSS, HENRY
1950, American
w&m/Henry Gross
Shannon

GROSS, WALTER
1909, American
m/Walter Gross
Tenderly
w/Jack Lawrence

GROUYA, THEODORE J. (Ted)
1910, Romanian/American
m/Theodore Grouya
Flamingo
w/Edmund Anderson
In My Arms
w/Frank Loesser

GRUBER, EDMUND L.
1882, American
w&m/Edmund L. Gruber
Caissons Go Rolling Along, the
(The Caisson Song)
(arrangement by John Philip
Sousa was entitled "The Field
Artillery March")

GRUBER, FRANZ XAVIER
German
m/Franz Xavier Gruber
w/Joseph Mohr
Silent Night! Holy Night!
 (Stille Nacht, Heilige Nacht)
 (1818)
GRUSIN, DAVE
American
m/Dave Grusin
Film scores:
Divorce American Style (1967)
Goodbye Girl, The (1977)
Goodbye Girl, the (1977)
Graduate, The (1967)
Heart Is A Lonely Hunter, The (1968)
Heaven Can Wait (1978)
TV theme:
Good Times

GUARALDI, VINCE
American
w&m/Vince Guaraldi
in co w/Carel Werber
Cast Your Fate To
 The Wind (1965)
Film score:
Boy Named Charlie Brown, A

GUIDRY, ROBERT
American
w&m/Robert Guidry
See You Later Alligator (1956)

GUION, DAVID WENDELL
DE FENTRESSE
1892, American
w&m/David Wendell De Fentresse
Guion
Harmonica Player, The
Million Dollar Mystery Rag
My Country Love Song
Texas Fox Trot
GULESIAN, GRACE WARNER
American
m/Grace Warner Gulesian
w/Sam Walter Foss
House By the Side Of The
 Road,The (1927)

GUMMOE, JOHN
American
w&m/John Gummoe
Rhythm Of The Rain (1973)

GUTHRIE, ARLO
1947, American
w&m/Arlo Guthrie
Alice's Restaurant
Comin' Into Los Angeles
Motorcycle Song, The

GUTHRIE, WOODY
(Woodrow Wilson Guthrie)
1912-1967, American
w&m/Woody Guthrie

Ain't Gonna Be Treated This Way
Bound For Glory
Dedorjee
 m/Martin Hoffman
Hard Ain't It Hard
Hey Lolly Lolly
Poor Boy
So Long It's Been Good To
 Know Yuh
This Land Is Your Land
Tom Joad
Union Maid
Vigilante Man
Worried Man Blues

Addenda:

GORE, MICHAEL
American
w&m/Michael Gore

Fame (1980)
 in co w/D. Pritchard

POPULAR COMPOSERS
& LYRICISTS

H

HADJIDAKIS, MANOS
Greek
m/Manos Hadjidakis
Never On Sunday (1960)
w/Billy Towne
Film scores:
Never On Sunday
Topkapi

HAGEMAN, RICHARD
1882-1966, American
w&m/Richard Hageman
I Hear America Calling
Film scores:
Fort Apache
Fugitive, The
If I Were King
Long Voyage Home, The
She Wore A Yellow Ribbon
Stagecoach (1939)

HAGGARD, MERLE
1937, American
w&m/Merle Haggard
Bottle Let Me Down, The
Branded Man
Colorado (Have You Ever Been
  Down To)
Daddy Frank (The Guitar Man)
Dark As A Dungeon
Everybody's Had The Blues
Fighting Side Of Me, The
Grandma Harp
Heaven Was A Drink Of Wine
  in co w/R. Lane
Hungry Eyes
I Can't Be Myself
I Take A Lot Of Pride
  In What I Am
I Wonder If They Ever Think
  Of Me
If We Make It
  Through December
It's All In The Movies
Jesus Takes A Hold
Legend Of Bonnie And Clyde
  in co w/Bonnie Owens
Livin' With The Shades
  Pulled Down
Mama Tried
My Own Kind Of Hat
  in co w/R. Lane
Okie From Muskogee
  in co w/Roy Edward Burris
Old Man From the Mountain, The
Sam Hill
Shoulder To Cry On, A
Someday We'll Look Back
Sing A Bad Song
Swinging Doors
Tulare Dust
(Today) I Started
  Loving You Again
  in co w/Bonnie Owens
Workin' Man Blues

HAGGART, ROBERT (Bob)
1914, American
m/Robert Haggart
Big Noise From Winnetka
  w/Ray Bauduc
What's New
  w/Johnny Burke

HAGUE, ALBERT
1920, American
m/Albert Hague
w/Arnold B. Horwitt
Young And Foolish

HALEY, ED
American
w&m/Ed Haley
Fountain In The Park, The
  (While Strolling In The Park
  One Day)

HALL, DARYL
1949, American
w&m/Daryl Hall
Back Together Again
  in co w/John Oates
Do What You Want, Be What
  You Are
  in co w/John Oates
It's A Laugh
  in co w/John Oates
Rich Girl
Sara Smile
  in co w/John Oates
She's Gone
  in co w/John Oates
Wait For Me

HALL, JOHN
1948, American
w&m/John Hall
in co w/Johanna Hall
Dance With Me
Still The One

HALL, TOM T.
1936, American
w&m/Tom T. Hall
Country Is
Day That Clayton Delaney
  Died, The
DJ For A Day
Faster Horses
Harper Valley P.T.A.
Hello Viet Nam
Homecoming
I Like Beer
I Love
I Washed My Face In
  The Morning Dew
If I Ever Fall In Love With
  A Honky Tonk Girl
Mad
Margie's At The Lincoln Park Inn
Me And Jesus
Old Dogs, Children And
  Watermelon Wine

One More Mile
Ravishing Ruby
That Song Is Driving Me Crazy
That's How I Got To Memphis
Week In A County Jail, A
What We're Fighting For
You Show Me Your Heart
Your Man Loves You Honey

HALL, WENDELL WOODS
1896, American
w&m/Wendell Woods Hall
It Ain't Gonna Rain No Mo' (1923)
  (based on an old folk tune of
  America's southern region)

HAM, PETER
1947-1975, English (Wales)
w&m/Peter Ham
in co w/Thomas Evans
Baby Blue
Come And Get It
Without You

HAMBLEN, STUART
1908, American
w&m/Stuart Hamblen
It Is No Secret
  (What God Can Do)
King Of All Kings, The
My Mary
Texas Plains
These Things Shall Pass
This Ole House
Until Then

HAMILTON, ARTHUR
1928, American
w&m/Arthur Hamilton
Cry Me A River

HAMILTON, NANCY
1908, American
w/Nancy Hamilton
m/Morgan Lewis
How High The Moon
Old Soft Shoe, The

HAMLISCH, MARVIN
1944, American
m/Marvin Hamlisch
Better Than Ever
  w/Carole Bayer Sager
If You Remember Me
  w/Carole Bayer Sager
Last Time I Felt Like This, The
  w/Alan & Marilyn Bergman
Life Is What You Make It
  w/Johnny Mercer
My Love Goes With You
  w/Carole Bayer Sager
Nobody Does It Better
  w/Carole Bayer Sager
One
  w/Edward Kleban
They're Playing Our Song
  w/Carole Bayer Sager

Through The Eyes Of Love
(theme from Ice Castles)
   w/Carole Bayer Sager
Sunshine, Lollipops
 And Rainbows
   w/Howard Liebling
Way We Were, The
   w/Marilyn & Alan Bergman
What I Did For Love
   w/Edward Kleban
Film scores:
April Fools, The
Chapter Two (1979)
Fat City
Kotch
Swimmer, The
Take The Money And Run

HAMMERSTEIN II, OSCAR
1895-1960, American
w/Oscar Hammerstein II
All At Once You Love Her
   m/Richard Rodgers
All The Things You Are
   m/Jerome Kern
Bali Hai
   m/Richard Rodgers
Can't Help Lovin' Dat
 Man Of Mine
   m/Jerome Kern
Carefully Taught (You
 Have To Be)
   m/Richard Rodgers
Climb Ev'ry Mountain
   m/Richard Rodgers
Cockeyed Optimist, A
   m/Richard Rodgers
Desert Song, The (Blue Heaven)
   co-lyricist Otto Harbach
   m/Sigmund Romberg
Don't Ever Leave Me
   m/Jerome Kern
Do-Re-Mi
   m/Richard Rodgers
Edelweiss
   m/Richard Rodgers
Everybody's Got A Home But Me
   m/Richard Rodgers
Fellow Needs A Girl, A
   m/Richard Rodgers
Folks Who Live On The Hill, The
   m/Jerome Kern
Gentleman Is A Dope, The
   m/Richard Rodgers
Getting To Know You
   m/Richard Rodgers
Happy Talk
   m/Richard Rodgers
Hello Young Lovers
   m/Richard Rodgers
Honey Bun
   m/Richard Rodgers
I Caint Say No
   m/Richard Rodgers

I Enjoy Being A Girl
   m/Richard Rodgers
I Have Dreamed
   m/Richard Rodgers
I Whistle A Happy Tune
   m/Richard Rodgers
I Won't Dance
   co-lyricist Otto Harbach
   m/Jerome Kern
If I Loved You
   m/Richard Rodgers
I'll Take Romance
   m/Ben Oakland
I'm Gonna Wash That Man Right
 Outa My Hair
   m/Richard Rodgers
I'm In Love With A
 Wonderful Guy
   m/Richard Rodgers
I've Told Every Little Star
   m/Jerome Kern
Indian Love Call
   co-lyricist Otto Harbach
   m/Rudolf Friml
It Might As Well Be Spring
   m/Richard Rodgers
It's A Grand Night For Singing
   m/Richard Rodgers
June Is Bustin' Out All Over
   m/Richard Rodgers
Kiss To Build A Dream On, A
   co-lyricist Burt Kalmar
   m/Harry Ruby
Last Time I Saw Paris, The
   m/Jerome Kern
Life Upon The Wicked Stage
   m/Jerome Kern
Love, Look Away
   m/Richard Rodgers
Lover Come Back To Me
   m/Sigmund Romberg
Make Believe
   m/Jerome Kern
Maria
   m/Richard Rodgers
Mist Over The Moon, A
   m/Ben Oakland
My Favorite Things
   m/Richard Rodgers
No Other Love
   m/Richard Rodgers
Oh, What A Beautiful Morning
   m/Richard Rodgers
Oklahoma
   m/Richard Rodgers
Ol' Man River
   m/Jerome Kern

One Alone
   co-lyricist Otto Harbach
   m/Sigmund Romberg

One Kiss
   m/Sigmund Romberg

People Will Say We're In Love
   m/Richard Rodgers
Riff Song, The
   co-lyricist Otto Harbach
   m/Sigmund Romberg
Romance
   m/Sigmund Romberg
Rose-Marie
   co-lyricist Otto Harbach
   m/Rudolf Friml
Shall We Dance
   m/Richard Rodgers
Softly As In a Morning Sunrise
   m/Sigmund Romberg
Soliloquy
   m/Richard Rodgers
Some Enchanted Evening
   m/Richard Rodgers
Something Wonderful
   m/Richard Rodgers
Song Is You, The
   m/Jerome Kern
Song Of The Flame
   co-lyricist Otto Harbach
   m/George Gershwin,
   Herbert Stothar
Song Of The Vagabonds
   m/Rudolf Friml
Sound Of Music, The
   m/Richard Rodgers
Stouthearted Men
   m/Sigmund Romberg
Sunny
   co-lyricist Otto Harbach
   m/Jerome Kern
Surrey With The Fringe
 On Top, The
   m/Richard Rodgers
That's For Me
   m/Richard Rodgers
There Is Nothing Like A Dame
   m/Richard Rodgers
This Nearly Was Mine
   m/Richard Rodgers
Wanting You
   m/Sigmund Romberg
We Kiss In A Shadow
   m/Richard Rodgers
What's The Use Of Wond'rin
   m/Richard Rodgers
When I Grow Too Old To Dream
   m/Sigmund Romberg
Who
   co-lyricist Otto Harbach
   m/Jerome Kern
Why Do I Love You
   m/Jerome Kern
Why Was I Born
   m/Jerome Kern
Wonderful Guy, A
   m/Richard Rodgers
You Are Beautiful
   m/Richard Rodgers

You Are Love
m/Jerome Kern
You Are Never Away
m/Richard Rodgers
You Are Sixteen
m/Richard Rodgers
You'll Never Walk Alone
m/Richard Rodgers
Younger Than Springtime
m/Richard Rodgers

HAMMOND, ALBERT LOUIE
1942, English
w&m/Albert Louie Hammond
Gimme Dat Ding
in co w/Mike Hazelwood
Good Morning Freedom
(Blue Mink)
in co w/Mike Hazelwood
It Never Rains In
Southern California
in co w/Mike Hazelwood
Little Arrows
in co w/Mike Hazelwood
Make Me An Island
in co w/Mike Hazelwood
Oklahoma Sunday Morning
in co w/Mike Hazelwood,
Tony Macaulay
Shame, Shame
in co w/Mike Hazelwood
Train, The (Colors Of Love)
in co w/Mike Hazelwood
When I Need You
in co w/Carole Bayer Sager
HAMPTON, GLADYS
American
w&m/Gladys Hampton
in co w/Regina Adams, Ace Adams
Everybody's Somebody's
Fool (1950)
HAMPTON, LIONEL
1913, American
w&m/Lionel Hampton
Beulah's Boogie
Evil Gal Blues
in co w/Leonard Feather
Flyin' Home
in co w/Benny Goodman
Midnight Sun
in co w/Joseph F. (Sonny) Burke
Red Top
in co w/Ben Kynard
Salty Papa Blues
in co w/Leonard Feather
HANBY, BENJAMIN RUSSELL
American
w&m/Benjamin Russell Hanby
Darling Nellie Gray (1856)

HANCOCK, HERBERT
JEFFREY (Herbie)
1940, American
w&m/Herbie Hancock
Canteloupe Island
Chameleon

Hang Up Your Hang Ups
I Thought It Was You
Maiden Voyage
Ready Or Not
Tell Everybody
Waltermelon Man

HANDY, W.C.
1873-1958, American
m/W. C. Handy
Aunt Hagar's Blues
w/J. Tim Brymn
Beale St. Blues
w&m/W.C. Handy
East Of St. Louis Blues
w&m/W. C. Handy
Joe Turner Blues
w&m/W.C. Handy
John Henry Blues
w&m/W. C. Handy
Memphis Blues, The
w/George A Norton
St. Louis Blues
w&m/W.C. Handy

HANIGHEN, BERNARD D.
1935, American
m/Bernard D. Hanighen
Bob White (Watcha Gonna
Swing Tonight?)
in co w/Johnny Mercer
Mountain High, Valley Low
in co w/Raymond Scott

HANKEY, KATHERINE
English
w/Katherine Hankey
m/William G. Fischer
I Love To Tell The Story (1874)

HANLEY, JAMES FREDERICK
1892-1942, American
m/James Frederick Hanley
Back Home Again In Indiana
w/Ballard MacDonald
Just A Cottage Small
By A Waterfall
w/Buddy De Sylva
Rose Of Washington Square
w/Ballard MacDonald
Second Hand Rose
w/Grant Clarke
Zing! Went The Strings
Of My Heart
w&m/James Frederick Hanley

HARBACH, OTTO ABELS
1873-1963, American
w/Otto Harbach
Allah's Holiday
m/Rudolf Friml
Cossack Love Song, The
co-lyricist Oscar Hammerstein II
m/Herbert Stothart
Cuddle Up A Little
Closer, Lovey Mine
m/Karl Hoschna

Desert Song, The (Blue Heaven)
co-lyricist Oscar Hammerstein II
m/Sigmund Romberg
Every Little Movement Has
A Meaning All Its Own
m/Karl Hoschna
Giannina Mia
m/Rudolf Friml
I Won't Dance
co-lyricist Oscar Hammerstein II
m/Jerome Kern
Indian Love Call
co-lyricist Oscar Hammerstein II
m/Rudolf Friml
Love Nest, The
m/Louis A Hirsch
No No Nanette
m/Otto Harbach
One Alone
co-lyricist Oscar Hammerstein II
m/Sigmund Romberg
Rose-Marie
co-lyricist Oscar Hammerstein II
m/Rudolf Friml
Riff Song
co-lyricist Oscar Hammerstein II
m/Sigmund Romberg
Romance
co-lyricist Oscar Hammerstein II
m/Sigmund Romberg
Sunny
co-lyricist Oscar Hammerstein II
m/Jerome Kern
Song Of The Flame
co-lyricist Oscar Hammerstein II
m/George Gershwin,
Herbert Stothart
She Didn't Say Yes
m/Jerome Kern
Smoke Gets In Your Eyes
m/Jerome Kern
Sympathy
m/Rudolf Friml
Touch Of Your Hand, The
m/Jerome Kern
Who
co-lyricist Oscar Hammerstein II
m/Jerome Kern
Yesterdays
co-lyricist Oscar Hammerstein II
m/Jerome Kern

HARBURG, E.Y. (Yip)
1898, American
w/E.Y. Harburg
April In Paris
m/Vernon Duke
Begat, The
m/Burton Lane
Brother Can You Spare A Dime
m/Jay Gorney
Buds Won't Bud
m/Harold Arlen

Ding Dong The Witch Is Dead
  m/Harold Arlen
Down With Love
  m/Harold Arlen
Eagle And Me, The
  m/Harold Arlen
Evelina
  m/Harold Arlen
Fun To Be Fooled
  co-lyricist Ira Gershwin
  m/Harold Arlen
Happiness Is A Thing Called Joe
  m/Harold Arlen
How Are Things In Glocca Morra
  m/Burton Lane
I Could Go On Singing
  m/Harold Arlen
**I Don't Think I'll End
 It All Today**
  m/Harold Arlen
I Got A Song
  m/Harold Arlen
I Like The Looks Of You
  m/Vernon Duke
If I Only Had A Brain
  m/Harold Arlen
If This Isn't Love
  m/Burton Lane
In Your Own Quiet Way
  m/Harold Arlen
It's Only A Paper Moon
  co-lyricist Billy Rose
  m/Harold Arlen
Lat Night When We Were Young
  m/Harold Arlen
**Let's Take A Walk Around
 The Block**
  co-lyricist Ira Gershwin
  m/Harold Arlen
Look To The Rainbow
  m/Burton Lane
Lydia The Tatooed Lady
  m/Harold Arlen
Over The Rainbow
  m/Harold Arlen
Right As The Rain
  m/Harold Arlen
Suddenly
  m/Vernon Duke
Take It Slow Joe
  m/Harold Arlen
That Old Devil Moon
  m/Burton Lane
**There's A Great Day
 Coming Manana**
  m/Burton Lane
We're Off To See The Wizard
  m/Harold Arlen
What Is There To Say
  m/Vernon Duke
**When I'm Not Near The Girl I
 Love**
  m/Burton Lane

You're A Builder Upper
  co-lyricist Ira Gershwin
  m/Harold Arlen

HARDIN, TIM
1940, American
w&m/Tim Hardin
If I Were A Carpenter
Lady Came From Baltimore, The
Morning Dew
Reason To Believe

HARLINE, LEIGH
1907, American
m/Leigh Harline
w/Ned Washington
Give A Little Whistle
Hi Diddle Dee Dee
Jiminy Cricket
When You Wish Upon A Star
Film scores:
Broken Lance
Desert Rats
Farmer's Daughter, The
Johnny Angel
**Mr. Blandings Builds His
 Dream House**
Pinocchio
Pride Of The Yankees
Snow White And The Seven Dwarfs
Ten North Frederick
**Wonderful World Of The
 Brothers Grimm, The**

HARLING, W. FRANKE
1887-1958, American
m/W. Franke Harling
Beyond The Blue Horizon
  co-composer Richard Whiting
  w/Leo Robin
Corps, The (West Point Hymn)
  w&m/W. Franke Harling
Sing You Sinners
  w/Sam Coslow

HARMATI, SANDOR
1892-1936, Hungarian/American
m/Sandor Harmati
w/Edward Heyman
Blue Bird Of Happiness

HARMS, DALLAS
American
w&m/Dallas Harms
Old Man And His Horn
Paper Rosie

HARNEY, BENJAMIN R.
1871-1938, American
w&m/Benjamin R. Harney
Cakewalk In The Sky, The
I Love My Little Honey
**Mister Johnson Turn Me
 Loose (1896)**
**You've Been A Good Wagon
 But You Done
 Broke Down (1894)**

HARNICK, SHELDON
1924, American
w/Sheldon Harnick
in co with music by Jerry Bock. See
list of selections under Jerry Bock.
Add't. Songs/Sheldon Harnick
Someone Is Sending Me Flowers
  m/David Baker

HARRIS, ART
American
w&m/Art Harris
in co w/Fred Jay
What Am I Living For (1958)

HARRIS, CHARLES K.
1867-1930, American
w&m/Charles K. Harris
After The Ball (1892)
Always In The Way (1903)
**Break The News
 To Mother (1897)**
For Old Times Sake (1900)
Goodbye My Lady Love (1904)
  in co w/Joseph E. Howard
**Hello, Central, Give Me
 Heaven (1901)**
**I've A Longing In My Heart For
 You, Louise (1900)**
**I've Just Come Back To Say
 Goodbye (1897)**
**Nobody Knows, Nobody
 Cares (1909)**
One Night In June (1899)
Would You Care (1905)

HARRIS, EMMYLOU
1949, American
w&m/Emmylou Harris
in co w/Rodney Crowell
Boulder To Birmingham

HARRIS, ROLF
Australian
w&m/Rolf Harris
**Tie Me Kangaroo Down
 Sport (1960)**

**HARRIS, WILLARD
PALMER (Bill)**
1916-1974, American
m/Bill Harris (instr.)
Bijou
Everywhere
Your Father's Moustache
  in co w/Woody Herman,
  Chubby Jackson

HARRISON, GEORGE
1943, English
w&m/George Harrison
All Things Must Pass
Apple Scruffs
Art Of Dying, The
Awaiting On You All
Ballad Of Sir Frankie Crisp

Bangla Desh
Behind That Locked Door
Beware Of Darkness
Blow Away
Crackerbox Palace
Dark Horse
Deep Blue
Ding-Dong, Ding-Dong
Give Me Love
  (Give Me Peace)
Govinda
Hear Me Lord
Here Comes The Sun
I Don't Care Anymore
If I Needed Someone
Isn't It A Pity
Living In The Material World
Maya Love
My Sweet Lord
Something
This Guitar
What Is Life
While My Guitar Gently Weeps
World Of Stone
You

HARRISON, WILBERT
American
w&m/Wilbert Harrison
Let's Work Together (1941)

HARRY, DEBORAH
English
w&m/Deborah Harry
Call Me (1979)
  in co w/Georgio Moroder
Dreaming (1979)
  in co w/Chris Stein
Heart Of Glass (1978)
  in co w/Chris Stein
One Way Or Another (1978)
  in co w/Nigel Harrison

HART, FREDDIE
1933, American
w&m/Freddie Hart
Bless Your Heart
  in co w/Jack Lebsock
Easy Loving
Got The All Overs For You
Hang In There Girl
If You Can't Feel It
My Hang Up Is You
Trip To Heaven
Wall, The

HART, LORENZ (Larry)
1895-1943
w/Lorenz (Larry) Hart
m/Richard Rodgers
Babes In Arms
**Bewitched, Bothered And
  Bewildered**
Blue Moon
Blue Room

Dancing On The Ceiling
Easy To Remember, Its
Everything I've Got
Falling In Love With Love
Girl Friend, The
Have You Met Miss Jones
Here In My Arms
I Could Write A Book
I Didn't Know What Time It Was
I Married An Angel
I Wish I Were In Love Again
Isn't It Romantic
It Never Entered My Mind
It's Easy To Remember
Johnny One Note
Lady Is A Tramp, The
Little Girl Blue
Love Me Tonight
Lover
Manhattan
Mimi
Most Beautiful Girl In
  The World, The
Mountain Greenery
My Funny Valentine
My Heart Stood Still
My Romance
On Your Toes
Over And Over Again
Ship Without A Sail, A
Sing For Your Supper
Spring Is Here
Ten Cents A Dance
There's A Small Hotel
This Can't Be Love
Thou Swell
Tree In The Park, A
Wait Till You See Her
Where Or When
Where's That Rainbow
Why Can't I
With A song In My Heart
You Took Advantage Of Me
You're Nearer
Zip
HARTFORD, JOHN
1937, American
w&m/John Hartford
Gentle On My Mind
HASTINGS, THOMAS
American
m/Thomas Hastings
w/Augustus Montague Toplady
Rock Of Ages (1832)

HATCH, TONY
1933, English
w&m/Tony Hatch
Call Me
Don't Sleep In The Subway
  in co w/Jackie Trent
Downtown
I Know A Place
Look At Mine
My Love

HAWKINS, COLEMAN
1904-1969, American
m/Coleman Hawkins
Queer Notions
Rifftide

HAWKINS, SCREAMIN' JAY
American
w&m/Screamin' Jay Hawkins
I Put A Spell On You

HAWKINS, WALTER
American
w&m in co w/Tremayne Hawkins
He's That Kind Of Friend

HAVEZ, JEAN
1874-1925, American
w&m/Jean Havez
Darktown Poker Club
**Everybody Works But
  Father (1905)**
**Sailing Down The Chesapeake
  Bay (1913)**
    m/George Botsford

HAWKS, ANNIE SHERWOOD
1835, American
w/Annie Sherwood Hawks
m/Robert Lowry
I Need Thee Ev'ry Hour

HAYMES, BOB
American
w&m/Bob Haymes
in co w/Alan Brandt
That's All

HAYES, ISAAC
1942, American
w&m/Isaac Hayes
Deja Vu
  in co w/Adrienne Anderson
Hold On I'm Coming
  in co w/David Porter
I Thank You
  in co w/David Porter
Soul Man
  in co w/David Porter
Theme from "Shaft"

HAYES, JERRY
American
w&m/Jerry Hayes
Rollin' With The Flow (1979)

HAYMAN, RICHARD
1920, American
m/Richard Hayman
Carriage Trade
Dansero
No Strings Attached

HAYS, J.H. (Red)
American
w&m/J.H. (Red) Hays
in co w/Jack Rhodes
Satisfied Mind, A (1955)

**HAYS, WILLIAM
SHAKESPEARE**
1837-1907
w&m/William Shakespeare Hays
Drummer Boy Of Shiloh
Early In De Mornin'
Evangeline
Little Old Log Cabin In The Lane
Mollie Darling
Number Twenty Nine
Roll Out, Heave That Cotton
Susan Jane
Walk In De Middle Of The Road
We Parted By The River
Write Me A Letter

**HAYTON, LEONARD
GEORGE (Lennie)**
1908-1970, American
m/Leonard George Hayton
Film scores:
Battleground
Harvey Girls, The
Hello Dolly (1968)
    in co w/Lionel Newman
Hucksters, The
On The Town
    in co w/Roger Edens
Pirate, The
Singin' In The Rain
Yank On The Burma Road, A

HAYWARD, JUSTIN
1946, English
w&m/Justin Hayward
Dawning Is The Day
Driftwood
Had To Fall In Love
It's Up To You
Lovely To See You
Never Comes The Day
Nights In White Satin
Question
Story In Your Eyes, The
You Can Never Go Home

HAZLEWOOD, LEE
1929, American
w&m/Lee Hazlewood
Guitar Man
    in co w/Duane Eddy
Houston
Rebel Rouser
    in co w/Duane Eddy
Summer Wine
**These Boots Are Made
  For Walkin'**

**HAZELWOOD,
MICHAEL E. (Mike)**
1942, English
Many songs written in co w/Albert
Louie Hammond. See list of
selections under Albert
Louie Hammond.

HAZZARD, TONY
English
w&m/Tony Hazzard
Fox On The Run (1969)

HEATH, WALTER HENRY (Hy)
1890-1965, American
m/Walter Henry Heath
Clancy Lowered The Boom
    w/Johnny Lange
Mule Train
    w/Johnny Lange, Fred Glickman
Somebody Bigger Than You And I
    w/Johnny Lange, Sonny Burke
**Take These Chains
  From My Heart**
    w/Fred Rose

HEATHERTON, FRED
English
w&m/Fred Heatherton
**I've Got A Lovely Bunch Of
  Cocoanuts (1949, U.S.A.)**

HEBB, BOBBY
1939, American
w&m/Bobby Hebb
Sunny (1970)

HEFTI, NEAL
1922, American
m/Neal Hefti (instr.)
Batman Theme
Coral Reef
Girl Talk
Good Earth, The
Wildroot
Film scores:
Barefoot In The Park (1967)
Harlow (1965)
How To Murder Your Wife (1965)
Sex And The Single Girl (1964)
Odd Couple, The (1968)

HEINDORF, RAY JOHN
1908-1980, American
m/Ray John Heindorf
Pete Kelly's Blues (instr.)
Some Sunday Morning
    co-composer M.K. Jerome
    w/Ted Koehler
Sugarfoot (instr.)
Film scores:
Finian's Rainbow (1968)
Hollywood Canteen (1944)
Jazz Singer, The
Look For the Silver Lining
Music Man, The (1963)
Rhapsody In Blue
Star Is Born, A
This Is the Army (1943)
Up In Arms
    in co w/Louis Forbes (1945)
West Point Story, The
Yankee Doodle Dandy
    in co w/Heinz Roemheld (1942)
Young Man With A Horn (1950)

HENDERSON, MICHAEL
American
w&m/Michael Henderson
Take Me I'm Yours (1978)
Valentine Love
You Are My Starship (1977)

HENDERSON, RAY
1896-1970, American
m/Ray Henderson
Alabamy Bound
    co-composer Bud Green
    w/Buddy DeSylva
Animal Crackers In My Soup
    w/Ted Koehler, Irving Caesar
Best Things In Life Are Free, The
    w/Buddy DeSylva, Lew Brown
Birth Of The Blues
    w/Buddy DeSylva, Lew Brown
Black Bottom
    w/Buddy DeSylva, Lew Brown
Button Up Your Overcoat
    w/Buddy DeSylva, Lew Brown
Bye Bye Blackbird
    w/Mort Dixon
Don't Bring Lulu
    w/Billy Rose, Lew Brown
Five Foot Two, Eyes Of Blue
    w/Samuel M. Lewis,
    Joseph Young
Good News
    w/Buddy DeSylva, Lew Brown
If I Had A Talking Picture Of You
    w/Buddy DeSylva, Lew Brown
I'm A Dreamer, Aren't We All
    w/Lew Brown, Buddy DeSylva
I'm Sitting On Top Of The World
    w/Samuel M. Lewis,
    Joseph Young
It All Depends On You
    w/Buddy DeSylva, Lew Brown
Just A Memory
    w/Buddy DeSylva, Lew Brown
Life Is Just A Bowl Of Cherries
    w/Buddy DeSylva, Lew Brown
Lucky Day
    w/Buddy DeSylva, Lew Brown
Lucky In Love
    w/Buddy DeSylva, Lew Brown
My Sin
    w/Buddy DeSylva, Lew Brown
Oh You Nasty Man
    w/Jack Yellen, Irving Caesar
So Blue
    w/Buddy DeSylva, Lew Brown
Sonny Boy
    w/Buddy DeSylva, Lew Brown,
    Al Jolson
Sunny Side Up
    w/Buddy DeSylva, Lew Brown
Thank Your Father
    w/Buddy DeSylva, Lew Brown
That Old Gang Of Mine
    w/Billy Rose, Mort Dixon

This Is The Missus
w/Lew Brown
Thrill Is Gone, The
w/Buddy DeSylva, Lew Brown
Together
w/Buddy DeSylva, Lew Brown
Varsity Drag, The
w/Buddy DeSylva, Lew Brown
You're The Cream In My Coffee
w/Buddy DeSylva, Lew Brown

HENDRIX, JIMI
1942-1970, American
w&m/Jimi Hendrix
All Along The Watchtower
Are You Experienced
Bold As Love
Fire
Foxy Lady
Freedom
Hey Joe
If 6 Was 9
Manic Depression
Purple Haze
Up From The Skies
Wind Cries Mary, The
You Got Me Floatin'

HENDRICKS, FREDERICK WILMOTH (Wilmouth Houdini)
1901, Trinidad/American
w&m/Frederick Wilmoth Hendricks
Gin And Cocoanut Water
Stone Cold Dead In The Market

HENLEY, DON
1947, American
w&m in co w/Glenn Frey
After The Thrill Is Gone
Best Of My Love
in co w/J.D. Souther
Heartache Tonight
in co w/J.D. Souther, Bob Seger
Hotel California
in co w/Don Felder
I Can't Tell You Why
in co w/T. Schmit
James Dean
in co w/J.D. Souther, Jackson Browne
Lead On
Life In The Fast Lane
in co w/Joe Walsh
Long Run, The
Lyin' Eyes
New Kid In Town
in co w/J.D. Souther
On The Border
in co w/J.D. Souther
One Of These Nights
Sad Cafe
Victim Of Love
in co w/J.D. Souther, Don Felder

HENRY, FRANCIS
1905-1953, American
m/Francis Henry
Little Girl
w/Madeline Hyde

HERBERT, VICTOR
1859-1924, American
m/Victor Herbert
Ah! Sweet Mystery Of Life
w/Rida Johnson Young
All For You
w/Henry Blossom
Angel Face
w/Robert B. Smith
Angelus, The
w/Robert B. Smith
Gypsy Love Song
w/Harry B. Smith
I Want What I Want When I Want It
w/Henry Blossom
I'm Falling In Love With Someone
w/Rida Johnson Young
Indian Summer
w/Al Dubin
Isle Of Our Dreams, The
w/Henry Blossom
Italian Street Song, The
w/Rida Johnson Young
Kiss In The Dark, A
w/Buddy DeSylva
Kiss Me Again (If I Were On The Stage)
w/Henry Blossom
Neapolitan Love Song
w/Henry Blossom
'Neath The Southern Moon
w/Rida Johnson Young
Sweethearts
w/Robert B. Smith
Thine Alone
w/Henry Blossom
To The Land Of My Own Romance
w/Harry B. Smith
Toyland
w/Glen MacDonough
Tramp! Tramp! Tramp!
w/Rida Johnson Young
When You're Away
w/Henry Blossom

HERMAN, JERRY
1932, American
w&m/Jerry Herman
Before The Parade Passes By
Dear World
Hello Dolly
If He Walked Into My Life
It Only Takes A Moment

Mame
Milk And Honey
Open A New Window
Put On Your Sunday Clothes
Shalom
So Long Dearie
We Need A Little Christmas

HERMAN, WOODROW WILSON (Woody)
1913, American
w&m/Woody Herman
Apple Honey
At The Woodchopper's Ball
in co w/Joe Bishop
Blues On Parade
in co w/Toby Tyler
Early Autumn
in co w/Ralph Burns, Johnny Mercer
Northwest Passage
in co w/Ralph Burns
Wildroot
in co w/Neal Hefti
Your Father's Moustache
in co w/Greig Stewart (Chubby) Jackson, Bill Harris

HERNANDEZ, RAFAEL
Puerto Rican
w&m/Rafael Hernandez
Lamento Borincano

HERRMANN, BERNARD
American
m/Bernard Herrmann
Film scores:
All That Money Can Buy (1944)
Citizen Kane (1941)
Fahrenheit 451 (1966)
Ghost And Mrs. Muir, The (1946)
Hatful Of Rain, A (1957)
Jane Eyre (1944)
Journey To The Center Of The Earth (1959)
Man In the Gray Flannel Suit, The (1956)
Magnificent Ambersons, The (1942)
North By Northwest (1959)
Psycho (1960)
Snows Of Kilimanjaro (1952)
Tender Is The Night (1962)

HERRON, JOEL
1916, American
w&m/Joel Herron
I'm A Fool To Want You

HERSHEY, JUNE
American
w&m/June Hershey
in co w/Don Swander
Deep In The Heart Of Texas

HEWITT, JOHN HILL
1801-1890, American
w&m/John Hill Hewitt, except as noted
All Quiet Along The Potomac (1864)
  w/Lamar Fontaine
Carry Me Back To the Sweet Sunny South
Minstrel's Return From The War, The (1825)
Mountain Bugle, The
Our Native Land
Take Me Home Where The Sweet Magnolia Blooms

HEYMAN, EDWARD
1907, American
w/Edward Heyman
Blame It On My Youth
  m/Oscar Levant
Body And Soul
  co-lyrists Robert Sour, Frank Eyton
  m/John Green
Bluebird Of Happiness
  m/Sandor Harmati
Boo-Hoo
  m/Carmen Lombardo, John J. Loeb
Drums In My Heart
  m/Vincent Youmans
Easy Come, Easy Go
  m/John Green
I Cover The Waterfront
  m/John Green
I Wanna Be Loved
  co-lyricist Billy Rose
  m/John Green
My Silent Love
  m/Dana Suesse
Out Of Nowhere
  m/John Green
They Say
  m/Paul Mann, Stephen Weiss
Through The Years
  m/Vincent Youmans
When I Fall In Love
  m/Victor Young
You Ought To Be In Pictures
  m/Dana Suesse

HEYMAN, WERNER
American
m/Werner Heyman
Film scores:
Ninotchka (1939)
One Million B.C. (1940)
Our Hearts Were Young And Gay (1944)
Shop Around The Corner, The (1940)
Topper Returns (1941)

HEYWARD, DuBOSE
1885-1940, American
w/DuBose Heyward
Bess You Is My Woman Now
  co-lyricist Ira Gershwin
  m/George Gershwin
I Got Plenty O' Nuthin'
  co-lyricist Ira Gershwin
  m/George Gershwin
I Loves You Porgy
  co-lyricist Ira Gershwin
  m/George Gershwin
My Man's Gone Now
  m/George Gershwin
Summertime
  m/George Gershwin
Woman Is A Sometime Thing, A
  m/George Gershwin

HILDEBRAND, RAY
American
w&m/Ray Hildebrand
Hey, Paula (1963)

HILL, BILLY
(William Joseph Hill)
1899-1940, American
w/Billy Hill
Call Of The Canyon
  w&m/Billy Hill
Down The Old Oregon Trail
  m/Peter De Rose
Empty Saddles
  w&m/Billy Hill
Glory Of Love, The
  w&m/Billy Hill
In A Mission By The Sea
  m/Peter De Rose
In The Chapel In The Moonlight
  w&m/Billy Hill
On A Little Street In Singapore
  m/Peter De Rose
Last Roundup, the
  w&m/Billy Hill
Lights Out
  w&m/Billy Hill
Old Spinning Wheel, The
  w&m/Billy Hill
Rock-A-Bye Your Baby Blues
  w/Larry Yoell
  m/Billy Hill
There's A Cabin In The Pine
  w&m/Billy Hill
There's A Home In Wyoming
  w&m/Billy Hill
They Cut Down The Old Pine Tree
  in co w/William Raskin

HILL, ROBERT
American
w&m/Robert Hill
in co w/Lester Allen

Kiss Of Fire (1952) (music adapted from A.G. Villoldo's Argentine tango "El Choclo")

HILLIARD, BOB
1918-1971, American
w/Bob Hilliard
Be My Life's Companion
  m/Milton Delugg
Big Brass Band From Brazil
  m/Carl Sigman
Bouquet Of Roses
  m/Steve Nelson
Careless Hands
  m/Carl Sigman
Civilization (Bongo, Bongo, Bongo)
  m/Carl Sigman
Coffee Song, The
  m/Richard Miles
Dear Hearts And Gentle People
  m/Sammy Fain
Dearie
  m/David Mann
I'm Late
  m/Sammy Fain
Every Street's A Boulevard In Old New York
  m/Jule Styne
In The Wee Small Hours Of the Morning
  m/David Mann
Moonlight Gambler
  m/Philip Springer
My Little Corner Of The World
  m/Lee Pockriss
Our Day Will Come
  m/Mort Garson
Red Silk Stockings And Green Perfume
  m/Sammy Mysels
Seven Little Girls
  m/Lee Pockriss
Somebody Bad Stole De Wedding Bell
  m/David Mann
Stay With The Happy People
  m/Jule Styne
Thousand Island Song, The (Florence)
  m/Carl Sigman

HILL, MILDRED J.
1859-1916, American
m/Mildred J. Hill
Happy Birthday To You (originally Good Morning To All)
  w/Patty Smith Hill

HILLMAN, ROC
w&m/Roc Hillman
in co w/Johnny Napton
My Devotion (1942)

HIMBER, RICHARD
1907, American
w&m/Richard Himber
It Isn't Fair

HINE, STUART K.
English
w/Stuart K. Hine
Music attributed to Carl Boberg of
Sweden, with some contention that
melody was adapted from Franz
Schubert's "The Almighty")
How Great Thou Art

HINES, EARL
KENNETH (Fatha)
1905, American
m/Earl Kenneth (Fatha) Hines
Deep Forest
Earl, The
Everything Depends On You
Jelly, Jelly
Mad House
Rosetta
Stormy Monday Blues

HIRSCH, LOUIS ACHILLE
1887-1924, American
w&m/Louis Achille Hirsch
Bacchanal Rag, The
Gaby Glide, The
Hello Frisco Hello
  in co w/Gene Buck

HIRSCH, WALTER
1891, American
w/Walter Hirsch
Bye Bye Baby
  m/Lou Handman
'Deed I Do
  m/Fred Rose
Strange Interlude
  m/Phil Baker, Ben Bernie
Was It Rain
  m/Lou Handman
Who's Your Little Whoo-Zis
  m/Ben Bernie, Al Goering

HIRSCHHORN, JOEL
American
w&m/ Joel Hirschhorn
in co w/Al Kasha
Candle On The Water (1977)
Higher And Higher (1967)
Morning After, The (1972)
Saturday Night In
  The Summertime
We May Never Love Like This
  Again (1974)
Will You Be Staying After
  Sunday (1968)

HODGES, JAMES S. (Jimmy)
1885-1971, American
w&m/James S. Hodges

Someday (You'll Want Me
  To Want You)

HODGES, KENNETH
American
w&m/Kenneth Hodges
And She's Mine (1969)

HODGSON, ROGER
Australian
w&m/Roger Hodgson
in co w/Rick Davies
Bloody Well Right
Give A Little Bit
Goodbye Stranger
Logical Song, the
Take The Long Way Home

HOFFMAN, AL
1902-1960, American
w&m/Al Hoffman
Allegheny Moon
  in co w/Dick Manning
Auf Wiedersehn, My Dear
  in co w/Ed Nelson, Al Goodhart,
  Milton Ager
Bibbidi, Bobbidi, Boo
  in co w/Mack David,
  Jerry Livingston
Chi Baba, Chi Baba
  in co w/Mack David,
  Jerry Livingston
Dream Is A Wish Your Heart
  Makes, A
  in co w/Mack David,
  Jerry Livingston
Everything Stops For Tea
  in co w/Al Goodhart
Fit As A Fiddle
  in co w/Arthur Freed,
  Al Goodhart
Hawaiian Wedding Song, The
  in co w/Charles E. King,
  Dick Manning
Heartaches
  in co w/John Klenner
Hot Diggety
  in co w/Dick Manning
I Apologize
  in co w/Al Goodhart,
  Ed G. Nelson
If I Knew You Were Coming I'd
  Have Baked A Cake
  in co w/Bob Merrill, Clem Watts
I'm Gonna Live Till I Die
  in co w/Mann Curtis, Walter Kent
I'm In A Dancing Mood
  in co w/Maurice Sigler
Little Man You've Had A Busy
  Day
  in co w/Maurice Sigler, Mabel
  Wayne

Mairzy Doats
  in co w/Milton Drake,
  Jerry Livingston
Papa Loves Mambo
  in co w/Bix Reichner,
  Dick Manning
Romance Runs In The Family
  in co w/Al Goodhart, Mann Curtis
Takes Two To Tango
  in co w/Dick Manning
There's No Tomorrow (adapted
  from E. DiCapua's "O Sole Mio")
  in co w/Leo Corday, Leon Carr
What's The Good Word
  Mr. Bluebird
  in co w/Jerry Livingston
Who Walks In When I Walk Out
  in co w/Al Goodhart

HOLIDAY, BILLIE
1915-1959, American
w&m/Billie Holiday
Billie's Blues
Don't Explain
Fine And Mellow
God Bless The Child
Left Alone
Riffin' the Scotch
Strange Fruit
  w/Lewis Allan
Tell Me More And More
  And Then Some
Your Mother's Son-In-Law

HOLINER, MANN
1897-1958, American
w&m in co w/Alberta Nichols
(Mrs. Mann Holiner)
Until The Real Thing
  Comes Along

HOLLAND, BRIAN
American
Many songs written in co w/Eddie
Holland and Lamont Dozier. See list
of selections under Eddie Holland.

Please Mr. Postman
w&m in co w/Robert Bateman,
Freddie Gorman, Georgia Dobbins
and William Garret.

HOLLAND, EDDIE
1939, American
w&m/Eddie Holland
Ain't That Peculiar
  in co w/Norman Whitfield
Ain't Too Proud To Beg
  in co w/Norman Whitfield
All I Need
  in co w/Frank Wilson,
  R.Dean Taylor

Baby I Need Your Loving
  in co w/Brian Holland,
  Lamont Dozier
Baby Love
  in co w/Brian Holland,
  Lamont Dozier
Back In My Arms Again
  in co w/Brian Holland,
  Lamont Dozier
Beauty Is Only Skin Deep
  in co w/Norman Whitfield
Bernadette
  in co w/Brian Holland,
  Lamont Dozier
Can I Get A Witness
  in co w/Brian Holland,
  Lamont Dozier
Come See About Me
  in co w/Brian Holland,
  Lamont Dozier
Happening, The
  in co w/Brian Holland,
  Lamont Dozier
(Love Is Like A) Heat Wave
  in co w/Brian Holland,
  Lamont Dozier
**How Sweet It Is (To Be
  Loved By You)**
  in co w/Brian Holland,
  Lamont Dozier
Heaven Must Have Sent You
  in co w/Brian Holland,
  Lamont Dozier
I Can't Help Myself
  in co w/Brian Holland,
  Lamont Dozier
I Hear A Symphony
  in co w/Brian Holland,
  Lamont Dozier
I Know I'm Losing You
  in co w/Norman Whitfield,
  Cornelius Grant
I'm Ready For Love
  in co w/Brian Holland,
  Lamont Dozier
It's The Same Old Song
  in co w/Brian Holland,
  Lamont Dozier
Jimmy Mack
  in co w/Brian Holland,
  Lamont Dozier
Mickey's Monkey
  in co w/Brian Holland,
  Lamont Dozier
My World Is Empty Without You
  in co w/Brian Holland,
  Lamont Dozier
Nothing But Heartaches
  in co w/Brian Holland,
  Lamont Dozier

Nowhere To Run
  in co w/Brian Holland,
  Lamont Dozier

Reach Out, I'll Be There
  in co w/Brian Holland,
  Lamont Dozier
Reflections
  in co w/Brian Holland,
  Lamont Dozier
Road Runner (I'm A)
  in co w/Brian Holland,
  Lamont Dozier
Seven Rooms Of Gloom
  in co w/Brian Holland,
  Lamont Dozier
Something About You
  in co w/Brian Holland,
  Lamont Dozier
**Shake Me, Wake Me
  (When It's Over)**
  in co w/Brian Holland,
  Lamont Dozier
Standing In The Shadows Of Love
  in co w/Brian Holland,
  Lamont Dozier
Stop! In The Name Of Love
  in co w/Brian Holland,
  Lamont Dozier
Too Many Fish In The Sea
  in co w/Norman Whitfield
**When The Lovelight Starts
  Shining Through His Eyes**
  in co w/Brian Holland,
  Lamont Dozier
Where Did Our Love Go
  in co w/Brian Holland,
  Lamont Dozier
You Can't Hurry Love
  in co w/Brian Holland,
  Lamont Dozier
You Keep Me Hanging On
  in co w/Brian Holland,
  Lamont Dozier
You're A Wonderful One
  in co w/Brian Holland,
  Lamont Dozier

HOLLER, DICK
American
w&m/Dick Holler
**Abraham, Martin And
  John (1964)**

HOLLOWAY, BRENDA
1947, American
w&m/Brenda Holloway
in co w/Patrice Holloway,
Berry Gordy Jr., Frank E. Wilson.
You've Made Me So Very Happy

**HOLLY, BUDDY
(Charles Hardin Holly)**
1938-1959, American
w&m/Buddy Holly
Early In The Morning
It Doesn't Matter Anymore
It's So Easy
  in co w/Norman Petty

Peggy Sue
Raining In My Heart
Rave On
That'll Be The Day
  in co w/Norman Petty,
  Jerry Allison

HOLMES, RUPERT
American
w&m/Rupert Holmes
Answering Machine
**Escape (The Pina Colada
  Song) (1979)**
Him (1979)
**People That You Never Get
  To Love, The**

HOLMES, WILLIAM H.
American
m/William H. Holmes
w/Charles W. Berkeley
**Hand That Rocks The
  Cradle, The (1895)**

HOLOFCENER, LAURENCE
1926, American
w/Laurence Holofcener
m/Jerry Bock
Mr. Wonderful
  co-lyricist George D. Weiss
Too Close For Comfort
  co-lyricist George D. Weiss

HOLT, WILL
1929, American
w&m/Will Holt
Daddy, Roll 'Em
Lemon Tree
One Of Those Songs
Sinner Man

HOLYFIELD, WAYLAND
American
w&m/Wayland Holyfield
I Met A Friend Of Yours Today
  in co w/Bob McDill
I'll Do It All Over Again
  in co w/Bob McDill
**Red Necks, White Socks And
  Blue Ribbon Beer**
  in co w/Bob McDill, Chuck Neese
She Never Knew Me
  in co w/Bob McDill
Some Broken Hearts Never Mend
Till The Rivers All Run Dry
  in co w/Don Williams

HOMER, BEN
1917, American
m/Ben Homer
Sentimental Journey
  in co w/Bud Green, Les Brown

HOOKER, JOHN LEE
1917, American
w&m/John Lee Hooker
Apologize
Baby I Love You

Birmingham Blues
Boogie Chillen'
Crawlin' King Snake
Hobo Blues
I'm In The Mood
   in co w/Jules Taub
Waterfront

HOPE, LAWRENCE
American
w/Lawrence Hope
m/Amy Woodford-Finden
**Kashmiri Song (Pale Hands
I Loved) (1902)**

HOPKINS, JOHN HENRY
American
w&m/John Henry Hopkins
**We Three Kings Of
Orient Are (1857)**

HOPKINS, KENYON
American
m/Kenyon Hopkins
Film scores:
Baby Doll (1956)
Downhill Racer (1969)
Lilith (1964)
Mr. Buddwing (1966)
Twelve Angry Men (1957)
Wild In The Country (1961)

HOPKINSON, JOSEPH
early 18th century, American
w/Joseph Hopkinson
m/Philip Phile
Hail Columbia

HORTON, JOHNNY
1929-1960, American
w&m/Johnny Horton
Honky Tonk Man
   in co w/Tillman Franks,
   Howard Hausey
Sink The Bismarck
   in co w/Tillman Franks
When It's Springtime In Alaska

HORTON, VAUGHN
1911, American
w&m/Vaughn Horton
Mocking Bird Hill
Sugar Foot Rag
   in co w/Hank Garland

HOSCHNA, KARL
1877-1911, German/American
m/Karl Hoschna
**Cuddle Up A Little Closer,
Lovey Mine (1908)**
   w/Otto A. Harbach
**Every Little Movement Has
A Meaning Of Its Own (1910)**
   w/Otto A. Harbach
Girl Of My Dreams, The
   w/Otto A. Harbach
Yama Yama Man, The (1908)
   w/George Collin Davis

**HOUSE, EDDIE,
JAMES JR. (Son)**
1902, American
w&m/Son House
Dry Spell Blues
Grinnin' In Your Face
Hobo
Mississippi County Farm Blues
My Black Mama
Preachin' The Blues
Son's Blues
Trouble Blues

HOWARD, BART
1915, American
w&m/Bart Howard
**Fly Me To The Moon
(In Other Words)**
My Love Is A Wanderer

HOWARD, HARLAN
1929, American
w&m/Harlan Howard
**Above And Beyond
(The Call Of Love)**
Blizzard, The
Busted
Chokin' Kind, The
**Don't Call Me From A Honky
Tonk**
**Excuse Me (I Think I've Got
A Heartache)**
   in co w/Buck Owens
Evil On Your Mind
Foolin' Around
   in co w/Buck Owens
Guy Named Joe, A
Heartaches By The Number
Heartbreak U.S.A.
Hurtin's All Over, The
**I Don't Believe I'll Fall
In Love Today**
I Fall To Pieces
   in co w/Hank Cochran
I Won't Forget You
It's All Over
   in co w/Jan Howard
I've Got A Tiger By The Tail
   in co w/Buck Owens
Mommy For A Day
   in co w/Buck Owens
No Charge
Odds And Ends (Bits And Pieces)
Pick Me Up On Your Way Down
**Second Hand Rose
(Second Hand Heart)**
She Called Me Baby
She's A Little Bit Country
Streets Of Baltimore
   in co w/Buck Owens
Three Steps To The Phone
Under The Influence Of Love
   in co w/Buck Owens
You Comb Her Hair
   in co w/Hank Cochran

You Took Her Off My Hands
   in co w/Wynn Stewart,
   Skeets McDonald
Your Heart Turned Left
Yours Love

HOWARD, JAN
1932, American
w&m/Han Howard
Dis-Satisfied
   in co w/Bill Anderson,
   Carter Howard
I Never Once Stopped Loving You
   in co w/Bill Anderson
Love Is A Sometimes Thing
   in co w/Bill Anderson
My Son

**HOWARD, JOSEPH
EDGAR (Joe)**
1878-1961, American
Goodbye My Lady Love
   w/Charles K. Harris
Hello My Baby
   Ida Emerson
I Wonder Who's Kissing Her Now
   co-composer Harold Orlob
   w/Will M. Hough,
   Frank R. Adams

HOWARD, RICHARD
1890, American
w&m/Richard Howard
**Somebody Else Is Taking
My Place (1937)**
   in co w/Russ Morgan,
   Bob Ellsworth
**When The Leaves Come
Tumbling Down (1922)**

HOWARD, ROLLIN
American
w&m/Rollin Howard
**You Never Miss The Water Till
The Well Runs Dry**

HOWE, JULIA WARD
1819-1910
w/Julia Ward Howe
Music from the melody of "John
Brown's Body", based on "Glory
Hallelujah", believed composed by
William Steffe.
**Battle Hymn Of The Republic,
The**

HUBBARD, FREDDIE
1938, American
w&m/Freddie Hubbard
Backlash
Buhaina's Delight
Can't Let Her Go
First Light
Free For All
Mosaic
Red Clay
Return Of The Prodigal Son, The

Sky Dive
Thermo
Windjammer

HUBBELL, RAYMOND
1879-1954, American
m/Raymond Hubbell
w/John Golden
Poor Butterfly

HUDSON, WILL
1908, American
m/Will Hudson
Moonglow
in co w/Eddie De Lange,
Irving Mills
Organ Grinder's Song, The
in co w/Mitchell Parish,
Irving Mills
Sophisticated Swing (instr.)

HUFF, LEON
American
w&m in co w/Kenneth Gamble

See list of selections under
Kenneth Gamble.
Do It Any Way You Wanna
w&m/Leon Huff

HUNTER, IAN
American
w&m/Ian Hunter
Ships (1979)

HUNTER, IVORY JOE
1923, American
w&m/Ivory Joe Hunter
Dancing In The Streets
in co w/William Stevenson,
Marvin Gaye
Empty Arms
I Almost Lost My Mind
I Need You So
I Quit My Pretty Mama
Since I Met You Baby

HUPFELD, HERMAN
1894-1951, American
w&m/Herman Hupfeld
As Time Goes By
**Let's Put Out The Lights
And Go To Sleep**
Sing Something Simple
**When Yuba Plays The
Rhumba On The Tuba**

HUSKY, FERLIN
(Simon Crum, Terry Preston)
1927, American
w&m/Ferlin Husky
Country Music Is Here To Stay

HYNDE, CHRISSIE
1953, American
w&m/Chrissie Hynde
in co w/Pete Farndon
Brass In Pocket (1979)
Kid (1979)
Up The Neck (1979)
Wait, The (1979)
Tatooed Love Boys (1979)

POPULAR COMPOSERS
& LYRICISTS

I , J

IAN, JANIS
1950, American
w&m/Janis Ian
At Seventeen
Society's Child

IBERT, JACQUES
1890-1962, French
m/Jacques Ibert (instr.)
Little White Donkey, The
(Le petit ane blanc)

IDRISS, RAMEZ (Ramey)
1911, American
w&m/Ramez Idriss
in co w/George Tibbles
Woody Woodpecker Song, The

INSETTA, PAUL PETER
1915, American
w&m/Paul Peter Insetta
Sitting By The Window (1949)

ISLEY, O'KELLY
1937, American
w&m/O'Kelly Isley
Don't Say Goodnight (1980)
in co w/Rudolph Isley,
Ronald Isley, E. Isley, M. Isley,
C. Jasper
It's Your Thing (1969)
in co w/Rudolph Isley,
Ronald Isley
Shout (1959)
in co w/Rudolph Isley,
Ronald Isley

JABARA, PAUL
1949, American
w&m/Paul Jabara
Enough Is Enough (1979)
Last Dance (1979)
No More Tears
in co w/Bruce Roberts

JACKSON, GEORGE HENRY
American
w&m/George Henry Jackson
in co w/Roe Hall
Find 'Em, Fool 'Em,
Forget 'Em (1969)

JACKSON, HOWARD MANUCY
1900, American
m/Howard Manucy Jackson
Lazy Rhapsody
Film scores:
Cry Terror (1958)
Hearts In Dixie (1929)
Meet Nero Wolfe (1936)
Merrill's Marauders (1962)
Mr. Deeds Goes To Town (1936)

JACKSON, JILL
1913, American
w&m in co w/Seymour (Sy) Miller
Let There Be Peace On Earth
(Let It Begin With Me)

JACKSON, JOE
1928, American
w&m/Joe Jackson
Is She Really Going
Out With Him (1979)
Fool In Love
Sunday Papers

JACKSON, MICHAEL JOE
1958, American
w&m/Michael Joe Jackson
Don't Stop 'Til You Get Enough

JACOBI, VICTOR
1883-1921, American
m/Victor Jacobi
All The Girls Love A Sailor Man
w/Adrian Ross, Arthur Anderson
Come Nestle In My Arms
w/Adrian Ross, Arthur Anderson
Deep In Your Eyes
w/William Le Baron
Golden Day Of Love, The
w/Adrian Ross, Arthur Anderson
I Know Now
w/Harry B. Smith
Just A Little Bit Of Love
w/Harry B. Smith
Little Girl Goodbye
w/William Le Baron
Love May Be A Mystery
w/Harry B. Smith, Harry Graham
Love Of Mine
w/Adrian Ross, Arthur Anderson
Sibyl
w/Harry B. Smith, Harry Graham
When Cupid Calls
w/Harry B. Smith, Harry Graham
You Are Free
w/William Le Baron

JACOBS, AL
1903, American
w&m in co w/Jimmy Crane
I Need You Now
If I Give My Heart To You

JACOBS, WALTER
American
w&m/Walter Jacobs
You're So Fine (1954)

JACQUET, ILLINOIS
1922, American
w&m/Illinois Jacquet
Port Of Rico (1952)

JAFFE, MOE
1901, American
w&m/Moe Jaffe
Bell Bottom Trousers
New lyrics by Jaffe, music from a
sea chantey of unknown origin.
Collegiate
in co w/Nat Bonx, Lew Brown
Gypsy In My Soul, The
in co w/Clay A. Boland

If I Had My Life To Live Over
in co w/Henry Tobias,
Larry Vincent
If You Are But A Dream
in co w/Nat Bonx, Jack Fulton
I'm My Own Grandpaw
in co w/Dwight B. Latham

JAGGER, MICK
1944, English
w&m/Mick Jagger
in co w/Keith Richard
Angie
Beast Of Burden
Brown Sugar
Emotional Rescue
Get Off My Cloud
Gimme Shelter
Going Home
Happy
Honky Tonk Woman
Hot Stuff
Jumpin' Jack Flash
Lady Jane
Let's Spend The Night Together
Midnight Rambler
Miss You
Not Fade Away
Paint It Black
Ruby Tuesday
(Can't Get No) Satisfaction
Sister Morphine
Street Fighting Man
Sympathy For The Devil
Tumbling Dice
Under My Thumb
Wild Horses
You Can't Always Get
What You Want

JAMES, BOB
American
m/Bob James (instr.)
Lucky Seven (1977)
(Theme from) Taxi
(Angela) (1977)

JAMES, HARRY
1916, American
m/Harry James
I'm Beginning To See The Light
in co w/Don George,
Johnny Hodges, Duke Ellington
Mole, The
in co w/Leroy Holmes
Two O'Clock Jump
in co w/William (Count) Basie,
Benny Goodman

JAMES, INEZ ELEANOR
1919
w&m/Inez James
Pillow Talk
in co w/Buddy Pepper
Vaya Con Dios
in co w/Buddy Pepper,
Larry Russell

JAMES, MARK
American
w&m/Mark James
Alone Too Long (1973)
 in co w/Cynthia Weil
**Everybody Loves A
 Rain Song (1978)**
 in co w/Chips Moman
**Eyes Of A New
 York Woman (1968)**
Hooked On A Feeling (1968)
It's Only Love (1969)
Moody Blue (1975)
One Hell Of A woman (1974)
 in co w/Mac Davis
Raised On Rock (1973)
Roller Coaster (1973)
Sunday Sunrise (1974)
Suspicious Minds (1968)

JAMES, SONNY (James Loden)
1929, American
w&m/Sonny James
For Rent
 in co w/Jack Morrow
You're The Only World I Know
 in co w/Robert F. Tubert

JAMES, TOMMY
1947, American
w&m/Tommy James
in co w/Bob King, except as noted.
Ball Of Fire
Crimson And Clover
Crystal Blue Persuasion
Draggin' The Line
Hanky Panky
I'm Coming Home
I Think We're Alone Now
Mony, Mony
Say I Am
Sweet Cherry Wine
Three Times In Love
 in co w/R. Serota

JANKOWSKI, HORST
German
m/Horst Jankowski
Simpel Gimpel (1965)
**Walk In The Black
 Forest, A (1965)**

JARRE, MAURICE
French
m/Maurice Jarre
**Marmalade, Molasses And Honey
 (1972)**
 w/Marilyn & Alan Bergman
**Theme From Lawrence
 Of Arabia (1962) (instr.)**
Somewhere My Love (1965)
 w/Paul Francis Webster
**(instr. version of Somewhere My
Love is known as "Lara's Theme
from Doctor Zhivago")**

Film scores:
Behold A Pale Horse (1964)
Collector, The (1965)
Doctor Zhivago (1965)
Is Paris Burning (1966)
Lawrence Of Arabia (1962)
Life And Times Of Judge
 Roy Bean, The (1972)
Night Of The Generals, The (1967)
Plaza Suite (1971)
Ryan's Daughter (1970)

JARREAU, AL
American
w&m/Al Jarreau
Burst In With The Dawn (1978)
Letter Perfect (1978)
Loving You (1978)
One Good Turn (1978)
So Long Girl (1978)
We Got By (1978)
You Don't See Me (1978)

JARRETT, KEITH
1942, American
m/Keith Jarrett
Arbour Zena
Dream Weaver
Facing You
Great Bird
In The Light
Kuum (Backhand)
Luminescence
Prayer (Death & The Flower)

JASEN, DAVID ALAN
1937, American
m/David Alan Jasen (instr.)
Dave's Rag
Festival Rag
Nobody's Rag
Shoe String Rag
Susan's Rag

JASON, WILL
1910, American
w&m/Will Jason
in co w/Val Burton
Penthouse Serenade

JENKINS, DAVID
1947, American
w&m in co w/Cory Lerios
See list of selections under
Cory Lerios.

JENKINS, GORDON
1910, American
w&m/Gordon Jenkins
Blue Prelude
 in co w/Joe Bishop
Future, The
Manhattan Tower (suite)
Married I Can Always Get
P.S. I Love You
 w/Johnny Mercer
San Fernando Valley
This Is All I Ask

JENNINGS, WAYLON
1937, American
w&m/Waylon Jennings
Anita You're Dreaming
 in co w/Don Bowman
**Are You Sure Hank Done
 It This Way**
Bob Wills Is Still The King
Come With Me
 in co w/C. Howard
Good Hearted Woman, A
 in co w/Willie Nelson
I'm A Ramblin' Man
Stop The World And Let Me Off
Suspicious Minds
**That's The Chance I'll
 Have To Take**
This Time

JENNINGS, WILL
1944, American
w&m/Will Jennings
If Love Must Go
I'll Never Love This Way Again
 in co w/Richard Kerr
Looks Like We Made It
 in co w/Richard Kerr
No Night So Long
 in co w/Richard Kerr
Somewhere In The Night
 in co w/Richard Kerr

JEROME, M.K.
1893, American
w&m in co w/Jack Scholl
My Little Buckaroo

**JEROME, MAUDE NUGENT
(Mrs. William Jerome)**
1877-1958, American
w&m/Maude Nugent Jerome
Sweet Rosie O'Grady

JEROME, WILLIAM
1865-1932, American
w/William Jerome
**And The Green Grass
 Grew All Around**
 m/Harry Von Tilzer
Bedelia
 w/Jean Schwartz
Chinatown My Chinatown
 m/Jean Schwartz
Mr. Dooley
 m/Jean Schwartz
On The Old Fall River Line
 m/Harry Von Tilzer
Row Row Row
 m/James V. Monaco

JESSEL, LEON
German
m/Leon Jessel (instr.)
w/Ballard MacDonald (1922)
**Parade Of The
 Wooden Soldiers (1911)**

JOBIM, ANTONIO CARLOS
1927, Brazilian
m/Antonio Carlos Jobim
Desafinado (Slightly Out Of Tune)
w/Jessie Cavanaugh
Spanish w/Newton Mendonca
Girl From Ipanema, The
w/Norman Gimbel
Spanish w/Vinicius De Moraes
How Insensitive (Insensatez)
Meditation
w/Norman Gimbel
Spanish w/Newton Mendonca
**One Note Samba (Samba De
Una Nota Só)**
**Quiet Nights Of Quiet
Stars (Corcavado)**
w/Astrud Gilberto
Wave

JOEL, BILLY
(B. William Martin Joel)
1949, American
w&m/Billy Joel
Angry Young Man
Big Shot
Captain Jack
Entertainer, The
52nd Street
Half A Mile Away
Honesty
Just The Way You Are
Movin' Out (Anthony's Song)
My Life
New York State Of Mind
Only the Good Die Young
Piano Man
Rosalinda's Eyes
She's Always A Woman
Stiletto
Stranger, The
Streetlife Serenade
You May Be Right

JOHN, ELTON
(B. Reginald Kenneth Dwight)
1947, English
m/Elton John
w/Bernie Taupin
Bennie And The Jets
Bitch Is Back, The
Border Song
Burn Down The Mission
Candle In The Wind
Caribou
Cold Highway
Country Comfort
Crocodile Rock
Crazy Water
Daniel
Day In The Life Of A Tree, A
Don't Go Breaking My Heart
Don't Let The Sun Go Down

**Don't Shoot Me, I'm Only The
Piano Player**
Ego
Elderberry Wine
First Episode
Friends
Goodbye Yellow Brick Road
Harmony
Have Mercy On The Criminal
High Flying Bird
Honky Cat
I Think I'm Gonna Kill Myself
Island Girl
I've Seen That Movie Too
Levon
One Day At A Time
Philadelphia Freedom
Take Me To The Pilot
Teacher I Need You
Teenage Idol
Tiny Dancer
Tonight
Rock And Roll Madonna
Rock Of The Westies
Rocket Man
Saturday Night's Alright
Sick City
Skyline Pigeon
Someone Saved My Life Tonight
**Sorry Seems To Be
The Hardest Word**
Suzie
Sweet Painted Ladies
Talking Old Soldiers
Tumbleweed Connection
Young Man's Blues
Your Song

JOHN, ROBERT
English
w&m/Robert John
Sad Eyes (1979)

JOHNS, LEO
w/Leo Johns
m/Henri Salvador
Melodie D'Amour

JOHNSON, CHARLES LESLIE
1876-1950, American
m/Charles Leslie Johnson (instr.)
Dill Pickles Rag
Iola
Porcupine Rag
Powder Rag
Sneeky Pete
Snookums
Sweet And Low

JOHNSON, GEORGE
1953, American
w&m/George Johnson
Brother Man
in co w/Dave Grusin,
Louis Johnson

Free Yourself, Be Yourself
in co w/Louis Johnson
Love Is
in co w/Louis Johnson,
Quincy Jones, Peggy Jones
Never Leave You Lonely
in co w/Louis Johnson,
Peggy Jones
Q
in co w/Louis Johnson
Right On Time
in co w/Louis Johnson,
Quincy Jones
Runnin' For Your Lovin'
in co w/Louis Johnson
Stomp
in co w/Rod Temperton,
Louis Johnson, V. Johnson

JOHNSON, GEORGE W.
American
w&m/George W. Johnson
m/J.A. Butterfield
**When You And I Were
Young Maggie (1866)**

JOHNSON, HOWARD E.
1887-1941, American
w/Howard E. Johnson
Georgia
m/Walter Donaldson
Ireland Must Be Heaven
co-lyricist Joseph McCarthy
m/Fred Fisher
**There's A Broken Heart For
Every Light On Broadway**
m/Fred Fisher
Siam
m/Fred Fisher
Sweet Lady
m/Frank Crumit, Dave Zoob
**M-O-T-H-E-R (A Word That
Means The World To Me)**
m/Theodore F. Morse
**What Do You Want To Make
Those Eyes At Me For**
co-lyricist Joseph McCarthy
m/James V. Monaco
**When The Moon Comes Over
The Mountain**
m/Kate Smith, Harry Woods
Where Do We Go From Here Boys
m/Percy Wenrich

JOHNSON, J. ROSAMOND
American
w&m in co w/Bob Cole
Under The Bamboo Tree

JOHNSON, JAMES P.
1891-1955, American
w&m/James P. Johnson
Caprice Rag (instr.)
Carolina Shout
Carolina Shout (instr.)

Charleston
in co w/Cecil Mack
(Richard C. McPherson)
Harlem Strut (instr.)
If I Could Be With You
One Hour Tonight
in co w/Henry Creamer
Runnin' Wild
in co w/Leo Wood, Joe Grey,
A.G. Gibbs
Sippi
in co w/Henry Creamer,
Clarence Todd

JOHNSON, JAMES WELDON
1871-1938, American
w&m/James Weldon Johnson
Lift Every Voice And Sing
in co w/J. Rosamond Johnson
Maiden With The Dreamy Eyes
in co w/Bob Cole
Oh Didn't He Ramble
in co w/J. Rosamond Johnson
Bob Cole
Since You Went Away
in co w/J. Rosamond Johnson
My Castle On The Nile
in co w/J. Rosamond Johnson,
Bob Cole

JOHNSON, JAY JAY (J.J.)
1924, American
m/Jay Jay Johnson
Blue Mode
El Camino Real
Elora
Perceptions
Poem For Brass
Teapot

JOHNSON, JAY W.
1903, American
w/Jay W. Johnson
m/Billy Hayes
Blue Christmas

JOHNSON, PETE K.H.
1904-1967, American
m/Pete Johnson
Boogie Woogie Prayer (Cafe
Society Swing & The
Boogie Woogie)
in co w/Albert C. Ammons,
Joe Turner
Barrelhouse Breakdown
Boss Of The Blues
in co w/Joe Turner
Cafe Society Rag
in co w/Albert C. Ammons,
Joe Turner
Dive Bomber
Johnson & Turner Blues
in co w/Joe Turner
627 Stomp
Rock It Boogie

Rock & Roll Boogie
Wee Baby Blues
Zero Hour
JOHNSON, WILLIAM
1912-1960, American
m/William Johnson
in co w/Erskine Hawkins,
Julian Dash
w/Buddy Feyne
Tuxedo Junction

JOHNSTON, ARCHIBALD
American
m/Archibald Johnston
w/Charles MacKay
Baby Mine (1878)

JOHNSTON, ARTHUR J.
1898-1954
m/Arthur J. Johnston
All You Want To Do Is Dance
w/Johnny Burke
Cocktails For Two
w/Sam Coslow
Day You Came Along, The
w/Sam Coslow
Down The Old Ox Road
w/Sam Coslow
Just One More Chance
w/Sam Coslow
Learn To Croon
w/Sam Coslow
Moon Got In My Eyes, The
w/Johnny Burke
Moon Song
w/Sam Coslow
Mr. Paganini
w/Sam Coslow
My Old Flame
w/Sam Coslow
Pennies From Heaven
w/Johnny Burke
So Do I
w/Johnny Burke
Thanks
w/Sam Coslow
Thanks A Million
co-lyricist Ted Fiorito
w/Gus Kahn

JOHNSTON, BRUCE
American
w&m/Bruce Johnston
I Write The Songs (1976)

JOHNSTON, THOMAS
1950, American
w&m/Thomas Johnston
Another Park,
Another Sunday (1974)
China Grove (1973)
Eyes Of Silver (1974)
Listen To The Music (1972)
Long Train Running (1973)
Natural Thing
Nobody (1974)

JOLSON, AL
1886-1950, American
w&m/Al Jolson
Anniversary Song, The
in co w/Saul Chaplin
Avalon
in co w/Vincent Rose,
Buddy De Sylva
Back In Your Own Back Yard
in co w/Billy Rose, Dave Dreyer
California, Here I Come
in co w/Buddy De Sylva,
Joseph Meyer
Keep Smiling At Trouble
in co w/Buddy De Sylva,
Lewis Gensler
Me And My Shadow
in co w/Billy Rose, Dave Dreyer
Sonny Boy
in co w/Buddy De Sylva,
Lew Brown, Ray Henderson
There's A Rainbow 'Round
My Shoulder
in co w/Billy Rose, Dave Dreyer
You Ain't Heard Nothin' Yet
in co w/Buddy De Sylva, Gus
Gus Kahn

JONES, GEORGE
1931, American
w&m/George Jones
Take Me
in co w/Leon Payne
Who Shot Sam
in co w/Darrell Edwards,
Ray Jackson
Why Baby Why
in co w/Darrell Edwards
Window Up Above

JONES, ISHAM
1894, American
m/Isham Jones
I'll See You In My Dreams
w/Gus Kahn
Indiana Moon
w/Benny Davis
It Had To Be You
w/Gus Kahn
Meet Me In Bubble Land
w/Casper Nathan, Joe Manne
My Best To You
w/Gene Willadsen
On The Alamo
w/Gus Kahn
One I Love Belongs To Somebody
Else, The
w/Gus Kahn
Spain
w/Gus Kahn
Swingin' Down The Lane
w/Gus Kahn
There Is No Greater Love
w/Marty Symes

JONES, MICK
1947, English
w&m/Mick Jones
Back Where You Belong
Cold As Ice
in co w/Ian Richard McDonald
Damage Is Done, The
Double Vision
in co w/Lou Gramm
Feels Like The First Time
in co w/Ian Richard McDonald
Hot Blooded
in co w/Lou Gramm
Long, Long Way From Home
in co w/Lou Gramm,
Ian Richard McDonald
Spellbinder
in co w/Lou Gramm

JONES, QUINCY
1933, American
m/Quincy Jones
Black Requiem
in co w/Ray Charles
Eyes Of Love, The
w/Bob Russell
For Love Of Ivy
w/Bob Russell
Love Is
w/Louis Johnson, Peggy Jones
Right On Time
w/Louis Johnson,
George Johnson
Stuff Like That (1978) (instr.)
Film scores:
Anderson Tapes, The (1971)
Bob And Carol And
 Ted and Alice (1969)
Cactus Flower (1969)
For Love Of Ivy (1968)
In Cold Blood (1967)
In The Heat Of The Night (1967)
John And Mary (1969)
McKenna's Gold (1969)
Pawnbroker, The (1965)
New Centurions, The (1972)
Wiz, The (1978)
TV themes:
Ironside (theme)
Sanford And Son (theme)
Roots (TV scoring) (1977)

JONES, RICHARD M.
1892-1945, American
w&m/Richard M. Jones
All Night Blues
Ball O' Fire
Red Wagon
Riverside Blues
Trouble In Mind

JONES, RICKIE LEE
American
w&m/Rickie Lee Jones
Chuck E's In Love (1979)
Last Chance Texaco, The (1979)

JONES, STAN
1914-1963, American
w&m/Stan Jones
Riders In The Sky

JONES, TOM
1928, American
w&m in co w/Harvey Schmidt
My Cup Runneth Over
Try To Remember

JONSON, BEN
1573-1637, English
w/Ben Jonson
Music of English traditional origin,
sometimes attributed to a "Colonel
R. Mellish."
Drink To Me Only
 With Thine Eyes

JOPLIN, JANIS
1943-1970, American
w&m/Janis Joplin
Down On Me (1972)

JOPLIN, SCOTT
1868-1917, American
m/Scott Joplin (instr.)
Bethena
Breeze From Alabama, A
Cascades, The
Chrysanthemum, The
Country Club
Easy Winners
Elite Syncopations
Entertainer, The
Eugenia
Euphoric Sounds
Favorite, The
Fig Leaf Rag
Gladiolus
Leola
Maple Leaf Rag
Magnetic Rag
Nonpareil
Original Rags
Palm Leaf Rag
Paragon Rag
Peacherine Rag
Pineapple Rag
Pleasant Moments
Ragtime Dance, The
Reflection Rag
Rose Leaf Rag
Searchlight Rag
Silver Swan Rag
Solace
Stoptime Rag
Strenuous Life, The
Sugar Cane

Sunflower Rag
Tremonisha (opera)
Wall Street Rag
Weeping Willow

JORDAN, LONNIE LEROY
1948, American
See list of selections and
collaborators under Lee Oskar.

JORDAN, LOUIS
1908-1975, American
w&m/Louis Jordan
Don't Burn The
 Candle At Both Ends
in co w/Benny Carter,
Irving Gordon
Early In The Morning
in co w/Leo Hickman,
Dallas Bartley
Is You Is Or Is You Ain't My Baby
in co w/Billy Austin
Saturday Night Fish Fry
in co w/Ellis Walsh

JOYNER, CAROLE
1940, American
w&m in co w/Ric Cartey
Young Love

JUDGE, JACK
English
w&m/Jack Judge
in co w/Harry Williams
It's A Long, Long Way
 To Tipperary (1912)

JULIA, AL
American
w&m/Al Julia
in co w/Fred Jacobson
I Cried A Tear (1959)

JURGENS, DICK
1911, American
w&m/Dick Jurgens
Careless
in co w/Eddy Howard,
Lew Quadling
Elmer's Tune
in co w/Sammy Gallop,
Elmer Albrecht
One Dozen Roses
in co w/Walter Donovan,
Roger Lewis, Country Washburn

JUSTIS, WILLIAM E. JR. (Bill)
American
w&m/William e. Justis Jr.
Raunchy
in co w/Sidney Manker
Release Me
in co w/Sidney Manker
Ways Of A Woman In Love
in co w/Charlie Rich

POPULAR COMPOSERS
& LYRICISTS

K

KAEMPFERT, BERT
1923, German
m/Bert Kaempfert
Afrikaan Beat
w/June Tansey
Danke Schoen
w/Kurt Schwabach, Milt Gabler
Lady
co-composer Herbert Rehbein
w/Charles Singleton, Larry Kusik
L-O-V-E
w/Milt Gabler
Spanish Eyes
w/Charles Singleton,
Eddie Snyder
Strangers In The Night
w/Charles Singleton,
Eddie Snyder
**World We Knew, The
(Over And Over)**
co-composer Herbert Rehbein
w/Carl Sigman

KAHAL, IRVING
1903-1942, American
w/Irving Kahal
By A Waterfall
in co w/Sammy Fain
I Can Dream Can't I
in co w/Sammy Fain
I'll Be Seeing You
in co w/Sammy Fain
Let A Smile Be Your Umbrella
in co w/Sammy Fain,
Francis Wheeler
**Night Is Young And You're So
Beautiful, The**
in co w/Dana Suesse, Billy Rose
**Wedding Bells Are Breaking Up
That Old Gang Of Mine**
in co w/Sammy Fain,
Willie Raskin
When I Take My Sugar To Tea
in co w/Sammy Fain,
Rev. Norman Connor
**You Brought A New Kind Of Love
To Me**
in co w/Sammy Fain,
Rev. Norman Connor

KAHN, GUS
1886-1941, American
w/Gus Kahn
Ain't We Got Fun
co-lyricist Raymond B. Egan
m/Richard Whiting
Beside A Babbling Brook
m/Walter Donaldson
Carioca, The
m/Vincent Youmans,
Edward Eliscu
Carolina In The Morning
m/Walter Donaldson

Charley My Boy
m/Ted Fiorito
Chloe
m/Neil Moret
Coquette
m/John Green,
Carmen Lombardo
Dream A Little Dream Of Me
m/Wilbur Schwandt,
Fabian Andre
Flying Down To Rio
co-lyricist Edward Eliscu
m/Vincent Youmans
Goofus
m/Wayne King, Burke Bivens
Guilty
m/Harry Akst, Richard Whiting
I Never Knew
m/Ted Fiorito
I'll Never Be The Same
m/Matt Malneck,
Frank Signorelli
I'll See You In My Dreams
m/Isham Jones
I'm Through With Love
m/Matt Malneck
It Had To Be You
m/Isham Jones
I Wish I Had A Girl
m/Grace Leboy Kahn
Josephine
m/Wayne King, Burke Bivens
**Little Street Where Old Friends
Meet, A**
m/Harry Woods
Liza
co-lyricist Ira Gershwin
m/George Gershwin
Love Me Or Leave Me
m/Walter Donaldson
Makin' Whoopee
m/Walter Donaldson
Memories
m/Egbert Van Alstyne
My Baby Just Cares For Me
m/Walter Donaldson
My Buddy
m/Walter Donaldson
My Isle Of Golden Dreams
m/Walter Blaufus
Nobody's Sweetheart
m/Billy Meyers, Ernie Erdman,
Elmer Schobel
No No Nora
m/Ted Fiorito
**One I Love Belongs To
Somebody Else, The**
m/Isham Jones
One Night Of Love
m/Victor Schertzinger
On The Alamo
m/Isham Jones

Orchids In The Moonlight
m/Vincent Youmans,
Edward Eliscu
Pretty Baby
m/Egbert Van Alstyne,
Tony Jackson
Sailin' Away On The Henry Clay
m/Edgert Van Alstyne
San Francisco
m/Bronislau Kaper,
Walter Jurmann
Side By Side
m/Harry Woods
Some Sunday Morning
co-lyricist Raymond B. Egan
m/Richard Whiting
Spain
m/Isham Jones
Swingin' Down The Lane
m/Isham Jones
That Certain Party
m/Walter Donaldson
Toot, Toot Tootsie, Goodbye
m/Robert King, Ernie Erdman,
Dan Russo, Ted Fiorito
Thanks A Million
m/Arthur Johnston, Ted Fiorito
Ukulele Lady
m/Richard Whiting
Waitin' At The Gate For Katy
m/Richard Whiting
Waltz You Saved For Me, The
m/Wayne King, Emil Flindt
**Where The Morning
Glories Grow**
co-lyricist Raymond B. Egan
m/Richard A. Whiting
Yes Sir, That's My Baby
m/Walter Donaldson
Your Eyes Have Told Me So
m/Egbert Van Alstyne,
Walter Blaufus
You Stepped Out Of A Dream
m/Nacio Herb Brown

KAILIMAI, HENRY
Hawaiian/American
m//Henry Kailimai
w/G.H. Stover
On The Beach At Waikiki (1915)

KALMAN, EMMERICH
1882-1953, Hungarian
m/Emmerich Kalman
Garden Of Romance, The (1916)
w/Guy Bolton
Love Has Wings (1912)
w/C.C.S. Cushing, E.P. Heath
Love's Own Sweet Song (1912)
w/C.C.S. Cushing, E.P. Heath
**Play Gypsies, Dance
Gypsies (1926)**
w/Harry B. Smith,
Alfred Gruenwald

My Faithful Stradivari (1912)
w/C.C.S. Cushing, E.P. Heath
Softly Thro' The
Summer Night (1912)
w/C.C.S. Cushing, E.P. Heath
Throw Me A Rose (1915)
w/P.G. Wodehouse,
Herbert Reynolds
We Two Shall Meet Again
w/Harry B. Smith
You Are Mine Evermore
w/Harry B. Smith

KALMAR, BERT
1884-1947, American
w/Bert Kalmar
A Kiss To Build A Dream On
co-lyricist Oscar Hammerstein II
m/Harry Ruby
Hooray For Captain Spaulding
m/Harry Ruby
I Love You So Much
m/Harry Ruby
I Wanna Be Loved By You
m/Herbert Sto thart, Harry Ruby
Keep On Doin' What You're Doin'
m/Harry Ruby
Nevertheless
m/Harry Ruby
So Long Oo-long
m/Harry Ruby
Take Your Girlie To The Movies
co-lyricist Edgar Leslie
m/Pete Wendling
Thinking Of You
m/Harry Ruby
Three Little Words
Harry Ruby
Who's Sorry Now
m/Ted Snyder, Harry Ruby
KAMAKAHI, DENNIS
American
w&m/Dennis Kamakahi
E. Hihiwai (1979)
KANDER, JOHN
American
m/John Kander
w/Fred Ebb
All I Need
Cabaret
How Lucky Can You Get
Maybe This Time
New York, New York
Willkommen
KANTNER, PAUL
1942, American
w&m/Paul Kantner
Jane
in co w/David Freiberg,
Craig Chaquico, J. McPherson
St. Charles
in co w/Craig Chaquico, Jessie
Barish, Thunderhawk
KAPER, BRONISLAU
1902, American
m/Bronislau Kaper

Cosi Cosa
w/Ned Washington,
Walter Jurmann
Follow Me (Love theme from
Mutiny On The Bounty)
w/Paul Francis Webster
Hi Lili, Hi Lo
w/Helen Deutsch
Invitation (instr.)
San Francisco
w/Gus Kahn
Film scores:
Auntie Mame (1958)
Barretts Of Whimpole
Street, The (1957)
Bataan (1943)
Brothers Karamazov (1958)
Butterfield 8 (1960)
Day At The Races, A
Green Dolphin Street (1947)
Green Mansions
Lili (1953)
Mrs. Parkington (1944)
Mutiny On The Bounty (1962)
Lord Jim (1965)
Our Vines Have Tender
Grapes (1945)
Red Badge Of Courage, The (1951)
San Francisco (1936)
Solid Gold Cadillac, The (1956)
Somebody Up There Likes Me
Song Of Love (1947)
Yank At Eton, A (1942)

KAPLAN, SOL
American
m/Sol Kaplan
Film scores:
Guns Of August, The (1964)
Halls Of Montezuma (1950)
I Can Get It For You
Wholesale (1951)
Living Free (1972)
Spy Who Came In
From The Cold, The
Titanic (1953)
Treasure Of The Golden
Condor (1953)

KARAS, ANTON
Austrian
m/Anton Karas
**Third Man Theme,The
(1949) (instr.)**

**KARLIN, FREDERICK
JAMES (Fred)**
1936, American
m/Frederick James Karlin
Come Follow-Follow Me
w/Tylwyth Kymry
Come Saturday Morning
w/Dory L. Previn

For All We Know
w/Robb Wilson, Arthur James
Film scores:
Baby Maker, The (1970)
in co w/Tylwyth Kymry
Little Ark, The (1972)
in co w/Tylwyth Kymry
Lovers And Other Strangers (1970)
Marriage Of A Young
Stockbroker (1971)
Sterile Cuckoo, The (1969)
Up The Down Staircase (1967)

KARMEN, STEVE
American
w&m/Steve Karmen
I Love New York

KASENETZ, JERRY
1946, American
w&m/Jerry Kasenetz
in co w/Jeff Katz
Goody Goody Gumdrops (1968)
Indian Giver (1969)
May I Take A Giant Step (1968)
1,2,3, Red Light (1968)
Quick Joey Small (1969)
Simon Says (1968)
Special Delivery (1969)
Train, the (1969)
Yummy, Yummy, Yummy (1968)

KASHA, AL
American
w&m/Al Kasha
in co w/Joel Hirschhorn
See selections under
Joel Hirschhorn.

KASSEL, ART
1896-1965, American
w&m/Art Kassel
Around The Corner
Don't Let Julia Fool Ya
in co w/Jerome Brainin
**You Never Say Yes, You Never
Say No**

KATSCHER, ROBERT
1894-1942, Austrian/American
m/Robert Katscher
**When Day Is Done (originally,
Viennese song
entitled "Madonna")**
w/Buddy DeSylva

KAUFMAN, ALVIN S. (Al)
American
m/Alvin S. Kaufman
Ask Anyone Who Knows
w/Edward Seiler, Sol Marcus
**How Many Hearts
Have You Broken**
w/Marty Symes

KAY, JOHN
1944, Canadian
w&m/John Kay
in co w/Michael Monarch,
Goldy McJohn
Born To Be Wild
Magic Carpet Ride

KAYE, BUDDY
1918, American
w&m/Buddy Kaye
"A" You're Adorable
 in co w/Sidney Lippman, Fred
 Wise
Full Moon And Empty Arms
 (based on Rachmaninoff's
 Second Piano Concerto)
 in co w/Ted Mossman
I'll Close My Eyes
 in co w/Billy Reid
Speedy Gonzales
 in co w/David Hill (Hess),
 Ethel Lee
This Is My Prayer
 in co w/Philip Springer
Till The End Of Time (based on
 Chopin's Polonaise In A Flat
 Major, Op.53)
 in co w/Ted Mossman

KEITH, VIVIAN
1928, American
w/Vivian Keith
m/Ben Peters
Before The Next Teardrop Falls

KELLER, JACK
American
w&m/Jack Keller
in co w/Howard Greenfield.
See list of selections under
Howard Greenfield.

KELLY, DANIEL E.
American
m/Daniel E. Kelly
w/Brewster (Bruce) Higley
Home On The Range (1904)
 (Oh, Give Me A Home Where
 The Buffalo Roam)
 (proof of authorship by Kelly and
 Higley has never been firmly
 verified, although most
 musicologists credit them as the
 originators)

KELLY, EDWARD HARRY
1879-1955, American
m/Edward Harry Kelly
Peaceful Henry (1901) (instr.)

KELLY, J.W.
American
w&m/J.W. Kelly
Throw Him Down,
 McCloskey (1890)

KEN, THOMAS
(Bishop) (also Kenn)
1637-1711, English
w/Bishop Thomas Ken
Music from a Psalter published in
Geneva (1551).
Praise God From Whom
 All Blessings Flow

KENDIS, JAMES
1883-1946, American
m/James Kendis
If I Had My Way
 w/Lou Klein
I'm Forever Blowing Bubbles
 co-composer John
 Williams Kellette
 w/James Brockman, Nat Vincent

KENNEDY, JAMES B. (Jimmy)
English
w/Jimmy Kennedy
And Mimi
 m/Nat Simon
Apple Blossom Wedding
 m/Nat Simon
April In Portugal
 (Coimbra) (1947)
 m/Raul Ferrao
Harbor Lights (1937)
 m/Will Grosz (Hugh Williams)
Isle Of Capri (1934)
 m/Will Grosz (Hugh Williams)
My Bolero
 m/Nat Simon
My Prayer (1939)
 m/Georges Boulanger
Istanbul (Not
 Constantinople) (1953)
 m/Nat Simon
Red Sails In The Sunset (1935)
 m/Will Grosz (Hugh Williams)
Roll Along Covered Wagon (w&m)
South Of The Border (1939)
 m/Michael Carr
Sweet Heartaches
 m/Nat Simon

KENNER, CHRIS
American
w&m/Chris Kenner
I Like It Like That (1961)
 in co w/Allen Toussaint
Land Of 1,000 Dances (1936)
Something You Got (1964)

KENNY, NICK
1895-1976, American
w&m/Nick Kenny
Gone Fishin'
 in co w/Charles Kenny
Love Letters In The Sand
 co-lyricist Charles Kenny
 in co w/J. Fred Coots (music)
There's A Gold Mine In The Sky
 in co w/Charles Kenny

KENT, WALTER
1911, American
m/Walter Kent
Endlessly
 w/Kim Gannon
Gertie From Bizerte
 w/James Cavanaugh, Bob Cutter
I'll Be Home For Christmas
 w/Kim Gannon, Buck Ram
I'm Gonna Live 'Til I Die
 w/Mann Curtis, Al Hoffman
Too Much In Love
 w/Kim Gannon
White Cliffs Of Dover, The
 w/Nat Burton

KENTON, STANLEY
NEWCOMB (Stan)
1912-1979, American
m/Stan Kenton
And Her Tears Flowed Like Wine
 in co w/Joe Greene
Artistry In Rhythm
Artistry Jumps
Opus In Pastels

KEPPEL, LADY CAROLINE
17th Century, English
w/Lady Caroline Keppel
Music from the traditional Irish air
"Eileen Aroon".
Robin Adair (1750)

KERKER, GUSTAVE A.
1857-1923, American
m/Gustave A. Kerker
Cynthia Jane
 w/Harry B. Smith
Golly Charlie
 w/Hugh Morton
Good Old Days, The
 w/Hugh Morton
I'm The Belle Of New York
 w/Hugh Morton
Is It A Dream
 w/Charles A. Byrne
It's Forty Miles From
 Schenectady To Troy
 w/Hugh Morton
It's Nice To Have A Sweetheart
 w/R.H. Burnside
Loud Let The Bugles Sound
 w/Frederick Ranken
Old Man Manhattan
 w/Joseph Herbert
Teach Me How To Kiss
 w/Hugh Morton
They All Follow Me
 w/Hugh Morton
What In The World Would
 Compare To this
 w/Charles A. Byrne
You're the Girl I'm Looking For
 w/Joseph Herbert

KERN, JEROME
1885-1945, American
m/Jerome Kern
All The Things You Are
   w/Oscar Hammerstein II
Bill
   w/P.G. Wodehouse
Can't Help Lovin' Dat
 Man Of Mine
   w/Oscar Hammerstein II
Dearly Beloved
   w/Johnny Mercer
Don't Ever Leave Me
   w/Oscar Hammerstein II
Fine Romance, A
   w/Dorothy Fields
Folks Who Live On The Hill, The
   w/Oscar Hammerstein II
I Dream Too Much
   w/Dorothy Fields
I Won't Dance
   w/Oscar Hammerstein II,
   Otto Harbach
I'm Old Fashioned
   w/Johnny Mercer
I've Told Every Little Star
   w/Oscar Hammerstein II
In Love In Vain
   w/Leo Robin
Last Time I Saw Paris, I
   w/Oscar Hammerstein II
Life Upon The Wicked Stage
   w/Oscar Hammerstein II
Look For The Silver Lining
   w/Buddy DeSylva
Long Ago (And Far Away)
   w/Ira Gershwin
Make Believe
   w/Oscar Hammerstein II
More And More
   w/E.Y. Harburg
Ol' Man River
   w/Oscar Hammerstein II
She Didn't Say Yes
   w/Otto Harbach
Smoke Gets In You Eyes
   w/Otto Harbach
Song Is You, The
   w/Oscar Hammerstein II
Sally
   w/Clifford Grey
Sunny
   w/Otto Harbach,
   Oscar Hammerstein II
They Didn't Believe Me
   w/Herbert Reynolds
   (real name: M.E. Rourke)
Till The Clouds Roll By
   w/P.G. Wodehouse
Touch Of Your Hand, The
   w/Otto Harbach
Way You Look Tonight, The
   w/Dorothy Fields

Who?
   w/Otto Harbach,
   Oscar Hammerstein II
Why Do I Love You
   w/Oscar Hammerstein II
Why Was I Born
   w/Oscar Hammerstein II
Yesterdays
   w/Otto Harbach
You Are Love
   w/Oscar Hammerstein II
You Couldn't Be Cuter
   w/Dorothy Fields
You Were Never Lovelier
   w/Johnny Mercer

KERR, RICHARD
1944, English
w&m/Richard Kerr
I'll Never Love This Way Again
   in co w/Will Jennings
Looks Like We Made It
   in co w/Will Jennings
Mandy (formerly "Brandy")
   in co w/Scott English
No Night So Long
in co w/Will Jennings
Somewhere In The Night
   in co w/Will Jennings

KEY, FRANCIS SCOTT
1779-1843, American
w/Francis Scott Key
Music adapted from an English song
"To Anacreon In Heaven".
Star Spangled Banner, The

KHACHATURIAN,
ARAM ILYICH
1903, Russian
m/Aram Ilyich Khachaturian
Sabre Dance (from the
   "Gayne Ballet") (1947, instr.)

KIBBLE, PERRY
1949, American
w&m/Perry Kibble
in co w/Janice Johnson
Boogie Oogie Oogie (1978)

KILGORE, MERLE
(Wyatt Merle Kilgore)
1934, American
w&m/Merle Kilgore
Dear Mama
Gettin' Old Before My Time
Johnny Reb
Love Has Made You Beautiful
More And More
   in co w/Webb Pierce
Old Records
   in co w/Arthur Thomas
Ring Of Fire
   in co w/June Carter Cash
Tiger Woman
   in co w/Claude King
Wolverton Mountain
   in co w/Claude King

KILMER, JOYCE
1886-1918, American
w/Joyce Kilmer
m/Oscar Rasbach
Trees

KIM, ANDY (Andrew Joachim)
Canadian/American
w&m/Andy Kim
Rock Me Gently (1974)
Sugar Sugar (1968)
   in co w/Jeff Barry

KING, B.B. (Riley B. King)
1925, American
w&m/B.B. King
Please Love Me
   in co w/Jules Taub
Sweet Little Angel
   in co w/Jules Taub
Three O'Clock Blues
   in co w/Jules Taub
Woke Up This Morning
   in co w/Jules Taub
You Know I Love You
   in co w/Jules Taub
You Upset Me Baby
   in co w/Joe Josea

KING, BEN E.
American
w&m/Ben E. King
in co w/Jerry Lieber, Mike Stoller
Stand By Me (1961)

KING, CAROLE
1942, American
w&m/Carole King
Beautiful
Been To Canaan
Believe In Humanity
Bitter With The Sweet
Brother, Brother
Chains
   in co w/Gerry Goffin
Child Of Mine
   in co w/Gerry Goffin
Corazon
Crying In The Rain
   in co w/Howard Greenfield
Don't Say Nothing Bad
 About My Baby
   in co w/Gerry Goffin
Eventually
   in co w/Gerry Goffin
Every Breath I Take
   in co w/Gerry Goffin
Go Away Little Girl
   in co w/Gerry Goffin
Goin' Back
   in co w/Gerry Goffin
Halfway To Paradise
   in co w/Gerry Goffin
Her Royal Majesty
   in co w/Gerry Goffin

Hey Girl
  in co w/Gerry Goffin
Hi-De-Ho
  in co w/Gerry Goffin
High Out Of Time
  in co w/Gerry Goffin
Home Again
I Can't Hear You
  in co w/Gerry Goffin
I Can't Stay Mad At You
  in co w/Gerry Goffin
I Feel The Earth Move
**I'm Going Back To Living
 In The City**
  in co w/Charles Larkey
I'm Into Something Good
  in co w/Gerry Goffin
**It Might As Well Rain
 Until September**
  in co w/Gerry Goffin
It's Going To Take Some Time
  in co w/Tony Stern
It's Too Late
  in co w/Tony Stern
Jazz Man
  in co w/David Palmer
Just Once In My Life
  in co w/Gerry Goffin,
  Phil Spector
Keep Your Hands Off My Baby
  in co w/Gerry Goffin
Loco-Motion (The)
  in co w/Gerry Goffin
Man Without A Dream, A
  in co w/Gerry Goffin
Natural Woman
  in co w/Gerry Goffin,
  Jerry Wexler
Nightingale
  in co w/David Palmer
No Easy Way Down
  in co w/Gerry Goffin
No Sad Song
  in co w/Tony Stern
Oh No, Not My Baby
  in co w/Gerry Goffin
One Fine Day
  in co w/Gerry Goffin
Only Love Is Real
Pleasant Valley Sunday
  in co w/Gerry Goffin
Smackwater Jack
  in co w/Gerry Goffin
Snow Queen
  in co w/Gerry Goffin
So Far Away

Some Kind Of Wonderful
  in co w/Gerry Goffin
Sweet Seasons
  in co w/Tony Stern
Sweet Sweetheart
  in co w/Gerry Goffin

Take A Giant Step
  in co w/Gerry Goffin
Take Good Care Of My Baby
  in co w/Gerry Goffin
Tapestry
To Love
  in co w/Gerry Goffin
Up On The Roof
  in co w/Gerry Goffin
Wasn't Born To Follow
  in co w/Gerry Goffin
Way Over Yonder
What Am I Gonna Do
  in co w/Tony Stern
When My Little Girl Is Smiling
  in co w/Gerry Goffin
Where You Lead
  in co w/Tony Stern
Will You Love Tomorrow
  in co w/Gerry Goffin
Yours Until Tomorrow
  in co w/Gerry Goffin
You've Got A Friend

KING, CHARLES E.
1874-1950, Hawaiian/American
w&m/Charles E. King
**Hawaiian Wedding Song
 (Ke Kali Nei Au)**
  in co w/Al Hoffman,
  Dick Manning
**Song Of The Islands
 (Na Lei O Hawaii) (1915)**

KING, CLAUDE
1933, American
w&m in co w/Merle Kilgore
Tiger Woman
Wolverton Mountain

KING, IRVING
English
w&m/Irving King
**Show Me the Way To Go
 Home (1925)**

KING, JONATHAN
1944, English
w&m/Jonathan King
Everyone's Gone To The Moon
Where The Sun Has Never Shone

KING, PEE WEE
(Frank "Pee Wee" King)
1914, American
w&m/Pee Wee King
Bonaparte's Retreat
  in co w/Redd Stewart
Slow Poke
  in co w/Redd Stewart,
  Chilton Price
Tennessee Waltz, The
  in co w/Redd Stewart
You Belong To Me
  in co w/Redd Stewart,
  Chilton Price

KING, ROBERT
(Robert Keiser)
1862-1932, American
m/Robert King
Beautiful Ohio
  w/Ballard MacDonald
**I Scream, You Scream, We
 All Scream For Ice Cream**
  w/Howard Johnson
**While Strolling Through The
 Park One Day**(w&m)
 (The Fountain In The Park)

KING, WAYNE
1901, American
m/Wayne King
Josephine
  co-composer Burke Bivens
  w/Gus Kahn
Waltz You Saved For Me, The
  co-composer Emil Flindt
  w/Gus Kahn

KINGSTON, LARRY
American
w&m/Larry Kingston
Lovin' Machine (1966)

KIPNER, STEVE
Australian
w&m/Steve Kipner
Is That The Way (1971)
  in co w/Fred Goodman
**Toast And Marmalade
 For Tea ((1971)**
  in co w/Fred Goodman
**Too Much Too Little Too Late
(1979)**
  in co w/John Vallins

KIRK JAMES
w&m/James Kirk
Voice Of Freedom (1980)

**KIRKE, SIMON FREDERICK
ST. GEORGE**
1949, English
w&m/Simon F. St. George Kirke
All Right Now
  in co w/Paul Rodgers
Can't Get Enough Of Your Love
  in co w/Paul Rodgers

KIRKMAN, TERRY
American
w&m/Terry Kirkman
Along Came Mary (1966)
Cherish (1966)
**Pandora's Golden
 Heebie Jeebies**
Never My Love

KIRWEN DANNY
1948, English
w&m/Danny Kirwen
One Sunny Day
Something Inside Of Me

KITTREDGE, WALTER
American
w&m/Walter Kittredge
**Tenting On The Old
Camp Ground (1864)**

KLAUBER, MARCY
1896-1960, Hungarian/American
w&m/Marcy Klauber
I Get The Blues When It Rains

KLEIN, LOU
1888-1945, American
w/Lou Klein
m/James Kendis
If I Had My Way

KLEIN, MANUEL
1876-1919, American
w&m/Manuel Klein
Home Is Where The Heart Is
In Siam
Love Is Like A Rainbow
Meet Me When the Lanterns Glow
Moon Dear

KLENNER, JOHN
1889-1955, American
w/John Klenner
m/Al Hoffman
Heartaches

KLOHR, JOHN N.
Billboard, The (march) (1901)

KNAUFF, GEORGE P.
American
m/George P. Knauff
Words: source unknown.
Wait For The Wagon (1851)

KNEASS, NELSON
American
m/Nelson Kneass
w/Thomas Dunn English
**Ben Bolt (Oh! Don't You
Remember) (1848)**

KNIGHT, BAKER
American
w&m/Baker Knight
Lonesome Town (1958)
**Never Be Anyone Else
But You (1959)**

KNIGHT, VICK
1908, American
w/Vick Knight
I Love Coffee, I Love Tea
m/Henry Russell
I Walk Alone
m/Walter Schumann

KNIPPER, LEV
Russian
m/Lev Knipper.
Russian w/Victor Gussey.
Separate English word translations
by (1) Olga Paul (2) Harold J. Rome.
**Meadowland (s) (Cavalry Of
The Steppes) (1939)**

KOEHLER, TED
1894-1973, American
w/Ted Koehler
Animal Crackers In My Soup
co-lyricist Irving Caesar
m/Ray Henderson
**Between The Devil And The
Deep Blue Sea**
m/Harold Arlen
Don't Worry About Me
m/Rube Bloom
Every Night About This Time
m/James V. Monaco
Get Happy
m/Harold Arlen
I Love A Parade
m/Harold Arlen
I'm Shooting High
m/Jimmy McHugh
I've Got The World On A String
m/Harold Arlen
**I've Gotta Right To
Sing The Blues**
m/Harold Arlen
Kickin' The Gong Around
m/Harold Arlen
Let's Fall In Love
m/Harold Arlen
Lovely Lady
m/Jimmy McHugh
Stormy Weather
m/Harold Arlen
Sweet Dreams, Sweetheart
m/M.K. Jerome
Truckin'
m/Rube Bloom
When The Sun Comes Out
m/Harold Arlen
Wrap Your Troubles In Dreams
m/Harry Barris, Billy Moll

KOHLMAN, CHURCHILL
1906, American
w&m/Churchill Kohlman
Cry

KORNFELD, ARTHUR
American
w&m/Arthur Kornfeld
in co w/Al Duboff
**The Rain, The Park And
Other Things (1968)**

**KORNGOLD, ERICH
WOLFGANG**
1897-1957, American
m/Erich Wolfgang Korngold
Film scores:
Adventures Of Robin Hood,
The (1938)
Anthony Adverse (1936)
Captain Blood (1935)
Green Pastures, The (1936)
Kings Row
Midsummer Night's Dream, A (1936)
Of Human Bondage (1946)

Sea Hawk, The
Prince And The Pauper, The (1937)
Story Of Louis Pasteur (1936)

KOTZWARA, FRANZ
Czechoslovakian
m/Franz Kotzwara (instr.)
Battle Of Prague, The (1793)

KRAMER, ALEX CHARLES
1903, Canadian/American
w&m in co w/Joan Whitney
(Mrs. Alex Kramer).
Candy
in co w/Mack Davis,
Joan Whitney
Comme Si, Comme Sa
Far Away Places
High On A Windy Hill
It All Comes Back To Me Now
Love Somebody
No Man Is An Island

KREISLER, FRITZ
1875-1962, Austrian/American
m/Fritz Kreisler (instr.) (1910)
Caprice Viennois
Letter Song
w/William Le Baron
Liebesfreud
Schön Rosmarin
Tambourine Chinois

KRESA, HELMY
1904, American
m/Helmy Kresa
w/Carroll Loveday
That's My Desire

KRISTOFFERSON, KRIS
1936, American
w&m/Kris Kristofferson
Best Of All Possible Worlds, The
Come Sundown
Delta Day
in co w/Marijohn Wilkin
For The Good Times
**Help Me Make It Through
The Night**
I've Got To Have You
Jesus Was A Capricorn
Loving Her Was Easier
Me And Bobby McGee
in co w/Fred Foster
Nobody Wins
Once More With Feeling
in co w/Shel Silverstein
One Day At A Time
in co w/Marijohn Wilkin
Silver Tongued Devil And I, The
Song I Like To Sing, The
Stranger
Sunday Morning Comin' Down
Why Me (Lord)

KUMMER, CLARE
(Clare Rodman Beecher)
1888-1958, American
w&m/Clare Kummer
Dearie

POPULAR COMPOSERS
& LYRICISTS

L

LAI, FRANCES
French
m/Frances Lai
Where Do I Begin (Theme from "Love Story")
　w/Carl Sigman
Film scores:
Bobo, The (1967)
Love Story (1970)
Man And A Woman, A (1966)
Mayerling (1968)

LAINE, DENNY
(Brian Haynes)
1944, English
w&m/Denny Laine
in co w/Michael Pinder
From The Bottom Of My Heart

LAINE, FRANKIE
1913, American
w&m/Frankie Laine
in co w/Carl Fischer
We'll Be Together Again

LAKE, GREGORY
1948, English
w&m/Gregory Lake
C'est La Vie

LAKE, SOL
American
w&m/Sol Lake
Crawfish (1963)
Lonely Bull, The (1962)
Cantina Blue (1966)

LAMB, ARTHUR J.
1870-1928, English/American
w/Arthur J. Lamb
Any Old Port In A Storm
　m/Frederic Allen (Kerry) Mills
Asleep In The Deep (1879)
　m/H.W. Petrie
Bird In A Gilded Cage, A
　m/Harry Von Tilzer
Bird On Nellie's Hat, The
　m/Alfred Solman
Mansion Of Aching Hearts, The
　m/Harry Von Tilzer

LAMB, JOSEPH FRANCIS
1887-1960, American
w&m/Joseph Francis Lamb
American Beauty Rag
Cotton Tail Rag
Ragtime Nightingale
Top Liner Rag

LAMBERT, DENNIS
American
w&m/Dennis Lambert
in co w/Brian Potter
Ain't No Woman Like The One I Got (1973)
Country Boy, You Got Your Feet In L.A.

Don't Pull Your Love (1971)
Look In My Eyes Pretty Woman (1970)
One Tin Soldier (The Legend Of Billy Jack) (1969)

LAMM, ROBERT
1945, American
w&m/Robert Lamm
Beginnings
Does Anybody Really Know What Time It Is
Fancy Colours
Saturday In The Park
25 Or 6 To 4

LANE, BURTON
1912, American
m/Burton Lane
Begat, The
　w/E.Y. Harburg
Come Back To Me
　w/Alan Jay Lerner
Everything I Have Is Yours
　w/Harold Adamson
Feudin' and Fightin'
　w/Al Dubin
How About You
　w/Ralph Freed
How Are Things In Glocca Morra
　w/E.Y. Harburg
How Could You Believe Me When I Said I Love You
　w/Alan Jay Lerner
I Hear Music
　w/Frank Loesser
If This Isn't Love
　w/E.Y. Harburg
Lady's In Love With You, The
　w/Frank Loesser
Look To The Rainbow
　w/E.Y. Harburg
Melinda
　w/Alan Jay Lerner
Moments Like This
　w/Frank Loesser
On A Clear Day
　w/Alan Jay Lerner
Says My Heart
　w/Frank Loesser
Swing High Swing Low
　w/Ralph Freed
That Old Devil Moon
　w/E.Y. Harburg
There's A Great Day Coming Manana
　w/E.Y. Harburg
What Did I Have That I Don't Have
　w/Alan Jay Lerner
When I'm Not Near The Girl I Love
　w/E.Y. Harburg

LANE, KERMIT (Ken)
1912, American
m/Kermit (Ken) Lane
Everybody Loves Somebody
　w/Irving Taylor

LANGE, JOHNNY
1909, American
w&m/Johnny Lange
Clancy Lowered The Boom
　in co w/Walter H. (Hy) Heath
He's Only A Prayer Away
I Asked The Lord
　in co w/Jimmy Duncan
I Found The Answer
I Lost My Sugar In Salt Lake City
　in co w/Leon T. Rene
Mule Train
　in co w/Walter H. (Hy) Heath, Fred Glickman
Somebody Bigger Than You And I
　in co w/Walter H. (Hy) Heath, Sonny Burke

LARA, AUGUSTIN
Mexican
w&m/Augustin Lara
Granada (1932)

LARDEN, LARY
1945, American
w&m/Lary Larden
in co w/Dennis Larden
Come On Down To My Boat

LARSON, NICOLETTE
American
w&m/Nicolette Larson
Lotta Love (1978)

LATOUCHE, JOHN
1917-1956, American
w/John Latouche
Ballad For Americans
　m/Earl Robinson
Cabin In The Sky
　m/Vernon Duke
Honey In The Honeycomb
　m/Vernon Duke
Lazy Afternoon
　m/Jerome Moross
Summer Is A-Comin' In
　m/Vernon Duke
Taking A Chance On Love
　m/Vernon Duke

LAUDER, HARRY (Sir)
1870-1950, Scottish
w&m/Sir Harry Lauder
I Love A Lassie (Ma Scotch Bluebell) (1906)
　in co w/Gerald Grafton
Roamin' In The Gloamin' (1911)
She Is Ma Daisy (1905)
　in co w/Frank Folley
Stop Yer Tickling, Jock (1904)
　in co w/J.D. Harper

**That's The Reason Noo I
Wear A Kilt (1906)**
   in co w/A.B. Kendal
Wee Deoch-An-Doris, A (1911)
   in co w/Gerald Grafton

LAWNHURST, VEE
1905, American
m/Vee Lawnhurst
w/Tot Seymour
Accent On Youth (1935)

LAWLOR, CHARLES B.
1852-1925, American
w&m/Charles B. Lawlor
in co w/James W. Blake
**Sidewalks Of New
York, The (1894)**

LAWRENCE, JACK
1912, American
w&m/Jack Lawrence
All Or Nothing At All
   in co w/Arthur Altman
Beyond The Sea (La Mer)
   in co w/Charles Trenet
Delicado
   in co w/Waldyr Azevedo
Hold My Hand
   in co w/Richard Myers
If I Didn't Care
**In An Eighteenth Century
Drawing Room**
   in co w/Raymond Scott
Johnson Rag
   in co w/Guy Hall,
   Henry Kleinauf
Linda
   in co w/Ann Ronnell
My One And Only Love
Play Fiddle Play
   in co w/Emery Deutsch,
   Arthur Altman
Poor People Of Paris
   in co w/Marguerite Monnot
Sleepy Lagoon
   in co w/Eric Coates
Sunrise Serenade
   in co w/Frankie Carle
Symphony
Tenderly
   in co w/Walter Gross
**With The Wind And The Rain
In Your Hair**
   in co w/Clara Edwards
   (Bernard Haig)

LAWSON, HERBERT HAPPY
American
w&m/Herbert Happy Lawson
Anytime (1948)

LECUONA, ERNESTO
1896, Cuban
   m /Ernesto Lecuona

Always In My Heart
   Eng. w/Kim Gannon
Another Night Like This
   Eng. w/Harry Ruby
**Breeze And I, The (adapted
from "Andalusia")**
   Eng. w/Al Stillman
Carnival Parade (La Comparsa)
   Eng. w/Albert Gamse
Dust On The Moon (Canto Indio)
   Eng. w/Stanley Adams
Gitanerias
Malaguena
Maria La O
Para Vigo Me Voy
Rhapsody Negra
Say Si Si
   Eng. w/Al Stillman,
   Frances Luban
Siboney
   Eng. w/Theodora (Dolly) Morse
**Two Hearts That Pass In
The Night (Dame De Tus
Fosas)**
   Eng. w/Forman Brown

**LEDBETTER, HUDDIE
WILLIAM (Leadbelly)**
1889-1949, American
w&m/Huddie William Ledbetter
Blind Lemon
Boll Weevil, The
Cotton Fields
Fort Worth And Dallas Blues
Goodnight Irene
   in co w/John Lomax
Midnight Special, The
Scottsboro Blues
Take A Whiff On Me
We Shall Be Free

LEDESMA, ISH
1952, American
w&m/Ish Ledesma
in co w/Richie Puente
Get Off

LEE, ALVIN
1944, English
w&m/Alvin Lee
**Baby Won't You Let Me Rock
And Roll You**
Choo Choo Mama
Circles
Hard Monkeys
Here They Come
I'd Love To Change The World
I'm Going Home
Love Like A Man
Once There Was A Time
One Of These Days
**Rock And Roll Music
To The World**
Standing At The Station

Sugar The Road
You Give Me Loving
Year 3000 Blues

LEE, DICKEY
American
w&m/Dickey Lee
She Thinks I Still Care (1962)

LEE, KUI
Hawaiian/American
w&m/Kui Lee
One Paddle, Two Paddle (1966)

LEE, LEONARD
American
w&m/Leonard Lee
Let The Good Times Roll (1956

LEE, LESTER
1905-1956, American
w&m/Lester Lee
Dreamer With A Penny, A
   in co w/Allan Roberts
Pennsylvania Polka
   in co w/Zeke Manners

LEE, PEGGY
1921, American
w&m/Peggy Lee
Don't Be So Mean To Baby
   in co w/Dave Barbour
He's A Tramp
   in co w/Sonny Burke
I Don't Know Enough About You
   in co w/Dave Barbour
It's A Good Day
   in co w/Dave Barbour
Just An Old Love Of Mine
   in co w/Dave Barbour
Manana
   in co w/Dave Barbour
So What's New
   in co w/John Pisano

LEEDS, MILTON
American
w/Milton Leeds
Perfidia
   m/Alberton Dominguez

LEGRAND, MICHEL
French
m/Michel Legrand
Brian's Song (instr.)
I Will Wait For You
   w/Norman Gimbel,
   Jacques Demy
Images (instr.)
**Summer Knows, The (Theme
from "Summer Of '42")**
   w/Alan Bergman,
   Marilyn Bergman
Watch What Happens
   w/Norman Gimbel

**What Are You Doing The
Rest Of Your Life**
w/Alan Bergman,
Marilyn Bergman
Windmills Of Your Mind, The
w/Alan Bergman,
Marilyn Bergman
Film scores:
Ice Station Zebra (1968)
Lady Sings The Blues (1972)
Portnoy's Complaint (1972)
Thomas Crown Affair, The (1968)
Summer Of '42 (1971)
Umbrellas Of Cherbourg, The (1964)
Wuthering Heights (1970)

LEHAR, FRANZ
1870-1948, Hungarian
m/Franz Lehar
**Frasquita Serenade (My Little
Nest Of Heavenly Blue)**
Eng. w/Sigmund Spaeth
Golden And Silver (waltz)
w/Adrian Ross
Maxim's (1907)
w/Adrian Ross
Merry Widow Waltz, The (1907)
w/Adrian Ross
Yours Is My Heart Alone
Eng. w/Harry B. Smith
German words "Dein Ist Mein
Ganzes Herz" by Alfred
Gruenwald, Fritz Loehner-Beda
Vilia (1907)
w/Adrian Ross

LEHMAN, LIZA
1862-1918, English
m/Liza Lehman
w/Edward Fitzgerald (adapted from
"The Rubaiyat Of Omar Khayyam)
**In A Persian
Garden (1896 in U.S.A.)**

LEIGH, CAROLYN
1926, American
w/Carolyn Leigh
Best Is Yet To Come, The
m/Cy Coleman
Doodlin' Song, A
m/Cy.Coleman
Firefly
m/Cy Coleman
Hey Look Me Over
m/Cy Coleman
I Walk A Little Faster
m/Cy Coleman
I'm Flying
m/Mark (Moose) Charlap
I've Gotta Crow
m/Mark (Moose) Charlap
Pass Me By
m/Cy Coleman
Real Live Girl
m/Cy Coleman

Witchcraft
m/Cy Coleman
You Fascinate Me So
m/Cy Coleman
Young At Heart
m/Johnny Richards

LEIGH, MITCH
1928, American
m/Mitch Leigh
Impossible Dream, The
w/Joe Darion
Dulcinea
w/Joe Darion

LEIGH, RICHARD
American
w&m/Richard Leigh
**Don't It Make My Brown
Eyes Blue (1977)**
Your Old Cold Shoulder

LEIP, HANS
German
w&m/Hans Leip
in co w/Norbert Schultze,
Tommie Connor.
Lilli Marlene (1944)

LEKA, PAUL
American
w&m/Paul Leka
Green Tambourine (1967)
in co w/Shelly Pinz
**I'm Gonna Make You Love Me
(1970)**
**Na Na Hey Hey Kiss Him
Goodbye (1969)**

LENDHURST, PEARL
American
w&m/Pearl Lendhurst
Be-Bop Baby (1957)

LENNON, JOHN
1940, English
w&m/John Lennon
in co w/Paul McCartney
See list of selections under
Paul McCartney.
w&m/John Lennon
in co w/Yoko Ono (1933, Japanese)
Ballad Of John And Yoko, The
Cold Turkey
**Give Peace A Chance/Remember
Love**
Mother
Power To The People
SomeTime In New York City
**Woman Is The Nigger Of The
World**
w&m/John Lennon
How Do You Sleep
Imagine
Mind Games
Number 9 Dream

Oh, Yoko
Out The Blue
**Whatever Gets You Through The
Night**

LENOIR, JEAN
French
m/Jean Lenoir
w/Bruce Siever
Parlez Moi D'Amour

LENZBERG, JULIUS
1878-1956, American
m/Julius Lenzberg
**Hungarian Rag (1913) (adapted
from Franz Liszt's "Hungarian
Rhapsody")**
**Operatic Rag (1914) (adapted
from classic operatic themes)**

LEONARD, EDDIE
(Lemuel Gordon Toney)
1875-1941, American
w/Eddie Leonard
m/Eddie Munson
Ida, Sweet As Apple Cider

LEONCAVALLO, RUGGIERO
1858-1919, Italian
Italian w&m/Ruggiero Leoncavallo
Mattinata (La)
Eng. w/Edward Teschemacher,
entitled "Tis The Day", 1904.
Eng. w/Sunny Skylar, Pat Genaro,
entitled "You're Breaking My
Heart", 1948.

LEONTOVICH, M.
Russian (Ukranian)
m/M. Leontovich
w/Peter J. Wilhousky
Carol Of The Bells (1936)

LERIOS, CORY
1951, American
w&m/Cory Lerios
Don't Want To Live Without It
in co w/David Jenkins
I Want You Tonight
in co w/David Jenkins,
Allee Willis
Love Will Find A Way
in co w/David Jenkins
Never Had A Love
in co w/David Jenkins
Place In The Sun, A
in co w/Bud Cockrell
Whatcha Gonna Do?
in co w/David Jenkins
LERNER, ALAN JAY
1918, American
w/Alan Jay Lerner
m/Frederick Loewe, except as noted.
Almost Like Being In Love
Camelot
Come Back To Me
m/Burton Lane

Come To Me, Bend To Me
Follow Me
Get Me To The Church On Time
Gigi
Heather On The Hill, The
Here I'll Stay
   m/Kurt Weill
How Could You Believe Me When
  I Said I Loved You
   m/Burton Lane
How To Handle A Woman
I Could Have Danced All Night
I Remember It Well
I Still See Elisa
I Talk To The Trees
If Ever I Should Leave You
I'll Go Home With Bonnie Jean
I'm Glad I'm Not Young Anymore
I've Grown Accustomed To Her
  Face
Melinda
   m/Burton Lane
Night They Invented Champagne,
  The
On A Clear Day
   m/Burton Lane
On The Street Where You Live
Rain In Spain, The
Thank Heaven For Little Girls
There But For You Go I
They Call The Wind Maria
With A Little Bit Of Luck
Wouldn't It Be Loverly

LERNER, SAMUEL M. (Sammy)
1903, American
w&m/Samuel M. Lerner
Falling In Love Again
   in co w/Frederick Hollander
I'm Popeye The Sailor Man
Is It True What They Say
  About Dixie
   in co w/Irving Caesar, Gerald Marks

LESLIE, EDGAR
1885-1976, American
w/Edgar Leslie
America I Love You
   m/Archie Gottler
Among My Souvenirs
   m/Horatio Nicholls
By The River Sainte Marie
   m/Harry Warren
Do You Know What It Means
  To Miss New Orleans
   m/Louis Alter
For Me And My Gal
   co-lyricist E. Ray Goetz
   m/George W. Meyer
He'll Have To Get Under,
  Get Out And Get Under
   co-lyricist Grant Clarke
   m/Maurice Abrahams
In A Little Gypsy Tea Room
   m/Joseph A. Burke

It Looks Like Rain In Cherry
  Blossom Lane
   m/Joseph A. Burke
Little Bit Independent, A
   m/Joseph A. Burke
Lonesome
   m/George W. Meyer
Moon Over Miami
   m/Joseph A. Burke
Moon Was Yellow, The
   m/Fred E. Ahlert
Oh What A Pal Was Mary
   co-lyricist Bert Kalmar
   m/Pete Wendling
Sadie Salome, Go Home
   m/Irving Berlin
Take Your Girlie To The Movies
   co-lyricist Bert Kalmar
   m/Pete Wendling
We Must Be Vigilant
  (American Patrol)
   m/Joseph A. Burke
You've Got Me In The
  Palm Of Your Hand
   m/James V. Monaco

LEVANT, OSCAR
1906, American
m/Oscar Levant
Blame It On My Youth
   w/Edward Heyman
Lady Play Your Mandolin
   w/Irving Caesar

LEVAY, SILVESTER
German
w&m/Silvester Levay
Fly Robin Fly (1975)
Get Up And Boogie (1976)
No No Joe (1976)

LEVIN, IRA
1929, American
w&m in co w/Milton Schafer
He Touched Me

LEVINE, IRWIN
American
w&m in co w/L. Russell Brown;
except for "Candida"

Am I Losing You
Candida
   in co w/Toni Wine
Knock Three Times
Say Has Anybody Seen My Sweet
  Gypsy Rose
Steppin' Out, I'm Gonna
  Boogie Tonight
Tie A Yellow Ribbon Round
  The Ole Oak Tree
Who's In The Strawberry
  Patch With Sally

LEVY, EUNICE
American
w&m/Eunice Levy
in co w/Forest Wilson, Jake Porter
Ko Ko Mo (I Love You So) (1955)

LEWIS, AL
1901, American
w&m/Al Lewis
Blueberry Hill
   in co w/Larry Stock
Gonna Get A Girl
   in co w/Howard Simon
Now's The Time To Fall In
  Love (Potatoes Are Cheaper,
  Tomatoes Are Cheaper)
   in co w/Al Sherman
Ninety Nine Out Of 100
  Wanna Be Loved
   in co w/Al Sherman
No No A Thousand Times No
   in co w/Al Sherman
Over Somebody Else's Shoulder
   in co w/Al Sherman
Rose O'Day (Filla-Ga
  Dusha Song)
   in co w/Charles Tobias
Tears On My Pillow
   in co w/Sylvester Bradford
You Gotta Be A Football Hero
   in co w/Al Sherman

LEWIS, BARBARA
American
w&m/Barbara Lewis
Hello Stranger (1963)

LEWIS, CALVIN H.
American
w&m in co w/Andrew Wright
When A Man Loves A Woman
  (1966)

LEWIS, DAVE
American
w&m in co w/Paul Schindler,
Bob Adams
Mother Pin A Rose On Me
  (Mother, Mother, Mother Pin A
  Rose On Me)

LEWIS, GARY (Gary Levitch)
1945 American
w&m/Gary Lewis
in co w/Al Kooper
This Diamond Ring

LEWIS, JOHN
1920, American
m/John Lewis (instr.)
Afternoon In Paris
Concorde
Django
Fontessa
Golden Striker, The
Milano
Sun Dance

Three Windows
Vendome
LEWIS, MARGARET
1940, American
w&m in co w/Mira Smith
Girl Most Likely, The
I Almost Called Your Name
Oh Singer
Reconsider Me
There Never Was A Time
Wedding Cake, The
LEWIS, MATTHEW GREGORY
17th Century, English
w/Matthew G. Lewis
m/John Dary, G. Gilbert
Crazy Jane (1800)

LEWIS, MEADE "LUX"
1905-1964, American
m/Meade "Lux" Lewis (instr.)
Bass On Top
Bearcat Crawl
Glendale Fire
Honky-Tonk Train
Lux Boogie
Rockin' The Clock
Yancey Special
LEWIS, JR., MORGAN (William)
1906
How High The Moon
w/Nancy Hamilton
Old Soft Shoe, The
w/Nancy Hamilton

LEWIS, ROGER
1885-1945, American
w/Roger Lewis
Down By The Winegar Woiks
m/Don Bestor
Oceana Roll
m/Lucien Denni (1886-1947)
One Dozen Roses
co-lyricist:Country Washburn
m/Dick Jurgens, Walter Donovan
LEWIS, SAMUEL M.
1885-1959, American
w/Samuel M. Lewis
Beautiful Lady In Blue, A
m/J. Fred Coots
Cryin' For The Carolines
co-lyricist Joseph Young
m/Harry Warren
Dinah
co-lyricist Joseph Young
m/Harry Akst
Five Foot Two, Eyes Of Blue
co-lyricist Joseph Young
m/Ray Henderson
For All We Know
m/J. Fred Coots
Gloomy Sunday
m/Rezjo Seress
Have A Little Faith In Me
co-lyricist Joseph Young
m/Harry Warren

Hello Central, Give Me No Man's Land
co-lyricist Joseph Young
m/Jean Schwartz
How Ya Gonna Keep 'Em Down On The Farm
co-lyricist Joseph Young
m/Walter Donaldson
I Heard A Forest Praying
m/Peter DeRose
I Kiss Your Hand Madame
co-lyricist Joseph Young
m/Ralph Erwin
I'm Sitting On Top Of The World
co-lyricist Joseph Young
m/Ray Henderson
In A Little Spanish Town
co-lyricist Joseph Young
m/Mabel Wayne
King For A Day
co-lyricist Joseph Young
m/Ted Fiorito
Laugh Clown Laugh
co-lyricist Joseph Young
m/Ted Fiorito
Lawd You Made The Night Too Long
m/Victor Young
My Mammy
co-lyricist Joseph Young
m/Walter Donaldson
My Mother's Rosary
m/George W. Meyer
One Minute To One
m/J. Fred Coots
Rockabye Your Baby With A Dixie Melody
co-lyricist Joseph Young
m/Jean Schwartz
Street Of Dreams
m/Victor Young
Then You've Never Been Blue
co-lyricist Joseph Young
m/Ted Fiorito
When You're A Long Long Way From Home
m/George W. Meyer
Where Did Robinson Crusoe Go With Friday On Saturday Night
co-lyricist Joseph Young
m/George W. Meyer
LEWIS, TED
(Theodore Leopold Friedman)
1892, American
w&m in co w/Andrew B. Sterling, Bill Munroe, Harry Von Tilzer.
When My Baby Smiles At Me

LIEBER, JERRY
1933, American
w&m/Jerry Lieber
Along Came Jones
in co w/Mike Stoller

Black Denim Trousers And Motorcycle Boots
in co w/Mike Stoller
Charlie Brown
in co w/Mike Stoller
Corn Whiskey
in co w/Mike Stoller
Down In Mexico
in co w/Mike Stoller
Drip Drop
in co w/Mike Stoller
Framed
in co w/Mike Stoller
Hard Times
in co w/Mike Stoller
Hound Dog
in co w/Mike Stoller
Is That All There Is
in co w/Mike Stoller
Jailhouse Rock
in co w/Mike Stoller
Kansas City
in co w/Mike Stoller
King Creole
in co w/Mike Stoller
Late Again
in co w/Mike Stoller
Man Who Robbed The Bank At Santa Fe, The
in co w/Mike Stoller, Billy Edd Wheeler
On Broadway
in co w/Mike Stoller, Cynthia Weil, Barry Mann
Riot In Cell Block No. 9
in co w/Mike Stoller
Ruby Baby
in co w/Mike Stoller
Spanish Harlem
in co w/Phil Spector
Stand By Me
in co w/Mike Stoller, Ben E. King
Stuck In The Middle With You
in co w/Mike Stoller
That's What The Good Book Says
in co w/Mike Stoller
There Goes My Baby
in co w/Mike Stoller, Benjamin Nelson, Lover Patterson, George Treadwell
True Love, True Love
in co w/Mike Stoller
Yakety-Yak
in co w/Mike Stoller
Young Blood
in co w/Mike Stoller, Doc Pomus

LIEURANCE, THURLOW
1878-1963, American
m/Thurlow Lieurance
w/J.M. Cavanass
By The Waters Of Minnetonka (1914)

LIGGINS, JOE
American
w&m/Joe Liggins
Don't Put Me Down (1949)
Drunk (1953)
I've Got A Right To Cry (1946)
Pink Champagne (1950)
Tanya (1946)

LIGHTFOOT, GORDON
1938, Canadian
w&m/Gordon Lightfoot
Carefree Highway
Circle Is Small, The
Cotton Jenny
Did She Mention My Name
Early Mornin' Rain
For Lovin' Me
If You Could Read My Mind
Rainy Day People
Ribbon Of Darkness
Summertime Dream
Sundown
**That's What You Get For
 Lovin' Me**
Way I Feel, The
Wreck Of The Edmund Fitzgerald

LILIUOKALANI, QUEEN
(Lydia Kamekeha Liliuokalani)
1838-1917, Hawaiian
w&m/Queen Liliuokalani
Aloha Oe! (Farewell To Thee)

LINCKE, PAUL
German
Music & German words/Paul Lincke.
Original English words by Lilla
Cayley Robinson. Newer English
words by Johnny Mercer (1952)
Glow Worm, The (1902)

LIND, BOB
1944, American
w&m/Bob Lind
Elusive Butterfly
Remember The Rain
Truly Julie's Blues

LINDEMAN, EDITH
(Edith Calisch)
1898, American
w&m in co w/Carl Stutz
Little Things Mean A Lot

LINDSAY, MARK
1944, American
w&m/Mark Lindsay
Arizona

LINGARD, WILLIAM HORACE
English
w/William Horace Lingard
m/T. MacLagan
**Captain Jinks Of The Horse
 Marines (1868)**

LINK, HARRY
1896-1956, American
m/Harry Link
I've Got a Feeling I'm Falling
 in co w/Thomas "Fats" Waller,
 Billy Rose
These Foolish Things
 in co w/Holt Marvell,
 Jack Strachey

LIPPMAN, SIDNEY
1914, American
m/Sidney Lippman
w/Sylvia Dee, except as noted.
"A" You're Adorable
 w/Buddy Kaye, Fred Wise
After Graduation Day
Chickery Chick
House With Love In It, A
My Sugar Is So Refined
Too Young

LINZER, SANDY
American
w&m/Sandy Linzer
in co w/Denny Randell
Keep the Ball Rollin' (1967)
Lover's Concerto, A (1965)
**(Music adapted from Johann
 Sebastian Bach)**
Native New Yorker (1977)
**Working My Way Back
 To You (1980)**

LITTLE, JACK (Little)
1900-1956, American
w&m/Little Jack Little
In A Shanty In Old Shanty Town
 in co w/Joseph Young, John Siros
Jealous
 in co w/Tommie Malie,
 Dick Finch

LIVINGSTON, HATTIE
American
m/Hattie Livingston
w/Frank Spencer
Young Folks At Home, The (1852)

LIVINGSTON, JAY HAROLD
1915, American
All w&m in co w/Raymond B. (Ray)
Evans. See listing of selections under
the name of Raymond B.
(Ray) Evans.

LIVINGSTON, JERRY
1909, American
m/Jerry Livingston
**A Dream Is A Wish Your
 Heart Makes**
 w/Al Hoffman, Mack David
Bibbidi, Bobbidi Boo
 w/Al Hoffman, Mack David
Blue And Sentimental
 w/Mack David

Casper The Friendly Ghost
 w/Mack David
Cat Ballou
 w/Mack David
Chi Baba Chi Baba
 w/Al Hoffman, Mack David
Close To You
 w/Al Hoffman
Fuzzy Wuzzy
 w/Al Hoffman, Milton Drake
Hawaiian Eye
 w/Mack David
I'm Through With Love
 in co w/Matt Malneck
It's The Talk Of The Town
 w/Al J. Neiburg, Marty Symes
**I've Got An Invitation To
 A Dance**
 w/Al J. Neiburg, Marty Symes
Mairzy Doats
 w/Al Hoffman, Milton Drake
So This Is Love
 w/Mack David
Story Of A Starry Night
 w/Al Hoffman
77 Sunset Strip
 w/Mack David
Twelfth Of Never, The
 w/Paul Francis Webster
Unbirthday Party, The
 w/Mack David
Under A Blanket of Blue
 w/Al J. Neiburg, Marty Symes
**Wake The Town And Tell The
 People**
 w/Sammy Gallop
**What's The Good Word
 Mr. Bluebird**
 w/Al Hoffman, Allan Roberts
When It's Darkness On The Delta
 w/Al J. Neiburg, Marty Symes

LIVINGSTON, JOSEPH A. (Fud)
1906-1957, American
w&m in co w/Matt Malneck
I'm Through With Love

LOCKHART, EUGENE (Gene)
1891-1957, American
w/Eugene Lockhart
**World Is Waiting For The
 Sunrise, The**
 m/Ernest Seitz

LOCKLIN, HANK
1918, American
w&m/Hank Locklin
Please Help Me I'm Falling
**Send Me The Pillow You Dream
 On**

LODGE, JOHN
1945, English
w&m/John Lodge
Eyes Of A Child

I'm Just A Singer In A
  Rock & Roll Band
Isn't Life Strange
One More Time To Live
Ride My See Saw
Send Me No Wine
Steppin' In A Slide Zone

LOEB, JOHN JACOB
1910
w&m/John Jacob Loeb
Boo Hoo
  in co w/Carmen Lombardo,
  Edward Heyman
It's Easier Said Than Done
  in co w/Carmen Lombardo
Rosie The Riveter
  in co w/Redd Evans
Sailboat In The Moonlight, A
  in co w/Carmen Lombardo
Seems Like Old Times
  in co w/Carmen Lombardo

LOESSER, FRANK
1910-1969,American
w&m/Frank Loesser
Adelaid's Lament
Anywhere I Wander
Baby It's Cold Outside
Ballad Of Rodger Young, The
Big D
Bushel And A Peck, A
Brotherhood Of Man
Can't Get Out Of This Mood
  in co w/Jimmy McHugh
Dolores
  in co w/Louis Alter
Fugue For Tin Horns
Grand Old Ivy
Guys And Dolls
**Happy To Make Your
  Acquaintance**
Heart And Soul
  in co w/Hoagy Carmichael
Hey, Good Looking
  in co w/Matt Malneck
Hoop-Dee-Doo
  in co w/Milton Delugg
I Believe In You
**I Don't Want To Walk
  Without You**
  in co w/Jule Styne
**I Fall In Love With You
  Every Day**
  in co w/Manning Sherwin
I Hear Music
  in co w/Burton Lane
I Wish I Didn't Love You So
I Wish I Were Twins
  in co w/Eddie DeLange,
  Joseph Meyer
If I Were A Bell
I'll Dance At Your Wedding
  in co w/Hoagy Carmichael

I'll Know
I'll Never Let A Day Pass By
  in co w/Victor Schertzinger
In My Arms
  in co w/Ted Grouya
Inchworm, The
I've Never Been In Love Before
Jingle, Jangle, Jingle
  in co w/Joseph J. Lilley
Joey, Joey, Joey
Just Another Polka
  in co w/Milton Delugg
Lady's In Love With You, The
  in co w/Burton Lane
Let's Get Lost
  in co w/Jimmy McHugh
Luck Be A Lady
Make A Miracle
Moments Like This
  in co w/Burton Lane
Moon Of Manakoora, The
  in co w/Alfred Newman
More I Cannot Wish You
Most Happy Fella, The
My Darling, My Darling
My Heart Is So Full Of You
My Time Of Day
Never Will I Marry
**New Ashmolean Marching
  Society, The**
No Two People

On A Slow Boat To China
Once In Love With Amy
**Praise The Lord And Pass
  The Ammunition**
Says My Heart
  in co w/Burton Lane
**See What The Boys In The
  Back Room Will Have**
  in co w/Frederick Hollander
Sing A Tropical Song
  in co w/Jimmy McHugh
**Sit Down, You're Rockin' The
  Boat**
Small Fry
  in co w/Hoagy Carmichael
**Spring Will Be A Little Late
  This Year**
Standing On The Corner
Summertime Love
Take Back Your Mink
Tallahassee
**There's A Great Day Coming
  Manana**
  in co w/Burton Lane
**They're Either Too Young Or Too
  Old**
  in co w/Arthur Schwartz
Thumbalina
Two Sleepy People
  in co w/Hoagy Carmichael
Warm All Over

**What Are You Doing New Year's
  Eve**
**What Do You Do In
  The "Infantry"**
Woman In Love, A
Wonderful Copenhagen

LOEWE, FREDERICK
1904,American
m/Frederick Loewe
All w/Alan Jay Lerner
Almost Like Being In Love
Camelot
Come To Me, Bend To Me
Follow Me
Get Me To The Church On Time
Gigi
Heather On The Hill, The
How To Handle A Woman
I Could Have Danced All Night
I Remember It Well
I Still See Elisa
I Talk To The Trees
If Ever I Should Leave You
I'll Go Home With Bonnie Jean
I'm Glad I'm Not Young Anymore
**I've Grown Accustomed To Her
  Face**
**Night They Invented Champagne,
  The**
On The Street Where You Live
Rain In Spain, The
Thank Heaven For Little Girls
There But For You Go I
They Call The Wind Maria
With A Little Bit Of Luck
Wouldn't It Be Loverly

LOGAN, FREDERICK KNIGHT
1871-1928, American
m/Frederick Knight Logan
w/James Royce Shannon
Missouri Waltz

LOGGINS, DAVE
1947, American
w&m/Dave Loggins
Pieces Of April
Please Come To Boston
Someday

LOGGINS, KENNETH
1948, American
w&m/Kenneth Loggins
Ain't Gonna Change My Music
  in co w/James Messina
Celebrate Me Home
Danny's Song
House At Pooh Corner
I Believe In Love
Love Song
Mr. Night
Nightwatch
Thinking Of You
  in co w/James Messina

This Is It
    in co w/Michael McDonald
Your Mama Don't Dance
    in co w/James Messina
What A Fool Believes
    in co w/Michael McDonald
Whenever I Call You Friend
    in co w/Melissa Manchester
Vaheval
    in co w/James Messina

LOHR, HERMAN
English
m/Herman Lohr
w/D. Eardley-Wilmot
**Little Grey Home In
  The West (1911)**

LLOYD, ROBERT
American
w&m/Robert Lloyd
**Good Morning Mr.
  Zip-Zip-Zip (1918)**

LOMBARDO, CARMEN
1903, American
w&m/Carmen Lombardo
Boo Hoo
    in co w/John J. Loeb, Edward
    Heyman
Coquette
    in co w/John Green, Gus Kahn
It's Easier Said Than Done
    in co w/John J. Loeb
Powder Your Face With Sunshine
    in co w/Stanley Rochinski
Sailboat In The Moonlight, A
    in co w/John J. Loeb
Seems Like Old Times
    in co w/John J. Loeb
Snuggled On Your Shoulder
    in co w/Joseph Young

LOUCHEIM, STUART F.
1892, American
w&m/Stuart Loucheim
Mixed Emotions

LOUDERMILK, JOHN D.
1934, American
w&m/John D. Loudermilk
Abilene
    in co w/Lester Brown,
    Bob Gibson, Albert Stanton
Amigo's Guitar
    in co w/Muriel D. Wright,
    Roy Botkin
Bad News
**Blue Train (Of The Heartbreak
  Line)**
Break My Mind
(He's My) Dreamboat
Ebony Eyes
Everything's Alright
Find Out

Grin And Bear It
    in co w/Marijohn Wilkin
Give Me A Sweetheart
I Wanna Live
I'm Looking (For A World)
Indian Reservation
Interstate Forty
James (Hold The Ladder Steady)
**Lament Of The Cherokee
  Reservation**
Language Of Love, The
Little Bird, The
Norman
Paper Tiger
Rose And A Baby Ruth, A
Sad Movies (Make Me Cry)
Short On Love
Sittin' In The Balcony
Stayin' In
Sunglasses
Talk Back Trembling Lips
Then You Can Tell Me Goodbye
Thous Shalt Not Steal
Torture
Waterloo
    in co w/Marijohn Wilkin
Windy And Warm

LOUVIN, IRA (Ira Loudermilk)
1924-1965, American
w&m/Ira Louvin
in co w/Charles Louvin (brother; born
Charles Loudermilk, 1927)
Are You Teasing Me
I Take The Chance
If I Could Only Win Your Love
Must You Throw Dust In My Face
When I Stop Dreaming

**LOVE, ANDREW
FAIRWEATHER**
English
w&m in co w/Allen Jones,
Richard Shann
Keep On Dancing (1963)

LOVEDAY, CARROLL
1898-1955, American
w&m/Carroll Loveday
That's My Desire
    in co w/Helmy Kresa
Shrine Of St. Cecelia, The

LOWE, RUTH
1914, Canadian/American
w&m/Ruth Lowe
I'll Never Smile Again
Put Your Dreams Away
    in co w/Paul Mann

LOWRY, REVEREND ROBERT
American
m/Reverend Robert Lowry
I Need Thee Ev'ry Hour (1872)
    w/Annie Sherwood Hawks

**Where Is My Wand'ring Boy
  Tonight (1877) (w&m)**

LUBOFF, NORMAN
1917, American
w&m/Norman Luboff
Yellow Bird

LUDERS, GUSTAV
1865-1913, American
m/Gustav Luders
Flutter Little Bird
    w/George Ade
Heidelberg Stein Song, The
    w/Frank Pixley
I Am Yours Truly
    w/George Ade
I'll Live For You
    w/George Ade
Message Of The Red Red Rose
    w/Frank Pixley
Message Of The Violet
    w/Frank Pixley
Tale Of The Bumblebee, The
    w/Frank Pixley
Tale Of The Kangaroo, The
    w/Frank Pixley
Tale Of The Sea Shell, The
    w/Frank Pixley

LYMAN, ABE
1897-1957, American
w&m/Abe Lyman
**(What Can I Say) After I
  Say I'm Sorry**
    in co w/Walter Donaldson
I Cried For You (1923)
    w/Arthur Freed
    co-composer Gus Arnheim
Mary Lou (1926)
    in co w/George Waggner,
    J. Russell Robinson

LYMON, FRANKIE
1942, American
w&m/Frankie Lymon
in co w/George Goldner
Why do Fools Fall In Love

LYNNE, JEFF
1946, English
w&m/Jeff Lynne
Can't Get It Out Of My Head
Do Ya
Evil Woman
Light In The City
Livin' Thing
Ma Ma Belle
Mr. Blue Sky
Showdown
So Fine
Strange Magic

318

Sweet Talkin' Woman
Telephone Line
10538 Overture
Turn To Stone
Xanadu

LYNN, LORETTA
1935, American w&m/Loretta Lynn
Coal Miner's Daughter
Dear Uncle Sam

Don't Come Home A-Drinkin'
 With Lovin' On Your Mind
Fist City
I Cried the Blue Out Of My Eyes
I Wanna Be Free
Rated X
To Make A Man
You Ain't Woman Enough
You're Lookin' At Country

LYTE, HENRY FRANCIS
(Reverend)
English
w/Henry Francis Lyte
m/William H. Monk (from the song
"Evening")
**Abide With Me (Fast Falls
 The Eventide)**
 (words 1820, music 1847)

POPULAR COMPOSERS & LYRICISTS

M

MACCAULAY, TONY
English
w&m/Tony MacCaulay
Don't Give Up On Us (1977)
Going In With My
  Eyes Open (1977)
Oklahoma Sunday
  Morning (1973)
    in co w/Albert L. Hammond,
    Michael Hazlewood
Smile A Little Smile
  For Me (1969)
    in co w/Geoff Stephens

MACCOLL, EWAN
Scottish
w&m/Ewan MacColl
First Time Ever I Saw
  Your Face, The (1972)

MACDERMOT, GALT
American
m/Galt MacDermot
w/James Rado, Gerome Ragni
African Waltz (instr.)
Aquarius
Frank Mills
Good Morning Starshine
Hair
I Got Life
Let The Sunshine In
  (The Flesh Failures)
What A Piece Of Work Is Man
Film scores:
Cotton Comes To Harlem
Hair (1979)

MACDONALD, BALLARD
1882-1935, American
w/Ballard MacDonald
Beautiful Ohio
    m/Robert A. King
Bend Down Sister
    m/Dave Silverstein,
    Con Conrad
Breeze (Blow My Baby Back
  To Me)
    co-lyricist Joe Goodwin
    m/James F. Hanley
Bring Back Those Minstrel Days
    m/Martin Broones
Clap Hands Here Comes Charley
    m/Billy Rose, Joseph Meyer
(Back Home Again In) Indiana
    m/James F. Hanley
Parade Of The Wooden Soldiers
    m/Leon Jessel
Rose Of Washington Square
    m/James F. Hanley
Trail Of The Lonesome Pine, The
    m/Harry Carroll

MACDOWELL, EDWARD
ALEXANDER
1861-1908, American
w&m/Edward Alexander MacDowell
("Woodland Sketches" - 1896)
At An Old Trysting Place
By A Meadow Brook
Deserted Farm, A
From An Indian Lodge
From Uncle Remus
In Autumn
To A Water Lily
To A Wild Rose
Told At Sunset
Will O' The Wisp

MACGREGOR, J. CHALMERS
(Chummy)
1903, American
w&m/J. Chalmers MacGregor
It Must Be Jelly ('Cause Jam
  Don't Shake Like That)

MACK, ANDREW
American
m/Andrew Mack
w/"Alice"
The Story Of The Rose (Heart
  Of My Heart I Love You)

MACK, CECIL
(Richard C. McPherson)
1883-1944, American
w/Cecil Mack
Charleston
    m/James P. Johnson
Down Among The Sugar Cane
    m/Chris Smith, Avery Hart
If He Comes In I'm Going Out
    m/Chris Smith
Runnin' Wild
    co-lyricist Leo Wood
    m/Arthur H. Gibbs
S-H-I-N-E
    m/Ford Dabney
Teasing
    m/Albert Von Tilzer

MACK, RONNIE
American
w&m/Ronnie Mack
He's So Fine (1963)

MACKENZIE JR., LEONARD C.
1915, American
w&m/Leonard C. MacKenzie Jr.
in co w/William Wirges,
Garth Montgomery
Chiquita Banana (1938)

MACLEAN, ROSS
1904, American
w&m/Ross MacLean
in co w/Arthur Richardson
Too Fat Polka

MACLELLAN, GENE
Canadian
w&m/Gene MacClellan
Call, The
Put Your Hand In
  The Hand (1971)
Snowbird (1970)

MACMURROUGH, DERMOT
Irish
m/Dermot MacMurrough
w/Josephine V. Rowe
Macushla (1910)

MADDEN, EDWARD
1878-1952, American
w/Edward Madden
Blue Bell
    m/Theodore F. Morse
By The Light Of The
  Silvery Moon
    m/Gus Edwards
Chanticleer Rag, The
    m/Albert Gumble
Consolation
    m/Theodore F. Morse
Daddy's Little Girl
    m/Theodore F. Morse
Down In Jungle Town
    m/Theodore F. Morse
Look Out For Jimmy Valentine
    m/Gus Edwards
Silver Bell
    m/Percy Wenrich
Up Up In My Aeroplane
    m/Gus Edwards

MADRIGUERA, ENRIC
1904, Spanish/American
m/Enric Madriguera
w/E. Woods
Adios

MAGIDSON, HERBERT (Herb)
1906, American
w&m/Herbert Magidson
Continental, The
    in co w/Con Conrad
Enjoy Yourself (It's Later Than
  You Think)
    in co w/Carl Sigman
Gone With The Wind
    in co w/Allie Wrubel
I'll Dance At Your Wedding
    in co w/Ben Oakland
I'm Stepping Out With A
  Memory Tonight
    in co w/Allie Wrubel
Masquerade Is Over, The
    in co w/Allie Wrubel
Midnight In Paris
    in co w/Con Conrad
Music Maestro Please
    in co w/Allie Wrubel
Pink Cocktail For A Blue Lady, A
    in co w/Ben Oakland

MAHONEY, JACK FRANCIS
1882-1945, American
w/Jack Francis Mahoney
m/Percy Wenrich
**When You Wore A Tulip And I
 Wore A Big Red Rose**

MAKOWICZ, ADAM
1941, Polish
m/Adam Makowicz (instr.)
Chopin's Willows
Jig Saw Puzzle

MALIE, TOMMY
American
w&m/Tommy Malie
in co w/Jimmy Stieger
**Looking At The World Thru Rose
 Colored Glasses (1926)**

MALKIN, NORMAN
1918-1979, American
w&m/Norman Malkin
in co w/Freddy Morgan
Hey Mr. Banjo

MALNECK, MATT (Matty)
1904, American
m/Matt Malneck
Goody, Goody
 w/Johnny Mercer
I'll Never Be The Same
 co-composer Frank Signorelli
 w/Gus Kahn
I'm Through With Love
 w/Joseph A. Livingston
Pardon My Southern Accent
 w/Johnny Mercer
Shangri La
 co-composer Robert Maxwell
 w/Carl Sigman
Stairway To The Stars
 co-composer Frank Signorelli
 w/Mitchell Parish

MALOTTE, ALBERT HAY
1895-1964, American
w&m/Albert Hay Malotte
Ferdinand The Bull
 in co w/Larry Morey
Lord's Prayer, The
 musical setting/Albert
 Hay Malotte
Song Of The Open Road
Twenty Third Psalm
 musical setting/Albert Hay
 Malotte
Ugly Duckling, The

MALTBY, RICHARD E. (Jr.)
1937, American
w&m/Richard E. Maltby Jr.
in co w/David Shire
I'll Never Say Goodbye
Manhattan Skyline
Starting Here Starting Now
With You I'm Born Again

MANCHESTER, MELISSA
1951, American
w&m/Melissa Manchester
Come In Out Of The Rain
 in co w/Carole Bayer Sager
Just Too Many People
 in co w/Vincent Poncia
Midnight Blue
 in co w/Carole Bayer Sager
Whenever I Call You Friend
 in co w/Ken Loggins

MANCINI, HENRY (Hank)
1924, American
m/Henry Mancini
All His Children
 w/Alan & Marilyn Bergman
Baby Elephant Walk
 w/Hal David
Charade
 w/Johnny Mercer
Come To Me
 w/Don Black
Days Of Wine And Roses
 w/Johnny Mercer
Dear Heart
 w/Jay Livingston, Ray Evans
It Had Better Be Tonight
 w/Johnny Mercer
It's Easy To Say (Song from '10')
 w/Robert Welles
Joanna (instr.)
Moment To Moment
 w/Johnny Mercer
Moon River
 w/Johnny Mercer
Mr. Lucky (instr. theme)
Peter Gunn (instr. theme)
Pink Panther Theme (instr.)
Sweetheart Tree, The
 w/Johnny Mercer
Whistling Away In The Dark
 w/Johnny Mercer

Film scores:
Arabesque (1966)
Bachelor In Paradise
Benny Goodman Story, The (1955)
Breakfast At Tiffany's (1961)
Charade (1963)
Dear Heart (1964)
Days Of Wine And Roses (1962)
Glenn Miller Story, The (1954)
Great Imposter, The (1960)
Great Race, The (1965)
Hatari (1962)
Moment To Moment
Mr. Hobbs Takes A Vacation (1962)
Pink Panther, The (1964)
Shot In The Dark, A (1964)
"10" (1979)
Touch Of Evil

**MANDEL, JOHN ALFRED
(Johnny)**
1925, American
m/Johnny Mandel
w/Paul Francis Webster
**Shadow Of Your
 Smile, The (1965)**
m/Johnny Mandel
Film scores:
Americanization Of
 Emily, The (1964)
Being There (1979)
Harper (1966)
M*A*S*H (1970)
Russians Are Coming, The (1966)
Sandpiper, The (1965)

**MANGIONE, CHUCK
(B. Charles Frank Mangione)**
1940, American
w&m/Chuck Mangione
Bellavia
Feels So Good
Freddie's Walking
Give It All You Got
Children Of Sanchez
Land Of Make Believe
Look To The Children
Main Squeeze
Side Street (theme)

MANILOW, BARRY
1944, American
w&m/Barry Manilow
Copacabana
 in co w/Bruce Sussman,
 Jack Feldman, Hector Garrido
**Could It Be Magic (adapted from
 Chopin's Prelude In C Minor)**
 in co w/Adrienne Anderson
Daybreak
 in co w/Adrienne Anderson
Even Now
 in co w/Marty Panzer
It's A Miracle
 in co w/Marty Panzer
This One's For You
 in co w/Marty Panzer

MANN, BARRY
1941, American
w&m/Barry Mann
Angelica
 in co w/Cynthia Weil
Blame It On The Bossa Nova
 in co w/Cynthia Weil
Bless You
 in co w/Cynthia Weil
Brown Eyed Woman
 in co w/Cynthia Weil
Born To Be Together
 in co w/Cynthia Weil,
 Phil Spector

Footsteps
in co w/Hank Hunter
Here You Come Again
in co w/Cynthia Weil
He's Sure The Boy I Love
in co w/Cynthia Weil
How Much Love
in co w/Leo Sayer
Hungry
in co w/Cynthia Weil
I Just Can't Help Believing
in co w/Cynthia Weil
I Love How You Love Me
in co w/Larry Kolber
If A Woman Answers
in co w/Cynthia Weil
I'm Gonna Be Strong
in co w/Cynthia Weil
I'm Gonna Love You
in co w/Cynthia Weil
It's Getting Better
in co w/Cynthia Weil
Just A Little Lovin' (Early In The Morning
in co w/Cynthia Weil
Kicks
in co w/Cynthia Weil
Last Blues Song, The
in co w/Cynthia Weil
Let Me Be The One
in co w/Larry Kolber
Looking Through The Eyes Of Love
in co w/Cynthia Weil
Long Way To Go, A
in co w/Cynthia Weil
Magic Town
in co w/Cynthia Weil
Make The Man Love Me
in co w/Cynthia Weil
Make Your Own Kind Of Music
in co w/Cynthia Weil
Mamacita
in co w/Cynthia Weil
My Dad
in co w/Cynthia Weil
New World Coming
in co w/Cynthia Weil
Nobody But You
in co w/Cynthia Weil
Nothing Good Comes Easy
in co w/Cynthia Weil
On Broadway
in co w/Jerry Lieber,
Mike Stoller, Cynthia Weil
Only In America
in co w/Jerry Lieber,
Mike Stoller, Cynthia Weil

Patches
in co w/Larry Kolber
Proud
in co w/Cynthia Weil

Rock And Roll Lullaby
in co w/Cynthia Weil
Saturday Night At The Movies
in co w/Cynthia Weil
Shape Of Things To Come, The
in co w/Cynthia Weil
She Say Oom Dooby Doom
So Long Dixie
in co w/Cynthia Weil
Sometimes When We Touch
in co w/Dan Hill
Songs
in co w/Cynthia Weil
(You're My) Soul And Inspiration
in co w/Cynthia Weil
Too Many Mondays
in co w/Cynthia Weil
Uptown
in co w/Cynthia Weil
Walking In The Rain
in co w/Cynthia Weil,
Phil Spector
We're Over
in co w/Cynthia Weil
We've Got To Get Out Of This Place
in co w/Cynthia Weil
When You Get Right Down To It
Who Put The Bomp (In The Bomp Ba Bomp Ba Bomp)
in co w/Gerry Goffin
You Turn Me Around
in co w/Cynthia Weil
You've Lost That Lovin' Feelin'
in co w/Cynthia Weil,
Phil Spector
Film score:
I Never Sang For My Father (1970)

MANN, DAVID
1916, American
m/David Mann
Dearie
w/Bob Hilliard
Don't Go To Strangers
w/Redd Evans
In The Wee Small Hours Of The Morning
w/Bob Hilliard
No Moon At All
w/Redd Evans
Somebody Bad Stole De Wedding Bell
w/Bob Hilliard
There I've Said It Again
w/Redd Evans
MANN, HERBIE
(Herbert Jay Solomon)
1930, American
m/Herbie Mann (instr.)
Comin' Home Baby

Hijack
Concerto Grosso
It's A Funky Thing
Memphis Underground
Nirvana
Right Now
Super Mann

MANN, KAL
1917, American
w&m/Kal Mann
Let's Twist Again
in co w/Dave Appell
Teddy Bear
in co w/Bernie Lowe

MANNING, DICK
1912, American
w&m/Dick Manning
Allegheny Moon
in co w/Al Hoffman
Fascination
musical adaptation of
F.D. Marchetti's "Valse Tzigane"
Hawaiian Wedding Song
in co w/Al Hoffman,
Charles E. King (Hawaiian title:
Ke Kali Nei Ao)
Hot Diggety
in co w/Al Hoffman
Papa Loves Mambo
in co w/Al Hoffman, Bix Reichner
Takes Two To Tango
in co w/Al Hoffman
The Three Bells (While The Angelus Was Ringing)
music by Jean Villard
(French title: "Les Trois Cloches")

MANNING, KATHLEEN LOCKHART
1890-1951, American
w&m/Kathleen Lockhart Manning
In The Luxembourg Gardens (1925)

MANTLER, MICHAEL
1939, American
m/Michael Mantler
Hapless Child, The (based on Edward Gorey)
How It Is (based on Samuel Becket)
No Answer (based on Samuel Becket)
Silence (based on Harold Pinter)

MANUS, JACK
1909, American
w&m/Jack Manus
in co w/Bernard Bierman,
Arthur Bierman
Midnight Masquerade (1946)

MANZANERO, ARMANDO
Mexican
m/Armando Manzanero
It's Impossible (Somios
  Novios) (1968)
    Eng. w/Sid Wayne
Yesterday I Heard The Rain
  (Esta Tarde Vi Llover) (1967)
    Eng. w/Gene Lees

MARCHETTI, FILIPO
1831-1902, Italian
m/Filipo Marchetti
Fascination (adapted from
  Marchetti's "Valse Tzigane")
    best-know lyric version—words by
    Dick Manning (many English-
    lyric versions have
    been published).

MARCUS, SOL
1912, American
w&m/Sol Marcus
Ask Anyone Who Knows
    in co w/Edward Seiler,
    Alvin Kaufman
Cancel The Flowers
    in co w/Edward Seiler,
    Bennie Benjamin
I Don't Want To Set The
  World On Fire
    in co w/Edward Seiler,
    Bennie Benjamin
Strictly Instrumental
    in co w/Edward Seiler,
    Bennie Benjamin
Till Then
    in co w/Edward Seiler
When The Lights Go On Again
  All Over The World
    in co w/Edward Seiler,
    Bennie Benjamin

MARESCA, ERNEST
1938, American
w&m/Ernest Maresca
Donna The Prima Donna
    in co w/Dion Di Mucci
Lonely World
    in co w/Dion Di Mucci
Lovers Who Wander
    in co w/Dion Di Mucci
Lover's Prayer, A
No One Knows
    in co w/Ken Hecht
Party Girl
    in co w/Louis J. Zerato
Runaround Sue
    in co w/Dion Di Mucci,
    Robert Schwartz

MARKS, EDWARD B.
American
w/Edward B. Marks
m/Joseph W. Stern

His Last Thoughts
  Were Of You (1894)
Little Lost Child, The (1894)
Mother Was A Lady (If Jack Were
  Only Here) (1894)

MARKS, GERALD
1900, American
m/Gerald Marks
All Of Me
    w/Seymour Simons
Is It True What They Say
  About Dixie
    w/Sammy Lerner, Irving Caesar
That's What I Want
  For Christmas
    w/Irving Caesar

MARKES, LARRY
1921, American
w&m/Larry Markes
in co w/Dick Charles
Along The Navajo Trail
    in co w/Edgar DeLange,
    Dick Charles
Mad About Him, Sad About Him,
  How Can I Be Glad Without
  Him Blues
May You Always

MARKS, JOHN D.
(Johnny)
1909, American
w&m/John D. Marks
Anyone Can Move A Mountain
I Heard The Bells On
  Christmas Day
Jingle Jingle Jingle
Holly, Jolly Christmas, A
Most Wonderful Day
  Of The Year, The
Rockin' Around The
  Christmas Tree
Rudolph The Red Nosed Reindeer
Silver And Gold

MARLEY, BOB
1945, Jamaican
w&m/Bob Marley
Get Up, Stand Up
I Shot The Sheriff
Is This Love
No Woman, No Cry
Roots, Rock, Reggae

MARSALA, JOE
1907, American
w&m/Joe Marsala
And So To Sleep Again
    in co w/Sunny Skylar
Don't Cry Joe
Little Sir Echo
    in co w/Beatrice Marsala,
    J.S. Fearis, L.R. Smith

MARSHALL, ED
American
w&m/Ed Marshall
Venus (1959)

MARSHALL, HENRY I.
1883-1958, American
m/Henry I. Marshall
w/Stanley Murphy
Be My Little Baby Bumble
  Bee (1912)

MARTI, JOSE
19th Century, Cuban
Spanish w&m/Jose Marti
Guantanamera (Lady Of
  Guantanamo)

MARTIN, FREDDY
American
m/Freddy Martin
in co w/Ray Austin (adapted from
  Tchaikovsky's First Piano Concerto)
w/Bobby Worth
Tonight We Love (1941)

MARTIN, HUGH
1914
w&m/Hugh Martin
all songs in co w/Ralph Blane
Boy Next Door, The
Buckle Down Winsocki
Connecticut
Have Yourself A Merry
  Little Christmas
Love
Pass That Peacepipe
    in co w/Ralph Blane,
    Roger Edens
Trolley Song, The
You Are For Loving

MARTIN, JOHN MOON
American
w&m/John Moon Martin
Bad Case Of Loving You (1979)
Cadillac Walk (1979)

MARTIN, TRADE
American
w&m/Trade Martin
Made For Each Other (1971)

MARTINE, LAYNG
American
w&m/Lavng Martine
Everybody Needs A
  Rainbow (1975)
Rub It In (1975)
Way Down (1977)

MASON, BARBARA
American
w&m/Barbara Mason
Yes, I'm Ready (1980)

MASON, LOWELL
1792-1872, American
m/Lowell Mason
Come Unto Me, Ye Weary (1839)
　w/Catherine H. Watterman
My Faith Looks Up
　To Thee (1830)
　w/Ray Palmer
Nearer, My God, To Thee (1859)
　(from the song "Bethany")
　w/Sarah Flower Adams

MASSER, MICHAEL
American
m/Michael Masser
Do You Know Where You're
　Going To (theme
　from "Mahogany")
　w/Gerry Goffin
Touch Me In The Morning
　w/Ronald Miller

MASSEY, D. CURTIS (Curt)
1910, American
w&m/D. Curtis Massey
Beverly Hillbillies
　(The theme from)
Honey Song, The
Petticoat Junction (The
　theme from)

MASSEY, GUY
American
w&m/Guy Massey
Prisoner's Song,The (1924)
　music adapted from a traditional
　folk air

MASSEY, LOUISE
American
w&m/Louise Massey
in co w/Lee Penny
My Adobe Hacienda (1941)

MATTHEWS, CHARLES
American
w&m/Charles Matthews
White Silver Sands (1973)

MAXWELL, ROBERT
1921, American
m/Robert Maxwell
Ebb Tide
　w/Carl Sigman
Shangri La
　co-composer Matt Malneck
　w/Carl Sigman
Song Of The Nairobi Trio (instr.)

MAY, BRIAN
1947, English
w&m/Brian May
Bohemian Rhapsody
It's Late
Killer Queen
Tie Your Mother Down
We Are The Champions

MAYALL, JOHN
1933, English
w&m/John Mayall
Blues City Shakedown
Don't Waste My Time
I'm Gonna Fight For You JB
Jenny
Laws Must Change, The
Sitting In The Rain
So Hard To Share

MAYFIELD, CURTIS
1942, American
w&m/Curtis Mayfield,
except as noted.
Beautiful Brother Of Mine
Freddy's Dead
Get Down
Gypsy Woman
If There's A Hell Down Below,
　We're All Gonna Go
He Don't Love Like I Do
　in co w/Jerry Butler
He Will Break Your Heart
　in co w/Jerry Butler,
　Calvin Carter
I Plan To Stay A Believer
Let It Be Me
　in co w/Jerry Butler
Let's Do It Again
Mighty, Mighty
Monkey Time, the
Move On Up
Need To Belong
Nothing Can Stop Me
People Get Ready
Stare And Stare
Superfly
We Got To Have Peace
We're A Winner

MAYFIELD, PERCY
American
w&m/Percy Mayfield
Hit The Road Jack (1961)

MAYHEW, WILLIAM
1889-1951, American
w&m/William Mayhew
It's A Sin To Tell A Lie

MCALPIN, VIC
American
w&m/Vic McAlpin
Almost (1952)
　in co w/Jack Toombs
Anymore (1960)
　in co w/Roy F. Drusky,
　Marie Wilson
Before This Day Ends (1961)
　in co w/Roy F. Drusky,
　Marie Wilson
I'm In Love Again (1959)
　in co w/George Morgan

Let's Have A Little (1951)
　in co w/Ruth E. Coletharp
What Is Life Without Love (1947)
　in co w/Eddy Arnold,
　Owen Bradley
What Locks The Door (1968)

MCBROOM, AMANDA
American
w&m/Amanda McBroom
Rose, The (1979)

MCCALL, C.W. (William Fries)
1928, American
w&m/C.W. McCall
And Keep On-A-Truckin'
Cafe
Convoy
Old Home Filler-Up
There Won't Be No
　Country Music
Wolfcreek Pass

MCCARRON, CHARLES
1891-1919, American
w&m/Charles McCarron
Blues My Naughty Sweetie
　Gives To Me
　in co w/Carey Morgan
Down Where The Swanee
　River Flows
　in co w/Albert Von Tilzer,
　Charles S. Alberte
Oh How She Could Yacki Hacki
　Wicki Wacki Woo
　in co w/Albert Von Tilzer,
　Stanley Murphy

MCCARTHY, JOSEPH
1885-1943, American
w/Joseph McCarthy
Alice Blue Gown
　m/Harry Tierney
Beatrice Fairfax
　co-lyricist Grant Clarke
　m/James V. Monaco
I Miss You Most Of All
　m/James V. Monaco
I'm Always Chasing Rainbows
　m/Harry Carroll
Ireland Must Be Heaven For My
　Mother Came From There
　m/Fred Fisher, Howard Johnson
Irene
　m/Harry Tierney
Kinkajou, The
　m/Harry Tierney
Ranger's Song, The
　m/Harry Tierney
Rio Rita
　m/Harry Tierney
They Go Wild Simply Wild Over
　Me
　m/Fred Fisher

**What Do You Want To Make
  Those Eyes At Me For**
  m/James V. Monaco,
  Howard Johnson
You Made Me Love You
  m/James V. Monaco

MCCARTNEY, PAUL
1942, English
w&m in co w/John Lennon
All You Need Is Love
And I Love Her
Can't Buy Me Love
Come Together, Oh Darling
Day Tripper
Eleanor Rigby
Fool On The Hill, The
From Me To You
Get Back
Got To Get You Into My Life
Hard Day's Night, A
Here, There And Everywhere
Hey Jude
I Feel Fine
I Want To Hold Your Hand
Let It Be
Long And Winding Road, The
Lucy In The Sky With Diamonds
Michelle
Norweigan Wood
Ob-La-Di, Ob-La-Da
Paperback Writer
Penny Lane
Please, Please Me
She's Leaving Home
She Loves You
Strawberry Fields Forever
Ticket To Ride
w&m in co w/Linda
Eastman McCartney
Band On The Run
Girl's School
Helen Wheels
I've Had Enough
Jet
Junior's Farm
Let 'Em In
Let's Love
Live And Let Die
Maybe I'm Amazed
Mine For Me
My Love
Sally G
Silly Love Songs
Uncle Albert/Admiral Halsey
With A Little Luck

MCCLEAN, DON
1945, American
w&m/Don McClean
American Pie
And I Love You So
Vincent

MCCOY, ROSEMARIE
American
w&m/Rosemarie McCoy
Don't Be Angry (1955)
  in co w/Nappy Brown,
  Fred Mendelsohn
Hurts Me To My Heart (1954)
  in co w/Charles Singleton
It's Gonna Work Out Fine (1961)
  in co w/Sylvia McKinney
Mambo Baby (1954)
  in co w/Charles Singleton

MCCOY, VAN
1940, American
w&m/Van McCoy
Baby Don't Take Your Love
Baby I'm Yours
Hustle, The
**Right On The Tip Of
  My Tongue**
So Much Love
When You're Young And In Love

MCDANIELS, EUGENE
1935, American
w&m/Eugene McDaniels
Feel Like Makin' Love

MCDILL, BOB
American
w&m/Bob McDill
Amanda (1979)
Door's Always Open, The
  in co w/Dickey Lee
I Met A Friend Of Yours Today
  in co w/Wayland Holyfield
I Wish I Was Crazy Again
  in co w/Wayland Holyfield
I'll Do It All Over Again
  in co w/Wayland Holyfield
**Red Necks, White Socks And
  Blue Ribbon Beer**
  in co w/Wayland Holyfield,
  Chuck Neese
Say It Again
She Never Knew Me
  in co w/Wayland Holyfield
Why Don't You Spend The Night
**You Never Miss A Real
  Good Thing**

MCDONALD, MICHAEL
American
w&m/Michael McDonald
Let Me Go, Love (1979)
  in co w/B.J. Foster
Minute By Minute (1979)
  in co w/Lester Abrams
Takin' It To The Streets (1976)
This Is It
  in co w/Kenneth Loggins
What A Fool Believes (1979)
  in co w/Kenneth Loggins

MCFADDEN, GENE
American
w&m/Gene McFadden
in co w/John Whitehead, Jerry Cohen
Ain't No Stoppin' Us Now (1979)

MCCREE, JUNE
1865-1918, American
w&m in co w/Albert Von Tilzer
Carrie
Put Your Arms Around Me Honey

MCDONALD, JOSEPH
(Country Joe McDonald)
1942, American
w&m/Joseph McDonald
Fish Cheer
  in co w/Barry "The Fish"Melton
Hey Bobby
I Feel Like I'm Fixin' To Die Rag
Not So Sweet Matha Lorraine
Return Of Sweet Lorraine, The

MCGUINN, ROGER
(James Joseph, "Roger"
McGuinn III)
1942, American
w&m/Roger McGuinn
Ballad Of Easy Rider
5D (Fifth Dimension)
Eight Miles High
Have You Seen Her Face
It Won't Be Wrong
Jesus Is Just Alright
Lady Friend
Mr. Spaceman
My Back Pages
Set You Free This Time

MCHUGH, JIMMY
1894-1969, American
m/Jimmy McHugh
Blue Again
  w/Dorothy Fields
Can't Get Out Of This Mood
  w/Frank Loesser
Clear Out Of This World
  w/Al Dubin
**Coming In On A Wing And A
  Prayer**
  w/Harold Adamson
Cuban Love Song
  w/Dorothy Fields
Diga Diga Doo
  w/Dorothy Fields
Dinner At Eight
  w/Dorothy Fields
Doing The New Low-Down
  w/Dorothy Fields
Don't Blame Me
  w/Dorothy Fields
Dream, Dream, Dream
  w/Mitchell Parish

Exactly Like You
w/Dorothy Fields
How Blue The Night
w/Harold Adamson
Hubba, Hubba, Hubba, A
w/Harold Adamson
**I Can't Believe That You're
In Love With Me**
w/Clarence Gaskill
**I Can't Give You Anything But
Love Baby**
w/Dorothy Fields
I Feel A Song Coming On
w/Dorothy Fields
I'd Know You Anywhere
w/Johnny Mercer
I'm In The Mood For Love
w/Dorothy Fields
I'm Shooting High
w/Ted Koehler
It's A Most Unusual Day
w/Harold Adamson
Lost In A Fog
w/Dorothy Fields
Lovely Lady
w/Ted Koehler
Lovely To Look At
w/Dorothy Fields
**Lovely Way To Spend
An Evening, A**
w/Harold Adamson
My Own
w/Harold Adamson
On The Sunny Side Of The Street
w/Dorothy Fields
Porgy
w/Dorothy Fields
Singin' The Blues
w/Dorothy Fields
Thank You For A Lovely Evening
w/Dorothy Fields
Too Young To Go Steady
w/Harold Adamson
**When My Sugar Walks Down
The Street**
w/Gene Austin, Irving Mills
You're A Sweetheart
w/Harold Adamson
You Say The Nicest Things Baby
w/Harold Adamson

MCINTIRE, LANI
1904-1951, American
w&m in co w/Del Lyon
**One Rose, The (That's Left
In My Heart)**

MCKUEN, ROD
1938, American
w&m/Rod McKuen
Alley Ally Oxen Free
in co w/Tom Drake,
Steven Yates

Another Country
in co w/Barry McGuire
Beautiful Stranger, The
Chasing The Sun
Doesn't Anybody Know My Name
If You Go Away
in co w/Jacques Brel
I'll Never Be Alone
Jean
Listen To The Warm
Loner, The
Love's Been Good To Me
Love Child
Only Love
Pastures Green
People Change
Seasons In The Sun
in co w/Jacques Brel
To Die In The Summertime
World I Used To Know, The
Film scores:
Joanna (1968)
Prime Of Miss Jean
Brodie, The (1969)

MCNEELEY, BIG JAY
American
w&m/Big Jay McNeeley
Deacon's Hop (1949)

MCPHATTER, CLYDE
1933, American
w&m/Clyde McPhatter
in co w/Jerry Wexler
Honey Love

MCVIE, CHRISTINE PERFECT
1943, English
w&m/Christine Perfect McVie
Chain
in co w/Stephanie (Stevie) Nicks,
Lindsay Buckingham
Don't Stop
Never Forget
Never Make Me Cry
Oh Daddy
Over And Over
Say You Love Me
Sugar Daddy
Over My Head
Warm Ways
World Turning
in co w/Lindsay Buckingham
You Make Loving Fun

MEDLEY, PHIL
American
w&m/Phil Medley
Million To One, A (1968)
Twist And Shout (1962)
in co w/Bert Russell

MEINKEN, FRED
1882-1958, American
m/Fred Meinken
w/Dave Ringle
Wabash Blues (1921)

MEINKEN, FRED
1882-1958, American
m/Fred Meinken
w/Dave Ringle
Wabash Blues (1921)

MELANIE
(Melanie Safka Schekeryk)
w&m/Melanie
Beautiful People
Bitter Bad
Brand New Key
Lay Down (Candles In The Rain)
Little Bit Of Me
Nickel Song, The
Peace Will Come
Ring The Living Bell
Shine The Living Light
Someday, I'll Be A Farmer
Together Alone
**What Have They Done To My
Song, Ma (Look What They've
Done To My Song)**
Will You Love Me Tomorrow

MELLIN, ROBERT (Bobby)
1908, American
w&m/Robert Mellin
I'm Yours
Stranger On The Shore
in co w/Acker Bilk

MELROSE, WALTER
1889-1969, American
m/Walter Melrose
Asia Minor
Copenhagen
in co w/Charlie Davis
High Society
in co w/Clarence Williams
Sugar Foot Stomp
in co w/Louis Armstrong,
Joe "King" Oliver
Tin Roof Blues
in co w/Leon Rappolo,
Paul Wares, George Brunes,
Mel Stitzler

MELSHER, IRVING
1906-1962, American
m/Irving Melsher
I May Never Pass This Way Again
w/Murray Wizell
Roses In The Rain
w/Remus Harris
So Long
w/Remus Harris, Russ Morgan

MENCHER, MURRAY
(Ted Murry)
1898, American
m/Murray Mencher
**Don't Break The Heart That
Loves You**
w/Benny Davis

Throw Another Log On The Fire
  w/Charles Tobias, Jack Scholl
**You Can't Pull The Wool Over My
  Eyes**
  w/Milton Ager

MENDES, SERGIO
1941, Brazilian
w&m/Sergio Mendes
Constant Rain
Mas Que Nada

MENENDEZ, NILO
Cuban
m/Nilo Menendez
English w/E. Rivera, E. Woods.
Spanish w/Adolfo Utrera
**Green Eyes (Aquellos Ojos
  Verdes) (1929)**

MENDELLSOHN, FELIX
1809-1847, German
Wedding March

MERCER, JOHN H. (Johnny)
1909-1976, American
w/Johnny Mercer
Ac-Cen-Tchu-Ate The Positive
  m/Harold Arlen
And The Angels Sing
  m/Harry (Ziggy) Elman
Anyplace I Hang My Hat Is Home
  m/Harold Arlen
**Arthur Murray Taught Me
  Dancing In A Hurry**
  m/Victor Schertzinger
Autumn Leaves
  m/Joseph Kosma
Bilbao Song, The
  m/Kurt Weill
Blues In The Night
  m/Harold Arlen
Bob White
  m/Bernard Hanighen
Come Rain Or Come Shine
  m/Harold Arlen
Day In, Day Out
  m/Rube Bloom
Days Of Wine And Roses
  m/Henry Mancini
Dearly Beloved
  m/Jerome Kern
Dream
  m/Johnny Mercer
Early Autumn
  m/Ralph Burns
Facts Of Life, The
  m/Johnny Mercer
Fancy Free
  m/Harold Arlen
Fools Rush In
  m/Rube Bloom
G.I. Jive
  m/Johnny Mercer

**Girl Friend Of The
  Whirling Dervish, The**
  co-lyricist Al Dubin
  m/Harry Warren
Goody-Goody
  m/Matt Malneck
Glow-Worm, The
  original lyric Lilla Caley Robinson
  m/Paul Lincke
Hit The Road To Dreamland
  m/Harold Arlen
Hooray For Hollywood
  m/Richard Whiting
How Little We Know
  m/Hoagy Carmichael
I'd Know You Anywhere
  m/Jimmy McHugh
I Remember You
  m/Victor Schertzinger
I Thought About You
  m/James Van Heusen
I Wanna Be Around
  m/Sadie Vimmerstedt
If I Had My Druthers
  m/Gene DePaul
I'm An Old Cowhand
  m/Johnny Mercer
**I'm Building Up To
  An Awful Let-Down**
  m/Fred Astaire, Hal Borne
I'm Like A Fish Out Of Water
  m/Richard Whiting
**In The Cool, Cool, Cool Of
  The Evening**
  m/Hoagy Carmichael
Jamboree Jones
  m/Johnny Mercer
Jeepers Creepers
  m/Harry Warren
Jubilation T. Cornpone
  m/Gene DePaul
June Comes Around Every Year
  m/Harold Arlen
Lazybones
  m/Hoagy Carmichael
Laura
  m/David Raksin
Let's Take The Long Way Home
  m/Harold Arlen
Life Is What You Make It
  m/Marvin Hamlisch
Lost
  m/Phil Ohman, Macy O. Teetor
Love Is Where You Find It
  co-lyricist Al Dubin
  m/Harry Warren
Love Of My Life
  m/Artie Shaw
Love With The Proper Stranger
  m/Elmer Bernstein
Moment To Moment
  m/Henry Mancini

Moon River
  m/Henry Mancini
Mr. Meadowlark
  m/Walter Donaldson
My Shining Hour
  m/Harold Arlen
Not Mine
  m/Victor Schertzinger
**On Behalf Of The
  Visiting Fireman**
  m/Walter Donaldson
**On The Atchison, Topeka And
  The Santa Fe**
  m/Harry Warren
One For My Baby
  m/Harold Arlen
Out Of This World
  m/Harold Arlen
Pardon My Southern Accent
  m/Matt Malneck
P.S. I Love You
  m/Gordon Jenkins
Satin Doll
  m/Duke Ellington,
  Billy Strayhorn
Skylark
  m/Hoagy Carmichael
Something's Gotta Give
  m/Johnny Mercer
Tangerine
  m/Victor Schertzinger
That Old Black Magic
  m/Harold Arlen
This Time The Dream's On Me
  m/Harold Arlen
Too Marvelous For Words
  m/Richard Whiting
**We're Working Our Way
  Through College**
  m/Richard Whiting
When The World Was Young
  m/M. Philippe-Gerard
When You're In Love
  m/Gene DePaul
Whistling Away In The Dark
  m/Henry Mancini
**You Grow Sweeter As The
  Years Go By**
  m/Johnny Mercer
**You Must Have Been A
  Beautiful Baby**
  m/Harry Warren
You Were Never Lovelier
  m/Jerome Kern

**MERCURY, FREDDIE
(Frederick Bulsara)**
1946, English/African
w&m/Freddie Mercury
**Crazy Little Thing Called Love
  (1980)**

MERRILL, BOB
1921, American
w&m/Bob Merrill
Belle, Belle (My Liberty Belle)
Candy And Cake
Don't Rain On My Parade
in co w/Jule Styne
Honeycomb
How Much Is That
Doggie In The Window
If I Knew You Were Comin' I'd've
Baked A Cake
in co w/Al Hoffman, Al Trace
Love Makes the World Go 'Round
Make Yourself Comfortable
Mambo Italiano
My Truly, Truly Fair
People
in co w/Jule Styne
Pittsburgh, Pennsylvania
Sparrow In The Tree Top
Take Me Along
Tina Marie
Walkin' To Missouri

MESHEL, WILBUR (Billy)
1939, American
w&m/Wilbur (Billy) Meshel
Come Live Your Life With Me
in co w/Nino Rota, Larry Kusik
Dear Mrs. Appleby
in co w/Phil Barr
Do You Ever Think Of Me
I Didn't Come To New York
To Meet A Guy From
My Hometown
in co w/Fred Anisfield
L. David Sloane

MERSON, BILLY
English
w&m/Billy Merson
Spaniard That Blighted
My Life, The (1911)

MESKILL, JACK
1897, American
w&m/Jack Meskill
Au Revoir Pleasant Dreams
in co w/Jean Schwartz
I Sent A Letter To Santa
in co w/Vincent Rose,
Larry Stock
I Was Lucky
in co w/Jack Stern
On The Beach At Bali Bali
in co w/Al Sherman,
Abner Silver
Pardon Me Pretty Baby
in co w/Vincent Rose
Santa Claus Is Riding The Trail
in co w/Archie Gottler
Rhythm Of The Rain
in co w/Jack Stern

Smile, Darn Ya, Smile
in co w/Charles O'Flynn, Max
Rich
There's Danger In Your
Eyes Cherie
in co w/Harry Richman,
Pete Wendling
Were You Sincere
in co w/Vincent Rose
When The Organ Played
'O Promise Me'

MESSINA, JAMES
1947, American
w&m/James Messina
Ain't Gonna Change My Music
in co w/Kenneth Loggins
Listen To A Country Song
Thinking Of You
in co w/Kenneth Loggins
Your Mama Don't Dance
in co w/Kenneth Loggins
Vahevala
in co w/Kenneth Loggins

METZ, THEODORE A.
1948-1936, American
m/Theodore A. Metz
w/Joe Hayden
There'll Be A Hot Time In The
Old Town Tonight (1896)

MEYER, CHARLES (Chuck)
1924, American
w&m/Chuck Meyer
in co w/Biff Jones
Suddenly There's A Valley (1955)

MEYER, GEORGE W.
1884-1959, American
m/George W. Meyer
Beautiful Annabelle Lee
w/Alfred Bryan
Brown Eyes Why Are You Blue
w/Alfred Bryan
Everything Is Peaches Down
In Georgia
co-composer Milton Ager
w/Grant Clarke
For Me And My Gal
w/Edgar Leslie, E. Ray Goetz
Lonesome
w/Edgar Leslie
My Mother's Rosary
w/Samuel M. Lewis
There Are Such Things
w/Stanley Adams, Abel Baer
When You're A Long, Long Way
From Home
w/Samuel L. Lewis
Where Did Robinson Crusoe Go
With Friday On Saturday Night
w/Samuel M. Lewis,
Joseph Young

MEYER, JOSEPH
1894, American
w&m/Joseph Meyer
California Here I Come
in co w/Buddy DeSylva,
Al Jolson
Clap Hands Here Comes Charley
in co w/Billy Rose,
Ballard MacDonald
Crazy Rhythm
in co w/Irving Caesar,
Roger Wolfe Kahn
Cup Of Coffee, A Sandwich
And You, A
in co w/Al Dubin, Billy Rose
Golden Gate
in co w/Billy Rose,
Dave Dreyer, Al Jolson
I Wish I Were Twins
in co w/Frank Loesser,
Eddie DeLange
If You Knew Susie
in co w/Buddy DeSylva
It's An Old Southern Custom
in co w/Jack Yellen
My Honey's Lovin' Arms
in co w/Joseph Meyer, Herman
Ruby

MEYERS, BILLY
1894, American
w&m/Billy Meyers
Bugle Call Rag
Nobody's Sweetheart
in co w/Gus Kahn,
Ernie Erdman, Elmer Schoebel

MICHAELS, LEE
1945, American
w&m/Lee Michaels
Do You Know What I Mean

MIEIR, AUDREY
American
w&m/Audrey Mieir
His Name Is Wonderful

MILES, ALFRED HART
1883-1956, American
w/Alfred Hart Miles
in co w/Royal Lovell
m/Charles A. Zimmerman
Anchors Aweigh (1906)

MILES, C. AUSTIN
1868-1946, American
w&m/C. Austin Miles
In The Garden (1912)

MILLER, BOB
1895-1955, American
w&m/Bob Miller
There's A Star-Spangled Banner
Waving Somewhere

MILLER, CHARLES WILLIAM
1939, American
See list of selections and
collaborators under Lee Oskar.

MILLER, EDDIE
1929, American
w&m/Eddie Miller
in co w/Dub Williams, Robert Yount
Release Me (1954)

MILLER, GLENN
1904-1944, American
m/Glenn Miller
w/Mitchell Parish
Moonlight Serenade

MILLER, HELEN
American
w&m/Helen Miller
Foolish Little Girl (1963)
    in co w/Howard Greenfield
It Hurts To Be In Love (1964)
    in co w/Howard Greenfield
**Love Takes A Long
  Time Growin' (1966)**
    in co w/Roger Atkins
Make Me Your Baby (1965)
    in co w/Roger Atkins
Rumors (1962)
    in co w/Howard Greenfield

MILLER, J.D.
American
w&m/J.D. Miller
**It Wasn't God Who Made
  Honky Tonk Angels (1952)**

MILLER, ROGER
1936, American
w&m/Roger Miller
Billy Bayou
Chug-A-Lug
Dang Me
Do-Wacka-Do
Engine, Engine Number Nine
England Swings
Home
Husbands And Wives
I Believe In Sunshine
Invitation To The Blues
King Of The Road
**Last Word In Lonesome Is Me,
  The**
My Ears Should Burn
Walkin' In The Sunshine
When Two Worlds Collide
    in co w/Bill Anderson

MILLER, RONALD
American
w/Ronald Miller
For Once In My Life (1965)
    m/Orlando Murden
Place In The Sun, A (1966)
    m/Bryan Wells

Touch Me In The Morning (1972)
    m/Michael Masser

MILLER, STEVE
1943, American
w&m/Steve Miller
Brave New World
Dear Mary
Fly Like An Eagle
Living In The U.S.A.
Quicksilver Girl
Rock'n Me
Seasons
    in co w/Ben Sidran
Space Cowboy
    in co w/Ben Sidran

MILLS, FRANK
Canadian
w&m/Frank Mills
Music Box Dancer (1979)
Peter Piper (1979)

**MILLS, FREDERICK ALLEN
(Kerry)**
1869-1948, American
w&m/Frederick Allen Mills
Any Old Port In A Storm
    in co w/Arthur J. Lamb
At A Georgia Camp Meeting
Meet Me In St. Louis, Louis
    w/Andrew Sterling
Red Wing
    w/Thurland Chattaway

MILLS, GORDON
English
w&m/Gordon Mills
in co w/Les Reed
It's Not Unusual (1965)

MILLS, IRVING
1894, American
w&m/Irving Mills
Caravan
    in co w/Duke Ellington,
    Juan Tizol
**I Let A Song Go Out Of
  My Heart**
    in co w/Duke Ellington,
    Henry Nemo
In A Sentimental Mood
    in co w/Duke Ellington
**It Don't Mean A Thing (If It
  Ain't Got That Swing)**
    in co w/Duke Ellington
Minnie The Moocher
    in co w/Cab Calloway
Mooche, The
    in co w/Duke Ellington
Mood Indigo
    in co w/Duke Ellington,
    Leon (Barney) Bigard
Moonglow
    in co w/Will Hudson,
    Eddie DeLange

Organ Grinder's Song, The
    in co w/Will Hudson,
    Mitchell Parish
Solitude
    in co w/Duke Ellington,
    Eddie DeLange
Sophisticated Lady
    in co w/Duke Ellington,
    Mitchell Parish
**When My Sugar Walks Down
  The Street**
    in co w/Gene Austin,
    Jimmy McHugh

MILTON, ROY
American
w&m/Roy Milton
R.M. Blues (1946)

MINGUS, CHARLES
1922-1979, American
m/Charles Mingus (instr.)
**Black Saint And The Sinner
  Lady, The**
Duke's Choice
Eat That Chicken
Foggy Day
Goodbye Pork Pie Hat
Haitian Fight Song
LoveChant
Pithecanthropus Erectus
Shadows (film score)
Tijuana Gift Shop
**Wednesday Night
  Prayer Meeting**
What Love
Ysabel's Table Dance

MITCHELL, JONE
1943, Canadian/American
w&m/Joni Mitchell
All I Want
Amelia
Big Yellow Taxi
Both Sides Now
Carey
Circle Game, The
Chelsea Morning
Court And Spark
Coyote
**Dry Cleaner From
  Des Moines, The**
Free Man In Paris
Hejira
He Played Real Good For Free
Help Me
Hissing Of Summer Lawns, The
**In France They Kiss
  On Main Street**
Ladies Of The Canyon
Mingus
My Old Man
Raised On Robbery
This Flight Tonight
Willie

Woodstock
You Turn Me On, I'm A Radio

MIZZY, VIC
1922, American
w&m/Vic Mizzy
in co w/Mann Curtis
Jones Boy, The
Loop De Loo
My Dreams Are Getting Better
  All The Time
Whole World Is Singing
  My Song, The

MOELLER, FRIEDRICH WILHELM
Austrian
m/Friedrich Wilhelm Moeller
Happy Wanderer, The (Val-De Ri,
  Val-De Rah) (1954)
  w/Antonia Ridge

MOLL, BILLY
1905, American
w&m/Billy Moll
I Scream, You Scream, We All
  Scream For Ice Cream
  in co w/Robert King,
  Howard Johnson
Wrap Your Troubles In Dreams
  in co w/Harry Barris, Ted Koehler

MOLLOY, JAMES LYMAN
American
m/James Lyman Molloy
Kerry Dance, The (1875 approx.)
  w/James Lyman Molloy
Love's Old Sweet Song
  w/G. Clifton Bingham

MOMAN, CHIPS
American
w&m/Chips Moman
(Hey Won't You Play) Another
  Somebody Done Somebody
  Wrong Song (1975)
  in co w/Larry Butler
Dark End Of The Street
  in co w/Dan Penn
Do Right Woman, Do Right Man
  in co w/Dan Penn
Everybody Loves A Rain Song
  in co w/Mark James
Luckenback, Texas
  in co w/Bobby Emmons
Wurlitzer Prize, The
  in co w/Bobby Emmons

MONACO, JAMES V.
1885-1945, American
m/James V. Monaco
Ain't It A Shame About Mame
  w/Johnny Burke
Apple For The Teacher, An
  w/Johnny Burke

Beatrice Fairfax
  w/Joseph McCarthy,
  Grant Clarke
Every Night About This Time
  w/Ted Koehler
For Dancers Only (Pigeon
  Walk) (instr.)
I Can't Begin To Tell You
  w/Mack Gordon
I Miss You Most Of All
  w/Joseph McCarthy
I've Got A Pocketful Of Dreams
  w/Johnny Burke
Hang Your Heart On A
  Hickory Limb
  w/Johnny Burke
My Heart Is Taking Lessons
  w/Johnny Burke
On The Sentimental Side
  w/Johnny Burke
Only Forever
  w/Johnny Burke
Row Row Row
  w/William Jerome
Sing A Song Of Sunbeams
  w/Johnny Burke
Six Lessons From
  Madam Lazonga
  w/Charles Newman
That Sly Old Gentleman
  w/Johnny Burke
That's For Me
  w/Johnny Burke
This Is My Night To Dream
  w/Johnny Burke
What Do You Want To Make
  Those Eyes At Me For
  w/Joseph McCarthy,
  Howard E. Johnson
You Made Me Love You
  w/Joseph McCarthy
You're Gonna Lose Your Gal
  w/Joseph Young
You've Got Me In The
  Palm Of Your Hand
  w/Edgar Leslie

MONDA, RICHARD
American
w&m/Richard Monda
Chick-A-Boom (1971)

MONEY, EDDIE
1949, American
w&m/Eddie Money
Baby Hold On
  in co w/Jimmy Lyon
Get A Move ON
  in co w/Paul Collins,
  Lloyd Chiate
Maybe I'm A Fool
  in co w/Lloyd Chiate,
  Lee Garrett, Robert Taylor
Two Tickets To Paradise

MONK, THELONIOUS SPHERE
1920, American
m/Thelonious Sphere Monk (instr.)
Blue Monk
Criss Cross
Episotrophy
Eronel
Evidence
I Mean You
Little Rootie Tootie
Monk's Dream
Monk's Mood
Mysterioso
Off Minor
Round Midnight
Straight No Chaser

MONROE, WILLIAM SMITH (Bill)
1911-1975, American
m/William Smith Monroe (instr.)
Blue Grass Breakdown
Blue Moon Of Kentucky
I'm Working On A Building
My Little Georgia Rose
Uncle Pen
Roanoke
Scotland
Walking In Jerusalem

MONROE, VAUGHN
1911, American
w&m/Vaughn Monroe
Racing With The Moon

MONTGOMERY, BOB
American
w&m/Bob Montgomery
Misty Blue (1967)

MONTGOMERY, MELBA
1938, American
w&m/Melba Montgomery
Don't Keep Me Lonely Too Long
We Must Have Been Out Of Our
  Minds

MONTGOMERY, WES
1925-1968
m/Wes Montgomery (instr.)
Airgun
Finger Pickin'
Four On Six

MOODY, JAMES
1925, American
m/James Moody (instr.)
I've Got The Blues
Moody's Workshop
Moody's Mood

MOONEY, JAMES A.
1872-1951, American
w&m/James A. Mooney
I Had A Hat When I Came In

MOONEY, RALPH
American
w&m/Ralph Mooney
in co w/Charles Seals
Crazy Arms (1956)

MOORE, DANNY
American
w&m/Danny Moore
Shambala

MOORE, FLEECIE
1915, American
w&m/Fleecie Moore
Beans And Cornbread
in co w/Freddie Clark
Beware Brother Beware
in co w/Morry Lasco, Dick Adams
Buzz Me
in co w/Dick Adams
Caldonia
Let The Good Times Roll
in co w/Sam Theard

MOORE, MARVIN
American
w/Marvin Moore
m/Bob Davie
Green Door, The (1956)

MOORE, PETE
American
w&m/Pete Moore
in co w/Billy Griffin
Love Machine (1968)

MOORE, PHIL
1918, American
w&m/Phil Moore
Shoo Shoo Baby (1943)

MOORE, THOMAS
1779-1852, Irish
w/Thomas Moore
**Believe Me If All Those
Endearing Young Charms (1808)**
m/from the traditional Irish
melody "My Lodging Is On The
Cold Ground"
Canadian Boat Song (1804)
m/from the French-Canadian folk
song "Dans Mon Chemin",
composer unknown.
**Harp That Once Thro' Tara's
Halls, The (1807)**
m/from the traditional Irish
melody "Gramachree"
**'Tis The Last Rose Of
Summer (1813)**
m/from the traditional Irish
melody "Groves Of Blarney"
**Let Erin Remember The Days
Of Old (1808)**
m/from the traditional Irish
melody "The Red Fox"

Minstrel Boy, The (1813)
m/from the traditional Irish
melody "The Moreen"
**Rich And Rare Were The Gems
She Wore (1807)**
m/from the traditional Irish
melody "The Summer Is Coming"

MORALI, JACQUES
French
w&m/Jacques Morali
Macho Man (1978)
Ready For The '80's (1979)
Y.M.C.A. (1978)

MOREHEAD, JAMES T.
1906, American
w&m/James T. Morehead
in co w/Jimmy Cassin
Sentimental Me (1950)

MOREY, LARRY
1905, American
w/Larry Morey
Ferdinand The Bull
in co w/Albert Hay Malotte
Heigh Ho, Heigh Ho
in co w/Frank E. Churchill
Lavender Blue (Dilly Dilly)
in co w/Eliot Daniel, after
an old English folk melody
One Song
in co w/Frank E. Churchill
Some Day My Prince Will Come
in co w/Frank E. Churchill
Whistle While You Work
in co w/Frank E. Churchill

MORGAN, CAREY
1885-1960, American
w&m/Carey Morgan
**Blues My Naughty Sweetie Gives
To Me**
in co w/Charles McCarron
Sippin' Cider Thru' A Straw
in co w/Lee David

MORGAN, DORINDA
1909, American
w&m/Dorinda Morgan
in co w/Harold Stanley,
Gerry Manners
Man Upstairs, The (1954)

MORGAN, GEORGE
1925, American
w&m/George Morgan
Candy Kisses (1948)
I'm In Love Again
in co w/Vic McAlpin

MORGAN, LEE
1938-1972, American
m/Lee Morgan (instr.)
Sidewinder, The (1963)

MORGAN, RUSS
1904, American
w&m/Russ Morgan
Does Your Heart Beat For Me
in co w/Arnold Johnson,
Mitchell Parish
So Tired
in co w/Jack Stuart
So True
in co w/Jack Stuart
**Somebody Else Is Taking
My Place**
in co w/Dick Howard,
Bob Ellsworth
**You're Nobody 'Til Somebody
Loves You**
in co w/Larry Stock,
James Cavanaugh

MORODER, GEORGIO
German
w&m/Georgio Moroder
Call Me (1980)
in co w/Deborah Harry
Heaven Knows
in co w/Pete Bellotte,
Donna Summer
I Feel Love (1977)
in co w/Pete Bellotte,
Donna Summer
I Love You (1978)
in co w/Pete Bellotte,
Donna Summer
I Remember Yesterday
in co w/Pete Bellotte,
Donna Summer
Love Passion (1980)
Night Drive (1980)
On The Radio
in co w/Donna Summer
Our Love
in co w/Donna Summer
Rumour Has It
in co w/Pete Bellotte,
Donna Summer
Spring Affair
in co w/Pete Bellotte,
Donna Summer
**Try Me I Know We Can
Make It (1976)**
in co w/Pete Bellotte,
Donna Summer
Winter Melody
in co w/Pete Bellotte,
Donna Summer
Film scores:
American Gigolo (1980)
Foxes (1980)
Midnight Express (1978)

MOROSS, JEROME
1913, American
m/Jerome Moross
w/John Latouche
Lazy Afternoon

MORRIS, CRAIG
American
w&m/Craig Morris
Mountains Don't Seem High, The

MORRIS, KENNETH
19th century, American
m/Kenneth Morris
**Just A Closer Walk With Thee
(various English word versions)**

MORRIS, LEE
1916, American
w&m/Lee Morris
in co w/Bernie Wayne
Blue Velvet

MORRISON, ROBERT (Bob)
American
w&m/Robert Morrison
Midnight Angel
  in co w/Bill Anthony
You Decorated My Life (1979)
  in co w/Debbie Hopp
**Are You On The Road To
 Lov'in Me Again**
  in co w/Debbie Hopp

MORRISON, VAN
1945, Irish
w&m/Van Morrison
Blue Money
Brown-Eyed Girl
Come Running
Domino
Gloria
  in co w/George Ivan Morrison
Into The Mystic
Jackie Wilson Said
Moondance
Moonshine Whiskey
Old Old Woodstock
Redwood Tree
St. Dominic's Preview
Tupelo Honey
Wavelenghth
Wild Night

MORSE, THEODORA
**(Dorothy Terriss, D.A. Esrom,
Dolly Morse)**
1890-1953, American
w/Theodora Morse
Blue Bell
  m/Edward Madden
Siboney
  m/Ernesto Lecuona
Three O'Clock In The Morning
  m/Julian Robledo

MORSE, THEODORE F.
1873-1924, American
m/Theodore F. Morse
Blue Bell
  w/Edward Madden,
  Theodora (Dolly) Morse
Consolation
  w/Edward Madden
Daddy's Little Girl
  w/Edward Madden
Dear Old Girl
  w/Richard Henry Buck
Down In Jungle Town
  w/Edward Madden
Hail Hail The Gang's All Here
  w/Theodore F. Morse
  (adapted from music by Sir
  Arthur Sullivan)
Keep On The Sunny Side
  w/Jack Drislane
Longing For You
  w/Jack Drislane
**M-O-T-H-E-R (A Word That
 Means The World To Me)**
  w/Howard Johnson
**MORTON, FERDINAND
JOSEPH LA MENTHE (JELLY
ROLL)**
1885-1941, American
m/Ferdinand (Jelly Roll) Morton
Bert Williams (Pacific Rag)
Black Bottom Stomp
Chant, The
Chicago Breakdown
Clarinet Marmalade
  in co w/Leon Rappolo,
  Paul Mares
Finger Breaker, The
Frances
Freakish
Frog-I-More Rag
Grandpa's Spells
Jelly Roll Blues (Doctor Jazz)
Kansas City Stomp
King Porter Stomp
London Blues
  in co w/Leon Rappolo,
  Paul Mares
Milenberg Joys
  in co w/Leon Rappolo,
  Paul Mares
Naked Dance, The
Pearls, The
Pep
Perfect Rag, The
Sidewalk Blues
Steamboat Stomp
Tom Cat Blues

MORTON, GEORGE A.
1880-1923, American
w/George A. Norton
Memphis Blues
  m/W.C. Handy

My Melancholy Baby
  m/Ernie Burnett
**MORTON, GEORGE
"SHADOW"**
American
w&m/George "Shadow" Morton
**Remember (Walkin' In The
  Sand) (1964)**
MOSSMAN, TED
1914, American
w&m in co w/Buddy Kaye
**Full Moon And Empty Arms
  (adapted from Rachmaninoff's
  Second Piano Concerto)**
**Till The End Of Time
  (adapted from Chopin's
  Polonaise In A-flat Major, Op.
  53)**

MOY, SYLVIA
1939, American
w&m/Sylvia Moy
I Was Made To Love Her
  in co w/Stevie Wonder,
  Henry Cosby,
  Lula Mae Hardaway
My Baby Loves Me
  in co w/William Stevenson,
  Ivy Hunter
My Cherie Amor
  in co w/Stevie Wonder,
  Henry Cosby
Nothing's Too Good For My Baby
  in co w/William Stevenson,
  Henry Cosby
Uptight (Everything's Alright)
  in co w/Stevie Wonder,
  Henry Cosby

MUIR, LEWIS F.
1884-1950, American
m/Lewis F. Muir
Hitchy Koo
  co-composer Maurice Abrahams
  w/L. Wolfe Gilbert
Play That Barber Shop Chord
  w/William Tracey
Ragtime Cowboy Joe
  co-composer Maurice Abrahams
  w/Grant Clarke
Take Me To That Swanee Shore
  w/L. Wolfe Gilbert
Waiting For The Robert E. Lee
  w/L. Wolfe Gilbert

MULLAN, RICHARD
American
w/Richard Mullan
m/Jack Richards
He

MULLIGAN, GERRY
1927, American
m/Gerry Mulligan (instr.)
Bark For Barksdale

Jeru
Line For Lyon
Rocker
Turnstile
Venus De Milo

MULLINS, JOHNNY
American
w&m/Johnny Mullins
Blue Kentucky Girl (1979)

MURDEN, ORLANDO
American
m/Orlando Murden
w/Ronald Miller
For Once In My Life (1965)

MURPHY, C.W.
English
w&m/C.W. Murphy
in co w/Will Letters
Revised American version by
William C. McKenna.
Has Anybody Here
Seen Kelly (1909)

MURPHY, STANLEY
1875-1919, American
w&m/Stanley Murphy
Be My Little Baby Bumble Bee
in co w/Henry I. Marshall
Put On Your Old Gray Bonnet
in co w/Percy Wenrich
Oh How She Could Yacki Hacki
Wicki Wacki Woo
in co w/Alvert Von Tilzer,
Charles McCarron
When We Meet In The
Sweet Bye And Bye
in co w/Harry Von Tilzer

MURRAY, FRED
English
w&m/Fred Murray
in co w/R.P. Weston
I'm Henry The VIII (1965)

MURRAY, JOHN
1906, American
w&m/John Murray
Two Loves Have I
If I Love Again
in co w/Ben Oakland

MURRAY, MITCH
English
w&m/Mitch Murray
How Do You Do It (1943)

MUSEL, BOB
1916, American
w/Bob Musel
m/Jack Taylor
Band Of Gold (1955)

MYDDLETON, W. H.
English
m/W.H. Myddleton (instr.)
Down South (1901)

MYERS, RICHARD
1901, American
w&m/Richard Myers
Hold My Hand (1950)
Jericho (1929)
w/Leo Robin

MYERS, SHERMAN
English
m/Sherman Myers
w/Chester Wallace
Moonlight On The Ganges (1926)

MYROW, JOSEF
1910 American
m/Josef Myrow
Autumn Nocturne
w/Kim Gannon
Five O'Clock Whistle
w/Kim Gannon
On The Boardwalk At
Atlantic City
w/Mack Gordon
Wilhemina
w/Mack Gordon
You Make Me Feel So Young
w/Mack Gordon

MYSELS, GEORGE
1915, American
w/George Mysels
Heaven Drops Her Curtain Down
m/Sammy Mysels
One Little Candle
m/J. Maloy Roach

MYSELS, SAMMY
1906, American
m/Sammy Mysels
Heaven Drops Her Curtain Down
w/George Mysels
His Feet's Too Big For De Bed
w/Dick Sanford
Mention My Name In Sheboygan
w/Dick Sanford
Red Silk Stockings And
Green Perfume
w/Bob Hilliard
Singing Hills, The
w/Dick Sanford
Walking Down To Washington
w/Dick Sanford, Redd Evans

POPULAR COMPOSERS
& LYRICISTS

N, O

NAEGELI, HANS GEORG
1773-1836, German
m/Hans Georg Naegeli
**Blest Be The Tie That Binds (from
the German song "Dennis")**
w/John Fawcett
**Life Let Us Cherish (from the
German song "Freut Euch
Des Lebens")**
w/source unknown for
English words

NASH, GRAHAM
1942, English
w&m/Graham Nash
Cathedral
Chicago
Cold Rain
Immigration Man
Just A Song Before I Go
Lady Of The Island
Marrakesh Express
Our House
Right Between The Eyes
Southbound Train
Teach Your Children

NASH, JOHNNY
1940, American
w&m/Johnny Nash
All I'll Ever Need Is You
Hold Me Tight
I Can See Clearly Now
Let Me Cry
Lonesome Romeo
My Merry Go Round
Ooh, What A Feeling
People In Love
What Kind Of Love Is This
Stir It Up
You Got Soul

NASH, OGDEN
1902, American
w/Ogden Nash
One Touch Of Venus
m/Kurt Weill
Out Of The Clear Blue Sky
m/Vernon Duke
Roundabout
m/Vernon Duke
Speak Low
m/Kurt Weill
That's Him
m/Kurt Weill
West Wind
m/Kurt Weill

MCNEALLY, BIG JAY
American
w&m/Big Jay McNeally
Deacon's Hop (1946)

NEIBURG, AL J. (Allen)
1902, American
m/Al J. Neiburg
in co w/Marty Symes,
Jerry Livingston
It's The Talk Of The Town
I've Got An Invitation To A Dance
Under A Blanket Of Blue
When It's Darkness On The Delta

NEIL, FRED
1938, American
w&m/Fred Neil
Blues On The Ceiling
Everybody's Talkin' (Echoes)
Little Bit Of Rain
Other Side Of Rain, The
Tear Down The Walls

NELSON, ED. G.
1895, American
w&m/Ed. G. Nelson
Auf Wiedersehn, My Dear
in co w/Al Hoffman,
Al Goodhart, Milton Ager
I Apologize
in co w/Al Hoffman,
Al Goodhart
**In A Shady Nook By A
Babbling Brook**
in co w/Harry Pease
**Josephine Please No Lean On
The Bell**
in co w/Harry Pease
Light A Candle In The Chapel
in co w/Harry Pease
Peggy O'Neill
in co w/Harry Pease,
Gilbert Dodge
Pretty Kitty Kelly
in co w/Harry Pease
Setting The Woods On Fire
in co w/Fred Rose
**Ten Little Fingers And Ten
Little Toes**
in co w/Harry Pease,
Ira Schuster
Why Do They Always Say No
in co w/Harry Pease

NELSON, OLIVER
1932, American
m/Oliver Nelson (instr.)
Hoedown
Stolen Moments
Swiss Suite

**NELSON, RICK (Ricky)
(Eric Hilliard Nelson)**
1940, American
w&m/Rick Nelson
Garden Party
Travelin' Man

NELSON, STEVE
1907, American
w&m in co w/Jack Rollins
Frosty The Snow Man
Peter Cottontail
Smokey The Bear

NELSON, WILLIE
1933, American
w&m/Willie Nelson
After The Fire Is Gone
Bloody Mary Morning
Crazy
Family Bible
Funny (How Time Slips Away)
Good Hearted Woman, a
in co w/Waylon Jennings
Hello Fool
in co w/James Coleman
Hello Walls
I Still Can't Believe You're Gone
Night Life
Party's Over, The
Pretty Paper
Pretend I Never Happened
So You Think You're A Cowboy
in co w/Hank Cochran
Three Days
in co w/Faron Young

NEMO, HENRY
1914, American
w&m/Henry Nemo
Blame It On My Last Affair
Don't Take Your Love From Me
I Let A Song Go Out Of My Heart
in co w/Duke Ellington,
Irving Mills
'Tis Autumn

NERO, PAUL
1917-1958, American
m/Paul Nero
Hot Canary, The (instr.)

NESMITH, MIKE
American
w&m/Mike Nesmith
Different Drum (1967
**I've Never Loved Anyone
More (1974)**
in co w/Linda Hargrove
Joanne (1970)
Silver Moon (1970)

**NEVIN, ETHELBERT
WOODBRIDGE**
1862-1901, American
m/Ethelbert Woodbridge Nevin
Mighty Lak' A Rose
w/Frank L. Stanton
Rosary, The
w/Robert C. Rogers

NEVINS, MORTY
1917, American
w&m/Morty Nevins
in co w/Al Nevins, Artie Dunn,
Buck Ram
Twilight Time

NEWBURY, MICKEY
1940, American
w&m/Mickey Newbury
American Trilogy, An
  m/adapted from folk songs of the
  American Civil War period
Frisco Mabel Joy
Funny Familiar
  Forgotten Feelings
Here Comes The Rain Baby
I Wonder If I Ever Said Goodbye
Just Dropped In
She Even Woke Me Up To
  Say Goodbye

NEWLEY, ANTHONY
1931, English
w&m in co w/Leslie Bricusse
Candy Man, The
Feeling Good
Goldfinger
  m/John Barry
Gonna Build A Mountain
Joker, The
Once In A Life Time
What Kind Of Fool Am I
Who Can I Turn To
Wonderful Day Like Today, A

NEWMAN, ALFRED
1901-1974, American
m/Alfred Newman
Airport Love Theme (instr.)
Anastasia
  w/Paul Francis Webster
Castle In The Sand
  w/Ralph Blane
Concentrate
  w/Otto Harbach
Girl Next Door, The
  w/Sammy Cahn
Moon Of Manikoora, The
  w/Frank Loesser
Someday You'll Find
  Your Bluebird
  w/Mack Gordon
Through A Long And
  Sleepless Night
  w/Mack Gordon
Voodoo Man
  w/Otto Harbach
Your Kiss
  w/Frank Loesser
Film scores:
Airport (1970)
Alexander's Ragtime Band (1938)
Black Swan, The (1942)

Call Me Madam (1953)
Camelot (1967)
  in co w/Ken Darby
Captain From Castile
Cowboy And The Lady, The (1938)
Diary Of Anne Frank, The
How Green Was My Valley (1941)
Keys Of The Kingdom, The (1945)
King And I, The (1956)
  in co w/Ken Darby
Love Is A Many-Spendored Thing
  /title song by Sammy Fain and
  Paul Francis Webster
Mother Wore Tights (1947)
My Gal Sal (1942)
Robe, The
Song Of Bernadette, The (1943)
Tin Pan Alley (1946)
With A Song In My Heart (1952)
Wuthering Heights (1939)

NEWMAN, CHARLES
1901, American
w/Charles Newman
Six Lessons From
  Madame La Zonga
  m/James V. Monaco
Why Don't We Do This
  More Often
  m/Allie Wrubel
You Can't Pull The Wool Over
  My Eyes
  m/Milton Ager,
  Murray Mencher (Ted Murry)
You've Got Me Crying Again
  m/Isham Jones

NEWMAN, HERBERT
1925, American
w&m in co w/Stan Lebowsky
Wayward Wind, The

NEWMAN, JOEL
American
m/Joel Newman
w/Paul Campbell
Kisses Sweeter Than Wine (1951)

NEWMAN, RANDY
1943, American
w&m/Randy Newman
Baltimore
I Think It's Going To Rain Today
Just One Smile
Little Criminals
Lonely At The Top
Mama Told Me (Not To Come)
Sail Away
Short People
You Can't Fool The Fat Man

NEWTON, EDDIE
American
m/Eddie Newton
w/T. Laurence Seibert
Casey Jones (1909)

NEWTON, JOHN
Mid-19th century, American
w/John Newton
Composer unknown; believed to
of 18th century origin in
southern U.S. rural regions.
Amazing Grace

NICHOLS, ALBERTA
(Mrs. Mann Holiner)
1898-1957, American
m/Alberta Nichols
w/Mann Holiner
Until The Real Thing
  Comes Along

NICHOLS, ROGER
American
w&m/Roger Nichols
in co w/Paul Williams
See list of selections under
Paul Williams.

NICKS, STEPHANIE (Stevie)
English
w&m/Stephanie (Stevie) Nicks
Chain
  in co w/Lindsay Buckingham,
  Christine McVie
Crystal
Dreams
Gold Dust Woman
I Don't Want To Know
Rhiannon
Sara
Storms

NILES, JOHN JACOB
1892-1980, American
w&m/John Jacob Niles
Carol Of The Birds, The
Go 'Way From My Window
I Wonder As I Wander
My Horse Ain't Hungry
Songs Of The Gambling Man

NILSSON, HARRY EDWARD
1941, American
w&m/Harry Edward Nilsson
Best Friend
Cuddly Toy
Coconut
Gotta Get Up Without Her
Joy
Jump Into The Fire
Me And My Arrow
One
Spaceman
Ten Little Indians
(I Guess) The Lord Must Be In
  New York City
Waiting
Without You
You're Breaking My Heart

NIMS, WALT
American
w&m/Walt Nims
Precious And Few (1972)

NOACK, EDDIE
American
w&m/Eddie Noack
These Hands (1955)

NOBLE, HARRY
1912-1966, American
w&m/Harry Noble
Hold Me, Thrill Me, Kiss Me
Little White Donkey, The

NOBLE, JOHN AVERY (Johnny)
1892-1944, Hawaiian/American
w&m/John Avery Noble
Hilo Hattie
  in co w/Don McDiarmid
My Little Grass Shack In
  Kealakekua, Hawaii
My Tane
Naughty Hula Eyes
  in co w/Andy Iona

NOBLE, RAY
1904, English/American
w&m/Ray Noble
By The Fireside
Cherokee
Good Night Sweetheart
  in co w/Jimmy Campbell,
  Reg Connelly
I Hadn't Anyone Til You
Love Is The Sweetest Thing
Love Locked Out
  w/Max Kester
Touch Of Your Lips, The
Very Thought Of You, The

NOLAN, BOB
1909, American
w&m/Bob Nolan
Cool Water
Cowboy Has To Sing, A
One More Ride
Song Of The Bandit
Trail Herding Cowboy
Tumbling Tumbleweeds
Way Out There

NOLAN, KENNY
American
w&m/Kenny Nolan
Back To Dreamin' Again (1978)
Get Dancin' (1974)
  in co w/Bob Crewe
I Like Dreamin' (1976)
Lady Marmalade (1974)
  in co w/Bob Crewe
Love's Grown Deep (1977)
My Eyes Adored You (1974)
  in co w/Bob Crewe

NOLAN, MICHAEL
American
w&m/Michael Nolan
Little Annie Rooney
  (1890, U.S.A.)

NORTH, ALEX
1910, American
m/Alex North
Long Hot Summer, The
  w/Sammy Cahn
Unchained Melody
  w/Hy Zaret
Film scores:
Agony and The Ecstasy, The (1965)
Bite The Bullet (1975)
Death Of A Salesman (1951)
Desireé
I'll Cry Tomorrow
Long Hot Summer, The
Member Of The Wedding
Misfits, The
Rainmaker, The (1956)
Rose Tatoo, The (1955)
Sound And The Fury, The
Spartacus (1960)
Streetcar Named Desire, A (1951)
Unchained Melody
Viva Zapata (1952)
Who's Afraid Of Virginia
  Woolf (1966)
Sharks (1974)
Shoes Of The Fisherman, The (1968)

NORWORTH, JACK
1879-1959, American
w&m/Jack Norworth
Come Along My Mandy
  in co w/Nora Bayes, Tom Mellor,
  Alfred J. Lawrence, Harry Gilford
Good Evening Caroline
  in co w/Albert Von Tilzer,
Honey Boy
  in co w/Albert Von Tilzer
Shine On Harvest Moon
  in co w/Nora Bayes
Smarty
  in co w/Albert Von Tilzer
Take Me Out To The
  Ball Game (1908)
  in co w/Albert Von Tilzer

NOVELLO, IVOR
1893-1951, English
m/Ivor Novello
w/Lena Guilbert Ford
Keep The Home Fires Burning

NUGENT, MAUD
American
w&m/Maud Nugent
Sweet Rosie O'Grady (1896)

NYRO, LAURA
1947, American
w&m/Laura Nyro
And When I Die
Blowin' Away
Eli's Coming
Save The Country
Stoned Soul Picnic
Stoney End
Time And Love
Sweet Blindness
Wedding Bell Blues

OAKLAND, BEN
1907, American
m/Ben Oakland
I'll Dance At Your Wedding
  w/Herbert Magidson
I'll Take Romance
  w/Oscar Hammerstein II
Pink Cocktail For A Blue
  Lady, A
  w/Herbert Magidson

OATES, JOHN
1948, American
w&m/John Oates
Back Together Again
  in co w/Daryl Hall
Do What You Want, Be What
  You Are
  in co w/Daryl Hall
It's A Laugh
  in co w/Daryl Hall
Outlaw Blues
Sara Smile
  in co w/Daryl Hall
She's Gone
  in co w/Daryl Hall

O'DAY, ALAN
1940, American
w&m/Alan O'Day
Angie Baby
Rock 'N' Roll Heaven
Undercover Angel

O'DELL, KENNY
(Kenneth Gist Jr.)
American
w&m/Kenny O'Dell
Beautiful People (1967)
Behind Closed Doors (1974)
I Take It On Home (1973)
Next Plane To London (1967)
Old Time Love
Springfield Plane (1968)
What I've Got In Mind

O'HARA, GEOFFREY
1882, American
m/Geoffrey O'Hara
Give A Man A Horse He
  Can Ride (1917)
  w/James Thomson

K-K-K-Katy (1918)
w/Geoffrey O'Hara

OLCOTT, CHAUNCEY
1858-1932, American
w&m/Chauncey Olcott
I Love The Name Of Mary
in co w/Ernest R. Ball,
George Graff
Mother Machree
in co w/Rida Johnson Young
My Wild Irish Rose
When Irish Eyes Are Smiling
in co w/Ernest R. Ball,
George Graff

OLDFIELD, MIKE
English
m/Mike Oldfield
Tubular Bells (instr.) (1974)

OLIVER, SY
1915, American
w&m/Sy Oliver
Opus One (instr.)
Yes Indeed

OLIVIERI, DINO
French
m/Dino Olivieri
French w/Louis Poterat
English w/Anna Sosenko
J'attendrai (I'll Be Yours) (1945)

OLMAN, ABE
1888, American
m/Abe Olman
**Down Among The
Sheltering Palms**
w/James Brockman
Down By The O-hi-O
w/Jack Yellen
**I'm Waiting For Ships That
Never Come In**
w/Jack Yellen,
William Raskin
Oh Johnny, Oh Johnny, Oh
w/Ed Rose

OPENSHAW, JOHN
English
m/John Openshaw
w/Leslie Cooke
**Love Sends A Little Gift
Of Roses (1919)**

ORBISON, ROY
1936, American
w&m/Roy Orbison
Blue Bayou
in co w/Joe Melson
Claudette
in co w/Joe Melson
Crying
in co w/Joe Melson
Only The Lonely
in co w/Joe Melson

Oh Pretty Woman
in co/William Dees
Oobie Doobie
in co w/Joe Melson
Running Scared
in co w/Joe Melson

**ORIGINAL DIXIELAND
JAZZ BAND**
**(Dominic James (Nick) La Rocca,
Larry Shields, Henry Ragas,
Edwin Bransford, Tony Spargo)**
American
w&m/Original Dixieland Jazz Band;
except "Clarinet Marmalade" by
Nick La Rocca, Larry Shields only.
At the Jazz Land Ball
Clarinet Marmalade
Livery Stable Blues (1917)
**Original Dixieland
One Step (1917)**
Ostrich Walk
Reisenweber Rag (1917)
Sensation
Tiger Rag (1917)

ORNANDEL, CYRIL
English
m/Cyril Ornandel
Portrait Of My Love
w/Norman Newell

ORTOLANI, RIZ
Italian
m/Riz Ortolani
**More (theme from
"Mondo Cane") (1962)**
w/Nino Oliviero, Norman Newell,
M. Ciorciolini
Forget Domani
w/Norman Newell

OSKAR, LEE
1946, Danish/American
w&m/Lee Oskar
in co w/Howard E. Scott, Charles
William Miller, Lonnie Leroy Jordan,
Morris DeWayne "B.B." Dickerson,
Thomas Sylvester "Papa Dee" Allen
and Harold Ray Brown.
All Day Music
in co w/Jerry Goldstein
Cisco Kid, The
Gypsy Man
Me And Baby Brother
Slippin' Into Darkness
Summer
in co w/Jerry Goldstein
Why Can't We Be Friends
in co w/Jerry Goldstein
World Is A Ghetto, The

OTIS, CLYDE
1929, American
Many songs in co w/Brook Benton.

See list of selections under
Brook Benton.
Additional songs by Clyde Otis.
Baby (You've Got What It Takes)
in co w/Murray Stein
Stroll, The
in co w/Nancy Lee
This Bitter Earth

O'SULLIVAN, GILBERT
1946, Irish
w&m/Gilbert O'Sullivan
Alone Again Naturally
Clair
Get Down
Ooh Baby

OTIS, JOHNNY
1921, American
w&m/Johnny Otis
Cry Baby
in co w/Marco De La Garde
Cupid's Boogie
Double Crossing Blues
Every Beat Of My Heart
Mistrustin' Blues
Rockin' Blues
**Wallflower (Dance With
Me Henry)**
in co w/Hank Ballard, Etta James
Willie And The Hand Jive

OTIS, SHUGGIE
American
w&m/Shuggie Otis
Strawberry Letter 23 (1977)

OVERSTREET, W. BENTON
American
m/W. Benton Overstreet
w/Billy Higgins
**There'll Be Some
Changes Made (1929)**

OWENS, BUCK
1929, American
w&m/Buck Owens
Before You Go
Big In Vegas
in co w/Terry Staffore
**Excuse Me (I Think I've Got A
Heartache)**
in co w/Harlan Howard
Foolin' Around
in co w/Harlan Howard
How Long Will by Baby Be Gone
**I Don't Care (Just As Long As
You Love Me)**
It Takes People Like You
I've Got A Tiger By The Tail
Kansas City Song
in co w/Red Simpson
**Let The World Keep
On A-Turning**
Love's Gonna Live Here

340

Mommy For A Day
in co w/Harlan Howard
My Heart Skips A Beat
Nobody's Fool But Yours
Only You (Can Break My Heart)
On The Cover Of The Music
City News
in co w/Shel Silverstein,
James B. Shaw

Open Up Your Heart
Rollin' In My Sweet Baby's Arms
Sam's Place
in co w/Red Simpson
Tall Dark Stranger
Together Again
Under The Influence Of Love
in co w/Harlan Howard

Waitin' In Your Welfare Line
in co w/Nathan Stuckey,
Don Rich
We're Gonna Get Together
Where Does The Good Times Go
Who's Gonna Mow Your Grass
Your Tender Loving Care

OWENS, D.H. (Tex)
1892-1962, American
w&m/D.H. Owens
Cattle Call

OWENS, HARRY
1902, American
w&m/Harry Owens
Hawaiian Paradise
Linger Awhile
in co w/Vincent Rose

O-Ko-Le Ma-Lu-Na
Princess Poo-Poo-ly
Sing Me A Song Of The Islands
Sweet Leilani
To You Sweetheart, Aloha

OWENS, JACK
1912, American
w&m/Jack Owens
Hi Neighbor (1941)
Hut Sut Song, The
in co w/Leo V. Killian,
Ted McMichael

OZEN, BARBARA LINDA
1941, American
w&m/Barbara Linda Ozen
You'll Lose A Good Thing (1962)

POPULAR COMPOSERS & LYRICISTS

P, Q

PACK, DAVID
1952, American
w&m/David Pack
in co w/Joe Puerta,
Burleigh G.A. Drummond
Holdin' On To Yesterday
How Much I Feel
Magical Mystery Tour

PADILLA, JOSE
Spanish
m/Jose Padilla
My Toreador (1926)
   w/William Cary Duncan
Paree! (1926)
   w/Leo Robin
**Princesita (Little
Princess) (1928)**
   w/Frederic Herman Martens
Valencia (1925)
   w/Clifford Grey

PAGE, JAMES
1945, English
w&m/James Page
Babe, I'm Gonna Leave You
Dancing Days
   in co w/Robert Plant
Dazed And Confused
   in co w/Robert Plant
Fool In The Rain
   in co w/Robert Plant,
   John Paul Jones
Going To California
   in co w/Robert Plant
Good Times, Bad Times
   in co w/Robert Plant,
   John Paul Jones, John
   "Bonzo" Bonham
Over The Hills And Far Away
   in co w/Robert Plant
Stairway To Heaven
Whole Lotta Love
   in co w/Robert Plant,
   John Paul Jones,
   John "Bonzo" Bonham

PAGE, LARRY
English
w&m/Larry Page
Wild Thing (1966)

PAICH, DAVID
1954, American
w&m/David Paich
Hard Time
   in co w/Boz Scaggs
Hold The Line
I'll Supply The Love
It's Over
   in co w/Boz Scaggs
Lido Shuffle
   in co w/Boz Scaggs
Lowdown
   in co w/Boz Scaggs

99
What Can I Say
   in co w/Boz Scaggs

PALMER, JACK
1901, American
w&m/Jack Palmer
**Everybody Loves My Baby (But
My Baby Don't Love Nobody
But Me)**
   in co w/Spencer Williams
I Found A New Baby
   in co w/Spencer Williams
Silver Dollar
   in co w/Clarke Van Ness

PALMER, ROBERT
1949, English
w&m/Robert Palmer
Every Kinda People

PANKOW, JAMES
1947, American
w&m/James Pankow
Baby What A Big Surprise
Colour My World
Feelin' Stronger Every Day
   in co w/Peter Cetera
If You Leave Me Now
Just You 'N' Me
Make Me Smile
(I've Been) Searchin' So Long
You Are On My Mind

PANELLA, FRANK
American
m/Frank Panella, adapted from an
1858 song "Down In Alabam",
composed by J. Warner.
w/source unknown
Old Grey Mare, The (1915)

PARDO, FRANK
American
w&m/Frank Pardo
in co w/Joseph Pardo,
Robert Hovorka
Rip Van Winkle (1960)

PARISH, MITCHELL
1900, American
w/Mitchell Parish
All My Love
   m/Paul Durand
American Waltz, The
   m/Peter DeRose
Belle Of The Ball
   m/Leroy Anderson
Blue September
   m/Peter De Rose
Blue Tango
   m/Leroy Anderson
Blue Skirt Waltz
   m/Vaclava Blacha
Ciao Ciao Bambino
   m/M. Modugno

Deep Purple
   m/Peter DeRose
Don't Be That Way
   m/Benny Goodman,
   Edgar Sampson, Chick Webb
Does Your Heart Beat For Me
   m/Howard Johnson,
   Russ Morgan
Dream, Dream, Dream
   m/Jimmy McHugh
Emaline
   m/Frank Perkins
Fiddle Faddle
   m/Leroy Anderson
Hands Across The Table
   m/Jean Delettre
Lamp Is Low, The
   m/Peter DeRose, Bert Shefter
Let Me Love You Tonight
   m/Rene Touzet
Lilacs In The Rain
   m/Peter DeRose
Moonlight Serenade
   m/Glenn Miller
Organ Grinder's Song, The
   m/Will Hudson, Irving Mills
Promenade
   m/Leroy Anderson
Riverboat Shuffle
   m/Hoagy Carmichael,
   Dick Yoynow, Irving Mills
Ruby
   m/M. Roamheld

Serenata
   m/Leroy Anderson
Sleigh Ride
   m/Leroy Anderson

Sophisticated Lady
   m/Duke Ellington,
   Irving Mills
Sophisticated Swing
   m/Will Hudson
Stairway To The Stars
   m/Matt Malneck,
   Frank Signorelli

Stardust
   m/Hoagy Carmichael
Starlit Hour, The
   m/Peter DeRose
Stars Fell On Alabama
   m/Frank Perkins
Sweet Lorraine
   m/Clifford R. Burwell
Tzena, Tzena, Tzena
   m/Issachar Miron, adapted by
   Julius Grossman
Volare
   m/Domenico Modugno
Washboard Blues
   m/Hoagy Carmichael

PARISSI, BOB
American
w&m/Bob Parissi
Play That Funky Music (1976)

PARKER, CHARLIE
1916-1955, American
m/Charlie Parker
Confirmation
Constellation
Dewey Square
Now's The Time
Ornithology
Yardbird Suite

PARKER, DOROTHY
1893, American
w&m/Dorothy Parker
How Am I To Know
in co w/Jack King
I Wished On The Moon
in co w/Ralph Rainger

PARKER, EULA
English
w&m/Eula Parker
Village Of St.
 Bernadette, The (1959)

PARKS, C. CARSON
American
w&m/C. Carson Parks
Cab Driver (1963)
Somethin' Stupid (1967)

PARKER, GRAHAM
English
w&m/Graham Parker
Between You And Me (1975)
Squeezing Out Sparks (1979)
Don't Ask Me Questions (1979)
Protection (1978)

PARMAN, CLIFF
1915, American
w&m in co w/Lew Douglas, Frank
Lavere
Pretend

PARSONS, ALAN
English
w&m/Alan Parsons
in co w/Eric Woolfson
Breakdown Days (The Show Must
 Go On)
Day After (1977)
Damned If I Do (1978)
Don't Let It Show (1977)
I Robot (1978)
I Wouldn't Want To Be
 Like You (1978)
Some Other Time (1977)

PARSONS, GEOFFREY
English
w&m/Geoffrey Parsons

Eternally (Terry Theme) (1953)
in co w/Charles Spencer Chaplin
If You Love Me (Really Love Me)
in co w/Marguerite Monnot
Smile
in co w/Charles Spencer Chaplin,
John Turner

PARSONS, GRAM (Cecil Connor)
1946-1973, American
w&m/Gram Parsons
Hickory Wind
Ooh Las Vegas
Sin City
Wheels

PARTON, DOLLY
1946, American
w&m/Dolly Parton
All I Can Do
Coat Of Many Colors
Daddy Was An Old Time
 Preacher Man
in co w/Dorothy Jo Hope
Dumb Blonde
God's Coloring Book
Heartbreaker
I Will Always Love You
It's All Wrong But It's
 All Right
Jolene
Joshua
Kentucky Gambler
Last One To Touch Me, The
Light Of A Clear Blue Morning
Love Is Like A Butterfly
Me And Little Andy
Please Don't Stop Loving Me
Put It Off Until Tomorrow
in co w/B.E. Owens
Seeker, The
Something Fishy
To Daddy
Travelling Man
Two Doors Down
We Used To

PATRICHALA, F.
Mexican
Mexican w&m/F. Patrichala
Mexican Hat Dance
 (Jarabe Tapatio)

PAXTON, GARY S.
American
w&m/Gary S. Paxton
Woman (Sensuous Woman) (1973)

PAXTON, THOMAS R. (Tom)
1937, American
w&m/Thomas R. Paxton
Bottle Of Wine
I Can't Help But Wonder (Where
 I'm Bound)

Last Thing On My Mind
Marvelous Toy, The
My Ramblin' Boy

PAYCHECK, JOHNNY
(Don Lytle)
1941, American
w&m/Johnny Paycheck
Apartment No. 9
(Stay Away From) Cocaine Train,
 The
Mister Lovemaker
Once You've Had The Best
You Can Take This Job
 And Shove It

PAYNE, JOHN HOWARD
1791-1852, American
w/John Howard Payne
m/Sir Henry Rowley Bishop (from his
opera "Clari, or The Maid of Milan")
Home Sweet Home (1823)

PAYNE, LEON
1917-1969, American
w&m/Leon Payne
Blue Side Of Lonesome
I Love You Because
Lost Highway
More Than Anything Else
 In The World
Take Me
in co w/George Jones
They'll Never Take Her
 Love From Me
You Can't Pick A Rose
 In December

PEACOCK, TREVOR
English
w&m/Trevor Peacock
Mrs. Brown You've Got A
 Lovely Daughter (1965)

PEASE, HARRY
1886-1945, American
w&m in co w/Ed. G. Nelson
See list of selections under
Ed. G. Nelson.

PENN, ARTHUR A.
1875-1941, English/American
w&m/Arthur A. Penn
Carissima (1907)
Smilin' Through (1919)
When The Sun Goes Down

PEPPER, BUDDY
1922, American
w&m in co w/Larry Russell, Inez
James
Vaya Con Dios (May God
 Be With You)

PERETTI, HUGO
1916, American
w&m/Hugo Peretti
Can't Help Falling In Love
in co w/Luigi Creatore,
George Weiss
**Lion Sleeps Tonight, The
(Wimoweh) (based on song
"Wimoweh, Hey Up Joe" by
Paul Campbell, Solomon Linda)**
in co w/Luigi Creatore, George
Weiss, Albert Stanton,
Paul Campbell, Solomon Linda

PERKINS, CARL LEE
1932, American
w&m/Carl Lee Perkins
Blue Suede Shoes
Boppin' The Blues
Daddy Sang Bass
**Everybody's Trying To Be
My Baby**
Honey Don't
Match Box Blues
Rise And Shine
**True Love Is Greater
Than Friendship**

PERREN, FREDERICK
1943, American
w&m/Frederick Perren
ABC
in co w/Berry Gordy Jr.,
Deke Richards, Alphonso Mizell
Boogie Fever
in co w/Keni St. Lewis
Cotton Candy
in co w/Keni St. Lewis
Don't Take Away The Music
in co w/Keni St. Lewis,
Christine Yarion
**Heaven Must Be Missing
An Angel**
in co w/Keni St. Lewis
Hot Line
in co w/Keni St. Lewis
I Pledge My Love
in co w/Dino Fekaris
I Will Survive
in co w/Dino Fekaris
**It's So Hard To Say Goodbye
To Yesterday**
in co w/Christine Yarion
Let Me Know (I Have A Right)
in co w/Dino Fekaris
Making It
in co w/Dino Fekaris
Reunited
in co w/Dino Fekaris
Roller Skatin' Mate
in co w/Dino Fekaris

Shake Your Groove Thing
in co w/Dino Fekaris
We've Got Love
in co w/Dino Fekaris
Who Done It? (Whodunit)
in co w/Keni St. Lewis

PERRY, BARNEY
1953, American
w&m/Barney Perry
Walking In Rhythm

PERRY, BETTY SUE
1935-1974, American
w&m/Betty Sue Perry
Before I'm Over You
Home You're Tearing Down, The
Other Woman, The
Roll Muddy River
Wine Women And Song

PERRY, JOE
1950, American
w&m in co w/Steve Tyler
Back In The Saddle
Draw The Line
Dream On
Home Tonight
Kings And Queens
Sweet Emotion
Walk This Way

PETERS, BEN
American
w&m/Ben Peters
Before My Time
Before The Next Teardrop Falls
in co w/Vivian Keith (1975)
Daytime Friends
Don't Give Up On Me (1974)
**I Can't Believe That It's
All Over (1974)**
**Kiss An Angel Good
Morning (1973)**
Perfect Match, A
in co w/Glenn Sutton (1973)
Tell Me What It's Like
That's A No No (1979)
**Turn The World Around The
Other Way (1968)**

**PETERSON, BETTY J.
(Mrs. Louis Blasco)**
1918, American
w&m in co w/Borney Bergantine
My Happiness

PETHER, HENRY E.
American
w&m in co w/Fred W. Leigh
**Waiting At The Church (My
Wife Won't Let Me)**

PETRIE, HENRY W.
1857-1925, American
m/Henry W. Petrie

Asleep In The Deep (1897)
w/Arthur J. Lamb
Davy Jones' Locker (1901)
w/Henry W. Petrie
**I Don't Want To Play In
Your Yard (1894)**
w/Philip Wingate

PETRILLO, CAESAR
1898-1963, American
m/Caesar Petrillo
in co w/Milton Samuels,
Nelson Shawn
Jim

PETTY, TOM
1952, American
w&m/Tom Petty
American Girl
Anything That's Rock 'N' Roll
Break Down
Century City
Don't Do Me Like That
Even The Losers
Fooled Again (I Don't Like It)
Here Comes My Girl
Listen To Her Heart
Louisiana Rain
Refugee
in co w/M. Campbell
**Shadow Of A Doubt (A
Complex Kid)**

PHILE, PHILLIP
American
m/Phillip Phile
w/Joseph Hopkinson (1798)
Words set to melody of "The
President's March", composed by
Phile in 1798.
Hail Columbia

PHILLIPS, JOHN
1935, American
w&m/John Phillips
California Dreamin'
in co w/Michelle Gilliam Phillips
Creeque Alley
in co w/Michelle Gilliam Phillips
Dancing In The Street
Go Where You Wanna Go
Got A Feeling
in co w/Dennis Doherty
Hey Girl
in co w/Michelle Gilliam Phillips
I Saw Her Again
in co w/Dennis Doherty
Look Through My Window
Monday, Monday
No Salt On Her Tail
**San Francisco (Be Sure To Wear
Flowers In Your Hair)**
Straight Shooter
Words Of Love

PHILLIPS, MIKE
American
w&m/Mike Phillips
North To Alaska (1960)

PIANTADOSI, AL
1884-1955, American
m/Al Piantadosi
Baby Shoes
   w/Joe Goodwin, Ed Rose
**Curse Of An Aching Heart, The
(You Made Me What I Am Today)**
   w/Henry Fink
**I Didn't Raise My Boy To
Be A Soldier**
   w/Alfred Bryan
Send Me Away With A Smile
   w/Louis Weslyn
**Where Was Moses When The
Lights Went Out**
   w/Edgar Leslie

PICKETT, WILSON
1941, American
w&m/Wilson Pickett
Don't Fight It
   in co w/Steve Cropper
Don't Knock My Love
   in co w/Brad Shapiro
If You Need Me
   in co w/Robert Bateman,
   Sonny Sanders
In The Midnight Hour
   in co w/Steve Cropper

PICONE, VITO
American
w&m in co w/Arthur Venosa
Little Star

PIERCE, WEBB
1926, American
w&m/Webb Pierce
Crazy Wild Desire
   in co w/Mel Tillis
How Do You Talk To A Baby
   in co w/Wayne P. Walker
I Don't Care
   in co w/Cindy Walker
Last Waltz, The
   in co w/Myrna Freeman
Leavin' On Your Mind
   in co w/Wayne P. Walker
Little Rosa
   in co w/Red Sovine
More And More
   in co w/Merle Kilgore
Bands Of Gold
   in co w/Hal Eddy, Cliff Parman
**That Heart Belongs To Me
Slowly**
   in co w/Tommy Hill
Those Wonderful Years
   in co w/Don Schroeder
Thousand Miles Ago, A
   in co w/Mel Tillis

You're Not Mine Anymore
   in co w/Doyle Wilburn, Teddy
   Wilburn

PIERPONT, JOHN S. (Rev.)
1785-1866, American
w&m/Rev. John S. Pierpont
**Jingle Bells (One Horse
Open Sleigh)**

PINDER, MICHAEL
1941, English
w&m/Michael Pinder
From The Bottom Of My Heart
   in co w/Denny Laine
Have You Heard
Melancholy Man
My Song
So Deep Within You

PINKARD, MACEO
1897-1962, American
m/Maceo Pinkard
Gimme A Little Kiss, Will Ya Huh
   w/Roy Turk, Jack Smith
Here Comes The Showboat
   w/Billy Rose
Sweet Georgia Brown
   w/Ben Bernie, Kenneth Casey
Them There Eyes
   w/William Tracey, Doris Tauber

PIRON, ARMAND JOHN
1888-1943, American
w&m/Armand John Piron
**I Wish I Could Shimmy Like
My Sister Kate (1919)**

PITNEY, GENE
1941, American
w&m/Gene Pitney
Hello Mary Lou
I Wanna Love My Life Away

PITTMAN, WAYNE
1947, American
w&m/Wayne Pittman
Girl Watcher (1968)

PITTS, WILLIAM S. DR.
American
w&m/Dr. William S. Pitts
**Little Brown Church In The Vale,
The (Come To the Church In
The Wildwood) (1864)**

PIPPIN, STEVE
American
w&m/Steve Pippin
Better Love Next Time (1979)
   in co w/Larry Keith, J. Slate
**My World Begins And Ends With
You**
   in co w/Larry Keith
Sharing (1979)
   in co w/J. Slate

**This Time I'm In It For
Love**
   in co w/Larry Keith, J. Sl

PLANT, ROBERT
1947, English
w&m/Robert Plant
in co w/James Page
See list of selections under
Page

POBER, LEON
1920, American
w&m/Leon Pober
Beyond The Rainbow
   in co w/Webley Edwards
Pearly Shells
   in co w/Webley Edwards
Tiny Bubbles (Hua Li'i)

POINTER, BONNIE
1951, American
w&m/Bonnie Pointer
in co w/Anita Pointer
Fairytale

POCKRISS, LEE J.
1927, American
m/Lee J. Pockriss
Calcutta
   w/Heino Gaze, Paul Vance
Catch A Falling Star
   w/Paul Vance
In My Room
   w/Paul Vance
**Itsy Bitsy Teenie Weenie Yellow
Polka Dot Bikini**
   w/Paul Vance
Johnny Angel
   w/Lyn Duddy
My Heart Is An Open Book
   w/Hal David
My Little Corner Of The World
   w/Bob Hilliard
**Seven Little Girls (Sitting
In The Back Seat)**
   w/Bob Hilliard
Starlight
   w/Paul Vance
What Is Love
   w/Paul Vance

POLA, EDWARD
1907, American
w&m/Edward Pola
**I Didn't Slip, I Wasn't
Pushed, I Fell**
   in co w/George Wyle
**I Said My Pajamas And Put
On My Prayers**
   in co w/George Wyle
Longest Walk, The
   in co w/Fred Spielman
Marching Along Together
   in co w/Franz K.W. Steininger,
   Mort Dixon

POLLA, W.C.
1876-1939, American
m/W.C. Polla
Dancing Tambourine
  (1927) (instr.)

POLLACK, BEN
1903, American
Make Love To Me
  melody of "Tin Roof Blues" with
  words by Bill Norvas,
  Allan Copeland
Tin Roof Blues
  co-composers: Walter Melrose,
  Leon Rappolo, Paul Wares,
  George Brunes, Mel Stitzler

POLLACK, LEW
1895-1946, American
w&m/Lew Pollack
Angela Mia
  in co w/Erno Rapee
At The Codfish Ball
  in co w/Jack Yellen,
  Sidney D. Mitchell
Charmaine
  in co w/Erno Rapee
Cheatin' On Me
  in co w/Jack Yellen
Diane
  in co w/Erno Rapee
Miss Annabelle Lee
  in co w/Sidney Clare,
  Harry Richman
Silver Shadows And
  Golden Dreams
  in co w/Charles Newman
Sing Baby Sing
  in co w/Jack Yellen
That's A-Plenty
  in co w/Ray Gilbert
Two Cigarettes In The Dark
  in co w/Paul Francis Webster
Weep No More My Mammy
  in co w/Sidney D. Mitchell,
  Sidney Clare

POLLOCK, CHANNING
1880-1946, American
w/Channing Pollock
m/Maurice Yvain
My Man (Mon Homme)

POMUS, DOC (Jerome)
1925, American
w&m in co w/Mort Shuman
Can't Get Used To Losing You
His Latest Flame
It's a Long, Long Lonely Highway
Little Sister
Mess Of Blues
Save The Last Dance For Me
Surrender
Teen Ager In Love, A
Viva Las Vegas
Young Blood

PONCE, MANUEL M.
Mexican
m/Manuel M. Ponce
w/Frank La Forge
Estellita (Little Star) (1911)

PONCIA, VINCENT
1942, American
w&m/Vincent Poncia
I Was Made For Loving You
  in co w/Paul Stanley,
  Desmond Child
Just Too Many People
  in co w/Melissa Manchester
Mind Excursion
  in co w/Pete Anders
New York's A Lonely Town
  in co w/Pete Anders
You Make Me Feel Like Dancing
  in co w/Leo Sayer

PONS, JAMES
1942, American
w&m/James Pons
in co w/William Rinehart
Hey Joe

POPP, ANDRE
French
m/Andre Popp
English w/Bryan Blackburn
French w/Pierre Cour
Love Is Blue
  (L'Amour Est Blue) (1966)

POST, MIKE
American
m/Mike Post
Rockford Files (1975) (instr.)

POREE, ANITA
American
w&m/Anita Poree
Boogie Down
  in co w/Jerry Eugene Peters
Going In Circles (1970)
  in co w/Jerry Eugene Peters
Keep On Truckin' (1973)
  in co w/Frank G. Wilson,
  Leonard Caston
Love Or Let Me Be
  Lonely (1970)
  in co w/Jerry Eugene Peters,
  Clarence A. Scarborough

PORTER, COLE
1891-1964, American
w&m/Cole Porter
Ace In The Hole
All Of You
All Through The Night
Allez-vous-en Go Away
Always True To You In My
  Fashion
Another Op'ning, Another Show
Anything Goes

As On Through The Seasons We
  Sail
At Long Last Love
Be A Clown
Begin The Beguine
Between You And Me
Blow Gabriel Blow
Brush Up Your Shakespeare
But In The Morning, No
Ca, C'est L'Amour
C'est Magnifique
Come Along With Me
Could It Be You
Do I Love You?
Don't Fence Me In
Down In The Depths (On The
  Ninetieth Floor)
Easy To Love
Ev'ry Time We Say Goodbye
Ev'rything I Love
Far Away
Farewell Amanda
Farming
Find Me A Primitive Man
Friendship

From Alpha To Omega
From This Moment On
Get Out Of Town
I Am Loved
I Concentrate On You
I Get A Kick Out Of You
I Hate You, Darling
I Love Paris
I Love You
I'm In Love Again
In The Still Of The Night
It's All Right With Me
It's De-Lovely
I've A Shooting Box In Scotland
I've Got My Eyes On You
I've Got You Under My Skin
I've Still Got My Health
Just One Of Those Things
Katie Went To Haiti
Let's Be Buddies
Let's Do It (Let's Fall In Love)
Let's Fly Away
Let's Not Talk About Love
Live And Let Live
Love For Sale
Make It Another Old Fashioned
  Please
Miss Otis Regrets
My Heart Belongs To Daddy
Night And Day
Old Fashioned Garden
Ours
Red, Hot And Blue
Ridin' High
Rosalie
Since I Kissed My Baby Goodbye
Something For The Boys
So In Love

So Near And Yet So Far
Stereophonic Sound
Too Darn Hot
True Love
Use Your Imagination
Were Thine That Special Face
What Is This Thing Called Love
Where Is The Life That Late I Led
Where Oh Where
Why Can't You Behave
Why Shouldn't I
Wouldn't It Be Fun
Wunderbar
Yale Bulldog Song
You Do Something To Me
You'd Be So Nice To Come Home
  To
You're Sensational
You're The Top
You've Got That Thing

PORTER, ROBIE
Australian
w&m Robie Porter in co w/Rick
Chertoff, Charles Fisher
Lost In Love (1980)

POULTON, GEORGE R.
American
m/George R. Poulton
w/W.W. Fosdick
Aura Lee (1861)
  Melody used with new lyrics for:
  Army Blue (West Point perennial)
  (1865)
  Love Me Tender (Elvis Presley,
  with new lyrics by Vera Matson)

POUNDS, JESSIE B.
American
w/Jessie B. Pounds
m/John S. Fearis
**Beautiful Isle Of Somewhere
  (1867)**

POWELL, FELIX
English
m/Felix Powell
w/George Asaf
**Pack Up Your Troubles In Your
  Old Kitbag And Smile Smile
  Smile (1915)**

POWERS, CHET
American
w&m/Chet Powers
**Get Together (C'mon People Now
  Smile On Your Brother) (1963)**

PRADO, PEREZ
1922, Mexican
w&m/Perez Prado
Caballa Negro (Black Horse)
**Mambo No. 5, Mambo No. 8,
  Mambo No. 10**
Patricia
Quel Rico El Mambo

PRESLEY, ELVIS
1935-1977, American
w&m/Elvis Presley
All Shook Up
  in co w/Otis Blackwell
Don't Be Cruel
  in co w/Otis Blackwell
Heartbreak Hotel
  in co w/Mae Axton, Tommy
  Durken
**Love Me Tender (based on the
  traditional folk melody
  "Aura Lee")**
  in co w/Vera Matson

PRESTON, BILLY
1946, American
m/Billy Preston
w/Bruce Fisher
Nothing From Nothing
You Are So Beautiful

PREVIN, ANDRE
1929, American
m/Andre Previn
w/Dory Langdon Previn
Faraway Part Of Town
Second Chorus
You're Gonna Hear From Me
Film Scores
Elmer Gantry (1960)
Irma La Douce (1963)
My Fair Lady (1964)
Porgy And Bess (1959)
  in co w/Ken Darby
Thoroughly Modern Millie (1967)
  in co w/Joseph Gershenson
Two For The Seesaw

PREVIN, CHARLES
1888, American
m/Charles Previn
Film scores
Bank Dick, The (1940)
Buck Privates
First Love (1939)
Mad About Music (1938)
One Hundred Men And A Girl (1937)

PREVIN, DORY LANGDON
1925, American
w/Dory Langdon Previn
Come Saturday Morning
  w/Fred Karlin
Faraway Part Of Town
  m/Andre Previn
Morning After, The
  m/Harold Arlen
Second Chorus
  m/Andre Previn
You're Gonna Hear From Me
  m/Andre Previn

PRICE, LLOYD
1933, American
w&m/Lloyd Price
Come Into My Heart
  in co w/Harold Logan
Just Because
I'm Gonna Get Married
  in co w/Harold Logan
Lawdy Miss Clawdy
Ooh, Ooh, Ooh
(You've Got) Personality
  in co w/Harold Logan
Stagger Lee
  in co w/Harold Logan (adaptation
  of the traditional folk song
  "Stack-O-Lee")
**Where Were You (On Our
  Wedding Day)**
  in co w/Harold Logan

PRIMROSE, JOE
American
w&m/Joe Primrose
St. James Infirmary (1930)

PRINCE
1960, American
w&m/Prince
I Wanna Be Your Lover
Sexy Dancer
**When We're Dancing Close And
  Slow**
With You

PRINCE, HUGH DENHAM
(Hughie)
1906-1960, American
w&m in co w/Don Raye
Beat Me Daddy Eight To The Bar
Boogie Woogie Bugle Boy
Rhumboogie

PRINE, JOHN
American
w&m/John Prine
Angel From Montgomery
**Come Back To Us Barbara Lewis
  Hare Krishna Beauregard (1975)**
Hello Out There
If You Don't Want My Love
  in co w/Phil Spector

PROVOST, HEINZ
Swedish
m/Heinz Provost
w/Robert Henning
Intermezzo (A Love Story) (1936)

PRYOR, ARTHUR
1870-1942, American
m/Arthur Pryor (Instr.)
Whistler And His Dog, The (1905)

PURDY, W.T.
American
m/W.T. Purdy
w/Carl Beck
On Wisconsin (1909)

PUTNAM, CURLY
American
w&m/Curly Putnam

Ballad Of Two Brothers
in co w/Buddy Killen, Bobby
Braddock
Blood Red And Going Down
Easy Look
in co w/Sonny Throckmorton

Green Green Grass Of Home

**If You Think I Love You Now
(I've Just Started)**
in co w/Billy Sherrill

I'll Be Coming Back For More
in co w/S. Whipple

My Elusive Dreams
in co w/Billy Sherrill

QUADLING, LEW
1908, American
w&m/Lew Quadling
Careless
in co w/Dick Jurgens, Eddy
Howard
Sam's Song
in co w/Jack Elliott
Do You Care
in co w/Jack Elliott

POPULAR COMPOSERS
& LYRICISTS

R

RABBITT, EDDIE
1941, American
w&m/Eddie Rabbitt
Drinkin' My Baby Off My Mind
in co w/Even Stevens
Drivin' My Life Away
in co w/Even Stevens, David Malloy
Hearts On Fire
in co w/Even Stevens, Don Tyler
I Can't Help Myself
in co w/Even Stevens
I Just Want To Love You
in co w/Even Stevens, David Malloy
Kentucky Rain
in co w/Dick Heard
Pour Me Another Tequila
in co w/Dave Malloy, Even Stevens
Pure Love
Rocky Mountain Music
Suspicions
in co w/Randy McCormick, David Malloy
We Can't Go On Livin' Like This
in co w/Even Stevens
What Do You Want
in co w/Even Stevens

RADO, JAMES
American
Co-lyricist with Gerome Ragni,
in co w/music of Galt MacDermot
See list of selections under Galt MacDermot

RAFFERTY, GERRY
c. 1943, Scottish
w&m/Gerry Rafferty
Baker Street
Day's Gone Down (Still Got The Light In Your Eyes)
Everyone's Agreed in co w/Joe Egan
Get It Right Next Time
Home And Dry
Right Down The Line
Royal Mile, The
Stealin' Time
Stuck In The Middle With You
in co w/Joe Egan
Tourist, The

RAGNI, GEROME
American
Co-lyricist with James Rado,
in co w/music of Galt MacDermot
See list of selections under Galt MacDermot

RAGOVOY, JERRY
American
w&m/Jerry Ragovoy
Get It While You Can

Piece Of My Heart
in co w/Bert Berns
You Got It
in co w/Linda Laurie

RAINEY, GERTRUDE ("MA")
1886-1939, American
w&m/Gertrude "Ma" Rainey
Countin' The Blues
Dead Drunk Blues
Deep Moanin' Blues
Hear Me Talking To You
Jelly Bean Blues
Leavin' This Morning
Mountain Jack Blues
Runaway Blues
See See Rider Blues
Shave 'Em Dry Blues
Sweet Rough Man
Rough Luck Blues
Trust No Man
Wringin' And Twistin'

RAINGER, RALPH
1901-1942, American
m/Ralph Rainger
Blue Hawaii
w/Leo Robin
Easy To Love
w/Leo Robin
I Wished On The Moon
w/Dorothy Parker
If I Should Lose You
w/Leo Robin
June In January
w/Leo Robin
La Bomba
w/Leo Robin
Love In Bloom
w/Leo Robin
Moanin' Low
w/Howard Dietz
Please
w/Leo Robin
Thanks For The Memory
w/Leo Robin
With Every Breath I Take
w/Leo Robin
You're A Sweet Little Headache
w/Leo Robin

RAITT, BONNIE LYNN
1949, American
w&m/Bonnie Lynn Raitt
Give It Up

RAKSIN, DAVID
1912, American
m/David Raksin
w/John H. (Johnny) Mercer

Laura
Film scores:
Bad And The Beautiful, The (1952)
Daisy Kenyon (1947)
Forever Amber (1947)
Laura (1944)
Magnificent Yankee The (1950)
The Secret Life Of Walter Mitty (1947)

RALEIGH, BEN
1918, American
w&m/Ben Raleigh
Bring A Little Sunshine (To My Heart)
in co w/Mark Barkan
Buenos Dias Argentina
in co w/V. Jurgens
Dead End Street
in co w/Dave Axelrod
Laughing On The Outside, Crying On The Inside
in co w/Bernie Wayne
Love Is A Hurtin' Thing
in co w/Dave Linden
Tell Laura I Love Her
in co w/Jeff Barry
Wonderful, Wonderful
in co w/Sherman Edwards

RAM, BUCK
1909, American
w&m/Buck Ram
Come Prima (For The First Time)
in co w/M. Panzeri
Enchanted
Great Pretender, The
I'll Be Home For Christmas
in co w/Walter Kent, Kim Gannon
Only You
in co w/Ande Rand
Twilight Time
in co w/Morty Nevins, Al Nevins, Artie Dunne

RAMIREZ, ROGER J. (Ram)
1913, American
w&m/Roger J. (Ram) Ramirez
Lover Man (Oh Where Can You Be)
in co w/Jimmy Davis, Jimmy Sherman

RANDALL, JAMES RYDER
American
w/James Ryder Randall
Music adapted from the German folk song "O Tannenbaum".
Maryland, My Maryland (1861)

RANDAZZO, TEDDY
American
w&m/Teddy Randazzo
Goin' Out Of My Head
   in co w/Bobby Weinstein
Hurt So Bad
   in co w/Bobby Wilding, Bobby
   Hart

RANDOLPH, BOOTS
American
w&m/Boots Randolph
Yakety Sax (1963)

RANEY, WAYNE
American
w&m/Wayne Raney
in co w/Lonnie Glosson
**Why Don't You Haul Off And
  Love Me (1949)**

RAPEE, ERNO
1891-1945, Hungarian/American
m/Erno Rapee
w/Lew Pollack
Angela Mia
Charmaine
Diane

RAPOSO, JOSEPH (Joe)
American
w&m/Joseph Raposo
Green (Bein' Green) (1972)
Rubber Duckie
Sing (1972)

RASKIN, GENE
1909, American
w&m/Gene Raskin
Those Were The Days

RASKIN, WILLIAM
1896-1942, American
w&m/William Raskin
**I'm Waiting For Ships That
  Never Come In**
   in co w/Abe Olman, Jack Yellen
**They Cut Down The Old Pine
  Tree**
   in co w/Billy Hill
**Wedding Bells Are Breaking Up
  That Old Gang Of Mine**
   in co w/Irving Kahal,
   Sammy Fain

RAVEL, MAURICE
1875-1937, French
m/Maurice Ravel (instr.)
Bolero (1929)
**Rapsodie Espagnole (Spanish
  Rhapsody)**

**RAZAF, ANDY (Andrea
Menentania Razafinkeriefo)**
1895, American
w/Andy Razaf
Many songs in co w/Thomas "Fats"
Waller. See list of selections under

Thomas "Fats" Waller.
Add't. songs by Andy Razaf.
**I'm Gonna Move To The Outskirts
  Of Town**
   m/William Weldon
In The Mood
   m/Joe Garland
Make Believe Ballroom
   m/Paul Denniker
Memories Of You
   m/Eubie Blake
My Handy Man
   m/Eubie Blake
Milkman's Matinee
   m/Paul Denniker
S'posin'
   m/Paul Denniker
Stompin' At The Savoy
   m/Benny Goodman,
   Chick Webb, Edgar Sampson
**That's What I Like About
  The South**
   w&m/Andy Razaf
**Twelfth Street Rag (original
  words James S. Sumner)**
   m/Euday L. Bowman
You're Lucky To Me
   m/Eubie Blake

RAY, JOHN ALVIN (Johnnie)
1927, American
w&m/John Alvin Ray
The Little White Cloud That Cried

RAY, HARRY
American
w&m/Harry Ray
in co w/Al Goodman
Special Lady (1980)

RAY, LILLIAN
English
m/Lillian Ray
w/Leonard Cooke
**Sunshine Of Your
  Smile, The (1915)**

**RAYE, DON (Donald MacRae
Wilhoite, Jr.)**
1909, American
w&m/Don Raye
Beat Me Daddy Eight To The Bar
   in co w/Hugh D. Prince
Boogie Woogie Bugle Boy
   in co w/Hugh D. Prince
Cow Cow Boogie
   in co w/Gene DePaul,
   Benny Carter
Domino
   in co w/Louis Ferrari
House Of Blue Lights, the
   in co w/Freddie Slack
**Milkman, Keep Those
  Bottles Quiet**
   m/Gene DePaul

Mister Five By Five
   in co w/Gene DePaul
I'll Remember April
   in co w/Gene DePaul,
   Patricia Johnson
Rhumboogie
   in co w/Hugh D. Prince
Star Eyes
   in co w/Gene DePaul
They Were Doing The Mambo
   in co w/Sonny Burke
This Is My Country
   in co w/Al Jacobs
Your Red Wagon
   in co w/Gene DePaul

RECORD, EUGENE
American
w&m/Eugene Record
in co w/William Sanders
Soulful Strut (1969)

REDDING, OTIS
1941-1967, American
w&m/Otis Redding
Groovin' Time
   in co w/Steve Cropper
I Can't Turn You Loose
I Want To Thank You
I've Been Loving You Too Long
   in co w/Jerry Butler
(Sitting On The) Dock Of The Bay
   in co w/Steve Cropper
Respect
Sweet Soul Music
   in co w/Arthur Conley,
   Sam Cooke

REDDY, HELEN
1942, Australian/American
w/Helen Reddy
m/Ray Burton
I Am Woman

REDMAN, DON
1900-1964, American
w&m/Don Redman
Cherry
   in co w/Ray Gilbert
Gee Baby Ain't I Good To You
Save It, Pretty Mama

REDMOND, JOHN
1906, American
w&m/John Redmond
Dream, Dream, Dream
   in co w/Louis Ricca
Gaucho Serenade, The
   in co w/James Cavanaugh,
   Nat Simon
Christmas In Killarney
   in co w/James Cavanaugh,
   Frank Weldon

REDNER, LEWIS H.
American
m/Lewis H. Redner (from the song
"St. Louis").
w/Phillips Brooks
O Little Town Of
 Bethlehem (1868)

REED, JERRY (Jerry Hubbard)
1937, American
w&m/Jerry Reed
Alabama Wild Man
Amos Moses
Crazy Legs
Georgia Sunshine
Guitar Man
Ko-Ko Joe
Misery Loves Company
Remembering
Talk About The Good Times
Thing Called Love
U.S. Male
When You're Hot You're Hot
You Took All The Ramblin' Out
 Of Me

REEVES, JIM
(James Travis Reeves)
1923-1964, American
w&m/Jim Reeves
Am I Losing You
Heartache
I'm Getting Better
Is It Really Over
It's Nothin' To Me
Yonder Comes A Sucker

REID, BILLY
English
w&m/Billy Reid
I'll Close My Eyes (1945)
 in co w/Buddy Kaye
I'm Walking Behind You (1953)
Gypsy, The (1945)
Tree In The Meadow, A (1947)

REID, CLARENCE
American
w&m/Clarence Reid
in co w/Willis Clarke
Clean Up Woman (1970)

REID, DON
1914, Canadian
w/Don Reid
m/Sammy Kaye
Remember Pearl Harbor

REID, DON
1945, American
w&m/Don Reid
Class Of '57
 in co w/Harold Reid
Do You Know You Are My
 Sunshine (1978)
 in co w/Harold Reid

Do You Remember These
 in co w/Harold Reid, Larry Lee
I Was There (1976)
I'll Go To My Grave
 Loving You (1974)
Monday Morning Secretary
Nothing As Original
 As You (1978)
So This Is Love
 in co w/Lew DeWitt
Susan When She Tried (1973)
That Certain Love
Whatever Happened To
 Randolph Scott (1973)
 in co w/Harold Reid

REID, HAROLD W.
1939, American
w&m/Harold W. Reid
Bed Of Roses
Class Of '57
 in co w/Don Reid
Do You Remember These
 in co w/Don Reid, Larry Lee
Whatever Happened
 To Randolph Scott

REINHARDT, DJANGO
1910-1953, French
m/Django Reinhardt (instr.)
Babik
Crepuscule
Moppin' The Bride
Nuages
Vendredi 13

REINHARDT, GLADYS
1920-1961, American
w&m in co w/Charles
"Red" Matthews
White Silver Sands

REISFELD, BERT
German
m/Bert Reisfeld
in co w/Mort Fryberg, Rolf Marbet.
English words by Dorothy Dick.
Call Me Darling (1931)

RENE, LEON T.
1902, American
w&m/Leon T. Rene
I Lost My Sugar In Salt Lake City
 in co w/Johnny Lange
I Sold My Heart To the Junkman
 in co w/Otis J. René Jr.
Someone's Rocking
 My Dreamboat
 in co w/Otis J. René Jr.
When It's Sleepytime
 Down South
 in co w/Clarence Muse,
 Otis J. René Jr.
When The Swallows Come Back
 To Capistrano

REVEL, HARRY
1905-1958
m/Harry Revel
w/Mack Gordon
College Rhythm
Did You Ever See A
 Dream Walking
Goodnight My Love
I Feel Like A Feather In
 The Breeze
I Played Fiddle For The Czar
Listen To The German Band
Loveliness Of You, The
Love Thy Neighbor
May I
Never In A Million Years
Paris In The Spring
She Reminds Me Of You
Stay As Sweet As You Are
Take A Number From One To Ten
There's A Lull In My Life
Underneath The Harlem Moon
Wake Up And Live
With My Eyes Wide Open
 I'm Dreaming
Without A Word Of Warning
You Can't Have Everything
You Hit The Spot

RICE, BILL
American
w&m in co w/Jerry Foster
Easy Part's Over, The
For A Minute There
I Hate Goodbyes
Just Long Enough To
 Say Goodbye
Love Survived
One To One
Rising Above It All
Satisfied Man, A
Someone to Give My Love To
Songs We Made Love To, The
Wonder Could I Live
 There Anymore
 w&m/Bill Rice
Your Pretty Roses Came Too Late

RICE, TIM
English
w/Tim Rice
m/Andrew Lloyd Webber
Buenos Aires (1977)
I Don't Know How To
 Love Him (1970)
Don't Cry for Me
 Argentina (1977)
High Flying, Adored

RICH, CHARLIE
1934, American
w&m/Charlie Rich
There Won't Be Anymore

Ways Of A Woman In Love
in co w/William E. Justis, Jr.

RICHARD, KEITH
1943, English
w&m/Keith Richard
in co w/Mick Jagger
See list of selections under
Mick Jagger.

RICHARD, LITTLE
(Richard Penniman)
1935, American
w&m/Little Richard
Jenny Jenny
in co w/Enotris Johnson
Long Tall sally
in co w/Robert A. Blackwell
Enotris Johnson
Lucille (1957)
in co w/Albert Collins
Slippin' And Slidin'
in co w/Albert Collins,
James Smith
Tutti Frutti
in co w/Joe Lubin,
Dorothy La Bostrie

RICHARDSON, ARTHUR
1899-1963, American
w&m in co w/Ross MacClean
**Too Fat Polka (She's
Too Fat For Me)**

RICHARDSON, J.P.
(Big Bopper)
1930-1959, American
w&m/J.P. Richardson
Chantilly Lace
Little Red Riding Hood
Running Bear
Treasure Of Love
White Lightning

RICHEY, GEORGE
American
w&m/George Richey
Good News
in co w/Billy Sherrill,
Norro Wilson
**Let's Get Together (One
Last Time)**
in co w/Billy Sherrill
Soul Song
in co w/Norro Wilson,
Billy Sherrill
Southern California
in co w/Billy Sherrill,
Roger Bowling

'Til I Can Make It On My Own
in co w/Tammy Wynette,
Billy Sherrill
You And Me

RICHIE, LIONEL
1949, American
w&m/Lionel Richie
Sail On
Still
Three Times A Lady

RICHMAN, HARRY
1895, American
w&m/Harry Richman
Singing A Vagabond Song
in co w/Sam Messenheimer,
Val Burton
**There Oughta Be A Moonlight
Saving Time**
in co w/Irving Kahal
**There's Danger In Your
Eyes, Cherie**
in co w/Jack Meskill,
Pete Wendling
Walkin' My Baby Back Home
in co w/Roy Turk, Fred E. Ahlert

RICKS, JIMMY
American
w&m/Jimmy Ricks
in co w/Billy Sandford
Rock Me All Night Long (1952)

RIDDLE, NELSON
1920, American
m/Nelson Riddle (instr.)
Film scores:
Great Gatsby, The (1974)
Paint Your Wagon (1969)

RILEY, MIKE
1904, American
w&m in co w/Edward Farley
**Music Goes Round And Round,
The**

RIO, CHUCK
American
w&m/Chuck Rio
Tequila (1958)

ROACH, JOSEPH MALOY
1913, American
w&m/Joseph Maloy Roach
in co w/George Mysels
One Little Candle (1951)

ROBBINS, MARTY
1925, American
w&m/Marty Robbins
Begging To You
Big Iron
Camelia
Chair, The
**Cowboy In The Continental
Suit, The**
Devil Woman
Don't Let Me Touch You
in co w/Billy Sherrill
Don't Worry
El Paso
I'll Go On Alone

It's Your World
Kate
My Woman, My Woman My Wife
White Sport Coat (And A
Pink Carnation), A

ROBERTS, BRUCE
1955, American
w&m/Bruce Roberts in co w/Paul Jabara
Main Event, The
No More Tears (Enough Is Enough)

**ROBERTS, CHARLES
LUCKEYTH**
1887-1968, American
w&m/Charles Luckeyth Roberts
Helter Skelter
Junk Man Rag
Massachusetts
Moonlight Cocktail
Music Box Rag
Pork And Beans
Railroad Blues
Ripples Of The Nile
Rosetime And You
w/Alex Rogers
Shy And Sly

ROBERTS, LEE S.
1884-1949, American
m/Lee S. Roberts
w/J. Will Callahan
Smiles (1917)

ROBERTS, PAUL
1915, American
w&m/Paul Roberts
in co w/Red River Dave,
Shelly Darnell
**There's A Star-Spangled Banner
Waving Somewhere (The Ballad
Of Francis Powers)**

ROBERTS, RICK
American
w&m/Rick Roberts
You Are The Woman (1976)

ROBERTS, RUTH
1926, American
w&m/Ruth Roberts
First Thing Every Morning, The
in co w/Jimmy Dean
Meet The Mets
in co w/William Katz
Mr. Touchdown, U.S.A.
in co w/William Katz

ROBERTSON, DON
1922, American
w&m/Don Robertson
Condemned Without Trial
in co w/Hal Blair
I Don't Hurt Anymore
in co w/Jack Rollins
I'm Yours
in co w/Hal Blair

I Really Don't Want To Know
in co w/Howard Barnes
Ninety Miles An Hour
in co w/Hal Blair
Not One Minute More
in co w/Hal Blair
Please Help Me, I'm Falling
in co w/Hal Blair
Please Help Me, I'm Falling
in co w/Hal Blair
Ringo
in co w/Hal Blair

ROBERTSON, J. ROBBIE
1944, Canadian
w&m/J. Robbie Robertson
Across The Great Divide
Chest Fever
Daniel And The Sacred Harp
Don't Do It
Life Is A Carnival
**Night They Drove Old
  Dixie Down, The**
Ophelia
Rag, Mama, Rag
Rumor, The
Shape I'm In, The
Stage Fright
Time To Kill
Up On Cripple Creek
Weight, the

ROBEY, DON
American
w&m/Don Robey
in co w/Ferdinand Washington
Pledging My Love (1955)

ROBIN, LEO
1900 American
w/Leo Robin
Beyond The Blue Horizon
m/Richard A. Whiting,
W. Franke Harling
Blue Hawaii
m/Ralph Rainger
Bye Bye Baby
m/Jule Styne
**Diamonds Are A Girl's
  Best Friend**
m/Jule Styne
Easy To Love
m/Ralph Rainger
Faithful Forever
m/Ralph Rainger
For Every Man There's A Woman
m/Harold Arlen
Gal In Calico, A
m/Arthur Schwartz
Hallelujah
co-lyricist Clifford Grey
m/Vincent Youmans
If I Should Lose You
m/Ralph Rainger

In Love In Vain
m/Jerome Kern
June In January
m/Ralph Rainger
La Bomba
m/Ralph Rainger
Little Girl From Little Rock, A
m/Jule Styne
Lost In Loveliness
m/Sigmund Romberg
Louise
m/Richard A. Whiting
Love In Bloom
m/Ralph Rainger
Love Is Just Around The Corner
m/Lewis E. Gensler
My Ideal
m/Richard A. Whiting,
Newell Chase
Oh But I Do
m/Arthur Schwartz
One Hour With You
m/Richard A. Whiting
Please
m/Ralph Rainger
Prisoner Of Love
m/Russ Columbo,
Clarence Gaskill
Rainy Night In Rio, A
m/Arthur Schwartz
So In Love
m/David Rose
Thanks For The Memorey
m/Ralph Rainger
What's Good About Goodbye?
m/Harold Arlen
Whispers In The Dark
m/Frederick Hollander
With Every Breath I Take
m/Ralph Rainger
You're A Sweet Little Headache
m/Ralph Rainger

**ROBINSON, SYLVIA
VANDERPOOL**
1936, American
w&m/Sylvia Vanderpool Robinson
Cry Cry Cry
Love Is Strange
in co w/Mickey Baker,
Ellas McDaniels
Pillow Talk
in co w/Michael Burton
Shame, Shame, Shame

**ROBINSON, WILLIAM JR.
(Smokey)**
1940, American
w&m/William Robinson Jr.
Baby Baby Don't Cry
in co w/Al Cleveland,
Terry Johnson
Brokenhearted
Cruisin'
Don't Mess With Bill

Everybody Gotta Pay Some Dues
Get Ready
Going To A Go-Go
in co w/Warren Moore,
Bobby Rogers, Marvin Tarplin
Got A Job
in co w/Berry Gordy,
Tyrone Carlo
I Like It Like That
in co w/Marvin Tarplin
I Second That Emotion
in co w/Alfred Cleveland
I'll Be Doggone
in co w/Warren Moore, Bobby
Rogers
I'll Try Something New
Let Me Be The Clock
Love She Can Count On, A
More Love
Mighty Good Lovin'
My Girl
in co w/Ronald White
My Guy
One Who Really Loves You, The
Shop Around
in co w/Berry Gordy Jr.
Since I Lost My Baby
in co w/Warren Moore
Tears Of A Clown, The
in co w/Stevie Wonder,
Henry Cosby
Tracks Of My Tears, The
in co w/Marvin Tarplin,
Warren Moore
Two Lovers
**Way You Do the Things You
  Do, The**
in co w/Robert Rogers
What's So Good About Goodbye
You Beat Me To The Punch
in co w/Ronald White
You've Really got A Hold On Me

ROBISON, CARSON J.
1890-1957, American
w&m/Carson J. Robison
Barnacle Bill The Sailor
**Carry Me Back To The
  Lone Prairie**
**I'm Going Back To Whur I
  Came From**
**In The Blue Ridge Mountains
  Of Virginia (My Blue Ridge
  Mountain Home)**
Left My Gal In The Mountains
Life Gets Teejus Don't It
Little Green Valley
Open Up Them Pearly Gates

ROBLEDO, JULIAN
American
m/Julian Robledo
w/Dorothy Terris
**Three O'Clock In The Morning
  (1922)**

RODDENBERRY, GENE
American
w/Gene Roddenberry
m/Alexander Courage
Star Trek (TV Theme)

RODGERS, JIMMY
1897 - 1933, American
w&m/Jimmy Rodgers
Any Old Time
Blue Yodels
Daddy And Home
Home Call
I'm Lonesome Too
In The Jailhouse Now
Jimmy The Kid
   in co w/Bob Neville
Lullaby Yodel
Mississippi Moon
Mother, The Queen Of My Heart
   in co w/Hoyt Bryant
Mule Skinner Blues
   in co w/George Vaughn
My Little Ol' Home Down In New
   Orleans
My Old Pal
Never No Mo' Blues
T For Texas
   in co w/George Thorn
Travelin' Blues
   in co w/Shelley Lee Alley
Treasures Untold
   in co w/Elsworth T. Cozzens
Waiting For A Train
Why Should I Be Lonely?
Yodeling Cowboy
You And My Old Guitar

RODGERS, NILE
1952, American
w&m/Nile Rodgers
Dance, Dance, Dance (Yowsah,
   Yowsah, Yowsah) (1978)
   in co w/Bernard Edwards, Kenny
   Lehman
Everybody Dance (1978)
   in co w/Bernard Edwards
Freak Le (1979)
   in co w/Bernard Edwards
Got To Love Somebody (1980)
   in co w/Bernard Edwards

Upside Down
   in co w/Bernard Edwards

We Are Family (1979)
   in co w/Bernard Edwards

RODGERS, PAUL
1949, English
w&m/Paul Rodgers
All Right Now
Can't Get Enough Of Your Love
   in co w/Simon F. Kirke

RODGERS, RICHARD
1902-1979, American
Instr. m/Richard Rodgers
Slaughter On Tenth Avenue
Victory At Sea (TV score)
Winston Churchill: The Valiant
   Years (TV score)
March Of The Siamese Children
   (from "The King And I")
w&m/Richard Rodgers
Look No Further
Maine
No Strings
Sweetest Sounds, The

m/Richard Rodgers
All At Once You Love Her
   w/Oscar Hammerstein II
Babes In Arms
   w/Lorenz Hart
Bali Hai
   w/Oscar Hammerstein II
Bewitched, Bothered And
   Bewildered
   w/Lorenz Hart
Blue Moon
   w/Lorenz Hart
Blue Room
   w/Lorenz Hart
Carefully Taught (You Have To
   Be)
   w/Oscar Hammerstein II
Climb Ev'ry Mountain
   w/Oscar Hammerstein II
Cockeyed Optimist, A
   w/Oscar Hammerstein II
Dancing On The Ceiling
   w/Lorenz Hart
Do I Hear A Waltz
   w/Stephen Soldheim
Do-Re-Mi
   w/Oscar Hammerstein II
Easy To Remember
   w/Lorenz Hart
Edelweiss
   w/Oscar Hammerstein II
Everybody's Got A Home But Me
   w/Oscar Hammerstein II
Everything I've Got
   w/Lorenz Hart
Falling In Love With Love
   w/Lorenz Hart
Fellow Needs A Girl, A
   w/Oscar Hammerstein II
Gentleman Is A Dope, The
   w/Oscar Hammerstein II
Getting To Know You
   w/Oscar Hammerstein II
Girl Friend, The
   w/Lorenz Hart
Happy Talk
   w/Oscar Hammerstein II
Have You Met Miss Jones
   w/Lorenz Hart

Hello Young Lovers
   w/Oscar Hammerstein II
Here In My Arms
   w/Lorenz Hart
Honey Bun
   w/Oscar Hammerstein II
I Caint Say No
   w/Oscar Hammerstein II
I Could Write A Book
   w/Lorenz Hart
I Didn't Know What Time It Was
   w/Lorenz Hart

I Enjoy Being A Girl
   w/Oscar Hammerstein II
I Have Dreamed
   w/Oscar Hammerstein II
I Married An Angel
   w/Lorenz Hart
I Whistle A Happy Tune
   w/Oscar Hammerstein II
I Wish I Were In Love Again
   w/Lorenz Hart
If I Loved You
   w/Oscar Hammerstein II

I'm Gonna Wash That Guy Right
   Right Outa My Hair
   w/Oscar Hammerstein II
I'm In Love With A Wonderful
   Guy
   w/Oscar Hammerstein II
Isn't It Romantic
   w/Lorenz Hart
It's Easy To Remember
   w/Lorenz Hart
It Might As Well Be Spring
   w/Oscar Hammerstein II
It Never Entered My Mind
   w/Lorenz Hart
It's A Grand Night For Singing
   w/Oscar Hammerstein II
Johnny One Note
   w/Lorenz Hart
June Is Bustin' Out All Over
   w/Oscar Hammerstein II
Lady Is A Tramp, The
   w/Lorenz Hart
Little Girl Blue
   w/Lorenz Hart
Love, Look Away
   w/Oscar Hammerstein II
Love Me Tonight
   w/Lorenz Hart
Lover
   w/Lorenz Hart
Manhattan
   w/Lorenz Hart
Maria
   w/Oscar Hammerstein II
Mimi
   w/Lorenz Hart
Most Beautiful Girl In The World,
   The
   w/Lorenz Hart

Mountain Greenery
w/Lorenz Hart
My Favorite Things
w/Oscar Hammerstein II
My Funny Valentine
w/Lorenz Hart
My Heart Stood Still
w/Lorenz Hart
My Romance
w/Lorenz Hart
No Other Love
w/Oscar Hammerstein II
Oh, What A Beautiful Morning
w/Oscar Hammerstein II
Oklahoma
w/Oscar Hammerstein II
On Your Toes
w/Lorenz Hart
Over And Over Again
w/Lorenz Hart
People Will Say We're In Love
w/Oscar Hammerstein II
Puzzlement, A
w/Oscar Hammerstein II
Shall We Dance
w/Oscar Hammerstein II
Ship Without A Sail, A
w/Oscar Hammerstein II
Sing For Your Supper
w/Lorenz Hart
Soliloquy
w/Oscar Hammerstein II
Some Enchanted Evening
w/Oscar Hammerstein II
Something Wonderful
w/Oscar Hammerstein II
Sound Of Music, The
w/Oscar Hammerstein II
Spring Is Here
w/Lorenz Hart
Stay
w/Stephen Sondheim
Surrey With The Fringe On Top, The
w/Oscar Hammerstein II
Take Him
w/Lorenz Hart
Take The Moment
w/Stephen Sondheim
Ten Cents A Dance
w/Lorenz Hart
That's For Me
w/Oscar Hammerstein II
There Is Nothing Like A Dame
w/Oscar Hammerstein II
There's A Small Hotel
w/Lorenz Hart
This Can't Be Love
w/Lorenz Hart
This Nearly Was Mine
w/Oscar Hammerstein II
Thou Swell
w/Lorenz Hart

Tree In The Park, A
w/Lorenz Hart
Two By Two
w/Stephen Sondheim
Wait Till You See Her
w/Lorenz Hart
We Kiss In A Shadow
w/Oscar Hammerstein II
What's The Use Of Wond'rin
w/Oscar Hammerstein II
Where Or When
w/Lorenz Hart
Where's That Rainbow
w/Lorenz Hart
Why Can't I
w/Lorenz Hart
With A Song In My Heart
w/Lorenz Hart
Wonderful Guy, A
w/Oscar Hammerstein II
You Are Beautiful
w/Oscar Hammerstein II
You Are Sixteen
w/Oscar Hammerstein II
You Are Never Away
w/Oscar Hammerstein II
You Took Advantage Of Me
w/Lorenz Hart
You'll Never Walk Alone
w/Oscar Hammerstein II
Younger Than Springtime
w/Oscar Hammerstein II
You're Nearer
w/Lorenz Hart
Zip
w/Lorenz Hart

RODRIGUEZ, G.H. MATOS
m/G.H. Matos Rodriguez
La Cumparsita (The Masked One)

ROE, TOMMY
1942, American
w&m/Tommy Roe
Dizzy
in co w/F. Wheeler
Heather Honey
Hooray For Hazel
Jam Up, Jelly Tight
Sheila
Sweet Pea

ROGERS, MILTON (Shorty)
1924, American
m/Shorty Rogers (instr.)
Cerveza
Coop De Graas
Infinity Promenade
Jazz Waltz
Jolly Rogers
Short Stop
Sugar Loaf
Sweetheart Of Sigmund Freud
That's Right

ROIG, GONZALO
Cuban
m/Gonzalo Roig
w/Jack Sherr
Yours (Quiérme Mucho)

ROLLINS, JACK
1906, American
m/Jack Rollins
Frosty The Snow Man
w/Steve Nelson
I Don't Hurt Anymore
w/Don Robertson
Peter Cottontail
w/Steve Nelson
Smokey The Bear
w/Steve Nelson

ROLLINS, SONNY
1930, American
m/Sonny Rollins (instr.)
Airegin
Blue 7
Come Gone
Freedom Suite, The
Jungoso
Oleo
St. Thomas
Shadow Waltz, The
Sonneymoon For Two
Tenor Madness
Valse Hot

ROMBERG, SIGMUND
1887-1951, Hungarian/American
m/Sigmund Romberg
Auf Wiedersehn
w/Herbert Reynolds
Close As Pages In A Book
w/Dorothy Fields
Deep In My Heart, Dear
w/Dorothy Donnelly
Desert Song, The (Blue Heaven)
w/Oscar Hammerstein II
Otto Harbach
Drinking Song, The
w/Dorothy Donnelly
Golden Days
w/Dorothy Donnelly
Lost In Loveliness
w/Leo Robin
Lover, Come Back To Me
w/Oscar Hammerstein II
One Alone
w/Oscar Hammerstein II
Otto Harbach
One Kiss
w/Oscar Hammerstein II
Riff Song, The
w/Oscar Hammerstein II
Otto Harbach
Romance
w/Oscar Hammerstein II
Otto Harbach

Serenade
w/Dorothy Donnelly
Silver Moon
w/Dorothy Donnelly
Softly As In A Morning Sunrise
w/Oscar Hammerstein II
Song Of Love
w/Dorothy Donnelly
Stouthearted Men
w/Oscar Hammerstein II
Wanting You
w/Oscar Hammerstein II
Will You Remember
w/Rida Johnsong Young
When I Grow Too Old To Dream
w/Oscar Hammerstein II

ROME, HAROLD
1908, American
w&m/Harold Rome
All Of A Sudden My Heart Sings
Adapted from the French song "Ma
Mie," by Jamblan and Herpin
Anyone Would Love You
Along With Me
Be Kind To Your Parents
Face On The Dime, The
Fanny
Franklin D. Roosevelt Jones
Have I Told You Lately
Mene, Mene Tekel
Money Song, The
South America, Take It Away
Sunday In The Park
Take Off The Coat
To My Wife
Where Did The Night Go

ROMEO, TONY
American
w&m/Tony Romeo
Candy Kid The (1968)
I Think I Love You (1970)
Indian Lake (1968)
It's One Of Those Nights (1971)
Poor Baby (1969)

ROMERO, CHAN
English
w&m/Chan Romero
Hippy, Hippy Shake, The (1964)

RONELL, ANN
1909, American
w&m/Ann Ronell
Baby's Birthday Party
**Who's Afraid Of The Big Bad
Wolf**
in co w/Frank Churchill
Linda
in co w/Jack Lawrence
Rain On The Roof
Willow Weep For Me

ROOT, GEORGE FREDERICK
1820-1895, American
w&m/George Frederick Root
Battle Cry Of Freedom, The
First Gun Is Fired, The
Hazel Dell, The
Jesus Loves The Little Children
w/C. H. Woolston (music based
on Root's "Tramp, Tramp,
Tramp")
Just Before The Battle, Mother
Rosalie The Prairie Flower
There's Music In The Air
w/Frances J. Crosby
**Tramp Tramp Tramp (The
Prisoner's Hope)**
Vacant Chair, The
w/H.S. Washburn

ROSE, BILLY
1899-1966, American
w/Billy Rose
Back In Your Own Backyard
m/Dave Dreyer, Al Jolson
Barney Google
w/Con Conrad
Cheerful Little Earful
co-lyricist Ira Gershwin
m/Harry Warren
Clap Hands Here Comes Charley
m/Joseph Meyer, Ballard
MacDonald
**Cup Of Coffee, A Sandwich
And You, A**
m/Joseph Meyer
Don't Bring Lulu
co-lyricist Lew Brown
m/Ray Henderson
**Does The Spearmint Lose Its
Flavor On The Bedpost
Overnight**
m/Ernest Breuer
**Fifty Million Frenchmen Can't Be
Wrong**
m/Fred Fisher
Great Day
co-lyricist Edward Eliscu
m/Vincent Youmans
Here Comes The Show Boat
m/Maceo Pinkard
House Is Haunted, The
m/Basil G. Adlam
**I Found A Million Dollar Baby In
A Five And Ten Cent Store**
co-lyricist Mort Dixon
m/Harry Warren
I Wanna Be Loved
co-lyricist Edward Heyman
m/John Green
It Happened In Monterey
m/Mabel Wayne

It's Only A Paper Moon
co-lyricist E.Y. Harburg
m/Harold Arlen
I've Got A Feeling I'm Falling
m/Thomas "Fats" Waller, Harry
Link
Me And My Shadow
m/Dave Dreyer, Al Jolson
More Than You Know
co-lyricist Edward Eliscu
m/Vincent Youmans
**Night Is Young And You're So
Beautiful, The**
co-lyricist Irving Kahal
m/Dana Suesse
Suddenly
co-lyricist E.Y. Harburg
m/Vernon Duke
That Old Gang Of Mine
co-lyricist Mort Dixon
m/Ray Henderson
**There's A Rainbow Round My
Shoulder**
m/Dave Dreyer, Al Jolson
Without A Song
co-lyricist Edward Eliscu
m/Vincent Youmans
Would You Like To Take A Walk
co-lyricist Mort Dixon
m/Harry Warren
**You've Got To See Momma Every
Night**
m/Con Conrad

ROSE, DAVID
1910, American
m/David Rose (instr. except as noted)
Betty
Dance Of The Spanish Onion
Holiday For Strings
w/Sammy Gallop
Holiday For Trombones
Nostalgia
Our Waltz
Winged Victory (score)
Just In Love
w/Leo Robin

ROSE, FRED
1897-1954, American
w&m/Fred Rose
Afraid
Before You Call
Be Honest With Me
in co w/Gene Autry
Blue Eyes Crying In The Rain
Crazy Heart
in co w/Maurice Murray
Deed I Do
in co w/Walter Hirsch
Don't Bring Me Posies
Foggy River

Hang Your Head In Shame
   in co w/Ed G. Nelson, Steve
   Nelson
Honest & Truly
I Wonder When We'll Ever Know
  (The Wonder Of It All)
I'll Never Stand In Your Way
   in co w/Hy Heath
It's A Sin
   in co w/Zeb Turner
Just Like Me
Kaw-Liga
   in co w/Hank Williams
Lesson Of Love, The
   in co w/Nat Vincent
Mansion On The Hill, A
   in co w/Hank Williams
Midnight Flyer
   in co w/Hy Heath
No One Will Ever Know
   in co w/Mel Foree
Red Hot Mama
Roly Poly
Setting The Woods On Fire
   in co w/Ed G. Nelson
Take These Chains From My
  Heart
   in co w/Hy Heath
Tears On My Pillow
   in co w/Gene Autry
Texarkana Baby
   in co w/Cottonseed Clark
We Live In Two Different Worlds
Worried Over You
   in co w/Ed G. Nelson, Steve
   Nelson
You Know How Talk Gets Around

ROSE, VINCENT
1880-1944, American
w&m/Vincent Rose
Avalon
   in co w/Al Jolson
Blueberry Hill
   in co w/Al Lewis, Larry Stock
Linger Awhile
   in co w/Harry Owens
Whispering
   in co w/John Schonberger,
   Richard Coburn, Malvin
   Schonberger

ROSENTHAL, LAURENCE
1926, American
m/Laurence Rosenthal
Film scores
Meteor
Man Of La Mancha (1972)
Raisin In The Sun, A
The Miracle Worker
Rashomon
Requiem For A Heavyweight

ROSS, BEVERLY
1937, Amnerican
w&m in co w/Julius Dixon
Lollipop
ROSS, JERRY
1926-1955, American
m/Jerry Ross
w/Richard Adler
A Little Brains, A Little Talent
Heart
Hernando's Hideaway
Hey There
I'm Not At All In Love
Rags To Riches
Small Talk
Steam Heat
Two Lost Souls
Whatever Lola Wants
Who's Got The Pain
ROSTILL, JOHN
d. 1977, English
w&m/John Rostill
I You Love Me (Let Me Know)
  (1975)
Let Me Be There (1974)
Please Mr. Please (1975)
ROTA, NINO
Italian
m/Nino Rota
Come Live Your Life With Me
   w/Larry Kusik, Wilbur (Billy)
   Meshel
Speak Softly Love (Love Theme
  From "The Godfather")
   w/Larry Kusik
Time For Us, A (Love Theme
  From "Romeo And Juliet")
   w/Larry Kusik, Eddy Snyder
ROTTER, FRITZ (M. ROTHA)
German
(In Dreams) I Kiss Your Hand
  Madame (1929)
   w/Fritz Rotter, Samuel M. Lewis,
   Joseph Young
   m/Ralph Erwin
Take Me In Your Arms
   w&m/Fritz Rotter
That's All I Want From You
   w&m/Fritz Rotter

ROUSE, ERVIN T.
American
w&m/Erwin T. Rouse
Orange Blossom Special (1964)
ROX, JOHN
American
w&m/John Rox
It's A Big Wide Wonderful World
  (1940)

ROZSA, MIKLOS
1907, American
m/Miklos Rozsa
Film scores
Ben Hur (1959)
Double Indemnity (1944)
Double Life, A (1947)
Four Feathers, The
Ivanhoe (1952)
Julius Caesar (1953)
Jungle Book, The (1942)
Killers, The (1946)
Lost Weekend, The (1945)
Lydia (1941)
Quo Vadis (1951)
Spellbound (1945)
Song To Remember, A
   in co w/Morris Stoloff (1945)
Thief Of Bagdad, The
Time After Time (1979)
ROSENFELD, MONROE H.
American
Take Back Your Gold
   m/Monroe H. Rosenfeld
   w/Louis W. Pritzkow
Those Wedding Bells Shall Not
  Ring Out
   w&m/Monroe H. Rosenfeld
With All Her Faults I Love Her
  Still
   w&m/Monroe H. Rosenfeld
RUBY, HARRY
1895-1977, American
m/Harry Ruby
A Kiss To Build A Dream On
   w/Oscar Hammerstein II, Bert
   Kalmar
Give Me The Simple Life
   w/Rube Bloom
Hooray For Captain Spaulding
   w/Bert Kalmar
I Wanna Be Loved By You
   in co/Herbert Stothart
   w/Bert Kalmar
I Love You So Much
   w/Bert Kalmar
Keep On Doin' What You're Doin'
   w/Bert Kalmar
Maybe It's Because
   w/Johnnie Scott
Nevertheless
   w/Bert Kalmar
So Long Oo-long
   w/Bert Kalmar
Thinking Of You
   w/Bert Kalmar
Three Little Words
   w/Bert Kalmar
Who's Sorry Now
   in co w/Ted Snyder
   w/Bert Kalmar

RUIZ, GABRIEL
Mexican
m/Gabriel Ruiz
English w/Sunny Skylar
Amor (1943)

RUNDGREN, TODD
1948, American
w&m/Todd Rundgren
Be Nice To Me
Black Maria
Can We Still Be Friends
Cold Morning Light
Couldn't I Just Tell You
Devil's Bite
A Dream Goes On Forever
Hello, It's Me
It Wouldn't Have Made Any
  Difference
Initiation
I Saw The Light
Long Flowing Robe
Love Is The Answer
We Got To Get You A Woman
You Cried Wolf

RUSHING, JAMES ANDREW
(JIMMY)
1902-1972, American
w&m/James Andrew Rushing
Baby Don't Tell On Me
Blues In The Dark
Evil Blues
Goin' To Chicago
Good Morning Blues
  in co w/William (Count) Basie,
  Eddie Durham
Jimmy's Blues
Sent For You Yesterday And Here
  You Come Today
  in co w/Eddie Durham
Take Me Back Baby
Thursday Blues
Undecided Blues

RUSKIN, HARRY
1894, American
w/Harry Ruskin
m/Henry Sullivan
I May Be Wrong But I Think
  You're Wonderful

RUSSELL, BOB (Sidney Keith
Russell)
1914-1970, American
w&m/Bob Russell
Ballerina
  in co w/Carl Sigman
Brazil
  in co w/Ary Barroso
Crazy He Calls Me
  in co w/Carl Sigman
Do Nothing Till You Hear From
Me
  in co w/Duke Ellington
Don't Get Around Much Anymore
  in co w/Duke Ellington
Eyes Of Love, The
  in co w/Quincy Jones
For Love Of Ivy
  in co w/Quincy Jones
Frenesi
  in co w/Albert Dominguez
He Ain' t Heavy ... He's My
  Brother
  in co w/Bobby Scott
I've Been Kissed Before
  in co w/Lester Lee
Maria Elena
  in co w/Lorenzo Barcelata
You Came A Long Way From St.
Louis
  in co w/John Benson Brooks

RUSSELL, BOBBY
American
w&m/Bobby Russell
Everlasting Love
  in co w/Buzz Cason (1967)
1432 Franklin Pike Circle Hero
Honey
Little Green Apples (1968)
Night The Lights Went Out In
  Georgia, The (1973)
Saturday Morning Confusion

RUSSELL, HENRY
1812-1900, English
w&m/Henry Russell
Indian Hunter, The
Life On The Ocean Wave, A
Old Arm Chair, The
Woodman Spare That Tree
  w/George Pope Morris

RUSSELL, JAMES I.
American
w&m/James I. Russell
Where The River Shannon Flows
  (1905)

RUSSELL, LEON
1941, American
w&m/Leon Russell
Back To The Island
Bluebird
Delta Lady
I Put A Spell On You
Lady Blue
Little Hideaway
Magic Mirror
Me And Baby
Of Thee I Sing
Rainbow In Your Eyes
Roll Away The Stone
  in co w/G. Dempsey
Song For You, A
Stranger In A Strange Land
Superstar
  in co w/Bonnie Bramlett
Sweet Emily
This Masquerade
Tight Rope

RUSSO, DAN
1885-1956, American
m/Dan Russo
w/Gus Kahn, Ernie Erdman
Toot, Toot Tootsie, Goodbye

RYAN, BEN
1892, American
w/Ben Ryan
Gang That Sang Heart Of My
  Heart, The
Inka-Dinka-Doo
  m/Jimmy Durante
M-I-S-S-I-S-S-I-P-P-I
  co-lyricist Bert Hanlon
  m/Harry Tierney
When Francis Dances With Me
  m/Sol Violinsky

Addenda:

ROGERS, KENNETH (KENNY)
1941, American
w&m/Kenny Rogers
Love Or Something Like It
  in co w/Steve Glassmeyer
Sweet Music Man

POPULAR COMPOSERS & LYRICISTS

S

SADLER, BARRY
American
w&m/Barry Sadler
Ballad Of The Green Berets
(1966)

SAGER, CAROLE BAYER
1944, American
w&m/Carole Bayer Sager
Better Than Ever
m/Marvin Hamlisch
Come In Out Of The Rain
m/Melissa Manchester
Everything Old Is New Again
m/Peter Allen
Groovy Kind Of Love, A
m/Tony Wine
I'd Rather Leave While I'm In Love
m/Peter Allen
If You Remember Me
m/Marvin Hamlisch
Midnight Blue
m/Melissa Manchester
My Love Goes With You
m/Marvin Hamlisch
Nobody Does It Better
m/Marvin Hamlisch
When I Need You
m/Albert Hammond
They're Playing Our Song
m/Marvin Hamlisch

SAHM, DOUGLAS SALDANA (DOUG)
1942, American
w&m/Doug Sahm
Mendocino (1969)
Rains Came, The (1966)
She's About A Mover (1965)

ST. LEWIS, KENI
American
w&m/Keni St. Lewis
Boogie Fever
in co w/Frederick Perren
Cotton Candy
in co w/Frederick Perren
Don't Take Away The Music
in co w/Frederick Perren,
Christine Yarion
Heaven Must Be Missing An Angel
in co w/Frederick Perren
Hot Line
in co w/Frederick Perren
Lover And Friend
in co w/Minnie Riperton, Dick
Rudolph, Gene Dozier
Who Done It? (Whodunit)
in co w/Frederick Perren

SAINTE-MARIE, BUFFY
1941, American
w&m/Buffy Sainte-Marie

Piney Wood Hills
Universal Soldier, The
Until It's Time For You To Go

SALVADOR, HENRI
French
m/Henri Salvador
w/Leo Johns
Melodie D'Amour (1957)

SAMPSON, EDGAR MELVIN (ED)
1907-1973, American
m/Edgar Melvin Sampson
Blue Lou (Instr.)
Blue Minor (instr.)
Don't Be That Way
in co w/Benny Goodman, Chick
Webb, Mitchell Parish
If Dreams Come True
w&m/Edgar Melvin Sampson
Light And Sweet (instr.)
Lullaby In Rhythm
in co w/Benny Goodman
Stompin' At The Savoy
in co w/Andy Razaf, Benny
Goodman, Chick Webb

SANDERS, JOE L.
1896-1965, American
w&m/Joe L. Sanders
Little Orphan Annie

SANDERS, WILLIAM
American
w&m in co w/Eugene Record
Soulful Strut (1969)

SANTAMAMARIA, MONGO
Cuban/American
w&m/Mongo Santamaria
Afro-Blue
Afro Roots
Yeh Yeh (1965)

SANTLY, JOSEPH H.
1886-1962, American
m/Joseph H. Santly
w/Cliff Friend
There's Yes Yes In Your Eyes

SANTLY, LESTER
1894, American
m/Lester Santly in co/Milton Ager
w/Benny Davis
I'm Nobody's Baby

SAUER, ROBERT
1872-1944, American
m/Robert Sauer
w/Mary Hale Woolsey, Milton
Taggart
When It's Springtime In The Rockies

SAXON, DAVID
1919, American
m/David Saxon
w/Sammy Gallop

There Must Be A Way
Vagabond Shoes

SAYER, LEO (B. GERARD HUGH SAYER)
1948, English
w&m/Leo Sayer
Giving It All Away
in co w/David Courtney
How Much Love
in co w/Barry Mann
Long Tall Glasses
in co w/David Courtney
Show Must Go On, The
in co w/David Courtney
Thunder In My Heart
in co w/Thomas Snow
You Make Me Feel Like Dancing
in co w/Vincent Poncia

SAYERS, HENRY J.
American
w&m/Henry J. Sayers
Ta-Ra-Ra-Boom-De-Re (1891)

SCAGGS, BOZ (WILLIAM ROYCE SCAGGS)
1944, American
w&m/Boz Scaggs
Breakdown Dead Ahead
Dinah Flo
Hard Time
in co w/David Paich
It's Over
in co w/David Paich
Lido Shuffle
in co w/David Paich
Lowdown
in co w/David Paich
My Friend
in co w/James Davis
Overdrive
Slow Dancer
What Can I Say
in co w/David Paich

SCANLAN, WILLIAM J.
1856-1898, American
w&m/William J. Scanlan
Jim Fisk (authorship considered
probable, but unverified)
Moonlight At Killarney
Molly O
My Maggie
My Nellie's Blue Eyes
Pekk-A-Boo
Peggy O'Moore
Remember Boy You're Irish
There's Always A Seat In The Parlor For You

SCHARF, WALTER
1911, American
m/Walter Scharf
w/Don Black
Ben

Film scores
Brazil (1944)
Hans Christian Andersen (1952)
Hit Parade Of 1943
In Old Oklahoma (1943)
Johnny Doughboy (1942)
Mercy Island (1941)
    in co w/Cy Feuer
Pocket Full Of Miracles
The Fighting Seabees (1944)
    in co w/Roy Webb
Willie Wonka And The Chocolate
  Factory
    in co w/Leslie Bricusse, Anthony
    Newley
Mahogany (1973)

SCHERTZINGER, VICTOR
1890-1941, American
m/Victor Schertzinger
Arthur Murray Taught Me
  Dancing In A Hurry
    w/Johnny Mercer
Dream Lover
    w/Clifford Grey
Fleet's In, The
    w/Johnny Mercer
I Remember You
    w/Johnny Mercer
If You Build A Better Mousetrap
    w/Johnny Mercer
I'll Never Let A Day Pass By
    w/Frank Loesser
Kiss The Boys Goodbye
    w/Frank Loesser
Marcheta
    w&m/Victor Schertzinger
Not Mine
    w/Johnny Mercer
One Night Of Love
    w/Gus Kahn
Sand In My Shoes
    w/Frank Loesser
Tangerine
    w/Johnny Mercer

SCHIFRIN, LALO
American
m/Lalo Schifrin (instr.)
Cat, The (instr.) (1964)
Jazz Suite On The Mass Texts
  (instr.) (1967)
Mission: Impossible, Theme
  From (1967)
Film scores
Amityville Horror, The (1979)
Cool Hand Luke (1967)
Fox, The (1968)
Voyage Of The Damned (1967)

SCHLITZ, DONALD ALAN
American
w&m/Donald Alan Schlitz
Gambler, The (1979)

SCHMIDT, HARVEY
1929, American
w&m in co w/Tom Jones
My Cup Runneth Over
Try To Remember

SCHOLL, JACK
1903, American
w/Jack Scholl
My Little Buckaroo
    m/M.K. Jerome
Throw Another Log On The Fire
    in co w/Charles Tobias, Murray
    Mencher

SCHOLZ, TOM
1947, American
w&m/Tom Scholz
Don't Look Back
Long Time
More Than A Feeling
Peace Of Mind

SCHONBERGER, JOHN
1892, American
m/John Schonberger
Whispering
    in co w/Vincent Rose, Richard
    Coburn, Malvin Schonberger

SCHRAUBSTADER, CARL
1902, American
m/Carl Schraubstader
w/Lew Brown
Last Night On The Back Porch

SCHROEDER, AARON
1926, American
w&m/Aaron Schroeder
Anyway You Want Me
    in co w/Cliff Owens
Because They're Young
    in co w/Wally Gold
Big Hunk O' Love, A
    in co w/Sid Wyche
Good Luck Charm
    in co w/Wally Gold
I Got Stung
    in co w/David Hill
It's Now Or Never
    (adapted from Eduardo di Capua's
    "O Sole Mio")
Mandolins In The Moonlight
    in co w/George D. Weiss
Stuck On You
    in co w/J. Leslie McFarland

SCHUBERT, FRANZ PETER
1797-1828, American
m/Franz Peter Schubert
w/based on Sir Walter Scott's
"Lady Of The Lake"
Ave Maria (Opus 52, No. 6)

SCHUMANN, WALTER
1913-1958, American
m/Walter Schumann

Dragnet (Theme)
I Walk Alone
    w/Vick Knight

SCHUSTER, IRA
1889-1945, American
w&m/Ira Schuster
Did You Ever Get That Feeling In
  The Moonlight
    in co w/Larry Stock
I Am An American
    in co w/Paul Cunningham,
    Leonard Whitcup
Shanty In Old Shanty Town, A
    in co w/Joseph Young, Little Jack
    Little
Ten Little Fingers And Ten
  Little Toes
    in co w/Ed Nelson, Harry Pease

SCHWARTZ, ARTHUR
1900, American
m/Arthur Schwartz
Alone Together
    w/Howard Dietz
By Myself
    w/Howard Dietz
Dancing In The Dark
    w/Howard Dietz
Day After Day
    w/Howard Dietz
Gal In Calico, A
    w/Leo Robin
I Guess I'll Have To Change My
  Plan
    w/Howard Dietz
I Love Louisa
    w/Howard Dietz
I See Your Face Before Me
    w/Howard Dietz
If There Is Someone Lovelier
  Than You
    w/Howard Dietz
Look Who's Dancing
    w/Dorothy Fields
Louisiana Hayride
    w/Howard Dietz
Love Is The Reason
    w/Dorothy Fields
Magic Moment
    w/Howard Dietz
Make The Man Love Me
    w/Dorothy Fields
Oh But I Do
    w/Leo Robin
Rainy Night In Rio, A
    w/Leo Robin
Shine On Your Shoes, A
    w/Howard Dietz
Somthing To Remember You By
    w/Howard Dietz
Spring Has Sprung
    w/Dorothy Fields

That's Entertainment
    w/Howard Dietz
**They're Either Too Young Or
Too Old**
    w/Frank Loesser
**You And The Night And The
Music**
    w/Howard Dietz

SCHWARTZ, JEAN
1878-1956, American
m/Jean Schwartz
Au Revoir Pleasant Dreams
    w/Jack Meskill
Bedelia
    w/William Jerome
Chinatown, My Chinatown
    w/William Jerome
**Hello Central Give Me No Man's
Land**
    w/Samuel M. Lewis, Joseph
Young
Mr. Dooley
    w/William Jerome
**Rockabye Your Baby With A
Dixie Melody**
    w/Samuel M. Lewis, Joseph
Young

SCHWARTZ, STEPHEN
American
w&m/Stephen Schwartz
Day By Day (1071)

SCOTT, CLEMENT
New Zealander
m/Clement Scott
English w/Dorothy Stewart
Maori w/Maewae Kaihau
**Now Is The Hour (Maori
Farewell Song) (1913)**

SCOTT, HOWARD E.
1946, American
See list of selections and
collaborators under Lee Oskar

SCOTT, JACK
American
w&m/Jack Scott
Leroy (1958)
My True Love (1958)
What In The World (1959)

SCOTT, JAMES SYLVESTER
1886-1938, American
m/James Sylvester Scott (instr.)
Climax Rag
Frog Legs Rag
Kansas City Rag
On The Pike
Ragtime Oriole

**SCOTT, LADY JOHN
MONTAGUE-DOUGLAS SCOTT
(Alicia Ann Spottiswoode)**
1810-1900, Scottish

m/Lady John Montague-Douglas
Scott
w/believed to be one William Douglas
c. 1688
Annie Laurie (1838)
Loch Lomond (1838)

SCOTT, MAURICE
American
m/Maurice Scott
w/Weston & Barnes
**I've Got Rings On My Fingers
(Mumbo, Jumbo, Jijiboo O'Shea)
(1909)**

**SCOTT, RAYMOND (HARRY
WARNOW)**
1909, American
m/Raymond Scott (instr., except as
noted)
All Around The Christmas Tree
**Dinner Music For A Pack Of
Hungry Cannibals**
Girl With The Light Blue Hair
Huckleberry Duck
**In An Eighteenth Century
Drawing Room**
    w/Jack Lawrence
Minuet In Jazz
Mountain High, Valley Low
    w/Bernard Hanighen
Powerhouse
Square Dance For Eight
Egyptian Mummies
Toy Trumpet, The
Twilight In Turkey
War Dance For Wooden Indians

SCOTT, ROBERT W. (BOBBY)
1937, American
m/Robert W. Scott
**He Ain't Heavy ... He's My
Brother**
    w/Bob Russell
Taste Of Honey, A
    w/Ric Marlow

SCOTT, ROBIN
American
w&m/Robin Scott
Pop Muzik (1979)

SCOTT, RONNIE
English
w&m/Ronnie Scott
in co w/Steve Wolfe
It's A Heartache (1977)
**Sitting On The Edge Of The
Ocean (1977)**

SCOTT, SIR WALTER
1771-1832, Scottish
w/Sir Walter Scott (from his
poem "The Lady Of The Lake)
(1810)

m/James Sanderson, between 1810
and 1820
Hail To The Chief

SCOTT, WINFIELD
American
w&m/Winfield Scott
Many Tears Ago (1961)
Tweedle Dee (1955)

SCOTTO, VINCENT
French
m/Vincent Scotto (from the French
song "La Petite Tonkinoise")
English w/Anna Held
It's Delightful To Be Married

SCRIVEN, JOSEPH
American
w/Joseph Scriven
m/Charles Crozat Converse (from his
song "Erie")
**What A Friend We Have In Jesus
(1855)**

**SCRUGGS, EARL (EARL
EUGENE SCRUGGS)**
1924, American
m/Earl Scruggs
in co w/Lester Flatt
Earl's Breakdown (instr.)
**Foggy Mountain Breakdown
(instr.)**

SEALS, DANNY WAYLAND
1948, American
w&m/Danny Wayland Seals
in co w/John Ford Coley
See list of selections under John
Ford Coley

SEALS, JAMES (JIMMY)
1941, American
w&m in co w/Dash Crofts, except
for "King Of Nothing" and "Unborn
Child"
Baby, I'll Give It To You
Diamond Girl
Get Closer
Hummingbird
I'll Play For You
It's Gonna Come Down (On You)
King of Nothing
    w&m/James Seals
My Fair Share
Ridin'Thumb
Summer Breeze
Unborn Child
    m/James Seals
    w/Lana Bogan
**We May Never Pass This Way
Again**
You're The Love

**SEARS, REV. EDMUND
HAMILTON**
1816-1876, American
w/Rev. Edmund Hamilton Sears
m/Richard Storrs Willis
**It Came Upon The Midnight
Clear (1850)**

SEBASTIAN, JOHN B.
1944, American
w&m/John B. Sebastian
Daydream
Do You Believe In Magic
**Did You Ever Have To Make Up
Your Mind**
I Had A Dream
Lovin' You
Rainbows All Over Your Blues
She's A Lady
Welcome Back
Younger Girl
You're A Big Boy Now

SEDAKA, NEIL
1939, American
w&m/Neil Sedaka
Bad Blood
in co w/Phillip Cody
Breaking Up Is Hard To Do
in co w/Howard Greenfield
Calendar Girl
in co w/Howard Greenfield
Diary, The
in co w/Howard Greenfield
Fallin'
in co w/Howard Greenfield
Frankie
in co w/Howard Greenfield
Happy Birthday Sweet Sixteen
in co w/Howard Greenfield
I Waited Too Long
in co w/Howard Greenfield
Immigrant, The
in co w/Phillip Cody
Laughter In The Rain
in co w/Phillip Cody
Little Devil
in co w/Howard Greenfield
Love Will Keep Us Together
in co w/Howard Greenfield
Next Door To An Angel
in co w/Howard Greenfield
Oh Carol
in co w/Howard Greenfield
One Day In My Life
in co w/Howard Greenfield
Puppet Man
in co w/Howard Greenfield
Rainy Jane
in co w/Howard Greenfield
Should've Never Let You Go
in co w/Phillip Cody

Solitaire
in co w/Howard Greenfield
Stairway To Heaven
in co w/Howard Greenfield
Steppin' Out
in co w/Phillip Cody
Stupid Cupid
in co w/Howard Greenfield
That's When The Music Takes Me
Where The Boys Are
in co w/Howard Greenfield
Working On A Groovy Thing
in co w/Roger Atkins

SEEGER, PETE
American
w&m/Pete Seeger
If I Had A Hammer
in co w/Lee Hays
Bells Of Rhymney, The
w/Idris Davies
Gotta Travel On
in co w/Paul Clayton, Lee Hays,
David Lazar, Fred Hellerman,
Ronnie Gilbert, Larry Ehrlich
Kisses Sweeter Than Wine
in co w/Joel Newman, Ronnie
Gilbert, Lee Hays, Fred
Hellerman
Turn! Turn! Turn!
w/from "The Book Of
Ecclesiastes"
We Shall Overcome
in co w/Zilphia Horton, Frank
Hamilton, Guy Carawan
**Where Have All The Flowers
Gone**
additional verses by Joe
Hickerson

SEELEN, JERRY
1912, American
w/Jerry Seelen
m/Henri Betti
C'est Si Bon

SEGAL, JACK
1918, American
w/Jack Segal
Hard To Get
w&m/Jack Segal
Here's To The Losers
m/Bob Wells
Scarlet Ribbons
m/Evelyn Danzig
When Joanna Loved Me
m/Bob Wells
When Sunny Gets Blue
m/Marvin Fisher

SEGER, BOB
1945, American
w&m/Bob Seger
Fire Lake
Heavy Music
Hollywood Nights

Katmandu
Looking Back
Mainstreet
Night Moves
No Man's Land
Nutbush City Limits
Ramblin' Gamblin' Man
Still The Same
We've Got Tonight
You'll Accompany Me

SEILER, EDWARD
1911-1952, American
w&m/Edward Seiler
in co w/Sol Marcus
See list of selections under Sol
Marcus

SERRADELL, MARCISO
Mexican
m/Narciso Serradell
Spanish w/B. Niceto de Zamacois
La Golondrina (The Swallow)

SEVERINSEN, CARL H. (DOC)
1927, American
w&m in co w/Mac Davis
Stop And Smell The Roses

SHAND, TERRY
1904, American
w&m/Terry Shand
**Dance With A Dolly With A Hole
In Her Stocking**
in co w/Jimmy Eaton, Mickey
Leader
I Double Dare You
in co w/Jimmy Eaton

SHANKLIN, WAYNE SR.
1916, American
w&m/Wayne Shanklin
Chanson d'Amour
Jezebel
Primrose Lane
in co w/George (Red) Callender

**SHANNON, DEL (CHARLES
WESTOVER)**
1941, American
w&m/Del Shannon
Hats Off To Larry
Keep Searchin'
Little Town Flirt
in co w/M. McKenzie
Runaway
in co w/Max T. Crook
Stranger In Town

SHANNON, JAMES ROYCE
1881-1946, American
w&m/James Royce Shannon
Missouri Waltz, The
Original music by John Valentine
Eppel; adapted by Frederic
Knight Logan

Too-Ra-Loo-Ra-Loo-Ra (That's An Irish Lullaby)

SHANNON, RONNIE
American
w&m/Ronnie Shannon
Baby I Love You (1967)
I Never Loved A Man The Way I Love You (1967)

SHAPIRO, JOSEPH (JOE)
American
w&m/Joe Shapiro
in co w/Lou Stallman
Round And Round (1956)
Treasure Of Love (1956)

SHARPE III, JOHN RUFUS (JACK)
1909, American
w/John Rufus (Jack) Sharpe III
m/Jerry Herbst
So Rare (1937)

SHAVERS, CHARLIE
1917, American
m/Charlie Shavers
Blues Petite (instr.)
Close Shave
in co w/John Kirby (instr.)
Dawn On The Desert (instr.)
It Feels So Good (instr.)
Jumping In The Pump Room (instr.)
Pastel Blue
w/Artie Shaw
Undecided
w/Sid Robin

SHAW, ARTIE
1910, American
m/Artie Shaw
Back Bay Shuffle
in co w/Teddy McCrae
Love Of My Life
w/Johnny Mercer
Pastel Blue
w/Artie Shaw
m/Charlie Shavers
Summit Ridge Drive (instr.)
Traffic Jam
in co w/Teddy McCrae

SHAW, TOMMY
1951, American
w&m/Tommy Shaw
Blue Collar Man (Long Nights)
Crystal Ball
Fooling Yourself (The Angry Young Man)
Mademoiselle
in co w/Dennis De Young
Man In The Wilderness
Renegade
Sing For The Day

SHAWN, NELSON H.
1898-1945, American
w&m/Nelson H. Shawn
in co w/Caesar Petrillo, Edward Ross
Jim

SHAY, LARRY
1897, American
w&m/Larry Shay
Get Out And Get Under The Moon
in co w/Charles Tobias, William Jerome
Everywhere You Go
in co w/Joe Goodwin, Mark Fisher
When You're Smiling
in co w/Mark Fisher, Joe Goodwin
When You're Smiling (The Whole World Smiles With You)
in co w/Mark Fisher, Joe Goodwin

SHAYNE, GLORIA
American
w&m/Gloria Shayne
Goodbye Cruel World (1961)

SHAYNE, LARRY (Ray Joseph)
1909, American
w&m/Larry Shayne
in co w/Mack David
Sinner Kissed An Angel, A

SHEARING, GEORGE
1919, English
m/George Shearing
w/George Weiss
Lullaby Of Birdland

SHEELEY, SHARI
1942, American
w&m/Shari Sheeley
Dum Dum
in co w/Jackie de Shannon
Great Imposter, The
in co w/Jackie de Shannon
Heart In Hand
in co w/Jackie de Shannon
He's So Heavenly
in co w/Jackie de Shannon
Poor Little Fool
So Deep
in co w/Jackie de Shannon

SHEPP, ARCHIE
1937, American
w&m/Archie Shepp
Attica Blues
Black Gypsy
Black Woman, A
Damn If I Know
Hambone
Los Olvidados
Magic Of Ju-Ju, The
Malcolm, Malcolm - Semper Malcolm
Mama Too Tight

Rain Forest
Things Have Got To Change
Yasmina

SHERMAN, AL
1897, American
w&m/Al Sherman
Ninety Nine Out Of A Hundred Wanna Be Loved
in co w/Al Lewis
No No A Thousand Times No
in co w/Al Lewis
Now's The Time To Fall In Love
in co w/Al Lewis
No No A Thousand Times No
in co w/Al Lewis, Abner Silver
Now's The Time To Fall In Love
in co w/Al Lewis
On The Beach At Bali Bali
in co w/Abner Silver
Over Somebody Else's Shoulder
in co w/Al Lewis
You Gotta Be A Football Hero
in co w/Al Lewis

SHERMAN, ALLAN
1924, American
w&m/Allan Sherman
Hello Muddah, Hello Faddah (music adapted from Amilcare Poincelli's "Dance Of The Hours")

SHERMAN, JOE
1926, American

SHERMAN, NOEL
1930, American
m/Joe Sherman
w/Noel Sherman
Graduation Day
Juke Box Baby
Ranblin' Rose
To The Ends Of The Earth

SHERMAN, RICHARD M.
American
w&m/Richard M. Sherman
in co w/Robert B. Sherman (brother)
Bedknobs And Broomsticks
Chim Chim Cheree (1964)
Chitty Chitty Bang Bang (1968)
Supercalifragilistic expialidocious (1964)
Spoonful Of Sugar, A
It's A Small World
You're Sixteen

SHERMAN, ROBERT B.
American
w&m/Robert B. Sherman
in co w/Richard M. Sherman (brother) See list of selections under Richard M. Sherman

SHERRILL, BILLY
1941, American
w&m/Billy Sherrill
Almost Persuaded
in co w/Glenn Sutton
Another Lonely Song
in co w/Tammy Wynette, Norro
Wilson
Bedtime Story
in co w/Glenn Sutton
Don't Let Me Touch You
in co w/Marty Robbins
Good Lovin'
Good News
in co w/Norro Wilson,
George Richey
Good Things
in co w/Norro Wilson,
Carmol Taylor
Have A Little Faith
in co w/Glenn Sutton
I Do My Swinging At Home
I Don't Wanna Play House
in co w/Glenn Sutton
I Don't Want To Lose You
in co w/Norro Wilson,
Steve Davis
I Love My Friend
in co w/Norro Wilson
If You Think I Love You Now
(I've Just Started)
in co w/Curly Putnam
I'm Down To My Last I Love You
in co w/Glenn Sutton
Kids Say The Darndest Things
in co w/Glenn Sutton
Let's Get Together
(One Last Time)
in co w/George Richey
Loving In A House Full Of Love
in co w/Glenn Sutton
Loser's Cathedral
in co w/Glenn Sutton
Most Beautiful Girl, The
in co w/Norro Wilson,
Rory Bourke
My Elusive Dreams
in co w/Curly Putnam
My Man
in co w/Norro Wilson,
Carmol Taylor
One Of A Kind
in co w/Steve Davis

My Woman's Good To Me
in co w/Glenn Sutton
Put Your Clothes Back On
in co w/Steve Davis
Reach Out Your Hand And Touch
Somebody
in co w/Tammy Wynette
Singing My Song
in co w/Glenn Sutton,
Tammy Wynette

Soul Song
in co w/George Richey,
Norro Wilson
Southern California
in co w/George Richey,
Roger Bowling
Stand By Your Man
in co w/Tammy Wynette
There's A Party Goin' On
in co w/Glenn Sutton
'Til I Can Make It On My Own
in co w/George Richey,
Tammy Wynette
Tonight My Baby's Coming Home
in co w/Glenn Sutton
Very special Love Song, A
in co w/Norro Wilson
Ways To Love A Man, The
in co w/Tammy Wynette,
Glenn Sutton
Woman Always Knows, A
Woman To Woman
You Mean The World To Me
in co w/Glenn Sutton
Your Good Girl's Gonna Go Bad
in co w/Glenn Sutton

SHERWIN, MANNING
1902, American
w&m/Manning Sherwin
I Fall In Love With You Every Day
Moment I Saw You, The
Nightingale Sang In Berkeley
Square, A

SHIELDS, REN
1868-1913, American
w&m/Ren Shields
In The Good Old Summertime
(1902)
in co w/George Evans
In The Merry Month Of May
in co w/George Evans
Steamboat Bill (1910)
in co w/The Leighton Brothers
Waltz Me Around Again
Willie (1906)
in co w/Will D. Cobb

SHILKRET, NATHANIEL
1895, American
m/Nathaniel Shilkret
Jeannine I Dream Of Lilac Time
w/L. Wolfe Gilbert
Lonesome Road, The
w/Gene Austin

SHIRE, DAVID
1937, American
m/David Shire
I'll Never Say Goodbye
in co w/Richard Maltby Jr.
It Goes Like It Goes
in co w/Norman Gimbel
Manhattan Skyline
in co w/Richard Maltby Jr.

Starting Here, Starting Now
in co w/Richard Maltby Jr.
With You I'm Born Again
in co w/Carol Connors
Film score:
Norma Rae (1979)

SHIRL, JIMMY
1909, American
w&m/Jimmy Shirl
Across The Wide Missouri (based
on "Shenandoah")
Castle Rock
in co w/Ervin M. Drake
Come To The Mardi Gras
in co w/Ervin M. Drake,
Max Bulhões, Milton de Oliveira
I Believe
in co w/Ervin M. Drake,
Al Stillman, Irvin Graham
Made For Each Other
in co w/Ervin M. Drake

SHOCKLEY, SHELBY
American
w&m in co w/L. Sylvers
And The Beat Goes On (1980)

SHORROCK, GLENN
1944, English/Australian
w&m/Glenn Shorrock
Cool Change
Happy Anniversary
Help Is On Its Way
It's A Long Way There
I'll Always Call Your Name
Reminiscing

SHORTER, WAYNE
American
m/Wayne Shorter
Children Of The Night
Dolores
Free For All
Lester Left Town
Nefertiti
Orbits
This Is For Albert

SHUMAN, MORT
1936, American
w&m in co w/Doc Pomus
See list of selections under
Doc Pomus.

SIECZYNSKI, RUDOLF
Austrian
m/Rudolf Sieczynski
English w/Irving Caesar (1937)
Vienna Dreams (1914)

SIGLER, MAURICE
1901-1961, American
w/Maurice Sigler
Everything Stops For Tea
m/Al Hoffman,
Al Goodhart

I'm In A Dancing Mood
m/Al Hoffman,
Al Goodhart
I Saw Stars
m/Al Hoffman,
Al Goodhart
**Little Man You've Had A
Busy Day**
m/Al Hoffman, Mabel Wayne

SIGMAN, CARL
1909, American
w/Carl Sigman
Answer Me My Love
m/Gerhard Winkler
Arrivederci Roma
m/R. Rascel
Ballerina
w&m in co w/Bob Russell
Big Brass Band From Brazil
w&m in co w/Bob Hilliard
Buena Sera
m/Peter DeRose
Careless Hands
w&m in co w/Bob Hilliard
**Civilization (Bongo,
Bongo, Bongo)**
w&m in co w/Bob Hilliard
Crazy He Calls Me
w&m in co w/Bob Russell
Day In The Life Of A Fool, A
m/Luiz Bonfa
Day The Rains Came, The
m/Gilbert Becaud
Dream Along With Me
m/Carl Sigman
Ebb Tide
m/Robert Maxwell
Enjoy Yourself
m/Herb Magidson
Hop Scotch Polka
m/William Whitlock,
Gene Rayburn
I Could Have Told You
m/James Van Heusen
It's All In The Game
m/Charles Gates Dawes
Love Story (Where Do I Begin)
m/Francis Lai
My Heart Cries For You
m/Percy Faith (adapted from
French folk song "Chanson
de Marie Antoinette")
My Way Of Life
m/Bert Kaempfert
Over And Over
m/Bert Kaempfert
Pennsylvania 6-5000
m/Jerry Gray
Robin Hood
m/Carl Sigman
Shangri La
m/Matt Malneck,
Robert Maxwell

Swedish Rhapsody
m/Percy Faith, Hugo Alfven
**Thousand Island Song, The
(Florence)**
w&m in co w/Bob Hilliard
Till
m/Charles Danvers
Twenty Four Hours Of Sunshine
m/Peter DeRose
What Now My Love
m/Gilbert Becaud

SIGNORELLI, FRANK
1901, American
m/Frank Signorelli
I'll Never Be The Same
co-composer Matt Malneck
w/Gus Kahn
Stairway To The Stars
co-composer Matt Malneck
w/Mitchell Parish

SILVER, ABNER
1899, American
w&m/Abner Silver
Farewell To Arms
in co w/Allie Wrubel
Have You Forgotten So Soon
How Did He Look
I Laughed At Love
No No A Thousand Times No
in co w/Al Lewis, Al Sherman
On The Beach At Bali Bali
in co w/Al Sherman
There Goes My Heart
in co w/Benny Davis
**When The Mighty Organ Played
'O Promise Me'**
With These Hands
in co w/Benny Davis
Young And Beautiful

SILVER, FRANK
1896-1960, American
w&m/Frank Silver
in co w/Irving Cohn
**What Do We Get From Boston?
Beans, Beans, Beans**
Yes, We Have No Bananas (1923)

SILVER, HORACE
1928, American
m/Horace Silver (instr.)
Cape Verdean Blues
Calcutta Cutie
Filthy McNasty
Home Cookin'
Let's Get To The Nitty Gritty
Preacher, The
Sweet Sweetie Dee

SILVERS, DOLORES (Vicki)
1925, American
w&m/Dolores Silvers
Learnin' The Blues

SILVERS, LOUIS
1889-1954, American
m/Louis Silvers
w/Buddy G. DeSylva
April Showers
Film scores:
In Old Chicago (1938)
Jazz Singer, The (1927)
Message To Garcia, A (1936)
Lloyds Of London (1937)
One Night Of Love (1934)
Road To Glory (1936)
Seventh Heaven (1937)
Under Two Flags (1936)

SILVERS, PHIL
1911, American
w/Phil Silvers
m/James Van Heusen
Nancy (With The Laughing Face)

SILVERSTEIN, SHEL
American
w&m/Shel Silverstein
A Boy Named Sue
Big Four Poster Bed
Couple More Years
Cover Of The Rolling Stone
Daddy What If
Danger Of A Stranger
in co w/Even Stevens
Here I Am Again
Hey Loretta
One's On The Way
Queen Of The Silver Dollar
Sylvia's Mother
Unicorn, The
Winner, The

SIMEONE, HARRY
1911, American
w&m in co w/Henry Onorati
Little Drummer Boy, The

SIMMON, PAUL
American
w&m/Paul Simmon
Black Water (1974)

SIMMONS, GENE
1949, American
w&m/Gene Simmons
Calling Dr. Love
Christine Sixteen
Flaming Youth
in co w/Paul "Ace" Frehley,
Paul Stanley, Bob Ezrin
Rock And Roll All Nite
in co w/Paul Stanley

SIMPSON, VALERIE
1948, American
w&m in co w/Nicholas (Nick) Ashford
Ain't No Mountain High Enough
Ain't Nothing Like
  The Real Thing
Anywhere
California Soul
Don't Cost You Nothin'
Found A Cure
Let's Go Get Stoned
Reach Out And Touch
You're All I Need To Get By

SIMON, CARLY
1944, American
w&m/Carly Simon
Anticipation
Attitude Dancing
Back Down To Earth
Boys In The Trees
Devoted To You
  in co w/James Taylor
Haven't Got Time For The Pain
Jesse
in co w/M. Manieri
Legend In Your Own Time
Mockingbird
  in co w/James Taylor
Right Thing To Do, The
That's The Way I've Always
  Heard It Should Be
  in co w/Jacob Brackman
Tranquillo (Melt My Heart)
  in co w/James Taylor,
  Arif Mardin
You Belong To Me
  in co w/Mike McDonald
You're So Vain

SIMON, HOWARD
1901-1948, Canadian/American
w&m in co w/Al Lewis
Gonna Get A Girl

SIMON, NAT
1900-1979, American
w&m/Nat Simon
And Mimi
  in co w/James B. Kennedy
Apple Blossom Wedding
  in co w/James B. Kennedy
Coax Me A Little Bit
  in co w/Charles Tobias
Crosstown
  in co w/John Redmond
Gaucho Serenade, The
  in co w/John Redmond,
  James Cavanaugh
Her Bathing Suit Never Got Wet
  in co w/Charles Tobias
In My Little Red Book
  in co w/Raymond A. Bloch,
  Al Stillman
Istanbul (Not Constaninople)
  in co w/James B. Kennedy

My Bolero
  in co w/James B. Kennedy
Old Lamplighter, The
  in co w/Charles Tobias
Poinciana
  in co w/Buddy Bernier
Wait For Me Mary
  in co w/Charles Tobias,
  Harry Tobias
SIMON, PAUL
1941, American
w&m/Paul Simon
America
At The Zoo
Boxer, The
Bridge Over Troubled Water
Cecilia
Dangling Conversation
El Condor Pasa
  w/Paul Simon
  m/Jorge Milch Berg,
  Daniel Robles
Fakin' It
50 Ways To Leave Your Lover
59th St. Bridge Song, The
  (Feelin' Groovy)
Homeward Bound
I Am A Rock
Kodachrome
Late In The Evening
Loves Me Like A Rock
Me And Julio Down By The
  Schoolyard
Mother And Child Reunion
Mrs. Robinson
My Little Town
Scarborough Fair/Canticle
Slip Sliding Away
Something So Right
Sounds Of Silence
Still Crazy After All
  These Years
SIMONS, SEYMOUR
1896-1949, American
w&m/Seymour Simons
All Of Me
  in co w/Gerald Marks
Breezin' Along With The Breeze
  in co w/Haven Gillespie,
  Richard A. Whiting
Honey
  in co w/Haven Gillespie
Just Like A Gypsy
  in co w/Nora Bayes

SINATRA, FRANK
(Francis Albert Sinatra)
1915, American
w&m in co w/Sol Parker,
  Hank Sanicola
This Love Of Mine

SINCLAIR, GORDON
1900, Canadian
w&m/Gordon Sinclair

Americans, The (1974) (narrative
  to musical setting of "The Battle
  Hymn Of The Republic")

SINCLAIR, J.L.
American
w&m/J.L. Sinclair
Eves Of Texas, The (1936)

SINDING, CHRISTIAN
1856-1941, Norwegian
m/Christian Sinding
Rustle Of Spring (instr.)
  ("Fruhlingstrauschen") (1896)

SINGER, ARTHUR
1919, Canadian/American
w&m in co w/David White Tricker,
  J. Medora
At The Hop

SINGER, GUY
American
w&m/Guy Singer
Whither Thou Goest

SINGER, LOUIS C.
1912, American
m/Louis C. Singer
w/Hy Zaret
One Meat Ball

SINGLETON, CHARLES
American
w&m/Charles Singleton
Apple Green (1960)
Don't Forbid Me
Hurts Me To My Heart (1954)
  in co w/Rosemarie McCoy
Mambo Baby (1954)
  in co w/Rosemarie McCoy
Wheel Of Hurt
  in co w/Eddie Snyder
Lady
  in co w/Bert Kaempfert,
  Herbert Rehbein, Larry Kusik

SINGLETON, MARGIE
(Mrs. Leon Ashley)
1937, American
w&m/Margie Singleton
in co w/Leon Ashley
Laura (What's He Got That
  I Ain't Got)
Mental Journey

SISSLE, NOBLE
1889-1975, American
w/Noble Sissle
m/Eubie Blake
Bandana Days
Gypsy Blues
I'm Just Wild About Harry
Love Will Find A Way
Shuffle Along
You Were Meant For Me

SLAY, FRANK C. JR.
1930, American
w&m/Frank C. Slay Jr.
Jump Over
   in co w/Bob Crewe,
   Freddie Cannon
Happy Shades Of Blue
   in co w/Bob Crewe,
   Freddie Cannon
Lah Dee Dah
   in co w/Bob Crewe
Silhouettes
   in co w/Bob Crewe
Tallahassee Lassie
   in co w/Bob Crewe,
   Freddie Cannon
Transistor Sister
   in co w/Bob Crewe,
   Freddie Cannon

SLICK, DARBY
American
w&m/Darby Slick
Somebody To Love (1967)
   in co w/Grace Slick

SLICK, GRACE WING
1940, American
w&m/Grace Slick
Somebody to Love
   in co w/Darby Slick
White Rabbit (1967)

SLOAN, A. BALDWIN
1872-1925, American
w&m in co w/Edgar Smith (1857-
1938)
**Heaven Will Protect
The Working Girl**

SLOAN, P.F.
American
w&m/P.F. Sloan
Child Of Our Times (1965)
Eve Of Destruction (1965)
Secret Agent Man (1966)
   in co w/Steve Barri
**You Baby (Nobody
But You) (1966)**
   in co w/Steve Barri

SKYLAR, SUNNY
1913, American
w&m/Sunny Skylar
Amor
   in co w/Gabriel Ruiz (music)
Besame Mucho
   in co w/Consuelo
   Velazquez (music)
Be Mine Tonight
Hair Of Gold, Eyes Of Blue
**Just A Little Bit South Of
North Carolina**
   in co w/Bette Cannon,
   Arthur Shaftel

Love Me With All Your Heart
   in co w/Carlos Rigual,
   Mario Rigual, Carlos A. Martinoli
Nola
   in co w/Felix Arndt
And So To Sleep Again
   in co w/Joe Marsala
**Waiting For The Train To
Come In**
   in co w/Martin Block
You're Breaking My Heart
   in co w/Pat Genaro
   (music based on Ruggiero
   Leoncavallo's "Mattinata")

SMALLS, CHARLIE
American
w&m/Charlie Smalls
Ease On Down The Road (1975)

SMITH, ARTHUR
1921, American
m/Arthur Smith
**Dueling Banjos (Feuding
Banjos) (instr.)**
Guitar Boogie (instr.)

SMITH, BEASLEY
1901, American
w&m/Beasley Smith
Beg Your Pardon
   in co w/Francis Craig
God's Country
   in co w/Haven Gillespie
Night Train To Memphis
Old Master Painter, The
   in co w/Haven Gillespie
That Lucky Old Sun
   in co w/Haven Gillespie

SMITH, CARL
American
w&m/Carl Smith
**Higher And Higher (Your Love
Has Lifted Me) (1977)**

SMITH, CHRIS
1879-1949, American
w&m/Chris Smith
Ballin' The Jack
   in co w/James Burris
Beans, Beans, Beans
   in co w/Elmer Bowman
Down Among The Sugar Cane
   in co w/Cecil Mack,
   Avery and Hart
He's A Cousin Of Mine
   in co w/Cecil Mack,
   Silvio Hein
**You're In The Right Church
But The Wrong Pew**
   in co w/Cecil Mack

SMITH, EDGAR
1857-1914, American
w/Edgar Smith

**Heaven Will Protect The
Working Girl**
   m/A. Baldwin Sloane
**Ma Blushin' Rosie (Ma
Posie Sweet)**
   m/John Stromberg

SMITH, HARRY B.
1860-1936, American
w/Harry B. Smith
Brown October Ale
   m/Reginald DeKoven
Do You Remember Love?
   m/Reginald DeKoven
Gypsy Love Song
   m/Victor Herbert
Moonlight Song
   m/Reginald DeKoven
Oh Promise Me
   m/Reginald DeKoven
Play Gypsies, Dance Gypsies
   m/Emmerich Kalman
Sheik Of Araby, The
   co-lyricist Francis Wheeler
   m/Ted Snyder
**To The Land Of My
Own Romance**
   m/Victor Herbert
Yours Is My Heart Alone
   m/Franz Lehar

**SMITH, HEZEKIAH LEROY
GORDON (Stuff)**
1909, American
w&m/Stuff Smith
Desert Sands
I Hope Gabriel Likes My Music
I'se A-Muggin'
Onyx Club Spree
Serenade For A Wealthy Widow
Time And Again

SMITH, NORMAN
1923, English
w&m/Norman Smith
**Oh Babe What Would
You Say (1972)**
Who Was It (1973)

SMITH, PATTI
1946, American
w&m/Patti Smith
Because The Night
   in co w/Bruce Springsteen
Rock 'N' Roll Nigger

SMITH, PINETOP
1904-1929, American
m/Pinetop Smith (instr.)
Pinetop's Boogie

SMITH, RICHARD B.
1901-1935, American
w/Richard B. Smith
**When A Gypsy Makes His
Violin Cry**
   m/Emery Deutsch,
   Jimmy Rogan

Winter Wonderland
m/Felix Bernard

SMITH, ROBERT BACHE
1875-1951, American
w/Robert Bache Smith
Angelus, The
m/Victor Herbert
Come Down, Ma Evenin' Star
m/John Stromberg
Day Dreams, Visions Of Bliss
m/Robert Hood Bowers
I Might Be Your Once In A While
m/Victor Herbert
Sweethearts
m/Victor Herbert

**SMITH, WILLIAM HENRY
JOSEPH BONAPARTE
BERTHOLOFF (Willie The Lion)**
1897, American
m/Willie The Lion Smith (instr.)
Echo Of Spring
Morning Air
Rippling Waters
Sneakaway

**SNOW, HANK (Clarence
Eugene Snow)**
1914, Canadian
w&m/Hank Snow
Golden Rocket, The
I Don't Hurt Anymore
I'm Moving ON
I'm Moving On
Marriage Vows
Rhumba Boogie, The

SNOW, PHOEBE (Phoebe Laub)
1952, American
w&m/Phoebe Snow
Poetry Man (1975)
Shaky Ground (1977)

SNYDER, TED
1881-1965, American
m/Ted Snyder
**I Wonder If You Still Care
For Me**
w/Harry B. Smith,
Francis Wheeler
Kiss Me My Honey Kiss Me
w/Irving Berlin
My Wife's Gone To The Country
w/Irving Berlin,
George Whiting
Sheik Of Araby, The
w/Harry B. Smith
Who's Sorry Now
w/Bert Kalman, Harry Ruby
Wild Cherries Rag
w/Ted Snyder

SOLOVYEV-SEDOY, VASILY
Russian
mVasily Solovyev-Sedoy
**Midnight In Moscow
(Moscow Nights) (instr.)**

SOMMERS, JOHN MARTIN
American
w&m/John Martin Sommers
**Thank God I'm A Country Boy
(1974)**

SONDHEIM, STEPHEN
1930, American
w/Stephen Sondheim
Ah Paree
m/Jule Styne
All I Need Is The Girl
m/Jule Styne
America
m/Leonard Bernstein
Anyone Can Whistle
m/Stephen Sondheim
Barcelona
m/Stephen Sondheim
Being Alive
m/Stephen Sondheim
Boy From.....The
m/Stephen Sondheim
Comedy Tonight
m/Stephen Sondheim
Company
m/Stephen Sondheim
Cool
m/Leonard Bernstein
Do I Hear A Waltz?
m/Richard Rodgers
**Everybody Ought To
Have A Maid**
m/Stephen Sondheim
Everything's Coming Up Roses
m/Jule Styne
Gee Officer Krupke
m/Leonard Bernstein
Getting Married Today
I Feel Pretty
m/Leonard Bernstein
I'm Still Here
Joanna
m/Stephen Sondheim
Let Me Entertain You
m/Jule Styne
**Little Things You Do Together,
The**
m/Stephen Sondheim
Lovely
m/Stephen Sondheim
Maria
m/Leonard Bernstein
Send In The Clowns
m/Stephen Sondheim
Side By Side
m/Stephen Sondheim
Small World
m/Jule Styne
Some People
m/Jule Styne
Something's Coming
m/Leonard Bernstein
Somewhere
m/Leonard Bernstein

Stay
m/Richard Rodgers
Take The Moment
m/Richard Rodgers
Together Wherever We Go
m/Jule Styne
Tonight
m/Leonard Bernstein
Two By Two
m/Richard Rodgers
What Would We Do Without You
m/Stephen Sondheim
With So Little To Be Sure Of
m/Stephen Sondheim

SOSENKO, ANNA
1910, American
w&m/Anna Sosenko
Darling Je Vous Aime Beaucoup
J'Attendrai (I'll Be Yours)
English w/Anna Sosenko
m/Dino Olivieri

SOURIRE, SOEUR - O.P.
(Sister Luc-Gabrielle)
Belgian
m/Soeur Sourire
English w/Noel Regney
Dominique

SOUSA, JOHN PHILIP
1854)1932, American
m/John Philip Sousa (marches)
Black Horse Troop
Boy Scouts Of America
El Capitan
Fairest Of The Fair
**Field Artillery (see Edmund L.
Gruber, "The Caissons Go
Rolling Along")**
Free Lance, The
Hands Across The Sea
High School Cadets
Invincible Eagle
King Cotton
Liberty Bell
Manhattan Beach
New York Hippodrome March
Nobles Of The Mystic Shrine
On Parade
Picador, The
Pride Of The Wolverines
Sabre And Spurs
Semper Fidelis
Solid Men To The Front
Stars And Stripes Forever, The
Thunderer, The
Washington Post March

SOUTH, JOE
1942, American
w&m/Joe South
Down In The Boondocks
Games People Play
How Can I Unlove You
Hush

**(I Never Promised
You A) Rose Garden**
These Are Not My People
Walk A Mile In My Shoes
SOUTHER, J.D.
(John David Souther)
1945, American
w&m/J.D. Souther
Best Of My Love, The
in co w/Glenn Frey,
Donald Henley
James Dean
in co w/Glenn Frey,
Donald Henley, Jackson Browne
Doolin' Patton
in co w/Glenn Frey,
Donald Henley, Jackson Browne
Faithless Love
Fallin' In Love
in co w/Richie Furay,
Chris Hillman
Heartache Tonight
in co w/Glenn Frey,
Donald Henley, Bob Seger
New Kid In Town
in co w/Glenn Frey,
Donald Henley
Prisoner In Disguise
Silver Blue
Victim Of Love
in co w/Glenn Frey,
Donald Henley
White Rhythm And Blues
You Never Cry Like A Lover
in co w/Donald Henley
You're Only Lonely
SOVINE, RED
(Woodrow Wilson Sovine)
1918-1980, American
w&m/Red Sovine
Giddyup go
in co w/Tommy Hill
Little Rosa
in co w/Webb Pierce
Missing You
in co w/Dale Noe
Teddy Bear
in co w/Tommy Hill, Billy Joe
Burnette, Dale Royal

SPAETH, SIGMUND
1888-1953, American
w/Sigmund Spaeth
m/Franz Lehar (adapted from
"Frasquita Serenade")
My Little Nest Of Heavenly Blue
SPANIER, FRANCIS JOSEPH
(Muggsy)
1906-1967, American
m/Muggsy Spanier
Relaxin' At Touro

SPARKS, RANDY
1933, American
w&m/Randy Sparks
in co w/Barry McGuire
Green Green
SPEAKS, OLEY
1874-1948, American
w&m/Oley Speaks
On The Road To Mandalay (1907)
in co w/Rudyard Kipling
Sylvia (1914)
in co w/Clinton Scollard
**Now The Day Is Over
Morning (1910)**
in co w/Frank L. Stanton
When The Boys Come Home
SPECTOR, PHIL
1940, American
w&m/Phil Spector
Be My Baby
in co w/Jeff Barry,
Ellie Greenwich
Born To Be Together
in co w/Barry Mann,
Cynthia Weil
**Da Doo Ron Ron (When He
Walked Me Home)**
in co w/Jeff Barry,
Eliie Greenwich
He's A Rebel
I Love You You Love Me
in co w/John Prine
If You Don't Want My Love
in co w/John Prine
Just Once In My Life
in co w/Carole King,
Gerry Goffin
Little Did I Know
Pretty Little Angel Eyes
River Deep, Mountain High
in co w/Jeff Barry,
Ellie Greenwich
Spanish Harlem
in co w/Jerry Lieber
Then He Kissed Me
in co w/Jeff Barry,
Ellie Greenwich
To Know Him Is To Love Him
There's No Other Like My Baby
Walking In The Rain
in co w/Barry Mann,
Cynthia Weil
You've Lost That Lovin' Feeling
in co w/Barry Mann,
Cynthia Weil
SPENCE, LEW
(Lewis Slifka)
1920, American
m/Lew Spence
Nice 'N' Easy
w/Alan & Marilyn K. Bergman

Sleep Warm
w/Alan & Marilyn K. Bergman
That Face
w/Alan & Marilyn K. Bergman
SPENCER, JEREMY
English
w&m/Jeremy Spencer
Evenin' Boogie
I've Lost My Baby
SPENCER, RICHARD
American
w&m/Richard Spencer
Color Him Father (1977)
SPENCER, TIM
1907-1972, American
w&m/Tim Spencer
Careless Kisses
**Cigareetes, Whiskey And Wild
Wild Women**
Room Full Of Roses
SPIELMAN, FRED (Fritz)
Austrian/American
Fred Spielman
**It Only Hurts For A
Little While**
in co w/Mack David
Longest Walk, The
in co w/Eddie Pola
Paper Roses
in co w/Janice Torre
SPIER, LARRY
1901-1956, American
w&m/Larry Spier
Memory Lane
in co w/Con Conrad,
Buddy DeSylva
SPINA, HAROLD
1906, American
w&m/Harold Spina
**Annie Doesn't Live Here
Any More**
in co w/Johnny Burke,
Joseph Young
Cumana
in co w/Barclay Allen
**I Still Love To Kiss
You Good Night**
in co w/Walter Bullock
**It's So Nice To Have A
Man Around The House**
in co w/Jack Elliott
This Is Where I Came In
in co w/Walter Bullock
SPRINGER, PHILIP
1926, American
m/Philip Springer
Moonlight Gambler
w/Bob Hilliard
Santa Baby
w/Joan Javits, Tony Springer

Teasin'
    w/Richard Adler

SPRINGFIELD, RICK
1949, Australian
w&m/Rick Springfield
American Girls
Speak To The Sky
What Would The Children Think

SPRINGFIELD, TOM
English
w&m/Tom Springfield
Georgy Girl (1966)
    in co w/Jim Dale
I'll Never Find Another You
**Silver Threads And Golden
    Needles (1963)**

SPRINGSTEEN, BRUCE
1949, American
w&m/Bruce Springsteen
Badlands
Blinded By The Light
Born To Run
E Street Shuffle, The
Growing Up
Promised Land, The
Prove It All Night
Rosalita (Come Out Tonight)
Spirit In The Night
Tenth Avenue Freeze Out

STAFFORD, JIM
1944, American
w&m/Jim Stafford
I Got Stoned And I Missed It
Jasper
My Girl Bill
Swamp Witch
Wildwood Weed
Your Bulldog Drinks Champagne

STALLINGS, JOHN
1933, American
w&m/John Stallings
Learning To Lean
One Day I Will
    in co w/Walt Mills
Touching Jesus
**You're All Invited To My
    Mansion**

STALLMAN, LOU
American
w&m/Lou Stallman
**Everybody's Got The Right To
    Love (1970)**
Round And Round (1956)
    in co w/Joseph Shapiro
Treasure Of Love (1956)
    in co w/Joseph Shapiro

STAMPER, DAVID
1883-1963, American
m/David Stamper
**Daddy Has A Sweetheart And
    Mother Is Her Name**
    w/Gene Buck

Garden Of My Dreams
    w/Gene Buck, Louis A. Hirsch
My Rambler Rose
    w/Gene Buck, Louis A. Hirsch
'Neath The South Sea Moon
    w/Gene Buck, Louis A. Hirsch
Sally Won't You Come Back
    w/Gene Buck
Some Sweet Day
    w/Gene Buck, Louis A. Hirsch
Sweet Sixteen
    w/Gene Buck
Tulip Time
    w/Gene Buck

STANLEY, PAUL
1950, American
w&m/Paul Stanley
Detroit Rock City
    in co w/Bob Ezrin
Flaming Youth
    in co w/Paul "Ace" Frehley, Gene
    Simmons, Bob Ezrin
God Of Thunder
Hard Luck Woman
Hotter Than Hell
I Was Made For Loving You
    in co w/Vincent Poncia, Desmond
    Child
King Of The Night Time World
    in co w/Kim Fowley, Mark
    Anthony, Bob Ezrin
Love Gun
Rock And Roll All Nite
    in co w/Gene Simmons

**STANTON, FRANCIS
HAYWARD**
1913, American
w&m/Francis Hayward Stanton
in co w/Del Sharbutt
A Romantic Guy, I

STANPHILL, IRA (Reverend)
American
w&m/Rev. Ira Stanphill
Mansion Over The Hilltop (1949)

STAPLES, ROEBUCK ("Pop")
1915, American
w&m/Roebuck "Pop" Staples
I'll Take You There
This World

STAPP, JACK
American
w&m/Jack Stapp
in co w/Harry Stone
**Chattanoogie Shoe Shine Boy
(1950)**

STATON, CANDI
American
w&m/Candi Staton
in co w/Calvin Carter
**I'd Rather Be An Old Man's
    Sweetheart (1969)**

STEELE, LOIS
1910, American
w&m/Lois Steele
in co w/Jack Fulton
Ivory Tower
Wanted

STEIN, WILLIAM
1918, American
w&m/William Stein
Orange-Colored Sky
    in co w/Milton DeLugg
Wave To Me My Lady
    in co w/Frank Loesser

STEINBERG, BILLY
American
w&m/Billy Steinberg
How Do I Make You (1980)

**STEINER, MAXIMILIAN
RAOUL (MAX)**
1888-1977, American
m/Max Steiner
**Dark At The Top Of The Stairs,
    The (theme)**
Honey Babe
    w/Paul Francis Webster
**It Can't Be Wrong (theme from
    "Now Voyager")**
    w/Kim Gannon
My Own True Love (Tara's Theme)
    w/Mack David
Summer Place, A (theme)
**Tara's Theme (from "Gone With
    The Wind")**
Film scores:
Battle Cry
Casablanca (not including "As Time
    Goes By" by Herman Hupfeld)
Dark At The Top Of The Stairs
Gone With The Wind
Informer, The
Now Voyager
Life With Father
Since You Went Away
Summer Place, A
Treasurer Of Sierra Madre

STEPHENS, GEOFF
English
w&m/Geoff Stephens
Winchester Cathedral (1966)

STERLING, ANDREW B.
1874-1955, American
w/Andrew B. Sterling
All Aboard For Blanket Bay
    m/Harry Von Tilzer
**Down Where The Cotton
    Blossoms Grow**
    m/Harry Von Tilzer
Meet Me In St. Louis, Louis
    m/Frederick Allen (Kerry) Mills
On A Sunday Afternoon
    m/Harry Von Tilzer

On The Old Fall River Line,
   m/Harry Von Tilzer
**Strike Up The Band, Here Comes
  A Sailor**
   m/Charles B. Ward
Wait Till The Sun Shines Nellie
   m/Harry Von Tilzer
**What You Goin' To Do When The
  Rent Comes 'Round (Rufus
  Rastus Johnson Brown)**
   m/Harry Von Tilzer
When My Baby Smiles At Me
   m/Ted Lewis, Bill Munro

STERN, JACK
1896, American
w&m/Jack Stern
I Want You To Want Me
   in co w/Harry Tobias
I Was Lucky
   in co w/Jack Meskill

STERN, JOSEPH W.
1890-1934, American
m/Joseph W. Stern
w/Edward B. Marks
His Last Thoughts Were Of You
Little Lost Child, The
My Mother Was A Lady
No One Ever Loved More Than I

**STEVENS, CAT (STEPHEN
DEMETRI GEORGIOU)**
1948, English
w&m/Cat Stevens
Another Saturday Night
Bad Breaks
Banapple Gas
Crazy
Father And Son
Fill My Eyes
First Cut Is The Deepest, The
Hard-Headed Woman
Hurt, The
Here Comes My Baby
I Love My Dog
Katmandu
Lady D'Arbaville
Lily White
Longer Boats
Morning Has Broken
   in co w/Eleanor Farjeon
Mona Bone Jakon
Moon Shadow
**(Remember The Days Of The) Old
  Schoolyard**
On The Road To Find Out
Peace Train
Sitting
Tea For The Tillerman
Two Fine People
Where Do The Children Play
Wild World

STEVENS, EVEN
American
Many songs, w&m in co w/Eddie
Rabbitt
See list of selections under Eddie
Rabbitt
Danger Of A Stranger
   in co w/Shel Silverstein

**STEVENS, RAY (RAY
RAGSDALE)**
1939, American
w&m/Ray Stevens
Ahab The Arab
Along Came Jones
Can't Stop Dancing
   in co w/John Pritchard Jr.
Everything Is Beautiful
Gitarzan
   in co w/Bill Everett
**Jeremiah Peabody's Polyun-
  saturated Quick Dissolving,
  Fast Acting, Pleasant Tasting
  Green And Purple Pills**
Mr. Businessman
Nashville
Streak, The
Turn Your Radio On

STEVENSON, B.W.
1949, American
w&m/B.W. Stevenson
My Maria (1973)

STEVENSON, WILLIAM
American
w&m/William Stevenson
Beechwood 4-5789
   in co w/Marvin Gaye, George
  Gordy
Dancing In The Street
   in co w/Ivy Hunter, Marvin Gaye
Hitch Hike
   in co w/Marvin Gaye, Clarence
  Paul
Jamie
   in co w/Barrett Strong
My Baby Loves Me
   in co w/Sylvia Moy, Ivy Hunter
Nothing's Too Good For My Baby
   in co w/Henry Cosby, Sylvia Moy
Once Upon A Time
   in co w/Clarence Paul, Dave
  Hamilton, Barney Ales
**What's The Matter With You
  Baby**
   in co w/Clarence Paul, Barney
  Ales

STEVENSON, W.S.
American
w&m/W.S. Stevenson
**Grass Is Getting Greener, The
(1945)**
   in co w/Cecil Gant

Let Me Be The One
   in co w/Paul Blevins, Joe Holson
Lonely Street (1956)
   in co w/Kenny Sowder, Carl
  Belew
**Stop The World (And Let
  Me Off)**
   in co w/Carl Belew
That's When I See The Blues
   in co w/Carl Belew

STEWART, AL
1945, Scottish
w&m/Al Stewart
Almost Lucy
Broadway Hotel
Carol
Come Closer To Me
   in co w/Oswaldo Farres
On The Border
Song On The Radio
Time Passages
   in co w/Peter White
Valentina Way
Year Of The Cat
   in co w/Peter Wood

STEWART, DOROTHY M.
1897-1954, Australian/American
w&m/Dorothy M. Stewart
in co w/Maewae Kaihau, Clement
Scott
Now Is The Hour

STEWART, ERIC
1945, English
w&m/Eric Stewart
in co w/Lol Creme, Graham
Gouldman
Art For Art's Sake
Good Morning Judge
I'm Mandy Fly Me
I'm Not In Love
Rubber Bullets
Things We Do In Love, The
People In Love

STEWART, JOHN
English
w&m/John Stewart
Daydream Believer (1979)
Lost Her In The Sun (1980)

**STEWART, REDD (HENRY
REDD STEWART)**
1921, American
w&m/Redd Stewart
Bonaparte's Retreat
   in co w/Pee Wee King
Slow Poke
   in co w/Pee Wee King, Chilton
  Price
Soldier's Last Letter
   in co w/Ernest Tubb
Tennessee Waltz, The
   in co w/Pee Wee King

You Belong To Me
in co w/Pee Wee King, Chilton
Price

STEWART, ROD
1945, English
w&m/Rod Stewart
Blondes Have More Fun
in co w/Jim Cregan
Do You Think I'm Sexy
in co w/Carmine Appice
Every Picture Tells A Story
in co w/Ron Wood
Gasoline Alley
in co w/Ron Wood
Hot Legs
in co w/Gary Grainger
I Was Only Joking
in co w/Gary Grainger
I Wouldn't Ever Change A Thing
If Loving You Is Wrong
I'm Losing You
Kiss Of Georgie, The
Maggie May
in co w/M. Quittendon
Mandolin Wind
Reason To Believe
Tonight's The Night
You Got A Nerve
You Wear It Well
in co w/M. Quittendon
You're In My Heart

STILLMAN, AL
1906, American
w/Al Stillman
And That Reminds You (My Heart
Reminds Me
in co w/Carmello Bargoni
(instr. version known as
"Autumn Concerto")
Bless 'Em All
Original w&m/Jimmie Hughes,
Frank Lee
Breeze And I, The
in co w/Ernesto Lecuona (based
on "Andalucia" by Lecuona)
Can You Find It In Your Heart
in co w/Robert Allen
Chances Are
in co w/Robert Allen
Enchanted Island
in co w/Robert Allen
Home For The Holidays
in co w/Robert Allen
If Dreams Come True
in co w/Robert Allen
It's Not For Me To Say
in co w/Robert Allen
In My Little Red Book
in co w/Nat Simon, Raymond A.
Bloch
Juke Box Saturday Night
in co w/Paul J. McGrane

Moments To Remember
in co w/Robert Allen
My One And Only Heart
in co w/Robert Allen
No Not Much
in co w/Robert Allen
Salud, Dinero y Amor
in co w/Rodolfo Sciammarella
Teacher, Teacher
in co w/Robert Allen
There's Only One Of You
in co w/Robert Allen
Who Do You Know In Heaven
in co w/Peter DeRose
Who Needs You
in co w/Robert Allen
You Alone
in co w/Robert Allen

STILLS, STEPHENS
1945, American
w&m/Stephen Stills
Blue Bird
Carry On
For What It's Worth
Love The One You're With
Rock And Roll Woman
Suite: Judy Blue Eyes
Wooden Ships
in co w/David Crosby, Paul
Kanter
You Don't Have To Cry

STOCK, LARRY
1896, American
w&m/Larry Stock
Blueberry Hill
in co w/Al Lewis, Vincent Rose
Did You Ever Get That Feeling In
The Moonlight
in co w/Ira Schuster
Morningside Of The Mountain,
The
in co w/Dick Manning
You're Nobody Till Somebody
Loves You
in co w/James Cavanaugh
You Won't Be Satisfied
in co w/Freddy James

STOLLER, MIKE
1933, American
w&m/Mike Stoller
in co w/Jerry Lieber
See list of selections under Jerry
Lieber

STOLZ, ROBERT
German
m/Robert Stolz
Englist w/Joseph Young
Two Hearts In Three Quarter
Time (1930)

STONE, JESSE
American
w&m/Jesse Stone
Idaho (1942)

STONE, SLY (SYLVESTER
STEWART)
1944, American
w&m/Sly Stone
Dance To The Music
Everybody Is A Star
Everyday People
Family Affair
Frisky
Hot Fun In The Summertime
I Want To Take You Higher
If You Want Me To Stay
Mojo Man
Runnin' Away
Smilin' Somebody's Watching
You
Stand
Swim
Thank You
You're The One

STONER, MICHAEL S.
(MICKEY)
1911, American
w&m/Michael S. Stoner
I Guess I'll Have To Dream The
Rest
in co w/Harold Green
Jamaican Rhumba

STORDAHL, AXEL
1913-1963, American
m/Axel Stordahl
in co w/Paul Weston
w/Sammy Cahn
Day By Day
I Should Care

STOOKEY, PAUL (NOEL PAUL
STOOKEY)
1937, American
w&m/Paul Stookey
A 'Soalin'
in co w/Tracy Batteast, Elena
Mezzetti
I Dig Rock And Roll Music
in co w/James Mason, Dave Dixon

STOTHART, HERBERT
1885-1949, American
m/Herbert Stothart
Bambalina
in co w/Vincent Youmans
w/Otto Harbach, Oscar
Hammerstein II
Cossack Love Song, The
w/Otto Harbach, Oscar
Hammerstein II
Cuban Love Song, The
w/Jimmy McHugh, Dorothy
Fields

Donkey Serenade, The
in co w/Rudolf Friml
    w/Robert Wright, George "Chet"
    Forrest
I Wanna Be Loved By You
in co w/Harry Ruby
    w/Bert Kalmar
Rogue Song, The
    w/Clifford Grey
Song Of The Flame
in co w/George Gershwin
    w/Otto Harbach, Oscar
    Hammerstein II
Totem Tom Tom
in co w/Rudolf Friml
    w/Otto Harbach, Oscar
    Hammerstein II
Wildflower
in co w/Vincent Youmans
    w/Otto Harbach, Oscar
    Hammerstein II

STRAUS, OSCAR
1870-1954, Austrian
m/Oscar Straus (from "The
Chocolate Soldier")
w/Stanislaus Stange
Letter Song, The (1909)
My Hero (1909)

STRAYHORN, BILLY
1915-1967, American
w&m/Billy Strayhorn
Chelsea Bridge
Grieving
    in co w/Duke Ellington
Lush Life
Satin Doll
    in co w/Duke Ellington, Johnny
    Mercer
Take The "A" Train
    in co w/Lee Gaines

**STREISAND, BARBRA
(BARBARA JOAN STREISAND)
(1942)**
1942, American
w&m in co w/Paul Williams
**Evergreen (Love Theme From A
Star Is Born)**

STROMBERG, JOHN
1853-1902
m/John Stromberg
w/Edgar Smith except as noted
Come Back My Honey Boy
Come Down Ma Evenin' Star
    w/Robert B. Smith
Dinah (Kiss Me Honey Do)
My Blushin' Rosie
My Best Girl's A Corker
    w&m/John Stromberg
When Chloe Sings A Song

STROUSE, CHARLES
1928, American
m/Charles Strouse
w/Lee Adams except as noted
Born Too Late
    w/Fred Tobias
Kids
Lot Of Livin' To Do, A
Once Upon A Time
Put On A Happy Face
Tomorrow
    w/Martin Charnin
While The City Sleeps
Yes I Can

**STRUNK, JUD (JUSTIN
RODERICK STRUNK JR.)**
1936, American
w&m/Jud Strunk
Daisy A Day, A
My Country
Biggest Parakeets In Town, The

STUART, LESLIE
American
w&m/Leslie Stuart
**Tell Me Pretty Maiden (Are There
Any More At Home Like You)**

STULTS, R.M.
American
w&m/R.M. Stults
**Sweetest Story Ever Told, The
(Tell Me Do You Love Me)**

STYNE, JULE
1905, American
m/Jule Styne
All I Need Is The Girl
    w/Stephen Sondheim
Anywhere
    w/Sammy Cahn
As Long As There's Music
    w/Sammy Cahn
Be A Santa
    w/Betty Comden, Adolph Green
Bye Bye Baby
    w/Leo Robin
Change Of Heart
    w/Harold Adamson
Comes Once In A Lifetime
    w/Betty Comden, Adolph Green
**Diamonds Are A Girl's Best
Friend**
    w/Leo Robin
Don't Rain On My Parade
    w/Bob Merrill
**Every Street's A Boulevard In
Old New York**
    w/Bob Hilliard
Everything's Coming Up Roses
    w/Stephen Sondheim
Five Minutes More
    w/Sammy Cahn
Funny Girl
    w/Bob Merrill

Give A Little, Get A Little
    w/Betty Comden, Adolph Green
How Do You Speak To An Angel
    w/Bob Hilliard
**I Don't Want To Walk Without
You**
    w/Frank Loesser
I Fall In Love Too Easily
    w/Sammy Cahn
I Still Get Jealous
    w/Sammy Cahn
I'll Walk Along
    w/Sammy Cahn
It's Been A Long, Long Time
    w/Sammy Cahn
It's Magic
    w/Sammy Cahn
**I've Heard That Song Before
(It Seems)**
    w/Sammy Cahn
Just In Time
    w/Betty Comden, Adolph Green
**Let It Snow, Let It Snow, Let
It Snow**
    w/Sammy Cahn
Let Me Entertain You
    w/Stephen Sondheim
Little Girl From Little Rock, A
    w/Leo Robin
Long Before I Knew You
    w/Betty Comden, Adolph Green
Make Someone Happy
    w/Betty Comden, Adolph Green
Never Never Land
    w/Betty Comden, Adolph Green
On A Sunday By The Sea
    w/Sammy Cahn
Papa Won't You Dance With Me
    w/Sammy Cahn
Party's Over, The
    w/Betty Comden, Adolph Green
People
    w/Bob Merrill
Poor Little Rhode Island
    w/Sammy Cahn

Put'Em In A Box
    w/Bob Hilliard
**Saturday Night Is The Loneliest
Night In The Week**
    w/Sammy Cahn

Small World
    w/Stephen Sondheim
Some People
    w/Stephen Sondheim

Stay With The Happy People
    w/Bob Hilliard
There Goes That Song Again
    w/Sammy Cahn
Things We Did Last Summer, The
    w/Sammy Cahn
Three Coins In The Fountain
    w/Sammy Cahn

Time After Time
w/Sammy Cahn
Together Wherever We Go
w/Stephen Sondheim
Who Am I
w/Walter Bullock
Who Are You Now
w/Bob Merrill
You Are Woman (I Am Man)
w/Bob Merrill
You're My Girl
w/Sammy Cahn

SUESSE, DANA
1911, American
m/Dana Suesse
Jazz Nocturne (1931) (Instr.)
My Silent Love (melody of "Jazz Nocturne")
w/Edward Heyman
Night Is Young And You're So Beautiful, The
w/Billy Rose, Irving Kahal
You Oughta Be In Pictures
w/Edward Heyman

SULLIVAN, SIR ARTHUR
1842-1900, English
m/Sir Arthur Sullivan
w/Sir William Schwenck Gilbert
(1836-1911)
(See listing under classical composers)
From the Operetta "The Goldoliers"
Dance A Cachuca
I Am A Courtier Grave And Serious
I Stole The Prince
In Enterprise Of Martial Kind
O My Darling O My Pet
Rising Early In The Morning
Roses White And Roses Red
Take A Pair Of Sparkling Eyes
There Lived A King
There Was A Time
We're Called Goldolieri
When A Merry Maiden Marries
From the operetta "H.M.S. Pinafore"
Carefully On Tiptoe Stealing
Farewell My Own
He Is An Englishman
I Am The Captain Of The Pinafore
I Am The Monarch Of The Sea
I'm Called Little Buttercup
Kind Captain I've Important Information
Maiden Fair To See, A
Never Mind The Why And Wherefore
Refrain Audacious Tar
Sorry Her Lot
Things Are Seldom What They Seem
We Sail The Ocean Blue
When I Was A Lad

From the operetta "Patience"
I Canot Tell What This Love MayBe
If You Want A Receipt
If You're Anxious For To Shine
Love Is A Plaintive Song
Magnet And The Churn, The
Prithee, Pretty Maiden
Silvered Is The Raven Hair
Twenty Love-Sick Maidens, We
When I First Put This Uniform On
When I Go Out Of Door
From the operetta "Iolanthe"
Faint Heart Never Won Fair Lady
Good Morrow, Good Lover
If We're Weak Enough To Tarry
Law Is The True Embodiment, The
Loudly Let The Trumpet Bray
None Shall Part Us
Of All The Young Ladies I Know
Oh Foolish Fay
Spurn Not The Nobly Born
We Are Dainty Little Fairies
When All Night Long
When Britain Really Ruled The Waves
When I Went To The Bar
When You're Lying Awake
Young Strephon Is The Kind Of Lout
From the operetta "The Mikado"
Behold The Lord High Executioner
Braid The Raven Hair
Brightly Dawns Our Wedding Day
Criminal Child, The
Flowers That Bloom In The Spring, The
For He's Going To Marry Yum Yum
From Every Kind Of Man
Here's A How-De-Do
If You Want To Know Who We Are
I've Got A Little List
Moon And I, The
My Object All Sublime
Three Little Maids From School
Tit-Willow
Wand'rng Minstrel, A
Were You Not To Ko-Ko Plighted
From the operetta "The Pirates Of Penzance"
Ah, Leave Me Not To Pine
Climbing Over Rocky Mountain
Model Of A Modern Major General
Oh Better Far To Live And Die
Oh, Is There Not One Maiden Breast
Policeman's Lot Is Not A Happy One, A
Poor Wandering One
When Frederic Was A Little Lad
With Catlike Tread

From the operetta "Princess Ida"
Expressive Glances
Ida Was A Twelvemonth Old
If You Give Me Your Attention
Would You Know The Kind Of Maid
From the operetta "The Sorcerer"
My Name Is John Wellington Wells
Now To The Banquet We Press
Time Was When Love And I
From the operetta "The Yeomen Of The Guard"
I Have A Song To Sing, O!
Is Life A Boon
Man Who Would Woo A Fair Maid, A
Oh, A Private Buffoon
Strange Adventure
Were I Thy Bride
When A Wooer Goes A-Wooing
When Maiden Loves
When Our Gallant Norman Foes
From the operetta "Ruddigore"
I Know A Youth
If Somebody There Chanced To Be
My Boy, You May Take It From Me
There Grew A Little Flower
When The Night Wind Howls
From the operetta "Trial By Jury"
Oh Gentlemen Listen
When First My Old, Old Love I Knew
When I Good Friends Was Call'd To The Bar
With A Sense Of Deep Emotion
Additional m/Sir Arthur Sullivan
Hail Hail The Gang's All Here
w/Theodora (Dolly) Morse
(music adapted from "With Catlike Tread" by Theodora Morse)
Lost Chord, The (1877)
w/Adelaide Proctor
Onward Christian Soldiers (1871)
w/Sabine Baring-Gould

SULLIVAN, JOSEPH J.
w&m/Joseph J. Sullivan
Where Did You Get That Hat

SUMMER, DONNA
1948, American
w&m in co w/Georgio Moroder, Pete Bellotte, except as noted
Bad Girls
in co w/Bruce Sudano, Joe Esposito, Eddie Hokenson
Dim All The Lights
w&m/Donna Summer
Heaven Knows
I Feel Love
I Love You

I Remember Yesterday
On The Radio
    w&m/Donna Summer, Georgio
    Moroder
Our Love
    w&m/Donna Summer, Georgio
    Moroder
Rumour Has It
Spring Affair
Try Me I Know We Can Make It
Winter Melody

SUN RA (SONNY BLOUNT)
1928, American
m/Sun Ra
Atlantis
Cosmic Chaos
Magic City, The
Sound Of Joy
Street Named Hell
Sun Myth, The
Sun Song

SULLIVAN, DAN J.
1875-1948, American
w&m/Dan J. Sullivan
Machushla
When It's Springtime In
  Killarney
You're As Welcome As The
  Flowers (1901)

SUTTON, GLENN
1937, American
w&m/Glenn Sutton
Almost Persuaded
    in co w/Billy Sherrill
Bedtime Story
    in co w/Billy Sherrill
Have A Little Faith
    in co w/Billy Sherrill

I Don't Wanna Play House
    in co w/Billy Sherrill
I'm Down To My Last I Love You
    in co w/Billy Sherrill
I'm Gonna Write A Song
I'm Still Loving You
    in co w/George Richey
Kids Say The Darndest Things
    in co w/Billy Sherrill
Living In A House Full Of Love
    in co w/Billy Sherrill
Loser's Cathedral
    in co w/Billy Sherrill
My Woman's Good To Me
    in co w/Billy Sherrill
Singing My Song
    in co w/Tammy Wynette, Billy
    Sherrill
Stay There Till I Get There
There's A Party Goin' On
    in co w/Billy Sherrill
Tonight My Baby's Coming Home
    in co w/Billy Sherrill

Ways To Love A Man, The
    in co w/Tammy Wynett, Billy
    Sherrill
What A Man My Man Is
What Made Milwaukee Famous
You Mean The World To Me
    in co w/Billy Sherrill
Your Good Girl's Gonna Go Bad
    in co w/Billy Sherrill
You're My Man

SUTTON, HARRY O.
American
m/Harry O. Sutton
w/Jean Lenox
I Don't Care (1905)

SWAN, BILLY
1944, American
w&m/Billy Swan
I Can Help
I'm Her Fool

SWANDER, DON
American
m/Don Swander
w/June Hershey
Deep In The Heart Of Texas
  (1941)

SWIFT, KAY
1905, American
m/Kay Swift
w/Paul James (James P. Warburg)
Can't We Be Friends
Fine And Dandy

SYLVERS, LEON
American
w&m/Leon Sylvers
    in co w/S. Shockley, W. Shelby
And The Beat Goes On (1980)

SYMES, MARTY
1904-1953, American
w/Marty Symes
    in co w/Al J. Neiburg, Jerry
Livingston, except for "There Is No
Greater Love," music by Isham Jones
It's The Talk Of The Town
I've Got An Invitation To A Dance
There Is No Greater Love
Under A Blanket Of Blue
When It's Darkness On The Delta

SZABO, GABOR
Hungarian/American
m/Gabor Szabo (instr.)
Breezin' (1975)

POPULAR COMPOSERS
& LYRICISTS

T , U , V

TALENT, LEO (JACK WINTERS)
1906, American
w/Leo Talent
m/J. Fred Coots
Me And My Teddy Bear

TAUB, JULES
American
w&m/Jules Taub
Bad Luck (1956)
in co w/Saul Ling
Please Love Me (1953)
in co w/B.B. King
Sweet Little Angel (1956)
in co w/B.B. King
"T" 99 Blues
in co w/Jimmy Nelson
Texas Hop (1948)
in co w/Pee Wee Crayton
Three O'Clock Blues (1951)
in co w/B.B. King
Woke Up This Morning
in co w/B.B. King
You Know I Love You
in co w/B.B. King

TAUBER, DORIS
1908, American
w&m in co w/Maceo Pinkard,
William G. Tracey
Them There Eyes

TAUPIN, BERNIE
English
Words to many songs, music of
Elton John.
See list of selections under Elton
John

TAYLOR, EARL
American
w&m/Earl Taylor
My Southern Rose (1909)

TAYLOR, IRVING
1914, American
w/Irving Taylor
m/Ken Lane
Everybody Loves Somebody
Kookie, Kookie (Lend Me Your Comb)
w&m/Irving Taylor
So Dear To My Heart
Something Sentimental
Three Little Sisters

TAYLOR, JAMES
1948, American
w&m/James Taylor
Carolina In My Mind
Country Road
Devoted To You
in co w/Carly Simon
Don't Let Me Be Lonely Tonight
Fire And Rain

Long Ago And Far Away
Mexico
Mockingbird
in co w/Carly Simon
Mudslide Slim
One Man Parade
Shower The People
Sweet Baby James
Tranquillo
in co w/Carly Simon, Arif Mardin
Your Smiling Face

TAYLOR, R. DEAN
Canadian
w&m/R. Dean Taylor
Ain't It A Bad Thing (1971)
Gotta See Jane (1974)
Indiana Wants Me (1970)
Love Child (1968)
Taos, New Mexico (1972)

TAYLOR, TELL
American
w&m/Tell Taylor
Down By The Old Mill Stream (1910)

TEAGARDEN, JACK
1905-1964, American
w&m/Jack Teagarden
Blues After Hours

TEETOR, MACY O.
1898, American
m/Macy O. Teetor
w/Johnny Mercer
Lost

TEMPERTON, ROD
English
w&m/Rod Temperton
Always And Forever (1969)
Boogie Nights (1977)
Give Me The Night (1980)
Groove Line, The (1978)
Off The Wall (1980)
Rock With You (1978)
Stomp (1980)
in co w/George Johnson, Louis
Johnson, V. Johnson
Treasure

TENNANT, H.M.
English
w&m in co w/R.H. Hooper
My Time Is Your Time

TENNEY, JACK B.
1898, American
m/Jack B. Tenney
w/Helen Stone
Mexicali Rose (1923)

TENNILLE, TONI
1943, American
w&m/Toni Tenille
Do That To Me One More Time
Way I Want To Touch You, The

TEPPER, SID
1918, American
w&m in co w/Roy C. Bennett
See list of selections under Roy C.
Bennett

TEX, JOE (JOSEPH ARRINGTON JR., JOSEPH X)
1933, American
w&m/Joe Tex
I Gotcha
Show Me
Baby You're Right
in co w/James Brown
Skinny Legs And All
Sweet Woman Like You

THALER, RUDOLF
w/Rudolf Thaler
m/A. Pestalozza
Ciribiribin

THARPE, ROSETTA (SISTER)
American
w&m/Rosetta Tharpe
Strange Things Happening Every Day (1945)
Up Above My Head, I Hear Music In The Air (1948)

THEARD, SAM
1904, American
w&m/Sam Theard
I'll Be Glad When You're Dead You Rascal You
in co w/Charles Davenport
Let The Good Times Roll

THOMAS, B.J.
1943, American
w&m/B.J. Thomas
Happy Man
Home Where I Belong

THOMAS, CARLA
1942, American
w&m/Carla Thomas
Gee Whiz (Look At His Eyes)

THOMAS, DICK
1915, American
m/Dick Thomas
w/Max C. Freedman
Sioux City Sue

THOMAS, HARRY
American
w&m/Harry Thomas
Hold 'Em Joe
Matilda, Matilda (1953)

THOMAS, JIMMIE
American
w&m/Jimmie Thomas
Rockin' Robin (1958)

THOMAS, JOE
American
w&m/Joe Thomas

Blue Shadows (1951)
in co w/George Rhodes
Got You On My Mind (1952)
in co w/Howard Biggs
I Don't Know (1952)
in co w/Willie Mabon

THOMAS, RAY
1941, English
w&m/Ray Thomas
Dear Diary
For My Lady
Lazy Day
Nice To Be Here
UnderMoonshine

THOMAS, TIMMY
1944, American
w&m/Timmy Thomas
People Are Changing
Why Can't We Live Together

THOMPSON, HANK (HENRY WILLIAM THOMPSON)
1925, American
w&m/Hank Thompson
Humpty Dumpty Heart
Lonely Heart Knows, A
Hangover Tavern
I've Come Awful Close
Movin' On
Oklahoma Hills
Swing Wide Your Gate Of Love
Today
Whoa Sailor

THOMPSON, H.S.
American
w&m/H.S. Thompson
Annie Lisle (1860)
Melody adapted later for the Alma Mater songs of Cornell University, "Far Above Cayuga's Waters"; New York University, "Oh Grim Grey Palisades;" University of North Carolina- verse to "Cause I'm A Tar Hell Born" and several other colleges

THOMPSON, WAYNE CARSON
American
w&m/Wayne Carson Thompson
Soul Deep
Letter, The (1967)

THORNHILL, CLAUDE
1909-1965, American
m/Claude Thornhill
Portrait Of A Guinea Farm
Snowfall

THORNTON, JAMES
1861-1938, American
w&m/James Thornton
Bridge Of Sighs, The
Don't Give Up The Old Love For The New
Irish Jubilee, The
m/Charles Lawlor

My Sweetheart's The Man In The Moon
On The Benches In The Park
She May Have Seen Better Days
Streets Of Cairo, The (Poor Little Country Maid)
There's A Little Star Shining For You
When You Were Sweet Sixteen

THROCKMORTON, SONNY
American
w&m/Sonny Throckmorton
Ain't No Way To Make A Bad Love Grow
Easy Look
in co w/Curly Putman
How Long Has It Been
I Wish I Was Eighteen Again
If We're Not Back In Love By Monday
in co w/Glenn Martin
Knee Deep In Loving You
Last Cheater's Waltz
Middle Age Crazy

TIBBLES, GEORGE F.
1913, American
w&m in co w/Ramey Idriss
Woody Woodpecker

TICHENOR, TREBOR JAY
1940, American
m/Trebor Jay Tichenor (instr.)
Chestnut Valley Rag
Show-Me Rag, The

TIERNEY, HARRY AUSTIN
1890-1965, American
m/Harry Austin Tierney
m/Joseph McCarthy except as noted
Alice Blue Gown (In My Sweet Little)
Castle Of Dreams (music adapted from Chopin's "Minute Waltz")
Honky Tonky Town
Irene
It's A Cute Little Way Of My Own
w/Alfred Bryan
Kinkajou, The
M-I-S-S-I-S-S-I-P-P-I
On Atlantic Beach
Rangers Song, The

TILLIS, MEL
1932, American
w&m/Mel Tillis
All The Time
Burning Memories
in co w/Wayne Walker
Crazy Wild Desire
in co w/Webb Pierce
Detroit City
in co w/Danny Dill

Heart Over Mind
Holiday For Love
in co w/Webb Pierce, Wayne Walker
Honky Tonk Song
in co w/A.R. Peddy
I Ain't Never
in co w/Webb Pierce
I'm Tired
in co w/Ray Price, A.R. Peddy
No Love Have I
One More Time
Ruby, Don't Take Your Love To Town
Sawmill
in co w/Horace Whatley
Thousand Miles Ago, A
in co w/Webb Pierce

TILLMAN, FLOYD
1914, American
w&m/Floyd Tillman
Daisy Mae
Each Night At Nine
I Love You So Much It Hurts
I'll Keep On Lovin' You
I'll Never Slip Around Again
It Just Tore Me Up
It Makes No Difference Now
Slipping Around

TIMBERG, SAMMY
1903, American
w&m/Sammy Timberg
It's A Hap Hap Happy Day

TIMMONS, BOBBY
American
w&m/Bobby Timmons
This Here (1966)

TIOMKIN, DIMITRI
1894-1979, American
m/Dimitri Tiomkin
Ballad Of The Alamo, The
w/Paul Francis Webster
Friendly Persuasion
w/Paul Francis Webster
Green Leaves Of Summer
w/Paul Francis Webster
Guns Of Navarone, The
w/Paul Francis Webster
Happy Time, The
w/Ned Washington
High And The Mighty, The
w/Ned Washington
Nigh Noon (Do Not Forsake Me)
w/Ned Washington
So Little Time
w/Paul Francis Webster

Film scores
Alamo, The
Friendly Persuasion
Giant
Guns Of Navarone, The

High And The Mighty, The (1954)
High Noon (1952)
Moon And Sixpence, The
Mr. Smith Goes To Washington
Old Man And The Sea, The (1958)
Young Land, The

TIZOL, JUAN
1900, American
m/Juan Tizol
Caravan
in co w/Duke Ellington
Perdido
in co w/Ervin Drake, Hans J.
Lengsfelder

TOBANI, THEODORE MOSES
French
m/Theodore Moses-Tobani
w/Mary D. Brine
Hearts And Flowers (Coeurs et Fleures) (1879)

TOBIAS, CHARLES
1898, American
w&m/Charles Tobias
Coax Me A Little Bit
in co w/Nat Simon
Don't Sit Under The Apple Tree
in co w/Lew Brown, Sam H. Stept
Don't Sweetheart Me
in co w/Cliff Friend
Her Bathing Suit Never Got Wet
in co w/Nat Simon
Miss You
in co w/Harry Tobias, Henry Tobias
Old Lamplighter, The
in co w/Nat Simon
Rose O'Day (The Filla-Ga-Dusha Song)
in co w/Al Lewis
Somebody Loves You
in co.w/Peter DeRose, Harry Tobias
Those Lazy, Hazy Crazy Days Of Summer
in co w/Hans Carste
Throw Another Log On The Fire
in co w/Jack Scholl, Murray Mencher
Time Waits For No One
in co w/Cliff Friend
Two Tickets To Georgia
in co w/Joseph Young, J. Fred Coots
We Did It Before And We Can Do It Again
in co w/Cliff Friend
When Your Hair Has Turned To Silver (I Will Love You Just The Same)
in co w/Peter DeRose

TOBIAS, FRED
1928, American
w&m/Fred Tobias
Banned In Boston
Born Too Late
in co w/Charles Strouse
It Isn't Your Heart That Breaks
in co w/Stan Lebowsky

TOBIAS, HARRY
1895, American
w&m/Harry Tobias
At Your Command
in co w/Harry Barris
I Want You To Want Me
in co w/Jack Stern
Miss You
in co w/Charles Tobias, Henry Tobias
Sail Along Silv'ry Moon
in co w/Percy Wenrich
Somebody Loves You
in co w/Charles Tobias, Peter DeRose
Sweet And Lovely
in co w/Gus Arnheim, Jules LaMare
Wild Honey
in co w/Neil Moret

TOBIAS, HENRY
1905, American
w&m/Henry Tobias
If I Had My Life To Live Over
in co w/Moe Jaffee, Larry Vincent
Miss You
in co w/Charles Tobias, Harry Tobias

TODD, CLARENCE E.
1897, American
w&m/Clarence E. Todd
Oooh Look-A-There Ain't She Pretty

TOLLERTON, NEIL
English
m/Neil Tollerton
w/Eily Beadell
Crusing Down The River (1945)

TOMLIN, PINKY
1908, American
w&m/Pinky Tomlin
Love Bug Will Bite You If You Don't Watch Out, The
Object Of My Affection, The
in co w/James W. Grier, Coy Poe
That's What You Think
What's The Reason
in co w/James W. Grier

TOOMBS, RUDOLPH
American
w&m/Rudolph Toombs
Crawlin' (1953)
Daddy, Daddy (1952)

One Mint Julep (1952)
One Scotch, One Bourbon, One Beer (1953)
Teardrops From My Eyes (1951)

TORME, MELVIN HOWARD (MEL)
1925, American
w&m/Mel Torme
in co w/Robert Wells
except as noted
Born To Be Blue
Christmas Song, The
County Fair
Stranger In Town
w&m/Mel Torme
Stranger Called The Blues
Welcome To The Club
w&m/Mel Torme

TOSELLI, ENRICO
1883-1926, Italian
m/Enrico Toselli
English w/Sigmund Spaeth
Serenade (Serenata, OP. 6, No. 1)

TOUSSAINT, ALLEN
1939, American
w&m/Allen Toussaint
All These Things
I Like It Like That
in co w/Chris Kenner
Java
in co w/Freddy Friday, Alvin, Tyler, Marilyn Schack
Southern Nights
What Do You Want The Girl To Do
Yes We Can Can

TOWNSEND, ED
American
w&m/Ed Townsend
For Your Love (1958)
Let's Get It On (1973)
in co w/Marvin Gaye
Love Of My Man, The (1963)

TOWNSHEND, PETER
1945, English
w&m/Peter Townshend
Acid Queen, The
Behind Blue Eyes
Gettin' In Tune
Goin' Mobile
Guitar And Pen
I'm Free
Kid's Are Alright, The
Love Ain't For Keepng
Love Is Coming Down
Magic Bus
My Generation
Music Must Change, The
Pinball Wizard
Pure And Easy

Sister Disco
Squeeze Box
Tommy Can You Hear Me
Shakin' All Over
We're Not Gonna Take It
Who Are You
Won't Get Fooled Again
Young Man Blues

TRACE, ALBERT J. (AL) (CLEM WATTS, BOB HART)
1901, American
w&m/Albert J. Trace
If I Knew You Were Comin' I'd Have Baked A Cake
    in co w/Al Hoffman, Bob Merrill
You Call Everybody Darlin'
    in co w/Ben L. Trace, Sam Martin

TRACEY, WILLIAM G.
1893-1957, American
w/William G. Tracey
Gee But It's Great To Meet A Friend From Your Home Town (1910)
    m/James McGavisk
Play That Barber Shop Chord (1910)
    m/Lewis F. Muir
Them There Eyes (1930)
    in co w/Maceo Pinkard, Doris Tauber

TRADER, BILL
1922, American
w&m/Bill Trader
Fool Such As I, A

TRAVIS, MERLE
1917, American
w&m/Merle Travis
Cincinatti Lou
    in co w/Shug Fisher
Dark As A Dungeon
Divorce Me C.O.D.
    in co w/Cliffie Stone
No Vacancy
Sixteen Tons
Smoke, Smoke, Smoke (That Cigarette)
    in co w/Tex Williams
So Round, So Firm, So Fully Packed
    in co w/Cliffie Stone, Eddie Kirk

TRENET, CHARLES
French
French w&m/Charles Trenet
Beyond The Sea (La Mer) (1947)
    English w/Jack Lawrence
I Wish You Love (1955) (Que reste-t'il de nos amours)
    English w/Albert A. Beach (Lee Wilson)

TRENT, JO
1892-1954, American
w/Jo Trent
I Just Roll Along
    m/Peter DeRose
Muddy Water
    m/Peter DeRose, Harry Richman
My Kinda Love
    m/Louis Alter

TRIPP, PAUL
1911, American
w/Paul Tripp
m/George Kleinsinger
Tubby The Tuba

TRIVERS, BARRY
1912, American
w/Barry Trivers
m/Ben Oakland
Two Loves Have I

TROUP, ROBERT WILLIAM (BOBBY)
1918, American
w&m/Bobby Troup
Baby Baby All The Time
Daddy
Girl Talk
Route 66
Snootie Little Cutie

TROXEL, GARY ROBERT
1939, American
w&m in co w/Barbara Laine Ellis, Gretchen Diane Christopher
Come Softly To Me

TUBB, ERNEST
1914, American
w&m/Ernest Tubb
Don't Just Stand There
    in co w/Cherokee Jack Henley
Letters Have No Arms
    in co w/Arbie Gibson
Soldier's Last Letter
    in co w/Redd Stewart
Tomorrow Never Comes
    in co w/Johnny Bond
Try Me One More Time
Walkin' The Floor Over You

TUBB, JUSTIN
1935, American
w&m/Justin Tubb
Be Better To Your Baby
Keeping Up With The Jones
Lonesome 7-7203
Love Is No Excuse
Take A Letter Miss Gray

TUCKER, HENRY
American
m/Henry Tucker
w/George Cooper
Sweet Genevieve (1869)

TUCKER, ORRIN
1911, American
w&m in co w/Phil Grogan
Especially For You

TOMMY TUCKER
1908, American
w&m/Tommy Tucker
I Love You
Man Who Comes Around, The
No, No, No

TURK, ROY
1892-1934, American
w/Roy Turk
Are You Lonesome Tonight
    m/Lou Handman
Contented
    m/Don Bestor
Gimme A Little Kiss Will Ya Huh
    m/Maceo Pinkard
I Don't Know Why
    m/Fred Ahlert
I'll Get By
    m/Fred Ahlert
Love You Funny Thing
    m/Fred Ahlert
Mean To Me
    m/Fred Ahlert
Walkin' My Baby Back Home
    m/Fred E. Ahlert, Harry Richman
Where The Blue Of The Night (Meets The Gold Of The Day)
    m/Fred E. Ahlert, Bing Crosby

TURNER, IKE
1933, American
w&m/Ike Turner
Fool In Love
Poor Fool
Tra La La La

TURNER, JOE ("Big Joe")
1911, American
w&m/Joe Turner
Boogie Woogie Prayer (Cafe Society Swing & The Boogie Woogie)
    in co w/Albert C. Ammons, Pete K.H. Johnson
Boss Of The Blues
    in co w/Pete K.H. Johnson
Cafe Society Rag
    in co w/Albert C. Ammons, Pete K.H. Johnson
Flip Flop And Fly
    in co w/Charles Calhoun
Honey Hush
Johnson & Turner Blues
    in co w/Pete K.H. Johnson

TUVIM, ABE
1895-1958, American
w in co w/Francia Luban
m/J.J. Espinosa
Gay Ranchero, A (Las Altenitas)

TWILLEY, DWIGHT
American
w&m/Dwight Twilley
I'm On Fire (1975)
Money (1979)

TWITTY, CONWAY (HAROLD LLOYD JENKINS)
1933, American
w&m/Conway Twitty
As Soon As I Hang Up The Phone
Baby's Gone
in co w/Billy Parks
Happy Birthday, Darlin'
in co w/C. Howard
Hello Darlin'
I Can't See Me Without You
It's Only Make Believe
in co w/Jack Nance
I've Already Loved You In My Mind
Linda On My Mind
Lost Her Love On Our Last Date
in co w/Floyd Cramer
Play Guitar, Play
To See An Angel Cry
Walk Me To The Door
You've Never Been This Far Before

TWOMEY, KATHLEEN G. (KAY)
Hey Jealous Lover
in co w/Sammy Cahn, Bee Walker
Johnny Doughboy Found A Rose In Ireland
in co w/Al Goodhart
Serenade Of The Bells
in co w/Al Goodhart

TYLER, STEVE
1948, American
w&m in co w/Joe Perry
See list of selections under Joe Perry

TYNER, McCOY
1938, American
m/McCoy Tyner
African Village
Fly With The Wind
Message From The Nile
Rebirth
Sama Layuca
Song Of Happiness
Song Of The New World
Valley Of Life
Vision

TYSON, IAN
American
w&m/Ian Tyson
Someday Soon (1969)

UDALL, LYN
American
m/Lyn Udall
Just As The Sun Went Down (1898)
w&m/Lyn Udall
Just One Girl (1898)
w/Karl Kennett

ULVAEUS, BJORN (BJORN KRISTIAN ULVAEUS)
1950, Swedish
m/Bjorn Ulvaeus
in co w/Benny Andersson
w/Stig Anderson
See list of selections under Benny Andersson

UNGER, STELLA
1905, American
w/Stella Unger
Don't Cry Baby
m/James P. Johnson
I'm All Dressed Up With A Broken Heart
m/Fred Fisher
Man With A Dream, A
m/Victor Young

URANGA, EMILIO D.
Cuban
m/Emilio D. Uranga
w/Bartley Costello
Alla En El Rancho Grande (My Ranch) (1934)

VALDES, MIGUELITO
Cuban
w&m/Miguelito Valdes
Babalú

VALENS, RICHIE (RICHARD VALENZUELA)
1941-1959, American
w&m/Richie Valens
Come On, Let's Go
Donna
Ooh My Head (Boogie With Stu)

VALLEE, RUDY (HERBERT PRYOR VALLEE)
1901, American
w&m/Rudy Vallee
Betty Co-ed
in co w/J. Paul Fogarty
Deep Night
in co w/Charles Henderson
I'm Just A Vagabond Lover
in co w/Leon Zimmerman
Stein Song, The
adaptation: Rudy Vallee
original music: E.A. Fenstad
original words: Lincoln Colcord

Whiffenpoof Song, The
adaptation: Rudy Vallee
original music: Guy Scull
original words: Meade Minnigerode, George S. Pomeroy

VAN ALSTYNE, EGBERT ANSON
1882-1951, American
m/Egbert Anson Van Alstyne
Back, Back, Back To Baltimore
w/Harry H. Williams
Cheyenne
w/Harry H. Williams
Drifting And Dreaming
w/Harry H. Williams
Good Night Ladies
w/Harry H. Williams
I'm Afraid To Go Home In The Dark
w/Harry H. Williams
In The Shade Of The Old Apple Tree
w/Harry H. Williams
Memories
w/Gus Kahn
Pretty Baby
w/Gus Kahn, Tony Jackson
Sailin' Away ON The Henry Clay
w/Gus Kahn
San Antonio
w/Harry H. Williams
That Old Girl Of Mine
w/Earle C. Jones
There Never Was A Girl Like You
w/Harry H. Williams
Won't You Come To My House
w/Harry H. Williams
Your Eyes Hve Told Me So
w/Gus Kahn, Walter Blaufus

VAN ALSTYNE, FANNY CROSBY
1820-1915, American
w/Fanny Crosby Van Alstyne
Blessed Assurance
m/Mrs. Joseph F. Knapp
Safe In The Arms Of Jesus
m/W.H. Doane

VAN BOSKERCK, FRANCIS SALTUS
American
w&m/Francis Saltus Van Boskerck
Semper Paratus (official U.S. Coast Guard Song (1928)

VAN HEUSEN, JAMES (EDWARD CHESTER BABCOCK)
1913, American
m/James Van Heusen
All The Way
w/Sammy Cahn

All This And Heaven Too
w/Eddie de Lange
Aren't You Glad You're You
w/Johnny Burke
Birds Of A Feather
w/Johnny Burke
But Beautiful
w/Johnny Burke
Call Me Irresponsible
w/Sammy Cahn
Come Blow Your Horn
w/Sammy Cahn
Come Fly With Me
w/Sammy Cahn
Darn That Dream
w/Eddie de Lange
Deep In A Dream
w/Eddie de Lange
Going My Way
w/Johnny Burke
Heaven Can Wait
w/Eddie de Lange
Here's That Rainy Day
w/Johnny Burke
High Hopes
w/Sammy Cahn
I Could Have Told You
w/Carl Sigman
I Thought About You
w/Johnny Burke
Imagination
w/Johnny Burke
Isn't That Just Like Love
w/Johnny Burke
It Could Happen To You
w/Johnny Burke
It's Always You
w/Johnny Burke
It's Anybody's Spring
w/Johnny Burke
Love And Marriage
w/Sammy Cahn
Moonlight Becomes You
w/Johnny Burke
My Kind Of Town
w/Sammy Cahn

Nancy
w/Phil Silvers
Oh You Crazy Moon
w/Johnny Burke

Personality
w/Johnny Burke
Polka Dots And Moonbeams
w/Johnny Burke

Road To Morocco
w/Johnny Burke
Second Time Around, The
w/Sammy Cahn

September Of My Years
w/Sammy Cahn
So Help Me
w/Eddie de Lange

Suddenly, It's Spring
w/Johnny Burke
Sunday Monday Or Always
w/Johnny Burke
Swinging On A Star
w/Johnny Burke
Tender Trap, The
w/Sammy Cahn
Welcome To My Dream
w/Johnny Burke

VAN RONK, DAVID (DAVE)
1936, American
w&m/David Van Ronk
Bad Dream Blues
Bamboo
Frankie's Blues
If You Leave Me
Pretty Mama
Sunday Street

VAN STEEDEN JR., PETER
1904, American
w&m in co w/Harry Clarkson, Jeff
Clarkson
Home (When Shadows Fall) (1931)

**VAN ZANT, RONALD WAYNE
(LYND SKYNYRD)**
w&m in co w/Garry Rossington,
Larken Allen Collins
Free Bird
Saturday Night Special
Sweet Home Alabama
What's Your Name
You Got That Right

VANCE, PAUL J.
1929, American
w/Paul J. Vance
m/Lee Pockriss except as noted
Calcutta
m in co w/Heino Gaze
Catch A Falling Star
Itsy Bitsy Teenie Weenie Yellow
Polka Dot Bikini
Playground In My Mind
w&m/Paul J. Vance
What Is Love

VANDA, HARRY
1947, English/Australian
w&m in co w/George Young
Friday On My Mind
St.Louis

VANNELLI, ROSS
1949, Canadian
w&m/Ross Vannelli
I Just Wanna Stop
People Gotta Move
in co w/Gino Vannelli

VAUGHN, BILLY
American
w&m/Billy Vaughn
Trying

VAUGHAN, SHARON
American
w&m/Sharon Vaughan
My Heroes Have Always Been
Cowboys (1979)

VELONA, ANTHONY (TONY)
1920, American
w&m/Anthony Velona
Lollipops And Roses

**VERA, BILLY (WILLIAM
McCORD JR.)**
1944, American
w&m/Billy Vera
Make Me Belong To You
Mean Old World
Storybook Children
in co w/Judy Clay
Country Girl-City Man
in co w/Judy Clay
With Pen In Hand

VERNOR, F. DUDLEIGH
1892, American
m/F. Dudleigh Vernor
w/Bryon D. Stokes
Sweetheart Of Sigma Chi, The

VICARS, HAROLD (MOYA)
English
m/Harold Vicars
English w/Clarence Lucas
French w/Maurice Vancaire
Song Of Songs, The (Chanson Du
Coeur Brisé) (1914)

VILLOLDO, A.G.
Argentinian
Spanish w&m/A.G. Villoldo
El Choclo (The Owl)

VINCENT, GENE
1935-1971, American
w&m in co w/Don Graves
Be Bop A Lula

**VINCENT, NATHANIEL
HAWTHORNE (JAAN
KENBROVIN, F.N. VINARD)**
1889, American
w&m/Nathaniel Hawthorne Vincent
I'm Forever Blowing Bubbles
in co w/James Kendis, James
Brockman
Strawberry Roan
in co w/Fred Howard
When The Bloom Is On The Sage
in co w/Fred Howard

**VINTON, BOBBY (STANLEY
ROBERT VINTON)**
1935, American
w/Bobby Vinton
Mister Lonely
m/Gene Allan
My Melody Of Love (English
and Polish)
German w/George Buschor
m/Henry Mayer

VON TILZER, ALBERT
w&m/Albert Von Tilzer
Au Revoir But Not Goodbye
in co/Lew Brown
Carrie
in co w/Junie McCree
Chili Bean
in co/Lew Brown
Dapper Dan
in co/Lew Brown
Down Where The Swanee River Flows
in co w/Charles McCarron, Charles S. Alberte
Give Me The Moonlight, Give Me The Girl
in co/Lew Brown
Good Evening Caroline
in co w/Jack Norworth
Honey Boy
in co w/Jack Norworth
I May Be Gone For A Long, Long Time
in co/Lew Brown
I Used To Love You But It's All Over Now
in co/Lew Brown
I'll Be With You In Apple Blossom Time
in co w/Neville Fleeson
I'm The Lonesomest Gal In Town
in co/Lew Brown
Kentucky Sue
in co/Lew Brown
My Little Girl
in co w/Samuel M. Lewis, William Dillon
Oh By Jingo
in co/Lew Brown
Oh How She Could Yacki Hacki Wicki Wacki Woo
in co w/Charles McCarron, Stanley Murphy

Put Your Arms Around Me Honey
in co w/Junie McCree
Roll Along Prairie Moon
in co w/Cecil Mack (Richard C. McPherson), Ted Fiorito
Say It With Flowers
in co w/Neville Fleeson
Smarty
in co w/Jack Norworth
Soldier Boy
in co/Lew Brown
Take Me Out To The Ball Game
in co w/Jack Norworth
Take Me Up With You, Dearie
in co w/Junie McCree
Teasing
in co w/Cecil Mack (Richard C. McPherson)

VON TILZER, HARRY
1871-1946, American
m/Harry Von Tilzer
Alexander Don't You Love Your Baby No More
w/Andrew B. Sterling
All Aboard For Blanket Bay
w/Andrew B. Sterling
All Alone
w/William Dillon
And The Green Grass Grew All Around
w/William Jerome
Bird In A Gilded Cage, A
w/Arthur J. Lamb
Cubanola Glide, The
w/Vincent P. Bryan
Don't Take Me Home
w/Vincent P. Bryan
Down On The Farm
w/Raymond A. Browne
Down Where The Cotton Blossoms Grow
w/Andrew B. Sterling

Down Where The Wurzburger Flows
w/Vincent P. Bryan
Go On And Coax Me
w/Andrew B. Sterling
I Want A Girl Just Like The Girl That Married Dear Old Dad
w/William Dillon
In The Sweet Bye And Bye
w/Vincent P. Bryan
Just Around The Corner
w/Dolf Singer
Jennie Lee
w/Arthur J. Lamb
Mansion Of Aching Hearts, The
w/Arthur J. Lamb
On A Sunday Afternoon
w/Andrew B. Sterling
On The Old Fall River Line
w/Andrew B. Sterling
Pardon Me, My Dear Alphonse, After You My Dear Gaston
w/Vincent P. Bryan
Please Go Way And Let Me Sleep
w&m/Harry Von Tilzer
Take Me Back To New York Town
w/Andrew B. Sterling
Under The Anheuser Busch
w/Andrew B. Sterling
Under The Yum Yum Tree
w/Andrew B. Sterling
Wait 'Til The Sun Shines Nellie
w/Andrew B. Sterling
What You Goin' To Do When The Rent Comes 'Round (Rufus Rastus Johnson Brown)
w/Andrew B. Sterling
Where The Morning Glories Twine Around The Door
w/Andrew B. Sterling
You'll Always Be The Same Sweet Girl
w/Andrew B. Sterling

POPULAR COMPOSERS
& LYRICISTS

W, Y, Z

WAINWRIGHT, LOUDON III
1946, American
w&m/Loudon Wainwright III
Dead Skunk

WAKELY, JIMMY (JAMES CLARENCE WAKELY)
1914, American
w&m/Jimmy Wakely
I'll Never Let You Go Little Darling
Too Late
You Can't Break The Chains Of Love

WALFORD, WILLIAM B.
English
w/William W. Walford (1945)
m/William Batchelder Bradbury (American)
Sweet Hour Of Prayer

WALKER, AARON THIBAUD (T-Bone)
1912-1975), American
w&m/T-Bone Walker
Ain't That Cold Baby
All Night Long Baby
Good Feelin'
I Want A Little Girl
Lonesome Woman Blues
Mean Bone Boogie (Blues)
Stormy Monday Blues (Call It Stormy Monday)
T Bone Blues
T Bone Shuffle
You Don't Love Me

WALKER, CINDY
1918, American
Anna Marie
Casa Manana
Distant Drums
Dream Baby (How Long Must I Dream)
Gold Rush Is Over, The
Heaven Says Hellow
Hey Mr. Bluebird
In The Misty Moonlight
Lone Star Trail
Take Me In Your Arms And Hold Me
Thank You For Calling
This Is It
Triflin' Gal
You Don't Know Me
    in co w/Eddy Arnold
You're From Texas

WALKER, JERRY JEFF (RONALD CROSBY)
1942, American
w&m/Jerry Jeff Walker
L.A. Freeway
Mr. Bojangles

WALKER, JAMES J. (JIMMY)
1881-1946, American
w/James J. Walker
Goodbye Eyes Of Blue
    m/Harry Armstrong
Will You Love Me In December As You Do In May
    m/Ernest R. Ball

WALKER, WAYNE
American
w&m/Wayne Walker
Other Cheek, The

WALLACE, OLIVER G.
1887-1963, English/American
w&m/Oliver G. Wallace
Der Fuehrer's Face
Hindustan
    in co w/Harold T. Weeks
When I See An Elephant Fly
    in co w/Ned Washington

WALLER, THOMAS ("Fats")
1904-1943, American
m/Thomas "Fats" Waller

Ace In The Hole
    w/Frank Crumit, Bartley Costello
Ain't Misbehavin'
    in co w/Harry Brooks
    w/Andy Razaf
All That Meat And No Potatoes
    w/Ed Kirkeby
Black And Blue (What Did I Do To Be So)
    in co w/Harry Brooks
    w/Andy Razaf
Blue Turning Gray Over You
    w/Andy Razaf
Can't We Get Together
    in co w/Harry Brooks
    w/Andy Razaf
Concentrating On You
    w/Andy Razaf
Fat Man Blues (instr.)
Find Out What They Like
    w/Andy Razaf
Georgia Bo Bo (instr.)
Handful Of Keys
    w/Andy Razaf

Honeysuckle Rose
    w/Andy Razaf
If You Like Me Like I Like You
    w/Clarence Williams, Spencer Williams

I've Got A Feeling I'm Falling
    w/Billy Rose, Harry Link
Jitterbug Waltz, The (instr.)
Joint Is Jumpin', The
    w/Andy Razaf

Keeping Out Of Mischief Now
    w/Andy Razaf
My Fate Is In Your Hands
    w/Andy Razaf
Prisoner Of Love
    w/Andy Razaf
Rollin' Down The River
    w/Stanley Adams
Squeeze Me
    w/Clarence Williams
Take It From Me, I'm Takin' To You
    w/Stanley Adams
There's A Man In My Life
    w/George Marion Jr.
Valentine Stomp (instr.)
Viper's Drag (instr.)
Willow Tree
    w/Andy Razaf
You're My Ideal
    w/Spencer Williams
Zonky
    w/Andy Razaf

WALSH, JOSEPH FIDLER (JOE)
1947, American
w&m/Joseph Fidler Walsh
Bomber, The
Funk #49
Life's Been Good To Me
Life In The Fast Lane
    in co w/Don Henley, Glenn Frey
Meadows
Rocky Mountain Way
    in co w/Joe Vitale, Ken Passerelli, Rocke Groce
So What
Turn To Stone
Walk Away
You Can't Argue With A Sick Mind

WALSH, STEVE
1951, American
w&m in co w/Kerry Livgren, Phillip Ehart, Robert Steinhardt, David Hope, Richard Williams
Carry On Wayward Son
Dust In The Wind
Point Of Know Return

WALTERS, ROGER
1947, English
w&m/Roger Walters
Money

WARD, CHARLES B.
1865-1917, American
m/Charles B. Ward
Band Played On, The (1895)
    w/John E. Palmer
Strike Up The Band, Here Comes A Sailor
    w/Andrew B. Sterling

WARD, EDWARD
1896, American
m/Edward Ward
w/Chick Endor
**Who Takes Care Of The
 Caretaker's Daughter**

WARD, WILLIAM (BILLY)
1921, American
w&m/William (Billy) Ward
Do Something For Me
 in co w/Rose Marks
Have Mercy, Baby
I'd Be Satisfied

WARE, DICK
American
w&m in co w/Shorty Allan
Rock And Roll Waltz, The
WARE, LEONARD
1909, American
w&m/Leonard Ware
Hold Tight-Hold Tight
WARREN, BOB
American
w&m/Bob Warren
City Called Heaven (1941)

WARREN, HARRY
1893, American
About A Quarter To Nine
 w/Al Dubin
Affair To Remember, An
 w/Harold Adamson, Leo
 McCarey
At Last
 w/Mack Gordon
Boulevard Of Broken Dreams
 w/Al Dubin
By The River Sainte Marie
 w/Edgar Leslie
Chattanooga Choo-Choo
 w/Mack Gordon
Cheerful Little Earful
 w/Ira Gershwin, Billy Rose
Chica Chica Boom Chic
 w/Mack Gordon
Cryin' For The Carolines
 w/Samuel L. Lewis, Joseph Young
Daydreaming
 w/Al Dubin
Don't Give Up The Ship
 w/Al Dubin
Down Argentine Way
 w/Mack Gordon
Forty Second Street
 w/Al Dubin
**Girl Friend Of The Whirling
 Dervish, The**
 w/Al Dubin, Johnny Mercer
Have A Little Faith In Me
 w/Samuel L. Lewis, Joseph
 Young
**I Found A Million Dollar Baby
 In A Five And Ten Cent Store**
 w/Mort Dixon, Billy Rose

I Had The Craziest Dream
 w/Mack Gordon
I Only Have Eyes For You
 w/Al Dubin
I Yi Yi Yi Yi Like You Very Much
 w/Mack Gordon
**I'll Sing You A Thousand Love
 Songs**
 w/Al Dubin
I'll String Along With You
 w/Al Dubin
It Happened In Sun Valley
 w/Mack Gordon
I've Got A Gal In Kalamazoo
 w/Mack Gordon
Jeepers Creepers
 w/Johnny Mercer
Keep Young And Beautiful
 w/Al Dubin
Lullaby Of Broadway
 w/Al Dubin
Lulu's Back In Town
 w/Al Dubin
More I See You, The
 w/Mack Gordon
My Dream Is Yours
 w/Ralph Blane
My One And Only Highland Fling
 w/Ira Gershwin
Nagasaki
 w/Mort Dixon
**On The Atchison, Topeka And
 The Santa Fe**
 w/Johnny Mercer
Pettin' In The Park
 w/Al Dubin
Remember Me
 w/Al Dubin
September In The Rain
 w/Al Dubin
Serenade In Blue
 w/Mack Gordon
Shadow Waltz
 w/Al Dubin
She's A Latin From Manhattan
 w/Al Dubin
Shuffle Off To Buffalo
 w/Al Dubin
Stanley Steamer, The
 w/Ralph Blane
That's Amore
 w/Jack Brooks
There Will Never Be Another You
 w/Mack Gordon
This Heart Of Mine
 w/Arthur Freed

We're In The Money
 w/Al Dubin
Where Do You Work - A John
 w/Charles B. Marks, Mortimer
 Weinberg
With Plenty Of Money And You
 w/Al Dubin

Would You Like To Take A Walk?
 w/Mort Dixon, Billy Rose
You'll Never Know
 w/Mack Gordon
**You Must Have Been A Beautiful
 Baby**
 w/Johnny Mercer
**You Say The Sweetest Things,
 Baby**
 w/Mack Gordon
**You're Getting To Be A Habit
 With Me**
 w/Al Dubin
You're My Everything
 w/Mort Dixon, Joseph Young

WASHBURNE, JOE (Country)
1904, American
w&m/Joe Washburne
One Dozen Roses
**You Don't Know What Lonesome
Is**

WASHINGTON, DINAH
1924-1963, American
w&m in co w/Richard Johnson
I Only Know

WASHINGTON, NED
1901, American
w/Ned Washington
Can't We Talk It Over
 m/Victor Young
Cosi-Cosa
 m/Bronislau Kaper, Walter
 Jurmann
Give A Little Whistle
 m/Leigh Harline
High Noon (Do Not Forsake Me)
 m/Dimitri Tiomkin
High And Mighty, The
 m/Dimitri Tiomkin
Hundred Years From Today, A
 m/Victor Young
**I Don't Stand The Ghost Of A
 Chance With You**
 m/Victor Young, Bing Crosby
**I'm Getting Sentimental Over
 You**
 m/George Bassman
Jiminy Cricket
 m/Leigh Harline
Major Dundee March
 m/Daniele Amfitheatrof
My Foolish Heart
 m/Victor Young
Nearness Of You, The
 m/Hoagy Carmichael
Smoke Rings
 m/H. Eugene Gifford
Stella By Starlight
 m/Victor Young
When You Wish Upon A Star
 m/Leigh Harline

WATERS, MUDDY (McKINLEY MORGANFIELD)
1915, American
w&m/Muddy Waters
Blues Had A Baby And They Named It Rock And Roll
 in co w/Brownie McGhee
Bus Driver
 in co w/Terry Abrahamson
Copper Brown
 in co w/Marva Brooks
Cross Eyed Cat
Deep Down In Florida
Got My Mojo Working
Hoochie Koochey Man
I Can't Be Satisfied
I Feel Like Going Home
Jealous Hearted Man
Little Girl
Long Distance Call
Mamie
 in co w/Jimmy Rogers
Man
 in co w/Ellas McDaniel, Melvin London
Rock Me
Rollin' Stone
Thirty Three Years
 in co w/Charles E. Williams
Trouble No More
Screamin' And Cryin'
Who Do You Trust
Why Don't You Live So God Can Use You
You're Gonna Miss Me When I'm Dead

WATERS, ROGER
1945, English
w&m/Roger Waters
Another Brick In The Wall (1979)

WATSON, DEKE
American
w&m in co w/William Best
I Love You
(For Sentimental Reasons) (1945)

WATTS, H. GRADY
1908, American
w&m/H. Grady Watts
Blue Champagne

WATTS, MAYME
American
w&m in co w/Robert Mosley
Midnight Flyer

WAYNE, BERNIE
American
w&m/Bernie Wayne
Blue Velvet
 in co w/Lee Morris
He Believes In Me
 in co w/Ervin Drake

Laughing On The Outside, Crying On The Inside
 in co w/Ben Raleigh
Magic Touch, The
Magic Island, The
 in co w/Johnny Mercer
Port Au Prince
There She Is, Miss America
Vanessa
Where Were You When I Need You
 in co w/Marvin Moore
You're So Understanding
 in co w/Ben Raleigh
You Walk By
 in co w/Ben Raleigh

WAYNE, DON
American
w&m/Don Wayne
Birmingham Blues
Country Bumpkin (1975)
Poor Little Jimmy
Saginaw, Michigan (1964)
 in co w/Bill Anderson
Walk Tall, Walk Straight
Belles Of Southern Bell (1966)

WAYNE, MABEL
1910, American
m/Mabel Wayne
Dreamer's Holiday, A
 w/Kim Gannon
I Understand
 w/Kim Gannon
In A Little Spanish Town
 w/Samuel M. Lewis, Joseph Young
It Happened In Monterey
 w/Billy Rose
Little Man You've Had A Busy Day
 w/Al Hoffman, Maurice Sigler
My Cathedral
 w/Hal Eddy
Ramona
 w/L. Wolfe Gilbert

WAYNE, SID
1923, American
w/Sid Wayne
It's Impossible (Somos Novios)
 m/A. Manzanero
See You In September
 m/Sherman Edwards
Two Different Worlds
 m/Al Frisch

WEATHERLY, FREDERICK EDWARD
English
w/Frederick Edward Weatherly
Danny Boy (1913)
 music adapted by Weatherly from an Irish traditional air "Farewell To Cuchulain," also known as "The Londonderry Air"

Holy City, The (1892)
 m/Michael Maybrick (Stephen Adams)
Roses Of Picardy (1916)
 m/Haydn Wood

WEBB, JIMMY
1946, American
w&m/Jimmy Webb
All I know
By The Time I Get To Phoenix
Carpet Man
Crying In My Sleep
Didn't We
Galveston
MacArthur Park
Paper Cup
Up Up And Away
Watermark
Where's The Playground Susie
Wichita Lineman
Worst That Could Happen, The

WEBBER, ANDREW LLOYD
1948, English
m/Andrew Lloyd Weber
w/Tim Rice
Buenos Aires (1977)
I Don't Know How To Love Him (1970)
Don't Cry For Me Argentina (1977)
High Flying, Adored

WEBER, CARL MARIA VON
1786-1826, German
m/Carl Maria Von Weber (instr.)
Invitation To The Dance (Aufforderung Zum Tanze) (1819)

WEBSTER, JOSEPH PHILBRICK
American
m/Joseph Philbrick Webster
Lorena (1857)
 w/Rev. H.D.L. Webster
Sweet By And By (1868)
 w/S. Fillmore

WEBSTER, PAUL FRANCIS
1907, American
w/Paul Francis Webster
Anastasia
 m/Lionel Newman
April Love
 m/Sammy Fain
Black Coffee
 m/Sammy Fain
Certain Smile, A
 m/Sammy Fain
Doctor, Lawyer, Indian Chief
 m/Hoagy Carmichael
Farewell To Arms, A
 m/Mario Nascimbene

Follow Me
m/Broislaw Kaper
Friendly Persuasion
m/Dimitri Tiomkin
Gift Of Love, The
m/Sammy Fain
Green Leaves Of Summer, The
m/Dimitri Tiomkin
How It Lies, How It Lies, How It Lies
m/Sonny Burke
I Got It Bad And That Ain't Good
m/Duke Ellington
Imitation Of Life
m/Sammy Fain
Jump For Joy
m/Duke Ellington
Lamplighter's Serenade, The
m/Hoagy Carmichael
Love Is A Many-Splendored Thing
m/Sammy Fain
Loveliest Night Of The Year, The
m/Juventino Rosas, Irving Aaronson
My Moonlight Madonna
m/William Scotti
Rainbow On The River
m/Louis Alter
Secret Love
m/Sammy Fain
Shadow Of Your Smile, The
m/Johnny Mandel
Somewhere My Love
m/Maurice Jarre
Strange Are The Ways Of Love
m/Sammy Fain
Tender Is The Night
m/Sammy Fain
Time For Love, A
m/Johnny Mandel
Twelfth Of Never, The
m/Jerry Livingston
Two Cigarettes In The Dark
m/Lew Pollack
Very Precious Love, A
m/Sammy Fain
World That Never Was, A
m/Sammy Fain
You And The Waltz And I
m/Walter Jurmann

WECHTER, JULIUS
American
w&m in co w/Cissy Wechter
Spanish Flea (1966)

WEIL, CYNTHIA
1943, American
w&m in co w/Barry Mann
See selection of many titles under Barry Mann
Additional song w/Cynthia Weil
m/Mark James
Alone Too Long

WEILL KURT
1900-1950 German/American
Bilbao Song, The
w/Johnny Mercer
Cry, The Beloved Country
w/Maxwell Anderson
Foolish Heart
w/Ogden Nash
Here I'll Stay
w/Alan Jay Lerner
Lost In The Stars
w/Maxwell Anderson
Mack The Knife
w/Marc Blitzstein
My Ship
w/Ira Gershwin
One Life To Live
w/Ira Gershwin
One Touch Of Venus
w/Ogden Nash
Saga Of Jenny, The
w/Ira Gershwin
September Song
w/Maxwell Anderson
Speak Low
w/Ogden Nash
Stay Well
w/Maxwell Anderson
That's Him
w/Ogden Nash

WEISS, GEORGE DAVID
1921, American
w&m/George David Weiss
Can Anyone Explain
in co w/Bennie Benjamin
Can't Help Falling In Love
in co w/Hugo Peretti, Luigi Creatore
Confess
in co w/Bennie Benjamin
Cross Over The Bridge
in co w/Bennie Benjamin
How Important Can It Be
in co w/Bennie Benjamin
I Want To Thank Your Folks
in co w/Bennie Benjamin
I'll Never Be Free
in co w/Bennie Benjamin
Lonesome And Blue
in co w/Bennie Benjamin
Lion Sleeps Tonight, The (Wimoweh)
in co w/Hugo Peretti, Luigi Creatore, Albert Stanton, Paul Campbell, Solomon Linda
Mr. Wonderful
in co w/Jerry Bock, Larry Holofcener
Oh What It Seemed To Be
in co w/Bennie Benjamin, Frankie Carle
Rumors Are Flying
in co w/Bennie Benjamin

Too Close For Comfort
in co w/Jerry Bock, Larry Holofcener
Wheel Of Fortune
in co w/Bennie Benjamin
What A Wonderful World
in co w/George Douglas

WEISS, LARRY
American
w&m/Larry Weiss
Rhinestone Cowboy

WEISS, STEPHAN
1899, Austrian/American
w&m/Stephan Weiss
And So Do I
in co w/Paul Mann
Music Music Music (Put Another Nickel In)
in co w/Bernie Baum
They Say
in co w/Paul Mann, Edward Heyman
While You Danced Danced Danced

WELCH, BOB
1946, American
w&m/Bob Welch
Ebony Eyes
Oh Jenny
Precious Love
Sentimental Lady

WELLS, KITTY (MURIEL DEASON WRIGHT)
1918, American
w&m/Kitty Wells
Amigo's Guitar
in co w/John D. Loudermilk, Roy Botkin
Whose Shoulder Will You Cry On
in co w/Billy Wallace

WELLS, ROBERT (BOB LEVINSON)
1922, American
w&m/Robert Wells
Ask Me No Questions
in co w/David Saxon
Born To Be Blue
in co w/Mel Torme
Christmas Song, The
in co w/Mel Torme
County Fair
in co w/Mel Torme
From Here To Eternity
in co w/Fred Karger
Here's To The Losers
in co w/Jack Segal
It's Easy To Say (Song From '10')
in co w/Henry Mancini
Mobile
in co w/David J. Holt

Stranger Called The Blues
in co w/Mel Torme
When Joanna Loved Me
in co w/Jack Segal

WENRICH, PERCY
1887-1952, American
m/Percy Wenrich
Moonlight Bay
w/Edward Madden
**Put On Your Old Gray Bonnet
(1909)**
w/Stanley Murphy
Red Rose Rag (instr.) (1911)
w/Harry Tobias
Sail Along Silv'ry Moon
w/Harry Tobias
Up In A Balloon
w/Ren Shields
**When You Wore A Tulip And I
Wore A Big Red Rose (1914)**
w/Jack Mahoney
Where Do We Go From Here Boys
w/Howard E. Johnson
**Way Out Yonder In The Golden
West (1914)**
w&m/Percy Wenrich

WESLEY, CHARLES
1707-1788, English
w/Charles Wesley
Jesus, Lover Of My Soul
m/Simeon Buckley Marsh
Love Divine, All Love Excelling
m/John Zundel

WEST, DOTTIE
1932, American
w&m/Dottie West
in co w/Bill West, except as noted
Country Sunshine
in co w/Bill Davis
Here Comes My Baby Back Again
I Was Born A Country Girl
Is This Me
Would You Hold It Against Me

WESTENDORF, THOMAS P.
American
w&m/Thomas P. Westendorf
**I'll Take You Home Again,
Kathleen (1876)**

WESTMORELAND, PAUL
American
w&m/Paul Westmoreland
Detour (1951)

WEXLER, JERRY
1917, Ameican
w&m/Jerry Wesler
Honey Love
in co w/Clyde McPhatter
Natural Woman, A
in co w/Gerry Goffin, Carole King

WHEELER, BILLY EDD
1932, American
w&m/Billy Edd Wheeler
Coal Tatoo
Coming Of The Roads
Jackson
Lonesome, Lovesick Puppy Dog
**Ode To The Little Brown Shack
Out Back**
Power Of Love
Reverend Mr. Black

WHITTAKER, ROGER
English
w&m/Roger Whittaker
Last Farewell, The
New World In The Morning
You Are My Miracle

WHITCOME, IAN
1941, English
w&m/Ian Whitcomb
N-E-R-V-O-U-S-
This Sporting Life
You Turn Me On

WHITCUP, LEONARD
1903, American
w&m/Leonard Whitcup
From The Vine Came The Grape
in co w/Paul Cunningham
I Am An American
in co w/Paul Cunningham, Ira
Schuster
**Take Me Back To My Boots And
Saddle**

WHITE, BARRY
1944, American
w&m/Barry White
**I'm Gonna Love You Just A Little
More**
**Can't Get Enough Of Your Love,
Babe**
I Belong To You And Only You
I'llDo Anything You Want Me To
**It's Ecstasy (When You Lay Down
Next To Me)**
I've Got So Much To Give
Let The Music Play
Love's Theme
Never, Never Gonna Give Ya Up
Oh What A Night For Dancing
in co w/Vince Wilson
Rhapsody In White
What Am I Gonna Do With You
**You're The First, The Last, My
Everything**

WHITE, CHARLES A.
1830-1892, American
w&m/Charles A. White

Come Silver Moon
Marguerite (1883)
My Love's A Rose
President Cleveland March, The
When The Leaves Begin To Turn
When 'Tis Moonlight

WHITE, CHARLES T.
American
w&m/Charles T. White
**Carry Me Back To Ole Virginny
(De Floating Scow) (1847)**

WHITE, COOL
c.1820, American
w&m/Cool White
Buffalo Gals (Lubly Fan)

**WHITE, JOSHUA DANIEL
(JOSH)**
1919-1969, American
w&m/Joshua Daniel White
Ball And Chain Blues
Can't Help But Crying Sometimes
Collins' Body Lies In Sound Cave
Delia
Hard Time Blues
I Had A Woman
I Know Moonlight
Jim Crow Train
Little Man Sittin' On A Fence
Silicosis Blues
Timber
Number 12 Train
Uncle Sam Says
Welfare Blues

WHITE, MAURICE
1941, American
w&m/Maurice White
Best Of My Love
in co w/Albert McKay, Wanda
Hutchinson
Devotion
in co w/Phillip Bailey
Fantasy
in co w/Verdine White, E. Del
Bamo
In The Stone
in co w/David Foster, Allee Willis
Mighty, Mighty
in co w/Verdine White
Reasons
in co w/Phillip Bailey, Larry Dunn
Saturday Nite
in co w/Phillip Bailey, Al McKay
September
in co w/Allee Willis, Alan McKay
Serpentine Fire
in co w/Verdine White, Sonny
Burke
Shining Star
in co w/Phillip Bailey, Larry Dunn
Sing A Song
in co w/Alan McKay

Star
in co w/Allee Willis, E. Del Bamo
That's The Way Of The World
in co w/Verdine White, Charles
Stepney

WHITE, TONY JOE
1943, American
w&m/Tony Joe White
Beouf River Road
Georgia Pines
Gospel Singer, The
I've Got A Thing About You Baby
Migrant, The
Polk Salad Annie
Rainy Night In Georgia, A
Roosevelt and Ira Lee
Save Your Sugar For Me
Sidewalk Hobo
Soul Francisco
Sundown Blues
Watching The Trains Go By
Willie And Laura Mae Jones

WHITFIELD, NORMAN
1940, American
w&m/Norman Whitfield
Ain't That Peculiar
in co w/Eddie Holland
Ain't Too Proud To Beg
in co w/Eddie Holland
Ball Of Confusion
in co w/Barrett Strong
Beauty Is Only Skin Deep
in co w/Eddie Holland
Car Wash
Cloud Nine
in co w/Barrett Strong
I Can't Get Next To You
in co w/Barrett Strong
**I Heard It Through The
Grapevine**
in co w/Barrett Strong
I Know I'm Losing You
in co w/Eddie Holland, Cornelius
Grant
I Wish It Would Rain
in co w/Barrett Strong, Rodger
Penzabene
**I Wanna Get Next To You
(I Know) I'm Losing You**
in co w/Eddie Holland, Cornelius
Grant
Just My Imagination
in co w/Barrett Strong
Masterpiece, The
Papa Was A Rolling Stone
in co w/Barrett Strong
Psychedelic Shock
in co w/Barrett Strong
Smiling Faces Sometimes
in co w/Barrett Strong
Superstar
in co w/Barrett Strong

That's The Way Love Is
in co w/Barrett Strong
**Too Busy Thinking About My
Baby**
in co w/Barrett Strong, Janie
Bradford
Too Many Fish In The Sea
in co w/Eddie Holland
War
in co w/Barrett Strong
You're My Everything
in co w/Rodger Penzabene,
Cornelius Grant

WHITING, RICHARD A.
1891-1938, American
m/Richard A. Whiting
Ain't We Got Fun
w/Gus Kahn, Raymond B. Egan
Beyond The Blue Horizon
in co w/W. Franke Harling
w/Leo Robin
Breezin' Along With The Breeze
in co w/Seymour Simons
w/Haven Gillespie
Eadie Was A Lady
in co w/Nacio Herb Brown
w/Buddy DeSylva
Guilty
in co w/Harry Akst
w/Gus Kahn
Honey
in co w/Seymour Simons
w/Haven Gillespie
Hooray For Hollywood
w/Johnny Mercer
I'm Like A Fish Out Of Water
w/Johnny Mercer
Japanese Sandman
w/Raymond B Egan
Louise
w/Leo Robin
My Future Just Passed
w/George Marion Jr.
My Ideal
in co w/Newell Chase
w/Leo Robin
On The Good Ship Lollipop
w/Sidney Clare
One Hour With You
w/Leo Robin
Roses In The Rain
w/Neil Moret
Sleepy Time Gal
in co w/Ange Lorenzo
w/Raymond B. Egan, Joseph R.
Alden
She's Funny That Way
w/Neil Moret
Some Sunday Morning
w/Raymond B. Egan, Gus Kahn
Sorry
w/Buddy Pepper

They Called It Dixieland
w/Raymond B. Egan
Till We Meet Again
w/Raymond B. Egan
Too Marvelous For Words
w/Johnny Mercer
Ukulele Lady
w/Gus Kahn
Waiting At The Gate For Katy
w/Gus Kahn
**We're Working Our Way Through
College**
w/Johnny Mercer
When Did You Leave Heaven
w/Walter Bullock
**Where The Morning Glories
Grow**
w/Gus Kahn, Raymond Egan
You're An Old Smoothie
in co w/Nacio Herb Brown
w/Buddy DeSylva

WHITNEY, JOAN
1914, American
w&m in co w/husband, Alex Charles
Kramer
See selections listed under Alex
Charles Kramer

WHITSON, BETH SLATER
1879-1930, American
w/Beth Slater Whitson
Let Me Call You Sweetheart
m/Leo Friedman
Meet Me Tonight In Dreamland
(w&m)

WHITTIER, HENRY
American
w&m in co w/Charles W. Noell, Fred
J. Lewey
Wreck Of The Old '97, The (1924)
Melody based on Henry C. Work's
"The Ship That Never Returned"

WILBURN, TEDDY
1931, American
w&m in co w/Doyle Wilburn, Don
Helms
Somebody's Back In Town

WILCOX, ELLA WHEELER
American
w/Ella Wheeler Wilcox
m/Louis F. Gottschalk
**Laugh And The World Laughs
With You (1896)**

WILDER, ALEC
American
w&m/Alec Wilder
I'll Be Around
While We're Young
in co w/William Engvick, Morty
Palitz

WILKIN, MARIJOHN
American
w&m/Marijohn Wilkin
Fallen Angel (1961)
    in co w/Wayne P. Walker, Webb
    Pierce
Grin And Bear It (1959)
    in co w/John D. Loudermilk
Long Black Veil, The (1959)
    in co w/Danny Dill
One Day At A Time (1975)
    in co w/Kris Kristofferson
PT 109 (1962)
    in co w/Fred Burch

WILKINSON, DUDLEY
1897, American
m/Dudley Wilkinson
w/Arthur Hammerstein
Because Of You

WILLET, SLIM
American
w&m/Slim Willet
**Don't Let The Stars Get In Your
  Eyes**

**WILLIAMS, BERT
(EGBERT AUSTIN WILLIAMS)**
1875-1922, British West Indian/
American
m/Bert Williams
Constantly
    w/Chris Smith, James Henry
    Burris
Let It Alone
    w/Alex Rogers
My Landlady
    w/F.E. Mierich, James T. Bryan
Nobody (1905)
    w/Alex Rogers
Somebody Lied
    w/Jeff T. Brainen, Evan Lloyd
That's A Plenty
    w/Henry Creamer

WILLIAMS, CLARENCE
1893-1965, American
w&m/Clarence Williams
**Baby Won't You Please Come
  Home**
    in co w/Charles Warfield
Gulf Coast Blues (instr.)
High Society
    in co w/Walter Melrose
If You Like Me Like I Like You
    in co w/Thomas "Fats" Waller,
    Spencer Williams
Royal Garden Blues (instr.)
Shout Sister Shout
Sugar Blues
    in co w/Lucy Fletcher
Swing Brother Swing

West End Blues (instr.)
Wildcat Blues
    in co w/Thomas "Fats" Waller
Wildflower Rag (instr.)

WILLIAMS, DENIECE
1951, American
w&m/Deniece Williams
Free
God Is Amazing

WILLIAMS, DOOTSIE
American
w&m/Dootsie Williams
Bobby Sox Blues

**WILLIAMS, HANK (HIRAM
KING WILLIAMS)**
1923-1953, American
w&m/Hank Williams (except where
indicated)
Alabama Waltz, The
Baby We're Really In Love
Cajun Baby
    in co w/Hank Williams Jr.
Cold Cold Heart
Half As Much
Hey Good Lookin'
Honky Tonkin'
**I Can't Help It (If I'm Still In
  Love With You)**
I Saw The Light
I Won't Be Home No More
I'm So Lonesome I Could Cry
I'm Sorry For You, My Friend
Jambalaya (On The Bayou)
Kaw-Liga
    in co w/Fred Rose
Long Gone Lonesome Blues
Lonesome Whistle
Mansion On The Hill
    in co w/Fred Rose
May You Never Be Alone
Moanin' The Blues
Movin' On Over
Nobody's Lonesome For Me
**On The Banks Of The Old
  Ponchartrain**
    in co w/Ramona Vincent
Pan-American
Ramblin' Man
**There'll Be No Teardrops
  Tonight**
Weary Blues From Waitin'
Why Don't You Love Me
You Win Again
Your Cheatin' Heart

WILLIAMS, HANK JR.
1949, American
w&m/Hank Williams, Jr.
Cajun Baby
    in co w/Hank Williams Sr.
Family Tradition
Last Love Song, The
Standing In The Shadows

Whiskey Bent And Hell Bound
Women I've Never Had

WILLIAMS, JOHN
1932, American
m/John Williams
Nice To Be Around
    w/Paul Williams
**Theme from "Close Encounters
  Of The Third Kind"**
Theme from "Jaws"
Theme from "Star Wars"
Film Scores
Cinderella Liberty (1973)
Close Encounters Of The Third Kind
  (1977)
Jaws
Jaws2
1941
Paper Chase
Poseidon Adventure (1972)
Reivers, The
Star Wars (1978)
Towering Inferno (1974)

WILLIAMS, LARRY
1933-1980, American
w&m/Larry Williams
Bony Maronie
Short Fat Fannie
Dizzy Miss Lizzy

WILLIAMS, LAWRENCE
1950, American
w&m/Lawrence Williams
Let Your Love Flow

WILLIAMS, MARY LOU
1910, American
m/Mary Lou Williams (instr.)
Bearcat Shuffle
Blues For John
**Black Priest Of The Andes
  (cantata)**
Camel Hop
Cloudy
Foggy Bottom
Fungus Amungus, A
In The Land Of Oo-Bla-Dee
Little Joe From Chicago
Morning Glory
Music For Peace
Pretty-Eyed Baby
Roll 'Em
Scratchin' In The Gravel
Steppin' Pretty
Walking And Swinging
What's Your Story Morning Glory
Zodiac Suite

WILLIAMS, MASON
1938, American
Baroque A Nova (1968)
Cinderella Rockefella (1966)
    w/Nancy Ames
Classic Gas (1968) (Instr.)

Saturday Night At The World
(1969)

WILLIAMS, MAURICE
1938, American
w&m/Maurice Williams
Little Darling
Stay

WILLIAMS, MENTOR
American
w&m/Mentor Wiliams
Drift Away (1973)

WILLIAMS, PATRICK M.
1939, American
m/PatWilliams
Film Scores
Breaking Away (1979)
Don't Drink The Wate (1969)

WILLIAMS, PAUL
1940, American
w&m/Paul Williams
Do You Really Have A Heart
   in co w/Roger Nichols
Evergreen
   in co w/Barbra Streisand
I Won't Last A Day Without You
   in co w/Roger Nichols
Let Me Be The One
   in co w/Roger Nichols
Life Goes On
   in co w/Crain Doerge
Little Bit Of Love, A
   in co w/Ken Ascher
Nice To Be Around
   in co w/John Williams
Old Fashioned Love Song, An
Out In The Country
   in co w/Roger Nichols
Rainbow Connection
   in co w/Ken Ascher
Rainy Days And Mondays
   in co w/Roger Nichols
Someday Man
   in co w/Roger Nichols
Trust
   in co w/Roger Nichols
Walking Up Alone
We've Only Just Begun
   in co w/Roger Nichols
You And Me Against The World
   in co w/Ken Ascher
You Know Me
   in co w/Ken Ascher

WILLIAMS, SPENCER
1889-1965, American
w&m in co w/Jack Palmer
Everybody Loves My Baby
I Found A New Baby

WILLIAMS, TEX (SOL
WILLIAMS)
1917, American

w&m in co w/Merle Travis
Smoke, Smoke,Smoke (That
   Cigarette)

WILLIAMS, W.R.
American
w&m/W.R. Williams
I'd Love To Live In Loveland
   (With A Girl Like You) (1910)

WILLIS, ALLEE
1948, American
w&m/Allee Willis
I Want You Tonight
   in co w/Cory Lerios, David
   Jenkins
Lead Me On
Love Me Again
   in co w/David Lasley
September
   in co w/Alan McKay, Maurice
   White
In The Stone
   in co w/David Foster, Maurice
   White
Star
   in co w/Maurice White, E. Del
   Bamo

WILLIS, CHUCK
1928-1958, American
w&m/Chuck Willis
C.C. Rider (adaptation of earlier
traditional folk song)
Don't Deceive Me
Door Is Still Open To My Heart,
   The
It's Too Late
My Story
What A Dream
You're Still My Baby

WILLS, BOB (JAMES ROBERT
WILLS)
1905-1975, American
w&m/Bob Wills
Faded Love
   in co w/John Wills
San Antonio Rose

WILLS, JOHNNIE LEE
American
w&m in co w/Deacon Anderson
Rag Mop (1950)

WILLSON, MEREDITH
1902, American
w&m/Meredith Willson
Arm In Arm
Belly Up To The Bar Boys
Dolce Far Niente
Goodnight My Someone
Here's Love
He's My Friend
I Ain't Down Yet
I'll Never Say No

Lida Rose
Look Little Girl
May The Good Lord Bless And
   Keep You
My Wish
Pine Cones And Holly Berries
Seventy Six Trombones
Till There Was You
Trouble
You And I

WILSON, ANN
1950, Amrican
w&m/Ann Wilson
Barracuda
   in co w/Nancy Wilson, Rodger
   Fisher, Michael Derosier
Crazy On You
   in co w/Nancy Wilson, Roger
   Fisher
Dreamboat Annie
   in co w/Nancy Wilson
Even It Up
   in co w/Nancy Wilson, S. Ennis
Heartless
   in co w/Nancy Wilson
Kick It Out
Little Queen
   in co w/Nancy Wilson, Roger
   Fisher
Love Alive
   in co w/Nancy Wilson, Roger
   Fisher
Magic Man
   in co w/Nancy Wilson
Straight On
   in co w/Nancy Wilson

WILSON, BRIAN
1942, American
w&m/Brian Wilson
Be True To Your School
California Girls
Caroline
Darlin'
   in co w/Mike Love
Dead Man's Curve
   in co w/Jan Berry, Roger
   Christian, Artie Kornfeld
Do It Again
   in co w/Mike Love
Don't Worry Baby
   in co w/Roger Christian, H.
   Jamiph
Drag City
   in co w/Jan Berry, Roger
   Christian
Fun, Fun, Fun
   in co w/Mike Love
God Only Knows
   in co w/Tony Asher
Good Vibrations
   in co w/Mike Love
Help Me Ronda

I Get Around
In My Room
    in co w/Gary Usher
Little Deuce Coupe
Little Honda
Ride The Wild Surf
    in co w/Jan Berry
Spirit Of America
    in co w/Roger Christian
Surf City
    in co w/Jan Berry
Surfer Girl
    in co w/Mike Love
Surfin'
    in co w/Mike Love
Surfin' Safari
    in co w/Mike Love
Surfin' U.S.A.
    in co w/Mike Love
Wendy
Wouldn't It Be Nice
    in co w/Tony Asher

WILSON, JACKIE
1932, American
w&m/Jackie Wilson
Baby Workout
    in co w/Alonzo Tucker
You Betta Know It
    in co w/Norm Henry

WILSON, MARIE
1926, American
w&m/Marie Wilson
Before This Day Ends
    in co w/Roy F. Drusky, Vic
    McAlpin
Price For Loving You, The
    in co w/Ray Price
Set Him Free
    in co w/Mary Depew, Helen
    Moyers

WILSON, NANCY
1954, American
w&m in co w/Ann Wilson (sister)
See list of selections under Ann
Wilson

WILSON, THEODORE (TEDDY)
1912, American
m/Theodore Wilson
Blues In C Sharp Minor

WINKLER, RAY
American
w&m in co w/John Hathcock
Welcome To My World (1964)

**WINNER, J.E. (pen name R.A.
Eastburn)**
w&m/J.E. Winner
Little Brown Jug, The (1869)
**WINNER, SEPTIMUS (ALICE
HAWTHORNE)**
1847-1902, American

w&m/Septimus Winner
**Ellie Rhee (Carry Me Back To
Tennessee)**
**Give Us Back Our Old
Commander (Little Mac, The
People's Pride)**
**Listen To The Mocking Bird
(1855)**
What Is Home Without A Mother
**Where, O Where Has My Little
Dog Gone** (music adapted from a
German folk song "Zu Lauter bach
hab' i mein Strump verlor'n"; also
known as "Der Deitcher's Dog")
Whispering Hope

WINTER, EDGAR
1946, American
w&m in co w/Ronnie Montrose
Frankenstein (1973)

WINWOOD, STEVE
1948, English
w&m/Steve
in co w/Jim Capaldi, except as noted
Can't Find My Way Home
w&m/Steve Winwood
Dear Mr. Fantasy
    in co w/Jim Capaldi, Chris Wood
Empty Pages
Every Mother's Son
Freedom Rider
Gimme Some Loving
    in co w/Muff Winwood,
    Spencer Davis
Glad
    w&m/Steve Winwood
Hole In My Shoe
Paper Sun
Stranger To Himself

WISE, FRED
1915-1966, American
w/Fred Wise
A-You're Adorable
    m/Sidney Lippman
I Won't Cry Anymore
    m/Al Frisch
Lonely Blue Boy
    m/Ben Weisman

WISEMAN, SCOTT
American
w&m/Scott Wiseman
**Have I Told You Lately That I
Love You (1946)**

WITHERS, BILL
1938, American
w&m/Bill Withers
Ain't No Sunshine
Grandma's Hands
Kissing My Love
Lean On Me
Lovely Day
Use Me

**WITHERSPOON, JAMES
"JIMMY"**
1923, American
w&m/Jimmy Witherspoon
Blue Spoon
Destruction Blues
Money's Getting Cheaper
No Rollin' Blues
Skidrow Blues
**Some Of My Best Friends Are The
Blues**
Spoon Calls Hootie

WITT, MAX S.
American
m/Max S. Witt
w/George Taggert
Moth And The Flame, The (1898)

WOLFE, JACQUES
1896, American
m/Jacques Wolfe
Glory Road, De (1928)
    w/Clement Wood
Short'nin Bread (1928)
    w&m/Jacques Wolfe

WOMACK, BOBBY
1944, American
w&m/Bobby Womack
I'm In Love
Midnight Mover

WONDER, STEVIE
1951, American
w&m/Stevie Wonder
All In Love Is Fair
Black Orchid
Boggie On Reggae Woman
Don't You Worry 'Bout A Thing
Earth's Creation
Finger Tips
Golden Lady
He's Mista Know It All
Higher Ground
**I Believe (When I Fall In Love
It Will Be Forever)**
    in co w/Yvonne Wright
I Was Made To Love Her
    in co w/Henry Cosby, Sylvia Moy,
    Lulu Mae Hardaway
Isn't She Lovely
Livin' For The City
Maybe Your Baby
My Cherie Amour
    in co w/Sylvia Moy, Henry Cosby
Outside My Window
Send One Your Love
Sir Duke
**Signed, Sealed, Delivered I'm
Yours**
    in co w/Lee Garrett, Syreeta
    Wright, Lulu Mae Hardaway
Superstition

Tears Of A Clown, The
in co w/William "Smokey"
Robinson, Henry Cosby
Tell Me Something Good
Tuesday Heartbreak
Uptight (Everything's Alright)
in co w/Sylvia Moy, Henry Cosby
You And I
You Are My Heaven
in co w/Eric Mercury
You Are The Sunshine Of My Life
You Haven't Done Nothin'

WOOD, BRENTON
1941, American
w&m/Brenton Wood
Gimme Little Sign
Oogum, Boogum Song, The

WOOD, CYRUS D.
1889-1942, American
m/Cyrus D. Wood
m/Dave Stamper, Harold Levy
Lovely Lady (Ain't Love Grand)
(1927)

WOOD, HAYDN
English
m/Haydn Wood
w/Rayden Barrie
Brown Bird Singing, A (1922)

WOOD, LAUREN
American
w&m/Lauren Wood
Please Don't Leave (1979)

WOOD, LEO
1882-1929, American
w&m/Leo Wood
Runnin' Wild
in co w/Arthur H. Gibbs, Joe Gray
Somebody Stole My Gal

WOOD, ROY
1946, English
w&m/Roy Wood
Blackberry Way
Brontosaurus
Fire Brigade
Flowers In The Rain
Night Of Fear

WOODS, HARRY MACGREGOR
1896-1970, American
w&m/Harry MacGregor Woods
I'll Never Say Never Again Again
I'm Looking Over A Four-Leaf
Clover
in co w/Mort Dixon
Just An Echo In The Valley
Little Kiss Each Morning, A
Little Street Where Old Friends
Meet, A
in co w/Gus Kahn

Paddlin' Madelin' Home
River Stay 'Way From My Door
in co w/Mort Dixon
Side By Side
in co w/Gus Kahn
Try A Little Tenderness
in co w/Jimmy Campbell, Reg
Connelly
When The Moon Comes Over The
Mountain
in co w/Howard Johnson, Kate
Smith
When The Red Red Robin Comes
Bob-Bob-Bobbin' Along

WOODWORTH, SAMUEL
American
w/Samuel Woodworth
m/George Kiallmark (adapted from
his English song "Araby's Daughter")
Old Oaken Bucket, The (1808)

WORK, HENRY CLAY
1832-1884, American
w&m/Henry Clay Work
Babylon Is Fallen
Come Home Father
Grandfather's Clock
Kingdom Coming (The Year Of
Jubilo)
Marching Through Georgia
Wake Nicodemus

WORTH, BOBBY
1921, American
w&m/Bobby Worth
Do I Worry
Don't You Know (music adapted
from Puccini's "Musetta's Waltz")

WRIGHT, GARY
1943, American
w&m/Gary Wright
Dream Weaver

WRIGHT, J.B.F.
19th Century, American
w&m/J.B.F. Wright
Precious Memories

WRIGHT, ROBERT CRAIG
1914, American
w&m in co w/George (Chet) Forrest
See list of selections under
George (Chet) Forrest

WRUBEL, ALLIE
1905, American
w/Allie Wrubel
As You Desire Me
w&m/Allie Wrubel
Everybody's Got A Laughing
Place
m/Ray Gilbert
Fare Thee Well, Annabelle
m/Mort Dixon

Farewell To Arms
m/Abner Silver
Flirtation Walk
m/Mort Dixon
I Met Her On Monday
m/Charles Newman
I'll Buy That Dream
m/Herb Magidson
I'm Stepping Out With A Memory
Tonight
m/Herb Magidson
Lady In Red, The
m/Mort Dixon
Mr. And Mrs. Is The Name
m/Mort Dixon
Masquerade Is Over, The
m/Herb Magidson
Music Maestro Please
m/Herb Magidson
Why Don't We Do This More
Often
m/Charles Newman
Zip-A-Dee-Doo-Dah
m/Ray Gilbert

WYCHE, SID
American
w&m/Sid Wyche
Talk That Talk (1963)
Woman, A Lover, A Friend (1960)

YAKUS, MILT
American
w&m in co w/Claire Rothrock, Allan
Jeffrey
Old Cape Cod (1956)

YANCY, MARVIN (REVEREND)
American
w&m in co w/Chuck Jackson
Inseparable
I've Got Love On My Mind
Not Like Mine
in co w/Natalie Cole, Chuck
Jackson
Sophisticated Lady
in co w/Natalie Cole, Chuck
Jackson
This Will Be

YARROW, PETER
1938, American
w&m/Peter Yarrow
Day Is Done
Puff (The Magic Dragon)
in co w/Leonard Lipton
Torn Between Two Lovers
in co w/Phillip Jarrell

YELLEN, JACK
1892, American
w/Jack Yellen
Ain't She Sweet
m/Milton Ager

Alabama Jubilee
m/George L. Cobb
Are You From Dixie
m/George L. Cobb
Are You Having Any Fun
m/Sammy Fain
Happy Days Are Here Again
m/Milton Ager
Happy In Love
m/Sammy Fain
Hard Hearted Hannah
in co w/Bob Bigelow, Charles
Bates
m/Milton Ager
I'm Waiting For Ships That Never Come In
m/Abe Olman, William Raskin
I Wonder What's Become Of Sally
m/Milton Ager
Mama Goes Where Papa Goes
m/Milton Ager
Oh You Nasty Man
in co w/Irving Caesar
m/Ray Henderson
Sing Baby Sing
m/Lew Pollack
Sweet And Hot
m/Harold Arlen
Yiddisha Momme, A
m/Lew Pollack

YON, PIETRO A.
Italian
Italian w&m/Pietro A. Yon
English w/Frederick Herman Martens
Gesù Bambino (1917)

YOST, DENNIS
American
w&m in co w/Wally Eaton
Spooky (1967)
Traces (1969)

YOUMANS, VINCENT
1898-1946, American
m/Vincent Youmans
Carioca, The
w/Edward Eliscu, Gus Kahn
Drums In My Heart
w/Edward Heyman
Flying Down To Rio
w/Edward Eliscu
Great Day
w/Billy Rose, Edward Eliscu
Hallelujah
w/Leo Robin, Clifford Grey
I Know That You Know
w/Anne Caldwell
I Want To Be Happy
w/Irving Caesar
More Than You Know
w/Billy Rose, Edward Eliscu
No No Nanette
w/Otto Harbach

Orchids In The Moonlight
w/Edward Eliscu
Rise 'N' Shine
w/Buddy DeSylva
Sometimes I'm Happy
w/Irving Caesar
Tea For Two
w/Irving Caesar
Through The Years
w/Edward Heyman
Time On My Hands
w/Harold Adamson, Mack Gordon
Without A Song
w/Billy Rose, Edward Eliscu

YOUNG, FARON
1932, American
w&m/Faron Young
All Right
Backtrack
in co w/Alex Zanetis
Goin' Steady
I Miss You Already
in co w/Marvin Rainwater
My Friend On The Right
in co w/Red Lane
Three Days
in co w/Willie Nelson
You're Still Mine
in co w/Eddie Thorpe
Your Old Used To Be
in co w/Hilda M. Young

YOUNG, JOHN PAUL
1953, Australian
w&m/John Paul Young
Love Is In The Air

YOUNG, JOSEPH
1889-1939, American
w/Joseph Young
Annie Doesn't Live Here Anymore
in co w/Johnny Burke
m/Harold Spina
Cryin' For The Carolines
in co w/Samuel M. Lewis
m/Harry Warren
Dinah
in co w/Samuel M. Lewis
m/Harry Akst
Five Foot Two Eyes Of Blue
in co w/Samuel M. Lewis
m/Ray Henderson
Have A Little Faith In Me
in co w/Samuel M. Lewis
m/Harry Warren
Hello Central Give Me No Man's Land
in co w/Samuel M. Lewis
m/Jean Schwartz
How Ya Gonna Keep 'Em Down On The Farm

in co w/Samuel M. Lewis
m/Walter Donaldson
Hundred Years From Today,
in co w/Ned Washington
m/Victor Young
I Kiss Your Hand Madame
in co w/Samuel M. Lewis
m/Ralph Erwin
I'm Gonna Sit Right Down And Write Myself A Letter
m/Fred E. Ahlert
I'm Sitting On Top Of The World
in co w/Samuel M. Lewis
m/Ray Henderson
In A Little Spanish Town
in co w/Samuel M. Lewis
m/Mabel Wayne
In A Shanty In Old Shanty Town
m/Ira Schuster, Little Jack Little
King For A Day
in co w/Samuel M. Lewis
m/Ted Fiorito
Laugh Clown Laugh
in co w/Samuel M. Lewis
m/Ted Fiorito
Life Is A Song
m/Fred E. Ahlert
Lullaby Of The Leaves
m/Bernice Petkere
My Mammy
in co w/Samuel M. Lewis
m/Walter Donaldson

Rockabye Your Baby With A Dixie Melody
in co w/Samuel M. Lewis
m/Jean Schwartz

Snuggled On Your Shoulder
m/Carmen Lombardo

Take My Heart
m/Fred E. Ahlert
Then You've Never Been Blue
in co w/Samuel M. Lewis
m/Ted Fiorito

Two Tickets To Georgia
in co w/Charles Tobias
m/J. Fred Coots
Was That The Human Thing To Do
m/Sammy Fain

Where Did Robinson Crusoe Go With Friday On Saturday Night
in co w/Samuel M. Lewis
m/George Meyer
You're Gonna Lose Your Gal
m/James V. Monaco
You're My Everything
in co w/Mort Dixon
m/Harry Warren

YOUNG, LESTER
1910-1959, American
m/Lester Young (instr.)
Jumpin' With Symphony Sid
Lester Leaps In
Nobody Knows
Taxi War Dance
Tickletoe
Up 'N Adam

YOUNG, NEIL
1945, Canadian
w&m/Neil Young
Broken Arrow
Cinnamon Girl
Cortez The Killer
Country Girl
Cowgirl In The Sand
Heart Of Gold
Helpless
I Am A Child
Like A Hurricane
Lotta Love
Look Out For My Love
Love Is A Rose
Mr. Soul
My, My, Hey, Hey
Ohio
Roll Another Number
Southern Man
Sugar Mountain
Tonight's The Night

YOUNG, RIDA JOHNSON
1869-1926, American
w/Rida Johnson Young
Ah Sweet Mystery Of Life
    m/Victor Herbert
I'm Falling In Love With
  Someone
    m/Victor Herbert
Italian Street Song
    m/Victor Herbert
Mother Machree
    m/Chauncey Olcott, Ernest R.
    Ball
'Neath The Southern Moon
    m/Victor Herbert
Tramp! Tramp! Tramp!
    m/Victor Herbert
Will You Remember
    m/Sigmund Romberg

YOUNG, VICTOR
1900-1956, American
m/Victor Young

Around The World
    w/Harold Adamson
Blue Star
    w/Edward Heyman
Can't We Talk It Over
    w/Ned Washington
Golden Earrings
    w/Jay Livingstone, Ray Evans
Hundred Years From Today, A
    w/Ned Washington, Joseph
    Young
I Don't Stand The Ghost Of A
  Chance With You
    w/Ned Washington, Bing Crosby
Lord, You Made The Night Too
  Long
    w/Sam M. Lewis
Love Is The Thing
    w/Ned Washington
Love Letters
    w/Edward Heyman
Mad About You
    w/Ned Washington
My Foolish Heart
    w/Ned Washington
My Love
    w/Ned Washington
Stella By Starlight
    w/Ned Washington
Street Of Dreams
    w/Sam M. Lewis
Sweet Madness
    w/Ned Washington
Sweet Sue (Just You)
    w/Will J. Harris
When I Fall In Love
    w/Edward Heyman
Written On The Wind
    w/Sammy Cahn

YRADIER, SEBASTIAN
1809-1865, Spanish
w&m/Sebastian Yradier
La Paloma (The Dove)

ZAMECNIK, J.C.
1872-1953, American
m/J.C. Zamecnick
w/Harry D. Kerr
Neapolitan Nights (1925)

ZANETIS, ALEX
American
w&m/Alex Zanetis
Backtrack
    in co w/Faron Young

Guilty
If The Back Door Could Talk
    in co w/Grady Martin
I'm Gonna Change Everything
I'm Saving My Love

ZAPPA, FRANK
1940, American
w&m/Frank Zappa
I Don't Want To Get Drafted
  (1980)
Dancing Fool
Film score:
200 Motels (1972)

ZARET, HY
1907, American
w/Hy Zaret
It All Comes Back To Me Now
    m/Joan Whitney, Alex Kramer
Lass With The Delicate Air
    m/Lou Singer
My Sister And I
    m/Joan Whitney, Alex Kramer
One Meat Ball
    m/Lou Singer
Unchained Melody
    m/Alex North

ZARITSKY, BERNARD
1924, American
w&m/Bernard Zaritsky
Little White Duck, The

ZAWINUL, JOSEF (JOE)
1938, Austrian/American
m/Joe Zawinul
American Tango
Black Thorn Rose
Dr. Honoris Causa
Gibralter In A Silent Way
Jungle Book
Mercy, Mercy, Mercy (1967)
Nubian Sundance
Orange Lady
Remark You Made, A

ZEVON, WARREN
1947, American
w&m/Warren Zevon
Carmelita
Empty Handed Heart
Poor, Poor Pitiful Me
Werewolves Of London
    in co w/Leroy P. Marinell, Robert
    Wachtel
Wild Age

BEST-KNOWN
CLASSICAL MUSIC
COMPOSERS

FROM ANTIQUITY TO 1980

INCLUDING
NATIONALITIES, YEARS OF BIRTH
AND/OR DEATH AND THE
PRINCIPAL WORKS
OF THE MAJOR 20TH CENTURY COMPOSERS
AND
PRE-20TH CENTURY COMPOSERS

In Alphabetical Order
PART I - From Antiquity to 1900
PART II - 20th Century (1900 - 1980)

BEST-KNOWN CLASSICAL MUSIC COMPOSERS

PART ONE

FROM ANTIQUITY TO 1900

404

ABEL, CARL FRIEDRICH
1723-1787, German
Principal Works - Symphonies and Chamber music; Pasticcios: *Love In A Village, Berenice;* Sonatas for Harpsichord.

ABT, FRANZ
1819-1885, German
Principal Works - Operas, Cantatas, Songs *(Wenn Die Schwalben Heimwarts Zieh'n).*

ADAM, ADOLPHE-CHARLES
1803-1856, French
Principal Works - Comic Opera: *If I Were King; The Postillion Of Longjumeau;* Ballet: *Giselle;* Song: *Cantique de Noel* (Christmas Song).

AGAZZARI, AGOSTINO
1578-1640, Italian
Principal Works - Masses and Motets; Madrigals and Drama (Eumelio); Figured Bass: *Del Sonare Sopra Il Basso.*

AGRICOLA, ALEXANDER
1446-1506, Flemish
Principal Works - Masses, Chansons, Motets.

AGRICOLA, JOHANN FRIEDRICH
1720-1774, German
Principal Works - Operas, organ and Piano Pieces.

AICHINGER, GREGOR
1564-1628, German
Principal Works - Masses And Sacred Chorals

ALBÉNIZ, ISAAC
1860-1909, Spanish
Principal Works- Opera: *The Magic Opal, Enrico Clifford, Pepita Jiménez, Merlin;* Rhapsody: *Catalonia;* Piano: *Iberia* (cycle); *San Antonio de la Florida;* Piano Concerto and other works including *Navarra; Cantos de Espana; Espana; Recuerdof de Viaje; Suite Espanola; Torre Bermeja, Rapsodia Espana.*

ALBERT, EUGÈNE D'
1864-1932, Scottish/German
Principal Works - Opera: *Die Abreise,* 1898, *Tiefland,* 1903, *Die Toten Augen,* 1916; Choral: *Der Mensch Und Das Leben;* Orchestral and Piano Pieces; Songs.

ALKAN, CHARLES-HENRI VALENTIN
1813-1888, French
Principal Works - Piano *Le Chemin de fer; L'incendie au village prochain;* etudes, concertos, chamber pieces.

ALLEGRI, GREGORIO
1582-1652, Italian
Principal Works - Sacred Masses, Motets; *Misserere* for mine voices.

ANERIO, FELICE
1560-1614, Italian
Principal Works - Sacred Chorals; Madrigals

ANERIO, GIOVANNI
1567-1630, Italian
Principal Works - Sacred Motets, Masses; Madrigals.

ANFOSSI, PASQUALE
1727-1797, Italian
Principal Works - Operas: *L'incognita perseguitata* (1773), *Le gelosie fortunate* (1786)

ANGLEBERT, JEAN-HENRI D'
1628-1691, French
Principal Works - *Folies d'Espagne* for harpsichord; *Pieces de clavecin.*

ANIMUCCIA, GIOVANNI
1514-1571, Italian
Principal Works - Masses, Madrigals, Magnificats

ANTES, JOHN
1740-1811, American
Principal Works - String Trios, Anthems

ARAJA, FRANCESCO
1709-1770, Italian
Principal Works - Operas: *Lo Matremmonejo pe'vennetta* (1729); *La forza dell'amore e dell'odio* (1734); *Cefal i Prokris* (1755).

ARCADELT, JACOB
1514-1568, Flemish
Principal Works - Motets, Masses, Madrigals

ARDITI, LUIGI
1822-1903, Italian
Principal Work - *Il Bacio (The Kiss).*

ARENSKY, ANTON STEPANOVICH
1861-1906, Russian
Principal Works - Piano Trio, D minor, Op. 32; Serenade, G major, Op. 30, No. 2 for violin and piano; Suite, Op. 15: *Romance, Waltz, Scherzo* for 2 pianos; Variations on a Theme Of Tchaikovsky for strings.

ARIOSTI, ATTILIO
1666-1740, Spanish
Principal Works - Operas, oratorios, Cantatas.

ARNE, MICHAEL
1740-1786, English
Principal Works - Operas: *Hymen* (1764); *Cymon (1767), The Choice Of Harlequin* (1781).

ARNE, THOMAS AUGUSTINE
1710-1778, English
Principal Works - Operas: *Rosamund, Opera Of Operas, Dido and Aenas, Zara, Comus, Alfred,* a masque including *"Rule Britannia"; The Judgment Of Paris, Eliza, Britannia, Artaxerxes, Olimpiade;* Oratorio: *Abel;* Pasticcio: *Love In A Village.*

ARNOLD, SAMUEL
1740-1802, English
Principal Works - Pasticcio: *The Maid Of The Mill* (1765); Oratorio: *The Prodigal Son* (1773).

ARRIAGA, JUAN CRISOSTOMO ANTONIO
1806-1826, Spanish
Principal Works - Symphony, string quartets and piano pieces; Opera: *Los esclavos felices* (1819).

ASIOLI, BONIFAZIO
1769-1832, Italian
Principal Works - Operas including *Cinna* (1793); Cantatas, motets, Masses; Oratorio: *Giacobbe in Galaad.*

ASTORGA, EMANUELE GIOACCHINO CESARE RINCON D'
1680-1757, Italian
Principal Works - Operas: *La moglie nemica* (1698); *Amor tirannico,* (1710); *Dafni* (1709); chamber pieces; sacred music.

ATTWOOD, THOMAS
1765-1838, English
Principal Works - Sacred Organ pieces; songs.

AUBER, DANIEL
1782-1871, French
Principal Works - Operas: *Masaniello* (1828); *Fra Diavolo* (1830); *The Bronze Horse* (1835); *The Black Domino* (1837); *The Crown Diamonds* (1841); *Manon Lescaut* (1856).

AUBERT, JACQUES
1689-1753, French
Principal Works - Violin and Bass Concertos.

AUDRAN, EDMOND
1842-1901, French
Principal Works - Many Operettas including *La Mascotte* (1880)

AVISON, CHARLES
1709-1790, English
Principal Works - Organ Concertos, Sonatas.

BACH, JOHANN CHRISTIAN
1735-1782, German
Principal Works - Operas including *Orione* (1763), *Lucio Silla* (1776); Symphonies and Chamber Music.

BACH, JOHANN CHRISTOPH
1642-1703, German
Principal Works - Motets, Cantatas, Fugues, Organ Pieces.

BACH, JOHANN CHRISTOPH FRIEDRICH
1732-1795, German
Principal Works - Sacred and secular music; Cantata: *Die Amerikanerin* (1776): Oratorios, Symphonies, Concertos; Songs.

BACH, JOHANN SEBASTIAN
1685-1750, German
Principal Works - **Organ**: *Five Fantasies in Bm: C: Cm: Gm; and Fugue in A minor; Fugues in Cm: D: G; Four Preludes in Am: C: C: G; Four Preludes and Fugues in Am: C: Cm: Em (Short); Toccata and Fugue in E; Variations on Chorales (Partitas); 1) "Christ, der du bist der helle Tag", 2) "O Gott, du frommer Gott", 3) "Sei gegrusset, Jesu gütig", "Alla breve pro organo pleno" in D; Four organ concertos (after Vivaldi and others) in Am: C: C:G; Two Fantasies and Fugues in Cm: Gm; Fantasy in C minor; Four Fugues in Bm: Cm: G "Jig": Gm; "Passacaglia" in C minor; "Pastorale" in F; Nine Preludes and Fugues in A: Am (Great): C: Cm (Great): D: Fm: G (Great): Gm; Eight Short Preludes and Fugues in C: Dm: Em: F: G: Gm: Am: B flat; Four Toccatas and Fugues in C: Dm (Dorian): Dm: F; Three Trios in Cm: Dm: F (Aria); Six sonatas (trios) in E flat: Cm: Dm: Em: C: G; Schübler's Book; "Canzona" in D Minor; Orgelbüchlein.* **Clavier:** *Fantasy in C minor; Fantasy (on a Rondo) in C minor; Fughetta in C minor; Five Fugues in C: Cm: Dm: Dm: Em; Two Preludes (Fantasies) in Am: Cm; Four Preludes and Fughettas in Dm: Em: F: G; Prelude and Fugue in A minor; Sonata in A minor (one movement); Five Toccatas in D: Dm: Em: G: Gm; Sonata in D; Fantasy in G minor; Fantasy (Prelude) in A minor; Five Fugues in A: A: A (on a theme by Albinoni): Am: Bm; Suite in A minor; Suite in E flat; Suite ("Ouverture") in F; "Canzona" in D minor; Orgelbüchlein; Fantasy and Fugue in A minor; Twelve Little Preludes; Prelude and Fugue in A minor; Six Preludes for Beginners; Suite in D; Two Toccatas in C minor; F sharp minor; Clavierbüchlein vor Wilhelm Friedemann Bach; Chromatic Fantasy and Fugue, in D minor; Clavierbüchlein vor Anna Magdalena Bachin; Six Suites (French) in Dm, Cm, Bm, E flat, G, E; The Well-Tempered Clavier, Book I; "Notenbuch vor Anna Magdalena Bachin"; Six Suites (English) in A; Am; Gm; F; Em; Dm; Six Partitas for clavier, in B flat: Cm: Am: D: G; Partita (Ouverture) in B minor; Fantasy (with unfinished Fugue) in C minor; Clavier Duets (two-part pieces for one player); Aria with thirty variations, "Goldberg Variations" for double-keyboard harpsichord; The Well-Tempered Clavier, Book II.*
Sonatas: Sonata In G for violin and continuo; Three sonatas for flute and continuo: No. 1 in C; No. 2 in E Minor, No. 3 in E; Sonata in C for two violins and continuo; Sonata in C minor for flute, violin and continuo; Sonata in E minor for violin and continuo; Sonata in C for violin and continuo; Sonata in G for flute, violin and continuo; Sonata in G for two flutes and continuo; Three Sonatas for clavier and flute: No. 1 in B minor, No. 2 in D, No. 3 in G minor; Three Sonatas for clavier and viola da gamba: No. 1 in G, No. 2 in D, No. 3 in G minor; Six Sonatas for clavier and violin: No. 1 in B minor, No. 2 in A, No. 3 in E, No. 4 in C minor, No. 5 in F minor and No. 6 in G; Six Sonatas (Partitas) for solo violin; No. 1 in G minor, No. 2 in A minor, No. 3 in C, No. 4 in B minor, No. 5 in D minor, No. 6 in E; Six Suites (Sonatas) for solo cello, No. 1 in G., No. 2 in D minor, No. 3 in C, No. 4 in E flat, No. 5 in C minor, No. 6 in D.
Concertos: The Brandenburg Concerti, No. 1 in F for violino piccolo, three oboes, two horns, bassoon, strings and continuo; No. 2 in F for violin, flute, oboe, trumpet, strings, and continuo; No. 3 in G for strings and continuo; No. 4 in G for violin, two flutes, strings and continuo; No. 5 in D for clavier, violin, flute, strings and continuo; No. 6 in B flat for strings (without violins and continuo); Concerto in C for two claviers with strings; Concerto in C minor for two claviers with strings; identical to the concerto for two violins in D minor; Concerto in C minor for two claviers with strings; Clavier Concerto in A with strings (& continuo); Clavier Concerto in D with strings (& continuo) (identical to violin concerto in E); Clavier Concerto in D minor with strings (& continuo) (probably originally a violin concerto); Clavier Concerto in E with strings (& continuo); Clavier Concerto in F with two flutes, strings (& continuo) (identical to Brandenburg Concerto No. 4 in G); Clavier Concerto in F minor with strings (& continuo); Clavier Concerto in G minor with strings (& continuo) (same as violin concerto in A minor); Concerto in A minor for clavier, flute and violin with strings; Concerto in C for three claviers with strings; Concerto in D minor for three claviers with strings; Concerto in A minor for four claviers with strings; Concerto in the Italian Style, for clavier, in F.
Choral: Magnificat in D, for solo voices, chorus, orchestra and continuo; Motet: "Jesu, meine Freunde", for five-part chorus; Passion according to St. John for soprano, contralto, tenor and bass soli, chorus, organ & continuo; Sanctus in D, for eight-part chorus, orchestra and organ; Variations on Chorale (Partita) "Vom Himmel hoch da Komm' ich her"; Five songs from Anna Magdalena Bach's "Notenbuch"; *Quodlibet,* for four voices and continuo; Motet: "Der Geist hilft unser Schwachheit auf", for eight-part chorus with accompaniment; **Psalms:** "Lobet den

Herrn, alle Heiden", for four-part chorus; "Singet dem Herrn ein neues Lied", for eight-part chorus.

Fugue, Suites (Overtures), Flute/Violin: *The Art of Fugue,* for unspecified instruments—Contrapunctus I—XIV; Four Canons; Two Fugues for two keyboards; Unfinished Fugue on three subjects; Overtures (Suites): in C for woodwind, strings (& continuo); in B minor for flute, strings (& continuo); in D for oboes, bassoons, trumpets, timpani, strings (& continuo); in D for oboes, bassoons, trumpets, timpani, strings (& continuo).

Sacred: Passion according to St. Matthew, for soprano, contralto, tenor and bass soli, double chorus, double orchestra and continuo; Mass in B minor for two sopranos, contralto, tenor, bass, chorus, orchestra and continuo; Christmas Oratorio (six cantatas) for solo voices, chorus, orchestra and organ; Easter Oratorio for solo voices, chorus, orchestra and organ; Lutheran Masses for solo voices, chorus, orchestra and organ: No. 1 in F: No. 2 in Gm: No. 3 in Am: No. 4 in G; Ascension Oratorio (Cantata No. 11 "Lobet Gott in seinen Reichen") (1735-36); Catechism Preludes (Clavierübung, Vol. III).

BACH, KARL PHILIPP EMANUEL
1714-1788, German
Principal Works - Symphonies, Concertos; Many oratorios, cantatas.

BACH, WILHELM FRIEDEMANN
1710-1784, German
Principal Works - Many organ pieces; Cantatas; Concertos, Sonatas for trio; Symphonies.

BACKER-GRONDAHL, AGATHE
1847-1907, Norweigan
Principal Works - Piano pieces, songs.

BAILLOT, PIERRE
1771-1842, French
Principal Works - Violin concertos and pieces.

BAKFARK, VALENTIN
1507-1576, Hungarian
Principal Works - Music for Lute.

BALAKIREV, MILY ALEXEYEVITCH
1837-1910, Russian
Principal Works - Piano: *Islamey* (1869); Symphonic: *Tamara* (1867); *Russia:* Second overture; on Russian themes (1864).

BALBASTRE, CLAUDE
1727-1799, French
Principal Works - Organ, harpsichord, piano pieces.

BALFE, MICHAEL WILLIAM
1808-1870, Irish
Principal Works - Opera: *The Bohemian Girl* (1843).

BANCHIERI, ADRIANO
1568-1634, Italian
Principal Works - Dramas: *La Pazzia Senile* (1598); Masses, Chorals, figured bass pieces.

BANISTER, JOHN
1670-1679, English
Principal Works - Music for violin.

BARBIERI, FRANCISCO ASENJO
1823-1894, Spanish
Principal Works - Comic Operas (Zarzuelas) including *"The Little Barber of Lavapies".*

BARNBY, JOSEPH
1838-1896, English
Principal Works - Part songs including "Sweet And Low".

BARNETT, JOHN
1802-1890, English
Principal Works - Symphony, operettas, operas including "The Mountain Sylph".

BARSANTI, FRANCESCO
1690-1776, Italian
Principal Works - Sonatas for violins and bass; flute solos with bass; concerti grossi.

BASSANI, GIOVANNI BATTISTA
1657-1716, Italian
Principal Works - Masses, motets, oratorios.

BATESON, THOMAS
1570-1630, English
Principal Works - Various madrigals.

BATTEN, ADRIAN
1591-1637, English
Principal Works - Sacred organ and choral pieces; Anthems including *Hear My Prayer O Lord* and *Out Of The Deep.*

BAZZINI, ANTONIO
1818-1897, Italian
Principal Works - Opera, string quartets and *La Ronde des Lutins (Dance Of The Goblins)* for violin and piano.

BEETHOVEN, LUDWIG VAN
1770-1827, German
Principal Works - Opera: *Fidelio,* Op. 72, 2 Acts (1805; 1806; 1814); **Incidental Music:** *The Creatures of Prometheus,* Op. 43, ballet (1801); *Egmont,* Op. 84 (1810), Overture, Entr'acte Nos. 1-3, *Clärchen's Death; Ruins of Athens,* Op. 113 (1811), Overture, *Dervish Chorus, Turkish March;* **Orchestral: Symphonies** — No. 1, C major, Op. 21 (1800); No. 2, D major, Op. 36 (1802); No. 3, E flat major, Op. 55 (1804) *(Eroica);* No. 4, B flat major, Op. 60 (1806); No. 5, C minor, Op. 67 (1805) *(Fate);* No. 6, F major, Op. 68 (1809) *(Pastoral);* No. 7, A major, Op. 92 (1812); No. 8, F major, Op. 93 (1812); No. 9, D minor, Op. 125 (1817-23) *(Choral);* Battle Symphony *(Wellington's Victory),* Op. 91 (1813).

Overtures — *Coriolanus,* Op. 62 (1807); *Consecration of the House,* Op. 124 (1822); *Fidelio,* Op. 72b (1814); *Leonora Overtures* (originally written for *Fidelio),* No. 1, Op. 138 (1807), No. 2, Op. 72a (1805), No. 3, Op. 72a (1806).

Dances — Contra-Dances (1803); 12 German Dances (1795).

Concertos - Piano: No. 1, C major, Op. 15 (published 1801); No. 2, B flat major, Op. 19 (1795); No. 3, C minor, Op. 37 (1800); No. 4, G major, Op. 58 (1805); No. 5, E flat major, Op. 73 (1809) *(Emperor);* Violin: Violin Concerto, D major, Op. 61 (1806); *Romances* for violin and orchestra, No. 1, G major, Op. 40 (1803), No. 2, F major, Op. 50 (1805); Triple Concerto in C major, Op. 56, for piano, violin, and cello (1804).

Chamber Music: Strings and Wind Instruments - Septet, E flat major, Op. 20 (1799); **Piano and Strings** - 3 Trios, Op. 1 (1794); 2 Trios, Op. 70 (1808); B flat major, Op. 97 (1811) *(Archduke).* **String Quartets** - 6 Quartets,

Op. 18; No. 1, F major (1798), No. 2, G major (1798), No. 3, D major (1798), No. 4, C minor (1799), No. 5, A major (1799), No. 6, B flat major (1799); 3 Quartets, Op. 59 (1806) *(Rasoumovsky),* No. 1, F major, No. 2, E minor, No. 3, C major; E flat major, Op. 74 (1809) *(Harp);* F minor, Op. 95 (1810); E flat major, Op. 127 (1824); B flat major, Op. 130 (1825); C sharp minor, Op. 131 (1826); A minor, Op. 132 (1825); Grosse Fuge, B flat major, Op. 133 (1825); F major, Op. 135 (1826).

Violin and Piano (Sonatas) - 3 Sonatas, Op. 12 (1798), No. 1, D major, No. 2, A major, No. 3, E flat major; A minor, Op. 23 (1800); F major, Op. 24 (1801) *(Spring);* 3 Sonatas, Op. 30 (1802); No. 1, A major, No. 2, C minor, No. 3, G major; A major, Op. 47 (1802) *(Kreutzer);* G major, Op. 96 (1812).

Cello and Piano - 2 Sonatas, Op. 5 (1796), No. 1, F major, No. 2, G major; Sonata in A major, Op. 69 (1809); 2 Sonatas, Op. 102 (1815), No. 1, C major, No. 2, D major; 12 Variations on Handel's *See, the Conquering Hero Comes* (1797); 12 Variations on *Ein Mädchen,* Op. 66 (1797); 12 Variations on *Bei Männern* (1801).

Piano: Sonatas - C minor, Op. 13 (1799) *(Pathêtique);* A flat major, Op. 26 (1802); C sharp minor, Op. 27, No. 2 (1802) *(Moonlight);* D major, Op. 28 (1801) *(Pastoral);* D minor, Op. 31, No. 2 (1802) *(Tempest);* E flat major, Op. 31, No. 3; C major, Op. 53 (1803-04) *(Waldstein);* F minor, Op. 57 (1806) *(Appassionata);* E flat major, Op. 81a (1811) *Les Adieux);* A major, Op. 101 (1816); B flat major, Op. 106 (1818-19) *(Hammerklavier);* E major, Op. 109 (1820); A flat major, Op. 110 (1821); C minor, Op. 111 (1822).

Variations - Variations on *Nel cor piu* by Paisiello (1795); F major, Op. 34 (1802); E flat, Op. 35 (1802) *(Eroica);* C minor (1806-07); C major, Op. 120 (1823) *(Diabelli).*

Other Works: *Für Elise* (Bagatelle in A minor); 8 Ecossaises in E flat major; Rondo a capriccio *(Rage over a lost penny),* Op. 129; *Andante Favori* in F major (1804); 7 Bagatelles, Op. 33 (1782-1802); 13 Bagatelles, Op. 119 (1821-22); 6 Bagatelles, Op. 126 (1823); Minuet in G (1796).

Vocal: Choral - *Fantasia,* for piano, orchestra and chorus, Op. 80 (1808); Mass, C major, Op, 86 (1807); Mass, D major, Op. 123 *(Missa Solemnis)* (1818-23).

Songs - *Ah! perfido,* Op. 65 (1796); *Adelaide,* Op. 46 (Matthisson) (1795); *An die ferne Geliebte,* Op. 98, cycle (1816); *Andenken* (Matthisson) (1810); *Die Ehre Gottes,* Op. 48, No. 4 (Gellert) (1803); *Ich liebe dich* (Herrosen) (1803); *In questa tomba oscura* (Carpani) 1807.

BERLIOZ, Hector
1803-1869, French

Principal Works - Operas: *Benvenuto Cellini* (1838); *Les Troyens* (1856-59); *(The Siege of Troy) (The Trojans at Carthage); Beatrice and Benedict* (1860-62). Orchestral: *King Lear* Overture (1831); *Fantastic symphony* (1831); *Harold in Italy,* with viola obbligato (1834); *Funeral and Triumphal Symphony* (1840) for military band, string orchestra and chorus ad lib; *Roman Carnival* Overture (1844). Choral: *Requiem* (1837); *Romeo and Juliet* (1838-39); *The Damnation of Faust* (1846); *L'Enfance du Christ* (1850-54); *Te Deum* (1849-50). Vocal: *Les Nuits d'Ete* (1834).

BISHOP, SIR HENRY ROWLEY
1786-1855, English

Principal Works - Opera: *Clari* (includes *Home Sweet Home*) Words: John Howard Payne.

BIZET, GEORGES
Principal Works - Opera: *The Pearl Fishers; The Fair Maid of Perth; Carmen; Don Procopio; La Petresse; Ivan The Terrible; Djarmileh; Le Docteur Miracle* (operetta); Piano: *Chasse Fantastique; Variations Chromatiques; Marine; Trois esquisses musicales;* Orchestral: *Symphony in C major; L'Arlesienne; Marche Funebre; Vasco da Gama; Petite Suite d'Orchestre ; Patrie,* Overture; *Jeux d'enfants,* 12 piano duets of which 5 were expanded into orchestral suites; *Clovis et Clothilde,* Cantata.

BOIELDIEU, FRANCOIS-ADRIEN
1775-1834, French

Principal Works - Operas: *The Caliph of Bagdad* (1800); *La Dame Blanche* (1825).

BORODIN, ALEXANDER
Principal Works - Opera: *Prince Igor* (completed and revised by Rimsky-Korsakov and Glazunov, 1890; containing the "Polovtzian Dances"); Bogatyry (1867); Orchestral: Symphony No. 2, B minor (1869-76); *In the Steppes of Central Asia* (1885); Chamber Music: Serenade from Petite Suite (1885); String Quartet No. 2, in D major (1881-87) Nocturne.

BOTTESINI, GIOVANNI
1821-1889, Italian

Principal Works - Opera: Ali Baba (1871); Erd e Leandro (1879); Cristoforo Colombo (1847); Oratorio: The Garden of Olivet (1887).

BOYCE, WILLIAM
1711-1779, English

Principal Works - (1750) Eight Symphonies in Eight Parts; (1758) Ode to the New Year; (1769) Ode to the King's Birthday; (1772) Ode to the New Year; Ballad: Heart of Oak (1759)

BRAHMS, JOHANNES
1833-1897, German

Principal Works - Orchestral: Symphonies - No. 1, C minor, Op. 68 (1876); No. 2, D major, Op. 73 (1877); No. 3, F major, Op. 90 (1883); No. 4, E minor, Op. 98 (1884-85); Variations on a Theme of Haydn, Op. 56a (1873); **Overture** - *Academic Festival Overture,* Op. 80 (1880); *Tragic Overture,* Op. 81 (1880-81); **Piano Concertos** - No. 1, D minor, Op. 15 (1854); No. 2, B flat major, Op. 83 (1881); **Violin Concerto** - D major, Op. 77 (1878); **Violin, Cello, and Orchestra** - Double Concerto in A minor, Op. 102 (1887).

Chamber Music: Clarinet and Strings - Quintet, B minor, Op. 115 (1891); **Piano and Strings** - Quintet, F minor, Op. 34 (1864); Quartet No. 1, G. minor, Op. 25 (1861); Quartet No. 2, A major, Op. 26 (1862); Quartet No. 3, C minor, Op. 60 (1855-75); Trio No. 1, B major, Op. 8 (1853-54); Trio No. 2, C major, Op. 87 (1880-82); Trio No 3 Piano - Sonata No. 1, G major, Op. 78 (1878-79); Sonata No. 2, A major, Op. 100 (1886); Sonata No. 3, D minor, Op. 108 (1886-88); Sonatensatz, C minor (1853); **Cello and Piano** - Sonata No. 1, F minor, Op. 120 (1894); Sonata No. 2, E flat major, Op. 120 (1894).

PIANO: Sonatas: *No. 1, C major Op. 1* (1852-53); *No. 2, F sharp minor, Op. 2* (1852); *No. 3, F. minor, Op. 5* (1853); Ballads: *D minor, Op. 10, No. 1* (1854), *Edward; G minor, Op. 118, No. 3* (1892); Capriccios: *B minor, Op. 76, No. 2* (1871-78); Intermezzos: *A flat, Op. 76, No. 3* (1871-78); *A minor, Op. 116, No. 2* (1892); *E major, Op. 116, No. 4*

(1892);*E flat major, Op. 117, No. 1* (1892); *B flat minor, Op. 117, No. 2* (1892); *A major, Op. 118, No. 2* (1892); *C major, Op. 119, No. 3* (1892);Rhapsodies: *B minor, Op. 79, No. 1* (1879);*G minor, Op. 79, No. 2* (1879);*E flat major, Op. 119, No. 4* (1892); Variations: *On a Theme of Handel, Op 24* (1861)' *On a Theme of Paganini, Op. 35* (1862-63); *On a Theme of Haydn for two pianos, Op. 56b* (1873); Waltzes: *Op. 39* (Original piano duet) (1865).

VOCAL: *Alto Rhapsody, Op. 53 (alto, male choir, and orchestra)* (1869); *Ein deutsches Requiem, Op. 45* (1861-67);*Liebeslieder Waltzer, Op. 52* (1868-69) (piano duet and vocal quartet); *Gypsy Songs (Zigeunerlieder), Op. 103* (1887);*An die Nachtigall* (Hölty), *Op. 46, No. 4; Botschaft* (Daumer) *Op. 47, No. 1; Wiegenlied (Cradle Song), Op. 49, No. 4; Vier ernste Gesänge (Four Serious Songs), Op. 121; Feldeinsamkeit* (Allmer), *Op. 86, No. 2; Der Gang zum Liebchen* (Wenzig), *Op. 48, No. 1;* Two Songs for Alto, Viola and Piano, *Op. 91; Immer leiser wird mein Schlummer, Op. 105, No. 2; Die Mainacht* (Hölty), *Op. 43, No. 2; Meine Liebe is grün* (F. Schumann), *Op. 63; Minnelied* (Hölty) *Op. 71, No. 5; Nicht mehr zu dir zu gehen* (Daumer), *Op. 32, No. 2; O wusst' ich doch den Weg zuruck* (Groth) *Op. 63; Sandmännchen* (The Little Sandman); *Sapphische Ode* (Scmidt) *Op. 94, No. 4;Der Schmied* (Uhland) *Op. 19, No. 4;Sonntag* (Uhland) *Op. 47, No. 3;Ständchen* (Kugler) *Op. 106, No. 1; Vergebliches Ständchen* (Zuccalmaglio) *Op. 84, No. 4; Von ewiger Liebe* (Wenzig) *Op. 43, No. 1;Wie bist du, meine Königin* (Daumer) *Op. 32, No. 9;Wie Melodien zieht es mir* (Groth) *Op. 105. No. 1.*

BRUCH , MAX
1838-1920, German

Principal Works - *Violin Concerto in G. Minor, Op. 26; Kol Nidrei, Op. 47* (cello).

BRUCKNER, ANTON
1824-1896, Austrian

Principal Works - Orchestral: Symphonies - No. 3, D minor (1873); No. 4, E flat major (1874), *Romantic;* No. 5, B flat major (1875-78); No. 6, A major (1879-81); No. 7, E major (1881-83); No. 8, C minor (1885-86); No. 9, D minor (unfinished) (1891-96); Overture, G minor (1863).
Chamber Music: String Quintet, F major (1879).
Choral: Mass No. 2, E minor (1866); Mass No. 3, F minor (1868-1890); *Ave Maria* (1885); Requiem, D minor (1849); *Te Deum* (1885).

BRUNEAU, ALFRED (LOUIS-CHARLES-BONAVENTURE)
1857-1937, French

Principal Works - Operas: *Messidor* (1897); *L'Ouragan* (1901); *L'enfant roi* (1905); *L'Attaque du Moulin* (1893); Ballet: Les Bacchantes (1912).

BUSONI, FERRUCIO
1866-1924, Italian

Principal Works - Dramatic: *Doktor Faust;Arlecchino* (Harlequin); Opera: *Die Brautwahl:.Turandot.*

BYRD, WILLIAM
1543-1623, English

Principal Works - Harpsichord (Virginal): *The Bells (Fitzwilliam Virginal Book 69);* Fantasia: *The Leaves Be Green; The Earl of Salisbury Pavanne; La Volta (Fitzwilliam Virginal Book 155).*
Choral - Masses: *Five Voices; Four Voices; Three Voices.*
Motets: *Ave, verum corpus; Justorum animae.* **Services:** *The Great Service; The Short Service.*

CHABRIER, EMMANUEL
1841-1894, French

Principal Works - Orch: *Espana* (Rhapsody); Opera: *Le Roi Malgré Lui ; Gwendoline ; Marche Joyeuse.*

CHARPENTIER, GUSTAVE
1860-1956, French

Principal Works - Opera: *Louise;* Orchestral suite: *Impressions d'Italie.*

CHERUBINI, LUIGI
1760-1842, Italian

Principal Works - Operas: *Medea,* 3 Acts (1797); *The Portuguese Inn (L'Osteria Portugese)* (1789); *The Water Carrier (Les Deux Journées)* (1800); *Anacreon* (1803). Orchestral: Symphony in D major (1815); Choral: Mass in C major; Requiem in C minor.

CHOPIN, FREDERIC
1810-1849, Polish

Principal Works - Orchestral: Piano Concertos: No. 1, E minor, Op. 11 (1830); No. 2, F minor, Op. 21 (1829); Variations on *Là ci darem la mano* (1827); Cello and Piano: Introduction and Polonaise, C major, Op. 3 (1833); Sonata, G minor, Op. 65 (1846); Piano: Ballades (4): No. 1, G minor, Op. 23 (1831-35), No. 2, F major, Op. 38 (1836-39), No. 3, A flat major, Op. 47 (1840-41), No. 4, F minor, Op. 52 (1842); *Barcarolle,* F sharp major, Op. 60 (1845); *Berceuse* D flat major, Op. 57 (1843); *Ecossaises,* Op. 72, No. 3 (1826); Etudes (12), Op. 10 (1828-33): No. 1, C major; No. 3, E major; No. 4, C sharp minor; No. 5, G flat major, *Black Keys;* No. 6, E flat minor; No. 8, F major; No. 10, A flat major; No. 11, E flat major; No. 12, C minor, *Revolutionary .*Etudes (12), Op. 25 (1831-37): No. 1, A flat major; No. 2, F minor; No. 7, C sharp minor; No. 9, G flat major; No. 11, A minor, *Winter Wind;* No. 12, C minor. Etudes (3 Nouvelles, 1839): No. 1, F minor; No. 2, A flat major; Impromptus (4): No. 1, A flat major, Op. 29 (1837); No. 2, F sharp major, Op. 36 (1839); No. 4, C sharp minor, Op. 66 (1834);*Fantaisie-Impromptu,* Mazurkas (58): No. 5, B flat major, Op. 7, No. 1 (1830); No. 7, F minor, Op. 7, No. 3 (1830); No. 13, A minor, Op. 17, No. 4 (1833); No. 21, C sharp minor, Op. 30, No. 4 (1837); No. 23, D major, Op. 33, No. 2 (1837-38); No. 32, C sharp minor, Op. 50, No. 3 (1841); No. 41, C sharp minor, Op. 63, No. 3 (1846); No. 45, A minor, Op. 67, No. 4 (1846); No. 47, A minor, Op. 68, No. 2 (1827); No. 49, F minor, Op. 68, No. 4 (1849); Nocturnes (20): No. 2, E flat major, Op. 9, No. 2 (1831); No. 5, F sharp major, Op. 15, No. 2 (1830-33); No. 6, G. minor, Op. 15, No. 3 (1830-33); No. 7, C sharp minor, Op. 27, No. 1 (1834-35); No. 8, D flat major, Op. 32, No. 1 (1836-37); No. 13, C minor, Op. 48, No. 1 (1841);No. 20, C sharp minor .Polonaises (12): No. 3, A major, Op. 40, No. 1 (1838-40); No. 5, F sharp minor, Op. 44 (1840-41); No. 6, A flat major, Op. 53 (1842); No. 7, A flat major, Op. 61 (1845) .Preludes (24), Op. 28 (1836-39): No. 3, G major; No. 4, E minor; No. 6, B minor; No. 7, A major; No. 15, D flat major, *Raindrop;* No. 16, B flat minor; No. 20, C minor; No. 23, F major; No. 24, D minor; Rondo, C major, Op. 73 (2 pianos) (1828) .Scherzos (4): No. 1, B minor, Op. 20 (1831-32); No. 2, B flat minor, Op. 31 (1837); No. 3, C sharp minor, Op. 39 (1839); No. 4, E major, Op. 54 (1842). Sonatas (3): No. 1, C minor, Op. 4 (1827); No. 2, B flat minor, Op. 35 (1837-39); No. 3, B minor, Op. 58 (1844);

Tarantella, A flat major, Op. 43 (1841) .Waltzes (14): No. 1, E flat major, Op. 18, *Grande valse brillante;* No. 2, A flat major, Op. 34, No. 1, *Valse brillante;* No. 3, A minor, Op. 34, No. 2 (1831); No. 4, F major, Op. 34, No. 3 ((1838); No. 5, A flat major, Op. 42 (1840); No. 6, D flat major, Op. 64, No. 1 *Minute valse;* No. 7, C sharp minor, Op. 64, No. 2 ((1846-47); No. 8, A flat major, Op. 64, No. 3 (1846); No. 9, A flat major, Op. 69, No. 1 (1835), *"L'adieu";* No. 10, B minor, Op. 69, No. 2 (1835), No. 11, G flat major, Op. 70, No. 1 (1835); No. 12, F minor, Op. 70, No. 2 (1843); No. 13, D flat major, Op. 70, No. 3 (1820); No. 14, E minor. Songs: Polish Songs (17), Op. 74 (1829-47) - *The Maiden's Wish* (Witwicki), *My Joys* (Mickiewicz), *The Betrothal* (Witwicki), *Lithuanian Song.*

COLERIDGE-TAYLOR, SAMUEL
1875-1912, English
Principal Works - *Symphony in A minor; Hiawatha's Wedding Feast,* cantata (Longfellow); *Ballade in A minor,* orchestra; *Death of Minnehaha,* cantata (Longfellow); *Solemn Prelude; Hiawatha's Departure,* cantata (Longfellow); *The Blind Girl of Castel-Cuille; Toussaint l'ouverture,* concert overture; *Idyll; Meg Blane; The Atonement,* oratorio; Five Choral Ballads; *Kubla Khan; Bon-Bon* suite; *Endymion's Dream,* for chorus; *A Tale of Old Japan,* cantata; *Bamboula,* rhapsodic dance; Violin Concerto in G minor.

CORELLI, ARCANGELO
1653-1713, Italian
Principal Works - Strings and Harpsichord: 12 Concerti Grossi, Op. 6 (1714; posthumous); No. 8, G minor, *Christmas* Concerto. Violin and Harpsichord: 12 Sonatas, Op. 5 (1700), No. 1, D major, No. 3, C major, No. 12, D minor, *La Folia.*

COUPERIN, FRANCOIS
1668-1733, French
Principal Works - Chamber Music: *4 Concerts Royaux* (1722); *Les Goûts Réunis* (1724); No. 9, E major (*Il ritratto dell'amore); La Sultane,* Sonata; Overture and Allegro (arr. orch.); Harpsichord: *Les Barricades Mystérieuses; Le Carillon de Cythère; Le Dodo ou l'amour au berceau; Les Fastes de la Grande et Ancienne Ménêstrandise; Le Roissignol en amour* (with flute or recorder); *Soeur Monique; Le Tic-toc-choc ou les maillotins.*

CUI, CESAR ANTONOVICH
1835-1918, Russian
Principal Works - Scherzo for orchestra, Nos. 1 and 2; *The Caucasian Prisoner,* opera; Tarantella; *The Mandarin's Son,* opera; *William Ratcliffe,* opera; *Angelo,* opera; Marche Solenelle; *Suite Concertante,* for violin and orchestra; *Deux Morceaux,* for cello and orchestra; *Le Filibustier,* opera.

DAQUIN, LOUIS-CLAUDE
1694-1772, French
Principal Works - Harpsichord: *The Cuckoo;* Organ: *Noëls.*

DARGOMYZHSKY, ALEXANDER
1813-1869, Russian
Principal Works - Symphonic: *Russalka* (The Watersprite); *The Stone Guest.*

DAVID, FELICIEN
1810-1876, French
Principal Works - Symphonic: *Le Désert;* Opera comique: *La Perle du Brasil; Lalla Rookh; Herculanum.*

DEBUSSY, CLAUDE
1862-1918, French
Principal Works - Opera: *Pelléas et Mélisande* (1902); Orchestral: *Danses* (harp and strings) (1904) - *Danse sacré; Danse profane; Images: Ibéria* (1907); *La Mer* (1903-05); *Nocturnes* (1894-99); *Prélude à l'après-midi d'un faune* (1894); *Printemps,* Suite (chorus and orchestra) (1886-87); Rhapsody for Saxophone (1903); Rhapsody for Clarinet (1910); Chamber Music: String Quartet in G minor, Op. 10 (1893); *Petite Pièce,* in B flat major (clarinet and piano) (1910); *Syrinx,* for unaccompanied flute (1912); Sonatas: D minor (cello and piano) (1915); flute, viola harp (1916); G minor (violin and piano) (1917); Piano: *Deux Arabesques* (1888); *Suite Bergamasque* (1890-1905); *Prélude; Menuet; Clair de lune; Passepied .Pour le piano,* Suite (1901) - *Prélude; Sarabande; Toccata .Estampes* (1903) - *Pagodes; Soirée dans Grenade; Jardins sous la pluie .L'Isle joyeuse* (1904) . *Images* - (1905) *Reflets dans l'eau; Hommage à Rameau . Mouvements;* (1907) - *Cloches à travers les feuilles; Et la lune descend sur le temple qui fut; Poissons d'or . Children's Corner,* Suite (1908): *Doctor Gradus ad Parnassium; Jimbo's Lullaby (Berceuse des éléphants); Serenade for the Doll (Sérénade à la poupée); The Snow Is Dancing (La Neige danse); The Little Shepherd (Le petit Berger); Golliwog's Cake-walk .La plus que lente,* Valse (1910). Preludes: Book I (1910): *Danseuses de Delphes; Voiles; Le Vent dans la plaine; Les sons et les parfums tournent dans; l'air du soir; Les Collines d'Anacapri; Des Pas sur la neige; Ce qu'a vu le vent d'ouest; La Fille aux cheveux de lin; La Sérénade interrompue; La Cathédral engloutie; La Danse de Puck; Minstrels .Book II* (1910-13): *Brouillards; Feuilles mortes; La Puerta del Vino; Les Fées sont d'exquises danseuses; Bruyères; General Lavine-eccentric; La Terrasse des audiences au clair de lune; Ondine; Hommage à S. Pickwick, Esq., P.P.M.P.C.; Canope; Les Tierces alternées; Feux d'artifice .Etudes* (12) (1915); *Petite Suite* (1889), for two pianos (arranged for orchestra by Busser) *Enbateau; Cortege; Ballet;* **Vocal:** Cantatas: *L'Enfant Prodigue; La Damoiselle élue* (Rossetti) ; *Le Martyre de St. Sébastien* (d'Annunzio) (1911) .Songs: *Ariettes oubliées* (Verlaine) (1888-1903) - *Il pleure dans mon coeur; Aquarelles-Green; 3 Ballades de François Villon* (1910).; *Ballade des femmes de Paris; Beau Soir* (Bourget) 1878); *3 Chansons de Bilitis* (P. Louÿs) (1898) - *La Flûte de Pan; La Chevelure; Fêtes Galantes* (Verlaine).

DE KOVEN, REGINALD
1859-1920, American
Principal Works - Opera: *The Canterbury Pilgrims; Rip Van Winkle .* Operetta: *Robin Hood* (O Promise Me and Brown October Ale); *The Begum; Don Quixote; Rob Roy; The Highwayman; Foxy Quiller; The Little Duchess; Maid Marian.*

DE LARA, ISIDORE (COHEN)
1858-1935, French/English
Principal Works - Opera: *The Light Of Asia; Amy Robsart; Moina; Messalina; Sanza; Solea; Les Trois Masques; Les Trois Mousquetaires.*

DELIBES, LEO
1836-1891, French
Principal Works - Operas: *Le Roi l'a Dit* (1873); *Lakmé* (1883); *Le Roi s'amuse* (Victor Hugo).*Ballet La Source* (1866); *Coppélia* (1870); *Sylvia* (1876).Orchestral: *Naïla valse (Pas des fleurs)* (1867); Songs: Ariose: *Omer, ouvre-toi* (Sylvestre); *Bonjour, Suzon* (de Musset); Boléro: *Les filles de Cadiz....*(de Musset).

DELIUS, FREDERICK
1862-1934, English
Principal Works - Opera: *Irmelin* (1890-92); *Koanga* (1895-97); *A Village Romeo and Juliet* (1900-01), Intermezzo:*The walk to the Paradise Garden; Fennimore and Gerda* (1908-10); Incidental Music to *Hassan* (Flecker) (1920).Chorus With Orchestra: *Appalachia*, Variations (1902); *Sea Drift* (Whitman), with baritone (1903); *A Mass of Life* (Nietzsche), with solo voices (1904-05); *Songs of Sunset* (Symons), with solo voices (1906-07); *Arabesk* (Jacobsen), with baritone (1911); *A Song of the High Hills* (wordless) (1911-12); *Requiem* (Nietzsche), with solo voices (1914-16); *Songs of Farewell* (Whitman) (1930-32). Piano Concerto (1906); Violin and Cello Concerto (1915-16); Violin Concerto (1916); Cello Concerto (1921); *Caprice and Elegy* (cello) (1925).Orchestral: *Florida* Suite (1886); *Over the Hills and Far Away*, tone poem (1895); *Paris: the Song of a Great City*, Nocturne (1899); *Brigg Fair*, an English Rhapsody (1907); *In a Summer Garden*, Fantasy (1908); *On Hearing the First Cuckoo in Spring* (1919); *Summer Night on the River* (1912); *North Country Sketches* (1913-14); *Dance Rhapsody No. 2 (1916); Evyntyr* (1917); *A Song before Sunrise* (1918).

DITTERSDORF, KARL DITTERS VON
1739-1799, Austrian
Principal Works - Opera: *Doktor und Apoteker;* 12 Symphonies; *Ovid's Metamorphoses;* Violin pieces, 30 operas, choral works.

DONIZETTI, GAETANO
1797-1848, Italian
Principal Works - Opera: *Anna Bolena; L'Elisir d'Amore; Lucrezia Borgia; Lucia di Lammermoor; La Fille du Regiment; Les Martyrs; Linda de Charmonix; Don Pasquale; Maria di Rohan; Dom Sebastien; Il Duca d'Alba.*

DRIGO, RICCARDO
1846-1930
Principal Works - Ballet: *Harlequin's Millions* (includes Serenade); *Valse Bluette.*

DUKAS, PAUL
1865-1935, French
Principal Works - *Polyeucte*, overture; Symphony in C major; *The Sorcerer's Apprentice,* symphonic poem; Piano Sonata in E flat minor; Variations, Interlude and Finale on a Theme by Rameau, for piano; *Villanelle*, for horn and piano; *Ariadne and Bluebeard*, opera *(Ariane et Barbe-bleue); Prélude élégiaque,* for piano; Vocalise; *La Péri—Poeme danse,* for orchestra (possibly 1921); *La Plainte, au loin, du faune,* for piano; *Sonnet de Ronsard,* for voice and piano.

DUPARC, HENRI
1848-1933
Principal Works - Songs: Sérénade (Marc); *Romance de Mignon* (Goethe); *Galop; Soupir* (Sully-Prudhomme); *Chanson triste; Extase; Serenade florentine* (Lahor); *Invitation au voyage; La Vie anterieure* (Baudelaire); *La Vague et la cloche* (Coppée); *La Manoir de Rosemonde* (de Bonnières); *Testament* (Silvestre); *Phydilé* de Lisle); *Lamento; Au pays où se fait la guerre* (Gautier); and *Elégie* (Moore).

DVORAK, ANTONIN
1841-1904,Czeckoslovakian
Principal Works - Operas: *The Devil and Kate* (1899); *The Jacobin* (1887-88); *Russalka* (1900). Choral: *Stabat Mater,* Op. 58 (1877); Mass in D Major, Op. 86 (1892); *Requiem,* Op. 89 (1890); *Te Deum,* Op. 103 (1892). Orchestral: Symphonies - E flat major, Op. 10 (1873); D minor, Op. 13 (1874), *English;*No. 1, D major, Op. 60 (1880); No. 2, D minor, Op. 70 (1884-85); No. 3, F major, Op. 76 (1875, rev. 1887); No. 4, G. major, Op. 88 (1889); No. 5, E minor, Op. 95 (1893), *New World;* Carnival Overture, Op. 92 (1891); Slavonic Dances (originally piano duets - Set I, Op. 46 (1878) - No. 1, C major, No. 1; No. 2, E minor, No. 2; No. 3, D major, No. 3; No. 4, F major, No. 4; No. 5, A major, No. 5; No. 6, A flat major, No. 6; No. 7, C minor, No. 7; No. 8, G minor, No. 8; Set II, Op. 72 (1886) - No. 9, B major, No. 1; No. 10, E minor, No. 2; No. 11, F major, No. 3; No. 12, D flat major, No. 4; No. 13, B flat minor, No. 5; No. 14, B flat major, No. 6; No. 15, C major, No. 7; No. 16, A flat major, No. 8; Serenade, E major, Op. 22, for string orchestra (1875).Concertos: Piano: G minor, Op. 33 (1876); Violin: A minor, Op. 53 (1879); Cello: B minor, Op. 104 (1895).Chamber Music: String Quartets - No. 3, E flat major, Op. 51 (1879-80); No. 6, F major, Op. 96 (1893), *American;* Piano and Strings - Quintet, A major, Op. 81 (1887); Trio No. 4, E minor, Op. 90 (1891), *Dumky;* Violin and Piano - *Humoresques* (8), Op. 101 (1894); No. 1, E flat minor, No. 2, B major, No. 7, G flat major. Songs: 10 Biblical Songs, Op. 99 (1894); 7 Gypsy Songs (Heyduk), Op. 55 (1880), No. 1, *My Song Tells of My Love;* No. 4, *Songs My Mother Taught Me; The Girl Mowed Grass,* Op. 73, No. 2; *In so Great Anxiety of Heart,* Op. 83, No. 2; *The Maiden's Lament,* Op. 73, No. 3; *My Darling, My Little Grass,* Op. 27, No. 2; *When Thy Sweet Glances,* Op. 83, No.7.

ELGAR, SIR EDWARD
1857-1934, English
Principal Works - Orchestral: Symphonies: No. 1, A flat major, Op. 55 (1908); No. 2, E flat major, Op. 63 (1911); Violin Concerto, B minor, Op. 61 (1910); Cello Concerto, E minor, Op. 85 (1919); *Enigma Variations,* Op. 36 (1899); *Falstaff:* Symphonic Study, Op. 68 (1913); *Pomp and Circumstance,* Op. 39, Marches; - 1. D major, *Land of Hope and Glory* (1901); 1. A minor (1901); 3. C minor (1905); 4. G major, *Song of Liberty* (1907); 5. C major (1930); Choral: *Coronation Ode,* Op. 44, soloists and chorus; No. 6, *Land of Hope and Glory* (1901); *The Dream of Gerontius,* Op. 38, oratorio (1900).

ENNA, AUGUST
1860-1939, Danish
Principal Works - Opera: *Helen* (The Witch); *Cleopatra; l'igenmed Svovlstikkerne* (The Little Match Girl).

ERKEL, FERENC
1810-1893, Hungarian
Principal Works - Opera: *Hunyady László; Bánk-Bán;* Hymn: Hungarian National Hymn.

ERLANGER, CAMILLE
1863-1919, French
Principal Works - Opera: *Le Juif Polonais; Aphrodite.*

ERNST, HEINRICH WILHELM
1814-1865, Moravian/French
Principal Works - Violin: Concerto In F sharp; Elégie; Rondo Papageno.

FARWELL, ARTHUR
1872-1952, American
Principal Works - Orch: Cabiban; Dawn; Symbolistic Studies. Piano: American Indian Melodies.

FAURE, GABRIEL
1845-1924, French
Principal Works - Orchestral: Ballade for piano and orchestra, Op. 19 (1881); Requiem for soloists, chorus, orchestra and organ, Op. 48 (1887); *Masques et Bergamasques Suite,* Op. 112 (1920).Chamber Music: Sonata No. 1 in A major for piano and violin, Op. 13 (1876); Piano Quartet No. 1 in C minor, Op. 15 (1879); *Berceuse,* Op. 16, violin and piano (1880); *Elégie* in C minor, Op. 24, cello and piano (1883); Piano Quartet No. 2 in G minor, Op. 45 (1886); *Papillon,* Op. 77, cello and piano (1898); *Sicilienne,* Op. 78, cello and piano (1898); Quintet for Piano and strings, No. 2, Op. 115 (1921). Piano: *Romance sans paroles,*No. 3, Op. 17 (1863); Nocturnes (13) - No. 3, A flat major,Op. 33 (1883); No. 6, D major, Op. 63 (1894); Theme and Variations,C minor, Op. 73 (1897); Preludes (9), Op. 103 (1911).Songs: *Après un rêve* (Bussine), Op. 7 (1865); *Automne* (Silvestre), Op. 18 (1884); *Clair de lune* Verlaine), Op. 46 (1887); *En prière* (Bordese) (1890); *En sourdine* Verlaine), Op. 58 (1890); *L'Horizon chimérique* (de Mirmont),Op. 118 (1922); *Les Berceux* (Prudhomme), Op. 23 (1882); *Le Secret* (Silvestre), Op. 23 (1882); *Les Roses d'Ispahan* (Leconte de Lisle), Op. 39 (1884); *Nell* (Leconte de Lisle), Op. 18 (1880); *Nocturne* (Villiers de L'Isle Adam), Op. 43 (1886).

FEO, FRANCESCO
1691-1761, Italian
Principal Works - Operas: *Siface; Ipermestra.*

FIBICH, ZDENEK
1850-1900, Czech.
Principal Works - Operas: *The Bride of Messina; Saika; Pad Arkuna; Hippodamia.*

FIORILLO, FEDERIGO
1755-unkn., German
Principal Works - Violin: Etudes pour violon (36 caprices).

FLOTOW, FRIEDRICH VON
1812-1883, German
Principal Works - Opera-comique: *Martha; Alessandro; Stradella;* Ballet: *Lady Henriette.*

FOOTE, ARTHUR
1853-1937, American
Principal Works - Cantata: *the Farewell of Hiawatha;* Orchestral: *Suite in E major*

FORSTER, JOSEPH
1845-1917, Austrian
Principal Works - Opera: Die Rose Von Ponteverda.

FRANCHETTI, BARON ALBERTO
1860-1942, Italian
Principal Works - Operas: *Asrael; Germania; Cristoforo Colombo;* Symph.: *Inno.*

FRANCK, CESAR
1822-1890, French
Principal Works - Orchestral: Symphony, D minor (1886-88); *Redemption,* symphonic poem (1871); *Le Chasseur Maudit,* symphonic poem (1882); *Variations Symphoniques* (piano and orchestra) (1885); *Psyché,* symphonic poem (1887-88). Chamber Music: Quartet in D major (strings) (1889); Quintet, F minor (piano and strings) (1878-79); Sonata, A major (violin and piano) (1886). Piano: *Prélude, Choral et Fugue* (1884); *Prélude, Aria et Finale* (1886-87); Organ: *Grande Pièce Symphonique,* Op. 17 (1860-62); *Pastorale,* Op. 19 (1860-62); *Pièce Héroïque,* B minor (1878); 3 Chorals (1890): E major; B minor; A minor. Songs: *Nocturne* (de Foucaud) (1884); *Panis Angelicu* (from *Messe Solennelle*)(1872); *La Procession* (Brizeux) (1888); *La Vierge à la crêche* (Daudet) (1888).

FRANZ, ROBERT
1815-1892, German
Principal Works - Lieder: *Die Widmung; Schlumerlied; Wonne der Wehmuth.*

FRESCOBALDI, GIROLAMO
1583-1643, Italian
Principal Works - Organ: *Aria detta la Frescobaldi* (harpsichord or organ); *Canzona dopo L'Epistola (Fiori musicali,* 1635); *Canzona,* F major (harpsichord and strings) (1637); *Gagliarde,* No. 2 (harpsichord and orchestra); *Toccata per l'elevazione (Fiori musicali,* 1635).

FUX, JOHANN JOSEPH
1660-1741, Austrian
Principal Works - Opera: *Constanza e Fortezza;* sacred choral: *Missa canonica.*

GADE, NIELS WILHELM
1817-1890, Danish
Principal Works - Overture: *Echoes of Ossian;* Symph: *First Symphony.*

GERMAN, SIR EDWARD
1862-1936, English
Principal Works - Dances: *Henry VIII; Nell Gwynn;* Incidental Music: *Richard III.*

GIBBONS, ORLANDO
1583-1625, English
Principal Works - Church anthems; *Hosanna, Lift Up Your Heads; O Clap Your Hands.*

GIORDANO, UMBERTO
1867-1948, Italian
Principal Works - Opera: *Andrea Chénier; Fedora; Madame Sano-Gêne.*

GLAZUNOV, ALEXANDER
1865-1936, Russian
Principal Works - Ballet Music: *The Seasons,* Op. 67 (1901); *Ruses d'Amour,* Op. 61 (1899); *Raymonda,* Op. 57 (1897); Orchestral: *Stenka Rasin,* Op. 13, symphonic poem (1885); *From the Middle Ages,* Op. 79, Suite (1903); Violin Concerto in A minor, Op. 82 (1904).

GLINKA, MICHAEL IVANOVITCH
1804-1857, Russian
Principal Works - Operas: *A Life for the Tsar (or Ivan Susanin* in the U.S.S.R.), (1836); *Russlan and Ludmila,* 5 Acts (1842); *Valse-Fantaisie* (1839); *Jota Aragonesa; Kamarinskaya - Wedding song, Dance song.*

GLUCK, CHRISTOPH
1714-1787, Bohemian
Principal Works - Opera: *Orfeo ed Euridice* (Italian 1762); *Alceste* (Italian 1767, French 1776); *Paris and Helen* (1770); *Iphigenia in Aulis* (1774); *Armide* (1777); *Iphigenia in Tauris* (1779).

GODARD, BENJAMIN
1849-1895, French
Principal Works - Opera: *Joselyn* (incl. Berceuse); Song: *Chanson de Florian.*

GOETZ, HERMANN
1840-1876, German
Principal Works - Opera: *The Taming Of The Shrew.*

GOLDMARK, KARL
1830-1915, Austrian/Hungarian
Principal Works - Opera: *The queen of Sheba.*

GOMES, ANTONIO CARLOS
1836-1896, Brazilian
Principal Works - Overture: *Il Guarany.*

GILBERT, SIR WILLIAM SCHWENK
1836-1911, English
See Sir Arthur Sullivan for Gilbert and Sullivan repertoire (librettos and lyrics by Gilbert)

GOTTSCHALK, LOUIS MOREAU
1829-1869, American
Principal Works - Piano: *Cakewalk.*

GOUNOD, CHARLES
1818-1893, French
Principal Works - Opera: *Faust* (1859); *Mireille* (1864); *Romeo and Juliet* (1867); Orchestral: *Funeral March of a Marionette;* Little Symphony for Wind Instruments, B minor; Vocal: *Ave Maria* (Meditation on Bach's Prelude in C major from *The Well-Tempered Clavier).*

GRAUN, KARL HEINRICH
1704-1759, German
Principal Works - *Passion Oratorio: Der Tod Jesus.*

GRÉTRY, ANDRÉ ÉRNEST MODESTE
1741-1813, Gelgian/French
Principal Works - Opera: *Zémire et Azor* (1771); *Céphale et Procris* (1773); *L'Amant Jaloux* (1778); *Richard Coeur de Lion* (1784).

GRIEG, EDVARD
1843-1907, Norweigan
Principal Works - Incidental Music: *Sigurd Jorsalfar* (1872) (play by Björnson) *The Norse People (Norrönafolktet)* (male chorus) *Homage March* (orchestra) *Peer Gynt* (1874-75) (play by Ibsen); Orchestral: Piano Concerto, A minor, Op. 16 (1868); *Peer Gynt* Suite No. 1, Op. 46 (1888); *Peer Gynt* Suite No. 2, Op. 55 (1891); (4) Norwegian Dances, Op. 35 (1881); (4) Symphonic Dances, Op. 64 (1898); *The Elegaic Melodies,* Op. 34 (1880-81); *Holberg Suite,* Op. 40 (strings) (1884); (2) Norwegian Melodies, Op. 53; *Lyric Suite,* Op. 54 (1891); Chamber Music: String Quartet, G minor, Op. 27; Sonatas (violin and piano) - No. 1, F major, Op. 8 (1865); No. 2, G major, Op. 13 (1867); No. 3, C minor, Op. 45 (1887) .Sonata (cello and piano), A minor, Op. 36 .Piano: *Pictures of Folk Life,* Op. 19 (1872); *Bridal Procession;* Ballade, G minor, Op. 24 (1875); *Lyric Pieces.*

HALEVY, JACQUES FRANCOIS
1799-1862, French
Principal Works - Opera: *La Juive (The Jewess).*

HANDEL, GEORGE FRIDERIC
1685-1759, English/German
Principal Works - Operas: *Rinaldo* (1711); *Teseo* (1712); *Il Pastor Fido* (1712; second version, 1734); *Floridante* (1721); *Guilio Cesare* (1723); *Rodelinda* (1725); *Alessandro* (1726); *Arianna* (1733); *Alcina* (1735); *Atalanta* (1736); *Berenice* (1737); *Serse (Xerxes)* (1738); *Imeneo* (1738-40); *Semele* (1743); Masque, *Acis and Galatea* (c. 1720). Orchestral: 6 Concerti Grossi, Op. 3, for winds and strings *(Haubois Concerti)* (1729); 12 Concerti Grossi, Op. 12, for strings (1739); 17 Organ Concertos (1738; 1740); Oboe Concerto, *G minor*; *Water Music* (c 1717); *Music for the Royal Fireworks* (1749). Instrumental Chamber Music: 6 Violin Sonatas (1724); 9 Flute (recorder) Sonatas (1724); 22 Trio Sonatas for 2 violins, oboes or flutes and continuo (1696; 1733; 1738).. Vocal Chamber Music: 77 Italian Cantatas (for solo voice or voices and instrumental accompaiment); 20 Italian Duets, with continuo (1707-08; 1741-45) .Harpsichord Works: 17 Suites (or Lessons), in 2 vols. (1720; 1733); 2 Sonatas, each in C major; Various short dance movements, fugues, and other occasional pieces; Oratorios: *Esther* (1720; revised 1732); *Tolomeo* (1728); *Deborah* (1733); *Athalia* (1733); *Israel in Egypt* (1738); *Saul* (1738); *Samson* (1741); *The Messiah* (1741); *Belshazzar* (1744); *Hercules* (1744); *Judas Maccabaeus* (1746); *Occasional Oratorio* (1746); *Joshua* (1747); *Susanna* (1748); *Solomon* (1748); *Theodora* (1749); *Jephtha* (1751). Additional Choral Works: *The Passion According to*

St. John (Ger. text) (1704); Utrecht *Te Deum and Jubilate* (1713); *Chandos Anthems* (1716-18); *Coronation Anthems* (1727) - *Zadok the Priest; The King Shall Rejoice; My Heart is Inditing; Let Thy Hand Be Strengthened;* Ode, *Alexander's Feast* (1736); *Funeral Anthem for Queen Caroline* (1737); *Ode for St. Cecilia's Day* (1739); Cantata, *L'Allegro ed Il Penseroso* (1740); Dettingen *Te Deum* (1743).

HARDELOT, GUY D'
(Mrs. Helen Rhodes)
1858-1936, French
Principal Works - Songs: *Because, Three Green Bonnets, I Know A Lovely Garden.*

HAYDN, FRANZ JOSEPH
1732-1809, Austrian
Principal Works - Symphonies (104): No. 45, F sharp minor (1772); *Farewell;* No. 49, F minor (1768), *La Passione;* No. 53, D major (1773), *Imperial;* No. 73, D major (1781), *La Chasse Paris* symphonies (Nos. 82-87): No. 83, G minor (1785), *La Poule;* No. 86, D major, Op. 52, No. 2 (1786); No. 88, G major, Op. 56, No. 2 (1786); No. 91, E flat major, Op. 66, No. 3 (1788); No. 92, G major, Op. 66, No. 2 (1788), *Oxford .* Orchestral: *London* symphonies (Nos. 93-104): No. 93, D major, Op. 83, No. 2 (1791-92); No. 94, G major, Op. 80, No. 1 (1791), *Surprise;* No. 96, D major, Op. 77, No. 2 (1791), *Miracle;* No. 97, C major, Op. 83, No. 1 (1791-92); No. 98, B flat major, Op. 82, No. 2 (1792); No. 99, E flat major, Op. 98, No. 3 (1793); No. 100, G major, Op. 90 (1794), *Military;* No. 101, D major, Op. 95, No. 2 (1794), *Clock;* No. 102, B flat major, Op. 98, No. 2 (1794-95); No. 103, E flat major, Op. 95, No. 1 (1795), *Drum-Roll;* No. 104, D major, Op. 98, No. 1 (1795), *London Toy Symphony* (1788). German Dances (*Deutsche Tänze*) (1792); Sinfonia concertante, B flat major, Op. 84 (1792); Piano Concerto, D major, Op. 21 (1784); Violin Concerto, C major, "No. 1" (1765); Cello Concerto, D major, Op. 101 (1783); Trumpet Concerto, E flat major (1796).

Chamber Music: String Quartets - B flat major, Op. 1, No. 1 (1755), *Hunt;* F major, Op. 3, No. 5 (1765), *Serenade;* E flat major, Op. 33, No. 2 (1781), *The Joke;* C major, Op. 33, No. 3 (1781), *The Bird;* D major, Op. 50, No. 6 (1784-87), *The Frog;* B flat major, Op. 64, No. 3; D major, Op. 64, No. 5 (1790), *the Lark;* E flat major, Op. 64, No. 6; G minor, Op. 74, No. 3 (1793), *The Rider;* D minor, Op. 76, No. 2 (1797-98), *Fifths;* C major, Op. 76, No. 3 (1797-98), *Emperor;* B flat major, Op. 76, No. 4 (1797-98), *The Sunrise;* D major, Op. 76, No. 5 (1797-98); String Trio, D major, Op. 32, No. 1 (c. 1760). Piano Trios - D major, Op. 63 (1790); G major, Op. 73, No. 2 (1795); E flat major, Op. 75, No. 3 (c. 1795); Harpsichord or Piano: Fantasy, C major, Op. 58 (1789); Sonatas - No. 20, C minor (1771); No. 37, D major (1780); Variations, F minor, Op. 83 (1793). Masses: *Paukenmesse (Kettledrum Mass; Missa in tempori belli),* C major (1796); *Nelsonmesse (Nelson Mass),* D minor (1798); *Theresienmesse (Theresa Mass),* B flat major (1799). Oratorios: *The Creation (Die Schöpfung)* (1798); *The Seasons (Die Jahreszeiten)* (1801); *The Seven Words (Die Sieben Worte).* Songs: *My Mother Bids Me Bind My Hair* (Hunter) (1794); *She Never Told Her Love* (Shakespeare) (1798); Austrian National Hymn (Austrian version: *Gott erhalte Franz den Kaiser;* German version: *Deutschland uber alles*).

HÉROLD, LOUIS JOSEPH FERDINAND
1791-1833, French
Principal Works - Opera: *Zampa; Le Pre Aux Clercs.*

HEUBERGER, RICHARD
1850-1914, Austrian
Principal Works - Operetta: *Der Opernball.*

HILLER, JOHANN ADAM
1728-1804, German
Principal Works - Opera: *(Singspiel); Die Jagd.*

HOFFMANN, ERNST THEODORE AMADEUS
1776-1822, German
Principal Works - Opera: *Undine.*

HOPKINSON, FRANCIS
1737-1791, American
Principal Works - Songs: *Ode To Music; My Days Have Been So Wondrous Free.*

HUBAY, JENÖ
1858-1937, Hungarian
Principal Works - Violin and Piano: *Hungarian Czardas Scenes* - No. 4, Op. 32 *(Hejre Kati),* No. 5, Op. 33 *(Waves of Balaton);* Intermezzo (from the opera the *Violin Maker of Cremona,* 1894); *The Zephyr,* Op. 5.

HUMPERDINCK, ENGELBERT
1854-1921, German
Principal Works - Orch: *Humoresque;* Opera: *Hänsel und Gretel; Königskinder.*

INDY, VINCENT D'
1851-1931, French
Principal Works - *Symphony on a French Mountain Air,* G major, Op. 25, No. 1 *(Symphonie cévenole)* (piano and orchestra) (1886); Introduction from the opera *Fervaal* (1897); *La Forêt enchantée,* symphonic ballad; *Istar,* symphonic variations.

IPPOLITOV-IVANOV, MICHAEL
1859-1935, Russian
Principal Works - Orch.: Caucasian Sketches; Songs: *Song To Stalin; Voroshilov March.*

ISQUARD, NOCOLO
1775-1818, Maltese
Principal Works - Opera-comique: *Joconde; Les Rendezvous bourgeois.*

IVANOVICI, J.
1848-1905, Romanian
Principal Works - Song: *Danube Waves* (Melody source of *The Anniversary Song*).

JOMMELLI, NOCCOLÒ
1714-1774, Italian
Principal Works - Sacred: Miserere for 2 voices.

JONES, SIDNEY
1861-1946, English
Principal Works - Operettas: *The Geisha; The Girl From Utah.*

JOSQUIN DES PRÉS
1440-1521, French
Principal Works - Masses: *Ave Maris Stellis; De Beata Vergine.*

KALINNIKOV, BASIL
1866-1901, Russian
Principal Works - Symphony No. 1 in G minor; Second Symphony.

KAMIEŃSKI, MACIEJ
1734-1821, Polish
Principal Works - Opera: *Misery Contented.*

KEISER, REINHARD
1674-1739, German
Principal Works - Opera: *Circe.*

KÉLER, BÉLA
1820-1882, Hungarian
Principal Works - Dance: Lustspiel Overture

KIENZL, WILHELM
1857-1941, Austrian
Principal Works - Opera: *Der Evangelimann*

KREUTZER, KONRADIN
1780-1849, German
Principal Works - Opera: *Der Verschwender.*

KREUTZER, RUDOLPHE
1766-1831, French
Principal Works - Violin: 40 Études

KUHNAU, JOHANN
1660-1722, German
Principal Works - Clavier: Biblical Sonatas.

LALO, EDOUARD
1823-1892, French
Principal Works - Ballet: *Divertissement; Nanouna;* Violin Concerto; *Symphonie Espagnol* (violin & orch.); Cello Concerto; *Rapsodie Norwegienne; Concerto Russe; Piano Concerto;* Opera: *Le Roi d'Ys.*

LANNER, JOSEPH
1801-1843, Austrian
Principal Works - Dances: (Waltz); *Trennungs Walzer* (Parting); *Pestherwalzer,* Op. 93; *Die Werber,* Op. 103; *Die Kosenden,* Op. 128; *Hofball-Tänze (Court Ball WAltzes),* Op. 161; *Steirische Tänze,* Op. 165; *Die Romantiker,* Op. 167; *Abendsterne,* Op. 180; *Die Mozartisten,* Op. 196; *Die Schönbrunner,* Op. 200; *Alt Wien Walzer* (potpourri-arranged by Kemser).

LASSO, ORLANDO DI
1530-1594, Flemish
Principal Works - Sacred Choral Works: *Requiem; St. Matthew Passion; Seven Penitential Psalms;* Mass, *Puisque j'ai perdu;* Secular Songs: *Audite Nova! (Die Martinsgans)* With Chorus); *Matona, mia cara (Landsknechtsstandchen)* (4 voices) (1581); *Mon coeur se recommande à vous* (5 voices) (1560); *Ola! O che bon eccho!* (8 voices) (1581); *Quand mon mari vienti du dehors* (1564); *Neue Teutsche Lieder.*

LECOCQ, ALEXANDRE CHARLES
1832-1918, French
Principal Works - Operetta: *La Fille de Mme. Angot.*

LEKEU, GUILLAUME
1870-1894, Belgian
Principal Works - Cantata: *Andromède;* Violin Sonata: *Ysaÿe.*

LEONCAVALLO, RUGGIERO
1858-1919, Italian
Principal Works - Opera: *I Pagliacci; Zaza;* Song: *La Mattinata.*

LE ROUX, GASPARD
1660-1707, French
Principal Works - Harpsichord: *Pieces de clavessin.*

LESUEUR, JEAN FRANCOIS
1760-1837, French
Principal Works - Opera: *Ossian; La Mort D'Adam.*

LIADOV, ANATOL
1855-1914, Russian
Principal Works - Piano: *A Musical Snuff-Box .* Symphonic: Eight Russian Folksongs; *Baba Yaga; The Enchanted Lake; Kikimora.*

LINLEY, THOMAS
1733-1795, English
Principal Works - Opera: *The Duenna.*

LISZT, FRANZ
1811-1886, Hungarian
Principal Works - Orchestral: Symphonies - *A Faust Symphony* (with tenor and chorus) (1853-57); *Dante Symphony* (with chorus) (1867). Symphonic Poems - *Prometheus* (1850); *Orpheus* (1854); *Hungaria* (1856); *Les Préludes* (1854); *Mazeppa* (1854); *Tasso* (1856); Two Episodes from Lenau's *Faust* (also arranged for piano) (1860-61); *Mephisto Waltzes* Nos. 1 and 2 (1860; 1880); Piano Concertos - No. 1, E flat major (1855); No. 2, A major (1861); *Hungarian Fantasy* (piano and orchestra) (1852); *Malediction* (piano and strings) (1830-40); *Totentanz* (piano and orchestra) (1859). Piano: 12 *Études d'exécution transcendante;* Sonata, B minor; 6 *Études d'exécution transcendante d'après Paganini; Feux follets; Ricordanza;* Concert Études; *Waldesrauschen; Gnomenreigen; Annees de Pèlerinage; Au bord d'une source;* 3 *Sonetti del Petrarca; Venezia e Napoli,* Suite; 6 *Consolations; Legend: St. Francis Walking on the Water;* Polonaise, E major; *Valse oubliées; Spanish Rhapsody;* 20 *Hungarian Rhapsodies* (also orchestral versions); *Valse Impromptu; Mazurka Brillante;* 12 *Grandes Études; Berceuse; Les Jeux d'eau à la Villa d'Este;* 2 *Mephisto Waltzes* (originally for orchestra); 2 *Légendes; Album d'un Voyageur;* Fantasie and Fugue on the theme B.A.C.H.; *Liebesträume,* Op. 62. Choral: **Christus** (solists, chorus, orchestra, and organ) (1855-67); *The Legend of St. Elizabeth* (soloists, chorus, orchestra and organ) (1857-62); *Missa Choralis,* in A minor (chorus and organ) (1865-69); *Missa Solemnis (Gran Festival Mass)* soloists, chorus, orchestra, and organ (1855); *Hungarian Coronation Mass* (soloists, chorus, organ, and orchestra) (1867)69).

LOEWE, CARL
1796-1869, German
Principal Works - Ballads: *Edward; Erlkonig; Die Uhr.*

LORTZING, GUSTAV ALBERT
1801-1851, German
Principal Works - Opera: *Undine; Zar und Zimmermann; Der Wildschültz.*

LOTTI, ANTONIO
1667-1740, Italian
Principal Works - Aria: *Pur dicesi.*

LOUIS FERDINAND (PRINCE)
1772-1806, Prussian
Principal Works - Rondo in B major.

LUIGINI, ALEXANDRE
1850-1906, French
Principal Works - Ballet: *Ballet Egyptien; Ballet russe; Carnaval truc.*

LULLY, JEAN-BAPTISTE
1632-1687, French
Principal Works - Opera: *Alceste* (1674); *Amadis de Gaule* (1684); *Armide et Renaud* (1686); *Acis et Galatee* (1686).

LUTHER, MARTIN
1483-1546, German
Principal Works - Hymn: *Ein' Feste Burg ist unser Gott (A Mighty Fortress Is Our God).*

LVOV, ALEXIS
1798-1870, Russian
Principal Works - The old national anthem of "Imperial Russia."

MACDOWELL, EDWARD ALEXANDER
1861-1908, American
Principal Works - Orchestral: *Hamlet and Ophelia*, symphonic poem, Op. 22 (1885); Piano Concerto No. 1, A minor, Op. 15 (1885); Piano Concerto No. 2, D minor, Op. 23 (1890); Suite No. 2, Op. 48 (1897), *Indian Legend; Love Song; In War-time; Dirge; Village Festival; The Saracens*, symphonic poem, Op. 30 (1891). Piano: A.D. 1620, Op. 55, No. 3; *Woodland Sketches*, Op. 51 (Also arranged for organ, piano duet, and orchestra); *To a Water Lily*, Op. 51, No. 6; *To a Wild Rose*, Op. 51, No. 1; *Witches' Dance*, Op. 17, No. 2; Piano Sonata No. 1, G minor, Op. 45, *Tragica*; Piano Sonata No. 2, G minor, Op. 50, *Eroica*; Song: *Thy Beaming Eyes* (Gardner), Op. 40, No. 3.

MAHLER, GUSTAV
1860-1911, German
Principal Works - Orchestral: *Das klagende Lied* (soloists and chorus) (1880); Symphony No. 1, D major, *"Titan"* (1888); Symphony No. 2, C minor, *"The Resurrection"* (1894); Symphony No. 3, D minor (1896); Symphony No. 4, G major, *"Ode to Heavenly Joy"* (1900); Symphony No. 5, C sharp minor, *"The Giant"* (1902); Symphony No. 6, A minor (1905); Symphony No. 7, E minor, *"Song of the Night"* (1905); Symphony No. 8, E flat major, *"Symphony of a Thousand"* (1907); *Das Lied von der Erde* (1908); Symphony No. 9, D major (1909); Symphony No. 10 (unfinished) (1910). Vocal: *Lieder und Gesänge aus der Jugendzeit* (1882); *Lieder eines fahrenden Gesellen* (orchestra) (1883); *Kindertotenlieder* (orchestra) (1902); 14 Songs from *Des Knaben Wunderhorn* (1888); 5 Songs to Poems by Rückert (1902).

MARSCHNER, HEINRICH AUGUST
1795-1861, German
Principal Works - Opera: *Hans Heiling.*

MASCAGNI, PIETRO
1863-1945, Italian
Principal Works - Opera: *Cavalleria Rusticana* (inc. Intermezzo); *L'Amico Fritz; Zanetto; Iris.*

MASSENET, JULES
1842-1912, French
Principal Works - Opera: *Herodiade; Manon; Le Cid; Werther; Thais; Le Jongleur de Notre Dame.* Songs: *Élégie* (Ballet) (based on the invocation from *Les Erinnyes* with violin obbligato); *Pensée d'automne* (A. Silvestre). Orchestral: *Phèdre*, Overture (1873); *Scènes pittoresques*, Suite No. 4 (1873); *Scènes alsaciennes*, Suite No. 7 (1884).

MÉHUL, ÉTIENNE
1763-1817, French
Principal Works - Opera: *Joseph.*

MENDELSSOHN, FELIX
1809-1847, German
Principal Works - Stage Music: *A Midsummer Night's Dream* (Shakespeare), Overture, Op. 21 (1826), Scherzo, Op. 61 (1843), *Wedding March*, Op. 61 (1843); *Athalie*, Op. 74 (Racine) (1843-45), *War March of the Priests.* Orchestral: Symphonies - No. 3, A minor, Op. 56 (1842), *"Scottish"*; No. 4, A major, Op. 90 (1833), *"Italian"*; No. 5, D major, Op. 107 (1830), *"Reformation"*; Overtures - *Fingal's Cave (Hebrides)*, Op. 26 (1832); *Calm Sea and Prosperous Voyage*, Op. 27 (1832); *Ruy Blas*, Op. 95 (1839); Piano Concerto No. 1, G minor, Op. 25 (1831); Capriccio brillant, B minor, Op. 22 (piano and orchestra) (1832); Rondo brillant, E flat major, Op. 29 (piano and orchestra); Violin Concerto, E minor, Op. 64 (1844). Chamber Music: Strings - Octet, E flat major, Op. 20 (1825); Quartets, Op. 12, 13, 44 (No. 3-5), 80; Cello and Piano - *Song without Words*, D major, Op. 109 (1845). Piano: *Songs without Words*, No. 25, G major, Op. 62, No. 1, *May Breezes*; No. 30, A major, Op. 62, No. 6, *Spring Song*; No. 34, C major, Op. 67, No. 4, *Bee's Wedding*; Rondo capriccioso, E major, Op. 14. Organ: Sonata No. 6 in D minor. Vocal: Oratorios - *Elijah*, Op. 70 (1846), *If with All Your Hearts* (tenor) *Baal, We Cry* (chorus), *Lord God of Abraham* (baritone), *It Is Enough* (baritone), *O Rest in the Lord* (contralto); *Saint Paul*, Op. 36 (1834-36), *But the Lord Is Mindful* (contralto), *How Lovely Are the Messengers* (chorus). Cantatas - *Festival Hymn, No. 2, Hark, the Herald Angels Sing* (chorus); *Hear My Prayer, O for the Wings of a Dove; Hymn of Praise*, Op. 52 (1840), *I Waited for the Lord* (2 sopranos and chorus). Songs - *On Wings of Song, Auf Flügeln des Gesanges* (Heine), Op. 34, No. 2; *Gruss* (Eichendorff), Op. 63, No. 3 (duet); *Ich wollt', meine Liebe ergösse sich* (Heine), Op. 63, No. 1 (duet).

MESSAGER, ANDRÉ
1853-1929, French
Principal Works - Operetta: *Monsieur Beaucaire; Les P'tites Michu; Véronique;* Ballet: *Les Deux Pigeons.*

MEYERBEER, GIACOMO
1791-1864, German
Principal Works - Operas: *Les Huguenots* (1836); *L'Africaine* (1864); *Le Pardon de Ploërmel* (1859)' *Le Prophète* (1849) Orchestral: *Torch Dance No. 1 B Flat major; Torch Dance No. 3, C minor;* Ballet: *Les Patineurs (The Skaters).*

MONTEVERDI, CLAUDIO
1567-1643, Italian
Principal Works - Operas: *Il Ritorno D'Ulisse in Patria* (1641); *L'Incoronazione di Poppea* (1642); *Orfeo,* (1607). Madrigals: *Chiome d'oro* (VII) (1619); *Ecco moromorar l'onde* (1590) ; *Lettera amorosa* (VII); *Maladetto sia L'aspetto* (1636); *Ohimê dov'e il mio ben* (VII) (1619); Sacred Works: *Vespers* (1610); *Sacta Maria* (sonata for solo and 8 instruments).

MORLEY, THOMAS
1587-1602, English
Principal Works - Songs: *Fire, Fire, My Heart; My Bonnie Lass, She Smileth; Now Is The Month of Maying; Sing We and Chant It; It Was A Lover and His Lass.*

MOSZKOWSKI, MORITZ
1854-1925, Polish
Principal Works - Piano: *Caprice espagnole,* Op. 37; *Guitare,* Op. 45, No. 2 (arr. violin and piano); *Serenata,* Op. 15 No. 1 (arr. violin and piano/orchestra/voice); *Spanish Dances,* Op. 12 (arr. piano 4 hands/orchestra), No. 2, G minor, No. 5, D major (Bolero).

MOZART, WOLFGANG AMADEUS
1756-1791, German
Principal Works - Opera: *Bastien and Bastienne* (1768); *Lan Finta Giardiniera; (The Girl In Gardener's Disguise)* (1775); *Il Rè Pastore (The King as Shepherd)* (1775); *Idomeneo, Rè di Creta (Idomeneus, King Of Crete)* (1781); *The Abduction from the Seraglio* (1782); *The Marriage of Figara (Le Nozze di Figaro)* (1786); *The Impresario* (1786); *Don Giovanni* (1787); *Così fan tutte* (1790); *La Clemenza di Tito* (1790); *The Magic Flute (Die Zauberflöte)* (1791). Sonatas: *E flat major; G major; G major; A major (Rondo alla turca); A minor; F major; C minor; C major; D major Trumpet Sonata;* 2 pianos, *Sonata D major.* Rondos: *D major; A minor.* Variations: *C major; G major.* Vocal: Masses: *C major, C minor, D minor;* Motets: *Ave verum corpus; Exultate, jubilate; Alleluia; Vespers (De confessore); Laudate Dominum.* Symphonies - No. 25, G minor, K. 183 (1773); No. 29, A major, K. 201 (1774); No. 31, D major, K. 297 (1778), *Paris;* No. 32, G major, K. 318 (1779); No. 33, B flat major, K. 319 (1779); No. 34, C major, K. 338 (1780); No. 35, D major, K. 385 (1782), *Haffner;* No. 36, C major, K. 425 (1783), *Linz;* No. 38, D major, K. 504 (1786), *Prague;* No. 39, E flat major, K. 543 (1788); No. 40, G minor, K. 550 (1788); No. 41, C major, K. 551 (1788), *Jupiter.* Serenades -D major, K. 239 (1776), *Serenata notturna;* D major, K. 250 (1776), *Haffner;* D major, K. 320 (1779), *Posthorn;* G major, K. 525 (1787), *Eine kleine Nachtmusik.* Piano Concertos -E flat major, K. 271 (1777), *Jeunehomme;* A major, K. 414 (1782); E flat major, K. 449 (1784); B flat major, K. 450 (1784); D major, K. 451 (1784); G major, K. 452 (1784); B major, K. 456 (1784); F major, K. 459 (1784); D minor, K. 466 (1785); C major, K. 467 (1785); E flat major, K. 482 (1785); A major, K. 488 (1786); C minor, K. 491 (1786); C major, K. 503 (1786); D major, K. 537 (1788), *Coronation;* B flat major, K. 595 (1791); Concerto with 2 pianos, E flat major, K. 365 (1779). Violin Concertos - G major, K. 216 (1775); D major, K. 218 (1775), *Strasbourg;* A major, K. 219 (1775), *Turkish .* Concertos - Sinfonia concertante, E flat major, K. 364 (violin, viola) (1779); Bassoon Concerto, B flat major, K. 191 (1774); Clarinet Concerto, A major, K.

622 (1791); Flute Concerto, D major, K. 314 (1778); Horn Concerto, E flat major, K. 447 (1783); German Dances *(Deutsche Tänze)* - K. 602, No. 3, *Der Leiermann;* K. 605, No. 3, *Die Schlittenfart;* Adagio, E major, K. 261 (1776); Adagio and Fugue, C minor, K. 546 (strings); *Masonic Funeral Music (Maurerische Trauermusik),* K. 477 (1785); Piano: Fantasias - C major, K. 394 (Prelude and Fugue) (1782); D minor, K. 397 (1782); C minor, K 475 (1785); Minuet, D major, K. 355 (New K. 594a) (1790); Songs - *Abendempfindung* (Campe), K. 523 (1787); *Abend ist's, die Sonne ist verschwunden; An Chloe* (Jacobi), K. 524 (1787); *Wenn die Lieb aus deinen blauen, hellen,...; Ridente la calma,* K. 152 (1775); *Ridente la calma nell' alma si desti; Sehnsucht nach dem Frühlinge,* K. 596 (1791); *Komm, lieber Mai und mache die Bäume wieder grun; Das Veilchen* (Goethe), K. 476 (1785); *Ein Veilchen auf der Wiese stand gebück; Warnung,* K. 433 (Bs) (1783), *Männer suchen stets zu naschen, lässt man sie allein; Wiegenlied,* K. 350 (See *Cradle Song); Schlafe, mein Prinzchen* (attributed to Mozart, but composed by a contemporary, Bernard Flies); Chamber Music: String Quintets - C minor, K. 406 (arranged from Serenade, K. 388) (1787); C major, K. 515 (1787); G minor, K. 516 (1787); D major, K. 593 (1790); E flat major, K. 614 (1791); String Quartets - E flat major, K. 171 (1773); G major, K. 387 (1782); D minor, K. 421 (1783); E flat major, K. 428 (1783); B flat major, K. 458 (1784), *The Hunt;* A major, K. 464 (1785); C major, K. 465 (1785); D major, K. 499 (1786); D major, K. 575 (1789); B flat major, K. 589 (1790); F major, K. 590 (1790); Divertimento, E flat major, for string trio, K. 563 (1788). Strings and 2 horns - D major, K. 251 (with oboe); B flat major, K. 287, "No. 15"; D major, K. 334, "No. 17", Minuette; *A Musical Joke (Ein Musikalischer Spass),* K. 522 (1787); Duo: B flat major, K. 424 (violin, viola) (1783). Piano Quartets - G minor, K. 478 (1785); E flat major, K. 493 (1786); Piano Trios - E major, K. 542 (1788); C major, K. 564 (1788); Serenades for Wind Instruments - B flat major, K. 361 (1781), *Grand Partita;* E flat major, K. 375 (1781); C minor, K. 388 (1782).

MUSSORGSKY, MODEST
1839-1881, Russian
Principal Works - Opera: *Boris Godunov* (1874); *Khovantschina* (1873); *Sarochintzy Fair* (1874). Orchestral: *A Night on Bald Mountain,* Fantasia (1872). Piano: *Pictures at an Exhibition* (1874) (orchestrated Maurice Ravel, 1922); 1. *The Gnome,* 3. *Tuileries (Children Quarreling at Play),* 5. *Ballet of Unhatched Chickens,* 7. *The Market Place at Limoges,* 9. *The Hut of Baba-Yaga,* 10. *The Great Gate of Kiev.* Songs: *Ballade* (Golenishchev - Kutuzov) with orchestra; *Hopak* (Shevchenko) with orchestra (1868); *The Little Star* (Grekov) (1858); *The Nursery* (cycle) (1868-72); *Song of the Flea* (Goethe), arranged for orchestra (1879); *Songs and Dances of Death,* cycle (1875)77).

NEVIN, ETHELBERT
1862-1901, American
Principal Works - Songs: *May In Tuscany, Mighty Lak A Rose, The Rosary; Piano Suite: Water Scenes (Narcissus).*

NICOLAI, KARL OTTO EHRENFRIED
1810-1849, German
Principal Works - Opera: *The Merry Wives of Windsor.*

OFFENBACH, JACQUES
1819-1880, French

Principal Works - Opera: *The Tales of Hoffman* (1881). Operettas: *La Belle Hélène* (1865), *La Grande Duchesse de Gérolstein* (1867), *Le Périchole* (1868), *Orpheus in the Underworld, (Orphée aux Enfers)* (1858), *La Vie Parisienne* (1866). Orchestral: *Gaité Parisienne*.

PADEREWSKI, IGNACE JAN
1860-1941, Polish
Principal Works - *Minuet In G,* Op. 14, No. 1; *Cracovienne; Fantastique* Op. 14, No. 6; Opera: *Manru* (1901).

PAGANINI, NICCOLO
1782-1840, Italian
Principal Works - Violin and Orchestra: Violin Concerto No. 1, E flat major, Op. 6; Violin Concerto No. 2, B minor, Op. 7 *"La Campanella";* Fantasia on the G string (after Rossini's *Mosè in Egitto*); Moto perpetuo *(Allegro di Concert),* Op. 11. Violin and Piano: Sonata No. 12, E minor, Op. 3, No. 6 (piano or guitar); Sonatina, *"Grande";* Variations; *Dal tuo stellato soglio* (from Rossini's *"Mosé in Egitto"*), *Nel cor più non mi sento* (from Paisiello's *La Molinara*). Violin: 24 Caprices, Op. 1 - No. 5, A minor, No. 9, E major, *"La chasse",* No. 13, B flat major, *"Le rire du diable",* No. 17, E flat major, *"Andantino capriccioso",* No. 20, D major, No. 24, A minor, *"Tema con variazioni".*

PAISIELLO, GIOVANNI
1740-1816, Italian
Principal Works - Opera: *Il Barbiere di Siviglia* (not to be confused with the Rossini opera of the same name).

PALESTRINA, GIOVANNI PIERLUIGI DA
1525-1594, Italian
Principal Works - *Marcellus Mass; Missa Papae Marcelli;* plus 90 Masses, 500 Motets, madrigals, songs, hymns.

PARKER, HORATIO WILLIAM
1863-1919, American
Principal Works - Oratorio: *Hora Novissima;* Opera: *Mona; Fairyland.*

PERGOLESI, GIOVANNI BATTISTA
1710-1736, Italian
Principal Works - Cantata: *Stabat Mater;* comic opera: *La Serva Padrona;* Opera: *Flaminio; Lo Frate Innamorato.*

PERI, JACOPO
1561-1633, Italian
Principal Works - Opera: *Dafne; Euridice.*

POLDINI, EDUARD
1859-1957, Hungarian
Principal Works - piano: *The Dancing Doll.*

PONCHIELLI, AMILCARE
1834-1866, Italian
Principal Works - Opera: *La Gioconda* (incudes ballet intermezzo: *Dance of the Hours*).

PUCCINI, GIACOMO
1858-1924, Italian
Principal Works - Opera: *Manon Lescaut* (1893); *La Bohème* (1896); *Tosca* (1900); *Madame Butterfly* (1904); *The Girl Of The Golden West* (1910); *Gianni Schicchi* (1918); *Turendot* (1926); Song: *Inno a Roma* (1919).

PURCELL, HENRY
1658-1695, English
Principal Works - Anthems: *Hear My Prayer* (1680-82); *Praise the Lord, O My Soul* (1682-85); *My Beloved Spake* (1683); *My Heart Is Inditing* (1685); *Blessed Is He That Considereth the Poor* (1688); *O, Sing unto the Lord* (1688). Hymns and Sacred Songs: *Great God and Just* (Taylor); *Lord, I Can Suffer* (Patrick); *In The Black Dismal Dungeon of Despair* (Fuller); *With Sick and Famished Eyes* (Herbert); *O, I'm Sick of Life* (Sandys); *Ah, Few and Full of Sorrows* (Sandys); Odes: *Fly, Bold Rebellion* (1683); *Arise, My Muse* (1690); *Hail, Bright Cecilia* (1692); *Celebrate This Festival* (1693); *Come, Ye Sons of Art, Away* (1694). Chamber Music: Fantasias for Strings in several parts; Sonatas of III Parts (1683); Sonatas of IV Parts (1697). Chamber Cantatas: *How Pleasant Is the Flowery Plain; If Ever I More Riches Did Desire* (Cowley); *In a Deep Vision's Intellectual Scene* (Cowley). Operas and Masques: *Dido and Aeneas* (1689); *The Fairy Queen* (1692); *The Indian Queen* (1695); *The Tempest* (1695). Songs: *In These Delightful Pleasant Groves; Ah, Cruel Nymph, You give Despair; What, O Solitude, My Sweetest Choice; I'll Sail upon the Dog-Star (A Fool's Preferment, 1688); There's Nothing So Fatal as Woman (AFool's Preferment, 1688); Nymphs and Shepherds, Come Away (The Libertine, 1692); Man Is for the Woman Made (The Mock Marriage, 1695).*

RAMEAU, JEAN PHILIPPE
1683-1764, French
Principal Works - Dramatic Works: *Hippolyte et Aricie* (1733); *Les Indes galantes* (1735); *Castor et Pollux* (1737); *Dardanus* (1739); *Les Fêtes d'Hébé* (1739); *Platée* (1745); *Les Paladins* (1760). Harpsichord: Suite No. 2, E minor - 3. Gigue en rondeau, 4. *Le Rappel des oiseaux,* 5. Rigaudon, 6. Musette en rondeau, 7. Tambourin; Suite No. 3, D minor - 8. *Les Cyclopes;* Suite No. 4, A minor - 7. Gavotte and 5 doubles.

REYER, ERNEST
1823-1909, French
Principal Works - Opera: *Sigurd Salammbo.*

REZNICEK, EMIL NIKOLAUS VON
1860-1945, Austrian
Principal Works - Opera: *Donna Diana.*

RIMSKY-KORSAKOV, NICOLAI ANDREYEVITCH
1844-1908, Russian
Principal Works - Orchestral: Symphony No. 2, Op. 9 (Antar) (1868); *Capriccio espagnol,* Op. 34 (1887); *Russian Easter Overture,* Op. 36 (1888); *Scheherazade,* Op. 35 (1888); *Dubinushka,* Op. 69 (1905); *Coq d'Or Suite; Tsar Saltan* Suite, Op. 57. Songs: *It Is Not the Wind,* Op. 43, No. 2; *The Rose and the Nightingale,* Op. 2, No. 2. Operas: *May Night* (1880); *The Snow Maiden* (1882); *Sadko* (1898); *The Tale of Tsar Saltan* (1900); *Le Coq d'Or* (1907); Revised version: *Moussorgsky's "Boris Godunov".*

ROSSINI, GIOACCHINO
1792-1868, Italian
Principal Works - Operas: *Marriage by Promissory Note (La Cambiale di Matrimonio), L'Italiana in Algeri* (1812); *Tancredi* (1812); *Il Signor Bruschino* (1813); *Il Turco in Italia* (1814); *Otello* (1816); *The Barber of Seville* (1816); *Cinderella (La Cenerentola)* (1817); *The Thieving Magpie (La Gazza Ladra)* (1817); *Semiramide* (1823); *Le Siège de Corinthe* (1826); *Moses (Moïse)* (1827); *Count Ory (Le Comte Ory)* (1828); *William Tell* (1829). Sacred Music: *Stabat Mater* (1842); *Petite Messe Solennelle* (1864); Vocal: *La Danza* (Pepoli) (1835) (Arranged for organ or piano);

Pieta, Signore (orchestra); *Cujus animam* (from *Stabat Mater*) (1824) (tenor).

RUBINSTEIN, ANTON GREGOROVITCH
1830-1894, Russian
Principal Works - Piano: *Melody In F,* Op. 3, No. 2; *Romance In E Flat,* Op. 44, No. 1; *Valse Caprice In E Flat.*

SAINT-SAENS, CAMILLE
1835-1921, French
Principal Works - Opera: *Samson et Dalila* (1877). Choral Music: *Christmas Oratorio,* Op. 12 (1863), No. 7, *Tecum principium* (trio), No. 10, *Tollite hostias* (chorus), *Le Déluge,* Op. 45 (oratorio) (1876) Prelude. Orchestral: *Le Rouet d'Omphale,* Op. 31 (1871); *Phaëton,* Op. 39 (1873); *Danse Macabre,* Op. 40 (1874); *Carnival of the Animals* (orchestra and two pianos) (1886), 3. *Tortues* (from Offenbach's *Orpheus in the Underworld),* 4. *L'Éléphant,* 6. *Aquarium,* 7. *Le Coucou au Fond des Bois,* 8. *Fossiles',* 9. *Le Cygne;* Symphony No. 3, C minor, Op. 78 (with organ) (1886); Piano concerto No. 2, G minor, Op. 22 (1868); Piano Concerto No. 4, C minor, Op. 44 (1875); Piano Concerto No. 5, F major, Op. 103 (1895); Violin Concerto No. 1, A major, Op. 20 (1859); Violin Concerto No. 3, B minor, Op. 61 (1880); *Havanaise,* Op. 83 (violin and orchestra) (1887); *Introduction and Rondo Capriccioso,* Op. 28 (violin and orchestra) (1863); Cello Concerto, A minor, Op. 33 (1873).

SARASATE, PABLO DE
1844-1908, Spanish
Principal Works - Violin and Piano: *Carmen Fantasia,* Op. 25 (for violin and orchestra) *Danzas Españolas,* No. 1, *Malagueña,* Op. 21, No. 1; No. 2, *Habañera,* Op. 21, No. 2; No. 3, *Romanza andaluza,* Op. 22, No. 1; No. 4, *Jota Navarra,* Op. 22, No. 2, No. 5, *Playera,* Op. 23, No. 1; No. 6, *Zapateado,* Op. 23, No. 2; *Introduction & Tarantella,* Op. 43; *Zigeunerweisen,* Op. 20, No. 1 (arranged for violin and orchestra).

SCANDELLO, ANTONIO
1517-1580, Italian
Principal Works - Passion According To St. John.

SCARLATTI, ALESSANDRO
1659-1725, Italian
Principal Works - Operas: (1679) *Gli equivoci nel sembiante;* (1683) *Pompeo; Psiche;* (1690) *Gli equivoci in amore;* (1694) *Pirro e Demetrio;* (1698) *Flavio cuniberto; La donna ancora e'fedele;* (1707) *Mitridate eupatore; Il trionfo della liberta;* (1715) *Tigrone;* (1718) *Telemaco;* (1719) *Marco attilo regolo;* (1720) *Tito O sempronio gracco;* (1721) *Griselda.* Other Works: (1699) 2 Sonatas for flute and continuo; (1706) *Il sedecia, re di Gerusalemme,* oratorio; (1710) Motet: Est dies tropael; *Informata vulnerate,* cantata. (1715) Twelve sinfonias; Four quartets for two violins, viola amd cello, plus more than 101 operas, 500 chamber cantatas, 200 masses, 14 oratorios.

SCARLATTI, DOMENICO
1685-1757, Italian
Principal Works - Opera: *Ottavia ristituta al rono; Giustina; Irene; La Sylvia; Orlando; Tolomeo e Alessandro; Tetide in sciro; Ifigenie in Aulide; Ifgenie in Tauride; Moses and Aron; Von Heute Hof Morgen; Serenade,* for septet and baritone; Quintet for wind instruments; string Quartet No. 3; Variations for orchestra; Suite in G major for strings.

SCHUBERT, FRANZ
1797-1828, Austrian
Principal Works - Operas: *Alfonso and Estrella* (1821); *Der Zwillingsbrüder* (1818); Incidental Music: *Rosamunde,* Op. 26 (1823). Symphonies - No. 1, D major (1813); No. 2, B flat major (1815); No. 3, D major (1815); No. 4, C minor (1816), *Tragic;* No. 5, B flat major (1816); No. 6, C major (1818), *Little;* No. 7, E major (1821) (orchestrated by Weingartner); No. 8, B minor (1822), *Unfinished;* No. 9, C major (old No. 7) (1828), *Great;* Overture in the Italian Style, C major, Op. 170 (1817); 5 German Dances and 7 Trios, strings (1813). String Quartets - No. 10, E flat major, Op. 125, No. 1 (1813); No. 12, C minor (Quartett-Satz) (1820); No. 13, A minor, Op. 29, No. 1 (1824); No. 14, D minor (1824), *Death and the Maiden;* No. 15, G major, Op. 161 (1826). Piano Trios - No. 1, B flat major, Op. 99 (1817); No. 2, E flat major, Op. 100 (1827). Violin and Piano -Sonata, A major, Op. 162 (1817), *Duo;* Sonatina, D major, Op. 137, No. 1 (1816); Sonatina, G minor, Op. 137, No. 3 (1816); Sonata, A minor, for arpeggione and piano (1824). Piano: Fantasia, C major, Op. 15, *The Wanderer* (1822); 12 Ländler, Op. 171 (1823): No. 3, F minor, *Air russe;* No. 6, A flat major. Impromptus, Op. 90 (1827): No. 2, E flat major; No. 3, G major; No. 4, A flat major. Impromptus, Op. 142 (1827): No. 2, A flat major; No. 3, B flat major, *Andante con variazioni;* No. 4, F minor; Allegretto, C minor (1827). Sonatas - B major, Op. 147 (1817); A minor, Op. 164 (1817); C major, *Unfinished* (1818); A major, Op. 120 (1819); A minor, Op. 143 (1823); D major, Op. 53 (1825); G major, Op. 78 (1826); C minor (1828); B flat major (1828); A major (1828). Waltzes - Op. 9 (1816-21); Op. 77, *Valses nobles* (1827) Songs: *die schöne Müllerin* (Muller), cycle of 20 songs, Op. 25 (1823) - No. 2, *Wohin?,* No. 6, *Der Neugierige,* No. 7, *Ungeduld,* No. 20, *Des Baches Wiegenlied; Die Winterreise* - - - cycle of 24 songs, Op. 89 (1827) - No. 5, *Der Lindenbaum;* No. 11, *Frühlingstraum;* No. 13, *Die Post; Schwanengesang* (Rellstab, Heine, Seidl), cycle of 14 songs (1828) - No. 1, *Liebesbotschaft* (Rellstab); No. 4, *Ständchen (Serenade)* (Rellstab), No. 12, *Am Meer* (Heine), No. 13, *Der Doppelgänger* (Heine), No. 14, *Die Taubenpost* (Seidl). *Die Allmacht* (Pyrker) (1825); *An den Mond* (Hölty) (1815); *An die Leyer* (Bruchmann) (1822); *An die Musik* (Schober) (1817); *Auf dem Wasser zu singen* (Stollberg) (1823); *Ave Maria* (Storck, after Scott) (1825); *Dass sie hier gewesen* (Rückert) (1823); *Du bist die Ruh;* (Rückert) (1823); *Der Einsame* (Lappe)(1825); *Erlkönig (The Erlking)* (Goethe) (1815); *Die Forelle (The Trout—* Schubart) (1817); *Frühlingsglaube* (Uhland) (1820); *Geheimes* (Goethe) (1821); *Gretchen am Spinnrade* (Goethe) (1814); *Gruppe aus dem Tartarus* (Schiller) (1817); *Hark! Hark! the Lark* (Shakespeare) (1826); *Heidenröslein* (Goethe) (1815), *Der Hirt auf dem Felsen* (Müller, Von Chézy) (1828); *Im Abendroth* (Lappe) (1824); *Im Frühling* Schulze) (1826), *Die Junge Nonne* (Craigher) (1825); *Der Jüngling an der Quelle* (Salis) (1821); *Lachen und Weinen* (Rückert) (1823); *Die Liebe hat gelogen* (Platen) (1822); *Litanei (For All Souls' Day)* (Jacobi) (1818); *Der Musensohn* (Goethe) (1822); *Nacht und Träume* (Collin) (1825); *Rastlose Liebe* (Goethe) (1815); *Sie mir gegrüsst!* (Ruckert) (1821); *Seligkeit* (Hölty) (1816), *Der Tod und das Mädchen* (Claudius) (1817); *Dem Unendlichen* (Klopstock) (1815); *Der Wanderer* (Schmidt) (1816), *Der Wanderer an den Mond* (1826); *Wander-*

ers Nachtlied I (Goethe) (1815); *Wanderers Nachtlied II* (Goethe) (1822); *Who Is Sylvia?* (Shakespeare) (1826); *Wiegenlied* (Claudius) (1816); *Wiegenlied* (Seidl) (1826). Piano Duets - 3 Marches militaires, Op. 51 (1821); Andantino varié, B minor, Op. 84, No. 1 (1825); *Lebenstürme*, Op. 44 (1828)Choral: Mass No. 1 in F major, D 105 (1814); Mass No. 2 in G major, D 167 (1815); Mass No. 3 in B flat major, Op. 141 (1815); Mass No. 4 in C major, Op. 48 (1816); Mass No. 5 in A flat major, D 678 (1819-22); Mass No. 6 in E flat major, D 950 (1828); German Mass, F major (1827); Psalm No. 23, Op. 132 (1820); *Song of the Spirits over the Water,* male chorus and strings (1820); *Ständchen* Op. 135, alto and female voices (1827).

SCHUMANN, ROBERT
1810-1856, German
Principal Works - Opera: *Genoveva,* 4 acts, Op. 81 (1847-50); **Orchestral:** Symphonies - No. 1, B flat major, Op. 38 (1841), *Spring;* No. 2, C major, Op, 71 (1845-46); No. 3, E flat major, Op. 97 (1850), *Rhenish;* No. 4, D minor, Op. 120 (1841, revised in 1851); Piano Concerto, A minor, Op. 54 (1845); Cello Concerto, A minor, Op. 129 (1850); Violin Concerto, D minor (1853). **Chamber Music:** 3 String Quartets, Op. 41 (1842: No. 1, A minor; No. 2, F major; No. 3, A major);Quintet for Piano and Strings, E flat major, Op. 44 (1842);Quartet for Piano and strings, E flat major, Op. 47 (1842); Andante and Variations for 2 pianos, 2 cellos, horn (1843); Trio No. 1 for violin, cello, piano, D minor, Op. 63 (1847); Trio No. 2 for violin, cello, piano, F major, Op. 80 (1847); *Fantasiestücke* for violin, cello, piano, Op. 88 (1842); Trio No. 3 for violin, cello, piano, G minor, Op. 110 (1851) ; *Märchenerzählungen* for clarinet, viola, piano, Op. 132(1853). **Piano and one additional instrument:** *Fantasiestücke* for clarinet, Op. 73 (1849); Violin Sonata No. 1,A minor, Op. 105 (1851); Violin Sonata No. 2, D minor, Op. 121 (1851). **Piano:** *Abegg* Variations, Op. 1 (1830); *Album für die Jugend,* Op. 68 (1848), 43 pieces No. 10, *FröhlicherLandmann (The Jolly Farmer); Albumblätter,* Op. 124 (1832-45), 20 pieces; *Arabesque,* C major, Op. 18 (1839); *Carnaval,* Op. 9 (1834-35), 20 pieces; *Davidsbündlertänze,* Op. 6 (1837), 18 pieces; Études in the form of variations *(Études Symphoniques),* Op. 13 (1834) 17 pieces; *Fantasia,* C major, Op. 17 (1836); *Fantasiestücke,* Op. 12 (1837) 9 pieces — No. 2, *Aufschwung (Soaring),* No. 3, *Warum? (Why?),* Kinderscenen *(Scenes of Childhood),* Op. 15 (1838) 13 pieces — No. 7, *Träumerei (Reverie); Kreisleriana,* Op. 16 (1838), 8 fantasies; *Papillons (Butterflies),* Op. 2 (1832), 12 pieces; Sonata No. 2, G minor, Op. 22 (1833-38); Sonata No. 3, F minor *(Concert sans orchestre),* Op. 11 (1833-35, revised in 1853); Toccata, C major, Op. 7 (1832); *Waldscenen (Wood Scenes),* Op. 82 (1848-49), 9 pieces No. 7, *Vogel als Prophet (The Prophet Bird),* **Piano Duets:** 12 Fourhanded pieces for children, Op. 85(1849); No. 9, *Am Springbrunnen (At the Fountain);* No. 12,, *Abendlied (Evening Song),* **Incidental Music:** *Manfred* Op. 115 (to Byron's play) (1848-51) Overture. **Choral:** *Paradise and the Peri,* Op. 50 (Moore) (soloists, chorus, orchestra) (1843); *Requiem für Mignon,* Op. 98b (Goethe) soloists, chorus, orchestra (1849); *Nachtlied,* Op. 108 (Hebbel) (chorus, orchestra) (1849); Mass, Op. 147 (chorus, orchestra) (1852); Requiem, Op. 148 (chorus, orchestra) (1852); Scenes from Goethe's *Faust* (soloists,

chorus, orchestra) (1844-53). **Vocal Quartets:** *Spanish Love Songs,* Op. 138 (1849), 10 pieces (solos, duets, quartets); *Zigeunerleben (Gypsy Life)* Op. 29, No. 4 (1840). **Partsongs:** *Romances:* Vol. I, Op. 69 (1849), six songs; Vol. II, Op. 91 (1849), six songs (women's voices); Six Songs, Op. 33 (1840) (men's voices); *Gute Nacht,* Op. 59, No. 4 (1846) (mixed voices). **Songs:** *Liederkreis* (9 songs: Heine), Op. 24 (1840); *Myrthen (Myrtles)* (26 songs) Op. 25 (1840 — 1, *Widmung (Dedication),* 3, *Der Nussbaum (The Nut Tree),* 7, *Die Lotosblume (The Lotus Flower),* 24, *Du bist wie eine Blume (Thou Art Like a Flower);* Twelve Poems (Kerner), Op. 37 (1840); — No. 3, *Wanderlust; Liebesfrühling (Love's Spring)* (1840) —— *Liederkreis* (12 songs: Eichendorff), Op. 39 (1840) — No. 3, *Waldesgespräch (Forest Dialogue);* No. 5, *Mondnacht (Night of the Moon); Frauenliebe und leben (Woman's Love and Life)* 8 songs: Chamisso), Op. 42 (1840); *Dichterliebe (Poet's Love)* (16 songs: Heine), Op. 48 (1840) — 1, *Im wunderschönen Monat Mai (In the Beautiful Month of May)* 7, *Ich grolle nicht (I Do Not Lament); Die beiden Grenadiere (The Two Grenadiers)* (Heine), Op. 49, No. 1 (1840).

SCHUTZ, HEINRICH
1585-1672, German
Principal Works - Church Choral: The Seven Words of Jesus Christ; The St. Matthew Passion; The Resurrection Oratorio; Christmas Oratorio.

SIBELIUS, JEAN
1865-1957, Finnish
Principal Works - Symphonies: No. 1, E minor, Op. 39 (1899); No. 2, D major, Op. 43 (1902); No. 3, C major, Op. 52 (1907); No. 4, A minor, Op. 63 (1910); No. 5, E flat major, Op. 82 (1915); No. 6, D minor, Op. 104 (1923); No. 7, C major, Op. 105 (1924); Violin Concerto in D minor, Op. 47 (1903); *En Saga,* Op. 9 (1892); *Karelia Suite,* Op. 11 (1893); *Spring Song,* Op. 16 (1894); *Lemminkäinen Suite,* four legends, Op. 22 (1893-99) - The Swan of Tuonela, *Lemminkäinen's Return; Scènes historiques I,* Op. 25 (1899) - *Festivo; Finlandia,* Op. 26 (1899); *Romance,* C major, Op. 42 (string orchestra) (1903); *Pohjola's Daughter,* Op. 49 (1906); *Pan and Echo,* dance intermezzo, Op. 53 (1906); *Night Ride and Sunrise,* Op. 55 (1909); *Canzonetta,* Op. 62a (1911); *Rakastava* (The Lover), Op. 14 (string orchestra) (1911); *Scènes historiques II,* Op. 66 (1912); *March of the Finnish Infantry,* Op. 91a (1918); *The Oceanides,* Op. 73 (1914); *Tapiola,* Op. 112 (1925); *Humoresque,* Op. 89, No. 4 (violin and orchestra) (1917); **Violin and Piano:** *Romance,* F major, Op. 78, No. 2 (1915); *Danses champêtres,* Op. 106 (1925). **Incidental Music:** *King Christian II* (A. Paul), Op. 27 (1898) — *Elegy; Musette; Fool's Song* (The Spider); *Kuolema* (Järnefelt), Op. 44 (1903) — 2Valse triste (arranged for orchestra); *Pelléas et Mélisande* (Maeterlinck), Op. 46 (1905); *The Tempest* (Shakespeare), Op. 109 (1926). **Songs:** *The Dream, Op. 13, No. 5* (Runeberg) (1891); *Jubal,* Op. 35, No. 1 (Josephson) (1907); *Black Roses,* Op. 36, No. 1 (Josephson); *Ingalill,* Op. 36, No. 4 (Fröding); *March Snow,* Op. 36, No. 5 (Wecksell) (1899); *The Tryst,* Op. 37, No. 5; *Autumn Night,* Op. 38, No. 1; *On a Balcony by the Sea,—* Op. 38, No. 2 (Rydberg) (1904); *In the Fields a Maiden Sings,* Op. 52, No. 3.

SINDING, CHRISTIAN
1856-1941, Norweigan
Principal Works - Piano: *Rustle Of Spring.*

SMETANA, BEDŘICH
1824-1884, Czech
Principal Works - Orchestral: *Wallenstein's Camp,* Op. 14 (1858); *My Country (Má Vlast)* 6 symphonic poems (1874-1879). **Chamber Music:** Trio, G minor, Op. 15 (piano, violin, cello) (1855); String Quartet No. 1, E minor, *From My Life* (1876); *From My Homeland* (violin and piano) (1878) — No. 1, Moderato; No. 2, Andantino; String Quartet No. 2, D minor (1882). **Opera:** *The Bartered Bride* (1866); *Dalibor* (1868); *The Kiss* (1876); *Libuše* (1881).

SMYTHE, ETHEL MARY
1858-1944, English
Principal Works - Opera: *Fantasio; Der Wald; The Wreckers; The Boatswain's Mate; Fete Galante; Entente Cordiale; The March Of The Women.* **Orchestral:** *Serenade; Anthony and Cleopatra; Mass In D Major.*

SOUSA, JOHN PHILIP
1854-1932, American
Principal Works - Marches: *Black Horse Troop; El Capitán* (1896); *The Corsican Cadets; Crusaders; The Diplomat; Fairest of the Fair; Gladiators* (1886); *Golden Jubilee; Gridiron Club; Hands Across The Sea* (1889); *Her Majesty The Queen; High School Cadets* (1891); *Invincible Eagle; King Cotton* (1895); *Liberty Bell* (1893); *Manhattan Beach* (1893); *Semper Fidelis* (1888); *Stars and Stripes Forever* (1897); *The Thunderer* (1889); *Washington Post* (1889).

SPOHR, LUDWIG
1784-1859, German
Principal Works - Symphonies: *The Conservation of Sound; The Earthly and Divine;* plus 15 violin concertos.

SPONTINI, GASPARO
1774-1851, Italian
Principal Works - Opera: *La Vestale; Ferdinand Cortez; Olympie; Agnes von Hohenstaufen.*

STAINER, SIR JOHN
1840-1901, English
Principal Works - Church Choral: *The Daughter of Jairus; The Crucifixion.*

STENHAMMER, WILHELM
1871-1927, Swedish
Principal Works - Opera: *Tirfing;* **Choral:** *Sverige.*

STRAUSS, RICHARD
1864-1949, German
Principal Works - Opera: *Salome* (1905); *Elektra* (1909); *Der Rosenkavalier* (1911); *Ariadne auf Naxos* (1912); *Die Frau ohne schatten* (1914); *Arabella* (1930); *Die schweigsame Frau* (1934); *Capriccio* (1940). **Orchestra:** *Alpine Symphony,* Op. 64 (1915); *Also sprach Zarathustra,* Op. 30 (1896); *Burleske* (piano and orchestra) (1883); *Don Juan,* Op. 20 (1888); *Don Quixote,* Op. 35 (cello and orchestra) (1897); *Ein Heldenleben,* Op. 40 (1898); *Sinfonia Domestica,* Op. 53 (1903); *Till Eulenspiegels lustige Streiche,* Op. 28 (1895): *Death and Transfiguration (Tod und Verk-*

lärung), Op. 24 (1888-89); *Metamorphosen* (1945); Concerto for oboe (1945). **Songs:** *Allerseelen,* Op. 10, No. 8 (von Gilm); *Befreit,* Op. 39, No. 4 (Dehmel); *Cäcilie,* Op. 27, No. 2 (Hrt); *Du meines Herzens Krönelein,* Op. 21, No. 2 (Dahn); *Freundliche Vision,* Op. 48, No. 1 (Bierbaum); *Heimkehr,* Op. 15, No. 5 (Schack); *Heimliche Aufförderung,* Op. 27, No. 3 (Mackay); *Ich trage meine Minne,* Op. 32, No. 1 (Henckell); *Morgen,* Op. 27, No. 4 (Mackey); *Die Nacht,* Op. 10, No. 3 (von Gilm); *Ruhe, meine Seele,* Op. 27, No. 1 (Henckell); *Ständchen,* Op. 17, No. 2 (Schack) See *Serenade; Traum durch die Dämmerung,* Op. 29, No. 1 (Bierbaum); *Wiegenlied,* Op. 41, No. 1 (Dehmel); *Zueignung,* Op. 10, No. 1 (von Gilm); *Four last songs* (voice and orchestra) (1950).

SULLIVAN, SIR ARTHUR
1842-1900, English
Principal Works - Operetta or Comic Opera: *Trial By Jury* (1875); *H.M.S. Pinafore* (1878); *The Pirates of Penzance* (1879); *Patience* (1881); *The Gondoliers* (1889); *Iolanthe* (1882); *Princess Ida* (1884); *The Mikado* (1885); *Ruddigore* (1887); *The Yeomen of the Guard* (1888). **Orchestral:** Symphony in E (1866) *Irish;* Overtures: *In Memoriam, Di Ballo, Sapphire Necklace;* Imperial March (1893); Incidental music to *The Tempest, The Merchant of Venice, The Merry Wives of Windsor, Henry VIII, Macbeth,* and *The Forresters* (Tennyson). **Oratorios and Cantatas:** *The Prodigal Son* (1869); *The Light of the World* (1873); *The Martyr of Antioch* (1880); *The Golden Legend* (1886). **Vocal:** *Onward! Christian Soldiers* (Baring-Gould); *The Long Day Closes* (Chorley) (chorus); *The Lost Chord* (Proctor) (tenor and organ); *Orpheus with his Lute* (Shakespeare) (soprano and piano. (See Listing Under Popular Composers).

SUPPE, FRANZ VON
1819-1895, Austrian
Principal Works - Operas: *Poet and Peasant* (1845); *Flotte Bursche* (1863); *Pique-Dame* (1864); *Beautiful Galathea* (1865); *Light Cavalry* (1865); *Banditenstreiche* (1867); *Morning, Noon and Night in Vienna; Boccaccio* (1879); *Donna Juanita* (1880).

SVENDSEN, JOHAN SEVERIN
1840-1911, Norweigan
Principal Works - Orchestral: Symphony No. 1, in D major, Op. 4; Symphony No. 2 in B flat major, Op. 15; *Carnival in Paris* (overture), Op. 9; *Zorahayde* (legend), Op. 11; *Festival Polonaise,* Op. 12; *Norwegian Rhapsodies,* Op. 17, 19, 21, and 22; Romance in G major for violin and orchestra, Op. 26.

SWEELINCK, JAN PIETERSZOON
1562-1621, Dutch
Principal Works - 250 vocal and instrumental compositions in counterpoint.

TARTINI, GIUSEPPE
1692-1770, Italian
Principal Works - Sonata: *Devil's Trill.*

TCHAIKOVSKY, PETER ILYITCH
1840-1893, Russian
Principal Works - Opera: *Eugene Onegin* (1878); *Joan of Arc* (1879); *Mazeppa* (1883); *Queen of Spades (Pique Dame)* (1890). **Ballets:** *Swan Lake*, Op. 20 (1876); *The Sleeping Beauty*, Op. 66 (1889) (includes *Aurora's Wedding*); *The Nutcracker (Casse-noisette)*, Op. 71 (1892). **Symphonies:** No. 1, G minor, Op. 13 (1868), *Winter Dreams;* No. 2, C minor, Op. 17 (1873), *Little Russian;* No. 3, D major, Op. 29 (1875), *Polish;* No. 4, F minor, Op. 36 (1878); No. 5, E minor, Op. 64 (1888); No. 6, B minor, Op. 74 (1893), *Pathetique; The Tempest*, Op. 18 (fantasy) (1873); *Francesca da Rimini*, Op. 32 (orchestral fantasy) (1876); *Manfred*, Op. 58 (symphonic poem); Suite No. 3, G major, Op. 55 (1884) Theme and Variations; Suite No. 4, G major, Op. 61 (1887), *Mozartiana; Nutcracker Suite (Caisse-noisette suite)*, Op. 71a *Miniature Overture; March; Dance of the Sugar-Plum Fairy; Trepak; Arab Dance; Dance of the Reed-Flutes; Waltz of the Flowers; Romeo and Juliet*, overture-fantasy (1870); *Capriccio Italien*, Op. 45 (1880); *Festival Overture 1812*, Op. 49 (1880); *Hamlet*, Overture-fantasy, Op. 67a (1885); *Marche Slav*, Op. 31 (1876); Serenade, C major, Op. 48, string orchestra (1880).

TELEMANN, GEORG PHILIPP
1681-1767, German
Principal Works - (1708) Trio Sonata in E flat major; (1715) Concerto in A major; Suite in D minor; (1716) *Die Kleine Kammermusik;* Six suites for violin, querflute and piano; (1718) Six trios for two violins and cello, with bass continuo; (1723) *Hamburger Ebb und Fluht*, overture in C major; (1725) *Pimpinone*, opera; (1728) *Der getreuer Musikmeister*, cantata; (1759) St. Mark Passion. **Plus:** 40 operas; 600 overtures; 44 liturgical passions; many oratorios, cantatas and psalms.

THOMAS, AMBROISE
1811-1896, French
Principal Works - Opera comique: *Le Caïd; Raymond; Mignon;* **Opera:** *Hamlet.*

TOSTI, FRANCESCO PAOLO
1846-1916, Italian/English
Principal Works - Songs: *Forever, At Vespers, Good-bye, Parted, Serenata, My Ideal.*

VECCHI, ORAZIO
1550-1605, Italian
Principal Works - Madrigal Opera: *L'Amfiparnaso.*

VERDI, GIUSEPPE
1813-1901, Italian
Principal Works - Opera: *Nabucodonosor (Nabucco)* (1842); *Ernani* (1844); *Macbeth* (1847); *Luisa Miller* (1849); *Rigoletto* (1851); *Il Trovatore* (1853); *La Traviata* (1853); *I Vespri Siciliani (Sicilian Vespers)* (1855); *Simon Boccanegro* (1857); *Un Ballo in Maschera (A Masked Ball)* (1859); *Aroldo* (1857); *La Forza del Destino* (1862); *Don Carlos* (1867); *Aida* (1871); *Otello* (1886); *Falstaff* (1893). **Orchestral:** *Messa da Requiem (Manzoni Requiem)*, four voices, chorus, orchestra (1874); *Inno delle Nazioni (Hymn of the Nations)*, soprano (or tenor), chorus, orchestra (Boito) (1862); Four Sacred Pieces: *Ave Maria; Stabat Mater; Laudi alla Vergine* (Dante); *Te Deum;* String Quartet in E minor (1873).

VIEUXTEMPS, HENRI
1820-1881, Belgian
Principal Works - Violin Concerto: No. 4 in D Minor, Op. 31.

VIVALDI, ANTONIO
1678-1741, Italian
Principal Works - Concerti for violin & orchestra, *The Four Seasons*, Op. 8 Nos. 1-4; *La Centra*, Op. 9; *L'Estro armonico*, Op. 3. **Oratorio:** *Juditha Triumphans.* **Choral:** *Gloria in D Major.* **Sonata:** *Violin Sonata in A major;* plus 400 concerti and 100 operas.

WAGNER, RICHARD
1813-1883, German
Principal Works - (1832) Symphony in C major; (1840) *Faust*, overture; (1842) *Rienzi*, opera; (1843) *The Flying Dutchman*, opera; (1845) *Tannhäuser*, opera; (1851) *Lohengrin*, opera; (1857-58) The *Wesendonck Lieder*, five songs with orchestra; (1865) *Tristan und Isolde*, music drama; (1868) *Die Meistersinger von Nürnberg*, opera; (1869) *Das Rheingold* (No. 1 of *Der Ring des Nibelungen*); (1870) *Die Walküre* (No. 2 of *Der Ring des Nibelungen*); (1876) *Siegfried* (No. 3 of *Der Ring des Nibelungen*); *Götterdämmerung* (No. 4 of *Der Ring des Nibelungen*); (1882) *Parsifal*, religious music drama. **Piano:** *Ein Albumblatt*, C major (1861) (Several arr.).

WALDTEUFEL, EMIL
1837-1915, French
Principal Works - Waltzes: *Acclamations*, Op. 223 *(Hoch lebe der Tanz); Dolores*, Op. 170; *España*, Op. 236 (On themes of Chabrier); *Estudiantina*, Op. 191; *Les Grenadiers; Mon rêve* (My dream), Op. 151; *Les Patineurs* (The Skaters), Op. 183; *Pluie de diamants*, Op. 160; *Les Sirènes*, Op. 154; *Toujours ou jamais* (Ever or never), Op. 156; *Très jolie (Ganz allerliebst)*, Op. 159; *Violettes*, Op. 148.

WALLACE, WILLIAM VINCENT
1812-1865, Irish
Principal Works - Opera: *Maritana; Lurline; The Amber Witch; Love's Triumph; The Desert Flower.*

WEBER, CARL MARIA VON
1786-1826 German
Principal Works - Opera: *Peter Schmoll und seine Nachbarn* (1801); *The Ruler of the Spirits (Der Beherrscher der Geister)* (1805); *Abu Hassan* (1811); *Der Freischütz* (1821); *Euryanthe* (1823); *Oberon* (1826). **Orchestral:** *Jubel-Ouvertüre*, E major, Op. 59 (1818); *Concertstück*, F minor, Op. 79 (piano and orchestra) (1821); Concertino, E flat major, Op. 26 (clarinet and orchestra) (1811). **Chamber Music:** *Grand duo concertant*, for clarinet and

piano, E flat major, Op. 48 (1816); Violin Sonata No. 3, D minor (1810). **Incidental Music:** *Preciosa,* Op. 78 (Play by A.P. Wolff) (1820) Overture. **Piano:** Piano Sonata No. 1, C major, Op. 24 (1812); Presto (Rondo—*Perpetuum mobile*); Piano Sonata No. 2, A flat major, Op. 39 (1816); Piano Sonata No. 4, E minor, Op. 70 (1822); *Rondo brillante,* E flat major, Op. 62 (1819); *Invitation to the Dance,* Op. 65 (1819).

WIDOR, CHARLES MARIE
1844-1937
Principal Works - Organ Symphony: Symphony No. 5 in F minor, Op. 42, No. 1.

WIENIAWSKI, HENRI
1835-1880, Polish
Principal Works - Violin Concerti: No. 1 in F sharp minor, Op. 14; No. 2 in D minor, Op. 22; *Legende; Souvenir de Moscou; Variations on Gounod's Faust.*

WILBYE, JOHN
1574-1638, English
Principal Works - Madrigals: *Adieu, Sweet Amaryllis, Stay, Corydon, Flora Gave Me Fairest Flowers, What Needeth All This Travail* and many others.

WOLF, HUGO
1860-1903, Austrian
Principal Works - Chamber Music: *Italian Serenade,* G major (string quartet, 1887, orchestra 1892). **Songs:** *Anakreons Grab* (Goethe); *Auch kleine Dinge (Italian Songbook); Das doch gemalt all'deine Reize wären (Italian Songbook); Eiphanias* (Goethe); *Er ist's* (Mörike); *Der Freund* (Eichendorff); *Fussreise* (Mörike); *Der Gärtner* (Mörike); *Gebet* (Mörike); *Gesang Weylas* (Mörike); *Heimweh* (Eichendorff); *In dem Schatten meiner Locken (Spanish Songbook); Mausfallen-sprüchlein* (Morike); *Nimmersatte Liebe* (Mörike); *Nun wandre, Maria (Spanish Songbook); Schlafendes Jesuskind* (Mörike); *Storchenbotschaft* (Mörike); *Und willst du deinen Liebsten sterben sehen?; Verborgenheit* (Mörike); *Das verlassene Mägdelein* (Mörike); *Verschwiegene Liebe* (Eichendorff).

ZELLER, CARL
1842-1898, Austrian
Principal Works - Operetta: *Der Vogelhändler (The Brideseller); Der Obersteiger (The Foreman).*

BEST-KNOWN
CLASSICAL MUSIC
COMPOSERS

PART II
20TH CENTURY
(1900 - 1980)

ÁBRÁNYI, EMIL
1882, Hungarian
Principal Works - Operas: *Monna Vanna, Paolo, Francesca, Don Quixote, Ave Maria, Singing Dervishes, The Prince With The Lilies, The Cantor of St. Thomas Church.*

ABSIL, JEAN
1893-1974, Belgian
Principal Works - Symphonies, ballets, concertos for piano and violin. String quartets and chamber music.

ADAMIS, MICHAEL
1929, Greek
Principal Works - *Apocalypse (The Sixth Seal)* for narrator, chorus, piano and tape; *Genesis* for narrator, 3 choruses and tape.

ADASKIN, MURRAY
1906, Canadian
Principal Works - Opera: *Grant, Warden of the Plains. Qalala and Nilaula of the North* for woodwind, strings, percussion.

ADDINSELL, RICHARD
1904, English
Principal Works-Film music including *Warsaw Concerto.*

ADDISON, JOHN
1920, English
Principal Works - Ballet: *Carte Blanche*; trumpet concert; film and theater music.

ADLER, SAMUEL
1928, American
Principal Works - Opera: *The Outcasts of Poker Flat;* **Cantata:** *The Vision of Isaiah,* 1949; 5 symphonies and other pieces.

AKHRON (ACHRON), JOSEPH
1886-1943, Lithuanian/American
Principal Works - Violin and orchestra: *Hebrew Melody,* 1911; 3 violin concertos; chamber pieces.

AKIMENKO, FEODOR STEPANOVICH
1876-1945, Russian
Principal Works - Orch. pieces; an opera, a ballet and chamber music.

AKIYAMA, KUNIHARU
1929, Japanese
Principal Works - *Music for Bells,* with glass bottles, stones and tape; *Music for Farting* for clarinet, trumpet, trombone and tuba.

ALAIN, JEHAN
1911-1940, French
Principal Works - Organ and choral music.

ALBRIGHT, WILLIAM
1944, American
Principal Works - Organ, piano and orchestral pieces. Multimedia composition: *Tic,* 1967.

ALBRIGHT, WILLIAM
1944, American
Principal Works - Organ, piano and orchestral pieces. Multimedia composition: *Tic,* (1967).

ALFANO, FRANCO
1876-1954, Italian
Principal Works - Opera: *Risurrezione* (1904), *La Leggenda di Sakuntala* (1921); ballets, symphonic pieces; chamber and piano.

ALFVEN, HUGO
1872-1960, Swedish
Principal Works - Rhapsody for orchestra: *Midsummer Vigil* (1904).

ALLENDE SARÓN, PEDRO HUMBERTO
1885-1959, Chilean
Principal Works - Symphony, concertos, choral, chamber. **Piano:** *12 tonadas de caracter popular chileno.*

ALPAERTS, FLOR
1876-1954, Flemish
Principal Works - Symphony: *Pallieter* (1921); **Opera:** *Shylock* (1913); **Orch. Suite:** *James Ensor Suite* (1929).

ALWYN, WILLIAM
1905, English
Principal Works - Concerto for harp and strings: *Lyra Angelica;* 5 symphonies, a violin concerto, string quartets, film music.

AMFITHEATROF, DANIELE
1901, Russian/American
Principal Works - Motion picture music composer.

AMRAM, DAVID
1930, American
Principal Works - Operas: *The Final Ingredient* (1965); *Twelfth Night* (1968); Trio for Tenor Sax, French Horn, and Bassoon (1958); Shakespearean Concerto for Small Orchestra (1959); Sonata Allegro for String Orchestra; *Lysistrata* (for solo flute) (1960); Sonata for Violin and Piano (1960); Piano Sonata (1960); Discussions for Flute, Piano, and Percussion; *Jazz Studio No. 6* (1962).

AMY, GILBERT
1936, French
Principal Works - *Cantata breve* (1960); *Antiphonies for 2 orchestras* (1963); *Trajectoires* for violin and orchestra (1966).

ANDREAE, VOLKMAR
1879, Swiss
Principal Works - Operas: *Ratcliff, Abenteuer des Casanova.*

ANDRIESSEN, HENRIK
1892, Dutch
Principal Works - Masses; cello sonata, 3 symphonies; song cycle *Miroir de Peine* (1923); **opera:** *Philomela* (1950).

ANDRIESSEN, JURRIAAN
1925, Dutch
Principal Works - 4 symphonies; symphonic ballet poem *Berkshire Symphonies* (1949); piano concerto; film music, chamber music, songs.

ANDRIESSEN, LOUIS
1939, Dutch
Principal Works - Opera: *Reconstructie* (1969); orchestral pieces, chamber and piano pieces, film music.

ANDRIESSEN, WILLEM
1887-1964, Dutch
Principal Works - A mass; piano and organ music; songs.

ANHALT, ISTVÁN
1919, Hungarian/Canadian
Principal Works - Electronic music; a symphony; piano and chamber pieces.

ANTHEIL, GEORGE
1900-1959, American
Principal Works - 6 symphonies; 3 string quartets, 2 violin sonatas; 4 piano sonatas; concertos for piano, for violin, for flute, bassoon and piano; chamber concerto for 8 instruments; **Operas:** *Transatlantic* (1930); *Helen Retires; Volpone; The Brothers; The Wish; Ballet mechanique* for pianos, percussion and airplane propeller (1927); **piano:** *Airplane Sonata* (1922); *Mechanisms; Crucifixion* for string orchestra; *Decatur at Algiers; McKonkey's Ferry; Overture; 2 Odes of Keats; Songs of Experience* after William Blake; *Tom Sawyer; 8 Fragments from Shelley; Valentine Waltzes.*

ANTILL, JOHN
1904, Australian
Principal Works - **Ballet:** *Corroboree.*

ANTONIOU, THEODORE
1935, Greek/American
Principal Works - **Orchestral:** *Mikrographien* (1964); *Events II* (1969); *Cassandra* for mixed media (1969).

APOSTEL, HANS ERICH
1901-1974, Austrian
Principal Works - *Variations on theme from Wozzeck;* a Requiem; 3 string quartets, piano pieces.

ARCHER, VIOLET
1913, Canadian
Principal Works - *Cantata Sacra* for solo vocals and chamber orch.; piano concerto, violin concerto.

ARDÉVOL, JOSÉ
1911, Cuban
Principal Works - Ballet; symphonies, concerto for 3 pianos; **Cantatas:** *Lenin* (1970); *Canton de la revolución* for chorus (1962).

AREL, BÜLENT
1918, Turkish
Principal Works - Electronic pieces; orchestral and chamber music.

ARGENTO, DOMINICK
1927, American
Principal Works - **Operas:** *Voyage of Edgar Allan Poe* (1976); *A Water Bird Talk* (1977); **orchestral:** *In Praise of Music* (1977); **songs:** *From The Diary of Virginia Woolf* (1975).

ARNELL, RICHARD
1917, English
Principal Works - **Cantata:** *The War God;* **ballet:** *Punch and The Child.*

ARNOLD, MALCOLM
1921, English
Principal Works - *Toy Symphony* and 7 other symphonies; **Ballet:** *Homage to the Queen* (1953); *Solitaire* (1956); Concertos for oboe, for clarinet, for harmonica; chamber and film music, songs.

ARRIGO, GIROLAMO
1930, Italian
Principal Works - *Infra-red* for 16 instruments; *From the mist to the mist* for 16 celli and 6 double basses; Vocal works.

ARUTIUNIAN, ALEXANDER GRIGORIEVICH
1920, Soviet/Armenian
Principal Works - **Opera:** *Sayat-Nova;* concertos for piano, for trumpet, for horn.

ASAFIEV, BORIS
1884-1949, Russian
Principal Works - **Ballet:** *The Fountain of Bakhchisarai;* Operas, 4 symphonies.

ASHLEY, ROBERT
1930, American
Principal Works - Electronic theater: *Kittyhawk (an Antigravity Piece)* (1964); *Untitled Mixes* (1965); *She Was A Visitor,* for chorus (1967).

ATTERBERG, KURT
1887-1974, Swedish
Principal Works - Symphony No. 6 (1928); *Värmland Rhapsody.*

AUBERT, LOUIS
1877-1968, French
Principal Works - **Opera:** *La Forêt bleue* (1913).

AURIC, GEORGES
1889, French
Principal Works - Ballets, orchestral works, chamber, piano and film scores.

AUSTIN, FREDERIC
1872-1952, English
Principal Works - Rescoring *The Beggar's Opera* (1920); *Polly* (1922).

AUSTIN, LARRY
1930, American
Principal Works - Improvisations for Orchestra and Jazz Soloists (1961); Open Style for orchestra and piano soloist (1965); *The Magicians* for mixed media (1968); *Catharsis: Open Style for Two Improvisation Ensembles Tapes and Conductor* (1967); Electronic: *Agape* (1970).

AVIDOM, MENAHEM
1908, Israeli
Principal Works - **Opera:** *Alexandra;* 7 symphonies; **Piano:** *Twelve Changing Preludes.*

AVNI, ZVI
1927, Israeli
Principal Works - **String quartet:** *Summer Strings; Collage* for voice, flute, percussion and electric guitar; **Orchestra:** *Thoughts On A Drama.*

AVSHALOMOV, AARON
1894-1965, Russian/American
Principal Works - Piano concerto on Chinese themes; other combined Chinese-Western pieces.

AVSHALOMOV, JACOB
1919, American
Principal Works - **Orchestra:** *Sinfonietta; Slow Dance; Inscriptions at the City of Brass* for narrator, chorus and orchestra; **symphony** *Tom O'Bedlam,* use of Chinese materials.

AXMAN, EMIL
1887-1949, Czech
Principal Works - Symphonies, choral pieces, etc.

AYALA PÉREZ, DANIEL
1908, Mexican
Principal Works - Symphonic suites, vocal, chamber. Use of Mayan materials.

BAAREN, KEES VAN
1906-1970, Dutch
Principal Works - Serial music; orchestra, piano, chamber music.

BABBITT, MILTON
1916, American
Principal Works - Twelve-tone and electronic music. *Composition for 4 Instruments* (1948); *Composition for 12 Instruments* (1948); song cycle *Du* (1951); **Jazz:** *All Set* (1957); **Piano:** *Partitions* (1957); **Orchestral:** *Relata I* and *II; Composition for Synthesizer* (1963); Soprano and tape: *Vision and Prayer* (1961), *Philomel* (1964); 4 string quartets; Tape: *Reflections* with piano (1974); *Phonemena* with soprano; *Concerti* with violin and orchestra; *More Phonemena* with soprano; *Concerti* with violin and orchestra; *More Phonemena* for mixed chorus (1977).

BABIN, VICTOR
1908, American
Principal Works - Concerto for 2 pianos.

BACEWICZ, GRAZYNA
1913-1969, Polish
Principal Works - Ballets; **Orchestral:** *Music for Strings, Trumpets and Percussion* (1958); *In una parte* (1967); 4 symphonies; concertos for violin, for cello, for piano, for viola; string quartets; violin sonatas.

BÄCK, SVEN-ERIK
1919, Swedish
Principal Works - String quartets; chamber music.

BACON, ERNST
1898, American
Principal Works - **Folk opera:** *A Tree On The Plains.*

BADINGS, HENK
1907, Dutch
Principal Works - Symphony No. 3 (1934); *Orpheus and Eurydice* ballet (1941); **Opera:** *The Night Watch* (1942); Oratorio; *Apocalypse* (1949); Symphony No. 5 (1949); Electronic music: *Cain and Abel,* ballet (1956); **Opera:** *Genese* (1958).

BAIRD, TADEUSZ
1928, Polish
Principal Works - Twelve-tone music. **Opera:** *Jutro* (1966); **Symphonic works:** *Sinfonia brevis,* 3 symphonies, 4 orch. *Essays* (1958); *Psychodrama* (1975), chamber music, songs.

BALADA, LEONARDO
1933, Spanish
Principal Works - **Orchestral works:** *Guernica* (1967), *Transparencias* (1973); concertos for piano, for guitar; *Maria Sabina* for orch. and narrator; *Geometrias* for 7 instruments (1966); *Cuatris* for 4 instruments (1969).

BALASSA, SANDOR
1935, Hungarian
Principal Works - *Iris* for orchestra; *Requiem for Lajos Kassak,* Trio for violin, viola and harp.

BALLIF, CLAUDE
1924, French
Principal Works - *Journey Of My Ear* for orchestra; *Double Trio* chamber work for flute, oboe, cello, violin, clarinet, horn.

BALOGH, ERNO
1897, Hungarian/American
Principal Works - Orchestral, violin and piano pieces.

BAMERT, MATTHIAS
1942, Swiss
Principal Works - **Orchestral:** *Septuaria lunnaris* (1970); *Mantrajana* (1971); *Inkblot* for band (1971); *Organism* for organ (1972).

BANFIELD, RAFFAELO DE
1922, Italian
Principal Works - **Opera:** *Lord Byron's Love Letter;* **Ballet:** *The Duel.*

BANKS, DON
1923, Australian
Principal Works - *Four pieces for orchestra;* Concerto for horn; Psalm 70 for soprano and chamber orchestra; Divertimento for flute and string trio; a violin sonata.

BANSHCHIKOV, GENNADY IVANOVICH
1943, Russian
Principal Works - 5 cello concertos; cantata with orch. in memory of Lorca; operas.

BANTOCK, GRANVILLE
1868-1946, English
Principal Works - **Operas:** *Caedmar* (1893); *The Seal Woman* (1924); **Ballet:** *Egypt* (1892); **symphonic poems:** *Fifine at the Fair* (1901); *Hebridean Symphony* (1915); *Omar Khayyam* (1906), choral with orchestra; **Unaccompanied choral:** *Atlanta in Calydon* (1911); **Piano:** *Songs from the Chinese Poets* (1918).

BARATI, GEORGE
1913, Hungarian
Principal Works - A symphony; concertos for cello, for guitar, for piano; chorus and orch: *The Waters of Kane* (1966); chamber and stage music.

BARBER, SAMUEL
1910, American
Principal Works - **Opera:** *Vanessa; A Hand Of Bridge; Antony and Cleopatra;* 2 symphonies; Symphony In One Movement; *Adagio* for strings; *Essay for orchestra;* Violin Sonata; *Overture to The School for Scandal;* Cello concerto; *Capricorn Concerto* for flute, oboe, trumpet and strings; Piano Sonata, Op. 26; *Dover Beach* for voice and strings; **Ballet suites:** *Medea, Souvenirs;* **cantata:** *Prayers of Kierkegaard; Knoxville: Summer of 1915;* Cello Sonata (1962); **Piano:** *Excursions.*

BARLOW, SAMUEL
1892, American
Principal Works - **Opera:** *Mon Ami Pierrot.*

BARLOW, WAYNE
1912, American
Principal Works - **Oboe and strings:** *The Winter's Passed;* **cantata:** *Wait for the Promise of the Father* (1968); **Chorus and organ:** *Missa Sancti Thomae* (1959); Concerto for saxophone and band (1970); Tape and orchestra, *Soundscapes;* Chorus, organ and tape: *Psalm 97* (1970); chamber and organ pieces.

BARRAQUE, JEAN
1928-1973, French
Principal Works - Piano sonata; concerto for clarinet, vibraphone, six instrumental ensembles; *Song after Song* for six percussionists, voice and piano.

BARRAUD, HENRY
1900, French
Principal Works - Comic opera: *La Farce de Maître Pathelin* (1948); *Le testament de Francois Villon,* cantata (1945); **Oratorio:** *Le mystère des Saints Innocents* (1946); **Chorus and winds:** *Te Deum* (1955); symphonies, vocal, stage music.

BARTOK, BELA
1881-1945, Hungarian
Principal Works - Two Suites for Orchestra (1905); **Piano Solo:** *Rhapsody, Two Elegies, Three Burlesques, Sketches;* 14 Bagatelles, Ten Easy Pieces for piano; Two Rumanian Dances; 85 children's pieces; First String Quartet (1908); **Opera:** *Bluebeard's Castle;* **ballet:** *The Wooden Prince* (1904); *The Miraculous Mandarin* (1918); *Dance Suite* (1923); *Cantata Profana* (1920); *Mikrokosmos* (1926); Fifth String Quartet (1934); Sonata for two Pianos and Percussion (1938); Music For Strings, Percussion and Celeste (1937); Concerto for orchestra (1943); Sonata for solo violin (1944); Third Piano Concerto (1945); Violin Concerto (1937); *Divertimento for String Orchestra* (1939); Sixth String Quartet (1940).

BARTOLOZZI, BRUNO
1911, Italian
Principal Works - Concerto for orchestra; *The Hollow Man* for woodwind; *Images* for women's voices and 17 instruments.

BARTOS, JAN ZDENĚK
1908-1973, Czech.
Principal Works - Concerto for horn, for accordion; *From Petrarch's Sonnets to Laura* for tenor, bass, violin, cello and harpsichord.

BASSETT, LESLIE
1923, American
Principal Works - Orchestral: *Variations for Orchestra* (1966); *Five Movements* (1962); *Echoes From An Invisible World* (1976); Concerto for 2 pianos and orch. (1977); *Five Pieces* (1957) for string quartet; chamber and choral works; **Tape:** *Three Studies in Electronic Sounds* (1965).

BATE, STANLEY RICHARD
1911-1959, English
Principal Works - Ballets, symphonies, concertos, film music.

BAUDRIER, YVES
1906, French
Principal Works - Film music, orchestral works, chamber music.

BAUER, MARION
1887-1955, American
Principal Works - Orchestral: *Sun Splendor* (1926); piano and choral pieces, songs.

BAULD, ALION
1944, Australian
Principal Works - *Exiles* for 4 actors, mezzo-soprano, tenor, chorus and instruments; *Mad Doll* for soprano; *Dear Emily* for soprano and harp; *Van Diemen's Land* for unaccompanied chorus.

BAX, ARNOLD
1883-1953, English
Principal Works - 7 symphonies; symphonic poems: *The Garden of Fand* and *Tintagel;* **choral:** *Mater ora Filium* for unaccompanied double chorus; **Ballet:** *The Truth about the Russian Dancers; Overture To A Picaresque Comedy;* piano solos.

BAZELON, IRWIN
1922, American
Principal Works -Symphonies, overtures, string quartets.

BEACH, AMY MARCY
1867-1944, American
Principal Works - *Gaelic Symphony* (1896); a Mass, 2 piano concertos; cantatas; a violin sonata, songs.

BECERRA SCHMIDT, GUSTAVO
1925, Chilean
Principal Works - Opera: *La muerte de Don Rodgrigo;* choral, ballet and film music; 3 symphonies, 2 guitar concertos, string quartets; tape works.

BECK, CONRAD
1901, Swiss
Principal Works - 7 symphonies, cantatas, oratorios, piano concerto, chamber.

BECKER, JOHN J.
1886-1961, American
Principal Works - 7 symphonies; choral and stage works: *A Marriage With Space* (1935); *Soundpiece* nos. 1 to 8 for various instruments; a violin concerto; 2 piano concertos, songs.

BECKWITH, JOHN
1927, Canadian
Principal Works - Chamber opera: *Night Blooming Cereus* (1959); *Canada Dash, Canada Dot* collage for singers, speakers and orchestra; *Circle with tangents* for harpsichord and 13 strings; *A Message to Winnipeg* for 3 speakers and instruments (1960).

BEDFORD, DAVID
1937, English
Principal Works - Choral: *Two Poems* (1963); *A Dream Of The Seven Lost Stars* (1964); *Music for Albion Moonlight* for soprano and instruments; *O Now The Drenched Land Awakes,* for baritone and piano duet; *That White and Radiant Legend* for soprano, speaker and instruments; *Come In Here Child* for soprano and amplified piano (1968); *Star*

Clusters, Nebulae and Places in Devon for mixed double chorus and brass (1971); *Nurse's Song With Elephants* for 10 acoustic guitars and singer (1971); *Some Stars Above Magnitude 2.9* for soprano and piano; *Holy Thursday with Squeakers* for soprano and instruments; **Orchestral:** *Piece for Mo* (1963); *This One For You* (1965); *Five* for violins and cellos; *Trona for 12; 18 Bricks Left on April 21* for two electric guitars (1967); *The Garden of Love, The Sword of Orion; When I Heard The Learned Astronomer* for tenor and instruments (1972); *A Horse, His Name Was Hunry Fencewaver Wadkins* for instruments (1973).

BEDFORD, HERBERT
1867-1945, English
Principal Works - Military band music, unaccompanied songs.

BEECROFT, NORMA
1934, Canadian
Principal Works - *Contrasts* for oboe, viola, harp, marimba, vibraphone, other percussion; **choral:** *The Living Flame of Love.*

BEESON, JACK
1921, American
Principal Works - **Operas:** *Hello Out There,* one-act chamber; *Jonah* and *The Sweet Bye and Bye,* both two-act operas; **symphonies:** *Lizzie Borden* (1957); *Captain Jenks of the Horse Marines* (1959); *Transformations* for orchestra (1959); **Opera:** *My heart's in the Highlands;* 5 piano sonatas, choral music, songs.

BEHRMAN, DAVID
1937, American
Principal Works - Electronic and mixed media (1974); *Net For Catching Big Sounds.*

BENGUEREL, XAVIER
1931, Spanish
Principal Works - *Successions* for wind quintet; violin concerto, organ concerto.

BEN-HAIM, PAUL
1897, Israeli
Principal Works - 2 symphonies; orchestral pieces; a piano concerto; chamber music; uses Jewish and Arabic materials.

BENJAMIN, ARTHUR
1893-1960, Australian
Principal Works - **Operas:** *A Tale Of Two Cities* (1953); *The Devil Take Her* (1931); **Ballet:** *Orlando's Silver Wedding* (1951); **orch. works:** *Jamaican Rumba* (1938) and others.

BENNETT, RICHARD RODNEY
1936, English
Principal Works - **Operas:** *the Mines of Sulphur* (1965); *Victory* (1970); **Cantata:** *The Approaches of Sleep* (1959); **orchestral:** symphony, *Aubade* (1964); concerto for horn, for piano; violin, flute, piano and guitar music; 4 string quartets, film music; *Calendar* for chamber group (1960).

BENSON, WARREN
1924, American
Principal Works - Solo wind and ensemble pieces; chamber music; string quartets.

BENTOIU, PASCAL
1927, Rumanian
Principal Works - **Opera:** *Hamlet;* symphony for 3 saxophones and orchestra; 2 piano concertos.

BENTZON, JORGEN
1897, Danish
Principal Works - *A Dickens Symphony; Racconti* for 3 to 5 instruments.

BENTZON, NIELS VIGGO
1919, Danish
Principal Works - **Ballet:** *The Courtesan; Napoleon* and 10 other piano sonatas; 9 string quartets; symphonic works.

BEREZOWSKY, NICOLAI
1900-1953, American
Principal Works - **Orchestral:** *Suite hebraique;* **cantata:** *Gilgamesh;* **children's opera:** *Babar the Elephant;* 4 symphonies; concertos for violin, for viola, for cello, for harp, for clarinet; chamber music.

BERG, ALBAN
1885-1935, Austrian
Principal Works - **Opera:** *Wozzeck;* Five Orchestral Songs Op. 4; **Opera:** *Lulu;* Chamber symphony; *Lyric Suite* for string quartet; violin concerto; *Der Wein,* aria; *Chamber Concerto* with piano, violin solos.

BERGER, ARTHUR
1912, American
Principal Works - *Serenade Concertante* for violin, woodwind quartet and small orchestra; *Ideas of Order* for orchestra; *Partita* for piano; chamber pieces, songs.

BERGER, THEODOR
1905, Austrian
Principal Works - *The Elements,* symphonic poem cycle; *Manual Concerto* for 2 pianos, percussion and strings; 2 string quartets.

BERGSMA, WILLIAM LAURENCE
1921, American
Principal Works - **Opera:** *The Wife Of Martin Guerre* (1956); two ballets; a symphony; chamber, piano and choral pieces.

BERIO, LUCIANO
1925, Italian
Principal Works - Serial, electronic, aleatory music. **Ballet:** *Mimomusique* (1954); **orchestral:** *Nones* (1954); *Differences* for 5 instruments and tape; **Tape:** *Omaggio a Joyce* (1958); *Circles* for soprano, harp, percussion ensembles; *Epiphanie* for soprano and orch. (1961); *Sinfonia* for reciters, chorus and orch. (1968); *Sequenza* for voice and solo instruments; works for electronic instruments; *Linea* for pianos and percussion (1979).

BERKELEY, LENNOX
1903, English
Principal Works - Opera: *Nelson* (1953); **oratorio:** *Jonah* (1935); *Domini est Terra* for chorus and orch.; *4 Sonnets of Ronsard* for tenor and orch. (1963); **ballet:** *The Judgement of Paris* (1938); *6 Preludes* for piano; 3 symphonies; piano and chamber pieces.

BERNERS, LORD GERALD HUGH
1883-1950, English
Principal Works - Ballets: *The Triumph of Neptune* (1926); *A Wedding Bouquet* (1936); an opera; piano works, songs.

BERNSTEIN, LEONARD
1918, American
Principal Works - Prominent serious and popular music composer; **Orchestral works:** *Jeremiah Symphony* (1944); *The Age of Anxiety* (1949); *Kaddish* (1963); *Chichester Psalms* with countertenor and chorus; **opera:** *Trouble in Tahiti;* **ballet:** *Fancy Free, Facsimile, Dybbuk;* **stage works:** *Candide* (1956); *West Side Story* (1957); *Mass* for singer, players and dancers; **film music:** *On The Waterfront; Songfest* for vocal solos and orchestra (1977); piano and chamber pieces, songs.

BENZANSON, PHILIP
1916, American
Principal Works - Opera: *Golden Child* (1960); Piano Concerto; chamber and vocal pieces.

BIBAO, ANTONIO
1922, Italian
Principal Works - Opera: *The Smile At The Foot of the Ladder;* piano and orchestral music.

BINKERD, GORDON
1916, American
Principal Works - *A Christmas Carol* and other choral works; 4 symphonies; string quartets; chamber and piano music.

BIRTWHISTLE, HARRISON
1934, English
Principal Works - *Refrains and Choruses* for wind quintet (1957); **Orchestral:** *Chorales* (1963); *The Triumph of Time* (1970); **chamber opera:** *Punch and Judy* (1968); *Tragoedia* for winds, strings and harp (1965); *Grimethorpe Aria* for brass band; *Chanson de Geste* for tape and solo instruments; *Chorales from a Toyshop* in five parts.

BLACHER, BORIS
1903-1975, German
Principal Works - Operas: *Furstin Tarakanowa* (1941); *Abstrakte Oper* (1953); *Rosamunde floris* (1960); **orchestral:** *Concertante Musik* (1937); ballet, film music, 3 piano concertos; *Jazzkoloraturen* chamber pieces; piano and songs.

BLACKWOOD, EASLEY
1933, American
Principal Works - *Chamber Symphony* (1955); 3 symphonies; concertos for clarinet, for violin, for flute, for piano; 2 string quartets; piano and chamber pieces.

BLAKE, DAVID
1936, English
Principal Works - Opera: *Toussaint;* Variations for piano; Chamber Symphony; choral works (unaccompanied).

BLECH, LEO
1871-1958, German
Principal Works - Operas: *Das var ich* (1902); *Versiegelt* (1908); *Alpenkonig und Menschenfeind* (1903); symphonic poems, piano and choral pieces.

BLISS, ARTHUR
1891-1975, English
Principal Works - *Madame Noy* for soprano and six instruments (1908); *Rhapsody* (1919); *Conversations* for flute, Eng. horn, string trio; *Rout* (1919); *Checkmate, Adam Zero, Morning Heroes; A Colour Symphony* (1922); *Music for Strings; Piano Concerto* (1938); *Miracle In The Gortals* (1944); Clarinet Quintet; Viola Sonata; film music.

BLITZSTEIN, MARC
1905-1964, American
Principal Works - Operas: *The Cradle Will Rock* (1937); *No For an Answer* (1941); *Regina* (1949); **cantata:** *This Is The Garden* (1957); **orchestral:** *Airborne Symphony* (1945); *Freedom Morning* (1943); film music, chamber pieces; adaptation of *Three-Penny Opera* (1953).

BLOCH, ERNEST
1880-1959, American
Principal Works - *Trois Poemes Juifs,* orchestra (1913); *Schelomo,* rhapsody for cello and orchestra (1916); *Israel,* symphony for orchestra and solo voices (1912-16); *The Psalms,* voice and orchestra (1912)14); Concerto grosso, for strings with piano (1924-25); *America,* epic rhapsody (1926); *Sacred Service* (1932-34), for baritone solo, choir, and orchestra; Piano Quintet (1923-24); String Quartet No. 3 (1945).

BLOMDAHL, KARL-BIRGER
1916-1968, Swedish
Principal Works - Operas: *Aniara* (1959); *Herr von Hancken* (1965); **Orchestral:** *Sisyphos* (1954); *Forma ferritonans* (1961); *Anabase* (1956); 3 symphonies; orchestral and voices; *Altisonans* (1966) with tape; chamber pieces.

BOATWRIGHT, HOWARD
1918, American
Principal Works - Operas: *Aniara* (1959); *Herr von Hancken* (1965); **Orchestral:** *Sisyphos* (1954); *Forma ferritonans* (1961); *Anabase* (1956); 3 symphonies; orchestral and voices: *Altisonans* (1966) with tape; chamber pieces.

BOATWRIGHT, HOWARD
1918, American

430

Principal Works - Choral, sacred and orchestral music; songs and chamber music.

BOGUSLAWSKI, EDUARD
1940, Polish
Principal Works - *Apocalypse* for narrator, chorus and orchestra; *Intonations* for orchestra.

BOLCOM, WILLIAM
1938, American
Principal Works - Serial and electronic music; **Pop opera:** *Dynamite Tonight* (1963); *Open House* for tenor and chamber orchestra (1975); string quartets, piano and chamber music.

BOONE, CHARLES
1939, American
Principal Works - Electronic and tape music; solo flute, solo clarinet; orchestral and small ensemble pieces, including *Shunt.*

BORKOVEC, PAVEL
1894-1972, Czech.
Principal Works - Operas; **Ballet:** *The Pied Piper* (1939), **orchestral:** *Start* (1929); 3 symphonies, 2 piano concertos; 4 string quartets; songs.

BOROWSKI, FELIX
1872-1956, American
Principal Works - **Ballet:** *A Century of the Dance* (1934); 2 ballet-pantomimes; **opera:** *Fernando del Nonsensico* (1935); 3 symphonies, chamber music, songs.

BOSCOVICH, ALEXANDER URIJA
1907-1964, Israeli
Principal Works - **Orchestral:** *Semitic Suite* (1947); **choral cantata:** *Daughter of Israel* (1960); **chamber:** *Concerto da camera* (1962); violin concerto, oboe concerto. Jewish sacred music and serial music.

BOSSI, (MARCO) ENRICO
1861-1925, Italian
Principal Works - **Orchestral:** *Tema e variazioni;* **choral:** *Canticum canticorum, Il Cieco, Il Paradiso perduto; Giovanna d'Arco.*

BOSSI, RENZO
1883-1965, Italian
Principal Works - **Opera:** *Volpino il calderaio;* **orchestral:** *Pinocchio;* ballets and chamber music.

BOUCOURECHLIEV, ANDRE
1925, French/Bulgarian
Principal Works - 4 aleatory pieces *Archipel.*

BOUGHTON, RUTLAND
1878-1960, English
Principal Works - **Opera:** *The Immortal Hours* (1914); chorus and orchestra: *Midnight.*

BOULANGER, LILI
1893-1918, French
Principal Works - **Cantata:** *Faust et Helene;* **Orchestral:** *Psalms;* music to Maeterlinck's *Princess Maleine.*

BOULANGER, NADIA
1887-1979, French
Principal Works - Director of the American Conservatory in Fontainbleau, France and faculty member of the École normale de musique in Paris. One of the most important forces in 20th century music in view of the incredible percentage of American and European composers who have

ascended under her tutelage. Her own compositions include: *Rhapsodie* for piano and orchestra; *La ville morte;* **cantata:** *La sirene* (1908).

BOULEZ, PIERRE
1925, French
Principal Works - *Visage Nuptial,* for soprano, alto and chamber orchestra; Piano Sonata No. 1; Sonatina for flute and piano (1946); *Soleil des eaux,* for voices and orchestra; Piano Sonata No. 2 (1947-48); *Livre pour cordes,* for string orchestra; *Livre pour quatour,* for string quartet (1949); *Polyphonie X,* for eighteen instruments; Second version of *Visage Nuptial,* for soprano, alto, choir and orchestra (1951); *Structures,* Book I, for two pianos (1952); *Le Marteau sans maitre,* for alto voice and six instruments (1954); *Symphonie Mecanique* (1955); *Doubles,* for three orchestral groups divisi; *Poésie pour pouvoir,* for reciter, orchestra and tape; *Deux Improvisations sur Mallarmé,* for soprano and instrumental ensemble; Piano Sonata No. 3 (1957); *Tombeau,* for orchestra (1959); *Pli selon pli,* Portrait de Mallarmé for soprano and orchestra (1960); Structures, Book II, for two pianos (1961); *Figures-Doubles-Prismes,* for orchestra; *Éclat,* for fifteen instruments (1964); *Domaines,* for clarinet and twenty-one instruments (1968); *Multiples,* for orchestra; *Cummings ist der Dichter,* for sixteen mixed voices and instruments (1970); *Explosante-Fixe...*for ensemble and live electronics (1972-74); *Rituel, in memoriam Maderna,* for orchestra (1974-75).

BOURGUIGNON, FRANCIS DE
1890-1961, Belgian
Principal Works - Polytonal works; piano concertos, chamber music, songs.

BOWEN, YORK
1884-1961, English
Principal Works - 3 piano concertos; piano solos.

BOWLES, PAUL
1910, American
Principal Works - **Ballet:** *Colloque Sentimental* (1944); **Opera:** *Denmark Vesey* (1937); *The Wind Remains* (1943); piano sonatas, concertos, songs, chamber music.

BOZAY, ATTILA
1939, Hungarian
Principal Works - *Outcries* for tenor and chamber ensemble; *Symphonic Piece* for orchestra; piano variations.

BRAND, MAX
1896, American
Principal Works - **Opera:** *Machinist Hopkins;* **oratorio:** *The Gate*(1944); **orchestral:** *the Wonderful One-Hoss Shay;* **one-act opera:** *Stormy Interlude.*

BRANSCOMBE, GENA
1881, Canadian/American
Principal Works - **Choral:** *Pilgrims of Destiny, The Phantom Caravan, Youth of the World; Sun and the Warm Brown Earth;* Royal Navy song *Arms That Have Sheltered Us.*

BRANT, HENRY
1913, American
Principal Works - 2 Symphonies (1931 and 1937); 4 Choral-Preludes (orchestra, 1932); **Concertos:** Double bass (1932); Flute and 10 instruments (1932); Clarinet (1939); saxophone (1940); *Gallopjig Colloquy* (orchestra,

1934); *Music for an Imaginary Ballet* (1947); *Millenium No. 2* brass and percussion (1954); *Poem and Burlesque* 11 flutes (1932); *Five-and-Ten Cent Store Music* piano and 20 instruments (1932); *My Father's House,* film score, expanded into a "symphony of Palestine," *The Promised Land* (1948).

BRAUNFELS, WALTER
1882-1954, German
Principal Works - Operas: *Prinzessin Brambilla* (1909); *Ulenspiegel* (1913); *Die Vogel* (1920); *Don Gil* (1924); *Der gläserne Berg* (1928); *Galathea* (1930); *Der Traum, ein Leben* (1937); *Verkündigung* (1936).

BRIAN, WILLIAM HAVERGAL
1876)1972, English
Principal Works - *Gothic Symphony;* 31 other symphonies; an opera; orchestral and choral works.

BRIDGE, FRANK
1879-1941, English
Principal Works - Children's opera: *The Christmas Rose* (1919); **orchestral suite:** *The Sea* (1911); string quartets; piano trios; violin, viola, cello, organ and chamber pieces.

BRINDLE, REGINALD SMITH
1917, English
Principal Works - *Cantata da Requiem;* **orchestral:** *Homage to H.G. Wells;* quintet for clarinet, piano and strings.

BRITTEN, BENJAMIN
1913-1976, English
Principal Works - Hymn to the Virgin (1930); Sinfonietta, for chamber orchestra; Phantasy Quartet, for oboe and string trio (1932); *A Boy Was Born,* choral variations; Two Part-songs for chorus and piano; *Friday Afternoons,* twelve children's songs with piano (1933); *Simple Symphony,* for string orchestra; Suite, for violin and piano; *Holiday Diary,* suite for piano; Te Deum in C major (1934); *Our Hunting Fathers,* song cycle; *Soirées musicales,* suite for piano; Te Deum in C major (1934); *Our Hunting Fathers,* song cycle; *Soirees musicales,* suite (1936); *Mont Juic, suite of Catalan Dances,* for orchestra; *Variations on a Theme of Frank Bridge,* for strings; *On This Island,* song cycle (1937); Piano Concerto No. 1 (1938); Violin Concerto; *Canadian Carnival,* for orchestra (1939); *Ballad of Heroes,* for high voice, choir and orchestra; *Les Illuminations,* song cycle; *Diversions on a Theme,* for piano (left hand) and orchestra; *Paul Bunyan,* operetta (c. 1940-41); *Sinfonia da Requiem; Seven Sonnets of Michelangelo,* for tenor and piano (1940); *Scottish Ballad,* two pianos and orchestra; *Matinées musicales,* for orchestra; String Quartet No. 1 (1941); Hymn to St.Cecilia, for five-part chorus with solos unaccompanied; *A Ceremony of Carols,* for treble voices and harp (1942); *Rejoice in the Lamb,* a Festival Cantata; Prelude and Fugue, for strings; *Serenade,* song cycle for tenor, horn and strings (1943); Festival Te Deum, for chorus and organ (1944); *Peter Grimes,* opera; *The Holy Sonnets of John Donne,* for high voice and piano; String Quartet No. 2 (1945); Variations and Fugue on a Theme of Purcell *(Young Person's Guide to the Orchestra),* for speaker and orchestra; *The Rape of Lucretia,* opera (1946); *A Albert Herring,* opera; Canticle No. 1, *My Beloved is Mine;* Prelude and Fugue on a Theme of Vittoria, for organ (1947); *St. Nicholas,* for tenor, choir, strings, piano and percussion; *The Beggar's Opera,* by John Donne — — — from original airs (1948); *The Little Sweep (Let's Make an Opera); Spring Symphony,* for three solo singers, mixed

choir, boys choir, boys' choir and orchestra; A Wedding Anthem, for soprano, tenor, chorus and organ (1949); *Lachrymae,* for viola and piano; *Five Flower Songs,* for unaccompanied chorus (1950); *Billy Budd,* opera; *Six Metamorphoses After Ovid,* for solo oboe (1951); Canticle No. 2, "Abraham and Isaac", for contralto, tenor and piano (1952); *Gloriana,* opera; *Winter Words, songs (1953); The Turn of the Screw,* opera; Canticle No. 3, *Still Falls the Rain,* for tenor, chorus and piano (1954); *Alpine Suite,* for recorder trio; Hymn to St. Peter, for choir and organ (1955); *The Prince of the Pagodas,* ballet; *Antiphon,* for mixed choir and organ (1956); *Noyes Fludde,* mystery play with music; *Songs from the Chinese,* for high voice and guitar (1957); *Nocturne,* song cycle for tenor, seven obbligato instruments and strings (1958);*A Midsummer Night's Dream,* opera (1960); War requiem for soloists, mixed chorus, boys' chorus and orchestra based on text of Roman Catholic Requiem Mass and poems by Wilfred Owen (1962).

BROTT, ALEXANDER
1915, Canadian
Principal Works - Ballet: *Le corriveau* (1967); Suite: *From Sea to Sea* (1946); violin concerto (1950); orchestral works; chamber music.

BROUWER, LEO
1939, Cuban
Principal Works - *Sonograma I* for prepared piano; *Sonograma II for orchestra* (1964); *Canticum* for guitar; *Dos conceptos del tiempo* for 10 players (1965); film music.

BROWN, EARLE
1926, American
Principal Works - Aleatory and tape pieces; *25 Pages for 1 to 25 pianos* (1953); *Folio, Available Forms I* and *Available Forms II; Event: Synergy II* for chamber ensemble (1968); *Corroboree* for 2 or 3 pianos (1964).

BRÜN, HERBERT
1918, German
Principal Works - Ballet: *Mobile for Orchestra (1958); Gesture for 11* chamber piece; electronic: *Futility 1964, Infraudibles* with computer (1968).

BRUNSWICK, MARK
1902-1971, American
Principal Works - Ballet: *Lysistrata* (1930); Symphony in B-Flat (1945); **Choral symphony:** *Eros and Death (1954);* string quartet, piano pieces and chamber music.

BUCCI, VALENTINO
1916-1976, Italian
Principal Works - Opera: *The Double-bass; Concerto Lirico* for violin and string orchestra; film music.

BUDD, HAROLD
1936, American
Principal Works - Amplified gongs: *Magnus Colorado* (1969); *Noyo for piano, vibraphone and chimes* (1966); *the Candy Apple Revision* (1970).

BURLAN, EMIL FRANTIŠEK
1904-1959, Czech.
Principal Works - Opera: *Maryša* (1940); ballets, cantatas; orchestral works; film music; songs.

BURKHARD, PAUL
1911, Swiss
Principal Works - Operetta: *O My Papa; Casanova In Switzerland* and others.

BURKHARD, WILLY
1900-1955, Swiss
Principal Works- Oratorios: *The Vision of Isaiah,* (1936); *The Year* (1942); a Mass (1951); opera: *Die Schwarze Spinne* (1949); choral, chamber, etc.

BUTTING, MAX
1888-1976, German
Principal Works - 10 symphonies; 10 string quartets; an opera; chamber music, etc.

BURT, FRANCIS
1926, English
Principal Works - *Iambics* for orchestra: opera: *Volpone;* ballet; cantata; 2 string quartets.

BUSH, ALAN
1900, English
Principal Works - Operas: *Wat Tyler* (1950); *The Sugar Reapers* (1964); *Joe Hill* (1968); *childrens' operas; 3 symphonies; Fantasia on Soviet Themes* (1945); string quartet, chamber music, piano pieces.

BUSH, GEOFFREY
1920, English
Principal Works - Operas: *Lord Arthur Savile's Crime;* 2 symphonies; overture: *Yorick; A Little Concerto* on T.A. Arne themes.

BUSSER, HENRI-PAUL
1872-1973, French
Principal Works - Operas: *Daphnis et Chloë* (1897); *Colomba* (1921); *Le carrosse du Saint-Sacrement* (1936); ballet; church music, piano pieces, songs.

BUSSOTTI, SYLVANO
1931, Italian
Principal Works - Voices and instruments: *La Passion Selon Sade; Five Piano Pieces for David Tudor* (1966); *Torso* (1959); *The Rara Requiem* (1963); *Due Voci* for soprano, Ondes Martenot and orchestra (1969).

BUTTERLY, NIGEL
1935, Australian
Principal Works - Violin concerto; *Meditations of Thomas Traherne* for children's recorders and orchestra; *Exploration* for piano and orchestra.

BUTTERWORTH, GEORGE SAINTON KAYE
1885-1916, English
Principal Works - 1909: *I Fear Thy Kisses,* song; 1911: Six Songs from Housman's *A Shropshire Lad;* Two English Idylls, for small orchestra; *Requiescat,* song; 1912: *A Shropshire Lad,* rhapsody for orchestra; *On Christmas Night,* for chorus; *We Get Up In The Morn,* arranged for male chorus; *In The Highlands,* arranged for female voices and piano; *Bredon Hill* and other songs; Eleven folk songs from Sussex; *Love Blows as the Wind Blows,* for baritone and string quartet; 1913: *Banks of Green Willow,* idyll for orchestra.

CADMAN, CHARLES WAKEFIELD
1881-1946, American
Principal Works - Opera: *Shanewis* (1918); symphonic suites and poems; cantatas, a piano sonata, violin music. Songs: *From The Land of The Sky Blue Water, At Dawning, Memories.*

CAGE, JOHN
1912, American
Principal Works - Aleatory and prepared piano pieces: *Wonderful Widow of Eighteen Springs* (1942); *Forever and Sunsmell* (1942); Ballet: The Seasons!; Amores for Prepared Piano & Percussion; Aria with Fontana Mix; Cartridge Music; *Silence, Indeterminacy,* Fontana Mix For Magnetic Tape; Double Music For Percussion; *Sixteen Dances* for six instruments and percussion (1951); *4'33* for any instruments (1952); *Imaginary Landscape no. 4 for 12 radios* (1951); *Atlas Eclipticalis* for orchestra (1961); *Renga with Apartment House 1776* for orchestra (1976); Piano: *Music of Changes* (1951); *HPSCHD for 1-7 harpsichords and 1-51 tape machines* (1969); *34' 46.776* for a Pianist (1954); *First Construction* (in Metal) for percussion sextet (1939); *Imaginary Landscape* No. 1 for variable-speed phonograph turntables, piano and cymbal (1939).

CAMILLERI, CHARLES
1931, Maltese
Principal Works - Opera: *Melita; Abongo* for wind quintet; organ: *Missa Mundi.*

CAMPBELL-TIPTON, LOUIS
1877-1921, American
Principal Works - Piano: *Sonata Heroic, The Four Seasons, Sea Lyrics.* Many songs.

CAMPO Y ZABALETA, CONRADO DEL
1879-1953, Spanish
Principal Works - Operas: *El final de Don Álvaro* (1911); *El Avapiés* (1919); *Capricios romantiques* for string quartets (1908).

CANNON, PHILIP
1929, English
Principal Works - *Songs to Delight* for women's chorus; concertino for piano and strings; songs.

CANTELOUBE, JOSEPH MARIE
1879-1957, French
Principal Works - French folk-songs; *Chants d'Auvergne.*

CAPDEVILLE, PIERRE
1906, French
Principal Works - Opera: *Les Amants Captifs* (1950); incidental music: *The Trachiniae;* chamber music.

CAPLET, ANDRÉ
1878-1925, French
Principal Works - Oratorio: *Mircir de Jésus* (1924); *Épiphanie* for cello and orch. (1923); *Le masque de la mort rouge* for harp and orchestra; choral and chamber music.

CARDEW, CORNELIUS
1936, English
Principal Works - Orchestral: *Autumn '60; First Movement for String Quartet* (1962); Piano: *3 Winter Potatoes* (1965); *Treatise* (1967) and *Schooltime Compositions* (1967) for various media.

CARPENTER, JOHN ALDEN
1876-1951, American
Principal Works - 1904: *Improving Songs for Anxious Children;* 1912: Violin Sonata; 1913: *Gitanjali,* song cycle on poems of Tagore; 1915: *Adventures in a Perambulator,* for orchestra; Concertino for piano and orchestra (revised

1947); 1917: Symphony No. 1; 1918: Four Negro Songs; 1919: *Birthday of the Infanta,* ballet; 1920: *A Pilgrim Vision,* for orchestra; 1921: *Krazy Kat,* ballet; 1925: *Skyscrapers,* ballet; 1928: String Quartet; 1932: *Patterns,* for piano and orchestra; *Song of Faith,* for chorus and orchestra; 1933: *Sea Drift,* symphonic poem; 1934: Piano Quintet; 1935: *Danza,* for orchestra; 1936: Violin Concerto; 1940: Symphony No. 2; 1941: *Song of Freedom,* for chorus and orchestra; 1942: Symphony No. 3; 1943: *The Anxious Bugler,* for orchestra; 1945: *The Seven Ages;* 1948: *Carmel Concerto.*

CARRILO, JULIÁN
1875-1965, Mexican
Principal Works - *Microtonal Sonido 13 system;* operas and symphonies; *Horizontes* for small Sonido 13 orchestra with conventionally tuned ensemble; *Missa de la restauración* (quarter tone).

CARTER, ELLIOTT
1908, American
Principal Works - Piano Sonata; Cello Sonata; Woodwind Quintet from Minotaur ballet; Three Songs based on Robert Frost poems; String Quartet No. 1; Variations for orchestra; String Quartet No. 2; Concerto for orchestra (1969); Double Concerto for harpsichord, piano, 2 chamber orchestras (1961); *Symphony of Three Orchestras* (1976); String quartets No. 2 (1959); and No. 3 (1973); Violin and piano duo (1974); brass quintet (1974); Soprano and chamber ensemble: *A Mirror on Which to Dwell* (1976).

CASADESUS, ROBERT
1899-1972, French
Principal Works - Noted pianist who composed symphonies, concertos for 1 and 2 pianos; sonatas.

CASALS, PABLO
1876-1973, Spanish
Principal Works - Noted cellist who composed *Sardanas* for cello ensemble; *La vision de Fray Martin* for chorus; Christmas oratorio, *El pesebre;* a Miserere and other sacred choral pieces.

CASANOVA, ANDRE
1919, French
Principal Works - *The Silver Key* for soprano, tenor, baritone and orchestra; *Three Poems by Rilke* for chorus; *Strophes* for xylophone, kettledrums and strings; a violin concerto.

CASELLA, ALFREDO
1883-1947, Italian
Principal Works - Opera: *La Favola d'Orfeo* (1932); Ballet; *La giara* (1924); orchestra: *Paganiniana* (1942); *Italia* (1910); oratorio: *The Desert Challenged; Scarlattiana* for piano and orchestra (1927); Sacred songs; Missa Solemnis; Concerto for String quartet (1924); *11 pezzi infantili* for piano.

CASSUTO, ALVARO (LEON)
1938, Portuguese
Principal Works - *Sinfonia breve* No. 1 and No. 2; *Canticum in tenebris* for soloists, chorus and orchestra.

CASTELNUOVO-TEDESCO, MARIO
1895-1968, Italian/American
Principal Works - Operas: *Mendragola; The Merchant of Venice;* Symphonic Variations for violin and orchestra; Three Chorales on Hebrew Melodies; Oratorio: *The Book of Jonah;* 2 violin concertos; guitar concerto, etc.

CASTIGLIONI, NICCOLÒ
1932, Italian
Principal Works - *Granulation* for 2 flutes, 2 clarinets; *Symphony in C with choral text.*

CASTRO, JUAN JOSÉ
1895-1968, Argentinian
Principal Works - Operas: *Preserpina y el extranjero* (1952); *La zapatera prodigiosa* (1943); *Bodas de sangre* (1956); Orchestral: *Corales criollos no. 3;* ballet; *Sonatina española* for piano.

CAZDEN, NORMAN
1914, American
Principal Works - Dramatic musical: *Dingle Hill* (1958); orchestral: *3 Ballads* (1949); *Concerto for 10 Instruments* (1937); symphonies; chamber music: *Elizabethan Suites,* No. 1 and No. 2 (1965); piano music.

CERHA, FRIEDRICH
1926, Austrian
Principal Works - Orchestral: *Espressioni fundamentali* (1957); *Spiegel I-VII* with tape (1960); violin and piano pieces; chamber music.

CHAGRIN, FRANCIS
1905-1972, English/Romanian
Principal Works - Piano concerto; piano solos; film music.

CHAILLY, LUCIANO
1920, Italian
Principal Works - Operas: *The Proposal, Trial by Tea-Party;* Chamber and Piano music.

CHAMPAGNE, CLAUDE
1891-1965, Canadian
Principal Works - *Altitude* for chorus, ondes martenot and orchestra, concerto for piano with small orchestra; French-Canadian folk-songs; *Suite canadienne* for chorus and orchestra.

CHANLER, THEODORE
1902-1961, American
Principal Works - Chamber opera: *The Pot of Fat* (1955); violin sonata; *The Children* for voice and piano (1945); *Eiptaphs* songs with text by de la Mare; piano music.

CHASINS, ABRAM
1903, American
Principal Works - Noted pianist who has composed 2 piano concertos; pieces for 1 and 2 pianos; chamber and orchestral works; *Shvanda Fantasy.*

CHAVEZ, CARLOS
1899, Mexican
Principal Works - Opera: *The Visitors* (1953); *Clio* symphonic ode (1969); Orchestral: *Discovery* (1969); *Sinfonia de Antigona* (1933); *Sinfonia India* (1935); *Fourth Symphony;* Ballet: *The New Fire, Lattija de Colquide (Dark Meadow);* Concerto for Four Horns (1937); Piano Concerto (1938); Violin Concerto (1948).

CHEVREUILLE, RAYMOND
1902-1976, Belgian
Principal Works - Ballet: *Cinderella;* orchestral: *Prayer for Those Condemned to Death* with narrator; 7 symphonies; concertos; string quartets; *Lilliputian Music* for four flutes.

CHILDS, BARNEY
1926, American
Principal Works - Concerto for clarinet (1970); *Nonet;* Quartet for clarinet and strings (1953); 2 symphonies; *Keet Seel* for chorus a capella (1970); choral and band: *When Lilacs Last in the Dooryard Bloom'd* after Walt Whitman; string quartets; chamber music.

CHOU, WEN-CHUNG
1923, Chinese/American
Principal Works - Orchestral: *And The Fallen Petals* (1954); *Landscapes, Riding The Wind* (1964); *Pien* for piano, wind, percussion (1966); *7 Poems of T'ang Dynasty.*

CHRISTOU, YANNIS
1926-1970, Greek
Principal Works - Serial and aleatory music. *The Strychnine Lady* for tapes, instruments, actors (1967); Oratorio: *Mysterion* for actors, chorus, speakers; Orchestral: *Enantiodromia; Praxis* (1966).

CIKKER, JAN
1911, Czech
Principal Works - Operas: *Juro Jánošik* (1954); *Prince Bajazid* (1957); *The Resurrection* (1962); *Mister Scrooge* (1963); symphonic poems; 2 string quartets.

CILÈA, FRANCESCO
1866-1950, Italian
Principal Works - Opera: *Adriana Lecouvreur, L'Arlesiana;* orch. suites: *Poema sinfonico* for solo, chorus, orchestra; chamber music, songs.

CLAFLIN, AVERY
1898, American
Principal Works - Operas: *The Fall of Usher; Hester Prynne;* Choral: *Lament For April 15.*

CLARKE, HENRY LELAND
1907, American
Principal Works - Chamber opera: *The Loafer and the Loaf* (1951); choral: *No Man Is an Island* (1951); orchestral and chamber music.

CLARKE, REBECCA
1886, English
Principal Works - Psalm for a capella chorus; psalm for voices; chamber and piano pieces.

CLEMENTI, ALDO
1925, Italian
Principal Works - Serial and aleatory music. Electronic: *Collage* 1-3 with 2 on tape; *Informel* 1-3 (1963); *3 studi* for chamber ensemble (1957); *Triplum* for flute, oboe and clarinet (1960).

CLUTSAM, GEORGE HOWARD
1866-1951, Australian
Principal Works - Composer stage music and inventor of *Clutsam* keyboard.

COATES, ERIC
1886-1957, English
Principal Works - Orchestral suites: *London Suite* (including Knightsbridge March); *Sleepy Lagoon, Four Centuries; Three Elizabeths; Miniature Suite,* Songs.

COELHO, RUI
1891, Portugese
Principal Works - Opera: *Belkiss* (1928); Ballets; symphony suites; concertos for piano and orchestra; piano music.

COHN, ARTHUR
1910, American
Principal Works - Orchestral: *4 Symphonic Documents* (1939); *Kaddish* (1964); chamber music: *Music for Ancient Instruments* (1939); *Quotations in Percussion I* (1958); Pianno: *Machine Music* for 2 pianos, 1937.

COLE, BRUCE
1947, English
Principal Works - Chamber orchestra: *Fenestrae Sanctae; Harlequinade; Pantomimes.*

COLE, ROSSETTER GLEASON
1866-1952, American
Principal Works - Opera: *The Maypole Lovers* (1919); *Pioneer Overture* (1919); cantatas; orch. pieces; songs.

COLGRASS, MICHAEL
1932, American
Principal Works - Orchestral: *As Quiet As* (1966); *the Earth's a Baked Apple* (1968) including chorus; *Virgil's Dream* for 4 actors, 4 mimes, singers and musicians; *Déjà vu* concerto for 4 percussionists and orchestra (1977); *Inventions on a Motive* for percussion (1955); *Variations* for drums and viola (1957).

COLLINGWOOD, LAWRANCE
1887, English
Principal Works - Opera: *Macbeth* (1934); a symphonic poem; instrumental and piano pieces.

COLLINS, ANTHONY
1893, English
Principal Works - Opera: *Catherine Parr* and other short operas.

CONE, EDWARD T.
1917, American
Principal Works - Cantata: *The Lotus Eaters* (1939); *La figlia che piange* for tenor and chamber ensemble; *Excursions* for chorus a capella; *Philomela* song cycle for soprano, flute, viola and piano; string quartets and chamber music.

CONNOLLY, JUSTIN
1933, English
Principal Works - *Anima* for viola and orchestra; *Triads* for various combinations of three instruments.

CONSTANT, MARIUS
1925, Rumanian
Principal Works - *The Flute Player* suite; short opera: *Pygmalion;* violin concerto; *Three Complexes* for piano and double-bass, woodwind trio; ballet: *Paradise Lost.*

CONVERSE, FREDERICK SHEPHERD
1871-1940, American
Principal Works - *Flivver 10,000,000* for orchestra; 4 operas; 6 symphonies; Opera *The Pipe Of Desire* (1906); Orchestral: *California* (1928):*American Sketches.*

COOKE, ARNOLD
1906, English
Principal Works - Opera: *Mary Barton;* 3 symphonies; chamber and piano music.

COPLAND, AARON
1900, American
Principal Works - Orchestral: *Dance Symphony* (1925); Concerto *(Jazz)* for Piano and Orchestra (1926); *Music for the Theatre* (1925); *El Salón Mexico* (1936); *Billy the Kid* (1938), Suite from the ballet; *An Outdoor Overture* (1938); *Our Town* (1940), music from the film; *Lincoln Portrait* (1942), for narrator and orchestra; *Rodeo,* Four Dance Episodes from the ballet (1942); *Music for the Movies* (1942)- - -(from the scores to *The City, Of Mice and Men,* and *Our Town); Appalachian Spring* (1944), Suite from the ballet; Third Symphony (1947); *The Red Pony* (1948), Suite from the film; Concerto for Clarinet (1948); *The Heiress* (1949) (film); *The Tender Land,* Orchestral Suite (1957); *Orchestral Variations* (1957); *Quiet Land* orchestral suite. Instrumental: Two Pieces for Violin and Piano (1926); Two Pieces for String Quartet (1928); *Vitebsk* (1929), for Violin, Cello and Piano; Piano Variations (1930); Sonata for Piano (1941); *Four Piano Blues* (1948); Piano Fantasy (1957); (1960) Nonet for Nine Solo Strings; Vocal: *Old American Songs,* Set I (1950); *Old American Songs,* Set II (1952); *Twelve Poems of Emily Dickinson* (1950).

CORIGLIANO, JOHN
1938, American
Principal Works - Orchestral: *Elegy* (1966); *Tournaments Overture* (1967); *The Cloisters* with voice (1965)*The Naked Carmen,* based on Bizet's Carmen, for Moog synthesizer and rock-pop group; violin sonata; clarinet concerto (1977); choral works and play music.

CORTÉS, RAMIRO
1933, American
Principal Works - Opera: *Prometheus* (1960); *Meditation:* x*ochitl* (1965); woodwind quintet (1968); chamber and choral pieces; piano works. Serial music.

COWELL, HENRY
1897-1965, American
Principal Works - Orchestral: *Celtic* Symphony; *Hymns and Fuguing Tunes;* Piano: *Aeolian Harp; The Banshee; Sinister Resonance;* opera: *O'Higgins of Chile;* chamber music: *Trickster Coyote; Action in Brass; Two Bits;* Piano: *Amiable conversation; Fabric; Advertisement; Dynamic Motion.* Almost 1000 works en toto.

CRAWFORD, ROBERT
1925, Scottish
Principal Works - Sinfonietta; string quartet; quintet for woodwinds and strings.

CRAWFORD, RUTH SEEGER (PORTER)
1901-1953, American
Principal Works - *Rissolty Rossolty* for 10 wind instruments, drums and strings; string quartet; songs with piano, oboe, percussion; collector and arranger folk-songs.

CRESTON, PAUL
1906, American
Principal Works - Symphonies No. 2, No. 4, No. 5 and symphonic sketch *A rumor;* Concertino for Marimba and Strings; Partita for flute, violin and strings; orchestral: *Threnody, Dance Variations, Frontiers,* Two Dances; fantasia for trombone and orchestra.

CRIST, BAINBRIDGE
1883-1969, American
Principal Works - Ballet: *Pregiwa's Marriage* (1920); orchestral: *American Epic, 1620* (1943); chamber and choral music, piano pieces, songs.

CROSS, LOWELL
1938, American
Principal Works - Television, laser and other visual devices for works: *Video II* and *Video/Laser II,* in collaboration with Carson Jeffries and Tudor (1970).

CROSSE, GORDON
1937, English
Principal Works - Childrens' pieces: *Meet My Folks!* (1964); *Ahmet the Woodseller;* orchestral works and chamber pieces.

CRUFT, ADRIAN
1921, English
Principal Works - Overture: *Actaeon;*Partita for small orchestra; sacred works.

CRUMB, GEORGE
929, American
Principal Works - Orchestral: *Echoes of Time and the River* (1968); *Starchild* with chorus (1977); Instrumental and choral: *Ancient Voices of Children* (text by Garcia Lorca) (1970); *Songs, Drones and Refrains of Death* (text by Garcia Lorca) (1971); Electric string quartet: *Black Angels* (1970); Amplified piano: *Makrokosmos I* and *II* (1972-1973); *Music for a Summer Evening* for 2 amplified pianos and percussion (1974).

CUSTER, ARTHUR
1923, American
Principal Works - Orchestral: *Sinfonia de Madrid* (1961); *Found Objects II* (1969); *Interface I* for 2 recording engineers and string quartet; *Rhapsodality Brown!* for piano (1969); choral and instrumental ensemble pieces; chamber music.

DAHL, INGOLF
1912-1970, American
Principal Works - *Andante and Arioso* for winds; *Music for Brass Instruments; Symphony Concertante* for 2 clarinets and orchestra; piano: *Sonata Seria;* symphonic: *The Tower of Santa Barbara.*

DALE, BENJAMIN JAMES
1885-1943, English
Principal Works - Choral: *Song of Praise* (1923); cantata: *Before The Paling of The Stars* (1912); sonata in D minor for piano (1905); violin and viola music; chamber pieces; orchestral works.

DALLAPICCOLA, LUIGI
1904-1975, Italian
Principal Works - Twelve tone music: *Tre Laudi* (1936-37), voice and chamber orchestra; *Liriche Greche* (192-45), voice and chamber orchestra; Two Pieces for Orchestra (1945-47); *Canti di Prigionia (Songs from Captivity),* for choir and instruments (1938-41); *Il Prigioniero (The Prisoner)* (1944-48), opera, based on story by Villiers de L'Isle-Adam; Variations for Orchestra (1954); *Cinque Canti* (1956); opera: *Volo di notte* (1940); *Canti di libera-*

zione (1955); *Requiescant* (1958); *Partita* (1933); Piano: *Quaderno musicale di Annalibera* (1952); became variations for orchestra, above.

DAN, IKUMA
1924, Japanese
Principal Works - Opera: *Yuzuru;* 5 symphonies; chamber and choral music; piano works; film music.

DANIELS, MABEL WHEELER
1878-1971, American
Principal Works - Orchestral: *Deep Forest* (1931); choral: *A Psalm of Praise* (1954); *Three Observations* for oboe, clarinet and bassoon (1943).

DAVID, JOHANN NEPOMUK
1895, Austrian
Principal Works - Organ and choral work: *Choralwerk;* 8 symphonies; concertos; motets; chamber music; songs.

DAVIDOVSKY, MARIO
1934, American
Principal Works - Electronic music. *Contrasts* No. 1 for strings and electronic sounds; *Synchronisms 1-7* of which *No. 6 for piano and electronic sound* won Pulitzer Prize (1971); chamber and orchestral works.

DAVIES, HENRY WALFORD
1869-1941, English
Principal Works - Organ: *Solemn Melody;* oratorio: *Everyman* sacred music.

DAVIES, PETER MAXWELL
1934, English
Principal Works - Operas: *Taverner* (1970); *The Martyrdom of St. Magnus* (1977); *Vesalii icones* for ensemble, cello and dancer-pianist; orchestral: *2 Fantasias on an In nomine of Taverner* (1962, 1964); *A Mirror of Whitening Light* (1977); choral: *O magnum mysterium* (1960); *8 Songs for a Mad King* (1969), for voice and instruments; *L'homme armé* for tape and instruments; piano music.

DEGEN, HELMUT
1911, German
Principal Works - Stage music: *Die Konferenz der Tiere* (1950); concertos; oratorios; piano pieces.

DEL TREDICI, DAVID
American
Principal Works - *Happy Voices* for piano and orchestra (1980).

DELANNOY, MARCEL
1898-1962, French
Principal Works - Opera: *Le Poirier de Misère* (1927); ballet: *Le Fou de la Dame* (1929); *La Pantoufle* (1935); *Ginevra* (1942); *Puck* (1949); *Serenade Concertante* for violin; a piano concerto; film music; 2 symphonies.

DELLO JOIO, NORMAN
1913, American
Principal Works - Operas: *Blood Moon* (1961); *The Ruby* (1955); *The Trial at Rouen* (1956) a reworking of the 1950 – Triumph of St. Joan. Ballet: *Prairie* (1942); *Duke of Sacramento* (1942); *On Stage* (1945); *Wilderness Stair* (1948); Choral: *Psalm of David* (1950); *Lamentation of Saul* (1954); Choral Mass (1969); Orchestral: Meditations on Ecclesiastes (1957); *Homage to Haydn* (1969); chamber music: Sextet for 3 recorders and string trio; trio for flute, cello and piano and *Duo Concertante* for cello and piano; piano pieces and songs.

DELVINCOURT, CLAUDE
1888-1954, French
Principal Works - Opera: *Lucifer;* musical comedy: *La femme à barbe* (1938); *Ce monde de rosée* for orchestra with vocals; piano and chamber pieces.

DENISOV, EDISON VASILIEVICH
1929, Russian
Principal Works - Symphony in D for 2 string orchestras and percuss.; *Plashi* for soprano, piano and percuss.; *Solntse inkov* for soprano and instruments; *crescendo e diminuendo* for harpsichord and strings; an opera; piano and chamber pieces; songs.

DES MARIAIS, PAUL
1920, American
Principal Works - Some serial music. *Epiphanies* chamber opera with film segments; *Le cimetière marin* for voice keyboards and percussion (1971); piano sonatas; sacred choral pieces; instrumental music.

DESSAU, PAUL
1894, German
Principal Works - Opera: *Das Veruteilung des Lukullus* (1951) with text by Brecht; symphonic music; oratorios; cantatas; piano and chamber music; choral works.

DETT, ROBERT NATHANIEL
1882-1943, Canadian/American
Principal Works - Oratorio: (1921) *The Chariot Jubilee;* (1937) *The Ordering of Moses, Piano Suite; In The Bottoms* (inc: Juba Dance) (1913).

DIAMOND, DAVID
1915, American
Principal Works - *Rounds* for string orchestra (1944); orchestral: *Psalm* (1936); *Romeo and Juliet* (1947); 8 symphonies; ballets; concertos; 10 string quartets; *Nonet* for 3 violins, 3 violas, 3 cellos (1962); choral and chamber music; piano works.

DICKINSON, CLARENCE
1873, American
Principal Works - Orchestral: *Storm King;* two operas; organ pieces.

DICKINSON, PETER
1934, English
Principal Works - Dramatic musical: *The Judas Tree; Winter afternoons* for 6 male voices plus double-bass; 2 string quartets; organ concerto; piano pieces.

DIEREN, BERNARD VAN
1936, Dutch/English
Principal Works - Comic opera: *The Tailor* (1917); *Diaphony* for voices and orchestra (text by Shakespeare); *Chinese Symphony* (1914); piano and chamber music; violin pieces, songs.

DISLTER, HUGO
1908-1942, German
Principal Works - Cantatas: concerto for harpsichord and string orchestra (1935); oratorio: *Die Weltalter* (1942); *Konzertstück* for 2 pianos; sacred and secular choral pieces; organ music.

DLUGOSZEWSKI, LUCIA
1931, American
Principal Works - *Orchestra Structure for the Poetry of*

Everyday Sounds (1952); *Delicate Accidents in Space* for unsheltered rattle quintet (1959); *Velocity Shells* for prepared piano, trumpet, invented percussion (1970); *Space Is A Diamond* for trumpet (1970); dance music for various ensembles.

DODGE, CHARLES
1912, American
Principal Works - *Rota* for orchestra (1966); *Changes,* computer-synthesized tape sounds (1970); *Folia* for chamber ensemble (1965); *Speech Songs* (1973); conventional instrumental works and computerized compositions.

DOHNANYI, ERNST VON
1877-1960, Hungarian
Principal Works - Orchestral: *Symphonic Minutes,* Op. 36; *Variations on a Nursery Song,* Op. 25 (with piano); Piano Concerto No. 2 (1946); Violin Concerto No. 2 (1952); Concertino for harp and orchestra (1952); *American Rhapsody* (1954); Piano: Rhapsodies, Op. 11, No. 3, in C; *Ruralia Hungarica,* Op. 32 (1924), suite for piano; Chamber music: Serenade in C major, Op. 10.

DONATO, ANTHONY
1909 - American
Principal Works - 2 symphonies; 3 string quartets; 2 violin sonatas; incidental music.

DONATONI, FRANCO
1927, Italian
Principal Works - Serial and aleatory music. Orchestral: *Sinfonia* for strings (1953); *Sezioni* (1960); *Doubles II* (1970); piano: *3 Improvisations* (1957); 4 string quartets; piano pieces.

DONOVAN, RICHARD
1891-1970, American
Principal Works - *Passacaglia on Vermont folk tunes* (1949); Mass (1955); Elizabethan Lyrics, 5 with instruments (1957); chamber music.

DRAGON, CARMEN
1914, American
Principal Works - *Santa Fe Suite.*

DRESDEN, SEM
1881-1957, Duth
Principal Works - Opera: *Francois Villon;* operetta: *Toto;* concertos for violin, for oboe, for piano, for flute, for organ; choral; *Chorus tragicus* (1928); chamber music; songs.

DRIESSLER, JOHANNES
1921, German
Principal Works - Oratorios: *Dein Reich komme* (1949); operas; symphonies; a capella choruses; etc.

DRUCKMAN, JACOB
1928, American
Principal Works - Orchestral: *Windows* (1972); *Mirage* (1976); *Chiaroscuro* (1977); instruments and voice: *The Sound of Time* (1965); *Lamia* (1974); *Animus, I, II, III* for voices, tape and/or instruments; *Incenters* for 13 players (1968); tape: *Synapse;* chamber and choral pieces.

DUBENSKY, ARCADY
1890-1966, Russian/American
Principal Works - *Fugue for 18 violins* (1932); operas; film music.

DUKELSKY, VLADIMIR
(Vernon Duke)
1903-1969, American
Principal Works - Ballets: *Zephyr et Flore;* operas; symphonies; piano concertos; choral, chamber and piano pieces. Many popular song hits (see popular listing).

DUNAYEVSKY, ISAAK OSIPOVICH
1900-1955, Russian
Principal Works - Operettas; film music; ballets; orchestral; choral.

DUNHILL, THOMAS FREDERICK
1877-1946
Principal Works - Operas: *The Enchanted Garden* (1927); *Tantivy Towers* (1931); orchestral; ballet; chamber and choral works.

DUPRÉ, MARCEL
1886-1971, French
Principal Works - Organ: *Symphonie-Passion* (1921); *Le chemin de la croix* (1931); oratorio: *Le Songa de Jacob;* sacred choral and organ pieces.

DUPUIS, ALBERT
1877-1967, Belgian
Principal Works - Opera: *La Passion* (1916); ballets; 2 symphonies; concertos; oratorios; chamber and choral music.

DUREY, LOUIS
1888, French
Principal Works - One of the progressive group of SIX; chamber music, opera; songs.

DURUFLÉ, MAURICE
1902, French
Principal Works - Orchestral: *Trois danses* (1936); motets, Requiem; chamber and organ pieces.

DUTILLEUX, HENRI
1916, French
Principal Works - Symphony (1951); ballet; chamber; film music.

DYSON, GEORGE
1883-1964, English
Principal Works - Choral cantata: *The Canterbury Pilgrims* (1931); concertos; chamber and piano pieces.

DZERZHINSKY, IVAN IVANOVICH
1909-1978, Russian
Principal Works - Opera: *Quiet Flows the Don* (1935); instrumental works.

EATON, JOHN
1935, American
Principal Works - Operas: *Heracles* (1971); *Myshkin* (1970); *Danton and Robespierre* (1978); *Concert Piece* for tape and jazz ensemble (1962); *Concert Piece* for Syn-Ket and symphonic group; choral and instrumental pieces; chamber music. *Mass* for soprano, clarinet and synthesizer; *Microtonal Fantasy* for piano (1965).

EFFINGER, CECIL
1914, American
Principal Works - 3 symphonies; marches; concertos; chamber music.

EGGE, KLAUS
1906, Norweigan

Principal Works - Symphony No. 1, Op. 17; Symphony No. 3; Violin Concerto; Piano Concerto No. 2; chamber and piano music.

EGK, WERNER
1901, German
Principal Works - Operas: *Peer Gynt; Irish Legend; The Government Inspector; Betrothal in Santo Domingo;* ballet: *A Summer Day;* Opera: *Die Zaubergeige* (1934); orchestral: *French Suite After Rameau* (1949); violin concerto; piano sonata; film music; choral works.

EICHHEIM, HENRY
1870-1942, American
Principal Works - Orchestral: *Oriental Impressions* (1922); *Chinese Legend* (1925); *Burma* (1926); *Java* (1929); chamber music, ballet.

EINEM, GOTTFRIED VON
1918, Austrian
Principal Works - Operas: *Dantons Tod* (1947); *Der Prozess* (1953); Ballet: *Prinzessin Turandot* (1944); orchestral: *Meditations* (954); choral cantata: *An die Nachgeborenen* (1975); chamber pieces; songs.

EL-DABH, HALIM
1921, Egyptian
Principal Works - Ballet: *Clytemnestra* (1958); *Lucifer* (1974); Orchestral: *Leiyla and the Poet,* tape (1962); symphonies; electronic pieces.

ELIZALDE, FEDERICO
1907, Spanish
Principal Works - Opera: *Paul Gauguin* (1948); Violin Concerto (1943); Piano Concerto (1947).

ELLSTEIN, ABRAHAM
1907-1963
Principal Works - Opera: one-act *The Thief and the Hangman;* full opera: *The Golem* (1962); oratorio: *The Redemption;* many Jewish operettas; film music and theater pieces.

ELOY, JEAN-CLAUDE
1938, French
Principal Works - Orchestral: *Etude III* (1962); *Équivalences* (1963); choral works with instruments; piano and chamber pieces.

ENESCU, GEORGE (ENESCO, GEORGES)
1881-1955, Rumanian
Principal Works - Opera: *Oedip* (1932); *Symphonie Concertante;* 3 more symphonies; 2 Rumanian rhapsodies, *Poème rumain;* 2 string quartets; concertos; violin sonatas; piano pieces; chamber music.

ELWELL, HERBERT
1898, American
Principal Works - Ballet: *The Happy Hypocrite* (1927); *The Forever Young* for voice and orchestra; choral works; string quartets; chamber music; songs.

ENGEL, A. LEHMAN
1910, American
Principal Works - Operas: *Malady of Love; The Soldier;* much incidental theater music; ballet and chamber music.

ENGELMANN, HANS ULRICH
1921, German
Principal Works - Serial, aleatory, electronic music.

Opera: *Der Fall van Damm* (1968); Ballet; Theater music, *Ophelia* (1969); *Modelle I* for electronic group; cantata; oratorio; chamber and piano pieces, songs.

ENGLERT, GIUSEPPE GIORGIO
1927, Italian
Principal Works - Electronic music. *Miranda,* visual music for orchestra; *Vagans animula* for organ and tape (1969); tape and instruments pieces; orchestral works with and without voices; chamber music.

ENRIQUEZ, MANUEL
1926, Mexican
Principal Works - Electronic music: *Movil I* for piano, *Movil II* for violin; 2 violin concertos; symphonies; film music, string quartets.

EPSTEIN, DAVID M.
1930, American
Principal Works - Orchestral:*Sonority-Variations* (1968); *Ventures* for symphonic wind ensemble (1971); a symphony; song cycle *The Seasons* (1956); piano pieces; chamber music.

ERB, DONALD (JAMES)
1927, American
Principal Works - Orchestral: *Symphony of Overtures* (1965); *Music for a Festive Occasion* with tape (1976); *Klangfarbenfunk I* for orch., rock group and electronic sounds (1970); *Christmasmusic* (1967); *Cummings Cycle* for orchestra and chorus; band pieces; piano and chamber music; *Fallout* for narrator, chorus, piano; *In No Strange Land* for tape, trombone, double-bass, String Trio for violin, electric guitar, cello.

ERB, JOHN WARREN
1887-1948, American
Principal Works - *An Early Greek Christmas; The Unfoldment* for strings.

ERICKSON, ROBERT
1917, American
Principal Works - Serial, electronic, free form music. Orchestral: *Chamber Concerto* (1960); *Pacific Sirens* on tape and with instruments; *General Speech,* tape and instruments; piano and chamber pieces; *Night Music* for solo trumpet and ensemble (1978).

ESCHER, RUDOLF (GEORGE)
1912, Dutch
Principal Works - Orchestral: *Musique pour l'esprit en deuil* (1943); symphonies; choral music; piano and chamber pieces.

ESCOBAR, LUIS ANTONIO
1925, Colombian
Principal Works - Ballets: *Preludes* for percussion and piano (1960); symphonies, operas, piano concertos, chamber works.

ETLER, ALVIN (DERALD)
1913-1973, American
Principal Works - Serial music. Orchestral: *Triptych* (1961); concertos for chamber orchestra; 2 string quartets; 2 wind quintets; choral pieces.

EVANGELISTI, FRANCO
1926, Italian
Principal Works - Electronic, graphic, free-form music.

Random or not random for orchestra 91962); *Spazio a 5* for voices and percussion (1961); *4!* for violin and piano (1955); *Campi integrati* on tape (1959); *Proporzioni* for flute (1958).

EVETT, ROBERT
1922-1975, American
Principal Works - 3 symphonies; concertos for cello, for piano, for bassoon, for harpsichord; choral music, sacred and secular; piano and chamber pieces.

FABINI, EDUARDO
1882, Uruguayan
Principal Works - Orchestral: *Campo* (1922); *La isla de los ceibos* (1926); chamber and piano music; songs.

FALL, LEO
1873-1925, Austrian
Principal Works - Operettas: *The Dollar Princess* (1907); *The Merry Peasant* (1907); *The Girl In The Train* (1908); *The Rose of Stamboul* (1916); *Madame Pompadour* (1922).

FALLA, MANUEL DE
1876-1946, Spanish
Principal Works - Opera: *La Vida Breve* (1904); *Master Peter's Puppet Show* (1922). Ballets: *El Amor Brujo (Love the Sorcerer;* includes the *Ritual Fire Dance* (1915); *The Three-Cornered Hat (El sombrero de tres picos)* (1919). Choral: *Atlantida,* for soloists, chorus, and orchestra (post-humously completed by Ernest Halffter) (1928-46). Orchestral: *Nights in the Gardens of Spain (Noches en los jardines de España)* (1909-15); Concerto for Harpsichord (1923)26). Piano: *4 Pièces Espagnoles* (1907-08); *Fantasia Bética (Andalusian Fantasy).* Songs: *7 Canciones populares españolas* (Blas de Laserne).

FARKAS, FERENC
1905, Hungarian
Principal Works - Opera: *The Magic Cupboard* (1942); orchestral works; ballet; film music; concertos; a cantata; an oratorio; chamber and piano pieces.

FARWELL, ARTHUR (GEORGE)
1872, American
Principal Works - Orchestral: *Dawn* (1901); *Symbolistic Studies; Caliban* for stage (1916); concerto for 2 pianos; concerto for string orchestra; *American Indian Melodies* for piano; choral pieces; chamber music; American Indian songs and arrangements.

FELDMAN, MORTON
1926 , American
Principal Works - Progressive, indeterminate and graphic techniques. *Projections I-V* (1951); *Marginal Intersection* (1951); *In Search of an Orchestration* (1967), for orchestra; *Structures* for string quartet (1951); *First Principles* for orch. ensemble (1967); choral: *The swallows of Salangan* (1960); electronic pieces.

FENNELLY, BRIAN
1937, American
Principal Works - *Divisions for a Violinist* (1968); *Evanescences* for chamber ensemble and tape (1969); quintet for winds; chamber pieces, etc.

FERGUSON, HOWARD
1908, Irish
Principal Works - Ballet: *Chauntecleer* (1948); Partita for orchestra; Serenade for string orchestra (also an octet for wind and strings); 5 Bagatelles for piano; piano concerto with string orchestra (1951); 2 violin sonatas; choral and chamber works.

FERRARI, LUC
1929, French
Principal Works - Musique concrète: *Visage V* (1959); *Tautologos II* (1961); *Presque rien; Tautologos III* for any instrumental group (1969); orchestral works; chamber music.

FERROUD, PIERRE-OCTAVE
1900-1936, French
Principal Works - Comic Opera: *Chirurgie* (1928); Symphony In A (1931); *Au Parc Monceau* for piano; several symphonic works; piano and chamber music; songs.

FEVRIER, HENRI
1875-1957, French
Principal Works - Opera: *Monna Vanna* (1909) and eight other operas; chamber music, songs.

FINE, IRVING
1914-1962, American
Principal Works - Orchestral: *Serious Song* (1955); a symphony (1962); *Fantasia* for string trio and other chamber pieces; Song cycle *Mutability* (1952); choral works and string quartet.

FINE, VIVIAN
1913, American
Principal Works - Ballets: *The Race of Life* (1937); *Alcestis* (1960); *A Guide To The Life Expectancy of a Rose* (1956) for voice with instruments; a piano concerto; piano and chamber music pieces; choral works.

FINKE, FIDELIO FRITZ
1891-1968, German
Principal Works - Operas; piano concerto; orchestra works; choral and chamber music: *Eine Reiterburleske: Romantische Suite* for piano; organ music.

FINNEY, ROSS LEE
1906, American
Principal Works - Serial music. *Still Are New Worlds* (1962) for chorus and orchestra; 4 symphonies; violin and piano concertos; string quartets; piano and other chamber-music pieces; songs.

FINZI, GERALD
1901-1956, English
Principal Works - Orchestral: *New Year Music,* nocturne; *Severn Rhapsody,* piano concerto; *Requiem da camera;* cello concerto; *Intimations of Immortality* for tenor, chorus and orchestra; cantata: *Dies natalis* for voice and string orchestra; songs.

FITELBERG, JERZY
1903-1951, Polish/American
Principal Works - Second and Fourth string quartets; two piano concertos; two violin concertos; concerto for strings; two suites for orchestra; cello concerto; chamber music and a piano sonata.

FLAGELLO, NICHOLAS
1928, American
Principal Works - Opera: *The Judgement of St. Francis* (1959); orchestral works and concertos; choral and chamber music; songs.

FLOTHUIS, MARIUS (HENDRIKUS)
1914, Dutch
Principal Works - Concertos for flute, for horn, for piano, for violin, for clarinet; orchestral and chamber orch. works; choral pieces.

FLOYD, CARLISLE
1926, American
Principal Works - Operas: *Susannah* (1955); *Wuthering Heights* (1958); *The Passion of Jonathan Wade* (1962); *Of Mice and Men* (1970); a ballet; choral and orchestral pieces; songs.

FORTNER, WOLFGANG
1907, German
Principal Works - Twelve tone music. Opera: *Bluthchzeit* (1957) (based on Garcia Lorca); ballet: *Die weisse Rose* (1950); cantata: *An die Nachgeborenen* (1948); Vocal work: *The Creation* (1954); Piano: 7 elegies (1950; *Kammermusik* (1944); a symphony and other works for orchestra; organ, violin, cello concertos; string quartets.

FOSS, LUKAS
1922, American
Principal Works - *The Prairie* (1941-42), for chorus, four soloists, orchestra; *Song of Anguish* (1945), for baritone solo and orchestra; *Song of Songs* (1946), for soprano solo and orchestra; String Quartet in G major (1947); *The Jumping Frog* (1949), one-act opera, based on the Mark Twain story; Second Piano Concerto (1951-53); *A parable of Death* (1953); *Psalms* (1957), cantata for chorus and orchestra; *Symphony of Chorales* (1958); *Time Cycle* (1961), for soprano and orchestra.

FRANÇAIX, JEAN (RENÉ)
1912, French
Principal Works - Opera; ballet; oratorio: *L'apocalypse de St. Jean* (1942); piano concerto; concertino for piano and orchestra (1934); quintet for winds; choral and chamber pieces.

FREEMAN, HARRY LAWRENCE
1869-1954, American
Principal Works - Operas: *The Octaroon* (1904); *American Romance,* jazz opera; *Voodoo* (1928); songs.

FREITAS, BRANCO, LUÍS
1890-1955, Portugese
Principal Works - Choral symphony *Manfred* based on Byron; five symphonies; violin concerto, two violin sonatas; a cello sonata; choral and piano pieces.

FRICKER, PETER RACINE
1920, English
Principal Works - Ballet: *Canterbury Prologue* (1951); *O longs desirs* for voice and instruments; piano: *4 Sonnets, 12 studies;* orchestral: *3 Scenes* (1966); 4 symphonies; film music; concertos for viola, for piano, for violin; choral and chamber pieces.

FULEIHAN, ANIS
1900-1970, American
Principal Works - Opera: *Vasco;* orchestral: *Three Cyprus Serenades* (1941); *Symphonie concertante* for string quartet and orchestra (1940); concerto for theremin; for piano, for cello, for violin; 2 symphonies; 5 string quartets; choral works.

GABURO, KENNETH (LOUIS)
1926, American
Principal Works - Choral improvisation and theater materials. Play music: *Lingua I-IV* (1970); *Antiphony I* for strings and tape (1957); *4 Inventions* for clarinet and piano (1954); *Line Studies* for flute, clarinet, trombone, viola (1957); electronic music; piano pieces.

GAL, HANS (JOHANN)
1890, Austrian/English
Principal Works - Opera: *Die heilige Ente* (1923); 3 symphonies; choral music: sacred and secular; concertos; piano pieces; chamber music.

GALINDO, BLAS
1910, Mexican
Principal Works - Orchestral: *Obra para orchestra mexicana* for native instruments (1938); 3 symphonies; ballets; concertos, cantatas; piano and chamber works.

GARCÍA ABRIL, ANTÓN
1933, Spanish
Principal Works - Concerto for strings (1967); piano concerto (1963); ballet, film music, choral and chamber pieces.

GARCIA CATURIA, ALEJANDRO
1906-1940, Cuban
Principal Works - Orchestral: *3 danzas cubanas* (1927); *La rumba* (1933); *Yamba-O* for chorus and orchestra (1931); piano and chamber pieces; songs.

GARDINER, HENRY BALFOUR
1877-1950, English
Principal Works - Orchestral: *Shepherd Fennel's Dance* (1911); *News from Whydah* , chorus; piano and chamber pieces; songs.

GARDNER, JOHN
1917, English
Principal Works - Operas: *The Moon and Sixpence* (1957); *The Visitors* (1972); a symphony; *Theme and Variations* for brass; choral secular and sacred works; piano music.

GATTY, NICHOLAS COMYN
1874-1946, English
Principal Works - Operas: *Greysteel* (1906); *Duke or Devil* (1909); *The Tempest,* based on Shakespeare (1920); *Prince Ferelon* (1921); orchestral: *Ode on Time* for chorus and soloists as well; piano and chamber pieces.

GENZMER, HARALD
1909, German
Principal Works - Symphonic music; ballet; cantatas; concertos for various instruments; chamber and choral works; piano, organ pieces.

GERHARD, ROBERTO
1896-1970, English/Spanish
Principal Works - Opera: *The Duenna* (1948); Ballet: *Don Quixote* (1950); oratorio: *The Plague* (1964); Concerto for Orchestra (1965); 4 symphonies; chamber: *Leo* (1969); music of the Zodiac signs; *7 Hai-Ku* for voice and instruments; *Impromptus* for piano (1950).

GERMAN, SIR EDWARD
(Edward German Jones)
1862-1936, English

Principal Works - Opera: *Merrie England* (1902); Incidental music *Richard III;* dances from *Henry VIII; Nell Gwynne* dances; 2 symphonies; sacred vocals; piano, organ and chamber pieces.

GERSHWIN, GEORGE
1898-1937, American
Principal Works - World-renowned serious and popular composer: **Classical works:** Opera: *Porgy and Bess* (1935); Orchestral: *Rhapsody In Blue* (1924); *An American In Paris*(1928); *Cuban Overture* (1932); *Piano Concerto in F* (1925); *Second Rhapsody* for piano and orchestra (1931); *3 Preludes* for piano (1936); film music. See popular composer listing for songs.

GESENSWAY, LOUIS
1906, American
Principal Works - *Suite for Strings and Percussion* (1935); Flute Concerto; orchestral works; chamber music for woodwinds.

GHEDINI, GIORGIO FEDERICO
1892-1965, Italian
Principal Works - Operas: *Maria d'Alessandria* (1937); *Billy Budd* (1949); *L'ipocrita felice* (1956); orchestral: *Architetture* (1940); *Concerto del'Albatro* (1945); *Sette Ricercari* for violin, cello and piano (1943); Partita for orchestra; *De l'Incarnazione del Verbo Divino* for women's choir, 2 sopranos and small orchestra.

GARANT, SERGE
1929, Canadian
Principal Works - Serial music. *Ennéade* for orchestra (1964); *Offrande I* for instruments and taped soprano (1969); *Cage d'oiseau* for soprano and piano (1962).

GIANNINI, VITTORIO
1903-1966, American
Principal Works - Operas: *The Taming of the Shrew; The Harvest; Beauty and the Beast; The Scarlet Letter.* *Frescobaldiana* for orchestra; Concerto for Trumpet; Canticle for Christmas; Prelude and Fugue for Strings; four symphonies.

GILBERT, HENRY FRANKLIN BELKNAP
1868-1928, American
Principal Works - Orchestral: *The Dance in Place Congo* (1906); Comedy Overture on Negro Themes (1905); *Negro Rhapsody* (1913); Indian Sketches (1921); opera; piano and vocal pieces; songs.

GILBOA, YAAKOV
1920, Israeli
Principal Works - *The 12 Chagall Windows at Jerusalem* for orch.; violin sonata; various ensemble pieces.

GILLIS, DON
1912, American
Principal Works - *No 5½ Symphony for Fun* (1947) and 11 other symphonies; opera, ballet; band pieces; a cantata; string quartets; piano works.

GINASTERA, ALBERT
1916, Argentinian
Principal Works - Ballet suites: *Panambí, Estancia; Argentinian Concerto* for piano and orchestra; *Variaciónes Concertantes* for chamber orchestra; symphonic: *Pampeana No. 3;* Overture: *Creole Faust;* a string quartet; operas: *Don Ridrigo; Bomarzo.*

GLANVILLE-HICKS, PEGGY
1912, Australian
Principal Works - Operas: *the Transposed Heads* (1954); *Nausicaa* (1961); orchestral: *Etruscan Concerto* for piano and chamber orchestra; choral music; film music; songs.

GLASS, PHILIP
1937, American
Principal Works - *Music in Similar Motion* (1969); *Music in Fifths; Music with Changing Parts* (1970); *Music in 12 Parts* (1973).

GLIERE, REINHOLD MORITZOVICH
1875-1956, Russian
Principal Works - Opera: *Shah-Senem* (1934); *Gulsara* (1936); *Leila and Medjun;* Ballet: *The Red Poppy* (1927); and other ballets; Symphony: *Ilya Murometz* (1911), plus two others; *The March of the Red Army* (1924); concerto for coloratura soprano and orchestra; concertos for horn, for harp, for violin, for cello; string quartets; piano and chamber music; songs.

GNESSIN, MIKHAIL FABIANOVICH
1883-1957, Russian
Principal Works - Opera: *The Youth of Abraham* (1923); *The Maccabees;* symphonic poems; chamber music; orchestral arrangements of Jewish folk music.

GOEB, ROGER
1914, American
Principal Works - *Prairie Song* for woodwind quintet; 4 symphonies; violin concerto; chamber music.

GOEHR, ALEXANDER
1932, English
Principal Works - Opera: *Areden muss sterben* (1967); *Triptych,* 3 theater pieces; cantata: *The Deluge* (1958); *Symphony* for small orchestra; *A Little Cantata of Proverbs,* after Blake; *Naboth's Vineyard* for theater; violin concerto; chamber and piano pieces; choral with instruments.

GOLDMARK, RUBIN
1872-1936, American
Principal Works - Noted teacher at Julliard School of Music. Orchestral works: *Hiawatha* (1900); *Samson* (1914); *A Negro Rhapsody* (1923); *Requiem Suggested by Lincoln's Gettysburg Address* (1919); chamber and piano pieces.

GOLESTAN, STAN
1875-1956, Rumanian
Principal Works - Orchestral: *Rhapsodie roumaine;* vocal: *10 chansons populaires roumaines* (1909); concertos; piano and chamber pieces.

GOLDMAN, EDWIN FRANKO
1878-1956, American
Principal Works - Famed bandmaster and composer of over 100 marches, including the well-known *On The Mall;* also pieces for symphonic band and wind instruments.

GOOSENS, SIR EUGENE
1893-1962, English
Principal Works - Operas: *Judith; Don Juan de Manara;* 2 symphonies; Concertino for string orchestra (also in string octet form); piano and chamber pieces; ballet.

GOTOVAC, JAKOV
1895, Yugoslavian

Principal Works - Operas: *Morana* (1930); *Ero the Joker* (1935); orchestral: *Symphonic Kolo* (1926); choral: *Koleda* (1925); piano and folk-music pieces.

GOULD, MORTON
1913, American
Principal Works - Third Symphony (1947); Ballets: *Fall River Legend* (1948); *Interplay* (1943); Concerto For Orchestra (1944); *Symphony of Spirituals* (1976); *Foster Gallery* (1940); *Venice* (1966); *Jekyll and Hyde Variations* (1955); chorus with speakers: *Declaration; Derivations* for band (1956); the well-known *Pavanne* for symphonic and popular orchestras; piano and chamber pieces; film music.

GRABOVSKY, LEONID ALEXANDROVICH
1935, Russian
Principal Works - *4 Ukranian Songs* for chorus and orchestra (1959); film music; piano and chamber pieces.

GRAINGER, PERCY
1882-1961, Australian/American
Principal Works - Electronic music with *free music* microtones and rhythms. Orchestral pieces: *Country Gardens; Handel in the Strand; Shepherd's Hey; Lads of Wamphray* for band; *Free Music* for string quartet; choral music; piano pieces.

GRANADOS, ENRIQUE
1867-1916, Spanish
Principal Works - Opera: *Goyescas,* (1916); Intermezzo (arranged for cello and piano); 6 other operas; Piano: *12 Danzas españolas,* Op. 37 (1893); *Goyescas* (1912); *Los requiebros; Elnajo discheto; El fandango del Candil; Quejas o la Maja y el Ruiseñor (The Maiden and the Nightingale); 10 Tonadillas al estilo antique.*

GRANDJANY, MARCEL
1891-1975, American
Principal Works - *Poème* for harp, horn and orch.; *Aria In Classic Style* for harp and strings; *Children's Hour Suite, Colorado Trail; Divertissement; Rhapsody* for harp; *Fantasia on a Theme of Haydn ; The Erie Canal.*

GRECHANINOV, ALEXANDER TIKHONOVICH
1864-1956, Russian
Principal Works - Opera: *Dobrinya Nikitich* (1903); 5 symphonies; Sacred: *Missa Oeucumenica* for chorus, solos and orchestra; stage pieces; chorus works; piano and chamber pieces. Songs: *Berceuse; The Captive; My Country; Night; Over The Steppe; Snowflakes.*

GREEN, RAY
1909, American
Principal Works - *Sunday Sing Symphony* and two other symphonies; vocal: *Quarter-tone madrigal* for male voices; dance scores for ballet; violin concerto; piano and chamber pieces.

GRIFFES, CHARLES TOMLINSON
1884-1920, American
Principal Works - Orchestral: *The Pleasure Dome of Kubla Khan,* after Coleridge (1920); *Poem for Flute and Orchestra* (1918); *The White Peacock* (1917) (also original piano piece); Piano sketches: *Four Roman Sketches* (1915); *Nightfall; The Fountain of Acqua Paolo; Clouds* and *The White Peacock* (as above); *Sketches on Indian Themes* for string quartet (1922).

GROFE, FERDE
1892-1972, American
Principal Works - Orchestral: *The Grand Canyon Suite; Mississippi Suite; Hollywood Suite;* piano pieces.

GROVLEZ, GABRIEL
1879-1944, French
Principal Works - Opera: *Le Marquis de Carabas* (1925); ballet; symphonic and vocal music; piano and chamber pieces; songs.

GRUEN, JOHN
1926, American
Principal Works - Art songs: *13 Ways of Looking at a Blackbird; Pomes Penyeach; Seven by cummings.*

GRUENBERG, LOUIS
1884-1964, American
Principal Works - Opera: *The Emperor Jones;* orchestral: *The Hill of Dreams* (1921); *Jazzberries* for piano; Violin Concerto; Dancel Jazz for tenor and 8 instruments.

GUARNIERI, CAMARGO MOZART
1907, Brazilian
Principal Works - Orchestral: *Brazilian Dance* for orchestra; 4 symphonies; 2 violin concertos; 5 piano concertos; choral music; piano and chamber pieces.

GUION, DAVID WENDEL FENTRESS
1895, American
Principal Works - Concert arrangements of *Home On The Range* and *Turkey In The Straw;* American folk-song arranger.

GURIDI, JESÚS
1886-1961, Basque/Spanish
Principal Works - Basque *zarzuelas: El caserío* (1926); Operas: *Mirentxu* (1910); *Maya* (1920); orchestral: *10 melodias vascas;* choral and piano pieces; chamber music; sacred music; organ works.

GUTCHE, GENE
1907, American
Principal Works - Twelve tone and microtone music. Orchestral: *Genghis Khan* symphonic poem (1963); *Gemini* (1966); 6 symphonies; concertos for varied instruments; 4 string quartets; piano sonatas.

HAAS, JOSEPH
1879-1961, German
Principal Works - Oratorio: *Die heilige Elisabeth;* operas; church music; orchestral and choral works.

HÁBA, ALOIS
1893-1973, Czech.
Principal Works - Twelve tone and mmicrotone music. Opera: *Matka* (1931); orchestral: *The Path of Life,* symphonic fantasy (1935); violin concertos; chamber and choral music; piano and guitar pieces.

HADLEY, HENRY KIMBALL
1871-1937, American
Principal Works - Opera: *Azora* (1917); *Bianca* (1918); *Cleopatra's Night* (1920); *The Four Seasons* symphony and 3 more symphonies; choral pieces; many songs.

HADLEY, PATRICK ARTHUR SHELDON
1899-1973, English
Principal Works - Choral works: *La Belle Dame Sans Merci; The Trees So High* (1931); *Scene from the Cenci*

(1951) for solo voice and orchestra; incidental music for *Antigone* and other Greek tragedies.

HAGEMAN, RICHARD
1882-1966, Dutch/American
Principal Works - Opera: *Caponsacch* (1937); film music; songs, including *Do Not Go, My Love.*

HAHN, REYNALDO
1875-1947, French
Principal Works - Operas: *La carmélite* (1902); *Ciboulette* (1923); Ballet, theater and orchestral music. Songs including *Si mes vers avaient des ailes (If My Words Only Had Wings).*

HAHN, REYNALDO
1875-1947, French
Principal Works - Operas: *La carmelite* (1902); *Ciboulette* (1923); Ballet, theater and orchestral music. Songs including *Si mes vers avaient des ailes (If My Words Only Had Wings).*

HAIEFF, ALEXEI
1914, American
Principal Works - Ballet: *Beauty and the Beast; Divertimento* (1944) (originally orchestral); symphonies; concertos; chamber and piano pieces; songs.

HALFFTER, CRISTOBAL
1930, Spanish
Principal Works - Opera: *Don Quijote* (1970); orchestral: *Secuencias* for orchestra (1964); *Anillos* for orchestra (1968); choral: *Simposion* (1966); *Misa ducal* (1956); cantata: *Yes, Speak Out Yes* for soprano, baritone, 2 choruses, 2 orchestras, 2 conductors (1970); *Sinfonia* for 3 instrumental groups; *Espejos* for tape and percussion; cello concerto (1974).

HALFFTER, ERNESTO
1905, Spanish
Principal Works - Opera: *The Death of Carmen;* ballet: *Sonatina* (1928); orchestral: *Sinfonietta* (1924); *Dos bocetos sinfónicos;* guitar concerto (1969); chamber and vocal pieces; piano music.

HALFFTER, RODOLFO
1900, Mexican/Spanish
Principal Works - Ballet: *Don Lindo de Almeria* (1940); Opera: *Clavileño* (1936); concertos for violin and piano; twelve tone music.

HALLEN, JOHAN ANDREAS
1846-1925, Swedish
Principal Works - Operas: *Harald der Wiking* (1881); *Waldermarsskatten* (1899); *Die Toteninsel,* symphonic poem; choral: *Missa Solemnis;* chamber works.

HAMBRAEUS, BENGT
1928, swedish
Principal Works - *Rota* for 3 orchestras and tape; *Responsorier* for solo vocals, chorus and instruments; *Microgram* for alto flute; *Constellations I-III* for organ and tape; *Interferences* for organ.

HAMILTON, IAIN
1922, Scottish
Principal Works - Serial music. Ballet *Clerk Saunders* (1951); Operas: *The Catiline Conspiracy; The Royal Hunt of the Sun* (1974); *Sinfonia for 2 orchestras* (1959); *Voyage* for

horn and orchestra; *Epitaph For this World; Time.* Organ: *Threnos: In Time Of War* (1966); *Sonata notturna* for horn and piano; concerto for clarinet; cantata: *The Bermudas.*

HANSON, HOWARD
1896, American
Principal Works - *Song of Human Rights* (1963); a cantata; *Lament for Beowulf* (chorus and orchestra); *Merry Mount* (opera); *Drum Taps* (chorus and orchestra); setting of three Walt Whitman Civil War poems: *Beat, Beat Drums; By the Bivouac's Fitful Flame; To Thee, Old Cause;* Four Symphonies: No. 1 (Nordic); No. 2 (*Romantic);* No. 3, written to celebrate the landing of the Swedes in Delaware; No. 4 *(Requiem); Cherubic Hymn* (chorus and orchestra).

HARBISON, JOHN
1938, American
Principal Works - *Sinfonia* for violin and double orchestra (1963); *Shakespeare Series* – soprano and piano (1965); *The Flower Fed Buffaloes* (1976), for baritone, chorus and instruments; *Cantata Sequence* for soprano and instruments (1968); *Parody Fantasia* for piano; *Bermuda Triangle* for tenor saxophone, amplified cello and electronic organ (1970).

HARRIS, ROY
1898-1979, American
Principal Works - 16 symphonies including Symphony No. 4 *Folk Song Symphony,* No. 3 (1938) and Symphony No. 7 (1951); Choral works: *Abraham Lincoln Walks at Midnight;* a Mass, a chamber cantata; and sacred pieces; *Elegy and Paean* for viola and orchestra, electronic piano; ballets; many concertos and sonatas.

HARRISON, LOU
1917, American
Principal Works - Serial, aleatory and Asiatic (gamelan) music. Ballet: *Solstice* (1950); opera: *Rapunzel;* orch.: *Symphony on G, Concerto in Slendro; Pakifika Rondo* for Western and Asian chamber orchestra; *Suite for Solo Violin,* solo piano and small orchestra (1951); *Canticle No. III* for percussion.

HARSANYI, TIBOR
1898-1954, Hungarian
Principal Works - Orchestral: *Suite hongroise* (1937); symphony violin concerto; piano concerto; nonet; film music; chamber opera; piano pieces.

HART, FRITZ BENNICKE
1874-1949, English
Principal Works - Operas; symphony; orchestral pieces; chamber works; songs and choral pieces.

HARTIG, HEINZ FRIEDRICH
1907-1969, German
Principal Works - Serial music. Chamber opera: *Escorial* (1961); Orchestral: *Variationen Uber enen siebentönigen Klang* (1962); concertos; choral: *Perche with guitar;* piano and chamber pieces.

HARTMANN, KARL AMADEUS
1905-1963, German
Principal Works - Twelve tone music. Opera: *Simplicius Simplicissimus;* 8 symphonies; 2 string quartets; *Gesangszene* for baritone voice and orchestra; concertos.

HARTY, SIR HAMILTON (HERBERT)
1879-1941, Irish

Principal Works - *Ode To A Nightingale* for soprano and orchestra (1907); Symphonic poem: *With The Wild Geese* (1910); Violin Concerto in D minor (1909); Irish Symphony (1910), (rewritten 1923); *Comedy Overture* (1907); arrangements and settings of Irish poems and folk songs.

HARWOOD, BASIL
1859-1949, English

Principal Works - Choral music; sacred music for services; motets; anthems; organ: *Dithyramb:Paean.*

HAUBENSTOCK-RAMATI, ROMAN
1919, Polish

Principal Works - Serial, electronic, graphic, aleatory music. Opera: *Amerika* (1966); *Tableaux* for orchestra; *Jeux,* works for percussionists; vocal: *Mobile for Shakespeare* (1959); *Interpolation* for flute and tape; *Recitative and aria* for harpsichord and orchestra; *Credentials* based on Beckett's *Waiting For Godot.*

HAUBIEL, CHARLES (TROWBRIDGE)
1892, American

Principal Works - Orchestral: *Brigands Preferred* (1925); *Portraits* (1934); *Karma* (1928); Mexican folk opera: *Sunday Costs Five Pesos* (1950); cantatas; chamber pieces.

HAUER, JOSEF MATTHIAS
1883-1959, Austrian

Principal Works - Twelve tone music; developed "trope" combinations based on 12-tone octave, independent of Schönberg. Cantata: *The Way of Humanity* (1953); Oratorio: *Wanlungen* (1928); *Nomoi* (1912) for piano; *Zwölftonspiel* for instruments.

HAUFRECHT, HERBERT
1909, American

Principal Works - *Square Set* for strings; *A Woodland Serenade* for wind quintet; orchestral, band, choral and piano pieces; songs and folk, jazz pieces.

HEIDEN, BERNHARD
1910, German/American

Principal Works - Opera: *The Darkened City* (1963); 2 symphonies; ballet; film music; choral and chamber pieces; piano sonatas.

HEILLER, ANTON
1923, Austrian

Principal Works - Masses, and other sacred and secular choral works; toccata for 2 pianos; organ works; instrumental pieces.

HENZE, HANS WERNER
1926, German/Italian

Principal Works - Twelve tone, electronic and microtone music. Operas: *Das Wundertheater* (1949); *Boulevard Solitude* (1952); *Ein Landarzt* (1953); *Der König Hirsch* (1956); Ballet: *Undine* (1958); *Elegie für junge Liebende; The Bassarids* (1966); *El cimarron* for voice, flute, guitar, percussion; symphonies;concertos for violin, for piano, for double bass.

HERRMAN, BERNARD
1911-1975, American

Principal Works - Opera: *Wuthering Heights;* cantata: *Moby Dick* film score for *Citizen Kane;* orchestral: *For the Fallen;* violin concerto; choral music.

HERRMANN, HUGO
1896-1967, German

Principal Works - Opera: *Vasantasena* (1930); 5 symphonies; concertos for organ, for harpsichord, for accordion; sacred music; chamber instrumentals and cantatas; piano, organ, accordion and harmonic pieces.

HILL, ALFRED
1870-1960, Australian

Principal Works - Opera: *The Weird Flute;* orchestral: *Maori Symphony;* Maori themes, cantata; piano and violin works; choral and chamber pieces; film music.

HILL, EDWARD BURLINGAME
1872-1960, American

Principal Works - Orchestral: *Lilacs* (1927); *The Fall of the House of Usher* symphonic poem (1920); 3 symphonies; violin concerto; *Music for English horn and orchestra;* piano pieces; choral and chamber music.

HILLER, LEJAREN
1924, American

Principal Works - Electronic, computer and visual music. *Illiac Suite for String Quartet (1957),* computer generated; *Machine Music,* electronic with instruments, for piano, percussion and tape (1964); *HPSCHD for 1-7 harpsichords and 1-51 tapes* (1968), a John Cage collaboration.

HINDEMITH, PAUL
1895-1963, German

Principal Works - Operas: *Cardillac* (1926); *Neues vom Tage* (1929); *Mathis der Maler* (1934); *The Harmony of the World* (1957); *The Long Christmas. Dinner* (1960); Ballet: *Nobilissima Visione* (1937); Orchestra: Concerto for Orchestra (1925); Philharmonic Concrto (1932); Symphonic Dances (1937); *Nobilissima Visione* (Suite) (1938); Concerto for Violin and Orchestra (1940); Concerto for Cello and Orchestra (1940); Symphony *Mathis der Maler* (1934); Symphony in E flat (1940); *The Four Temperaments,* for piano and string orchestra (1940); Symphonic Metamorphosis on Themes by Weber (1943); *Sinfonia Serena* (1946); Symphony, *the Harmony of the World* (1951), Chamber Orchestra: Five *Kammermusiker,* Concertos for Wind Instruments, Piano, Violin, Cello and Viola, Op. 36, Nos. 1-5 (1924-28); Concert Music for Viola and Chamber Orchestra, Op. 48 (1930); Concert Music for Piano, Brass Instruments and Harp, Op. 49 (1930); Concert Music for Strings and Brass Instruments, Op. 50 (1931); *Der Schwanendreher* (viola and orchestra) (1935). Chorus: *Apparebit Repentina Dies* (1947); 6 *Chansons* (a cappella) (1939); Requiem, *When Lilacs Last in the Door-yard Bloom'd* (1946).

HODKINSON, SYDNEY
1934, Canadian

Principal Works - Serial, aleatory music. Orchestral: *Caricatures, 1966; Valence* for chamber orchestra (1970); *Ritual* for chorus (1970); instrumental ensemble pieces.

HOFFDING, FINN
1899, Danish

Principal Works - Operas: *The Emperor's New Clothes* (1928); *Pasteur* (1938); 4 symphonies; orchestral *Evolution* (1939); concerto for oboe and strings; chamber and vocal pieces.

HOFFMANN, RICHARD
1947, Austrian/American
Principal Works - Orchestral: *Orchestra Piece* (1961); concertos for piano, for violin, for cello; Organ: *Fantasy and Fugue in memoriam Arnold Schoenberg* (1951); piano and chamber pieces.

HOIBY, LEE
1926, American
Principal Works - Operas: *The Scarf; Beatrice* (1959); *Natalia Petrovna; Summer and Smoke* (1971); Ballet: *After Eden* (1966); *The Tides of Sleep* for voice and orchestra; piano concerto (1958); stage music; chamber and choral music.

HOLBROOKE, JOSEPH
1878-1958, English
Principal Works - Opera triology: *The Cauldron of Annwen* (1912); Orchestral: *Three Blind Mice; Byron, The Raven, The Bells,* symphonic poems; concertos for piano, for saxophone, for violin, for piano; choral, chamber and clarinet pieces; piano works.

HÖLLER, KARL
1907, German
Principal Works - *Kammerkonzert* for harpsichord and small orchestra; *Variations on a Theme of Sweelinck;* symphony; concertos for violin, for cello, for organ; choral sacred and secular pieces; piano, organ and chamber music; film music.

HOLST, GUSTAV
1874-1934, English
Principal Works - Operas: *Savitri,* 1 Act (1916); *At The Boar's Head; the Perfect Fool,* Op. 39, 1 Act (1923); *Savitri,* Ballet music. Orchestral: *St. Paul's Suite* (strings), Op. 29, No. 2 (1913); *The Planets Suite,* Op. 32 (1916); *The Hymn of Jesus* (with chorus), Op. 37 (1917); First Choral Symphony. Songs *This Have I Done for My True Love,* Op. 34a, No. 1; *I Vow to Thee, My Country.*

HOMER, SIDNEY
1864-1953, American
Principal Works - Songs: *A Banjo Song: The Song of The Shirt; General William Booth Enters into Heaven;* orchestral pieces.

HONEGGER, ARTHUR
1892-1955, Swiss
Principal Works - A member of the *Les Six* group. Operas: *The Eaglet* (with Ibert); *Antigone* (1927); *King David; Judith; Joan Of Arc at the Stake* (oratorio); symphonies: No. 2 for strings (trumpet optional); No. 3 *Liturgical;* No. 5 *Di tre re* plus three others: orchestral works: *Pacific 231; Rugby* (1928); *Dance of the Goat* for flute; *Christmas Cantata* film music; concertos; choral and chamber pieces; piano music; ballet: *Semiramis* (1934).

HOVHANESS, ALAN
1911, American
Principal Works - Armenian, Oriental and Indian music influences. *Lousadzak* piano concerto with strings; *And God Created Great Whales* for tape humpbacked whale solo and orchestra; 25 symphonies; choral *Triptych* (1953); piano and chamber music.

HOWE, MARY
1882-1964, American
Principal Works - Orchestral: *Rock* (1955); choral: *Prophecy* (1943); *Chain Gang Song;* orchestral: *Stars and Sand* chamber music.

HOWELLS, HERBERT NORMAN
1892, English
Principal Works - Choral: Masses, anthems, sacred and secular: *Sine nomine* with orchestra; *Hymnus paradisi* (1938); piano and cello concertos; piano and organ pieces; chamber and clavichord works; songs.

HRISANIDE, ALEXANDRU
1936, Rumanian
Principal Works - Twelve tone, aleatory, folk music! Orchestral: *Passacaglia* (1959); *Volumes-Inventions* for cello and piano (1963); *Mers-Tefs II for 1-4 violins;* piano and choral music.

HUBAY, JENÖ
1858-1937, Hungarian
Principal Works - Opera: *A Cremonai hegodus* (1894); *Csardajelenet* for violin and orchestra; symphonies; ballet; 4 violin concertos; chamber and violin pieces.

HUBER, KLAUS
1924, Swiss
Principal Works - Sacred oratorios: *The Angels; Address To The Soul;* tenor, flute, clarinet, horn, harp pieces.

HUMEL, GERALD
1931, American
Principal Works - Twelve tone music! Ballet: *Die Folterungen der Betrice Cenci* (1971); operas; a symphony; chamber music.

IBERT, JACQUES
1890-1962, French
Principal Works - Orchestral: *Ballade de la geole de Reading,* after Oscar Wilde's poem; revised as ballet (1947); Suite: *Ports of Call (Escales)* (1920); Divertissement from *The Italian Straw Hat;* Concertino da Camera for alto saxophone and 11 instruments. Opera: *Angélique; Le Roi d'Yvetot; L'Aiglon* (with Honegger) after Rostand; *Les Petites Cardinal; Diane de Poitiers* (1934). Piano pieces: *Le Petit âne blanc* The Little White Donkey); String Quartet (1937); Ballet: *The Knight-Errant* (1950).

ICHIYANAGI, TOSHI
1933, Japanes
Principal Works - Electronic music, Oriental and Western instruments. *Distance,* stage music; *The Field* for bamboo, flute and orchestra; *Extended Voices* for chorus; *Music for Piano;* pieces; *Sapporo* for up to 15 instruments; tape collages.

IKENOUCHI, TOMOJIRO
1906, Japanese
Principal Works - *Mago Uta* for orchestra; string quartets; chamber pieces.

IMBRIE, ANDREW W.
1921, American
Principal Works - Opera: 3 symphonies; symphonic poem: *Legend* (1959); 2 violin concertos (1953); piano concerto (1973); flute concerto (1977); choral works; string quartets.

INGHELBRECHT, DÉSIRÉ-EMILE
1880-1965, French

Principal Works - Ballet: *El Greco* (1920); *Le cantique des créatures de Saint François,* chorus with orchestra; opera; chamber and piano pieces.

IRELAND, JOHN
1879-1962, English

Principal Works - Orchestral: *The Forgotten Rite; Mai-Dun; A London Overture; Satyricon; Concertino Pastorale* for strings; cantata:*These Things Shall Be;* piano concerto (1930); *Sea Fever* and many other songs; piano, organ and chamber pieces.

IVES, CHARLES (EDWARD)
1874-1954, American

Principal Works - Polytonal, tone cluster, aleatory music! Orchestral: Symphony No. 1 (1896); Symphony No. 2 (1897-1902); Symphony No. 3 (1901-04) *The Camp Meeting;* Symphony No. 4 (1910-16) *The Unanswered Question* (before 1908); *Three Outdoor Scenes* (1898-1911); 1. *Hallowe'en,* 2. *The Pond,* 3. *Central Park in the Dark; A Symphony: Holidays* (1904-13); 1. *Washington's Birthday,* 2. *Decoration Day,* 3. *Fourth of July,* 4. *Thanksgiving and/or Forefather's Day; Orchestral Set No. 1: Three Places in New England.* 1. *Boston Common,* 2. *Putnam's Camp,* 3. *Thee Housatonic at Stockbridge; Universal Symphony* (unfinished) (1911-16; 1927). Chamber music: String Quartet No. 1, *A Revival Service* (1896); String Quartet No. 2 (1907-13). Instrumental music: Sonata No. 1 (violin and piano) (1903-08); Sonata No. 2 (violin and piano) (1903-10); Sonata No. 3 (violin and piano) (1902-14); Sonata No. 4 (violin and piano) (1914-15); Piano Sonata No. 1 (1902-09); Piano Sonata No. 2 (*Concord*) (1909-15) 1. *Emerson,* 2. *Hawthorne,* 3. *The Alcotts,* 4. *Thoreau; Some Southpaw Pitching* (piano) (1908); *The Anti-Abolitionist Riots* (piano) (1908); *Variations on a National Hymn (America)* (1891). Choral Works: *Sixty-Seventh Psalm* (1898); *Three Harvest Home Chorales* (1898-1912); *General William Booth's Entrance into Heaven.* Songs: *Ann Street; Charlie Rutledge; The Children's Hour; Ich Grolle Nicht; In Flanders Fields; Serenity; Songs My Mother Taught Me.*

IVEY, JEAN EICHELBERGER
1923, American

Principal Works - Electronic music. *Hera, Hung from the Sky* for mezzo soprano, winds, percussion, piano and tape. Orchestral and chamber pieces.

JACOB, GORDON
1895, English

Principal Works - *Oranges and Lemons,* Passacaglia on a Well-Known Theme; Concerto for Oboe and Strings (1933); Variations for Orchestra (1935); Quintet for Clarinet and Strings (1940); Symphony No. 2 in C major; Concerto for Bassoon and Strings (1946); Symphonic Suite (1948).

JACOBI, FREDERICK
1891-1952, American

Principal Works - American-Indian and Jewish theme materials. Opera: *The Prodigal Son;* two symphonies; concertos; *Ballade* for violin and piano; piano, organ and chamber pieces.

JAMES, PHILIP
1890-1975, American

Principal Works - Overture: *Bret Harte;* Suite *Station WGZBX* (1932); 2 symphonies; symphonic poem: *Song of the Night;*choral, sacred and secular; piano and chamber works.

JANÁČEK, LEOŠ
1881-1888, Czech.

Principal Works - Operas: *Jenufa; Katya Kabanová; The Cunning Little Vixen; The Makropoulos Affair; From The House of the Dead;* Choral: *Glagolitic Mass* cantata; *Amarus;* orchestral: *Sinfonietta, Taras Bulba;* song cycle: *The Diary of One Who Vanished;* piano, organ and chamber pieces.

JARNACH, PHILIPP
1892, Spanish

Principal Works - *Sinfonia Brevis* for orchestra; *Musik mit Mozart,* symphonic variations; chambr music: *Musik zum Gedächtnis der Einsamen* for string quartet; piano solos and unaccompanied violin sonatas.

JARNEFELT, ARMAS
1869-1958, Swedish

Principal Works - Orchestral: *Praeludium; Berceuse;* choral works; cantatas; piano music.

JIRÁK, KAREL BOLESLAV
1891-1972, Czech.

Principal Works - *Overture to a Shakespearean Comedy;* 5 symphonies; 7 string quartets; operas; piano concerto; choral works; song cycles.

JOHANSEN, DAVID MONRAD
1888, Norweigan

Principal Works - *Voluspá* for large chorus; orchestral and chamber works.

JOHNSON, HUNTER
1906, American

Principal Works - Ballet: *Letter to the World* (1940); *Deaths and Entrances* (1943); symphony; piano concerto; piano sonata; chamber music.

JOHNSON, LOCKREM
1924, American

Principal Works - Chamber opera; six piano sonatas; violin sonatas; ballet; choral works.

JOHNSTON, BEN
1926, American

Principal Works - Aleatory, serial and microtone music! Dance-opera: *Gertrude, or Would She Be Pleased To Receive It; Gambit* for dancers and orchestra; *Quintet* for groups with orchestra; Sonata for Microtonal Piano; string quartets; jazz band pieces.

JOLAS, BETSY
1926, French

Principal Works - *Points of the Dawn* for contralto and 13 winds; *States* for violin and 6 percussionists; *4 Plages* (1967) for orchestra: *Quatuor II* for coloratura soprano and string trio; chamber pieces.

JOLIVET, ANDRÉ
1905-1974, French

Principal Works - Opera; two ballets; film and theater music! Oratorio: *the Truth About Joan of Arc.* Choral: *Les Trois complaintes du soldat;* 5 symphonies; concertos for Ondes Martenot, for trumpet, for harp, for piano, for flute, for bassoon; piano, organ and chamber pieces.

JONES, CHARLES
1910, Canadian/American
Principal Works - Ballet; orchestral works; chamber music.

JONGEN, JOSEPH
1873-1953, Belgian
Principal Works - Orchestral and concerto works; opera; ballet piano and organ and chamber pieces; quartet for saxophones.

JOSTEN, WERNER
1885-1963, German/American
Principal Works - *Concerto Sacro* for strings and piano; ballet; orchestral and choral works; chamber music; songs.

KABALEVSKY, DMITRI BORISOVITCH
1904, Russian
Opera: *The Master of Clamecy* (includes overture *Colas Breugnon*); *Taras' Family* after Gorbatov; Violin Concerto (1948); Cello Concerto, (1949); Orchestral: *Comedians, Op. 26; Piano Concerto No. 3; 24 Preludes for piano, Op. 38;* 3 piano concertos; songs.

KABELÁČ, MILOSLAV
1908, Czech.
Principal Works - Orchestral: *Improvisation on Hamlet; Mysterium času* (1957); *Ricercari* for 1-6 percussionists; choral cantatas; piano, organ and chamber pieces.

KADOSA, PAL
1903, Hungarian
Principal Works - Opera: *Huszti Kaland* (1950); 8 symphonies; 4 piano concertos; violin and viola concertos; cantata: *De amore fatali* (1940); string quartets; choral pieces; piano music.

KAGEL, MAURICIO
1931, Argentinian
Principal Works - Aleatory, musique concrète, electronic forms. *Sur scene* for mime, speaker, singer and instrumentalists; *Match* for 3 players on 2 cellos with percussion; *Tower Music* for taped instruments, musique concrète and visual projections; *Pas de cinq* for theater (1965); *Improvisation ajoutée for 3 organists* (1962); Transicion I and II for piano, percussion and tape (1958); film music.

KÁLMÁN, EMMERICH
1882-1953, Hungarian
Principal Works - Operettas: *The Gypsy Princess; Countess Maritza; The Gay Hussars; The Riviera Girl; The Circus Princess;* instrumental pieces and other stage music.

KAMINSKI, HEINRICH
1886-1946, Austrian
Principal Works - Operas: *Jürg Jenatsch* (1929); *Das Spiel vom König Aphelius* (1946); Concerto gross o – double orchestra (1922); *Triptych* for organ and voice; *Magnificat* for chorus (1925); sared and secular choral pieces; piano and organ works; songs.

KAPR, JAN
1914, Czech.
Principal Works - Twelve tone and aleatory forms. An opera; ballet; 7 symphonies; concertos; *Homage to the trumpet* for two trumpets with wind, piano and percussion. Film music; piano and chamber pieces.

KAREL, RUDOLF
1880-1945, Czech.
Principal Works - Operas: *Ilsea's Heart; Godmother Death.* Orchestral: *Scherzo Capriccio* (1904); oratorio; choral works; piano and chamber pieces; songs.

KASEMETS, UDO
1919, Estonian/Canadian
Principal Works - Serial, aleatory, graphic forms. *Calceolaria* time/space variations on a floral theme (1966); *Square root of 5* for 2 pianos and percussion; T^t computerized multi-media work; *Cumulus* for 2 tape recorders and instruments; vocal and instrumental ensemble music.

KASSERN, TADEUSZ
1904-1959, Polish
Principal Works - *Symphonic poem* after Pilsudski; concerto for soprano; piano and chamber pieces; songs.

KASTLE, LEONARD
1929, American
Principal Works - Opera: *The Pariahs, Deseret; A Whitman Reader* for voice and orchestra; a piano sonata; *Three Whale Songs from Moby Dick* for male chorus.

KAY, ULYSSES (SIMPSON)
1917, American
Principal Works - Opera: *The Juggler of Our Lady,* 1956; ballet; orchestral: *Markings,* (1966); *Sinfonietta;* concerto for oboe; film music; choral works; piano and chamber pieces; songs.

KELEMEN, MILKO
1924, Yugoslavian
Principal Works - Serial and aleatory music. Opera: *The Plague; König Ubu; Composé* for 2 pianos and 3 orchestras; *Surprise* for string orchestra; *Equilibriums* for 2 orchestras; concerto for bassoon.

KENNAN, KENT (WHEELER)
1913, American
Principal Works - Orchestral: a symphony; *Night Soliloquy* for flute with piano and/or orchestra; *Il campo dei filori* for trumpet (1937) choral works.

KERR, HARRISON
1897 American
Principal Works - *Sinfonietta* for chamber orchestra, (1968); opera; 3 symphonies; choral pieces; *Dance Sonata* for 2 pianos, percussion and dancers, string quartets; chamber pieces with piano.

KHACHATURIAN, ARAM ILYICH
1903, Russian
Principal Works - Piano Concerto (1937); *Poem for Stalin* (1938); Violin Concerto (1940); *Gayne* (1941) ballet (includes *Sabre Dance*); Cello Concerto (1947); Symphony No. 2 (1943); Three arias for solo voice with orchestra (1947); Music to the film *The Battle for Stalingrad* (1949); *Ode of Lamentation,* in memory of Lenin (1949); *Poem Overture* (1950).

KHRENNIKOV, TIKHON NIKOLAIEVICH
1913, Russian
Principal Works - Anti-formalist critic of Prokofiev. Operas: *Mother, Mother* (1957); ballet; piano concerto; 2 symphonies; film and theater music; piano works.

KILPINEN, YRJÖ (HENRIK)
1892-1959, Finnish
Principal Works - Suite for bass viol and piano: orchestral and choral works; many songs in Finnish, Swedish and German including *Fjeldliedern: Kanteletar.*

KIM, EARL
1920, American
Principal Works - *Dialogues* for piano and orchestra (1959); *Eatrh-light* for violin, piano, soprano and visual effects (1973); *Exercises en Route for chamber group and soprano, dancers, actors with film;* violin sonata; cello sonata; piano works.

KIRCHNER, LEON
1919, New York
Principal Works - Opera: *Lily* (1977) after Saul Bellow; 2 piano concertos; piano sonata; *Sinfonia* for orchestra (1952); *String Quartet No. 3 with tape,* and other string quartets.

KLAMI, UUNO
1900-1961, Finnish
Principal Works - Orchestral: *Kalevala* suite; two symphonies; overture to *King Lear;* concertos for violin, for piano; incidental play music, after Eugene O'Neill.

KLEBE, GISELHER
1925, German
Principal Works - Twelve tone music. Operas: *Die Räuber* (1957); *Alkmene; Figaro seeks a divorce; Jacobowsky and the Colonel,* after Franz Werfel. *Roman Elegies* for narrator and orchestra; Symphony for 42 strings and three other symphonies; choral and chamber pieces.

KLENAU, PAUL (AUGUST) VON
1883-1946, Danish
Principal Works - Operas: *Gudrun auf Island (1924); randt van Rijn* (1937); Ballet: *Klein-Idas Blumen;* 7 symphonies; choral and chamber works; piano pieces.

KLOSE, FRIEDRICH
1862-1942, German
Principal Works - Opera: *Ilsebill* (1905); oratorio: *Der Sonne-Geist (1918); symphonic poems; Mass in D-minor for chorus;* organ and chamber pieces.

KLUSÁK, JAN
1934, Czech.
Principal Works - Opera: *Proces (The Trial)* after Kafka (1964); *Invention I* for chamber orchestra; 3 symphonies; choral and chamber pieces; tape assemblages; pieces for individual instruments.

KOCH, ERLAND VON
1910, Swedish
Principal Works - Opera: *Lasse Lucidor* (1943); ballets; *Musica malinconica* for string orchestra (1952); 3 symphonies; concertos; choral and chamber works.

KODÁLY, ZOLTAN
1882-1967, Hungarian
Principal Works - Orchestal: Orchestral Suite from the opera *Háry János* (1926); *Dances of Marosszék* (1930); *Galánta Dances* (1933); Concerto for Orchestra; *Peacock Variations;* Theater Overture (1927); Symphony No. 1 (1961). Chamber music: Duo for Cello and Violin, Op. 7 (1914); Quartet No. 1, Op. 2 (1908); Quartet No. 2, Op. 10 (1916-18); Sonata for Cello, Op. 8 (1915); Sonata for Cello

and Piano, Op. 4 (1909). Piano: *It Is Raining in the Village,* Op. 11, No. 3. Choral: *Psalmus Hungaricus* (Psalm 55) (1923); *Jesus and the Traders* (1934); *Missa Brevis* (1945); *Te Deum* (1936).

KOECHLIN, CHARLES
1867-1951, French
Principal Works - Four Symphonic Poems based on Kipling's Jungle Book; Two Symphonies in homage to Bach; *Doctor Fabricius,* symphonic poem (1949); Sonatas for cello and piano, for violin and piano, for choir and piano; Piano pieces: *Landscapes; Sea Pictures; The Old Country House.*

KOHN, KARL
1926, American
Principal Works - *Concerto mutabile* for piano and orchestra; orchestral pieces; choral and chamber music; piano and organ pieces.

KOHS, ELLIS (BONOFF)
1916, American
Principal Works - Opera: *Amerika* after Kafka (1969); 2 symphonies; orchestral works; choral and chamber music; piano and organ pieces; *Concerto for Percussion Quartet.*

KOLB, BARBARA
1939, American
Principal Works - Tape assemblage. *Chansons bas* for voice, harp, percussion (1965); *Trobar Clus* for 12 instruments (1970); other instrumental pieces; piano music.

KOPPEL, HERMANN (DAVID)
1908, Danish
Principal Works - Opera: *Macbeth* (1968); ballet; film and theater music; 7 symphonies; concertos for piano, for clarinet, for cello; oratorio: *3 Psalms of David* for chorus, tenor and orchestra; piano and chamber pieces.

KORN, PETER JONA
1941, American
Principal Works - Opera: *Heidi* (1963); 3 symphonies; concerto for saxophone; orchestral works with solo instruments; choral and chamber music.

KORNGOLD, ERICH WOLFGANG
1897-1957, Austrian
Principal Works - Piano sonata; operas: *Violanta; Der Ring des Polykrates* (1916); *Die Tote Stadt* (1920); film music; orchestral and chamber music; Violin Concerto in D major, Op. 35.

KÓSA, GYÖRGY
1897, Hungarian
Principal Works - Opera: *Tartuffe,* after Molière; *Requiem Mass* (1949); Easter Oratorio; cantatas; 8 string quartets.

KOTÓNSKI, WLODZIMIERZ
1925, Polish
Principal Works - Electronic music. *Study on one cymbal stroke,* tape; *Concerto per quattro* for harp, guitar, harpsichord, piano and chamber ensemble; *Multiplay* for brass sextet (1971); Microstructures-musique concrète (1963); *Aeolian Harp* for soprano and 4 instruments; *Musica per fiati e timpani* (1963); *Die Windrose* for orchestra (1976); Chamber Music for 21 Instruments and Percussion (1958); trio for flute, guitar and percussion (1960); *Pezzo per flauto e pianoforte* (1962); *Music en relief* for 4 orchestra groups.

KRAFT, WILLIAM
1923, American
Principal Works - *Configurations* for jazz ensemble and 4 percussionists; *Silent Boughs* song cycle for soprano and string orchestra; pieces for percussion; *Avalanche* for orchestra.

KRAMER, ARTHUR WALTER
1890-1969, American
Principal Works - Orchestral: *Two Sketches* (1916); *Symphonic Rhapsody* for violin and orchestra (1912); choral: *In Normandy* (1925); chamber and piano music; songs.

KREIN, ALEXANDER ABRAMOVICH
1883-1951, Russian
Principal Works - Choral: *Kaddish* (1921); *U.S.S.R.* (1925); *Hebrew Sketches* for clarinet and string quartet; film and theater music; orchestral pieces; operas: *The Youth of Abraham; The Maccabees.*

KREIN, GRIGORY ABRAMOVICH
1879)1955, Russian
Principal Works - *Hebrew Rhapsody* for clarinet and orchestra: 2 piano concertos; orchestral pieces; piano and chamber music.

KREIN, JULIAN
1913, Russian
Principal Works - *Destruction,* symphonic prelude; ballet; piano and chamber pieces.

KREISLER, FRITZ
1875-1962, Austrian/American
Principal Works - Noted violinist; composed 2 operettas; concerto for violin; violin solos: *Caprice Viennois, Tambourin Chinois,* etc.; string quartets.

KRENEK, ERNST
1900, Austrian/American
Principal Works - Jazz opera: *Jonny Spielt Auf* (1927); Operas: *The Life of Orestes; The Golden Ram; Orpheus and Eurydice* (1923); *Karl V* (1933); String Quartet No. 7; *Lamentations of Jeremiah,* Op. 93 for chorus; 6 piano sonatas; 5 symphonies; *Symphonic Elegy for strings, Santa Fé Time-Table* for chorus; electronic music; chamber music; songs. *The Dissembler* for chamber group; *Flute piece in nine phases* (1959).

KUBELIK, (JERONYM) RAFAEL
1914, Czech.
Principal Works - Noted conductor; composed operas: *Veronika (1947) and four others; choral symphonies; a cantata; concerto for cello; Requiems; chamber and piano pieces.*

KUBIK, GAIL
1914, American
Principal Works - Folk opera: *Mirror for the Sky* (1947); *Symphonie concertante* for orchestra (1952); symphonies; choral works; violin concerto; cantata *In Praise of Johnny Appleseed;* film music including score of *Gerald McBoing-Boing* (1950).

KUPFERMAN, MEYER
1926, American
Principal Works - Opera: *The Judgement* (1967); ballet; *Cycle of Infinities* for varied instrumental groups; 4 symphonies; piano and choral pieces.

KURKA, ROBERT
1921-1957, American
Principal Works - Opera: *The Good Soldier Schweik* (1958); 2 symphonies; orchestral pieces with and without solo instruments; choral; string quartets and other chamber pieces; piano music.

KURTÁG, GYÖRGY
1926, Rumanian
Principal Works - Serial music. *Bornemisza Péter mondásai* for soprano, piano and orchestra (1968); concerto for viola; chamber and piano pieces.

KUULA, TOIVO (TIMOTEUS)
1883-1918, Finnish
Principal Works - A Stabat Mater; cantatas; orchestral works; piano, organ and chamber pieces.

KVAPIL, JAROSLAV
1892-1958, Czech.
Principal Works - *Victory* symphony and two other symphonies; cantata: *The Lion-Hearted;* opera; orchestral pieces; piano and chamber music, songs.

LA MONTAINE, JOHN
1920, American
Principal Works - Trilogy of Christmas operas: symphony *From Sea To Shining Sea* (1961); Piano Concerto (1959); *Birds of Paradise* for piano and orchestra; choral and chamber works; piano pieces.

LABROCA, MARIO
1896, Italian
Principal Works - A symphony; chamber and choral works.

LABUNSKI, FELIKS RODERYK
1892, American
Principal Works - Ballet: Suite For Strings; *Canto di aspirazione;* sacred and secular choral works; piano, organ and chamber pieces.

LACERDA, OSVALDO
1927, Brazilian
Principal Works - Orchestral and choral works; sacred music; chamber pieces; *Brasilianas* piano pieces.

LADERMAN, EZRA
1924, American
Principal Works - Opera: *Galileo Galilei* (1967); cantata: *And David Wept* (1971); film and stage music; symphonies; string quartets; piano pieces; songs.

LADMIRAULT, PAUL-ÉMILE
1877-1944, French
Principal Works - Orchestral: *Suite bretonne* (1903) for orchestra; operas; *Choeurs des ames de ta forêt* for chorus and orchestra; sacred and chamber music; piano pieces.

LAJTHA, LÁSZLÓ
1891-1963, Hungarian
Principal Works - Opera: 2 ballets; 9 symphonies; 10 string quartets; film music.

LAKNER, YEHOSHUA
1924, Czech.
Principal Works - *Ballet for Rina Schönfeld* (1962) for flute, cello, piano and percussion; musique concrète works; orchestral pieces; choral and piano music.

LAMBERT, CONSTANT
1905-1951, English
Principal Works-Ballet: *Romeo and Juliet* (1926); *Horoscope* (1937); *Tiresias* (1951); *The Rio Grande* for jazz chorus and orchestra; *Summer's Last Will and Testament* for baritone, chorus and orchestra; film music; orchestral works; piano concerto.

LANDOWSKI, MARCEL
1915, French
Principal Works - Ballet; operas; 3 symphonies; orchestra works with and without solo instruments; oratorio; film music; chamber pieces.

LANDRÉ, GUILLAUME (LOUIS-FREDERIC)
1905-1968, Dutch
Principal Works - Opera: Jean Lévecq, after Maupassant *De Snoek* (1938); 4 symphonies; *Sinfonia Sacra* for orchestra; violin concerto; concertos for cello, for clarinet; chamber and choral music.

LANGGAARD, RUED IMMANUEL
1893-1952, Danish
Principal Works - 16 symphonies; operas; *Music of the Spheres* for chorus and orchestra; piano, organ and chamber music.

LANZA, ALCIDES
1929, Argentinian
Principal Works - Electronic music. Orchestral works; piano concerto; choral and chamber pieces; piano music; mixed media compositions.

LAPARRA, RAOUL
1876-1943, French
Opera: *La Habanera; L'illustre Fregona*, after Cervantes; *Un dimanche basque* for piano and orchestra; piano and chamber music; songs.

LA PRADE, ERNEST
1889, American
Principal Works -Comic opera; orchestral works; songs.

LARSSON, LARS-ERIK
1908, Swedish
Principal Works - Opera: *The Princess of Cyprus;* Missa Brevis for chorus; Music for Orchestra; Intimate Miniatures for string quartet; Symphonic Sketch; suite: *The Disguised God;* a violin concerto; piano sonatas.

LAVRY, MARC
1903-1967, Israeli
Principal Works - Operas; oratorios; orchestral works with and without solos for instruments; harp music; choral works.

LAZZARI, SYLVIO
1857-1944, Italian
Principal Works - Operas: *Le sauteriot* (1918); *La lepreuse* (1912); *Rhapsodie Espagnole* for orchestra; *Rhapsodie* for violin and orchestra; choral and chamber music; piano pieces.

LE FLEM, PAUL
1881, French
Principal Works - Opera: *Le rossignol de Saint-Malo* (1942); film and stage music; choral and orchestral works; piano, harp and chamber pieces.

LE GALLIENNE, DORIAN
1916, 1963, Australian
Principal Works - Sonfonietta for orchestra; stage music; piano pieces; songs.

LEE, DAI-KEONG
1915, Hawaiian/American
Principal Works - Orchestral: *Golden Gate Overture* (1942); *Pacific Prayer* (1942); opera; ballet; symphonies; violin concerto; choral music; piano and chamber pieces; film music; songs.

LEES, BENJAMIN
1924, American
Principal Works - Operas: *The Oracle; The Gilded Cage;* choral: *Visions of Poets;* concertos for violin, for piano for oboe; *Etudes* for piano and orchestra; piano and chamber pieces; 3 symphonies.

LEEUW, TON DE
1926, Dutch
Principal Works - Opera: *De Droem* (1965); Ballets; *Haiku II* for soprano and orchestra; oratorio: *Hiob* (1956); *Spatial Music* for instrumental ensembles; electronic music pieces; string quartets; piano pieces.

LEFANU, NICOLA
1947, English
Principal Works - *Columbia Falls* for orchestra; *Collana* for 8 instruments; *Antiworld* for 2 voices, 3 instr.

LEGLEY, VICTOR
1915, French
Principal Works - Opera: ballet; 5 symphonies; concertos for harp, for violin, for viola, for piano; string quartets; solo sonatas; chamber music.

LEHAR, FRANZ
1870-1948, Hungarian
Principal Works - Operettas: *Der Rastelbinder* (1920); *The Merry Widow (Die lustige Witwe)* (1905); *The Count of Luxemburg (Der Graf von Luxemburg)* (1909); *Gypsy Love (Zigeunerliebe)* (1905); *Eva* (1911); *Frasquita* (1922); *Paganini* (1925); *Der Zarwitch* (1927); *Frederica* (1928); *The Land of Smiles (Das Land des Lächelns)* (1920); *Giuditta* (1934). Orchestral: *Gold and Silver Waltz* (1899); *Eva Waltz (Wär' es auch nichts...); Merry Widow Waltz (I Love You So...).*

LEHMANN, HANS ULRICH
1937, Swiss
Principal Works - *Quanti I* for flute and chamber orchestra; *Rondo* for soprano and orchestra (1967); chamber music; vocal pieces.

LEIBOWITZ, RENÉ
1913-1972, Polish/French
Principal Works - *Chamber Symphony; The Explanation of Metaphors* for speaker, 2 pianos, harp and percussion; operas; dramatic musical; symphonies; orchestral works with solo instruments; string quartets; choral and piano pieces. Twelve tone music!

LEIGHT, WALTER
1905-1942, English
Principal Works - Opera: *Jolly Roger* (1933); concertino for harpsichord and strings; *Aladdin* (1931), pantomime; film and stage music; chamber and choral pieces.

LEIGHTON, KENNETH
1929, English
Principal Works - 3 piano concertos; concertos for violin, for viola, for cello, for organ; Mass for chorus and organ; symphony; sacred cantatas; chamber music including string quartets; piano pieces.

LESSARD, JOHN AYRES
1920, American
Principal Works - Orchestral pieces; wind octet; partita for wind quintet; piano trio; string trio; harpsichord, piano and vocal pieces; songs.

LESUR, DANIEL
1908, French
Principal Works - Opera: *Andrea del Sarto* (1969); *The Inner Life* for organ; piano pieces; choral sacred and secular works; chamber music.

LETELIER, (LLONA) ALFONSO
1912, Chilean
Principal Works - *Los sonetos de la muerte* (1947) for voice and orchestra; guitar concerto; oratorio; a Mass; secular and sacred choral works; chamber music; piano pieces.

LEVY, MARVIN DAVID
1932, American
Principal Works - Opera: *The Tower; Sotoba Komachi; Escorial;* Oratorio: *For The Time being; Symphony No. 1; Mourning Becomes Electra; Kyros,* symphonic poem; *One Person* for alto and orchestra.

LIDHOLM, INGVAR
1921, Swedish
Principal Works - *Mutanza* for orchestra; *Nausicaa Alone* for soprano, chorus and orchestra; *Fitornello* (1955); *Poesis* (1963); choral and chamber music; piano sonata; opera: *The Dutchman;* Concertino for flute, oboe, English horn and cello.

LIEBERMANN, ROLF
1910, Swiss
Principal Works - Operas: *Penelope* (1954); *Leonora 40/45; School for Wives;* Concerto for jazz band and symphony orchestra; *Furioso* (1947) for orchestra; cantatas; film music; piano pieces.

LIGETI, GYÖRGY
1923, Hungarian
Principal Works - Electronic music including *Articulation* on tape; Theater music: *Adventures,* mime drama and *Novelle Aventures; Symphonic poem* for 100 metronomes; orchestral: *Atmospheres* (1961); *Lontano* (1967); *Melodien* (1971); *San Francisco Polyphony* (1974); concerto for cello (1966); choral: Requiem; *Lux aeterna* (1966).

LIPATTI, DINU
1917-1950, Rumanian
Principal Works - Symphonic suite: *Satrarii* (1933); *3 Rumanian Dances for orchestra* (1945); concertino for piano and orchestra; piano works; chamber music; songs.

LINCKE, PAUL
1866-1946, German
Principal Works - Operettas: *Venus auf Erden; Im Reiche des Indra; Frau Luna; Nakiris Hochzeit; Lysistrata; Berlinerluft.*

LOCKWOOD, NORMAND
1906, American

Principal Works - Operas: concertos for oboe, for piano; stage music; oratorios; *Out of the Cradle Endlessly Rocking* (1939) for voice and instruments; piano and chamber pieces; organ works.

LUCIER, ALVIN
1931, American
Principal Works - Electronic and non-conventional music! *Music for Solo Performer,* amplified brain waves and percussion; *Composition for pianist and mother; North American Time Capsule* for vocorder and voices; *Chambers* for sound environment; *Signatures* for orchestra (1970); *Action Music for Piano* (1962).

LUENING, OTTO
1900, American
Principal Works - Electronic music! *Fantasy In Space* for flute, tape, joint composition with Ussachevsky; *Poem in Cycles and Bells* for tape and orchestra Opera: *Evangeline* (1927); orchestral: 2 Symphonic Fantasias (1924, 1939); *Kentucky Concerto* (1951); Serenade for 3 horns and strings; *Music for Orchestra* (1952); *Synthesis* on tape; *Diffusion of Bells* (1962) colloborator, Halim El Dabh, Theater Piece No. 2 for tape, voice, brass, narrator, percussion; *Gargoyles* with violin.

LUTOSTAWSKY, WITOLD
1913, Polish
Principal Works - 1958: *Funeral Music,* for strings; Three Postludes for orchestra; 1959: *Dance Preludes, third version,* for instruments; 1961: *Jeux Vénitiens;* 1962: *Trois poèmes d'Henri Michaux,* for mixed chorus of twenty voices, wind instruments, two pianos, harp and percussion; 1964: String Quartet; 1965: *Paroles Tissées,* for voice and instruments; 1967: Symphony No. 2; 1969: Cello Concerto; 1972: *Preludes and fugue,* for thirteen solo strings; 1934: Piano Sonata; 1938: *Symphonic Variations,* for orchestra; 1941: *Variations on a Theme of Paginini,* for two pianos; Symphony No. 1; 1949: *Overture for Strings; Concerto for Orchestra;* 1950: *Concerto for Orchestra;* 1951: *Little Suite,* for orchestra; *Silesian Triptych,* for soprano and orchestra; 1954: *Dance Preludes,* first version for clarinet and piano.

LUTYENS, ELISABETH (AGNES)
1906
Principal Works - Twelve tone music! Operas: *Infidelio; Isis and Osiris.* Ballet: *The Birthday of the Infanta,* after Wilde; *Symphonic Preludes* (1942); concertos for horn, for viola; *And Suddenly It's Evening* for tenor and chamber group; unaccompanied motet; 6 chamber concertos; 6 string quartets; film music; piano and organ pieces.

LYBBERT, DONALD
1923, American
Principal Works - *Concert Overture for Orchestra* (1958); *Praeludium for brass and percussion* (1963); *Lines for the Fallen* for soprano; *2 pianos, a quarter tone apart* (1968); instrumental works; songs.

LYFORD, RALPH
1882-1927, American
Principal Works - Opera; piano concerto; chamber music.

MACMILLAN, ERNEST CAMPBELL
1893-1973, Canadian
Principal Works - *England* after Swinburne (1917) for chorus; orchestral works; chamber music; Indian and Canadian folk songs.

MACONCHY, ELIZABETH
1907, England
Principal Works - Operas; Ballets: *The Little Red Shoes* (1935); symphony; orchestral pieces with solo instruments; concertino for clarinet and strings; 9 string quartets; choral, piano and harpsichord music; songs.

MADERNA, BRUNO
1920-1973, Italian/German
Principal Works - Electronic and serial music. Opera: *Satyrikon* (1973); *Aria da Hyperion* for soprano, flute, orchestra; stage music: *Hyperion* (1964); *Oedipe-Roi* (1970) ballet; *Composizione in 3 tempi* for orchestra; concertos for piano, two pianos, for oboe; chamber music: *Serenata II* for 11 instruments: tape work: *Notturno, Continuo, Dimensioni II.*

MADETOJA, LEEVI ANTTI
1887-1947, Finnish
Principal Works - Operas; *Pohjalaisia* (1924); *Juha* (1935); 3 symphonies; ballet; stage music; *Kullervo,* symphonic poem; choral and chamber works; piano pieces.

MALER, WILHELM
1902-1976, German
Principal Works - Concerto grosso; oratorio; cantatas; concertos for violin, for harpsichord, for piano trio; choral and chamber pieces; piano music; German folk song arrangements.

MALIPIERO, GIAN FRANCESCO
1882-1973, Italian
Principal Works - Operas: *L'Orfeide* trilogy (1918); *Il miterio di Venezia* (1925); *I capricci di Callot* (1942); *Venere prigonera* (1957); 11 symphonies; *Pause del silenzio* for orchestra; ballets; concertos for violin, for cello, for piano; 7 string quartets; chamber and choral works; piano pieces.

MANZONI, GIACOMO
1932, Italian
Principal Works - Opera: *A tomtod* (1965); orchestral works; tape assemblage; vocal pieces.

MARCO, TOMÁS
1942, Spanish
Principal Works - *Ensemble,* jointly with Stockhausen, for instrumental ensemble (1967); mixed-media music; piano and guitar pieces; orchestral works.

MARKEVITCH, IGOR
1912, Russian/Swiss
Principal Works - *Concerto Grosso* (1929); Piano Concerto; Cantata; Ballet: *Rebus;* Oratorio: *Paradise Lost; Le nouvel âge* (1938) for piano and orchestra; chamber pieces; music for voice and instruments.

MARTIN, FRANK
1890-1959, Swiss
Principal Works - Opera: *The Tempest* (1956); *Monsieur de Pourceaugnac* after Molière; *Le Vin herbé* (1938); for 12 singers and instrumental accompaniment; *Der Cornet* (1942) for contralto and small orchestra; oratorio: *In Terra Pax* (1944); *Petite Symphonie Concertante* (1944) for piano, harp, harpsichord and two string orchestras; oratorio: *Golgotha* (1945); *The Mystery of the Nativity; Six Monologues from Everyman* for voice and piano accompaniment, later for orchestra.

MARTINŮ, BOHUSLAV
1890-1959, Czech.
Principal Works - Operas: *Juliette* (1938); *What Men Live By* after Tolstoy (1953); *Comedy On a Bridge* (1937); *The Marriage* (1953); *The Greek Passion,* after Kazantzakis (1955); Double Concerto for strings and piano (1938); 3 *Ricercari* for chamber orchestra (1936); Symphony No. 6 (1955); oratorio: *The Prophecy of Isaiah* (1959); ballets; 6 symphonies; 7 string quartets; choral and chamber music; piano pieces; Symphonic poems: *Tumult; Half-Time.*

MARTIRANO, SALVATORE
1927, American
Principal Works - Chamber opera: *Prelude for orchestra* (1950); Choral: *a capella Mass* (1953); *O O O O That Shakespearian Rag* with instruments; tape and chamber pieces; *Cocktail Music* for piano (1962); *L's GA* (1968) for stage.

MASON, DANIEL GREGORY
1873-1953, American
Principal Works - Overture: *Chanticleer* (1928); 3 symphonies; string quartet and other chamber pieces; piano music; songs.

MATA, EDUARDO
1942, Mexican
Principal Works - Aleatory and serial music! Tape ballet; 3 symphonies; orchestral works; *Improvisations* for chamber ensembles; vocal music; piano pieces.

MATHER, BRUCE
1939, Canadian
Principal Works - *Symphonic Ode* (1964); *Ombres* (1967) for orchestra; piano concerto; chamber music; vocal music with instrumental accompaniment; *Orphee* (1963); *Madrigal* (1968).

MATSUDARIA, YORITSUNE
1907, Japanese
Principal Works - *Metamorphosis* for soprano and orchestra; Ancient Japanese dance (1953); 2-piano concerto; piano solos; songs.

MATTON, ROGER
1929, Canadian
Principal Works - *Mouvements symphoniques* no. 1 and 2; concertos for 2 pianos and saxophone; *Suite on Gregorian Themes* for piano; choral and chamber pieces.

MAW, NICHOLAS
1935, English
Principal Works - Serial music! Operas: *One Man Show; The Rising of the Moon* (1970); *Scenes and arias* for 3 female singers and orchestra; *Nocturne* for mezzo-soprano and chamber group; *Essay* for organ; Sinfonia for orchestra (1966); chamber pieces.

MAXFIELD, RICHARD
1927-1969, American
Principal Works - Electronic and serial music! Opera; ballet; instrumental pieces; varied electronic compositions with and without instruments.

MAYER, WILLIAM
1925, American
Principal Works - Electronic music! Opera; ballet; orchestral: *Overture for an American* (1958); *Octagon* for piano,

orchestra (1966); *Brief Candle* for small chorus and small orchestra (1965); piano and chamber music; songs.

MAYUZUMI, TOSHIRO
1929, Japanese
Principal Works - Ballet: *Bugaku* (1962); opera; oratorio; *Mandala Symphony* for orchestra; symphonic poem, *Samsara* (1962); *Campanology* (1959) tape work; *Bacchanal* for orchestra: *Divertimento for 10 instruments; Tonepleromas 55* for wind, percussion instruments, musical saw; film music; choral pieces; chamber pieces.

MCBRIDE, ROBERT (GUYN)
1911, American
Principal Works - Ballet: *Jazz Symphony* (1953); *Brooms of Mexico* for soprano and chamber group (1970); *March of the Be-bops* for orchestra (1948); orchestral: *Mexican Rhapsody; Prelude To A Tragedy; Pumpkin Eater's Little Fugue; Work-out for Small Orchestra; Hill Country Symphony;* choral and chamber pieces; film music, songs.

MCDONALD, HARL
1899-1955, American
Principal Works - 4 symphonies; concertos for 2 pianos, for harp, for violin; chora works with and without orchestra; chamber pieces.

MCEWEN, JOHN BLACKWOOD
1869-1948, Scottish
Principal Works - 5 symphonies; concerto for viola; 17 string quartets; choral and chamber pieces.

MCKINLEY, CARL
1895-1966, American
Principal Works - *Masquerade: An American Rhapsody* (1925); orchestral works; choral pieces; string quartets and other chamber music.

MCPHEE, COLIN
1901-1964, Canadian
Principal Works - Orchestral: toccata: *Tabuh-Tabuhan* (1936); *Nocturne* (1958); Concerto for Wind Orchestra (1959); *Balinese Ceremonial Music* for flute and 2 pianos; concerto for piano and wind octet.

MEFANO, PAUL
1937, Iraqi
Principal Works - Electronic and tape music! *Incidences* for piano and orchestra (1960); *Paraboles* for soprano, piano and chamber ensemble (1964); *Interferences* for horn, piano and chamber group (1966); *Aurélia* for 3 choruses, 3 orchestras and 3 conductors (1968); *Old Oedip* for narrator, actress, contact amplifiers, modulator and tape.

MELLERS, WILFRID HOWARD
1914, English
Principal Works - An opera; *Alba* for flute and orchestra; cantata: *Yggdrasil; Life Cycle* for 3 choirs and 2 orchestras; *Yeibichai* for chorus, orchestra, jazz trio, soprano, tape; string trio; chamber pieces; piano music; Latin motets.

MENASCE, JAQUE DE
1905-1960, Austrian/American
Principal Works - Ballet; orchestral works; two piano concertos.

MENNIN, PETER
1923, American

Principal Works - *Canto* (1963) for orchestra; 8 symphonies; *Concertato* for orchestra; cantata: *The Christmas Story;* concertos for piano, for cello; 2 string quartets; piano pieces; songs.

MENOTTI, GIAN-CARLO
1911, Italian/American
Principal Works - Operas: *Amelia Goes To the Ball* (1937); *The Old Maid and the Thief* (1939); *The Medium; The Telephone; The Consul; Amahl and the Night Visitors; The Saint of Bleeker Street* (1954); *The Last Savage; Help, Help the Globolinks;* ballets: *Sebastian* (1944); *The Unicorn, the Gorgon and the Manticore;* concerto for piano, for violin; piano pieces; songs.

MERCURE, PIERRE
1927-1966, Canadian
Principal Works - Electronic and aleatory music. *Kaleidoscope* for orchestra (1947); *Cantata pour une joie* for chorus, soprano and orchestra; ballet: *Incandescence* (1961) with tape; musique concréte pieces; film music; chamber ces.

MESSIAEN, OLIVIER
1908, French
Principal Works - Multi-media materials; Indian and Oriental rhythms; *Turangalila Symphony* (1948) for string quintet, 13 percussion instruments; 8 tubular bells; vibraphone; Ondes Martenot; celeste, brass, wood winds; *Chronochromie* (1960) for orchestra; *Visions de l'Amen* for 2 pianos; *Trois petites liturgies* for string orch., female choir, vibraphone and percussion, ondes martenot; *Vingt regards sur l'enfant Jesus* for piano; *Harawi, chant d'amour et de mort* for soprano and piano; choral works: *5 rechants* (1948); *La transfiguration de Notre Seigneur Jésus-Christ* with orchestra; *Quatuor pour la fin du temps* for violin, clarinet, cello, piano; *Oiseau exotiques* for piano, 2 clarinets, percussion, and chamber winds; *Couleurs de la cité céleste* for piano, winds and percussion; many organ works including *Apparition de l'Eglise éternelle; Messe de la pentecôte,* etc.

MEYEROWITZ, JAN
1913, German/American
Principal Works - Opera: *The Barrier* (1950); *The Glory Round His Head* (1953) for soloists, chorus and orchestra; Symphony: *Midrash Esther* (1954); orchestral: *6 Pieces, 1965;* piano and chamber music; songs.

MIASKOVSKY, NIKOLAI YAKOVIEVICH
1881-1950, Russian
Principal Works - Cantata: *Kirov Is With Us* (1942); Violin concerto (1938); 27 symphonies; choral and chamber works.

MIGNONE, FRANCISCO
1897, Brazilian
Principal Works - Opera: *O contractador dos diamantes including Cogada* (1924); ballet: *Yara* (1946); *Festa das Igrejas* from his opera for orchestra; *4 fantasias brasileiras* for piano and orchestra; *Seresta* for cello and orchestra; symphonic poem: *Four Churches.*

MIGOT, GEORGES (ELBERT)
1891-1976, French
Principal Works - Opera: *Le rossignol en amour* (1926); ballet: *Hagoromo* (1921); oratorio: Saint Germain d' Auxerre (1947); 12 symphonies; *Sinfonia da chiesa* for 85 wind

instruments; *La jungle* for organ and orchestra; piano, harpsichord and chamber pieces; songs.

MIHALOVICI, MARCEL
1898, Rumanian
Principal Works - Opera: *Les Jumeaux* (1963); *Krapp,* after Beckett; *Concerto quasi una fantasia* for violin and orchestra; 5 symphonies; violin sonatas; string quartets; choral works; piano pieces.

MILHAUD, DARIUS
1892-1974, French
Principal Works - Operas: *L'Orestie* trilogy (1913) after Aeschylus; *Esther de Carpentras* (1925); *Les Malheurs d'Orphée* (1924); *Le Pauvre Matelot* (1926); *Christophe Colomb* (1928); *Maximilien* (1932); *Bolivar* (1943); *David* (1954); Ballet: *L'homme et son désir* (1918); *Le boeuf sur le toit* (1919) with Cocteau text; *La création du monde* (1923); orchestral: *Suite provençale* (1937); *Suite française* (1945); *Corcovado* for clarinet and orchestra; *Symphony No. 3* (1946); *Saudades do Brasil* (1921); 11 more symphonies: including Symphony No. 6 for chorus without words and oboe and cello; 15 string quartets and other chamber pieces including *Pastorale* (1936); *La Cheminée du roi René* (1942); *Scaramouche* for 2 pianos (1937); *Brasileira* for 4 pianos; film music; songs.

MIROGLIO, FRANCIS
1924, French
Principal Works - Aleatory and serial music. *Espaces* for large orchestra (1962); *Phases* in various versions for 4 chamber groups; *Insertions* for harpsichord (1969).

MOMPOU, FEDERICO
1893, Spanish
Principal Works - Piano works: *Scénes d'enfants* (1915); *Canción y danza,* nos. 1-12; *Combat del somni* (1951); *Llueve solve el río* (1945); *Suite compostelana* for guitar.

MOÓR, EMANUEL
1863-1931, Hungarian
Principal Works - Operas; 7 symphonies; concertos for piano, for violin; string quartets; violin sonatas; chamber and piano pieces; inventor of two-manual piano *Duplex Coupler,* each keyboard an octave apart, with coupling facility.

MOORE, DOUGLAS (STUART)
1893-1969, American
Principal Works - Operas: *The Devil and Daniel Webster* (1951); *Giants in the Earth* (1951); *Ballad of Baby Doe* (1958); *Gallantry* (1958); *The Wings of The Dove* (1961); *Carrie Nation* (1966); Orchestral: Symphony in A (1945); *Farm Journal; Pageant of P.T. Barnum;* choral and chamber music; pieces for amateurs.

MORAN, ROBERT (LEONARD)
1937, American
Principal Works - Graphic and mixed media music! *Interiors* for orchestra or chamber group with percussion; *Hallelujah* for 20 marching bands, drum and bugle corps, choruses, carillons.

MORAWETZ, OSKAR
1917, Czech.
Principal Works - *From the Diary of Anne Frank* for soprano and orchestra (1970); symphonies; piano concerto; string quartets and other chamber music; choral pieces.

MOREL, FRANCOISE D'ASSISE
1926, Canadian
Principal Works - *Antiphonie* (1953); *Rituel de l'espace* (1958); orchestral works; string quartets; music for jazz ensemble.

MOROI, MAKOTO
1930, Jpanese
Principal Works - *Développements raréfiants* (1968); *Piano Concerto* (1966).

MOROI, SABURO
1903, Japanese
Principal Works - 5 symphonies; piano concertos; concertos for violin and cello; chamber pieces.

MOROSS, JEROME
1913, American
Principal Works - Operas: *Susanna and the Elders* (1940); *Gentlemen, Be Seated!;* symphony (1941); *A Tall Story* for orchestra; choral and chamber music.

MORRIS, HAROLD
1890-1964, American
Principal Works - *Poem,* after Tagore (1918) for orchestra; 3 symphonies piano concerto (1931); violin concerto (1939); chamber music; piano pieces.

MORTARI, VIRGILIO
1902, Italian
Principal Works - Opera: *La figlia del diavolo* (1954); ballet; concerto for piano; orchestral works; choral and solo instrument pieces.

MORTENSEN, FINN (EINAR)
1922, Swedish
Principal Works - *Evolution* (1961) for orchestra; a symphony; piano concerto (1963); piano and chamber pieces.

MOSS, LAWRENCE
1927, American
Principal Works - Operas: *The Brute* (1960); *The Queen and the Rebels* (1965); *Scenes for Small Orchestra; Timepiece* for violin, piano, percussion; *Auditions* for woodwind quintet and tape (1971); piano pieces; *3 Rilke Songs* (1963) and other songs; *Nightscape* for mixed media.

MOSSOLOV, ALEXANDER VASILIEVICH
1900-1973, Russian
Principal Works - *Iron Foundry* (1928) for orchestra with a shaken metal sheet; concertos for piano, for harp, for cello; operas; 6 symphonies; *Kirghiz Rhapsody* for soprano, chorus and orchestra; chamber and choral works; songs.

MOTTE, DIETHER DE LA
1928, German
Principal Works - Opera; concerto; symphony; orchestral pieces; piano and flute concertos; choral and chamber pieces; tape works; organ music.

MOYZES, ALEXANDER
1906, Czech
Principal Works - Opera; 9 symphonies; concerto for violin, for flute; opera; piano and chamber pieces; songs.

MUMMA, GORDON
1935, American
Principal Works - Electronic and aleatory music! Live electronics entitled *cybersonics! Gestures II* for 2 pianos (1958); *Mograph* for various pianos (1962); *Mesa* for bandoneon and *cybersonic* equipment (1966); *digital pro-*

cess for mixed electronic and acoustic instruments.

MUSGRAVE, THEA
1928, Scottish
Principal Works - Operas: *The Decision* (1964); *The Voice of Ariadne* (1974); *Mary, Queen of Scots* (1977); Ballets: *A Tale for Thieves* (1953); *Beauty and the Beast* (1969) with tape; *Festival Overture* for orchestra; Concerto for Orchestra (1967); concertos for horn, for clarinet, for viola; *The Five Ages of Man* for chorus and orchestra with optional brass; *Night Music* for 2 horns and chamber orchestra; *Soliloquy* for guitar and tape (1969); chamber concertos with varied instruments; piano and guitar pieces; songs.

NABOKOV, NICHOLAS
1903-1978, Russian/American
Principal Works - Opera: *Rasputin* (1958); *Love's Labour Lost* (1973); Ballet: *Union Pacific* (1934); *Ode* (1928); *Don Quixote* (1965); *Vista Nuova* (1951); oratorio: *Job* (1933); 3 symphonies; concertos for flute, for cello, for piano; choral, chamber pieces; piano music; songs.

NELHYBEL, VACLAV
1919, Czech.
Principal Works - Operas; ballets; *Étude symphonique* 1949) and *3 Modes* (1952) for orchestra; string quartets; choral and chamber pieces; piano music.

NELSON, RON J.
1929, American
Principal Works - Opera: *The Birthday of the Infanta* (1956); oratorio: *What Is Man?* (1964); choral works: *Triumphal Te Deum* (1962); orchestral pieces.

NEVIN, ARTHUR FINLEY
1871-1943, American
Principal Works - Opera: *A Daughter of the Foret* (1918); orchestral works; choral and chamber pieces.

NIELSEN, CARL (AUGUST)
1865-1931, Danish
Principal Works - Operas: *Maskarade* (1906); *Saul and David;* 6 symphonies, including No. 1 beginning in one key and ending in another (progressive tonality); No. 2 *The Four Temperaments;* No. 3 *Sinfonia Espansiva;* No. 4 *The Unquenchable.* Concertos for flute, for clarinet, for violin; choral: *Hymnus amoris* for soloists, chorus and orchestra; *Commotio* for organ; string quartets; wind quintet and other chamber pieces; piano music.

NIGG, SERGE
1924, French
Principal Works - Symphonic poems: *Timur; For a Captive Potet;* Ballet: *L'étrange aventure de Gulliver à Lilliput* (1958); *Jérôme Bosch Symphony* (1960); symphonic poems; concertos for violin, piano, for flute; piano sonata; choral and chamber pieces; songs.

NILSSON, BO
1937, Swedish
Principal Works - *Frequenzen* for clarinet, flute, vibes, xylophone, guitar, bass; *Quantitäten* for piano; *Grüppen für Bläser* for piccolo, oboe, clarinet; *Reaktionen* for 4 percussionists; *Versuchungen* for orchestra (1963); vocal and instrumental music; choral pieces.

NOBRE, MARLOS
1939, Brazilian
Principal Works - Orchestral: *Mosaico* (1970); *Concerto breve* (1969); Rhythmic Variations for piano and Brazilian instruments; *Ukunmakrinjkin* for soprano and instruments.

NONO, LUIGI
1924, Italian
Principal Works - Serial and electronic music! Opera: *Intoleranza* (1960); *Epitaph for Federico Garcia Lorca* for speaker, singers and orchestra; *Incontri* for 24 instruments; *On The Bridge of Hiroshima,* cantata for soprano, tenor and orchestra; a ballet; *Il canto sospeso* for chorus, solo vocals and orchestra; *Polifonica-Monodia-Ritmica* for piano, winds, and percussion; *La fabrica illuminata* for soprano and tape (1964); *Contrappunto dialettico alla mente* on tape (1968).

NORDHEIM, ARNE
1931, Norweigan
Principal Works - Ballet: *Katharsis* with orchestra and tape; *Epitaffio* for orchestra with tape; *Solitaire* (1968) on tape with electronic sounds and musique concrète; string quartets; songs; *Dinosaurus* for accordion and tape; Partita for viola, harpsichord and percussion.

NORDOFF, PAUL
1909-1977, American
Principal Works - Opera: *The Masterpiece* (1951); *Winter Symphony* (1954) and other orchestral works; 2 piano concertos; a violin concerto; choral works; 2 string quartets; a piano quintet; songs.

NØRGARD, PER
1932, Danish
Principal Works - Oratorio: *Babel;* Opera: *Labyrinth* (1967); a ballet; *Fragment 6* for six orchestral groups; *The Enchanted Forest* on tape (1968); *Constellations* for 12 solo strings or groups of strings; chamber piece: *Voyage into the golden screen;* piano pieces; songs. Serial music and graphic notation!

NOWAK, LIONEL
1911, American
Principal Works - *Concert Piece* for kettledrums and string orchestra (1961); Ballet scores; choral and chamber music; piano pieces, songs.

OBUKHOV, NICOLAS
1892-1954, Russian/French
Principal Works - An original twelve tone music form; electronic instrument innovator. *Le livre de vie* for chorus, soloists, 2 pianos and orchestra; electronic works.

OHANA, MAURICE
1914, French
Principal Works - Choral settings to Garcia Lorca verse; guitar concerto (1950); opera; ballet: *Llanto por Ignacio Sachez Mejias* for baritone, speaker, chorus and chamber orchestra (1950); *Tres gráficos* for guitar and orchestra (1950); *Études choréographiques* for 6 percussionists (1955); *Tombeau de Claude Debussy* for soprano, zither, tapes, piano and chamber orchestra (1961).

OLDBERG, ARNE
1874-1962, American
Principal Works - *St. Francis of Assissi* for baritone and orchestra (1954); 5 symphonies; violin concerto; 2 piano concertos; piano and chamber pieces.

OLIVEROS, PAULINE
1932, American
Principal Works - Electronic music, tape and mixed media works! *Outline* for flute, percussion, string bass (1963); *Aeolian Partitions* chamber piece for stage (1969); tape: *Beautiful Soop* (1967); *Festival House* for chorus, orchestra, mime, film and visual effects (1968) *Phantom fathom,* mixed-media (1972).

O'NEILL, NORMAN
1875-1934, English
Principal Works - Theater music: Incidental music to Barrie's *Mary Rose;* ballets; orchestral works; piano and chamber pieces, songs.

ORBÓN, JULIAN
1925, Spanish
Principal Works - *Danzas sinfónicas* for orchestra (1956); *concerto gross* for string quartet and orchestra (1958); Partita no. 3 (1966); choral and chamber music; piano and guitar pieces.

ORFF, CARL
1895, German
Principal Works - Scenic oratorio: *Carmina burana,* based on ancient minstrel lays and drinking songs from monastic archives (1935); cantatas: *Catulli carmina* (1943); *Trionfo di Afrodite* (1951); operas: *Der Mond* (1939); *Die Kluge* (1943); *Antigonae* (1949); *Oedipus der Tyrann* (1959); *Prometheus* (1968); Easter cantata; Incidental music *A Midsummer Night's Dream;* *Musikalishes Hausbuch,* children's music for brass, percussion, hand-clapping.

ORNSTEIN, LEO
1892, American
Principal Works - *Hebraic Fantasy* for violin and piano (1929); orchestral: *The Fog* (1915); a symphony; piano concerto (1925); piano works: *3 Moods* (1913); *6 Water Colors* (1935); 4 sonatas; children's songs; string quartet, string quintet and other chamber pieces.

ORR, ROBIN (ROBERT KEMSLEY)
1909, Scottish
Principal Works - Opera: *Full Circle* (1968); Symphony In One Movement (1963); prelude and fugue for string quartet; anthems; chamber and choral works; organ music.

ORREGO-SALAS, JUAN
1919, Chilean
Principal Works - Opera-oratorio: *El retablo del rey pobre* (1952); *Five Castilian Songs* for voice and chamber orch.; cantata *America, we do not invoke your name in vain;* Mass (1969); 4 symphonies; piano concerto; concerto for piano trio and orchestra (1962); piano and chamber pieces; songs.

OSTERC, SLAVKO
1895-1941, Yugoslavian
Principal Works - Quarter-tone forms. Ballet: *The Masque of the Red Death* (1930) after Poe; *Passacaglia Symphony* (1939); *Mouvement symphonique* (1938); 6

operas; choral and chamber works; piano and organ pieces.

OSTRČIL, OTAKAR
1879-1935, Czech.
Principal Works - Operas: *The Bud* (1911); *Johnny's Kingdom* (1934); symphony; symphonic poems; cantatas; chamber pieces; songs.

OVERTON, HALL (FRANKLIN)
1920-1972, American
Principal Works - Opera: *Huckleberry Finn* (1971); Ballet: *Nonage* (1951); *Symphony For strings* (1955); *Fantasy For Brass, Piano and Percussion;* 3 string quartets; piano and chamber pieces; songs.

PACCAGNINI, ANGELO
1930, Italian
Principal Works - Electronic music. Opera: *Mosè;* ballet; *Gruppi concertanti* (1960) for orchestra; *Sequenze e strutture* tape works (1962); choral music; string quartet; piano pieces.

PAHISSA, JAIME
1880-1969, Spanish
Principal Works - Opera: *La Princesa Margarida* (1928) originally *La presó de Lleida; Gala Placidia* (1913); ballet; *Monodia* for orchestra (1925); *Suite intertonal* (1926) for orchestra (1926); chamber and choral music; piano pieces; songs.

PAIK, NAM JUNE
1932, Korean
Principal Works -*hommage à john cage* for 2 pianos, 3 tape recorders, mixed media effects (1959); 5 symphonies; *Opera Sextronique* (1967); Electronic Opera No. 1; *Etude for pianoforte;* cello sonata.

PALAU, MANUEL
1893-1967, Spanish
Principal Works - Orchestral: *Gongoriana; Homenaje a Debussy; Concierto levantino* for guitar and orchestra (1949); *Beniflors,* a zarzuela (1920) and other *Zarzuelas;* ballets; 3 symphonies; choral and chamber music; piano pieces; songs.

PALESTER, ROMAN
1907, Polish/French
Principal Works - Opera: *The Living Stones* (1944); *Song of the earth,* a ballet (1937); 4 symphonies; concertos for piano, for violin, for alto saxophone; choral sacred and secular works; string quartets; piano pieces; film and theater music.

PALMER, ROBERT (MOFFETT)
1915, American
Principal Works - Oratorio: *Nabuchodonosor* (1960); cantata: *Of Night and the Sea* (1957); *Variations, Chorale and Fugue* for orchestra (1947); *Organon II* for strings (1975); *Chorie Song and Toccata* for winds (1968); 2 symphonies; other choral works; 4 string quartets; piano quintet; 2 quartets, a trio; a wind quintet; piano pieces.

PALMGREN, SELIM
1978, Finnish
Principal Works - *Refrain du Berceau* (lullaby); Opera: *Daniel Hjort* (1910); *A Night In May* and other piano pieces; ballet; 5 piano concertos; operas; cantatas, etc.

PANUFNIK, ANDRZEJ
1914, Polish

Principal Works - Orchestral: *Sinfonia rustica* (1948); *Heroic Overture* (1952); *Sinfonia sacra* (1963); piano concerto (1962); cantatas: *Universal Prayer,* after Pope (1968) and 2 others; choral and chamber music; piano pieces; songs.

PAPAIOANNOU, IANNIS
1911, Greek

Principal Works - Serial music. 5 symphonies; symphonic poems; ballet; piano concerto; concertino for piano and strings; *3 Byzantine Odes* for voices and orchestra; string quartet; guitar and piano pieces; chamber music.

PAPINEAU-COUTURE, JEAN
1916, Canadian

Principal Works - Orchestral: *Oscillations* (1969); *Poème* (1952); *Landscape* for 8 narrators, 8 singers and orchestral ensemble; piano concerto; *Psaume CL* for soloists, chorus and orchestra (1945); *5 pieces concertantes* for orchestra and various ensembles; *Suite* for violin (1956); chamber music; piano pieces; compositions for voice and orchestra, for voice and piano.

PARKER, HORATIO (WILLIAM)
1863-1919, American

Principal Works - Oratorio: *Hora Novissima* and others; Operas: *Mona* (1912); *Fairyland* (1915); masque: *Cupid and Psyche* (1916); a symphony; symphonic poem; overtures; choral and chamber music; string quartets; piano and organ pieces; songs.

PARRIS, ROBERT
1924, American

Principal Works - Concerto for 5 kettledrums (1955); concertos for violin (1959); for viola (1956); for trombone (1964); *The Book of Imaginary Beings* (1972); chamber pieces and other chamber music; 2 string quartets; choral works, including pieces for voice and instruments.

PARTCH, HARRY
1901-1974, American

Principal Works - Inventor microtonal system (43 tones to an octave) and instruments designed for system...*Cloudchamber bowls, bamboo marimba, quadrangularis reversum* and others . Stage works: *Windsong; Water, Water; And on the Seventh Day Petals Fell in Petaluma* (1963); *The Bewitched* (1955); *Revelation in the Courthouse Park* (1960); *Delusion of the Fury* (1963); setting of Oedipus Rex after Yeats translation of Sophocles.

PAZ, JUAN CARLOS
1901-1972, Argentinian

Principal Works - Twelve tone music. Orchestral: *Movimiento sinfónico* (1930); *Ritmica ostinata* (1942); *Continuidad* (1960); *3 Jazz Movements for piano; Composición dodecafónica* for chamber group; piano and organ pieces; songs.

PECK, RUSSELL
American

Principal Works - *Automobile* (1966).

PEDRELL, FELIPE
1841-1922, Spanish

Principal Works - Operas: *Los Pirineos,* trilogy (1902); *La Celestina* (1904); *Excelsior, I trionfi* for orchestra; 8 more operas; choral sacred and secular music with and without orchestra; piano and chamber pieces; songs.

PEETERS, FLOR
1903, Belgian

Principal Works - Organ concerto (1944); *Hymn Preludes for the Liturgical Year* (1959) for organ; Masses and other choral sacred pieces with organ accompaniment; piano pieces; songs.

PEIKO, NIKOLAI IVANOVICH
1916, Russian

Principal Works - Ballet: *Zhanna d'Ark* and others; an opera; 6 symphonies; string quartets; piano and chamber pieces; film music; songs.

PENDERECKI, KRZYSTOF
1933, Polish

Principal Works - Serial music. Opera: *The Devils of Loudun* (1969); Orchestral: *Canon* for 52 string instruments and tape; *To The Victims of Hiroshima-Threnody* for 52 strings (1960); *Fluorescences* (1961); *Emantionen* for 2 string orchestras (1959); *De natura sonoris* for orchestra (1967); choral works: *The Psalms of David* with percussion (1958); *stabat mater* for 3 choruses (1962); *St. Luke Passion* for narrator, soloists, and orchestra (1965); *Utrenja* for soloists, 2 choruses, and percussion (1970); string quartet (1960).

PENTLAND, BARBARA
1912, Canadian

Principal Works - Chamber opera: *The Lake* (1954); 4 symphonies; ballet; violin concerto (1942); piano concerto (1956).

PÉPIN, CLERMONT
1926, Canadian

Principal Works - Ballet: *The Gates of Hell* and others; 2 symphonies; 2 piano concertos; orchestral works; *Monologue* for chamber orchestra; *Les quasars* for chorus and orchestra (1967); string quartets; piano and other chamber pieces: songs.

PEPPING, ERNST
1901, German

Principal Works - Masses and other sacred choral music; 3 symphonies; piano and organ concertos; piano and organ pieces; *St. Matthew Passion,* unaccompanied motets.

PERAGALLO, MARIO
1910, Italian

Principal Works - Opera, *La gita in campagna* (1954); *La collina* a madrigal after Edgar Lee Masters (1947); concerto for orchestra, for piano, for violin; string quartets and other chamber music; piano and organ pieces.

PERKINS, JOHN MACIVOR
1935, American

Principal Works - Orchestral: *Music for Orchestra* (1964); chamber opera; *Music for 13 Players* (1964); piano pieces; songs.

PERKOWSKI, PIOTR
1902, Polish

Principal Works - Ballet: *Balladyna* (1961); opera; symphonies; *Nocturne* for orchestra (1955); concerto for piano, for violin; piano pieces; songs.

PERLE, GEORGE
1915, American

Principal Works - Twelve tone music. *3 Movements for Orchestra* (1960); *Songs of Praise and Lamentation* for chorus and orchestra (1975); 2 symphonies; concerto for cello (1966); string quartets, a string quintet; *6 Preludes* for piano (1946); *Sixetudes* (1976); *Toccata* for piano (1969). Serial composition.

PERSICHETTI, VINCENT
1915, American
Principal Works - Ballet: *King Lear;* oratorio: *The Creation* (1970); 9 symphonies; piano concerto; concerto for piano duet and orchestra; violin and cello sonatas.

PETERSON-BERGER, OLOF WILHELM
1867-1942, Swedish
Principal Works - Opera: *Arnljot* (1910); *Frösöblomster,* for piano (1914); 5 symphonies; violin concerto; choral and chamber music; songs.

PETRASSI, GOFFREDO
1904, Italian
Principal Works - Operas: *Il cordovano* (1949); *La morte dell-aria* (1950); ballet: *Le Portrait de Don Quichotte* (1945); *Partita for Orchestra* (1932); *Psalm IX* for chorus and orchestra (1934); 7 orchestral concertos; concertos for flute, for piano; choral sacred and secular music; chamber pieces; included are *Orlando's Madness* ballet; *Nonsense* for chorus after Edward Lear.

PETRIDIS, PETRO
1892, Greek
Principal Works - Oratorio: *St. Paul* (1951); opera; ballet; 5 symphonies; 2 piano concertos; concerto for violin, for cello, for 2 pianos.

PETROV, ANDREW PAVLOVICH
1930, Russian
Principal Works - Opera: *Peter I* (1974); ballet:*Creation of the World* (1971); Orchestral poem for strings, organ, trumpet and percussion (1966).

PETTERSON, ALLAN
1911, Swedish
Principal Works - 13 symphonies; 3 concertos; piano and chamber pieces.

PFITZNER, HANS
1869-1949, German
Principal Works - Opera: *Palestrina* and 4 others; cantata: *Of The German Soul;* 2 symphonies; concertos for piano, for violin; string quartets and other chamber works; piano trio; songs.

PHILIPPOT, MICHEL (PAUL)
1925, French
Principal Works - Tape, musique concrète and electronic music. *Etude,* 3 musique concrète pieces; *Ambiance,* 2 musique concrète pieces 91962); *Composition* for piano (1958); for double orchestra (1959); *Transformations triangulaires* for 12 instruments (1962).

PHILLIPS, BURRILL
1907, American
Principal Works - Ballet: *Play Ball* (1938); opera; *Selections from McGuffey's Reader* (1934); for orchestra; *Tom Paine Overture* (1947); *Canzona III* for poet and 7 instruments (1970); concertos for piano (1942) for viola, for clarinet, for piano and orchestra (1952); 2 string quartets; quartet for oboe and strings (1967); piano and organ pieces; film music; songs.

PIERNE, GABRIEL
1863-1937, French
Principal Works - Opera: *La Fille de tabarin* (1901); Ballet: *Cydalise et le chevrepied* (1919); Oratorio: *La croisade des enfants* (1905); piano concerto (1887); *Konzertstück* for harp and orchestra.

PIJPER, WILLEM
1894-1947, Dutch
Principal Works - Opera: *Halewijn* (1933); 3 symphonies; concertos for cello, for piano, for violin; 4 string quartets; piano trios; choral and chamber works; songs.

PISK, PAUL AMADEUS
1893, Austrian/American
Principal Works - Ballet: *American Suite* (1948); *Passacaglia* fororchestra (1948); *3 Ceremonial Rites* (1958); choral and chamber music; piano pieces; songs.

PISTON, WALTER
1894-1976, American
Principal Works - Ballet: *The Incredible Flutist* (1938); Symphony No. 3 (1947); Symphony No. 7 (1960) and six other symphonies; concerto for orchestra (1933); concertino for piano and chamber orchestra (1933); 2 violin concertos; concerto for viola (1957); for 2 pianos (1959); for clarinet (1967); Variations for cello and orchestra (1967); *Fantasy* for violin and orchestra (1973); concerto for string quartet and orchestra (1974); String Quartet No. 3 (1946) and other quartets for strings; *Divertimento* for Nine Instruments (1946) Quintet for Piano and Strings (1949); Prelude and Allegreo for Organ and Strings (1943); piano and organ pieces.

PIZZETTI, ILDEBRANDO
1880-1968, Italian
Principal Works - Operas: *Fedra,* after D'Annunzio (1915); *Debora e Jael* (1922); *Fra Gherardo* (1928); *Lo straniero* (1930); *Orseolo* (1935); *Vanna Lupa* (1949); *Ifigenia* (1950); *Cagliostro* (1953); *La figlia di Iorio* after D'Annunzio (1954); *Assassinio nella cattedrale* after T.E. Eliot (1958); orchestral: *Concerto dell'estate* (1928); concertos for violin, for cello; *Prelude to another Day;* choral and chamber works; piano pieces; songs, including *I pastori* after D'Annunzio.

POLDINI, EDE
1869-1957, Swiss
Principal Works - Comic opera: *The Vagabond and The Princess* (1903) and 3 others; ballet; piano pieces including *The Dancing Doll.*

PONCE, MANUEL
1882-1948, Mexican
Principal Works - Orchestral: *Chapultepec* (1929); Suite en estilo centiguo (1935); *Concierto del sur* for guitar and orchestra; chamber and piano pieces; song *Estrelita.*

PONIRIDY, GEORGES
1892, Turkish/Greek
Principal Works - Dramatic musical: *Lazaros* (1960); ballet; symphonies; Greek folk songs.

POOT, MARCEL
1901, Belgian
Principal Works - Symphonic poem: *Charlot;* 4 symphonies; operas; ballets; piano concerto; concerto grosso for piano quartet and orchestra; oratorios; piano and chamber music; songs.

POPOV, GAVRIIL NIKOLAIEVICH
1904-1972, Russian
Principal Works - Operas; 6 symphonies; violin concerto; choral and chamber pieces; piano music; film music.

PORTER, QUINCY
1897-1966, American
Principal Works - *New England Episodes* (1958) for orchestra; *Concerto concertante* for 2 pianos and orchestra (1954); 2 symphonies; 10 string quartets; piano and organ pieces; songs.

POULENC, FRANCIS
1899-1963, French
Principal Works - 1917: *Rhapsodie negre* for cello, piano, flute, string quartet; 1918: Sonata for 2 clarinets, for piano; 3 perpetual movements for piano; *Toreador* songs; 1919: *Valse* for piano; songs: *Le Bestaire au cortège d'Orphée; Cocardes;* 1920: *Cinq Impromptus* and *Suite in C Major* for piano; 1922: Sonata for trumpet, horn, trombone; for clarinet and bassoon; *Chanson a boire,* for male a capella choir; 1923: Ballet: *Les Biches;* 1924: *Promenade* and *Poemes de Ronsard:* piano; 1925: *Napoli Suite* for piano; 1926: Trio for oboe, bassoon and piano; *Chansons gaillardes; Concert champêtre,* for harpsichord and orchestra; *Deux novelettes,* for piano; *Airs chantés.* 1928: *Trois pièces,* for piano; 1929: *Aubade,* for piano and eighteen instruments; *Hommage à Roussel,* and *Huit Nocturnes,* for piano. 1930: *Epitaphe,* song; 1931: *Bagatelle,* for violin and piano; *Trois poèmes de Louise Lalane,* songs; 1932: Concerto in D minor, for two pianos and orchestra; Sextet for piano and wind quintet; Improvisations for piano; *Intermezzo,* in D minor, for piano; *Le Bal masque,* cantata. 1933: *Feuillets d'album,* for piano (Ariette, Rêve, Gigue); *Villageoises,* children's piano pieces.
1934: *Intermezzo,* in D flat major; *Intermezzo,* in C major; *Presto, Badinage* and *Humoresque,* for piano. Huit chansons polonaises; Quatre chansons pour enfants; 1935: *Suite francaise,* for chamber orchestra; Cinq poèmes (Paul Eluard); *A sa guitare,* song.
1936: *Sept chansons,* for a cappella mixed choir; *Litanies à la Vierge noire,* for women's or children's voices and organ; *Petites voix,* for a cappella children's choir; *Les Soirées de Nazelles,* for piano; 1937: *Deux marches et un intermède,* for chamber orchestra; Mass in G major; *Secheresses,* cantata; *Bourée d'Auvergne,* for piano; *Tel jour telle nuit,* songs; 1938: *Concerto in G major,* for organ, strings and timpani; Four penitential Motets; 1939: *Fiancailles pour rire,* songs; *Mélancolie* for piano; *Banalities,* songs; *Histoire de Babar le petit éléphant,* for piano and narrator; Cello Sonata; 1941: *Salve regina,* and *Exultate Deo,* for four-part a cappella mixed choir; *Les Animaux modèles,* ballet; *La Fille du jardinier,* incidental music.
1942: Violin Sonata; *Chansons villageoises,* songs; 1943: *Figure humaine,* cantata; *Metamorphoses, Deux poèmes, Montparnasse,* songs; 1944: *La Mamelles de Tiresias,* opera buffe; *La Voyageur sans bagage, La Nuit de la Saint-Jean,* incidental music; *Un Soir de neige,* cantata.
1945: *Chansons françaises,* for a cappella mixed choir; *Le Soldat et la Sorcière,* incidental music; 1947: Flute Sonata; 1948: *Quatre petites prières (St. Francis),* for a cappella male choir; 1949) Piano Concerto; 1950: *Stabat Mater,* for soprano, mixed choir and orchestra; 1953: Sonata for two pianos; *Dialogues des Carmelites,* opera; 1956: *Le Travail*

du peintre, song cycle; *Deux mélodies,* songs; 1957: *Elegy,* for horn and piano; 1958: *La Voix humaine,* monodrama for soprano;1959: *Gloria,* for soprano, mixed choir and orchestra; 1960: *Elegy,* for two pianos; 1961: *La Dame de Monte Carlo,* monologue for soprano and orchestra; 1962: *Sept Repons des ténèbres,* for soprano, choir and orchestra; Oboe Sonata; Clarinet Sonata.

POUSSEUR, HENRI
1929, Belgian
Principal Works - Electronic. aleatory and serial music. *Quintette à la mémoire de Webern* (1955); *Mobile* for 2 pianos (1958); *Scambi* (1957) and 3 visages de Liège (1961) on tapes; *Votre Faust* for actors, singers, chamber group and tapes (1961); *Madrigal III* for clarinet, cello, piano, violin and percussion (1962).

POWELL, JOHN
1882-1963, American
Principal Works - Opera: *Rapsodie negre* for piano and orchestra (1918); *Virginia Symphony;* piano concertos; a violin concerto; chamber and choral music; piano pieces; songs.

PREVIN, ANDRE
1929, American
Principal Works - *Overture to A Comedy* for orchestra (1960); Ballet: *Invitation to the Dance;* Guitar Concerto; Portrait for Strings; String quartet; Flute Quintet; Cello Sonata, *Impressions* for piano.

PROKOFIEV, SERGIE SERGEIEVICH
1891-1953, Russian
Principal Works - Opera: *The Love for Three Oranges,* 4 Acts (1921); *The Gambler,* (1916); *The Flaming Angel (1922); Semyon Kotko* (1940); *Duenna* (1940); *War and Peace,* after Tolstoy (1943). Orchestral: Symphony No. 1, D major, Op. 25, *Classical* (1917); Symphony No. 5, B flat major, Op. 100 (1944); Symphony No. 6, E flat major, Op. 101; Piano Concerto No. 3, C major, Op. 26 (1921); Violin Concerto No. 1, D major, Op. 19 (1913); Violin Concerto No. 2, G minor, Op. 63 (1935); March, Op. 99 (1943); *Peter and the Wolf,* Op. 67 (with narrator and orchestra) (1936); *Scythian Suite,* Op. 20 (1914); *The Love for Three Orange Suite,* Op. 33a; *Lieutenant Kijé Suite,* Op. 60 (1934). Dramatic: Incidental music: to *Boris Godunov* (1936), to *Eugene Onegin* (1936); to *Hamlet* (1938). Piano: Suite, Op. 75; *Masques* (various arrangements); Gavotte , Op. 32, No. 3 (1918); March, Op. 12, No. 1; *Pieces for Children,* Op. 65 (1935), *Summer Day Suite;* Prelude, C major, Op. 12, No. 7 (1908-13); Sonata No. 3, A minor, Op. 28 (1917); Sonata No. 6, A major, Op. 82 (1940); Sonata No. 7, B flat major, Op. 83 (1942); *Suggestion diabolique,* Op. 4, No. 4; Toccata, D minor, Op. 11 (1912); *Visions fugitives,* Op. 22 (1915) . Film Music: *Alexander Nevsky* (1938). Ballets: *Romeo and Juliet* (1936); *Chout* (1920); *Le pas d'acier* (1927); *Cinderella* (1941); *The Prodigal Son* (1929); *The Stone Flower* (1950). Chamber Music: Quartet No. 1, B major, Op. 80 (1938-46); Quartet No. 2, F major, Op. 92 (1941). Film Music: *The Queen of Spades* (1938); *Alexander Nevsky* (1938) (later expansion into cantata);*Ivan the Terrible* (1945).

PYLKKANEN, TAUNO (KULLERVO)
1918, Finnish

Principal Works - Opera: *The Wolf's Bride* (1950); symphonic poems; concerto for cello and other symphonic works; choral and chamber music including string quartet; songs.

QUILTER, ROGER
1877-1953, English
Principal Works - Shakespearean song settings including *Twelfth Night; As You Like It* and many others; light opera: *Julia* (1936); orchestral: *A Children's Overture; Serenade* and others; choral and chamber works; piano pieces.

QUINTANAR, HECTOR
1936, Mexican
Principal Works - Electronic music. Orchestral: *Sideral II* (1969); choral and chamber music; electronic and conventional instrumental pieces.

RABAUD, HENRY (BENJAMIN)
1873-1949, French
Principal Works - Opera: *Mârouf, savetier du Caire* (1914); *Riders to the Sea* after Synge; 2 symphonies; *La procession nocturne* for orchestra; symphonic poems, oratorio and choral pieces; film music; songs.

RACHMANINOV, SERGEI VASSILIEVICH
1873-1943, Russian
Principal Works - Orchestral: Symphony No. 1, D minor, Op. 13 (1895); Symphony No 2, E minor, Op. 27 (1907); Symphony No. 3, A minor, Op. 44 (1936); *The Bells* (choral symphony), Op. 35 (1913); *The Isle of the Dead*, Op. 29 (1907); Symphonic Dances (1940); Piano Concerto No. 1, F sharp minor, Op. 1 (1980; revised 1917); Piano Concerto No. 2, C minor, Op. 18 (1901); Piano Concerto No. 3, D minor, Op. 30 (1909); Piano Concerto No. 4, G minor, Op. 40 (1927; revised 1938); *Rhapsody on a Theme of Paganini*, Op. 43 (1934). Piano: Five Pieces, Op. 3 (1892): No. 2, C sharp minor, No. 5, Serenade; Moments Musicaux, Op. 16 (1896): Oriental Sketch, Polka de W.R.; Ten Preludes, Op. 23 (1901): No. 1, F sharp minor, No. 3, D minor, No. 4, D major, No. 5, G minor, No. 6, E flat major, No. 7, C minor, etc.; Thirteen Preludes, Op. 32 (1910): No. 3, E major, No. 5, G major, No. 6, F minor, No. 12, G sharp minor, etc.; Etudes Tableaux (6), Op. 33 (1911); Etudes Tableaux (9), Op. 39 (1916-17). Songs: *Before My Window*, Op. 26, No. 10(Galina); *Christ Is Risen*, Op. 26, No. 6 (Merezhlovsky); *Daisies*, Op. 38, No. 3 (Severyanin); *Spring Waters*, Op. 14, No. 11 (Tyutchev); *How Fair This Spot*, Op. 21 (Galina); *In theSilent Night*, Op. 4, No. 3 (Fet); *Lilacs*, Op. 21, No. 5 (Beketova); *O Never Sing to Me Again (Chanson Georgienne)*, Op. 4, No. 4 (Pushkin); *To the Children*, Op. 26, No. 7 (Khomyakov); *Vocalise*, Op. 34, No. 14. Opera: *Aleko*, after Pushkin (1893) and 2 others.

RAINIER, PRIAULX
1903, South African
Principal Works - Cello concerto; *Barbaric Dance Suite* for piano; *Incantation* for clarinet and orchestra; 3 string quartets; *Cycle for Declamation* for unaccompanied high voice, after Donne; other choral and chamber pieces; songs.

RAITIO, VÄINÖ
1891-1945, Finnish
Principal Works - 5 operas; 2 ballets; symphonic poems; piano concerto; a symphony; double concerto for violin and cello; chamber and choral music; songs.

RAMIN, GUNTHER
1898-1956, German
Principal Works - Organ and choral music; chamber pieces.

RANDALL, JAMES K.
1929, American
Principal Works - *Improvisation on a Poem of e.e. cummings* for voice and instruments; *Mudgett: Monologues by a Mass Murderer* (1965); *Lyric Variations for violin and computerized tape* (1967).

RANGSTRÖM, TÜRE
1884-1947, Swedish
Principal Works - Opera: *Kronbruden* (1919); Symphony No. 1 *In Memoriam August Strindberg* and 3 other symphonies; choral, chamber and piano pieces; more than 50 songs.

RANDS, BERNARD
1935, English
Principal Works - *Wildtrack I* for orchestra; *Espressiones* for piano (1960); *Action for 6* for chamber ensemble; *Per esempio* for orchestra (1967); compositions for youth orchestra; *Metalepsis 2,* Requiem Mass (1972).

RANKL, KARL FRANZ
1898-1968, Austrian
Principal Works - Opera: *Deidre of the Sorrows* (1951); 8 symphonies; oratorio; other choral works; chamber pieces; songs.

RANTA, SULHO
1901-1960, Finnish
Principal Works - Symphonies; ballet; cantata *Kalevala* (1935); choral and chamber pieces.

RAPHAEL, GÜNTER
1903-1960, German
Principal Works - 5 symphonies; concerto for violin, for cello, for organ; piano and organ pieces.

RATHAUS, KAROL
1895-1954, Polish
Principal Works - Opera: *Fremde Erde* (1930); *Prelude* for orchestra (1953); *Vision dramatique* for orchestra; ballets; 3 symphonies; piano concerto; choral pieces; 5 string quartets; piano music; songs.

RAVEL MAURICE (JOSEPH)
1875-1937, French
Principal Works - Operas: *L'Heure espagnole*, 1 Act (1907); *L'Enfant et les sortilèges* (1920-25). Ballets: *Daphnis et Chloë* (1910); *Ma Mère l'Oye (Mother Goose)* 1915); *Adelaide*. Orchestral: *Pavane for a Dead Infanta (Pavane pour une Infante défunte)* (1899); *Alborado del Gracioso* (Miroirs No. 4) (1905); *Rapsodie espagnole* (1907); *Ma Mère l'Oye Suite (Mother Goose)* (1908); *Tombeau de Couperin*, after the piano suite (1917); *Daphnis et Chloë*, 2 suites from the ballet (1911); *La Valse, Poème choréographique* (1920); *Boléro* (1928); Piano Concerto, D major (left hand) (1931); Piano Concerto, G major (1931); Transcription of Mussorgsky's *Pictures at an Exhibition;* Overture: *Sheherazade*. Chamber Music: Quartet for Strings, F major (1903); *Introduction and Allegro*, G flat major (septet) (1906); Piano Trio, A minor (1915); *Tzigane* for violin and piano *(Gypsy)* (1924) (also for violin and

orchestra); *Chansons madécasses* (1926) (voice, flute, cello, and piano). Piano: Menuet Antique (1895); *Pavane for a Dead Infanta (Pavane pour une Infante défunte); Jeux d'eau* (1901); Sonatine, F sharp major (1905); *Miroirs* (1905); *Noctuelles - Oiseaux tristes - Une Barque sur l'océan, Alborado del gracioso - La Vallée des Cloches; Gaspard de la Nuit,* suite (1908): *Ondine - Le Gibet - Scarbo; Valses nobles et sentimentales* (1911) (also for orchestra); Prelude (1913); *Tombeau de Couperin* (1914-17), *Ma Mère l'Oye (Mother Goose),* 4 hands (1908). Songs: *Shéhérazade* (Klingsor) (with orchestra) (1903), *Histoires naturelles* (J. Renard) (1906), *Don Quichotte à Dulcinée* (P. Morand) (1932). *Épigrammes de Clément Marot* (1898); 5 popular Greek melodies (1907); *Chants Populaire* (1910); 2 Hebrew melodies (1914); *3 chansons* (1915).

RAWSTHORNE, ALAN
1905-1971, English
Principal Works - Overture *Street Corner;* overture *Cortèges;* concerto for strings; 2 piano concertos; ballet: *Madame Chrysanthème* (1957); *Symphonic Studies* for orchestra; 2 violin concertos; concerto for oboe, for clarinet; 3 string quartets; clarinet quartet; piano bagatelles; film music; concerto for 2 pianos.

READ, GARDNER
1913, American
Principal Works - *A Bell Overture; Sketches of the City* for orchestra; *Prelude and Toccata* (1937); *Pennsylvania* (1947); cello concerto; opera: *Villon* (1967); 4 symphonies; chamber and organ pieces; piano music, songs.

RAXACH, ENRIQUE
1932, Spanish/Dutch
Principal Works - *Metamorphose I* (1956); *Inside Outside* for orchestra and tape (1969); 2 string quartets; *The Looking Glass* for organ.

REDA, SIEGFRIED
1916-1968, german
Principal Works - *Marienbilder* (1952); choral sacred music; organ concertos; choral concertos; sonatas; organ pieces.

REED, H. (HERBERT) OWEN
1910
Principal Works - Opera: *Michigan Dream* (1955); pantomime ballet: *The Masque of the Red Death,* after Poe (1936); *The Turning Mind* (1968) for orchestra; symphony; oratorio: *A Tabernacle for the Sun* (1963); string quartet; piano pieces; songs.

EGER, MAX
1873-1916, German
Principal Works - *Symphonischer Prolog zu einer Tragödie; Variations on a Teme of Mozart;* concerto for violin, for piano; choral works including liturgy; 5 string quartets; 2 piano trios; organ pieces; songs.

REICH, STEVE
1936, American
Principal Works - Electronic and tape works. *It's Gonna Rain* (1965) on tape; *Phase Patterns for 4 electric organs* (1970); *Drumming* for bongo drums, marimbas, glockenspiels and voices; *Music for 18 Musicians* (1976); *Music for 3 or more pianos and tape; Piano Store* for a store full of pianos.

REINER, KAREL
1910, Czech.
Principal Works - A symphony (1960); *Suite Concertante* (1967); concertos for piano, for violin, for bass clarinet; choral and piano works; film music.

REIZENSTEIN, FRANZ
1911-1968, German/English
Principal Works - Oratorio: *Genesis* (1958); cantata: *Voices of Night* (1951); *Jolly Overture* (1952); 2 piano concertos; cello concerto; piano pieces; chamber music.

RESPIGHI, OTTORINO
1879-1936, Italian
Principal Works - Opera: *La Campana Sommersa,* 4 Acts (1924-1927); *Maria Egiziaca* (mystery), 1 Act (1930-1931); *Belfagor* (1923); *La Fiamma* (1934); *Lucrezia* (1937). Orchestral: *La Boutique fantasque* (Ballet suite after Rossini) (1919); *Gli uccelli* (The Birds) (1927); *Brazilian Impressions* (1927); *Trittico botticelliano* (1927); *Vetrate di chiesa* (1927); *Fountains of Rome* (1917); *Pines of Rome* (1924); *Rossiniana* (1925); *Roman Festivals* (1929); *Ancient airs and dances* (1917, 1924, 1932); Suite No. 1 (1917); Ballet: *Belkis* (1932); Galilei: *Gagliarda;* Anon: *Villanella;* Suite No. 3 (1932): Besard: *Arie di corte;* Anon: *Siciliana.* Songs: *Nebbie* (Negri); *Pioggia* (Pompei).

REVUELTAS, SILVESTRE
1899-1940, Mexican
Principal Works - Ballets: *Esquinas* for orchestra (1930); *Sensemayá* for orchestra; 3 string quartets; film music including *Redes* (1935); chamber pieces and songs; *Homenage a Garcia Lorca* for orchestra.

REYNOLDS, ROGER
1934, American
Principal Works - Mixed media and graphic techniques. *The Emperor of Ice Cream* for 8 singers, piano, percussion, double bass (1962); *Ping* for flute, piano, harmonium, bowed cymbal, tam-tam with film and tape and electronics; *Masks* for chorus and orchestra; *Quick Are The Mouths of Earth* for chamber group (1965); *Blind Men* for chorus, brass, percussion, piano (1966); *Threshold* for divided orchestra (1967); *From Behind the Unreasoning Mask* for trombone, percussion and tape (1975); *Eclipse* with video tape and pre-recorded voices (1980).

REZNIČEK, EMIL NIKOLAUS VON
1860-1945, German
Principal Works - Operas: *Donna Diana* (1894); *Ritter Blaubart* (1920); Mass; Requiem; 5 symphonies; violin concerto; string quartet; other chamber pieces; piano music; songs.

RHODES, PHILLIP
1940, American
Principal Works - Opera-oratorio: *From Paradise Lost;* ballet: *About Faces; The Lament of Michal* for soprano and orchestra (1970); choral sacred and secular music; *Autumn Setting* for soprano and string quartet (1969); string trio; chamber music.

RICHTER, MARGA
1926, American
Principal Works - *Lament for String Orchestra;* piano concerto; *7E-Quintet for Winds in Five Movements* (1951); *Two Short Suites for Young Pianists.*

RIDKY, JAROSLAV
1897-1956, Czech.
Principal Works - 7 symphonies; concertos for piano, for cello, for violin; cantatas; chamber pieces including 5 string quartets; piano music.

RIDOUT, GODFREY
1918,, Canadian
Principal Works - Ballet: *La prima ballerina* (1966); *Esther* for soloists, orchestra and chorus (1953); *In Memoriam Anne Frank* (1965); *Cautiones mysticae* for soprano and orchestra (1953); *Fall Fair* (1961) for orchestra; piano and chamber pieces; organ works; songs.

RIEGGER, WALLINGFORD
1885-1961, American
Principal Works - Twelve tone music, partially employed. Orchestral: Variations for Piano and Orchestra (1954); Variations for Violin and Orchestra, Op. 71 (1959); Symphony No. 3, Op. 42 (1946); Dance Rhythms; Now Dance (1934); Romanza: Symphony No. 4; *Dichotomy* for piano, percussion and strings (1931); Choral and instrumental setting: Keats' *La Belle Dame Sans Merci*; Chamber music works: String Quartet No. 2, Op. 43 (1948); Quintet for Winds, Op. 51; Trio for Piano, Violin and Cello, Op. 1 (1919); Suite for Flute Alone, Op. 8; Sonatina for Violin and Piano; Duos for Flute, Oboe and Clarinet (1943); Dance scores and ballet: Theater Pieces (1935); *New Dance* and *With My RedFires* (1936); *Chronicle* (1936); *The Pilgrim's Progress* (1938); *Candide* (1937); *Case History* (1937); *Machine Ballet* and *Trojan Incident* (1938); *Trend*, in collaboration with Edgar Varèse.

RIETI, VITTORIO
1898, Italian/American
Principal Works - Opras: *Don Perlimplin* after Lorca;*The Pet Shop*; ballet: *Barabau, Le Bal*; orchestral: 5 symphonies; *Introduction and Game of the Hours* (1954); concerto for piano, violin and cello; 4 string quartets; choral works; film music.

RIISAGER, KNUDAAGE
1897, Danish
Principal Works - *Concertino for Trumpet and Strings*; Little Overture for Strings; ballet; choral and chamber works; vocal and piano pieces.

RILEY, TERRY
1935, American
Principal Works - Electronic music! *In C* for any number of instruments; *A Rainbow In Curved Air* for electronic keyboards; freely-structured works.

RIVIER, JEAN
1896, French
Principal Works - *Don Quixote Overture* (1929); Symphony in D for large orchestra (1932); Symphony No. 3 in G, for strings (1938); *Provencal Rhapsody*; Psalm 56 for soprano voice, orchestra and chorus (1937); Piano Concerto (1940); violin concerto; Requiem; chamber works.

ROBERTSON, LEROY (JASPER)
1896-1971, American
Principal Works - Oratorio: *The Book of Mormon* (1953); *Punch and Judy Overture* for orchestra (1946); *Trilogy* (1947); choral works; concertos for piano, for cello, for violin; string quartet and other chamber pieces; piano and organ music; songs.

ROCHBERG, GEORGE
1918, American
Principal Works - Some twelve tone music. Symphony No. 3 *A 20th-century Passion* and two other symphonies; *Night Music* (1949); *Time-Span (1960); Music for the Magic Theater* (1965); *Imago mundi* (1974); violin concerto; *Contra mortem et tempus* for violin, flute, clarinet and piano; *Apocalyptica* for band (1964); *Black Sounds* for winds and percussion (1965); *Zodiac* (1965) for orch. called 12 Bagatelles in piano version (1952); 3 string quartets; 3 Psalms for chorus; piano trio (1963); other chamber and piano pieces.

RODRIGO, JOAQUIN
1902, Spanish
Principal Works - Ballets; *zarzuelas;* orchestral works; con cierto de Aranjuez for guitar and orch. *Fantasy for a gentleman* for guitar and orchestra (1954); *Concierto heroico* for piano and orchestra; *Concierto de estio for violin and orchestra; Concierto galante* for cello and orchestra (1949); *Concierto-serenata* for harp and orchestra (1952); *Concierto andaluz* for 4 guitars and orchestra; *Concierto madrigal* for 2 guitars and orchestra; choral and chamber music; piano works; songs.

ROGERS, BERNARD
1893-1968, American
Principal Works - Operas: *The Warrior* (1947); *The Veil* (1950); *The Passion* (1942) for orchestra and chorus; Symphony No. 4 (1946); *A Letter from Pete* (1947); *The Emperor's Nightingale* (1939), orchestral: *To The Fallen; The Faithful; The Supper at Emmaus; In Memory of Franklin Delano Roosevelt;* 5 fairy tales; *Once Upon A Time* (1934); *Soliloquy for Flute and Strings (1922); Three Japanese Dances (1933); Leaves from the Tale Of Pinocchio; The Plains; Three Landscapes;* Symphony No. 3 (1936); Choral: *The Raising of Lazarus; The Exodus;* (1932).

ROLAND-MANUEL, ALEXIS
1891-1966, French
Principal Works - Opera: *Isobelle et Pantalon* (1922); Ballets: *Le Tournoi Singulier* (1924); *L'Ecran des Jeunes Filles* (1929); symphonic poem, piano pieces; film and theater music; songs.

ROLDÁN, AMADEO
1900-1939, Cubam
Principal Works - Ballet: *La rebambaramba* (1928); *3 toques* (1931) for orchestra; *Motivos de son* for voice and 9 instruments: *Rítmicas,* a series including some pieces for percussion only; choral and chamber music.

ROLÓN, JOSÉ
1883-1945, Mexican
Principal Works - Orchestral: *Zapotlán* (1895); a symphony; *El festin de los enanos* (1925); *Cuauhtémoc* (1929); piano concerto; string quartets and other chamber works; piano works; songs.

ROOTHAM, CYRIL BRADLEY
1875-1938, English
Principal Works - Opera: *The Two Sisters* (1922); *Brown Earth* for chorus and orchestra (1921); 2 symphonies; chamber music including string quartets; piano and organ pieces, songs.

ROPARTZ, GUY (JOSEPH-MARIE)
1864-1955, French
Principal Works - Opera: *Le pays* (1912); 5 symphonies; Masses, motets, and other choral sacred music; organ and piano works; 5 string quartets; orchestral works for solos by oboe, violin and by cello; songs.

ROREM, NED
1923, American
Principal Works - Operas: *A Childhood Miracle* (1952); *The Robbers; Miss Julie,* after Strindberg (1965); *Bertha* (1969); *Air Music* for orchestra (1976); and 3 symphonies; 3 piano concertos; choral and chamber works; piano pieces; 9 song-cycles, for piano and other instruments, after Whitman, Herrick, Koch and others; *Design for Orchestra* (1955).

ROSENBERG, HILDING (CONSTANTIN)
1892, Swedish
Principal Works - Operas: *Resan till America* (1932); *Marionetter* (1933); ballets; 6 symphonies; 12 string quartets; oratorio tetralogy, after Thomas Mann's *Joseph;* piano solos; - - - Ballets and symphonies, no. 4 symphony *The Revelation of St. John* for chorus and orchestra, one ballet entitled *Orpheus in Town;* concertos for violin, for viola, for cello, for trumpet.

ROSENTHAL, MANUEL
1904, French
Principal Works - Symphonic suite *Joan of Arc oratorio: St. Francis of Assisi* (1939); choral sacred pieces; chamber music; songs.

ROUSSEL, ALBERT (CHARLES PAUL MARIE)
1869-1937, French
Principal Works - Opera-ballet: *Padmâvâtî* (1914); ballets: *Bachus et Ariane* (1930); *Aenéas* (1935); *Le festin de l'araignée* (1912); 4 symphonies; orchestral *Suite en fa* (1926); *Pour une fête de printemps* (1920); piano concerto (1927); concertino for cello (1936); *Evocations* for chorus with soloists and orchestra (1910); chamber and piano pieces; songs.

ROWLEY, ALEC
1892-1958, English
Principal Works - 2 piano concertos; concerto for oboe; orchestral works; choral and chamber music; piano and organ pieces.

RÓZSA, MIKLÓS
1907, Hungarian/American
Principal Works - Ballet: *Hungaria* (1935); symphony; concertos for piano, for cello; choral and chamber works; piano pieces; songs; noted film music composer.

ROZYCKI, LUDOMIR
1884-1953, Polish
Principal Works - Operas: *Eros und Psyche* (1923); *Casanova* (1923); ballet: *Pan Twardowski* (1921); symphonic works and poems; concertos for violin, for piano; choral and chamber pieces; songs.

RUBBRA, (CHARLES) EDMUND
1901, English
Principal Works - 10 symphonies; Sinfonia Concertante for piano and orchestra; 2 Masses, Catholic and Anglican; concertos for piano and orchestra; for piano; for viola; choral secular works; 3 string quartets; piano trio; piano solos; songs.

RUDHYAR, DANE
1895, French/American
Principal Works - Symphonic poems: *To the Real* (1920); *Soul Fire* (1922); dance poems: *Poèmes ironiques* and *Vision végétale* (1917); piano: *4 Pentagrams* 1924); *Paeans* (1927); *Granites* (1932).

RUGGLES, CARL (CHARLES SPRAGUE)
1876-1971
Principal Works - Modernist! Symphonic poems: *Men and Mountains* (1921);*The Sun-Treader* (1927); *Organum* for orchestra (1945); *Toys* for voice and piano (1919); *Men and Angels* for brass (1920); *Portals* for strings (1925); *Evocations* for piano (1937); hymn: *Exaltation* (1958).

RZEWSKI, FREDERIC (ANTHONY)
1938, American
Principal Works - Electronic music! *Composition for 2* for any 2 instruments (1964); *Self-portrait* for one person, with any sounds; *Nature morte* for chamber group (1965); *Zoologischer Garten* on tape; *Spacecraft* for group inprovisation (1965); *Portrait* for actor, lights, tapes, visuals (1967); *Coming Together; Attica* for narrator and ensemble (1972); *The People United Will Never Be Defeated,* for piano (1975); *Falling Music* for piano and tape; *Song and Dance* for flute, bass clarinet, double bass and vibraphone (1978).

SABATA, VICTOR DE
1892-1967, Italian
Principal Works - *Suite for Orchestra* (1912); operas: *Il Macigno* (1917); *Lysistrata;* symphonic poems: *Juventus* (1919); *La notte di Platon* (1924); *Gethsemane* (1925); ballets.

SALLINEN, AULIS
1935, Finnish
Principal Works - Opera.*The Horseman; Chorali* for 32 winds, percussion, harp and celesta; concerto for violin; 3 string quartets.

SALZEDO, CARLOS
1885-1961, American
Principal Works - Concert harpist with many compositions for harp, with orchestra; with ensembles; with other instruments; solos. Developed harp-percussion sonorities; music for two harps: *Four Preludes to the Afternoon of a Telephone,* etc.

SALZMAN, ERIC
1933, American
Principal Works - Electronic music; opera a cappella: *Voices* (1971); *Inventions for Orchestra* (1958); *Foxes and Hedgehogs* for voices, instruments and sound systems (1967); *Queen's Collage* (1966) on tape; *The Nude Paper Sermon* for Renaissance instruments, actor, chorus, electronic materials (1969); *Noah,* collaboration with Mort Sahl (1978).

SAMINSKY, LAZARE
1882-1959, American
Principal Works - Operas: *The Vision of Ariel* (1916); *The Gagliarda of a Merry Plague* (1925); *the Defeat of Caesar Julian* (1933); ballet-opera *Jephta's Daughter;* ballet: *The Lament of Rachael* (1913); 5 symphonies; choral works for synagogue and secular use; heavy use of Jewish materials modernist setting

SANCHEZ DE FUENTES, EDUARDO
1874-1944, Cuban

Principal Works - Operas: *Dolorosa* (1910); *Kabelia* (1942); orchestral and choral music; piano and chamber pieces; songs, including *Tú.*

SANDERS, ROBERT L.
1906-1974, American
Principal Works - Dance: *L'Ag'ya* (1944); Little Symphony No. 1 and No. 2; band music; choral and chamber pieces.

SANTA CRUZ (WILSON), DOMINGO
1899, Chilean
Principal Works - 4 symphonies; *5 piezas for strings* (1937); *Cantata de los rio de Chile* for chorus and orch. (1941); choral works; 3 string quartets and other chamber pieces; piano music; songs.

SANTORO, CLAUDIO
1919, Brazilian
Principal Works - Opera; ballets; 8 symphonies; *Brasil-iana* for orchestra (1954); 3 piano concertos; 2 violin concertos; *Ode a Stalingrado* for chorus (1947); chamber music including 6 string quartets; piano pieces; film and television music; many songs.

SATIE, ERIK (ALFRED LESLIE)
1866-1925, French
Principal Works - Ballets: *Relâche; Parade* with Cocteau; *Mercure* with Picasso and Massine (1924); *Le piège de Méduse* (1913) for stage; *Socrate,* symphonic drama for 4 sopranos and small orchestra; piano pieces: *3 sarabandes* (1887); *3 gymnopedies* (1988), two of which orchestrated by Debussy; *6 gnossiennes* (1890); *3 Preludes from Le fils des étoiles (1891);* a Péladan play; *3 morceaux en forme de poire* for piano four-hands (1893); *En habit de cheval* for four-hand piano (1911); *Sports et divertissements* (1914); *Sonatine Bureaucratique.*

SAUGUET, HENRI
1901, French
Principal Works - Operas: *Le plumet du colonel* (1924); *La chartreuse de Parme* (1939); *La gargeuse imprévue* (1944); 25 ballets including *La chatte;* orchestral works for violin, for cello, for ensemble; some musique concrète; string quartets and other chamber pieces; piano music; film music.

SAYGUN, AHMED ADMAN
1907, Turkish
Principal Works - Opera: *Tas Bebek* (1934); *Kerem* (1953); symphonies; concertos for piano, for violin; choral and chamber music.

SCALERO, ROSARIO
1870-1954, Italian
Principal Works - Orchestral works; violin concerto; chamber and sacred choral music; piano pieces.

SCHAFER, R. MURRAY
1933, Canadian
Principal Works - Electronic and aleatory music! Operas; *Requiems for the Party Girl,* for soprano and 9 instruments; *Son of Heldenleben* for orchestra and tape (1968); *No Longer than Ten (10) Minutes* for orchestra (1970); *From the Tibetan Book of the Dead* for soprano, instruments, chorus and tape.

SCHAFFER, BOGUSLAW (JULIEN)
1929, Polish

Principal Works - Serial and graphic music; Polish folk materials. *Nocturne* for strings (1953); *Tertium datur,* graphic composition for harpsichord and orchestra; *Non-Stop,* 8 hours of piano music; *Little Symphony; Collage and Form* for 8 jazz musicians and symphony orchestra; *Monosonata* for 6 string quartets (1959); *Equivalenze sonore* for percussion (1959); *Communicazione audiovisiva,* theatrical, audio-visual composition (1970); tape works.

SCHELLING, ERNEST (HENRY)
1876-1939, American
Principal Works - *A Victory Ball* (1923) and *Morocco* (1927) for orchestra; a violin concerto (1916); *Impressions from an Artist's Life,* for piano and orchestra; piano and chamber pieces; songs.

SCHIBLER, ARMIN
1920, Swiss
Principal Works - Operas: *Der spanische Rosenstock* (1950); *Die Füsse im Feuer* (1955); symphonic variations; 3 symphonies; fantasy for viola; oratorio *Media in vita* (1958); concertos for piano, for violin and ensemble groups; string quartets; a Psalter for the home; piano and choral pieces; songs.

SCHIDLOWSKY, LEÓN
1931, Chilean
Principal Works - Serial, aleatory and graphic music! *Nueva York* (1965) for orchestra; *La noche de cristal* for tenor and orchestra (1961); *Erostrato* for percussion; *Cantata negra* (1957); chamber pieces.

SCHILLINGER, JOSEPH
1895-1943, American
Principal Works - Inventor of mathematical system of composition which enjoyed some notoriety in '30's and '40's, but waned subsequently due to alleged abstruse complexity of the principles! Composed *First Airphonic Suite* for Theremin and orchestra (1929); chamber and piano pieces; songs.

SCHMITT, FLORENT
1870-1958, French
Principal Works - Ballets: *The Tragedy of Salome; Oriane and the Prince of Love;* Psalm XLVII for chorus and orchestra (1907); incidental music *Antoine et Cleopatre* (1920); Sonata for violin and piano (1919); *Le Petit Elfe Ferme-l'oeil* (1924); Trio for strings (1944); Quartet (1947); *Le palais hante,* after Poe, for orchestra; chamber music; piano pieces, including works for four hands; songs; film music.

SCHNABEL, ARTHUR
1882-1951, Austrian
Principal Works - Famed pianist who composed some symphonies, an orchestral rhapsody, and piano concertos.

SCHNEBEL, DIETER
1930, German
Principal Works - *Versuche I to III* for stringed instruments and percussion; *für stimmen für 12 vocal groups* (1958); Concert without orchestra (1964); *Ki-no* for projector and listeners (1967).

SCHOECK, OTHMAR
1886-1957, Swiss
Principal Works - Opera: *Penthesilea* (1927)*Gaselen* song cycle for baritone with instruments (1923); *Elegie* for voice

and chamber orchestra (1924); *Lebendig begraben* for baritone and large orchestra (1926); *Notturno* for baritone and string quartet (1933); concertos for violin, for horn, for cello; string quartets; orchestral works;other choral works with orchestra; piano pieces; many songs.

SCHOENBERG, ARNOLD (FRANZ WALTER)
1874-1951, Austrian/American
Principal Works - World-famed iniator of twelve tone music forms! Operas: *Erwartung* monodrama); *Die glückliche Hand; Von Heute auf Morgen* (1 act); *Moses und Aron* (3 acts), Orchestral: *Pelléas et Mélisande* (1902)03); Chamber Symphony in E major, Op. 9 (1906); Five Pieces for Orchestra, Op. 16 (1908); Variations for Orchestra, Op. 31 (1928); Chamber Symphony No. 2, Op. 38 (1940); *Ode to Napoleon*, Op. 41b (1947); Theme and Variations for Band, Op. 43b (1943) (arranged for orchestra); Violin Concerto, Op. 36 (1936); Piano Concerto, Op. 42 (1942). Choral: *Gurrelieder* (soloists, chorus, and orchestra); *Kol Nidre* (speaker, chorus, and orchestra) (1938); *A Survivor from Warsaw*, Op. 46 (1947) (cantata); *Die Jakobsleiter* (1913); Unf. Oratorio; Chamber Music: *Verklärte Nacht*, Op. 4 (1899; string orchestra, 1917; revised, 1943); Quartet No. 1, D minor, Op. 7 (1904-05); Quartet No. 2, F sharp minor, Op. 10 (1907-08); *Pierrot Lunaire*, Serenade for Septet and Baritone, Op. 24 (1923); Quintet for Wind Instruments, Op. 26 (1924); Suite, Op. 29 (1926); Quartet No. 3, Op. 30 (1926); Quartet No. 4, Op. 37 (1936); String Trio, Op. 45 (1946); Piano: 3 Pieces, Op. 11 (1908); 6 Little Pieces, Op. 19 (1911); 5 Pieces, Op. 23 (1923); Suite, Op. 25 (1925). Songs: *Das Buch der hängenden Gärten* (1908); Variations on a recitative for organ (1910).

SCHREKER, FRANZ
1878-1934, Austrian
Principal Works - Operas: *Der ferne Klang* (1912); *Der Schatzgräber* (1920); ballet: *Der Geburtstag der Infantin*, after Wilde (1908); orchestral and choral works; chamber and piano pieces; songs.

SCHULLER, GUNTHER
1925, American
Principal Works - Serial music and jazz influences! Opera: *The Visitation* (1966); *American Triptych* (1969); *Variants* for jazz quartet: *Conversations* for jazz quartet and string quartet; orchestral: *Spectra* (1958); 7 *Studies on Themes of Paul Klee* (1959); symphony (1965); concerto for horn, for cello, for piano, for double bass; Concertino for jazz quartet and orchestra (1959); ballet, band and chamber music; jazz ensemble pieces; songs.

SHUMAN, WILLIAM
1910, American
Principal Works - Symphony For Strings, No. 5 and nine other symphonies; opera: *the Mighty Casey* (1953); orchestral: *American Festival Overture; William Billings Overture; New England Triptych; In Praise of Shahn* (1969); concertos for piano, for violin; *A Song of Orpheus* for cello and orchestra; *Concerto on Old English Rounds for viola, female chorus and orchestra (1973)*; choral: *A Free Song* (1943); 4 string quartets; *The Young Dead Soldiers* (text by Archibald MacLeish) for soprano, horn, woodwinds and strings (1976); dance scores: *Night Journey* (1947); *Judith* (1948); *Undertow* (1945).

SCOTT, CYRIL MEIR
1879-1970, English
Principal Works - Opera: *The Alchemist* (1925); *La belle dame sans merci* for chorus (1916); Piano pieces: *Lotus Land* (1905); *Danse nègre* (1908); *Impressions of the Jungle Book*, after Kipling (1912); 3 symphonies; ballet; concertos for violin, for piano, for cello, for harpsichord; for oboe; chamber music and many songs.

SCRIABIN, ALEXANDER NIKOLAIEVICH
1872-1915, Russian
Principal Works - Modernist use of whole-tone scale; *mystic chord;* Symphony No. 3 *The Divine Poem;* Symphony No. 4 *The Poem of Ecstasy* (1908); Symphony No. 5 *Prometheus: The Poem of Fire* (1910) and two other symphonies; piano concerto; 10 piano sonatas; many mazurkas, preludes, etudes, impromptus for piano.

SCULTHORPE, PETER (JOSHUA)
1929, Australian
Principal Works - Orchestral: *Sun Music Ballet* (1968); pieces entitled *Sun Music; Music for Japan* (1970); *Love 200* for 2 singers, pop group and orchestra; 7 string quartets; choral and other chamber pieces; film and theater music.

SEARLE, HUMPHREY
1915, English
Principal Works - Operas: *The Diary of a Madman*, after Gogol (1958); *The Photo of the Colonel*, after Ionesco (1964); *Hamlet* (1968); ballet: *Noctambules* (1956); 5 symphonies; Trilogy for speakers and orchestra: *Gold Coast Customs* (text Edith Sitwell),*The Riverrun*, after James Joyce, *The Shadow of Cain*, after Edith Sitwell; *Poem for 22 solo strings;* piano sonata; Setting of Lear's *The Owl and the Pussycat* for flute, cello, guitar and speaker (1968); piano and chamber pieces; film music; tv and theater pieces; songs.

SEIBER, MÁTYÁS GYÖRGY
1905-1960, Hungarian/English
Principal Works - Twelve tone music and jazz forms. Cantata: *Ulysses;* 4 string quartets; clarinet concertino; violin concerto; 2 orchestral suites from old lute materials; opera; Missa brevis for chorus; 3 string quartets; *Permutazioni a 5* for chamber group (1958); piano pieces; folksong arrangements; film music and songs.

SEKLES, BERNHARD
1872-1934, German
Principal Works - Opera: *Sheherazade* (1917); ballet: *Aus den Gärten Semiramis*,Passacaglia and Fugue for organ and orchestra; choral and chamber works; piano pieces.

SENDER, RAMON
1934, Spanish
Principal Works - Mixed media and tape works. *4 Sanskrit Hymns for 4 sopranos, instruments and tapes* (1961); *Time Fields* for any 6 instruments (1963); *World Food I-XII* for drone tapes (1963).

SEREBRIER, JOSE
1938, American
Principal Works - *Elegy for Strings* (1954); *Partita* (1958) for orchestra; a symphony; *Colores magicos for harp and chamber orchestra, including visuals (1971); Variations on a theme from Childhood* for trombone with string orchestra

or quartet; *Erotica* for soprano, trumpet and wind quintet; choral works; piano and chamber pieces; songs.

SEROCKI, KAZMIERZ
1922, Polish
Principal Works - Serial and aleatory music. Symphony No. 2 for soloists and chorus and orchestra; *Forte e piano* for 2 pianos and orchestra; *Niobe* for 2 narrators, chorus and orchestra; *Symphonic Frescoes* (1964); piano, trombone, and organ pieces; other symphonies, choral and chamber works; songs.

SESSIONS, ROGER (HUNTINGTON)
1896, American
Principal Works - Twelve tone music. Operas: *The Trial of Lucullus* and *Montezuma;* 8 symphonies; cantata: *Turn O Libertad,* after Walt Whitman; *When Lilacs Last in the Door-yard Bloom'd,* after Whitman (1970); *Divertimento for Orchestra* (1960); *Rhapsody for Orchestra* (1970); concertos for violin, for piano, for viola, for cello; *Idyll of Theocritus* for soprano and orchestra (1954); Mass (1955) for chorus; piano: *From My Diary* (1939); 3 sonatas; organ works; 2 string quartets and other chamber pieces; songs.

SETER, MORDECAI
1916, Russian
Principal Works - Serial music and use of Jewish sacred materials; Ballet: *Judith* (1962); *The Daughter of Jephtah* for orchestra; *Sabbath Cantata* (1947); *Jerusalem* (1966); piano and chamber pieces.

SÉVERAC, DÉODAT DE
1873-1921, French
Principal Works - Opera: *Coeur du moulin* (1909); *Le chant de la terre* (1900) and *En Languedoc* (1904) for piano; chamber works, songs.

SHAPERO, HAROLD
1920, American
Principal Works - *Symphony for classical orchestra* (1947); *Credo* for orchestra (1955); Partita (1960); *Hebrew Cantata* (1954); string quartet (1940); *Nine minute Overture;* synthesizer and piano pieces.

SHAPEY, RALPH
1921, American
Principal Works - Orchestral: *Rituals* (1959); violin concerto (1959); oratorio: *Praise* (1976); *Songs of Ecstasy* (1967); *Incantations for soprano and 10 instruments* (1961); 7 string quartets; *Evocation* for viol, piano and percussion.

SHAPORIN, YURI ALEXANDROVICH
1887-1966, Russian
Principal Works - Opera: *The Decembrists* (1930); cantata: *A Tale of the Battle for the Russian Land* (1944); cantata-symphony: *On the Kulikov Field* (1939); 2 piano sonatas; suite for the play *The Flea;* piano and choral pieces; songs; film music.

SHCDREDRIN, RODION KONSTANTINOVICH
1932, Russian
Principal Works - Operas: *Not Love Alone* (1961); *Dead Souls* (1977); Ballet: *The Little Hump-Backed Horse* (1959); *Carmen Ballet* after Bizet (1967); *Anna Karenina* (1972); 2 symphonies; *The Chimes* for orchestra; 3 piano concertos; piano and choral pieces; songs.

SHEBALIN, VISSARION YAKOVIEVICH
1902-1963, Russian
Principal Works - Opera: *The Taming of the Shrew* (1955); ballet; *Lenin* for soloists, chorus and orchestra; cantata: *Moscow* (1936); 9 string quartets; piano and other chamber pieces; songs.

SHEPHERD, ARTHUR
1880-1958, American
Principal Works - 2 symphonies including *Horizons;* violin concerto; choral works; 3 string quartets; cantatas.

SHERIFF, NOAM
1935, Israeli
Principal Works - Serial music and Oriental and Jewish influences. *Chaconne* for orchestra (1968); *Heptaprisms* for chamber orchestra (1965); Dance: *Cain* on tape (1969); *Metamorphoses on a Galliard* for orchestra; piano sonata; choral pieces; piano and chamber pieces.

SHIFRIN, SEYMOUR
1926, American
Principal Works - *Chamber Symphony* for orchestra (1954); *3 Pieces* (1958); *Satires of Circumstance* for mezzo-soprano and 6 instruments (1964); *Responses* for piano; *Serenade for 5 Instruments* (1954); other piano and chamber works.

SHINOHARA, MAKOTO
1931, Japanese
Principal Works - Electronic music. *Visions II* for orchestra (1970); *Alternance* for percussion (1961); *Mémoires* on tape (1966); *Tendance* for piano (1969).

SHNITKE, ALFRED
1934, Russian
Principal Works - Electronic music. *the Yellow Sound,* for 9 instruments, tape, chorus and visuals (1973); oratorio *Nagasaki* (1958); 2 violin concertos; concerto for piano, for oboe, for harp and strings (1970); string quartet; chamber music including violin sonata; piano pieces and songs; electronic works; film and theater music; *Pianissimo* for orchestra.

SHOSTAKOVICH, DMITRI DMITRIEVICH
1906-1975, Russian
Principal Works - Operas: *The Nose,* Op. 15, based on Gogol (1927) ; *Lady Macbeth of Misensk,* Op. 29 (1930-32); Ballets: *The Age of Gold,* Op. 22 (1930); *Bolt ,* Op. 27 (1931); *The Limpid Stream,* Op. 39 (1935); Cantata: *Songs of the Forests.* Orchestral: Symphony No. 1, F major, Op. 10 (1924-25); Symphony No. 5, D major, Op. 47 (1937) (A composer's answer to just criticism); Symphony No. 6, B minor, Op. 53 (1939); Symphony No. 7, C major, Op. 60 (1941), *Leningrad;* Symphony No. 9, E flat major, Op. 70 (1945-46); Symphony No. 10, E minor, Op. 93 (1953); Symphony No. 11, Op. 103 (1957), *Year 1905;* Symphony No. 12 (1961); Symphony No. 13 *Babi Yar,* Chorus and text by Yevtushenko (1962); Festive Overture, Op. 96; Concerto for Piano, Trumpet, and Strings, Op. 35 (1933); Piano Concerto No. 2, Op. 101 (1957); and one other piano concerto; Violin Concerto, Op. 99 (1956) and 2 other violin

concertos; Cello Concerto in E flat major, Op. 107; *Poem of Fatherland* (1948).

Chamber Music: 13 String Quartets (1938, 1944, 1946, 1949, 1952, 1956, 1973, 1974); Quintet, G minor, Op. 57 (piano and strings) (1940); Trio, E minor, Op. 67 (piano, violin, cello) (1944), Piano: 24 *Preludes,* Op. 34 (1932-33); 2 Sonatas (1926, 1942). Songs: From Jewish Folk Poetry (1948); From Pushkin (1936); From Raleigh, Shakespeare, Burns (1942); From Michelangelo (1974); Film music.

SICILIANOS, YORGO
1922, Greek
Principal Works - Ballet: *Bacchantes* (1959); a symphony (1958); concerto for orchestra (1954) for cello (1963); choral works; string quartets and other chamber pieces; piano music; theater music.

SIEGMEISTER, ELIE
1909, American
Principal Works - 5 symphonies; theater works including *Sing Out Sweet Land, The Western Suite;* orchestral: *Ozark Set; Sunday in Brooklyn; Abraham Lincoln Walks at Midnight; Prairie Legend.* Opera: *The Plough and the Stars* after O'Casey; sextet for brass and percussion; American folk songs.

SILVESTROV, VALENTIN VASILIEVICH
1937, Russian
Principal Works - Twelve tone music! 2 symphonies; *Monodia* (1965); *Hymn* for 5 chamber groups (1967) and other chamber pieces; piano works; songs; film music.

SIMS, EZRA
1928, American
Principal Works - Microtonal music, musique concrète, tape collages. Theater and dance pieces, some on tapes; string quartets including no. 3 with quarter tones (1962); vocal and other chamber pieces.

SINIGAGLIA, LEONE
1868-1944, Italian
Principal Works - *Danze piemontesi* (1905) for orchestra; *Rapsodia piemontese* for violin and orchestra; violin concerto; chamber music; piano pieces including Piedmont folk songs; other songs.

SKALKOTTAS, NIKOS
1904-1949, Greek
Principal Works - Twelve tone music! Orchestral: *36 Greek Dances* (1936); *Symphonic Suite no. 2* (1944); 3 piano concertos; choral pieces; chamber music including 4 string quartets; piano suites and other piano pieces; songs.

SKILTON, CHARLES SANFORD
1868-1941, American
Principal Works - American Indian materials. Opera: *Kalopin* (1930); *Suite Primeval* for orchestra; *Indian Dances* (1915); *Shawnee Indian Hunting Dance* (1930); choral and chamber pieces.

SMITH, DAVID STANLEY
1877-1949, American
Principal Works - 4 symphonies; *Overture:Prince Hal* (1912); *Epic Poem* (1935); Requiem for violin and orchestra (1939); *Visions of Isaiah* for chorus, soloists and orchestra (1927); 10 string quartets; piano pieces.

SKROWACZEWSKI, STANISLAW
1923, Polish
Principal Works - Ballet, 4 symphonies; concerto for English horn; choral works; string quartets; piano pieces.

SLAVENSKI, JOSIP
1896-1955, Croatian
Principal Works - Orchestral: *Balkanphonia* (1929); violin concerto; *Symphonie des Orients* for orchestra and chorus; chamber music; piano pieces; film music.

SLONIMSKY, SERGE (MIKHAILOVICH)
1932, Russian
Principal Works - Opera: *Virineia* (1967); *Master and Margarita;* Ballet: *Ikar* (1969); Cantata: *A Voice from the Chorus;* a symphony; Concerto Buffo (1965); choreographic miniatures; Concerto for 3 electric guitars and orchestra (1974); *Antiphonies* for string quartets, with free moving performers in and about the audience (1968); *Coloristic Fantasy* for piano (1972); piano and organ pieces; film music; songs.

SMITH, HALE
1925, American
Principal Works - *Rituals and Incantations* for orchestra (1974); *In Memoriam-Beryl Rubinstein* (1953) for chorus; band music; *Evocation* for piano; chamber and other piano pieces; songs with text by Langston Hughes.

SMITH, JULIA
1911, American
Principal Works - Opera: *Daisy* (1973); *Folkways Symphony* (1948); piano concerto (1939); band music; choral works; string quartet (1964); piano and chamber pieces; songs.

SMITH, LELAND
1925, American
Principal Works - Opera: *Santa Claus,* libretto by e.e. cummings (1957); *Machines of Loving Grace* for computer, bassoon and narrator (1970); orchestral pieces; chamber music.

SMITH, RUSSEL
1927, American
Principal Works - Opera: *The Unicorn in the Garden,* after Thurber (1956); ballet; orchestral pieces; 2 piano concertos; *Anglican Service in G* (1954); piano, organ and chamber pieces; film and tv music; songs.

SMITH, WILLIAM OVERTON
1926, American
Principal Works - Jazz materials! Concerto for jazz clarinet and orchestra; concertino for trumpet and jazz ensemble; chamber music including string quartet; *Quadrodram* for clarinet, trombone, piano, percussion, dancer, film (1970).

SMITH-BRINDLE, REGINALD
1917, English
Principal Works - Chamber opera: *Antigone* (1969); *Symphonic Variations* for orchestra; *Apocalypse* (1970) for orchestra; vocal solos with instrumental accompaniment; chamber pieces; film music.

SMYTH, ETHEL MARY
1858-1944, English
Principal Works - Opera: *The Wreckers* (1906); *The Boatswain's Mate* (1916); Mass in D (1893); *The Prison* for chorus (1930); orchestral works; piano and chamber pieces; organ music; songs.

SOLLBERGER, HARVEY
1938, American
Principal Works - *Chamber Variations for 12 players and conductor* (1964); Impromptu for piano (1968); *Musica transalpina* for soprano, baritone and 6 players (1964); Divertimento for flute, cello, piano (1970); string quartet and other chamber pieces.

SOMERS, HARRY (STEWART)
1925, Canadian
Principal Works - Twelve tone music and electronic music. Operas: *Louis Riel,* with tape (1967) and others; 3 ballets including *The House of Atreus* (1964); orchestral: *Passacaglia and Fugue* (1954); *Stereophony* (1962); 2 symphonies; piano concerto; 3 string quartets and other chamber pieces; choral and piano pieces; songs; film and tv music.

SOMERVELL, ARTHUR
1863-1937, English
Principal Works - Oratorio: *The Passion of Christ* (1914); cantata; *Christmas, 1926;* song cycles *Maud* and *A Shropshire Lad;* 4 children's operettas; orchestral works including a symphony, concertos; piano and violin solos; sacred and secular choral pieces.

SOMMER, VLADIMIR
1921, Czech.
Principal Works - *Vocal Symphony No. 1* with speaker, chorus and orchestra and 2 other symphonies; concertos for piano, for violin, for cello; choral pieces; chamber music including string quartets; film and theater music; songs.

SORABJI, KAIKHOSRU SHAPURJI
1892, English
Principal Works - Prohibits public performance of his works! 3 symphonies for orchestra and 3 for organ; 5 piano oncertos; choral and chamber pieces; 5 piano sonatas; *Opus clavicembalisticum* for 2 hours of piano; songs.

SORO, ENRIQUE
1884-1954, Chilean
Principal Works - Orchestral: *Sinfonia romántica* (1920); *Aires chilenos* (1942); *Suite en estilo antiguo* (1943); piano concerto (1919); choral and chamber pieces; piano music; songs.

SOURIS, ANDRÉ
1899-1970, Belgian
Principal Works - Orchestral: *Symphonies* (1939); *Hommage a Babeuf* for winds (1934); *Avertissement* for speakers and percussion (1926); choral music; chamber pieces for vocal and instrumental ensembles; film music.

SOUSTER, TIM (ANDREW JAMES)
1943, English
Principal Works - Electronic music! *Titus Groan Music* for wind quintet, tape and electronic instruments (1969); *Pelvic Loops,* tape work (1969); *Chinese Whispers* for percussion and 3 synthesizers (1970); *Triple Music II* for 3 orchestras (1970); *Music for Eliot's Waste Land* for piano, electric organ, soprano saxophone, 3 synthesizers (1970).

SOWERBY, LEO
1895-1968, American
Principal Works - 5 symphonies; concertos for piano, for cello, for organ, for violin; choral: *The Canticle of The Sun* (1944) with orchestra; oratorio: *Christ Reborn* (1950).

SPELMAN, TIMOTHY MATHER
1891-1970, American
Principal Works - *Saint's Days* (1925) for orchestra; *Pervigilium veneris* for chorus (1931); operas; piano and chamber pieces; songs.

SPIEGELMAN, JOEL (WARREN)
1933, American
Principal Works - Electronic music! *2 Movements* for orchestra (1957); *Kousochki* for four-hand piano; *The 11th Hour,* tape ballet (1969); Jewish sacred service with tape (1969); *Daddy* for actress, soprano, flute, oboe, conga drums and synthesizer.

STALVEY, DORRANCE
American
Principal Works - For Brass and Percussion: *Celebration - Principium* (1967); *Celebration - Sequent IV* (1980).

STARER, ROBERT
1924, Austrian
Principal Works - Opera: *The Intruder* (1956); ballets: *The Dybbuk* (1960); *Samson Agonistes* (1961); *Mutabili* for orchestra (1965); 3 symphonies; 3 piano concertos; *Concerto a 3* for clarinet, trumpet, trombone and strings (1954); chamber and choral music; piano pieces; songs.

STAROKADOMSKY, MIKHAIL LEONIDOVICH
1901-1954, Russian
Principal Works - Opera; operettas; concerto for orchestra (1937); violin concerto (1937); choral and chamber music; songs.

STEIN, RICHARD HEINRICH
1882-192, German
Principal Works - Quarter tone techniques! Opera; 2 *Konzertstücke* for cello and piano (1906); opera; symphonic pieces; piano music; songs.

STEINBERG, MAXIMILIAN OSSEIEVICH
1883-1946, Russian
Principal Works - *Tursib* Symphony No. 5 and 4 other symphonies; Ballet, after *Till Eulenspiegel;* violin concerto; 2 string quartets and other chamber pieces; piano music; songs and choral works.

STENHAMMER, KARL WILHELM EUGEN
1871-1927, Swedish
Principal Works - Operas: *Tirfing* (1898); *Das Fest auf Solhaug* (1899); 2 symphonies; 2 piano concertos; string quartets; choral and chamber works; piano pieces; songs.

STEUERMANN, EDUARD
1892-1964, Russian/American
Principal Works - Cantata: *Auf der Galerie,* after Kafka (1964); orchestral pieces; 2 string quartets and other chamber works; choral music; piano pieces; songs.

STILL, WILLIAM GRANT
1895-1978, American
Principal Works - First black symphonic composer who began as a popular band arranger: *Afro-American* symphony (1931); *Poem for Orchestra* (1944); Fourth Symphony (1949); *Troubled Island* (1938); opera: *Costaso* (1949); *Darker America* (1924); *From The Black Belt* (1926); cantata: *And They Lynched Him On a Tree* (1940); *In Memoriam: The Colored Soldiers Who Died for Democracy* (1944) for orchestra; *Festive Overture* (1947); chamber music; *Lenox Avenue* for speaker, chorus and orchestra, also as a ballet.

STOCKHAUSEN, KARLHEINZ
1928, German

Principal Works - Worldwide recognition as influence in electronic, serial, aleatory, graphic, musique concréte and spatial concepts of musical composition! *Kreuzspiel* for orchestra (1951); *Formel* for orchestra (1951); *Punkte* for orchestra (1952); *Kontrapunkte* for 10 instruments (1952); *mobile Klavierstücke XI* (1956); *Gesang der Jünglinge* (1956); *Zyklus* for a percussionist beginning on any page; *Stimmung*, atmosphere tuning for vocal ensemble; *Inori* (adorations) for stage, for soloist and orchestra; *Carré* for 4 orchestras and 4 choruses (1959); *Kontakte* for piano, tape and percussion; *Mikrophonie I* for electronics, tamtam and 2 microphones; *Mikrophonie II* for Hammond organ, chorus, and electronics; *Prozession* for electric viola, tamtam, piano and electronics; *Hymnen*, national anthems, on tape only (1966); with soloists (1967); with orchestra (1969); 17 texts for *intuitive music*, unspecified instruments; *Mantra* for 2 pianos and electronics; *Trans* for orchestra (1971); *Ylem* for 19 or more players and singers; *Musik im Bauch* for 6 percussionist and music boxes (1975).

STOESSEL, ALBERT FREDERIC
1894-1943, American

Principal Works - *Suite antique* for 2 violins and piano (1922), opera; orchestral pieces; choral and chamber works; piano pieces; songs.

STOUT, ALAN
1932, American

Principal Works - 4 symphonies; a Passion and other choral works; 10 string quartets; cello sonata; chamber pieces.

STRANG, GERALD
1908, American

Principal Works - Electronic music pieces; 2 symphonies; cello concerto; Percussion Music for 3 players (1935).

STRAUSS, OSCAR
1870-1054, German

Principal Works - Operettas: *A WaltzDream (Ein Walzertraum)* (1907); *The Chocolate Soldier (Der tapfere Soldat)* (1908); Waltz: *My Hero, The Letter Song, Sympathy; The Last Waltz (Der letzte Walzer)* (1920); *Teresina* (1925); *The Three Waltzes (Drei Walzer)* (1936). Orchestral: *Der Traum ein Leben*, Overture; *Alt-Wiener Reigen; Love's Roundabout (Liebeskarusell); Serenade.*

STRAUSS, RICHARD
1864-1949, German

Principal Works - Operas: *Gantram* (1894); *Feuersnot* (1901); *Salome; Elektra: Der Rosenkavalier; Ariadne auf Naxos; Die Frau ohne Schatten; Intermezzo* (1924); *Die ägyptische Helena* (1928); *Arabella: Die schweigsame Frau* 91935); *Friedenstag* (1938); *Daphne* (1938); *die Liebe der Danae* (1940); *Capriccio* (1914); ballet: *Josephslegende* (1914).Orchestral: Symphony in F minor (1884); *Aus Italien, Macbeth, Don Juan* (1890); *Symphonia domestica, Ein Heidenleben; Don Quixote; Also sprach Zarathustra; Till Eulenspiegel's lustige Streiche; Tod under Verklärung;* violin concerto; 2 horn concertos; an oboe concerto; choral works; *4 Last Songs* with orchestra (1948); string quartet; cello sonata; piano quartet; violin sonata; woodwind pieces; piano pieces; songs.

STRAVINSKY, IGOR (FEODOROVICH)
1882-1971, Russian/American

Principal Works - Opera and stage music: *The Firebird (L'Oiseau de feu)* (1910)–New orchestral suite (1945); *Petrouchka* (1911)– Orchestral suite (new version, 1946); *The Rite of Spring (Le Sacre du printemps)* (1913)–orchestral suite 1914); *Le Rossignol* (1914); *Renard* (1916-17); *Les Noces* (1917-23); *The Soldier's Tale (L'Histoire du soldat)* (1918); *Pulcinella* (1920) (after Pergolesi)–Suites (arr. for orchestra) 1924; *Suite Italienne;* violin and piano, 1934); *Oedipus Rex* (1921); *Mavra* (1921-22); Russian maiden's song (Parasha); *Apollon Musagete (Apollo, Leader of the Muses)* (1928); *Le Baiser de la fée* (themes from Tchaikovsky) (1928); Divertissement (Concert Suite); *Persèphone* (1934); Jeu *des Cartes (The Card Party)*(1937); *Orpheus* (1948); *The Rake's Progress* (1951); *Agon* (1957); *The Flood* (1962). Orchestral: *Fireworks* (Feu d'artifice) (1908); *Song of the Nightingale (Chant du rossignol)* (1913-14); *Ragtime for Eleven Instruments* (1918); *Symphonies of Wind Instruments* (1920); Concerto for Piano and Wind Orchestra (1923-24); Caprices for Piano and Orchestra (3) (1929); Concerto, D major (violin and orchestra) (1931); Concerto, E flat, *Dumbarton Oaks* (1938); *Symphony of Psalms* (1930); Symphony in C (1940); *Circus Polka* (1942); *Norwegian Moods* (1942); Symphony in Three Movements (1945); *Ebony Concerto* for clarinet and swing band (1945); Concerto in D for strings (1946); *Canticum Sacrum* (1956); *Threni* (1957-58); *Monumentum pro Gesualdo* (1960); *Movements* for piano and orchestra (1960); *A Sermon, Narrative and Prayer* (1962); *Abraham and Isaac* for baritone and chamber orch. (1963). *Requiem Canticles* for soloists, chorus and orchestra (1966). Chamber Music: *Elegy for J.F.K.* (1964) for baritone and instruments; Three Pieces for String Quartet (1914); Octet for Wind Instruments (1923); Tango for Violin and Piano (1941); Septet (strings, wind, and piano) (1953), *In Memorian Dylan Thomas.* Choral: Mass (1948); Cantata (1952); *Tres Sacrae Cantiones* (1957-59). Vocal: *Three ShakespeareSongs* (1953). Piano: 2 Sonatas (1904) (1924); Serenade in A (1925); Concerto for 2 Pianos (1935); Sonata for 2 Pianos.

STRINGFIELD, LAMAR
1897-1959, American

Principal Works - Folkdrama: *Carolina Charcoal* (1952); *From The Southern Mountains* including *Cripple Creek* (1928) for orchestra; *The Legend of John Henry* for orchestra; chamber and choral pieces.

STRINGHAM, EDWIN JOHN
1890-1974, American

Principal Works - *The Ancient Mariner* for orchestra (1928); symphony (1929); choral and chamber works; songs.

STRUBE, GUSTAV
1867-1953, German/American

Principal Works - Operas; 2 symphonies; violin concertos and other orchestral works; choral and chamber pieces.

STÜRMER, BRUNO
1892-1958, German

Principal Works - *Die Messe des Maschinenmenschen* for chorus (1932); orchestral works, some for stage; concertos for cello, for violin, for piano; chamber music; piano pieces; songs.

SUBOTNICK, MORTON
1933, American
Principal Works - Prominent modernist in electronics, mixed media, *Ghost* techniques, including film and tapes! *Play,* 4 pieces for varied combinations of instruments, electronics, and film (1962); serenades for instruments and tape (1959); *Silver Apples of the Moon* on tape (1967); *The Wild Bull* tape (1968); *Touch* tape (1969); *Ritual Game Room* for tape, dancer, 4 game players, with lights and no audience; *After the Butterfly* for solo trumpet; 7 instruments and electronic score (1979); *The First Dream of Light* for tuba, piano and electronic ghost score (1979).

SUCHOŇ, EUGEN
1908, Czech.
Principal Works - Opera: *The Whirlpool; Svatopluk;* cantata: *Psalm of the Carpathian Land; Pictures of Slovakia* piano and violin pieces with orchestra; choral and chamber music; piano pieces; songs.

SUDERBURG, ROBERT
1936, American
Principal Works - *Orchestra Music I, II, III (1969, 1971, 1973);* concerto for piano (1974); Concert Mass for chorus (1960); 2 cantatas with orchestra; piano and chamber pieces.

SUK, JOSEF
1874-1935, Czech.
Principal Works - Symphonies: *Asrael, Prague* and other symphonic poems; *Things Lived and Dreamed* (Zivotem snem), a piano cycle; other piano and chamber pieces.

SURINACH, CARLOS
1915, Spanish/American
Principal Works - Opera; Dance music: *Ritmo jondo* (1953); *Embattled Garden* (1958); *Feast of Ashes;* 3 symphonies; *Symphonic Variations* (1963); piano concerto (1974); *Songs of the soul* for chorus; *Flamenco meditations* for voice and piano; chamber and other choral pieces; piano music; songs.

SUTER, HERMANN
1870-1926, Swiss
Principal Works - Oratorio: *Le laudi di San Francesco d'Assisi* (1924); violin concerto; symphony; chamber music and other choral works; piano pieces, songs.

SUTERMEISTER, HEINRICH
1910, Swiss
Principal Works - Operas: *Romeo und Juliet*(1940); *Die Zauberinsel; Raskolnikoff* (1948); *Madame Bovary* (1967); 3 piano concertos; concerto for 2 pianos; cello concerto; other orchestral works; choral and chamber pieces; songs.

SVIRIDOV, GEORGY VASSILIEVICH
1915, Russian
Principal Works - *Oratorio pathétique* (1958); *Miniature Triptych* for piano; musical comedies; orchestral works; choral and chamber music; piano pieces; film music; songs.

SWANSON, HOWARD
1909, American
Principal Works - *Short Symphony* (1948); Symphony No. 3 (1970); 4 preludes to T.S. Eliot poems (1947) for piano; chamber music.

SWIFT, RICHARD
1927, American
Principal Works - Serial music. Opera: *The Trial of Tender O'Shea* (1964); *A Coronal* (1956); *Extravagance* (1962) for orchestra; symphony (1970); concertos for piano, for violin; *Stravaganza* chamber works and 4 string quartets; piano pieces.

SYDEMAN, WILLIAM (JAY)
1928, American
Principal Works - Serial music and tape and visual materials. *Orchestral Abstractions* (1958); *Oecumenicus* (1966); *Studies for Orchestra;* concerto for four-hand piano with chamber orchestra and tape; *concerti da camera* for chamber groups; *Projections no. 1* for amplified violin, tape, slides (1968).

SZABO, FERENC
1902-1969, Hungarian
Principal Works - Opera; ballet: *Ludas Matyi* (1960); oratorio: *The Sea Is Rising* (1955); orchestral works including concerto for orchestra; string quartets; film music; piano pieces.

SZALONEK, WITOLD
1927, Polish
Principal Works - *Les sons* (1965); *Mjtazioni* (1966); for orchestra; choral and chamber works; piano pieces.

SZELIGOWSKI, TADEUSZ
1896-1963, Polish
Principal Works - Opera: *The Revolt of the Schoolboys;* ballet: *The Peacock and the Girl;* orchestral: *Epitaph for Szymanowski;* concertos for violin, for piano, for clarinet; sacred choral; string quartets; piano music; songs.

SZERVÁNSZKY, ENDRE
1911, Hungarian
Principal Works - Twelve tone music! Ballet suite: *Oriental Tale* (1949); concerto for orchestra (1954); *6 pieces* (1959); *Variations* (1965); concertos for flute, for clarinet, string quartets; choral pieces; piano music, songs.

SZOKOLAY, SÁNDOR
1931, Hungarian
Principal Works - Operas: *Vérnász* (1964); *Hamlet* (1968); ballets; concertos for piano, for trumpet, for violin; choral works including oratorios; piano and chamber pieces.

SZYMANOWSKI, KAROL (MACIEJ)
1882-1937, Polish
Principal Works - Operas: *Hagith* (1922); *Król Rober* (1926); ballet: *Harnasie* (1935); orchestral works including 4 symphonies; 2 violin concertos and a *Symphonie Concertante* for piano and orchestra; a Stabat Mater and other choral orks; string quartets and more chamber pieces; Polish folk materials, mazurkas and piano pieces; songs.

TAILLEFERRE, GERMAINE
1892, French
Principal Works - Opera: *Il etait un petit navire* (1951); ballet and theater music; concertino for harp and orchestra; piano concerto; piano and chamber pieces; film music; songs.

TAKAHASHI, YUJI
1938, Japanese

Principal Works - Stochastic and computer techniques. *Metatheses* for piano (1968); *Orphika* for orchestra (1969); *Time* tape work; *6 Stoicheia* for 4 violins (1967).

TAKEMITSU, TORU
1930, Japanese
Principal Works - Some tape works: *November Steps No. 1* for shaku hachi, biwa and orchestra; *Requiem* for strings; *Coral Island* for soprano and orchestra; *Music of Tree (1961); Asterism* for piano and orchestra; piano and chamber pieces; vocal pieces.

TAL, JOSEF
1910, Polish-Israeli
Principal Works - Opera: *Ashmedai* 1973); electronic ballet music; 2 symphonies cantata: *Call Of The Fallen Soldiers;* 5 piano concertos including 1 on tape; concertos for harpsichord, for viola; choral and chamber music; piano pieces; songs.

TANSMAN, ALEXANDRE
1897, Polish/French
Principal Works - Symphony No. 5 (1942); *In Memoriam* Symphony No. 6 (1943); Symphony No. 7 (1944); Music for orchestra (1948); oratorio: *The Prophet Isaiah* (1950); *Triptyque* for strings (1930); *Suite Divertissement* (1928); String quartets No. 5, 6, 7; Piano Sonata no. 4; *2 Symphonic Moments* for orchestra; *Capriccio* for orchestra (1955); pieces for 1 and 2 pianos; 5 other symphonies; ballet.

TARP, SVEND ERIK
1908, Danish
Principal Works - Opera: *Prinsessen i der Fjerne* (1953); 3 symphonies; ballets; *Te Deum* for chorus; other choral and chamber pieces; piano music; film music.

TATE, PHYLLIS
1911, English
Principal Works - Opera: *The Lodger* (1960); concerto for saxophone; *A Secular Requiem* for voices, orchestra, and organ; concerto for cello; choral and chamber pieces.

TAURIELLO, ANTONIO
1931, Argentinian
Principal Works - Opera and orchestral music; *Transparencias* for 6 instrumental groups (1965); 2 piano concertos; orchestral works featuring violin and clarinet; piano and chamber music.

TAYLOR, (JOSEPH) DEEMS
1885-1966, American
Principal Works - Noted music critic! Composed operas: *The King's Henchman* (1926); *Peter Ibbetson* (1931), orchestral: *Through The Looking Glass* (1919); *Jurgen* (1925); cantata: *The Chambered Nautilus* (1914); piano and chamber pieces; songs.

TCHEREPNIN, ALEXANDER NIKOLAIEVICH
1899-1977, Russian
Principal Works - Ballet: *Ajanta's Frescoes* (1923); operas; ballets; 4 symphonies; 6 piano concertos; other orchestral works; piano and chamber music; choral pieces; string quartets; songs.

TENNEY, JAMES C.
1934, American
Principal Works - *13 Ways of Looking at a Blackbird* for tenor and 5 instruments (1958); *Collage no. 1, Blue Suede Shoes, after Elvis Presley,* musique concrète (1961); *Erogdos I* for 2 tapes and computer, forward or reverse, solo or simultaneous, with or without accompaniment; *Fabric for Che,* computerized tape (1967).

THOME, JOEL
American
Principal Works - *Savitri: Traveler of the Worlds* (1980) for mezzosoprano, percussion, winds, strings, electronic sound modifiers, short wave radios.

THOMPSON, RANDALL
1899, American
Principal Works - Opera: *Solomon and Balkis; The Peaceable Kingdom* for chorus, and *Americana, Alleluia ,The Testament of Freedom* for chorus; 3 symphonies; orchestral works; piano and chamber music; songs.

THOMSON, VIRGIL
1896, American
Principal Works - Music critic! Composed operas: *Four Saintys in Three Acts, The Mother Of Us All* (1947); *Lord Byron* (1970); ballet: *Filling Station* (1937); orchestral: *Four Portraits* (1931); *Arcadian Songs and Dances* (1949); Cello Concerto (1949); *Three Pictures* (1948-1952); String quartet No. 2 (1948); *Stabat Mater* for soprano and string quartet (1932); *Five Songs from William Blake* (1952).

THORNE, FRANCIS
1922, American
Principal Works - Serial and jazz forms! *Liebesrock* for 3 electric guitars and orchestra (1969); *6 Set Pieces for 13 players* (1967); 3 symphonies; a one-movement symphony; concerto for piano (1966); piano pieces.

TIESSEN, (RICHARD GUSTAV) HEINZ
1887-1971, German
Principal Works - Ballet: *Salambo* (1929); 2 symphonies; orchestral works; piano and violin music with orchestra; choral music; piano and chamber pieces; songs.

TIGRANIAN, ARMEN
1879-1950, Armenian
Principal Works - Operas: *Anush, David-Beg;* piano music with orchestra; Armenian folk music; chamber pieces.

TIPPETT, MICHAEL (KEMP)
1905, English
Principal Works - Operas:*The Midsummer Marriage* (1955); *The Knot Garden* (1970); *Ice Break* (1977); *King Priam* (1962); 4 symphonies; Concerto for double string orchestra; Concerto for orchestra; Fantasia Concertante on a Theme of Handel, and another on a Theme of Corelli. oratorio: *A Child Of Our Time* (1944); cantata: *The Vision of St. Augustine* (1965); *Boyhood's End* song cycle; piano concerto; 3 piano sonatas; 3 string quartets; piano and organ pieces; chamber works; songs.

TISHCHENKO, BORIS IVANOVICH
1939, Russian
Principal Works - Ballets: *The Twelve* (1964); *Yaroslavna* (1974); cantata *Lenin Lives* (1959); 3 symphonies; concertos for piano, for cello, for violin; chamber works; film and theater music; songs.

TOCH, ERNST
1887-1964, Austrian/American
Principal Works - Symphony No. 3 (1955) and 6 other symphonies; *Big Ben Variations* for orchestra; *Notturno* (1953); and *Peter Pan, Op. 76, 1956* for orchestra; piano and cello concertos; *Geographical Fugue* for chorus (1930); 13 string quartets; other chamber pieces; piano music; film music; songs.

TOMASI, HENRI (FREDIEN)
1901-1971, French
Principal Works - Operas; *Sampiero Corso; The Silence of The Sea*; ballets; symphonic poems; concertos for over 13 individual instruments of the orchestra; choral and chamber pieces; piano music; songs.

TOMMASINI, VINCENZO
1878-1950, Italian
Principal Works - Ballet: *Le donne di buon amore,* after Scarlatti (1917); and two other ballets; operas; concertos for piano, for violin and for string quartet, and other orchestral works; string quartets and chamber pieces; piano music; film music; songs.

TOSAR ERRECART, HECTOR ALBERTO
1923, Uruguayan
Principal Works - *Toccata* (1940); 3 symphonies and other orchestral works; *Te Deum* (1959) and other works for chorus; *Stray Birds* for baritone and 11 instruments (1963) and other chamber music; piano pieces.

TOURNEMIRE, CHARLES (ARNAUD)
1870-1939, French
Principal Works - *L'orgue mystique,* 51 offices for the liturgical year and many other organ works; operas; 8 symphonies; choral sacred and secular music; cantata: *Le sang de la sirène* (1904); piano pieces; songs.

TOVEY, DONALD FRANCIS
1875-1940, English
Principal Works - Opera: *The Bride of Dionysus;* cello concerto in honor of Casals; a symphony; piano concerto; choral and chamber works; string quartets; piano pieces; songs.

TRAPP, (HERMANN EMIL ALFRED) MAX
1887-1971, German**Principal Works** - 7 symphonies; 3 orchestral concertos and other symphonic pieces; piano concerto; concertos for violin and cello; a cantata; string quartets and other chamber works; piano pieces; songs.

TRAVIS, ROY (ELIHU)
1922, American
Principal Works - Opera: *The Passion of Oedipus* (1965); *Symphonic Allegro* (1951) and *Collage* (1968) for orchestra; piano concerto (1969); pre-recorded: *Switched-On Ashanti* for synthesizer, flute and African instruments (1973); *African Sonata* (1966) for chamber group; piano pieces; songs.

TREMBLAY, GILLES
1932, Canadian
Principal Works - Electronsic music. *Phases et réseaux* for piano (1958); *Sonorization* on 24 tape channels (1967); *Kekoba* for 3 voices with ondes martenot and percussion (1965); *Cantile of durations* (cantique des durees) for orchestra (1960); *Champs II - Souffle* for winds, double bass, piano and percussion (1968); piano solos.

TRIMBLE, LESTER (ALBERT)
1923, American
Principal Works - *5 Episodes* for orchestra (1962); concerto for violin (1955); *Duo concertante* for 2 violins and orchestra (1963); opera; 3 symphonies; string quartets and other chamber pieces; choral music; *4 Fragments from the Canterbury Tales* for soprano, flute, clarinet and harpsichord (1958).

TRYTHALL, RICHARD
1939, American
Principal Works - Orchestral: *Composition for Piano and Orchestra* (1965); *Construzione per orchestra* (1967); *Coincidences* for piano (1969); *Variations on a Theme of Haydn* for woodwind quintet, tape (1975);Noah And The Flood.

TUDOR, DAVID (EUGENE)
1926, American
Principal Works - Modernist; aleatory and electronic/visual techniques; *Bandoneon!* with projections by Lowell Cross (1966); *Rainforest* for Merce Cunningham (1968); *Video/Laser II,* withCross and Carson Jeffries (1970).

TURINA, JOAQUIN
1882-1949, Spanish
Principal Works - Symphonic poem: *The Procession of the Virgin of the Dew (La Procesión del Rocio)* (1912); *Sevilliana Symphony* (1920); string quartet: *The Bull-Fighter's Prayer (La Oración del Torero);* piano pieces; songs.

UHL, ALFRED
1909, Austrian
Principal Works - *Konzertante Sinfonie* for clarinet and orchestra (1944); oratorio: *Gilgamesch;* opera; ballets; cantata and other choral music; chamber works including string quartets; *48 Études for clarinet.*

URIBE HOLGUIN, GUILLERMO
1880-1971, Colombian
Principal Works - 11 symphonies; opera; 2 violin concertos and a concerto for piano; choral and chamber works including string quartets; many *Trozos en el sentimento popular,* piano pieces; songs.

URRUTIA BLONDEL, JORGE
1905, Chilean
Principal Works - Ballet: *La guitarra del diablo* (1942); orchestral and other dance music; chamber and choral pieces; piano music; Chilean folk songs.

USANDIZAGA, JOSÉ MARIA
1887-1915, Spanish
Principal Works - Opera: *Mendy-Mendiyan (1910); Las golondrinas* (1914); vocal and orchestral pieces; 2 string quartets; many piano pieces; organ music.

USSACHEVSKY, VLADIMIR
1911, Russian/American
Principal Works - Modernist, electronic music! Choral: *Jubilee Cantata* for baritone, chorus, narrator and orchestra (1938); *The Creation,* prologue for 4 choruses, orchestra and tape (1961); piano concerto (1951) and other orchestral works; electronic: *Sonic Contours* for tape and instruments (1952); *Incantation* on tape with Luening (1953); *Poem of Cycles and Bels* for orchestra and tape, with Luening (1954); *Piece for Tape Recorder* (1956); *Computer Piece No. 1* (1969); *We,* computer-synthesized tape score.

VAINBERG, MOISSEI SAMUILOVICH
1919, Polish/Russian
Principal Works - *Moldavian Rhapsody* for violin and orchestra; operas; ballets; 11 symphonies; concerto for trumpet, for cello; chamber works including string quartets; piano pieces; film music; songs.

VARESE, EDGARD (VICTOR ACHILLE CHARLES)
1883-1965, French/American
Principal Works - Modernist: electronic music and

techniques, usage of non-conventional instruments and dissonance! *Amériques* for orchestra (1921); *Offrande* for orchestra and soprano (1922); *Octandre* for 7 winds and double bass; *Density 21.5* for flute solo; *Hyperprism* for woodwinds, brass and percussion (1925); *Arcana* for orchestra (1927); *Ionisation* for percussion and 2 sirens (1931); *Equatorial* for bass, brass, piano, organ, percussion and Theremin (1934); *Déserts* for winds, brass, percussion, tape (1954);   *Poème électronique* tape (1958); *Nocturnal* for soprano, chorus of basses and orchestra (1961), posthumously completed by Chou Wen-Chung (1968).

VASSILENKO, SERGEI NIKIFOROVICH
1872-1956, Russian
Principal Works - Opera: *Buran* (1939); 5 symphonies; *Circus Nocturnus, No. 9* for orchestra; *Chinese Suite* and *Hindu Suite* (1927); *Uzbek Suite* (1942); concertos for cello, for trumpet, for violin, for balalaika; piano and chamber pieces.

VAUGHAN WILLIAMS, RALPH
1872-1958, English
Principal Works - Orchestral: Symphonies: No. 1, *A Sea Symphony* (1910); No. 2, *A London Symphony*, G major (1914); No. 3, *A Pastoral Symphony* (1922); No. 4, F minor (1934); No. 5, D major (1943); No. 6, E minor (1945)47); No. 7, *Antarctica* (1952); No. 8, D minor (1956); No. 9, E minor (1958); *Fantasia on Greensleeves* (1929); *Fantasia on a Theme by Tallis* (double string orchestra) (1910); *Folk Song Suite* (military band; orchestra) (1924); *The Lark Ascending* (violin and chamber orchestra) (1914); *The Wasps* (incidental music to Aristophanes) (1909); Concerto, two pianos and orchestra; *Concerto Academico*, D minor, violin and orchestra (1925); Concerto, bass tuba and orchestra (1954). Choral: Mass, G minor (1922); *Flos Campi* (viola obbligato, chorus, small orchestra) (1925); *Five Tudor Portraits* (cantata) (1936); *Serenade to Music* (Shakespeare) (1938); *This Day* (Christmas cantata) (1954); Oratorio: *Sancta Civitas* (1926); Cantata: *Hodie* (1953). Operas: *Hugh the Drover* (Child), 2 Acts (1911–14); *The Shepherds of the Delectable Mountains* (Bunyan) (1922); *Sir John in Love*, 4 Acts (Shakespeare) (1929); *Job, a Masque for Dancing* (1931);*The Poisoned Kiss*, 3 Acts (Sharpe) (1936); *Riders to the Sea*, 1 Act(Synge) (1937); *Pilgrim's Progress* (Bunyan) (1952). Songs: *Linden Lea* (Barnes) (1902); *Silent Noon* (No. 2 of the cycle *The Hosue of Life)* (Rossetti) (1918); *Songs of Travel*, 2 sets (1905; 1907); *On Wenlock Edge* (tenor and piano quintet) (Housman) (1909); Motets; string quartets; piano and organ pieces; film music.

VEGA, AURELIO DE LA
1925, Cuban/American
Principal Works - Some serial music! *Overture to a serious Farce* (1950); *Symphony in 4 Parts* (1960); *Intrata* (1972); *Structures for piano and string quartet* and other chamber works; *Segments for piano and violin* (1964); electronic: *Vectors*, tape (1963); *Tangents* for violin and tape (1973).

VERESS, SÁNDOR
1907, Hungarian
Principal Works - *Homage to Paul Klee,* 7 movements, 7 pictures for 2 pianos and strings; Hungarian folk-music; Concerto for violin; *Sinfonia Minneapolitana; Songs of The Seasons* for chorus; ballets; 2 symphonies; concertos for string quartet and orchestra, for piano; piano and chamber pieces; songs.

VIANA DA MOTA, JOSE
1868-1948, Portugese
Principal Works - Symphony A patria; *Invocação dos Lusiadas for chorus and orchestra; 5 Portuguese Rhapsodies* for piano; chamber works and other choral pieces; other piano pieces; songs.

VIERK, LOIS
American
Principal Works - *Gingko* for piano and vibraphone.

VIERU, ANATOL
1926, Rumanian
Principal Works - *Sanduhr* for orchestra (1969); concerto for orchestra (1954); concertos for violin, for cello; *Jeux* for piano and orchestra (1963); oratorio: *Miorita* 91957); other choral pieces; chamber music including string quartets; piano pieces; some electronic music.

VILLA-LOBOS, HEITOR
1887-1959, Brazilian
Principal Works - Symphonic poems: *Amazonas* (1917), *Uirapurú* (1917); *Papagaio do Moleque* (1932); Symphonies: No. 1 (The Unexpected, 1916), No. 2 (Resurrection, 1917), No. 4 (Victory, 1921), No. 5 (Peace, 1921), No. 6 (1944), No. 7 (*America*, 1945). Oratorios: *Manducarara* (1940); *Vidapura* (1919); *The Discovery of Brazil (1937);* 16 choral song sequences (1920-29); Trios Nos. 2 and 3 for violin, cello, and piano (1915, 1918); String quartets: No. 2 (1915), No. 3 (1916), No. 4 (1917), No. 6 (1938), No. 7 (1942), No. 8 (1944), No. 9 (1945), No. 10 (1946), No. 11 (1947), No. 12 (1950); *Studies and Preludes for Guitar;* Nonet (1923). *Bachianas Brasileiras:* No. 1 (cello and orchestra, 1930), No. 5 (soprano and celli, 1938), No. 7 (orchestra, 1942), No. 8 (orchestra, 1944), No. 9 (string orchestra, 1945), No. 2 *The Little Train of the Caipira.*

VINCENT, JOHN
1902-1977, American
Principal Works - *Symphony In D* (1955); *Symphonic Poem after Descartes* (1958); opera: *Primeval Void* (1969); another symphony; ballet; *Benjamin Franklin Suite* with glass harmonica (1962); *Rondo Rhapsody* (1965) and *The Phoenix* (1965) for orchestra; 2 string quartets; choral works; other chamber pieces; songs.

VIVES, AMADEO (ROIG)
1871-1932, Spanish
Principal Works - Opera: *Maruxa* (1914); *Dona Francisquita* (1923) and many other *zarzuelas;* piano and choral pieces; songs.

VLAD, ROMAN
1919, Rumanian/Italian
Principal Works - Some twelve tone music! Operas; ballets; film and theater music; choral and chamber works; piano pieces; orchestral works: *Sonnet to Orpheus* for harp and orch.; Variations on theme from *Don Giovanni* for piano and orch.; dance: *Lady of the Camellias.*

VLADIGEROV, PANTCHO
1899, Bulgarian
Principal Works - Opera: *Tsar Kaloyan* (1936); ballet; 5 symphonies; piano and violin concertos; chamber works; piano music; songs.

VLASOV, VLADIMIR ALEXANDROVICH
1903, Russian

Principal Works - Operas; ballets; orchestral works; concertos for cello; choral works including cantatas and ortorios; chamber music; songs.

FLIJMAN, JAN VAN
1935, Dutch

Principal Works - Some twelve tone music! Opera: *Reconstructie* (1969) with others; *Interpolations* for tape and orchestra; *Sonata* for orchestra and piano, 3 groups (1966); *Gruppi* for 20 instruments and percussion, 1962; wind quintet (1959); songs.

VOGEL, WLADIMIR
1896-1935, Russian/Swiss

Principal Works - Twelve tone music! *Sprechstimmen* for chorus and orchestra; *Thyl Claes* for speaking chorus; *Die Flucht* (1964) for speaking chorus; concertos for cello, for violin; *12 varietudes* for violin, flute, clarinet, cello (1940); piano music; songs.

VOLKONSKY, ANDREI
1933, Russian/Swiss

Principal Works - Concerto for orchestra (1953); *Wanderer* concerto for soprano, violin, percussion and orchestra (1968); 2 cantatas; piano quintet (1954); string quartet (1955); piano pieces; songs.

VOORMOLEN, ALEXANDER
1895, Dutch

Principal Works - *The Three Horsemen* for orchestra, for Dutch folk song (1927); *Arethusa* (1947); *Chaconne en Fuga* (1958); concertos for 2 oboes, 1 oboe, for cello, for 2 harpsichords; string quartets; ballets; other chamber pieces; piano music; songs.

VYCPÁLEK, LADISLAW
1882-1969, Czech.

Principal Works - *Czech Requiem* for chorus and orchestra (1940); piano and chamber works; folk materials.

VYSHNEGRADSKY, IVAN
1893, Russian/French

Principal Works - Microtonal music, particularly quarter tones, with innovative quarter-tone piano. Orchestral works in microtonal technique; choral pieces; chamber music including string quartets; piano pieces, some for 2 pianos tuned a quarter-tone apart.

WAGENAAR, bernard
1894-1971, American

Principal Works - Opera: *Pieces of Eight* (1944); 4 symphonies; 5 *Tableaux* for cello and orchestra; triple concerto for flute, cello, harp; 4 string quartets; other orchestral and chamber works; piano pieces; songs.

WAGNER, JOSEPH FREDERICK
1900-1974, American

Principal Works - Orchestral and chamber works; piano pieces and string quartets; songs.

WAGNER-REGENY, RUDOLF
1903-1969, German

Principal Works - Operas: *Der Günstling* (1935); *Die Bürger von Calais* (1939); *Das Bergwerk zu Falun* (1961); ballets; orchestral works; choral and chamber pieces.

WALKER, GEORGE
1922, American

Principal Works - A symphony; *Variations; Passacaglia* for orch.; concerto for trombone; choral and chamber music including 2 string quartets; 2 sonatas for piano and other pieces; *Spatials; Spektra* for piano.

WALKER, ERNEST
1870-1949, English

Principal Works - Choral: *Ode To A Nightingale* for baritone, chorus and orchestra; sacred and secular works; orchestral pieces; chamber and piano music; organ works; songs.

WALLACE, WILLIAM
1860-1940, Scottish

Principal Works - *The Passing of Beatrice* (1892) and *Francois Villon* (1909), symphonic poems; orchestral and chamber works; choral music and *Freebooter Songs* for orchestra (1899).

WALTON, WILLIAM (TURNER) SIR
1902, English

Principal Works - 1916: Piano Quartet; *Facade—An Entertainment,* for reciter and chamber ensemble; 1925: *Portsmouth Point,* overture; 1926: *Siesta,* for orchestra; 1927: Viola Concerto; *Sinfonia Concertante,* for piano and orchestra; *Belshazzar's feast,* for baritone, chorus and orchestra; 1935: Symphony No. 1; *Escape Me Never,* film ballet; 1937: *Crown Imperial,* coronation march for orchestra; *In Honour of the City,* for chorus and orchestra; 1939: Violin Concerto; 1940: *The Wise Virgins,* ballet from the music of J.S. Bach; 1941: *Scapino,* overture; 1942: *Prelude and Fugue (The Spitfire),* for orchestra; 1943: *Henry V,* incidental music for film; *The Quest,* ballet; 1947: *Hamlet, incidental music for film; String Quartet in A minor; 1949 Violin Sonata; 1953 Orb and Sceptre,* coronation march for orchestra; Coronation Te Deum; 1954: *Troilus and Cressida,* opera; 1955: *Richard III,* incidental music for film; *Johannesburg Festival Overture;* 1956: Cello Concerto; 1957: *Partita,* for orchestra; 1960: Symphony No. 2; *Anon. in Love,* six songs for tenor and guitar; 1961: *Gloria,* for contralto, tenor and bass, chorus and orchestra; 1962: *A Song for the Lord Mayor's Table,* cycle of six songs for soprano and piano; 1963: *Variations on a Theme of Hindemith,* for orchestra; 1965: *The Twelve,* for choir and orchestra, or organ.

WARD, ROBERT (EUGENE)
1917, American

Principal Works - Operas: *The Crucible* after Arthur Miller (1961); *The Lady From Colorado* (1964); *He Who Gets Slapped;* 4 symphonies; other orchestral works; piano concerto (1968); chamber and choral music; piano pieces; songs; *Euphony for Orchestra* (1954).

WARD-STEINMAN, DAVID
1936, American

Principal Works - Some electronic and mixed-media works! Opera; ballets; a symphony and other orchestral works; *Prelude and Toccata* (162); *Arcturus* with tape and synthesizer; concerto for cello (1966); oratorio: *The Song of Moses;* othr choral pieces; chamber and vocal music; music for band; electronic music with and without instruments, and mixed-media pieces.

WARLOCK, PETER
(Pseudonym for British composer Philip Heseltine)

1894-1930

Principal Works - Much use of Elizabethan materials; edited *Elizabethan Lute Songs;* composed *The English Ayre, The Curlew* song cycle; *Capriol Suite* for orchestra (1926); many songs and choral works.

WARNER, HARRY WALDO
1874-1945, English

Principal Works - Opera; *Hampton Wick* for orchestra (1932); string quartet; 3 piano trios; choral pieces; piano music; songs.

WATTS, WINTER
1884, American

Principal Works - Symphonic poems (1909, 1923); many songs.

WEBER, BEN
1916, American

Principal Works - Some twelve tone music! Ballet: *The Pool of Darkness* (1949); *Symphony on Poems of William Blake* (1952); Violin Concerto (1954); Prelude and Passacaglia for orchestra; *Dolmen, an Elegy* (1964); concerto for piano (1961); Concert Poem for violin and orchestra (1970); choral works.

WEBERN, ANTON
1883-1945, Austrian

Principal Works - Disciple of Schoenberg, noted for his individual development of twelve tone music, his *Klangfarbenmelodie!* Orchestral: Passacaglia, op. 1 (1908); *6 Pieces* op. 6 (1910); *5 Pieces,* op. 10 (1913); *Symphony for small orchestra,* Op. 21 (1928); *Variations,* op. 30 (1940); *Das Augenlicht,* op. 26 (1935); cantata 1, op. 29 (1940) and 2, op. 31 (1943); *5 Movements* for string quartet, op. 5 (1909); *6 Bagatelles* for string quartet, op. 9 (1913); string trio, op. 20 (1927); quartet for violin, clarinet, saxophone and piano, op. 22 (1930); concerto for 9 instruments, op. 24 (1934); string quartet, op. 28 (1938); *4 Pieces for violin and piano* (1910); piano pieces, op. 27 (1936); *3 Little Pieces for piano and cello* (1914); *Variations* op. 27 for piano (1936); songs; arrangements of Bach pieces.

WEIGEL, EUGENE
1910, American

Principal Works - Operas and orchestral works; *Prairie Symphony* (1953); *Requiem* (1956); chamber and piano music; songs.

WEIGL, KARL
1881-1949, Austrian

Principal Works - Concertos for violin, for cello, for piano; 6 symphonies; 8 string quartets; choral and other chamber music.

WEILL, KURT
1900-1950, German/American
(also see listing under Best-
Known Popular Music Composers
and Writers)

Principal Works - Operas: *Der Protagonist* (1926); *Aufstieg und Fall der Stadt Mahagonny,* text by Brecht (1927); *Der Zar lässt sich photographieren* (1928); *Der Jasager* (1930); *Die Dreigroschenoper* (The Threepenny Opera) (1930); *Der Silbersee* (1933). Several American musical comedies including *Knickerbocker Holiday* and *Street Scene;* orchestral works; 2 cantatas; piano and chamber pieces; other vocal works.

WEINBERG, HENRY
1931, American

Principal Works - *Sinfonia* for chamber orchestra (1957); *Cantus commemorabilis I* (1966) for chamber group; other chamber pieces, including 2 string quartets; choral works.

WEINBERGER, JAROMIR
1896-1967, Czech./American

Principal Works - Operas: *Schwanda the Bagpiper* (1927); *The Beloved Voice* (1930); *Outcasts of Poker Flat,* after Bret Hrte (1932); *Wallenstein* (1937); orchestral: *Don Quixote;* Variations and Fugue on *Under The Spreading Chestnut Tree* (1939); *A Czech Rhapsody* (1941); *A Lincoln Symphony* (1941); piano and violin pieces; choral and band music; some sacred vocal pieces.

WEINER, LAZAR
1897, Russian/American

Principal Works - Much use of Jewish folk materials! An opera; ballets, after Jewish folk-lore; Sabbath Services for synagogues; cantatas; orchestral works; piano and chamber music; songs.

WEINZWEIG, JOHN (JACOB)
1913, Canadian

Principal Works - Somer serial music; also jazz and folk materials! A symphony (1940); *Symphonic Ode* (1958); *Dummiyah* (1969) for orchestra; concertos for piano, for in, for harp; string quartets, divertimenti and other chamber pieces; piano pieces; *Around the stage in 25 minutes during which a number of instruments are struck,* for percussionist; film music; songs.

WEIS, KAREL
1862-1944, Czech.

Principal Works - Opera: *Der polnische Jude* (1901); symphony and symphonic works; piano and chamber music; songs and folk arrangements.

WEISGALL, HUGO
1912, Czech./American

Principal Works - Opras: *The Tenor* (1952); *The Stronger* after Strindberg; *Six Characters in Search of an Author,* after Pirandello (1956); *Purgatory,* after Yeats (1961); *Athaliah* after Racine (1964); *Nine Rivers from Jordan* (1968); *Graven Images* for chamber group and other chamber pieces; ballets.

WEISMANN, JULIUS
1879-1950, German

Principal Works - Opera: *Leonce und Lena* (1925); *Der Pfiffige Magd* (1939); 3 symphonies; orchestral pieces; ballets; concertos.

WEISS, ADOLPH
1891-1971, American

Principal Works - *American Life* for orchestra (1928); dance music; string quartets and other chamber pieces.

WELLESZ, EGON
1885-1974, Austrian

Principal Works - Opera: *Alkestis* (1924); *Die Bakchantinnen* (1931); 9 symphonies, concertos for piano, for violin; choral sacred and secular works; *The Leaden Echo and the Golden Echo* for soprano and 4 instruments.

WERNICK, RICHARD
1934, American

Principal Works - Orchestral: *Aevia* (1965); *Haiku of*

Basho (1967); *Moonsongs from the Japanese* for 1 or 3 sopranos (1969); *Visions of Terror and Wonder* (1977); *Requiem-Kaddish: A Prayer for Jerusalem* (1971); chamber pieces including string quartets.

WESTERGAARD, PETERE
1931, American
Principal Works - Chamber operas: *Charivari* (1953); *Mr. and Mrs. Discobbolos* (1965); 5 Movements for small Orchestra (1958); cantata: *Leda and the Swan* for mezzo-soprano, clarinet, viola, vibraphone, marimba (1961) chamber music.

WETZ, RICHARD
1875-1935, German
Principal Works - Operas; 3 symphonies; a Kleist-Ouverture; concerto for violin; choral works including a Christmas oratorio; chamber pieces; piano music; many songs.

WETZLER, HERMANN HANS
1870-1943, American
Principal Works - *Assisi* for orchestra (1925); opera; choral and chamber works; songs.

WHITE, CLARENCE CAMERON
1880-1960, American
Principal Works - Opera: *Ouanga* (1932); Symphony (1928); *Elegy* (1954); other orchestral pieces; violin and piano music; chamber and choral pieces.

WHITHORNE, EMERSON
1884-1958, American
Principal Works - Orchestral: *New York Days and Nights* (1926); *Moon Trail* (1933); Incidental music to *Marco's Millions* (1928); *The Aeroplane* for piano (1920) chamber pieces.

WHITTENBERG, CHARLES
1927, American
Principal Works - *Fantasy* (1962); *Games of Five* (1968) for wind quintet; *Tryptich* for brass quintet (1962); *Variations* for 9 Players (1965); string quartet (1965); *Polyphony* for Solo Trumpet (1965); *The Run Off,* electronic collage.

WIDOR, CHARLES-MARIE
1844-1937, French
Principal Works - Operas: *Les pêcheurs de Saint-Jean* (1905); 4 symphonies and other orchestral pieces; concerto for cello, for piano; choral sacred music; piano and chamber pieces; *Symphonie gothique* and *Symphonie romaine* for organ and 6 other symphonies ; edition of Bach's organ works in collaboration with Albert Schweitzer.

WIGGLESWORTH, FRANK
1918, American
Principal Works - 2 symphonies and other orchestral pieces; choral and chamber music; stage music.

WIHTOL, JOSEPH
1863-1943, Latvian
Principal Works - A symphony (1887); Latvian fairy tale *Spriditis* (1908); choral and chamber music; piano pieces; much use of Latvian folk materials.

WILDBERGER, JACQUE
1922, Swiss
Principal Works - Some serial music! *Mouvements* for orchestra (1964); concerto for oboe (1963); *Épitaphe pour*

Evariste Galois for speaking chorus, soloists, orchestra and tape; other choral works; *La notte* for mezzo-soprano, 5 instruments and tape (1967) and other chamber works.

WILLAN, HEASLEY
1880-1968, English
Principal Works - *Deidre* (1946) and two other operas; orchestral music including 2 symphonies; Anglican church music; chamber and other choral music; piano and organ pieces: songs.

WILSON, OLLY
1937, American
Principal Works - *Akwan,* for piano, electric piano, amplified strings and orchestra (1970); *In memoriam—Martin Luther King Jr.* choral work with tape (1969); pieces for vocals and instruments; tape works.

WILSON, RICHARD
1941, American
Principal Works - Orchestral and choral works; Music for Violin; Music for Solo Flute; Concert Piece for violin and piano; string quartet.

WIREN, DAG IVAR
1905, Swedish
Principal Works - Operas; ballets; 5 symphonies; *Serenade* for strings; other orchestral works; concertos for piano, for cello, for violin; chamber music including string quartets; piano pieces; film music; songs.

WOLF-FERRARI, ERMANNO
1876-1948, Italian
Principal Works - Operas: *Ilcampiello* 91936); *Dama Boba* (1939); *Le donne curiose* (1903); *I quattro rusteghi (School For Fathers)* (1906); *Il segreto di Susanna* (1909) (Susanna's Secret); *I gioielli della Madonna* (The Jewels of the Madonna) (1913); *Cinderella ;* chamber and choral music; piano pieces: songs.

WOLFF, CHRISTIAN
1934, American
Principal Works - Some aleatory music, tape and prepared piano and non-conventional notation! *Dance Scores* for Merce Cunningham; *For Prepared Piano* (1951); *Summer* for string quartet (1961); *For 1, 2, or 3 People on any instruments* (1964); *Burdocks* for one or more orchestras, any instruments or sources of sound, 1971; *Trio One* for flute trumpet and cello (1951); *Braverman Music* for flute, clarinet, horn, trumpet, trombone piano, celesta and two cellos (1978); *Nine* for nine instruments (1951).

WOLPE, STEFAN
1902-1972, German/American
Principal Works - Some twelve tone music, jazz materials! Semitic music: Ballet: *The Man from Midian* (1942); 2 operas; 5 symphonies; other orchestral and dance works; *Chamber Piece No. 1 and No. 2 for 14 players; Enactments for 3 pianos* (1953); songs.

WOOD, CHARLES
1866-1926, Irish
Principal Works - Cantatas; chuirch music; 8 string quartets; orchestral pieces and other choral works; organ music; songs; Irish folk-song arrangements.

WORDSWORTH, WILLIAM (BROCKLESBY)
1908, English
Principal Works - 5 symphonies; 6 string quartets;

concertos for violin, for cello, for piano; piano, organ and chamber pieces; songs.

WUORINEN, CHARLES
1938, American
Principal Works - Contemporary and electronic techniques! *Octet; Concerto for Tuba, 12 winds, 12 drums;* Piano Duet: *Making Ends Meet; The Winds; Time's Encomium* (1969); other electronic pieces.

WYNER, YEHUDI
1929, American
Principal Works - Jewish liturgical music; *Da camera* for piano and orchestra (1967); *Serenade for 7 instruments* (1958); *Passover Offering* for flute, clarinet, trombone and cello; *Cadenza* for clarinet and harpsichord (1970).

XENAKIS, YANNIS
1922, Rumanian
Principal Works - *Stochastic* mathematical and computerized procedures! *Duel* for 2 orchestras, follows game theory, with unpredicted results based on prescribed rules; *Eonta* for piano and 5 brass, with computer; *Metastaseis* for 61 individual instrumentalists(1954); *Pithprakta* for similar (1956); *Akrata* for 16 winds; *Polytrope* (1967), for 4 orchestras of 17 players each, placed among the audience; *Nomos Gamma* (1968); *ST4* for string quartet.

YAMADA, KOSAKU
1886-1965, Japanese
Principal Works - Opera: *Kurofune* (Black Ships) (1940); 5 symphonies; choral and chamber music.

YANNAY, YEHUDA
1937, Rumanian
Principal Works - Aleatory, electronic music! *Wraphap* for actress, amplified aluminum sheet and Yannachord (1969); *Houdini's 9th* for double bass, escape artist, etc.; *Coheleth* (1970) for electronic instrument and chorus.

YOUNG, LA MONTE
1935, American
Principal Works - Advanced sound/light environmental works! Use of long, sustained sounds with only slight changes at extremely long intervals; theatrical *modernist* techniques: *Word scores; Draw A Straight Line and Follow It; The Tortoise, His Dreams and Journeys* for *continuous performance* with strings, voices and projections, executed over several days.

YON, PIETRO ALESSANDRO
1886-1943, Italian
Principal Works - *Concerto gregoriano* for organ and orchestra; *Gesu Bambino* for organ (1917); other church music; Masses; motets; oratorios; piano and chamber pieces; songs.

YUN ISANG
1917, Korean
Principal Works - Serial music, and some Oriental elements! Opera: *Der Traum des Liu Tung* (1965); *Music for 7 Instruments* (1959); *Loyang* for 8 instruments and percussion (1962); and other chamber works; choral and other orchestral works; piano pieces.

ZANDONAL, RICCARDO
1883-1944, Italian
Operas: *Giulitta e Romeo,* after Shakespeare; *Francesca da Rimini,* after D'Annunzio (1914); *Conchita* (1911); orchestral works; concertos for cello and viola; choral music including a Requiem; piano and other chamber pieces: film music.

ZEMLINSKY, ALEXANDER VON
1871-1942, Austrian/American
Principal Works - Opera: *Es War Einmal* (1900); 3 symphonies; string quartets; ballet; chamber and choral works; piano music; songs.

Addenda:

SIEBERT, WILHELM PIETER
German
Opera: *The Sinking Of The Titanic* (1979)

ACADEMY AWARDS

FOR

"BEST SONG"

"OSCAR" Winners and "Other Nominated Songs"
In Chronological Order From 1934 Until 1980

"OSCARS" are awarded by
The Academy Of Motion Picture Arts and Sciences
in the year of initial motion picture release.

The Academy began its "Best Picture" awards in 1929
but the "Best Song" and "Best Musical Score"
categories did not begin until 1934.

ACADEMY AWARDS FOR "BEST SONG"

"Oscar-Winning Best Song"	Written by:	From the film:	Other Nominations:	Written by:	From the film:
			1934		
Continental, The	Con Conrad Herb Magidson	The Gay Divorcee	Carioca	Vincent Youmans Edward Eliscu Gus Kahn	Flying Down To Rio
			1935		
Lullaby Of Broadway	Harry Warren Al Dubin	Gold Diggers Of 1935	Cheek To Cheek	Irving Berlin	Top Hat
			Lovely To Look At	Jerome Kern Dorothy Fields Jimmy McHugh	Roberta
			1936		
The Way You Look Tonight	Jerome Kern Dorothy Fields	Swing Time	Did I Remember	Walter Donaldson Harold Adamson	Suzy
			I've Got You Under My Skin	Cole Porter	Born To Dance
			A Melody From The Sky	Louis Alter Sidney Mitchell	Trail Of The Lonesome Pine
			Pennies From Heaven	Arthur Johnston Johnny Burke	Pennies From Heaven
			When Did You Leave Heaven	Richard A. Whiting Walter Bullock	Sing Baby Sing
			1937		
Sweet Leilani	Harry Owens	Waikiki Wedding	Remember Me	Harry Warren Al Dubin	Mr. Dodd Takes The Air
			That Old Feeling	Sammy Fain Lew Brown	Vogues Of 1938
			They Can't Take That Away From Me	George Gershwin Ira Gershwin	Shall We Dance
			Whispers In The Dark	Frederick Hollander Leo Robin	Artists and Models
			1938		
Thanks For The Memory	Ralph Rainger Leo Robin	Big Broadcast Of 1938	Always And Always	Edward Ward George (Chet) Forrest Robert Wright	Mannequin
			Change Partners And Dance With Me	Irving Berlin	Carefree
			Cowboy And The Lady	Lionel Newman Arthur Quenzer	Cowboy And The Lady

"Oscar-Winning Best Song"	Written by:	From the film:	Other Nominations:	Written by:	From the film:
			Dust	Johnny Marvin	Under Western Stars
			Jeepers Creepers	Harry Warren Johnny Mercer	Going Places
			Merrily We Live	Phil Craig Arthur Quenzer	Merrily We Live
			A Mist Over The Moon	Ben Oakland Oscar Hammerstein II	The Lady Objects
			My Own	Jimmy McHugh Harold Adamson	That Certain Age
			Now It Can Be Told	Irving Berlin	Alexander's Ragtime Band

1939

"Oscar-Winning Best Song"	Written by:	From the film:	Other Nominations:	Written by:	From the film:
Over The Rainbow	Harold Arlen, E.Y. Harburg	Wizard Of Oz	I Poured My Heart Into A Song	Irving Berlin	Second Fiddle
			Faithful Forever	Ralph Rainger, Leo Robin	Gulliver's Travels
			Wishing	Buddy DeSylva	Love Affair

1940

"Oscar-Winning Best Song"	Written by:	From the film:	Other Nominations:	Written by:	From the film:
When You Wish Upon A Star	Leigh Harline, Ned Washington	Pinocchio	Down Argentine Way	Harry Warren Mack Gordon	Down Argentine Way
			I'd Know You Anywhere	Johnny McHugh Johnny Mercer	You'll Find Out
			It's A Blue World	George (Chet) Forrest Robert Wright	Music In My Heart
			Love Of My Life	Artie Shaw Johnny Mercer	Second Chorus
			Only Forever	James Monaco Johnny Burke	Rhythm On The River
			Our Love Affair	Roger Edens Georgie Stoll	Strike Up The Band
			Waltzing In The Clouds	Robert Stolz Gus Kahn	Spring Parade
			Who Am I	Jule Styne Walter Bullock	Hit Parade Of 1941

482

"Oscar-Winning Best Song"	Written by:	From the film:	Other Nominations:	Written by:	From the film:
1941					
The Last Time I Saw Paris	Jerome Kern Oscar Hammerstein II	Lady Be Good	Baby Mine	Frank Churchill Ned Washington	Dumbo
			Be Honest With Me	Gene Autry Fred Rose	Ridin' On A Rainbow
			Blues In The Night	Harold Arlen Johnny Mercer	Blues In The Night
			Boogie Woogie Bugle Boy Of Company B	Hugh Prince Don Raye	Buck Privates
			Chattanooga Choo Choo	Harry Warren Mack Gordon	Sun Valley Serenade
			Dolores	Louis Alter Frank Loesser	Las Vegas Nights
			Out Of The Silence	Lloyd B. Norlind	All American Coed
			Since I Kissed My Baby Goodbye	Cole Porter	You'll Never Get Rich
1942					
White Christmas	Irving Berlin	Holiday Inn	Always In My Heart	Ernesto Lecuona Kim Gannon	Always In My Heart
			Dearly Beloved	Jerome Kern Johnny Mercer	You Were Never Lovelier
			How About You	Burton Lane Ralph Freed	Babes For Broadway
			(It Seems) I Heard That Song Before	Jule Styne Sammy Cahn	Youth On Parade
			I've Got A Gal In Kalamazoo	Harry Warren Mack Gordon	Orchestra Wives
			Love Is A Song	Frank Churchill Larry Morey	Bambi
			Pennies For Peppino	Edward Ward George (Chet) Forrest Robert Wright	Flying With Music
			Pig Foot Pete	Gene De Paul Don Raye	Hellzapoppin'
			There's A Breeze On Lake Louise	Harry Revel Mort Greene	Mayor Of 44th St.

"Oscar-Winning Best Song"	Written by:	From the film:	Other Nominations:	Written by:	From the film:
1943					
You'll Never Know	Harry Warren Mack Gordon	Hello, Frisco Hello	Change Of Heart	Jule Styne Harold Adamson	Hit Parade Of 1943
			Happiness Is A Thing Called Joe	Harold Arlen E.Y. Harburg	Cabin In The Sky
			My Shining Hour	Harold Arlen Johnny Mercer	The Sky's The Limit
			Saludos Amigos	Charles Wolcott Ned Washington	Saludos Amigos
			Say A Prayer For The Boys Over There	Jimmy McHugh Herb Magidson	Hers To Hold
			That Old Black Magic	Harold Arlen Johnny Mercer	Star Spangled Rhythm
			They're Either Too Young Or Too Old	Frank Loesser Arthur Schwartz	Thank Your Lucky Star
			We Musn't Say Goodbye	James Monaco Al Dubin	Stage Door Canteen
			You'd Be So Nice To Come To	Cole Porter	Something To Shout About
1944					
Swinging On A Star	James Van Heusen Johnny Burke	Going My Way	I Couldn't Sleep A Wink Last Night	Jimmy McHugh Harold Adamson	Higher and Higher
			I'll Walk Alone	Jule Styne Sammy Cahn	Follow The Boys
			I'm Making Believe	James Monaco Mack Gordon	Sweet And Lowdown
			Long Ago And Far Away	Jerome Kern Ira Gershwin	Cover Girl
			Now I Know	Harold Arlen Ted Koehler	Up In Arms
			Remember Me To Carolina	Harry Revel Paul Francis Webster	Minstrel Man
			Rio De Janeiro	Ary Barroso Ned Washington	Brazil
			Silver Shadows And Golden Dreams	Lew Pollack Charles Newman	Lady Let's Dance

"Oscar-Winning Best Song"	Written by:	From the film:	Other Nominations:	Written by:	From the film:
			Sweet Dreams Sweetheart	M.K. Jerome Ted Koehler	Hollywood Canteen
			Too Much In Love	Walter Kent Kim Gannon	Song Of The Open Road
			The Trolley Song	Ralph Blane Hugh Martin	Meet Me In St. Louis

1945

"Oscar-Winning Best Song"	Written by:	From the film:	Other Nominations:	Written by:	From the film:
It Might As Well Be Spring	Richard Rodgers Oscar Hammerstein	State Fair	Accentuate The Positive	Harold Arlen Johnny Mercer	Here Comes The Waves
			Anywhere	Jule Styne Sammy Cahn	Tonight And Every Night
			Aren't You Glad You're You	James Van Heusen Johnny Burke	The Bells Of St. Mary's
			Cat And Canary	Jay Livingston Ray Evans	Why Girls Leave Home
			Endlessly	Walter Kent Kim Gannon	Earl Carroll Vanities
			I Fall In Love Too Easily	Jule Styne Sammy Cahn	Anchors Aweigh
			I'll Buy That Dream	Allie Wrubel Herb Magidson	Sing Your Way Home
			Linda	Ann Ronell Jack Lawrence	G.I. Joe
			Love Letters	Victor Young Edward Heyman	Love Letters
			More And More	Jerome Kern E.Y. Harburg	Can't Help Singing
			Sleighride In July	James Van Heusen Johnny Burke	Belle Of The Yukon
			So In Love	David Rose Leo Robin	Wonder Man
			Some Sunday Morning	M.K. Jerome Ray Heindorf Ted Koehler	San Antonio

"Oscar-Winning Best Song"	Written by:	From the film:	Other Nominations:	Written by:	From the film:
1946					
On The Atchison, Topeka And Santa Fe	Harry Warren Johnny Mercer	The Harvey Girls	All Through The Day	Jerome Kern Oscar Hammerstein II	Centennial Summer
			I Can't Begin To tell You	James Monaco Mack Gordon	The Dolly Sisters
			Ole Buttermilk Sky	Hoagy Carmichael Jack Brooks	Canyon Passage
			You Keep Coming Back Like A Song	Irving Berlin	Blue Skies
1947					
Zip-A-Dee-Doo-Dah	Allie Wrubel Ray Gilbert	Song Of The South	A Gal In Calico	Arthur Schwartz Leo Robin	The Time The Place And The Girl
			I Wish I Didn't Love You So	Frank Loesser	The Perils Of Pauline
			Pass That Peace Pipe	Ralph Blane Hugh Martin Roger Edens	Good News
			You Do	Josef Myrow Mack Gordon	Mother Wore Tights
1948					
Buttons And Bows	Jay Livingston Ray Evans	The Paleface	For Every Man There's A Woman	Harold Arlen Leo Robin	Casbah
			It's Magic	Jule Styne Sammy Cahn	Romance On The High Seas
			This Is The Moment	Frederick Hollander, Leo Robin	That Lady In Ermine
			The Woody Woodpecker Song	Ramey Idriss George Tibbles	Wet Blanket Policy (cartoon)
1949					
Baby It's Cold Outside	Frank Loesser	Neptune's Daughter	It's A Great Feeling	Jule Styne Sammy Cahn	It's A Great Feeling
			Lavender Blue	Eliot Daniel Larry Morey	So Dear To My Heart
			My Foolish Heart	Victor Young Ned Washington	My Foolish Heart
			Through A Long Sleepless Night	Alfred Newman Mack Gordon	Come To The Stable

"Oscar-Winning Best Song"	Written by:	From the film:	Other Nominations:	Written by:	From the film:
1950					
Mona Lisa	Ray Evans Jay Livingston	Captain Carey, U.S.A.	Be My Love	Nicholas Brodszky Sammy Cahn	The Toast Of New Orleans
			Bibbidy-Bobbidi-Boo	Mack David Al Hoffman Jerry Livingston	Cinderella
			Mule Train	Fred Glickman Hy Heath Johnny Lange	Singing Guns
			Wilhemina	Josef Myrow Mack Gordon	Wabash Avenue
1951					
In The Cool Cool Cool Of The Evening	Hoagy Carmichael Johnny Mercer	Here Comes The Groom	A Kiss To Build A Dream On	Bert Kalmar Harry Ruby Oscar Hammerstein II	The Strip
			Never	Lionel Newman Eliot Daniel	Golden Girl
			Too Late Now	Burton Lane Alan Jay Lerner	Royal Wedding
			Wonder Why	Nicholas Brodszky Sammy Cahn	Rich, Young And Pretty
1952					
High Noon	Dimitri Tiomkin Ned Washington	High Noon	Am I In Love	Jack Brooks	Paleface
			Because You're Mine	Nicholas Brodszky Sammy Cahn	Because You're Mine
			Thumbelina	Frank Loesser	Hans Christian Anderson
			Zing A Little Zing	Harry Warren Leo Robin	Just For You
1953					
Secret Love	Sammy Fain Paul Francis Webster	Calamity Jane	The Moon Is Blue	Herschel Burke Gilbert Sylvia Fine	The Moon Is Blue
			My Flaming Heart	Nicholas Brodszky Leo Robin	Small Town Girl
			Sadie Thompson's Song (Blue Pacific Blues)	Lester Lee Ned Washington	Miss Sadie Thompson
			That's Amore	Harry Warren Jack Brooks	The Caddy

"Oscar-Winning Best Song"	Written by:	From the film:	Other Nominations:	Written by:	From the film:
1954					
Three Coins In The Fountain	Jule Styne Paul Francis Webster	Three Coins In The Fountain	Count Your Blessings Instead Of Sheep	Irving Berlin	White Christmas
			The High And The Mighty	Dimitri Tiomkin Ned Washington	The High And The Mighty
			Hold My Hand	Jack Lawrence Richard Myers	Susan Slept Here
			The Man That Got Away	Harold Arlen Ira Gershwin	A Star Is Born
1955					
Love Is A Many-Splendored Thing	Sammy Fain Paul Francis Webster	Love Is A Many-Splendored Thing	I'll Never Stop Loving You	Nicholas Brodszky Sammy Cahn	Love Me Or Leave Me
			Something's Gotta Give	Johnny Mercer	Daddy Long Legs
			(Love Is) The Tender Trap	James Van Heusen Sammy Cahn	The Tender Trap
			Unchained Melody	Alex North Hy Zaret	Unchained
1956					
Whatever Will Be Will Be (Que Sera Sera)	Jay Livingston Ray Evans	The Man Who Knew Too Much	Friendly Persuasion (Thee I Love)	Dimitri Tiomkin Paul Francis Webster	Friendly Persuasion
			Julie	Leith Stevens Tom Adair	Julie
			True Love	Cole Porter	High Society
			Written On The Wind	Sammy Cahn Victor Young	Written On The Wind
1957					
All The Way	James Van Heusen Sammy Cahn	The Joker Is Wild	An Affair To Remember	Harry Warren Harold Adamson Leo McCarey	An Affair To Remember
			April Love	Sammy Fain Paul Francis Webster	April Love
			Tammy	Ray Evans Jay Livingston	Tammy And The Bachelor
			Wild Is The Wind	Dimitri Tiomkin Ned Washington	Wild Is The Wind

"Oscar-Winning Best Song"	Written by:	From the film:	Other Nominations:	Written by:	From the film:
1958					
Gigi	Frederick Loewe Alan Jay Lerner	Gigi	Almost In Your Arms	Jay Livingston Ray Evans	Houseboat
			A Certain Smile	Sammy Fain Paul Francis Webster	A Certain Smile
			To Love And Be Loved	Sammy Cahn James Van Heusen	Some Came Running
			A Very Precious Love	Sammy Fain Paul Francis Webster	Marjorie Morningstar
1959					
High Hopes	Sammy Cahn James Van Heusen	A Hole In The Head	The Five Pennies	Sylvia Fine	The Five Pennies
			The Best Of Everything	Alfred Newman Sammy Cahn	The Best Of Everything
			The Hanging Tree	Jerry Livingston Mack David	The Hanging Tree
			Strange Are The Ways Of Love	Dimitri Tiomkin Ned Washington	The Young Land
1960					
Never On Sunday	Manos Hadjidakis	Never On Sunday	The Facts Of Life	Johnny Mercer	The Facts Of Life
			Faraway Part	Andre Previn Dory Langdon Previn	Pepe
			The Green Leaves Of Summer	Dimitri Tiomkin Paul Francis Webster	The Alamo
			The Second Time Around	James Van Heusen Sammy Cahn	High Time
1961					
Moon River	Henry Mancini Johnny Mercer	Breakfast At Tiffany's	Bachelor In Paradise	Henry Mancini Mack David	Bachelor In Paradise
			Love Theme From El Cid	Miklos Rozsa Paul Francis Webster	El Cid
			Pocketfull Of Miracles	Sammy Cahn James Van Heusen	Pocketfull of Miracles
			Town Without Pity	Dimitri Tiomkin Ned Washington	Town Without Pity

"Oscar-Winning Best Song"	Written by:	From the film:	Other Nominations:	Written by:	From the film:
			1962		
Days Of Wine And Roses	Henry Mancini Johnny Mercer	Days Of Wine And Roses	Love Song From Mutiny On The Bounty	Bronislau Kaper Paul Francis Webster	Mutiny On The Bounty
			(Song From Two For The Seesaw) Second Chance	Andre Previn Dory Langdon Previn	Two For The Seesaw
			Tender Is The Night	Sammy Fain Paul Francis Webster	Tender Is The Night
			Walk On The Wild Side	Elmer Bernstein Mack David	Walk On The Wild Side
			1963		
Call Me Irresponsible	James Van Heusen Sammy Cahn	Papa's Delicate Condition	Charade	Henry Mancini Johnny Mercer	Charade
			It's A Mad Mad Mad Mad World	Ernest Gold Mack David	It's A Mad Mad Mad Mad World
			More	Riz Ortolani Norman Newell	Mondo Cane
			So Little Time	Dimitri Tiomkin Paul Francis Webster	55 Days In Peking
			1964		
Chim Chim Cher-ee	Richard M. Sherman Robert B. Sherman	Mary Poppins	Dear Heart	Henry Mancini Jay Livingston Ray Evans	Dear Heart
			Hush...Hush, Sweet Charlotte	Frank DeVol Mack David	Hush...Hush, Sweet Charlotte
			My Kind Of Town	James Van Heusen Sammy Cahn	Robin And The 7 Hoods
			Where Love Has Gone	James Van Heusen Sammy Cahn	Where Love Has Gone
			1965		
The Shadow Of Your Smile	Johnny Mandel Paul Francis Webster	The Sandpiper	The Ballad Of Cat Ballou	Jerry Livingston Mack David	Cat Ballou
			I Will Wait For You	Michel Legand Jacques Demy Norman Gimbel	Umbrellas Of Cherbourg
			The Sweetheart Tree	Henry Mancini Johnny Mercer	The Great Race
			What's New Pussycat?	Burt Bacharach Hal David	What's New Pussycat?

"Oscar-Winning Best Song"	Written by:	From the film:	Other Nominations:	Written by:	From the film:
1966					
Born Free	John Barry Don Black	Born Free	Alfie	Burt Bacharach Hal David	Alfie
			Georgy Girl	Tom Springfield Jim Dale	Georgy Girl
			My Wishing Doll	Elmer Bernstein Mack David	Hawaii
			A Time For Love	Johnny Mandel Paul Francis Webster	An American Dream
1967					
Talk To The Animals	Leslie Bricusse	Doctor Doolittle	The Bare Necessities	Terry Gilkyson	The Jungle Book
			The Eyes Of Love	Quincy Jones Bob Russell	Banning
			The Look Of Love	Burt Bacharach Hal David	Casino Royale
			Thoroughly Modern Millie	James Van Heusen Sammy Cahn	Thoroughly Modern Millie
1968					
The Windmills Of Your Mind	Michel Legrand Alan Bergman Marilyn Bergman	The Thomas Crown Affair	Chitty Chitty Bang Bang	Richard M. Sherman Robert B. Sherman	Chitty Chitty Bang Bang
			For Love Of Ivy	Quincy Jones Bob Russell	For Love Of Ivey
			Funny Girl	Jule Styne Bob Merrill	Funny Girl
			Star!	James Van Heusen Sammy Cahn	Star!
1969					
Raindrops Keep Fallin' On My Head	Burt Bacharach Hal David	Butch Cassidy And The Sundance Kid	Come Saturday Morning	Fred Krlin Dory L. Previn	The Sterile Cuckoo
			Jean	Rod McKuen	The Prime Of Miss Jean Brodie
			True Grit	Elmer Bernstein Don Black	True Grit
			What Are You Doing The Rest Of Your Life	Michel Legrand Alan Bergman Marilyn Bergman	The Happy Ending

"Oscar-Winning Best Song"	Written by:	From the film:	Other Nominations:	Written by:	From the film:

1970

(In 1970 the category heading was amended to read "Best Song - Original For The Picture)

"Oscar-Winning Best Song"	Written by:	From the film:	Other Nominations:	Written by:	From the film:
For All We Know	Fred Karlin Robb Wilson Arthur James	Love And Other Strangers	Pieces Of Dreams	Michel Legrand Alan Bergman Marilyn Bergman	Pieces Of Dreams
			Thank You Very Much	Leslie Bricusse	Scrooge
			Till Love Touches Your Life	Riz Ortolani Arthur Hamilton	Madion
			Whistling Away The Dark	Henry Mancini Johnny Mercer	Darling Lili

1971

The Way We Were					
Theme From Shaft	Isaac Hayes	Shaft	The Age Of Believing	Richard M. Sherman Robert B. Sherman	Bedknobs And Broomsticks
			All His Children	Henry Mancini Alan Bergman Marilyn Bergman	Sometimes A Great Notion
			Bless The Beasts And Children	Barry DeVorzon Perry Botkin Jr.	Bless The Beasts And Children
			Life Is What You Make It	Marvin Hamlisch Johnny Mercer	Kotch

1972

The Morning After	Al Kasha Joel Hirschhorn	The Poseidon Adventure	Ben	Walter Scharf Don Black	Ben
			Come Follow Follow Me	Fred Karlin Tylwyth Kymry	The Little Ark
			Marmalade, Molasses And Honey	Maurice Jarre Alan Bergman Marilyn Bergman	The Life And Times Of Judge Roy Bean
			Strange Are The Ways Of Love	Sammy Fain Paul Francis Webster	The Stepmother

1973

The Way We Were	Marvin Hamlisch Alan Bergman Marilyn Bergman	The Way We Were	All That Love Went To Waste	Sammy Cahn George Barrie	A Touch Of Class
			Live And Let Die	Paul And Linda McCartney	Live And Let Die
			Love	George Bruns Floyd Huddleston	Robin Hood
			Nice To Be Around	John Williams Paul Williams	Cinderella Liberty

"Oscar-Winning Best Song"	Written by:	From the film:	Other Nominations:	Written by:	From the film:
			1974		
We May Never Love Like This Again	Al Kasha Joel Hirschhorn	The Towering Inferno	Benji's Theme: I Feel Love	Euel Box Betty Box	Benji
			Blazing Saddles	John Morris Mel Brooks	Blazing Saddles
			Little Prince	Frederick Loewe Alan Jay Lerner	The Little Prince
			Wherever Love Takes Me	Elmer Bernstein Don Black	Gold
			1975		
I'm Easy	Keith Carradine	Nashville	How Lucky Can You Get	Fred Ebb	Funny Lady
			Now That We're In Love	George Barrie Sammy Cahn	Whiffs
			Richard's Window	Charles Fox Norman Gimbel	The Other Side Of The Mountain
			Theme From Mahogany (Do You Know Where You're Going To)	Michael Masser Gerry Goffin	Mahogany
			1976		
Evergreen	Barbra Streisand Paul Williams	A Star Is Born	Ave Satani	Jerry Goldsmith	Omen
			Come To Me	Henry Mancini Don Black	The Pink Panther Strikes Again
			Gonna Fly Now	Bill Conti Carol Connors Ayn Robbins	Rocky
			A World That Never Was	Sammy Fain Paul Francis Webster	Half A House
			1977		
You Light Up My Life	Joseph Brooks	You Light Up My Life	Candle On The Water	Al Kasha Joel Hirschhorn	Pete's Dragon
			Nobody Does It Better	Marvin Hamlisch Carole Bayer Sager	The Spy Who Loved Me
			The Slipper And The Rose Waltz	Richard M. Sherman Robert B. Sherman	The Slipper And The Rose
			Someone's Waiting For You	Sammy Fain Carol Connors Ayn Robbins	The Rescuers

"Oscar-Winning Best Song"	Written by:	From the film:	Other Nominations:	Written by:	From the film:
			1978		
Last Dance	Paul Jabara	Thank God It's Friday	Hopelessly Devoted To You	John Farrar	Grease
			Ready To Take A Chance Again	Charles Fox Norman Gimbel	Foul Play
			The Last Time I Felt Like This	Mrvin Hamlisch Alan Bergman Marilyn Bergman	Same Time Next Year
			When You're Loved	Richard M. Sherman Robert B. Sherman	The Magic Of Lassie
			1979		
It Goes Like It Goes	David Shire Norman Gimbel	Norma Rae	The Rainbow Connection	Paul Williams Ken Ascher	The Muppet Movie
			Song From '10' (It's Easy To Say)	Henry Mancini Robert Wells	'10'
			Theme From "Ice Castles" (Through The Eyes Of Love)	Marvin Hamlisch Carole Bayer Sager	Ice Castles
			Theme from "The Promise" (I'll Never Say Goodbye)	David Shire Richard Maltby, Jr.	The Promise

ACADEMY AWARDS

FOR

"BEST MUSICAL SCORE"

"OSCAR" Winners and
"Other Nominated Scores"
In Chronological Order
From 1934 Until 1980

"OSCARS" are awarded by
THE ACADEMY OF MOTION
PICTURES ARTS AND
SCIENCES
in the year following the
year of initial motion
picture release.

The Academy began its "Best Picture" awards in 1929 but the "Best Musical Score Category" did not begin until 1934.

In 1938, the "Best Musical Score" category was divided into two categories: "Best Score" and "Best Original Score". The latter category applied only to music composed originally for a motion picture.

In 1941, the categories were re-defined as "Best Score Of A Dramatic Picture" and "Best Score Of A Musical Picture.

In 1957, two categories as above were combined into one category "Best Score".

In 1958, the two-category system, begun in 1941, was resumed.

In 1962, the two categories were changed again to become "Best Music Score — substantially original" and "Best Scoring Of Music—adaptation or treatment".

In 1966, the category "Best Music Score—substantially original" was redefined as "Best Original Score—for which only the composer shall be eligible".

In 1967, the category "Best Scoring Of Music—adaptation or treatment" was extended by the phrase "for which only the adaptor and/or music director shall be eligible". Subsequent changes in category definitions continued and are indicated in the text beginning with the year 1968.

ACADEMY AWARDS FOR BEST MUSICAL SCORE

Oscar-Winning Score	Composed by:	Other Nominations:	Composed by:
		1934	
One Night Of Love	Louis Silvers	Gay Divorcee	Max Steiner
		Lost Patrol	Max Steiner
		1935	
The Informer	Max Steiner	Mutiny On The Bounty	Herbert Stothart
		Peter Ibbetson	Nat W. Finston
		1936	
Anthony Adverse	Leo Forbstein	Charge Of The Light Brigade	Max Steiner
		The Garden Of Allah	Max Steiner
		The General Died At Dawn	Werner Janssen
		Winterset	Nathaniel Shilkret
		1937	
One Hundred Men And A Girl	Charles Previn	Hurricane	Alfred Newman
		In Old Chicago	Louis Silvers
		The Life Of Emile Zola	Max Steiner
		Lost Horizon	Dimitri Tiomkin
		Make A Wish	Hugo Fiesenfeld
		The Prisoner Of Zenda	Alfred Newman
		Quality Street	Roy Webb
		Snow White And The Seven Dwarfs	Frank Churchill Leigh Harline Paul J. Smith
		Souls At Sea	Bernard Kaun
		Something To Sing About	C. Bakaleinikoff
		Way Out West	Marvin Hatley

1938

(In 1938, the "Best Musical Score" category was divided into two categories:
(1) Best Score and (2) Best Original Score. The latter category was limited
to music composed originally for a motion piecure score.)

Best Score	Composed by:	Other nominations:	Composed by:
Alexander's Ragtime Band	Alfred Newman	Carefree	Victor Baravalle
		Girls School	Morris Stoloff, Gregory Stone
		Goldwyn Follies	Alfred Newman
		Jezebel	Max Steiner

		Other Nominations:	
		Mad About Music	Charles Previn, Frank Skinner
		Storm Over Bengal	Cy Feuer
		Sweethearts	Herbert Stothart
		There Goes My Heart	Marvin Hatley
		Tropic Holiday	Boris Morros
		Young In Heart, The	Franz Waxman

Best Original Score

The Adventures Of Robin Hood	Erich Wolfgang Korngold	Army Girl	Victor Young
		Blockade	Werner Janssen
		Blockheads	Marvin Hatley
		Breaking The Ice	Victor Young
		Cowboy And The Lady, The	Alfred Newman
		If I Were King	Richard Hageman
		Marie Antoinette	Herbert Stothart
		Pacific Liner	Robert Russell Bennett
		Suez	Louis Silvers
		Young In Heart, The	Franz Waxman

1939

Best Score

Stagecoach	Richard Hageman Frank Harling John Leipold Leo Shuken	Babes In Arms	Roger Edens George E. Stoll
		First Love	Charles Previn
		The Great Victor Herbert	Phil Boutelje, Arthur Lange
		The Hunchback Of Notre Dame	Alfred Newman
		Intermezzo	Lou Forbes
		Mr. Smith Goes To Washington	Dimitri Tiomkin
		Of Mice And Men	Aaron Copland
		The Private Lives Of Elizabeth And Essex	Erich Wolfgang Korngold
		She Married A Cop	Cy Feuer
		Swanee River	Louis Silvers

| | | They Shall Have Music | Alfred Newman |
| | | Way Down South | Victor Young |

Best Original Score

The Wizard Of Oz	Herbert Stothart	Dark Victor	Max Steiner
		Eternally Yours	Werner Janssen
		Golden Boy	Victor Young
		Gone With The Wind	Max Steiner
		Gulliver's Travels	Victor Young
		The Man In The Iron Mask	Lud Gluskin Lucien Moraweck
		Man Of Conquest	Victor Young
		Nurse Edith Cavell	Anthony Collins
		Of Mice And Men	Aaron Copland
		The Rains Came	Alfred Newman
		Wuthering Heights	Alfred Newman

1940

Best Score

Tin Pan Alley	Alfred Newman	Arise My Love	Victor Young
		Hit Parade Of 1941	Cy Feuer
		Irene	Anthony Collins
		Our Town	Aaron Copland
		The Sea Hawk	Erich Wolfgang Korngold
		Second Chorus	Artie Shaw
		Spring Parade	Charles Previn
		Strike Up The Band	George E. Stoll Roger Edens

Best Original Score

Pinocchio	Leigh Harline Paul J. Smith Ned Washington	Arizona	Victor Young
		The Dark Command	Victor Young
		The Fight For Life	Louis Gruenberg
		The Great Dictator	Meredith Willson
		The House Of Seven Gables	Frank Skinner
		The Howards Of Virginia	Richard Hageman
		The Letter	Max Steiner
		The Long Voyage Home	Richard Hageman

		Other Nominations:	
		The Mark Of Zorro	Alfred Newman
		My Favorite Wife	Roy Webb
		Northwest Mounted Police	Victor Young
		One Million B.C.	Werner Heymann
		Rebecca	Franz Waxman
		The Thief Of Bagdad	Miklos Rozsa
		Waterloo Bridge	Herbert Stothart

1941

((In 1941, the "scoring categories were re-defined as:
(1) Best Score Of A Dramatic Or Comedy Picture and
(2) Best Score Of A Musical Picture)

Best Score Of A Dramatic Or Comedy Picture

Oscar Winner		Other nominations:	
All That Money Can Buy	Bernard Herrman	Back Street	Frank Skinner
		Ball Of Fire	Alfred Newman
		Cheers For Miss Bishop	Edward Ward
		Citizen Kane	Bernard Herrman
		Dr. Jekyll And Mr. Hyde	Franz Waxman
		Hold Back The Dawn	Victor Young
		How Green Was My Valley	Alfred Newman
		King Of The Zombies	Edward Kay
		Ladies In Retirement	Morris Stoloff, Ernst Toch
		The Little Foxes	Meredith Willson
		Lydia	Miklos Rozsa
		Mercy Island	Cy Feuer, Walter Scharf

Best Score Of A Musical Picture

Dumbo	Frank Churchill Oliver Wallace	All American Co-Ed	Edward Ward
		Birth Of The Blues	Robert Emmett Dolan
		Buck Privates	Charles Previn
		The Chocolate Soldier	Herbert Stothart Bronislau Kaper
		Ice-Capades	Cy Feuer
		The Strawberry Blonde	Heinz Roemheld
		Sun Valley Serenade	Emil Neuman

		Other Nominations:	
		Sunny	Anthony Collins
		You'll Never Get Rich	Morris Stoloff

1942

Best Score Of A Dramatic Or Comedy Picture Oscar Winner

		Other Nominations:	
Now Voyager	Max Steiner	Arabian Nights	Frank Skinner
		Bambi	Frank Churchill Edward Plumb
		The Black Swan	Alfred Newman
		The Corsican Brothers	Dimitri Tiomkin
		Flying Tigers	Victor Young
		The Gold Rush	Max Terr
		I Married A Witch	Roy Webb
		Joan Of Paris	Roy Webb
		Jungle Book	Miklos Rozsa
		Klondike Fury	Edward Kay
		Pride Of The Yankees	Leigh Harline
		Random Harvest	Herbert Stothart
		The Shanghai Gesture	Richard Hageman
		Silver Queen	Victor Young
		Take A Letter Darling	Victor Young
		Talk Of The Town	Frederick Hollander Morris Stoloff
		To Be Or Not To Be	Werner Heyman

Best Score Of A Music Picture

Yankee Doodle Dandy	Ray Heindorf Heinz Roemheld	Flying With Music	Edward Ward
		For Me And My Gal	Roger Edens George E. Stoll
		Holiday Inn	Robert Emmett Dolan
		It Started With Eve	Charles Previn, Hans Salter
		Johnny Doughboy	Walter Scharf
		My Gal Sal	Alfred Newman
		You Were Never Lovelier	Leigh Harline

1943

Best Score Of A Dramatic Or Comedy Picture
Oscar Winner

Other Nominations:

The Song Of Bernadette	Alfred Newman	The Amazing Mrs. Holliday	Hans J. Salter
			Frank Skinner
		Casablanca	Max Steiner
		The Commandos Strike At Dawn	Louis Gruenberg
			Morris Stoloff
		The Fallen Sparrow	C. Bakaleinikoff
			Roy Webb
		For Whom The Bell Tolls	Victor Young
		Hangmen Also Die	Hanns Eisler
		Hi Diddle Diddle	Phil Boutelje
		In Old Oklahoma	Walter Scharf
		Johnny Come Lately	Leigh Harline
		The Kansan	Gerard Carbonara
		Lady Of Burlesque	Arthur Lange
		Madame Curie	Herbert Stothart
		The Moon And Six Pence	Dimitri Tiomkin
		The North Star	Aaron Copland
		Victory Through Air Power	Edward H. Plumb, Paul J. Smith Oliver G. Wallace

Best Score Of A Musical Picture

This Is The Army	Ray Heindorf	Coney Island	Alfred Newman
		Hit Prade Of 1943	Walter Scharf
		The Phantom Of The Opera	Edward Ward
		Saludos Amigos	Edward H. Plumb Paul J. Smith Charles Wolcott
		The Sky's The Limit	Leigh Harline
		Something To Shout About	Morris Stoloff
		Stage Door Canteen	Frederic E. Rich
		Star Spangled Rhythm	Robert Emmett Dolan
		As Thousands Cheer	Herbert Stothart

1944

Best Score Of A Dramatic Or Comedy Picture
Oscar Winner

		Other Nominations:	
Since You Went Away	Max Steiner	Address Unknown	Morris Stoloff
		The Adventures Of Mark Twain	Max Steiner
		The Bridge Of San Luis Rey	Dimitri Tiomkin
		Casanova Brown	Arthur Lange
		Christmas Holiday	H.J. Salter
		Double Indemnity	Miklos Rozsa
		The Fighting Seabees	Walter Scharf Roy Webb
		The Hairy Ape	Michel Michelet Edward Paul
		It Happened Tomorrow	Robert Stoiz
		Jack London	Frederic E. Rich
		Kismet	Herbert Stothart
		None But The Lonely Heart	C. Bakaleinikoff, Hanns Eisler
		The Princess And The Pirate	David Rose
		Summer Storm	Karl Hajos
		Three Russian Girls	Franke Harling
		Up In Mabel's Room	Edward Paul
		Voice In The Wind	Michel Michelet
		Wilson	Alfred Newman
		Woman Of The Town	Miklos Rozsa

Best Score Of A Musical Picture

Cover Girl	Carmen Dragon Morris Stoloff	Brazil	Walter Scharf
		Higher And Higher	C. Bakaleinikoff
		Hollywood Canteen	Ray Heindorf
		Irish Eyes Are Smiling	Alfred Newman
		Knickerbocker Holiday	Kurt Weill Werner R. Heymann
		Lady In The Dark	Robert Emmett Dolan

Other Nominations:

Lady Let's Dance	Edward Kay
Meet Me In St. Louis	George E. Stoll
The Merry Monahans	H.J. Salter
Minstrel Man	Leo Erdody Ferde Grofe
Sensations Of 1945	Mahlon Merrick
Song Of The Open Road	Charles Previn
Up In Arms	Louis Forbes, Ray Heindorf

1945

**Best Score Of A Dramatic Or Comedy Picture
Oscar Winner**

Spellbound	Miklos Rozsa

Other Nominations:

The Bells Of St. Mary's	Robert Emmett Dolan
Brewster's Millions	Lou Forbes
Captain Kidd	Warner Janssen
Enchanted Cottage	Roy Webb
Flame Of The Barbary Coast	Dale Butts
G.I. Honeymoon	Edward Kay
G.I. Joe	Louis Applebaum, Ann Ronell
Guest In The House	Werner Janssen
Guest Wife	Daniele Amfitheatrof
The Keys Of The Kingdom	Alfred Newman
The Lost Weekend	Miklos Rozsa
Love Letters	Victor Young
Man Who Walked Alone	Karl Hajos
Objective Burma	Franz Waxman
Paris-Underground	Alexander Tansman
A Song To Remember	Miklos Rozsa, Morris Stoloff
The Southerner	Werner Janssen
This Love Of Ours	H.J. Salter
Valley Of Decision	Herbert Stothart
Woman In The Window	Hugo Friedhofer, Arthur Lange

Best Score Of A Musical Picture

Anchors Aweigh	Georgie Stoll	Belle Of The Yukon	Arthur Lange
		Can't Help Singing	Jerome Kern, H.J. Salter
		Hitchhike To Happiness	Morton Scott
		Incendiary Blonde	Robert Emmett Dolan
		Rhapsody In Blue	Ray Heindorf, Max Steiner
		State Fair	Charles Henderson, Alfred Newman
		Sunbonnet Sue	Edward J. Kay
		Three Caballeros	Edward Plumb, Paul J. Smith Charles Wolcott
		Tonight And Every Night	Marlin Skiles Morris Stoloff
		Why Girls Leave Home	Walter Greene
		Wonder Man	Lou Forbes Ray Heindorf

1946

Best Score Of A Dramatic Or Comedy Picture
Oscar Winner:

Other Nominations:

The Best Years Of Our Lives	Hugo Friedhofer	Anna And The King Of Siam	Bernard Herrmann
		Henry V	William Walton
		Humoresque	Franz Waxman
		The Killers	Miklos Rozsa

Best Score Of A Musical Picture

The Jolson Story	Morris Stoloff	Blue Skies	Robert Emmett Dolan
		Centennial Summer	Alfred Newman
		The Harvey Girls	Lennie Hayton
		Night And Day	Ray Heindorf Max Steiner

1947

Best Score Of A Dramatic Or Comedy Picture
Oscar Winner:

Other Nominations:

A Double Life	Miklos Rozsa	The Bishop's Wife	Hugo Friedhofer
		Captain From Castile	Alfred Newman
		Forever Amber	David Raksin
		Life With Father	Max Steiner

Best Score Of A Musical Picture

Mother Wore Tights	Alfred Newman	Fiesta	Johnny Green
		My Wild Irish Rose	Ray Heindorf, Max Steiner
		Road To Rio	Robert Emmett Dolan
		Song Of The South	Daniele Amfitheatrof Paul J. Smith Charles Wolcott

1948

Best Score Of A Dramatic Or Comedy Picture

Oscar Winner: **Other Nominations:**

The Red Shoes	Brian Easdale	Hamlet	William Walton
		Joan Of Arc	Hugo Friedhofer
		Johnny Belinda	Max Steiner
		The Snake Pit	Alfred Newman

Best Score Of A Musical Picture

Easter Parade	Johnny Green	The Emperor Waltz	Victor Young
		The Pirate	Lennie Hayton
		Romance On The High Seas	Alfred Newman
		When My Baby Smiles At Me	Alfred Newman

1949

Best Score Of A Dramatic Or Comedy Picture

Oscar Winner: **Other Nominations:**

The Heiress	Aaron Copland	Beyond The Forest	Max Steiner
		Champion	Dimitri Tiomkin

Best Score Of A Musical Picture

On The Town	Roger Edens, Lennie Hayton	Jolson Sings Again	Morris Stoloff, George Duning
		Look For The Silver Lining	Ray Heindorf

1950

Best Score Of A Dramatic Or Comedy Picture

Oscar Winner: **Other Nominations:**

Sunset Boulevard	Franz Waxman	All About Eve	Alfred Newman
		The Flame And The Arrow	Max Steiner
		No Sad Songs For Me	George Duning
		Samson And Deliliah	Victor Young

506

Best Score Of A Musical Picture

Annie Get Your Gun	Adolph Deutsch Roger Edens	Cinderella	Oliver Wallace Paul J. Smith
		I'll Get By	Lionel Newman
		Three Little Words	Andre Previn
		The West Point Story	Ray Heindorf

1951

Bet Score Of A Dramatic Or Comedy Picture
Oscar Winner:

Other Nominations:

A Place In The Sun	Franz Waxman	David And Bathsheba	Alfred Newman
		Death Of A Salesman	Alex North
		Quo Vadis	Miklos Rozsa
		A Streetcar Named Desire	Alex North

Best Score Of A Musical Picture

An American In Paris	Johnny Green Saul Chaplin	Alice In Wonderland	Oliver Wallace
		The Great Caruso	Peter Herman Adler Johnny Green
		On The Riviera	Alfred Newman
		Show Boat	Adolph Deutsch Conrad Salinger

1952

Best Score Of A Dramatic Or Comedy Picture
Oscar Winner:

Other Nomintions:

High Noon	Dimitri Tiomkin	Ivanhoe	Miklos Rozsa
		Miracle Of Fatima	Max Steiner
		The Thief	Herschel Burke Gilbert
		Viva Zapata	Alex North

Best Score Of A Musical Picture

With A Song In My Heart	Alfred Newman	Hans Christian Andersen	Walter Scharf
		The Jazz Singer	Ray Heindorf, Max Steiner
		The Medium	Gian-Carlo Menotti
		Singin' In The Rain	Lennie Hayton

1953

Best Score Of A Dramatic Or Comedy Picture
Oscar Winner:

		Other Nominations:	
Lili	Bronislau Kaper	Above And Beyond	Hugo Friedhofer
		From Here To Eternity	Morris Stoloff, George Duning
		Julius Caesar	Miklos Rozsa
		This Is Cinerama	Louis Forbes

Best Score Of A Musical Picture

Call Me Madam	Alfred Newman	The Bandwagon	Adolph Deutsch
		Calamity Jane	Ray Heindorf
		5000 Fingers Of Dr. T.	Frederick Hollander, Morris Stoloff
		Kiss Me Kate	Andre Previn, Saul Chaplin

1954

Best Score Of A Dramatic Or Comedy Picture

The High And The Mighty	Dimitri Tiomkin	The Caine Mutiny	Max Steiner
		Genevieve	Muir Mathieson
		On The Waterfront	Leonard Bernstein
		The Silver Chalice	Franz Waxman

Best Score Of A Musical Picture

Seven Brides For Seven Brothers	Adolph Deutsch, Saul Chaplin	Carmen Jones	Herschel Burke Gilbert
		The Glenn Miller Story	Joseph Gershenson, Henry Mancini
		A Star Is Born	Ray Heindorf
		There's No Business Like Show Business	Alfred Newman, Lionel Newman

1955

Best Score Of A Dramatic Or Comedy Picture
Oscar Winner:

		Other Nominations:	
Love Is A Many-Splendored Thing	Alfred Newman	Battle Cry	Max Steiner
		The Man With The Golden Arm	Elmer Bernstein
		Picnic	George Duning
		The Rose Tatoo	Alex North

Best Score Of A Musical Picture

Oklahoma   Robert Russell Bennett
Jay Blackton
Adolph Deutsch

Other Nominations

Guys & Dolls   Jay Blackton
Cyril J. Mockridge

It's Always Fair Weather   Andre Previn

Love Me Or Leave Me   Percy Faith
George E. Stoll

1956

**Best Score Of A Dramatic Or Comedy Picture
Oscar Winner**

Around The World
In 80 Days   Victor Young

Other Nominations:

Anastasia   Alfred Newman

Between Heaven And Hell   Hugo Friedhofer

Giant   Dimitri Tiomkin

The Rainmaker   Alex North

Best Score Of A Musical Picture

The King And I   Alfred Newman,
Ken Darby

The Best Things In
Life Are Free   Lionel Newman

The Eddy Duchin Story   Morris Stoloff,
George Duning

High Society   Johnny Green,
Saul Chaplin

Meet Me In Las Vegas   George Stoll,
Johnny Green

1957
(In 1957, the two categories for "Best Score" were combined into
one category designated as "Best Score")

**Best Score
Oscar Winner:**

Bridge On The River Kwai   Malcolm Arnold

Other Nominations:

An Affair To Remember   Hugo Friedhofer

Boy On A Dolphin   Hugo Friedhofer

Perri   Paul Smith

Raintree County   John Green

1958

(In 1958, the designation of two categories for (1) Best Score For A Dramatic
Or Comedy Picture and (2) Best Score For A Musical Picture was resumed)

Best Score Of A Dramatic Or Comedy Picture
Oscar Winner

		Other Nominations:	
The Old Man And The Sea	Dimitri Tiomkin	The Big Country	Jerome Moross
		Separate Tables	David Raksin
		White Wilderness	Oliver Wallace
		The Young Lions	Hugo Friedhofer

Best Score Of A Musical Picture
Oscar Winner:

		Other Nominations:	
Gigi	Andre Previn	The Bolshoi Ballet	Yuri Faier G. Rozhdestvensky
		Damn Yankees	Ray Heindorf
		Mardi Gras	Lionel Newman
		South Pacific	Alfred Newman Ken Darby

1959

Best Score Of A Dramatic Or Comedy Picture
Oscar Winner:

		Other Nominations:	
Ben Hur	Miklos Rosza	The Diary Of Anne Frank	Alfred Newman
		The Nun's Story	Franz Waxman
		On The Beach	Ernest Gold
		Pillow Talk	Frank DeVol

Best Score Of A Musical Picture

Porgy And Bess	Andre Previn, Ken Darby	The Five Pennies	Leith Stevens
		Li'l Abner	Nelson Riddle, Joseph J. Lilley
		Say One For Me	Lionel Newman
		Sleeping Beauty	George Bruns

1960

Best Score Of A Dramatic Or Comedy Picture
Oscar Winner:

		Other Nominations:	
Exodus	Ernest Gold	The Alamo	Dimitri Tiomkin
		Elmer Gantry	Andre Previn
		The Magnificent Seven	Elmer Bernstein
		Spartacus	Alex North

Best Score Of A Musical Picture

		Other Nominations:	
Song Without End	Morris Stoloff Harry Sukman	Bells Are Ringing	Andre Previn
		Can-Can	Nelson Riddle
		Let's Make Love	Lionel Newman, Earle H. Hagen
		Pepe	Johnny Green

1961

Best Score Of A Dramatic Or Comedy Picture
Oscar Winner:

		Other Nominations:	
Breakfast At Tiffany's	Henry Mancini	El Cid	Miklos Rozsa
		Fanny	Morris Stoloff, Harry Sukman
		The Guns Of Navarone	Dimitri Tiomkin
		Summer And Smoke	Elmer Bernstein

Best Score Of A Musical Picture

West Side Story	Saul Chaplin Johnny Green Sid Ramin Irwin Kostal	Babes In Toyland	George Bruns
		Flower Drum Song	Alfred Newman, Ken Darby
		Kovanshchina	Dimitri Shostakovich
		Paris Blues	Duke Ellington

1962

(In 1962, the two "scoring categories were re-defined as (1) Best Music Score - substantially original and (2) Best Scoring Of Music - adaptation or treatment.)

Best Music Score - substantially original
Oscar Winner:

		Other Nominations:	
Lawrence Of Arabia	Maurice Jarre	Freud	Jerry Goldsmith
		Mutiny On The Bounty	Bronislau Kaper
		Taras Bulba	Franz Waxman
		To Kill A Mockingbird	Elmer Bernstein

Best Scoring Of Music - adaptation or treatment

The Music Man	Ray Heindorf	Billy Rose's Jumbo	George Stoll
		Gigot	Michel Magne
		Gypsy	Frank Perkins
		Wonderful World Of The Brothers Grimm	Leigh Harline

1963

Best Music Score - substantially original
Oscar Winner:

		Other Nominations:	
Tom Jones	John Addison	Cleopatra	Alex North
		55 Days At Peking	Dimitri Tiomkin
		How The West Was Won	Alfred Newman, Ken Darby
		It's A Mad, Mad, Mad Mad World	Ernest Gold

Best Scoring Of Music - adaptation or treatment

Irma La Douce	Andre Previn	Bye Bye Birdie	Johnny Green
		A New Kind Of Love	Leith Stevens
		Sundays And Cybele	Maurice Jarre
		Sword In The Stone	George Burns

1964

Best Music Score - substantially original
Oscar Winner

		Other Nominations:	
Mary Poppins	Richard M. Sherman, Robert B. Sherman	Becket	Laurence Rosenthal
		The Fall Of The Roman Empire	Dimitri Tiomkin
		Hush...Hush Sweet Charlotte	Frank DeVol
		The Pink Panther	Henry Mancini

Best Scoring Of Music - adaptation or treatment

My Fair Lady	Andre Previn	A Hard Day's Night	George Martin
		Mary Poppins	Irwin Kostal
		Robin And The 7 Hoods	Nelson Riddle
		The Unsinkable Molly Brown	Robert Armbruster, Leo Arnaud, Jack Elliot, Jack Hayes, Calvin Jackson, Leo Shuken

1965

Best Music Score - substantially original

Other Nominations:

Doctor Zhivago	Maurice Jarre	The Agony And The Ecstasy	Alex North
		The Greatest Story Ever Told	Alfred Newman

		Other Nominations:	
		A Patch Of Blue	Jerry Goldsmith
		The Umbrellas Of Cherbourg	Michel Legrand Jacques Demy

Best Scoring Of Music - adaptation or treatment

The Sound of Music	Irwin Kostal	Cat Ballou	Frank DeVol
		The Pleasure Seekers	Lionel Newman, Alexander Courage
		A Thousand Clowns	Don Walker
		The Umbrellas Of Cherbourg	Michel Legrand

1966

(In 1966, the category "Best Music Score - substantially original" was re-defined
as "Best Original Score—for which only the composer shall be eligible". The
category "Best Scoring Of Music - adaptation or treatment" was retained without change.)

Best Original Score - for which only the composer is eligible

Oscar Winner:		Other Nominations:	
Born Free	John Barry	The Bible	Toshiro Mayazumi
		Hawaii	Elmer Bernstein
		The Sand Pebbles	Jerry Goldsmith
		Who's Afraid Of Virginia Woolf	Alex North

Best Scoring Of Music - adaptation or treatment

A Funny Thing Happened On The Way To The Forum	Ken Thorne	The Gospel According To St. Luke	Luis Enrique Bacalov
		Return Of The seven	Elmer Bernstein
		The Singing Nun	Harry Sukman
		Stop The World - I Want To Get Off	Al Ham

1967

Best Original Score - for which only the composer is eligible

Oscar Winner:		Other Nominations:	
Thoroughly Modern Millie	Andre Previn, Joseph Gershenson	Cool Hand Luke	Lalo Schifrin
		Doctor Doolittle	Leslie Bricusse
		Far From The Madding Crowd	Richard Rodney Bennett
		In Cold Blood	Quincy Jones

(In 1967, the statement "for which only the adaptor and/or music director
shall be eligible" was added to the category "Best Scoring Of Music - adaptation
or treatment".)

**Best Scoring Of Music - adaptation or treatment
for which only the adaptor and/or music director
is eligible.**

Other Nominations:

Camelot	Alfred Newman, Ken Darby	Doctor Doolittle	Lionel Newman, Alexander Courage
		Guess Who's Coming To Dinner	Frank DeVol
		Thoroughly Modern Millie	Andre Previn, Joseph Gershenson
		Valley Of The Dolls	John Williams

1968

(In 1968, both "scoring" categories were once again re-defined as
shown in the captions below.)

**Best Original Score, for a non-musical
motion picture for which only the
composer shall be eligible.
Oscar Winner:**

Other Nominations:

The Lion In Winter	John Barry	The Fox	Lalo Schifrin
		Planet Of The Apes	Jerry Goldsmith
		The Shoes Of The Fisherman	Alex North
		The Thomas Crown Affair	Michel Legrand

**Best Score Of A Motion Picture -
Original Or Adaptation, for which the
composer, lyricist, and the adaptor shall
be eligible if the music score was written
directly for the screen, but only the adaptor
shall be eligible if the score is an adaptation
from another medium.
Oscar Winner:**

Other Nominations:

Oliver	Johnny Green	Finian's Rainbow	Ray Heindorf
		Funny Girl	Walter Scharf
		Star	Lennie Hayton
		The Young Girls Of Rochefort	Michel Legrand Jacques Demy

1969

**Best Original Score, for a non-musical
motion picture for which only the
composer shall be eligible.**
Oscar Winner: **Other Nominations:**

Butch Cassidy And The Sundance Kid	Burt Bacharach	Anne Of The Thousand Days	Georges Delerue
		The Reivers	John Williams
		The Secret Of Santa Vittoria	Ernest Gold
		The Wild Bunch	Jerry Fielding

**Best Score Of A Motion Picture - Original Or Adaptation,
for which the composer, lyricist, and the adaptor
shall be eligible if the music score was written
directly for the screen, but only the adaptor shall
be eligible if the score is an adaptation from
another medium.**

Hello Dolly	Lennie Hayton, Lionel Newman	Goodbye Mr. Chips	Leslie Bricusse, John Williams
		Paint Your Wagon	Nelson Riddle
		Sweet Charity	Cy Coleman
		They Shoot Horses, Don't They	Albert Woodbury

1970
(In 1970, both "scoring" categories were re-defined once again
as shown below.)

**Best Original Score For Which The Composer
And Collaborator, If Any, Shall Be Eligible**
Oscar Winner: **Other Nominations:**

Love Story	Francis Lai	Airport	Alfred Newman
		Cromwell	Frank Cordell
		Patton	Jerry Goldsmith
		Sunflower	Henry Mancini

**Best Original Song Score - for which the
song writer or writers and adaptor, if any,
shall be eligible.**
Oscar Winner: **Other Nominations:**

Let It Be	The Beatles	The Baby Maker	Fred Karlin, Tylwyth Kymry
		A Boy Named Charlie Brown	Rod McKuen, John Scott Trotter, Bill Melendez, Al Schean, Vince Guaraldi

Other Nominations:

Darling Lili	Henry Mancini
	Johnny Mercer
Scrooge	Leslie Bricusse
	Jan Fraser
	Herbert W. Spencer

1971
(In 1971, both "scoring" categories were re-defined again
as shown in the text below.)

**Best Original Score - for which only
the composer shall be eligible.
Oscar Winner:**

Other Nominations:

Summer Of '42	Michel Legrand	Mary, Queen Of Scots	John Barry
		Nicholas And Alexandra	Richard Rodney Bennett
		Shaft	Isaac Hayes
		Straw Dogs	Jerry Fielding

**Best Scoring: Adaptation and Original Song Score,
for which the composer, lyricist and adaptor shall
be eligible if the song score was written or first
used in a motion picture but only the adaptor will
be eligible if the material (song score or otherwise)
is an adaptation from another medium or has been
previously used.**

Fiddler On The Roof	John Williams	Bedknobs And Broomsticks	Richard M. Sherman
			Robert B. Sherman
			Irwin Kostal
		The Boy Friend	Peter Maxwell Davies
			Peter Greenwell
		Tchaikovsky	Dimitri Tiomkin
		Willy Wonka And The Chocolate Factory	Leslie Bricusse,
			Anthony Newley,
			Walter Scharf

1972

**Best Original Dramatic Score - for which only
the composer shall be eligible.
Oscar Winner:**

Other Nominations:

Limelight	Charles S. Chaplin	Napoleon And Samantha	Buddy Baker
	Raymond Rasch		
	Larry Russell	Sleuth	John Addison
		The Poseidon Adventure	John Williams
		*The Godfather	Nino Rota

*nomination was withdrawn on the grounds that portions of
the music had been used previously by Rota in the score of
Fortunella, a 1958 Italian picture.

Best Scoring: Adaptation and Original Song Score, for which the composer, lyricist and adaptor shall be eligible if the song score was written or first used in a motion picture but only the adaptor will be eligible if the material (song score or otherwise) is an adaptation from another medium or has been previously used.

Cabaret	Ralph Burns	Lady Sings The Blues	Gil Askey
		Man Of La Mancha	Laurence Rosenthal

1973
(In 1973, the "scoring" categories were simplified as shown in the text below)

Best Original Dramatic Score
Oscar Winner:

Other Nominations:

The Way We Were	Marvin Hamlisch	Cinderella Liberty	John Williams
		The Day Of The Dolphin	George Delerue
		Papillon	Jerry Goldsmith
		A Touch Of Class	John Cameron

Best Scoring - Original Song Score And Adaptation Or Best Scoring - Adaptation
Oscar Winner:

Other Nominations:

The Sting	Marvin Hamlisch	Jesus Christ Superstar	Andre Previn Herbert Spencer Andrew Lloyd Webber
		Tom Sawyer	Richard M. Sherman Robert B. Sherman John Williams

1974

Best Original Dramatic Score
Oscar Winner

Other Nominations:

The Godfather Part II	Nino Rota Carmine Coppola	Chinatown	Jerry Goldsmith
		Murder On The Orient Express	Richard Rodney Bennett
		Sharks	Alex North
		The Towering Inferno	John Williams

Best Scoring - Original Song Score And Adaptation Or Best Scoring - Adaptation

The Great Gatsby	Nelson Riddle	The Little Prince	Alan Jay Lerner, Frederic Loewe Angela Morley Douglas Gamley
		Phantom Of The Pradise	Paul Williams, **George Alliceson Tipton**

1975

Best Original Dramatic Score
Oscar Winner:

Jaws | John Williams

Other Nominations:

Birds Do It, Bees Do It	Gerald Fried
Bite The Bullet	Alex North
One Flew Over The Cuckoo's Nest	Jack Nitzsche
The Wind And The Lion	Jerry Goldsmith

Best Scoring - Original Song Score And Adaptation
Or Best-Scoring - Adaptation

Barry Lyndon	Leonard Rosenman	Funny Lady	Peter Matz
		Tommy	Peter Townshend

1976

Best Original Dramatic Score
Oscar Winner:

Omen | Jerry Goldsmith

Other Nominations:

Obsession	Bernard Herrmann
The Outlaw Josie Wales	Jerry Fielding
Taxi Driver	Bernard Herrmann
Voyage Of The Damned	Lalo Schifrin

Best Scoring - Original Song Score And Adaptation
Or Best-Scoring - Adaptation
Oscar Winner:

Other Nominations:

Bound For Glory	Leonard Rosenman	Buggsy Malone	Paul Williams
		A Star Is Born	Roger Kellaway

1977

Best Original Dramatic Score
Oscar Winner: **Other Nominations:**

Star Wars | John Williams

Close Encounters Of The Third Kind	John Williams
Julia	Georges Delarue
Mohammed - Messenger Of God	Maurice Jarre
The Spy Who Loved Me	Marvin Hamlisch

Best Scoring - Original Song Score and Adaptation
Or Best-Scoring - Adaptation

Other Nominations:

A Little Night Music   Jonathan Tunick

Pete's Dragon   Al Kasha
                                       Joel Hirschhorn

The Slipper and the   Robert B Sherman
Rose - The Story   Richard M. Sherman
of Cinderella

1978

Best Original Dramatic Score
Oscar Winner:

Other Nominations:

Midnight Express   Georgio Moroder

The Boys From Brazil   Jerry Goldsmith

Days Of Heaven   Enno Maricone

Heaven Can Wait   Dave Grusin

Superman   John Williams

Best Scoring - Original Song Score And Adaptation
Or Best-Scoring - Adaptation
Oscar Winner:

Other Nominations:

The Buddy Holly Story   Joe Renzetti

Pretty Baby   Jerry Wexler

The Wiz   Quincy Jones

1979

Best Original Dramatic Score
Oscar Winner:

Other Nominations:

A Little Romance   Georges Delerue

The Champ   David Grusin

Star Trek, The Motion   Jerry Goldsmith
Picture

The Amityville Horror   Lalo Schifrin

'10'   Henry Mancini

Best Scoring - Original Song Score And Adaptation
Or Best-Scoring - Adaptation
Oscar Winner:

Other Nominations:

All That Jazz   Ralph Burns

The Muppet Movie   Paul Williams,
                                       Kenny Ascher

Breaking Away   Patrick Williams

THE
NATIONAL ACADEMY OF
RECORDING ARTS
AND SCIENCES

GRAMMY
AWARDS
FOR

RECORD OF THE YEAR

SONG OF THE YEAR

BEST INSTRUMENTAL
COMPOSITION/THEME
(composer's award)

BEST COUNTRY SONG
(songwriter's award)

BEST RHYTHM AND BLUES SONG
(songwriter's award)

BEST ORIGINAL SCORE
WRITTEN FOR MOTION PICTURE OR TV
(composer's award)

BEST SCORE FROM AN ORIGINAL
CAST SHOW ALBUM
(composer's award)

BEST ORIGINAL JAZZ COMPOSITION

GRAMMY AWARD FOR RECORD OF THE YEAR

Year	Song	Recorded By	Written By
1958	Nel Blu Dipinto Di Blu (Volare)	Domenico Modugno	Domenico Modugno Mitchell Parish
1959	Mack The Knife	Bobby Darin	Kurt Weill Marc Blitzstein
1960	Theme From A Summer Place	Percy Faith	Max Steiner
1961	Moon River	Henry Mancini	Henry Mancini Johnny Mercer
1962	I Left My Heart In San Francisco	Tony Bennett	George Cory Douglass Cross
1963	The Days Of Wine And Roses	Henry Mancini	Henry Mancini Johnny Mercer
1964	The Girl From Ipanema	Stan Getz Astrud Gilberto	Antonio Carlos Jobim Newton Mendonca Norman Gimbel
1965	A Taste Of Honey	Herb Alpert And The Tijuana Brass	Robert W. Scott Ric Marlow
1966	Strangers In The Night	Frank Sinatra	Bert Kaempfert Charles Singleton Eddie Snyder
1967	Up, Up And Away	5th Dimension	Jimmy Webb
1968	Mrs. Robinson	Simon And Garfunkel	Paul Simon
1969	Aquarius/Let The Sunshine In	5th Dimension	Galt MacDermot James Rado Gerome Ragni
1970	Bridge Over Troubled Water	Simon And Garfunkel	Paul Simon
1971	It's Too Late	Carole King	Carole King Toni Stern
1972	The First Time Ever I Saw Your Face	Roberta Flack	Ewan MacColl
1973	Killing Me Softly With His Song	Roberta Flack	Charles Fox Norman Gimbel
1974	I Honestly Love You	Olivia Newton-John	Peter Allen, Jeff Barry
1975	Love Will Keep Us Together	Captain and Tennille	Neil Sedaka, Howrd Greenfield
1976	This Masquerade	George Benson	Leon Russell
1977	Hotel California	Eagles	Glenn Frey, Don Felder, Don Henley
1978	Just The Way You Are	Billy Joel	Billy Joel
1979	What A Fool Believes	The Doobie Brothers	Kenny Loggins Michael McDonald

GRAMMY AWARD FOR SONG OF THE YEAR
(Songwriter's Award)

1958	Nel Blu Dipinto Di Blu (Volare)	Domenico Modugno (English words: Mitchell Parish)
1959	The Battle Of New Orleans	Jimmy Driftwood
1960	Theme From Exodus	Ernest Gold (words by Pat Boone)
1961	Moon River	Henry Mancini Johnny Mercer
1962	What Kind Of Fool Am I	Leslie Bricusse Anthony Newley
1963	The Days Of Wine and Roses	Henry Mancini Johnny Mercer
1964	Hello, Dolly!	Jerry Herman
1965	The Shadow Of Your Smile (Love Theme From The Sandpiper)	Johnny Mandel Paul Francis Webster
1966	Michelle	John Lennon Paul McCartney
1967	Up, Up And Away	Jimmy Webb
1968	Little Green Apples	Bobby Russell
1969	Games People Play	Joe South
1970	Bridge Over Troubled Water	Paul Simon
1971	You've Got A Friend	Carole King
1972	The First Time Ever I Saw Your Face	Ewan MacColl
1973	Killing Me Softly With His Song	Charles Fox Norman Gimbel
1974	The Way We Were	Marilyn and Alan Bergman Marvin Hamlisch
1975	Send In The Clowns	Stephen Sondheim
1976	I Write The Songs	Bruce Johnston
1977	Love Theme From "A Star Is Born" (Evergreen)	Barbra Streisand Paul Williams
1978	Just The Way You Are	Billy Joel
1979	What A Fool Believes	Kenny Loggins Michael McDonald

GRAMMY AWARD FOR BEST COUNTRY SONG
(Songwriter's Award)

Year	Song Title	Written by:
1964	Dang Me	Roger Miller
1965	King Of The Road	Roger Miller
1966	Almost Persuaded	Billy Sherrill Glenn Sutton
1967	Gentle On My Mind	John Hartford
1968	Little Green Apples	Bobby Russell
1969	A Boy Named Sue	Shel Silverstein
1970	My Woman, My Woman, My Wife	Marty Robbins
1971	Help Me Make It Through The Night	Kris Kristofferson
1972	Kiss An Angel Good Mornin'	Ben Peters
1973	Behind Closed Doors	Kenny O'Dell
1974	A Very Special Love Song	Billy Sherrill Norro Wilson
1975	(Hey, Won't You Play) Another Somebody Done Somebody Wrong Song	Chips Moman, Larry Butler
1976	Broken Lady	Larry Gatlin
1977	Don't It Make My Brown Eyes Blue	Richard Leigh
1978	The Gambler	Donald Schlitz
1979	You Decorated My Life	Robert Morrison Debbie Hupp

GRAMMY AWARD FOR BEST INSTRUMENTAL COMPOSITION/THEME
(Composer's Award)

Year	Composition	Written by:
1961	African Waltz	Galt MacDermot
1962	A Taste Of Honey	Bobby Scott Ric Marlow
1963	More (Theme from Mondo Cane)	Riz Ortolani, Nino Oliviero Norman Newell
1964	The Pink Panther Theme	Henry Mancini
1965	No Award	
1966	Batman Theme	Neal Hefti
1967	Classical Gas	Mason Williams

1969	Midnight Cowboy	John Barry
1970	Airport Love Theme	Alfred Newman
1971	Theme From Summer Of '42	Michel Legrand
1972	Brian's Song	Michel Legrand
1973	Last Tango In Paris	Gato Barbieri
1974	Tubular Bells (from The Exorcist)	Mike Oldfield
1975	Images	Michel Legrand
1976	Bellavia	Chuck Mangione
1977	Star Wars (Main Title Theme)	John Williams
1978	Theme From "Close Encounters Of The Third Kind"	John Williams
1979	Theme From "Superman"	John Williams

GRAMMY AWARD FOR BEST RHYTHM AND BLUES SONG
(Songwriter's Award)

Year	Song Title	Written by
1968	(Sittin' On) The Dock Of The Bay	Otis Redding Steve Cropper
1969	Color Him Father	Richard Spencer
1970	Patches (I'm Depending On You)	Ronald Dunbar General Johnson
1971	Ain't No Sunshine	Bill Withers
1972	Papa Was A Rolling Stone	Norman Whitfield Barrett Strong
1973	Superstition	Stevie Wonder
1974	Livin' For The City	Stevie Wonder
1975	Where Is The Love	Harry Wayne Casey Richard Finch Willie Clarke Betty Wright
1976	Lowdown	Boz Scaggs David Paich
1977	You Make Me Feel Like Dancing	Leo Sayer Vini Poncia
1978	Last Dance	Paul Jabara
1979	After The Love Has Gone	David Foster Jay Graydon Bill Champlin

GRAMMY AWARD FOR BEST ORIGINAL SCORE WRITTEN
FOR MOTION PICTURE OR TELEVISION
(composers's award)

Year	Title	Composer
1959	Anatomy Of A Murder	Duke Ellington
1960	Exodus	Ernest Gold
1961	Breakfast At Tiffany's	Henry Mancini
1962	No Award	
1963	Tom Jones	John Addison
1964	Mary Poppins	Richard M. Sherman Robert B. Sherman
1965	The Sandpiper	Johnny Mandel
1966	Dr. Zhivago	Maurice Jarre
1967	Mission: Impossible	Lalo Schifrin
1968	The Graduate	Paul Simon additional music by Dave Grusin
1969	Butch Cassidy And The Sundance Kid	Bert Bacharach Hal David
1970	Let It Be	John Lennon, Paul McCartney George Harrison, Ringo Starr
1971	Shaft	Isaac Hayes
1972	The Godfather	Nino Rota
1973	Jonathan Livingston Seagull	Neil Diamond
1974	The Way We Were	Marvin Hamlisch Alan and Marilyn Bergman
1975	Jaws	John Williams
1976	Car Wash	Norman Whitfield
1977	Star Wars	John Williams
1978	Close Encounters Of The Third Kind	John Williams
1979	Superman	John Williams

GRAMMY AWARD FOR BEST SCORE FROM AN
ORIGINAL CAST SHOW ALBUM
(composer's award)

Year	Show	Words and music by
1958	The Music Man	Meredith Willson
1959	Tie: Gypsy Redhead	Jule Styne, Stephen Sondheim Albert Hague, Dorothy Fields
1960	The Sound Of Music	Richard Rodgers, Oscar Hammerstein II
1961	How To Succeed In Business Without Really Trying	Frank Loesser
1962	No Strings	Richard Rodgers
1963	She Loves Me	Jerry Bock, Sheldon Harnick
1964	Funny Girl	Jule Styne, Bob Merrill
1965	On A Clear Day	Alay Jay Lerner, Burton Lane
1966	Mame	Jerry Herman
1967	Cabaret	Fred Ebb, John Kander
1968	Hair	Gerome Ragni James Rado Galt MacDermot
1969	Promises, Promises	Burt Bacharach Hal David
1970	Company	Stephen Sondheim
1971	Godspell	Stephen Schwartz
1972	Don't Bother Me, I Can't Cope	Micki Grant
1973	A Little Night Music	Stephen Sondheim
1974	Raisin	Judd Woldin John Brittan
1975	The Wiz	Charlie Smalls
1976	Bubbling Brown Sugar	Emmerlyne Kemp Danny Holgate Lillian Collazo
1977	Annie	Charles Strouse Martin Charnin
1978	Ain't Misbehavin'	title song and other songs by Thomas "Fats" Waller and Andy Razaf (additional songs by Jimmy McHugh, Dorothy Fields, etc.)
1979	Sweeney Todd	Stephen Sondheim

GRAMMY AWARD FOR BEST ORIGINAL JAZZ COMPOSITION
(composer's award)

Year	Title	Composer
1960	Sketches Of Spain	Miles Davis, Gil Evans
1961	African Waltz	Galt MacDermot
1962	Cast Your Fate To The Winds	Vince Guaraldi
1963	Gravy Waltz	Steven Allen, Ray Brown
1964	The Cat	Lalo Schifrin
1965	Jazz Suite On The Mass Texts	Lalo Schifrin
1966	In The Beginning God	Duke Ellington
1967	Category eliminated	

THE
AMERICAN THEATRE WING
ANTOINETTE PERRY AWARDS
"TONY"
FOR DISTINGUISHED ACHIEVEMENT IN
THEATRE

TONY AWARDS
BEST MUSICAL PLAY
AND AUTHOR

BEST MUSICAL PLAY DIRECTOR
BEST MUSICAL PLAY COMPOSER
AND LYRICIST
BEST PRODUCER, MUSICAL PLAY

From 1949 to 1980

TONY AWARDS
BEST MUSICAL PLAY AND AUTHOR

Year	Musical Play	COMPOSER AND LYRICIST OR SCORER	AUTHOR	DIRECTOR (Began 1960)
1949	Kiss Me, Kate	Cole Porter	Bella Spewack Samuel Spewach	
1950	South Pacific	Richard Rodgers Oscar Hammerstein II	Oscar Hammerstein II Joshua Logan	
1951	Guys And Dolls	Frank Loesser	Jo Swerling Abe Burrows	
1952	The King And I	Richard Rodgers Oscar Hammrstein II	Oscar Hammerstein II	
1953	Wonderful Town	Leonard Bernstein Betty Comden Adolph Green	Joseph Fields Jerome Chodorov	
1954	Kismet	Aleksandr Borodin George (Chet) Forrest Robert C. Wright	Charles Lederer Luther Davis	
1955	The Pajama Game	Jerry Ross Richard Adler	George Abbott Douglass Wallop	
1957	My Fair Lady	Frederick Loewe Alan Jay Lerner	Alan Jay Lerner	
1958	The Music Man	Meredith Willson	Meredith Willson Frank Lacey	
1959	Redhead	Albert Hague Dorothy Fields	Herbert Fields Dorothy Fields Sidney Sheldon David Shaw	
1960	**Tie:**			
	Fiorello	Jerry Bock Sheldon Harnick	Jerome Weidman George Abbott	George Abbott
	The Sound Of Music	Richard Rodgers Oscar Hammerstein II	Howard Lindsay Russel Crouse	
1961	Bye Bye Birdie	No Award	Michael Stewart	Gower Champion
1962	How To Succeed In Business Without Really Trying	Award To Richard Rodgers for "No Strings"	Abe Burrows Jack Weinstock Willie Gilbert (for "How To Succeed", etc.)	Abe Burrows (How To Succeed, etc.)
1963	A Funny Thing Happened On The Way To The Forum	Award To Lionel Bart for "Oliver"	Bert Shevelove Larry Gelbart (for "A Funny Thing, etc. /)	George Abbott (for "A Funny Thing, etc.")
1964	Hello, Dolly!	Jerry Herman	Michael Stewart	Gower Champion
1965	Fiddler On The Roof	Jerry Bock Sheldon Harnick	Joseph Stein	Jerome Robbins

1966	Man Of La Mancha	Mitch Leigh Joe Darion	No Award	Albert Marre
1967	Cabaret	John Kander Fred Ebb	No Award	Harold Prince
1968	Hallelujah, Baby!	Jule Styne Betty Comden Adolph Green	No Award	Gower Champion (for "The Happy Time")
1969	1776	No Awrd	No Award	Peter Hunt
1970	Applause	No Award	No Award	Ron Field
1971	Company	Stephen Sondheim	George Furth	Harold Prince
1972	Two Gentlemen Of Verona	Stephen Sondheim	John Guare Mel Shapiro	Harold Prince, Michael Bennett (for "Follies")
1973	A Little Night Music	Stephen Sondheim	Hugh Wheeler	Bob Fosse (for "Pippin")
1974	Raisin (words and music by Judd Woldin and John Brittan)	Frederick Loewe Allan Jay Lerner (for "Gigi")	Hugh Wheeler	Harold Prince (for "Candide")
1975	The Wiz	Charlie Smalls	James Lee Barrett Peter Udell Philip Rose	Geoffrey Holder
1976	A Chorus Line	Marvin Hamlisch Edward Kleban	James Kirkwood Nicholas Dante	Michael Bennett
1977	Annie	Charles Strouse Martin Charnin	Thomas Meehan	Gene Sacks (for "I Love My Wife")
1978	Ain't Misbehavin'	Cy Coleman, Betty Comden Adolph Green (for "On The Twentieth- Century Limited")	Betty Comden Adolph Green (for "On The Twentieth-Century Limited")	Richard Maltby Jr. (for "Ain't Misbehavin' ")
1979	Sweeney Todd	Stephen Sondheim	Hugh Wheeler	Harold Prince
1980	Evita	Andrew Lloyd Webber, Tim Rice	Tim Rice	Harold Prince

TONY AWARDS

YEAR	MUSICAL DIRECTOR	(PLAY DIRECTED)	PRODUCER	(PLAY PRODUCED)
1949	Max Meth	As The Girls Go	Saint-Subber Lemuel Ayers	Kiss Me, Kate
1950	Maurice Abravanel	Regina	Oscar Hammerstein II Richard Rodgers Joshua Logan Leland Hayward	South Pacific
1951	Lehman Engel	The Consul	Cy Feuer Ernest Martin	Guys And Dolls
1952	Max Meth	Pal Joey	Richard Rodgers Oscar Hammerstein II	The King And I

1953	Lehman Engel	Wonderful Town The Gilbert And Sullivan Season	Robert Fryer	Wonderful Town
1954	Louis Adrian	Kismet	Charles Lederer	Kismet
1955	Thomas Schippers	The Saint Of Bleeker Street	Frederick Brisson Robert Griffith Harold S. Prince	The Pajama Game
1956	Hal Hastings	Damn Yankees	Frederick Brisson Robert Griffith Harold S. Prince Albert B. Taylor	Damn Yankees
1957	Franz Allers	My Fair Lady	Herman Levin	My Fair Lady
1958	Herbert Greene	The Music Man	Kermit Bloomgarden Herbert Green Frank Productions	The Music Man
1959	Salvatore Dell'Isola	Flower Drum Song	Robert Fryer Lawrence Carr	Redhead
1960	Frederick Dvonch	The Sound Of Music	Robert Griffith Harold S. Prince tied with Leland Hayward Richard Halliday	Fiorello The Sound Of Music
1961	Franz Allers	Camelot	Ed Padula	Bye Bye Birdie
1962	Elliot Lawrence	How To Succeed In Business Without Really Trying	Cy Feuer Ernest Martin Frank Productions	How To Succeed In Business Without Really Trying
1963	Donald Pippin	Oliver	Harold S. Prince	A Funny Thing Happened On The Way To The Forum
1964	Shephard Coleman	Hello Dolly	David Merrick	Hello Dolly

(after 1964 no further awards were given for musical director)

			PRODUCER	**PLAY**
1965			Harold Prince	Fiddler On The Roof
1966			No Award	
1967			No Award	
1968			Albert Selden, Hal James, Jane C. Nussbaum Harry Rigby	Hallelujah, Baby!
1969			No Award	
1970			No Award	
1971			Harold Prince	Company

The
Elements
of
Music

Contents:

Musical Notation
(Staffs and Clefs, Accidentals, Notes, Rests)

Notation Marks
(Dynamic, Performance and Expression)

Terms of Acceleration / Deceleration, Dynamics and Volume

Octaves and Scales

Octave Notation

Time Signatures, Time and Meter

Measures or Bars
(Accents & Beats)

Intervals

Chords

Harmonic Analysis

MUSICAL NOTATION
STAFFS and CLEFS

Notes above or below the staff are placed on or between added short ledger lines.

STAFF

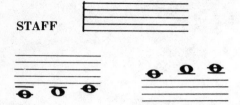

Added ledger lines The five lines and spaces on which notes are placed to indicate pitch. The lines are called "ledger" or "leger": The lines and spaces on a staff also are referred to as "degrees":

treble clef or **G clef** or **violin clef** The G clef places the note G above middle C (c′) on the second line of the staff counting from the bottom. Also called **treble clef** or **violin clef**:

bass clef or **F clef** The F clef or bass clef places the F below middle C (c′) on the fourth line of the staff counting from the bottom.

tenor clef — one of the C clefs The tenor C clef places the middle C (c′) on the fourth line of the staff counting from the bottom.

alto clef — one of the C clefs The soprano C clef places middle C (c′) on the third line of the staff counting from the bottom.

soprano clef — one of the C clefs The alto C clef places middle C (c′) on the first line of the staff counting from the bottom.

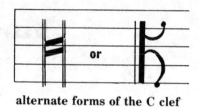

alternate forms of the C clef

ACCIDENTALS

Signs that affect the note immediately following, and all similar notes within the same measure, except those in another octave. A bar line at the end of a measure cancels the effect of all accidentals except for those that appear in the key signature.

	American, English	Italian	German	French	Spanish
♯ a sign indicating that the line or space on the staff (on which it is placed) will be pitched one half-tone higher than otherwise	sharp	diesis	kreuz	dièse	sostenido
♭ a sign indicating that the line or space on the staff (on which it is placed) will be pitched one half-tone lower than otherwise.	flat	bemolle	be	bémol	bemol
𝄪 or ♯♯ a sign indicating that the pitch is to be raised by two half-tones or semitones.	double sharp	doppio diesis	doppel-kreuz	double dièse	doble sostenido
♭♭ a sign indicating that the pitch is to be lowered by the two half-tones or semitones.	double flat	doppio bemolle	doppel-be	double bémol	doble bemol

	American, English	Italian	German	French	Spanish

♮ a sign that cancels the effect of all other accidentals preceding it in the same measure and cancels the effect of all accidentals in the key signature as well. The affect *does* apply to notes in a following measure linked by a tie (⌣) to a preceding measure. — natural — bequadro — auflö-sungs-zeichen — becarre — becuadro

♮♯ a sign that returns a double sharp note to a single sharp note: for the same purpose, the ♯ by itself is frequently used.

♮♭ a sign that returns a double flat to a single flat note: for the same purpose, the ♭ by itself is frequently used.

NOTES

The duration of a musical tone — its time value — is indicated in notation by a "note".
(Americans use the words "note" and "tone" interchangeably on an informal basis; formally, they use "note" for notation and "tone" for the sound: The British use "note" for both notation and sound:)

U.S.A. Name	Sign	Value	British	Italian	Names Used By German	French	Spanish
breve	𝄴	2 whole notes	breve				
whole note (semibreve)	𝅝	2 half notes	semibreve	semibreve	ganze note	ronde	redonda
half note	𝅗𝅥 or	2 quarter notes, ½ whole note	minim	bianca	halbe note	blanche	blanca
quarter note	𝅘𝅥 or	2 eighth notes, ½ half note	crotchet	nera	viertel	noire	negra
eighth note	𝅘𝅥𝅮 or	2 sixteenth notes, ½ quarter note	quaver	croma	achtel	croche	corchea
sixteenth note	𝅘𝅥𝅯 or	2 thirty-second notes ½ eighth note	semi-quaver	semi-croma	sech-zehntel	double-croche	semi-corchea
thirty-second note	or	2 sixty-fourth notes ½ sixteenth note	demi-semi-quaver	bis-croma	zweiund-dreissig-stel	triple-croche	fusa
sixty-fourth note	or	½ thirty-second note	hemidemi-semi-quaver	semibis-croma	vierund-sechszeg-stel	quadruple-croche	semifusa

The physical parts of a note are:

| — the stem

●○ — the note head attached to the stem

𝅘𝅥𝅮 𝅘𝅥𝅮 — the "hook" or "flag" attached to the stem, each of which cuts the original note value in half.

The stems of a group of eighth notes are joined by a thick, horizontal line called a "beam"

The stems of a group of sixteenth notes are joined by two "beams", etc. ("hooks" and "flags" are eliminated by beam connections)

RESTS

The duration of *silence* is indicated in notation by a "rest". The time value for the silent pause corresponds to the value of the note for which the "rest" is named.

U.S.A. Name	Sign	Value & Position	British and German names for "rests" correspond to "note" names. See "Notes":		
			Italian	French	Spanish
breve rest		two whole rests. placed between 3rd and 4th lines of the staff counting from bottom			
whole rest		hangs down from 4th line of the staff counting from bottom	pausa di semibreve	pause	silencio de rendonda
half rest		½ whole rest. placed above 3rd line of staff counting from bottom	pausa di bianca	demipause	silencio de blanca
quarter rest		½ half rest. position as shown	pausa di nera	soupir	silencio de negra
eighth rest		½ quarter rest. position as shown	pausa di croma	demi- soupir	silencio de corchea
sixteenth rest		½ eighth rest. position as shown	pausa di semicroma	quart de soupir	silencio de semicorchea
thirty-second rest		½ sixteenth rest. position as shown	pausa di biscroma	huitième de soupir	silencio de fusa
sixty-fourth rest		½ thirty-second rest.	pausa di semibiscroma	seizième de soupir	silencio de semifusa

An extended rest is abbreviated in any of the following ways. The "rest" applies to the amount of measures indicated by the number: **8** **16** **16** **3**

NOTATION MARKS
Dynamic Marks, Performance Marks, and Expression Marks

Dotted Notes:

A dot after a note or rest increases the time value of the note or rest by one-half. A double dot adds three-quarters to the time-value and a triple dot adds seven-eighths to the time-value. A dotted half-note, therefore, equals three quarter-notes, or a half-note plus a quarter-note. A dotted quarter-note equals a quarter-note plus an eighth note, etc. In current practice, dotted notes are used only when they do not cross over a bar-line. For this purpose, "tied" notes are used.

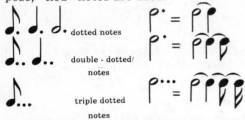

dotted notes

double - dotted notes

triple dotted notes

A dot over or under notes indicates they are to be played *staccato*:

A wedge-shaped mark over or under notes indicates they are to be played with a sharper, more abrupt type of *staccato*:

A dot in a slur, over or under the notes, indicates they are to be played *mezzo staccato* or *portato* (half-way between *staccato* and *legato:*)

A dot under a dash, over or under a note, indicates the note is to be played *non-legato* (in accented or sustained manner) or *marcato* or sforzando. Similarly, a dotted note under or over a slur indicates the note(s) should be played *non-legato* or *half-legato (portato)*:

Slur — over or under two or more notes of different pitch; indicates they are to be played *legato!* Also *portato:*

also used to indicate a melodic phrase:

vocal music: indicates notes to be sung in one breath or notes to be sung to one syllable of text: for bowed strings: notes to be played in one stroke.

Tie — Not to be confused with a slur: A tie connects two notes of the same pitch, and indicates that the two notes are to be sounded as one tone for the time value of both notes combined:

Tenuto — A small horizontal dash over or under a note calls for sustaining the note to its full value: *Tenuto*, the opposite of staccato:

Accent Marks — Indicates especially stressed or emphasized notes or chords: *(marcato):*

Breath Marks — Indicates where or when a breath should be taken in vocal music:

Pause or Hold *(Fermata)* — The sign over or under a note or rest which means sustaining either at the discretion of the performer. Also used over a double bar to stress the end of a composition. The pause sign ⌒ or the sign ⊕ also may indicate the end of a portion of music to be repeated.

division marks — placed over or under groups of notes to indicate they are to be played in the time-value of even notes (the next smallest even number): Thus, 3,5,7 notes are played in time of 2,4,6 notes:

crescendo a gradual increase of loudness: abbreviated *cresc.* or cr.

decrescendo or diminuendo } a gradual decrease of loudness: abbreviated { *decresc.* or decr. dimin. or dim.

swell a gradual crescendo followed by a gradual decrescendo:
In vocal music: *messa di voce.* In piano music: smoothly resonant.
also rinforzando; calls for added stress or accents over notes or chords.

Segno *(Presa)* The sign that indicates the beginning or the end of a portion of music that is to be repeated. Also used to indicate the entrance of a lead part in a series of vocal parts

"al segno" . . . repeat up to the sign.

The sign that indicates the beginning of a portion to be repeated:

D.C., da capo The sign that means "repeat from the beginning of the music to the end (the word *fine*) or to the pause (fermata) sign ⌒ or the ⊕ sign," marking the end of a portion: *D.C.*

D.S., dal segno or dal segno al fine The sign that means "repeat from the sign 𝄋 or 𝄉 to the word *fine* or to the pause (fermata) ⌒ or ⊕ sign:

Octave The sign above a note that indicates the note an octave higher is to be sounded along with the original note. The same sign below a note indicates the note an octave lower is to be sounded along with the original note: **8**

all' ottava "at the octave" or coll' ottava "with the octave" Either sign above the staff indicates the note(s) are to be played one octave higher than written (not including the note as written). Either sign below the staff indicates the note(s) will be played one octave lower than written (not including the note as written): *8va*

Direct (custos) The direct sign placed at the end of a staff indicates the position of the upcoming, first note on the next page:

Octave Indicates an octave or the extension of a trill which is a a shorter sign:

trill Indicates the rapid alternation of two notes. Also used with other *ornaments.* See *Trill:*

Short Grace Note A short appoggiatura marking:

Long Grace Note An appoggiatura: (long)

arpeggio "Broken chord"; play the notes of a chord one after the other, usually beginning with the lowest:

tremolo Rapid repetition of the same note (same pitch) with alternating loud-soft patterns:

glissando Quickly moving up or down a scale:

coda A closing section of music, usually an added conclusion: ⊕

mordents A) A special "grace" marking. See *mordent (definition).* B) Inverted mordent: *Pralltriller.*

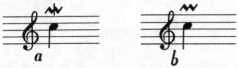

a   b

turn & inverted turn A particular "ornament" marking. See turn (definition): A) Turn B) Inverted Turn.

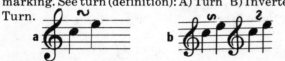

a   b

D.M. Destro mane (Italian) **or** Mane destra (Italian) **M.D.** Main droite (French) Use right hand:

M.S. Mano sinistra (Italian) **or M.G.** Main gauche (French) Use left hand:

L.H. abbreviation left hand

R.H. abbreviation right hand

Repeat Marks
Repeat preceding measure:

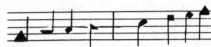

Repeat preceding eight-note group: /

Repeat preceding sixteenth-note group: //

Repeat preceding thirty-second note group: ///

Pedal Marks
Press down the piano damper pedal (right pedal):

Release the piano damper pedal (right pedal):

Use piano damper pedal for duration of the marking:

Organ pedal . . . play connected notes with alternate toe and heel of one foot:
∧— heel
∨— toe

Changes toes on organ pedal: ∧—∨

Slide toe to next note on organ pedal: ∨ ∨

+ or' an augmented chord: III₊, augmented minor triad III⁷ augmented minor seventh C+, augmented C chord or C'

+ also indicates *stopped* notes for the French horn:

+ also used sometimes to indicate a *trill!*

o indicates a diminished chord: II° diminished minor triad; VII⁷ diminished seventh

o also indicates a note to be played on an *open* (unstopped) string.

also indicates a note is to be played as a *harmonic.*

heavy, and firmly sustained (*pensante*):

shaped notes or *patent notes,* used in some sacred music notation (mostly in southern states of the U.S.A.)

Abbreviated note marks

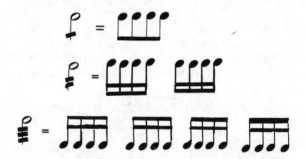

Bowing Marks—Violin, etc.

down-bow or tiré (arm moves away from body)

up-bow or pousse (arm moves towards body)

martelé (small arrowheads)

sautillé or spiccato

détaché (short dashes over or under the notes)

grand détaché (longer dashes over or under the notes)

ricochet or jeté

portato or louré (dashes or dots connected by slur . . . over or under notes)

staccato

staccato volante

arpeggio

tremolo

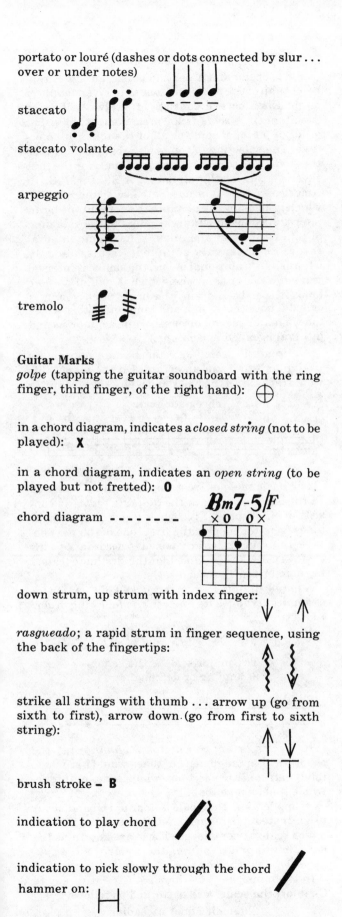

Guitar Marks

golpe (tapping the guitar soundboard with the ring finger, third finger, of the right hand): ⊕

in a chord diagram, indicates a *closed string* (not to be played): **X**

in a chord diagram, indicates an *open string* (to be played but not fretted): **O**

chord diagram - - - - - - - -

Bm7-5/F

down strum, up strum with index finger: ↓ ↑

rasgueado; a rapid strum in finger sequence, using the back of the fingertips:

strike all strings with thumb . . . arrow up (go from sixth to first), arrow down (go from first to sixth string):

brush stroke - **B**

indication to play chord

indication to pick slowly through the chord

hammer on:

trill; play the note as written but alternate rapidly with next highest tone as follows, for example: ∿

down stroke, up stroke ⊓ ⊔

slide up to indicated note (from one fret back; do not lift finger)

slide down to indicated note (from one fret higher; do not lift finger)

rapid slide down several frets after playing indicated note

long dash between two notes indicates a slide from one to the other without lifting finger:

a "bend" or "smear"; after playing note, sliding along the fret and returning to original position: ∿∿∿∿

P.I.M.A. or T.I.M.R. finger designations:

In Spanish, pulgar
indice
medio
annular

In English, thumb
index
middle
ring

Tempo Marks
slowest to fastest

Larghissimo   as slowly as possible; very, very slow
Largo   very slow and stately
Largamente   slow and broad
Larghetto   a bit faster than *largo*
Grave   slow, solemn, stately; slower than *adagio*
Lento   slow
Adagissimo   a bit slower than *adagio*
Adagio   slow, easy, graceful
Andantino   a bit slower than andante; sometimes ambiguously translated as "a bit faster"
Andante   moving along moderately slow; leisurely
Moderato   moderately; the middle tempo between *largo* and *presto*
Allegretto   lively, but a bit slower than *allegro*
Allegro   fast, with animation; lively
Vivace   a bit faster than allegro; with vivacity
Presto   very fast; rapid (for 17th & 18th century music, *presto* means *fast*, but *not as fast as the modern meaning*)
Prestissimo   extremely fast; very rapid

Tempo Accelerations

Accelerando gradually increasing speed; *poco a poco*, little by little

Affrettando or Stringendo swift or hurried increase in speed

Doppio movimento twice as fast, double speed

Incalzando more rapid and warmer

Piu allegro more lively, and then constant

Piu Mosso or Piu Moto faster, and then constant

Rubato free, elastic tempo

Veloce rapidly, hurrying

Velocissimo extremely rapid, hurried

Metronome Marks (Maelzel Metronome) Abbreviated M.M.)

M.M. ♩ = 66 Calls for 66 quarter-notes in one minute

M.M. ♪ = 80 Calls for 80 half-notes in one minute (hence, each note = ¾ of a second)

Tempo Decelerations

Allargando or Ritardando or Rallentando or Tartando or Slentando gradually more slowly; sometimes louder or building to a crescendo

Molte Meno Mosso much slower; much less quickly

Meno Mosso or Meno Moto less quickly

Strascinando dragging, almost sliding

Slargando slowing down (by extending the time)

Calando or Mancando or Moremdo gradually slower and fading away

Rattenuto or Trattenuto holding back, delaying the tempo

DYNAMICS/VOLUME

	Abbreviation
Double Pianissimo as soft as possible	ppp
Pianissimo very soft	pp
Piano soft	p
Mezzo Piano half soft; moderately soft	mp
Mezzo Forte half loud; moderately loud	mf
Forte loud	f
Fortissimo very loud	ff
Double Fortissimo as loud as possible	fff
Forte-piano loud, then immediately soft	fp
Rinforzando reinforced, abruptly accented; sometimes louder than before	rf or rfz or inf.
Sforzando or Sforzato sharp loud accents, followed by softer	sf or sfz

Octaves and Scales

In European and American music, an *octave* represents all of the notes and tones in a given family of pitch. Each octave consists of twelve half-tones (semitones)! A *scale* is an arrangement, in rising order of pitch, of some or all of the tones in an octave. The selection of tones in a scale is known as the *mode*. The tones or notes are named for the first seven letters of the alphabet: A,B,C,D,E,F,G. In America, a tone is a note, a basic sound of pitch which is measured in distance to another tone by an *interval*. A melodic interval refers to the sounding of tones one after the other; a harmonic interval refers to intervals sounded simultaneously (chords). In traditional music, the smallest interval is a *half-tone* or semitone, which is half of a *whole tone*. (Note: In Britain, the basic pitch sound is called a note (not tone), and tone refers to a whole tone, a major second interval, while a minor second interval is called a semitone.)

A chromatic scale (dodecuple scale) contains all twelve half-tones in an octave. On the piano, this would include all the black and white keys from c' to c''.

chromatic scale

c' c# d d# e f f# g g# a a# b c''

The basic scale of Western music (American and European) however, is the *diatonic scale!* It consists of eight tones: Five whole tones and two half-tones (semitones) plus the first tone of the next octave. Diatonic scales are named in accordance with their keys! A key is named for the first note (called keynote or tonic) of each scale.

A *major* diatonic scale, in the key of C-major for example, arranges its tones in the following order:

whole tone	whole tone	half tone	whole tone	whole tone	whole tone	half tone

c' ∧ d ∧ e ∧ f ∧ g ∧ a ∧ b ∧ c''

The major scale is the same ascending or descending:

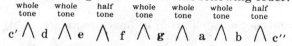

In a *pure* or *natural diatonic minor scale*, the theoretical arrangement of tones would be: Whole tone, half-tone, whole tone, whole tone, half-tone, whole tone, whole tone!

In application, this scale is impractical and never used. Instead, three modified forms of the natural minor scale are employed. These are known as the *melodic minor ascending*; the *melodic minor descending*, and the *harmonic minor*.

In the minor key of A-minor (the relative key to C-major) the scales are patterned as follows:

Melodic minor ascending

whole tone	half tone	whole tone	whole tone	whole tone	whole tone	half tone

a ∧ b ∧ c ∧ d ∧ e ∧ f# ∧ g# ∧ a'

Melodic minor descending

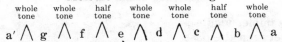

whole tone | whole tone | half tone | whole tone | whole tone | half tone | whole tone

a′ ∧ g ∧ f ∧ e ∧ d ∧ c ∧ b ∧ a

The harmonic minor scale is the same ascending as descending:

Harmonic minor

whole tone | half tone | whole tone | whole tone | half tone | Whole tone and a half | half tone

a ∧ b ∧ c ∧ d ∧ e ∧ f ∧ g# ∧ a′

Harmonic
A-minor

Other scales derived from the chromatic scale include:

whole tone scale — C-D-E-F#-G#-A#-C′ or C#-D#-F-G-A-B-C#′

...a six-tone scale which can begin only on C or C#; it omits the perfect fifth, perfect fourth and leading tone; popularized by Debussy at the beginning of the 20th century but has declined in usage!

pentatonic scale — C D F G A C′

...a five-tone primitive scale used in China, Africa and among the American Indians and Celts of Britain!

gypsy scale — C D Eb F# G Ab B C′

...with its two augmented seconds, this scale has a synthetic link to Hungarian music culture! It was imported into Hungary by the gypsies but owes its origin to Near East countries—India, Turkey—from which the gypsies migrated to Hungary. Not to be confused with natural Hungarian music scales.

In non-Western music ... India, the Orient, Near East ... microtone scales which contain intervals smaller than half-tones (microtones) are traditionally utilized. In addition, some European and American modern composers have written important pieces using microtones.

All **diatonic scales** ... major or minor ... may be transposed to begin on any note in Western music's chromatic scale. As a result, there are twelve major scales and twelve minor scales, one for each key. These are all listed under KEYS

Octave Notation

There are some variations in the method of notating octaves but the most widely-used system uses accent marks, lower-case letters, capital letters and small numerals as follows:

Contra octave	C_1 to C	Two-line Octave	c″ to c‴
Great octave	C to c	Three-line Octave	c‴ to c⁗
Small octave	c to c′ (c′ is middle C)	Four-line Octave	c⁗ to c⁗′
One-line Octave	c′ to c″		

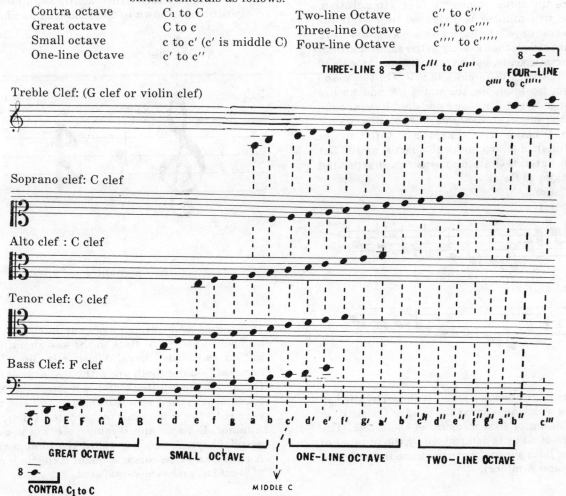

Treble Clef: (G clef or violin clef)

Soprano clef: C clef

Alto clef : C clef

Tenor clef: C clef

Bass Clef: F clef

THREE-LINE 8 — c‴ to c⁗   FOUR-LINE 8 — c⁗ to c⁗′

C D E F G A B c d e f g a b c′ d′ e′ f′ g′ a′ b′ c″ d″ e″ f″ g″ a″ b″ c‴

GREAT OCTAVE   SMALL OCTAVE   ONE-LINE OCTAVE   TWO-LINE OCTAVE

8 — CONTRA C_1 to C

MIDDLE C

In notation, a scale appears on the bass and treble clefs as follows:

    (key of C-major is used as an example; middle c′ is placed on the ledger line between the bass and treble staffs as a reference)

    All tones are whole tones except those marked half-tone!

Keys and Key Signatures

A **key** is an expression of tonality! It is a selected group of tones, relating to a tonic center ... the tonic or keynote ... which governs the components of composition. The key's tones, in rising order of pitch, make up a **scale**, but key and scale are not identical. The former allows for chromatic variations that may use notes foreign to the given scale.

Since there are 12 major and 12 minor scales, there are the same number of keys. (In notation, however, this number is increased to provide for **"enharmonic keys"**. Enharmonic keys or tones are those that are pitched exactly in the same degree of the chromatic scale, but have different names and are written with different symbols. On the piano keyboard, for example, the notes g# and ab are identical, as are the notes c# and db! These are called **"enharmonic equivalents"**! The enharmonic keys are B-major (five sharps) and C-flat major (seven flats); F-sharp major (6 sharps) and G-flat major (6 flats); C-sharp major (seven sharps) and D-flat major (5 flats)!

In notation:

B-major =

C-flat major =

The **key** of any written music is shown by the **key signature** which appears at the head of the staff ... the beginning or first measure of the music! The signature of a key is determined by the number of sharps or flats shown (there are none in the key of C-major and A-minor)!

When used in a key signature, a sharp or flat applies to all the octaves (all ledger lines and spaces) until cancelled by a natural sign (♮). In the body of music, a sharp or flat applies only to the one degree of its location, and only to the one measure in which it appears. The natural sign's effect applies in the same way unless it is used to alter the key signature itself.

The key signature is placed between the treble clef and the time signature at the beginning of a composition as shown in the following example:

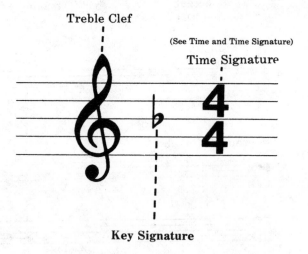

All major and minor keys that have the same number of sharps or flats in the key signature as known as **relative keys**! A-minor is the relative minor of C-major (both are without sharps or flats); D-major is the relative major of B-minor (both have two sharps in their signature)! All major and minor keys with the same tonic or keynote (A-major and A-minor, B-major and B-minor, etc. are known as **parallel keys**. A-major is called the tonic major of A-minor, and vice-versa; B-minor is the tonic minor of B-major, and vice-versa, etc.!

All twenty-four major and minor keys and scales (plus six enharmonic keys and scales) are shown in the following list:

Major Scale	Signature	Scale: ∧ = ½ tone all others are whole tones	Relative Minor Scale
C major	no sharps no flats	c d e f g a b c'	A minor — a b c d e f g a'
G major	one sharp	g a b c d e f g'	E minor — e f# g a b c d e'
D major	two sharps	d e f# g a b c# d'	B minor — b c# d e f# g a b'
A major	three sharps	a b c# d e f# g# a'	F sharp minor — f# g# a b c# d e f#'
E major	four sharps	e f# g# a b c# d# e'	C sharp minor — c# d# e f# g# a b c#'
B major	five sharps	b c# d# e f# g# a# b'	G sharp minor — g# a# b c# d# e f# g#'
C flat major	seven flats	cb db eb fb gb ab bb cb'	A flat minor — ab bb cb db eb fb gb ab'

enharmonic with (bracket joining B major and C flat major)

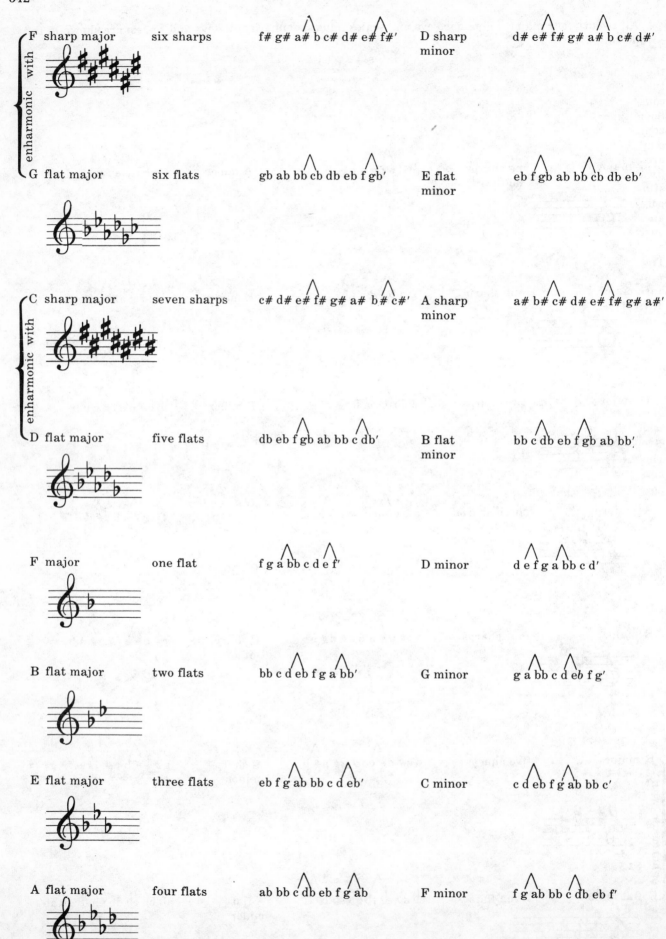

Time Signatures, Time and Meter

The **time** or **meter** of a composition is dictated by the time signature. This appears at the beginning of the music immediately after the clef and accidentals (if any) in the key signature. The **time signature** consists of two numbers placed one above the other. Sometimes, the numbers are separated by a horizontal dash, or a diagonal stroke, but these are only a matter of typographical preference. When there are two sets of vertically paired numbers shown (two time-signatures) this indicates one of two possibilities: Either the music is multitoned or polyphonic, with one meter in the treble staff and another meter in the bass staff applied simultaneously, or one meter applies simultaneously to all staffs but shifts back and forth to another meter. Time and meter are not to be confused with **tempo**, which is an expression of the rapidity of performance. Time and meter refer to time-value and the division of **beats** to a measure, not to speed.

A time signature appears as follows:

The **upper number** indicates the number of beats to each measure. Measures are separated by vertical bar-lines.

The **bottom number** indicates the time-value of the note (type of note . . . half-note, quarter-note, eighth note, etc.) that receives one beat!

Examples

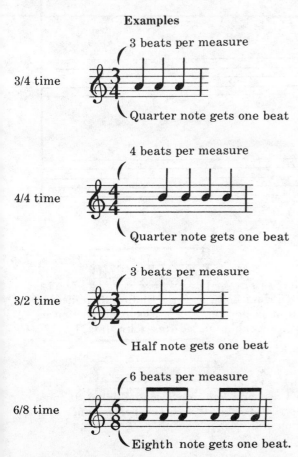

3 beats per measure

3/4 time

Quarter note gets one beat

4 beats per measure

4/4 time

Quarter note gets one beat

3 beats per measure

3/2 time

Half note gets one beat

6 beats per measure

6/8 time

Eighth note gets one beat.

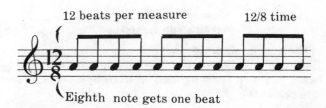

12 beats per measure   12/8 time

Eighth note gets one beat

INFREQUENTLY SEEN

4 3 2

etc.

same meaning as 4/4 4/4 2/4 etc.

Two survivors of historical notation still are frequently used in modern notation and may be seen in time signatures in place of numbers, or, sometimes, along with the numbers.

The symbol **C** which stands for "**common time**" or "**common measure**" is used to indicate $\frac{4}{4}$ meter.

The symbol **¢** which stands for "**cut time**" or "**alla breve**" (Italian) is used to indicate $\frac{2}{2}$ or $\frac{2}{2}$ meter. In contemporary use, it simply means that the half-note is the time unit, instead of the more common quarter-note.

Meter is also classified as follows:

SIMPLE METERS

Duple meter — $\frac{2}{2}$ $\frac{2}{4}$ $\frac{2}{8}$

Triple meter — $\frac{3}{2}$ $\frac{3}{4}$ $\frac{3}{8}$

Quadruple meter — $\frac{4}{2}$ $\frac{4}{4}$ $\frac{4}{8}$

COMPOUND METERS (three times the simple meter.)

Compound duple — $\frac{6}{2}$ $\frac{6}{4}$ $\frac{6}{8}$

Compound triple — $\frac{9}{4}$ $\frac{9}{8}$ $\frac{9}{16}$

Compound quadruple — $\frac{12}{4}$ $\frac{12}{8}$ $\frac{12}{16}$

Quintuple meter — $\frac{5}{4}$

(can be $\frac{2}{4}$ + $\frac{3}{4}$ or vice-versa as per accent)

In **duple meter**, an accent usually falls on every other beat (See Accents). The first and third beats in a standard march!

In **triple meter**, an accent usually falls on the first beat of each group of three beats (as in the standard waltz).

Metronome marks:

M.M. ♩ = 66   indicates Maelzel Metronome marking 66 quarter-notes per minute.

M.M ♪ = 88   indicates Maezel Metronome marking 88 eighth notes per min. (In modern practice the M.M. is eliminated!)

544

Measures or Bars
(Accents and Beats)

The terms **measure** and **bar** are synonomous! Either refers to a group of units of musical time ... **beats** ... which are separated on **staffs** by a vertical line called the "**bar-line**"!

Each **measure** or **bar** may contain two, three, four, five **beats** which repeat regularly throughout a musical composition. Measures are of equal duration, and each measure has regular accents (emphasis on particular beats) which repeat regularly throughout the other measures. Meter, therefore, simply is a statement of the amount of beats and accents and their duration. (The British use **measure** as another name for **meter**).

In notation, the following markings are employed:

Two thin lines usually are used when a key change or time signature change occurs in the body of music.

A single thick line is used in choral or hymn music to end a single verse or lyric line.

The sign 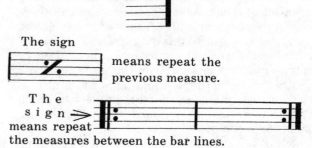 means repeat the previous measure.

The sign means repeat the measures between the bar lines.

Measures appear on staffs or staves

Staffs are connected by a brace or bracket

The brace or bracket indicates that the music of the staffs is related and is to be played simultaneously. The bar lines separating measures cut across the connected staffs (unless a different time signature in the lower clef appears, as compared to the upper clef's time signature).

Double bar lines—A double bar line indicates the end of an entire composition, or a section, phrase, division or movement.

One thin line and one thick line usually indicate the end of a phrase or section.

Two thick lines usually indicate the end of an entire work.

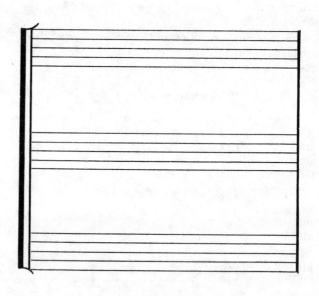

The sign 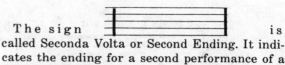 is called Prima Volta or First Ending. It indicates the first performance of a repeating portion of music. Also abbreviated Ima volta, Ima, I

The sign is called Seconda Volta or Second Ending. It indicates the ending for a second performance of a portion of music.

Intervals

An interval is both

...the name given to two tones, or notes, *sounded simultaneously*, and

...the name given to the *distance in pitch between two tones or notes*:

The intervals on the scale c,d,e,f,g,a,b,c′ are named as follows: (the same names apply to the intervals between any two notes ... d to f and g to b are thirds, e to f and b to c′ are seconds, etc.)

Distance	American or English name	Italian	German	French	Spanish
c	unison or prime	prima	Prime	unisson	unísono
c to d	second	seconda	Sekunde	seconde	segunda
c to e	third	terza	Terz	tierce	tercera
c to f	fourth	quarta	Quarte	quarte	cuarta
c to g	fifth	quinta	Quinte	quinte	quinta
c to a	sixth	sesta	Sexte	sixte	sexta
c to b	seventh	settima	Septime	septième	séptiema
c to c′	octave	ottava	Oktave	octave	octava

(larger than an octave)
Compound Intervals

Distance	American or English name	Italian	German	French	Spanish
c to d′	ninth (compound second)	nona	None	neuvième	novena
c to e′	tenth (compound third)	decima	Dezime	dixième	décima
c to f′	eleventh (compound fourth)	undicesima	Undezime	enzième	undécima
c to g′	twelfth	duodecima	Duodezime	douzième	duodécima

Since the half-tones and whole tones are arranged in a different order in the *major scales* as compared to the *minor scales*, the intervals are further categorized as follows:

PERFECT — The *unison*, the *fourth*, the *fifth* and the *octave* are called "perfect intervals" since they remain the same size in any key (in the sequence of half-tones and whole tones).

MAJOR —An interval based on a major scale! One half-tone (semitone) larger than the minor interval of the same name!

MINOR — An interval based on a minor scale! One half-tone (semitone) smaller than the major interval of the same name!

AUGMENTED — Every *perfect* or *major* interval can be *augmented* by raising the uppermost note by one half-tone (semitone) which is called *sharping the uppermost note*; or by lowering the lowest note by one half-tone (semitone) which is called *flatting the lowest note*. All *augmented intervals* (except the *augmented fourth*, the so-called *tritone)* must use a note that is not included in their key!

In notation: the augmented sign is a "+" (C+, Bb+); diminished is a small "o" next to, and to the top of,the note-sign (C° , C#°)!

DIMINISHED — Every *perfect* or *major interval* can be *dimished* by raising the lowest note by one half-tone (semi-tone) which is called *sharping the lowest note*; or by lowering the highest note which is called *flatting the uppermost note.*

LOWER INTERVAL — When the second note of an interval is pitched lower than the first note, it is a *"lower interval"!*

Interval Measurement
(Temperament)

In acoustic science, the pitch of a tone is a function of its frequency vibration per second. In the 6th century B.C., the Greek mathematician Pythagoras first discovered "pure" measurement in music by analyzing the vibrating string. He set down the physical law: The frequency of vibration (of a string) is inversely proportional to its vibration length. From this, he concluded the ratios of intervals to be: For the *octave* 2:1 ... for the *fifth* 3/2:1 ... for the *third* 5/4:1. Assuming c to be 1, the ratios for the complete scale were measured as c=1, d=9/8, e=5/4, f=4/3, g=3/2, a=5/3, b=15/8 and c′=2.

In more than 2500 years since Pythagoras, the scientific and aesthetic investigations of interval measurement have been complex and any attempt at full documentation would be simplistic. In brief: The Pythageran system, although "pure", is useful pragmatically only for the C-major scale and a few other tones and is generally inadequate for the complete chromatic scale! By the end of the Middle Ages, compromise systems of "temperament" for musical scales (changes in the tuning) began to evolve. A "just intonation" system used a formula based on the natural harmonic scale (intervals were based on the "pure" fifth and the "pure" third) but this proved awkward for key changes, making modulation virtually impossible. Next, came a "mean tone" system which represented a compromise between the Pythagorean and the "just intonation" temperament systems! "Mean tone" used some "pure" intervals but introduced some deviations as well; the fifth, for example, in "mean-tone" was smaller than the "pure" fifth"! The "mean tone" system soon also proved awkward and inadequate for advancements in key ranges and complex harmonies, and in the 17th century the "equal temperament" system evolved! This is the system which is still used in contemporary practice.

The "equal temperament" system modifies all of the "pure" interval measurements except for the "octave"! The principle: Make all the half-tones equidistant by dividing the octave into twelve equal half-tones (semitones)! The deviations are illustrated by the following:

Measured in frequencies

	c''	d''	e''	f''	g''	a''	b''	c'''
Equal temp.	520	584	655	694	779	874	982	1040
Pythagorean	520	585	658	693	780	877	987	1040

The mathematical complexities of adding or subtracting intervals were further simplified by a modern, widely-used system based on logarithms. This system measures the twelve equal parts of the "equal temperament" octave in terms of its logarithmic frequency, and uses a basic unit called "cent". The measurement of an octave by "cents" is as follows:

c'''' = 4800 cents
c''' = 3600 cents
c'' = 2400 cents
c' = 1200 cents   f# = 600 cents
c = 0 cents
C = −1200 cents

The scale in *cents:* c=0; c#=100; d=200; d#=300; e=400; f=500; f#=600; g=700; g#=800; a=900; a#=1000; b=1100; c'=1200

Comparing the intervals in "Cents"

	Equal temperament	Pythagorean
Semitone	100	90
Whole tone	200	204
Minor third	300	294
Major third	400	408
Fourth	500	498
Aug. fourth	600	612
Dim. fifth	600	588
Fifth	700	702
Minor sixth	800	792
Major sixth	900	906
Minor seventh	1000	996
Major seventh	1100	1110
Octave	1200	1200

Table of Intervals
(the numerals indicate the amount of half-tones in the interval)

	Unison or Prime	Second	Third	Fourth	Fifth	Sixth	Seventh	Octave	Ninth
Major		c to d 2	c to e 4			c to a 9	c to b 11		c to d' 14
Minor		c to db 1	c to eb 3			c to ab 8	c to bb 10		c to d'b 13
Perfect	c 0			c to f 5	c to g 7			c to c' 12	
Augmented	c to c# 1	c to d# 3	c to e# 5	c to f# 6	c to g# 8	c to a# 10	c to b# 12	c to c#' 13	c to d#' 16
Diminished		c# to db 0	c# to eb 2	c# to f 4	c# to g 6	c# to ab 7	c# to bb 9	c# to c' 11	

Inverted Intervals

Inversion is a process, in music, of changing tones or notes so that higher tones replace lower tones or, conversely, lower tones replace higher tones . . . all in correspondence with each other. The technique is exemplified in serious music by almost all major fugues and by many portions of symphonic works.

The inversion process is either *melodic* or *harmonic!* With a single-line melody, for example, successive intervals are inverted by substituting a descending interval for the corresponding ascending interval! A fifth (going up seven steps on the chromatic scale) such as c to g, goes down seven steps to become c to F! This is a *melodic inversion* (also known as *contrary motion*). When the reversal of half-tones is exactly the same in terms of the "number" of half-tones, this is called "strict" or "real" inversion.

To preserve tonality, however, most inversions use the degrees of a given scale and do not employ "strict" or "real" equality in the number of half-tones unless dealing with twelve-tone, atonal or Serial music. Inverting by degrees of a scale, for example, causes c-d'-e' to become c-b-a, whereas "strict" inversion would produce c-b♭-a♭! One of Bach's famous inversions C B A G# B A C following C D E F D E C, obviously is "tonal" and not "strict"!

Harmonic inversion of simultaneous-sounded intervals is achieved by raising the lower note of the interval one octave, or lowering the higher note of the interval by one octave . . . d to a becomes a to d' or A to d, for example! Inversion changes a *fifth* to a *fourth*, a *third* to a *sixth*, a *second* to a *seventh*, etc. The sum of the half-tones is always nine! See the preceding Table of Intervals!

By inversion: The *perfect* interval *(prime, fourth, fifth and octave)* remains *perfect!* The *major* intervals become *minor;* the *minor* become *major;* the *augmented* become *diminished,* and the *diminished* become augmented.

Chords

Chords are groups of *three* or *more tones or notes sounded simultaneously!* They are the building blocks of harmony, and harmonic analysis!

In traditional music, when chords are pleasant or agreeable (a subjective opinion) they are "consonant". All major and minor triads and their inversions are consonant. Subjectively unpleasant or disagreeable chords are *dissonant* . . . the seventh, ninth, fourth, augmented sixth, for example! In modern music, the formalities of "consonant, dissonant" are dismissed by many composers as irrelevant because they are only subjective. The rules of classical harmony and key signatures are observed in the main, but are neither worshipped nor adhered to by many 20th century modernists.

Every chord is comprised of intervals based on the tones or notes (degrees) of a scale! See *Table of Intervals!*

A *triad* is a *three-note chord* whose lowest or bottom note is called the *root* or *fundamental.* The *middle* note is located a third above the root; hence it is known as the *third!* The *top* note is known as the *fifth;* it is a fifth above the root!

Triads are described in four categories:

DIATONIC
consonant
Major triads — (major plus a minor third)
> Every major key can generate seven diatonic triads! In the C-major scale, for example, c-e-g is a *major* triad . . . e is a *major third* above the root c, and g is a *perfect fifth* above c.

Minor triads — (minor plus a major third)
> Every minor key can generate even more triads than the major key, since the minor scale can utilize variations of the scale degrees that are uniquely its own. In the C-minor scale, for example, both A♮ and A♭, B♮ and B♭ are utilized. In C-major, d-f-a is a *minor* triad . . . f is a minor third above the root d, and a is a perfect fifth above the root d.

dissonant
Diminished Triads (minor plus a minor third)
> When the root is grouped with a minor third and a diminished fifth, the result is a diminished triad! In a b-d-f triad, for example, d is a minor third above b and f is a diminished fifth above b!

CHROMATIC
Augmented Triads (major plus a major third)
> When the root is grouped with a major third and an augmented fifth, the result is an augmented triad! There are *no* augmented triads actually based on major scales! An augmented triad must use a note which is outside a major scale . . . for example, in the augmented triad c-e-g#, the note g# is *not* in the C-major scale!

A *diatonic triad* consists only of notes that belong to a given key!

A *chromatic triad* uses a note that is outside (foreign to) the notes of a given key!

A *seventh chord* is a *four-note chord* (adding another third to a triad) consisting of a root with a third, a fifth and a seventh above it in rising order of the scale!

A *ninth chord* is a *five-note chord* (adding another third to a seventh chord) consisting of a root with a third, a fifth, a seventh and a ninth above it in rising order of the scale.

Fourth chords (built on *fourths* instead of thirds) and "tone cluster" chords are *dissonant chords* utilized in "modern" music!

Triads

major	minor	augmented	diminished
g	a	g#	f
e	f	e	d
c	d	c	b

Seventh
C Scale

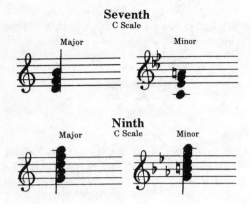

Major   Minor

Ninth
C Scale

Major   Minor

Chords are also classified as:

DOMINANT — Any chord built on the fifth degree of the diatonic scale! It is named for its "dominating" importance in harmony and melody!

DOMINANT TRIAD — The root is "dominant"! Example: g-b-d in the C scales!

DOMINANT SEVENTH — A dominant triad plus an added third! Example: g-b-d-f in the C scales!

TONIC — Any chord built on the first degree of the diatonic scale is called a "tonic" chord, since the first note (the keynote or main note) of a scale is called the "tonic"!

TONIC TRIAD — The root is tonic! Example: c-e-g in C-major key!

SUBDOMINANT — Any chord built on the fourth degree of the diatonic scale! The name "subdominant" arises because the fourth degree is a *fifth below* the tonic . . . the dominant is a *fifth above* the tonic!

Triad Example: f-a-c in the C-major key! The root is subdominant!

MEDIANT — Any chord built on the third degree of the diatonic scale! It is named for its position half-way between the tonic and the dominant!

Triad Example: e-g-b in the C-major key! The root is mediant!

SUBMEDIANT or SUPERDOMINANT — Any chord built on the sixth degree of the diatonic scale! *Triad example:* a-c-e- in the C-major key! The root is submediant or superdominant!

SUPERTONIC — Any chord built on the second degree of the diatonic scale! *Triad example:* d-f-a in the key of C-major. The root is supertonic!

LEADING TONE or SUBTONIC — Any chord built on the seventh degree of the diatonic scale! *Triad example:* b-d-f in the C-major key! The root is the subtonic *b*, called the leading tone because of its tendency to resolve up from its position (one half-tone below the tonic) to the tonic *c* thus creating a sense of finality.

DOMINANT NINTH — A dominant seventh chord plus an added third. Example: g-b-d-f-a in the C-major and C-minor keys!

By adding a third to a ninth chord, an *eleventh chord* is created! Adding still another third creates a *thirteenth chord*. This is the largest chord to be created (without redundancy) from the seven tones of the diatonic scale.

Inverted Chords

When the bottom note (lowest) of a chord is *not in the root position*, the chord is said to be *inverted*. Every triad takes two inversions (since it is a three-note chord); every four-note chord takes three inversions and so on up to and including the thirteenth chord with its seven notes!

Inversions of a *triad*

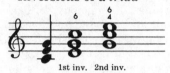

1st inv.   2nd inv.

Inversions of a *seventh* chord

1st inv.   2nd inv.   3rd inv.

Harmonic Analysis
(chords and harmony)

Harmonic analysis deals with the study of chords and harmonies, and their relationship to each other. In classical music, it represents the formal notational system for analysing "tonality" of traditional Western music composed in the 18th and 19th centuries. Following are the tenets of the system:

Any chord is said to be in its *"root position"* when the original lowest tone of the chord (bass tone) is in the lowest (bass) position!

When the *third* of the original chord is moved to the lowest (bass) position, the chord is in its *first inversion!*

When the *fifth* of the original chord is moved to the lowest (bass) position, the chord is in its second inversion.

When the *seventh* is moved to the bass, the chord is in its *third inversion*, etc.!

The *triads* in each *key* are given Roman numerals (I, II, III, IV, V, VI, VII) which identify the *scale degree* of the *root tone* in the *chord* (not necessarily the *bass tone*.)!

Arabic numerals (1, 2, 3 etc.) are used to designate either the content of a *chord* or its *added inversions* or *tones!* Similar to the *figured-bass* notation system, these numbers are placed next to, and to the top or bottom, of the Roman numeral. They indicate the *intervals* above the *lowest pitched tone*, not the root tone, of the *inversion position!*

V_1, V_2, V_3, for example, indicate the *first, second* and *third* inversions of the *dominant triad* V in a *given key!*

Sixth chords are I_6, *seventh* chords I_7, six-four chords I_4^6; I^7, I^9, for example, means that a *third* added to a *triad* has formed a *seventh*, or a *ninth* chord!

V_2^7, for example, means the *second inversion* of a *dominant seventh chord* . . . . in the *key* of *C-major*, the chord D-F-G-B! The "V" explains the *dominant G-B-D*, the *"7"* explains a *third* has been *added* to form *G-B-D-F* and the *"2"* explains that this *chord* has received its *"second" inversion* to finally become *D-F-G-B!*

I or I_3^5, for example, depicts the tonic triad *C-E-G* in the *key of C-major!* The *"E"* is *"3"*, the *third above C*, and the *"G"* is 5, the *fifth above C!* The sign + means augmented (II+) ... the sign ° means diminished (II°)

C scale Examples

Major Triads

I II III IV V VI VIIº

Minor Triads

I IIº III+ IV V VI VII°

Major Seventh Chords

I_7 II_7 III_7 IV_7 V_7 VI_7 $VII°_7$

Minor Seventh Chords

I_7 $II°_7$ $III+_7$ IV_7 V_7 VI_7 $VII°_7$

When chords use *accidentals* outside or foreign to their key, but proper to their tonality, they are called *"chromatic* chords" or *"altered"* chords. These include:

The Neapolitan Sixth — the first inversion of the sixth chord on the *flatted supertonic.* In C-major, f-a_b-d_b is the inversion of d_b-f-a_b, the *flatted supertonic* triad.

The "augmented sixths" — also known as the *Italian sixth, German sixth* and *French sixth!* (variations of the first inversion of the triad)

SIXTH   NEAP.   ITAL.   GER.   FR.

I^6 II^{6+} II^{6+}_4 IV^{6+}_5 IV^{6+}_4

Main Chords in Each Key	TONIC
	I Chord
	SUBDOMINANT
	IV Chord
	DOMINANT
	VII Chord

Modulation

Modulation is the process of changing from one key to another in a given composition, or section of a composition!

Modulations are:

Chromatic ... when chromatic chords are used to make the transition from one key to another. The *Neapolitan sixth chord*, for example, frequently is utilized!

Diatonic ... when diatonic chords common to both keys are utilized!

Enharmonic ... when "enharmonic notes" are used to replace notes of an original key! The *diminished seventh* and *augmented sixths* chords are utilized frequently for enharmonic modulation!

Modulations are also considered:

"Passing" or *"false"* (also *transient, transitory*) when a new key is employed only briefly, giving way to a third key. When the third key remains operative for any period of time, it is a "passing" modulation! When the third key speedily returns to the original, it is a "false" modulation! When the key change (to the second key, etc.) is retained for some duration other than "brief", it is often called "final"!

When multiple key changes are made in a series of progressions, it is known as *"sequential modulation"!*

Note: Most of the "rules" of tonality in modulation are no less subjective than the laws of consonance and dissonance and the devotion to triadic composition! These constantly have been "declassicized" by late 19th-century and 20th century composers who dismissed many techniques of tonality as irrelevant.

Use of *pivot chords!* These are chords common to both keys that alter their harmonic function when shifted to the new key. The C-major triad, *g-b-d*, for example modulates to G-major easily ... it is the *dominant* triad in C-major and the *tonic* triad in G-major! The C-major triad is a I chord in C, becomes a IV in G, a V in F, a III in A-minor, a VI in E-minor, a Neapolitan II in B and a VII chord in D-minor!

In a key change of short duration, the key signature usually is not changed. The notes outside, or foreign to, the new key are indicated, instead, by accidentals. When the key change is of long duration, a new key signature usually is appended.

Closely related keys are the most effective for easy or smooth modulation. Distant keys make the most abrupt and perhaps distracting modulations. Related keys (major or minor) are those that are adjacent on the Circle of Fifths, differing from each other by only one sharp or flat. See *Circle of Fifths!*

BASIC CHORDS

Table of the Main Chords in Each Key

Major Key	Tonic I Chord	Subdominant IV Chord	Dominant VII Chord	Minor Key Relative	Tonic I Chord	Subdominant IV Chord	Dominant VII Chord
C	C	F	G7	Am	Am	Dm	E7
G	G	C	D7	Em	Em	Am	B7
D	D	G	A7	Bm	Bm	Em	F♯7
A	A	D	E7	F♯m	F♯m	Bm	C♯7
E	E	A	B7	C♯m	C♯m	F♯m	G♯7
B	B	E	F♯7	G♯m	G♯m	C♯m	D♯7
F♯	F♯	B	C♯7	D♯m	D♯m	G♯m	A♯7
F	F	B♭	C7	Dm	Dm	Gm	A7
B♭	B♭	E♭	F7	Gm	Gm	Cm	D7
E♭	E♭	A♭	B♭7	Cm	Cm	Fm	G7
A♭	A♭	D♭	E♭7	Fm	Fm	B♭m	C7
D♭	D♭	G♭	A♭7	B♭m	B♭m	E♭m	F7

A
DICTIONARY
OF
POPULAR AND
CLASSICAL
MUSIC

ILLUSTRATED

OVER 4,000 TERMS
WITH PRONUNCIATION
GUIDE

PRONUNCIATION KEY

Vowels and Diphthongs

Phonetic Symbol   As in

ā   dāy, āpe, vāpor
ă   făt, răsh, căttle
â   dâre, âir, pârent
ä   ärt, fäther, därk, cälm
a̍   a̍ct, a̍fter, gra̍ss
ē   bē, mēre, hēar
ĕ   gĕt, dĕn, sĕnse
e̱   pe̱r, telle̱r, speake̱r
ē   rēlax, dēpart, bēside

ī   dīce, rīght, īdle, mīne
ĭ   sĭt, mĭddle, thĭn

ō   ōpen, bōld, echō
ŏ   lŏt, tŏtter, sŏck
ô   bôre, ôrder, ôrphan
ȯ   tȯmato, pȯtential, syncȯpate

ōō   rōōm, fōōd, ōōze
o͞o   bo͞ok, wo͞ol, push (po͞osh)
ou   out, round, loud
oi   oil, boil, boy

ū   tūbe, lūte, ūse
ŭ   ŭnder, stŭdy, ŭp
û   ûrge, lûrk, bûrst
ü   German *umlaut* sound, close to:
1. Pronouncing the English ē with the mouth shaped as if pronouncing o͞o
   or
2) Pronouncing the English ĭ with the mouth shaped as if pronouncing o͞o

Consonants

All unmarked consonants follow standard rules of phonetic English.

Special attention should be paid to:

j   both "j" and "soft g" sounds as in jump, jerk, giant, gesture
g   for "hard g" sounds as in go, get, guard
k   for "hard c" and "hard ch" sounds as in cattle, conquer, chord (kôrd), keep, kitchen.
s   for sibilant "s" or "ss" or "soft c" or sibilant "sc" sounds as in sell, sit, miss, cease, civil, scene.
ch   as in choke, etch, catch
sh   as in shape, should, action (ăk′ shŭn) ocean (ō′shŭn)
f   as in fool, fail, enough (ēnŭf) cough (kŏf)
z   for "z" and "soft s" sounds as in daze, cozy, wise, is, days
zh   as in azure, pleasure, genre

Note: There are many Italian, German, French and some Spanish terms in the daily language of music! Each of these languages have standard International phonetic symbols, normally used to depict sounds that are not found in exact English equivalents. After careful consideration, the author believes that the use of these symbols, except for the German umlaut (¨) over the letter "u", would defeat its own purpose. Pronunciation for this specialized dictionary would be made only more complex, and probably no more exact for any reader except the expert linguist. We have studied three of these languages for several years, and believe that the system used herein is simpler, but completely rigorous, for authentic comprehension and communication. If some lexicographers and linguists will challenge our "common sense" approach, we can only say as Samuel Johnson said: "We that live to please must please to live."

J.R.C.

DICTIONARY

A

— A —

A. (1) The *sixth tone* in the *C-major scale*, and the *first tone* of the *A-major* and *A-minor scales!* (2) For *triad chords*, a *capital A* indicates an *A-major triad*; the small *a* indicates the *a-minor triad!* (3) The *A above middle C* is used for *tuning* to *concert pitch*, since it is accepted as the *international standard* for *pitch (440 cycles per second frequency)!* (4) The *tone one half-step below A* is *A-flat* or *G-sharp (enharmonic equivalents)*; the *tone one-half step above A* is *A-sharp* or *B-flat* (5) In *vocal music*, *A* designates the *alto voice or part!*

A.A.B.A., A.B.A.B. Traditional construction forms of *popular songwriting*, which were common to many "*standard*" *songs* of yesteryear, but which today probably are more honored in the breach! The *A.A.B.A.* form referred, usually, to a *32-bar song* which started with *A.*, a *main 8-bar melody*; *A. again*, repeated the *8 bars*; *B.* introduced a new *theme* called the "*release*" or "*bridge*" or "*middle*" or "*channel*" for *another 8 bars*, and *A. finally*, returned to the *main theme* for *8 more bars*, with some *variation!* The *A.B.A.B.* form simply alternated *two 8-bar themes* for a total of *32 bars*, with some *variation* in the final *8 bars!* In *theater* or *production songwriting*, a *verse* often preceded the *main body* or *refrain* of a *song* with from *8 to 24 bars* of *verse* sometimes leading into the refrain! For *songs* originating on "*pop*" *recordings* (due to radio broadcasting "*time*" limitations) *verses* usually were not even *composed!*

a ballata *(ä bäl lä'tä)* from the Italian: In ballad style!

ab *(äp)* from the German: "off", "take away"!

abat-sons *(ä'bä'sôn')* from the French: Any device that propels sound in a downward direction!

a battuta *(äh bät tōō' tä)* The Italian term for *strict time*; literally, "with the beat"!

abat-voix *(ä'bä'vwä')* from the French: The *sounding board* over a rostrum or pulpit!

abbandono *(äb bän dō'nō)* from the Italian: A direction to play with abandon or passion or with deep emotional feeling!

abbellimenti *(äb bĕl lē mĕn'tē)* from the Italian: Musical embellishments!

abend musik *(ä'bĕnt mōō zēk')* from the German: Music for an evening performance!

a bene placito *(äh bā'nĕ plä'chē tō)* from the Italian: At the player's discretion! ... an indication that the performer can change *tempo*, add *grace notes*, substitute *instruments*, etc. as he pleases!

abgemessen *(ap' gĕ mĕs'sĕn)* from the German: Strictly measured .... see *a battuta!*

abgestossen *(ap' gĕ shtō' sĕn)* from the German: "Struck off", *detached notes, staccato!*

absolute music — Music intelligently combined and expressed, independently of explanation by title or text! Usually refers to non-vocal, non-program composition!

absolute pitch. (1) As measured by its independent rate of frequency vibration, the sound or position of a *tone* in relation to the entire standard *scale!* (2) Sometimes used to refer to one's ability to hear and identify *tones* with total accuracy ... "the maestro has absolute *pitch*"! (also *perfect pitch*)!

absonant *(ăb' sō nănt).* Discordant sound quality!

a cappella *(ä käp pĕl'lä)* from the Italian: "As in chapel"; *Choral singing* without *accompaniment!*

a capriccio *(ä kä prēt' chō)* from the Italian: A direction to play in accordance with one's own caprice or fancy!

accelerando *(ä chĕ lĕ rän'dō)* from the Italian: "Accelerating", a direction to speed up gradually! Abbreviated *accel.*

accent *(ăk sĕnt')* The greater stress placed on a *note* or *tone* as compared to the other *notes* or *tones* in a given group!

accent mark. Any symbol indicating stress, such as < for *sforzando*, or the "*degree*" mark (') placed after a musical *note* which locates its *octave* position or "*degree*" .... *a'* is *A* in the *octave rising from middle C*, which is *c'* ... an *octave* higher brings one to *c''* etc!

accentor *(ăk sĕn' tĕr)* The performer who plays or sings the leading part; sometimes used to designate the director or conductor!

accessory stop. A stop-knob on an *organ* that controls a mechanical device or *coupler* rather than a *register* of *pipes!*

acciaccatura *(ä chäk'kä tōō'rä)* An *ornament* used in 17th century *keyboard* music which usually consisted of a dissonant *note* sounded together with a *chord*, but the *note* would be immediately cut off (released) while the *consonant tones* of the *chord* were sustained!

An Acciaccatura (D added to C-E-G) Written Played Double Acciaccatura

accidental *(ăk'sĭ dĕn'täl)* Any *sharp, flat (single or double)* or *natural* that appears after the *key signature* in a composition. The *accidental* changes the *pitch* of the *note* to which it is appended throughout a composition ... the *sharp* ♯ raises the *pitch* one *half-tone*; the *flat* ♭ lowers the *pitch* one *half-tone*; the *double-sharp* ✗ raises the *pitch* two *half tones*; the *double flat* ♭♭ lowers the *pitch* two *half-tones*; the *natural* ♮ cancels all previous *accidentals!* An *accidental* applies not only to the *note* before which it appears in a *measure* or *bar* but to all *notes* of the same *pitch* in the given *measure* or *bar* (not to different *octaves*, however). The *bar*-line, ending a *measure*, cancels all previous *accidentals*, except for the *key signature*, unless there is a *tie* across the *bar*-line.

accolade(*ăk'ō lād*) A *brace*, or *brace line* (see *brace*).

accompaniment (*ă kŭm' pá nĭ mĕnt*) Playing along with another performer; usually refers to subordinate *keyboard* or *orchestral* support for a principal player or singer! Also, the *instrumental part* or *parts* written in support of a *solo instrumental* or *vocal part*.

accompaniment figure. A *melodic* or *harmonic* line which supports a principal *melody*:

accompanist. The musician who plays a supporting *part* for a *vocal* or *instrumental* solo:

accordatura (*ăk kôr' dä tōo'rä*) The *tuning* order of *stringed instruments* by *tonal degrees* . . . *g, d', a', e''* for the *violin's* four strings, etc!

accordion (*ă kôr' dī ŭn*) A portable, *wind-instrument* invented in 1829 which consists of two flattened boards at opposite ends of a bellows which squeezes air pressure across metallic *reeds*. The right-hand board of the instrument has *keys* similar to a *piano on which melody* is played; the left-hand board is studded with buttons that are pressed to sound *chords* and *bass notes*. The *accordion* is hung around the performer's neck and the *bellows* is drawn out and squeezed together while the fingers manipulate the keys and buttons of both boards. A smaller and simpler relative of the *accordion* is the *concertina* (see *concertina*)!

Accordion

achromatic(*ăk' rō măt'ĭk*) Without *modulations* and with no *accidentals*!

achtel(*äkh'tĕl*) The German word for an *eighth note* or the British *quaver*!

Acid Rock — See "Rock", "Rock 'n' Roll"!

acocotl (*ăk' ō kŏt'l*) A *clarin*; a *wind-instrument* similar to a *trumpet* used in ancient Mexico!

acoustic (*á kōo'stĭk*) The *timbre* or quality of a *tone*!

acoustic guitar. See *Guitar*!

acoustics. The science of musical sound or *tones*! (See *temperament, tone, pitch, frequency, vibration*, etc.) The term generally is used to describe the clarity and quality of sound that is heard in a concert hall, recording studio or other performance medium, and involves sound-engineering criteria such as absorption, reflection, echo and the physical structure of a hall or studio.

acoustic bass. A 32-foot or 64-foot *organ register*!

action (*ăk'shŭn*) The mechanical operation of the component parts of an instrument by the fingers or feet; in the *piano* and other *keyboards*, the levers connecting the *keyboard* to the striking *hammers* are called the *action*!

acute (*á'kūt*) High pitched; the opposite of *grave*.

acute mixture. A *compound organ stop* that sounds bright, high-ranged harmonics (also known as *sharp mixture*)!

adagio (*á dä'jō*) from the Italian: A direction to play in a slow, easy, graceful manner; also, the name given to the slow section of a *symphonic work*!

adagissimo (*á dä jīs' sē mō*) from the Italian: A direction to play a bit slower than *adagio*.

added sixth. A *subdominant* chord with a *sixth* added from the *root*; In C major, *C-E-G-A*!

added voice. Combining another voice with the principal *melody* or *harmony*; for example, when adding *counterpoint* to a Gregorian chant or *plainsong*!

addolorato (*ähd dō lō räh' tō*) from the Italian: A direction to play in a plaintive manner expressing grief!

adiaphone (*ăd' ĭ á fōn'*) A *keyboard instrument* developed in 1882 which resembled the *adiaphonon* (see next listing) but substituted *tuning forks* for steel bars!

adiaphonon (*ăd' ĭ áf'ō nŏn*) A *keyboard instrument* dating from 1819 which was similar to a *piano* but which used steel bars instead of *strings* to produce tones!

adjacent tone (*ă jā' sĕnt tōn*) An auxiliary tone (see *auxiliary tone*)!

adjunct note (*ăj' ŭngkt nōt*) An unaccented, *auxiliary tone* or *note*!

ad lib. (*ăd' lĭb*) from the Latin "ad libitum": "at will", "at one's pleasure" (1) To improvise music vocally or instrumentally which is not previously written out in a *score*. (2) A passage of music which the performer may interpret variably to his own taste or preference (3) A *cadenza* which may by option either be deleted or altered (4) an *accompaniment* which may be deleted by option as opposed to an accompaniment that is *obbligato*!

a due (*ā dōo'ā*) from the Italian: (1) A direction to two performers to play or sing the same *part* together in *unison*. (2) A direction to a group of performers to divide into two sections, each playing a different part (since the two meanings are ambiguous, the preferred term for this meaning of *a due* is called *divisi*)! *A due corde*, depress the *piano's soft pedal* half-way down: See *corda*!

A dur (*ā dōōr*) The *German* term for A major!

Aeolian attachment.(*ā ō' lē ăn ä tăch'mĕnt*) A device connected to a *piano* which increases the vibration of the strings, and the volume of sound produced, by directing an airstream upon the *strings*.

Aeolian harp, Aeolian lyre. An instrument with silk or gut *strings* stretched in or on a box and tuned in *unison*. Usually placed at an open window, the instrument gives off audible sweet pitched sounds when activated by a wind current.

Aeolian mode One of the *authentic church* modes, beginning on *A* in a *diatonic scale* (see *mode*).

aerophone(*ā'ēr ō fōn*) A classification for any musical instrument which produces pitched sounds as the result of vibration of a stream or column of air (*woodwinds, brass winds, organ, harmonica, harmonium*, etc.)!

aerophor (*ā' ēr ō fôr*) A contrivance for a *wind instrument* that can be used to extend a sustained tone!

affabile *(ăf fă' bē lē)* from the Italian: A direction to play in a graceful, sweet manner!

affetuoso *(ăf'fĕt tū ō'sō)* from the Italian: A direction to play with tenderness to create a sentimental mood!

affrettare *(ăf frĕt tā'rĕ)* from the Italian: To hurry or hasten ... *senza affrettare*, without hastening!

A.F.M. — The abbreviation for the American Federation of Musicians, the national union that represents all professional musicians in the United States. The A.F.M. national organization is comprised of many local groups who enjoy considerable autonomy. Locals 802, New York; 47 Los Angeles and 10, Chicago are the largest and most influential!

after beat *(ăf'tēr bĕt')* Usually refers to an *accompaniment note* which follows the *beat;* technically, the two notes (*principal* and lower *auxiliary*) which are used as an ending for a *trill!*

after note *(ăf'tēr nōt')* An *unaccented, grace note* which takes its *time-value* from the preceding *note* in a *measure* (see *appoggiatura*)!

agevolmente *(ȧ jā vōl mĕn'tĕ)* from the Italian: A direction to play light and easy!

agitato *(ȧ' jē tä'tō)* from the Italian: A direction to play in an agitated, hurried, restless manner!

agon *(ăg'ōn)* from Greek antiquity: A public contest which included music as one of the areas of competition!

agraffe *(ă grăf')* A small, metal piece in the *piano,* connecting the *bridge* and *pin,* which helps to control string vibration!

agrément *(ȧ grā män')* The French word for an *ornament, grace* or *embellishment!*

A-instrument. A *transposing instrument* pitched in A (the *clarinet,* for example, whose music is written a *minor third* above the sound)!

air (1) An *Elizabethan song* with *homophonic accompaniment* of the *melody* (2) Any popular *melody* or *tune* (3) The *dominant melody* or *voice-part* of a *hymn* or *choral work* (4) A specific piece for one instrument (5) Generally, a *movement* of a *suite* (6) In French, a type of song described by the following words ... *air champetre*, a country song; *air detaches* ... song from *opera*, etc!

alba *(äl'bä)* In medieval times, the musical *accompaniment* of a *lyric poem!*

Alberti bass *(äl bĕr'tē bäs).* Named after its originator, Domenico Alberti who died in 1739, this consists of a left-hand *bass part* using *broken chords* in close proximity!

Albumblatt *(äl'bōōm blät)* The German word for "after-leaf"; a short piece for *vocal* or *instrumental* (usually *keyboard*)!

aleatory music *(ā'lē ă tō rē)* A modern term describing *avant* music which applies "contingent" or "chance" possibilities to composition, allowing for variation in performance at the discretion of the performer. Time value, pitch, volume, attack may be chosen at random by a John Cage, for example, or defined under algebraic laws of probability by a Yannis Xenakis!

aliquot *(äl'ĭ kwŏt)* A *partial tone* or *harmonic! Aliquot strings* in *keyboards* are added strings that will vibrate sympathetically to the *pitched tone* of the *standard strings;* hence, augmenting the *instrument's tone.*

alla breve *(äl'lä brä'vä)* from the Italian: The tempo mark **𝄵** indicating quick duple time, with the *half-note* used as the *beat* instead of the *quarter-note* ... essentially a $\frac{2}{2}$ meter instead of $\frac{4}{4}$. Also known as *CUT TIME !*

alla polacca *(äl'lä pō läk' kä)* from the Italian: A direction to play like a *polonaise!*

allargando *(äl'lär gän'dō)* from the Italian: A direction to play gradually more slowly while increasing the loudness!

alla zingara *(äl'lä tsĭn' gä rä)* from the Italian: A direction to play in *gypsy style!*

allegramente *(äl'lĕ grä mĕn'tĕ)* from the Italian: Vivacious, quick, cheerful!

allegretto *(äl'lĕ grĕt'tō)* from the Italian: A lively *tempo* midway between *andante* and *allegro;* also, a composition or movement in *allegretto tempo!*

allegro *(äl lĕg'rō)* from the Italian: (1) A fast, lively *tempo* midway between *andante* and *presto* and faster than *allegretto.* (2) Usually designates the first and last *movements* of *symphonic works.* (3) Used in many phrases of direction ... *allegro ma non troppo,* "fast, but not too much"; *allegro di molto,* "very fast"; etc.

allemande *(äl'ē mänd')* The *French* word for "German": (1) *German* dance music in a brisk *duple meter* popular in the 1500-1700 period; in the 17th century, often used as the first *movement* of the old *suite* form! By the 18th century, *allemande* had reappeared in Germany as a lively dance in $\frac{3}{4}$ meter!

allentando *(äl'lĕn tän'dō)* from the Italian: A direction to slow down or relax the *tempo!*

allentato *(äl lĕn tä' tō)* from the Italian: A direction to slacken the *tempo*, or hold it back or *retard* the music!

al fine *(äl fē'nĕ)* from the Italian: "To the end or finish"; frequently used in notation by itself or in phrases ... *Dal segno al fine,* "from the sign to the end (marked *Fine)!*

al loco *(äl lō'kō)* SEE *LOCO!*

all'ottava *(äl'lōt tä'vä)* from the Italian: A direction, with the marking *8va- - - -*, to play an *octave* higher or lower depending on whether the *8va* appears above or below the *staff!*

all'unisono *(äl'ōō nē sō'nō)* from the Italian: "In unison"; a direction to sing or play in *unison!*

alphorn, alpine horn. A Swiss, wood, *wind-instrument* varying from a ten-foot-long straight *horn* version to a three-foot, bent-back version resembling an elongated *trumpet* with no *valves.* The *alphorn* has a *bell* and *cupped mouthpiece* but its *notes* are limited to the *harmonics* of the tube. Traditionally used by shepherds in the Swiss Alps!

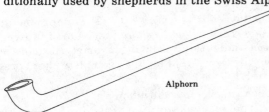

Alphorn

al segno *(äl sā'nyō)* from the Italian: A direction to return to the sign 𝄋 or :𝑆: and begin again, continuing on to the marking *FINE* or *FIN* or to the marking ⌒ appearing over a *double bar!*

al solito *(äl sō'lē tō)* from the Italian: A direction to play as usual!

althorn *(ält'hôrn)* An *alto horn* . . . . . *pitched in E flat* with a *range* from *A* to *e♭''* . . . which is used frequently in *bands* instead of the *French horn.* A *transposing instrument,* whose circular-shaped version is known as the *mellophone* (See *Mellophone*)!

alt *(ält)* from the Italian: "High"; *Notes* "*in alt*" are high-pitched, running from *f''* up one octave to *G above* the *treble staff. Notes* above the *G* are "*in altissimo*", the highest pitched!

In Alt

alt *(ält)* The German word for *alto!*

alto *(äl'tō)* (1) At one time the highest male *voice-part* but today the *part* usually sung by the lowest female voice: (2) Any *alto* singer or voice; a *contralto:* (3) A short name for the *tenor violin* or *viola,* or the *alto saxhorn* or *althorn!*

alto clarinet. An *E flat clarinet* that is larger than the standard *B flat clarinet* but smaller than the *bass clarinet!* A *transposing instrument,* it sounds a *major sixth* lower than its written music!

alto clef. The *C clef* or *viola clef;* the sign that designates the middle line of the *staff* as *middle C* (also called the *counter-tenor clef*).

alto flute. A *flute pitched* in *G* with a *three-octave range* to *G''''!* The *alto flute* (also called the *bass flute*) is a *transposing instrument* which sounds a *fourth* below its written music!

alto horn. Another name for *althorn!*

alto saxhorn. Another name for *althorn!*

alzati *(äl tsa'tē)* from the Italian: A direction to "*remove the mutes*" from *instruments!*

A major. The *major key* or *scale* with *A* as the *keynote* and a *signature* of *three sharps!*

key of **A major**

amarevole *(ä'mä rā'vō lä)* from the Italian: A direction to create a mood of bitter, sharp emotion!

Amati *(ä mät'tē)* A famous *violin* model made by the Amati family during the 16th and 17th centuries in Cremona, Italy!

ambitus *(ăm'bĭ tŭs)* from the Latin: In *Gregorian music,* the *compass* of the *melody!*

Ambrosian chant. The *antiphonal psalm-chants* or *plainsongs* established and introduced into the Western Church by St. Ambrose!

American organ. An *organ* which uses air drawn in through the *reeds* by a *bellows!*

A minor. The *minor key* or *scale* which has no *flats* or *sharps* in the *signature!*

Amphionic *(ăm'fē ŏn' ĭk)* from Greek mythology: Referring to Amphion and his music! According to legend, Amphion was a son of Zeus who fortified the city of Thebes by playing his *lyre* and charming the stones into forming a wall-like structure!

amusia *(ȧ mū zĭ ȧ)* A brain condition which causes inability to appreciate or comprehend music!

Ancora *(än kô'rä)* from the Italian: Again, still, continue . . . *ancora piu mosso,* still faster: *ancora piano,* continue to play or sing softly!

andante *(än dän' tä)* from the Italian: Moving along moderately slow; between *larghetto* and *allegretto!* Also, the name given to a *section* or *movement* of a *symphonic work* which is in *andante tempo!*

andante moderato *(mō'dä rä'tō)* A little quicker than *andante!*

andantino *(än'dän tē'nō)* Most often used to conform to its technical meaning "a little slower than *andante*"; some musical authorities, citing an ambiguity in the definition of *andante,* approve the frequent use of *andantino* to mean "a little faster than *andante*"!

andare *(än dä rĕ)* from the Italian: To go, to move on . . . . *andare in tempo,* keep *strict time!*

anesis *(ăn'ē sĭs)* Dropping from a higher *tone* to a lower; *tuning strings* to a lower *pitch!*

anfang *(än fängk)* The German word for "beginning" . . . *vom Anfang,* the German term for *Da Capo!*

angelot *(ăn'jĕ lŏt)* An ancient *lute,* now obsolete!

angemessen *(än'gĕ mĕss'n)* from the German: Suitable, appropriate, fit!

angenehm *(ăn' gĕ nām)* from the German: Pleasing, agreeable!

anglaise *(äng'glāz)* The *French* word for "*English*": A 17th century type of *English country dance* or *air* in fast *duple meter.* Later, the *anglaise* evolved into an instrumental form . . . a *movement* in a *suite,* etc.! The title *anglaise* also sometimes was given to the *hornpipe!*

Anglican chant. A *harmonized chant,* used in the Anglican service, which was made up of successive *seven-bar sections* with several *voice parts* to each, along with some rather simple *chords!* Each section was divided into a *three-bar phrase,* followed by a *phrase* of *four bars!* The first *bar* of each section contained a single, reciting note: the other *bars* used a *cadence* sung in strict *rhythm!*

anhang *(än' häng)* The *German* word for *CODA!*

animato *(ä nē mä' tō)* It. / **animè** *(ä nē mä')* Fr. / **animoso** *(ä nē mō'sō)* It. / A direction to play with animation and spirit!

anklong *(äng'klŏng)* A musical instrument from *Malaya* (consisting of hanging tubes of bamboo) used for *percussion* in an *Indonesian gamelan (orchestra).*

anomaly *(ä nŏm'á lē)* Applied to music, the reference usually is to the small variation from *perfect pitch* caused by the *tempered intervals* played by given *instruments!* (see *TEMPERAMENT*)

anlaufen *(än'lou f'n)* from the German: To increase the volume, to swell!

ansatz *(än'säts)* from the German: (1) The *embouchure* of a *wind-instrument* (2) The *attack* of a *phrase* in performance!

anschlag *(än shläg)* from the German: (1) A *double grace note!* (2) An *appoggiatura!* (3) A *stroke*, or *striking* of a *chord!* (4) The performer's *touch* while playing *piano!*

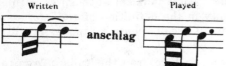

answer *(än'sēr)* In a *fugue*, a reproducing *response*, in the *dominant*, to the main *subject theme*. This continues as an alternating pattern so that the second, fourth, etc. *sections* are *answers*, usually set a *fifth* above the *subject!* If the *answer* is an exact reproduction (not counting the *fifth* displacement) this is called a *real answer*; if the *interval* values are altered (to stay within a *key*) this is called a *tonal answer!*

Fugue 9, Bach, Well Tempered Clavier II

antecedent *(ăn'tē sēd'ĕnt)* (1) The opening *theme* (*subject*) of a *fugue* or *canon!* (2) The *section* of a *periodic passage* of music that is followed by a *responding section* (*consequent*)!

anthem *(ăn'thĕm)* (1) *Sacred choral music* with lyrics from the *Scriptures!* (2) A song or *hymn* of joy or praise!

anticipation *(ăn tĭs'ĭ pā' shŭn)* (1) Playing one or more *notes* of a *following chord* just before the given *rhythm* indication, creating a brief *dissonance* within the *chord!* (2) Playing a complete chord prematurely!

antiphon *(ăn'tĭ fōn)*, antiphony *(ăn tĭf'ō nē)* In a *choir*, the *response* of one *section* of voices to another; alternate *singing* and *chanting!*

antithesis *(ăn tĭth'ĕ sĭs)* (1) A *corresponding* or *following part* in a musical work! (2) Another name for the *answer* portion of a *fugue!*

anvil *(ăn'vĭl)* A steel bar which sounds like an *anvil* when struck!

aphonic *(ā'fŏn'ĭk)* With neither voice nor sound!

apotome *(á pŏt' ō mē)* In Greek music, the larger of two *intervals* dividing an entire *step!* The *vibration ratio* of two *tones* so divided is 2187: 2048 in terms of *cycles per second frequency!*

appassionato *(äp päs'syō nä'tō)* from the Italian: A direction to play with passionate, deeply-emotional feeling!

appoggiatura *(á pŏj'á tōō'rá)* An *embellishing note* (*ornament*, *grace note*) that precedes a *following tone* and is written in notation as a note of smaller size (also known as "*leaning note*")! (1) The *long appoggiatura* is played on the *strong beat* and takes away a portion of the *time-value* of the *note* it precedes . . . generally one-half the value of an *even note* and two-thirds the value of a *dotted* note. The *long appoggiatura* is seldom used today!

(2) The *short appoggiatura* is a *grace note* played quickly just before the *following note* and *accenting* the *main note*. In classical composition a *short appoggiatura* was sometimes notated by a *stroke* across the *stem* of a small-sized *note*. The *appoggiatura* should not be confused with the *acciaccatura!*

(3) The *double appoggiatura* consists of two *grace notes* quickly played before the *main note* . . . the two *notes* are usually a *third* apart, the first *grace note* being lower!

a punta d'arco *(á pōōn'tä där'kō)* from the Italian: "With the point of the *bow*"!

à quatre mains *(ă kă'trĕ măn)* from the French: "For four hands"; a direction to play *duets* on *keyboard instruments!*

arabesque *(ăr' å bĕsk')* An ornate musical passage with intricate, imaginative melodic lines!

architectonic *(är'kĭ tĕk tŏn'ĭk)* A description for music that emphasizes structural design!

arco *(är' kō)* from the Italian: A direction to *bowed-instrument* players to use the *bow!* Particularly, after a *pizzicato* segment where the fingers are used instead of the *bow!*

arco saltando *(är' kō säl tän'dō)* from the Italian: "*The bounding bow*"; a *staccato* technique for *strings* wherein the *bow* rebounds from the *string* at each *note!*

Arentinian *(ăr'ē tĭn'ĭ ăn)* Referring to Guido d'Arezzo, Italian composer of the 11th century, whose *Arentinian syllables ut, re, mi, fa, sol, la* formed the basic structure for the voice exercises known as *solmization* or *solfeggio!*

aria *(ä'rĭ å)* An elaborate *single-voice melody part* sung with *accompaniment* in *operas* or other staged works!

aria buffa *(ä'ryå'bōōf'fä)* from the Italian: A comic or whimsical *aria!*

aria cantabile *(-kän tä'bē lä)* from the Italian: A slow-moving *aria* with a lyric style designed to express tragedy or longing!

aria da capo *(-dä kä'pō)* from the Italian: As contrasted to a simple *song* or recitative *air*, this is the grandest form of *aria!* It consists of three sections (1) The *complete theme!* (2) A new relaxed, fully *harmonized statement* and (3) A *da capo* repetition of the *theme* with much added *ornamentation!*

aria da chiesa *(-kyĕ'zä)* from the Italian: An *aria* using sacred lyrics!

aria di bravura *(-dē brä vōō' rä)* from the Italian: A fast *aria* with rich, difficult passages calling for much vocal virtuosity and strong expression of emotional feelings . . . joy, frustration, etc.!

aria d'imitazione *(-dē' mē tät syō' nä)* from the Italian: An *aria* in which the music or voice tend to imitate nature!

aria parlante *(pär län' tä)* from the Italian: A melodic *aria* but one characterized by a *rhetorical* or *declamatory* style.

arioso *(ä ryō'sō)* from the Italian: (1) A *vocal solo* midway between an *aria* and a *recitative* (2) A musical passage within a *recitative* (3) An *instrumental piece* with the melodic quality of an *air!*

a rovescio *(ä rō vĕsh' ō)* from the Italian: "Upside down"; a direction to reverse the course of performance, or *invert* a passage, or move in an opposite direction to the previous notation!

arpeggiando *(är'pĕ jän'dō)* from the Italian: A direction to play in *arpeggio* style!

arpeggio *(är pĕj'ō)* from the Italian: Literally "to play on a *harp*", but actually used to denote the playing of the *notes* of a *chord* in rapid consecutive manner on any *instrument.* An *arpeggio* is abbreviated in notation by a wavy vertical line drawn before the *chord!*

Written   Played

ARP ODYSSEY. A trademarked name for a *monophonic synthesizer* produced by the ARP company and used in conjunction with a *keyboard instrument* (see *SYNTHESIZER, INSTRUMENT*)!

arrangement *(å rānj'mĕnt)* The adaptation of a composition for any instrumental or vocal purpose other than that for which the music was originally written!

arsis *(är'sĭs)* The Greek name for "*upbeat*", the *weak* or *non-accented part* of the *measure* (the opposite of *thesis*, the "*downbeat*")!

artificial harmonics. A term for *harmonic tones* sounded by *stopped strings* (on stringed instruments such as *violin, guitar*, etc.) as opposed to the *natural harmonics* produced on *open strings!*

ars nova *(ärz'nō vä)* from the Latin: "New art", a description of 14th century music which advanced *polyphonic* complexities far beyond the music of *ars antiqua* ("old art") produced in the earlier 12th and 13th centuries.

art song. A lyrical song, usually of a single mood, but highly expressive in its structure! The *art song* is a term found in "serious composition" and is distinguished from songs written for popular commercial use or songs generated from folk origins!

as *(äs)* The *German* word for the note *A flat!*

a.s. The abbreviation for *al segno*, "up to the sign" (see *SEGNO*)!

ASCAP *(ăss kăp)* The abbreviation of American Society of Composers, Authors and Publishers, a non-profit membership society composed of two groups, songwriters and music publishers. Founded in 1914 by Victor Herbert and other composers, ASCAP today collects over $90,000,000 per annum from radio and television stations and other media for the "public performance of music" owned or written by its members. A large administrative staff supervises the "logging" of statistical samples of airplay and allocates the proceeds to the writers and publishers on the basis of several criteria, primarily the frequency of a given song's broadcast performance!

asor *(ăs'ôr)* A ten-stringed *Hebrew lyre* played with a *plectrum!*

A sharp. The *note* one *half-tone above A* and one *half-tone below B. A-sharp* is *enharmonically equivalent* to *B-flat* on *keyboards!*

aspiration *(ăs'pĭ rā'shŭn)* A rarely-used alternate name for the *dotted-note* marking for *staccato* (see *STACCATO*)!

a tempo *(ă těm'pō)* from the Italian: "Play in time"; a direction, after any *tempo* change, to return to the original *tempo!* In notation, **a tempo!**

atonal *(ā tōn'ăl)* Without any musical *tonality!*

attaca *(ăt tăk'kä)* from the Italian: "To attack"; a direction, at the end of a passage of music, to begin the next passage at once!

attaco *(ăt tăk' kō)* A brief *phrase* in simulated *counterpoint* which is used either as the main character of a *fugue* or as further *development!*

attack *(ă tăk')* (1) The characterization of the start of any performance, in terms of the precision or "togetherness" of the *ensemble!* (2) The vigor and accuracy of *pitch* of the beginning of a *solo performance*, particularly vocal, or at the outset of a given new *tone* or *phrase* (3) In computer technology, one of the components of sound as translated electronically; one of the generator controls of a *synthesizer* ... others are *sustain, decay* and *release* ... which govern the output and character of electronic sound!

attendant keys. The *relative major* or *minor keys* in terms of a given *key!* The *attendant keys* of the *C major key* are *a minor, G major, F major, e minor,* and *d minor!* (See *KEYS*)

attune *(ă tŭn')* To make sound melodious by bringing it into proper *pitch*, or *harmony*; to *tune* a *musical instrument!*

aubade *(ō'bäd)* from the French: Music celebrating the dawn; a *morning concert!*

audition *(ô dĭsh' ŭn)* "A hearing"; generally used to signify a "try out" for a musical or theatrical performance!

augment *(ôg měnt')* (1) Increasing a *major interval* by one *half-step* (2) *Doubling* the *note values* of a *theme* in *symphonic works* ... *augmentation* means *quarter-notes* become *half-notes, half-notes* become *whole-notes,* etc! The opposite technique, halving the *note-values,* is called *diminution!* Both are common to *classical variations* on a *theme!*

a una corda *(ä ōō'nä kôr'dä)* from the Italian: "With one *string*", a direction to use the *soft pedal* on the *piano* (left pedal)!

authentic *(ô thěn'tĭk)* (1) One of the church *modes* (SEE *MODE*)! (2) A *cadence* in which the *dominant* chord progresses to the *tonic* (SEE *CADENCE*)!

Autoharp *(ô'tō härp)* A trademarked name for an *instrument* resembling a *zither* or miniature harp which uses *chord bars* depressed by buttons to *stop* the *strings,* or leave them open, while they are strummed with the fingers or a *plectrum*; a favorite instrument for folk song and country music accompaniment!

autophon *(ô'tō fŏn)* An *instrument*, similar to a *barrel organ*, which sounds notes selected by pin holes in a hardboard sheet!

auxiliary tone. A *note* or *tone* which is not *harmonic* but which is only one *step* above or below a significant *note* to which it relates (*adjacent* or *neighboring*); used to describe *ornamentation* by such a *note* or *tone* (also called *neighboring tone*)!

axe *(ăks)* A colloquial "hip" expression used by popular, folk or jazz musicians to describe their *instrument*; particularly used by *guitarists!*

DICTIONARY

B

— B —

B. (1) The *seventh tone* in the *diatonic scale* of *C-major*, and the *first tone* of the *B-major* and *B-minor scales!* The *note* one *half-tone above B* is called *B-sharp* or *C;* the *note* one *half-tone below B* is called *B-flat* or *A-sharp* (*B-sharp* and *C; B-flat* and *A-sharp* are *enharmonic equivalents* on a *keyboard*)! (2) The abbreviation for the *BASS* voice or *part* in *choral music* . . . the *B* in *SATB,* for example! (3) The designation of a *second* stanza, *section* or *movement* in any musical sequence . . . the pattern *ABAB* would indicate the repetition of the first, second, first, second portions in that order. (4) The *German notation* for *B-flat; B-natural* is written as *H!*

Bach trumpet. A high-pitched *trumpet* originally constructed to accommodate the performance of Johann Sebastian Bach's voicings for *trumpet!*

backfall *(băk'fôl')* (1) One of the *levers* in a *piano, organ* or *pipe organ!* (2) An appoggiatura!

back-up *(băk ŭp)* In popular or jazz music, a colloquial term for any *supporting accompaniment!*

bagatelle *(băg'ȧ tĕl')* A lightly fashioned, brief musical piece!

bagpipe *(băg'pīp')* A *Scottish wind-instrument* of ancient origin, popular today throughout the world! A valved tube is used to blow into a pigskin or leather bag, out of which pressed air flows into three or more pipes that emit the characteristic *reedy, screechy bagpipe* sound! One eight-holed, *oboe-like pipe* plays *melody* and is called the *chanter;* the other *pipes* are used for sustained lower tones and are known as **drones!**

Blowpipe

Chanter   Drones

Bagpipe

baile *(bä'ē lä)* A Spanish country dance!

balafo *(băl'ȧ fō)* An *instrument* similar to the *xylophone,* used by the natives of West Africa!

balalaika *(băl'ȧ lī 'kȧ)* A *Russian guitar-like instrument* with a wooden body shaped in a triangle and with two to four *fretted strings!* Plucked with a *plectrum,* the *balalaika* comes in several sizes, the most common being a three-string version that is tuned *EEA* above middle *C!*

Balalaika

ballad *(băl'ăd)* (1) A popular, romantic song which may repeat the melody several times or use a narra-

tive form with no repeats! Usually limited, as a description, to compositions of a leisurely *tempo!* (2) A simple dance tune! (3) A *folk song* with text for recitation by a chorus and an orchestral background! (4) An *instrumental* piece with a narrative implication! (5) In the 14th and 15th centuries, a secular vocal song with *polyphonic, instrumental* background!

ballade *(bȧ läd')* from the French: (1) A poetic piece for *piano!* (2) An orchestral composition resembling a *tone poem!*

ballad horn. Another name for the *althorn* (see *ALTHORN*)!

ballad opera. A frothy, melodic type of *opera,* beginning with The Beggar's Opera (1728), which used popular or folk *airs* in conjunction with augmented text and dialogue!

ballerina *(băl'ĕ rē'nȧ)* A professional, female ballet dancer!

ballet *(băl'ā)* The highly aesthetic "fine art" of the dance, for which appropriate music is composed or adapted for theatrical presentation. "Ballet music" frequently has achieved such world-wide recognition as to be featured in orchestral programs independent of any dance or staging!

bamboula *(băm bōō' lä)* An indigenous *voodoo drum* used in the West Africa and the West Indies!

band *(bănd)* Any group of musicians who play *brass-wind, wood-wind* and *percussion instruments* in *ensemble* (sometimes augmented by *stringed instruments*). A complete *military-style band* uses *trumpets, cornets, trombones, saxophones, clarinets, flutes, piccolos, oboes, bassoons, tubas* and variations thereof, in addition to many *percussion instruments* including *drums, cymbals, glockenspiel, chimes, bells,* etc. A *concert band* may augment the above with *strings, harp* and other "non-marching" instruments; other modifications of band styles include the *dance band (five reed, five brass, four rhythm* type of format) *corps style band* (emphasis on marching instruments as opposed to "show-time" marching bands of larger size) and *"string" bands (banjos* and *glockenspiels* predominant)!

band major. A *bandmaster!*

bandmaster *(bănd'măs'tĕr)* The *leader* of a *band!*

bandora *(băn dôr'ȧ)* A *stringed instrument* of the *lute* family widely used in Europe during the 16th century! With a unique *"scalloped"* body, the *bandora (Italian, pandora; French, bandore)* was *multi-fretted* with seven pairs of *wire strings* tuned *G', C D G c e a!*

Bandora

band shell. A *bandstand* featuring a large shell-shaped structure at the rear of the platform which acts as a sounding board to re-inforce the sound and project it into the audience area!

bandstand *(bănd'stănd')* Usually an outdoor, raised platform with a roof and open sides to direct sound in all directions for a *concert!*

bandurria *(bän dōōr'ryä)* A *Spanish* form of *lute!*

Bandurria

banjo *(băn'jō)* A favorite American *stringed instrument* (with African roots), particularly popular among folk musicians, the *banjo* has a *fretted, guitar-shaped neck* and a *tambourine-shaped body*. Usually equipped with five strings (there are several variations in models and number of strings) it is strummed or plucked with *picks* or fingers. The five-string version is tuned to *D,B,G,C,E*, respectively!

Banjo

banjorine *(băn'jō rēn')* A short-necked *banjo* tuned a *fourth* above a conventional *banjo!*

bar *(bär)* Used loosely to denote one *measure* of music! The *bar-line* is a vertical line across the *staff*

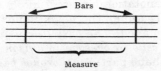

Bars

Measure

which separates the *measures* into equal, time *intervals*. A *double-bar-line* marks the end of a complete section of music!

A double bar with one thin and one heavy line indicates the end of a composition.

A double bar with two thin lines indicate the end of a musical phrase.

barbershop harmony. A colloquial term for *"close harmony" part-singing* which was a *singing style* employed by *American barbers* at the end of the 19th century! It favored what today is considered a *trite array of seventh chords (dominant* and *diminished)* and sixth chords (augmented)!

barcarole, barcarolle *(bär'kä rōl)* Any popular song sung in *Venice* by the *gondoliers!* The *barcarolle* has been made famous in serious music by such composers as Chopin and Mendelssohn and, particularly, Offenbach for his *Barcarolle* from *Les Contes d'Hoffman* (The Tales of Hoffman)!

bard *(bärd)* From medieval days, a Celtic singing poet who composed, sang or recited the deeds and legends of the heroes of his time! (See *CROUD*, the *instrument* used by *bards*)!

bariolage *(bä rē ŏh lä'zh)* from the French: A medley; a group of *notes* played on more than one string in the same *violin position!*

baritone *(băr'ĕ tōn)* (1) The male singing voice between *tenor* and *bass* with a *range* that averages *A* to *f'!* (2) A *B-flat tuba* with a range of *E* to *c'!* (3) Another name for the *viola di bordone!* (4) See *SAXOPHONE* for the *E-flat baritone saxophone!*

baritone horn. A type of enlarged *Flugelhorn* (with three *valves)* that comes in two models, one with the *bell* pointing up, the other with the *bell* facing backwards! The *baritone's* range is one *octave* below the *cornet* (the *cornet range* is *e* to *b-flat")* A four-*valve* version is called the *euphonium* (see *euphonium*)! The *baritone horn* is a *transposing instrument* . . . the music is written a *ninth* higher than the sound!

baritone horn

barn dance. A 4/4 dance, resembling a *schottische* that was popular in American rural areas and, as the name indicates, was held in a barn!

baroque *(bă'rōk')* A term borrowed from architecture to characterize a period of musical style dating about 1600 to 1750. *Baroque* music is known as elaborate and complex composition, although it was first developed as an *anti-polyphonic* movement. Later, *baroque* composers developed the art of *counterpoint* to intricate degrees and gave life to such forms as the *fugue* and the *toccata*. The great *baroque* composers included Monteverdi, Frescobaldi, Vivaldi, Purcell, Handel, Bach, and others!

barré *(bär rā')* from the French: In *guitar* music, the holding down (*stopping*) of all the *strings* with the left-hand forefinger while the remaining fingers form a *chord*. In a *half-barré*, the forefinger (index finger) does not *stop* all of the *strings*. To barré all the *strings* is called *CAPO* (see *CAPO*); to *barré* half the *strings* is called *CAPOSTRASTO*, barred chord. In *guitar* notation, a *chord* which calls for holding down (*stopping*) more than one *string* at a time. The held-down strings are indicated by a *slur* ⌒ over the given *strings* to be *stopped!*

barrel organ. A rudimentary *organ* used by street musicians! The instrument consists of a crank-turned, barrel-body into which a bellows squeezes air through a set of *pipes!*

baryton *(bă'rē tōn)* (1) An 18th century variation of the *viola de gamba,* the *baryton* was a *bowed, string-instrument* with added *sympathetic strings* (up to 40) to reinforce the six *melody strings* (a feature of the *viola d'amore*)! The *instrument* had a short life but gained its brief popularity due to the writings of Haydn, whose patron in court favored the *baryton!* (2) The *German* word for the *EUPHONIUM!* (3) The *French* word for the *baritone* voice or the *baritone range* for *instruments!*

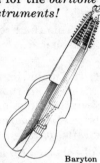

Baryton

bass *(bās)* The lowest *range* in *harmonic music!* (1) The lowest range for *male vocalist,* averaging *E* to *e'!* (2) the lowest *range* and largest size for many *instruments (bass drum, bass recorder, bass flute)* with the *contrabass* of other *instrument* families still lower and larger! (3) A shortened name for the *double bass* or *bass fiddle!*

bassa *(băs'sä)* from the Italian: "Low"; used in the direction, *8va bassa (ottava bassa),* to play the designated notes an *octave lower* than as written!

bass bar *(bās'băr')* The wooden strip running the length of, and within, a *violin* or its family members. The strip supports the *bridge* and tends to even out the vibration!

bass clarinet *(-klăr' ĭ nĕt')* A larger version of the *clarinet* that is pitched an *octave* lower than the standard *B-flat instrument.* (see *CLARINET*)!

Bass Clarinet

bass clef. The *F clef:* The marking that places *F* on the fourth line of the musical *staff!* The *bass clef* always appears below the *G clef (treble clef)!*

bass clef

bass drum The largest member of the standard *drum* family! The *bass drum* is circular-shaped (approximately three feet in diameter) and is played while held or rested vertically. The *drum* has two *heads* (skin covered sides), although sometimes only one *head* is struck, emitting a deep, low "boom"! The *instrument* is most often struck with a padded *beater (drum stick)!*

Bass Drum

bass flute. The *alto flute* (see *FLUTE, ALTO*)!

basset horn. A *tenor-range* version of the *alto clarinet,* shaped longer than the standard *clarinet* and with an upturned metal *bell! Pitched in F* (below the *alto clarinet),* the *basset horn* has a *compass* from *low F* to the *E above middle C!*

Basset Horn

bass oboe, Another name for the *heckelphone* (see *HECKELPHONE*)!

basso *(bäs'ō)* from the Italian: A male, *bass*-voiced singer!

basso buffo *(-bōōf'fō)* A low-voiced, male singer of comic roles in *opera!*

basso cantante *(-kän tän'tä)* A higher *bass* voice, between *baritone* and *basso profundo!*

basso continuo *(kōn tē nuō)* from the Italian: "Continuous bass" or "thorough Bass"; in *baroque music,* a "shorthand" notation for a *continuing bass part* with numerals under the *notes* indicating the *chords* to be played! The *bass line* usually was played by the *cello* or *bassoon* in *unison* with the *keyboard,* left-hand part! See *thorough bass* for *notation detail!*

basso de camera *(-dä kä'mä rä)* A small *double bass!*

Bassoon

bassoon *(bă soon')* A *double-reed, wind-instrument* (in the *oboe* family) with a long, thin curving *mouthpiece* and a long tube bent back upon itself! Requiring both fingers and *keys* to cover various holes, the *bassoon* is considered the natural *bass* for the *oboe* or *clarinet*! It has a *range of B-flat to D''*!

basso ostinato *(-ōs'tē nä'tō)* The continuous repetition of a *bass passage* behind changing *melodies* and/or *harmonies*!

basso profundo *(-prō fŭn'dō)* The lowest or deepest male *bass* voice with a *range* that reaches down to *C* or *D* below the *bass staff*!

bass saxhorn. Another name for the *bass tuba* (see *TUBA* and *SAXHORN*)!

bass trombone. The *trombone (pitched in F)* midway in size between the *tenor trombone* and the *contrabass trombone* (See *TROMBONE*)!

bass trumpet. A special-purpose *trumpet* which is *pitched an octave lower* than the standard *trumpet* (See *TRUMPET*)!

bass viol *(bās vē ôl).* Another name for the *double bass*, or *string bass*, or *vìola da gamba* (See *DOUBLE BASS*)!

baton *(bă tŏn').* The *conductor's* stick or wand!

battuta *(băt too'tä)* from the Italian: A *beat* or *pulse*; also a *measure* or *bar*!

batyphone *(băt'ĭ fōn)* A 19th century, *single-reed instrument* tuned a *fifth below* the *bass clarinet*!

Bayreuth Festival *(bī'roit)* A *Wagnerian* festival conducted every summer in the town of Bayreuth in Bavaria!

BB-flat bass (1) A *baritone bugle* (mostly used in bands) with a *range from D to A*! (2) Another name for the *helicon*! (3) An infrequently used name for the *contrabass Saxhorn*!

Be *(bā)* The German word for the flat sign (♭)!

b.c. The abbreviation for *basso continuo*!

beam *(bēm)* The thick, horizontal line connecting the *stems* of groups of *eighth* or *sixteenth notes*! One *beam* connects eighth notes, two *beams* for *sixteenth notes*, etc!

eighth notes   *sixteenth notes*

beat *(bēt).* (1) The division of a *measure (bar)* which regularly repeats as *accents* or *throbs*! The *strong* beat receives the most *accent*; the *weak beat* receives the least! (2) The moving of a hand, foot or wand to mark or *beat off* the time! (3) An *ornamental trill* used in older composition . . . similar to *MORDENT*! (4) In acoustical science, the change in apparent loudness caused by interfering vibrations of adjacent notes!

beating reed. The *oscillating reed* in *woodwind* instruments (such as the *clarinet)* which beats against the sides of the instrument's aperture. A *free reed* strikes no surface or edge of an aperture; a *double reed* consists of two *beating reeds* which strike each other!

bebung *(bĕ'boo'nkh)* from the German: A *vibrato* on string instruments, particularly, the *clavichord*! It is notated:

be-bop *(bē'bŏp).* See *BOP*!

bel canto *(bĕl kän'tō)* from the Italian: "Beautiful song"; a form of vocalizing, stemming from classic Italian *opera* of the 17th and 18th centuries, which stressed a "beautiful style" as contrasted to a "declamatory style" of singing!

bell *(bĕl)* (1) A *percussion instrument* constructed of varying-size metal tubes or bars which sound bell-like *tones* when struck with a metal rod or *beater*! (2) The flared end of a *wind instrument*! (3) Occasionally used as an informal name for the *glockenspiel*!

bell harp. A box-shaped, *harp-like instrument* which is swung like a bell at the same time that its strings are plucked!

bémol *(bā'môl')* The *French* word for *B-flat*; also the French word for a *flat tone*!

ben marcato *(bĕn' mär kä'tō)* from the Italian: "Well marked"; an indication to observe the *accents* of *rhythm*!

berceuse *(bĕr'sûz')* from the French: A *cradle song* or *lullaby*, or a short composition with similar qualities!

bergerette *(bĕr'zhē rĕt')* from the French: A pastoral, folk song!

bergamasca *(bĕr'gă mä'skă)* A form of song and dance (popular in Bergamo, Italy) which was adapted by serious composers! The *bergamasca* is identified by a strict harmonic sequence of *tonic*, *subdominant*, *dominant* and *return to tonic*!

bergamasca

berloque *(bĕr'lôk)* from the French: A military *drum beat* in which one stick plays two *beats* to the other's one. (2) A military *trumpet call*!

B-flat. The *tone* one *half-step below B* and one *half-step above A*! The *B-flat* on *keyboards* is the *enharmonic equivalent* of *A sharp*!

B-flat instrument. Any *transposing instrument* such as the *trumpet, clarinet, saxophone*, etc.!

B-flat major. The *key signature* for the *scale* which has *two flats* and begins on *B-flat*! The *G-minor scale* is the *relative minor* to the *B-flat major scale*!

B-flat minor. The *key signature* for the *scale* which has *five flats* and begins on *B-flat*! The *B-flat minor scale* is *relative* to the *D-flat major*!

bichord (bī'kôrd) "With two strings"; *bichord* instruments include *mandolin*, *lute* and certain *keyboards* which used *paired (double) strings* that are tuned in *unison* to each other!

bignou (bē'nyoo') from the French: A Breton *bagpipe* with only one *drone* pipe, and one *chanter* which has seven holes!

binary (bī'nà rē) A mathematical term used in music to describe a two-part *theme*, or one *theme* with an extension which may be contrasted but is still related! Today, the *SONATA* is classified as a *compound binary* construction!

binary measure. A *measure* in *common time* which alternates the *upbeat* and *downbeat* in regular order!

bind (bīnd) A *tie* marked ⌢ or ⌣ which connects two *notes* of the same *pitch* and indicates that the "combined" note is to be played once and held for the *time-value* of both *notes*! The *tie* should not be confused with a *slur* which uses the same marking or with the larger, similar curve that marks a *phrase*!

binding. A description for a *note* common to successive *chords* and held through both!

bis (bĭs). From the French; A direction to repeat a portion of music, the same direction as *encore*!

bit (bĭt). An extra-short tube used in *cornets* and similar instruments to alter the *fundamental pitch*!

bitonal (bī tō năl) Using two *keys* at the same time regardless of the *key signature*!

biwa (bē'wä) A Japanese *lute*! See *pyibar*!

block (blŏk) A *percussion instrument* made of a hollow, wooden block that is struck with a *drumstick*!

block chords. Consecutive, similar *chord groups* played with no specific tie-in to the *lead vocal-part* (sometimes, not related to any *assigned mode*)!

blowhole (blō'hōl). The opening or *mouth hole* in the side of a *flute*!

blues (blooz) The world-famous American music form that evolved from black work songs, spirituals and other folk music to become popular during the turn of the century! Most *blues* are slow in *tempo* but almost all are *syncopated*, using many "half-flatted" notes in the *third, fifth* and *seventh degrees*! A *blues* usually features a *twelve-bar section* with the *melody (solo)* distinguished by brief *phrases* or *statements* with regular *phrases* between! In the modern popular music idiom, *blues* has fused to many forms, including Jazz, rock, soul, etc.!

B-major. The *key signature* for the *major scale* that begins on *B* and has *five sharps*! The *relative minor* to the *B-major scale* is *G-sharp minor*.

B-minor. The *key signature* of the *minor scale* that begins on *B* and has *two sharps*! *B-minor* is *relative* to the *D-major scale*!

B.M.I. The abbreviation for Broadcast Music, Inc., the second largest American collection society which competes with the older and larger A.S.C.A.P. Unlike A.S.C.A.P., B.M.I. is a privately incorporated entity, but like A.S.C.A.P. it licenses and collects fees for the public performance of music, primarily from radio and television stations or networks. The proceeds are distributed (less expenses) to B.M.I. songwriters on the basis of a statistical analysis, of the frequency of air play, taken from "sample" logs of the actual broadcasts!

bobization (bō'bĭ zā' shŭn) An obsolete system that used the syllables *bo, ce, di,* etc. as a *scale*!

bocal (bō'kăl). A *brass instrument's mouthpiece*!

Boehm system (bōm sĭs't'm). A system invented by a German *flutist* in the 1830's which arranged the *finger holes* and *keys* for the *flute* (later for other *woodwinds*) to make them more easily accessible to the finger, yet holding closely to the order of the *chromatic scale*!

bois (bwäh) from the French: The *wood-winds*!

bolero (bō lâr'ō) A *Spanish* dance, usually in ¾ *time* that merges swift body-turns, clicking *castanets* and a syncopated foot-stamping which moves along as illustrated! The most famous *bolero* is the dramatic Ravel *Bolero* which was composed in 1928!

Bolero Rhythm

bombardon (bŏm'bêr dŏn) (1) Currently designates a *bass saxhorn* (originally, a low-toned forerunner of the *bassoon*)! 2) A low-toned *organ stop*! (3) Sometimes used as another name for the tuba!

bonang (bō năng) A *Javanese percussion instrument* consisting of a row of *gongs*!

bone (bōne) (1) A colloquial term (somewhat dated) among professional musicians for the *trombone* (2) The plural "bones" was used to describe a percussion instrument (popular in black minstrel shows of the turn of the century) which entailed the clicking together of two small bones with the fingers.

bongo (bŏng'gō) A small drum with one *head* used in percussion ensembles for Latin rhythms and usually employed in pairs, or as a set of three. Some versions of the *bongo* can be tuned, depending on the construction of the given model.

Bongo Drums

boogie-woogie (boogee woog'ee) (1) A dated piano style, pioneered by Meade Lux Lewis and Ammons and Johnson, (popular in the 1930's) usually in the form of a rapid blues variation! The right band played *melody* against a "rolling" *ostinato bass* from the left hand with eight beats to each *bar (measure)*. (2) In the late 1970's, the single word *boogie* has become a colloquial reference to dancing, or a dance step, particularly *disco* dancing.

bop *(bŏp)* also called be-bop. A jazz style of the 1940's, pioneered by renowned instrumentalists such as Dizzy Gillespie and Charlie Parker. *Be-bop* was characterized by swift and complicated solos accompanied by complex rhythm changes and frequent dissonant chords.

bottleneck guitar *(bŏt'l'nĕk)*. A colloquial name for *slide guitar*, on which the left hand of the player uses the neck of a bottle, or a metal tube, as a cover for the 3rd or 4th fingers, which slide across the strings! see *Guitar!*

bourrée *(bōō'rā')*. A brisk, 17th century French dance in *duple meter*, which later evolved into an instrumental music form common to the 18th century *suite!*

bout *(bout)*. The curve on the side of *violin-type instruments* that shapes the *waist* of the given *instrument!*

boutade *(bōō'tàd')*. An old, capricious French dance!

bow *(bō)*. The elongated, wooden stick (from end to end of which horsehairs are stretched) used to play *instruments* of the *violin* family!

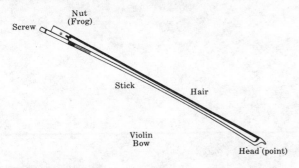

Screw · Nut (Frog) · Stick · Hair · Violin Bow · Head (point)

bowing. The art of using the *bow*. "*Down-bow*" ... sign ⊓ ... means the *bow-arm* strokes down and away from the body; "*up-bow*" ... sign ∨ ... means the *bow-arm* strokes up and towards the body. For examples of *bowing* techniques, see *slur, staccato, spiccato, détaché, flautato, pizzicato, sautillé, jeté, louré, martelé, viotti, arpeggio, tremolo, sul ponticello, sul tasto, col legno, ondulé, etc!*

brace *(brās)* The marking which connects two *staves* and indicates simultaneous performance of both! (also called *bracket)!*

Brace

branle *(brän''l)*. A French dance of the 16th century in *duple* and *triple meter*. Frequently accompanied by vocals, the *branle*, later in the 18th century, was used instrumentally in composition of *suites!*

brass band *(brās bănd)* A term for a *band* using "*brass wind-instruments*" with *mouthpieces* that omit *reeds*. Technically, the term "*brass band*" is a misnomer since the instruments are made of many metals, or other substances, and not necessarily of brass. A similar "misnomer' applies to "*woodwinds*" which are frequently made of metal, or other substances apart from wood!

bravura *(brä vū'rà)* Highly florid music designed to showcase virtuosity of a performer or performance!

brawl *(brôl)* The *English* version of the French *branle* (see *branle)!*

break *(brāk)*. (1) In popular and jazz music, an improvised *solo* or non-standard *rhythm pattern* (from 2 to 16 *bars*) inserted between sections of previously rehearsed or arranged music . . . a *drum break* gives the *solo* chore to the *drummer!* (2) The point where a particular *vocal* or *instrumental register* meets another! (3) An *organ stop* which suddenly reverts notes to a lower *octave*, or the point at which *organ pipes* change *pitch!* (4) Short for a "break-down" in the quality of music or performance! (5) A change in the *register* of some *wind-instruments!*

breve *(brēv)*. The equivalent of two *whole notes*, often called a *double whole note:* ⎜𝅝⎜ or ⎜ ⎜

bridge *(brĭj)*. (1) The thin wooden arch that raises and stretches the *strings* on the *body of stringed instruments* such as the *violin, guitar*, etc., and transmits the vibrations to the instrument's *belly!* (2) A wooden or metal ridge in a *piano soundboard* over which the *strings* are stretched, and through which the vibrations are transmitted!

bridle tape *(brī'd'l tap)*. A leather strip attached to a small wire which is used in *piano action* to restrain the motion!

brillante *(brēl län'tā)* from the Italian: Brilliant, flashy; a showy style of music or performance!

brindisi *(brĭn'dē zē)* from the Italian: A drinking song, or the musical accompaniment to a toast!

brio, con *(kôn brē'ô)* / **brioso** *(brē oh'sŏh)* It. / A direction to play in a spirited, fiery manner!

broken chord *(brō'kĕn kôrd)* A *chord* whose *tones* are sounded one at a time in any order! A *chord* whose *tones* are sounded in a rapid, orderly succession is called an *arpeggio!*

buccina *(bŭk'sĭ nà)* In the days of the old Roman Empire, a *C-shaped trumpet* used by the military!

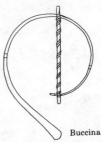

Buccina

buffo *(bōōf'fō)* from the Italian: A male singer of *operatic*, comic roles *(basso buffo, tenor buffo, etc.)!*

bugle *(bū'g'l)*. A *brass wind-instument*, with a *cupped-mouthpiece*, used for military signals and calls! *Bugles* sometimes are equipped with *keys (key-bugle)* or with *valves* (see *Saxhorn*) but without such added devices, the *instrument* can play only one *tone* and its related overtones! *Bugles* are *pitched in B-flat* or *C!*

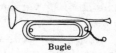
Bugle

buglet *(bu'glet)* A small *bugle!*

bull fiddle. A dated colloquialism among popular musicans for the *contrabass* or *double bass!*

burden *(bûr'd'n)* (1) A repeating refrain after each verse of a song. (2) A *droning bass figure* in a written or performed *accompaniment!* (3) The *drone* of a *bagpipe* (see *bagpipe*)!

bushing *(boosh'ing)* The padding used in *pianos* and *organs* to reduce vibration!

busker *(bŭs'kēr)* From English slang, a singing or playing beggar!

butt *(bŭt)* In a *piano*, the *heel* which holds a *hammer* (see *piano*)!

buzuki *(bŭ zoo'kē)* A *Greek guitar-like instrument* popular in many Near-East countries! The buzuki has a pear-shaped *body* and a long *neck* and normally comes with two *sets (courses)* of *three-metal-strings* each!

bylina *(bĭ lē'na)* A Russian folksong!

DICTIONARY

C

— C —

C (1) The *keynote* (first note) of the *natural C major scale*, which has no *flats* and no *sharps* in the *signature!* C also is the first *note* of the *C-minor scale* which has three *flats* in the *signature!* C is the third *note* of the *A-minor scale* which is the *relative minor* to the *C-major!* (2) A capital *C* indicates the *C major triad;* a small *c* the *c minor triad!* (3) On a *piano keyboard*, the note *c'* is the *middle C;* in the *tenor voice* range, *C* is the lowest note! (4) A *C instrument* usually is a *non-transposing instrument* that sounds at the *pitch* of the music written for it *(C flute, oboe, recorder* etc.)! (5) An *ornamental* **C** after the *clef* in a *key signature* indicates "*common time* $\frac{4}{4}$"; when the figure has a vertical line **¢** this is known as "*cut time*" or "*alla breve*" time, $\frac{2}{2}$ or $\frac{4}{2}$!

cabaletta *(kä'bä lĕt'tä)* from the Italian: A short *operatic* piece featuring *triplets* in the *background accompaniment!*

caccia *(kät'chä)* from the Italian: A chase or hunt! *Alla caccia* means to play in hunting style with *accompaniment* from the *horns!*

cacophony *(kă kŏf'ō nĭ)* When used in a musical reference, *cacophony* means a series of discordant, strident or dissonant *tones!*

cadence *(kā'dĕns).* (1) A closing strain! (2) An *ornamental* closing *trill:* (3) A *perfect* or *authentic cadence* is formed by the progression of harmony from the *dominant* to the *tonic!* (4) A *plagal cadence* is formed when the *tonic harmony* is preceded by the *subdominant chord!* (5) When the final note of a verse is the *keynote*, this is called a *complete* or *full cadence!* (6) When the *dominant chord* is followed by a *harmony* other than the *tonic*, this is called a *deceptive cadence!* (7) A *half-cadence* or *imperfect cadence* occurs when the *common chord* of the *tonic* precedes the *dominant harmony!*

cadenza *(kȧ dĕn'zȧ)* (1) An *ornamental flouish* to a *solo piece*, usually placed just before the closing *cadence!* (2) A technically brilliant passage (closing the first or last movement of a *concerto)* performed by a *solo instrument!*

cakewalk *(kak'wôlk)* A 19th-century form of black *ragtime* or *minstrel* music, performed with a high-stepping strut in 2/4 time, with a slightly syncopated single-note melody shifting from minor to major key as it progressed.

calando *(cȧ lan dō)* from the Italian: A direction to gradually soften and slow down as if fading away!

calcándo *(käl kän'dō)* from the Italian: "Pressing", a direction to hurry the *tempo!*

calliope *(kȧ lī'ō pē)* A *steam organ* that emits a series of whistles or shrill sounds from a small *range of keys!*

calliophone *(kȧ lē'ō fōn)* A variation of the *calliope* which uses air pressure instead of steam!

callithump *(kăl ĭ thŭmp)* A boisterous *concert* or *parade* with much discord and *tin horns!*

calmato *(käl mä'tō)* from the Italian: A direction to play in a calm or tranquil manner!

caloróso *(käl ō rō zō)* from the Italian: A direction to play with passion or warmth!

camera *(kä' mĕh rȧh)* from the Italian: "Chamber" or "room"; a description of *chamber music!*

camminando *(käm mē nän'dô)* from the Italian: A direction to play with an easy, flowing *andante* movement!

campana *(kăm pā'nȧ)* from the Italian: "A bell"!

campanella *(käm'pȧ nĕl'lä)* from the Italian: "A small bell"!

cancel *(kăn'sĕl)* Another word for the *natural*, the *accidental* symoblized by ♮ !

cancion *(kän thē ōn)* from the Spanish: "A song"!

cancrizans *(kăng'krĭ zănz)* from the Latin: "Going backwards"; the stating of a *musical theme* and repeating it backwards!

canon *(kăn'ŭn)* The strictest form of musical composition wherein a *following voice-part* exactly imitates the *melody* sung in the original *part!* The only distinction of the imitation (compared to the original) would be a few *beats* at the start with varying *intervals* thereafter!

cantabile *(kän tä' bē lä)* / **cantando** *(kän tän dō)* / **cantante** *(kän tän tĕ)* It. / A direction to sing or play in a smooth, melodious style!

cantata *(kän tä' tȧ)* (1) A *choral composition* with various movements of *recitatives, solos, choruses* and *airs!* (2) In its original use, a poem set to music!

canticle *(kăn tĭ k'l)* A brief *song* or *hymn* of sacred or biblical origin!

cantilena *(kăn'tĭ lēnȧ)* from the Italian: (1) A short *song!* (2) A graceful, *song-like instrumental piece!* (3) Sometimes used as a direction to play in *legato* style!

cantillation *(kăn'tĭ lä shŭn)* A *chant* or *intonation* without *accompaniment!* The *cantor* in a synagogue usually improvises vocal *tones* to a recitation from sacred text!

canto *(kăn'tō)* The highest part in a *choral* or *instrumental passage* . . . the *soprano part!*

cantor *(kăn'tôr)* See *cantillate.*

cantus *(kăn'tŭs)* A *song* or a *melody;* also the *principal, soprano part!*

cantus firmus *(fŭr'mŭs)* from the Latin: A fixed *melody;* simple *Gregorian chant* that follows prescribed church rules for *counterpoint!*

canzone *(kän tsō'nä)* (1) An Italian *lyric song* dedicated to romance or beauty! (2) A *melody* with polyphonic components in *madrigal* style!

canzonet *(kän'zō nĕt)* A little *song* or *air:* a *madrigal!*

capo *(kä pō)* from the Italian: (1) "Top", "head", "beginning": *Da Capo al segna* means "from the beginning to the sign **𝄋** or ⊕! (2) A familiar word in *guitar music*, actually short for *capotasto!* In the noun form, *capo* is a *bar-like clamp* or mechanical device made of rubber, metal, ivory, wood, cloth, etc. which is attached to the *neck* of a *guitar* and creates a movable *nut* across the *finger board!* The *capo* serves to *raise the pitch of all strings* uniformly, by acting as a *barre!* In the verb form, *capo* is used to describe the act of *barreing the strings*, either with the forefinger or a mechanical device (see *barre)!* (3) The *nut* of any *stringed instrument* with a *fingerboard!*

Capo

capricetto *(kä'prēt chĕt'tō)* from the Italian: A short *capriccio!*

capriccio *(kä'prēt'chō)* from the Italian: A free, fanciful composition played in a capricious style!

capriccioso *(kä'prēt chō'sō)* from the Italian: A direction to play in a free and capricious manner!

caprice *(kä prēs)* from the French: Same as *capriccio!*

carillon *(kăr'ĭ lŏn)* (1) A *glockenspiel*, or *chimes*, or set of *fixed bells* usually with a *three-octave range* and *tuned* to the *chromatic scale!* (2) An *organ stop* with *carillon* sound! (3) A composition designed for the *carillon* or suggesting the sound of *bells!*

carita *(kä rē'tä)* from the Italian: A direction to play with tenderness and expressive feeling!

carmen *(kär'mĕn)* from the Latin: A *song* . . . plural, *carmina!*

carol *(kăr'ŭl)* (1) A *song* of religious joy or praise . . . a *Christmas song!* (2) Generally, a happy, exultant *song!*

cassa *(kăs'ä)* from the Italian: A *drum!*

cassation *(kä sä'shŭn)* An 18th century *instrumental composition!*

castanets *(kăs'tä nĕts')* A *rhythm instrument* consisting of ivory shells *(clappers)* which are tied to the thumb and clapped by a finger or fingers; used in Spain to accompany the *flamenco* and *bolero* dancers! *Orchestral Castanets* are spring-mounted on a handle for easy operation by a *person!*

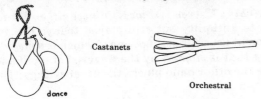

Castanets

dance   Orchestral

castrato *(käs trä'tō)* from the Italian: A male singer, *castrated* in childhood to preserve his *soprano* voice!

catch *(kăch)* A *round* for at least three voices with each singer taking up a *part* in turn! In modern times, *catches* are usually comic or humorous!

catgut *(kăt gŭt')* A popular vernacular name for *instrument strings* made of animal gut!

cavatina *(kä'vä tē'nä)* from the Italian: A short *air* with only one simple strain!

C-clef *(C klĕf)* The sign that designates both the *alto clef (viola clef)* and the *tenor clef!* The *alto clef* sign

indicates the *middle line of the staff* as *middle C!* The *tenor clef* indicates the *second line from the top of the staff* as *middle C!* The *tenor clef* is used for the *high-register notes* of the *cello* and *bassoon* as well as the *tenor trombone!* The *C-clef* sign also is written as

C dur *(C dōōr)* The *German* term for the *key of C major!*

cebell *(sē bĕl')* An old *air* in common time which featured rapid, alternating high and low *tones!*

cedendo *(sē dĕnd'ō)* from the Italian: Slowing down!

cédez *(sā dā')* from the French: To slow the *tempo!*

célere *(sā lĕr)* It. / **celerita** *(sē lĕr ĭ tä)* It. / **celerite** *(sā lär i tä)* Fr. / To play with velocity; rapidly!

celesta *(sē lĕs'tä)* A *percussion instrument* invented in 1886 by Mustel in Paris! It consists of *tuned* steel bars that are struck by *hammers* activated from a *keyboard!* The range is four *or more octaves up* from *middle C*; the *music sounds* an *octave higher* than *as written!*

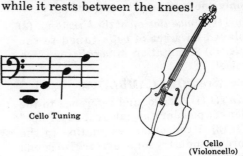

Celesta

cello *(chĕl'o)* One of the major orchestral instruments, the *cello* is the popular name for the rarely used designation *violoncello*, which is the *bass* member of the *violin* family! About twice the size of a *violin*, it is *bowed* in a seated position, with the spiked end of the instrument resting on the floor, while it rests between the knees!

Cello Tuning

Cello
(Violoncello)

A *cello* has a *compass of almost four octaves* (from *low C* to an *A two octaves above middle C*) and is *tuned one octave and a fifth below the violin*, and exactly *one octave below the viola!* The four *strings* of the *cello* are tuned *C, G, d, a!*

cembalo *(sĕm'bä lō)* from the Italian: The *harpsichord* or *pianoforte;* also an old Italian designation for *dulcimer!*

ces *(sĕss)* The *German* word for the note *C-flat!*

Ces dur *(sĕss dōōr)* The *German* term for the *key of C-flat major!*

ceses *(sĕss ĕss)* The *German* word for the note *C-double-flat.*

C-flat *(C flăt)* The musical *tone a half-tone below C* and *a half-tone above B-flat! C-flat* and *B* are identical on the *piano (enharmonic equivalents)!*

cents *(sĕnts)* *Units of measurement* for *intervals* that are used in *musicology!* Each *cent* is *equal to 1/100th of a half-tone* in the *well-tempered scale:* 1200 *cents* to the *octave* and 100 cents to each *interval!* The *scale of measurement by cents* is valuable in cross-referencing interval relationships *in all musical scales . . . . Pythagorean, just, mean-tone, equal temperament, non-Western,* etc. The *scale by cents* follows: c = 0; c# = 100; d = 200; d# = 300; e = 400; f = 500; f# = 600; g = 700; g# = 800; a = 900; a# = 1000; b = 1100; c' = 1200!

cesura, caesura *(sē zū'rä)* A *pause* dividing the *rhythm* in a melodic *strain* or between *strains!* A *cesura* is characterized as *masculine* or *feminine . . .* the former if it follows a *strong beat,* the latter if it follows a *weak beat!*

chaconne *(shä'kôn)* A slow *Spanish dance* in 3/4 time, closely resembling the *passacaglia!*

chalumeau *(shä'lü'mō')* An old form of *clarinet* used prior to the 17th century! The original *chalumeau* was a *shaum* from antiquity (see *shaum*)! The lowest *octave* of contemporary *clarinets* is still called the *chalumeau register!*

Chalumeau

chamber music *(chăm'b'r)* Any music suitable for performance in a small-audience area or *chamber!*

chamber orchestra. A *miniature orchestra* usually containing only one *instrument per part!*

change *(chānj)* (1) A *modulation* of the *harmony!* (2) A *melody* played on a set of *bells* tuned to the *diatonic scale!* (3) A mutation in *vocalizing . . .* a change of voice!

changing note. (See *NOTA CAMBIATA*)!

channel *(chăn'ĕl)* (1) A colloquial reference to the middle section of a popular song (also called *"bridge"* or *"release"*)! (2) A colloquial designation in the popular recording industry for one *"track"* of sound on *multi-track* recording tape or on a recording studio console board!

chanson *(shăn'sŏn)* from the French: A song!

chant *(chant)* A short, *sacred song* featuring the rhythmic recitation of many syllables to one *tone* which is almost sung! Part of a *chant* may be non-metrical with the other part sung in *strict time!*

Usually, a *chant* is *harmonized* in *four-part* fashion except for the *five-part Gregorian chant!*

chantant *(shän'tän)* from the French: Singing, melodious, tuneful music!

chanter *(chän'tēr)* The *melody pipe* of the bagpipe, also called the *chalumeau pipe!*

chanterelle *(shänt't' rĕl)* The *highest string* for *instruments* of the *violin, banjo* or *lute* family, particularly, the *treble string (E string)* of the *violin!*

chanteuse *(shän'tûz')* from the French: A female singer; usually applied to a concert or music hall *soloist!*

chantey (see *SHANTY*)!

charango *(chär'än gō)* A small guitar used by the Indians of South America!

charivari *(shä'rē vä'rē)* A mock *serenade* of dissonant noises such as those made by tin horns, pots and pans, etc.!

Charleston *(chärlz't'n)* A fast-moving popular dance of the American "roaring 20's" set to *4/4 time;* performed by couples, with alternate leg kicks and cross-hand knee-touching typical of the movements!

chart *(chärt)* (1) A colloquial term used by popular music professionals to designate an *arrangement* or *score!* (2) Also used colloquially as a reference to the best-selling record charts in various trade journals!

chef-d'oeuvre *(shĕf'dû'vr)* from the French: A *masterpiece* or *prestigious composition!*

chef d'orchestre *(shĕf'dôr'kĕs'tr')* from the French: The *conductor* of an *orchestra!*

chevalet *(shē vä'lĕ)* from the French: The *bridge* of a *stringed instrument; au chevalet,* a direction in French to *bow* the strings over or close to the *bridge!*

cheville *(shē vē'y)* A *peg* of any *stringed instrument!*

chiaramente *(kyä'rä mĕn'tē)* from the Italian: A direction to play distinctly and clearly!

chiave *(kyä'vä)* The *Italian* word for *"key"* or *"clef"!*

chime *(chīm)* (1) A *set of bells tuned* to a *musical scale!* (See *Tubular bells, Tubular chimes!*) (2) The harmonious sound of a musical passage or *instrument!*

chime-in — To join a musical or vocal performance either *harmonically* or in *unison!*

ch'in *(chīn)* A *seven-stringed, Chinese zither* dating back to antiquity but still played today. The instrument uses silk strings, one of which is a *melody string* that is *stopped* by the finger(s) of one hand while the other hand plucks the other strings! The

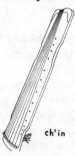

ch'in

stop positions are indicated by circular studs on the soundboard underneath the *melody string.* (also called CHYN). The new, official, romanized spelling announced by MAINLAND CHINA in 1979 is "GU QIN", pronounced *chĭn* as above!

Chinese drum. A gaudily-decorated, little *drum* with two *heads;* used by so-called *dance bands!*

chin rest. A shaped piece on top of a *violin* or other *stringed instrument* which is used to hold the *instrument* snugly under the chin!

chitarra *(kē tär'rä)* from the Italian: A *guitar!*

chitarrino *(kē tär rē'nō)* from the Italian: A small *guitar!*

chitarrone *(kē tär rō'nā)* from the Italian: A large *bass guitar!*

chiuso *(kē'ōō zō)* from the Italian: "Closed", (1) A direction to *horn players* to *mute* the *instrument* by inserting their hand into the *bell!* (2) A *choral* instruction to hum with the mouth closed!

choir *(kwīr)* (1) A group of singers, frequently those used in church services! (2) A group of instruments in the same family ... the *woodwind choir,* etc!

choke *(chōk)* To suddenly cut off, or suppress, a *tone* on a *musical instrument,* particularly on *percussion instruments* such as the *timpani;* sometimes used as an alternate expression for *dampen* or *muffle!* In *guitar notation,* the *sign "CH"!*

choral *(kō'răl)* Music relating to a chorus of singers!

chorale *(kō răl)* A simple *hymn* or *sacred tune* sung in Protestant churches since the 16th century! Dating from Bach (1685-1750), a *chorale* is characterized by the *sustained notes* at the end of musical *phrases* sung in *four-part harmony!*

chord *(kôrd)* The combination of two or more *tones* which sound *harmonious* when heard at the same time! *Chords* in *harmony* sound at least three separate *tones* with the lowest *tone* known as the *root* or *fundamental!* The *triad* is the simplest and most common *chord* ... its *bottom note* is the *root;* the *middle note* which is *a third above the root* is called the *third* and the *top note* which is a *fifth above the root* is called the *fifth!* See *Elements of Music, CHORDS!*

chord, dominant. A *chord* built on the *fifth note* of any *major* or *minor scale.* G is *dominant* in the *key of G-major;* A is *dominant* in the *key of A-minor,* etc. In the *C-major* or *C-minor keys,* the *dominant triad* is *G-B-D.* In the same *keys,* the *dominant seventh* is constructed by adding a *third* to the *dominant triad* ... *G-B-D-F.* In the same keys, the *dominant ninth* is constructed by adding a *third* to the *dominant seventh* ... *G-B-D-F-A!*

chord, inverted. A *chord* whose *notes* are placed so that the *root note* is *not* the lowest *note!*

chordophone *(kôr dō fōn)* A classification for any stretched *string instrument.* See Instruments! (violin, guitar, harp, piano, etc.)!

chord, tonic. A *chord* built on the *tonic,* which is the *keynote* or first *note* of any *major* or *minor scale!*

chorist *(kō'rĭst)* A member of a *chorus* or *choir!*

chorister *(kōr'ĭs tēr)* The *leader* of a *choir!*

chorus *(kō'rŭs)* (1) A group of *singers in concert!* (2) Music composed for *voices in concert!* (3) In popular music, the main *melody* or *refrain* of a *song,* sometimes introduced by a *verse!*

Christe eleison *(krĭs'tē ĕ lā ĭ sŏn)* "Christ have mercy"; a portion of the Kyrie, first movement in a Mass!

chromatic *(krō măt'ĭk)* Used in reference to *notes* with *half-step intervals* that form a *chromatic scale;* hence, the use of *notes* not in the *diatonic scale!*

chromatic scale. The *scale* consisting of the *12 half-steps* in an *octave* which appear between every *whole-step* of the *diatonic scale* (on a *piano keyboard,* every white and black key between *C* to *C')!*

chromatic signs — *Sharps, flats* and *naturals* (the *accidentals)* which indicate a *pitch* (for the *note* to which they are appended) that is different than the *key signature's* normal indication! The signs are notated as ♯, the *sharp;* ♭, the *flat* and ♮, the *natural.* Also 𝄪 for the *double sharp* and ♭♭ for the *double flat!*

church modes. A *scale* system on which *church music* and some *secular music* were based during the Middle Ages. These were grouped under two divisions: the *authentic* and the *plagal modes!* (see *MODE)!*

chyn *(chĭn)* A variant spelling of *Ch'in* (see *Ch'in),* a Chinese instrument!

cimbalom *(chĭm bă lōm)* A Hungarian version of the *dulcimer!*

Cimbalom

cinelli *(chĭn ĕl lē)* The Italian word for *cymbals!*

cipher *(sī'fēr)* A persistent *tone* sounded on *organ pipes* when the *keys* are still, arising from some fault in the *action!*

Circle of fifths. A circular system describing the *key signatures* of the *major* and *minor* scales! Going clockwise by *fifths* (the *keynotes* of succeeding *keys* all follow each other by the interval of a *fifth)* the number of *sharps* increase! Going counterclockwise by *fifths,* the number of *flats* increase! See *Illustration* On Following Page !

MAJOR KEYS AND THEIR RELATIVE
MINOR KEYS
ARRANGED ACCORDING TO:

CIRCLE OF FIFTHS — A *fifth* between each scale and the next *clockwise* scale! An added *sharp* is found in each successive key signature.

Counterclockwise, an added *flat* is found in each successive key signature!

The *harmonic* minor scale is depicted below; hence, the seventh tone of each *"pure"* or *"natural" minor scale* has been raised by one half step. See *ELEMENTS OF NOTATION, Key Signature* for all scales in their natural state.

*On piano and other instruments the following are enharmonically identical:

Key of F-sharp major (six sharps) and G-flat major (six flats); also D-sharp minor (6 sharps) and E-flat minor (6 flats)

Key of B-major (5 sharps) and C-flat major (seven flats)

Key of D-flat major (5 flats) and C-sharp major (seven sharps)

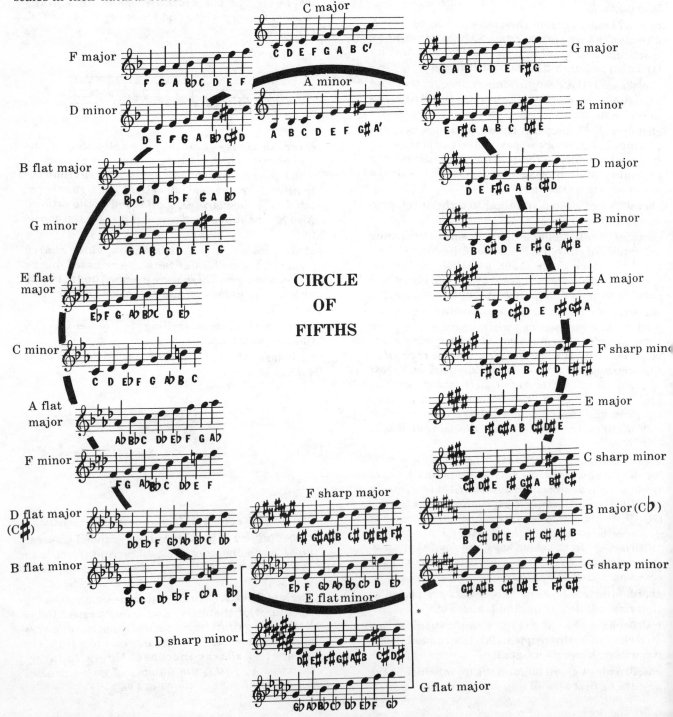

CIRCLE

OF

FIFTHS

cithara *(sĭth'á rá)* or **cither** *(sĭth'ēr)* A *musical instrument* similar to the *lyre* which dates back to ancient Greece! Better known as *kithara!* See *kithara!*

cittern *(sĭt'ērn)* A wire-strung, *fretted instrument* of the 16th and 17th centuries, which was similar to a *lute* and plucked by the fingers or a *plectrum!*

cittern

clarinet *(klăr'ĭ nĕt')* One of the best known and most important *wind instruments!* Shaped like a cylinder, it has a *mouthpiece* at one end and a moderately-flared *bell* at the other end! Played by manipulating a series of keys that open or close *finger holes*, the *clarinet* comes in various sizes and ranges! The *clarinets* in *B-flat, A* and *C* are commonly used, especially the *B-flat clarinet!* The *B-flat clarinet's* compass is from the *D below middle C* to the *B-flat above high-C!* All *clarinets* are *transposing instruments*, except for the *C clarinet!* The *B flat clarinet* sounds one complete *tone* lower than as written! The *A clarinet* sounds a *minor third* lower than as written, and the *E-flat clarinet* sounds a *minor third* higher than as written!

Clarinet

clarinet, clarinet flute. *Organ reed stops* (eight foot type) whose tone resembles the *wind instruments* of the same name!

clarinet, bass. A large-size *clarinet* that plays one *octave lower than the C or B-flat clarinets* and is shaped much like a *saxophone* (See *BASS CLARINET*)!

clarinet, alto. The "in-between" *clarinet* that plays in E-flat, a *fifth* below the *B-flat clarinet!* It sounds a *major sixth* lower than the music as written!

clarino *(klă'rē'nô)* It. / **clarion** *(klăr'ĭ ŭn)* U.S. / (1) A high-pitched *trumpet* with clear, shrill tones (also called *Bach trumpet*) that is used to play 18th century music with special *clarino* parts! (2) The name for the technique of composition written for the

trumpet or for the *parts* written for same! (3) A *reed organ stop* of four foot *scale!*

classic *(klăs'ĭk)*, **classical** *(klăs'ĭ kăl)*. The term applied to music which by test of time appeals to advanced taste and critical review! Usually designating an established musical art form *(concerto, symphony, fugue, suite, sonata,* etc.) classical music emphasizes formal elegance and intellectual exposition and precision, as contrasted with romantic and popular music which most often are linked to individual and transitory emotions! The great classical composers ... Beethoven, Haydn, Mozart, Wagner, Bach, Brahms, Tchaikovsky, etc. ... are those considered both timeless and universal in their appeal!

clausula *(klô' zū lá)* In *medieval music*, a reference to a short section of music taken from *Gregorian chant* and sung in regular rhythm to only one word or syllable; also a *cadence* or *close!*

clavecin *(klăv' ē sĭn)* (1) The *harpsichord!* (2) The keys of a *carillon!*

claves *(klä'vĭs)* from the Spanish: Two hardwood tubes about seven inches in length, used in the percussion section of Latin-American *orchestras*. The *percussionist* simply strikes one tube with the other!

claviature *(klăv' ĭ á tūr)* (1) The piano or organ keyboard! (2) The fingering technique for *keyboards!*

clavichord *(klăv'ĭ kôrd)* The predecessor of the *piano!* This *keyboard* instrument featured horizontal strings usually placed in a rectangular wooden casing! Small brass *tangents*, operated by *keys*, struck the strings whose vibrations were conducted through a *bridge* to a *soundboard*. The *clavichord* was widely used from the 16th through the 18th centuries, finally giving way to the *piano!* See *Instrument* for illustration!

clavier *(klä'vĭ ēr)* Fr. / *(klä' vēer)* Ger. / The French name for *keyboard*, and the German name for *harpsichord*, *spinet* and in modern times the *piano!* (also spelled *Klavier* in German).

clef *(klĕf)* The sign at the beginning of musical composition which determines the *pitch* of all the *lines* and *spaces* that follow! The four basic *clefs* are: The *treble clef* (also called the *G clef* or *violin clef*) which is used on the *top staff* in musical notation and designates the *second line from the bottom* as *G above middle C;* the *bass clef* (also called the *F clef*) which is used on the *bottom staff* and designates the *fourth line from the bottom* as *F below middle C;* the *tenor clef* (also called the *C clef*) which designates the *fourth line from the bottom of a staff* as *middle C;* the *alto clef* (also called the *C clef* or *viola clef*) which designates the *middle line* of a *staff* as *middle C!*

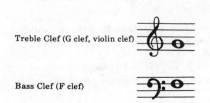

Treble Clef (G clef, violin clef)

Bass Clef (F clef)

576

Tenor Clef (C clef)

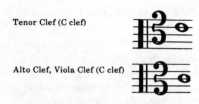

Alto Clef, Viola Clef (C clef)

Alternate Signs for the C Clef

cloche *(klōsh)* from the French: A bell!

close *(klōz)* (1) Same as *cadence!* (2) The ending of a portion of music! (3) To choke or muffle a tone!

close harmony. *Harmony* consisting of *chords* whose *notes* are close to one another in terms of *interval* distance . . . . in *four-part harmony*, the *four notes* of a *chord* lie within the *interval* of one *octave* or in closer proximity!

coda *(kō'dá)* from the Italian: "Tail"; a concluding portion of music, or a portion added to the closing of a composition which re-inforces or enhances the *close!*

coda sign. The symbol ⊕ which marks the point where the performer must skip over subsequent *bars* of music and go direct to the *coda!*

codon *(kō'dŏn)* (1) The *bell-shaped* end of a *trumpet!* (2) A small *bell!*

colascione *(kō'lä shō'nĕ)* An Italian *lute!*

col, colla *(kōl, Cōl lä)* from the Italian: "With the" . . . . *col arco*, a direction to *violinists* and other *string players* to use the *bow* as contrasted to *pizicato* string plucking; *col basso*, a direction to play the same music as the *bass*; *colla destra*, a direction to play with the right hand; *colla parte*, an indication in notation that a *part*, which is not written out, should be played in the identical fashion of an existing *part* for another *instrument* or *voice*; *colla voce*, a direction to the *accompaniment* to follow the *time* set by a *solo player* or *vocalist*; *colla sinistra*, a direction to play with the left hand; *col legno*, a direction to *string players* to use the wooden back of the *bow* to tap out *tones* on the *strings!*

collery horn *(kŏl'ēr ĭ hôrn)*. A long *brass horn* from *India!*

coll ottava *(kōl lōt tä'vä)* from the Italian: A direction to play above or below the *octave* as marked by the words *coll ottava* or the abbreviation *coll'* !

coloratura *(kŭl'ēr á tū'rá)* Florid music with elaborate *ornaments* including rapid passages, *trills*, *arpeggios*, etc!

coloratura soprano. Usually a high *female soprano voice* suitable for *coloratura* music; hence, an especially clear and flexible *soprano voice!*

come *(kō'mä)* from the Italian: "As", "The same as", "Like"!

come prima *(- prē'mä)* A direction to play or sing again as the music was played or sung the first time, or the time before!

come sopra *(- sō prä)* A direction to play "as above" or "as before" . . . . repeat a previous portion!

come sta *(- stä)* "As it stands"; a direction to play the music as written!

comma *(kŏm'a)* (1) A tiny distinction in *pitch* or *interval* based on the mathematical measurement of musical vibrations but difficult for the human ear to distinguish! (2) The comma sign (,) which is used to indicate a *breathing pause* in *vocal music!*

common chord. A *major* or *minor triad (chord)* in the *root position*; e.g., *C-E-G* or *C-E♭-G!*

common measure or common time. Music in which each *measure* has an even number of *parts* . . . . usually designates *4/4 time* which is notated by the sign

common meter. A four-line *stanza* in *iambic measure*, alternating the number of syllables of each line in regular order . . . 4,3,4,3, etc!

Communion *(kō mūn'yŭn)* The *psalm* sung last during the Roman Catholic Communion Mass!

comodo *(kô'mō dō)* from the Italian: A direction to play the music comfortably with ease and composure!

comp, comping. (1) In popular music, a colloquial expression for the *improvisation of accompaniment* . . . usually a direction to *ad lib chord progressions* in support of a written or familiar *solo part* or *melody!* (2) A direction from a *conductor* or an *arranger* in popular music recording sessions, or in band rehearsals, for the improvisation of background chords to accommodate so-called "*head*" *arrangements!* (see *HEAD*)!

compass *(kŭm'pás)* The *range* of *notes* or *tones* within the capacity of an *instrument* or *voice!*

complement *(kŏm'plē mĕnt)* The *interval* which when added to a given *interval* completes the *octave!*

completorium *(kŏm'plē tō'rĭ ŭm)* (1) A *complin!* (2) An Anarosian liturgical *anthem!*

complin *(kŏm'plĭn)* The last prayer of the day in Catholic services: "night song"!

composition *(kŏm'pō zĭsh'ŭn)*. Any musical piece written or arranged in *harmonic order* or the process of creating such a piece!

compound interval *(kŏm'pound ĭn'tēr vál)*. An *interval* larger than an *octave* which consists of two or more *intervals* each of which is smaller than an *octave* . . . an *octave* plus a *fourth* is the *compound interval* of a *twelfth!*

compound meter. Any *meter* whose number of *beats per measure* is a multiple of three, such as *compound duple* 6/2, 6/4, 6/8; *compound triple* 9/4, 9/8; *compound quadruple*, 12/4, 12/8, 12/16; *Quintuple meter*, 5/4 *(2/4 plus 3/4 or the reverse*, depending on the *accent!)*

compound stop. A mixture of three or more *organ stops* which can be sounded simultaneously by pressing one *key!*

con *(kŏn)* from the Italian: "With" . . . used in combination with other words for various musical directions including the following:

con abbandono *(äb'bän dō'nō)* With abandon!

con agilita *(ä jē'lē tä)* With agility; lightly!

con agitazione *(ä'jē tä tsyō'nä)* With agitation!

con alcuna licenza *(äl kōō'nä lē chěn'tsä)* With some freedom . . . not strict as to *tempo* or performance!

con amore *(ä mō'rä)* "With love"; play tenderly!

con anima *(ä'nē mä)* "With animation"!

con bravura *(brä vōō' rä)* "With boldness"!

con brio *(brē'ō)* "With spirit"!

concento *(kŏn chěn'tō)* The *simultaneous harmony* of *chords* by *voices* or *instruments;* the opposite of *arpeggio!*

concentus *(kŏn sěn tŭs)* *Church-service music* sung by an entire *choir!*

concert *(kŏn sûrt)* Any public music performance of music (excluding *opera* or *sacred services*) with two or more performers or vocalists! *Solo* or *duet* performances are usually termed *recitals!*

concertante *(kŏn'chěr tän'tä)* from the Italian: (1) A *concert!* (2) The type of music which allows for solo virtuosity in a *duo* or *ensemble* performance!

concert grand. The largest size of *grand piano!*

concertina *(kŏn'sěr tē'nä)* A small *instrument* built on the *bellows* principle of an *accordion* but shaped with *hexagonal heads* at each end which have buttons but no *keyboard!* It has a *four-octave range!*

Concertina

concertmaster *(kŏn'sûrt mäs'tēr)* Eng. / **concertmeister** *(kŏn'sûrt mīs'tēr)* Ger. / The first or chief *violinist* of the *strings* in an *orchestra!*

concerto *(kŏn chěr'tō)* A composition for one or more *solo instruments* with *orchestral accompaniment!* In *symphonic form,* the *concerto* usually consists of three *movements:* The *sonata* which ends in a *cadenza;* a slow middle *movement,* and finally a livelier *rondo* or variation on the *theme* for a closing *movement!*

concerto grosso *(-grôs'sō)* from the Italian: An orchestral *concerto* from the *baroque period* with frequent alternating *solos* by separate *instruments* accompanied by the full *orchestra!*

concert overture. An *orchestral piece* similar to an *operatic overture* but designed for performance in a concert hall!

concert pitch. SEE *PITCH!*

concertstück *(kŏn tsěrt'shtük)* from the German: A form of the *concerto!* An elaborate piece of music composed for public performance!

concitato *(kŏn'chě tä'tō)* from the Italian: A direction to play in an **agitated** or **excited** style!

concord *(kŏn'kôrd)* A combination of *harmonious* sounds, as opposed to *dissonant* sounds!

conductor *(kŏn dŭk'tēr)* The *leader* of an *orchestra* or *chorus* whose function is all-important to performance! The *conductor* is rated in direct proportion to his skill at commanding *tempo, instrument balance,* and the expressive qualities that constitute proper interpretation of a composition!

conductus *(kŏn dŭk'tŭs)* A medieval form of *vocal music* based on *Latin* poems of the era and using as many as four *vocal parts* in *strict tempo!*

conjunct degrees *(kŏn'jŭngkt dē'grēz).* The *adjacent degrees* in the *scale* as compared to a given *degree* . . . all in the order of progression of successive *tones* of the *scale!*

conjunct motion *(- mō'shŭn).* The movement of a *melody* at regular *intervals* of a *scale!*

connecting note. A *note* found in two successive *chords!*

consecutive *(kŏn sěk' ū tǐv)* The term describing a *parallel movement* of music; *consecutive fifths,* for example, refer to two or more *fifths* that follow each other in immediate succession!

consecutive intervals. *Intervals* that progress in pairs to *succeeding tones* that bear the same *interval* relationship!

consequent *(kŏn'sē kwěnt)* In a *canon* or *fugue,* an *answer to* (or *restatement of*) a preceding musical *phrase,* the *antecedent!*

conservatory *(kŏn sûr vá tō'ry)* A public school or institution offering specialized instruction in music!

console *(kŏn'sōl)* (1) The desk or cabinet case of an *organ* from which the *keyboards, stops* and *pedals* are manipulated! (2) In a recording studio, the housing for the *sound-mixing* controls *(knobs, slides,* etc.) manipulated by the *audio engineer!*

consonance *(kŏn'sō näns).* A combination of agreeable *tones!* A *consonant tone* or *chord* seems pleasant to the listener as opposed to a *dissonant tone* or *chord!* The definition of *consonance,* however, is always subject to changing taste and opinion as to what sounds are agreeable!

con sordino *(kŏn sŏr dē'nō)* from the Italian: "With the *mute*". The direction to play an instrument with its *mute* affixed!

contanto *(kŏn'täh nō)* from the Italian: A direction for *players* or *singers* of given *parts* to rest while other *parts* of the music may continue!

continued bass. SEE *BASSO CONTINUO!*

continuo *(kŏn tē nwō)* Short for *basso continuo, continued bass!*

contra *(kŏn'trá)* from the Italian: A prefix which designates the largest *instrument* of a class which is usually pitched an *octave below* the standard *instrument* in the class or family . . . for example, *contrabass (double bass)* or *contrabassoon (double bassoon)!*

contrafagotto *(-fäh gŏt'tō)* (1) The *Italian* name for the *contrabassoon.* (2) An *organ reed stop* of 16 or 32 foot scale!

contralto *(kŏn trăl'tō)* The *lowest female voice range* ... about *two octaves up from F* and frequently synonymous with the *male alto range!*

contraposaune *(-pō zou'nĕ)* An *organ reed stop, one or two octaves lower* than the *normal posaune* (see *POSAUNE*)!

contrapuntal *(kŏn'trä pŭn'tăl)* Pertaining to the rules of *counterpoint!* (see *counterpoint*).

contrary motion *(kŏn'trĕr ē mō'shŭn)*. The upward motion of one musical *part* in contrast to the downward motion of another *part!*

contrasto *(kŏn trăs' tō)* from the Italian: A romantic *song* that features a quarrelsome exchange between a man and a woman!

contra tenor *(tĕn'ēr)* The *counter tenor* or *contralto!*

contredanse *(kôn'trē däns)* A country dance in which the participants are lined up in opposite, facing ranks. Popular in France and Germany during the latter half of the 18th century, the *contredanse motif* appears in many Beethoven orchestral works!

coperto *(kŏh pâr'tō)* from the Italian: "Covered" or "muffled"!

coplas *(kō'pläs)* from the Spanish: Popular Spanish songs, frequently narrated with musical accompaniment and dancing!

cor *(kŏr)* from the French: A *horn;* commonly known as the *French horn!*

cor anglais *(kŏr än glā)* The French term for the *English horn!*

coránte *(kŏh răn tĕ)* / **coránto** *(kŏh răn tō)* / **corrente** *(kŏh rĕn tĕ)* It. / An Italian country dance in 3/2 time! In French, called the *courante!*

corda *(kôr dä)* from the Italian: A *string* ... *una corda,* *(ōō'nä kôr'da)* one string; *due corde (dōō ĕ -),* play on two *strings; tutte corde (tōōt tĕ),* use all the *strings!* In *piano music,* as a result of the *pedal's* effect on the *hammer* action, *una corda* means to depress the *soft (left) pedal; tre corda* means release the *soft pedal; a due corde* means depress the *soft pedal* half way down! *Corda vuota,* use an *unstopped (open) string!*

cornet *(kôr'nĕt)* A *brass instrument* in the *trumpet* family with three *valves* and a cupped *mouthpiece!* The *cornet pitched in B-flat* (the version most often used) has a *two-octave range from E below middle C to the B-flat below high C.* The *B-flat cornet* is a *transposing instrument* which sounds one *tone* lower than the music as written. An *E-flat cornet* is sometimes used in *brass bands!*

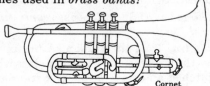

Cornet

cornet stop. *A compound organ stop* with three to five *pipes* sounding a *tone!*

corno, corno di caccia *(kôr nō)(-de kät'chä)* The Italian short and full terms for the *French horn!*

corno Inglese *(-ĕn gläs sĕ)* The *Italian* term for the *English horn!*

cornopean *(kôr nō'pĕ ăn)* (1) The *valve cornet!* (2) An eight-foot *organ reed stop!*

corny *(kôr'nĭ)*. A colloquialism in popular music circles that describes old-fashioned, cliched or dated music or style of performance. The term *corny* itself has become dated, giving way in current vernacular to such expressions as "square" or "Un-hip".

corona *(kŏ rō'na)* A rarely used *Italian term* for the *pause* or *hold* sign (⌢)!

cotillion *(kŏ tĭl'yŭn)* An elaborate ballroom dance similar to the *quadrille!*

cottage organ. A portable small *reed-organ!*

cottage piano. A small upright *piano!*

coulé *(kōō'lä)* A *slur* connecting two or more *tones!*

count *(kount)* The measurement of the *pulses* or steady *beats* of music, expressed in numeral fashion ... 1,2,3,4, etc.!

counter *(koun'tēr)*. Any *part* sung or played against another ... such as the *counter tenor* or *bass counter!*

counterpoint *(koun'tēr point')*. The technique of using one *melody* to accompany another! Formal *counterpoint* includes such musical forms as the *fugue* or *canon,* etc. *Double counterpoint* provides for the *inversion* of two musical parts; *quadruple counterpoint* could involve as many as 24 *inversions.* (see *INVERSION*)

counter-subject. A *secondary melody* contrasting to a *primary melody!* In a *fugue,* the *counter-subject* follows the *subject theme* in the same *part!*

counter-tenor. The highest male voicing, usually sung in *falsetto;* the male *alto!*

country-dance. A rustic English dance in a brisk tempo with two lines of partners facing each other!

coup d'archet *(kōō'där shĕ')* The French term for "a *stroke* of the *bow*"!

coupler *(kŭp'lēr)* The connection of two or more *digital keys* of a *keyboard* (particularly in an *organ*) that allows the *keys* to sound together when only one is depressed!

couplet *(kŭp'lĕt)* In *triple time,* two equally-valued *notes* replacing three of the same *notes* in regular *rhythm!*

courante *(kōō ränt')* A French dance in bright 3/2 time with many *dotted notes* and shifts to and from 6/4 time!

cow bell *(kou'bĕl)* A *percussion instrument,* once popular with dance-band *drummers,* that produced a rather harsh *bell tone* of no specific *pitch* when struck!

cracovienne *(krä kō'vĭ ĕn')* A *Polish* dance in 2/4 time!

credo *(krē'dō)* from the Latin: "I believe"; the third section of the Ordinary of the Catholic Mass sung between the Gloria and the Sanctus!

Cremona *(krĕ mō'na)* A renowned *violin* model made in Cremona, Italy during the 17th and 18th centuries, usually by Stradivarius, Guarnerius or the Amati clan!

crescendo (*krě shěn'dō*) A gradual increase in the loudness of sound, or a direction to play in such a manner. In notation, designated by the sign ⟨ or the abbrev. *cresc!*

crescendo pedal. The *organ pedal* which can bring all the *organ stops* up or down to the fullest or least volume in regular order!

crescent (*krĕs'ĕnt*). A Turkish military instrument consisting of small *bells* hung from *crescent-shaped* metal plates!

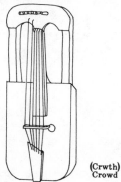

Crescent

cromorna (*krŏ môr'nä*). An *organ reed stop;* in German, the *krummhorn;* in French, the *cromorne!*

crook (*krŏŏk*). A small tube, most often curved, which is fitted to the large tube of a *horn* or *trumpet* to lower the *pitch;* the term is also used to denote the curved section of the *bassoon's mouthpiece!*

croon (*krŏŏn*). A dated expression for a style of popular singing in a low register, with exaggerated phrasing that emphasized sentiment and romantic appeal! First credited to Russ Colombo and Bing Crosby during the 1930's in the U.S.A.!

cross flute (*krŏs'flŏŏt*). The *transverse flute* held across the mouth and blown from its side!

cross relation. Another term for *false relation!* (see *FALSE RELATION*)!

cross rhythm. Two conflicting *rhythms* used at the same time!

crotchet (*krŏch'ĕt*) An old name for the quarter note ♩ !

crowd (*kroud*) also known as *crwth* (*krŏŏth*) or *croud* or *crouth:* An ancient Gaelic or Welsh instrument with a rectangular body extended by two arms which are joined by a crossbar. *Strings* extended from the center of the cross bar over the open area and across the middle of the body. Originally plucked, the *strings* later were *bowed!*

(Crwth)
Crowd

crucifixus (*krŏŏ'sǐ fǐks ŭs*) Part of the *Credo* in the Catholic *Mass!*

crumhorn (*krŭm'hôrn*) An old *double-reed woodwind* used in the sixteenth and seventeenth centuries! Shaped like a *long tube* ending in a *hook,* the *crumhorn* had seven *finger holes* and a cup-type *mouthpiece!*

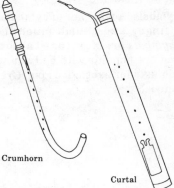

Crumhorn

Curtal

C-sharp (C♯) The *tone one half-step* above the *tone* C.

C-sharp minor (C♯m) The *minor key* or *scale* related to *E-major* and bearing the same *signature* of *four sharps!*

csardas (*chär'däsh*) also czardas. A brisk *Hungarian* or *Magyar dance* in 2/4 or 4/4 *time* usually starting slowly and accelerating to a fast pace!

cue (*kū*) Several small notes of a musical *phrase* inserted after a long *rest* to guide a *vocalist* or *player* to a proper entrance! The expression "cue in" generally means to insert *notes* that act as a cue!

cupo (*kŏŏ'pŏ*) from the Italian: Dark, veiled, obscure!

curtal (*kûr'tăl*) An early form of the *bassoon;* also an *organ stop!*

custos (*kŭs'tŏs*) The symbol ⌐ or ⌐ at the end of a music line or page that indicates, by its position on the *staff,* the position of the first *note* that appears on the following page!

cut (*kŭt*) A popular music colloquialism that means to make a recording ... "cut a record", "cut a session", "cut a demo" (*demonstration record*), etc.; dates from the pre-tape era, when sound recordings were cut direct into vinyl master discs by a stylus!

cut time. The popular equivalent of *alla breve* (see *alla breve*) which is indicated by the sign ¢ !

cycle forms, cyclical forms. Complete *movements* of music placed in a *cycle* relative to each other ... such as the *sonata, symphony, concerto, suite,* etc.!

cymbals (*sǐm'bălz*) A pair of thin brass plates (with handles on the back surfaces) which are clashed together to produce a strident, resonant sound. Cymbals in most ensemble-playing have no specific tuning! A single *cymbal* (the *ride cymbal*) is played by a drummer while it hangs suspended from its center. In marching bands, frequently, one *cymbal* is affixed to the *bass drum* and is struck by another *cymbal* held in one hand by the drummer who uses his other hand, meanwhile, to strike the *drum* surface with a *beater* or *drumstick!* Jazz and dance band drummers use a *hi hat cymbal* which is actually two small *cymbals* positioned vertically on a metal pole so that the lower *cymbal* remains stationary. The upper *cymbal* moves up or down in accordance with the action of a *foot pedal* which is operated by the drummer!

finger cymbals. A tiny pair of cymbals manipulated by one finger and thumb much like *castanets*. *Finger cymbals* are often tuned about *one half-tone apart* and are popular with belly dancers and with percussionists for exotic Turkish, Greek or African dance music!

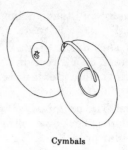

Cymbals

czardas. An optional spelling of *csardas* (see *csardas*)!

DICTIONARY

D

— D —

D. (1) The *second tone* in the *C-major scale* and the *fourth tone* of the latter's *relative minor scale* of *A-minor*. Both the *D major* and *D minor scales* begin on *D*! The *note one half tone* above *D* is *D-sharp* or *E-flat (enharmonic equivalents)* and the *note one half tone* below *D* is *D-flat* or *C-sharp* (also *enharmonically equivalent)*! (2) The abbreviation for the *Italian da . . . D.C.* for *da Capo*, and for *dal . . . D.S.* for *dal Segno!* (3) The abbreviation for *dominant*, which is the *fifth* note of any *diatonic scale!* (4) The abbreviation for the Italian *destra* or the French *droite* ("right" as in right hand)! (5) The abbreviation for *discantus* (see discantus)!

da *(dä)* from the Italian: "By", "for", "from", "in"!

da ballo *(bäl'lō)*. from the Italian: In dance style!

da capo *(kä'pō)*. from the Italian: "From the beginning"; the direction to go back to the beginning and repeat . . . frequently stated in the abbreviated form of *D.C.!*

da capo al fine *(äl fē'nä)*. from the Italian: The direction to repeat from the beginning to the end or to the word *Fine*, or to a *hold sign* ⌒ !

da capo al segno *(sā'nyō)*. from the Italian: The direction to repeat from the beginning up *to* the sign 𝄋 or :S: or ⊕ !

da capo dal segno. from the Italian: The direction to repeat *from* the sign 𝄋 or :S: or ⊕ to the end *(Fine.)*!

da capo e poi la coda. from the Italian: The direction to play from the beginning to the *coda sign* ⊕, then, play the *coda!*

da capo senza replica *(sĕn'zä rĕp li kä)* from the Italian: The direction to play from the beginning without paying attention to the *repeats!*

d'accord *(dä'kôr)* from the French: "In tune"!

dal segno *(däl sā'nyō)* from the Italian: "From the sign": a direction to repeat music from the sign 𝄋 or :S: or ⊕ . . . usually up to *"FINE"*!

damp *(dămp)* To muffle the sound or check the vibration of a *string!* The *dampers* of a piano are felt-covered wood blocks resting on the *strings!* The blocks raise up when the appropriate *piano key* is struck (releasing a full sound) and they drop down when the key is *released* (terminating the sound.) The *damper pedal* on a *piano* is the *right hand pedal* which, when depressed by the foot, raises all the *dampers* and allows the *strings* to continue vibrating until the *pedal* is released!

dämpfer *(dămp'fĕr)* from the German: A *mute* or any device that deadens a tone!

dance *(dăns)* Any instrumental music which is written primarily for dancing; e.g., *polka, waltz, minuet, foxtrot*, etc.!

dance band. In the "popular music" sense, a group of musicians who play for ballroom dancing! In the 30's and 40's, in the U.S.A., the term "dance band" was linked to the "name band" or traveling band which played in dance halls as well as theaters and concert halls. The "name band" usually consisted of basic sections of about five *brass*, five *woodwinds* and 5 *rhythm (piano, bass, guitar, drums* and *percussion)* To these, *violins* in varying numbers were added by so-called "society dance bands" who stressed milder, less syncopated performance! In the contemporary era of *disco dancing* and *rock-jazz-soul concert music*, the "dance band" expression has become limited to a description of ensembles playing for society or senior citizen affairs!

dark *(därk)* An expression for the *bottom tones* or the grave, deep quality, of certain *instruments* and *voices* . . . the *dark* sound "of an *English horn*" or "a low *contralto*"!

dash *(dăsh)* The wedge-shaped mark (▾) which is placed over or under a note to indicate the note is to be played staccato ♪♩ !

db. The abbreviation for *decibel* (see *decibel*)!

d.c. The abbreviation for *da capo* (see *da capo*)!

débile *(dā'bĭl ä)* / **débole** *(dā bōl ä)* It. / "Weak", "faint", "feeble"!

debut *(dā'bū)* The first public appearance or performance of a musician, singer, actor or composition!

decachord *(dĕk'ä kôrd)* A *ten-stringed musical instrument* related to the *lute* or *harp* family!

decibel *(dĕs'ĭ bĕl)* A tenth of a *bel;* the technical, acoustic unit for measurement of the loudness of sound!

decima *(dĕs'ĭ mä)* (1) A *tenth* interval . . . an *octave* and a *third!* (2) An *organ stop* that tunes the pipes a *tenth* above a given *key!*

decimole *(dĕs'ĭ mōl)* A decuple! (see *DECUPLE*)!

deciso *(dā'chē'zō)* from the Italian: "With decision", boldly, energetic!

declamando *(dā'klä män'dō)* from the Italian: In declamatory style!

declamation *(dĕk'lä mā' shŭn)* The vocal rendition of lyrics with an emphasis on clear, almost melodramatic precision!

decrescendo *(dā'krĕ shĕn'dō)* from the Italian: A gradual decrease in the loudness of sound or a direction to play in such a manner; usually designated by the sign ——▷; abbreviated *decresc.* !

decuple *(dĕk'ū p'l)* A *ten-note group* (each *note* of *equal value*) played in the time given to *eight notes* of *equal value* or to *four equal notes* of the next highest *value*. A *decuplet* is marked in notation by a *slur* and the *figure 10*. (also called *decimole*)!

defective *(dē fĕk'tĭv)* An outmoded expression that meant the same as *diminished* as in *"defective fifth"*!

degli *(dĕl'yē)* from the Italian: "Of the" or "than the"!

degree *(dē grē')* (1) Each *line* and *space* on the *staff* represents one *degree!* (2) One of the eight successive *tones* in the *diatonic scale*, or the *interval (step)* between two such *tones*. In dealing with *intervals* of two *notes*, the lower *note* is considered the *first de-*

gree (regardless of its position in any given *scale*) and numerically ascends through each *line* and *space* alternately up to the highest *note* of the *interval*. C to A, for example, would be a *sixth interval* as would *E* to *C* since both span six *diatonic degrees!*

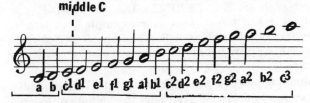

dehnen (*dā'něn*) from the German: A direction to *extend* or *prolong!*

dehors, en (*än dē'ôr*) from the French: To "stand out"; to play a given *note* or portion of music with emphasis!

dei(*dā'ē*), **del**(*děl*), **dell'**(*děl*), **della**(*děl ä*), **delle**(*děl ē*), **dello** (*děl lō*) from the Italian: "Of the", "than the"!

deliberamente (*děl ĭ bě rä měn'tē*) / **deliberato** (*dē lē bē rä'tō*) It. / A direction to play deliberately!

delicatamente (*děl ĭ kä tä měn'tē*) / **delicatezza, con** (*děl'ĭ kä tě tsä, kôn*) / **delicato** (*děl ĭ kä'tō*) It. / A direction to play with delicacy in a smooth, refined manner!

delirio, con(*děl ĭrĭ ō, kôn*) / **delirante**(*děl ĭr än tě*) It. / A direction to play in an agitated, frenzied, delirious manner!

demi(*dē mĭ'*) from the French: A prefix that means *half!*

demicadence (*-kā'děns*) A *half cadence!*

demilegato (*-lā gä'tō*) A direction to play halfway between *legato* and *staccato!*

demisemiquaver (*-sěm'ĭ kwā'věr*) A *thirty-second note*

demisemitone (*-tōn*) A quarter tone!

demitone. A *half-tone* or *semitone!*

depress(*dē prěs'*) (1) To *lower* or *flatten* a tone! (2) To push down a *key or a valve* or a *pedal* on an *instrument!*

derb (*děrp*) from the German: A direction to play in a vigorous, rough manner!

derivative (*dē rĭv'ä tĭv*) A *derivative chord* results from the *inversion* of another *fundamental chord!*

des (*děs*) The German word for the note *D-flat!*

descant (*děs'kănt*) (1) The upper *part* of any *vocal music* with more than one *part* (polyphonic vocal arrangement). (2) The *soprano part(s)* sung in *counterpoint* above a familiar *hymn* or *folk tune!* (3) In earlier times, a simple *counterpoint melody* imposed over the *tenor part!* (4) A simple *song* or melodic *strain!* (5) To sing or vocalize! (6) An old musical description for the highest-toned member of an *instrument* family, such as the *descant viol* (the *treble viol*)! (also known as *discant*)!

descant clef. The *C clef* when it appears on the first line of the *staff* ... the *soprano* clef!

des dur (*-dūr*) The German term for *D-flat major!*

des moll (*-mōl*) The German term for *D-flat minor!*

deses (*děs ěs*) The German word for *D-double flat!*

desiderio, con (*děs'ĭ dē'rē ō, kôn*) from the Italian: "With desire" or "with yearning"!

desterita (*děs těr ē'tä*) from the Italian: "With dexterity"!

désto (*děs tō*) from the Italian: "Lively", "brisk"!

déstra (*děs trä*) from the Italian: "Right" as in "right hand"; *destra mano* or *mano destra* or *colla destra* ... "play with the right hand"; abbreviated *M.D.* or *D.M.!*

détaché(*dā' ta'shā*) from the French: A direction to *violinists* to play with short, alternating, *down-bow* and *up-bow* strokes ... not as in *staccato*. "*Detached*" *notes* are marked with a *dash* over or under the notes ; *grand détaché*, a direction to use a *long bow stroke* for each *note* in an alternating, up and down direction!

determinato(*dā tûr'mē nätō*) from the Italian: "Determined", "forthright"!

detto (*dā tō*) from the Italian: "The same", or "ditto"!

deutlich (*doit'lĭkh*) from the German: The direction to play clearly and distinctly!

deux (*dū*) from the French: "Two"!

deux, à. from the French: (1) For two *instrumental* or *voice parts!* (2) The indication that a piece is to be played by two *instruments* or two groups of *instruments*, or to be sung by two *singers* or two *singing groups!*

deux mains, à (*măns*) from the French: "For two hands"!

deux temps, à (*tŏm*) from the French: "In two steps!" ... *valse a deux temps*, a two-step waltz!

development (*dē věl ŭp'ment*) (1) The elaboration of a *theme* by the use of *harmonic, melodic* or *rhythmic re-arrangement* of a central or starting musical idea! (2) The second section of a *Sonata* following the *exposition!*

dévot (*dā'vō*) Fr. / **devóto** (*dā'vō tō*) It. / "Devout", "pious", "religious"!

devozióne, con (*dā'vō tsĭ ō ně*) from the Italian: "With devout, religious feeling!"

dextra (*děks'trä*) / **dextrad** (*děks'trăd*) / **dextral** (*děks'trăl*) L. / Of or pertaining to the *right hand!*

di (*dē*) from the Italian: "Of", with, from, to, by!

diabolus in musica (*dī äb'ō lŭs ĭn mū'zĭ kä*) "The devil in music" ... the name given in medieval times to the *augmented fourth!*

dian(*dī'än*) Fr. / **diana** (*dē ä'nä*) Sp. / A *drum roll* or *trumpet call* that sounds *reveille!*

diapason (*dī'ä pā'zŭn*) (1) The sound or interval of an *octave!* (2) A standard of *pitch* ... the "*normal diapason*"! (3) Either of the two *foundation stops* of an *organ* ... the *open diapason* with metal *pipes* open at the top, or the *stopped diapason* with wooden *pipes* closed at the top! (4) The French word for "*tuning fork*"!

diatonic *(dī'á tŏn'ĭk)* (1) Describing any standard *major* or *minor scale* with eight *tones* to the *octave*. In the *key of C major*, the *white piano keys* form a *diatonic scale;* the other *keys* are *chromatic!* (2) A measurement by *degrees of a scale!* (3) *Diatonic harmony* consists mainly of *chords* in one *scale ... diatonic intervals* consist of *two tones* from the same *scale!* (4) A *diatonic instrument* is one which plays only the *scale* whose *fundamental tone* is its *key-note!*

di colta *(dī kôl tä)* from the Italian: "At once", "suddenly"!

Dies Irae *(dī'ēz ī'rē)* from the Latin: (1) "Day of wrath" ... the universally familiar section of the Roman Catholic Requiem Mass (2) The principal movement of a *requiem!*

diesis *(dī ā sĭs)* It. / **diese** *(dī āz)* Fr. / The *sharp!* (𝄪)!

difficile *(dĭf'ĭ sēl)* Fr./ *(dēfē chē lĕh)* It./"Difficult!"

dig *(dĭg)* A colloloquialism in popular and jazz music circles used as an expression of "comprehension" or "understanding", and optionally of "pleasurable reaction". .... "do you dig it?" could mean "do you understand?" or "do you like it?".... shortened to the one word, "dig" (following some positive statement) would imply a question as to understanding what was said, not necessarily calling for an opinion or approval of the commentary!

di gala *(dē gă lă)* from the Italian: "With merriment", gaily!

digital recording. The newest advance in professional sound recording! Using new equipment, built on computer principles (mainly researched at Stanford University), recorded sound is converted to "*digital*" information ("*bits*" and "*bites*") and stored until a later reproductive process is required! Currently, the information, equivalent to 32 tracks of conventional recording, is re-converted to *analogue* electrical information on magnetic tape and reduced to the end product ... a "two-track stereo master tape". Once "digital" playback systems are manufactured and distributed to the homes as is contemplated, however, the analogue conversion would be eliminated. New "end-product recordings in the form of chips or pieces of plastic" would replace tapes and records. The new "end-products" would be played by using optical lens or laser-beam scanning. The *digital* system eliminates most of the inherent, extraneous noise and hiss of standard magnetic tape, and is being installed in recording studios throughout the world as quickly as the equipment can be capitalized and acquired!

dignita *(dēn yĭ tä)* from the Italian: "With dignity"; in a grand manner!

dilettante *(dīl'ĕ tăntĕ)* from the French: An amateur art lover!

diligénza, con *(dē lē jĕn tsä, kôn)* from the Italian: "With diligence"; a direction to play in a careful manner!

diluendo *(dĕ lwĕn'dō)* from the Italian: A direction to play gradually softer until almost vanishing away!

diminish *(dĭ mĭn'ĭsh)* To reduce a *major interval* by making it a *half-tone* smaller! *Diminished chords* are *chords* which contain one or more *diminished intervals* (SEE *INTERVAL*). The chord B-D-F is a *diminished triad* chord, for example .... add a *minor third* such as *A-flat* and the *B-D-F-A-flat* combination becomes the *diminished seventh chord!*

diminuendo *(dĭ mĭn'ū ĕn'dō)* from·the Italian: A direction to decrease gradually the volume or intensity of the music! The notation sign is $>$; abbreviated *dim.* or *dimin!*

diminuition *(dĭm ĭ nū'ĭ shŭn)* Used in *counterpoint* (particularly in *fugues*) to describe the *reply* or *restatement* of a *theme* which decreases the *note values* of the original *theme* by a *half* or *quarter-tone*. *Half-notes* become *quarter-notes*, *quarter-notes* become *eighth-notes*, etc. Reversing the process is called *augmentation!* (SEE *INTERVAL* and *INVERSION*)!

di molto *(dē mōl'tō)* from the Italian: "Very much" ... giving extra emphasis to *molto*, "much"!

direct *(dĭ rĕkt')* The sign〰or ⌒ placed in position at the end of a *staff* on one page, to show the player or singer where the first note of the next *staff line*, on the next page, is located!

direct motion. *Musical parts* ascending or descending in *parallel* or *similar motion* and *direction!*

dirge *(dûrj)* A musical composition of a mournful or grievous quality played at funerals or at commemorations of the dead!

diritta *(dē rēt'tä)* / **diritto** *(dē rē'tō)* It. / "Direct"; A direction to play straight ahead / *alla diritta*, in direct motion!

dis *(dēs)* The German word for the note *D-sharp!*

discant *(dĭs kănt')* A variation of *descant* (SEE *DESCANT*)!

disciólto *(dĭ shē ōl tō)* from the Italian: A direction to play skillfully, with dexterity!

disco *(dĭs kō)* The latest popular dance music and rhythm *craze* with worldwide penetration! Disco music usually is recorded and played in 4/4 time at about 130 beats to the minute. Innovative, *disco* dance-steps include such as the *hustle* and the *boogie*, which provide a form of "touch" dancing for couples that permits much twirling and body muscle movement! What were once called *night clubs*, *cafes* or *cabarets* are now being termed "*discos*" ... the implication, of course, being that *disco music* and *dancing* are offered within!

discord *(dĭs kôrd)* Lacking agreeable harmony or sound! Dissonant! Harsh musical sounds caused by incompatible vibrations of the sound producing media!

Discreto *(dĭs krä'tō)* from the Italian: "Discreet", subdued!

dis dis *(dĭs dĭs)* The German term for *D-double-sharp* (also called *dises*)!

disinvolto (dĭs ĭn vōl'tō) /
disinvolturato (dĭs ĭn vōl'tōō'rä tō) It. / "Free", "natural"; a direction to play in an unforced manner!

disjunct motion (dĭs jŭnkt) Progressing by *skips* or *leaps*!

dis moll (dĭs mōl) The German term for the key of *D#-minor (D-sharp minor)*!

di sopra (dē sŏprä) from the Italian: "Above" (1) *come sopra*, as above . . . a direction to play a designated section or note as played before! (2) *Sopra* is used in *piano music* to direct playing in *cross-hand style* . . . *mano sinistra sopra (m.s. sopra)*, "cross the left hand over the right"; *mano dextra sopra* (m.d. sopra) "cross the right hand over the left!"

disperato (dĕs pä rä'tō) from the Italian: A direction to play in a manner creating a desperate or despairing mood!

dispersed harmony. (dĭs pŭrs't) An *open form* of *harmony* which features *chords* separated from each other by wide *intervals*!

dissonance (dĭs'ō năns) SEE DISCORD! It should be noted that *classic* definitions of *dissonance* or *discord* have withered and shrunk in modern times almost to the vanishing point . . . . due to the many *serious* and *popular music* explorations of new usages! Today, the *avant* theory holds that "*agreeable harmony*" is a relative, subjective quality that "lies in the ears of the beholder". In formal, *classical* terms, however, *dissonant intervals* are considered to be the *seconds*, *sevenths* and all *diminished* or *augmented intervals*!

distanza (dĭs'stŏn zä) from the Italian: "Distance"; *in distanza*, a direction to play so that the sound seems to be distant or far away!

distinto (dĭs tĭn'tō) from the Italian: "Distinct", "clear"!

dital (dī'tăl) A key on a *guitar harp (ital harp)* which raises the *pitch* one *half-tone*!

ditty (dĭt'ĭ) Any brief *song* (usually *vocal*) of a simple, folkish nature!

divertimento (dē vĕr'tĭ mĕn tō) It. /
divertissement (dē'vĕr'tēs'män) Fr. / (1) A light, sometimes humorous composition or *air*! (2) A short *ballet piece* for between-the-acts entertainment! (3) A short *classical* composition in several *movements*, scored for a small group!

divisi (dē vē'zē) from the Italian: The direction to *play* or *sing*, separately, *two or more parts* that would normally be performed as one *part*. Most commonly used by *string sections*, the *first strings* separate from the other *strings* when the music is marked *div.* (abbreviation for *divisi*) and continue to play separately until they reach the notation marking *unisono* or *uni*, at which point they resume playing *one part*!

division (dĭ vĭzh'ŭn) (1) In *classical music*, a constantly repeated pattern of *chords* and *notes* appearing in the *bass* (see *ostinato, basso ostinato* or *ground bass*)! (2) A "*dividing*" of the *tones* in a rapid *phrase* so as to allow them to be sung in one breath!

division mark The number marking placed over or under *slurs* or *brackets* to mark *triplets, quadruplets*, or other *groups* of notes!

division viol. Another name for the *viola da gamba (bass viol)* which is the *string-instrument* family member that is slightly smaller than the normal *bass*!

divoto (dē'vō tō) from the Italian: "Devout"; A direction to play with religious feeling (also spelled *devoto*)!

D-major. The *major scale* or *key* with a *signature* of *two sharps*!

D-minor. The *minor scale* or *key* relative to *F-major* with the same *signature* of one *flat*!

do (dō) (1) The first of the well-known *seven syllables* used in *solmization* or *solfeggio* . . . *do, re, mi, fa, sol, la, ti* (see SOLMIZATION and SOLFEGGIO). (2) In the *movable do* system, *do* is always the *keynote* or *first note* of any *scale* . . . . in the *fixed do* system, *do* always refers to the *C notes* whether or not they are *keynotes*!

dobro guitar (dō'brō gĭtär') See *Guitar*!

dodecuplet (dō dĕk'ŭ plĕt) A *group* of *twelve notes* of *equal value* played in the *time* of *eight equal notes* of the *same value*!

dodecuple scale. A *scale* that divides the *octave* into *twelve equal parts*!

doigté (dwä'tä') from the French: "Fingering"!

doina (doi'nä) A type of *Roumanian* folk song!

Dolby (dŏl bē) Dolby System. A trademarked, electronic noise-suppressor system which when installed on both the original recording equipment and the consumer's stereo receiver eliminates much of the "tape hiss" and other extraneous noise inherent in the reproduction of phonograph records and tape recordings.

dolce (dōl'chä) from the Italian: (1) A direction to play smoothly, softly or with ease! (2) A soft-toned *flute organ stop*!

dolcian (dŏl'tsĭ ăn') Ger. / **dolciana** (dŏl chĭ ä nä) It. / **dolciano** (dŏl chĭ ä nō) It. / (1) A type of small *bassoon* used in the 17th century (2) Currently, an *organ reed stop*, eight or sixteen foot *pitch*!

dolcissimo (dōl chēs's'ē mō) from the Italian: (1) A direction to play *very* smoothly, very softly! (2) A *very* soft-toned *organ stop*!

dominant (dŏm'ĭ nănt) The *fifth note* of any *major* or *minor scale* (the *fifth degree* of the *diatonic scale*)! *G* is the *dominant* note of the *key* of *C major*; *A* is the *dominant* note of *D major*, etc!

dominant chord. Any *chord* built on the *dominant*! The most used *dominant chords* are: (1) The *dominant triad* (the *major triad* whose *root* is the *dominant*) such as *G-B-D* in the keys of *C major* or *C minor*. (2) The *dominant seventh* (the *dominant triad* with an added *third*) . . . such as *G-B-D-F* in the *key of C major* or *C minor.* (3) The *dominant ninth* (the *dominant seventh* with an *added third*)... such as *G-B-D-F-A* in the *key of C major* or *C minor!* (also see *SECONDARY DOMINANT*)! In *harmonic analysis,* the *Roman numeral V* indicates a *chord* built on the *dominant!*

dominant harmony. *Harmony* founded on the *dominant* chord or the *dominant seventh* chord or their *inversions!*

doodlesack (dōō'd'l săk) The *Scotch bagpipe!*

dopo (dō'pō) from the Italian: "After."!

doppel (dŏp'ĕl) from the German: "Double"!

doppelflöte (flû'tĕ) The *German* term for "*double flute*", an eight-foot *flute organ stop!*

doppel-be (bā) The German term for *double flat* (♭♭) which drops a *note* by *two half-tones!*

doppelgriffe (grĭ'fĕ) The German term for a *double stop* on *violin-family instruments!*

doppelkreuz (kroi'ts) The German term for *double sharp* (✖) or (✳) which raises a *note* by two *half-tones.*

doppelt (dŏp'ĕlt) from the German: "Twice"... used as a direction in conjunction with other words... *doppelt so schnell,* "play twice as fast"; *doppelt so langsam,* "twice as slow", etc!

doppio (dŏp'pyō) From the Italian: "Double", a direction used in conjunction with other words.... *doppio tempo, double time,* etc. (see following terms)!

doppio bemolle. The Italian term for double flat (♭♭)!

doppio diesis. The Italian term for double sharp (✖) or ♯♯ !

doppio movimento. The Italian term for "*double speed*", twice as fast!

doppio pedale. The Italian term for playing *two notes* on *organ pedals* at the same time, usually in *octaves!*

doppio valore. The Italian term for "twice as slow" ...*doubling* the *time value* of each *note* (the opposite or reverse of *doppio movimento*)!

dot (dot) (1) The *point* appearing after a *note* or *rest* which extends the *time-value* by one half...a *dotted quarter note* equals a *quarter plus* an eighth note (♩=♩♪) Two *dots extend* the *value* by three-fourths of the original *value* ... a *double-dotted quarter note* equals a *quarter note* plus an *eighth note* and *one sixteenth note* ♩.. = ♩♪♪ (2) A *vertical pair* of *dots* just before a *double bar line* is a direction to repeat the previous portion of music! Appearing after the *bar line*, the same *pair of dots* directs repetition of the following portion of music! (3) A *dot* placed over or under a *note* indicates that the note is to be played *staccato!*

double (dub'l) (1) A term used to describe a musician's ability to play a *second* instrument ... the

"*saxophone*" player *doubles* on "*clarinet*"; the "*flute*" doubles on "*piccolo*", the "*oboe*" doubles on "*English horn*", etc.! (2) A term used to describe playing in *unison* with other *instruments* in the same *section* of an *orchestra*, or with other *sections* of *instruments* ... the *woodwinds* may *double* the *violins* ... if all the *horns* are playing in *unison*, the *second* and *third horns* are said to be *doubling* the first horn! (3) To play the part played by another *instrument* but an *octave higher or lower*, as when the *piccolo doubles* the *flute*, or the *double bassoon* doubles the *bassoon!* (4) In 17th and 18th century *suite music*, a term that indicates a *variation!* (5) A sixteen-foot *organ stop!* (6) Generally, to *play* or *harmonize* a *note or notes an octave below or above* an *accompanying note or notes.*

double bar. Two vertical *lines* through the *staff* indicating the end of a portion of music or the end of a complete section or composition! (1) A *double bar line* can appear within a *measure* when a *key change* or *change* in the *time signature* occurs! (2) A *thin line* preceding a *thicker line* specifies the end of a *section* or *phrase!* (3) Two *equally-thick* lines specify the end of a *complete work!* (See *DOT* for *bar signs* with *pairs* of *dots*).

double bass. The *contrabass* or *bass viol*, also called the *string bass* (in slang, known as the *bull fiddle*)... the largest and lowest-toned member of the *violin family.* The *double bass* is both *bowed (arco)* and *plucked*, the latter almost always the style adopted by popular and jazz music ensembles! The American and English version of the *double bass* has *four strings* which are pitched *E-A-D-G* (the *Italian version* has only *three strings*) but the music for the *double bass* is written an *octave higher than its sound* to avoid using too much notation below the *bass clef staff.*

Double Bass

double bassoon. The *contrabassoon!* The largest and *lowest-toned* member of the *double reed* family, pitched an *octave below* the standard bassoon!

double chant. An *Anglican chant* with fourteen *measures* and two *verses!*

double chorus. A *choral composition* for two full *choirs!*

double concerto. A *concerto* for *orchestra* with two *solo instruments!*

double counterpoint. *Invertible counterpoint! Counterpoint music* which is structured for two *parts* in such a manner that either *part* may be played above or below the other!

double drum. A large *drum* struck on both *sides* (*heads*)!

double flageolet. A *wind-instrument* with two *tubes* emanating from the same *mouthpiece!*

double flat. The *accidental* (♭♭) that drops the *pitch* of a *note* by two *half-tones*. On *keyboards*, the *double flat* is identical to the *note* one *full-tone below* . . . *A-double flat* is the same as *G; B-double-flat* is the same as *A*, etc! (See *ACCIDENTAL*)!

double fugue. A *fugue* with two *themes!*

double note. A *breve* which is a *note double* the length of a *whole note* . . . the sign   !

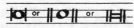

double octave. A *two-octave interval*, a *fifteenth!*

double pedal. Playing two *parts* with the feet on a *pedal organ!*

double pedal point. Sustaining two *tones* against successive *harmonies!*

double quartet. A group of *eight* (or *two sets of four*) *musicians* or *singers*, or a *composition* written for *eight solo parts* (or two sets of *4 solo parts*)!

double reed. A *mouthpiece*, formed by two *reeds* or two pieces of cane bound together, used by the *oboe* family of *instruments!*

double sharp. The sign ✖ or ✳ before a *note* which raises the *note* two *half-tones!* On *keyboards*, the *double sharped* note is identical to the *note* one *tone higher!*

double sonata. A *sonata* for two *solo instruments!*

double stem. A *note* with a *double stem*, ♪ one *stem* turning up, the other down that indicates two separate *parts* will sound the same *note* in *unison!*

double stop. *Stopping* two *strings* of the *violin* (or similar *instruments*) at the same time, resulting in *two-part harmony!*

double time. A direction to play twice as fast as a given *tempo!*

doublet. A *French organ stop* of two foot *pitch!*

double tongueing. In playing the *trumpet, cornet, flute*, etc, the use of *tongue action*, employing the silent pronunciation of the consonats *t* and *k*, with vibrations from the upper teeth to the palate. This enables an especially clear *staccato* or rapid repetition of a single *note!* (SEE *TONGUING*)!

doublette. Same as *doublet!*

douce *(dōōs)* / **doux** *(dōō)* / **doucement** *(dōōs mŏn)* Fr. / A direction to play softly and sweetly!

downbeat *(down'bēt).* The initial, accented *beat* in a given *bar*, normally indicated to an *orchestra* by a *conductor's downward movement* of the *hand* or *baton!*

down-bow *(down'bō)* Playing a *bow* (in *violin music*) with the *stroke* drawn down from *nut* to *point*, and vice-versa with the *up-bow stroke!* "Down-bow" is marked by the sign ⊓ and "up-bow" by ⋁ !

doxology *(dŏks ŏl'ō gē)* A form of *hymn*, or praise to God, sung in Christian churches traditionally at the end of a prayer or *psalm!*

drag *(drăg)* (1) In *drumbeating*, the effect created when two rapid light *beats* are played before the *heavy* or *accented beat* or *stroke!* (2) In *lute* playing, *drag* describes a downward-gliding *portamento!*

dramatic music. Music designed to accompany staged drama! Sometimes, the term is used to describe *program music* with especially dramatic features!

dramma per musica. An early type of lyric drama that led to the *opera* form!

drammático *(drä mät ē kō)* from the Italian: A direction to play in a dramatic manner!

drängend *(drĕng'ĕnt)* from the German: A direction to play in a driving, hurried manner as if pushing on to a rapid conclusion!

drawstop *(drô'stôp)* Any *organ stop* drawn by the hand which admits air into the *pipes* or *reeds!*

dreher *(drā'ēr)* An *Austrian folk dance* or *tune* in *triple time!*

drei *(drī)* from the German: "Three", *eins, zwei, drei*, one, two, three!

dreifach *(drī'fäkh)* from the German: "Triple", "thrice"!

dreist *(drīst)* from the German: A direction to play with confidence, boldly!

dritta *(drĭt'tä)* It. / **dritto** *(drĭt'tō)* It. / **droite** *(drwä)* Fr. / "Right"! A direction to play with the right hand; an abbreviated form of *mano dritta (Italian)* or *main droite (French)*, both meaning "right hand"!

drone *(drōn)* (1) Giving out a monotonous, continuous sound or murmur! (2) A general reference to a *bagpipe* or related *instrument;* a specific reference to the largest *tube* or *pair of tubes* in the *bagpipe* which sound a continuing *bass tone* against the *melody* played on the *chanter* tube (See *BAGPIPE*)! (3) Another name for *pedal point* (See *PEDAL POINT*)! (4) Any *instrument* which sounds a single, continuing tone as *accompaniment* to any other *instruments* or *voices!*

drum *(drŭm)* A *percussion instrument* consisting of a hollow cylinder, over one end or both ends of which a *skin* or *vellum* (the *head*) is stretched, hooped and tightened with clamps, cords, rods or screws. The three common classes of *drums* are: (1) the *bass drum* (the largest standard size *drum*) which is held or mounted vertically and struck with a *knobbed mallet* (*beater*); (2) The *side drum* and *snare drum*, which are much smaller than the *bass drum*, and which are held or mounted laterally (but at a tipped angle) . . . the *side* drum has two similar *heads* (top and bottom) while the *snare drum* frequently has *catgut strings* drawn across its *bottom head* in a criss-cross pattern something like a net. Both *drums* are played with a pair of *drum sticks* or *wire brushes!* (3) The *kettle drum* . . . a metal hemisphere shell over which a *parchment head* is hooped and clamped! The *kettle drum's tuning* can be altered by tightening or loosening the head clamps by hand or by a connecting *foot pedal*. (See *TIMPANI*). Almost all other *drums* can not be changed in pitch!

(2) drum

D.S. The abbreviation for *dal segno*, "repeat from the sign"! In notation, D.S.!

D-sharp. The tone (D) which is a *half-step above D!* On *keyboards*, D-sharp is the same as E-flat!

D-sharp minor. The *minor scale (relative to F-sharp major)* with six *sharps* in its *signature!*

D string. The *third string* of a *violin* or the *second string* of the *viola, cello* and *double bass!*

dub, dubbing (*dŭb, dŭb'ing*). A term used in the popular recording and music publishing industries to denote a copy (tape or disk) of a previously recorded composition. Publishers and songwriters usually consider a "*dub*" to be equivalent to a demonstration recording of a song or performance, not necessarily up to professional standards. Sometimes, however, and particularly among recording personnel, a "*dub*" simply refers to a hand-engineered copy of a single recording . . . professional or otherwise!

due (*dōō'ā*) from the Italian: "Two" . . . *a due*, for two *parts* or *voices; due corde*, "two strings", a direction to play the same *note* on *two strings* (of a *violin, cello*, etc.) at the same time; also, a direction for *keyboards* to depress the *soft pedal* halfway between *una corda (one string)* and *tre corde (three strings);* also, *due pedali*, a direction to use *two pedals* on the *piano!*

duet (*dü̆ ĕt*) A composition for *two performers (vocal* or *instrumental)* with or without *accompaniment!*

duettino (*dōō'ĕt tē'nō̇*) from the Italian: A brief *duet!*

duetto (*dōō'ĕt ō*) from the Italian: "*Duet*"!

due volte (- *vôl'tā̇*) from the Italian: "Two times", twice!

dulcet (*dŭl'sĕt*) An *organ stop one octave higher* than the *dulciana!*

dulciana (*dŭl'sĭ ăn'à*) (1) An *organ stop* with a soft, sweet *string quality!* (2) a *reed stop* on the *organ!* (3) A small *bassoon!*

dulcimer (*dŭl'sĭm ēr*). An *instrument* with metallic strings stretched over a *soundboard* which historically was flat-shaped and trapezoidal, but which today comes in a variety of shapes! The Asian or European *dulcimer* (also called *cimbalon, santouri,*

hackbrett, etc.) is struck by a pair of "*hammers*". The *Appalachian dulcimer* in the United States (a folk instrument actually indigenous to the southern mountain areas of the U.S.) probably belongs more to the *zither* family than the *dulcimer*, since it uses only *three strings* which are *plucked* and *stopped* by the player's fingers!

dumka (*dōōm'kà*) from the Polish: A *funeral song* or *elegy!*

dump or dumpe (*dŭmp*) An old *English* dance in a slow *4/4 rhythm!*

duo (*dōō'ō*) (1) A *composition* for *two instrumental soloists*, infrequently used for *piano* or *vocal duets!* (2) The Italian name for "two", as in "*two parts*" or a *duet!*

duodecimo (*dōō'ō dē'chē mō*) / **duodecima** (*dōō' ō dā'chē mà*) It. / (1) The *interval* of a *twelfth:* (2) An *organ stop*, the *twelfth!*

duole (*dū'ōl*) Two *equally-valued notes* played in the *time value* usually given to *three notes* of *equal value!*

duolo, con (*dōō ō'lō, kôn*) from the Italian: With sadness or grief!

duple (*dū'p'l*) "*Double*"; *duple rhythm*, two *beats* to a *measure; duple time*, either two *beats* to a *measure* or a number of *beats* to a *measure* divisible by two!

dur (*dōōr*) The German word for "*Major*" . . . *C dur* means *C major!*

dur (*dür*) from the French: "*Harsh*", "brittle"!

duramente (*dōōr ă mĕnt'ĕ*) / **durezza, con** (*dōōr ĕ'tsà, kôn*) It. / "*Stern*", "harsh"; A direction to play in a strong, firm manner!

durchcomponirt (*dōōrch'kôm'pō nĕrt*) from the German: "*Through composed*"; a reference to poetic songs in which each *section* or *stanza* receives a different musical setting!

durchfuhrung (*dōōrch'fewr'ōōng*) from the German: (1) The *exposition* of a *fugue!* (2) The *developing* portion of a *sonata!*

durch spielen (*dōōrch'shpēl ĕn*) from the German: A direction to play to the end!

duro (*dōō rō*) from the Italian: "*Hard*", "harsh", "rude"!

duster (*dŭs tēr*) from the German: "*Gloomy*", "sorrowful"!

Dutch Concert. A colloquialism for a babel of sounds where all participants are singing or playing their own music without regard to one another!

dynamics (*dī năm'ĭks*) The variations and contrast in the degrees of loudness or softness of *musical tones!*

dynamic marks. Signs or abbreviations which indicate the *dynamics* or *volume* recommended for performance (See *ELEMENTS OF NOTATION, DYNAMICS/VOLUME*)!

abbreviation or marking	dynamic indication (from the Italian)	English translation
ppp	double pianissimo	as soft as possible
pp	pianissimo	very soft

p	piano	soft
mp	mezzo piano	moderately soft
mf	mezzo forte	moderately loud
f	forte	loud
ff	fortissimo	very loud
fff	double fortissimo	as loud as possible
fp	forte piano	loud to soft

sf, sfz	sforzando or sforzato	sharply accented
cres.,cresc.	crescendo (sign $<$)	gradually louder (swell)
decresc.	decrescendo (sign $>$)	gradually softer (shrink)
dim.,dimin.	diminuendo	gradually smaller or softer

DICTIONARY

E

— E —

E. The *third tone* of the *scale* of *C-Major* and the *fifth tone* of *C-Major's relative minor* scale, the *key* of *A-minor.* The *E-major* and *E-minor* scales begin with the *E* tone! The *major* scale has four *sharps* in the *key signature,* and the *minor scale* has one *sharp* in its *signature!*

e, ed *(ā)* from the Italian: "And"!

ear training *(ēr trān'ing)* The technique of teaching the ear to identify *pitch, interval, rhythm,* etc. The most popular teaching processes are known as *solfege (French), solfeggio (Italian)* and *solmization* (English) which uses the *do, re, mi, fa,* etc. *syllable system!*

ebollimento *(ā bōl lĕ mĕnt' ō)* / **ebollizione** *(ā bōl lĭ tsē ō'nĕ)* It. / A sudden spilling over of passion or feeling!

eccheggiare *(ĕk kĕ jĕä'rĕ)* from the Italian: "Echoing", "resounding"!

eccitato *(ĕtch ē tä'tō)* from the Italian: "Excited"!

ecclesiastical modes *(ĕ klē' zĭ ăst tĭ kăl mōds)* (See *MODES* and *GREGORIAN*).

echelle *(ā' shĕl)* from the French: "Ladder"; the *French* expression for a *full scale!*

echo *(ĕk'ō)* (1) The soft repetition of a *musical phrase!* (2) An *organ stop* with echoing quality! (3) The *echo organ* is an *organ* with echoing qualities! (4) An *organ stop* with a soft, delicate sound! (5) In professional recording terms, the reverberation of a *tone or sound* induced either by mechanical transmission of the *tone* or *sound* through an "*echo chamber*" or by the natural resonance provided by the studio's own *acoustics!*

echo cornet. An *organ stop* with a soft, delicate sound!

eclat *(ā klä)* / **eclatant** *(ā klä tän)* Fr. / A direction to play with dash and brilliance!

éclisses *(ā'klēs)* from the French: The side ribs of a *violin!*

eco, ecco *(ĕk ō)* The *Italian* names for "*echo*"!

ecossaise *(ā kô'sâs)* An old *French/English dance* (misnomered "*Scottish*") that was written in *2/4 time!*

edel *(ā d'l)* from the German: "Distinguished", "noble"!

E dur *(ā dōōr)* The *German* term for the *key of E-major!*

effeto *(ĕ fĕt ō)* from the Italian: The impression or effect created by music!

effusione, con *(ĕ fū'zē ō nē, kon)* from the Italian: A direction to play with effusion or warmth!

E-flat. The tone (E♭) which is a *half-step* below *E* and a *half-step* above *D.* On *keyboards, E-flat* is the same as *D-sharp (enharmonic equivalents). E-flat* is the *first note* of both the *E-flat major* and the *E-flat minor scales!* The former has a *key signature* of *three flats,* and the latter has *six flats* in its *signature!*

E-flat instrument. Any *transposing instrument* such as the *alto sax* or *E-flat clarinet,* etc. These sound notes higher or lower than "as written" .... the *alto sax* sounds a *major sixth* lower than the written note and the *E-flat clarinet* sounds a *minor third* higher than the written note. Fingering of the *C* note in *E-flat instruments* sounds an *E-flat pitch.*

eguaglianza, con *(ā gwäl yän tsă, kôn)* from the Italian: A direction to play with smoothness! *Con molta eguaglianza (kôn mōl tă)* .... a direction to play *very* smoothly!

eguale *(ā gwä lĕ)* from the Italian: "Equal" or "even"; a direction to play the same as other *instruments* or *voices* of a related *group!*

egualment *(ā gwäl mĕn'tĕ)* from the Italian: A direction to play smoothly or evenly!

eighth *(āth).* An *octave!*

eighth note. The note ♪ which is 1/8th the *time value* of a *whole note!* Two successive *eighth notes* are joined by *beams* ♫ ! The English call an *eighth* note a *quaver!*

eighth rest. The *rest* 𝄾 directing *silence* for the *time value* of an *eighth note!*

eilen *(ī lĕn)* / **eilend** *(ī lĕnt)* Ger. / A direction to play with haste ... hurriedly or rapidly!

ein *(īn)* / **eins** *(īns)* Ger. / "One"!

einfach *(īn făk)* from the German: A direction to play in simple, unadorned fashion!

eingang *(īn găng)* from the German: An *introduction* or *prelude!*

einhalt *(īn hält)* from the German: A *pause!*

einheit *(īn hīt)* from the German: "Unity"!

einklang *(īn klăng)* from the German: "Unison", "consonance", "harmony"!

einlage *(īn lăg ĕ)* from the German: An inserted *portion* or *interpolation!*

einleitung *(ī līt ōōng)* from the German: An *introduction* or *prelude!*

einmal *(īn mäl)* from the German: "Once"; *noch einmal* .... one more time!

einsatz *(īn zŏts)* from the German: The *attack!* Also, the *entrance* of a musical *part!*

einschlafen *(īn shläf'n)* from the German: *Slackening* the *time* or making the *tone* die away! The literal meaning: "to fall asleep"!

einstimmig *(īn shtĭm ĭg)* from the German: With *one voice* or *one sound!*

einstimmen *(īn shtĭm'n)* from the German: To be *in tune* together! Also, to join in!

eintritt *(īn trĭt)* from the German: The *entrance,* or beginning!

eis *(ā'is)* The German word for the note *E-sharp* (E#).

eisis *(ā'is is)* The German word for the note *E-double sharp* (E##).

elan *(ā län)* / **elan, con** *(kôn)* Fr. / A direction to play with dash, eagerly and with ardor!

elegante *(ā lā gŏn tĕ)* / **elegantemente** *(-mĕn tĕ)* / **eleganza** *(-gŏn ză)* It. / A direction to play elegantly or gracefully or with refinement!

electrophone *(ē lĕk'tră fŏn')* A classification for any musical instruments that produce sound as a result of electronic vibrations! (synthesizers, novachord, theremin, electric organ, electric piano, electric guitar, etc.)

elegy *(ĕl ĕ jĭ')*. A *composition* with a mournful or melancholy mood!

elevatio *(ĕl ĕ vā'shĭ ō)* from the Latin: A *composition* during the portion of the Mass which celebrates the rising of the Host!

elevato *(ā lâ vä'tō)* from the Italian: A direction to play in an elevated or sublime manner!

eleventh *(ē lĕv ĕnth)* An *interval* consisting of an *octave* and a *fourth (spanning eleven diatonic degrees)*!

embellishment *(ĕm bĕl ĭsh mĕnt)* A musical *ornament*; a *grace* note *(trill, appoggiatura, acciaccatura,* etc.)!

embouchure *(ŏm bōō shōōr')* (1) The *mouthpiece* of a *wind-instrument!* (2) The shaping of the lips, mouth, tongue, jaw, etc. while blowing in or around or through the *mouthpiece* to achieve *tone*, *pitch* and *attack!*

emozione *(ā mō tsē ō'nĕ)* from the Italian: "Emotion", "agitation"!

empfindung *(ĕmp fĭn'dōōng)* / **empfindungsvoll** *('dōōngz fōl)* Ger. / "Emotion", "feeling", "passion"!

emphasis *(ĕm fă sĭs)* To put *stress* or *accent* on a given *tone, chord* or *portion of music!*

emphase, avec *(ăn făz', ă vĕk')* Fr. / **emphase, mit** *(ĕm făz, mĭt)* Ger. / "With emphasis"!

empressé *(än prĕ sā')* from the French: A direction to play hurriedly, pressing on to the conclusion!

ému *(ā mŏe)* from the French: A direction to play with much feeling and expression!

en *(än)* from the French: "In"!

enchainez *(än shā nā')* from the French: A direction to go on, without stopping, to the next section of music!

encore *(än kôr')* from the French: (1) A direction to play again! (2) An additional performance or repeated performance in response to audience applause! (3) A recall to the stage; see *BIS!*

ende *(ĕn dĕ)* from the German: "The end"; a *concluding composition!*

en dehors *(än dā ôr')* from the French: A direction to emphasize a *note* or portion of music in performance!

energia, con *(ā nâr jē' ă, kôn)* / **energicamente** *(ā nâr jē kă mĕnt' ĕ)* / **energico** *(ā nâr'jē kō)* It. / **énergie, avec** *(ā nâr jē', ă vĕk')* Fr. / **energisch** *(ā nâr' jĭsh)* Ger. / (1) A direction to perform in a vigorous, energetic fashion (2) To *accent* or *decisively phrase* marked portions of a *composition!*

enfasi *(ĕn' fă zē)* / **enfatico** *(ĕn fă' tē kō)* It. / "Emphatic"; a direction to play with emphasis!

enfler *(än flă)* from the French: A direction to increase the *tone* or swell the *sound!*

English horn. (1) The *alto oboe* which is pitched one *fifth* below the conventional *oboe!* A *transposing instrument,* the *English horn* (in *French, cor anglais*) is a *double reed instrument* identical in *keys* and *finger positions* to the *oboe* but sounding a *fifth* lower than its music as written. The *English horn's range* goes from *E below middle C* to the *second A above middle C* . . . slightly exceeding two *octaves!* (2) An *organ stop* with the sound quality of an *English horn!*

English Horn

enharmonic equivalents *(ĕn'här mŏn'ĭk ĕk kwĭ văl ĕnts).* The term which describes *notes, chords, intervals,* etc. which have different symbols in notation but which sound identical on given *instruments* . . . on *piano* and *organ, C-sharp* and *D-flat,* or *B-sharp* and *C* are *enharmonic equivalents* . . . on *bass guitar, E-sharp* and *F-natural,* and *F-flat* and *E-natural* are *enharmonic equivalents* as well!

enharmonic change. Using the *same keys* of an *instrument* to play *differently written notes!* Moving from *D-sharp* to *D-natural,* for example (instead of *E-natural*) actually means the *D-sharp* is stated as an *E-flat!* An *enharmonic chord* and *enharmonic modulation* (see following terms) are also said to be "*enharmonically changed*"!

enharmonic chord. A *chord* that sounds like another but is written with *different notation!*

enharmonic interval See *Interval!*

enharmonic key. One of the three *major keys* which can be notated either by *sharps* or *flats:*

(1) *B-major* with *five sharps* is identical to *C-flat major* with seven *flats.* The *minor key* of *G-sharp* also has five *sharps!*

(2) *F-sharp major* with six *sharps* is identical to *G-flat major* with six *flats.* The *minor key E-flat* also has six *flats!*

(3) *C-sharp major* with seven *sharps* is identical to *D-flat major* with five *flats!* The *minor key F-flat* also has five *flats!*

enharmonic modulation. Changing keys by passing from one enharmonic chord to another; for example, modulating from *G-flat* in the *key of D-flat* to *F-sharp* in the *key of G*.

ensemble (*än som' b'l*) (1) A general description for all the members of an *orchestra* or *chorus*! (2) A specific reference to a *quartet*, *quintet* or small group of *players* or *singers*! (3) A general term for the act of several *musicians* or *singers playing or singing together* with smoothness and precision!

entr'acte (*än'trăkt*) from the French: "Between the acts"! *Music* performed between two *acts*, also known as *intermezzo, interlude, intermission music*, etc.!

entrance (*ĕn trăns*) The place in *ensemble composition* where a *solo part* (*vocal or instrumental*) makes it *first entry*, frequently after a *rest* sign ( )!

entrée (*än' trä*) from the French: The *opening movement* of *opera* or *ballet music* which follows the *overture*.

entscheiden (*ĕnt shī d'n*) / **entscheidung** (*ĕnt shī dōōng*) / **entschlossen** (*ent shlōs'n*) Ger. / A direction to play resolutely with a decisive manner!

entusiasmo, con (*ĕn tōō zē äz'mō, kôn*) from the Italian: A direction to play with enthusiasm!

episode (*ĕp ĭ sōd*) (1) A *portion* of a *composition* which digresses from the *main theme* (a subdivision)! (2) In *fugues* or *rondos*, the *episode* is inserted between repetitions of the *main theme* and may or may not itself be a *variation on the theme*!

epitasis (*ĕ pĭt ă sĭs*) Raising the *pitch* of *voices* or *stringed instruments* (the opposite of *anesis*)!

equabile (*ā kwä'bē lĕ*) / **equabilemente** (*- mĕn tĕ*) It. / "Equal", uniform, even!

equal counterpoint. Composed music in two or more *parts* which consists of *equally valued notes*!

equal temperament. Equalizing the different sounds of an *octave* by *tuning the instrument* (usually *keyboards*) so that all the *half-tones* have the same mathematical difference in frequency vibration. The *intervals*, except for the *octave*, therefore, are slightly *out of tune* to the "pure ear" but sound normal for conventional listening. "*Equal temperament*" *intervals* have the same *value* in any *key* which allows for unrestricted *modulation*!

equal voices. *Voices* of the same *class* or *range*; that is, either men's or women's voices or either *tenors* or *sopranos*!

electric, electronic instruments. See *INSTRUMENTS, ELECTRONIC*!

ergriffen (*är grĭf'n*) from the German: A direction to play with stirring, highly emotional expression!

erhaben (*är hä'b'n*) from the German: A direction to play in a sublime, lofty or exalted manner!

erklingen (*är klĭng'n*) from the German: "Resonant", "ringing"!

erlöschend (*är lō 'shänt*) from the German: A direction to gradually soften and fade away!

ermattend (*är mät' ĕnt*) from the German: A direction to gradually soften and weaken the sound!

ermattet (*är mät'ĕt*) from the German: "Exhausted", "weary"!

ernst (*ärnst*) / **ernsthaft** (*ärnst häft*) Ger. / A direction to play in an earnest, serious or grave manner!

eroico (*ā rô ē kŏ*) / **eroica** (*- kă*) It. / "Heroic", strong, stately!

erschuttert (*är shŭt'ärt*) from the German: "Upset", agitated!

erweitert (*är vī'tärt*) from the German: "Extended" or developed!

erzählung (*är tsäl 'ŭng*) from the German: A story or narration!

es (*ĕss*) The *German* word for *E-flat* (*E♭*)!

es dur (*dōōr*) The *German words* for the *key of E-flat major*!

es es (*ĕs ĕs*) The *German words* for the *note E-double flat* (*E♭♭*)!

es moll (*mōl*) The *German words* for the *key of E-flat minor*!

escapement (*ĕs kăp'mĕnt*) A part of the *"action"* of a *piano*, the *escapement* is the mechanism which allows the *hammer* to rebound from a *string* after each *stroke*, although the *key* which activates the *hammer* may still be depressed! A *double escapement*, thus, facilitates the rapid repetition of a note, since the *hammer* does not rebound all the way back to its original position and each new *stroke* is shortened!

esclamato (*ĕs klă mä'tō*) from the Italian: "Exclaimed"; a direction to state forcefully!

E-sharp. The *note* that is *one half-tone* above *E* and *one half-tone* below *F-sharp*! On *keyboards*, *E-sharp* is the same as *F* (*enharmonic equivalents*)!

espandendosi (*ĕs spän dĕn'dō sē*) from the Italian: Growing in intensity or expanding in fullness of sound!

espansione, con (*ĕs păn sē ō'nĕ, kôn*) / **espansivo** (*ĕs păn sē'vō*) It. / A direction to play with intensity or expanded feeling!

espirando (*ĕs pē răn'dō*) from the Italian: (1) "Expiring" or "dieing away"! (2) Heavy gasping or deep breathing!

espressivo (*ĕs prĕs sē'vō*) from the Italian: A direction to play in an expressive manner!

essential (*ĕ sĕn shăl*) (1) Any *flat* or *sharp* specific to a *key signature*! (2) *Notes* that determine *chords* as opposed to *passing tones* or *ornamental tones* . . . an *essential seventh*, the *dominant seventh chord*!

estinto (*ĕs tēn'tô*) from the Italian: A direction to play very softly, almost to the point of not being heard . . . *ultra pianissimo*!

estremamente (*ĕs trä mä mĕn'tĕ*) from the Italian: "Extreme" or "extremely"!

étouffé (*ā tōō fā*) from the French: A direction to *dampen* or "*smother*" particular notes emanating from *harps, French horns, violins, percussion instruments* and others!

étude (*ā tūd*) from the French: "Study"; a musical piece designed as an exercise to improve the player's technique! Certain *etudes* (particularly those of Chopin) although technically motivated, have won lasting fame for their aesthetic public appeal.

euphone *(ū fōn)* A sixteen-foot *organ stop* with a soft *clarinet-like* sound!

euphonium *(ū fōn nĭ ŭm)* Considered either a *tenor tuba* or a *bass saxhorn*, the *euphonium* resembles a *baritone horn* except that the former has *four valves* and the *baritone* has a larger *wide-belled bore!* The *euphonium* is a *transposing instrument* for which music is written a *ninth* higher than the sound! It normally is pitched in *B-flat* with a *three-octave* range from *B-flat* above *middle C down to the B-flat, two octaves below middle C!*

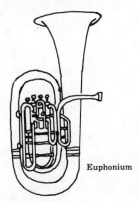

Euphonium

euphonium, double. A *euphonium* with two *"bells"*, to either of which the player can switch by operating a *valve!*

eurhythmics *(ū rĭth mĭks)* A method of using *timed body-movements* to provide *musical education!* Mainly developed by the Swiss composer Jacques Dalcroze, who translated *intervals* and *rhythm* into various physical movements!

evensong, evening song *(ēvĕn sông)* In the Anglican church, the *sung* version of the *evening prayer!* In the Roman Catholic church, the Vespers (sixth of the seven canonical hours) which are sung just before sunset!

exercise *(ĕk sēr sīz)* A brief portion of music designed to improve technical skills *(finger dexterity, embouchure, vocalization,* etc.)! (2) Generally, a portion of music primarily used for teaching purposes or practice!

exposition *(ĕks pō zĭsh ŭn)* The *initial section* of a *sonata* which states the *theme*(s)! In a *fugue*, the opening presentation of the *theme* by the individual players or vocalists!

expression *(ĕks prĕsh ŭn)* Using appropriate details of musical performance *(tempo, intensity, dynamics,* etc.) to bring out the intent of the composer or the emotionalism of the performer!

expressionism. Inspired by the "Expressionist" painters, a modern musical movement which began a few years after the beginning of the 20th century! It describes *composition* that reflects contemporary realities (complete with its stresses and anxieties) in its use of *atonal melody* and uneven, restless rhythm constructions!

DICTIONARY

F

— F —

F. The *fourth tone* of the *C-major scale* and the *sixth tone* of its *relative A-minor scale!* The *scales* that begin with *F* are known as *F-major (key signature, one flat)* and *F-minor (key signature, four flats)* ... "f" is the abbreviation for *forte;* "ff" or "fff" are optional abbreviations for *fortissimo!* An *F instrument (French horn, F trumpet,* etc.) is a *transposing instrument* ... the *French horn* plays its notes a *fifth lower than as written* while the *F trumpet plays a fourth higher than as written!* Both sound an *F pitch* when the *C note* is played!

fa *(fä)* In *solmisation* (and *solfeggio*) the *fourth note* of the familiar sequence *do, re, mi, fa, sol, la* and *ti!*

facile *(fä sēl')* Fr. / **facile** *(fä'chē lä)* It. / A direction to play in a fluent, easy manner!

fackeltanz *(fäk'l'tänts)* from the German: A dance with torches!

fado *(fä'dōō)* A world-renowned Portugese song-form, famous for its plaintive quality!

fagott *(fä gôt')* The German word for *bassoon.*

fagótto *(fä gōt'tō)* The Italian word for *bassoon;* also an *organ stop!*

fagótto contra *(-kôn trä)* / **fagottone** *(fä gōt tō'nä)* / The Italian term for *contrabassoon* or *double bassoon!*

faiblement *(fä blĕ män')* from the French: A direction to play feebly or softly!

fake *(fāk)* In popular music, a professional colloquialism describing the *improvising of accompaniment* to a *melody line,* for which appropriate *chords* (not necessarily original to the *composition*) may or may not be indicated!

fake book. A collection of *single-stave, melodic lines* from popular songs which facilitate *improvising accompaniment* for a *solo singer* or *instrumentalist,* or which help guide *ensemble performance* when no *arrangement parts* are available!

fala fala *(fä lä)* An early English refrain made up of *parts* featuring "fala la la" *syllables* in repeated variations!

false *(fôls)* *Out of tune!* Inaccurately *played* or inaccurately *notated!*

false accent. Placing the *accent* on the second or fourth *beat* of a *bar* of music instead of on the first *beat!*

false relation. A discrepancy caused by sounding a given *tone* and its *chromatic derivative* (its *sharp* or *flat*) during the simultaneous voicing of different music *parts!* (Also called *cross-relation*)!

falsetto *(fôl sĕt' ō)* (1) A *false* or *artificial voice* (usually used by a male) which lies above the *natural human range!* (2) The *upper* or *head* register of the voice, as opposed to the *lower* or *chest register!* (3) The *male alto* or *countertenor voice* popular in 16th and 17th century England! The *range* was equivalent to a *female alto,* up to the *second E* above *middle C!*

family *(fǎm'ĭ lĭ)* Any group of similar musical instruments (for example: *violin, viola, cello,* etc.)!

fancy *(fǎn sĭ)* See *fantasia* (also known as *ricetar* or *tiento*)!

fandango *(fǎn dǎng'gō)* (1) A lively Spanish dance in *triple meter* performed by couples playing *castanets* to *guitar accompaniment!* (2) In Mexico, a colloquial term for any ball or dance party!

fanfare *(fǎn'fâr)* A short passage of music in which the *brass* instruments are *flourished!* Usually a simple melodic *strain* based on one easy *chord,* a *fanfare* is used to announce the arrival of a VIP (very important person) or to herald the beginning of a parade. *Fanfares* are frequently employed in opera or theatre to dramatize similar events!

fantasia *(fǎn tä'zhä)* It. / **fantaisie** *(fǎn tä zē)* Fr.

fantasie *(fǎn tä zē)* Ger. / (1) An instrumental composition written to the composer's *fancy* and free of any restrictions of form or precedent. (also known as *fancy, ricetar, tiento,* etc.) (2) A mélange of familiar airs or melodies! (3) The middle portion of a *sonata* is frequently termed *free fantasia!*

fantasiren *(fǎn tä'zē rĭn)* from the German: A direction to *extemporize* or *improvise!*

fantastico *(fǎn tǎs'tĭ kō)* from the Italian: A direction to play with fanciful, capricious, or fantastic style!

farandole *(fǎr ǎn dōl')* from the French: An old, sprightly dance still performed in Provence, France! The *farandole,* typically, is in *6/8 time* and features a long chain of dancers preceded by musicians playing *pipes* and *tabors!*

farce *(färs)* (1) A *composition* with broad humor or burlesque! (2) A *one-act operetta* in such style!

farsa *(fär sä)* from the Italian: "Farce"!

fastosaménte *(fäs tō zō mǎn'tĕ)* / **fastoso** *(fäs tō zō)* It. / A direction to play in a dignified, pompous manner!

fauxbourdon *(fō bōōr dôn)* from the French: "False bass"! An old form of *three-part music* in which a simple *melody* lies in the *treble* or *soprano* part, while a *middle part* moves along *one fourth below the treble,* and a *tenor* part simultaneously moves *one sixth below the treble.* In England today, *fauxbourdon* describes *hymn singing* in which a *descant melody* is *sung by a choir above the part sung by the congregation!*

F clef. The *bass clef* (see *CLEF*)!

F dur *(ĕf dōōr)* The German term for the *key of F-major!*

"feedback" (1) The high-pitched *howl* or *buzz* heard in an electric-amplifier speaker when a connected microphone inadvertently picks up the speaker sound and recycles it in an endless output-input signal rotation! (2) A stylized technique in "rock" music, of deliberately feeding back (through the originating amplifier) music to reinforce the sound. This may be induced by sympathetic string vibration at particular pitches, with the instrument acting as an added amplifier or microphone. Deliberate "fuzz tones", "wah wah" sounds and "tape echo" reverberation are other manifestations of the "feed-back" principle!

feier *(fī ĕr)* from the German: "Festival" or celebration!

feierlich *(- lĭk)* from the German: A direction to play in a stately, solemn, ceremonial manner!

férma *(făr mä)* / **fermanénte** *(- näntē)* / It. / "Firm", steady, with resolution!

fermáta *(fĕr mä tä)* It. /**fermate** *(făr mä tĕ)* Ger. / The sign ⌢ which indicates a *rest* or *hold*. Used to indicate a *hold*, it directs that a *note be held longer than its time value!* A *fermata* over a *bar* line signals a *pause* before starting the next *bar!*

fermo *(făr'mō)* from the Italian: "Firm", unchanging!

fern *(fărn)* / **ferne** *(făr'nĕ)* Ger. / A direction to play or sing in a soft, distant manner ... *wie aus der Ferne,* "as if from a distance"!

feroce *(fä rō'chē)* It. / **ferocemente** *(- mĕn'tĕ)* It. / **ferocita, con** *(fä rō chē tä', kôn)* It. / A direction to play with ferocity and passion!

fertig *(fĕr'tĭg)* from the German: "Quick", nimble!

fervente *(făr vĕn'tĕ)* / **fervore** *(făr vō' rĕ)* It. / A direction to play with fervor and passion!

fes *(fĕs)* The *German* word for the note *F-flat* (F♭)!

feses *(fĕs ĕs)* The *German* word for the note *F-double flat* (F♭♭)!

fest *(fĕst)* from the German: (1) A festival! (2) A direction to play in a fixed and steady manner (also *festiglich*)!

festivamente *(fĕs tē vä mĕn'tĕ)* / **festività, con** *(fĕs tē vē tä', kôn)* / **festivo** *(fĕs tē'vō)* It. / **festlich** *(fĕst'lĭkh)* Ger. / **festoso** *(fĕst ō'sō)* It. / A direction to play in a gay, merry, festive manner!

feuer, mit *(foi'ĕr, mĭt)* / **feurig** *(foi'rĭg)* Ger. / "With fire"; a direction to play with fervor and passion!

ff. or fff. The abbreviations (either is optional) for *fortissimo!*

F-flat. The note F♭ which is a half-tone below *F!*

F holes. The *sound holes* on the top of *violins* (or other *string instruments*) so-called because they are *ƒ* shaped!

F horn. The *French horn* in *F!*

fiácco *(fē äk ō)* from the Italian: "Weak", languishing, feeble!

fiato *(fē ă tō)* from the Italian: "Breath" or "wind"; *stromenti a fiato,* "wind instruments"!

fieramente *(fē ĕr ä mĕn'tĕ)* / **fierezza, con** *(fē ĕr ĕts ä, kôn)* / **fiero** *(fē ĕr ō)* It. / A direction to play in a bold, wild, vigorous manner!

fife *(fīf)* A small, simple, shrill type of *cross-flute* used chiefly in military or *"fife and drum corps"* bands. The modern *fife* has *six finger-holes* and *one or more keys!*

fifteenth *(fĭf tēenth)* (1) An *interval* of two *octaves!* (2) An *organ stop* that sounds two *octaves* higher than the written music!

fifth *(fĭfth)* (1) The *interval* spanning five *diatonic degrees* (also known as the *perfect fifth*) ... the span of the *first* and *fifth* ascending notes in any *major* or *minor scale* (see *INTERVAL*)! (2) The *fifth* note of a *diatonic scale,* the *dominant* counting up from the *tonic!* (3) The *augmented fifth* is the *interval one-half-tone above the perfect fifth;* the *diminished fifth* (the *false fifth*) is one-half tone below the perfect fifth!

figura *(fĭ gū rä)* In olden days, a name for a *musical note!*

figuration *(fĭg ū rä shŭn)* *Ornamental* music using rapid *figures, passing tones* and *changing notes* to vary repeated *melodic* or *rhythmic patterns!*

figure *(fĭg ūr)* Generally, any particular *group of notes* (two or more) that have a special character in a *composition* either due to their frequent repetition or to their *melodic* or *rhythmic* uniqueness! (see *motive, motif, leit-motif*).

figured bass. A feature of the *baroque period* in music (1600-1750) which used numerical notation over or under the *bass-part notes* to indicate the appropriate *chords* for *accompaniment!* (see *thoroughbass* or *basso continuo*).

filar la voce *(fē lär'lä vō'chē)* It. / **filer la voir** *(fē lā'lä vwăh)* Fr. / A direction to draw out or prolong a *tone* or to slowly expand and diminish the sound in alternate order!

filato *(fē lä'tō)* from the Italian: A direction to draw out the music at length!

fill *(fĭl)* (1) An expression in popular music circles, generally used to denote music which is inserted between gaps or openings in written *compositions* or *arrangements* ... frequently employed as a direction to a *rhythm section* to improvise its performance! (2) More specifically, a term of direction for popular *drummers* to use a *one-or-two bar "break"* of *non-standard rhythm* performance to *fill* a gap in the written music!

fin *(făn)* from the French: The "end" ... *a la fin,* play to the end!

fin'al *(fē näl)* from the Italian: "End here", or "play as far as"!

fin'al segno *(sĕn yō)* from the Italian: "As far as the sign"; a direction to repeat the music from the beginning until the sign marked 𝄋 !

finale *(fĭ nä'lē)* (1) The last *portion* or *movement* of a *sonata, concerto, symphony,* etc.! (2) The last *portion* of an *act* in *opera,* usually involving *soloists* and *chorus.* (3) The closing number in any public performance!

fine *(fē'nă)* from the Italian: The "end" of a *composition,* or the end of a *repeat* following the *dal segno* or *da capo* markings! In notation *Fine!*

finger *(fĭng ĕr)* To play an *instrument* by using the fingers on the *strings, keys* or *holes!*

fingering. Signs or marks to indicate finger placements! American or English *fingering (piano)* uses the X sign for the thumb placement, with the numerals 1, 2, 3, 4 for the other fingers! German, French, Italian *fingering* usually assigns the number 1 to the thumb, and the numerals 2, 3, 4, 5 to the other fingers!

flügelhorn (*flü'gĕl hôrn*) (1) A *brass instrument* in the *saxhorn* family and similar to a *cornet* except for its larger *bore* and *bell* . . . . the *B-flat flügelhorn* version most popular for its velvety sound! (2) A *keyed bugle* is sometimes called a *flügelhorn!*

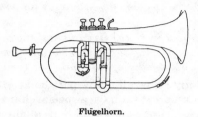

Flügelhorn.

flüssig (*flü' sĭkh*) from the German: A direction to play smoothly with an even flow!

flute (*flōōt*) A *wind instrument*, of major importance, played by blowing a column of air against a sharp edge at one end of a narrow *tube*. The modern orchestral *cross-flute* (developed by Theobald Boehm in the 1840's) is held laterally and played by blowing across the *embouchure* near the *tube end!* The *tube* is closed at *one end* and features a series of *holes* (14) which are kept *open* or *closed* by a number of *keys*, The *flute's compass* is about three *octaves* above *middle C!*

flute

flute, alto. Larger than the standard *flute*, the *alto flute* (also known as *bass flute*) is pitched in *G*, a *fourth* below the standard *flute!*

flute, contrabass. The largest *flute*, pitched a full *octave* below the standard *flute!*

flute, piccolo. A smaller-size *flute* which sounds one *octave* above the standard *flute!*

flûte à bec (*flü tä bĕk*) from the French: "Flute with a beak", the French term for the *recorder* or a *fipple flute!*

fluted (*flōōt'ĕd*) Referring to thin, clear, *flute-like* notes!

flûte d'amour (*flüt dä mōōr*) from the French: (1) An old *flute* which sounded a *minor third* below the *Boehm flute!* (2) An *organ stop!*

flute douce (*flōōt dōōs*) from the French: (1) A *recorder!* (2) An *organ stop!*

flutework (*flōōt'wûrk*) All of the *flue stops* in an *organ* that are not included in the *principal-work* or *gedecktwork!*

flutter tongue (*flŭt'ĕr tŭng'*) Creating special *flute* sounds by rapid insertion of the tongue into the *keyhole!* Speeded up variations are known as *double tonguing* and *triple tonguing:* The German term is *flatterzunge* (*flăt ĕr tsōōn gĕ*)!

flying staccato. In *violin music*, skipping the *bow* across the strings . . . *arco saltando!*

F-major. The *major key* or *scale* with one *flat* in the *signature!*

F-minor The *minor key* or *scale* (relative to the *key of A-flat major*) with four *flats* in the *signature!*

F moll (*mol*) The *German* term for the *key* of *F-minor!*

fois (*fwä*) from the French: "Time" . . . *encore une fois*, "one more time" or "play again" . . . *a la fois*, "at the same time" . . *une fois*, "once" . . . *deux fois*, "twice," etc.!

folgend (*fŏl'gĕnt*) from the German: "Following (see *colla parte* or *colla voce*)!

folia (*fô lē'ä*) (1) A chord pattern for *bass harmony* often used in 16th and 17th century *composition*, and later developed as a *melody* for the *bass* (*folia bass)!* (2) A *Spanish* solo dance in *slow waltz time!*

folk song (*fōk sŏng*) A *song* emanating from the common people of a nation, usually characterizing their native traditions and feelings, and composed in *simple ballad form!*

foot (*fŏŏt*) (1) A *group of syllables* with one distinct *metrical accent!* (2) An old term for a *drone bass accompaniment!* (3) The part of an *organ pipe* below the *mouth!* (4) The unit of measure for the *"pitch"* of *organ stops:* An eight-foot *organ stop* means the longest *pipe* is eight feet long and sounds a *C* when its corresponding *key* is depressed! A four-foot *stop* sounds an *octave* higher; a two-foot *stop* sounds two *octaves* higher, and conversely, a sixteen-foot *stop* sounds an *octave* lower!

forlana (*fôr lä'nä*) It. / **forlane** (*fôr lăn'*) Fr. / A lively Italian dance, in *6/8* or *6/4 time*, used by gondoliers, with adaptations found in the 16th and 17th century music of Bach and Ponchielli, and in various *ballet suites* of other composers!

form (*fôrm*) The *arrangement* of the elements of *composition* into symmetrical or organized order or structure! The basic elements are the *notes (pitch)*, their sequence *(melody)* and their *time relative to each other (rhythm)*. In formal music terms, there is the *binary (two-part* form); *ternary (three-part* form which includes an added middle section) and the *sonata, rondo, variation* and *strophic* forms. In larger works the expression *compound form* embraces the *symphony, concerto, sonata, cantata, oratorio, suite, quartet,* etc!

fort (*fôrt*) from the German: Used in *organ music* to signify "off"!

forte (*fôr'tā*) from the Italian: A direction to play loudly with power (abbreviated *f* or F)!

fortement (*fôr tĕ män*) Fr. / **fortemente** (*fôr tĕ mĕn'tĕ*) It. / A direction to play loudly and strongly!

fortepiano (*fôr'tĕ pĕ ä' nō*) from the Italian: (1) A direction to play loudly, but immediately diminishing to a soft sound (abbreviated *fp*) (2) The original *Italian name* for the *pianoforte!*

forte possibile (*- pōs sĕ'bĭlĕ*) from the Italian: A direction to play as loudly as possible!

fortissimo (*fôr tĭs'ĭ mō*) from the Italian: (1) A very loud tone or portion of music! (2) A direction to play

fingersatz *(finger sätz)* The *German* word for *"fingering"*!

fingerboard. (1) In *stringed instruments*, the narrow, wooden base over which the *strings* are stretched, and against which the fingers press down to change *pitch* by *damping the vibration* of the *string(s)*. (2) The *keyboard* of a *piano* or *organ-type instrument*!

finger cymbals. *Castanets!* (see *cymbals*).

finger hole. In various *wind instruments*, the hole in the *tube* which changes *tones* depending on whether it is covered or left open by a *finger or key*!

fino *(fĭ nō)* from the Italian: "Going as far as", "up to" (see *fin'al*)!

fioritura *(fē ō rē tōō rä)* from the Italian: "Flowering ... *musical embellishments or ornaments* such as *trills, turns, grace notes*, etc.!

fipple flute *(fĭp'l flŭt)* An obsolete name for the *recorder, flageolet, whistle flute* or any *wind instrument* which is blown into at one end of the *tube*. The *"fipple"* is a plug in the *mouthpiece* end of the *tube* which is narrowly slitted to allow air to pass through and strike the sharp edge of a hole just below the *"fipple"*. The vibration of air in the *tube* produces sound variation!

fis *(fĭs)* The *German* word for the note *F-sharp*!

fis dur *(dōor)* The *German* term for the *key of F-sharp major*!

fisis *(fĭs ĭs)* The *German* word for the *note F-double sharp*!

fis moll *(mōl)* The *German* term for the *key of F-sharp minor*!

fit *(fĭt)* An old term for a *strain of music*!

FIVE, The. The name given to a group of Russian composers who sought together to develop a *nationalist* school of composition. The members were Mily Balakirev, Modest Mussorgsky, Cesar Cui, Alexander Borodin and Nikoly Rimsky-Korsakov!

fixed do *(dō)* The system of *solmisation* in which the *tone* C and its *chromatic derivatives* (C#, C♭, C✗, C♭♭) are named *"do!"* (dō)! The *tone* D and its *derivatives* are named *"re"* (rā), and so on up the *scale*, regardless of *key* or *harmonization*!

fixed-tone instruments. Any *instruments (piano, organ, harp*, etc.) whose *tones* cannot be altered by the *player* as opposed to *violin-family instruments* (for example) whose *pitch* can be modified in use!

flag *(flăg)* The *hook* on the *stem* of a *note* ♪

flageolet *(flaj'o let)* A shrill, small *fipple flute* played through a *mouthpiece* and equipped with *six finger holes*! The *range* is similar to the *piccolo (from treble G up over two octaves to b-flat)*!

flageolet tones. *Harmonic tones* derived from the *stopping* of *stringed instruments (violin, zither*, etc.) by touching the appropriate *nodal points*!

flam *(flăm)* A *drumbeat* similar to a rapid *grace note* just preceding the *accented stroke* of a stick on the *drum head*! ♪

flamenco *(flä měn kō)* A form of *Andalusian gypsy music* usually featuring heel-stomping dancers who manipulate *castanets* to the *accompaniment* of *guitar music*!

flamenco guitar. A slightly-altered, *classical guitar* (with more *frets* and a sharper sound) frequently equipped with an inset plate, adjacent to the *sound hole*, on which the player taps for *percussive, rhythm variation*!

flat *(flăt)* (1) The symbol ♭ , an *accidental* which *lowers the pitch of the note* to which it is appended by one half-tone ...A-flat is one half-tone below A, for example. (2) When used in a *key signature*, the *flat* (♭) indicates that all *tones* of the same *degree* are to be *lowered one half-tone* unless *cancelled by a natural* (♮) sign! (3) On *keyboards*, the black keys *B-flat, D-flat, E-flat, G-flat* and *A-flat* are all *flat* notes but the white key *B* also sounds *C-flat* and the white key *E* also sounds *F flat* (the latter two are *enharmonic equivalents)*!

flautando *(flou tän'dō)*/ **flautato** *(flou tä'tō)* It. / A direction to play *"flutelike"* tones; in *violin music* to *bow* swiftly but softly near the *fingerboard*!

flautino *(flou tē'nō)* from the Italian: (1) A small *flute* or *piccolo*! (2) A small *accordion*! (3) An *organ stop*!

flautist *(flou' tĭst)* A player on the *flute*; a *flutist*!

flauto *(flou'tō)* from the Italian: A flute!

flauto amabile *(ä mä bē lä)* from the Italian: An *organ stop* with a sweet tone!

flauto piccolo. The *Italian* term for *piccolo* or *octave flute*!

flauto traverso *(trä vâr'sō).* The *Italian* term for the contemporary *transverse flute* which is held laterally in performance!

flebile *(flĕb'il ĕ)* from the Italian: Fearful, mournful, sad!

flehend *(flā'hĕnt)* from the German: "Pleading"!

flessibile *(flĕs sē'bē lĕ)* from the Italian: "Flexible", bending!

flicorno *(flē kôr'nô)* The *Italian* name for *flügelhorn*!

fliessend *(flē'sĕnt)* from the German: A direction to play with a smooth flow from sound to sound (see *scorrendo)*!

fling *(flĭng)* A lively *Scottish dance* in *quadruple time*!

florid *(flŏr'ĭd)* Highly embellished or elaborated! Full of *musical ornamentation*!

flote *(flō'tĕ)* The *German* word for *flute*!

flott *(flôt)* from the German: A direction to play briskly and decisively!

flourish *(flûr'ĭsh)* A *fanfare* of *trumpets*! More generally, any specially theatrical or elaborate musical portion !

flüchtig *(flükh'tĭkh)* from the German: A direction to play lightly, airily or in nimble fashion!

flügel *(flü'gĕl)* from the German: "Wing"; the *grand piano (pianoforte)* or *harpsichord*, both of which are "wing"-shaped!

very loud (abbreviated $\textit{ff}$)!

forza *(fôr'tsăh)* from the Italian: "Force", power . . . *con forza,* "with force or power"!

forzando *(fôr tsän'dō)* / **forzato** *(fôr tsä'tō)* It. / A direction to play with force or to heavily *accent* a *chord* or *note* (abbreviated *fz* or notated by the marks $\wedge$ or $>$)!

foundation stop *(foun dă shŭn stŏp)* (1) Any *organ stop* whose sound is the same or in exact *octave* ratio to the corresponding *piano* keys! (2) Any one of the basic *flue stops* of an *organ* as opposed to the *reed stops!*

four-hand *(fôr hănd)* Arranged or composed for *two players (four hands)! Piano pieces* for *four hands* are usually divided into *treble* and *bass parts* . . . *four-hand* instruction and performance has waned in popularity almost to the point of current non-existence!

fourteenth *(fôr'tēnth)* The interval of an *octave* plus a *seventh!*

fourth *(fôrth)* (1) The *interval* spanning the *first four diatonic degrees* of a *scale* (see *Interval*)! (2) The *fourth tone* of a *diatonic scale* counting up from the *tonic!* (3) The *subdominant* . . . the *perfect fourth* (see *Interval* for *augmented* and *diminished fourth*)!

fourth chord. A *chord* consisting of *two fourths* or a *fourth* and other *tones* (see *Interval*)!

four-three chord. The *second inversion* of a *seventh* chord (see *Inversion*)!

four-two chord. The *first inversion* of a *seventh* chord (see *Inversion*)!

fox trot *(fŏks trŏt)* A *ballroom dance* in *4/4 time,* popular in the "*name-band*" era but usually heard today only at formal adult or senior-citizen affairs!

fp. The abbreviation for *forte piano!*

française *(frăn săz)* A French country dance in *3/4 time!*

francamente *(frăn kă mĕn'tĕ)* / **franchézza** *(frăn kä'tsă)* It. / A direction to play confidently, with boldness and freedom!

frase larga *(frä ză lär gă)* from the Italian: "Broad phrase", same as *largamente!*

freddamente *(frĕd dă mĕn' tĕ)* / **freddeza** *(frĕd dä'tsä)* / **freddo** *(frä'dō)* It. / "Cold", "frigid", without passion!

free canon *(frē kăn ŭn)* A *canon* in which one or more of the similar, melodic parts is somewhat altered . . . omitting or adding *accidentals,* etc.

free composition. Music composed in free-style, ignoring the strict rules of form!

free counterpoint. *Counterpoint harmony* which came later than (and did not conform to) the strict rules of *counterpoint* stated by Johann Fux in the 1700's. Bach is the acknowledged master of *free counterpoint!*

free fugue. A *fugue* which disregards strict rules for the *subject* and *counterpoint,* and introduces unrelated, *melodic episodes!*

free jazz. A broad term for a style of *ensemble improvisation* developed by black *jazz musicians* in the last two decades, which is undoubtedly linked sociologically to the expanding and improving black ethnic culture! As the name implies, the music is characterized by its avoidance of formal structure!

free part. A part added to a *fugue* or *canon!*

frei *(frī)* from the German: "Free"; a direction to play in an *open style!*

fremente *(frä mĕn'tĕ)* from the Italian: A direction to play in a furious manner!

French horn (1) A *brass wind instrument* of importance in an *orchestra* and consisting of a long, conical, spiral-shaped *tube* with a funnel-shaped *mouthpiece* at one end and a wide-flared *bell* at the other. The *French horn* is pitched either in *F* or *B-Flat* and features *three valves* which provide a *range* from *low B* to *high F.* A transposing instrument, the *French horn* sounds a *fifth* lower than its written music (except for *bass clef notes* which sound a *fourth* lower than as written.) A *double horn* is frequently used in current performance which combines the sounds of the *F* and *B-flat* horns. The *double horn* has a *fourth valve* which can shift the *F* pitch to a *B-flat.*

french horn

French sixth. One variation of an *augmented sixth chord* which consists of an *augmented sixth,* a *major third* and an *augmented fourth!*

French overture. Dating from the seventeenth century, the *French overture* form was first developed by Lully who composed his *overtures* in two *parts* . . . a slow *first part* followed by a rapid *second part,* re-stating the same *melody* but frequently adding a *coda* as a *third part!* The *coda* returned to the slow *tempo* of the initial *part* (see *Overture*)!

frets *(frĕts).* Narrow ridges of metal, ivory or wood (laid across the *fingerboard* of a *guitar, banjo, mandolin,* etc.) on which the fingers are pressed to "*stop*" the *strings* at a point which creates an exact change in *pitch!* See *Guitar Illustration!*

fretta *(frĕt'tă)* / **frettolosamente** *(frĕt tō lō să mĕn 'tĕ)* / **frettoloso** *(frĕt tō lō'sō)* It. / A direction to play with haste, hurriedly!

freude *(froi'dĕ)* / **freudig** *(froi'dĭkh)* Ger. / "Joy", "joyous", "joyfully"!

frisch *(frĭsh)* from the German: A direction to play briskly with vigor *(brioso)!*

friss *(frĭs)* The fast portion of a Hungarian *csardas!*

frog *(frŏg)* The *nut* of the *violin bow,* used to tighten the *bow-hairs!*

fröhlich *(frō'līkh)* from the German: A direction to play in a joyful, gay manner!

frosch *(frōsh)* The German word for *"frog"*, the *nut* of the *violin bow!*

frosch, am *(- ăm)* from the German: A direction to play on the *violin strings* with the *bow-part (nut)* nearest the hand.

frottola *(frōt'tō lä)* from the Italian: One of the 15th-century forerunners of the *madrigal!* The *frottola (frottole)* generally consisted of *secular, choral* compositions in *four parts*, with the *melody* in the *soprano* part and *harmonies* of *fourths* and *fifths* in the other *parts!*

fruhlingslied *(frü'līngs lēd)* from the German: *"Spring song"!*

F-schlüssel *(ĕf shlü s'l)* The German term for the *F clef* or *bass clef!*

F-sharp. The tone *F#*, one *half-step* above *F!*

F-sharp major. The *major scale* or *key* with six *sharps* in its *signature!*

F-sharp minor. The *minor scale* or *key* (relative to *A-major)* with three *sharps* in its *signature.*

fuga *(fōo' gä)* from the Italian: A *fugue!*

fugara *(fōo gä'rä)* An *organ stop* with 8-foot or 4-foot *pipes* sounding *"string-like"*, sharp tones!

fugato *(fōo gä'tō)* from the Italian: In the style of a *fugue* but not conforming strictly to the rules of *fugue* form!

fuge *(fōo'gĕ)* The *German* word for *fugue!*

fugha *(fōo'gä)* The *Italian* word for fugue! (also *fuga*).

fughetta *(fōo gĕt' tä)* The *Italian word* for a short *fugue* or *exposition!*

fugue *(fūg).* A *multi-parted composition* based on a short *theme*, or *themes*, and constructed according to strict rules of *counterpoint!* The *fugue* is a famous form of *imitative contrapuntal music* which can vary from the *strict* to the *free* but always develops from a *subject theme (dux)* which is the opening statement of every *fugue.*

The general formula for a *fugue* is as follows: After the *subject* (usually presented in the *tonic* by a *first voice)*, the *second voice* repeats with the *answer* in the *dominant*, and at a *fifth* or *fourth interval* from the *subject theme*, sometimes with slight variations. A *third voice* now takes up the *subject* an *octave above or below the original key.* At this point, the *first voice* states a *compatible melody* in *counterpoint* to the *subject.* A *countersubject* may now be introduced by the *second voice* following the *counterpoint* of the *first voice*, while the *third voice* is repeating the *subject.* NOTE! The term *voice* above applies to either an instrumental *voicing* or to actual singing by human voice(s).

The *fugue* now continues with various *episodes* of interwoven complexity (sometimes featuring *key changes*, *augmented* or *diminished intervals*, *inversions*, *stretto*, etc.) and usually concludes with a *coda* which often includes *stretto variations* against *pedal point* background.

Formal musical terms for divisions of a *fugue* also are known as the *exposition, development* and *conclusion.* *Fugues* also are characterized by (1) *Mode* ... *diatonic, Dorian*, etc. (2) Adherence to the *subject* ... in a *Tonal fugue*, the *subject* is modified by the *answer* (3) Form or style ... a *strict fugue* is strictly symmeterical and "follows the rules"; a *free fugue* departs from the rules at the wish of the composer.

Historically, the *fugue* was first implanted in the classical music culture by Sweelinck, followed by Buxtehude, Pachelbel, Fischer and others, but the renowned masters of the form, dating from the *baroque period* are Bach and Handel. Later contributions to the art of *fugue* were made by such masters as Beethoven, Brahms and Mozart!

fugue, double. A *fugue* which develops from two beginning *subject themes!*

full *(fōol).* A description for the *total combination* of *instruments* and *voices!*

full anthem. An *anthem* in four or more *parts* for *full chorus* without *solos!*

full cadence. Another name for *perfect cadence* or *authentic cadence!*

full choir. See *full organ!*

full chord. A *chord* in which some, or all, *tones* are *doubled* in the *octave!*

full orchestra *(full band).* An *orchestra (band)* with a complete complement of *instruments* for *symphonic performance!*

full organ. An *organ* with all of its *stops* drawn and all of its *registers* in use! *Full choir, full great, full swell* are equivalent directions! *Full to fifteenth* means drawing all *stops* except *reeds* and *mixtures!*

full score. A *complete orchestral and/or vocal arrangement* with individual *parts written out on separate staves!*

fundamental *(fŭn dä mĕn'täl)* (1) The *root* or *lowest note* of a *chord!* (2) The *first* or *lowest note* of a *harmonic series!*

funèbre *(fŭ nā'br)* Fr. / **funebre** *(fōo' nĕ brĕ)* It. / **funerale** *(fōo nĕ rä'lĕ)* It. / A direction to play in a mournful, funereal manner!

funeral march. A slow, *minor-key march* in *4/4 meter* (also called *dead march)!* The slow portion of Chopin's *piano sonata in B-Flat minor* is the most renowned example of *funeral, processional marches!*

funk, funky. A modern-day colloquialism for the *"raunchy"*, high-energy sound of *black soul music* fused with *rhythm and blues* and *jazz.* "Funky" is a black-American description of uninhibited, almost visceral *soul/jazz* that followed after the more sophisticated, nuance-filled jazz of the *cool, be-bop* or *avant* schools developed by Charlie Parker, Dizzy Gillespie, Miles Davis, et al. in the '40's and early '50's!

fuóco *(fōo ō'kō)* / **fuocóso** *(fōo ō kō'sō)* It. / A direction to play with fire and passion!

furia *(fōo'rē ă)* / **furiosamente** *(fōo rē ōs ă mĕn'tĕ)* /

604

furioso *(foo rē ō'sō)* It. / A direction to play furiously or madly!

furiant *(foo'rē änt)* A brisk *Bohemian dance* in *3/4 time* with changing *accents* and frequent *syncopation!*

furniture stop. An *organ mixture stop!*

furóre *(foo rō'rĕ)* from the Italian: Fury, rage, passion!

futurism *(fū tūr 'ĭz'm)* A rebellious movement in the arts, originating in Italy about 1910, which clamored for personal expression in music, to the point of utilizing noise and discord. Futurists demanded relevance to current life styles, and rejected traditionalism or convention *en toto!*

fuzzy *(fŭz ē)* Not clear, inexact *musical tones!* Often used to describe muddy, amplified sound which occurs when the electronics are not adjusted or functioning properly!

fz. The abbreviation for *forzando!*

DICTIONARY

G

— G —

G. (1) The *fifth tone* of the *C-major scale* and the *seventh tone* of its *relative A-minor scale*. The *scales* that begin with a *G* are the *G-major* and *G-minor scales* whose *key signatures* are one *sharp* for the *G-major* and two-*flats* for the *G-minor!* (2) A *G* instrument (alto flute, etc) is a *transposing instrument* which plays its *notes* one *fourth* lower than as written! (3) *G* is an abbreviation for *"gauche"* (French for "left")... *main gauche*, left hand! (4) *G* or *G.O.* also are abbreviations for *grand-orgue* or *great organ!* (5) *G* is also the letter name for the *treble clef* (see *clef*)!

gagaku (*gä gä' kōō*) Orchestral music of Japan, dating back to the 8th century, and based on earlier forms emanating in China and Korea! Gagaku can be "left" (Chinese) or "right" (Korean); performed solo, it is *kangen;* as accompaniment *bugaku!* It is the "imperial" music of Japan!

gagliarda (*gäl yär'da*) / It. / **gagliarde** (*gäl yär'dĕ*) Ger. / A *galliard!*

gai (*gā*) Fr. / **gaiamente** (*gā ä mĕn' tĕ*) It. / **gaiement** (*gā mǎn'*) Fr. / **gaio** (*gā'ō*) It. / Gay, lively, brisk!

gain (*gān*) The amplification of sound by raising the electrical power in a circuit. Used by recording studio and sound engineering personnel to describe generally the loudness of the sound output!

galliarde (*gä yärd*) The French word for a *galliard!*

galliard (*gäl'yĕrd*) A gay, spirited 16th century *French dance* in *triple time* with five steps to each *phrase;* hence, also known as *cinque pace!*

galop (*gäl'ŭp*) A lively 19th century dance in *fast 2/4 time!* It is danced in a circle with hops or sliding steps that somewhat resemble a horse's gallop!

Galop

gamba (*gäm'bá*) Short for *viola da gamba!*

gamba bass A 16-foot *organ stop* with the quality of a *viola da gamba!*

gambang (*gäm'báng*) A *Javanese xylophone* of major importance in *Indonesian music* and the *gamelan orchestras* of Java, Bali, etc.! Also called *Saron!*

Gambang
(Saron)

gamme (*gäm*) from the French: A *scale!*

gamut (*gäm'ŭt*) (1) The *scale!* (2) The *range* of an *instrument or voice!* (3) The *staff!* (4) The *first note* of Guido d'Arezzo's *"great scale"* which was used in early church music (the *lowest note!*)

gamelan (*gäm'ĕ län*) / **gamelang** (*gäm'ĕ läng*) / (1) The name for various types of *Indonesian orchestras*, most of which are construed of *percussion instruments (gongs, drums, cymbals,* etc.) augmented by indigenous *strings* and *woodwinds!*

ganz (*gänts*) from the German: "Whole" ... *ganze note, whole note...ganze langsam,* very slowly!

gapped scale. A *scale* excerpted from the tones of a *larger scale!* The *pentatonic scale*, for example, is a *gapped scale* consisting of *five of the seven tones* of a *diatonic scale!*

garbamente (*gär bä mĕn'tĕ*)/**garbato** (*gär bä'tō*)/ **garbo, con** (*gär'bō, kôn*) It./A direction to play with refinement in a graceful or elegant manner!

gas, gasser, gassy (*gäs, -ĕr,-ē*) A popular, American slang-expression for appreciation of an outstanding performance, work or sound! "It's a gas" ... "that's a gasser" ... "it was gassy" ... indicate extremely favorable reactions!

gathering note. During a *chant*, the holding of the last syllable of the *recitation!*

gauche (*gōsh*) from the French: "Left"; a direction to play with the left hand!

gavotta (*gä vôt'tä*) It./ **gavotte** (*gä vôt'*) Fr./A French theatrical dance, usually in bright *4/4 time*, consisting of a *four bar section* of *melody* followed by a *second section of eight bars*, with repetitions of both sections thereafter!

G clef. The *treble clef* or *violin clef!* The sign for the *G clef* (derived from the letter "G") always swirls in the second line of the staff (see *Clef*)!

G dur (*gä dōōr*) The *German* term for the *key of G-major!*

gebrauchsmusik (*gē brouks'mū zik*) from the German: "Music to be used"; a reference to music intended for amateur use at home performances! Usually, this consists of short, simple *compositions* for small groups, with provision for optional *instruments!*

gebunden (*gē bōōn'd'n*) from the German: A direction to play the *notes* as if *connected* ... in *legato* style!

gedackt (*gē dŏkt'*) from the German: "Stopped", a reference to *closed organ pipes!*

gedämpft (*gē dĕmft'*) from the German: A direction to muffle, *mute* or "dampen" the tone!

gedeckt (*gē dĕkt'*) A *flute-like organ stop* from 2-foot *pitch* to 32-foot *pitch!*

gedehnt (*gē dänt'*) from the German: A direction to play in a slow, stately manner, drawing out or sustaining each *note!* Same as *steso, largamente!*

gefällig (*gē fĕl'lĭg*) from the German: "Pleasant", "agreeable"!

gefühl, mit (*gē fül'mĭt*) / **gefühlvoll** (*gē fül fôl*) / Ger. / A direction to play with feeling or to perform with much sentimental expression!

gehalten (*gē häl't'n*) from the German: "Sustained" or "held", giving each *note* full value!

gehaucht (*gē houcht'*) from the German: "Sighed"; A direction to play or whisper very softly!

geheimnisvoll *(gĕ hīm'nĭs fôl)* from the German: A direction to play in a "mysterious" or secretive manner!

gehend *(gā'ĕndt)* The German word for *andante!*

geige *(gī'gĕ)* The *German* word for *violin!*

geist *(gīst)* The *German* word for *"soul"* or *"spirit"!*

geistlich *(gīst'lĭk)* The *German* word for spiritual or religious types of music!

gelassen *(gĕ lä'sĕn)* from the German: A direction to play in an easy, quiet fashion!

geläufig *(gĕ loi'fĭk)* from the German: "Fluent", "easy"!

gemächlich *(gĕ mĕk'lĭk)* from the German: A direction to play in an easy, comfortable tempo *(comodo)!*

gemässigt *(gĕ mĕ'ss'ĭkt)*/**gemessen** *(gĕ mĕss'n)* Ger. / A direction to play in a moderate *tempo!*

gemisch *(gĕ mĭsh')* from the German: "Mixed"!

gemischte stimmen *(gĕ mĭsh'tĕ shtĭ'mĕn)* from the German: *"Mixed voices!"*

gemshorn *(gĕmz'hôrn)* An *organ flute-stop* with 8, 4 or 2-foot pitch on the *manuals* and 16-foot on the *pedals!*

gemütlich *(gĕ müt'lĭk)* from the German: Genial, cheerily (similar to *disinvolto, comodo)!*

generalbass *(gĕ nĕ räl'bäs)* from the German: *Thorough bass, basso continuo!*

generalpause *(- pow zŭ)* from the German: A *rest* or *tacet* for all *parts* of an *orchestra;* abbreviated *g.p.!*

generator *(jĕn'ĕr ā tĕr)* The *root* or *fundamental* tone of a *triad* or any other *chord* or *harmonic series!*

generoso *(jen ĕr ō'sō)* from the Italian: Free or abundant!

gentile *(jĕn tē'lĕ)* / **gentilezza** *(jĕn tē lĕt'sä)* / **gentil-ménte** *(jĕn tīl mĕn' tĕ)* It. / A direction to play in a graceful, elegant or stylish manner!

German flute. A name for the *transverse flute* or *cross flute,* originally used to distinguish it from the *recorder* which was called the *English flute!*

German sixth. An *augmented sixth chord* which contains, in addition to a *major third,* an *augmented sixth* tone!

ges *(gĕs)* The *German* word for the *note G-flat!*

gesang *(gĕ zäng')* from the German: "Singing"; a *song, melody* or a *vocal part!*

gesangreich *(gĕ zäng'rīk)* / **gesangvoll** *(gĕ zäng'fôl)* Ger. / In a singing, melodious manner *(cantabile)!*

geschick *(gĕ shĭk)* from the German: Skill, agility!

geschleift *(gĕ shlīft')* from the German: *Slurred, legato!*

geschwindt *(ge shvĭndt')* from the German: A direction to play rapidly!

gĕs dur *(ges'dōor)* The *German* term for *G-flat major!*

geses *(gĕs'ĕss)* The *German* word for *G-double flat!*

gesteigert *(gĕ stī'gĕrt)* from the German: A direction to play with increasing intensity *(rinforzato)!*

gestopft *(gĕ shtŏ'pft)* from the German: A direction to *"stop"* a *French horn* . . . raising the *pitch* a *half-tone* by inserting a hand or *mute* into the *bell!*

gestossen *(gĕ shtōs'n)* from the German: Detached, separated, *staccato!*

geteilt *(gĕ tīlt')* from the German: Divided, separated . . . *violinen geteilte, divisi violins!*

getragen *(gĕ trä'gĕn)* from the German: A direction to play in a sustained, slow manner *(sostenuto)!*

gewiss *(gĕ vĭss')* from the German: Resolute, firm!

gezogen *(gĕ tsō'gĕn)* from the German: A direction to draw out the *notes (largamente, steso)!*

G-flat. The *note G♭* which is a *half-step* below G!

G-*flat major. The *major key* or *scale* with a *signature* of *six flats!*

ghiribizzoso *(gē rē bĭd zō'sō)* from the Italian: Whimsical!

gig *(gĭg)* A colloquial term among popular music professionals used to denote any money-making job, such as a recording session, club date, tv broadcast, etc!

giga *(jē'gä)* It. / **gigue** *(jĭg)* Fr. / **gige** *(gē'g'ĕ)* Ger. / A lively *dance* or *jig* almost always in *two sections* and both in *6/8* or *12/8 time!* Probably derived from the German word *"geige"* (violin) although an old French *viol* was known as a *gigue!*

giochévole *(jē ō kĕ'vō lĕ)*
gioco, con *(jē ō' kō, kôn)*
giocóndo *(jē ō kōn'dō)*
giocondamente *(jē ō kōn dă mĕn'tĕ)*
giocosamente *(jē ō kō să mĕn'tĕ)*
giocoso *(jē ō kō'sō)*
gioia *(jē ō'yă)*
gioióso *(jē ō yō'sō)*
gioiosamente *(jē ō yō să mĕn'tĕ)*
gioviale *(jē ō vĕ â'lĕ)* It./A direction to play merrily, cheerfully, joyfully or gaily!

gis *(gĭs)* The *German* word for G-sharp!

gisis *(gĭs'ĭs)* The *German* word for G-double sharp!

gis moll *(gĭs mōl)* The *German* term for *G-sharp minor!*

gitana *(jē tä'nä)* from the Italian: A *Spanish dance!*

giubilante *(jē ōō bĭl ăn'tĕ)*
giubilazione *(jē ōō bĭl ătsē ō' nĕ)*
giubilio *(jē ōō bĭl ē'ō)*
giubilo *(jē ōō'bĭl ō)* It./A direction to play jubilantly, in a rejoicing manner!

giustamente *(jē ōō stă mĕn'tĕ)* / **giustezza, con** *(jē ōō stĕts'ă, kôn)* It. / "Exactly" . . . with precision as to *tempo!*

giusto *(jē ōō'stō)* from the Italian: Correct, strict or proper! *Tempo giusto,* strict time. . . . *allegro giusto,* moderately fast!

glass harmonica. An invention of Benjamin Franklin in 1761 which mechanized the use of *musical glasses* to sound different pitches when rubbed by hand! Franklin's contribution was to design a series of tuned glass bowls rotating around a lateral axle which received its spinning power from a foot treadle!

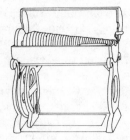

glass harmonica

glee *(glē)* An English song for three or more unaccompanied male voices, usually brief and with simple chords!

glee club. In modern times, an organized *club* or *group* devoted to *choral music* (usually associated with schools or colleges)!

glide *(glīd)* A *slur* or *slide* from one tone to another *(portamento)!*

gliss *(glĭs)* An abbreviation for *glissando!*

glissando *(glĭs än'dō)* "Slurred", "gliding", also *portamento!* On *bowed instruments, glissando* calls for flow and movement without *accents!* On *keyboards, glissando* is achieved by sliding the thumb, or any other finger, across the *keys!*

glocke *(glŏk'ĕ)* The German word for *bell!*

glockenspiel *(glŏk'ĕn spēl')* (1) A *percussion instrument* comprised of a set of metal bars tuned to a *chromatic scale* and struck with one or two *hammers.* The *range* usually is *two and one half octaves* from *G''* to the *C* two *octaves* above *high C.* To stay in the *staff,* the music for *glockenspiel* is written two *octaves* lower than its sound! A portable variation used in *marching bands* is also called the *bell lyre!* (2) A *percussion organ stop* with a *bell-like* sound! (3) A *carillon!*

glockenspiel

Gloria *(glō'rĭ ȧ)* The *"greater doxology".* .... the *"Angelic hymn"* sung or recited in a *Mass* following the *Kyrie!*

glottis *(glŏt'ĭs)* The space between the *vocal cord* and the *larynx* which expands and contracts to form *voice modulations!*

G-moll *(gā mōl)* The *German* term for *G-minor!*

G-major. The *major key* or *scale* with a *signature* of one *sharp!*

G-minor. The *minor key* or *scale* (relative to the *key* of *B-flat major*) with a *signature* of two *flats!*

golpe *(gŏlp)* Tapping the *guitar-soundboard* with the ring finger of the right hand! The notation marking is ⊕ !

G-sharp minor. The *minor key* or *scale* (relative to *B-major*) with a *signature* of five *sharps!*

gondellied *(gŏn'dĕl lēd)* Ger. / **gondoliera** *(gŏn dō lē â'rȧ)* It. / Song of the gondoliers, a *barcarolle!*

gong *(gŏng)* A large, circular, bronze plate which is struck with a *mallet* to produce a long-resounding sound of indefinite *pitch!* Also known as *tam-tam!*

Gong

gonzo *(gŏn'zō)* An *American* colloquialism for small, independent *"rock"* record companies *("labels")* whose "cult interest" or limited capital place them in an *"underground"* status! *"Gonzo"* labels are considered more adventurous sources for the exposure of new and unknown *"rock"* talents and concepts!

gopak *(gō'pȧk)* A *Ukranian peasant dance* in brisk *2/4 meter!* Also known as *hopak!*

gospel music. Protestant *church hymns* which are frequently *syncopated* in modern church ceremonies, largely due to the influence of American blacks who were probably first to add *rhythm* to *religious music!*

gothic *(gŏth'ĭk)* An architectural term used to describe music of the late Middle Ages (1000-1500)!

G.P. The abbreviation for *generalpause!*

grace note *(grās nōt)* Any *embellishing note* which is not basic to the *harmony* or *melody* of a *composition!* An *ornamental* note usually written small-size (see *trill, turn, appoggiatura, mordent, acciaccatura,* etc.)! A *grace note* is played just before the *beat,* and *accents* the *following main note;* hence the *grace note* has no distinct *time value* of its own in a given *bar* of music. It "steals" its *time* from the *note* before or after!

gradatamente *(grȧ dȧ tȧ mĕn'tĕ).* from the Italian: Proceeding gradually in *degrees!*

gradation *(grȧ dā'shŭn)* A *series* of *chords* that are *diatonically sequenced!*

gradevole *(grȧ dā'vō lĕ)* / **gradevolmente** *(grȧ dȧ vōl mĕn'tĕ)* It. / A direction to play in a pleasant, agreeable, easy manner!

grado *(grä'dō)* from the Italian: One *degree* or *step* of a *scale!*

gradual *(grăd'ū ăl)* (1) In the Roman Catholic Mass, the *antiphon* sung after the *Epistle* but before the *Gospel!* (2) A book of the *choral chants* sung during the *Mass!*

Gramophone *(grăm'ō fŏn)* A trademarked name for a *phonograph* or "talking machine"!

gran *(grän)* / **grand'** *(gränd)* / **grande** *(gröndĕ)* It. / Great, grand, big, full!

gran cassa *(grän căssȧ)* from the Italian: The *bass drum* (also *gran tambuco*)!

grand-barré *(grän bä'rā)* from the French: A *guitar* term for the *player* to "*stop*" all of the *guitar strings* (or at least three) with one finger of the left hand.

grand détaché *(gränd dā tă shä')* from the French: A direction for a *violinist* to "*bow*" the instrument with long, up and down strokes (a *bow-long* stroke to each note). ... see *detache!*

grandezza, con *(grän dĕt'să, kôn)* / **grandiosità, con** *(grän dē ō sē tä')* / **grandioso** *(grän dē ō'sō)* It. / A direction to play in a stately, lofty or grand manner!

grand opera. Currently used to describe full, elaborate *operas* as distinguished from *operettas, musical comedies* or *plays!* In former times, *grand opera* referred to *serious opera* which was completely *scored* and used no spoken dialogue!

grand orgue *(grän dôrg')* from the French: (1) "*Great organ*", "*full organ*"! (2) A *pipe organ!*

grand piano. A wing-shaped *piano* with *strings* and *soundboard* in a horizontal plane parallel to the floor! A *grand piano* can range from the smaller *baby grand* to the largest *concert grand* which exceeds nine feet in length (see *Piano*)!

gran tamburro. See *gran cassa!*

grave *(grä'vĕ)* from the Italian: (1) A direction to play in a solemn, slow, stately manner! (2) Low-pitched, serious sound!

gravemente *(grä vĕ mĕn'tĕ)* / **gravita** *(grä vē tä')* It. / Gravely, slowly, stately!

grazia *(grä 'tsē ă)* / **graziosamente** *(grä tsē ō să mĕn 'tĕ)* / **grazioso** *(grä tsē ō 'sō)* It. / Gracefully, with elegance!

great octave. The *octave* that begins on *C* (two *ledger lines* below the *bass clef staff*) and ascends to the "*small octave*", thus encompassing *C* through *B* on the *bass clef staff!*

great organ. The chief *keyboard* of a *pipe organ* including all the loud or full-sounding *stops!* On a *pipe organ* with more than two "*manuals*" (*keyboard rows*), the "*great organ*" is always the second row from the bottom!

gregorian chant *(grĕ gō'rĭ ăn chant)* The *cantus firmus* or ritual *plain chant* (a style of *choral music*, almost like *unison*, that is sung in Roman Catholic services. The *chant*, and its eight medieval musical *modes*, probably owes its original form to the editing and arranging of Pope Gregory (590-604) but it was enormously expanded after he expired. The *Gregorian chant* normally features *one melody* vocalized by a *choir* or *soloist* (without *accompaniment, rhythm* or *time values*) in a *droning unison* that matches *meters* to the *chanted* words!

grob-gedacht *(grōb gĕ däkt')* from the German: A large, *full-toned diapason organ stop!*

groove *(grōōv)* (1) The circular "*track*" or "*rut*" cut into a phonograph recording, in which the needle "*rides*", thereby translating sound back through the *tone-arm* and on to the *amplifier* and *speakers!* (2) A popular American slang expression for "smooth" or "agreeable" performance, sound or composition! "*In the groove*", "*groovy*" are expressions of critical approval by popular music fans!

gross-gedacht *(grōs gĕ däkt')* from the German: A 16-foot, *double diapason organ stop!*

grosse caisse *(grōs käs)* from the French: The *bass drum!*

grosse trommel *(grō'sĕ trô'mĕl)* The *German* term for the *bass drum!*

grosso *(grō'sō)* from the Italian: Full, grand, great!

grottesco *(grō tĕs'kō)* from the Italian: "Grotesque"!

ground bass. A *basso ostinato!* A *bass phrase* which is constantly repeated while the other parts of an *arrangement* (the *higher voicings*) vary *contrapuntally!* Featured in a *chaconne, passacaglia*, etc!

ground note. The *root* or *fundamental* note of a *chord!*

group *(grōōp)* (1) A brief series of rapid notes usually notated with a *tie* joining the *stems!* (2) A *section* of an *orchestra* embracing one family of *instruments;* e.g. the *woodwinds*, the *strings*, etc.!

gruppeto *(grōō pĕ'tō)* / **gruppo** *(grōōp'pō)* It. / (1) A *turn!* (2) A group of *grace notes!*

G schlüssel *(gä shlüs'l)* The German term for the *G-clef* or *treble clef!*

G-sharp. The *note G#* which is *one half-tone above G!*

G-sharp minor. The *minor key* or *scale* (relative to *B-major*) with a *signature* of *five sharps!*

G string. A string tuned to *G*, the *lowest string* on the *violin!* On the *viola* and *cello*, it is the *second string* above the *lowest string!* On the *double bass*, it is the *highest string!*

guaracha *(gwă ră'chă)* An old, lively *Spanish dance!*

guerrièro *(gwĕ rē ā'rō)* from the Italian: Warlike, martial!

guida *(gwē dä)* / **guide** *(gwē dĕ)* It. / (1) The *subject* of a *fugue* or a *canon's antecedent!* (2) A *direct* sign ∿ or ∿! (3) A *sign* designating the entrances into a *round* or *canon!*

guitar *(gĭ tär')*. In the contemporary, popular music world, probably the fastest-growing *instrument* in terms of popularity! A *stringed instrument* (related to the *lute*) with a long, narrow *neck* and six *strings* (usually three *strings* are wound with silken wire, and three with gut or nylon)! The *guitar's compass* is *three octaves*, running up from *E* in the *great octave to the second A* above the *staff!* The strings are tuned to *E, A, D, G, B, E'* but the music is written one *octave* higher than the sound. The basic unamplified, *nylon-string, acoustic guitar* (also known as the *Spanish guitar* or *classical guitar*) has been electronically adapted for use in *blues, jazz, rock* and other forms of modern music. At least nine separate *guitar variations* are in popular use: *Nylon string acoustic; steel string acoustic; steel guitar, electric; F-hole acoustic (auto-harp); hollow-body electric; solid-body electric; semi-hollow electric* and *12-string acoustic!*

The nomenclature for various *guitar models* in *popular music* includes:

(1) *"Bottleneck guitar"*... a *standard acoustic guitar* with *steel strings* on which the player *slides* a *metal plectrum* or a *plectrum* made from the *neck of a glass bottle*, etc.!

(2) *"Dobro guitar"* ... Named after the *American*, Dopyera brothers, who invented the model! An *acoustic guitar* with *steel strings* stretched high over a *fretboard* with *metal resonator* beneath! The *Dobro* is played by *sliding* a *metal plectrum* along the *strings!*

(3) *"Steel guitar"* ... An *electric, solid-body guitar* with *steel strings* stretched over a *"slab of wood"* on which *electrical "pick-ups"* are *located!* A *metal plectrum slides* over the *strings!* Early versions (in *country music*) were known as *"Hawaiian* guitars": Currently, still popular with country music players!

(4) "Slide guitar" ... A general term for any *guitar* (*acoustic* or *electric*) that uses a *plectrum sliding* on *steel strings* to produce *pitched sounds!*

(5) *"Pedal steel guitar"* ... A variation of the *"steel guitar"* (usually with *added strings*) that uses *pedals* and *knee levers* to change the *tuning* of the *strings* in performance! Also *played* by *sliding* a *plectrum* across the *strings!* See *Illustration* for identification of all of the components of a basic *guitar!*

guitar fiddle. The *vielle!*

gu qin *(gōo chēn)* The new, romanized name and spelling for *Ch'in* or *Chyn*, the ancient *Chinese zither*, still popular in the People's Republic of China! (see *Ch'in*)!

gusla *(gōos lä)* / **gusle** *(gōos lĕ)* / A Serbo-Croatian name for a simple, *one-stringed, bowed instrument* with a bowl-shaped *body* and a long *neck!* Used in *Yugoslavia* and the *Balkans* ... a similar *Russian instrument* is called *gusli!*

gusto *(gōo'stō)* / **gustoso** *(gōo stō' sō)* It. / A direction to play with taste and artistic expression!

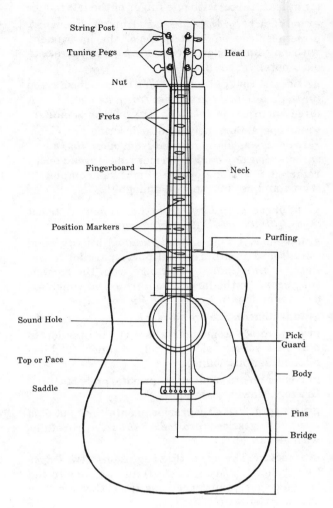

The Guitar!
(Basic Acoustic)

String Post
Tuning Pegs
Head
Nut
Frets
Fingerboard
Neck
Position Markers
Purfling
Sound Hole
Pick Guard
Top or Face
Body
Saddle
Pins
Bridge

DICTIONARY

H

— H —

H. (1) The *German* letter for the note *B-natural* (B♮), or the *key of B-natural!* (2) The *heel* in *organ* music! (3) In orchestral *scores*, the abbreviation for *horn!*

habanera *(hä bä nä' rä)* A *Cuban dance* (probably imported from Africa) named for the city of *Havana!* The music has a distinctive *syncopation* in *2/4 time* and became extremely popular in 19th-century Spain when it inspired the renowned *Habanera* from Bizet's opera *Carmen.* Bizet's version was adapted from an earlier melody!

Habanera
Rhythms

halb *(hälb)* The *German* word for "half"!

half-cadence. An alternate term for *imperfect cadence* (see *Cadence*), when the *dominant chord* or *subdominant* is preceded by the *common tonic!*

half-note. The *note* ♩ which is *one-half the time-value* of a *whole note!* In Britain, the *half-note* is known as a *minim!*

half-rest. A *rest* ▬ indicating a *silent pause* equal in time value to a *half-note!*

half-step. The smallest *interval* of *pitch* in contemporary music . . . sounded by any *two adjacent keys* on *keyboards!* (The same as *half-tone, semitone* or *minor second*)!

hallelujah *(hăl'ĕ lōō' yä)* from the Hebrew: "Praise Jehovah", adapted to "*Praise ye, the Lord*", a song of *thanksgiving!*

Hallelujah Chorus. The famous *chorus* composed by Handel which repeats the word "*Hallelujah*"!

halling *(hä' ling)* A *Norweigan dance* in bright *2/4 time* frequently *accompanied* by an indigenous *folk instrument* called the *hardanger fiddle!*

"hammer-on" *(hăm'ĕr ŏn)* In *guitar* playing, the rapid depression of a *string* with the finger or hand (after the *string* has been picked) to raise the *pitch* of the *tone!* The *guitar notation* is "H"!

hand horn. A *hunting horn* (see *French horn*)!

Hand Horn

hardanger fiddle *(här'däng'r).* An indigeous Norwegian instrument which resembles a violin but uses sympathetic strings (4 or 5) stretched under four melody strings! Bowing of the melody strings produces drone-like sound vibrations from the sympathetic strings in accompaniment to the melody notes!

hardingfele *(hôr'dĭng fä lĕ)* The *Norwegian name* for the *hardanger fiddle!*

Hardanger
Fiddle

harmonic *(här mŏn'ĭk)* (1) Generally related to any pleasing sounds in concord! (2) Specifically relating to *harmony* as distinguished from *melody* or *rhythm!* (3) An *overtone (upper partial tone)* produced, for example, by a *secondary vibration* at a frequency rate which is the precise multiple of an initial *generator* or *fundamental* vibration rate. (4) A *flute-like* tone *(flageolet tone)* produced on *stringed instruments* by light touching of a *vibrating string* at given *nodal points!* The points of contact determine the *pitch!* Light contact at *center-string* produces a note one *octave* above normal (the *second harmonic* or *first overtone* (see *harmonic series*)! Similar contact at one-third of the length of the *string* sounds a *note* an octave and a *fifth* above normal (the *second overtone*)! The sign for *harmonic* "touching" is a (°) set over the *note,* or a *diamond shape* given to the *note* itself ◇.

harmonica *(här mŏn'ĭ kä)* (1) A small *wind instrument* (also called *mouth organ*) played by moving a narrow metal box, housing a series of square holes, across the mouth and tongue tip! The player's airstream (inhale/exhale) vibrates one of a pair of *reeds* behind each hole; each *reed-pair* normally is *pitched* to *adjacent notes!*

A more sophisticated *harmonica* (the *chromatic harmonica*) includes another set of *reeds,* manipulated by a *slide,* that is pitched a *half-tone* higher than the first set, accommodating the full *chromatic scale!* The *compass* of the many models of *harmonica* that are marketed usually starts about *middle C* and *ranges upward* depending on the size of the given model.

harmonic analysis. The study of chords and harmonies and their relationship to each other. See "THE ELEMENTS OF MUSIC", HARMONIC ANALYSIS for details!

harmonic minor scale. A *minor scale* in which the *seventh tone* is raised by *one half-step!*

harmonic series. The entire *series* of *partial tones* starting with the *prime* or *fundamental tone* and progressing to the *overtones* which run an *octave* above the *fundamental,* a *fifth* above that, a *fourth* still higher, a *major third* higher, a *minor third* higher and so on! With *C* as the *fundamental,* the *harmonic series* would run:

C	c	g	c'	e'	g'	b '	c'',	etc.
1	2	3	4	5	6	7	8,	etc.

harmonic triad. The *major triad* or the *common chord!* A *triad* with a *major third* above the *root!*

harmonium *(här mō'nĭ ŭm)* A small, *organ-type instrument* which uses the *harmonica* principle of an airstream blown across a set of *reeds* causing them to vibrate! The *harmonium*, however, adds one or two *keyboards* to govern *reed* selection *(tone)!* The air-pressure is supplied by *pedals* which manipulate a *pair of bellows!* Also known as the *reed organ!*

Harmonium

harmony. (1) The study of *musical consonance* or agreeable sounds! (2) The structuring of *simultaneous tones* into *chords* or *triads!* The *dominant triad* has the *fifth tone* of the *major* or *minor scale* as its *root tone* (the *main note* in the *bass*)! See *Chords, Intervals,* etc. In *vocal music,* the number of *voice parts* dictates *two-part harmony, three-part harmony,* etc. (3) *Chromatic harmony* utilizes the *chromatic scale* and *chromatic modulations!* (4) *Close harmony* deals with the structuring of *three vocal parts* (in a *four-part* arrangement) within the *compass* of one *octave!* (5) *Open, spread, extended* or *dispersed harmony* refers to the placement of one or more *vocal parts* in *four-part harmony,* so that a *one-octave transposition* would result in the *part(s) falling between two others!* The original *three upper voices,* therefore, must have a total *range* exceeding *one octave!* (6) *Compound harmony* doubles two or more essential *chord tones!* (7) *Plain harmony* uses only essential *tones; figured harmony* includes variations such as *passing tones, suspensions,* etc. (8) *Diatonic harmony* employs only the *tones* of a *diatonic scale; Chromatic harmony* involves the use of many *sharps, flats, naturals,* etc.! (9) *Essential harmony* deals with *fundamental triads* without *embellishments!* (10) *False harmony* refers to *discords* produced by wrong notes or inaccurate performance! (11) *Pure harmony* deals with pure *pitch* as employed by an *a cappella chorus* or a *string quartet* where no accompanying *intonation* tempers the *produced tone!* (12) *Classical harmony* lays down rules prescribing a *tonic* or a *tonic center,* with each *chord* strictly positioned to the *tonic* of a given *key!* The basic *interval* is the *third,* two of which make up a *triad!* Each *chord* receives varying *harmonic* application in various *keys* following the rules of *modulation.* In *contemporary music,* many of the rules of *classical harmony* have been ignored or by-passed by the liberal use of *dissonance, key combinations, atonal scales* and other devices of *modern composition.*

harp *(härp)* A *stringed instrument* set in an open, triangular frame with a tapered, large, hollow back (the *soundboard*), an upright *pillar* and a curved *neck* on top connecting the *pillar* to the *back,* which at the bottom rests on a *pedestal! Plucked* by the fingers are *46 strings,* tuned diatonically in the *key* of *C-flat major!* The *harp* has a *compass* of 6½ *octaves with seven strings for each octave.* At the *foot* of the *harp* there are seven *pedals* which can be depressed in two stages or notches *(double action harp)* to produce either a *half-tone* or *full tone* above the *tuned string sound!* Special *harp* effects are achieved by rapid sliding of the finger(s) across the *strings (glissando)* or by a light touch at the center of a *string* which produces a *tone* one *octave* higher than the original!

harpsichord *(härp'sĭ kôrd)* A *keyboard, stringed* instrument (dating from the 16th century) shaped like a *grand piano* but with *strings* that are *plucked* by a *quill* or *leather plectrum* attached to a *felted, wooden jack* at the end of each *key.* When the *key* is depressed, the *jack* lifts up and the *string* is *plucked* by the *plectrum!* When the *key* is released, the *jack* returns to its *"down"* position, *"dampening"* the *string* so that it no longer resounds! Historical versions of the *harpsichord* used *hand-operated stops* to alter the volume of sound; modern *harpsichords* use *pedals* exclusively to change *stops!* The older *harpsichord* versions used *two keyboards,* with a combined *5-octave compass* running from *F below low C to F above high C!*

Harpsichord

haupt *(houpt)* The *German* word for "Head" or "principal"!

hauptsatz *(-sätz)* from the German: The principal *theme, movement* or *motive* of a *composition!*

hauptwerk *(-värk)* The *German* word for the *great organ* or for the *main work* or *manual* of an *organ!*

hautbois *(ōbwa)* The *French* word for *oboe* or *hautboy!*

H-dur *(hä dōo'r)* The *German* term for the *key* of *B-major!*

head *(hĕd)* (1) The point of a *violin bow!* (2) In the *lute*, or *violin*, the combined *scroll* and *peg box!* (3) In the *drum*, *tambourine*, etc., the membrane stretched over the end(s) of the *instrument!* (4) In music notation, the oval portion of a *note* without its *stem!* (5) In popular or jazz music vernacular, an improvisation ... *made up in the head* ... "a head arrangement" ... used to describe an *extemporaneous*, *ensemble performance* without any written *arrangement* or previously-rehearsed concept, except perhaps for a simple *melody line!*

head tones. The higher tones of the *vocal register!*

head voice. The highest *register* of the *voice!* In male voices, the *falsetto!*

heckelphone *(hĕk'lfōn')* A *wood-wind* of the *double-reed* family invented by Wilhelm Heckel about 1904 in Germany! With almost the same *compass* as the *baritone oboe (3 octaves from B below middle C to the second G above middle C*, the *heckelphone* produces a much louder, *cello-like tone* than the *oboe!*

Heckelphone

heftig *(hĕf'tĭkh)* / **heftigkeit** *(kīt)* Ger. / A direction to play in an impetuous, vehement manner!

heimlich *(hīm'lĭk)* from the German: A direction to play in a mysterious, furtive manner *(misterioso)!*

heiter *(hī'tēr)* from the German: A direction to play cheerfully or with serenity *(gioioso)!*

helicon *(hĕl'ĭ kŏn)* An extra-large *bass tuba* (used in *military* and *marching bands*) with a circular shape to facilitate carrying around the body or on the shoulders while marching! Somewhat similar to the *sousaphone*, the *helicon* comes in an *E-flat* or F *(bass size)* or a *C* or *B-flat (double-bass size)!* The *double bass* version also is called the *double B-flat bass!*

Helicon

hell *(hĕl)* from the German: A direction to play in a clear, bright manner!

hemidemisemiquaver *(hĕm'ē dĕm'ē sĕm'ē kwā'vēr)*

A *sixty-fourth* note ... ♬ ... a *British* term almost obsolete in modern *American* usage!

hemiola *(hĕm'ī ō lä)* / **hemiolia** *(hem'ī ō lē ä)* / (1) From the age of *medieval music*, the substitution of a *triplet (three notes)* in place of *two notes*, in alternate *bars*, resulting in a *series of measures* with successive 6/8, 3/4, or 6/4, 3/2 *meters*, or a *Bach shift* from 3/4 to 3/2! (2) A *perfect fifth interval!*

hervogehoben *(hār fōr'gĕ hō'bēn)* from the German: A direction to emphasize, or to play with emphasis!

herrotretend *(hār fōr'trā tĕnt)* from the German: (1) A direction to play in a prominent or distinctive manner! (2) An indication that a particular *part* should be prominently heard during *ensemble performance!*

herzig *(hār'tsĭk)* / **herzlich** *(hārts'lĭkh)* Ger. / Tenderly, heartfelt!

heterophony *(hĕt'ĕrōfō nē)* Variations of the same melody in simultaneously-sounded, separate *voice parts!* A common device in *Oriental music!*

hexachord *(hĕk'sä kôrd)* (1) The *six diatonic tones* used in *solmization: do* (or *ut*), *re, mi, fa, sol, la* ... which are equivalent of the white keys *(C to A)* in a *piano octave!* Historically, these are credited to Guido d'Arezzo in the 11th century! (2) A *major sixth!* (3) A *six-string musical instrument!*

hi fi *(hī fī)* A colloquial abbreviation for *high fidelity!*

hidden fifths or **octaves.** *(hĭd'n) Consecutive fifths* or *octaves (resultant)* which are implied but not sounded when two *progressions* move together towards an *open fifth* or *octave!* Although forbidden in *strict harmony*, these are acceptable in other musical forms!

high fidelity *(hī fĭd ĕl'ĭ tē)* The precursor of the newer term "*stereo*," this expression was a recording-industry coinage popularly used to describe "superior", recorded sound. First designated as a label for better-grade or stereo-sound components such as amplifiers, turntables and speakers and the records produced for same .... and publicly used in phrases such as "*hi fi sound*" or "*hi fi equipment*".... the expression and its broad connotations are gradually being replaced by the term *stereo* (short for *stereophonic*)!

hi hat. See *Cymbals!*

hillbilly *(hĭl bĭl ē)* A colloquial term for *American country music*, or its performers or performances ... particularly of Tennessee and Kentucky origin!

hip *(hĭp)* In popular and jazz music vernacular, a slang term for a *performance* or *composition* whose professional quality reflects knowledgeable modern or advanced style and technique .... as opposed to *trite* or *clichéd music* which is deemed "*corny*" or "*square*"!

his *(hĭs)* The *German* word for the note *B-sharp!*

H moll *(hä mōl)* The *German* term for the *key of B-minor!*

hoboe *(hō bō'e)* The *German* word for *oboe!*

hochzeitlied *(hōks'tsīt lēd)* from the German: *A wedding song!*

hocket *(hŏk ĕt)* A *medieval music* device in which a hiccup-like *(hocket) voice* interrupts another *voice part* in *spasmodic intervals!*

hohlflöte *(hōl'flô'te)* from the German: An eight-foot or four-foot *organ stop* with a *wood-flute* quality!

hold *(hōld)* The *fermata* or *pause* indicated by the sign ⌢ over or ⌣ under a note which directs the prolongation of the *time value!* Used over a *bar* of music, it calls for a slight *pause* or *breath* before going on to the next *bar!*

holding note. A *note* that is *sustained* in *one part* while the *other parts continue their motion!*

holzblasinstrument *(hôlts'bläs'ĭn strōō mĕnt)* The German term for a *woodwind instrument!*

homophony *(hō mŏ'fŏ nē)* Music in which *one dominating melody part* is *accompanied* by *other parts* consisting primarily of *chords!* The opposite of *polyphony* which uses *multi-melody parts!*

hook *(hook)* The *stroke (flag, pennant,* etc.) attached to the *stems* of notes. . . . the *eighth note* ♪ *(one hook),* the *16th note* ♫ *(two hooks),* etc. ♩

hora, horah *(hō'rä)* An ancient *Israeli folk dance* or *folk song* still popular at modern Israeli and American-Jewish ceremonies!

horn *(hôrn)* (1) In modern music, an all-embracing term for *brass wind instruments* (See *cornet, trumpet, trombone, English horn,* etc.)! (2) A specific reference to the *French horn!*

horn band. A *group* of *trumpeters!*

horn band, Russian. A *group* that plays *single-toned, hunting horns!*

hornpipe *(hôrn'pīp)* (1) A lively old *dance* in *3/2* or *4/4 time,* popular with sailors! (2) An old *Welsh instrument* consisting of a *wooden pipe* (with *holes* and a *single reed*) ending in a *bell* that was made frequently of animal horn!

house band. A *popular music* colloquialism for a musical *band* or *group* that regularly works for one establishment (cabaret, theater, TV show, etc.), as opposed to a visiting or travelling *band* or *group* that plays only limited-period engagements.

humoresque *(hū mĕr ĕsk')* A humorous, light or capricious *composition* used frequently as a title by 19th century *classical composers!*

hurdy-gurdy *(hûr'dī gûr'dī)* (1) An old *stringed instrument* that used a hand-cranked, rosined wheel to rub across the *strings!* The sounds produced were varied in pitch by rod-connected *keys* which operated to "stop" the *strings!* The *hurdy-gurdy* is also called the *symphonia, simphonie, lyra* or *vielle à roue,* etc.! (2) The name "hurdy-gurdy" is also used for an unrelated "steet organ" which is rare today but sometimes used at carnivals or by street peddlers!

Hurdy Gurdy

hurtig *(hōōr'tĭkh)* from the German: A direction to play hurriedly in headlong fashion *(allegro)!*

hydraulic organ / **hydraulos** *(hī'drô lōs)* / An ancient, Greek *keyboard-organ* that used water power to send wind-pressure through a series of *pipes* that produced *pitched sounds!*

hymn *(hĭm)* Any song or ode in praise or adoration of God!

hypo *(hī'pō)* In the *church-mode, plagal* system, the prefix denoting a *mode* that starts a *fourth below its tonic; hypoaeolian* starts on *E; hypodorian* starts on *A; hypoionian* starts on *G; hypolidian* starts on *C; hypomixolydian* starts on *D* and *hypophrygian* starts on *B* (see *Mode*)!

DICTIONARY

I

— I —

I *(ē).* In Italian, the masculine plural for "the"!

iambic *(ī ăm'bĭk)* / **iambus** *(ī ăm bŭs)* / *A musical, metrical foot of one short, unaccented note,* and *one long accented note ...*   !

ictus *(ĭk'tŭs)* An *accent* or *separation* sign used in *Gregorian chant* to stress an important *note!*

idée fixe *(ēdā'fĕks')* from the French: "Fixed idea!"; a recurring *theme* in a *symphonic work!* The term was first used by Berlioz to describe his *Symphonie fantastique!*

idiophone *(ĭd'ē ō fōn)* A classification for all percussion instruments consisting of any elastic material that produces sound when struck (gong, xylophone, triangle, castanets, cymbal, etc.)!

idyl *(ī'dĭl)* Eng. / **idillio** *(ĭ dĭl'ē ō)* It. / **idylle** *(ē dĭl')* Fr. / **idylle** *(ē dĭl'lĕ)* Ger. / A *pastoral* or *romantic piece of music!*

il *(ēl)* In Italian, the masculine singular for "the"!

il piu *(ēl pĕ ōō)* The *Italian* term for "the most"!

im *(ēm)* The *German* word for "in the"!

imitando *(ē mē tän'dō)* from the Italian: Imítating!

imitation *(ĭm ĭ tā'shŭn)* The repetition in *one part of music (consequent)* of a *theme, phrase* or *motive* from *another part (antecedent)! Free imitation* allows changes in the *consequent! Strict imitation* or *canonic imitation* calls for identical *notes* and *intervals* in *antecedent* and *consequent!* Variations of *free imitation* include *augmentation, diminuition, retrograde, inversion,* etc.!

immer *(ĭm'ēr)* from the German: Always, continuously!

impaziente *(ĭm pă tsē ĕn'tĕ)* / **impazientemente** *(ĭm pă tsē ĕn'tĕmĕnte)* It. / A direction to play in an impatient, hurried manner!

imperfect cadence. See *Cadence!*

imperioso *(ĭm pĕ rē ō'sō)* from the Italian: Imperious, lofty, pompous!

impeto *(ĭm'pē tō)* / **impetuosamente** *(ĭm pĕ tōō ō să mĕn'tĕ)* / **impetuosità** *(ĭm pĕ tōō ō sē tă')* / **impetuoso** *(ĭm pĕ tōō ō'sō)* It. / A direction to play with an impetuous, vehement or eager attack!

imponente *(ĭm po nĕn'tĕ)* from the Italian: Imposing, lofty, impressive!

impresario *(ĭm prĕ sä' rē ō)* from the Italian: The manager or producer (sometimes designating the *conductor* of an *orchestra*) of an *opera* or *concert company!*

impressionism *(ĭm prĕsh'ŭn ĭz'm)* Borrowed from the 19th century, French-painting movement of Renoir, Monet and others, the term was applied to music with highly descriptive impressions created by new, rich *harmonies* and *scales!* A feeling of formless, emotional mood was intended to be evoked! Debussy, Ravel, Delius, de Falla, Respighi, etc., were considered *impressionists* in the world of music!

impromptu *(ĭm prŏmp'tū)* (1) A *piece of music composed* or *played extemporaneously!* (2) A loosely-structured, musical form with extempore development; a *Fantasia!*

improvisation *(ĭm prŏ vĭ zā'shŭn)* The act of *extemporizing music (vocal or instrumental)* while it is being played or performed; hence, impromptu!

incalzando *(ĭn kăl tsăn'dō)* from the Italian: "To pursue hotly"; a direction to play with growing vehemence and rapidity!

incidental *(ĭn sĭ dĕn' tăl)* A *grace note* or *tone* not related to a *chord!*

incidental music. *Music* composed for *performance* during a play or other dramatic presentation but without which the play could still be presented! Ironically, *incidental music* often has emerged as *classic masterpieces* which are played long after the original *dramas* have been forgotten!

inciso *(ĭn chē'sō)* from the Italian: "Incisive"; a direction to play in a hesitant, irresolute manner!

inconsonant *(ĭn kŏn'sō nănt)* Not agreeable, discordant!

indeciso *(ĭn dĕ chē'sō)* from the Italian: "Indecisive"; a direction to play in a hesitant, irresolute manner!

indifferente *(ĭn dĭf fĕ rĕn'tĕ)* / **indifferentemente** *(- mĕn'tĕ)* / **indifferenza, con** *(ĭn dĭ fĕ rĕn'tsă, kon')* It. / A direction to play indifferently, or in a careless manner!

infino *(ĭn fē'nō)* from the Italian: "As far as", "until reaching a given point", "up to"!

inflection *(ĭn flĕk'shŭn)* A change or *modulation* in the *pitch* or *tone* of the voice!

innig *(ĭn'ĭkh)* from the German: A direction to play with deep feeling, sincerely!

innocente *(ĭn nō chĕn'tĕ)* / **innocentemente** *(ĭn nō chĕn tĕ mĕn'tĕ)* / **innocenza, con** *(ĭn nō chĕn'tsă, kôn)* It. / A direction to play innocently, in an artless or unaffected fashion!

inquieto *(ĭn kwē ē'tō)* from the Italian: Restless, agitated!

insensibile *(ĭn sĕn sē'bĭ lĕ)* It. / **insensibilemente** *(ĭn sĕn sē bĭ lĕ mĕn'tĕ)* It. / Imperceptible, or little by little in small degrees!

insistendo *(ĭn sē stĕn'dō)* / **instante** *(ĭn stăn'tĕ)* / **instantemente** *(ĭn stăn tĕ mĕn'tĕ)* It./ **inständig** *(in shtĕn'dĭkh)* Ger. / Urgent, pressing!

INSTRUMENT *(ĭn'strōō mĕnt).* (*See individual instruments by name: piano, organ, guitar, violin,* etc.) Any object or contrivance which produces musical sounds! The families of *instruments* are generally classified according to the manner in which the originating sound is produced or vibrated! The main categories consist of:

WESTERN MUSIC
(European/American)

A. *Stringed Instruments*
1. *Bowed* as with the *violin, viola, cello, contrabass,* etc.!
2. *Plucked* as with the *guitar,* ukulele, banjo, harp, mandolin, zither, etc.!

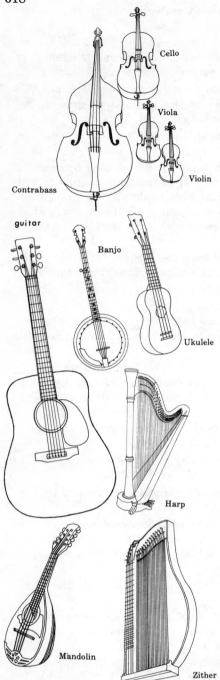

Cello

Viola

Violin

Contrabass

guitar

Banjo

Ukulele

Harp

Mandolin

Zither

Bass Clarinet

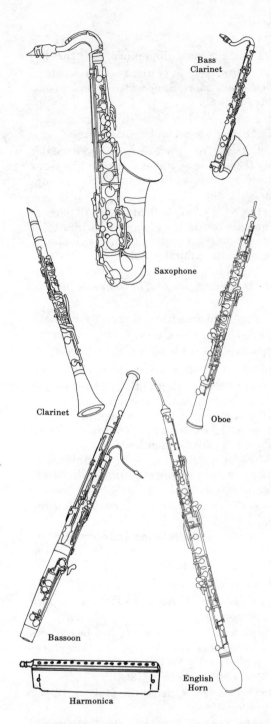

Saxophone

Clarinet

Oboe

Bassoon

English Horn

Harmonica

B. *Wind Instruments*
   1. *Woodwinds.* . . . where a column of air is vibrated by a *single* or *double reed*, as with a *saxophone, bass clarinet, clarinet, oboe, bassoon, English horn, harmonica*, etc.!

   2. *Woodwinds.* . . . where no *reed* is used as with *flute, piccolo, recorder, fife*, etc.!

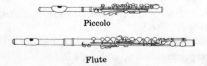

Piccolo

Flute

3. *Brass wind instruments* . . . . where the player's own lips substitute for any reed, as with *trumpet, cornet, trombone, French horn, tuba, bugle*, etc!

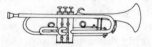

Trumpet

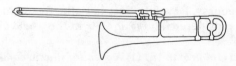

Trombone

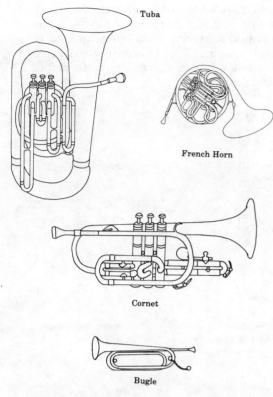

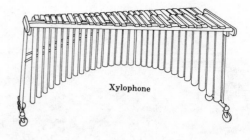

Xylophone

b. *Fixed-pitch percussion* as with *snare* and *bass drums, cymbals, triangle, tambourine, castanets, gong, maracas, etc!*

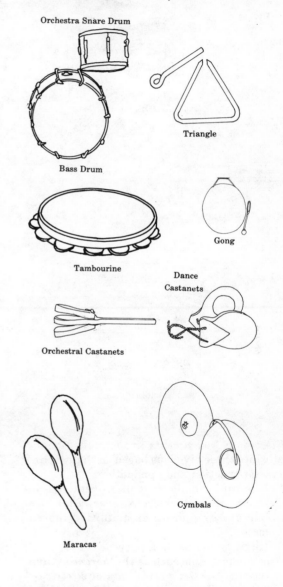

C. *Percussion Instruments* are classified in two categories according to whether the *struck instruments* can or can not be *tuned to different pitches!*

    a. *Variable-pitch percussion* as with *xylophone, timpani, glockenspiel, chimes, celesta (see keyboard) etc!*

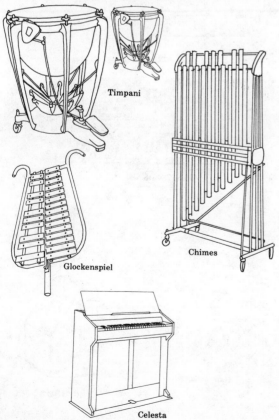

D. *Keyboard Instruments,* whose properties may fall under A, B or C categories above, but which also utilize a *fingerboard* (the *keyboard*) to initiate sound-producing action!

    1. *Piano, clavichord,* etc. uses strings that are *struck!*

    2. *Harpsichord* uses strings that are *plucked!*

    3. *Organ* uses *pipes* with or without *reeds!*

    4. Celesta uses metal bars that are *struck!*

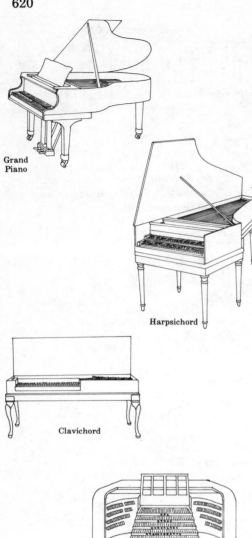

Grand Piano

Harpsichord

Clavichord

Organ

and popularity with working musicians, and are closing the gaps between the manual-dexterity techniques applied to *electronic oscillators* as contrasted to conventional *keyboard* or *guitar* performance and composition!

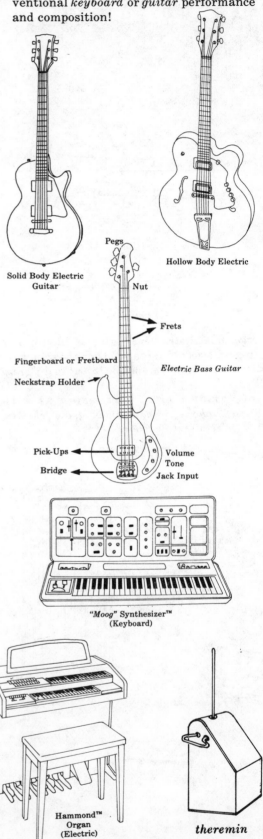

Solid Body Electric Guitar

Hollow Body Electric

Pegs

Nut

Frets

Fingerboard or Fretboard

Neckstrap Holder

Electric Bass Guitar

Pick-Ups

Bridge

Volume
Tone
Jack Input

"Moog" Synthesizer™ (Keyboard)

Hammond™ Organ (Electric)

theremin

E. *Electronic Instruments* are classified generally into three divisions based on their technical construction and application!

1. *Electronic adaptations* of conventional instruments such as *electric bass guitar, electric guitar* and other amplified instruments!

2. Instruments using a pure *electronic oscillation* principle such as the *theremin*, thantonium, the *electronic organ* or *electric organ*, the *Hammond organ*, the *novachord*, the *ondes Martenot*, etc.

3. Computer-technology *"Synthesizers"* which produce "original" sounds similar to conventional instruments but with the capability of extending the compass to unconventional extremes! Trademarked *synthesizers* such as the *Moog, Minimoog, Arp*, etc. are gaining rapidly in versatility

Another system of classifying instruments —
especially useful for the inclusion of non-Western
sources — includes the following:

CHORDOPHONES: All stretched-string instruments!

AEROPHONES: All wind instruments (vibrating
or moving column of air)!

IDIOPHONES: All percussion instruments of
any elastic material that makes a sound when
struck!

MEMBRANOPHONES: All stretched-skin or
stretched-parchment instruments (drums,
etc.)!

ELECTROPHONES: All instruments whose vibrations are produced electronically!

CHORDOPHONES

CHINA	JAPAN	INDIA	(JAVA/BALI) INDONESIA	PERSIA/IRAN	KOREA	AFRICA	GREECE(G) TURKEY (T) ARABIA (A) EGYPT (E)
gu quin	koto	vinà	tjelempung	setar	kayagum	valiha	kithara (G)
or	biwa	sitar	rebab	tar	komungo		'ud (A)
chin	shamisen	sarangi		santour	a-jaeng		qānūn (A)
or	kokyū	sarod		kamanche	yanggum		rabāb (A)
chyn	sō	dilruba		chank	haequm		
		esraj					
		tambura					
		shannai					

AEROPHONES

sheng	shō			nay	piri	bompate	aulos (G)
	shamisen				taegun	endere	hydraulos (G)
	wŏteki				t'aepyong so	imanza	
	hichiriki				tanso	bullroarer	
	shakuhachi						
	fue						

IDIOPHONES

cheng	dōbyōshi	j'al tarang	gambang		ching	adawuraa	duff (A)
pyiba	suzu		gamelan		pak	nnawuta	sistrum (E)
	bin-zasara		kemanak		p'yon kyong	kende	
	suri zasara		gender pending bwa		p'yon-jong	slit drum	
			malimba			lukumbi	
			limba				
			sanza				
			saron demung				
			saron barung				
			saron panerus				
			bonang				
			gender panemburg				
			gender barung				
			gender panerus				
			gongageng				
			kenong				
			kempul				
			ketuk				
			kempyang				

MEMBRANOPHONES

	taiko	mridanga	kendang–	tombak	janggo	earth drum	darbukka (A)
	kakko	tablas	gending			ndunger	
	shōko	khol	ketipung			ngoma	
		dholaka	batangan			dúndún	
			bedug			igbin	
						ganda	
						bompili	
						mantshomene	

intenzionato *(ĭn tĕn tsē ō nă'tō)* **intenzione, con** *(ĭn tĕn tsē ō ' nē, kôn)* It. / A direction to play with emphasis or stress!

interlude *(ĭn'tĕr lūd)* (1) A short *instrumental* piece played between portions of a *song* or *hymn*, or between the acts of a play or other dramatic presentation, or the segments of church service! (2) Sometimes, used to describe an *intermezzo* or *entr'acte!*

intermezzo *(ĭn tĕr mĕd'zō)* (1) A short *playlet with music (piano* solo or *orchestral)* that was performed between the acts of *serious opera* or *drama!* By the 17th century, most *intermezzi* were used only as comic or humorous reliefs. (2) A *movement* in a *symphonic work!* (3) *Incidental music* composed for modern drama! (4) A "catch-all" title for brief, *instrumental* diversions which may or may not have a humorous quality!

interruzione, sensa *(ĭn'tĕr rōō tsī ō nĕ, sĕn tsă)* from the Italian: A direction to play without interruption!

INTERVAL *(ĭn'tĕr vǎl)* The *distance* or *difference* in *pitch*, between two *tones!*

The smallest *interval* is a *half-tone!* A *whole tone* consists of two *half-tones!*

All *intervals* are measured by the number of *half-tones* or *whole tones* contained between the *lowest* and *highest tones* of the *interval.*

All *intervals* are:

MELODIC, when two *tones* are sounded in succession!

HARMONIC, when two *tones* are sounded simultaneously!

A *chord* consists of two or more *harmonic intervals! Harmony* refers to the succession of *intervals* and *chords* in a musical passage!

Intervals also describe the *degrees* of the *major* and *minor modes* of a *diatonic scale.* Each *mode* simply defines a given combination of *whole tones* and *half tones!* (see *Mode)!*

Intervals describe the "distance" of the *tones* they contain regardless of where the *pitch* begins:

In the *C Major scale*, for example, the *first note C* is called *prime* or *unison* when played with another note!

The *intervals* between *C* and the other notes in the *C Major* scale are called:

second . . . . . . C-D
third . . . . C-E (C,D,E)
fourth . . . . . . C-F (C,D,E,F)
fifth . . . . C-G (C,D,E,F,G)
sixth . . . . . . C-A(C,D,E,F,G,A)
seventh . . . . . C-B(C,D,E,F,G,A,B)
octave . . . . . . C-C'(C,D,E,F,G,A,B,C')

The *third, sixth* and *seventh intervals* are one *half-tone* smaller in a *minor scale!* The *second* interval consists of two *half-tones (major scale)* and one *half-tone (minor scale)!*

Major and *minor intervals* are:

major second..C-D minor second C-Db
major third ...C-E minor third C-Eb

major sixth ...C-A minor sixth C-Ab
major seventh .C-B minor seventh C-Bb

Perfect intervals remain the same in any *key!* The *unison, fourth,fifth* and *octave intervals* are called *perfect intervals!*

Perfect intervals can be *Augmented* or *Diminished (enlarged* or *condensed) by* one *half-tone!*

Enlarging any *major interval* by one *half-tone*, we arrive at *Augmented Second, Augmented Third, Augmented Fourth, Augmented Fifth* and *Augmented Sixth intervals!*

Conversely, when we condense *minor intervals* by one *half-tone*, we arrive at *Diminished Third, Diminished Fourth, Diminished Fifth* and *Diminished seventh intervals!*

All of these *intervals* involve a pair of notes, one higher (above), one lower (below)! A *lower interval* means the second note of the *interval* is pitched lower than the first!

Consonant intervals are those considered pleasing and harmonious!

Dissonant intervals are those which sound harsh and require *resolution!*

Chromatic intervals include all *augmented* or *diminished intervals* except for the *augmented fourth, diminished fifth* and *diminished seventh!*

Compound intervals are those that span more than one *octave!*

Diatonic intervals include all *tone pairs* in the same *key* except for an *augmented second* or an *augmented fifth* in the *harmonic minor scale!*

Inverted intervals are those which raise the lower tone, or lower the higher tone, by one *octave!*

INTERVALS, ENHARMONIC. *Intervals* which are almost identical in pitch on *keyboard instruments* but which are considered *different intervals* in *different keys!* These *enharmonic intervals* sound different from each other when played on *non-keyboard instruments!*

On the *piano*, for example, the *Augmented Fourth (C-F#)* is identical to the *Diminished Fifth (C-Gb)!* The *Diminished Seventh (C#-Bb)* is identical on the *piano* to the *Major Sixth (C#-A#)!*

Other *enharmonic intervals* include:

Augmented Unison = Minor Second
Major Second = Diminished Third
Augmented Second = Minor Third
Major Third = Diminished Fourth
Augmented Fifth = Minor Sixth
Augmented Sixth = Minor Seventh

intimissimo *(ĭn tē mĭs'ē mō)* from the Italian: Very warm and tender!

intimo *(ĭn'tē mō)* from the Italian: A direction to play with deep, heartfelt expression!

intonation *(ĭn'tō nā'shŭn)* (1) The accurate production or performance of a *pitched tone (vocal* or *instrumental)* . . . "in tune"! (2) The beginning *psalm-tones* of *Gregorian chant!* (3) The vocal technique used in *"Plain-chant"!*

intrada *(ĭn trä'dȧ)* from the Italian: A brief *intro-duction* or *prelude!*

intrepidamente *(ĭn trĕ pĕ dä mĕn'tĕ)* / **intrepidezza** *(ĭn trĕ pĕ dĕ'tsa)* It. / "Intrepid", bold!

introduction *(ĭn'trō dŭk'shŭn)* A short *phrase* or *movement* which prepares the way for the *main body* of a *composition!*

introit *(ĭn trō'ĭt)* (1) In the Roman Catholic *Mass,* the first part of the *Proper* which is sung or chanted as the priest approaches the altar! (2) In the Anglican church, a *psalm* or *hymn* played or sung at the beginning of *Communion!*

invention *(ĭn vĕn'shŭn)* A short piece using *free counterpoint!* Stemming from the baroque period (1600-1750), *invention* was an old title particularly identified with Bach's *keyboard-compositions!*

INVERSION. The general term for the act of *trans-posing* a note of an *interval* or *chord* so that the lowest note becomes the upper note!

Any *interval* can be *inverted* by raising the lower note up one *octave,* or by dropping the higher note down one *octave!*

The sum of two *inverted intervals* is always *nine!* Together, the *intervals* form an *octave!*

By *inversion:*

A *fifth* turns into a *fourth!*
A *second* turns into a seventh!
A *third* turns into a *sixth!*
A *fourth* turns into a *fifth!*

By *inversion:*

The *perfect intervals (unison, fourth, fifth* and *octave)* are still *perfect* but....

a. An *inverted major interval* becomes a *minor interval!*
b. An *inverted minor interval* becomes a *major interval!*
c. An *augmented interval* becomes a *di-minished interval!*
d. A *diminished interval* becomes an *aug-mented interval!*

To *invert* a *chord,* one moves up the *chord's root note* (the lowest note) one *octave!* When only the *root* is moved, the *chord* is in its *first inversion!*

for example: The *triad chorc C-E-G* becomes *E-G-C* in the *first inversion!*

First inversion triads also are known as *sixth chords* or *six-three chords* since the higher notes are a *sixth and a third* above the *bass!*

The *first inversion* of a *triad* with a *flatted supertonic* is called a *Neapolitan sixth.* In the *C major key,* the *flatted supertonic* is *D-flat*...the *triad* is *D –F-A* and the *first inversion* is *F-A –D ,*

When the first note above the *root* also moves up an *octave,* the *chord* is in its *second inversion!*

for example: The triad *C-E-G* becomes *G-C-E* in the *second inversion!*

Second inversion triads also are called *six-four chords* since the higher notes are a *sixth* and a *fourth* above the *bass!*

There are only *two possible inversions* of a *triad chord,* but a *seventh chord* (made up of *four notes*) takes *three inversions!*

for example: *C-E-G-B* in its *first inversion* becomes *E-G-B –C.* This is known as a *six-five chord* since the higher notes are a *sixth* and a *fifth* above the *bass!*

C-E-G-B in its *second inversion* becomes *G-B –C-E,* known as a *four-three chord!*

C-E-G-B in its *third inversion* becomes *E –C-E-G,* known as a *four-two chord!*

Inversion of Counterpoint *(invertible counterpoint* or *double counterpoint)!*

When musical parts are moved, so that the *treble* and *bass* are interchanged, this is known as *coun-terpoint inversion!* The parts are most often moved up or down a complete *octave,* but occasionally a different interval *(fifth, tenth, twelfth)* may be employed!

Inversion of melody *(contrary motion)* means changing the *direction* of each *interval!*

When the *melody* goes up a *third,* the *inversion* goes down a *third!*

When the *melody* goes down a *half-tone (minor second),* the *inversion* goes up a *half-tone!*

In *traditional tonal music,* melody inversions need not correspond exactly opposite to the number of *half-tones* in each *interval! Melody in-versions* (to remain *tonal)* are based on the *scale degrees* of the *given key,* rather than on the pre-cise size of the *intervals!*

Inversion of melody is often employed in *fugues* and various *sonata* movements! *Inversion of melody* in a *second voice* part (prior to the comple-tion of the *melody* by the *first voice)* is known as *canon by inversion* or *canon by contrary motion!*

Ionian mode *(ī ō nĭ ȧn mōd)* (1) Another name for the *Greek hypophrygian mode,* one of the *subordinate* species of *diatonic octave scales* in which the *con-junct fourth* and *fifth* appear in *inverted order!* (2) One of the *authentic church modes* beginning on *C!*

ira *(ē rȧ)* / **irato** *(ē rȧ'tō)* It. / Passionately, angrily!

Irish harp. A variation on the *concert harp,* with about 30 to 50 *brass strings* usually pitched in the *key of G!* Without *pedals,* triangular, and only three-feet high, the *Irish harp* is used in traditional *Hibernian* folk music!

irlandais *(ēr lăn dä')* / **irlandaise** / The French terms for *Irish* or *Hibernian!*

ironia *(ē rō nē'ȧ)* / **ironicamente** *(ē rō nē cȧ mĕn'tĕ)* / **ironico** *(ē rō'nē kō)* It. / "Ironically"!

irresoluto *(ēr rĕ sŏ lōō'tō)* from the Italian: A direc-tion to play in a wavering, hesitant manner!

isorhythm *(ī'sō rĭth'm)* A *rhythm pattern* that re-peats throughout portions of a *melody* but with dif-ferent values (usually shorter)! It was first used in the 14th century as a *variation* for the composition of *motets!*

istesso tempo *(ē stĕs'sŏ tĕm'pō)* from the Italian: "The same *tempo*"; a direction to remain in the *same* *tempo* despite any change in the *time signature!* Also used to indicate the resumption of an earlier portion of music whose *tempo* was interrupted!

Italian overture. The Italian musical form that serves as an *introduction* to *dramatic, complete works!* Contrasted to the *French overture* form with its two sections, slow and fast, the *Italian overture* which is also known as *sinfonia* consists of three *sections*, fast, slow and fast again!

Italian sixth. A *sixth chord* with an *augmented sixth* and a *major third* above the *bass*. . . . A♭-C-F#, for example!

ite, missa est(*ē'tä mĭs'sä ĕst*) from the Latin: "*Go, ye are dismissed*", the last words of the *Mass!*

DICTIONARY

J, K

— J —

jack (*jăk*) (1) The *quill* or *hard-leather bit* that *strikes* or *plucks* the *strings* of the *harpsichord* or *chavichord!* (2) The *"hopper"* or *escapement lever* used in the *piano* to *strike the strings!*

jadghorn (*yät'hôrn*) from the German: *Hunting horn!*

jagdstück (*yät'shtük*) from the German: *Hunting piece!*

jägerchor (*yă'gĕr kôr'*) from the German: *Hunters' chorus!*

jaleo (*hä lā'ō*) from the Spanish: A lively, *solo Spanish dance* featuring *castanets* and allowing for frequent *improvisations!*

jam session. Any *impromptu performance* by a *group of musicians* (usually *jazz-oriented*) or a group of *folk performers!*

Janizary music (*jăn'ĭ zĕr'ĭ*) Also known as *Turkish music* (from the *military, Turkish Janizary* infantry), the term is used to describe shrill, crude and noisy *band music* in which *drums, triangles, cymbals,* etc. predominate!

Jankò keyboard (*yäng'kō*) A *piano keyboard* invented in 1882 by Paul von Janko! With *six rows* of *keys,* it could sound any *tone* on every other *row;* thus, shortening the *octave span!* It also allowed for the *identical fingering* of *chords* and *scales* in all *keys* and facilitated the playing of *chromatic scales.* Despite its "convenience" advantages, the *keyboard* never received any popular acceptance!

jarábe (*hä rä'bā*) from the Spanish: (1) A *Spanish dance!* (2) A *jarábe gatuno* ... a modern *Mexican dance* in which a couple are costumed as male cavalier and female peasant!

JAZZ (*jăz*). The outstanding, if not the only, indigenous American music! Jazz has risen from primitive African roots and early ethnic denigration to the level of concerts in the White House and tributes to the art-form from the American president and his entire cabinet.

Black America's place in jazz was never seriously doubted, although only in recent years has the improved rigor of international research removed most of the stereotypes and historical inaccuracies. Various jazz critics and scholars ... Willis Conover, John Mehegan, Leonard Feather, Rudi Blesh, Marshall Stearns, Nat Hentoff, Norman Connors, Don Heckman, Arnold Shaw, Dave Dexter, et al., and mentors such as John Hammond, George Wien, Norman Granz, Creed Taylor, Bob Thiele, etc. ... have helped to widen the jazz lens and sharpen its focus on the black musician's role. For whatever reason—God-given talent, a scientifically-doubtful genetic advantage or selective reaction to social pressures—the black facility with *microtones* ("ear" for *syncopation*) and free harmonic expression are now recognized as basic elements that makes "all that jazz" possible.

Jazz traces its American chronological develop-ment back to the slave trade of the early 17th century, and to the "plantation" cultures of the Southern states, where a melange of French, English, German, Irish and Spanish settlers forcibly imported African blacks to work the fields.

From the 17th to 19th centuries, primitive instruments (earth drums, single-string "bass fiddles", jugs and bottles, washboards, kazoos, etc.) gradually merged with the European piano, banjo, guitar, cornet, clarinet and multi-sized drum sets. The music, itself, represented the cross-breeding of African, *antiphonal* tribal-chanting with the Western *diatonic-scale* harmonics common to the music of the American colonial settlers.

The black ear, accustomed to *quarter-tones* and probably bemused by the Western *third, fifth* and *seventh tones,* sent its own signals to black fingers which picked through the social fabrics of slave, sea, railroad, levee, work-gang, field and harvest, sacred and profane songs to create a new tonal quality called "blues". Linking *quarter-tone* beats with the more traditional *half-tones* or *whole-tones,* and speeding up the melodic line (with *eighths* and *sixteenths*) the folk blues standardized a *12-bar* structure, broken into three *sections* of four *bars* each. The simple I-IV-V *chord harmony* of the gospel church echoed in the "blues" *harmony;* the first section used the *tonic chord* behind a *melody;* the second section brought forth the *subdominant* with a *cadence* in the *tonic,* and the third section a *dominant close* on the *tonic.* A vocal blues, traditionally, was sung in 4/4 with the accompaniment in 12/8. A piano, cornet and trombone trio, for example, would improvise the open-end of a *four-bar phrase,* since the lyrics usually did not extend through the full *measure.* This improvisation became known as a *"riff".* The singers used a singular word-rhythm that anticipated the actual *beats* or *afterbeats* with *flatted thirds* and *sevenths, slurs* and *portandos* while the accompanists added *sevenths* to the *chords.*

The question of exactly how "jazz" derives may still be moot — some scholars insist on separating ragtime and minstrel roots from the folk blues, and no one yet can verify the specific origin of the word "jazz"—but the order of evolvement: folk blues, gospel, stomps, minstrel, cakewalk, ragtime, one-steps, boogie-woogie and stride piano, rhythm and blues and "race" records and finally "jazz" seems abundantly clear.

Actually, according to musical theatre authority Lehman Engel, the earliest popular minstrel shows dated back to 1828 when Thomas Dartmouth Rice sang *Jim Crow* and *Clare de Kitchen,* and to 1848 when the First Virginia Minstrels were led by Daniel Emmett (composer of *Dixie*) and the Christy Minstrels performed Stephen Foster compositions. But these were all by white men in black-face using burnt cork! It was not until 1898 that an all-black cast presented *Clorindy (The Origin Of The Cakewalk)* on New York's Broadway.

The earliest, significant jazz-shaping scene, however, surely must be laid in New Orleans, circa 1880, where the basic jazz-ensemble format was drawn. This consisted of two cornets, a clarinet, a trombone, tuba and drums (presumably borrowed from the French marching-band model)! In later years, a first and second alto saxophone was added to produce the "big jazz band sound" as was a trumpet and trombone to create the *five brass, five reed* *swing* orchestra.

Playing in sporting houses and bars, at funerals, weddings and the perennial Mardi Gras, legendary "jazz names" emerged, particularly from the bawdy "Storyville" area of New Orleans. These included the Zenith Brass Band, Buddy Bolden's Ragtime Band, The Olympic Band, The Eagle Band, Bunk Johnson's Original Superior Band, The Original Dixieland Jazz Band, Joe "King" Oliver and the Creole Jazz Band, Ferdinand "Jelly Roll" Morton, Sidney Bechet, Edward "Kid" Ory and Louis Armstrong.

Concomitantly, ragtime piano (including New Orleans' Buddy Bolden) was flourishing in the St. Louis area where Louis Chauvin, Tom Turpin and Scott Joplin gathered fame. Joplin, the "giant" of ragtime, published his Maple Leaf Rag in Sedalia, Missouri, becoming the first ragtime composer to put his musical thoughts into notation and "print". Ragtime differed from the blues in *bar-structure* (conventional *8, 16 or 32 measure* sections were utilized) and called for a more formal, consistent *syncopation* with harmonies in strict *duple meter*. Joplin's notation was exact (no improvisation) and showed technical familiarity with a *military march* or *classical scherzo*. "Jelly Roll" Morton's style was *"jazzier"*, with *sixths* in the left hand mixing with a trombone-like counterpoint.

From 1910 to 1920, blacks began a mass migration to Chicago, New York and other urban centers, seeking better job opportunities and drawing along with them the bulk of the "jazz players". This trend accelerated, particularly, when "Storyville" was closed down by the authorities in 1917.

The Chicago hegira, circa 1920-1930, lit the "hot jazz" cauldron! Joe "King" Oliver and the Creole Jazz Band introduced trumpeter/cornetist Louis Armstrong, clarinetists Leon "Barney" Bigard and Jimmy Noone, trombonist Edward "Kid" Ory, drummer "Baby" Dodds and other legendary figures. Solo improvisation soared in free flight as ensemble disciplines loosened! A host of white adherents and emulators rallied around! Joining the white New Orleans emigres (the Original Dixieland Band, and pioneers George Brunis and Leon Rappolo) were new forces such as Bix Beiderbecke, Benny Goodman, Eddie Condon, Jack Teagarden, Frank Teschemacher, Pee Wee Russell, Gene Krupa and others. In the same period, the vocal blues of Big Bill Broonzy, the folk blues of Huddie (Leadbelly) Ledbetter, the rural-rooted pianistics of Tampa Red and Leroy Carr, the guitar-picking of Lonnie Johnson and Big Maceo, and towards the end of the decade, the boogie-woogie piano stylists

such as Pinetop Smith, Meade Lux Lewis, Albert Ammons and Pete Johnson (with their eight-to-the-bar *ostinatos* and right-hand *riffing*) lent their assets to the black jazz bank.

In New York, the "jazz, blues and rag" scene from 1920 to 1930 was no less dynamic, when seen in retrospect. Fletcher Henderson innovated "big band" jazz by writing for (and forming) his own orchestra, which turned on hordes of "flapper dancers" (parallel contributions also were introduced by Chick Webb and Ella Fitzgerald). Duke Ellington raised the "jazz orchestra" to levels of virtuosity that broke down all barriers with respect to jazz as an art form. It was also the era of "race records", female blues singers such as Mamie Smith, Bessie Smith, Ma Rainey; Bertha Hill; etc.) rag-piano (Eubie Blake, Charles "Lucky" Roberts, James P. Johnson followed by jazz-piano stylists (Willie The Lion Smith, Thomas "Fats" Waller, Art Tatum and others) male blues singers (Jimmy Rushing, Joe Turner, Jimmy Witherspoon, etc.) and the "hot little bands" of Eddie Condon, Bud Freeman and Louis Armstrong (the latter in Chicago and New York). Jazz or blues prevailed from Harlem on down to the mid-town cabarets, clubs and dance-halls.

In 1924, Paul Whiteman became the "white" exponent of "symphonic jazz", forming a large orchestra that led to the debut of George Gershwin's rhapsodic works. From this time forward, the philosophical dilemna—can jazz, an improvisational form, be called jazz when it is formally notated and orchestrated—led to the ultimate cleavage between so called *swing, name* or *symphonic* bands and the oncoming progressive jazz movements. The *swing* and *name* band leaders from 1935 to 1950 (the Benny Goodmans, Glen Millers, Count Basies, Tommy Dorseys, Woody Hermans) embraced and advanced much "jazz flavor," but new purist voices began to come forth. The electric guitar emerged with exponent Charlie Christian advancing new ideas and techniques. Disdaining the commercial boundaries of the formalized bands, an avant group ... Charlie Parker and Lester Young on saxophone, Dizzy Gillespie on trumpet, Jimmy Blanton on double-bass, Jo Jones on drums brought the *progressive jazz and bop revolution* into view and vogue.

Charlie Parker, the "Bird," expressed the growing boredom with stereotyped chord changes as follows: "I found that by using the higher intervals of a chord as a melody line and backing them with appropriately related changes, I could play the thing I'd hear. I came alive". Trumpeters Miles Dewey Davis and Dizzy Gillespie, along with Parker, instigated the "bop" or "bebop" revolution with their emphasis on dissonant, dazzingly intricate short-phrased rhythm patterns and harmonies behind a solo, improvisational flow replete with crisp, almost stuttered *attacks* and *changes*. This *bop* or *cool* jazz (as distinguished from the *hot* little bands of predecessors) in its beginning period often used vocalized nonsense syllables in performance, which probably explains the origin of the term "bop" or "bebop".

With the progressive jazz movement came a serious-art quest that borrowed (and repaid) post-impressionist advancements from Stravinsky, Hindemith, Schonberg and other classicists of the 20th Century. Thirty-second and sixty-fourth notes became common to small-group polyphonies, which replaced conventional "big band" quarter notes and octave chords. An intellectualized "concert jazz" set the direction for departures in the '50's and '60's that embraced modern 12-tone or serial music (*third-stream* jazz).

In New York, during the '50's and '60's, key figures building on the initial "bop" framework included John Lewis, Oscar Peterson, and Horace Silver on piano, Stan Getz, Lee Konitz, Serge Chaloff on saxophone, the omnipresent Miles Davis on trumpet, J. J. Johnson on trombone, Art Blakey on drums, and Charlie Mingus and Oscar Pettiford on bass. These are summed up by jazz scholar John Mehegan as "*Hard* Groups..." the biting rhythmic character of the *rear line* (bass, piano, drums) supporting equally incisive trumpet or saxophone soloists comprising the *front line* and exemplified by the Miles Davis Quintet, Horace Silver Quintet, Art Blaky's Jazz Messengers and the Max Roach-Clifford Brown Quintet... "*Chamber* groups, such as the Modern Jazz Quartet, Lennie Tristano Quintet and the Red Norvo trio, which explored new areas of counterpoint and harmony along modern classical lines ... and the Experimental Groups: Charlie Mingus, John Coltrane, Cecil Taylor, Bob Prince, William Russo, Ornette Coleman who plumbed new dimensions of free form, atonality and modal extension."

On the West Coast, in the same time period, the late Stan Kenton and Gerry Mulligan created a "white" modernized "big band" jazz sound, with Mulligan foregoing orthodox writing for sections, applying open *fourths* and *fifths* rather than *thirds* to his charting. This same technique was further exploited by Miles Davis (a literal "giant of jazz" through all of its chronological history and variation) and others. Dave Brubeck and Paul Desmond advanced a more formalized "white" exposition, with stress on intricate counterpoint.

In the late '60's and through the '70's, modern jazz has moved along esoteric concert lines, divorced almost completely from popular, rock or "soul" music except for the latest jazz-tinged stylings of pop-rock groups such as Earth Wind And Fire, The Crusaders and others of high popularity. The "synthesizer" has made its mark on jazz performance and is skillfully employed by a Herbie Hancock, Chick Corea and other modern pianists. Long-time veterans enjoy new jazz-prominence as their work is recognized.... Dexter Gordon, Woody Shaw, Larry Coryell, for example. Indian music forms (Ravi Shankar inspired), Brazilian and other Latin chromatics, and Near East intricacies of the non-diatonic scale are interpolated frequently by young jazz performers and composers. The sacred field has attracted and encouraged many new-jazz exponents, following the example set by Duke Ellington in the '60's, when he began composing jazz concertos for church services.

jeté (*zhē tā'*) from the French: "Thrown"; a direction to *violin players* to *bow* on the *strings* so that the *down-bow stroke* bounces a few times! Also known as *ricochet!*

jeu (*zhû*) from the French: The style of performance! (2) An *organ stop!* (3) *Grand jeu* or *plein jeu* ... *full-organ, full-power; demi jeu ... half-organ, half-power!*

Jew's harp. A small, rigid, metal *instrument* with a *lyre shape* and a thin, vibrating *metal tongue!* It is played by placing the frame between the teeth and striking the metal tongue with a finger. The *pitch* is varied by the mouth-position while the *intensity* is governed by the force of breath!

jig (*jĭg*) (1) A lively *dance* in *triple time!* The *Irish jig* is commonly known and practiced! (2) See *Gigue!*

jingling johnny. See *Turkish crescent!*

jodel (*yō'd'l*) The German word for *yodel!* See *yodel!*

jongleur (*zhôn'glûr*) An itinerant *minstrel* in medieval times who *doubled* as an acrobat or juggler!

jota (*ho'ta*) from the Spanish: A Spanish dance of the northern peasantry, usually executed in *triple time* by couples, with the female partner playing *castanets* at the same time.

just intonation. "True pitch"! The precise, *mathematically-exact pitch* based on the *measured frequency of vibration!* This is the opposite of *tempered intonation* which makes adjustments that are more suitable for practical modulation in music. See *Temperament!*

The C scale in "Just" terms with ratio of intervals

	c	d	e	f	g	a	b	c'
c = 1	1	9/8	5/4	4/3	3/2	5/3	1⅞	2
c = 24	24	27	30	32	36	40	45	48

9/8 10/9 16/15 9/8 10/9 9/8 16/15

— K —

K. or K.V. The abbreviation for "Köchel" or "Köchel-Verzeichnis"! The first complete chronological catalog of Mozart's compositions was undertaken by Ludwig von Köchel (1800-1877). Each "K" or "KV" number is important in identifying specific Mozart pieces! (In German, "Verzeichnis" itself is translated as "catalogue number").

kammer (*käm'ĕr*) from the German: "chamber"! *Kammermusik ... chamber music!*

kantele (*kän'tā lā*) The national instrument of Finland! A *harp* or *psaltery* with five strings in older models, but with many more strings in modern versions.

kanteletar (*kän'tā lā tär*) Old *Finnish folk songs!*

kanun *(kä'nōōn)* from the Arabic: An *Egyptian psaltery!* See *Qanun!*

kapelle *(kä pĕl'ĕ)* from the German: Literally "chapel"; (1) A name given to the *choir* or *ensemble* which was attached to the *chapel* of a royal prince in the 17th and 18th centuries! (2) In modern usage, any *orchestra* or *musical group!*

kapellmeister *(kä pĕl'mīs tēr)* from the German: An *orchestra conductor* or *choirmaster!*

kastagnetten *(käs tä'nyĕt'n)* The *German* word for *castanets!*

kazoo *(kȧ zōō')* A toy *wind-instrument* consisting of a short metal *tube* with a membrane at each end! The player hums into the *tube* to produce a rude, nasal tone which actually is a modification of his own voice. It is also known as *mirliton* or *eunuch flute!*

keck *(kĕk)* / **kecheit** *(kĕk'hīt)* Ger. / Bold, confident!

Kent bugle *(kĕnt)* Another name for the *key bugle!* (See *key bugle!*)

keraulophon *(kĕ rô'lō fōn)* An eight-foot *organ stop* with a smooth, "reedy" sound!

kettledrum *(kĕt'l drŭm)* A hollow, hemispherically-shaped *drum* in a copper or metal casing over which a *parchment* "head" is stretched and clamped! The tension of the "head" can be adjusted by hand screws or by foot pedals which enables changing the *tuning* of the *drum* to various *pitches!* Usually played in *pairs* (*three* are used in *symphony orchestras*, however), the *kettledrums* in *orchestras* and *concert bands* are known as the *timpani* (frequently misspelled *tympani*) and are struck with *padded-head mallets.* Modern *kettledrums* can be *pitched* from the *second C below middle C* to the *second A above middle C!*

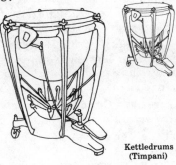

Kettledrums
(Timpani)

key *(kē)* (1) In *keyboard instruments*, one of the *levers* (depressed by the player's fingers) that actuates a device which *strikes* or *plucks a string*, producing a *pitched tone!* (2) In *woodwind instruments*, a *valve-lever* which is fingered by the player to open or close a *hole* (or *series of holes*) in the side of the *instrument!* A *closed key* normally is in the "shut" position and is opened by *finger action!* An *open key* normally is open, and closed by *fingering!* (3) A *scale, or series of tones*, progressing *diatonically* from the *keynote* (the *first note* or *tonic*) in *ordered degrees* of *whole tones* and *half-tones!* There are 12 *major* and 12 *minor keys* which are indicated at the beginning of any *composition* by the *key signature.* A *major key* has a *major third* and *sixth* in the *signature!* A *minor key* has a *minor third* and *sixth!* A *change of key* most often is achieved by *modulation* to a *common chord (pivot)* shared with another *key!*

Other definitions of *key* include:

Attendant keys. Scales with the sounds most common to a given *key ....*the *relative keys!* The *attendant keys* of *C-Major*, for example, are *A-Minor* (its *relative minor*); *G-major* (the *dominant*) and *E-minor* (the *dominant's relative minor*); *F-Major* (the *sub-dominant*) and *D-minor* (the *sub-dominant's relative minor*)!

Chromatic keys. Those with *sharps* or *flats* in the *key signature!*

Natural keys. Those with *no sharps* and *no flats* in the *key signature!*

Parallel keys. Major and *minor keys* with the same *keynote (tonic)*... *A-Major* is the *tonic major* of *A-minor*, and *A-minor* is the *tonic minor* of *A-major!*

Related keys. Major and *minor keys* that differ by only one *sharp* or *flat* in the *key signature* such as *C-Major* (no *sharps* or *flats*) and *E-minor* (one *sharp*)!

Relative keys. Major and *minor keys* with the same *key signature!* A *major key* is *relative* to the *minor key* whose *tonic* is a *minor third* below the *major!* Conversely, a *minor key* is *relative* to the *major key* whose *tonic* is a *minor third* above the *minor!* Examples: *C-Major* and *A-Minor*; *G-Major* and *E-minor*, etc! See *ELEMENTS OF MUSIC, Keys!*

keyboard *(kē'bôrd)* The row of *keys* on a *piano, organ, harpsichord, clavichord, accordion,* etc. which are activated by the player! The *standard piano keyboard* has 88 keys (seven *diatonic white keys* and 5 *chromatic black keys* in each *octave*) with a total span of seven and one-third *octaves!*

Middle C

A to b ← ←   → → d"to c'''''

Piano Keyboard

key bugle. The first *brass instrument* invented (Ireland, 1810) on which a full, *chromatic scale* could be sounded! Also known as the *Kent bugle* or *Kent horn*, the *key bugle* has been obsoleted by the *valved cornet!*

Key bugle

keynote *(kē'nōt)* The first note of a *key* or *scale (tonic)!*

key signature *(kē sĭg'nă tūr).* The *sharps* or *flats* placed at the beginning of every *composition....* immediately after the *Clef sign* at the *head* of the *staff....* which indicate the *key* of the *music* to follow!

The position of the *sharp* or *flat* in the *key signature....in* the given *space* or *on* the given *line* of the *staff...* indicates the *note* that is influenced regardless of *octave!*

The *key signature* does not distinguish between a *major* or *minor key* but the omission of a *key signature* means that the composition is written in *C-major* or *A-minor*, or that an *atonal* approach has been employed!

Key signatures usually are repeated at the head of each *staff* on a *score*, but *brief modulations* normally are indicated only by *sharp, flat,* or *natural signs....the accidentals...* which precede the notes to be influenced. A long-running *key change* often shows a new *key signature* following a *double-bar line!*

The Key Signatures

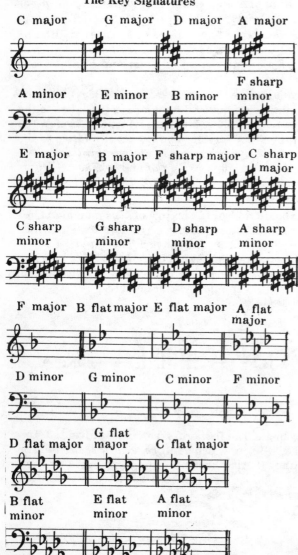

key stop. A *key* fastened to the *fingerboard* of a *violin* to control the "*stopping*" of the *strings!*

key tone. Same as *keynote!* The *tonic* or *first note* of a *scale* or *key!*

key trumpet. A *trumpet* equipped with *keys* which are operated to vary the *pitch!*

kill *(kĭl)* A colloquial expression used in popular music circles to "*stop*", "turn off" or "eliminate" the sound in a studio, hall or office...."*kill the gain*", in a recording studio, means to turn off the sound; "*kill the tape*" means to shut down the tape recorder and "*kill the rehearsal*" means to put an end to rehearsing!

kindlich *(kĭnt'lĭk)* from the German: Graceless, infantile!

kirchenmusik *(kĭr'kĕn mōō zĭk)* from the German: "*Church music*"!

kit *(kĭt)* A small, 16-inch *violin* once used by dancing masters!

kithara *(kĭth'ă rä)* An ancient *Greek instrument*, in the *lyre* class, consisting of a shallow, wooden box housing from five to eleven *strings* which were *plucked!* Also known as *cithara (sĭth'ă rä)!*

Kithara

klagend *(klä'g'nt)* from the German: A direction to play in a plaintive or mournful manner!

klang *(kläng)* from the German: A *fundamental tone* and its *harmonic overtones. Klangfarbe* (-färbĕ), "*tone color*"; *dreiklang* (drī-), a *triad chord!*

klangfarbenmelodie *(kläng' färb'n' mĕl' ō dē)* Arnold Schoenberg's 20th-century *German* expression for *melodies* with *wide, dissonant tone colors* that did not change *pitch!*

klappe *(kläp'pe)* from the German: The *key* or *valve* of any *wind instrument! Klappenhorn*, a *key bugle!*

klar *(klär)* from the German: A direction to play clearly and brightly!

klarinette *(klä rē nĕt'tĕ)* The *German* word for *clarinet!*

klavier *(klä vēr')* The *German* word for *piano* (also *clavier)!*

klavierauszug *(klä vēr'ous'tsōōk)* The *German* word for a *piano arrangement!*

klaviermässig *(–'mĕ'sĭk)* from the German: Styled, or suitable, for the *piano!*

klavierstück *(–'shtük)* The *German* word for a short *piano* piece or composition!

kleine Flöte *(klīn'e flō'te)* The *German* term for a *piccolo!*

kleine Trommel *(–trô'm'l)* The *German* term for *snare drum!*

kleingedackt *(klīn'gĕ dăkt)* The *German* word for a *flute organ stop!*

klesmor, klezmor *(klĕz'môr)* Yiddish music, or a Yiddish musician! Familiar to many Jewish immigrants of the Ellis Island era (early 20th century), the musical form is an amalgam of Hungarian, Rumanian, Slavic and Gypsy elements that penetrated the Jewish diaspora, and traces its beginnings back to the Rhine basin one thousand years ago. Mostly minor-key melodies are played by small groups in a "hora" like rhythm. The style is heard most often only at orthodox Jewish weddings or other ceremonies, although some attempts are being made to develop "klesmor" as a modern Jewish folk art.

knabenstimme *(knă'bĕn shtĭ' mĕ)* The *German* word for a boy's voice; *counter tenor!*

knarre *(knä'rĕ)* The *German* word for *rattle!*

knee stop. A *knee lever* under the *reed organ's manual! Three knee levers*: (1) Control the *wind supply!* (2) Open or close the *swell box!* (3) *Draw all the stops!*

kniegeige *(knē'gī gĕ)* The *German* word for *viola da gamba,* the "knee" violin!

kontrafagott *(kôn'trä fä gôt')* The *German* word for *double bassoon!*

konzert *(kôn tsärt')* The *German* word for (1) A *Concerto!* (2) A concert!

konzertmeister *(–'mī stĕr)* The *German* word for a *Concertmaster!*

konzertstück *(-'shtĭk)* The *German* word for a *concert piece* or a *short concerto!*

koto *(kô'tô)* A *Japanese* form of the *zither!*

kraft *(krăft)* / **kräftig** *(krĕf'tĭk)* Ger. / A direction to play with force and vigor *(con forza).*

krakowiak *(krä ō'vē äk)* A bright *Polish dance, in 2/4 time,* named after the city of Cracow (also *cracovienne)!*

kreuz *(kroyts)* The *German* word for a *sharp* (#)!

kujawiak *(kŭ yäv'ē äk)* A *Polish dance* resembling an *accelerated mazurka!*

kurz *(kōōrts)* from the German: Short, *detached, staccato!*

Kyrie eleison *(kĭr'ēä' ā'lä ēē sŭn)* from the Latin: "Lord have mercy upon us", the first movement in the *Mass!*

DICTIONARY

L

— L —

L. The abbreviation for "left" in *English*, and *linke*, *links* in *German*, meaning "left", and used in *l.h.*, "left hand"!

la *(lä)* In *solmization*, the *syllable* indicating the *sixth note* of the *scale*, *do, re, mi, fa, sol, la, ti*!

lacrymosa *(lăk rĭ mō'să)* from the Latin: One of the *stanzas* in the hymn *Dies Irae*, part of the *requiem Mass*!

lacrimoso *(lăk rē mō'sō)* from the Italian: A direction to play in a sad, tearful manner (also *lagrimoso*)!

lage *(lä'gĕ)* from the German: The "position" . . . of a *chord* or of the *hand*! *Enge lage*, closed position . . . . *weite lage*, open position!

lamentabile *(lä mĕn tä'bē lĕ)* / **lamentabilmente** *(lä mĕn tä bēl mĕn'tĕ)* / **lamentando** *(lä mĕn tăn'dō)* / **lamentazione** *(lä mĕn tä tsē ō'nĕ)* / **lamentevole** *(lä mĕn tĕ'vō lē)* / **lamentevolmente** *(lä mĕn tĕ vōl mĕn'tĕ)* / **lamento** *(lă mĕn'tō)* / **lamentoso** *(lă mĕn tō'sō)* It. / Plaintive, lamenting!

lancio, con *(län'chô, kôn)* from the Italian: A direction to play in a lively, energetic manner!

landler *(lĕnt'lēr)* from the German: An *Austrian country dance* in *3/4 or 3/8 time*, similar to the *Tyrolienne*!

langsam *(läng'zäm)* from the German: "Slow" . . . . similar to *adagio* or *lento* as a *tempo* indication . . . . *langsamer*, slower!

languendo *(lăn gwĕn'dŏ)* / **languente** *(lăn gwĕn'tĕ)* / **languidamente** *(lăn gwē dă mĕn'tĕ)* / **languido** *(lăn'gwē dō)* / **languore** *(lăn gô'rĕ)* It. / Languishing, plaintive!

largamente *(lär gä mĕn'tĕ)* / **largamento** *(lär gä mĕn'tō)* It. / A direction to play in a slow, broad, large manner without changing *tempo*!

largando *(lär gän'dō)* from the Italian: A direction to play more slowly and more loudly, often suggesting a *crescendo* (also *allargando*)!

larghetto *(lär gĕt'ō)* from the Italian: A direction to play at a *slow tempo* but faster than *largo* and slower than *andante*!

larghissimo *(lär gēs'sē mō)* from the Italian: A direction to play as slowly as possible!

largo *(lär'gō)* from the Italian: (1) A direction to play very slowly, and stately but broadly . . . *largo* is the *slowest tempo indication* of all *tempi signs*! (3) A *composition* in *largo tempo*!

larigot *(lär ĭ gŏt')* from the French: (1) A type of *flageolet* or *shepherd's pipe*! (2) An *organ stop* of one-and-one-third-foot *pitch*!

laud *(lôd)* / **lauda** *(lôd'ä)* / **laude** *(lô'dĕ)* L. / (1) A *hymn* in praise of the Lord! (2) A *song* in praise of any subject! (3) A form of *lute* or *cittern*!

laudamus te *(lou'dä mŭs tā)* from the Latin: "We praise Thee"; part of the *Gloria* of the *Mass*!

lau'te *(lou'tĕ)* The *German* name for *lute*!

lavolta *(lä vŏl'tä)* from the Italian: "*The turn*"; an old *Italian dance* popular in 16th century England!

lay *(lā)* A simple *song* or *melody*!

lead *(lēd)* (1) In popular music vernacular the "*lead*" refers to the *instrumental* or *vocal part*, *performer* or *performance* that carries the "*melody line*"! (2) The statement of a *theme* in one *part* that is taken up or repeated by other *parts*! (3) A *cue* for the *entrance* of a *part*!

leader *(lēd'ēr)* (1) The *conductor* or *director* of an *orchestra* or *band*! (2) The leading *player* or *singer* in an *instrumental* or *choral* section of an *orchestra* or *band*, such as the *first violin*, *first trumpet* or *first soprano*, etc.

leading chord *(lēd ĭng kôrd)* The *dominant seventh chord*!

leading note, or **leading tone.** The *seventh note* in any *major* or *minor scale*, one *half-tone* below the *keynote* or *tonic*! The name derives from the *tone's* tendency to "*lead*" up to the *tonic*, usually in a sense of finality! Also known as *subtonic*!

leaning note. Same as *appoggiatura*!

leap *(lēp)*. A *melodic skip* over any *degree(s)* in a *scale progression*!

lebendig *(lā b'n'dĭk)* / **leb'haft** *(lāb'häft)* Ger. / A direction to play with vivacity!

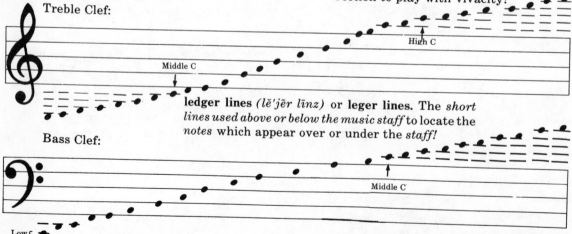

Treble Clef:

High C

Middle C

ledger lines *(lĕ'jēr līnz)* or **leger lines.** The *short lines* used *above* or *below* the music *staff* to locate the *notes* which appear over or under the *staff*!

Bass Clef:

Middle C

Low c

legando (*lĕ găn'dō*) from the Italian: Literally "binding": (1) A direction to perform *legato!* (2) A *sign* directing a *singer* or *instrumentalist* to complete two successive *tones* with one action of the *glottis, tongue* or *bow!*

legato (*lĕ gä'tō*) from the Italian: "*Slurred*", "*bound*"; a direction to play in a smooth, sustained manner without *pausing* between *notes*. *Legato* frequently is marked by a *slur* ⁀ ⌣ over or under the appropriate *notes*. The opposite of *legato* is *staccato*, which calls for distinctly *detached notes!*

legend (*lĕj'ĕnd*) Eng. / **legende** (*lĕ gĕn'dĕ*) / Ger. **légende** (*lā zhänd'*) Fr. / A romantic *composition* (*vocal* or *instrumental*) based on a legendary story!

légèrement (*lā zhĕr män'*) Fr. / **leggeramente** (*lĕd jĕ rä mĕn'tĕ*) It. / **leggero** (*lĕd jĕ'rō*) It. / A direction to play in a light, brisk, delicate manner!

leggiadra (*lĕd jĕ'ä drä*) / **leggiadramente** (*– mĕn'tĕ*) / **leggiadro** (*lĕd je'ä drō*) It. / A direction to play gracefully, neatly or with elegance!

leggiero (*lĕd jē ĕrō*) from the Italian: Same as *leggero!*

legno, col (*lān yô, kôl*) from the Italian: "*With the stick*"; a direction to *strike* the *strings* of a *violin* with the wooden portion of the *bow* (or bounce it) instead of brushing the *strings* with the *bow-hairs!*

leicht (*līkt*) from the German: A direction to play light and easy!

leidenschaft, mit (*lī'd'n shäft, mit*) / **leidenschaftlich** (*–lĭk*) Ger. / A direction to play with passion!

leise (*lī'zĕ*) from the German: A marking for soft and low, equivalent to *piano!*

leiser (*lī zĕr*) from the German: "Softer" .... *immer leiser*, "softer and softer"!

leitmotiv, leitmotif (*līt'mō tēf'*) from the German: From a larger work, a short, re-appearing, markedly-melodic *phrase* or *theme* that identifies a particular person, place, situation or idea! Introduced in *Wagnerian opera*, the "*leading motive*" form of composition became popular with many other composers.

leno (*lā'nō*) from the Italian: Faint, weak, quiet!

lentamente (*lĕn tä mĕn'tĕ*) from the Italian: Slowly!

lentando (*lĕn tän'dō*) from the Italian: Becoming slower, retarding!

lentement (*länt män'*) from the French: Slowly!

lentezza, con (*lĕn tĕt'să, kôn*) from the Italian: A direction to play with slowness, in a delayed manner!

lentissimo (*lĕn tēs sē'mō*) from the Italian: A direction to play "*very slow*"!

lento (*lĕn'tō*) from the Italian: A direction to play in *slow tempo* .... between *andante* and *largo!* *Adagio non lento* .... *slowly without dragging!*

lesson (*lĕs'n*) (1) A musical exercise or composition used for instruction! (2) An obsolete term for an *organ* or *harpsichord piece!*

lesto (*lĕs'tō*) from the Italian: Lively, quickly!

liberamente (*lē bĕ rä mĕn'tĕ*) / **libero** (*lē bĕ'rō*) It. / Freely, without restraint!

libretto (*lē brĕt'ō*) from the Italian: "A little book"! (1) The text of an *opera* or any long *choral work!* (2) The booklet containing such text!

licenza (*lē chĕn'tsă*) from the Italian: License or freedom!

lick (*lĭk*) In *popular* or *jazz music*, a colloquialism for a melodic *break* or *excerpt* played by a *lead instrument!*

lieblich (*lēb'lĭk*) from the German: Lovely, charming!

lied (*lēd*) from the German: A *German lyric* or *lay* with a sentimental, poetic quality to the *verses!* Originally *folk music*, the *lieder* (plural of *lied*) elaborated into *art songs* .... particularly those composed by Schubert and Schumann .... in which the music followed poetic forms! Frequently, famous poems (such as some authored by *Goethe, Heine,* etc.) were converted to *Kunstlieder (art songs)* by the composers!

liederkranz (*lē'dĕr krănts'*) from the German: "Wreath of songs"; (1) A *group of songs!* (2) The name for a *German singing society!*

liedertafel (*lē'dĕr tä'fĕl*) A *German* name for a *male choir!*

lieto (*lē ĕ'tō*) from the Italian: A direction to play joyfully or gaily!

lievo (*lē ā vō*) from the Italian: A direction to play light and easy!

ligature (*lĭg'ā tūr*) (1) A *slur!* (2) The *curved line* or *sign* connecting *two notes* ... a *tie* ♩ (3) A *group of notes* connected by a *tie* or by *syncopation!* (3) *Compound notes* sung to *one syllable* or with *one breath* or with *legato* execution! (4) The "*clamp*" with which the *reed* is attached to the *mouthpiece* of various *woodwinds* (*saxophone, clarinet,* etc.)!

light opera. Another term for *operetta* or *musical comedy!*

limpido (*lĭm'pē dō*) from the Italian: "Limpid", clear!

linke hand (*lĭn'kĕ hänt*) from the German: "*Left hand*", abbreviated *l.h.!*

lip (*lĭp*) The flat surface above and below the mouth of an *organ flue pipe!*

lipping, lip. The technique of adjusting a player's lips to the *mouthpiece* of a *wind instrument* to secure the best *tone!* See *Embouchure!*

lira (*lē'rä*) from the Italian: (1) A *lyre* or other *instrument* in the *lyre* family! (2) A *hurdy-gurdy!*

lira da braccio (*lē'rä da brät'chē ō*) from the Italian: "*Lyre* of the arm"; a *seven-string, bowed-instrument* of the 15th century! A predecessor of the *violin!*

Lira da braccio

636

lira da gamba *(lē'rä da gäm'bä)* from the Italian: A larger variation of the *lira da braccio* with many more *strings* and a lower *compass!* It rested on the floor between the player's knees while it was *bowed* . . . . a predecessor of the *viola da gamba!*

lira tadesca *(lē'rä tä dĕs'kä)* from the Italian: "The *German lyre*"; a *bowed instrument* of the *viol* class, dating from the 15th century!

liscio *(lē'shē ō)* from the Italian: A direction to play in a smooth, simple manner!

l'istesso *(lēs tĕs'sō)* from the Italian: "The same". . . . *l'istesso tempo*, the same *tempo!*

litany *(lĭt'á nī)* A *liturgical prayer* or *supplication* *sung* or *chanted* by *priests* and *choir* in a solemn procession!

liturgy *(lĭt'ĕr jī)* The public rites and services of the Christian churches!

lituus *(lĭt'ū ŭs)* (1) an *ancient Roman trumpet!* (2) Another name for the *crumhorn!*

liuto *(lē ōō'tō)* The Italian word for *lute!*

lobgesang *(lōb'gĕ zäng)* from the German: A *hymn* or song of praise!

loco *(lō'kō)* from the Italian: A direction to play the *notes* as written after the *notes* have been played in a *higher* or *lower octave!* The *higher* or *lower octave* is indicated by the sign   or "*ottava*"! *Loco* or *al loco* simply means: "Return to the original *octave!*"

locrian mode *(lō'krī ăn mōd)* One of the church modes, the *locrian* is structured on the *seventh note* of the *major scale!* See *Mode!*

lontano *(lŏn tä'nō)* from the Italian: A direction to play softly as if from a distance!

loud pedal. The *right pedal* on the *piano.* . . . also called the *damper pedal*, since it is the *pedal* which lifts the *dampers* off the *piano strings* when depressed!

loure *(lōōr)* from the French: (1) A 16th century *French* name for the *bagpipe!* (2) An old *dance* in *6/4* or *3/4* time with *slow* to *moderate tempo* and *strong downbeats!*

louré *(lōō rā)* from the French: A direction to play on the *violin* a series of *legato, slurred, non-staccato notes* (perhaps *slightly detached*) in *one sweep of the bow* . . . . similar to *piqué!*

luftig *(loof'tik)* from the German: Light, airy!

lugubre *(lōō gōō'brĕ)* from the Italian: "Lugubrious", sad, mournful!

lullaby *(lŭl'á bī)* A song to lull babies to sleep . . . a *cradle song!*

lunga *(lōōn'gä)* from the Italian: "Long"; a direction to take a *long pause* or *rest!* Usually, *lunga* is written over or under the *hold sign*   lunga   or   !

It is also written out as *pausa lunga*, long pause!

lur, lure *(lōōr, lōō'rĕ)* An ancient, bronze *Danish* or *Norwegian trumpet* with a twisted, long *tube* and a conical *bore* which ended in a flat-disk shape! It used a *cup-shaped mouthpiece!*

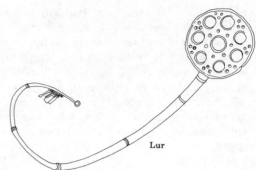

Lur

lusingando *(lōō zēn gän'dō)* / **lusingante** *(lōō zēn gän'tĕ)* / **lusinghevole** *(lōō zēn gĕ'vō lĕ)* / **lusinghiero** *(lōō zēn gĕ'ĕrō)* It. / Coaxing, seductive, persuasive, soothing!

lustig *(lōōs'tĭk)* from the German: A direction to play cheerfully or merrily!

lute *(lūt)* A *stringed instrument* with a *pear-shaped body*, a *long neck* with a *fingerboard* and a *pegbox head* that bends down and out from the top of the *neck*. The *lute* reached the height of its popularity in the 16th century, when the *instrument* was constructed with about seven *frets* and five *double strings (pairs)*, plus one *single string*, which were plucked by the finger(s)! The strings were tuned G-e-f-a-d'-g' . . . the *double strings* tuned in *fourths*, with the *single string* a *third* in the middle! In later centuries, the *lute* began to phase out into obsolescence, being replaced by the *guitar* and the *mandolin!* For other members of the *lute* family, see *tanbur, pandora*, etc!

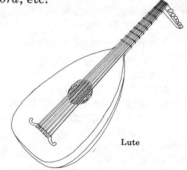

Lute

luttosamente *(lōōt ō sä mĕn'tĕ)* / **lottoso** *(lōōt ō'sō)* / **luttuoso** *(lōōt tōō ō'sō)* / **luttuosomente** *(lōōt tōō ō sō mĕn'tĕ)* It. / Sorrowful, mournful, plaintive!

lyre *(līr)* (1) A *stringed instrument* of the *harp* class used by the ancient Greeks to accompany *songs and recitations!* The *bodies* of some *lyres* are bowl-shaped while others are *box-shaped!* All *lyres* usually drop a *series of strings* vertically from a *crossbar* mounted on *two arms* extending from the *body!* The strings are "*stopped*" with one hand, while the other plucks with finger(s) or *plectrum*. Today, *lyres* generally are obsolete although folk versions persist in Africa, Finland, Siberia, etc. (2) A *percussion instrument* (found in *marching bands*) similar to the *glockenspiel* or *bell lyre!* Usually consisting of *tuned, metal bars* (mounted in a *lyre-shaped* frame) the *lyre* is held in one hand while parading, and struck by a "*hard beater*" or rod with the other hand.

Ancient Lyre

lyric *(lĭr'ĭk)* (1) In *popular music,* the *words* to a *song!* (2) "Pertaining to the *lyre*".... hence, *suitable for singing,* as contrasted to *dramatic* or *epic* which are suitable for the *narrative* form! (3) *Opera* is also called *lyric drama! Lyric drama* is dominated by the *lyric form!* (4) Generally, describing any emotional or tender quality!

DICTIONARY

M

— M —

M. m. The abbreviation: (1) For *Major (M)* or *minor (m)!* (2) For the French *main* or the Italian *mano*, either of which mean *hand!* (3) For *Mediant!* (4) For the *organ's Manual!* (5) For *Metronome*.... *M.M.* means *Maelzel Metronome.* See *Metronome!*

ma *(mä)* from the Italian: "But"; *ma non troppo*, but not too fast!

machete *(mä chā'tā)* A *small Portuguese guitar* with *four strings!*

mächtig *(mäkh'tĭkh)* from the German: Mighty, strong!

madrigal *(măd'rĭ găl)* A lyric, romantic poem set to music, using three or more *contrapuntal parts!* In the fourteenth century, the model *madrigal* repeated the same music in each of several *stanzas* .... the *high voice part* usually was more *ornamental* than the *low part(s)* ...... and ended with a shorter *stanza* known as the *ritornello!* In the 16th century, the *Dutch* or *Flemish* composers introduced more complex *voice parts*, expanding both the *chromatic* and *contrapuntal* techniques!

maestà, con *(mä ĕs tä', kôn)* / **maestade, con** *(mä ĕs tä'dĕ)* / **maestevole** *(mä ĕ stä'vō lĕ)* / **maestoso** *(mä ĕ stō'sō)* It. / A direction to play in a majestic, stately manner!

maestro *(mä ĕs'trō)* A *teacher* or *master* in the *arts*; a *conductor* or *eminent composer*.... *maestro di cappella*, the *choirmaster* or *conductor* of a *choir* or *chamber orchestra!*

magadis *(măg'à dĭs)* (1) An ancient *Greek dulcimer!* (2) A *Lydian flute* that played *octaves!* (3) A *monochord!*

magadize *(măg'à dīz)* An ancient *Greek* expression for *playing* or *singing in octaves*.... playing upon the *magadis!*

magas *(mä'găs)* (1) The *Greek* term for the *bridge* of a *stringed instrument!* (2) a *Greek monochord!*

maggiore *(măd jō'rā)* The Italian word for "*major*" or "*major key*"!

maggot *(măg'ŭt)* An old *English* term for an impromptu, romantic type of *madrigal!*

magnificat *(măg nĕf'ē kăt)* from the Latin: (1) from the Virgin Mary canticle "*magnificat anima mea dominum*".... "*my soul doth magnify the Lord*", sung at the Roman Catholic *Vespers service!* (2) A *sacred song* of praise!

main droite *(măn d'rwàt)* from the French: "Right hand", abbreviated *M.D.!*

main gauche *(măn gōsh)* from the French: "Left hand", abbreviated *M.G.!*

maitrix *(mâ trēz')* from the French: A church-affiliated school for vocalists!

major *(mä'jĕr)* A sequence of *tones (a mode)* which is greater than the *minor sequence* by a *half-step interval!* Major second.... an *interval* of two *half-steps (half-tones)*; *major third*.... an *interval* of two *whole steps (tones)*; *major seventh*.... an *interval* one *half-step (half-tone)* less than the *octave* span! See *Intervals!*

major chord. Any *triad* or *chord* with a *major third* and a *perfect fifth!*

major flute. *An open, flute-stop,* on the *organ*, of eight-foot *pitch!*

major scale. Any *scale* in the *major mode* which is sequenced in the order of *two whole tones, a half tone, three whole tones,* and *a half-tone!* Major scales generally are associated with a "happy" or "pleasant" sound, while *minor scales* are deemed appropriate for tragic or sad music! These generalities, however, are contradicted frequently by uninhibited composers!

major triad. See *Major chord!*

malaguena *(ma lä gwän'yäh)* A *Spanish dance* in *triple time* named after the city and province of Malaga where it originated!

malincono *(mä'lēn kôn ē kō')* from the Italian: A direction to play in a melancholy, sad manner!

mallet *(măl'ĕt)* A *drumstick* with a knobbed head in varying degrees of thickness and hardness (sometimes *padded*), used to strike such instruments as *xylophone, timpani,* etc.

mambo *(măm'bō)* A *Latin rhythm* or *dance* imported into the U.S. from the Caribbean and popular in ballrooms during the '60's!

mancando *(män kän'dō)* from the Italian: A direction to play gradually softer, as if dying away!

mandola *(măn dō'lä)* A large, *tenor mandolin* tuned like the *viola!* Also called *mandore (măn'dōr)!*

Mandola

mandolin *(măn'dō lĭn)* A *stringed instrument* (in the *lute* family) with a *pear-shaped bowl* and a *fretted neck.* The most popular *mandolin (Neapolitan)* has four *pairs* of *strings (double strings)!* Five or six *pairs* of *strings* are seen on other models (*Milanese*, etc.). The *mandolin* is tuned like a *violin* and is plucked with a *plectrum*. It's *range is approximately three octaves running up from G below* the *staff!*

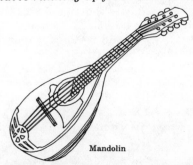

Mandolin

maniera *(mä nē ä'rä)* from the Italian: Manner, style!

mano *(mä'nō)* from the Italian: "Hand"!

mano destra *(dĕs'trä)* from the Italian: "The right hand"!

mano sinistra *(sē nĭs trä)* from the Italian: "The left hand"!

manual *(măn'ūăl)* (1) A *keyboard* (to be played by the hands)! (2) In *organ* music, the use of the *keyboard* without *pedals!* (3) An individual *key* of a *keyboard!*

maraca *(mä rä'kä)* A *Latin-American percussion instrument* usually played in pairs *(maracas)!* The *maraca*, simply stated, is a *gourd* with dry seeds which produces a scraping, hissing sound when rattled!

Maracas

marcando *(mär kän'dō)* from the Italian: A direction to play in an *accented*, distinct and emphatic manner!

marcatissimo *(mär'kä tĭs'sē mō)* from the Italian: A direction to play *very marcato!*

marcato *(mär kä'tō)* from the Italian: Same as *marcando!*

march *(märch)* A *composition* with heavily-structured *rhythm* appropriate for *marching! Marches*, most frequently, are in *double time, 2/4, 4/4*, with an occasional *6/8* variation! *Marches*, usually, are designed in *three sections:* (1) The *opening section!* (2) The *middle section (trio)* generally *sounds* a *fourth higher* than the *opening key!* (3) A *final section* which *reprises* the *opening!* A fast-moving *march* is known as a *quickstep* or *military march!* In slow *tempo*, there is the *processional march*, the *funeral march*, *dead march*, *wedding march*, etc.!

marcia *(mär'chä)* The *Italian* word for *march! Alla marcia*, in *march style!*

marcia funebre *(foo nä brĕ)* The *Italian* term for *funeral march!*

marimba *(mä rĭm'bä)* A modern, motorized *percussion instrument* with *tuned resonators* underlying *two banks* of *wooden bars* that are struck with *mallets!* A primitive *marimba* is native to Central America and Africa, and resembles a *xylophone* with *gourds* placed beneath the *bars* to add *resonance!* The modern *marimba* might loosely be described as an *electrified xylophone* in appearance, although its sound is much less brittle and much more "*smooth toned*" than the *non-electric xylophone!* The *marimba* has a *range* of *four octaves* from low C to high C!

marimba

marsch *(märsh)* The *German* word for *march!*

markiert *(mär kērt')* From the German: "*Marked*", accented!

martelé *(mär tĕl ā')* from the French: (1) In *violin music*, the use of abrupt, distinct *strokes* (frequently with the *point of the bow*) that are quickly released to achieve an emphatic *staccato!* Also called detaché, martelé usually is notated by small black triangles placed over or under the *notes!* (2) In *keyboard music*, *martelé* means to attack the *keys* with *hammering*, stiff and forceful strokes!

martellato *(mär tĕl lä'tō)* from the Italian: "*Hammered*", *martelé!*

masque *(măsk)* An old *English dramatic entertainment* with *musical accompaniment!* A predecessor of the *opera!*

Mass *(măs)* The *Eucharistic* rite of the *Latin church!* The central *sacred service* of the *Roman Catholic church!* The Mass consists of two sections, the *Ordinary* and the *Proper*, both with *text* and *music!* In the *Roman Catholic* church, the *music* is prescribed in *Gregorian chant* or *plainsong* and the best-known *musical sections* of the *Ordinary* are: (1) The *Kyrie (Kyrie eleison*, "Lord have mercy") (2) The *Gloria (Gloria in excelsis Deo*, Glory to God on high") (3) The *Credo* ("I Believe") (4) The *Sanctus (Sanctus* "Holy") and *Benedictus qui venit* ("Blessed Is He Who Comes") (5) The *Agnus Dei* ("Lamb of God")!

The word "Mass" comes from the conclusion of the *Ordinary* where the Latin *missa* (Mass) appears within the phrase *Ite, missa est* which signals the dismissal of the congregation at the end of the services! *Music* from the *Proper* includes the *Introit, Gradual, Alleluia, Offertory* and *Communion! High Mass*, with *music*, is celebrated at large church festivals .... *Low Mass* is conducted *without music!*

mässig *(mä'sĭkh)* from the German: "*Moderate*", a *tempo* indication equal to *moderate.* ... *mässig bewegt*, "moderately lively"; *mässig langsam*, "moderately slow"!

matins *(măt'ĭnz)* *Music of the morning prayer!* The *first service* of the eight Canonical Hours comprising the *Roman Catholic office!*

mazurka *(mä zûr'kä)* A *Polish dance* in *triple time* with unique, sliding and side-hopping steps that are *accompanied* by varied *accents* on the *second and third beats* of each bar!

m.d. The abbreviation for the *French* "*main droite*", or the *Italian* "*mano destra*", either of which translates to "*right hand*"!

measure *(mĕzh'ēr)* Also known as *bar*, the *measure* is the *basic unit of meter*, comprised of a *group of notes and rests (beats)* that are separated on the *staff* by *vertical bar lines!* The number of *beats* is indicated in the *time signature....* for example, *6/8* means each *measure* has *6 eighth notes!* See *Time* and *Meter!*

medesimo *(mĕ dā'zē mō)* from the Italian: "The same"!

medesimo tempo *(tĕm'pō)* from the Italian: A direction to play in the same *tempo* despite any change in the *time signature!* In a change from *2/4* to *4/4*, for example, the *tempo* is kept the same by playing *four quarter-notes* in the *same time* that *two quarter-notes* previously received!

mediant *(mē'dĭ ănt)* The *third degree* of a *diatonic scale!* Since it is centered between the *tonic (first degree)* and the *dominant (fifth degree)* it became known as the *mediant!* The *Roman numeral III*, in *notation*, indicates a *triad* built on the *mediant!*

medley *(mĕd'lē)* In *popular music*, a combination of *two or more songs* or *excerpts* which *segue* from one into the other! In *serious music* a loose collection of portions of several *works* mixed into one *composition!* "Medley" usually refers to *vocal pieces!* Potpourri would be the equivalent for *instrumental music!*

mehr *(mār)* from the German: "More"; mehr bewegt, "more lively"!

meistersinger *(mī'stēr zĭng'er)* from the German: "Master" members of an old *German* guild devoted to *poetry* and *music*. They were the middle-class successors to the aristocrat *minnesingers* who dominated the *arts* during the 12th to 14th centuries! The pedantic, almost rigid *compositions* of the *meistersinger* were both satirized and immortalized by Wagner in his opera *Die Meistersinger von Nürnberg!*

melange *(mă län'zh)* from the French: *A medley* or *potpourri!*

mele *(mā'lā)* A Hawaiian *vocal song* or *chant!*

melisma *(mĕ lĭz'mä)* (1) A *group of notes* or a *complete melody* sung to *one syllable* of *lyric*, particularly in *Gregorian chant!* (2) A *grace* or *ornament!* (3) A loose, infrequent substitution for *cadenza!*

mellophone *(mĕl'ō fōn)* A *brass althorn* that substitutes for the *French horn* in *school* and *marching bands!* A *three-valved, wind instrument*, the *mellophone* has a *compass of two and one half octaves* and can be *pitched* in *F* or *E-flat!* It is a *transposing instrument* that sounds a *sixth below as written!*

Mellophone

melodeon *(mĕ lō'dē ŭn)* An *early, small American reed organ* equipped with treadles to operate a suction bellows which drew air in through a *set of reeds!*

melodia *(mē lōd ĕ'ä)* from the Italian: (1) *A melody!* (2) An eight-foot *organ stop!*

Melodica *(mĕ lō'dĭ kä)* (1) A trademarked name for a *chromatic harmonica* with a *recorder-like mouthpiece* and a *two-octave keyboard!*

melodion *(mĕl ō'dĭ ŏn)* A *keyboard instrument* invented in *Germany*, 1806! It used a revolving cylinder to press against a set of metal bars, thereby producing *pitched sounds!*

melody *(mĕl'ō dĭ)* Any *single tones in succession* that are structurally related to *key* and *tempo!* *Harmony* deals with *combined tones in succession* that are structurally related to *key* and *tempo!*

melograph *(mĕl'ō gräf)* A device that records the *action* of *piano keys....* the *length* and *succession of the notes!*

melologue *(mĕl'ō lŏg)* *Vocal* or *instrumental music* that *accompanies*, or is interspersed throughout, a *spoken recitation!*

melomania *(mĕl'ō mā'nĭ ä)* An excessive passion (mania) for *music!*

melophone *(mĕl'ō fōn)* An *instrument* in the *accordion/concertina family* but shaped like a *guitar!*

Melophone

melopoeia *(mĕl'ō pē'yä)* The *art* of composing *melody!*

melos *(mēlŏs)* from the Greek: "Song"; a term used by Wagner to characterize the "singing style" of his *symphonic compositions* and the *vocal style* of his later *operas!*

melotrope *(mĕl'ō trōp)* A *piano*, mechanically equipped to play the music of a *melograph!* See *Melograph!*

membranophone *(mĕm brā' nă fōn')* A classification for any stretched-skin or stretched-parchment instrument such as a *drum* or *mirliton*.

même *(mĕm)* from the French: "The same"; *le même chose...* the same thing; *à la même ....* at the same *tempo* or *tempo primo!*

meno *(mā'nō)* from the Italian: "Less"; *meno allegro, meno mosso, poco meno* or simply *meno ....* a direction to play less quickly or more slowly!

mensurable music. *Music measurement*, dating back to the 12th century, when *notation* was based on *complex time-values! Eight basic notes (large, long, breve, semibreve, minim, semiminim, fusa* and *semifusa)* were employed without *bar lines,* with *each note valued at twice or three times the next note's value! If twice, it was called imperfect time; thrice, perfect time!* A *major mode* divided the *large* into *longs;* a *minor mode* divided the *long* into *breves,* etc! *Symbols of notation* consisted mainly of *vertical and horizontal lines!*

menuet *(mûn wā')* Fr. / **menuett** *(mĕ'nōō ĕt')* Ger. / A minuet!

messa *(mĕs'sä)* It. / **messe** *(mĕss)* Fr. / **messe** *(mĕs'sĕ)* Ger. / A Mass!

messa di voce *(mĕs'sä dē vô'chĕ)* from the Italian: A *direction* for a *vocalist to sustain* and *swell* a *tone* from *pianissimo to fortissimo and slowly back to pianissimo!* The *notation* would appear as:

Originally a *virtuoso feature* of *bel canto singers,* it usually is used in modern times only as a *voice-training technique!*

messe des morts *(mäss dā môr)* The *French* name for the *Requiem Mass!*

mesto *(mĕs'tō)* from the Italian: A *direction* to play in a sad, pensive manner!

meter, metre *(mē'tēr)* (1) The *division of musical composition* into *beats, measures* and *accents! Meter* is indicated by the *time-signature* at the *head of the staff* which states the *beats per measure* and the *note-value for each beat....* $\frac{3}{4}$ *....means* that in *each measure* there are *three beats* with *each quarter note* assigned *one beat! (See Elements of Music!). Meter* actually deals only with the *pattern of a group of measures; rhythm* relates to both *meter* and *time-value* within a *given measure!* The two best-known *meters* are the *duple* and the *triple!* The latter features *3 beats to a measure with the accent usually on the first beat;* the former has *2 beats* to a measure with the accent usually on every other beat! (2) *Simple meter ...* any *meter* whose *number of beats in a measure* is *two, three* or *four; 2/2, 2/4, 2/8, 3/2, 3/4, 3/8, 4/2, 4/4, 4/8! Compound meter...* any *simple meter multiplied by three; compound duple, 6/2, 6/4, 6/8; compound triple 9/4, 9/8; compound quadruple, 12/4, 12/8, 12/16. Quintuple meter* is 5/4, either via 2/4 plus 3/4 or the reverse, based on where the *subordinate accent* is placed! (3) The division of *poetic verse* into *groups of syllables* or *metrical feet!* The *metrical classification* of *hymns* is based on the number of *feet (iambic, trochaic, dactylic)* and the *order of the syllables!* These include:

Iambic:

Common meter ....4 lines with 8,6,8,6 syllables in order!

Long meter ....4 lines with 8,8,8,8 syllables in order!

Sevens and sixes..........4 lines with 7,6,7,6 syllables in order!
(sometimes used in *trochaic verse*)

Short meter ....4 lines with 6,6,8,6 syllables in order!

Hallelujah meter ....6 lines with 6,6,6,6,8,8 syllables in order!

Trochaic:

Sixes ....4 lines with 6,6,6,6 syllables in order!

Sixes and fives............4 lines with 6,5,6,5 syllables in order!

Sevens ....4 lines with 7,7,7,7 syllables in order!

Eights and sevens ....4 lines with 8,7,8,7 syllables in order!
(sometimes used in *iambic verse*)

Dactylic:

Elevens ....4 lines with 11,11,11,11 syllables in order!

Elevens and tens ......4 lines with 11,10,11,10 syllables in order!

method *(mĕth'ŭd)* A book of *instruction and/or exercises* for a particular *instrument* or *voice* or *technique!*

metronome *(mĕ'trō nōm')* A standard device for *marking time in music!* The familiar, but outdated *Maelzel Metronome* (introduced by J.N. Maelzel in 1816) features a clock-driven pendulum-bar which sounds a loud *click* at the end of each swing! The bar has a weight at the low end, and a sliding weight at the upper end which is adjusted to produce the desired number of *clicks per minute! Instructions for performance* in accordance with *metronome timing* are given as *110 M.M.,* for example, which is the abbreviation for *110 clicks per minute according to the Maelzel Metronome,* or can be written as $\downarrow = 100$ which means *100 quarter notes per minute* according to the *metronome.* In modern music usage (especially at professional levels) *mechanical "watch"* or *electronic "watch", "solid state" metronomes without pendula* have replaced the *Maelzel!* Compact and portable (some are shaped like stopwatches), these are used by many conductors and musicians to check their *tempo settings!*

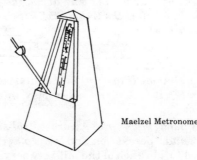

Maelzel Metronome

"Watch" Metronome
Sets small hand to
desired tempo;
large hand counts
the *beats!*

mezza, mezzo (*měd'zä, měd'zō*) from the Italian: "Half", middle, moderate!

mezzo voce (*měd'zo vō chā*) from the Italian: "Half the power of the voice"; softly!

mezzo forte, mezzo piano (*fôr'tě, pē ä nō*) from the Italian: "Half-loud, half-soft"! Abbreviated mf, mp!

mezzo soprano (*sô prä'nō*) from the Italian: A *female voice* in a *medium range* between *soprano* and *contralto* with a *limited compass* running *from A below middle C up to G''!* Frequently, shortened to just *mezzo!*

mezzo soprano clef. The *C clef* on the *second line of the staff!*

mezzo staccato (*stä kä'tō*) Same as *portato* or *demilegato!*

mezzo tenore (*tě nō'rě*) A *baritone* with some capability in the *tenor range!*

mf. The abbreviation for *mezzo forte!*

m.g. The abbreviation for "*main gauche*", the *French* term for "*left hand*"!

mi (*mē*) In *solmization*, the *third note* of the *diatonic scale* (do, re, mi, etc.)!

microphone (*mī'krō fōn'*) The familiar electronic device used in every form of theatrical and musical entertainment or recording studio to *receive sound-input from any instruments or voices.* The *microphone*, simply stated, converts the waves of air pressure created by the *performer* into electrical waveforms which are modified and transmitted through *amplifiers* to the final reproducing media (*speakers*)!

microtone (*mī'krō tōn'*) An *interval smaller* than a *half-tone*, experimentally used by "*modern composers*" such as Charles Ives!

Middle C. The *C* located at the *center of the piano keyboard*, appearing *one line above the bass staff* and *one line below the treble staff!* (See *Keyboard* and *Leger Lines*)!

militare, alla (*mē'lē tä'rě, äl'lä*) / **militarmente** (*mē lē tär měn'tě*) It. / A direction to play in a military manner!

military band (*mǐl'ǐ těr'ē*) An *orchestral-sized group of woodwinds, percussion* and *brass players* usually attached to a branch of the military services or to a military school!

military music. *Compositions* for *military bands* such as *quicksteps, marches*, etc. These are usually written for *woodwinds, percussion, cornets, saxophones*, etc. with *strings, keyboards* and *oboes* usually eliminated!

minim (*mǐn'ǐm*) The *British word* for *half-note!*

minnesänger, minnesinger (*mǐn'ě zěng'ēr, mǐn'ě sǐng'ēr*) from the German: The *lyric poets* and *musicians* of the *German aristocrat class*, during the 12th to 14th centuries! A *minnelied* described any *love song* or *other song* styled for the *minnesinger!*

minor (*mī'nēr*) Smaller by a *half-tone* than the *corresponding major interval* or *scale!* A *natural* or *pure minor scale* always *spans an octave* in the order of a *whole tone, a half-tone, two whole tones, a half-tone* and *two whole tones!* The *harmonic minor scale* raises the *seventh tone* of the *minor scale* by a *half-tone*, placing an *augmented second between the sixth and seventh tones!* The *melodic minor scale* raises the *seventh and sixth tones going up the scale* and reverses the process *going down* (the *second and third tones* are the *augmented tones* in a *descending melodic minor scale*)!

minor interval. *An interval distant* by one *half-tone smaller* than the *corresponding major interval!* (See *Interval!*)

minor mode. The *arrangement* of *tones* in the *minor scale!*

minor second. A *half-tone interval!* (See *Interval!*)

minor third. A *tone-and-a-half interval!* (See *Interval!*)

minor triad. A *triad chord* with a *minor third above the root!* (See *Chord!*)

minstrel (*mǐn'strěl*) (1) A *medieval musical entertainer* who usually *accompanied* his own *singing* on a *lute* or *harp* or *related-type instrument!* (2) In 19th century America, one of a *group of entertainers* (usually white men in blackface, impersonating blacks) who presented *song, dance* and *comedy shows!*

minuet (*mǐn'ū ět*) from the French: A *moderate* or *slow French dance* in *triple time* which was popular in royal courts for two hundred years beginning about 1650 (See *scherzo*)! The *minuet* became an important form in *classical composition!*

minuetto (*mǐ'ū ět'tō*) The *Italian* word for *minuet!*

mirliton (*měr'lē tôn*) from the French: Any member of a *group of instruments* which contain a *membrane* that *vibrates* in response to the *human voice* or *another instrument!*

miserere (*mǐz'ě rē'rē*) from the Latin: "Have mercy"; the *50th psalm* in the *Vulgate!* It is the best-known of the *supplicating psalms!*

missa (*mǐs'sä*) The Latin word for "Mass"; *missa bassa* . . . . "low Mass"; *missa brevis* . . . . "short Mass"; *missa solemnis* . . . . "high Mass"!

misteriosamente (*mē stě rē ō sä měn'tě*) / **misterioso** (*mē stě rē ō'sō*) / **mistero, con** (*mē stě'rō, kôn*) It. / A direction to play in a mysterious or secretive manner!

misura, alla *(mĕ zoō'rä, ăl lä) / **misurata** (mĕ zoō'rä tä)* It. / A direction to play in *strict time!*

misura, senza *(sĕn'tsä)* from the Italian: "Without measure"; a direction to play freely without exact conformance to the *time values!*

mit *(mĭt)* from the German: "With" ... *mit Kraft,* with power, the same as *con forza!*

mix *(mĭks)* In *professional recording studios,* the term for the combined sound of individual *"tracks"* of *multi-channel tape recordings!* The engineer's *console* or *"mixing"* board picks up each microphone's signal on a separate tape "track" and combines or reduces or *"mixes"* the combined tracks (when completed) down to a final *"two track" stereo master tape!* In the "mixing" process, each channel can be separately *equalized, augmented* or *echoed* to improve the *fidelity! "Mixer"* is used as an expression for both the "console board" or the sound engineer who presides over the *mixing* "console board"!

mixed cadence. See *Cadence!*

mixed chorus. A *vocal group* that combines *male and female voices* or *music* written for same!

mixolydian mode *(mĭk'sō lĭd ĭ ăn mōd)* The *authentic mode* which *runs from G to G* on the *white keys* of the *piano keyboard!*

mixture stop. An *organ stop* that *sounds* several *banks* of *pipes* (*pitched* to *various harmonies* of the *basic keys*) which add *harmonics* to the *diapason!*

m.m. The abbreviation for *Maelzel metronome!* (See *Metronome*)!

mode *(mōd)* A *sequence* of *tones* in *patterns,* first developed in ancient Greece, then evolving into *codified church scales* during the *Middle Ages,* and continuing to add elaboration until the 17th century, when the less complicated *major* and *minor* scales took their place as the new basic forms for organized music!

Modes may be classified in three ways:

(1) *The Church Modes,* developed from the ancient Greeks! Seven *principal modes based on the diatonic scale* include:

The Ionian	from C to C
The Dorian	from D to D
The Phrygian	from E to E
The Lydian	from F to F
The Mixolydian	from G to G
The Aeolian	from A to A
The Locrian	from B to B

Three *subordinate modes* begin a *fourth below* the *principal's* tonic:

The hypodorian
The hypophrygian
The hypolydian

(2) All of the *church modes* (whether *ecclesiastical, Gregorian* or *medieval-secular*) are classified as either *authentic modes* ... when the *lowest note of the octave is the keynote,* or as *plagal modes* ... when the *fourth note of the octave is the keynote!*

(3) Contemporary *major and minor modes:* The *major* corresponds to the *Lydian,* while the *minor* is *equivalent* to the *hypodorian* when the *scale is descending!*

moderato *(mŏd ĕ rä'tō)* from the Italian: "Moderate"; a direction to play at *moderate tempo!* Also used as a modifying term ... *allegro moderato,* for example, means moderately fast!

modulation *(mŏd'ū lā'shŭn)* The process of *changing from one key to another* in one *composition or portion of same!* The transition, in order to be smooth and flowing, most often involves the use of *chords common to the keys involved!* A *temporary key change* is indicated by the *accidentals* (*sharps, flats,* and *naturals*)! A *long-lasting key change* will be indicated by a *new key signature!* The simplest *modulations* are made by going from the *original key* to the *keys* of the *dominant* or *subdominant* of the *original,* or to their *relative minors!* For example, going from *C-Major* to *G* or *F-Major,* or from *C-Major* to *E, D,* or *A-minor!*

möglich *(mö'glĭck)* from the German: "Possible" ... *so rasch wie möglich,* as quickly as possible!

moll *(môl)* The German word for "Minor"; *C-moll* means *C-minor!*

molle *(môl'ĕ)* from the French: "A half-tone lower", or a "flat"; *B-molle* means *B-flat!*

molto *(môl'tō)* from the Italian: "Much, very"; a direction used in many musical terms! For example, *molto adagio* .... very slow; *molto allegro* .... very fast; *con molto* .... "with much"; *molto molto* .... extremely; *molto molto adagio* .... very, very slow!

monaural *(mŏn ô'răl)* Pertaining to, or using *one ear,* as contrasted to *binaural* or *stereophonic* (for *two ears*)! In *recording terms, monaural* refers to *single-channel* or *one-track tape recording* which is *reproduced* through only *one speaker!*

monochord *(mŏn ō kôrd)* An *ancient instrument* used by the *Greeks* to measure the mathematics of *musical sounds and intervals!* It consisted of a *single string stretched over a sound box* with a *movable bridge* to *divide* the *string* into *vibrating parts* for measurement. In the *Middle Ages,* more *strings* were added to the simple *monochord!* These medieval versions were used for performance, and continued to develop until the first *clavichord* emerged!

monody *(mŏn'ō dĭ)* (1) A *style of composition* with *only one voice part* for the *melody accompanied* by the *lute* or *continuo!* (2) *Monody* also refers to *music* (developed in Italy about 1600 for individual *songs* as well as *operas* and *oratorios*) which broke away from the *complicated contrapuntal composition* of *earlier times!*

monophonic *(mŏn'ō fŏn ĭk)* The equivalent of *monaural.* See monaural!

monophonous *(mŏn ŏf'ō nŭs)* Uttering *single tones,* one at a time!

monophony *(mŏn ŏf'ō nē) Music* with an *unaccompanied, single voice-part* for *solo* or a *group* in *unison!*

monotone (*mŏn'ō tŏn*) (1) A *single, unvarying tone!* (2) *Singing or chanting or reciting to a single tone!*

Moog (*mōg*) The trademarked name for one of the modern *electronic synthesizers*, named after Robert Moog, its inventor! (See *Synthesizer*)!

morbido (*môr'bēd ō*) / **morbidezza** (*môr bē dĕt'să*) It. / A direction to play softly, with tenderness!

morceau (*môr sō'*) from the French: "Piece"; *morceau de piano* . . . *a piano composition; morceau de genie* . . . *a characteristic piece; morceau d'ensemble* . . . *a composition for a group, etc!*

mordent (*môr'dĕnt*) from the German: A *grace* or *ornament* consisting of the quick alternation of a *principal tone* with an *auxiliary tone one half-tone below!* An *inverted mordent* alternates the *principal tone* with an *auxiliary tone one half-tone higher!*

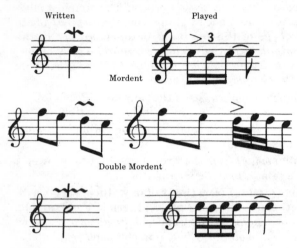

Written   Played

Mordent

Double Mordent

Inverted Mordent

morendo (*mō rĕn'dō*) from the Italian: A direction to play gradually more softly as if dying away!

moresca (*mŏ rĕs'kă*) from the Italian: *A Moorish dance!*

mormorando (*môr môr răn'dō*) / **mormoroso** (*môr mō rō ' sō*) It. / "Murmuring"; a direction to play with a gentle or soft tone!

mosso (*môs'sō*) from the Italian: "Moved"; a direction to play in a rapid, fairly excited manner; *meno mosso* . . . less rapid; *più mosso* . . . faster; *poco mosso* . . . somewhat quickly, etc!

motet (*mō'tĕt*) (1) *Sacred vocal music* usually composed for *polyphonic counterpoint* without *accompaniment!* In earlier centuries (1300-1600) the *cantus firmus* style of *motet* led to the *Protestant chorale* (1600-1750) *forms* of J.S. Bach, Mozart, Brahms, etc! (2) *English-style anthems* are loosely known as *motets!*

motif (*mō tēf'*) from the French: See *motive!*

motion (*mō' shŭn*) (1) The *progression of melody!* (2) *Conjunct motion* . . . *progressing by single successive tones!* (3) *Disjunct motion* . . . the *progression skips various tones!* (4) *Similar motion* . . . when *two or more parts progress in the same direction!* (5) *Parallel motion* . . . when *two or more parts progress in the same direction with the same intervals!* (6) *Oblique*

motion . . . when one of the *parts* remains *fixed* and the other *moves up or down!* (7) *Contrary motion* . . . when the *parts progress opposite to each other!* (8) *Mixed motion* . . . when *two or more of the previously stated motions occur simultaneously in the parts!*

motive (*mō'tĭv*) A short *leading phrase of music* (the *theme* or *subject*) which is *reproduced or developed* in a *whole work* or *composition!*

moto (*mô'tō*) from the Italian: "Movement" or *tempo; con moto*, "with quick movement"!

moto perpetuo (*–pâr pā'tū ō*) from the Italian: "Perpetual motion"; used to describe *extremely rapid, short rondos!* In *Latin, perpetuum mobile!*

mouth organ. (1) Another name for *harmonica!* (2) The *Panpipe!* (3) Sometimes referred to as *mouth harp!*

mouthpiece (*mouth pēs*) The *part* of the *wind instrument* that goes between, on or around the lips of a *player!*

mouvement (*mōōv'män*) from the French: "Motion", or *tempo!*

movable do (*dō*). A *solfeggio system* wherein the *tonic* or keynote of every *major scale* is "*Do*", the *second tone* "*Re*", and so forth, following the Guido d'Arezzo *syllable scale!* (See *Do* and *Solfeggio*!)

movement (*mōōv'mĕnt*) (1) A *distinct section* of a *suite, sonata* or *symphony* (the *allegro* or *andante movements*, for example)! (2) The *tempo* or *motion* of a *composition* or *performance!*

movimento (*mō vē mĕn'tō*) from the Italian: Same as *mouvement!*

mp. The abbreviation for *mezzo piano!*

m.s. The abbreviation for *mano sinistra (left hand)!*

munter (*mōōn'tēr*) from the German: A direction to play in a gay, animated manner!

musette (*mū zĕt'*) from the French: (1) A *small French bagpipe* dating from the 18th century! (2) A *small, simple oboe!* (3) An *organ reed-stop!* (4) A *short country air*, usually set to a *drone bass* suitable for the *musette bagpipe!*

music (*mū'zĭk*) Any *combination of tones* structured in *composition* or *performance* to conform to any law or theory of *melody* and *harmony* which is considered intellectually authoritative! Such "*authority*", of course, is subject to the influence of invention and "*free expression*"!

musica (*mū'zĭ ká*) from the Italian: "*Music*"; *dramma per musica* . . . . *opera!*

musica ficta (*fĭk'tá*) from the Italian: "Artificial" or "feigned" *music!* The name given to *contrapuntal music* during the Middle Ages when *accidentals* were *eliminated* or "questionable" *chromatics* were *utilized!*

musica fracta (*frăk'tá*) from the Latin: An *abrupt* or *alien change* in *pitch* or *tone!*

music box. A *clockwork-driven musical instrument* which produced *tones* by rotating a cylinder of pins against a series of *pitched* metal prongs!

musical comedy. The most popular form of *American musical theater*, derived from *European light opera* of the 19th century, and exploited in America ... in the *Broadway theater* ... by such *composers* and *lyricists* as Rudolf Friml, Jerome Kern, Sigmund Romberg, Victor Herbert, Richard Rodgers, Lorenzo Hart, Irving Berlin, George and Ira Gershwin, Cole Porter, Kurt Weill, Leonard Bernstein, Frank Loesser and many others! The first *original-cast recording (Oklahoma, 1946)* began the "world-wide" exposure of *Broadway music on records.* International recognition via the turntable has promoted an every-growing commercial audience for the *theater-music art form!*

music drama. The name given to *opera* that develops *music* and *text* in equal dimensions without interruption of the *dramatic flow* by *arias, duets,* etc. The later *operas* of Richard Wagner exemplify the *music drama* format!

musicology *(mū'zǐ kǒl'ō jǐ)* The *history or science of musical knowledge,* particularly in relation to its *documentation, source study* and the *collection and cataloguing* of its *data!*

music paper. Blank manuscript paper pre-printed with *music-staff lines!*

musique concrète *(mū zēk' kôn krĕt')* A *French* term for *music* consisting of *"real (concrete) sounds* that are adapted for various *tape-recording techniques! Street-traffic sounds, thunder, lightning* and other *"natural" sounds* usually are *"collaged"* into a final *tape* which can then be *performed only by reproduction through a tape recorder!*

muta *(mōō' tä)* from the Italian: "Change"; a direction to *change instruments* or to *change the tuning of an instrument,* or the *tuning* of its *"crooks"; muta la in si,* change the *timpani* tuning from *A (Italian la)* to *B (Italian si)!*

mutation *(mū tā'shŭn)* (1) *Voice change* at *puberty!* (2) *Shifting* of the *hand position* on a *violin!* (3) An *organ stop* that *modifies the tone* of *other stops* pitched to *basic tones!*

mute *(mūt)* Any device that *deadens* or *muffles* the *tone* of an *instrument!* In the *violin family,* the *mute* is *clamped* to *the bridge!* In the *brass family, mutes* include *pear, cup* and *coneshaped cylinders* that are inserted into the *bell* of the *instrument! French horns* frequently are *muted* by *hand, drums* by a *cloth* on the *drumhead,* etc!

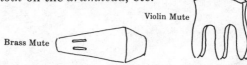

Violin Mute

Brass Mute

muthig *(mōō'tǐkh)* from the German: Spirited, bold!

DICTIONARY

N, O

— N —

nach *(näkh)* from the German: "After", "in accordance with"!

nachahmung *(näkh ä'mōōng)* from the German: "Imitation"

nachdruck *(näkh"drōōk)* from the German: "Emphasis", *accent; nachdrucklich,* a direction to play in a strong, emphatic fashion.

nachlassend *(näkh'lä'sĕnt)* from the German: A direction to play slower and slower, *rallentando!*

nachschlag *(näkh'shläkh)* from the German: (1) *"Afterbeat",* a *grace note (or notes)* added to a *non-accented note in the bar* which uses the *time value* of a *preceding note!* (2) *Auxiliary notes* added to the end of a *trill!*

Nachschlag

Written   Played

nachthorn *(näkht'hôrn)* from the German: An *organ stop* with 2, 4, or 8-foot *pitch!*

nachtmusik *(näkht' mōō zĭk)* from the German: "Night music", *serenade!*

nach und nach. from the German: Little by little, or gradually!

nanga *(năng'gȧ)* A small African harp!

narrante *(när rän'tā)* from the Italian: "Narrating, a direction to play as if *narrating* or *declaiming!*

natural *(năt'ū răl)* (1) The sign (♮) which negates the influence of any *sharp* or *flat* which *precedes* it in a *given measure* or in the *key signature!* (2) Without *flats* or *sharps....* the *natural scale of C-major,* for example! All of the *white keys* of the *keyboard* are *natural notes!* (3) Designating those *instruments* that have no *valves, stops, slides, keys,* etc. to alter their *pitch!*

natural harmonic. A *harmonic* produced on the *open string* of *stringed instruments!*

natural harmony. The *harmony* of the *common triad chord* without *modulations* or *derivated chords!*

natural horn. A simple form of *horn* without *valves* or *keys!*

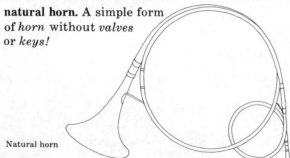

Natural horn

natural minor. The *scale* whose *third, sixth* and *seventh tones* are *one half-tone below* those in the *relative major scale!*

natural tone. Any *open tone* played on *wind* and *brass instruments* without *keys, valves* or *stops,* or any *open tone* played on *stringed instruments* without "stopping", or *holding down!*

Neapolitan sixth *(nē'ȧ pŏl'ĭ tăn)* The *first inversion* of a *sixth-chord triad* on the *lowered supertonic!* In the *key of C-major* or *minor,* for example, the first inversion of d♭-F-a♭ (the D♭ triad on the *flatted supertonic,* or the *flat-two chord,* ♭II) becomes F-a♭-d♭!

Neapolitan sixth

neck *(nĕk)* The part of a guitar, violin or similar instrument extending from the *head* to the body!

negligente *(nĕg lĭ jĕn'tē)* / **negligenza** *(nĕg lĭ jĕn'tsä)* It. / A direction to play in a manner that expresses negligence or carelessness!

nei *(nā'ē)* / **nel** *(nĕl)* / **nella** *(nĕl'lä)* / **nelle** *(nĕl lĕ)* / **nello** *(nĕl lō)* It. / "In the" or "at the"!

neighboring tone *(nā'bĕr ĭng)* (1) A *dissonant tone,* one degree *above* or *below* a *principal tone!* (2) A *grace* or *embellishment* using a *neighboring tone!* (3) Also called *auxiliary tone* or *returning tone!*

nettamente *(nĕt tä mĕn'tĕ)* / **netto** *(nĕt'tō)* It. / A direction to play in a neat, clear and distinct style!

neumes *(nūmz)* The *medieval signs* and *symbols* used as *notation* to indicate *pitch changes* in *Gregorian plainsong!* Examples of the "square-shaped" *neumes* (earlier versions used simpler *dash, hook* and *curve* marks) which appeared in the 13th century, include:

nicht *(nĭkht)* from the German: "Not"; *nicht zu langsam,* not too slow; *nicht zu schnell,* not too fast!

niente *(nē ĕnt'ĕ)* from the Italian: "Nothing"; *a niente,* a direction to play gradually softer until dying away; *quasi niente,* almost inaudible!

ninth. The *interval* of an *octave plus a second!* See *Interval!*

nobile *(nŏ'bē lĕ)* / **nobilità, con** *(nō bē lĭ tä', kŏn)* It. / direction to play in a dignified, grand manner!

noch *(nŏkh)* from the German: "Still", "yet"!

noch einmal *(–īn'mäl)* from the German: "Once again"; a direction to play *one more time!*

nocturne *(nŏk tûrn')* A dreamy, romantic *composition* considered appropriate for a *nighttime serenade!*

node *(nōd)* From the science of physics, a *point* or *line* in a *vibrating body* or *string* which *marks* the *absence of vibration,* as contrasted to the other portions of the *body* or *string!* A *single-stretched string in vibration* produces a *fundamental tone* with *nodes only* at the *two ends!* "Stopping" the *string* with a *finger at mid-point* creates a *central node* causing the *string to vibrate* in *two segments* and sound an octave!

noel *(nō'ĕl)* from the French: A *Christmas carol* or *joyful hymn!*

non *(nŏn)* from the Italian: "Not"; *non troppo,* not as much!

nonet *(nōn'ĕt)* A *composition* for *nine singers* or *instrumentalists* with an *individual part* for each in the style of *chamber music!* There may be an *occasional exception* when a *part* may *double another* in the *same or another octave!*

nota cambiata *(nô'tä käm bĭ' ä'tä)* from the Italian: *"Changed note"*, sometimes shortened to *cambiata!* The expression refers to *notes inserted between chords* to which they are *dissonant*, usually *rising* or *falling* in the same manner as the *chords themselves!*

notation *(nō tā'shŭn)* The system or process of *writing music* by the use of *notes or signs* which indicate *pitch or harmony* or *meter* or *tempo*, and other salient data for *performance!*

note *(nōt)* A *symbol* placed on a *staff* which details the *pitch* by its *position*, and the *time-value (duration)* by its *shape!* See *Elements of Music, Notes and Rests!*

notturno *(nôt tōōr nô)* The *Italian term* for *nocturne!*

novachord *(nōva kôrd)* An *electronic keyboard in-* *strument* with *twelve oscillators* to *reproduce* each *note* of a *chromatic scale!* The *oscillators* can be altered or blended by the use of *controls* and *pedals*.

nuance *(nū'äns)* In *performance*, a *shading* or *subtle variation* in *timbre* or *tempo* or *intensity* not indicated in the *arrangement* of a *composition!*

number opera. *Opera* divided into *musical pieces* (*duets, arias, ensemble chorus,* etc.) called *"numbers"* which are tied together by *dialog! Number opera* was common until the mid-19th century, when Wagner brought forth the *all-music, operatic form!*

nun's fiddle. A *trombo marina*, a *form* of *novachord!* In German, *nonnengeige!*

nuovo, di *(nōō ō'vē, dē)* from the Italian: "Again"; a direction to play again or anew!

nut *(nŭt)* (1) In *stringed instruments*, the *ridge* towards the *head* of the *fingerboard* over which the *strings* are *stretched!* (2) The *movable slide* at the end of a *violin bow* which tightens or loosens the *bow hairs!*

— O —

O. (1) A small ᵒ *sign*, inserted over or under *notes* in *written music* for *stringed instruments*, which indicates that the *notes* are *to be played* on an *open (unstopped)* string or that a *harmonic* should be employed. The *sign* is also used in so-called "*chordgrid*", *guitar-diagrams* to signify an *open string*! (2) For *brass instruments*, the ᵒ *sign* indicates an *unstopped, unmuted note*! (3) For *woodwinds*, the ᵒ *sign* indicates a *harmonic* should be played by *overblowing*!

obbligato *(ŏb lĭ gä'tō)* (1) An *indispensable part* in the *performance* of a *composition* .... as opposed to an *optional part* termed *ad libitum*! (2) A *melodic accompaniment part* to a *melody* with other *concerted accompaniment;* for example, a *solo violin obbligato* to a *vocal lead* with *piano accompaniment*!

oblique motion. See *Motion*!

oboe *(ō'bō)* One of the *four basic woodwinds* with a *double reed* and a *slender, conical tube* complete with *six finger holes* and a *complicated array of keys*! A *non-transposing instrument* with a *range of about two and a half octaves (B-flat to G''')*, the *oboe* dates back to ancient history! The present form, however, stems from the mid-17th century reign of French royalty when the *oboe* was known as the *hautbois*! The *oboe* is variously known as the *hautboy, schalmei, chalumeau,* etc.

oboe, alto. An obsolete version of the *oboe* with a *pitch* that is a *fifth below* the *modern instrument*! Another obsolete *alto* or *tenor* (with a *curved tube*) *version* is called *oboe da caccia*, which also sounds a *fifth below* its *modern descendant*! The *alto oboe* has another obsolete variation which is called the *oboe d'amore*, pitched a *minor third* below the *modern oboe*!

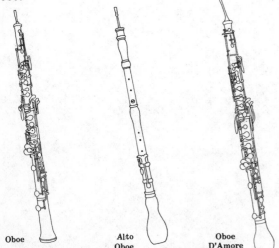

Oboe   Alto Oboe   Oboe D'Amore

ocarina *(ŏk'ȧ rē'nȧ)* "A goose pipe"! A simple, toylike *wind instrument* of terra-cotta construction with *finger holes* and *mouthpiece* that produce *whistling tones*. Colloquially known as *sweet potato* or *hot potato*!

ocarina

octave *(ok'tāv)* (1) The *eight diatonic tones* of any *major or minor scale* (see *Interval*)! (2) The *interval* between the *first* and *last notes* of an *octave scale*! (3) The *harmonic combination* of *two notes*, wherein the *frequency* of the *higher note* is *exactly double* the *frequency* of the *lower note*! (4) An *organ stop* with *pipe tones* an *octave above* the *digital keys*!

octave coupler. An *organ-device* which add (to the *notes* being *played*) the *tones* of an *upper* or *lower octave*!

octave flute. Another name for the *piccolo*!

octave key. A *key* on *wind instruments* that raises the *sound* of *other keys* by *one octave*!

octavina *(ŏk tȧ vē nȧ)* A small *spinet pitched* an *octave higher* than the usual *spinet*!

octavo *(ŏk'tä vō)* Denotes the 6 x 9½ size of paper commonly used for *printed choral music*!

octet,-tette *(ŏk'tĕt)* (1) A *composition* for *eight instrumental* or *vocal soloists*! (2) Any *group* of *eight instrumentalists* or *vocalists*!

ode *(ōd)* A *poem* set to *music*, usually honoring a particular person or occasion!

oder *(ō'dĕr)* from the German: "Or", "or else"!

off. (1) A direction to an *organist* to use a *stop* or *coupler*! (2) "Off pitch"; *false pitch*, "out of tune", etc.!

offertory *(ŏf ĕr tō'rē)* (1) The fourth section of the *Proper* from the Roman Catholic *Mass*! (2)

ohne *(ō'nĕ)* from the German: "Without"!

oliphant *(ŏl'ĭ fȧnt)* A medieval ivory horn made from an elephant's tusk!

oliphant

ondeggiamento *(ŏn dĕ jä mĕn'tō)* / **ondeggiando** *(ŏn dĕ jän'dō)* / **ondeggiante** *(ŏn dĕ jän'tĕ)* It. / A direction to a *violinist* to *rock* his *bow* in *performance*, creating an *undulating* or *wavy shading* of the *pitch intensity*!

ondes Martenot *(ônd mär tĕn ō')* An *electronic instrument* (named after the French inventor Maurice Martenot) that used a *single oscillator* to *produce pitched tones one at a time*! The *range* was *seven octaves* but limited, of course, *to single note melody without chords*! Also known as *ondes musicales*!

ondulé *(ôn dŭ lā')* The *French* equivalent of *ondeggiando*!

one-step. An old *American dance* (off-shoot of the *turkey trot*) which was popular in ballrooms from 1910 until 1929!

ongarese, all' *(ôn gä rā'zĕ, äl)* from the Italian: "*Hungarian style*"; a direction to play with the flavor of *Hungarian gypsy music*!

op. The abbreviation for *Opus*!

open pedal (*ō'pĕn pĕd'ăl*) The *damper pedal* on the piano ("*right*" *pedal*)!

open string. A *string* that sounds its *full tone* without being *stopped* or *fretted*! A *note* on an *open string* is indicated by a *small zero sign* ^{o} *placed above* or *below* the *note*, or *above* a *guitar* "*chord-grid*" *diagram* which depicts the *chordal tuning*!

Unstopped Notes on Violin, etc.

"Chord Grid"
Guitar tuned to E-A-D-G-B-E in this E-Minor Chord: E-G-B-E strings are "Open"!

Em

open tone. The *tone* produced by *unstopped fingering* on a *string instrument*, or by *blowing* on a *wind instrument* without the use of *keys, finger holes, valves, stopping,* etc.

opera (*ŏp'ĕr à*) A *musical drama* which is almost completely *sung* with *orchestral accompaniment*! The *vocals* may include *solo arias, duets, trios, sextettes, ensemble chorus,* etc.! The *instrumental music* may include *overtures, preludes* and *interludes*! Usually *staged* with *full theatrical costuming, lighting, scenery* and *direction, opera* probably began in *sixteenth century Italy* from where it spread its cultural appeal to *France, Germany, Russia,* etc., producing in the next two centuries much of the world's greatest *classical composition*! Noted *operatic composers* include the *Italian* Verdi, Donizetti, Rossini; the *French* Bizet, Debussy; the *German* Wagner, Beethoven, Weber, Richard Strauss; the *Russian* Tchaikovsky, Rimski-Korsakov, Moussorgsky, Borodin!

opera ballet. *Opera* which features *ballet dancing*!

opéra bouffe (*ō'pä rà bōof'*) Fr. / **opera buffa** (*ô'pä rä bōof'ä*) It. / *Light, comic opera* tending towards farce or burlesque!

opéra comique (*ō'pä rà kō mēk'*) from the French: "*Comic opera*"; the *French* term for *opera* using *spoken dialogue intermittently*, as contrasted to *grand opera* which is *completely sung*! *Opera comique* need *not* be *comical* or *humorous*; the literal meaning was applicable only in the eighteenth century!

opera house. A theater devoted mainly to the *performance of opera*!

operetta (*ŏp ĕr ĕt'à*) from the Italian: "*Little opera*"; a *light, humorous* or *satiric plot* or *poem*, set to appropriately *cheerful* and *lively music*, with occasional *spoken dialogue*!

ophicleide (*ŏf'ĭ klīd'*) A rarely-used form of *key bugle* with a *bass* or *baritone range*!

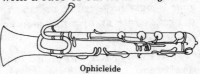

Ophicleide

opus (*ō'pŭs*) A *composition* or *work*, frequently numbered to identify the order of a *series of works* . . . . *opus number 3*, for example, would mark the third in a series of *one composer's publications*!

oratorio (*ô rä tô' rē ō*) An *extended Scriptural text* which includes *vocal arias, duets, quartets, chorus ensemble,* etc., set to *orchestral accompaniment*, but designed for *concert performance* without *drama, costume* or *scenery*! The *oratorio form* may be used, infrequently, in *secular music*!

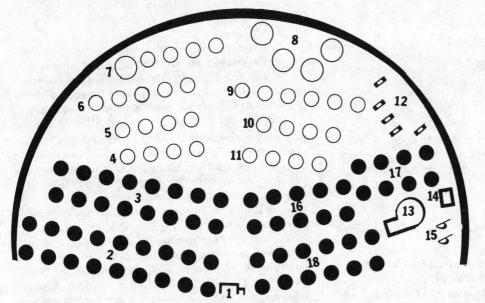

1	Conductor
2	18-First Violins
3	16-Second Violins
4	3-Flutes 1-Piccolo
5	3-Clarinets 1-Bass Clarinet
6	5-Trumpets
7	4-Trombones 1-Tuba
8	4-Timpani
9	6-French Horns
10	3-Bassoons 1-Contrabassoon
11	3-Oboes 1-English Horn
12	5-Percussion
13	1-Piano
14	1-Celesta
15	2-Harp
16	10-Cellos
17	8-Double Bass
18	12-Violas

Although there are no strict rules, a *full-size symphonic orchestra* usually is *positioned for performance* as shown above!

orchestra (ôr'kĕs trá) All of the *musicians* playing any, or all of the *string, brass, woodwind* and *percussion instruments in ensemble*, constitute an *orchestra*, which is almost always directed by a *conductor!* The number of *musicians* in a *symphonic orchestra* can range from a condensed group of about 50 to 60 to a complete group of about 115 to 120 members! A *modern dance band orchestra* would consist of perhaps 22 to 32 members with 5 *brass*, 5 *reeds*, 4 *rhythm*, and various percussion and violins making up the remainder! *Optional instruments* added to *symphonic orchestras* to meet the needs of a composition include *saxophones, harpsichord, recorder, flügelhorn, cornet, bugle, euphonium, xylophone* and a vast assortment of *percussive* variations . . . *blocks, bells, maracas, claves*, etc.

orchestration. The *art* of *writing music* for *orchestral performance (arrangement* or *arranging)!* Many *composers* have produced their own *detailed orchestrations!* Others have relied on "*specialized*" associates to *orchestrate* an *original composition!*

orchestral score. See *Score!*

orchestrion (ôr'kĕs trē ŏn) A large, mechanically-operated *barrel organ*, with many *stops* to simulate various *instruments* of an *orchestra!*

ordinary (ôr'dĭ nĕr'ē) The fixed portion of all *Roman Catholic* services regardless of time or occasion!

organ (ôr'găn) Probably the most versatile, powerful and complicated of all *musical instruments*, the *organ* is a *keyboard, wind-instrument* (known in modern times as the "*pipe organ*" or "*church organ*") which uses *keyboards* and *pedals* to selectively transmit compressed air through a *set of pipes* and produce *pitched tones*. It consists, basically, of the following components:

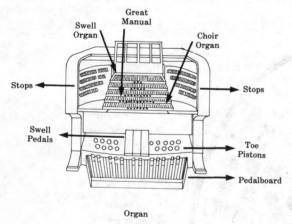

Organ

(1) *Console:*
One or more *rows of keyboard manuals!* A set of *pedals (pedalboard)!* A series of *stops, couplers* and a large, varied assortment of similar devices!

(2) *Action:*
The equipment operated from the *console (pallets* or *sliders)* which forwards air to and through the *pipes* and the *wind chests!* The *action* can take either *tracker* or *pneumatic*

form! The latter in modern times almost always is *electropneumatic* (electricity is required to activate the *pallets* and *sliders*)! The *tracker action* is completely *mechanical!*

(3) *Pipes:*
The *pipework* is arranged in various sizes and shapes (producing the *pitch changes*) and is divided into *stops* or *registers!* The *shorter* the *pipe*, the *higher* its *pitch!* An *open pipe*, two feet long, *sounds middle C!* A four-foot *open pipe* will sound an *octave lower! Couplers* make it possible to use the *stops* of *one register* from the *keyboard* of another!

Two distinct categories of "pipes" are the "*Flue Pipes*" and the "*Reed Pipes*"! *Flue pipes* are cylindrical pipes of varying thickness with slit openings at the top, over which air passes, vibrating the air column within! *Reed pipes* normally are conical and equipped with a brass, beating reed that is vibrated by passing air, transmitting the vibration to the air column within the pipe. Flue pipes include: (a) *Diapason* . . . a complete range of pitch and size, including "open diapason (principal)" and "flautino diapason", "violin diapason", etc. (b) *Flute pipes* . . . including "stopped flute" pipes and "open flute" pipes (spindle, block, chimney, etc.) (c) *String pipes* . . . various pipes with names matching the violin family—viola, cello, gamba, etc. (d) *Hybrid pipes* . . . pipes that blend string, flute, principal sounds (gemshorn, spitzflute, etc.)! *Reed pipes* are comprised of *chorus* and *solo pipes* . . . the chorus pipes are named for the brasses (trombone, trumpet, etc.) and the solo pipes are named for the woodwinds (bassoon, oboe, etc.)!

(4) *Wind Conveyors:*
A series of *bellows, blowers* or other *devices* which convey air streams to the *wind chests*, which are connected to each *pipe* by *pallets* and *slides!* The *wind chests* react to the *keyboard controls*, emitting air to selected *pipes* to produce *pitched sound(s)!*

The organ undoubtedly is the monarch of all instruments, with an enormous *nine-octave range* possible when all combinations of *pipe ranks* are taken into account. The *range* of a normal, modern *organ manual* is *five octaves* from *C to c''''* but the addition of *pipe ranks* to the *standard, 8-foot pitch, unison rank* (the *16-foot suboctave pitch* and *three superoctave pitches* of *4-foot, 2-foot* and *1-foot ranks* respectively) brings the *range* up to the *total* of *nine octaves!* The "*manuals*" or "*organs*" are classified individually as *great organ* (the *largest manuals*); *choir organ* (softer stops suitable for *accompaniment*); *solo organ* (suitable stops for *solo performance*); *pedal organ* (deeptoned stops *played* by the *feet*); *echo organ* (soft, echoing stops) and *swell organ* (pipes with *movable shutters*, controlled by *pedals*, to *increase volume* or "*swell*" the *volume*)!

organette *(ôr'găn ĕt)* (1) A *small, portable organ;* a form of the *medieval Portative organ*, known in *Italian* as the *organetto!* (2) A large *accordion!*

organ point. A *sustained pedal tone* over which a *harmonic chord progression* is *structured!* Also known as *pedal point!*

organum *(ôr'gä nŭm)* from the Latin: *Polyphonic music* in its most primitive form, dating from medieval times! A *Plainsong melody (cantus firmus)* would be *accompanied* by other *voice parts* moving in *parallel* at a *fourth, fifth* or *octave below the melody!*

orgel *(ôr'gĕl)* The *German* word for *organ!*

orgue *(ôrg)* The *French* word for *organ!*

orgue de barbarie *(–dē bär bē rē')* The *French* term for a *street organ* or *barrel organ* which produces a *"barbarous" sound!*

ornament *(ôr'nă mĕnt)* An *embellishing note* or *notes* added by the *performer* or *composer* to the *basic composition!* Ornament styles include a *trill, turn, mordent, appoggiatura, acciaccatura, grace note,* etc., each of which is indicated by special signs in a score: The mordent ⌇ or ～ ; the trill

 the turn

; *acciaccatura* [musical notation] ; grace note [musical notation]

osservanza, con *(ŏs sĕr vänts'ă, kôn)*/**osservato** *(ŏs sĕr vä'tō)* It. / A direction to play carefully, observing all the *signs* and keeping *strict time!*

ossia *(ŏs sē'ă)* from the Italian: "Or", "or else"; an indication to use an alternate way to *play* a *portion* of *music*, usually a modified, easier way around any *performance* difficulty!

ostinato, basso *(ôs tē nä'tō, bä'sō)* The *Italian* term for *"ground bass"!* Sometimes shortened to *ostinato!* See *ground bass!*

otez *(ō tā')* from the French: "Take off"; *otez les sourdines,* take off the *mutes; otez les boutons,* take off the *stops!*

ottava *(ōt tä'vä)* from the Italian: An *octave* which is designated in *notation* by the *sign* 𝟴*va*- - - - or

𝟴 - - - - - (1) Placed *over a note*, the *sign* means "*play one octave higher than as written!* Also called *all'ottava, ottava alta* or *ottava sopra!* (2) Placed *under a note*, the sign means "*play one octave lower than as written*"! Also called *ottava bassa* or *ottava sotto!* (3) Placed *under the bass clef*, the 𝟴*va* or 𝟴 means all the *notes* in the *bass staff* should be played an *octave lower than as written!* Placed under the *treble clef*, the same *sign* means all the *notes* in the *treble staff* should be *played* an *octave higher than written!*

ottavino *(ōt tä vē'nō)* The *Italian* term for *piccolo!*

ouverture *(ōō vâr tür')* Fr. / **ouvertüre** *(ōō vâr tü'rĕ)* Ger. / Overture!

overblowing *(ō'vĕr blō'wĭng)* The technique of producing *harmonic overtones* with *wind instruments* by *blowing harder* than *usual* and/or *altering* the *mouth and lip position!* Generally, *overblowing the oboe, English horn, bassoon* and *open organ pipes* results in a *tone one octave higher than usual!* *Overblowing the clarinet* or *closed organ pipe* will produce a *tone higher than usual by an octave and a fifth (a twelfth)!*

overtone *(ō'vĕr tŏn)* One of the *harmonic tones* sounding above the *fundamental tone.* See *Harmonic series!*

overture *(ō'vĕr tür)* A *composition* which *musically introduces* an *opera, oratorio* or similar "*whole work*"! A *concert overture* is an *independent composition*, usually in the form of a *sonata!*

DICTIONARY

P , Q , R

P. (1) An abbreviation for the Italian direction "*piano*", meaning "soft"! (2) An abbreviation ℘. or ℘ for *pedal* on *keyboards!* (3) An abbreviation for the *French* "*Pointe*", "toe"; or the *French* "*Positif*", "choir-organ"!

padovana *(pă dō vä'nă)* The *Italian* name for *pavane!*

paduane *(pä'dōō ä'nä)* The *German* name for *pavane!*

pallet *(păl'ĕt)* An *organ part* which links the *wind chests* with the *pipes!* See *Organ!*

pandean *(păn dē'ăn)* A member of a Panpipe band! See *Panpipe!*

pandora *(păn dō'rä)* An *Italian bandora!*

pandore *(păn dōr')* A *French bandora!*

pandura *(păn dū'rä)* Another name for the *Italian bandore!*

panharmonic *(păn'här mŏn'ĭk)* Applicable to all *modes* and *harmonics!*

panharmonicon *(păn'här mŏn'ĭk ŏn)* An *instrument* similar to an *orchestrion*, invented in 1900 by J. N. Maelzel, who also invented the *metronome!*

panmelodion *(păn'mĕ lō'dĭ ŭn)* A *keyboard instrument* that rotates *wheels* against a series of *metal bars* to produce *pitched tones!*

panpipe *(păn'pīp)* An *ancient, elementary wind instrument* (in *Greek* mythology, credited to the god *Pan*) consisting of a *series of connected pipes* of *graduated size!* Each *pipe* is *closed at the end*, has *no finger holes* and produces simply *one tone!* Harmonics are made possible only by *overblowing!* It is *played* by *blowing across* the *top* of the *pipes!*

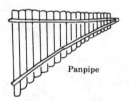

Panpipe

pantomime *(pan'tō mīm)* "All imitating"; a *dramatic performance* using only *physical dance movement* or *gestures* with no *sung* or *spoken word* ("*dumb show*")!

parallel chords, parallel intervals. When *chords* and *intervals* of *two or more parts* move along in consecutive repetition, they are deemed *parallel!* In *traditional harmony, parallel thirds* and *sixths* are *permissible* while *parallel fifths* and *octaves* are considered taboo! Many *modern composers*, starting with the *Impressionists*, have ignored the tradiţional limitations on *parallel chords* and encourage what is termed "*expressive dissonance*"!

paraphrase *(păr'ă frāz)* A *transcription* or *rearrangement* of a *composition* (written for *particular instrument(s)* or *vocal(s)*) which is to be used by *other instruments* (or *vocalists* of a *different range*) than those intended in the original writing! Considerable latitude for variation is common in "*music paraphrasing*"!

parlando *(pär län'dō)* / **parlente** *(pär län'tĕ)* It. / "Speaking"; (1) A direction to *sing* with crisp clear enunciation! (2) A direction for *instrumentalists* to *play* in a crisp, *distinctly-marked* manner as contrasted to a smooth *legato!*

parody *(pär'ō dē)* (1) A *burlesque imitation* of a *musical work* or *style!* (2) In olden times, *parody* referred to a *serious re-working* of a *simpler composition*, changing it into a *more complicated* or *extended work* with neither burlesque nor humour intended!

part *(pärt)* (1) The *melodic* or *harmonic notes* written for a particular *instrument* or *voice* to be *played in concert*, such as the *violin part, piano part, soprano part*, etc! (2) In all *music* using *more than one melodic line* (homophony, polyphony), a *part* refers to *each melodic line's development*, as in the terms *three-part fugue* or *four-part "barbershop" harmony!*

parte *(pär'tĕ)* The *Italian* word for *part!*

parte, colla *(kôlä)* from the Italian: A direction to play "*with the part*", meaning the *accompaniment* should follow and adjust to the *soloist's discretionary rendition* in terms of *tempo, phrasing*, etc.!

partial stop. A *half-stop!*

partial tone. An *overtone* or *harmonic tone!*

partita *(pär tē'tä)* from the Italian: (1) A *variation* or *series of variations!* (2) One of the initial forms of a *suite!*

partition *(pär tĭsh ôn')* Fr. / **partitur** *(pär'tĭ tōōr)* Ger. / **partitura** *(pär tē tōō'rä)* It. / A *score*, or *full score!*

part music. *Vocal music* with *harmonized multiple parts!*

part song. *Multiple-part vocal music*, in which the *highest part* usually carries the *melody* and the *remaining parts* offer *accompanying chord harmony!*

paspy *(päs'pē)* Another name for *passepied!* See *passepied!*

passacaglia *(päs sä käl'yä)* An old *Italian dance* almost identical to the *chaconne!* Usually written with a slow, stately *triple time movement over a ground bass* (basso ostinato) divided into *four-bar sections!* The precise distinctions between *chaconne* and *passacaglia* are a matter of dispute among musical authorities to this day!

passacaille *(pă sä kä'ĕ)* The French word for *passacaglia!*

passage *(päs'ĭj)* (1) A *short portion* of a *composition!* (2) A series of *rapid notes* usually requiring some virtuosity! See *run, flourish, arpeggio*, etc.!

passaggio *(päs säd'jō)* from the Italian: (1) A *modulation!* (2) An *ad lib embellishment* not written in the *score!* (3) A system of voice-training which concentrates on the throat areas that shape resonance, and tends to improve the muscular ability required to sing in smooth transition from low notes to high notes, or vice-versa!

passamezzo *(pä sä mĕ'tsō)* An old *Italian* dance in *double time!* The *passamezzo* is very similar to the *pavane* but perhaps taken more often at a *livelier tempo!*

passepied *(päs pyā')* A lively French dance of the 17th century in *3/4* or *3/8 time!* Somewhat resembles a sped-up *minuet!* Also known as *paspy!*

passing note, passing tone. A *note* or *tone* which is *foreign to the chord it accompanies* but which *passes on step-wise* to connect essential notes in the *harmony! Passing tones* usually are *not accented!*

Passion, Passion music. Any musical setting of *Biblical* text depicting *Christ's* suffering and death on the cross!

passionato *(päs syō nä 'tō)* from the Italian: A direction to play in a "passionate", fervent manner!

pasticcio *(päs tĭt'chō)* It. / **pastiche** *(päs tĕsh')* Fr. / A *musical work* consisting of excerpts from different works *(potpourri)!*

pastoral music. *Music* expressing rural life! *Shepherd* and *country sounds,* etc!

pastorale *(päs tō rä'lĕ)* from the Italian: (1) A *short cantata* representing rural life! (2) An *instrumental work* which expresses an idyllic, rural environment.

patch *(păch)* A *diagram* of the *electronic settings* of a *synthesizer* which *"charts"* the *settings* of *various controls* to produce a particular *sound* or *"tone"!* Individual *patches* are drawn for *trademarked synthesizer models* such as *Arp* and *Moog,* while a *generalized Universal patch* may be applied to any type of *synthesizer!*

SYNTHESIZER "PATCH" DIAGRAMS

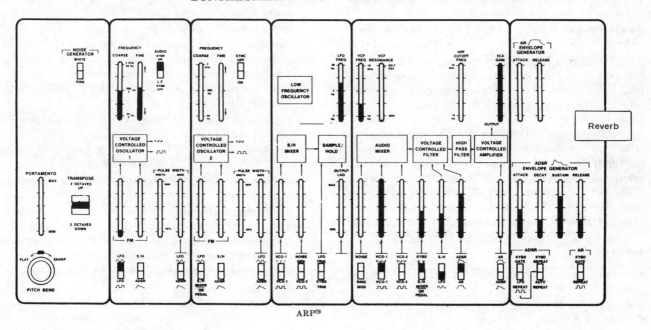

ARP®

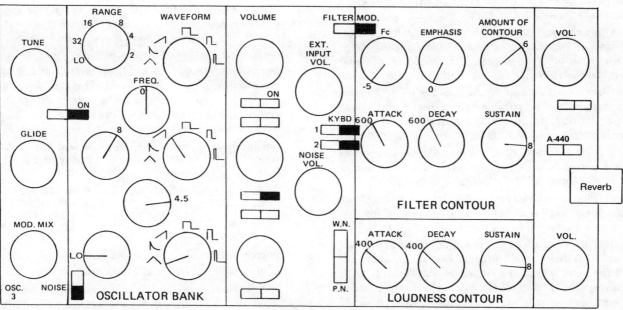

MOOG™

©Almo Publications Used by permission

660

patent notes *(păt'ĕnt nōts).* Same as *shaped notes!* See *shaped notes!*

patetico *(pä tä tē'kō)* It. / **pathetique** *(pä tä tēk')* Fr. / **pathetisch** *(pa'tä tĭsh)* Ger. / A direction to perform with deep, "pathetic" feeling!

patter song *(păt'ēr)* A *comic opera song* which is *sung rapidly* or *half-recited* in *parlando* fashion! The *flow of the patter,* as much as the *lyric content,* contributes to the humorous quality of the *composition!*

pauken *(pou'kĕn)* The *German* word for *timpani* or *kettledrums* (singular, "pauke")!

pausa *(pou'zä)* It. / **pause** *(pōz)* Fr. / **pause** *(pôz)* Eng. / A *rest* or *hold! See fermata,* and *see Elements of Music Notes and Rests!*

pausa generale *(pou'zä jĕn ēr ă lĕ)* from the Italian: A *pause* for the *entire ensemble!*

pausa lunga *(–lŭn'gă)* from the Italian: A *long pause!*

pavan *(păv ăn')* Eng. / **pavana** *(pä vä'nä)* It. / **pavane** *(pä vän')* Fr. / An old, stately *dance* in *moderate double-time, alla breve!* Authorities come up with two conflicting versions as to the source.... one school claims that the *16th century court dance* began in Padua, Italy which was another name for "Pava", whence comes *pavana!* The other version contends that the *dance* was executed in *ceremonial costumes;* hence, in "peacock" garb! Since the *Latin* and *French* roots for "peacock" are *pavus* and *pavo,* one can give some credence to this version! Nevertheless, most authorities lean to the *Paduan-to-Pava* etymology as the accurate explanation!

pavenne *(pä vĕn nĕ)* Another Italian name for *pavan!*

paventato *(pä vĕn tä'tō)* / **paventoso** *(pä vĕn tō'sō)* It. / Timidly, with fear or embarrassment!

pavillon *(pä vē yôn')* from the French: The *bell* of a *brass instrument!*

pavillon chinois *(–shē nwä')* from the French: An *instrument* consisting of *small bells hanging* from *crosspieces* on a rod or pole. The simple act of shaking the *instrument* created the *bell sounds.*

pavillions en l'air *(pä vē yôn'zän'lâr')* The French expression for playing an *instrument* with its *bell* end pointing up, above the horizontal; thus, *increasing the volume.*

peal *(pēl)* A *series of bells tuned* to the *major scale!* (2) A *set of changes upon a prescribed number of bells!* (3) Generally, the *sound of ringing bells!*

ped. The abbreviation for *pedal!* Indicates the *damper (right) pedal* should be depressed for the indicated *notes!* Usually notated in script as 𝒫𝑒𝒹!

pedal *(pĕd'ăl)* Refers to the employment of *foot action!* (1) With *organs,* the *pedal keyboard* consists of all the *keys* which are played by the *feet!* (2) With *pianos,* one of the *foot levers* ... the *damper pedal (right pedal),* which is erroneously called the *loud pedal,* lifts the *damper off* the *strings* to *maintain a*

struck-sound vibration; the *soft pedal (left pedal)* places a *muffler* between the *hammer* and *string* that *shortens* the *stroke* and *decreases* the *volume!* See *piano* for explanation of the *third pedal* found on some *pianos (sostenuto pedal)!* (3) With *harps,* a *foot lever* (there are *seven, en toto) stops a group of strings* and *raises* the *pitch* by a *half-tone* or a *whole-tone* when operated! (4) With *timpani,* a *pedal* loosens or tightens the *drumhead* to achieve a given *pitch!*

pedal point. A *bass note* or *pedal note* which is *sustained,* while a variety of *higher notes* or *chords* are *played!* If a *high note* is used as a *pedal point,* this is called *inverted pedal!* When a *middle-range note* is the *pedal point,* the term employed is *internal pedal!* Other names for *pedal point* include *bourdon, drone bass* or simply *drone* or *pedal!*

pedal tone. The *lowest tone* produced by *brass wind instruments,* the *fundamental tone!* Certain *brass instruments (trumpet, trombone, tuba, etc.)* usually are played at least *one octave* above the *pedal tone,* since the *fundamental tone* may be difficult to execute for the most *skillful players!*

pegs *(pĕgs)* In *stringed instruments,* the *wooden pins* at the *top* of the *neck* which *tighten* or *loosen* the *tension* of *each string!* The *player* turns each *peg* to adjust the *pitch* of *each string!*

peg box. The *part* of the *neck* of *stringed instruments* into which the *pegs* are set!

pentatonic scale *(pĕn'tä tŏn'ĭk skāl)* A *five-tone scale* which eliminates *half-tone steps* by omitting the *fourth* and *seventh tones* of the *major scale* as well as the *second* and *sixth tones* of the *minor scale!*

per *(pĕr)* from the Italian: "For", "by", "in", "from", "through"!

percussion *(pĕr kŭsh'ŭn)* The *sound* or *striking* of a *dissonant tone* or *chord!* (2) The collective group of *percussion instruments* which include *those that can be tuned* .... *timpani, xylophone, celesta, glockenspiel, chimes,* etc. .... and *those that cannot be tuned* .... *snare, tenor, bass drums, triangle, maracas, cymbals, triangle, tambourine,* etc.

percussion stop. (1) A *reed organ stop* which activates a device to strike a *reed* as it is *sounding,* adding *force* and *promptness* to the *tone quality!* (2) An *organ stop (xylophone stop,* etc.) which produces a *tone* by a *striking mechanism!*

perdendosi *(pĕr dĕn'dō sē)* from the Italian: "Losing itself!"; a direction to play gradually more softly and slowly as though dying away!

perfect cadence. See *Cadence!* A *dominant triad chord* preceding the *tonic triad chord!*

perfect interval. See *Interval!* The *fourth, fifth* and *octave intervals!*

perfect pitch. Absolute *pitch!* See *Absolute Pitch!*

perfect trill. A *trill* that *closes* with a *turn!*

perigordino *(pĕ rē gôr dē'nō)* It. / **périgourdine** *(pä rē gōōr dĕn')* Fr. / An old *Flemish dance* named after *Perigord,* a *former province of France!*

period *(pĕr ĭ ŭd)* A *complete musical thought (sentence)*, consisting of two or more *phrases (8 or 16 bars each)*, that end with a *cadence!*

perpetuum mobile *(pĕr pĕt'ū ŭm mō'bĭ lē)* from the Latin: "Perpetual motion"; usually designates a *short, fast composition* with a *repeating rhythm structure!* In *Italian, moto perpetuo!*

pesante *(pä sän'tĕ)* from the Italian: A direction to play in a heavy, impressive manner!

petite *(pĕ tēt')* from the French: Small, little!

petite flute *(-flüt)* The French name for piccolo!

peu *(pû)* from the French: "Little" ... *un peu,* "a little"!

peu à peu from the French: "Little by little"!

pezzo *(pĕt'sō)* from the Italian: A *"piece"*, a bit; *pezzi,* "pieces"; *pezzi staccati, detached pieces of music!*

pf. (1) The abbreviation for *piano forte,* the direction to "begin soft and follow rapidly to loud"! (2) An abbreviation of the older, more formal name for a *piano,* the *pianoforte!*

phase *(fāz)* The *measurement* of the *cycles of air-pressure (sound vibrations)* in *electronic waveform units* called *radians* or *degrees!* An analogued electrical signal is used to determine if magnitudes are *in phase* (the *sound's sine curve relationships are equal*) or *out of phase (unequal)! Phase measurement* is important not only in the use of *modern electronic synthesizers* but affects conventional recording equipment as well. The *"speakers"* in any *stereo component system,* for example, must be *"in phase"* to obtain *accurate "playback".* Mismatched wiring to the terminals of two *"speakers"* may create *"out of phase"* sound!

philharmonic *(fĭl'ĕr mŏn'ĭk)* from the Greek: Literally "loving harmony", which explains the application to *orchestral* names such as the *New York Philharmonic Society* or the *London Philharmonic Orchestra,* etc.!

phonograph *(fō'nō gräf)* An *instrument* for *playing back recorded sound* involving the use of a motor-driven *turntable!* A *"tone-arm"* containing a *stylus* (needle) *tracks* in the *groove* of a *rotating record* and *transmits* the *frequency vibration signal* through the *"tone-arm",* on to the *amplifier* and finally, after conversion, to the *"speakers"* which emit the *finished sound!*

phrase *(frāz)* (1) A *brief musical passage,* usually *four bars ending in a cadence!* (2) Any *melodic figure* in a *larger work* that expresses a *self-contained complete thought!*

phrasing. The art or technique of *grouping notes* for *distinctive performance* or *rendition! A singer's* "style" often relates to the way he takes his *breaths (before, after* or *during a phrase)* and frequently explains the public identification of his "phrasing"! *Composers* indicate their preference for *"phrasing"* by *instrumentalists* and *vocalists* with *articulation signs:* Slurs (‿ ⁀), dotted notes for staccato, etc. (See *Elements of Notation!*)

Phrygian mode *(frĭj'ē ăn)* The *church mode* that begins on *E,* spanning the *white-keys-only* of the *piano* from *E to E* (See *Mode*)!

piacere, a *(pyä châr'ā, ä)* from the Italian: A direction to play "at one's pleasure"! The *performer* may choose his own *tempo* or vary from the *written score (ad lib, ad libitum)!*

piacevole *(pyä chĕ'vōl ē)* from the Italian: A direction to play in a graceful, pleasing manner!

piangendo *(pyän jĕn'dō)* from the Italian: "Weeping"; a direction to play in a plaintive, mournful manner!

pianissimo *(pyä nēs'ē mo)* from the Italian: A direction to play *"very soft"!* Abbreviated ***pp***

piano *(pyä'nō)* from the Italian: A direction to play *"softly"!* Abbreviated ***p***

piano *(pĭ ăn'ō)* A less-formal name for the *pianoforte,* the *piano* universally is recognized as the most familiar of all *keyboard instruments!* In simplistic terms, the *piano* has *keys* which, when depressed, compel *hammers* to strike *strings* and produce *pitched tones!* Differing from its forerunners *(harpsichord, clavichord,* etc.) by its ability to play *soft* or *loud* (hence, *pianoforte*), the *piano* has the *largest range* of all *instruments except for the organ!* There are *88 keys* to the *keyboard,* spanning *seven and one-third octaves,* running from *A to C'''''!*

All *pianos* have two or three *foot-pedals!* The *left pedal (soft pedal)* and the *right pedal (damper pedal,* sometimes *misnomered* as the *loud pedal)* are standard! If there is a *third, center pedal (sostenuto pedal),* it is used to *sustain previous tones while new tones are added!* The signs ℛ or ℒℰⅅ appear in *piano scores* to designate use of the *damper pedal!* An *asterisk* (*) indicates that the *pedal* should be released! *Brackets*⎿_⎾ or ⎾‾⏋ are used to indicate *pedal action* for *groups of piano notes!*

piano duet. A *composition* for *two pianists* to *play* on *one piano!* Infrequently refers to a *piece* for *two pianos!*

piano, grand. The *grand piano* has a *harp-shaped case* with a flat *soundboard* and *horizontal strings!* The sizes range from a *five-foot baby grand* to a *nine-foot concert grand!*

piano quartet. A *composition* for an *individual piano, violin, viola* and *cello,* with an occasional substitution of a *wind instrument (clarinet, oboe,* etc.) for one of the *stringed instruments!*

piano quintet. A *composition* for *piano* and *string quartet (two violins, one viola* and *one cello)* with occasional substitutions of a *wind instrument* for a *stringed instrument!*

piano trio. A composition for an *individual piano, violin* and *cello!*

piano, upright. A *rectangular* or *square-shaped piano* with an *upright soundboard* and *vertical strings!* The sizes range from a *three-foot-high spinet* model to a *42-inch-high console* model or a *46-inch-high studio* model!

PIANO

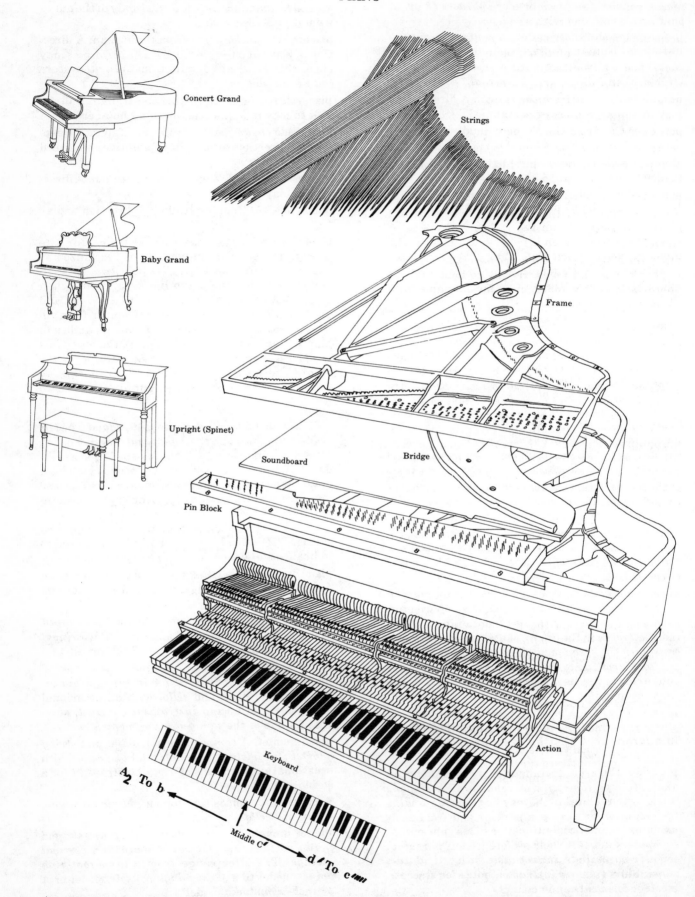

Concert Grand

Baby Grand

Upright (Spinet)

Strings

Frame

Soundboard

Bridge

Pin Block

Action

Keyboard

A₂ To b

Middle C′

d′ To c′′′′′

pianola *(pē'á nō'lă)* A trademarked name for a *player piano!* The *pianola* is a *mechanical piano* that uses a roll of perforated paper to direct an air flow against the *hammers* of a *piano,* thus producing *music!* No human presence is required!

piatti *(pyä'tē)* The Italian name for *cymbals!*

pibroch *(pē'brō)* A *set* of *variations* for the *bagpipe,* unique to the *Scottish highlands!*

Picardy third *(pĭk'ēr dē)* In *baroque music,* the ending of a *minor-key composition* with a *major chord,* the *third!*

picchettato *(pē kē tä'tō)* / **picchiettato** *(pē'kyē tä'tō)* It. / *Detached, staccato;* a direction to *string players* to play a *light, sharp staccato,* using the *bow* in one direction only! Same as the *French "piqué"!*

piccolo *(pĭk' ō lō)* From the Italian: "Small"; the small *octave flute* which is *pitched* an *octave higher* than the *conventional flute!* The *range* is *two octaves up from high C,* but *piccolo music is written* an *octave below its sound!* Also known as *flauto piccolo, ottavino,* etc.!

 Piccolo

pick *(pĭk)* (1) In *guitar* or *stringed-instrument music,* "pick" as a verb refers to the *plucking, pulling* or *twanging* of the *strings!* (2) Used as a noun, "pick" is the same as a *plectrum!* (3) "*Picker*" is the colloquial name for a *guitar-player!* Also called *finger-picker!*

piece *(pēs)* (1) A short *musical* composition! In *French,* "piece" (p'yess)! (2) One *instrument* in an *orchestral assortment!*

pieno *(pyá'nō)* from the Italian: "Full"! (1) Using all the *instrumental* or *vocal power; voce pieno, full voice!* (2) An *organ stop; organo pieno, full organ!*

pietoso *(pyĕ tō'sō)* / **pietosamente** *(pyē tō sä měn'tĕ)* It. / "With pity"; a direction to play in a manner expressing compassion!

piffero *(pēf'fä rō)* from the Italian: (1) A *fife!* (2) A primitive *shawm* or *oboe!* (3) A *tremolo organ stop,* also called *bifara!*

pincé *(păn sā')* from the French: (1) *Plucked* or *pinched!* (2) In the *violin family,* same as *pizzicato!*

pinched *(pĭncht)* (1) *Harmonics* created on *wind instruments* by *overblowing* or by the use of *finger stops!* (2) A *plucked string* is said to be "pinched"!

pipa *(pē'pä)* The new, official romanized spelling of "pyiba", the Chinese lute. See *pyiba.*

pipe *(pīp)* (1) A primitive *oboe* or *flageolet,* or any *crude reed* or *wood tube;* e.g., a *shepherd's pipe!* (2) One of the *open* or *closed tubes* in the *pipework* of an *organ!* (3) A *fipple flute* (similar to a *recorder*) played along with a *tabor!*

Pipe

piqué *(pē kā)* The *French* term for *picchiettato!*

piston *(pĭs'tŭn)* (1) A *sliding valve* (moving in a cylinder) found on *brass instruments* which, when depressed, directs the air column into an *extension* tube ("crook") attached to the *main tube!* This "lengthening" of the air column *lowers* the *pitch!* (2) A *movable knob* on an *organ keyboard,* used to *alter* the *registration!*

pitch *(pĭch)* (1) The *relative* or *absolute position* of a *tone* as compared with other *tones! Pitch* is determined by the *rate of vibration of the sound waves!* The *faster the number of vibrations per second,* the *higher the pitch of the tone,* and vice versa! *Relative pitch* refers to the *position* of a *tone* in a *scale! Absolute pitch* deals with the *position of a tone in a fixed-octave scale* that is organized according to mathematical measurement of the *vibrations per second* called the *vibration number!* See *Elements of Music: Octaves!* The *standard vibration number* (*concert pitch*) is almost universally recognized today as *440 double vibrations* for *treble A* (also called *philharmonic pitch*) although the *French* sometimes revert to an historical *435 double vibrations* for *a'* (the *old international pitch*)! *British military bands* may adhere to their "concert high pitch" which is *450 double vibrations for a'!* (2) The *pitch* of an *instrument* refers to its *fundamental tone!* A *B-flat instrument* is constructed to *produce B-flat* as its *fundamental tone* when *blown!*

pitch pipe *(pĭch pīp)* A *small reed pipe* which sounds the *distinct, pitched tones* of an *octave!* At one time popular as a *tuning guide* for *choral,* or *instrumental groups,* it has given way professionally to the *tuning fork!*

più *(pyōō)* from the Italian: "More"! Used in various directions such as *più allegro,* more lively; *più lento,* slower! By itself, *più* signifies "faster" which is also the meaning of *più mosso or più moto; più mosso ancora,* still faster!

piuttosto *(pyōō tôs'tō)* from the Italian: "Somewhat", "rather"; used in directions such as *piuttosto lento,* rather slow!

pivot chord *(pĭv'ŭt kôrd)* A *chord* used in *modulation* from one *key to another* but *harmonically pivoted* to both!

pizzicato *(pĭt'sē kä tō)* from the Italian: "Pinched", a direction to *string-players* to *pluck* the *strings(s)* instead of using the *bow!* Abbreviated *pizz.!*

placidamente *(plä'chē dä měn'tā)* / **placido** *(plä'chē dō)* It. / A direction to play in a calm, "placid" manner!

plagal cadence. See *Cadence!*

plagal mode. See *Mode!*

plainchant *(plān chänt)* plainsong *(-sŏng).* The *old, unison chant* music of a *church service,* structured in one of the *church* or *ecclesiastical modes* (see *Mode*)! *Plainsong melody* is used as a *cantus firmus* in *counterpoint* and therefore, sometimes, itself is called *cantus firmus!*

player piano. The general term for a *pianola type* of *piano* (see *Pianola*)!

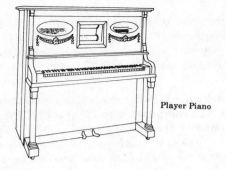

Player Piano

plectrum *(plĕk'trŭm)* A *pick!* A small piece of *ivory, quill, plastic, wood, metal, bone* or *horn* which is *held* by the *fingers* and used to *pluck* a *guitar, mandolin, zither* or similar *instrument!*

plein *(plăn)* from the French: "Full"; *plein-jeu (-zhü), full organ,* a *combination organ stop!*

pochette *(pŭ shĕt')* from the French: A *very small violin!*

pochettino *(pō kĕt'tē nō)* from the Italian: "Very little", used as a direction to mean "even less than *poco*"!

poco *(pô'kō)* from the Italian: "Little", "slightly"; *poco piu allegro,* slightly faster; *poco largo,* somewhat slow; *poco meno mosso,* a little slower! Frequently contracted to *po'* (po) as in *alzando un po' la voce,* raising the voice a little!

poco a poco *(ä pô'kō)* from the Italian: "Little by little", gradually!

podium *(pō'dē ŭm)* A *platform* or *one-man dais* on which the *orchestral conductor stands!*

poi *(pō'ē)* from the Italian: "Then", "after", "afterward"; *piano poi forte,* soft, then loud; *poi la coda,* after the given section, play the *coda!*

point d'orgue *(pwăn dôrg)* from the French: (1) The *pause* ⌢ ! (2) *Pedal point!* (3) A *cadenza* in a *concerto* (which has a *pause sign* over the *chord preceding its start*)!

pointe *(pwănt)* from the French: (1) a *dot* or *point!* (2) The *head* of the *violin bow!*

polacca *(pō läk'kä)* The *Italian* name for *polonaise,* the *Polish national dance!* See *polonaise!*

polka *(pōl'kä)* A *spirited, hopping dance* in *2/4 time* with an *accent* on the *second beat* (the *third eighth note*)! *Bohemian* in origin, the *polka* (literally, "*Polish woman*") has been particularly popular in *Polish* circles as a *ballroom favorite.*

Polka

polo *(pō'lō)* An *Andalusian gypsy dance* in *3/8 meter* with frequent *syncopation* and *declamatory vocalized expressions* such as "*Olé*", "*Ay*", etc.!

Polo

polonaise *(pŏl'ō nāz')* from the French: A *courtly Polish dance* in 3/4 time with a distinctive repeated rhythm pattern and frequent "weak-beat" cadences (feminine cadence)! Probably immortalized by *Chopin's Polonaise militaire!*

Polonaise

poly *(pŏl'ĭ)* A combining prefix that adds the meaning "many" or "multiple" to its following suffix!

polyacoustic *(pŏl'ĭ ȧ kōōs'tĭk)* Multiplying or increasing sound!

polychord *(pŏl'ĭ kôrd)* (1) With many *strings!* (2) A *ten-string instrument* (shaped like an old *viol*) with a moving *fingerboard!*

polyphonic *(pŏl'ĭ fŏn'ĭk)* (1) *Contrapuntal music* with *two or more melodies combined!* (2) Able to produce more than *one tone simultaneously* (*organ, harp,* etc.)!

polyphony *(-'fō nē)* (1) Multiple sounds! (2) The *harmonized progression* of *two or more independent melodies* in *counterpoint* to *each other!*

polytonality *(pŏl'ĭ tō năl'ĭ tē)* The *simultaneous use* of *two or more tones or keys!*

pomposo *(pŏm pō'sō)* from the Italian: A direction to play in a "pompous", stately manner!

ponderoso *(pŏn dĕ rō'sō)* from the Italian: A direction to play in a heavy "ponderous" style!

ponticello *(pŏn tĭ chĕl' ō)* (1) The *bridge of a violin* or other *instrument* using a *bow! Sul ponticello,* "use the *bow* over the *bridge*"! (2) A direction to guitarists to strum close to the bridge, achieving a metallic sound ("metallico")!

pop or **popular music.** *Music* for the *masses!* The category of *music* that sells the most records or occupies the most air time and constitutes the commercial, less-intellectualized "escapist entertainment" levels as contrasted to "*serious*" or "*classical*" music which is considered more conformed and committed to authoritative rules of art! Some degree of pretentiousness or "snobbery" invariably clouds the *classical* view of *popular music* since the latter can, and often does, project much artistic merit. Broadly, however, the *serious composer* or *performer* probably does represent a more timeless concern for the *art of music* than the *popular writer* or *performer* whose impact may be only temporal. *Popular music* in reverse chronological order has produced varied American vogues such as *disco, rock, country, soul, jazz, theater* and *film music, dance band, crooning, rhythm and blues, ragtime, work songs, folk songs, spiritual* and *sacred,* etc.!

popping *(pŏp'ĭng)* (1) A colloquial term for an *electric bass-guitar technique* of *thumping* the *low strings* with the *thumb* while *picking* the *high strings* with the *first* and *second fingers!* (2) A vernacular term for the *percussive distortions* caused by singing or playing straight into (and too close to) a microphone, as opposed to projecting the voice or instrument slightly across the microphone head! "Popping" is particularly chronic with hard, consonant-type sounds!

portamento *(pōr tä měn'tō)* from the Italian: *Sliding from one tone to another* with *rapid slurring* of the *intermediate tones!* Mainly used as a direction for *vocalists* or *bowed string-instrument players!* The French equivalent is *port de voix!*

portando *(pōr tän'dō)* from the Italian: "To carry", the same as *portamento; portando la voce, sing portamento* style!

portative *(pōr'tä tǐv)* A small *portable organ* from medieval times . . . the *Italian organetto!*

portato *(pōr tä'tō)* from the Italian: A direction to play somewhere between *legato* and *staccato* . . . usually designated by a *slur sign* under *dotted note groups!* With *strings, portato notes are played in one stroke of the bow!*

posato *(pŏ sä'tō)* from the Italian: A direction to play in a *dignified, placid manner!*

posaune *(pō zou'ne)* (1) The *German name* for *trombone!* (2) An *organ reed-stop* with a *trombone tone!*

position *(pō zǐsh'ŭn)* (1) Any of the *points* on the *fingerboard* of *stringed instruments* where the *fingers* are "positioned" to *stop* the *string(s)* and *produce pitch changes!* In the first *position*, the *first finger (forefinger* or *index finger)* of the *left hand* is placed on the *fingerboard point closest to the pegs!* This produces a *tone* on the *stopped string* that is *one whole tone higher than the tone of the open string(s).* On the *G string* of *violins*, for example, the *first position* means *G* is the *open string* and the *a, b, c', d' strings* are *stopped successively* by the *four fingers of the left hand*, beginning with the *index finger!* In *subsequent positions*, the *left hand moves (shifts) down the fingerboard!* In the *second position*, the *index finger* is placed on *b*, and the other *fingers on c', d', e';* in the *third position* the *index finger* is placed on *c'* and so on! On the *cello*, the *thumb* is used for *higher positions!* (2) The *placement* of the *slide* on the *slide trombone!* In the *first position*, the *slide* is *drawn in fully!* Subsequent *positions* are *graduated up* to the *fully-extended position*, the *seventh position!* (3) The *location of notes* in a *chord relative to each other!* In the *fundamental first position*, the *lowest part takes the root!* In the *second position*, the *lowest part takes the third*, etc.!

possible *(pŏs sē'bē lě)* from the Italian: "Possible"; *il più forte possible*, as loud as possible; *pianissimo possible*, as soft as possible!

post horn. A *brass-wind horn*, with a *straight tube* and a *cupped mouthpiece*, that plays *simple tones* with no *keys or valves!* Originally used on mail coaches!

postlude *(pōst'lūd)* A *closing passage* of *music;* particularly, a *concluding voluntary* to a *church service!*

potpourri *(pō pōo'rē')* from the French: A *medley!*

poussez *(pōo sā')* The *French word* for "up-bow" (see *bowing*)!

pp. The abbreviation for *pianissimo!*

ppp. The abbreviation for *pianissississimo!*

pralltriller *(präl'trǐl ēr)* An *upper auxiliary note* of a *mordent;* sometimes called *inverted mordent.* (see *Mordent*)!

Pralltriller

precentor *(prē sěn'tér)* The *leader* and *musical director* of a *choir* or *congregation*, particularly for a *church* or *cathedral!*

precipitando *(prě chē pē tän'dō)* / **precipitato** *(prě chē pē tä'tō)* / **precipitoso** *(prě chē pē tō'sō)* It. / A direction to play in a *precipitous, hurried manner!*

preciso *(prě chē'zō)* from the Italian: A direction to *play* with *precision*, in *exact time* and *distinctly accented!*

prelude *(prĕl'ūd)* A *musical introduction* to *another work* (usually larger) such as an *opera* or *fugue!* In *Italian, preludio* (prě lōo'dē ō)!

première *(prē myâr)* Fr. / **premier** *(prē'mǐ ěr)* Eng. / The *first performance* of a *composition* or *theatrical production!*

preparation *(prěp'à rā'shŭn)* Anticipation of a *dissonant tone (preparing)* by *sounding* that *tone* in the *preceding consonant chord!*

prepared chord. A *chord* with a *dissonant note* which is *consonant* in the *preceding chord!*

prepared piano. A *piano* whose *timbre* is *deliberately altered* by placing objects on or between the *strings!* John Cage and Karlheinz Stockhausen, *modernist composers*, are notorious for their non-conventional use of nuts, bolts, screws, bottle caps, etc. to "prepare" a *piano* before *performance!*

pressando *(prě sän'dô)* / **pressante** *(prě sän'tě)* It. / A direction to "press on" and *speed up performance!*

prestissimo *(prěs tē'sē mō)* from the Italian: A direction to *play* in a *very rapid* manner!

presto *(prěs'tō)* from the Italian: A direction to *play* in a *rapid* manner!

prima,-o *(prē'mä,-o)* from the Italian: "First"!

prima buffa *(-bōō'fä)* from the Italian: The *leading female singer* in *comic opera (opera bouffe)!*

prima come *(-kô'mě)* from the Italian: "As at first", play the *music as played before* . . . in the *same tempo*, etc.!

prima donna *(-dŏn'à)* from the Italian: The *leading female singer* in an *opera!*

prima vista *(-vǐs'tä)* from the Italian: "At first sight"; *sight-reading!*

prima volta *(-vôl'tä)* from the Italian: "The first time"; a direction in *written music* to *play* the *first* of *two or more endings* for a *repeating section of music!* The *sign* for *prima volta* usually is a *bracket*

666

over the ending bar(s) marked with the numeral 1
... also written as *ima volta* or I! The *second ending (seconda volta)* would be marked or II *da volta* or just II!

primo *(prē'mō)* from the Italian: "The first" ... the *leading part* or *first part* in a *duet!* The *first* of a *group of players* in the *same instrument family* ... *violino piano, first violin; flauto primo, first flute,* etc.

primo tenore *(-tā nō'rē)* from the Italian: The *leading male tenor* in an *opera!*

primo womo *(-wô'mô)* from the Italian: The *leading male singer* in an *opera!*

primo volta *(-vôl'tä)* from the Italian: Same as *prima volta!*

principal *(prĭn'sĭ p'l)* An *organ stop* of *4-foot pitch* on the *manual,* and *8-foot pitch* on the *pedal!*

processional *(prō sĕsh'ŭn ăl)* A *hymn sung* at the *beginning* of a *church service* while the *choir* and *clergy enter in procession!*

program music. *Music* written with (1) A definite narrative quality, or (2) Expressing a series of images or emotions or (3) A combination of the *tonal structures* of (1) and (2)! Also called *descriptive music!* Examples include Debussy's *La Mer;* Beethoven's *Pastoral Symphony, Berlioz' Symphonie Fantastique,* etc.!

progression *(prō grĕsh'ŭn)* The successive movement of *tone to tone,* or *chord to chord!* The former is termed *melodic progression;* the latter, *harmonic progression!*

pronto *(prŏn'tō)* from the Italian: Quick, prompt!

pronunziato *(prō nōōn tsē ä'tō)* from the Italian: "Pronounced", enunciated!

Proper *(prŏp'ēr)* The special *Mass,* or *part of the Mass,* that varies according to the particular holiday or special clerical occasion!

proportion *(prō pôr'shŭn)* In *mensurable music* of medieval times, a term applied to *changes in the time value (duration) of notes!*

proposition *(prŏp'ō zĭsh'ŭn)* The *subject* or *theme* of a *fugue!* Sometimes, used generally to describe any *musical composition!*

propósta *(prō pōs'tä)* from the Italian: A proposition!

ps. The abbreviation for (1) *Psalm!* (2) The *German name* for *trombone, posaune!*

psalm *(säm)* A *hymn* or *sacred song* based on the *text* of the *Old Testament (The Book of Psalms)!*

psaltery *(sôl'tēr ĭ)* An ancient *stringed-instrument* (also called *zither*) with a *flat soundboard* and many *tuned strings!* It is *plucked* by the *fingers* or a *plectrum,* as contrasted to a *dulcimer* which is *struck with hammers! Psalteries* usually were either *trapezoidal* or *harp-shaped!* See *Zither!*

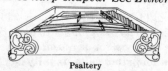
Psaltery

"pull off". In *guitar music,* a term for the *rapid removal of the finger* from a *stopped string!* A slight "pulling" action is employed after a *note* has been *plucked!* The guitar notation sign is "P"!

pulse *(pŭls)* The *accent* or *beat* of musical rhythm!

punk rock *(pŭnk).* A latter-day form of *English "rock music"* characterized by *high-energy sound* and *lyrics* offering social statements in the most unabashed and uninhibited form! Some critics deem *punk rock* tasteless and vulgar, but its protagonists hail it as the *non-commercial "true rock",* an alleged mirror of frenetic, modern living!

punta *(pōōn'tä)* from the Italian: "*Point*", "*point of the bow*"; used in the directions *colla punta dell'arco* or *a punta d'arco* which inform the *string-player* to use the *point of the bow!*

pupitre *(pü'pētr)* The *French* word for a *music stand!*

pyiba, pyipar *(pē'pä)* A *Chinese lute* with *silk strings* and a *short neck!* The *Japanese* version is called *biwa (bē'wä)!* In the new *Romanized* spelling of the *People's Republic of China,* the *pyiba* is officially spelled *pípa* but pronounced the same!

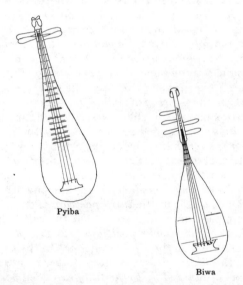
Pyiba
Biwa

pyramidon *(pĭ răm'ĭ dŏn)* An *organ stop* of *16* or *32-foot pitch,* sounded by *short pipes* that are much wider at the top than at the mouth!

Pythagorean tuning. *(pĭ thăg'ō rē'ăn tūn'ĭng)* A *tuning method* allegedly invented by the *Greek mathematician,* Pythagoras! Based on the principle that *two-thirds of a single string vibration creates a tone one-fifth above the tone produced by the vibration of the entire string,* this method determined the *interval ratio for a whole tone* to be *8:9!* The *perfect-fifth ratio* was *2:3;* the *half-tone ratio* was *243:256!* The system proved useless for *enharmonic intervals* and was replaced in medieval times by "*mean-tone tuning*" (many *perfectly tuned intervals* but a *restricted number* of *keys*)! In the mid-18th century, "*mean-tone tuning*" was obsoleted by the "*equal-tempered* or *equal temperament*" system which still persists today! See *Temperament!*

qānūn (*kä'nōōn*) from the Arabic! An *Egyptian psaltery* popular in contemporary Egypt as well as Syria and Turkey! A *lap-held instrument* with as many as *25 sets* or *courses* of *three strings each*, the *qanun* is *plucked* with *plectra* placed on *both forefingers!*

Qanun

quadrille (*kwŏ'drĭl'*) An old *French square dance* with *five or more movements* set to *2/4* or *6/8 time!* Popular in the early 19th century, the *dance* rarely is seen today except in some historical or dramatic context!

quadruplet (*kwŏd'rŏŏ plĕt*) A *group* of *four equal-value notes* which are *played* in the *time* regularly given to *three notes of equal value*. In *notation*, the *quadruplet* is indicated by a *bracket* and the *numeral 4!*

Quadruplet

quadruple counterpoint. *Counterpoint* with *four parts* that are *interchangeable!*

quadruple time, meter, measure. Any *rhythm* in which there are *four beats per measure* with *accents* on the *first and third beats!*

quarter note (*kwôr'tēr*) A *note* equal in value to *one-fourth* of a *whole note*, *one-half* of a *half-note* or *twice* the *value* of an *eighth note!* In *Britain*, the *quarter-note* is called a *crotchet!*

quarter rest. A *rest* indicating *silence for the same duration of time as that given to a quarter note!* Designated *in notation by the sign* or !

quarter tone. An *interval* of *one-half* of a *half-tone*; hence, a *microtone!* There are 24 *quarter-tones* to the *octave!*

quartet, quartette (*kwôr'tĕt*) (1) A *composition* with *four individual parts* for *voices* or *instruments* ... *chamber music*, etc! (2) A *composition* for *four players* or *singers* in *concert!* (3) A *group* of *four players* or *singers!* (4) A *string quartet* normally consists of *two violins* (*1st* and *2nd*), a *viola* and a *cello!* A *piano quartet: piano, violin, viola, cello!* *Brass quartet: two trumpets, horn and trombone!* *Woodwind quartet: flute, clarinet, oboe, bassoon*

with variations thereof! Vocal quartet: commonly, a *soprano*, *alto*, *tenor* and *bass!* *Variations* of a *vocal quartet* include *two sopranos* and *two altos*; or *two tenors*, a *baritone* and a *bass!*

quasi (*kwä'zē*) from the Italian: "*As if*", "*nearly*", "*almost*"; *quasi niente*, "almost nothing" or "scarcely audible"; *andante quasi allegretto*, "moderately", almost lively!

quatre (*kă'tr'*) The *French* word for "four"!

quattro (*kwä'trō*) The *Italian* word for "four"!

quaver (*kwä'vĕr*) The *British term* for an *eighth note!*

quickstep (*kwĭk'stĕp*) (1) A *lively march* for *bands* in *military 6/8 tempo!* (2) A *dance step* similar to a *marching gait!*

quint (*kwĭnt*) (1) The *interval* of a *fifth!* (2) The *E string* of the *violin!* (3) A small *viola da braccio!* (4) An *organ stop sounding a fifth higher* than the *digital's normal pitch!*

quintadena (*kwĭn'tä dē'nä*) / **quintadene** (*kwĭn'tä dĕn*) / An *organ stop* (4, 8 or 16-foot *pitch*) that *sounds* its *fundamental tone* as well as a *harmonic fifth* in the *second octave above the fundamental!*

quintet, quintette (*kwĭn'tĕt'*) (1) A *composition* with *five individual parts* for *voices* or *instruments* ... *chamber music* (see *quartet*)! (2) A *composition* for *five singers* or *players* in *concert!* (3) A *group* of *five players* or *singers* in *concert!* (4) A *string quintet* usually consists of *two violins*, *two violas* and a *cello!* A *piano quintet: piano, plus string quartet!*

quintole (*kwĭn'tōl*) from the Italian: A *group* of *five notes of equal value executed in the normal time value of four of the same notes!*

quintuplet (*kwĭn'tŭplĕt*) The same as a *quintole!* In *notation*, the *quintuplet* is indicated by a *bracket* and the *numeral 5*

quodlibet (*kwŏd'lĭ bĕt*) A *whimsical* or *humorous medley* or *popourri* of *two or more familiar melodies!*

— R —

R. r. The abbreviation for "right" (*rechte*, in German); *r.h.*, *right hand* (*rechte Hand*, in *German*)! In *French organ music*, the abbreviation for *clavier de recit*, "swell manual"!

rabbia (*räb'bē ä*) from the Italian: A direction to play with angry passion, furiously!

raccoglimento (*räk kōl yē mĕn'tō*) from the Italian: A direction to play in a calm, thoughtful manner!

raccontando (*räk kōn tän'dō*) from the Italian: A direction to *sing* in a *narrative* or *recitative* manner!

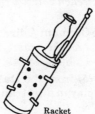

Racket

racket, rackett *(răk'ĕt)* An old *bassoon-like wind instrument* with a *double-reed mouthpiece* and *finger holes!* It encases a short, squat wooden *tube* that internally bends upon itself; thus, producing a *longer air column* and the capability for *low tones!*

raddolcendo *(räd dōl chĕn'dō)* / **raddolcente** *(räd dōl chĕn'tĕ)* / **raddolcito** *(räd dōl chē'tō)* It. / A direction to play gradually more gently and softly!

raga *(rä'gä)* From the *Sanskrit* word "color", *raga* is the native term for the *melody scale* common to the *Hindu music* of *India!* *Ragas* are almost infinite in number and are *performed* both *vocally* and *instrumentally!* They are never written but passed along from teacher to student! The best-known *ragas* use a *scale* of from *five* to *seven tones!* One *keynote tone drones* steadily while other *tones* at *distant intervals* sound *improvised variations* of memorized predecessor *ragas!* The *improvisation* is limited by strict *rhythmic* rules, with whose compliance the "*improviser*" displays his virtuosity! *Ragas* frequently use *rhythm meters* such as *14/4* that are unfamilar to *European* and *American* ears!

ragtime *(răg'tīm)* An indigenous American art form, *ragtime* was the early-19th-century *syncopated music* that sprang from black roots in honky tonks, riverboats and bordellos to become a *pre-jazz, ballroom, dance-band* craze! It also has passed down a *piano style* that has influenced *musical composition* world-wide! *Ragtime piano* stresses a *driving, thumping, left-hand rhythm* with a *heavily-syncopated right-hand melody part* that *shifts beats* and *accents* almost without regard to the *2/4* or *4/4 meter!* The re-discovery of Scott Joplin, "Jelly Roll" Morton and other "*composers*" of the era has assured *ragtime* of a continuing place in the *musical culture!*

rallentando *(räl ĕn tän'dō)* A direction to gradually slow down the *tempo!* Also *ritardando!*

ram's horn. The "*shofar*" of the *Hebrew* or *Judaic synagogue* ceremonies! See *shofar!*

range *(rānj)* All of the *notes* or *tones* that are within the capacity of a *voice* or *instrument* to *perform,* from the lowest *tone* of the lowest *register* to the highest! Same as *compass!*

rank *(rănk)* One series of *organ pipes* controlled by *one stop,* except for *mixture stops* which *control several ranks!*

rant *(rănt)* A rural name for an old, gay *century dance* or *reel!*

ranz des vaches *(räns dä väsh)* A *melodic call* to the cattle *played* by *Swiss herdsmen* on the *alpenhorn!*

rapidamente *(rä pē dä mĕn'tä)* / **rapido** *(rä'pē dō)* It. / A direction to *play rapidly!*

rappel *(rä pĕl')* The *French call to arms* sounded on the *drum!*

rasch *(räsh)* from the German: A direction to *play* in a *fast, rapid tempo* . . . *rascher, faster!* So *rasch wie möglich,* as fast as possible!

rattenuto *(rät tĕ nōō'tō)* from the Italian: "Holding back"; a direction to play in a restrained manner in regard to the *tempo!*

rattle *(rat'l)* (1) A general term for any *percussion instrument* (containing loose, hard objects) that gives off a "*rattling*" *sound* when *shaken, struck* or *rubbed!* See *gourd, maracas, sistrum,* etc.! (2) Specifically, a *rattle* is an *orchestral percussion instrument* which strikes a *wooden* or *metal tongue* against a *rotating ratchet wheel* producing a "*rattling*" sound! Other "*rattles*" are called *cog rattle, watchman's rattle,* etc.!

ravvivando *(räv vē vän'dō)* from the Italian! A direction to *accelerate* the *performance!*

re *(rā)* (1) In *solmization* the *syllable name* for the *second note* of the *diatonic scale (do, re, mi, fa,* etc.)! (2) The *French* and *Italian* name for the note *D!*

rebec, rebeck *(rē'bĕk)* A pear-shaped, *short-necked stringed-instrument* with *three strings* and a *bow,* thought to be the *European* ancestor of the *violin!* The *rebec* is quite similar to the *Arab rabab* which differs from its European relative only in the *bowing technique!* Also called *rubebe, ribab, rebab!*

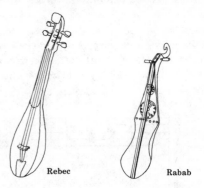

Rebec   Rabab

re bop *(rē'bŏp)* A variation of the colloquial *bop* or *bebop!* (See *bop)!*

recapitulation *(rē'kà pǐt'ū lā'shŭn)* The *third part* or *section* of a *sonata* which consists of (1) *Exposition* (2) *Development* and (3) *Recapitulation!* See *Sonata!*

recessional *(rē sĕsh'ŭn ăl)* (1) A *hymn sung* in *church* while the *clergy* and *choir depart in recession!* (2) Any *composition* played at the *end* of a *theatrical performance* while the *audience departs!*

recht *(rĕkht)* from the German: "Right", *rechte Hand,* right hand!

recital *(rē̆ sīt'ăl)* (1) A *public performance* by one or two *singers* or *instrumentalists!* (2) Sometimes designates a *concert* devoted to one *composer's works!*

recitando *(rā chē tän'dō)* from the Italian: A direction to play in a *free, declamatory manner!*

recitante *(rā chē tän'tĕ)* It. / (1) A *free-style* of *singing* which is almost *declamative!* / **recitative** *(rĕs'ĭ tà tēv')* It. / (2) *Music* composed for an *instrument* or *orchestra* to accompany declamatory vocals! *Recitative secco; unaccompanied recitative* except for a *few chords* and *pitch changes* that are *scored for accompaniment! Recitative stromentato, recitative* with *fully-scored instrumental accompaniment.* See *arioso* for *Recitative Arioso!*

reciting note. In *Gregorian chant,* the *dominant note* over which most of the *syllables* of *verse* are *sung!*

recorder (rē kôrd'ēr) An *end-blown fipple flute* with *eight finger holes* and a *mouthpiece!* The four commonly-used *recorders* are (1) The *soprano* or *descant recorder* (*C pitch, range C'' to d''''*)! (2) The *alto* or *treble recorder* (*F pitch, range f' to G'''*)! (3) The *tenor recorder* (*C pitch, c' to d'''*)! (4) The *bass recorder* (*F pitch, F to G''*)! Other less-common *recorders* include the *sopranino* and the *contrabass!*

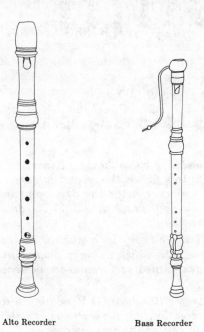

Alto Recorder   Bass Recorder

reed (rēd) A thin *strip (tongue)* of *wood, cane* or *metal* which is attached to the *mouthpiece* of various *wind instruments* (*saxophone, clarinet, oboe,* etc.), or to the *pipe* of a *reed organ*, or to the *keyboard* of an *accordion!* An *air column blown* by the *woodwind player* vibrates the *reed* and produces *pitched sound* in proportion to the length of the *instrument*, as modified by its *keys* and *fingerholes!* In a *reed organ* or *accordion*, the reed usually is a stiff, free *metal tongue* which vibrates to the *air column* produced by the *pedal bellows* of the *organ*, or the *hand-compressed bellows* of the *accordion! Reed* semantics include: *Free reed*, a reed with one end *vibrating freely within* an *aperture; Beating* or *Striking reed*, a reed that *overlaps* and *strikes the edges* of an *aperture; Double reed*, two attached *reeds* (or one folded into two strips) whose *ends vibrate against each other* (used in the *oboe, bassoon, English horn*, etc.)!

reed organ. A *keyboard organ* using *free reeds!* Examples include the *harmonium* whose *bellows* forces compressed air *out* against the *reeds*, and the *American organ* whose *bellows* sucks air *in* through the *reeds!*

reed pipe. An *organ pipe* that uses *reed vibration* to produce sound!

reed stop. An *organ knob* which is *"drawn"* and controls an *entire series* of *reed pipes!*

reel (rēl) A lively *dance* of Scottish origin, usually in *4/4* or *2/4 time*, with *repeating eight-bar phrases!* It is usually *danced* in gliding circles by two or more couples! The *American adaptation* is well-known as the *Virginia reel!*

refrain (rē'frān) (1) In *serious vocal music*, a *regularly recurring phrase* at the end of each *stanza* or *verse* of a *song* or *poem!* When both the *refrain* and the *verses* are *unchanging*, the *music form* is known as *strophic!* (2) In *serious instrumental music*, *refrain* frequently designates a recurring portion of *music* in a *larger composition!* (3) In *popular songwriting*, the *refrain* usually refers to the *main body* or *chorus* of a *song* as contrasted to its *verse* or *introduction.* See *A.A.B.A., A.B.A.B.!*

regal (rē'găl) A *small, portable reed organ* used in the 16th and 17th centuries!

reggae (rĕg'gā) A contemporary *Jamaican dance-rhythm* with a distinctive *4/4 repeating rhythm pattern* that combines *calypso* and *rock* influences! *Reggae* has gained international identity in *popular music*, mainly through its leading exponent, Bob Marley, whose own *lyric statements* are linked to the *socio-religious Rasterian philosophy!*

register (rĕj'ĭs tēr) (1) The *compass* or *range* of a *voice* or *instrument!* Vocalists have a *head register* for *high notes* and a *chest register* for *low notes!* Instruments have different *tone colors* or *registers*, such as the *chalumeau register* of the *clarinet*, its *lowest octave!* (2) An *organ stop* or *series of stops*, or a *series of organ pipes* with a common quality!

registration (rĕj'ĭs trā'shŭn) For *organs*, the *setting* or *selection* of *organ stops;* usually pre-determined in contemporary practice by the *composer* or *arranger!* Organ manufacturers also provide "*recommended registrations*" for various *styles* of *music!*

related keys, scales. Not to be confused with "*relative keys*", which is a term applied only to *major* and *minor keys* with the same *key signature!* "*Related keys*" refer to *keys* or *scales* with frequent *common notes* that are *easily modulated!* The *most closely related keys* are those (*closest to each other* in the "*circle of fifths*"; see *Circle Of Fifths*), which differ from each other *by only one flat or sharp;* hence, *share the same pitch for six of their seven notes!* Music in the *keys* of the *dominant* and *subdominant* and their "*relative*" *minor keys* are *related:* C-major is *related to* F and G-major and to A, D and E-minor, for example! See *Elements of Music*, "*Scales and Clefs*"!

relative (rĕl'ă tĭv) A term applied to *keys* with the same *key signature!* A *major key* is *relative* to a *minor key* whose *tonic* is a *minor third below* the *major* (for example, *G-major* and *E-minor*)! Conversely, a *minor key* is *relative* to a *major key* whose *tonic* is a *minor third above* the *minor!*

Relative Keys

Major	Minor	Sharps or Flats
C	Am	None
G	Em	One sharp .. F♯
D	Bm	Two sharps .. F♯, C♯
A	F♯m	Three sharps .. F♯, C♯, G♯
E	C♯m	Four sharps .. F♯, C♯, G♯, D♯
*B or C♭	*A♭m or G♯	Five sharps .. F♯, C♯, G♯, D♯, A♯,
		or seven flats D♭, E♭, F♭, G♭, A♭, B♭, C♭
*F♯ or G♭	D♯m or E♭m	Six sharps .. F♯, C♯, G♯, D♯, A♯, E♯
		or six flats B♭, E♭, A♭, D♭, G♭, C♭
F	Dm	One flat .. B♭
B♭	Gm	Two flats .. B♭, E♭
E♭	Cm	Three flats .. B♭, E♭, A♭
A♭	Fm	Four flats .. B♭, E♭, A♭, D♭
*D♭ or C♯	B♭m	Five flats .. B♭, E♭, A♭, D♭, G♭, or
*Enharmonic keys		seven sharps C♯, D♯, E♯, F♯, G♯, A♯, B♯

relative pitch. See *Pitch!*

religioso *(rĕ lē jō'sō)* from the Italian: A direction to play in a manner expressing religious feeling!

remote key. The opposite of related key! See *related key!*

Renaissance *(rĕn'ĕ säns)* Historically, the transitional period between *medieval times (middle ages)* and the *baroque era*, from about 1400 to 1600! The *Renaissance* was a time of *vocal music .... heavily clerical* although some *secular* contributions were made .... and a time for advancement of *polyphonic innovation*, particular with *secular madrigals!* *Instruments* were mostly variant forms of *lute, harpsichord, rebec, viol, recorder, church organ* and *military brass! Dances* included the *pavane, passamezzo, galliard,* etc.!

repeat *(rē pēt')* (1) A *section* of *music* that is to be *played again! Repeat signs* in *musical notation* use two or *four vertical dots* and *bar lines* as follows:

a. the *sign* ∶‖ at the *end* of a *section* or an *entire composition* indicates that the *section* or *composition* is to be *repeated from the beginning up to the sign!*

b. the *signs* ‖∶ and ∶‖ appearing *before and after* a *section within a composition* indicate that the *section* is to be *repeated from the* ‖∶ *sign to the* ∶‖ *sign!*

c. If there are *different endings* for the *first* and *second sections (first ending, prima volta* and *second ending, seconda volta)*, these are indicated by *brackets* with appropriate *numerals* ⌐1⌐ or ⌐2⌐

d. The *signs* ⫸ or ⫷ indicate that the *preceding* and *following sections* of *music* are to be repeated!

(2) The *sign D.C. (da capo)* "from the beginning", indicates that the *first section* of a *composition* is to be *repeated* after a *subsequent section* is *played!* (3) The *sign D.S. (dal segno)* "from the *sign*" indicates that a *section* of a *composition* is to be *repeated beginning at the sign* 𝄋 or ∶𝄋 and *continuing until the sign* **Fine** *(end)* or 𝄐 or ⊕ !

repercussion *(rē'pŭr kush'ŭn)* (1) *Repeating* a *tone* or *chord!* (2) In a *fugue,* the *second entrance* of the *subject* and *answer* after the *development* of an *episode following the exposition!* (3) The *dominant* in *Gregorian chant!*

repertoire *(rĕp'ĕr twär)* In a *musical context,* the *compositions* with which a *singer, player, group* or *orchestra* has gained *performance experience* and *skill!*

repetition *(rĕp'ē tĭsh 'ŭn)* (1) *Repeating* a *tone* or *chord* in *succession!* (2) An *instrument's ability* to *play tones* or *chords* in *rapid succession!*

répétition *(rĕ pĕ tē sē ōn')* The *French* word for *rehearsal!*

répétition générale *(-jĕn ĕr äl')* The *French* term for *dress rehearsal!*

replica *(rĕp'lē kă)* from the Italian: A *repeat* or *reprise! Senza replica, without repeats!*

reprise *(rē prēz')* from the French: (1) A *repeat* of an *earlier section of music after* a *later section has been completed!* (2) In the *sonata form,* a *repercussion* or *recapitulation!* (3) The *resumption* of a *theme* after a *rest* or *hold!*

requiem *(rē'kwĭ ĕm)* (1) The *musical setting* of the *Roman Catholic Mass* for the dead which begins with the word *Requiem (rest) .... "give eternal rest to them O Lord"!* The *Requiem Mass* includes the *Introit,* the *Kyrie (Kyrie eleison,* "Lord, have mercy upon us"), the *Dies irae hymn,* the *Offertory (Domine Jesu Christe),* the *Sanctus (Sanctus, sanctus, sanctus,* "holy, holy, holy"), the *Benedictus,* the *Agnus Dei* (O Lamb of God) and the *Communion* or *Lux Aeterna* (Eternal Light)! (2) Any stately *music* or *hymn* which honors the deceased!

resolution *(rĕz'ō lū'shŭn)* / **resolve** *(rē zŏlv')* / Moving from a *dissonant interval* or *chord* to one that is *consonant!* A *successive movement* to *consonance* is *direct resolution!* A *delayed movement* to *consonance ... with intermediate dissonance ...* is called *indirect resolution!*

resonance *(rĕz'ō nǎns)* The "*echoing*" or *reinforcement* and *enrichment of a tone,* produced by *auxiliary vibrations* which are normally *sympathe-*

tic to a *fundamental tone's frequency of vibration!* Such *auxiliary vibrations* also can be *mechanically* or *electronically* added to the *fundamental tone!*

resonance box (1) The *box* formed by the *body of a violin*, or the *chamber* of any *musical instrument* which *heightens* the *sonority!* (2) A *box* in which a *tuning fork* is placed!

resonator (*rĕz'ō nā tēr*) (1) Any *part* of an *instrument* that *vibrates* to *produce sound!* (2) Any *soundboard box*, *instrument body* or *attachment* which contributes to *resonance* .... such as the *resonator tubes* beneath a *marimba!*

response (*rē spŏns'*) (1) In *church services*, the *singing* or *spoken reply* by the *choir* and/or *congregation* to the *chant*, *song* or *speech* of the *clergyman* or *priest!* (2) Sometimes used in *folk songs* to describe the *chorus* or *refrain!*

rest (*rĕst*) A *pause* or *silence* in any *musical part!* Various *signs* designate the *duration of silence* for a *rest* which correspond to *note values!* See *Elements of Music, "Notes and Rests"!*

Whole Rest
Half Rest
Quarter Rest
Eighth Rest
Sixteenth Rest
Thirty-Second Rest
Sixty-Fourth Rest

restez (*rĕs tā'*) from the French: "Remain there" or "stay there"; a direction for *string players* to *bow* on the *same string* or to *remain in the same hand position* or *"shift"!*

retard (*rē tärd'*) A direction to *hold back* the *tempo* and play gradually more slowly (*rallentando, ritardando*)!

retardation (*rē tär dā'shŭn*) (1) A *suspension* that resolves *upwards!* See *Suspension!* (2) A *holding-back* or *dragging behind* the *tempo!*

retrograde (*rĕt'rō grād*) *Playing* a *melody* in *exact reverse order* ... *last note*, *next-to-last note*, etc.!

retrograde inversion. Not only *reversing* the *order* of the *notes in a melody*, but *changing* the *direction* of the *pitch changes* as well ... *up* for *down*, *down* for *up!*

reveille (*rĕv'ĕ lē*) The *military call* for *morning awakening*, usually *sounded* on a *bugle*, but sometimes supplemented with, or replaced by, a *fife* or *drum!*

rf., rfz. Abbreviations for *rinforzando!*

r.h. The abbreviation for "*right hand*", or the *German* "*rechte hand*"!

rhapsody (*răp'sō dē*) A *short, instrumental composition* in a somewhat *free form of fantasia!* In older times, *rhapsody* indicated a *musical setting* based on the characteristics of a *nation* or its *people!* In modern times, the term is applied to *similar styles of composition* that are not necessarily "nationalistic"!

rhythm (*rĭth'm*) (1) The *regular movement of groups of* tones determined by the *speed of performance* (*tempo*), the *time value of each tone* (*meter*) and the *structuring* of the *accents of each tone* (*beat* or *pulse*)! *Beats are divided* into *measures* or *bars* which contain *notes of varying time value* (♩ or *quarter-note;* ♪ or *half-note*, etc.)! The *notes* in each *bar* are *accented* in accordance with the *time signature* at the *head of the staff!* A ¾ *notation sign* means the *quarter-notes* in *each measure* are *grouped in threes* with every *third note accented* .... called *triple time!* A ²⁄₄ *notation sign* means the *quarter-notes* in *each measure* are *grouped in twos* with *every other note accented* .... called *duple* or *double time!* (2) *Rhythm* frequently is generalized to refer to any *group of tones* that has distinctive regularity ... Latin-American *rhythms*, for example, including *rhumba*, *samba*, *baion*, *mambo*, etc! The newest *pop disco rhythm* usually is patterned ⁴⁄₄ with approximately *130 M.M. beats* to the *minute!*

rhythm and blues. A catch-all "label" affixed to *black, urban popular music* prior to the advent of *rock and roll* in the 1950's and '60's! Considered by some critics to be a demeaning "tag" for the *black energy, beat,* and *free, emotional expression* that goes into the *music*, "the label" gave way in the 1970's to such classifications as "*soul music*" and "*jazz*-rock", and to the growing crossover of *black composers* and *performers* into the "non-tagged" mainstream of *best-selling records!*

rib (*rĭb*) (1) The *curved side* of a *violin* or *guitar-type instrument!* (2) The *hoop* in the *bellows* of an *organ!*

ricecare (*rēchĕr kä'rā*) from the Italian: An *instrumental, contrapuntal composition* of the 16th and 17th centuries, imitative of a *vocal motet!*

ricochet (*rĭk'ō shā'*) from the French: A direction to *violin players* to *strike the bow* on the *string(s)* in a *bouncing, down-bow, staccato manner.* Also *jeté!*

riddle ballad, riddle song. An old *English song* which poses a *riddle* or explains the solution of a *riddle!*

ride cymbal. A *percussion instrument* or *attachment!* See *cymbals!*

ride out (*rīd owt*) A professional "popular music" expression which designates "ad lib" accompaniment, usually in up-tempo, or "hot", or "syncopated" style .... e.g. "ride-out" chorus or "ride-out" ending.

riff (*rif*) The improvised accompaniment through the open-end of a four bar phrase. A vernacular term in Jazz. (See JAZZ)

rigadoon (*rĭg'ä dōōn'*) A *lively French dance* of the 17th and 18th centuries in *double or quadruple time,* said to have been invented by a dancing master from Marseilles named Rigaud! Also *rigaudon, rigodón!*

rigor *(rē gôr')* / **rigore** *(rē gôr'ĕ)* / **rigoroso** *(rē gôr ō'sō)* It. / Rigorous, strict! *Rigore di tempo,* a direction to play in *strict time!*

rilasciando *(rē lä shăn'dō)* / **riasciante** *(rē lä shăn'tĕ)* It. / A direction to play more slowly *(rallentando)!*

rimettendo *(rē mĕt tĕn'dō)* from the Italian: A direction to return to an *earlier tempo* after a *speed-up* or *slow-down!*

rinforzando *(rēn fôr tsän'dō)* from the Italian: (1) A direction to *sharply* and *strongly accent* a *note* or *chord* (same as *sforzando*)! (2) Sometimes used generally to direct an abrupt increase in *volume* or *intensity* by the *orchestra* or *performer!*

rinforzare, senza *(sĕn'tsä rĭn fôr tsä'rĕ)* from the Italian: "Without getting louder"!

ring cycle. The name given to *Wagner's four dramatic operas* which are based on the story of the *Ring of the Nibelung!* The *operas* are *Rheingold, Die Walkürie, Siegfried* and *Götterdämmerung!*

ripieno *(rē pyā'nō)* from the Italian: "Filling up", "supplementary"! (1) A *ripieno part* or *performer* is one that *doubles another part* or *supplements the harmony!* (2) A *score direction* for the entrance of a *full orchestra* or a *full section of instruments!* (3) A *combination stop* on the *organ* which *draws the full register* of a *manual!*

ripigliando *(rē pēl yän'dō)* / **ripigliare** *(rē pēl yä'rĕ)* It. / "Resume", "resuming", "to resume"! Also *riprendendo!*

riposo *(rē pō'sō)* from the Italian: "Reposefully"; a direction to play in a calm, peaceful manner!

risentito *(rē sĕn tē'tō)* from the Italian: A direction to play in a forceful, energetic manner!

risoluto *(rē zō lōō'tō)* from the Italian: A direction to play with *decided accents* in a resolute manner!

risonáre *(rē zō nä'rĕ)* from the Italian: Resounding, echoing!

risposta *(rē spōs'tä)* from the Italian: The *answer* or *consequent* in a *fugue* or *canon!*

ritardando *(rē tär dän'dō)* from the Italian: A direction to gradually slow down the tempo! Same as *retard, rallentando! Senza ritardare (sĕn'tsä rē tä dä'rĕ),* without slowing down! Abbreviated *rit.* !

ritenuto *(rē tä nōō'tō)* from the Italian: "Held back", a direction to *slow down at once!*

ritmico *(rĭt'mē kō)* from the Italian: A direction to *maintain* the *rhythm* in *exact time!* Same as *alla misura!*

ritornello *(rĭt ôr nĕl'ō)* from the Italian: (1) A *short instrumental part* used as a *prelude* to, or an *ending* for, a *vocal composition* or an *operatic work!* (2) A *burden* for each *vocal stanza* in a *song!* (3) In *concerto music,* a *repeating refrain* by the *full orchestra!*

rock, rock 'n' roll. *America's rock'n'roll music* first evolved in the 1950's as an amalgam of *black musical influences* rooted in *blues, gospel, jazz, folk,* and *ragtime. Black players* shaped a *driving, eight-beat rhythm,* unloosed *uninhibited variations* on a *few simple chords* by adding *unorthodox meters* and *new harmonic progressions,* and created a *music form* that with *small groups* and *soloists* virtually obliterated the *sounds* of *large orchestras, formal arrangements* and *smooth, bland pop vocals* that were in vogue! First promoted in the early '50's by *disk jockey* Alan Freed on a radio station in Cleveland, Ohio, the *black rock 'n' roll* of a Chuck Berry and a Little Richard quickly picked up white emulators ... Bill Haley, Buddy Holly, Jerry Lee Lewis et al; and later in the '50's, Sam Phillips of Sun Records in Memphis discovered a "white man who sang authentic *rock'n'roll,* Elvis Presley"! Now, *rock* began to pour into the mainstream!

In the early 1960's, a historical *segue* from "rock 'n' roll" to "*rock*" was being bundled in *Britain!* In Manchester, Liverpool and London, the sounds of Berry, Presley, Holly, Haley, Little Richard, The Drifters, The Coasters, The Supremes and all of the Motown artist roster were fascinating to British youth. Inevitably, there appeared the *all-time, best-selling, most-heard vocal group,* The Beatles! They added *melody* and *lyric nuance* to *rock* but they "*rocked*", and paved the way for *more raucous British groups* such as the Rolling Stones, Led Zeppelin, and *more complex-harmonic groups* such as Procol Harum, The Who, etc! In America, Bob Dylan contributed folk-rock variations with anti-war and social-injustice statements that touched the worldwide conscience of youth. As per Dylan, "the times were changing"! By the '70's, Woodstock had come and gone, and fusions with other musical forms were pell-melling onto the scene! These included "*Acid Rock*" (galvanized *amplification* of the *electric guitars* and alleged *mind-expanding words and music*) with its obvious *colloquial derivation* from the "*acid*" name for *LSD,* a *hallucinogenic drug;* "Soul music", a "*funky*", almost *improvised kind of black, rhythmic semi-jazz,* and currently "*Disco music*", the incorporation of *black and white sound* into *dance-beat* patterns that have compelled the *concert rock stars* .... Fleetwood Mac, The Eagles, Paul McCartney, Peter Frampton, Billy Joel, etc .... to share their honors with the new *disco* royalty, such as Donna Summer, Georgio Moroder, the Village People, Gloria Gaynor, etc. This co-existence now awaits the arrival of new stimuli and new sounds for the 1980's!

rococco *(rō kō'kō)* A term from *architecture* and the *fine arts,* used in *music* to characterize *ornamental composition* of the 18th century! The period was *transitional* between *late Baroque* and *early Pre-classic!*

Rohr-flote *(rōr'flû'tĕ)* from the German: "Reed flute", an *organ diapason stop!*

Rohr-quint *(-kwĭnt)* from the German: "Reed fifth", an *organ stop* which sounds the *fifth* above the *diapasons!*

roll *(rōl)* (1) *Rapid, alternating strokes,* with *two hands,* using *two sticks* on a *drum head!* Also called *drum roll!* The effect is similar to *tremolo* or *trill* and is indicated in *notation* as .... (2) A fast *arpeggio* on the *organ!*

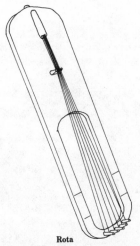

Rota

romance *(rō măns')* from the French: A *short, lyrical composition* for *vocal* or *instrumental performance*, usually in *ballad* style!

romanesca *(rô măn ĕsk' ä)* from the Italian: A 17th century *court dance* or *song* (from the area around *Rome*) with a distinctive *bass harmonic structure!*

romantic, romanticism *(rō măn'tĭk, -'tĭ sĭz'm)* A *school of composition* that took over from *classicism* in the early 19th century! The *romantic composers,* following similar trends in other *arts,* expressed their *passionate, emotional* and *subjective feelings* in a compulsive departure from the *formalized, realistic music* of *earlier periods!* The *romantic period* brought forth *Beethoven, Wagner, Schubert, Sibelius, Richard Strauss* and other geniuses of *melody* and *chromatic harmony!* Although it ultimately yielded to the *atonality* of the *20th Century,* the *romantic period* still is considered one of the richest eras in all of *serious music!*

rondeau *(rŏn dō')* A *French medieval form* of *vocal music* with *solo verses* and *choral refrains,* or *all-choir renditions* with *instrumental accompaniment! Rondeau* also was used in the 17th century to describe *instrumental music* with *repeating refrains!*

rondo *(rŏn dō')* from the Italian: A *lively composition,* or *section of a composition,* with a *theme* or *refrain* that *repeats three or more times* throughout the *piece* or *section,* with "in-between" *contrasting themes!*

root *(rōōt)* The *lowest note* of a *chord* in its *normal* or *fundamental position* (the *root position)!*

rosalia *(rō zäl'yä)* from the Italian: A *melodic pattern* that uses *successive repeating portions,* each of which *modulates* a *half-tone* or *whole-tone higher* into the *following portion!*

rose *(rōz)* The name given to the *decorated sound-hole* of a *guitar* or *lute!*

rota *(rō'tä)* from the Latin: (1) A *medieval name* for a *round!* Chaucer's "Summer is icumen in", set to a *melody,* particularly! (2) A *medieval name* for an *instrument* that is classified as either a *psaltery* or a *forerunner* of the *"hurdy gurdy"*. Also called *rotta* or *rotte!*

roulade *(rōō läd')* from the French: A *vocal* or *instrumental ornament . . . an arpeggio, run, flourish* or *grace!*

round. (1) A *multi-part, vocal composition* in which each *part* follows the other in a form of *unison canon!* (2) In *popular music,* a simple *melody* or *folk song* in which several *parts* in *unison* follow each other with each *part entering* and *remaining two* or *four bars* behind the *earlier entry!*

roundelay *(roun'dĕ lā)* from the French: A *simple folk air* which repeats a *brief theme* frequently, at a *lively tempo!*

rovescio *(rō vĕsh'o)* from the Italian: "Upside down", a direction to play in *contrary motion . . .* by *inversion of the intervals* or by *reversal of the intervals!* Also called *a rovescio!*

rubato *(rōō bä'tō)* from the Italian: "Robbed", a direction to *play in almost free, elastic tempo . . .* theoretically *"robbing" time from one note* to make up for the time given another!

ruff *(rŭff)* An *embellishment* used by *drummers* on the *side drum* or *snare drum!* In *serious music,* *"ruff"* generally applies to a rapid, *roll* of *drum strokes* before an *accented note!* Also called *drag! Popular music drummers* may *"ruff"* with *sixteenth-note triplets* on the *snare drum* against *quarter notes* on *cymbal!*

rumba *(rōōm'bē)* A *syncopated Cuban dance* imported into U.S. ballrooms during the 1930's! It was popular until the era of *mambo, cha cha* and *meringue* took over in the late '50's!

run *(rŭn)* (1) A *rapid-scale passage* in *vocal music,* frequently *sung* on *one syllable!* (2) A *rapid succession* of *notes,* a *roulade!*

rustico *(rōōs'stē kō)* from the Italian: Pastoral, rustic!

ruvido *(rōō vĭd ō)* from the Italian: A direction to play in a harsh, rough manner!

 **DICTIONARY**

S

— S —

S. The abbreviation for *schola, segno, senza, sinistra, solo, soprano, sordini, subdominant, subito, superius,* etc!

saccade *(să kăd')* from the French: (1) An abrupt *press-down* with the *violin bow* producing a *multi-string tone!* (2) A general term for abrupt, spasmodic movements!

salsa *(săl să)* A contemporary term for popular Latin dance or disco music (usually considered "hot", "spicy" and played in "up" tempo) which originated in Cuba and Puerto Rico, emigrated to the New York Puerto Rican community, thence across the U.S.! Literally meaning "sauce" (*con salsa,* with sauce), the basic meter is 4/4 with complicated variations in strong beat/weak beat accents supplied by Latin rhythm instruments such as the *bomba* and *bongo drums,* the *claves, cencerro, conga drum, maraccas, güiro, shekere, timbales* and varied Latin guitars!

sackbut *(săk'bŭt)* (1) A medieval ancestor of the slide trombone! (2) A Biblical reference to an instrument that probably was a form of primitive harp!

saite *(zī'tě)* The German name for a string of any stringed instrument!

salicet *(să lǐ să')* / **salicional** *(să lē'sǐ ŏ năl')* Fr. / An *organ stop* (*8-foot* or *16-foot pitch*) with *open-flue pipes* that produce a *smooth, reedy tone!*

saltando *(săl tăn'dō)* from the Italian: A direction to *bounce* the *violin bow* on the *string(s)* in a *springing, skipping, staccato* manner! Also *saltato, sautillé* or *arco saltando!*

saltarella *(săl tă rěl'ä)* / **saltarello** *(săl tă rel'ō)* / **salteretto** *(săl tă rět'ō)* It. / A *brisk, Italian dance* of the 16th Century, usually in *triple time,* with a "skipping" type of *rhythm pattern* . . .

Saltarella

saltato *(săl tă'tō)* from the Italian: Same as *saltando!*

salto *(săl'tō)* from the Italian: A *"leap, "jump",* or *"skip"!* *Di salto,* by a *leap!*

samba *(săm'bä)* A *bright Latin-American dance* (popular in the 1940's in the *U.S.* when it was imported from *Brazil)* in *2/4 time* with *unorthodox* but *prominent syncopation!*

samisen *(săm'ǐ sěn)* One of the *major instruments* in *Japanese music!* A *banjo-like, lute* with a *long neck* and *three strings* that are *struck (rather than plucked)* by an *ivory plectrum* that is shaped like an *axe blade!* Also *shamisen!*

Samisen

Sanctus *(sănk'tŭs)* Part of the *Roman Catholic Mass* and the *Anglican communion service!* See *Mass, para. 4!*

sanft *(zänft)* from the German: A direction to play in a *soft, smooth manner!*

sans *(sän)* from the French: "Without"!

santouri *(Sän tōōr'ē)* A *Greek instrument* (similar to the *European dulcimer*) which is played *solo* or in *small ensembles* along with the *Greek-Arabic 'ud* or *oud (al'ud), buzuki, tanbur,* etc. Also called *santir!*

saraband *(săr á bănd')* (1) A *slow, stately court dance* in *triple time* (originally, however, a *lively, sensuous Spanish dance* using *castanets*), important in the *baroque suites* of *Handel* and *Bach!* The *saraband* usually *accented* the *second beat* of a *measure* with *phrases* that concluded on *weak beats!*

Saraband

sarangi *(să rŭng gē')* A *Hindu, bowed string-instrument* with a *wide neck* and *three, gut melody strings,* to which a number of *added, metal strings vibrate sympathetically* when the *melody strings* are *bowed!*

sardana *(săr dä'nä)* from the Spanish: *Catalonian dance music!*

sarod *(să rōd')* A *short-necked Hindu lute* that is *bowed!* Similar to the *rebec!*

sarrusophone *(să rōōz'ō fōn)* A *double-reed brass instrument* in the *oboe family!* With a *mouthpiece* and a *metal pipe,* the *contrabass C model* is used in *European orchestras!* Named after its inventor, Sarrus, a *Parisian bandmaster* is the 1850's!

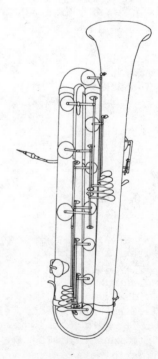

Sarrusophone

S.A.T.B., SATB. The abbreviation for parts in choral music: Soprano, Alto, Tenor, Bass!

satz *(säts)* The *German* word for a *symphonic movement!*

sautillé *(sō tē yā')* from the French: The technique of *bouncing* the *violin bow rapidly* but *slightly* on the *strings* in the *middle of the bow,* at the *beginning and for the duration of one bow stroke! Dotted notes* are used to indicate *sautillé* in notation! Same as *saltando!*

saw, sawing *(sô, -'ĭng)* An *American* country-colloquialism for the *playing* of a *violin* or *"fiddle"!*

saw, musical. A familiar *amateur instrument* consisting of an *ordinary carpenter's saw* which is *bowed* across its teeth!

saxhorn *(săks'hôrn)* A *valved, brass wind-instrument* named after Adolphe Sax (real name, Antoine Joseph Sax of Belgium) its inventor about 1840! With a *conical bore* and *large bell,* it is similar to an *enlarged bugle* (except for its *"funnel"* mouthpiece) and is popularly known in America as the *C* and *B-flat flügelhorn! Saxhorns* come in a broad range of sizes from *soprano* and *alto* to the *contrabass (double bass)! The bass saxhorn (bass tuba)* is used in almost all *marching bands* today! There is a great deal of confusion in the nomenclature of *saxhorns* . . . the German and American viewpoints are at considerable variance in the classification of various *saxhorn* models as *flügelhorns!*

In America, the optional names for *saxhorns* include:

high E-flat, F models — soprano Flügelhorn, sopranino saxhorn, soprano saxhorn.

low E-flat, F models — saxhorn, alt horn, alto saxhorn, tenor saxhorn.

high B-flat, C models — soprano saxhorn, alto saxhorn, alt flügelhorn.

low B-flat, C models — baritone saxhorn (euphonium), althorn, tenor horn.

BB-flat bass models — contrabass saxhorn or double bass tuba.

EE-flat or FF models — sax tuba or bass tuba.

Alto Saxhorn

saxophone *(săk'sō fōn)* A *wind instrument* (also invented about 1840 by Adolphe Sax; see *saxhorn*) with a *single-reed, clarinet-type mouthpiece* and a *thick metal tube! The bottom* of the *instrument curves up to a flared bell* which is *bent out from the upward extension!* The top of the instrument bends back to a crook-fitted mouthpiece! A complicated *series of keys* (similar to the *Boehm-system* array on the *clarinet*) decorate almost the full length of the

tube, and these are *fingered* to produce variations of a *sound* that is both penetrating and mellow. The *saxophone* is of major importance in *popular* and *jazz music* circles as well as for *serious band music* and occasional *symphonic performance!* With over a dozen historical models recognized, three *saxophones* are best known in modern times:

(1) The *E-flat alto sax*
(2) The *B-flat tenor sax*
(3) The *E-flat baritone sax*

Each of these *instruments* is a *transposing instrument* with a *range* of about *two and one half octaves!* Other more specialized *saxophones* include the *soprano* and *contrabass models!* The *soprano sax* is the only model that has no *bends* or *curves* and is *straight-shaped* like the *clarinet.* Most professional *musicians* (not all) *"double"* on *clarinet* and *saxophone,* or vice versa!

Saxophone

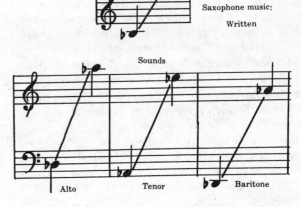

Saxophone music:

Written

Sounds

Alto   Tenor   Baritone

saxotromba *(săk'sō trŏm'bà)* Another Adolphe Sax invention (see *saxophone, saxhorn*)! A *valved brass instrument* somewhere between the *saxhorn* and *trombone* but obsolete in *contemporary music performance!*

saxtuba *(săks'tūba)* Another name for the *bass tuba!*

scale *(skāl)* A *European* and *American (Western music)* designation for a *succession* of *tones* or *half-tones* which make up *one octave* in any *diatonic* or *chromatic series!* The *diatonic scale* is *divided into major* and *minor keys* which determine the *eight-tone pattern* of *whole tones* and *half-tones!* The *chromatic scale* consists only of *half-tones, 12* of which *comprise an octave!* Other *modern "scale"* designations include (1) *The whole tone scale*, which contains only *whole intervals* and begins on *only one of two tones, C* or *D-flat!* (2) The *pentatonic scale*, with *only five tones* and (3) The *"gypsy" scale* which includes *two augmented seconds!* In *Near Eastern, Eastern* and *African music*, many *other scales* in *diverse modes* are known, frequently with *"microtones"* . . . *tones smaller than a half-tone! Western modernists* in the 20th century have introduced several *microtone scales* into *composition*, notably Charles Ives.

scale degrees. The system of *naming* and *numbering* the *tones* in a *major* or *minor scale* in terms of their *order of ascendance from the first note* or *tonic of the scale!* The *tones* are *named* and *numbered (Roman numerals)* as shown! The *tonic* is the *first degree*, the *supertonic* is the *second degree*, and so on! In a *given key*, the *scale degree always is the same* regardless of the *octave* that is used!

Scales

chromatic	C C# D D# E F F# G G# A A#B C′
major	C D E F G A B C′
minor melodic (ascending)	C D Eb F G A B C′
minor melodic (descending)	C D Eb F G Ab Bb C′
minor harmonic	C D Eb F G Ab B C′
whole tone	C D E F# G#A# C′
gypsy	C D Eb F# G Ab B C′
pentatonic	C D F G A C′

Degree Name	Degree #	C-major scale ← Example → A-minor scale	
Tonic (keynote)	I	C	A
Supertonic	II	D	B
Mediant	III	E	C
Subdominant	IV	F	D
Dominant	V	G	E
Submediant or Superdominant	VI	A	F
Subtonic or Leading Tone	VII	B	G#

scat *(skăt)* A *colloquial* term for the *singing* of *artificial* or *nonsense syllables* in *improvised jazz progression!* Ella Fitzgerald, Anita O'Day, "Scat Man" Crothers and others are noted for their "scat" abilities! Although the style is considered almost passé today, a sentimental regard is still retained by many *jazz* "buffs" for its *performance!*

scena *(shā'nă)* from the Italian: (1) An *opera scene!* (2) A *dramatic recitation*, with *accompaniment*, which *precedes a full aria!* (3) *Instrumental music* that *follows* the *style* of a *vocal scena!*

schalkhaft *(shälk'häft)* from the German: A direction to play in a roguish, frolicsome manner!

scherzando *(skĕr tsän'dō)* from the Italian: A direction to perform in a jesting, lively, playful manner! In the style of a *scherzo!*

scherzo *(skĕr'tsō)* (1) A jesting, lively, playful *instrumental composition* usually in *rapid 3/4 time* with *surprise contrasts* in both *harmony* and the *accents!* (2) The *rapid third movement* of a *sonata* or *symphony!*

schietto *(skē ĕt' tō)* from the Italian: Simple, neat, plain!

Schillinger system. A highly controversial system of *composition, based* on allegedly "pure mathematical principles" taught by Joseph Schillinger (1895-1943) in the 1920's and 1930's, and published in complex detail in 1946. Initial attention and some acclaim for the system was engendered by George Gershwin's participation as a student, but these diminished after Schillinger's demise, with many modernists dubious as to Schillinger's mathematical scholarship. Other critics simply objected to the abstruse nature of the theory.

schlag *(shläk)* The *German* word for *beat* or *strike! Schlaginstrumente, percussion instruments!*

schleppen *(shlĕp'ĕn)* / **schleppend** *(shlĕp'ĕndt)* Ger./ A direction to *retard*, or to play in a dragging, *retarding* manner! *Nicht schleppen*, "do not *retard* or *drag*, and *maintain a bright tempo*"!

schluss *(shlōōs)* from the German: The *end* or *cadence!*

schlussel *(shlŭs'sĕl)* The *German* word for *clef!*

schmachtend *(schmäkh'tĕndt)* from the German: Languishing, plaintive!

schmeichel *(shmī'khĕl)* from the German: To flatter, coax, caress!

schmerzhaft *(shmĕrts'häft)* from the German: Painfully, sorrowful!

schmetternd *(shmĕt'tĕrndt)* from the German: A direction to the *brass* to *increase* its *wind pressure*, and produce a harsher, *"brassier" tone!*

schnell *(shnĕl)* from the German: A direction to play fast, quick, rapid! *Schneller*, faster!

schottische, schottish *(shŏt'ish)* A 19th-century *circling dance* in *2/4 time* with *polka-like steps* but in a *slower tempo than the polka!* Also known as the *German polka!*

schwach (*shväkh*) from the German: "Weak"; a direction to play softly! Same as the *Italian* direction, *piano!*

schwegel (*shvä'gĕl*) from the German: (1) A *wind instrument!* (2) An *organ flue-pipe!*

schweige (*shvī'gĕ*) from the German: A *rest* or *pause!*

schwer (*shvâr*) from the German: "Hard", "difficult", ponderous!

schwermüthig (*shvâr'mü tĭkh*) from the German: A direction to play in a manner expressing a melancholy, sad mood!

schwindend (*shvĭn'dĕndt*) from the German: A direction to play gradually more softly until dying away! In *Italian, morendo!*

scioltezza (*shôl tĕt'sä*) / **sciolto** (*shôl'tō*) It. / A direction to play with fluency, freely or *detached*, not *legato!*

scordatura (*skôr'dä tōō'rä*) from the Italian: *Unorthodox tuning* of a *stringed instrument* to accommodate a special purpose, such as a *composer's instruction* to achieve a particular *sound effect* or *unique solo sound!*

score (*skōr*) A complete *arrangement* of *all the notes and parts* of a *composition* (*vocal* or *instrumental*) written out on *staves* in *vertical alignment* of the *time values!* "Score" generally refers to an *arrangement* or *transcription* which is "*scored*" for *particular voicings!* A *full score* or *orchestral score* depicts *every orchestral part on a separate staff* and is used by a *conductor!* A *full score* normally lists *woodwinds* at the *top of the page* and then *proceeds down* the *score* in the following order: *brass, percussion, keyboards, voices* and finally *strings!* A *short score* refers to *abbreviated transcriptions* or *2-stave, 4-voice choral arrangements!* A *vocal score* depicts all the *voice parts* with the *accompaniment* limited to a *2-stave piano part!* A *piano score* is an *arrangement* of the *orchestral score* reducing the *parts* to two staves for *piano* with any *lyrics appearing above the stave* .... or *between the staves* in a *piano/vocal arrangement!*

scorrendo (*skôr rĕn'dō*) / **scorrevole** (*skôr rĕ'vō lĕ*) It. / A direction to play in a smooth, gliding-from-note-to-note manner!

Scotch snap. A *two-beat rhythm figure* common to *many Scottish compositions!* It is actually an *inversion* of *normal dotted-note rhythm*, since its *dotted note* (*long note*) *follows* the *short undotted note* rather than *preceding* it!

 Scotch Snap

scozzese (*skŏ tsä'zĕ*) from the Italian: A direction to play in Scottish style!

S.C.T.B. SCTB. One of the abbreviations for *parts* in *choral music: soprano, contralto, tenor, bass!* See *SATB!*

sdegno (*sdĕn'yō*) / **sdegnoso** (*sdĕn yō'sō*) It. / A direction to play in a manner expressing anger, scorn or indignation!

se (*sā*) from the Italian: "If", "as"!

sec (*sĕk*) from the French: "Dry"; a direction to play in a dry, crisp manner without *delaying* the *note attack!*

secco (*sĕk'ō*) The Italian equivalent of the French *sec!*

second. (1) The *interval* of the *first two tones* (*degrees*) in any *ascending major or minor scale!* (2) The *alto part* in *vocal music!* (3) Relative to *first* ... as with an *instrument playing* a *lower-pitched part* than its colleague; *second violin, second clarinet,* etc.!

second, augmented. The *interval* that is a *half-tone larger* than a *major second.* Used prominently in *Oriental music!*

second, minor. The *interval* that is a *half-tone smaller* than the *major second!*

secondary chord. Any *chord* whose *root* is *not* the *tonic* nor the *dominant* or *subdominant* of the *key!* A *subordinate chord!*

secónda volta (*sĕ kôn'dä vôl'tä*) from the Italian: "Second time"; the term used to designate a "*second ending*"! *Prima volta,* "first time", designates the *first ending!* See *Repeat!* In notation:

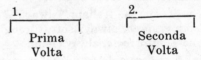

secóndo, -a (*sĕ kôn dō, -ä*) The *Italian* word for "second"!

section (*sĕk'shŭn*) (1) A *portion of music* (longer than a *period*) that has a clearly separated *rhythmic* or *harmonic structure relative to an entire composition!* (2) A *group* of the *same instruments* ... *horn section, flute section,* etc. or a *group of instruments* in the *same family* ... *string section, brass section, woodwind section,* etc.!

secular music. *Music not intended* for *spiritual* or *religious* services or purpose! The *opposite of sacred music!*

segno (*sā'nyō*) from the Italian: "Sign"; the sign 𝄋 or :S: that indicates the *beginning* or *end* of a *repeating section of music! Al segno,* means "repeat up to the sign"; *dal segno,* (*D.S.*), means "repeat from the *sign to the end marked fine* or to a *double-bar* with a *hold*

segue (*sā'gwĕ*) from the Italian: "Follows"; (1) A direction to immediately go on to a following *section of music* without *pause* or *interruption! Segue l'aria,* the *aria* follows; *segue la coda,* the *coda* follows, etc.! (2) A direction to *play in the same style* as a *preceding portion!*

seguendo (*sā gwĕn'dō*) from the Italian: "Following!"

sequidilla (*sā'gē dĕl'yä*) from the Spanish: A *Spanish dance,* based on *freely repeated lines* from *poetry*, executed in *brisk, triple time* with *guitar* and *castanets accompaniment*! The *tempo* may vary from province to province, but most often the sound resembles a faster version of the *bolero*!

sehnsuchtig(*zān'zōōkht'ĭk*) from the German: Play with a style expressing desire, longing, yearning, or ardor!

sehr (*zā'r*) from the German: "Very", "extremely"; *sehr schnell*, very fast; *sehr langsam*, very slow!

semibiscroma. The *Italian* word for a *sixty-fourth note*!

semibreve. The *British* word for a *whole note*!

semiclassic. A vague term to describe *music halfway* between *popular* and *classical*! Usually applied to *light operetta pieces* or *popularized program music* from *serious composers*, and, *conversely, serious efforts from popular music composers*! The characterization has so much inconsistency as to belittle its intellectual authority!

semicroma. The *Italian* word for a *sixteenth note*!

semiquaver. The *British* word for a *sixteenth note*!

semitone. An alternate term for *half-tone*!

semplice.(*sĕm'plē chĕ*) from the Italian: A direction to play in a simple, unaffected manner!

sempre (*sĕm'prę*) from the Italian: "Always", "continually"! *Sempre piano*, always soft (throughout the *music*) and *sempre forte*, always loud!

sentence (*sĕn'tĕns*) A complete *musical expression* or *period*!

sentito (*sĕn tē'tō*) from the Italian: A direction to play with feeling and expression!

senza (*sĕn'tsä*) from the Italian: "Without"; *senza battuta* . . . without *measure*, not *strict time*!

senza di slentare . . . *without retarding*!
senza misura . . . same as *senza battuta*!
senza passione . . . *quietly, without passion*!
senza piatti . . . *without cymbals, drums only*!
senza rallentando . . . *without slowing down*!
senza rallentare . . . same as *senza di slentare*!
senza sordini . . . *without mutes*!
senza suono . . . *without tone, recited*!
senza tempo . . . same as *senza battuta*!

septet, septette(*sĕp tet'*) (1) A *composition* for *seven voices* or *seven instruments*!

septime (*sĕp'tēm*) An old *Latin* name for a *seventh interval* (see *seventh*)!

septimole (*sĕp'tĭ mōl'*) A *group* of *seven notes* of *equal value* which are *played* in the *time value* of *four* or *six notes* of *equal value* without *changing the rhythm*! It is indicated by the *numeral seven* and a *bracket or slur*!

septole (*sĕp'tō lĕ*) The *German* word for a *septimole* or *septuplet*!

septuplet (*sĕp'tŭ plĕt*) Same as *septimole*!

sequence(*sē'kwĕns*) (1) The *multiple repetition* of a *melodic portion* of *music* at *different pitches* is a *melodic sequence*! A *sequence* is *real* or *chromatic* when the *intervals* of the *repeats* are the *same as* those of the *initial portion*, and *tonal* or *diatonic* when the *intervals* of the *repeats* are *altered to keep them in the same key as the original*! (2) The *repetition of a chord sequence* (rather than *melody notes*) is called a *harmonic sequence*!

serenade(*sĕr'ĕ nād'*) (1) A *romantic composition*, or *love song*, designed for *male singing* in the evening below a lady's window! (2) An *instrumental piece* for general evening entertainment! (3) A *light orchestral work* in *several movements* that preceded the *symphony form*! This type of *serenade* was developed by Mozart and his contemporaries! (4) For a "*mock serenade*", see *charivari*!

serenata (*sĕr ĕ nä'tä*) from the Italian: (1) A *serenade*! (2) A *short dramatic cantata* or *opera*, probably first developed in any importance by Handel!

serano (*sĕ rä'nō*) from the Italian: A direction to play in a "serene", calm manner!

serial music. A *modern form* of *composition* that uses a *series* of *tones* and *dynamics* without regard for traditional organization of *keys and scales*! It was first championed by Arnold Schoenberg in the first decade of the 20th century! His "*serialism principle*" used the *12 tones of the chromatic scale (dodecaphonic)* as a *particular series constantly repeating throughout a composition*! According to the system, *each row of notes or tones* always appears in *proper, consecutive order* regardless of *key*, or *scale* or *octave*! Schoenberg's "rules", however, allowed for *inversion of a series* (up or down in *pitch*) or for *retrograde reversal* of a *series*, or for a *combined retrograde inversion (going backwards and upside down)*! The *12 tone principle* has been employed by many *modern composers*! Alban Berg, Anton Webern, Milton Babbitt and many others have applied *serial music technique* to *rhythm* and *dynamics* in the '20's and '30's. Further extension into the areas of *time-value, attack, loudness*, etc. were "*serialized*" in the 1950's by such as Boulez and Berio.

serio(*sā'rē ō*) / **serioso**(*sā rē ō'sō*) It. / A direction to play in a serious, grave manner!

Serpent

Sextuplet

serpent *(sûr'pĕnt)* (1) An *obsolete bass, wind-instrument* from the 16th century, so named because of its *snake-like shape!* With a *long, reverse "S" twisting tube and finger holes* (later augmented with a few *keys*) the *serpent* sounded somewhat like the *bass cornet!* Its function is performed in modern times by the *tuba!*

sesquialtera *(sĕs kwĭ ăl'tēr ȧ)* from the Latin: (1) A *perfect fifth interval!* (2) An *organ stop* controlling *two or more ranks!*

session *(sĕsh'ŭn)* In *professional recording circles,* the *time allotted* to any *one period* of *studio recording time* based on *union standards.* Historically, a *recording session* is conducted for *three hours,* at *minimum AFM union scale* for *musicians,* after which overtime is charged for each additional half-hour utilized. A three-hour *session* normally will produce about 15 minutes of final *recorded music!*

set *(sĕt)* (1) To *"fit"* with *music . . . words "set"* to *music,* for example, or vice-versa! (2) To prepare *voices* or *instruments* or an *orchestra* for *performance!* (3) Sometimes, used in *popular music* as a colloquial term to describe the *unity* of the *players* in an *ensemble,* in terms of *tempo* and *rhythm!*

settima *(sĕt'tē mä)* / **settimo** *(sĕt' tē mō)* It. / A *seventh interval!*

seventh *(sĕv'ĕnth)* (1) An *interval* of *seven degrees* on the *diatonic scale!* (2) The *harmony* of *two simultaneous tones* a *seventh apart!* (3) The *seventh tone* of an *ascending scale!*

seventeenth *(sĕv'ĕn tēenth')* (1) An *interval* of *two octaves and a third!* (2) An *organ stop, 2 and 1/3 octaves above the diapason!* Same as *tierce!*

seventh chord. A *chord* consisting of a *root* or *fundamental tone,* along with the *third, fifth* and *seventh tones* above it! Every *key* has *seven "seventh" chords,* one for each *scale degree!* A *major seventh chord* consists of a *major triad* and a *major seventh tone!* A *minor seventh chord* consists of a *minor triad* and a *minor seventh tone!* The *most important chord* is the *dominant seventh,* the *chord* built on the *fifth degree . . .* in the *key of C major,* for example, the *chord g, b, d', f' numbered V⁷!* A *diminished seventh chord* consists of a *diminished triad* and a *minor third, usually on the seventh tone of the relative major!* In *C major or minor,* for example, the *chord b, d', f', a-flat!* See *Elements Of Music, Chords!*

sextet, sextette *(sĕks tĕt'* (1) A *composition* in *six parts* for *six voices* or *instruments!* (2) A *group* of *six performers* of a *composition . . .* a *string sextet* usually is comprised of *two violins, two violas* and *two celli!* Other *"famous" sextets* have been *written* for *two horns* and a *string quartet,* or for an *all-winds sextet* (2 horns, 2 clarinets, 2 bassoons)! There are many other variations!

sextuplet *(sĕks' tŭ plĕt)* A *group of six notes* of *equal value* which are *played* in the *time value of four notes* of the *same value without changing the rhythm!* It is indicated by the *numeral 6* and a *bracket* or *slur!* Also called *sextolet, sextole!*

sfogato *(sfō gä'tō)* from the Italian: "Exhaled"; (1) A direction to *sing* in a light, airy manner! (2) A very *high soprano voice . . . soprano sfogato!*

sforzando *(sfōr tsän'dō)* / **sforzato** *(sfōr tsä'tō)* It. "Forced"; A direction to sharply and loudly accent a note or chord! In notation indicated by the abbreviations **sf**: sfz. or > or ∧ or ⌄ over a note!

sforzando piano. from the Italian: A *sharp, loud accent* on a *note or chord,* abruptly or immediately followed by a *soft note or chord!* Abbreviated *sfp!*

sfumate *(sfoo mä'tĕ)* / **sfumato** *(sfoo mä'tō)* It. "Smoky"; a metaphoric direction (from the *graphic arts*) to *play* in an *extremely light manner,* akin to disappearing smoke trails!

shade *(shād)* (1) A *shutter* in the *swell box* of a *pipe organ,* or any object at the top of an *organ pipe* that regulates the *air column vibration* (the *pitch*) within the *pipe!* (2) A *nuance* or *effect* achieved by subtle, unwritten *variation* in the *dynamics* of *performance!*

shake *(shāk)* (1) A *jazz, brass* technique of *"shaking"* an *instrument's mouthpiece across the lips* while *blowing* a *fast, series of alternating harmonic tones!* (2) A *trill; fast alternation of the fundamental note* and a *note that is a half-tone* or a *whole tone above!* See *trill!*

shakuhachi *(shä koo hä'chē)* An *end-blown Japanese bamboo flute* with *four finger-holes* and a *thumb hole!*

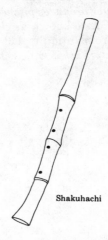

Shakuhachi

shamisen. See *samisen!*

shanty, shantey *(shän'tē)* A *folk song* of the *sea, sung* by *sailors* while they performed nautical chores such as rope-pulling, anchor-hoisting, etc.! Also *chanty, chantey!*

shaped notes *(shāpt nōts) Musical notes,* each of which is uniquely *shaped* to help identify its *position* on the *scale! Shaped notes* date from the mid-19th century as a form of *notation,* and are still used in some sections of the southern U.S.A., particularly for *semi-sacred* and *sacred music!* Also called *patent notes!*

Shaped Notes or Patent Notes

sharp *(shärp)* (1) An *accidental,* the *sign* ♯ for a *note* that is *one half-tone higher than the note* to which it is *appended* ... for example, *C-sharp (C#)* is the *sharp* of *C,* etc! (2) A *sharp (#)* in a *key signature* indicates that all *tones of the same degree* in a *composition* are to be *raised one half-tone higher* unless *cancelled* by a *natural sign* (♮)! A general term for *singing* or *playing* that *sounds higher* than the *intended (true) pitch!* (4) On the *keyboards,* the *black notes C#, D#, F#, G#, A#* are all *sharp,* but *B#* *(enharmonically identical* to the *white key C)* and *E#* *(enharmonically identical* to the *white key F)* are both *white keys!*

shawm *(shôm)* A *double-reed wind instrument,* forerunner of the *oboe* and *clarinet,* that dates back to ancient times! The *shawm* has a *conical bore* which *flares* to a *bell* at the *bottom!* At the *top,* the *mouthpiece* (to which the *reed* is *attached*) is in the form of a *small bent tube inserted into* the *main body* of the *instrument!* Imported into Europe from the Near East, various sizes of *shawms* were utilized until the 17th century, when they gave way to the *oboe!*

sheng *(shĕng)* A *Chinese wind instrument (mouth organ)* with a *bowl-shaped body* around which a *set of bamboo tubes* of *varying sizes* are *bound!* Each *tube* has a *reed,* an *air hole* and a *finger hole* which is *covered for sound!* A *spout* on *the side* serves as a *mouthpiece* and the *player produces pitched sounds* by *blowing* or *inhaling!* Also known as *cheng,* the *instrument* dates back from antiquity, but is still in use! The *Japanese counterpart* is called *sho* (shō)!

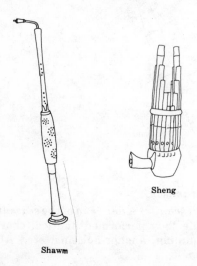

Sheng

Shawm

shift *(shĭft)* (1) A *change* of *the hand position* on *stringed instruments!* With *violins,* the *second position* represents a *half-shift;* third position, *whole shift,* and *fourth position, double shift!* See *Position!* (2) A *change* of the *"slide"* position on a *trombone!*

shimmy *(shĭmī)* A *popular ragtime dance* of the roaring '20's!

sho *(shō)* The *Japanese* counterpart of the *Chinese sheng!* See *sheng!*

shofar, shophar *(shō'fär)* The *ram's horn* of the *ancient Hebrews,* used in modern synagogues during services for *Yom Kippur,* the *Day of Atonement!* A simple, hollow, *animal horn,* the *shofar* sounds only *two harsh, brassy tones* about a *fifth* apart!

shuffle rhythm *(shŭf'l rĭth'm)* In *popular* and *"blues" music,* a *"skipping"* type of *rhythm pattern* which usually uses a *series* of *triplets* with a *rest on the middle beat!* The *drum* may play *dotted eighth* and *sixteenth notes* between the *hands* and *feet* or *play triplets* against *quarter notes* on the *cymbals!* The *rhythm guitar* emphasizes the *downbeat,* alternating *up and down strokes* and the *bass (guitar) plays* the *triplets* with a *middle beat rest,* or *dotted eighth* and *sixteenth notes (3 beats* to the *eighths* and *1 beat* to the *sixteenths)!*

Shuffle Rhythm

(Triplets-Middle Beat Rest)

Shuffle Rhythm

(Dotted Eighths and Sixteenths)

si *(sē)* In *solmization,* the same as *ti,* the *seventh* of the *syllables* in the *Guido d'Arezzo scale!* See *solmization!*

siciliana *(sē chēl yä'nä)* from the Italian: A *Sicilian country dance* in *6/8* or *12/8 meter* which was adapted for use as a *slow movement* in *serious sonatas* and *operas,* usually in a *minor-key type* of *pastorale!*

side drum *(sīd drum)* Same as *snare drum!* See *snare drum!*

sightreading *(sīt'rēd'ing)* The ability to *read* and *perform written music* without having seen or studied the *music* before!

signature *(sĭg'na tŭr)* The name for the *signs* at the *head* of the *first staff* of a *musical composition!* The *sharps (#)* and *flats* (♭) comprise the *key signature* (the *C-major* and the *A-minor keys* have no *sharp* or *flats*) while the vertical numbers **3/4** or **4/4** etc. make up the *time signature!* See *Elements Of Music, Keys!*

silenzio *(sē lĕn'tsē ō) from the Italian: "Silence", a rest or pause! Lunga silenzio, a long pause!*

similar motion. Two or more *parts moving* in the *same direction, up* or *down,* at the *same time!*

simile *(sē'mē lĕ) from the Italian: "Same", a direction to continue playing music that follows,* in the *same manner as the preceding music* . . . such as a *broken-chord style* or a *particular bowing technique!* Also *simile!* In *notation* the *simile mark,* abbreviated *sim.,* is ⸦ or ⸧ a *bar* or *group* is repeated as often as marked!*

simphonie *(sĭm'fōn ē') A French* name for the *hurdy-gurdy!*

simple *(sĭm'p'l) (1)* In regard to *notes* and *intervals, not compound* . . . just *simple measure! (2)* In regard to *rhythm* or *counterpoint,* an *unvarying, uncomplicated form* as opposed to *complicated* or *compounded!*

simple meter. Any *meter* whose *number of beats* in a *measure* is *two, three* or *four;* 2/2, 2/4, 2/8, 3/2, 3/4, 3/8, 4/2, 4/4, 4/8! *Multiples* of a *simple meter* are *compound!* See *compound meter!*

sin'al *(sēn'äl) from the Italian: "Up to", "as far as";* used in *directions to repeat portions of music! Sin'al fine,* up to the end; *sin'al segno,* up to the sign. See *segno!*

sinfonia *(sĭn fō nē'ä) from the Italian: (1)* A *symphony! (2)* The name given to the *overture* of some *early Italian baroque operas!* By 1700, a consistent form of *sinfonia* was characterized as *"Italian overture"!*

sinfonietta *(sĭn fō nyĕ'tä) from the Italian:* "Little symphony"; *(1)* A *short symphony* usually performed by a *small (chamber) orchestra! (2)* A term sometimes applied to the *small (chamber) orchestra* itself!

singbar *(zēnkh'bär)* / **singend** *(zēnkh'ĕndt)* Ger. / Singing, melodious *(cantabile)!*

singspiel *(zēnkh'shpēl)* A form of *German comic opera* popular in the 18th century which included *spoken dialogue* among the *songs!* The term in previous times had been more broadly applied to *serious opera,* as well!

sinistra *(sē nēs trä) from the Italian: "Left",* a direction to *play with the left hand! Mano sinistra,* left hand (abbreviated *m.s.)! Colla sinistra,* with the left hand!

sino *(sē'nō) from the Italian: "Up to"* or *"to", "as far as", "until"!* Also *sin'!* See *sin'al!*

sistrum *(sĭs'trŭm)* An ancient *Egyptian rattle,* shaped like a paddle, with horizontal rods that would *jingle* when *shaken!* Varying shapes have been found in ancient areas far from Egypt, such as in Brazil, Mexico, etc!

sitar *(sĭ'där)* A *long-necked, Indian lute* of major importance in almost all *Hindu music!* Thanks to the international exposure by artists such as Ravi Shankar, the *sitar* has become known and used both in *serious, modern, Western music* as well as in *new jazz-fusion performances!* The *sitar* has a *pear-shaped bowl* extending from the *end of a very long fretboard* with *up to eighteen frets!* Some *sitars* have *as many as 20 strings,* of which *more than a dozen, separately-pitched strings* are *not plucked* but simply *vibrate sympathetically* when the *melody strings* (up to seven strings which are *stopped)* or *two drone strings (unstopped)* are *plucked* with a *finger-plectrum!* The *strings* are *tuned by tightening* the *pegs* in *guitar fashion!*

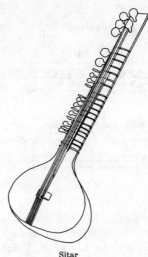

Sitar

Sistrum

six-four chord. The *second inversion* of a *triad chord.* See *inversion!*

sixteenth. An *interval* of *two octaves* and a *second!*

sixteenth note. The *note* ♪ with a *time-value* of *one sixteenth* of a *whole note! Eight sixteenth notes* equal *one half-note! Four sixteenth notes* equal a *quarter note,* and *two sixteenth notes* equal *one eighth note. Successive sixteenths* are written with *double crossbars* or *beams* ♬ (also called *semiquavers*)!

sixteenth rest A *rest* 𝄿 whose *silence* is held for the same time as a *sixteenth note!*

sixth. *(1)* The *interval spanning six diatonic degrees!* Also known as *major sixth! (2)* The *simultaneous sound of two tones a sixth apart! (3)* The *sixth tone* of a *rising scale! (4) Augmented sixth:* The *interval* a *half-tone larger than a major sixth!* In the *C-major scale,* the *interval C to A#* which is a *half-tone larger* than *C to A! (5) Minor sixth:* The *interval* that is a *half-tone smaller* than a *major sixth (C# to A)!*

sixth chord. The *first inversion* of a *triad!* Also called the *six-three chord.* See *Inversion!*

sixth, augmented *(chord).* A *sixth chord* that includes a *sixth* that is one *half-tone larger than a major sixth!* Three important categories of *augmented sixth chords* include: (1) *The Italian sixth* .... a *tone* with the *major third* and *augmented sixth* above it! (2) *The French Sixth* .... a *tone* with the *major third, augmented fourth,* and *augmented sixth* above! (3) *The German sixth* .... a *tone* with a *major third, perfect fifth* and *augmented sixth* above!

Augmented Sixths

Italian   French   German

sixth, Neapolitan *(chord)* The *first inversion* of the *triad* on the *lowered* or *flattened supertonic* .... in the *key of C-major,* the *chord D-flat, F, A-flat (D-flat* is the *supertonic)* becomes *F, A-flat, D-flat,* for example!

sixty-fourth note. The *note* ♬ with a *time-value* of *one sixty-fourth* of a *whole note!* Thirty-two *sixty-fourth notes* equal *one half-note!* Sixteen *sixty-fourth notes* equal *one quarter note!* Eight *sixty-fourth notes* equal *one eighth note,* etc.! When successive *sixty-fourth notes* are written, they appear with *quadruple crossbars* or *beams*

In *Britain,* a *sixty-fourth* note is known as a *hemidemisemiquaver!*

sixty-fourth rest. The *rest* 𝄿 whose *silence* is *held for the same time-value* as a *sixty-fourth note!*

ska *(skä)* A term for Jamaican music popular in the mid-'60's! Combining New Orleans jazz and native *(mento)* calypso rhythms, it was the forerunner of the more political and religious "rock steady" and "reggae" music trends that followed.

skip *(skĭp)* Any *melodic progression* that exceeds *one step* or *interval (second)* between *conjunct degrees* of a *scale!* A *disjunct progression!*

slancio, con *(slän'chō, kôn)* from the Italian: "With dash"; a direction to play in a dashing, strong, impetuous manner! Also *con islancio!*

slargando *(slär gän'dō)* from the Italian: A direction to *play slower* by *extending* or *enlarging* the *time!*

slargato *(slär gä'tō)* from the Italian: "Slower"! Same as *piu sostenuto,* which literally means *"more sustained"!*

slentando *(slĕn tän'dō)* from the Italian: A direction to *play gradually more slowly!*

slide *(slīd)* (1) The *movable portion* of *U-shaped tubing* in a *trombone* that changes the *tones* by *extending* or *contracting* its *"slide" position,* thus *lengthening* or *shortening* the *air column* that *vibrates within!* (2) A *portamento!* (3) A *grace* or *ornament* ... an *appoggiatura,* for example! (4) An *organ slider!* (5) The *part* of the *violin bow's nut* or *frog* which *slides* along the *stick!* (6) One of the variations of *guitar models* is called *"slide guitar"!* See *Guitar!*

slur *(slûr)* A curved line ⌐ or ⌐ which is placed *over* or *under notes of different pitch* to indicate that they are to be *played as a group!* Placed over a *few notes,* the *slur* indicates the *notes* are to be *played legato!* In *vocal music,* the *slur* designates *notes* to be *sung in one breath!* For *bowed strings,* the *slur* indicates *notes* that are to be *played with one stroke!* A *slur* with *staccato dots* over each *note* indicates the *notes* are to be played in *demilegato* or *portato* style! A curved line *over* or *under notes of the same pitch* is a *tie,* not to be confused with a *slur!*

smaniante *(smän ē än'tĕ)* / **smanioso** *(smän ē ō'sō)* It. / A direction to play in a furious, passionate raging manner!

smorzando *(smôr tsän'dō)* / **smorzato** *(smôr tsä'tō)* It. / A direction to play gradually more slowly and softly as if dying away!

snare drum *(snär drŭm)* The small, double-headed, cylinder-shaped *drum* which is common to *orchestras, marching bands, dance bands, rock groups* and *jazz ensembles.* Also called the *side drum,* it is a key member of the *percussion section* or the *"rhythm section"!* The *snare drum* has a *metal* or *plastic* frame covered at top and bottom with a *skin* or *vellum* or *plastic membrane!* The top of the *snare drum,* the *"batter"* head, is struck with a pair of *drumsticks* or *wire brushes!* Across the *bottom,* the *"snare"* head, a *series* of *metal, gut* or *plastic strings* are *stretched* and *clamped!* These *vibrate* when the *"batter head"* is *struck* and produce more *resonance* and *tone-brightness* for the *drum sound!* Loosening the *snares dulls* or *lowers* the *sound, tightening* brightens or *raises* the *sound!* A *muffled sound* often is produced by *placing a cloth over the "batter head"* to intercept the *drum strokes.* The *snare drum,* however, is classified as an *instrument* with an *indefinite pitch* that cannot be *tuned,* or as a *fixed-pitch instrument* whose *pitch cannot be varied!*

Snare drum (side drum)

soave *(sō ä'vĕ)* / **soavemente** *(sō ä vĕ mĕn'tĕ)* It. / A direction to play in a suave, sweet, soft manner!

soffocato *(sŏf ō kä'tō)* from the Italian: Choked, muffled, damped!

soft pedal. The *left pedal (una corda pedal)* of the *piano!* When depressed, the *soft pedal shifts* the *keyboard action slightly to the right*, so that only *two out of three strings* in the *higher registers* and *one out of two in the middle registers* (leaving *one for the bass tones*) are struck by *hammers* when the *notes* are *played!*

sol *(sōl)* (1) In *solmization*, the *fifth syllable* representing the *fifth tone of a diatonic scale (do, re, mi, fa, sol,* etc.) (2) The *French* and *Italian* name for the *note G!*

solenne *(sō lĕn'nĕ)* / **solennemente** *(sō lĕn nĕ mĕn'tĕ)* It. / A direction to play in a solemn manner!

sol-fa *(sōl fä)* (1) To *sing solfeggio!* (2) *Solmization*, or an *exercise using solmization syllables!*

solfege *(sŏl'fädj')* Fr. / **solfeggio** *(sŏl'fĕdg ō)* It. / A *technique* in *musical education* that *develops sight-singing ability* and the *recognition* of *related elements of musical notation!* The system *translates musical tones* into *vocal sounds!* The *solmization syllables do, re, mi, fa, sol, la, ti* or *si* are frequently employed in *solfeggio* training! (2) A short, vocal exercise that uses *solmization syllables* or *is sung to one vowel!* The latter technique is better known as *vocalizing* or *vocalization!*

soli *(sō'lē)* (1) The *Italian plural* of *solo!* (2) A direction in *music* to *use only one performer for each part!*

solmization *(sŏl mĭzä'shŭn)* The *system* of *denoting* the *notes* of a *scale* by *syllables!* The familiar *do, re, mi, fa, sol, la, ti* or *si* are descendants of a *hexachord tone-pattern* incepted by an 11th century monk, Guido D'Arezzo! Two forms of *solmization* are utilized today: The *"fixed-do"* system is used in France and Italy and it assigns to *each note* an *unchanging syllable regardless of key!* C is always *do*, D is always *re*, and so on! In the *"movable do"* system (used in the U.S. and Britain) *do* is C in a *C-major* or *C-minor key*, but A-flat in the *A-flat key*, or G in the *G-major* or *G-minor key!* The *other syllables* follow the *order of scale degrees* after *do!*

solo *(sō'lō)* from the Italian: (1) A *composition* for *one voice*, or *one instrument with or without* accompaniment! (2) A *performance* by *one singer*, or *one instrumentalist!* (3) A *portion of music* from a *larger work* (opera, symphony, etc.) *performed by one voice or instrument!* In a *solo concerto*, the *soloist* has a *key part* contrasted to the *orchestral accompaniment!*

solo organ. A *fourth manual* in *large organs* that *controls solo stops!*

solo pitch. Another term for *scordatura!*

sonata *(sō nä'ta)* One of the important forms of *classical instrumental music!* The *sonata* traditionally was designed for *solo performance* by a *piano (piano sonata)*, or by a *violin (violin sonata)* or by *cello, flute*, etc. It is, however, sometimes *played* as

chamber music! A *sonata* consists of *three or four typical movements* which are *contrasted* in *rhythm, theme* and *mood*, but *retain* some *sense of relationship* in the *tonality* and *style!* The movements are known as: (1) The *Allegro.... a fast movement*, sometimes preceded by a *short, slow introduction*, states the *theme(s)* in *prescribed "sonata form"!* (2) The *adagio* or *andante* or *largo movement .... a slow movement* usually quite *lyrical* in its *melodic variations!* (3) The *scherzo* or *minuet ....* the *presto* or *allegro movement* in a definite *dance-type* style; often with a *brisk rondo finale!* (4) If a *fourth movement* is *present*, it would return to *allegro* in the *pure sonata form*, or a *rondo form* with new variations! The classic *sonata* was nurtured in the early 18th century by Bach, Scarlatti, and others, and flourished during the Mozart and Beethoven years of the late 18th century!

sonata form. The name for the *musical structure characterized* by the *first movement* of a *sonata!* The *sonata form* usually consists of *three sections* in the following order: (1) The *exposition!* Two or more individual *themes* or *subjects* are *expounded;* first, the *principal subject* (written in the *tonic key*) and then, the *secondary subject* (written in the *dominant key*, or the *relative major key* if the *principal key* is a *minor key*)! (2) The *development!* The *extension* and *elaboration* of the *subject themes* with intricate *key changes, counterpoint, fugue* and, perhaps, *multiple variations* which *close* by *returning* to the *tonic key!* (3) The *recapitulation!* The *subject themes* are *repeated in order*, but they are written in the *tonic key*, and they *close usually* with a *coda* that varies in its length and detail!

song *(sŏng)* (1) Any *vocal composition!* (2) A *lyric poem* or *story set to music!* (3) A *short composition* for *solo voice* with or without *accompaniment!* (4) Categories of *songs* in *serious music* include *folk songs* and *art songs (lied, recitative, aria*, etc.); in the *popular music* area, there are *ballads, novelties, sacred* and *inspirational songs*, as well as *country* (the vernacular *hillbilly*), *"blues", "rock", and "disco", songs*, etc.

song form. A term for characterizing a *serious song* or *"songlike" instrumental composition* (also called the *primary* or *lied form*)! The *song form* usually has two divisions: (1) The *binary (two-part) form* which uses two *repeating sections*, one of which *modulates* to *related keys*, while the other continues in the *original key!* (2) The *ternary (three-part) form* which consists of *three sections*, the *third restating* the *opening section* or *theme* with a *contrasting second theme in between!*

sóno *(sō'nō)* from the Italian: *Sound*, or *tone!*

sonore *(sŏn ō'rĕ)* / **sonoro** *(sŏn ō'rō)* It. / Sonorous, resonant, resounding!

sonority *(sō nŏr'ĭ tē)* The *quality* of *sound*, particularly in regard to *fullness, loudness, resonance* and *projection!*

sons bouchés *(sŏn bōō shä')* from the French: *"Stopped notes"* in *brass* or *horn music!*

sons étouffés (sôn'zā tōō fā') from the French: "Stopped notes" in *harp music!*

sopra (sō'prä) from the Italian: "Above", "before", over, on; a direction in *keyboard music* to *play cross-handed! Mano sinistra sopra (m.s. sopra);* cross the left hand over the right hand! *Mano dextra sopra (m.d. sopra);* cross the right hand over the left hand!

sopra, come (sō'prä, kô'mĕ) from the Italian: "As above", a direction to *play a note or phrase* as it was *played before!*

sopranino (sō'prä nē'nō) from the Italian: "Little soprano"; any *instrument* that *is smaller* and *higher-pitched* than the *soprano size!*

soprano (sō prä'no) (1) the *highest range* of *human voice* (usually female) *ranging more than two octaves up from middle C! Operatic sopranos* are called: *Dramatic* . . . . powerful, gusty quality! *Lyric sopranos* . . . . sweet, emotional quality! *Coloratura sopranos* . . . . technically-skilled, clear, flexible quality! The *males* who can duplicate the *soprano range* usually fall under the heading of (a) *Young boys (boy sopranos)* whose *voices* are still in "pre-change" *registers* or (b) *Male adults singing* in *falsetto register,* or (c) The *castrati . . . young men* in the 17th and 18th centuries who were *castrated* to keep their *voice range* in a *feminine register!* (2) In some *families of instruments,* the *soprano model* usually is the *highest-pitched* and *shortest* . . . for example, *soprano saxophone, soprano recorder,* etc. (3) In *harmony notation,* the *treble range* or *treble part!*

soprano clef. Same as the *descant clef!* See descant clef! Not to be confused with *treble clef!*

sordini (sôr dēn'ē) plural / **sordino** (sôr dēn'ō) singular It. / "Mute" or "damper"! *Con sordino,-i,* with the *mute(s)! Senza sordino,-i,* without the *mute(s)!* Directions normally given to the *strings* or *wind instruments,* but sometimes ambiguously applied to the *una corda (soft) pedal* of the *piano!* Actually, the *left piano pedal* "mutes" the *tones,* while the *right pedal releases* the *dampers* to *sustain tones!*

sorda-o (sôr'dä-ō) from the Italian: "Muted" or a muted tone! *Tromba sorda, muted trumpet!*

sortita (sôr tē'tä) from the Italian: "Coming out"; (1) An *opening aria* in *opera!* (2) A *closing voluntary!*

sospirando (sōs pē rän'dō) from the Italian: A direction to *play* in a sighing, tearful manner!

sostenuto (sōs tĕ nōō'tō) from the Italian: "Sustained"; a direction to *hold* the *tones* for their *full time-value* which usually compels a *slight slowing of the tempo!*

sostenuto pedal. The *central pedal on pianos (pianos that have three pedals)* used to *sustain notes played just before the pedal is depressed!*

sotto (sō'tō) from the Italian: "Under", "below"!

sotto voce (sō'tō vō'chĕ) from the Italian: "Under the breath"; In a *low voice* or *undertone, directed aside* . . . . a "stage whisper"! A *faintly audible murmur!* A direction to *play* in the *softest of undertones!*

soul music. A contemporary term for *popular, rhythmic black music* that probably has helped to obsolete the label "*rhythm and blues*"! The latter term has been deemed demeaning and narrow by many critics, and the advanced *black contribution* to *rock, jazz, gospel, disco* may be more significantly categorized as "*soul music*"! Vernacular expressions such as "funky" and "raunchy" have compounded the task of precisely defining "soul" . . . . the standard cliche: "If it has to be explained to you, you don't have soul"! . . . . but certainly it relates to the moods described variously as expressive "soul" of modern black society and its fusion of historic, black-music, *blues lament, gospel fervor, jazz freedom* and innate-rhythm "feel" (the latter often overstated as a stereotype)! The most easily recognizable signs of "*soul music*", in any event, would be the uninhibited, *pulsing, microtonic rhythm patterns (electric bass* and *amplified lead guitars* at *peak levels)* and the simple, repeated *language of the streets* for *lyrics! Nuance* and *sophistication* are completely *secondary* to *intensity* and *sensuosity,* but with undoubted, if informal, virtuosity! The *subject matter* may be romance, social injustice or religious joy, but the *musical attack* of "*soul music*" is unfettered . . . complete with *heavily-accented beats,* and *effects* such as *note-bending, clapping,* and *stomping!* In the late 1970's, *soul music styles* have crossed over into the so-called "*disco*" market simply by adding "*danceability*", in the *form of 130 beats per minute,* to the *rhythm structure!*

sound. Anything heard as the result of *regular, repeated vibrations* which are transmitted to the *ear* and its *inner membrane!* The *type* of *vibration* determines the nature of *sound! Irregular vibrations* produce *noise; regular vibrations* (with *frequencies measured* by the *cycle of vibration per second)* produce *musical tones!*

soundboard (sound'bôrd) A thin, wooden board placed in *stringed instruments* (the *violin* "belly"; *under or behind* the *piano, harpsichord,* etc.) which *re-inforces* and *sustains tones* by *sympathetic vibration with the strings!*

sound hole (-'hōl) The *opening* in the *soundboard* or *belly* of *stringed instruments* which re-inforces *symphathetic string vibrations! Violins, violas, celli* and *double basses* have a *pair* of *F-holes* in their *bellies* (in the shape of a *scripted letter* 𝑓). *Guitars* and *lutes* have *one round, sound hole* in the middle of the top surface of the *body* which is usually decorated with a design called the *rose!*

soundpost (-'pōst) In *violins, viols* and other *related instruments,* the *small, wooden rod* between the *belly* and the *back,* just under the *treble foot* of the *bridge!* When the *strings* are *played,* the *soundpost* picks up the *symphathetic vibrations* of the *belly* and carries them to the *back,* creating more *sound re-inforcement!*

sourdine (sōōr dēn') from the French! "Mute". See the *Italian, sordine! Avec les sourdines,* the *French direction* to use *mutes! San les sourdines,* play without *mutes!*

sousaphone (*sōō'zä fŏn'*) A *large, circular bass tuba* (*helicon*) with a *huge, flared bell* that faces forward! The *instrument*, named after the renowned *bandmaster John Philip Sousa*, is designed to coil around the player's body! The *bass sousaphone* is *pitched in E-flat*, and the *contrabass* or *double bass sousaphone* is *pitched in B-flat!*

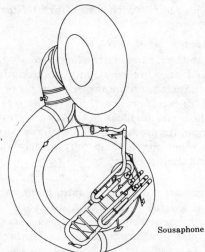

Sousaphone

space (*spās*) In *musical notation* the *open area* between the *horizontal lines on the staff* (including any *ledger lines*); hence, the *interval between the lines!*

spasshaft (*shpäs'häft*) The *German* word for *scherzando!*

speaker key. A *key* or *hole* in *woodwinds* (*oboe, clarinet*, etc.) that implements the production of *harmonics* by *overblowing!* Oboes usually have two *speaker keys!* One *raises* the *sound* of a *note* by a *full octave* (the *octave key*) and the *other raises the sound by an octave and a fifth!* Clarinets normally have only *one speaker key* that *raises* a *note* by an octave and a fifth!

sp anato (*spē yä nä ' tō*)from the Italian: A direction to play in a smooth, even, *legato* manner!

spiccato (*spē kä'tō*) from the Italian: "*Detached*"; a direction to players of bowed-string instruments to lightly spring the center of the bow on and off the string for each note! *Spiccato* is a sharper variation of "*staccato*" with more "*wrist stroke*" for each *detached note!* In notation, dotted notes are used (same as sautillé)

spinet (*spĭn'ĕt*) (1) The *smallest model* of *upright piano*; with *shorter strings* and a *more-indirect key action!* The *spinet* concedes some degree of *superior*

Spinet Piano

tone quality to *larger piano uprights!* (2) An *obsolete form* of *small harpsichord* with a *single-key, single-string action* and a *compass* from *low C to high F!*

spirito (*spē'rē tō*) / **spiritoso** (*spē rē tō'sō*) It. / A direction to play with spirit. Lively, animated! *Con spirito*, with spirit!

spiritual (*spĭr'ĭt ū ăl*) (1) A form of *religious song* developed by American blacks in the U.S. southern states during the latter half of the 19th century. Simple melodies with *complicated, syncopated rhythm patterns* are characteristic of the so-called "*Negro spirituals*" and reflect the mixed influences of African roots and white evangelism in *indigenous gospel music!* *Black college choirs*, travelling in the 1870's, popularized the "*spiritual*" for the masses, which led to timeless adaptation, thereafter, by various *popular composers!* In constant use today are such *spirituals* as *Go Down, Moses; Joshua Fought The Battle Of Jericho; Swing Low, Sweet Chariot; Lift Every Voice and Sing; Deep River; Sometimes I Feel Like A Motherless Chile; O Happy Day, Amen* and many others! (2) A more-secular type of *folk-song*, inspired by *black-spiritual music*, is credited to the *immortal white American composer Stephen Collins Foster* (1826-1864) who authored such *compositions* as *Massa's In de Cold, Cold Ground, Old Black Joe, Old Folks At Home (Swanee River), Jeanie With The Light Brown Hair, Beautiful Dreamer, Oh Susanna, My Old Kentucky Home* and many others!

spitze (*shpĭt'sĕ*) "*Point*", the *German* word for the *point* of the *violin bow!*

Spitzflöte (*shpĭts'flô'te*) from the German: An *open flue organ stop* (*1, 2, 4, 8-foot pitch*) with a *soft, flute tone!* The term derives from the *pointed top of the conical-shaped organ pipes!*

splice (*splīs*) In *professional recording* jargon, any one *cut* and *re-joining* of an *edited portion of magnetic recording tape* is called a "*splice*"! The artful "*splicing*" of *music tapes* at *record sessions* to expedite "*overdubbing*" by *vocalists* and *instrumentalists*, and to *extract* and *combine* the best qualities of various "*takes*" (*performances*), has become a combined *engineer/musican* craft indispensable to *multi-track recording!*

sprechstimme (*shprĕkh'shtĭm mĕ*) from the German: "*Speaking voice!*" The *German term* for a type of *spoken-singing recitation* (following *specially-notated, approximate pitches*) that *slides rapidly* from *one note to the next!* First credited to *composer Arnold Schoenberg* (1874-1951), the technique was adapted by others including *Schoenberg's disciple, Alban Berg* (1885-1935).

springing bow. A technique for *bowing* used by *violinists!* See *sautillé, saltando*, and *staccato!*

springer (*sprĭng'ēr*) Another *German* word for a *Nachschlag!* See *Nachschlag!*

spur (*spûr*) One of the pointed *clamps* on the *hoop* of a *bass drum!* The *clamps* keep the *drum* off the floor and prevent rolling!

square dance *(skwâr dăns)* An early American country dance still popular in the U.S.! Typically, it is danced in quadrille style with four couples interchanging in response to *"calls"* which are *"sung-spoken"* by a *"caller"!* The *music* usually is in *2/4* or *6/8 time,* and a *rural-flavored "fiddle"* frequently is prominent in the *accompaniment!*

square time. Another term for *march time,* or *4/4 time!*

squillante *(skwēl yän'tĕ)* from the Italian: A direction to play in a clear, ringing manner!

sruti *(shrŭ'tĭ)* from Sanskrit: "What is heard"! The *smallest audible interval* in *Hindu music,* which *divides* the octave into *22 sruti!*

Stabat Mater *(stä'băt mä'tēr)* from the Latin: "The Mother was standing"; a *Latin hymn* commemorating the Crucifixion which is *sung* in *Roman Catholic liturgy!*

stabile *(stä' bē lĕ)* from the Italian: Stable, steady, firm!

staccatissimo *(stăk kä'tēs sē mō)* from the Italian: An extremely *sharp, detached staccato!* See *staccato!* In *notation,* usually indicated by *wedge-shaped markings over or under the notes!*

staccato *(stăk kä'tō)* from the Italian: A direction to play *designated notes* in a *disconnected, detached manner* that actually *cuts short* the *time-value* of the *notes* (the opposite of *legato)!* A *quarter note* becomes an *eighth note,* etc! A *dot over or under a note* indicates *staccato!* A *wedge-shaped marking* instead of a *dot* usually suggests *staccatissimo! Staccato* sometimes is abbreviated **stacca.**! For *string players* using a *bow,* there are many variations of *staccato technique:* See *martelé, picchetato, saltando, sautillé* and *"springing bow"!*

staff *(stăf)* The *set of five, horizontal, parallel lines* used in *musical notation* to indicate *tones (notes)* and *key signatures!* Also called *stave!* The plural of *staff* is *"staves"! Instrumental music* for *keyboards* usually is *written* on *two staves coupled* by a *brace* or *bracket! Organ music* is *written* on *three staves (one for pedal)! Other instruments* may require only a *single stave! The key signature (clef)* indicates *pitch* and the *vertical pair of numbers* indicates *time-value . . .* both appear at the *head* of the *first staff* of a *musical composition! Notes* that *rise above or drop below the staff* are placed on or between *"ledger lines"! The top staff* of a *bracketed two-stave arrangement* is called the *treble clef! The bottom staff* of the *bracketed stave* is called the *bass clef!* See *Elements of Notation, Scales* and *Clefs!*

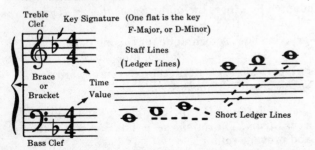

Treble Clef — Key Signature (One flat is the key F-Major, or D-Minor) — Staff Lines (Ledger Lines) — Brace or Bracket — Time Value — Short Ledger Lines — Bass Clef

stanchezza *(stän kĕ'tsä)* from the Italian: A direction to play in a weary, dragging manner!

ständchen *(stĕndt'chĕn)* The *German* word for *"serenade"!*

stanza *(stän'ză)* A *group* of *symmetric measures* which *recur, in series,* in a *poetic song!*

stark *(shtärk)* from the German: "Strong"; a direction to play loudly with power *(forte)! Starker,* more loudly!

stave *(stāv)* Same as *staff!*

steel band *(stēl bănd)* In the *Caribbean* (particularly *Trinidad* and *Jamaica),* any indigenous *musical group* that plays on the *surface of whole* or *shortened steel oil drums, in concert!* Skilled *players* bend and dent the *drum surfaces* so that *drum strokes* at different points produce different *fixed pitches!* The native ingenuity lends a particularly appropriate and enhancing effect to the *calypso* and *reggae* rhythms.

steel guitar. An *electric, solid-body variation* of *popular guitar!* Basically, no more than *steel strings* stretched over a *"slab of wood"* on which *electrical "pick ups"* are located! See *Guitar!*

steg *(shtĕg)* The *German* word for the *bridge* on *stringed instruments! Am steg,* a direction to *bow over* or *near the bridge!*

stem *(stĕm)* The short, vertical line attached at its

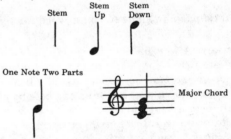

Stem — Stem Up — Stem Down — One Note Two Parts — Major Chord

top or bottom to the *head* of a *note!* When the *note-head* is at the *bottom (stem going up),* the *stem* is attached at the *right of the head!* When the *note-head* is at the *top (stem going down)* the *stem* is attached at the *left of the head!* Usually, the *stem* goes down when the *note* is located on the *top half of a staff,* and conversely, goes up when the *note* is located on the *bottom half!* The only *note* that has *no stem* is the *whole note* ○ ! Sometimes, when *two separate instrumental* or *vocal parts* are written on *one staff,* and *both parts* are to *play the same note,* only the *one note* will appear with both an *upward* and a *downward stem,* one for each part! In *chord notation, three or more notes* may appear to share the same *stem,* although the *position of each notehead* determines the *pitch* of the *individual note* in the *chord!*

step *(stĕp)* The *interval* between *two successive notes* on a *scale!* "Step" is frequently (if incongruously) used interchangeably with the term *"tone"!* In *European* and *American music, scales* consist of *patterns* of *whole steps (tones)* and *half-steps (half-tones)!* A *whole step* is also called a *major second,* and a *half-step* a *minor second!*

stereo (stĕ'rē ō) An *American* expression (an obvious shortening of "*stereophonic*") which has almost replaced "*hi-fi*" as a common expression for a *record-player* or for the *components* of a *record-playing system (turntable, tape machine, amplifier, speakers, etc.*)! "*Hi-fi*" generally applied to *improved fidelity*, including *monaural playback*, but "*stereo*" in its application to *recorded play-back* means at least two *reproducing* "*speakers*" must be used! See *stereophonic*!

stereophonic (stĕ'rē ō fŏn'ĭk) Binaural sound (for two ears) as opposed to *monaural* (for one ear)! Since the 1950's, *stereophonic sound* has described the *sound of music or voices* that is "*picked up*" by *two or more microphones* during *performance* and *reproduced* through *two or more* "*speakers*"! In the recording industry, the *stereophonic sound* is "*mixed*" or "*reduced*" from *multi-channel* "*tracks*" down to *two* "*master*" *channels* which become the source for *mass duplication* of *disks* and *tapes*! These are sold to the public for *reproduction* through *at least two* "*speakers*"! In modern recording practice, as many as *24 channels (tracks)* may be used in *professional studios* which go through various processes of *equalization, overdubbing, phase adjustment,* "*stacking*" and other *sound-engineering techniques* before arrival at the final "*two-track*" *master stereo tape*! Newer additions to *stereophonic equipment* include the *Dolby noise-suppressor system* (which reduces *tape hiss*) and the current, advanced *digital tape machines* which introduce *computer technology* to the business of "*stereo*"!

stessa, stesso (stĕs'sä, -ō) from the Italian: "The same"; a direction to play as before! *L'istesso tempo* or *lo stesso tempo, play* at the *same tempo regardless* of any *change* in the *time signature*!

stick (stĭk) (1) Short for *drumstick*! (2) The *wooden part* of the *violin bow*! (3) A *baton*!

stile (stē'lĕ) from the Italian: "Style"! *Stile rappresentativo,* "representational style," refers to an *early operatic form* of *recitative music*! *Stile osservato,* "observed style", means that *careful attention* should be paid to the *music,* particularly to *vocal parts*!

stimme (shtĭm'mĕ) from the German: (1) The *voice*! (2) A *soundpost*! (3) An *organ stop*! (4) A *vocal* or *instrumental part; mit der Stimme, with the part* (same as *Colla Parta*)!

stimmung (shtĭm'mo͞onkh) from the German: (1) "Mood" or "intonation"! *Traurige Stimmung,* unhappy mood! *Heitere Stimmung,* happy mood! *Stimmung halten,* to stay in tune! *Stimmungsbild,* a short, moody *composition*! (2) *Pitch* or *tuning, accordatura*!

stock arrangement (stŏk ă rānj'mĕnt) In the *popular music industry,* a term for all *all-purpose band* or *orchestral arrangement* usually commissioned or printed by a *music publisher* and kept in inventory stock! The term sometimes is used demeaningly to indicate a trite or commonplace *arrangement* as opposed to one that is new or singular!

stop (stŏp) (1) Controlling the *pitch* of a *stringed instrument* by using a *finger,* or a mechanical device, to press down a *string* at given points of its *length* . . . a "*stopped*" *string,* as contrasted to an "*open*" *string*! *Double stopping* means pressing down on *two strings simultaneously; triple stopping, three strings*! (2) Controlling the *pitch* of *wind instruments* by using a *finger,* or a *key,* to *close a finger hole* and *alter* the *air pressure*! (3) Changing the *tone quality* of *wind instruments* in the *French horn family* by inserting a hand or fist or *mute* into the *bell.* This technique produces *stopped notes* which are indicated by a *+ sign* in *notation*! See *son bouches*! (4) In *guitar music,* a *barre (bar)* means the first finger of the left hand "*stops*" all the *strings,* while the other fingers form a *chord*! A *half-barre* means only *2 to 5 strings* are *stopped*! The *capo (capostasto)* is a *mechanical device* which acts as a "*barre*"! *Capo* also is used as a verb meaning to *barre (stop)* the *strings* with a *finger* or a *mechanical device*!

stop, organ. (1) A *graduated row* of *pipes* in a *family of tones* and *quality* which is connected to the given *organ device* supplying air pressure! The *stop knobs* or *levers* on the *organ manuals* (equal in number to the *rows* of *pipes*) are "*drawn*" or moved by the *organist* to produce selected sound-combinations! The categories of *pipe rows (ranks)* are known as (1) *Speaking* or *Sounding stops* which include the *reed pipes (reed work)* and the *flue pipes (flue work)*! The latter include the *principal stops* with *full octave (diapason sound)*; the *Gedackt pipes* (stopped pipes covered at one end), and the *open-flue flute pipes (flute work)* that are too narrow or too broad for *diapason sound,* or are *stopped pipes* with *chimneys* or whose *entire pipe-length is shaped* with *three or four sides*! Other *stops* include: (2) *Mixture stops* . . . *stops* that elicit *sound* from two or more *rows* of *pipes*! Two or more *notes (chords)* are *sounded* by depressing a single *key* on the *manual keyboard.* Also called *compound stops*! (3) *Mechanical stops* . . . *stops* that are not connected to any *pipes* (producing no *tone*) but which operate a device such as a *coupler* or a *tremulant*! See *tremolo stop*! (4) *Auxiliary stops* . . . *stops* used in *conjunction* with *other stops*! (5) *Complete stops* . . . *stops* with *at least one pipe* for each *manual key*! (6) *Foundation stops* . . . all the *stops* of *normal pitch (unison)* and the *related principal stops* are called *foundation stops*! The *pitch* of *organ pipes* is designated by its size . . . an *eight-foot (8') pipe sounds* the *normal pitch;* a *sixteen-foot (16') pipe sounds* one octave *lower* and *4', 2', 1' sound* one, *two* and *three octaves higher* than *normal* in that order. (7) *Mutation stops* . . . *Stops played together* with *other tones*! The function of a *mutation stop* is to add *overtones (harmonics)*! A *quint stop* supplies a *twelfth* to the *basic tone;* a *tierce* adds a *seventeeth*! (8) *Pedal stops* . . . *stops* located on or just above the *pedal board*! See *ORGAN*!

strad *(străd)* An abbreviation, and a colloquial name, for a *Stradivarius violin!*

stradivarius *(stră'dĭ vâ'ĭ ŭs)* The *Latin name* for each of the *world-renowned violins* made by Antonio Stradivari in Cremona, Italy (1644-1737)!

strain *(strān)* (1) A *short division* of a *composition!* (2) A *song, air* or *melodic passage!* (3) A *theme,* or *motive,* or *period!*

strascicando *(stră shē kän'dō)* / **strascinando** *(stră shē nän'dō)* It./ "Dragging"; used in directions such as *strascinando l'arco,* "draw the *violin bow* across the *strings* in an *unbroken glide from tone to tone*"; *strascinando la voce,* the *vocalist* should *sing* the *notes* in an *extremely smooth legato,* almost *portamento!* Also *strascinare la voce!*

strathspey *(străth spā')* A *lively Scottish dance* in *4/4 time,* similar to a *reel* but *slower,* and characterized by the *rhythm* of a *Scotch snap* or *catch!* See *Scotch snap!*

street organ Another term for *barrel organ!*

strepitoso *(strĕ pē tō'sō)* from the Italian: A direction to play in a noisy, boisterous manner!

stretta, stretto *(strĕt'tä, -'tō)* from the Italian: "Squeezed" or hurried! (1) A direction to *play* the *notes* of a *theme more rapidly* to *compress the time!* Most often used for an *ending* or *coda!* (2) In *fugues,* gaining an effect by overlapping *answer* and *subject* with a deliberately *rapid performance!* Usually employed as an *ending portion!* (3) *Andante stretto,* a hurried *andante tempo!* (4) *Stretto pedale, rapid movement* of the *loud pedal on the piano* to increase *harmonic intensity!*

strict measure, strict time. In exact accordance with the *rhythmic division* of the *measure* into *beats* and *notes!* Adherence to the *time signature.* . . . $\frac{3}{4}$ means *3 quarter notes to the measure, each quarternote getting one beat;* $\frac{6}{8}$ means *6 eighth notes to the measure,* each *eighth note* ♪ *getting one beat.* . . .should not be confused with the *speed of performance (tempo)* of the *notes!*

stride piano. A ragtime, jazz-piano style made famous in early-20th century Harlem. The name derives from the muscular proficiency — large hands, thick wrists — required to prolong rapid ostinatos with the left hand while making swift shifts of syncopation with the right.

stridente *(strĕ dĕn'tĕ)* from the Italian: "strident" same as *martelé, martellato!*

string *(strĭng)* (1) A thin cord of *gut, wire* or *nylon* that is fastened to various *instruments* (violin, piano, guitar, harp, etc.) and *vibrates* when *struck, plucked, strummed* or *bowed!* The *frequency of vibration determines the pitch,* which varies in accordance with the *length* and *thickness* of the *strings* and the *tension* of the *strings at rest! Strings* that *vibrate* (without being directly activated) in *reaction* to the *vibration of other strings* are called *sympathetic strings!* When a *string vibrates* along its

full length, it is an *open string!* When a *string* is *shortened* (by *pressing a finger down at a fret position,* for example) the *string* is *called a stopped string!* The expression "*strings*" (or *string section*) refers to the *violins, violas, celli* and *double basses* in an *orchestra!* The *highest-pitched string part* is called *first string;* next highest, the *second string,* etc. (3) *Soprano string,* the *violin's E string!*

string bass. Another term for the *double bass!*

stringed instruments. All the "*strings*", or the *string section,* of an *orchestra* as well as the *piano, guitar, harpsichord, clavichord, harp, lute, sitar, mandolin, balalaika,* et al.! The *symphony orchestra* limits the term "*strings*" to the *violin, viola, cello* and *double bass* and groups these in a *symphonic score! Dance bands* and *military* or *marching bands* rarely use "*strings*", except for special *concert performance* with *augmented parts,* or for so-called "*society dance bands*" which regularly include *strings* for *ballroom dancing!*

stringéndo *(strēn jĕn'dô)* from the Italian: A direction to *play faster,* usually in anticipation of a *climax,* or an *oncoming section of music* that calls for a *swifter tempo!* Abbreviated *string.!*

stringere *(strēn jĕ'rĕ)* from the Italian: "To hasten" or to rush! *Senza stringere,* without rushing!

string orchestra. An *instrumental orchestra* consisting only of *stringed instruments,* usually *members* of the *bowed-string family!* Also called *string ensemble* or *chamber orchestra,* although a *chamber orchestra* actually does not play *chamber music!* The latter applies only to *music* played with an *individual part* for *each instrument in a group!*

string quartet. (1) A *group* of *four stringed instruments* . . . *first* and *second violins, viola,* and *cello!* The *music* is *written* with *separate parts* for *each instrument!* (2) A *composition* with *individual parts* for *four stringed instruments!*

string quintet. (1) A *group* of *five stringed instruments* . . . *first* and *second violins,* one *viola* and a *first* and *second cello* with *separate parts* for *each instrument!* A variation would include *first* and *second violin,* one *viola,* one *cello* and one *double-bass!* (2) A *composition* with *individual parts* for *five stringed instruments!*

string trio (1) A *group* of *three stringed instruments* . . . a *violin, viola* and a *cello* with *separate parts* for *each instrument!* (2) A *composition* with *individual parts* for *three stringed instruments!*

strisciando *(strĕ shē än'dō)* from the Italian: *Smooth gliding from note to note* in *legato* or *glissando* fashion!

stromente di legno *(strô mĕn'tĕ dē lĕn'yō)* The Italian phrase for "*woodwind instruments*"!

strophic *(strŏf'ĭk)* Describing a *song* that uses the same *music* in *successive, equal-length stanzas* (many *folk songs, hymns,* etc.), or which alternates *stanzas* with the *refrain of another melody!* The opposite of *strophic* is called "*through-composed*", applied to a *song* in which the *music of a stanza* *changes* with the *lyrics!* Many *lieder* by *Brahms, Schubert*, etc. are "*through-composed!*

stück *(shtŭk)* from the German: "*Piece*"; a *musical composition! Klavierstück*, a *piano piece!*

study *(stŭd'ĭ)* An *etude* or a *composition* useful as a *teaching exercise!*

stürmisch *(shtürm'ish)* from the German: A direction to play in a *stormy, furious manner!*

stürze *(shtür'tsĕ)* The *German* word for the *bell* of a *horn! Stürze hoch*, the *bell turned up!*

stylus *(stī'lŭs)* (1) The "*needle-like*" *metal tool* that "*cuts*" *grooves* into "*master*" *disk recordings* from which *mass-produced records* (after *plating* and *coating processes*) are ultimately "*pressed*"! (2) The *needle*, or its *tip* (housed in a *cartridge*) located in the *tone-arm* of a *phonograph turntable!* The *stylus* rotates in the *record groove*, sending "*sound signals*" back through the *tone-arm* to the *amplifier* and *speakers!*

styrienne *(stē rē ĕn')* from the French: A slow-moving *air* in *2/4 time* with a *yodel (Jodler)* after each *verse!*

su *(sū)* from the Italian: "On," "above," "upon," "by," "near"! *Arcata in su*, up-bow!

subbass *(sŭb'bås)* / **subbourdon** *(sŭb'boor d'n)* Ger. / "*Underbass*"; an *organ stop* of *16* or *32-foot pitch*, usually on the *pedalboard!*

subdominant *(sŭb dŏm'ĭ nånt)* The *fourth degree*, *note* or *tone* in a *diatonic scale!* The *subdominant* is *F* in the *C-major key, G* in *D-major, D* in *A-minor*, etc.

subdominant chord. Any *chord built* on the *fourth degree* of the *diatonic scale!* The *root* is the *subdominant* in a *subdominant triad! F-A-C* in the *key of C-major*, for example, is the most important *subdominant chord!* In *harmonic analysis*, the *Roman numeral IV* indicates a *chord* built on the *subdominant!* See *Elements of Music, CHORDS* and *INTERVALS!*

subito *(soo'bē tō)* from the Italian: "At once", "suddenly"; used in directions such as: *piano subito* (**p** *subito*), to *abruptly* and *suddenly play softly*; as opposed to *forte subito* (**f** *subito*), to *abruptly* and *suddenly play loudly! Volti subito*, "*quickly turn over the music page*," etc!

subject *(sŭb'jĕkt')* A *melodic phrase* or *theme* which forms the *structural basis of a composition* or *movement!* Longer than a *figure* or *motive*, the *subject* is common to *fugues* and *sonatas* and "*themes with variations*"! See *fugue, sonata!*

submediant *(sŭb mē'dĭ ănt)* The *sixth degree, note* or *tone* in a *diatonic scale; A* in the *C-major key; B* in the *D-major key; F* in the *A-minor key!* Also called *superdominant!*

submediant chord. Any *chord built* on the *sixth degree* of a *diatonic scale!* The *root* is the *submediant* in a *submediant chord! A-C-E* in the *C-major key* is the most important *submediant chord!* In *harmonic analysis*, the *Roman numeral VI* indicates a *chord* built on the *submediant!*

suboctave *(sŭb'ŏk tāv)* (1) The *octave below a given tone!* (2) An *organ coupler* that *sounds a tone simultaneously* with the *tone* that is *one octave below!*

subordinate chords *(sŭ bôr'dĭ nĭt kôrdz)* A term for those *chords* that are *neither basic* nor *principal! Chords* built on the *second, third, sixth* and *seventh degrees (supertonic, mediant, submediant, subtonic)!* The *dominant seventh*, however, is of major importance and is *not* in the *subordinate-chord category!*

subprincipal. A *subbass, organ pedal-stop* of *32-foot pitch!*

subtonic. The "*leading tone*"! The *seventh note* in any *major* or *minor scale*, one *half-tone below the tonic!* It derives the name "*leading tone*" from its tendency to *finalize* by *leading up* to the *tonic note!*

subtonic chord. Any *chord* built on the *seventh degree* of a *diatonic scale!* One of the least used of all *triad chords!* In *harmonic analysis*, the *Roman numeral VII* indicates a *chord* built on the *subtonic!*

suite *(swēt)* from the French: (1) In modern usage, an *instrumental composition* in a *series of movements!* Almost *symphonic* in size but *lighter* and *freer* in quality, *suites* are often related to *folk airs, ballets, opera* or some form of *narrative, program music!* In the *baroque era (1600-1750)*, a *suite* usually grouped a *set of dances* in one *key* (or *related keys*) with an occasional, important *prelude!* The *formal suite* included *dance movements* in the following order: *Allemande, courante, saraband, gigue* with supplementing *intermezzi* such as the *bourée, gavotte, minuet, passepied, pavane* and others!

suivez *(swē vä')* from the French: "Follow"! (1) A direction to an *orchestra* or *ensemble* to *follow* the *tempo* of the *soloist!* Same as *colla parte!* (2) A direction to *continue on to a following portion of music without pause or interruption!*

sul *(sool)* / **sull** *(sool)* / **sulla** *(sool'å)* / **sulle** *(sool'ĕ)* It. / "On", "at", "upon"! *Sul G*, on the *G string! Sulla corda La* or *sul A*, on the *A string! Sul tasto* or *sulla tastiera*, on or near the *fingerboard of a stringed instrument! Sul ponticello*, a direction to *bow over the bridge of a violin* or other *stringed instrument!*

superdominant. Another name for *submediant!*

superoctave. (1) The *octave above a given tone!* (2) An *organ coupler* that *sounds a tone simultaneously* with a *tone* that is *one octave higher!* (3) An *organ stop* tuned a *fifteenth (two octaves)* above the *diapason!*

supertonic. The *second degree* of a *diatonic scale! D* in the *key of C-major, E* in the *key of D-major, B* in the *key of A-minor*, etc.!

supertonic chord. Any *chord* built on the *second degree* of a *diatonic scale!* The *root* is *supertonic* in a *supertonic chord*, for example, *D-F-A* in the *key of C-major!* In *harmonic analysis*, the *Roman numeral II* indicates a *chord* built on the *supertonic!*

supplicando *(soo plē kän'do)* / **supplichevole** *(soo plē kĕ vō'lĕ)* / **supplichevolmente** *(soo plē kĕ vōl mĕn'tĕ)* It. / A direction to play in a manner expressing supplication, pleading or entreaty!

sur *(sŭr)* from the French: "On", "over", "upon"! *Sur la touche, play over the fingerboard* of *stringed instruments!*

suspension *(sŭs pĕn'shŭn)* (1) *Holding over one or more tones of a chord (preparation)* into a *following chord* which is *dissonant* to the *previous chord!* The *dissonance (percussion)* usually *resolves downward* to a *consonant note* in a *following chord (resolution)!* An infrequent, *upward resolution* is known as *retardation!*

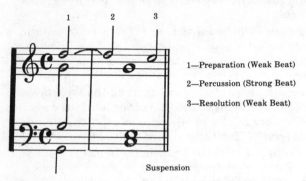

1—Preparation (Weak Beat)
2—Percussion (Strong Beat)
3—Resolution (Weak Beat)

Suspension

süss *(zŭs)* from the German; "Sweet or "sweetly"!

sustaining pedal. Another name for the *damper pedal* on a *piano!* See *Pedal, Piano!*

Suzuki method *(sōō zōō'kē mĕth'ŭd)* A *technique of instructing* young children to *play music by ear* (particularly *violin*) and to recall what is heard *without* the need or ability to *read written music!* Invented by Shinichi Suzuki of Japan (1897-), the *method* has become increasingly popular among American and European teachers and parents after observing *string-orchestra performances* by Suzuki-trained children! Special *small-sized violins* have been manufactured to abet the efforts of pre-school children enrolled in Suzuki courses!

svegliato *(svĕl yä'tô)* / **svegliando** *(svĕl yän'dô)* It. / A direction to play in a brisk, lively fashion!

swan song. From the ancient fable that alleges a *swan sings* just before dying: Any *musical work* or *performance* completed just before death! Sometimes the term is applied to a *final performance* or *final achievement* (before retirement, for example) without any implication of tragedy or sadness!

swell organ. One of the most important *manuals* on the *organ*, or the *rows of pipes (stops)* controlled by the *swell manual!* The *volume* of "swell" *stops* is controlled by the *shutters* framing the box that houses the *pipes!* A *pedal-stop lever (swell pedal)* opens the shutters to *swell* the *volume* and closes the shutters to *shrink* the *volume.* Abbreviated *sw.!* In notation, *crscendo* is marked   and *decrescendo*   !

swing *(swing)* (1) An obsolete term for a type of *name band music* of the 1930's that featured *full arrangements* (in *quasi-jazz style*) of *popular songs for dancing and/or concert presentation!* (2) The expression "swing" also is used as a verb in popular slang to express favorable reception .... in a *musical context,* for example, "the *tenor sax* really

swings", etc! Not to be confused with the more modern slang use of *"swing"* or *"swinger"* to imply uninhibited moral behavior or sexual activity!

syllabic *(sĭ lăb'ĭk)* Vocal music in which each *syllable* of the *lyrics* is accorded *one note!* The opposite of *melismatic*, which accords *many notes* to *one syllable!*

sympathetic strings *(sĭm'pă thĕt'ĭk strĭngs)* Strings that are *not directly sounded* by a *player*, but react to the *vibrations* of *other strings* that are *directly activated!* See *String!*

symphonia *(sĭm fŏn' yä)* A *Latin* name for the *hurdy-gurdy!*

symphony *(sĭm'fŏ nē)* One of the *major forms* of *classical music*, the *symphony* traditionally is thought of as a *long composition for orchestra* with *four, distinct, important movements* or *sections!* These usually are heard in the order of: (1) *Allegro;* a *fast movement* sometimes preceded by a *slow introduction!* The *allegro* movement usually appears in *sonata* form! (2) *Adagio;* a *slow, song-like movement!* (3) *Minuet* or *Scherzo;* a *movement* in *moderate tempo* but *brighter* in the *Beethoven scherzo form*, than the *Haydn* or *Mozart form* of *minuet* or *scherzo!* (4) *Allegro* or *Presto;* a *rapid, closing movement!*

syncopation *(sĭnk' ō pā'shŭn) Musical rhythm* that *shifts* the *orthodox patterns* of *metered accents or beats!* In *formal Western music*, normal *rhythm groups* equal *beats* into *pairs* or *triplets*, with an *accent* on the *first beat!* Syncopation deviations include: (1) Starting a *tone* on an *accented beat (strong beat)* and *holding it past the following unaccented beat* .... *skipping the second beat!* (2) *Skipping the first beat* (treating it as a *rest*) and *starting* the *tone* on the *next beat!* (3) *Starting* a *tone* with an *unaccented (weak) beat* and *accenting* the *following (strong) beat! Syncopation* in *serious music* usually is *formally notated*, but in *ragtime, jazz* and *much rock music* the *subtle variations*, as well as some of the *abrupt departures*, from *patterns of accent* are almost impossible to accurately *notate!* Generally, in the *pop, jazz, rock* area, however, the *beats* are shifted ... in *4/4 time*, for example, the *2* and *4 after-beats* are felt but not really played, yielding to *accent changes* with a *"rest"* inserted in *dotted eighth* and *sixteenth groups!*

Syncopation Examples

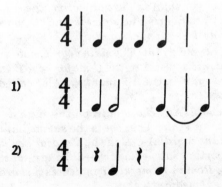

3)

3)

1)

2)

3)

Sample Drum Syncopation (Pop.)

symphonic *(sĭm fŏn'ĭk)* (1) Referring to the style of a *symphony!* (2) *Harmonious* in *sound!*

symphonic ode. A *lyrical composition* for *chorus* and *orchestra!*

symphonic poem. A *form* of *19th century program music*, generally consisting of *one continuous movement* with *various themes!* A *descriptive title* (occasionally *augmented* by *program notes*) usually indicates the *subject matter* or *program* of the *themes!*

synthesizer *(sĭn'thĕ sīz'ĕr)* An *electronic instrument* that uses *electric oscillator* principles to produce an infinite variety of *synthetic sounds, pitched* or *unpitched* as desired! Rapid advancement in the technology has made the *synthesizer* familiar to all *professional musicians*, and almost commonplace on the *popular-concert stage* as well as in the *recording studio.* See *INSTRUMENTS, ELECTRONIC!*

syrinx *(sĭr'ĭnks)* The *Greek* name for the *Panpipe!* See *Panpipe!*

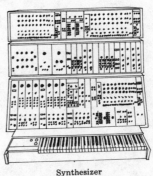

Synthesizer

DICTIONARY

T

— T —

T. The abbreviation for *tasto, tempo, tenor, toe, tonic, t.c.* or *tre corde, trill, tutti,* and *tutti le corde!*

tabla *(däb lä′)* One of a pair of *Indian drums* used in *Hindu rhythm patterns,* the *tabla* is made from a section of almost-hollow log with a *skin* stretched over the *open end!* The other *drum,* the *baya,* is a *metal cylinder* with *one end sealed* and a *skin* stretched over the *other end!* The *drums* are *tuned* by *side braces,* with a black circle of ground rice mashed in a mixture with metal bits, daubed on the *skinhead* to *affect* the *pitch!* Both drums are played together and are called by the plural name *tablas!*

tablas

tablature *(tăb′lá tŭr)* A set of ostentatious rules and procedures which governed the artistic efforts of the 15th and 16th century *German guilds* known as the *Meistersinger!* These were satirized by *Wagner* in his *famous opera Die Meistersinger von Nürnberg!* See *Meistersinger!*

tablature, classical. In *classical music, tablature* describes old systems of *notation* (for a broad range of *keyboard* and *stringed instruments*) that were used in the 15th, 16th and 17th centuries! Generally, *tones* were identified by *letters, numbers, symbols* or a *combination of all three* (*instead* of *notes* on a *staff*) .... particularly for the *lute tablatures of Italy, Spain* and *France,* which indicated *finger positions* for the *strings* including *stops* and *frets* instructions! *German lute tablature* was a complex mixture of *letters* and *signs* that included some *tone indications* with *finger position numerals!* *Keyboard tablature* varied in *Germany* and *Spain,* the former using *notes* for an *upper stave* with *letters on the lower; Spanish organ tablature* used *numbers* for the *diatonic scale* and placed them on *lines* that represented *separate voice parts!* The various *lute tablatures* led the way to *modern guitar tablature;* the *keyboard tablatures* became dead-ends except for the contribution of the concept of a *staff* with *notes!*

tablature, guitar. In *modern guitar notation,* the individual assignment of *numbers* to each "*string*" and "*fret*" position on a *six-line staff* (corresponding to the *six strings positioned* on the *guitar*)! The system usually works as follows:

The time signatures are conventional:

$\frac{4}{4}$ means: four beats to each measure, and each quarter note is accorded one beat!

$\frac{6}{8}$ means: six beats to each measure, and each eighth note is accorded one beat! (quarter-note, therefore, gets two beats)

One quarter note is indicated by a stem without a note head.

One eighth note is indicated by a stem with one flag or hook.

One sixteenth note is indicated by a stem with two flags or hooks.

Two or more eighth notes are connected with a beam.

Two or more sixteenth notes are connected with a double beam!

Rests are:

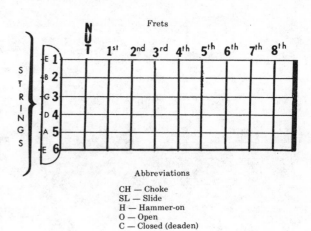

| Quarter rest | Eighth rest | Sixteenth rest | Half rest | Whole rest |

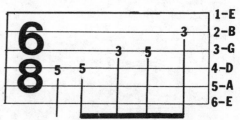

Abbreviations

CH — Choke
SL — Slide
H — Hammer-on
O — Open
C — Closed (deaden)

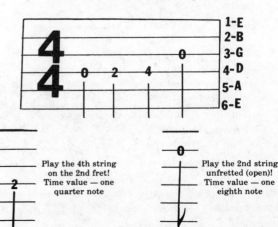

Numbers over the *stems* indicate *fret* positions.

Play the 4th string on the 2nd fret! Time value — one quarter note

Play the 2nd string unfretted (open)! Time value — one eighth note

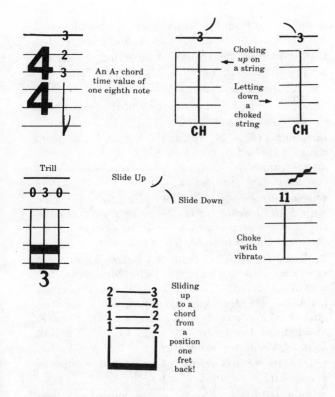

An A₇ chord time value of one eighth note

Choking *up* on a string

Letting down a choked string

Trill

Slide Up

Slide Down

Choke with vibrato

Sliding up to a chord from a position one fret back!

Conventional Notation (Guitar)

Corresponding Tablature (Guitar)

tabor *(tā'bĕr)* A small type of *snare drum* used to *accompany* a *pipe* or *fife played at the same time* by the same individual who *plays* the *drum!*

tabor

tacet *(tā'sĕt)* / **tacit** *(tā'sĭt)* Lt. / A direction for a *part (vocal or instrumental)* to remain *silent* during a *marked portion* of a *composition!*

tail *(tāl)* Another name for the *stem* of a *note!*

takt *(täkt)* from the German: A *beat,* a *measure* or *tempo! Streng im Täkt, strictly in time!*

talon *(tä lôn)* from the French: The *frog end (heel)* of the *bow! Au talon,* a direction to *play* at the *frog end of the bow!*

tambour, tambor *(tăn bōōr'-'bĕr)* The *French* word for *drum!*

tambour de Basque *(–dĕ bäsk)* The *French* term for *tambourine!*

tambourin *(tän bōō răn')* from the French: (1) A small, narrow type of *tabor drum* used by an individual to *accompany* himself on a *flute* or *recorder!* (2) A *small zither* without *strings* that was struck by a *drum stick!* (3) Old *French provincial dance music* that featured a *tambourin* or *geloubet!*

tambourine *(tăm bōō rēn)* The familiar *percussion instrument* used by *gypsies,* the *Salvation Army, dance bands, rock groups* and *symphony orchestra* alike! The *tambourine* is a shallow, *one-sided circular drum* with *pairs* of *metal disks,* called *"jingles",* loosely attached around the side of the *drum hoop! Striking, shaking* or *rubbing* the *drumhead,* produces a *"jingling," rattling* sound from the *disks* as well as a *percussive sound* from the *skin membrane!*

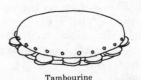

Tambourine

tambura *(dŭm bōō'rä)* A *Hindu lute* with a *long, narrow neck* extending from a *gourd-shaped body! Four metal strings* are *stretched over* the *unfretted instrument,* each *sounding only one open tone!* The *tambura* is a *drone* whose main function is to *accompany* the *sitar* and other *instruments* during *Indian raga performances!*

tamburo *(tăm bōō'rō)* The *Italian* word for *drum!*

tamburone *(tăm bōō rō nä)* The *Italian word* for *bass drum* or *big drum!*

tam tam *(tăm tăm, tŭm tŭm)* (1) Another name for the *gong!* (2) A *Hindu drum,* not to be confused with the *tom tom!*

tanbur *(tän bōōr')* A long-necked Persian lute also found in the Balkans which is similar to the Greek *buzuki!* Also *tunbur!*

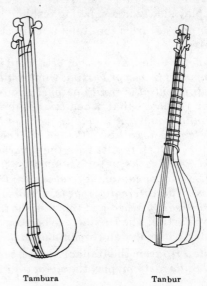

Tambura   Tanbur

tango *(tăng'gō)* A world-renowned dance that originated at the turn of the century in Argentina. Usually, the tango is set in 2/4 meter with a strongly-syncopated rhythm pattern taken at semi-slow dance tempo! Somewhat similar to the *habanera*, the tango features two separate and distinct musical phrases of equal length!

tanto *(tän'tō)* from the Italian: "So much", "as much"! Used in directions to mean "not too much"! *Allegro non tanto*, not too fast! *A tanto possibile*, as much as possible!

tanz *(tänts)* The *German* word for "dance"!

taps *(tăps)* A U.S. military term for the *bugle call* that signifies "lights out and go to sleep"! It is played also at memorial services or military funerals!

tarogato *(tă rō'gä tō)* An ancient *Hungarian wooden instrument* which first began as a *wooden horn*, evolved into a *shawm* with *finger holes* and a *mouthpiece*, and in modern times is constructed as a *wooden saxophone* with a *clarinet mouthpiece!*

Tarogato

tarentella *(tăr ăn tĕl'ă)* from the Italian: A brisk *Neapolitan folk dance* in *6/8 time* that is performed traditionally at Italian weddings and other festive occasions! Characteristics include *acceleration*, and *alternating major and minor keys!* Probably, the name derives from Taranto in Southern Italy, although legend persists that the tarantula spider's bite is neutralized by the spirited dance!

tardamenta *(tăr dä mĕn'tĕ)* / **tardo** *(tăr'dō)* It. / A direction to play slowly in a delaying fashion!

tardando *(tăr dän'dō)* from the Italian: A direction to *delay* or *retard!*

Tartini's tone. Named after the 17th century *violinist/composer*, Guiseppi Tartini, who first discovered the *differential* or *resultant tone!* Acoustic science later revealed that when *two tones are sounded simultaneously* at a *loud-enough level*, a *combination tone* is heard! Such a *tone* is either a *differential tone* (which results from the *difference* in the *frequencies* of *each tone*) or a *summation tone* (which results from the *sum* of the *frequencies* of the *original tones*)! The *differential tone* (also called *resultant*) is *more easily heard* and this was the *tone* discovered by Tartini! The *Tartini tone* is recognizable particularly in *violin* and *organ music!*

tastiera *(tä stē â rä)* from the Italian: A *fingerboard* or *keyboard! Sulla tastiera*, play the *violin* over the *fingerboard!*

tasto *(tăs'tō)* from the Italian: A *key*, a *fret*, a *touch*, a *fingerboard! Sul tasto*, same as *sulla tastiera!*

tasto solo. from the Italian: A direction to play the *bass part* without *chord accompaniment!*

tbn. Abbreviation for *trombone!*

t.c. Abbreviation for *tutte corde*, or *tutte le corde*, *all the strings!* See *corda!*

technique *(tĕk nēk')* In music, a "catch-all" word usually applied to technical skills with an *instrument (manual dexterity, embouchure*, etc.) or a *voice (breath control, projection*, etc.)!

tedesco, -a *(tĕ dĕs'kō, -ä)* The *Italian* word for "German"! *Alla tedesca*, in the *German style...*connoting a *3/4 waltz rhythm* with *moderate tempo changes! Danza tedesca*, German dance!

Te Deum *(tā dā'ōōm)* from the Latin: An *ancient, sacred hymn* which begins *Te Deum laudamus*, "We praise thee, God". Used in the daily services of the *Roman Catholic, Anglican* and *Episcopalian* churches! Famous *musical settings* to this *timeless hymn* have been *composed* by Handel, Berlioz, Dvořák, Verdi and others!

teil *(tīl)* from the German: A *part, portion, section* or *movement!*

telltale *(tĕl'tāl)* An *indicator* attached to an *organ*, showing the amount of *air pressure* furnished by the *bellows!*

tema *(tā'mä)* The *Italian* word for a *theme!*

temperament *(tĕm'pĕr ä mĕnt)* The system of *slight modification of tones in a "pure" scale (mathematically* or *acoustically exact scale)* to accommodate the *adding of chromatic tones* as well as for *modulation convenience! A compromise tone* solves the problem of dealing with those *"pure" scales* which have few *exactly-coinciding tones!* The *"pure" C-sharp* and *D-flat tones*, for example, are *compromised* into one *slightly-dissonant tone* which is acceptable to the *human ear.* The current system of *dissonant compromise* is known as *equal temperament*, wherein the *octave* is *divided* into *twelve equal parts (based on the frequency rate of vibration* which *produces pitched sounds)!* This makes the *interval between each half tone and the next tone identical* – C to C-sharp, D-sharp to D, D to D-sharp, etc. Previous systems, now replaced by the *equal temperment system*, include *Pythagorean Tuning (all intervals measured precisely from an originating tone), Just Intonation* which required *constant changes of keys* since it was based on the *natural harmonic series*, and the *MEAN TONE system* which combined the *Pythagorean* and the *Just* but which proved completely awkward for *keys* with *several accidentals!* See *Elements of Music!*

tempered *(tĕm'pĕrd)* Conforming to the *equal temperament system!* Applied to *scales* and *half-tones*, as well as to the *intonation of instruments!*

tempestoso *(tĕm pĕ stō'zō)* from the Italian: A direction to *play* in a manner expressing a stormy, tempestuous mood!

temple block *(tĕm'p'l blŏk)* An *accessory percussion instrument* which although ornamentally designed is simply a *hollow, resonant block of wood* that is struck by the *drumstick!* Also called *Chinese block!*

tempo *(tĕm'pō)* from the Italian: The *rate of speed* at which *music* is *performed!* Not to be confused with *meter!* See *Elements of Music, TEMPO! A tempo,* "return to the original *tempo*"! *Tempo commodo, moderate speed! Tempo di ballo, dance tempo! Tempo guisto, proper tempo* or *strict time! Tempo primo, return to the first tempo,* abbreviated *tempo 1°!*

tempo mark. (1) In modern *music notation,* a *marking* indicating a *metronome-measured tempo recommendation!* For example, presto ♩=120 M.M. means a *fast movement* with *120 metronome "ticks" to the minute, two ticks to each second,* for *each quarter note!* The *quarter note,* therefore, gets a *time-value* of *one-half second!* (2) *Tempo marks* spelled out in traditional *Italian* are universally used in *music notation* . . . these include *largo, adagio, andante, allegro, presto* and many others! See *Elements of Music, Tempo Marks* for complete list!

temps *(täm)* from the French: Literally "*time*", but also used to mean "*beat*"! *Temps fort, strong beat! Temps faible, weak beat!*

ten. The abbreviation for *tenuto!*

teneramente, -o *(tĕ nĕ rä mĕn'tĕ,-ō)* / **tenerezza, con** *(tĕ nĕ rĕts'ä, kôn)* It. / A direction to play tenderly with softness and delicacy!

tenor *(tĕn'ẽr)* (1) The *highest male voice* (except for the *unnatural falsetto*) with an *average range from C in the bass clef to G in the treble*. . .easily exceeded by some professionals! In *opera,* a *lyric tenor voice* has a *sweeter, lighter tone quality* than a *dramatic tenor voice* which is more *powerful* and *expressive!* (2) The *tenor part* in *four-part choral music* which is the *next part up from the bass!* The *choral tenor part* often is *written an octave higher than it sounds!* (3) A short term for the *tenor saxophone,* the *B-flat saxophone* which is prominent in *jazz music!* Also used as a prefix for *tenor violin (the viola)* which is *tuned a fifth below* the *standard violin!*

tenor C. The *small c* 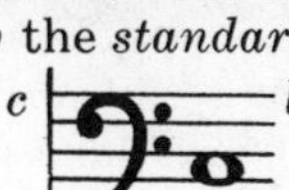 *lowest c* in the *tenor voice range* and the *lowest string on the viola!*

tenor clef. The *clef* 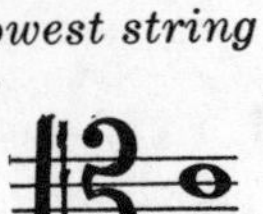 that marks the *fourth-from-the-bottom-line* of the *staff* as *middle C!* Used for the *bassoon, tenor trombone* and *high register of the cello,* etc.!

tenor drum. A *military* or *marching-band drum* of *medium size between* the *bass drum* and the *snare drum!* The *tenor drum* has no *snares* and is struck with *soft mallets!*

tenor horn. A *valved, brass instrument* with a *cone-shaped interior (bore)* that comes in various sizes and shapes, some of which are circular and confusingly similar to, if not identical with, some members of the *tuba* family! A *B-flat tuba* is known as a *tenor horn* in the U.S.A. and France, but is called a *baritone horn* in Britain! *E-flat tenor horns,* however, are used in U.S. brass bands! The *British* and *German E-flat tenor horn* is called an *alto horn* in the *U.S.A.* and *France.* The *B-flat tenor horn* has a *two-octave range* from *low E to B-flat above middle c!* (2) Another name for the *tenor saxhorn!*

tenth *(tĕnth)* (1) The *interval* of an *octave plus a third on the diatonic scale!* (2) The *organ stop* that *sounds* a *tenth above the diapasons!* Also known as *decima* or *double tierce!*

tenuto *(tĕ nōō'tō)* from the Italian: "Held"; a direction to *hold a tone or chord* to its *full value* (usually the same as *legato*) as opposed to *staccato!* Abbreviated *ten.* Frequently marked with a horizontal dash *over* or *under* the *notes* or *chord* to be *held* ( )!

tercet *(tûr'sĕt)* An infrequently used, alternate name for a *triplet!*

ternary *(tûr'nȧ rē)* Consisting of *threes! Ternary form* in *music* is a general term for *any music in three sections,* in *ABA order*. . .which means the *first section A* and the *third section A* are *identical*. . .and specifically applies to such *compositions* as the *minuet, scherzo* and *rondo* in *serious music!* The *third section* usually is not written out in *notation,* but is indicated by *da capo* or *dal segno signs!*

ternary measure. *Triple time!*

terzett *(târ tsĕt')* Ger. / **terzetto** *(tĕr tsĕt'tō)* It. / (1) A composition for three voices with individual parts! (2) A vocal trio!

tessitura *(tĕs sē tōō'rä)* (1) The *general range . . . high or low register* . . . of a *vocal part, judged* by *omitting* the *few highest or lowest tones from consideration* and then *appraising the location* of the *remaining notes!* (2) The same "*averaging*" principle applied to the *voice capability of a performer . . . high tessitura, low tessitura,* etc.! (3) The application of the same principle to the "*range*" of *instrumental parts!*

tetrachord *(tĕt'ra kôrd)* An *interval* of a *perfect fourth* between the *first* and *last notes* of a *four-note series* in a *diatonic scale!* The *C-major scale* contains *two tetrachords C-D-E-F* and *G-A-B-C!*

tetrad *(tĕt'răd)* Any *four-tone note chord* such as the *seventh!*

tetradiapason *(tĕt'rȧ dī'ȧpā'zŭn)* A *twenty-ninth!* A *four-octave interval* in *organ music!*

text *(tĕkst)* A general reference to the *lyrics* or *words* of a *musical composition!*

theme *(thēm)* (1) The *subject* of a *composition!* See *Subject!* (2) A *short, melodic* statement!

theme and variations. A *classic form of composition* which begins with a simple, *harmonized melody* that is *repeated* in *several* or *many elaborated variations!*

theme song. In *popular music,* a term applied to the *main melody* or *song* from a *motion picture (main title), theater production, television series,* etc.!

Also, an identifying, introductory *song* for a *"star" performer* or *group!* When *"name bands"* were in vogue, the *"signature" music* that would open the *performance program!*

theorbo *(thē ôr'bō)* A large, *double-neck* type of *bass lute* used in the 17th and 18th centuries but now obsolete!

thesis *(thē'sĭs)* The *Greek* name for *"downbeat"*, the *accented part* of a *measure!* The opposite of *"arsis"*, *upbeat!*

theremin *(thĕr'ă mĭn)* An *electronic instrument* invented by the *Russian* Leon Theremin in the 1920's! The *theremin* produced *electronic tones* when one passed a hand across a *vertical-rod antenna*, which was connected to *oscillators* and a *speaker!* Limited to the output of a *single tone at a time*, and difficult to control because of its tendency to generate *glissando-like interference* with the *pitch*, the *theremin* gained little popularity!

third *(thûrd)* (1) The *interval* of the *first* and *third tones (rising in pitch)* of a *major* or *minor scale!* In the *C-major scale*, *C-E* is the *third* or *major third!* (2) The *third degree* of a *scale*, the *mediant!*

third, diminished. The *interval smaller* than a *major third* by a *whole tone*, and *smaller* than a *minor third* by a *half-tone!* *C#-E♭* or *C-E♭♭* , for example!

third, minor. The *interval smaller* than a *major third* by a *half-tone!* *C#-E* or *C-E♭* , for example!

thirteenth *(thûr'tēnth')* The *interval* consisting of an *octave* and a *sixth!*

thirty-second note. The *note* with the *time-value* of *one thirty-second* of a *whole note* (called *demi-semiquaver* in Britain)! The *note singly* has a stem and *three hooks* (pennants)! *Successive notes* are joined by *triple beams!*

thirty-second rest. A rest with the same time-value as a thirty-second note! Sign:

Theorbo

thorough bass *(thûr'ō bās)* Dating from the *baroque period* (1600-1750), a *system* of *notating accompaniment* by indicating only the *bass part* and placing *numerals, symbols* or *signs* under the *bass note* to indicate the appropriate *chords* and *intervals* to be used in the *harmony!* Also called *basso continuo, figured bass*, etc.!

Example

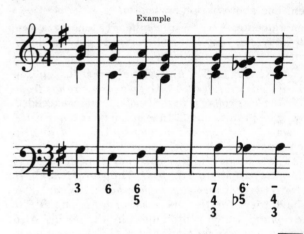

Basic Rules of "thorough-bass "shorthand"!

numerals and/or signs under the bassnote	*application*
no numeral, no sign	use the common chord of the note!
one numeral, 5 or 6 by itself, for example	use the *corresponding interval* in the *indicated key!* In *E-flat major*, for example, the number 5 under a *C* would call for a *G* which is a *fifth* above *C!* In the *A-flat major* key, the number 6 under a *G* would call for *E-flat* which is a *sixth* above *G!* In the *G-Major key*, the number 6 under *E* would call for *C!*
when there are two or more numerals positioned vertically such as 6 or 6 4 5	use the corresponding intervals in the indicated key! In *E-flat major*, the $\begin{smallmatrix}6\\4\end{smallmatrix}$ under a *C* calls for *F* and *A-flat* which are a *sixth* and a *fourth* above *C!* In *A-flat major*, a $\begin{smallmatrix}6\\5\end{smallmatrix}$ under a *G* calls for *D-flat* and *E-flat* which are a *sixth* and a *fifth* above *G!* In the *G-major key*, a $\begin{smallmatrix}6\\5\end{smallmatrix}$ under an *F* calls for *C* and *D* which are a *sixth* and a *fifth* above *F!*

where there is a *sharp* or *flat* or *natural* standing alone

Use a *major third* for the sharp, a *minor third* for the *flat!* Apply the *natural* in conventional manner!

when a stroke appears through a numeral, such as 5̸

raise the *interval* by a *half-tone (sharping)!*

when a numeral appears with an *accidental* placed after or before, such as 5#, 5♭ , 5♮

raise or lower the *interval* in accordance with the *effect* of the *sign!*

when there is a horizontal dash —

continue the *harmony* of the *previous chord* even if the *bass note changes!*

when there is a + sign

this indicates a *chord abbreviation:* 6+, an *Italian sixth;* 6+5, the *German sixth!*

when there is a 0

the *bass note* is *solo,* and there should be no accompaniment!

---

three step. A colloquial term for the *standard Viennese waltz!*

through composed. The opposite of *strophic! A composition* in which the *music changes for each of the verses!*

tie *(tī)* A *curved line* ⌣ connecting *two identically pitched notes* which indicates they are to be played as one *note* to be held for the *time-value* of the two notes combined! A *tie* will *connect notes, separated by a bar line* ♩♩ or, when the *time values cannot be expressed by a single note* . . . . *five quarter notes for example:*

Enharmonic
tie.

A *tie* should not be confused with a *slur* which links *notes* of *different pitch!* The *tie* is also called a *bind!*

tierce *(tērs)* (1) A *third!* (2) A *mutation organ stop, two and one third octaves above the diapason!*

tierce de Picardie *(tērs dŭ pē kär'dē)* The *French* term for a "*Picardy third*" *chord!* See *Picardy third!*

timbale *(tăn băl')* The *French* name for the *kettledrum!*

timballo *(tĭm băl ō)* The *Italian* name for the *kettledrum!*

timbre *(tĭm'bēr)* The *English* and *French (tăn'br)* word for *tone color* and *quality* of sound! In technical terms, *timbre* is determined by the *amplitude ratio* of *harmonic* or *partial tones* to the *fundamental tone!*

"three over four". A popular rhythm pattern identified with American, black ragtime or blues music! The expression refers to a three-note sequence in each *measure* of *four-beat value,* with a different note receiving the *accent* each time the *measure* is repeated.

time *(tīm)* The *grouping* of *beats* into *equal measures* which determines the *meter* of any *composition!* Each *measure* is marked off by a *bar line!* The *duration* of *each beat* in a *measure* is called the *time-value* and is indicated by a *note!* A *whole note* 𝅝 is held twice as long as a *half-note* 𝅗𝅥 ; a *half-note* is held twice as long as a *quarter-note* ♩ , which is held twice as long as an *eighth note* ♪ etc. The *time signature* at the *head* of the *staff* of any *musical composition* 3/4 - 4/4 - 6/8 explains the *meter!* The *upper number (numerator)* in 3/4 , for example, says there are *three beats* to each *measure!* The *lower number* says there is *one beat* for *every quarter note* . . . . 6/8 means there are *six beats* to *each measure* with *one beat* for *every eighth note! Time signatures* with a *2* or *3* in the *numerator* are classified as "*simple time*" or "*simple measure*"! In *notation,* the *tempo mark* ₵ , known as *alla breve,* is used to indicate 2/2 *meter!* The *tempo mark* ₵ , known as *common time,* indicates 4/4 *meter.* When *numerators* indicate a *multiple* of *two* or *three beats* . . . . 4/4 , 9/8 , 12/8 , etc. these are classified as "*compound time*" or "*compound measure*"!

Any *meter* with *two units to the measure* . . . .

702

$\frac{2}{2}, \frac{2}{4}, \frac{2}{3}$, etc. . . . is called *simple duple meter* or *simple duple time!* When multiples of 2 are indicated in the *numerator* . . . . $\frac{4}{4}, \frac{4}{8}$, etc. . . . the *meter* is called *compound duple meter* or *compound duple time!*

When the *numerator* indicates *three units to the measure* . . . $\frac{3}{2}, \frac{3}{4}, \frac{3}{8}$, etc., this is called *simple triple measure* or *simple triple time!* When the *numerator* indicates a *multiple of three beats* . . . $\frac{9}{4}, \frac{9}{8}$, etc., . . . it is called *compound triple measure* or *compound triple time!*

Meter refers only to the *structure of rhythmic beats!* It is not to be confused with the actual *speed of performance* which is called *tempo! Tempo markings* usually are indicated by *Italian-word equivalents* such as *largo* (slow), *andante* (moderate), *allegro* (fast) and many others! When two different *time signatures* are shown *together at the head of a staff*, the *music* is either in *polymeter form* ($\frac{2}{4}$ in the *treble stave*, for example, and $\frac{3}{4}$ in the *bass stave*, both *played simultaneously*) or there is a *shifting*, at a given point in the composition, of one *meter to the other!*

timoroso *(tē mŏ rō'sŏ)* from the Italian: A direction to play in a manner expressing timidity or hesitation!

timpani *(tĭm'pă nē)* The *kettledrums!* See *kettledrum!*

timpani coperti *(kŏ pâr'tī)* / **timpani sordi** *(sôr dē')* It. / A direction to *muffle* the *kettledrums!* Also *notated* as *t. coperti, t. sordi!*

tirer, tirez, tiré *(tē rā')* (1) The *French* word for "*down-bow*", the *downstroke* of a *violin bow!* (2) The *French* expression for *drawing* an *organ stop!* (3) A *French* direction to *slow down the tempo!*

toccata *(tō kä'tä)* from the Italian: Usually a *brilliant, technical piece* for *keyboard* (historically written for *harpsichord, organ* or *clavichord*) with many free, elaborate *arpeggios* and *runs*, and sometimes some *fugue forms!* Bach's *organ toccatas* (17th century) are world-renowned as are later *toccata* pieces from such as Schumann and Debussy which were designed for *virtuoso performance!* There has been some critical dismissal of the *toccata* as an *exercise* in "*virtuosity*", but most authorities consider this viewpoint narrow, and disrespectful of the highly *expressive* and *meaningful music* found in many *toccata* contributions!

toccatina *(tō kä tē'nä)* from the Italian: A short *toccata!*

todesgesang *(tō'dĕs gĕ zängk)* / **todeslied** *(tō'dĕs lēdt)* Ger. / A *funeral song* or *dirge!*

tom-tom *(tŏm'tŏm)* (1) One of a *set of higher-register, dance-band drums* which can be *tuned* to *various definite pitches!* The *sound quality*, regardless, is reminiscent of the *hollow-dull tone* of *African drums!* (2) A *drum* of the *American Indians*, played by *drumsticks* despite popular misconception that the *drum* was *struck* by *hand!* Neither *drum* is to be confused with the *Tam Tam*, which is a *gong!*

ton *(tōn)* The *German* word for a *tone, key, mode, pitch, octave* or *scale!*

ton *(tôn)* The *French* word for a *tone, key, mode, pitch, octave* or *scale!*

tonada *(tō nä'dä)* The *Spanish* word for "*song*" or "*tune*"!

tonadella *(tō nä dē'yä)* A *light, brief comic opera* popular in Spain during the 18th and 19th centuries!

tonal *(tōn'ăl)* Referring to *music* which has a specific *tone, key* or *mode!*

tonal answer. See *answer* or *fugue!*

tonality *(tō năl'ĭ tē)* The *principle* of *grouping* all *tones* and *chords* in accordance with their *relationship* to a *central tone* called the *tonic* or the *keynote!* In the evolution of *music* from antiquity until the end of the 19th century, this principle of "*tonality*" maintained world-wide dominance! In the 20th century, more and more composers have explored and embraced *atonality (composition* with *no key signature* and *little regard* for *traditional modes* or *structure)* travelling a path first pioneered by Arnold Schoenberg and followed by such as Charles Ives, Alban Berg, Anton Webern, Milton Babbitt, Henry Cowell, Edgar Varese, and many others.

tonante *(tō nän 'tē)* from the Italian: A direction to play in a thundering, loud, vigorous manner!

tonart *(tō'närt)* An alternate *German* word for *key, scale* or *mode!* Also *ton!*

tone *(tōn)* (1) Any *sound* whose *frequency-vibration* produces a *definite pitch!* "*Note*" and "*tone*" are interchangeably used in the U.S.A., although "*tone*", more frequently, is applied to *performance* and "*note*" to *notation! Tones* are classified as: *Simple*, a *tone* arising from *one simple vibration* at a *steady frequency; complex*, all *compound* or *composite tones* made up of *two or more component tones* which include a *fundamental tone* (the *lowest tone*, or *root tone* and most *dominating tone)* and the *overtones* (the *higher, partial tones)!* The *overtones* add *timbre, tone color, quality* and other special characteristics to "*tone*" by *vibrating* in *exact multiple ratios* (2, 3, 4, 5, etc. times faster) compared to the *fundamental tone!* (2) The "*pitched*" *sound-quality* of any *instrument* or *voice*, or any *group of instruments* or *voices!* (3) Frequently used to designate an *interval* or *step* between *two pitched sounds*, such as a *whole tone, half-tone*, etc., or a *major tone, minor tone*, etc.!

tone cluster *(klŭs'tĕr) A group of successive notes on any scale which are sounded simultaneously regardless of dissonance!* Keyboard tone-clusters were first introduced in the 20th century by Henry Cowell, the *American composer!*

tone color *(kŭl'ĕr) The timbre or quality of "pitched" sounds,* usually resulting from the character and deployment of *harmonic overtones!*

tone poem *(pō'ĕm) A symphonic poem!* See *symphonic poem!*

tone row *(rō) A basic group of tones used in a twelve-tone scale!* See *serial music!*

tonguing *(tŭng'ĭng)* Using the *tongue on wind instruments* to produce an *articulate series of rapid notes or specific staccato effects!* The teaching of "tonguing" employs the device of silently pronouncing the consonants "t" and "k" while making *rapid tongue thrusts* into a mouthpiece! *Single tonguing* repeats a "t,t,t,t,t" order of *thrusts! Double tonguing* repeats "tk,tk,tk,tk,tk" and is most effective on *instruments without reeds! Triple tonguing* is the *most rapid articulation,* using a "ttk, ttk, ttk, ttk, ttk," series which most often is applied to *trumpet* and other *brass instruments,* as well as *flute!* Another technique, known as "flutter tonguing" calls for *repeated tongue thrusts* to the silent pronunciation of the letter "r" which produces a unique, type of *tremolo ... a "fluttering"* sound especially effective on the *flute!*

tonic *(tŏn'ĭk)* (1) The *keynote of any scale!* The *first degree or note of any major or minor scale: C* in the *C-major* and *C-minor keys, D* in the *D-major key,* etc. See *tonality!*

tonic chord. Any *chord built on the tonic! A tonic triad chord* has the *tonic note* as its *root;* for example, *C-E-G* in the *key of C-major,* etc.! In *harmonic analysis,* the *Roman* numeral I indicates a *chord built on the tonic!*

tonic sol-fa *(-sōl,fä)* The *British method* of teaching *vocalists* to *sight-sing* by a system of *solmization* similar to the *movable dō!* The *tonic sol-fa system* uses the *syllables doh, ray, me, fah, soh, lah, te* for the *degrees* of the *scale! Doh* is the *first note (tonic)* in every *key! Fah* is the *fourth note (subdominant)* in every *key,* etc.! A *vowel change* in the *syllable* is used to indicate *sharps* and *flats .... De* is *C-sharp* in the *key of C, da* is *C-flat* in the *key of C,* etc.! In notation, only the *first letter* of the *syllable* is written .... *d, r, m, f,* etc.! See *movable dō, solfeggio, solmization!*

tonkunst *(tōn'kŭnst)* from the German: *Composed music! Tonkünstler,* a composer!

tonleiter *(tōn'lītĕr)* The *German* word for *scale!*

tonsatz *(tōn'zăts)* The *German* word for a *composition!*

tonus *(tŏ'nŭs)* The *Latin* word for *"whole tone"!* A prefix designation for many of the church modes and plainsong formulas from the Middle Ages such as *tonus peregrinus, tonus lectionum, tonus authenticus, tonus plagalis,* etc.!

torch song. Once a *popular colloquialism* applied to any *highly sentimental song* of unrequited love sung by a female! It derived from the idiomatic expression "carrying a torch for the guy", and a so-called *torch singer* was noted for her skill in *performing such songs!* Today, the expression is considered somewhat "dated"!

tornando *(tôr nän'dō)* from the Italian: "Returning"! *Tornando come prima, return to the original tempo!*

tostamente *(tŏs tä mĕn'tä)* from the Italian: A direction to play rapidly with boldness!

tosto *(tōs'tō)* from the Italian: Quickly, rapidly, at once! *Piú tosto,* more quickly!

touch *(tŭch)* (1) The manner in which the *fingers* press the *keys* of *keyboard instruments:* A *heavy touch, light touch, staccato touch, firm touch,* etc.! (2) Describing the resistance of *keyboard instruments* to *finger pressure!* A *piano* that requires much *finger pressure* has a *heavy touch,* etc.!

touche *(tōōsh)* (1) The *French* word for *fingerboard! Sur la touche,* a direction to a *violinist* to *bow over* the *fingerboard!* (2) A *key* on a *piano keyboard!* (3) An *old expression* for a *fret!*

tpt. Abbreviation for *trumpet!*

tranquillo *(trän kwēl'ō)* from the Italian: A direction to play in a tranquil, quiet manner!

transcription *(trän skrĭp'shŭn)* An *arrangement* or *adaptation* of a *previously arranged composition!* A *transcription* is used by *instruments* or *voices* for which the *original arrangement* was not *intended!*

transition *(trän zĭsh'ŭn)* (1) A *modulation* in the *sonata form* (also called *bridge)* or any *modulation,* particularly of a *transient* or *temporary* type! (2) An *abrupt key change!* (3) In *tonic sol-fa, changing the key* without *changing the mode!*

transpose *(trăns pōz')* To *re-write,* or *perform extemporaneously,* a composition in a *higher* or *lower key* than as *originally written!* The act of *transposing* is called *transposition!*

transposing instrument. (1) An *instrument* which *sounds* a *pitch* or *octave* that is different from the *written music notation!* Most *transposing instruments* are *members* of the *wind family,* whose *pitch* is frequently in *keys* with *many accidentals: B-flat, E-flat,* etc., or which have a *high* and *low compass* that requires too many *ledger lines* for *non-transposed notation!* The *B-flat clarinet,* for example, *sounds* a *whole tone lower* than its *written notation* in the *C-major key!* The *E-flat clarinet sounds one and a half tones* (a *minor third) higher than as written,* and the *A clarinet sounds one and a half tones* (a *minor third) lower than as written!* Other important *transposing instruments* include the *E, E-flat* and *B-flat trumpets* for which the *music is written in C major,* a *whole tone higher* than the *sound!* The *English horn (in F)* and the *French horn (in B-flat) sound a fifth below* their *written music,* but *French horn notes set in the bass clef sound a fourth below as written! Piccolo* and *soprano record-*

er sound an octave higher than as written! Contra bass and contra bassoon sound an octave lower than as written! Cornets sound one tone below as written! With saxophones, the E-flat alto sax transposes up a major sixth, the B-flat tenor sax transposes up a major ninth, and the E-flat baritone sax transposes up an octave and a major sixth! (2) Any *instrument* provided with a *mechanical device,* such as a *keyboard shifter,* which automatically converts the *music as written to the sound of another key!*

transverse flute *(trăns vŭrs' flūt)* Another name for the *cross flute,* or *orchestral flute* which is *held towards the horizontal* and *side-blown* by the *flautist!*

traps. A somewhat *"dated" colloquial term* for the *drum set* in a *dance* or *jazz band,* or *rock group!*

trascinando *(trä shē năn'dō)* from the Italian: A direction to gradually *slow down* or *"drag"* the *tempo!*

trattenúto *(trä tĕ nū'tō)* from the Italian: *"Slowed down," "holding back"!* Same as *rattenúto!*

trauermusik *(trou'ĕr mōō'zĭk)* from the German: *Funeral music! Trauermarsch, funeral march!*

träumerisch *(troi'mĕr ĭsh)* from the German: "Dreamy"!

traurig *(trou'rĭkh)* from the German: A direction to play in a sad, melancholy manner!

tre *(trä)* The Italian word for "three"! *A tre, "for three",* an expression *denoting one part for three instruments! A tre voce,* a composition *with three parts! Tre corde,* literally *"three strings",* but serves as a direction to *pianists to release the soft pedal!*

treble *(trĕb'l)* (1) The *highest voice part* in *choral music!* (2) A *high-pitched voice: Female soprano, male alto* or *young boy soprano!* (3) The *higher strings* or *keys* of *violins* and *keyboards: treble string, treble register,* etc.! (4) Relatively, a *higher range* of *pitch,* the *treble range!*

treble clef. The *G clef* or *violin clef* , not to be confused with *the soprano clef!*

treibend *(trī'bĕnt)* from the German: A direction to play in a hurried, urgent manner!

tremolo *(trĕm'ō lō)* (1) A *fluttering sound produced* on *instruments* by *repeating the same tone rapidly,* with no distinct breaks! *A tremulous effect results* from *alternating changes in volume,* as opposed to *vibrato,* which is *created by changes in pitch!* (2) With *stringed instruments* of the *violin family, tremolo* or *"bowed tremolo"* is created by the *rapid repetition* of a *tone* induced by *speedy up-and-down strokes of the bow!* It is marked in *notation with bars across the stem of the given note* ! In the same *instrumental family, "fingered tremolo"* is achieved by *rapid alternation of two notes in a chord,* produced by *bowing on a string* that is *stopped at two positions!*

tremolo stop, tremulant. An *organ stop* which actually produces a *vibrato-like effect* by *rapidly alternating two different rates of air pressure;* hence, *two different pitches!*

trepak *(trĕ păk')* A *Russian Cossack dance* in *brisk 2/4 meter!*

tres *(trä)* The *French* word for "very"; equivalent to the *Italian molto! Tres animé,* very animated; *tres lentement,* very slow, etc.!

triad *(trī'ăd)* A *chord* consisting of *three tones (notes)* which includes a basic *root tone* and the *third* and *fifth tones* above it in the *ascending order of a scale!* Four categories of *triads* are used in music: (1) *Major triads (a major plus a minor third)!* (2) *Minor triads (a minor plus a major third)!* (3) *Augmented triads (a major plus a major third)!* (4) *Diminished triads (a minor plus a minor third)!* Categories (1) and (2) are *consonant chords;* (3) and (4) are *dissonant chords!* There are *two inversions* for *each triad,* the *sixth chord* and the *six-four chord!* See *Elements Of Music, Chords* and see *Inversion!*

triangle *(trī ăng'l)* A *percussion instrument constructed* by bending a *steel rod* into a *triangle* which is *slightly open at one angle!* The *triangle* normally is *suspended freely, usually by a gut string attached to one of the closed angles!* It is struck by a *metal rod* or *mallet,* producing a *clear, pleasant ring* without a *specific pitch!*

Triangle

trill *(trĭl)* One of the most-frequently used *musical ornaments,* the *trill* is produced by the *rapid alternation of two adjacent tones,* a *major* or *minor second apart!* In modern usage, the *trill* usually *begins* on the *lower tone (principal)* and *alternates* with the *higher tone (auxiliary)!* A *trill* frequently will end with an *accompanying ornament* called the *Nachschlag!* See *Nachschlag!* In *notation,* the *trill sign* may appear as ∿ or *t* ∿ or *t* or *tr* or the symbol +! The *sign* appears *over* or *under the note* which is to be *alternated* with the *next higher note* in the *time value* of the *initial note!*

trinklied *(trĭngk'lēd)* The *German* word for a *drinking song!*

trio *(trē'ō)* (1) A *composition* for *three voice parts,* or *three parts for three instruments! Piano, violin, cello* constitute a *piano trio! Violin, viola, cello* a *string trio,* etc.! (2) A *secondary, middle portion* of a *minuet, scherzo* or *march,* usually written in a more *subdued key* than the *initial* or *primary section!*

trio sonata. The best-known form of *baroque chamber music!* Usually consisting of *three instrumental parts* with *two higher parts* for *violin,* and a *basso continuo part* for the *cello!* Sometimes the *basso continuo part* also is played by an *added keyboard instrument!*

triole *(trē ō'lĕ)* Ger. / **triolet** *(trē ō lā')* Fr. / A *triplet!*

trionfale *(trē ōn fä'lē)* / **trionfo** *(trē ōn'fō)* It. / "Triumph"; a *triumphant processional!*

triplet *(trĭp'lĕt)* A *group* of *three notes* of *equal value played* in the *same time value* as *two of the same* notes *individually!* In *notation,* a *triplet* is marked by the numeral 3 placed within a *slur* or *bracket,* or as shown:

3 ③ ⌐3⌐ ∴3 —3—

a half-note triplet equals two half-notes or one whole note!

○ = ♩♩♩

a quarter note triplet equals two quarter-notes or one half-note!

♩ = ♩♩♩

an eighth-note triplet equals two eighth-notes or one quarter-note!

♩ = ♪♪♪

a sixteenth-note triplet equals two sixteenth-notes or one eighth-note!

♪ = ♬♬♬

triple time. The same as *triple meter,* the *meter* with *three units* indicated in the *numerator* of the *time signature...* 3/2 3/4 3/8 etc.! See *Meter!*

triple tonguing. See *Tonguing!*

triste *(trĭs'tē)* A *sad, romantic song* of *Spanish/Indian* flavor whose form originated in *Peru* and spread to *Argentina* and other *South American* regions!

triste *(trēst)* Fr. / **tristo** *(trē'stō)* It.: A direction to play in a manner expressing sadness or melancholy!

tritone *(trī'tōn)* An interval of *three whole steps* or *tones* (an *augmented fourth* or *diminished fifth*):

Tritones were an anathema to *composers* in earlier centuries but are used in modern times without restraint! In *classical harmony,* however, the *tritone* can be used only together with other *intervals* or their *inversions!*

trochee *(trō'kē)* From *poetry:* A *metrical foot* of *two syllables,* with the *accent* on the *long, first syllable* and an *unaccented, short second syllable.* Notated —‿!

tromba *(trōm bä')* (1) The *Italian* word for *trumpet!* (2) An *organ stop* with a *trumpet-like* quality!

tromba da tirarsi *(-dä tē rär'sē)* The *Italian* term for a *"slide" trumpet,* or a *small trombone!*

trombone *(trōm'bōn)* One of the *important* members of the *brass, wind-instrument group!* The *trombone* consists of a long, U-shaped, metal tube (*the slide*) which moves in and out of another stationary U-shaped tube that flares into a *bell* at its end! The *slide tube* has an attached, cupped *mouthpiece* into which the *player blows* while he moves the *slide* to and from one of the *seven basic positions!* These replace the function of *valves* in other *brass instruments!* In the *first position (slide all the way in),* the *note B-flat above middle C* is produced in the *tenor trombone;* and an *F above middle C* is produced in a *bass trombone!* In the *second position (slide pulled out slightly),* the *note* is a *half-tone lower; in third position,* a *whole tone lower,* and so on until the *seventh position* which *produces a note three whole tones lower!* The *tenor trombone* is equipped with a *thumb valve* and *added tubing,* which can *lower the pitch to F from the basic B-flat!* The *compass* of the *tenor trombone* is *from E below the bass staff to the second B-flat above! Written music* for the *tenor trombone appears in the bass clef,* but frequently, to avoid excessive *ledger lines,* the *tenor clef* is used for the *top of the range! Music* for *bass trombone* is always *written in the bass clef!* The *lowest-pitch* and *largest trombone* is the *contrabass model,* which is rarely seen today! It is *pitched* a *full octave below the tenor!* Neither the *tenor* nor the *bass trombone* is a *transposing intrument!*

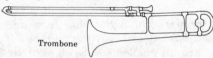

Trombone

trommel *(trôm'ĕl)* The *German* word for *drum!*

trompete *(trôm pā'tĕ)* The *German* word for *trumpet!*

trompette *(trôn pĕt')* The *French* word for *trumpet!*

tronco, -a *(trōn'kō, -ä)* from the Italian: A direction to *cut short the music* or *sound!* An *abrupt stop!*

trope *(trōp)* A portion of *music* or *text* added to *Gregorian chant* which in *medieval* times *varied from a change in the words to the insertion* of a *new melody* or to the *appendage* of a *new song* to an old one!

troppo *(trôp'pô)* from the Italian: "Too" or "too much"! *Non troppo presto* or *allegro non troppo,* not too fast! *Adagio, ma non troppo,* slow, but not too slow!

troubadour *(trōō'bä dôr)* A member of a *group* of *poet-musicians* which flourished in *Southern France* and *Northern Italy* during the 12th and 13th centuries! *The romantic musical texts* of the *troubadours* were written in the common people's tongue, although many *troubadours* were of the nobility and performed at court! In *Northern France,* the *troubadours* were imitated by a mixture of nobles and commoners called the *trouvères!* In *Germany,* similar *minstrel groups* were known as the *minnesingers!*

trüb *(trüb)* from the German: Gloomy, sad, melancholy!

trumpet *(trŭm'pĕt)* Another important member of the *brass, wind-instrument group!* The *trumpet* consists of a *long, metal tube, curved twice on itself into an oval,* with a *cupped mouthpiece at one end,* and a *flared bell at the other! Three valves,* centered on the *instrument,* are used to produce all the *pitched tones,* while the *player blows* through pursed lips into the *mouthpiece!* The *modern trumpet* usually is a *B-flat instrument,* with a *range from*

E below middle C to the B-flat below high C! Professional *jazz trumpeters* can *extend the top of the range to high G!* A few are able to go up a *full octave from high C!* The *trumpet* is a *transposing instrument* with its *music written one whole tone higher than the sound of the instrument.* Frequently, it is played with a variety of *mutes* which give a broad versatility of sound and effect! *Special-purpose trumpets,* still seen today, include the *bass trumpet (pitched in C or B-flat, an octave below* the *standard B-flat trumpet;* and the *trumpet in F,* which *sounds a fourth lower* than the *trumpet in B-flat!* Abbreviation: *tpt.!* See *Valve!*

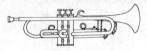

trumpet

tuba *(tū'bä)* Another important *orchestral member* of the *brass, wind-instrument group!* The *tuba* is a *bass saxhorn* whose three most common sizes are: *Tenor (euphonium),* the *E-flat bass tuba* and the *BB-flat double-bass tuba!* The *E-flat* and the *BB-flat double bass* are also called *bombardons! Circular models* of the *bombardons* (which *encircle the player's body)* are known as *helicons* or *sousaphones!* The *tuba* is *large-bodied* with a *double-curved, wide conical bore flaring into a huge bell!* It is played by manipulating *three, four or five valves* while *blowing* through *pursed lips into a cupped mouthpiece!* Purists consider the *only true tuba* to be the *euphonium or bombardon versions* whose *bells point straight up!* The *helicon* and *sousaphone bells point forward* and *away from the player's body!* The *standard orchestral tuba is pitched in B-flat* with a *two-octave range from low E to B-flat below middle C.!* Experts can reach *F above middle C!*

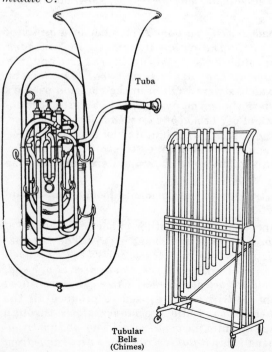

Tuba

Tubular
Bells
(Chimes)

tubular bells, tubular chimes *(tū'bū lẽr bĕlz, chīmz)* A series of *hollow metal tubes* (usually 18) of graduated length which are *suspended from a bar* and *struck* with a *hammer!* The *bells* or *chimes* are *chromatically tuned* with an *attached pedal dampener used to stop the ring!* The *compass of halftones* usually *extends from middle C to the F two octaves up!*

tune *(tūn)* (1) An *air* or *melody!* In *popular music,* a casual or generalized reference to a *song!* (2) Referring to *intonation* or *pitch accuracy* such as in the expressions *"in tune"* or *"out of tune"* or *"tune an instrument",* etc.! See *tuning!*

tuning *(tūn'ĭng)* (1) The adjustment of an *instrument* ... the *strings* of a *violin, guitar, piano,* etc., the *pipes* of an *organ,* or any *slides, clamps, valves* or other *devices* on the *instrument* ... to *produce* an *exact pitch as desired!* (2) The *accordatura* of a *stringed instrument (correct pitch)* ... g-d-a-e for the *violin strings,* for example!

tuning cone. A hollow, metal cone used to *tune organ flue-pipes!*

tuning fork. A two-pronged *instrument* of tempered steel which, when *struck, sounds* an extremely accurate *single pitch* with almost no *overtones!* The *single-pitched tone* is the *current international concert pitch: A above middle C, 440 vibrations per second!* This *pitch* determines the *absolute pitch* which is the reference for *tuning instruments* or *voices* to any *desired pitch!*

Tuning Fork

turca, alla *(toor'kä, ä lä)* from the Italian: A direction to *play in Turkish style,* emulating a noisy, exotic type of 18th century *Turkish band music (Janissary music)!*

turkish crescent. See *crescent!*

turn. A *musical ornament* or *grace* consisting of *four or five tones* which *"turn"* around a *principal tone!* The *common, four-note turn* uses the *principal tone twice* with the *two auxiliary tones, one step above* and *one step below* the *principal tone,* in the order of *high auxiliary, principal, low auxiliary, principal!* In *notation,* the *turn* is marked by the symbol

for example!
a *tone* so marked is written
and played

An inversion of a turn (*inverted turn*) is written

and played

tusch *(tōōsh)* from the German: An *orchestral flourish* or *fanfare* (usually *played* by the *brasswinds* and *percussion*) used as a gesture of applause, honoring a *conductor* or *soloist!*

tutti *(tōōt'tē)* from the Italian! "All", a direction for *all voices* and *all instruments to perform!* "*Full orchestra*"!

twelfth. (1) The *interval* of an *octave plus a fifth!* (2) A *mutation organ stop* which *sounds* a *twelfth above the diapason!*

twelve-tone technique. The basis of "*serial music*"! A *method of composition* wherein the *music is structured on a repeated pattern of 12 tones in the chroma-* *tic scale (dodecuple scale) in an order elected by the composer!* The technique gained 20th century prominence from the works of Arnold Schoenberg! See *Serial music!*

two step. A *popular dance* of the first two decades in the 20th century, *played* in *march* or *polka time!*

tympani. See *kettledrums, timpani!* An improperly spelled version of *timpani!*

tyrolienne *(tē rō lyĕn')* from the French: A *popular folk dance* from the *Austrian Tyrol,* usually in *3/4 meter* and characterized by the *vocal yodeling part* that *accompanies* the *dance music!*

**DICTIONARY**

U , V , W

— U —

üben *(ü'bĕn)* from the German: To *practice!*

über *(ü'bēr)* from the German: "Over", "above"! *überblasen* (u'ber bla z'n), to *overblow; übergreifen* (-grī f'n), a *transition; übermässig* (ü'ber mās'sikh), *augmented,* excessive!

übung *(ü'bōōnkh)* from the German: An *exercise* or *étude!* Also the *act of practicing music!*

u.c. Abbreviation for *"una corde",* a direction to use the *piano's* "soft pedal"!

'ud *(ōōd)* An *Arabian lute* (al 'ud, "the wood") dating from the seventh century and still popular in Greece, Turkey and the Near East! It is also popular in America among ethnic groups from these countries! The *'ud* may have up to a *dozen gut strings (some paired to one pitch)* which may or may not be *fretted!* Also anglicized in some circles as "oud"!

'Ud

ukulele *(ū'kŭ lā'lē)* The world-renowned *Hawaiian instrument* that is probably *Portugese* in origin! The typical *"uke"* is a *small, classical guitar* or *lute* with *four gut* or *nylon strings, strung over a fretted fingerboard,* and *plucked* with either the fingers or a *plectrum!* The *strings* normally are *tuned either, A,D,F#,B* or *G,C,E,A! Ukulele notation* normally is *written* in *tablature form,* with a *four-line staff marked with dots* and other *symbols* to show the *"stopping" positions!*

Ukulele

umfang *(ōōm'fäng)* The *German* word for the *compass* or *range* of a *voice* or *instrument!*

un *(ŭn)* feminine, **une** *(ōōn).* The *French* words for "a", "an", "one"! *Un peu,* or *un poco,* a little; *encore une fois,* one more time, etc!

un *(ōōn),* **uno** *(ōōn'ō)* The Italian words for "a", "an", "one"! *Una corda;* one string, a *piano* direction to employ the *soft pedal; uno a uno,* one by one!

und *(ōōndt)* The *German* word for "and"!

unda maris *(ŭn'dä mā'rĭs)* from the Latin: "Sea wave"; an *eight-foot organ stop* with an *undulating tone produced* by *using pipe rows* that are *slightly varied in pitch* to each other!

undecuplet *(ŭn'dĕk ŭ plĕt)* A group of *eleven equal notes, performed* in the *time-value* of *eight or six notes of equal value,* while maintaining the *original rhythm!*

undulation *(ŭn dū lā'shŭn)* (1) A *vibrato* or *tremolo!* On *bowed instruments,* a *tremulous tone* induced by *rapid finger-stopping* of a *string!* (2) The *pulsing sound (beat)* of *two vibrating strings* whose *tones* are *slightly out of unison!*

unis *(yū'nē)* The *French word* for *unison!*

unis. Abbreviation for unison!

unison *(ū'nĭ sŭn)* (1) *Sounding* the *same tones* or *parts* by *instruments* or *voices,* either in the *identical pitch* or in *different octaves* of *identical notes!* The *opposite* of *performance using harmony* or *harmonic tones!* (2) The *interval* of the *perfect prime! Two notes* whose *frequency vibrations* are in exact *one-to-one ratio;* hence, *identically pitched!* (3) In *piano music, two* or *three strings tuned* to the *same note,* and called a *unison!* (4) In *organ music,* the *standard eight-foot pitch, sounding notes* in the *same octave as written!*

universal notation. A *system of notation* for *fretted instruments* which modifies the *G clef* and *eliminates* the *F* and *C clefs!* The *standard G clef* 𝄞 with

a *stroke through it* 𝄞 is used to indicate the *tenor clef* and *all notes* are *sounded one octave lower!* The *bass clef* has *two strokes* 𝄞 and *all notes* are

sounded two octaves lower!

unruhig *(ōōn'rōō'ĭkh)* from the German: A direction to play in a *restless, almost frantic fashion!*

unter *(ōōn'tēr)* from the German: Under, below! Commonly used as a *prefix* to mean "one step lower than the connecting suffix"! *Unterdominante, subdominant; untermediante, submediant; unterstimme, lower voice (part)* etc.!

upbeat *(ŭp'bēt)* The *unaccented (weak) beat* of a *measure* which *precedes* the *downbeat* (the *first accented beat of a measure)!* The *upbeat* frequently appears in the *measure preceding a measure* whose *first beat* is a *downbeat!* A *conductor* raises his *hand* or *baton* for the *upbeat, lowers either* for the *downbeat!* Also called *arsis* or *anacrusis.* In German, *"auftakt"!*

up-bow *(ŭp-bō)* Stroking the *bow* of a *violin* from the *point* to the *nut* in the *direction towards the body!*

"*Up-bow*" is indicated in *notation* by the *sign* $\lor$
See *bowing!*

upright piano. The *piano model* whose *strings* and *soundboard* are mounted vertically in a *rectangular casing!* In contrast, the *grand piano's soundboard* and *strings* are mounted horizontally in a *wing-shaped casing!*

ut *(ŭt)* (1) Another name for the *dō* or *doh* used as the *first note* in a *solmization scale!* The *French* word *(üt) for the C note!*

ut supra *(ŭt sūp'rä)* The Latin term for "as above"! Also used to signify "as before"!

— V —

V. Abbreviation for *vide, violin, voce, voice, volti,* etc.!

va *(vä)* from the Italian: "It continues" or "it goes on"; a direction that usually extends a previous direction: *Va crescendo, continue to increase the volume,* etc.!

vaccilando *(vä tshē län'dō)* from the Italian: "Vacillating"; a direction to *play* in a hesitant, wavering manner!

vaghezza, con *(vä gĕt'tsä, kon)* from the Italian: A direction to *play* with charm in an easy, graceful manner!

valse *(vals)* The *French* word for *waltz!* In *Spanish, vals!*

value *(văl'ū)* The *duration* of a *note* or *tone!* A *whole note* equals *four quarter-notes*, a *quarter-note* equals *two eighth notes*, etc.! See *Elements of Music, Notes and Rests,* See *note!*

valve *(vălv)* A *mechanical piston* or *rotary device* used on all *brass instruments* except the *trombone!* The *valves* on *trumpets, horns* and *tubas,* etc. change the *extent of tubing (length)* through which the *air column travels,* producing an *increased range* of *pitched tones!* Without *valves;* the *brass* would be limited to the "*natural*" sound of a *fundamental tone* and its *overtones!* Usually the *horns* and *trumpets* have *three descending valves (sometimes four)* to *open up added tube-length!* The *first valve lowers* the *pitch* by a *whole tone;* the *second valve* by a *half-tone,* and the *third valve* by a *minor third!* The *valves* make the *complete chromatic scale* possible *in combination use* by *lowering* a *total of six half-tones!* The *trumpet's three valves* function as follows:

Notes:	Valves:
C above middle C	No Valve
B	2
B-flat	1
A	1 & 2 or 3 alone
A-flat	2 & 3
G	No Valve
G-flat	2
F	1
E	1 & 2 or 3 alone
E-flat	2 & 3
D	1 & 3
D-flat	1, 2 & 3
Middle C	No Valve

valve trombone. A version of the *trombone* which uses three *piston valves* instead of a *slide!* Since professionals consider the *tone-quality* of the "*slide trombone*" to be superior, the *valve trombone* is rarely seen!

valve trumpet. An old, formal name for the modern *trumpet!*

vamp *(vămp)* An *improvised series* of *chords* and *rhythm* used by *popular* and *jazz-band groups* to "*fill time*" until a scheduled or belated *solo entrance* or *performance* is made! "*Vamp 'til ready*", is a common colloquialism for a direction issued by the *band leader!*

variation *(vâr'ī ā'shŭn)* A *basic technique* of *composition,* which *expounds* a *theme* or *melody* (the *subject* or *motif*) and proceeds to *repeat same* with *ornamentation* and/or *modification,* including *changes in the mode, key, melody, rhythm,* etc. or *harmonic shifts, inverted* and *retrograded parts,* etc.! The repeated portions are designed to create new interest in the *music* while *retaining* a *unifying character!*

varsovienne *(vär sō vyĕn')* The *French* name for Warsaw, and the name given to a *popular 19th cen-*

tury dance which resembled the *polka* or *mazurka!* The *varsovienne* usually was *played* in *slow or moderate ¾ time* with a *strong downbeat* on *every other measure!*

vaudeville *(vōd'vĭl)* (1) The name given to *"live" American variety shows* that were prominent in the U.S.A. during the early decades of the 20th century! These were presented in *established national theater circuits* with tremendous popularity that waned only after *talking movies* and *television* appeared! Although *vaudeville* is obsolete, it is still fondly remembered by senior adults as the training grounds for many of the great, if older, *movie* and *tv stars* still enjoying prominence today! (2) A *comical* or *satirical popular song* or *presentation* named for the *Normandy* village of *Vau de Vire (in France)* where the *type* of *music* originated!

vcl. Abbreviation for *cello (violoncello)!*

veemenza, con *(vā ĕ mĕn'tsä, kôn)* from the Italian: A direction to play with vehemence! Passionate, forceful!

veil *(vāl)* The term applied to a *vocalist's tone* when the *clarity* is obscured by some individual quirk, such as *huskiness, unusual breathiness* or *muffled projection,* etc.! *Voce velata,* a *veiled voice!*

velato-a *(vĕ lä'tō-ä)* from the Italian: A direction to *sing,* or *play,* in a veiled, obsure fashion!

vellutato *(vĕl lōō tä'to)* from the Italian: A direction to *play* in velvety, smooth manner!

veloce *(vĕ lō'tshĕ)* from the Italian: A direction to *play rapidly;* in a *hurried tempo!*

velocissimo *(vĕ lō tshĕ'sē mō)* from the Italian: A direction to *play very rapidly;* in an *extremely hurried tempo!*

vent *(vän)* The *French* word for *"wind"!* *Instruments a vent,* wind instruments!

venusto *(vĕ nōō'stō)* from the Italian: A direction to play in an elegant, graceful manner!

verismo *(vā rēz' mō)* from the Italian: *"Realism",* the theory of *verism,* as applied to 19th century *Italian opera!* In the *verismo school of opera,* plots were based on everyday realities . . . evil with the good, ugly with the beautiful, etc.! . . . *Musically,* this brought forth *distinctly contrasting harmonies,* to support the melodramatic gamut of realities portrayed!

vergrösserung *(fâr grös'sĕr ōōngk)* The *German* word for *augmentation!*

verhallend *(fâr häl'ĕndt)* The *German* word for fading away, or dying away!

verkleinerung *(fâr klīn'âr ōōngk)* the *German* word for *diminuition!*

vermindert *(fâr mĭn'dârt)* The *German* word for *diminished!*

verschiebung, mit *(fâr shē'bōōngk)* from the German: A direction in *keyboard music* to use the *soft pedal: Una corda!*

verschwindend *(fâr shvĭn'dĕndt)* from the German: A direction to *play gradually more softly* until *dying away!*

verse. (1) In *vocal music,* a *section* of an *anthem* or *service* with *solo vocal part(s)!* (2) Generally, a *quantified portion* of a *lyric composition!* Sometimes, used to describe a *stanza,* although *technically a verse* is *only a line within a stanza!* (3) In *popular music,* the *introduction* to the *main body* of a *song! Verses* are *common* in *"production songs"* written for *musical theater* or *cinema!* They are often performed *rubato* or *ad lib* until the *entrance* of the *"chorus"* or *"refrain"!* Verses of *popular standard songs,* although highly regarded by *"buffs"* of *Lorenz (Larry) Hart* and *Ira Gershwin,* etc., are rarely heard on *radio* and *records* in *modern times!* The *"time limitation"* of *top-40 broadcasting* has prompted *songwriters, music publishers* and *record executives* to *market songs* without any *verses* in their own commercial self-interest!

verset,-to *(vûrsĕt,-'tō)* A *short, organ interlude* or *fugue* sometimes briefly inserted into *Gregorian chant* or a *Mass service!*

versetzung *(fâr zĕts'ōōngk)* The *German* word for transposition! **Versetzungzeichen,** an *accidental!*

Vespers *(vĕs'pĕrz)* The *evening service (sixth canonical hour)* of the *Roman Catholic church,* as well as many other churches including the *Anglican!*

vezzoso *(vĕt tsō'zô)* from the Italian: A direction to play in a graceful, *sweet-toned* manner!

via *(vīa)* from the Italian: *"Away",* "take away"! *Via sordini, take away (remove)* the mutes!

vibes. (1) A colloquial shortening for the *vibraphone* or *vibraharp!* (2) A slang term for *"vibrations",* used as a general reference! *"Good vibes"* results from anything pleasant and agreeable; *"bad vibes",* just the opposite! The expression probably developed from public awareness that *musical sounds* were *derived* from *frequency vibrations!*

vibraharp *(vī'brä härp)* or **vibraphone** *(vī'brä fōn).* A *percussion instrument,* which in principle, is simply an *electrified xylophone* or *marimba!* With *two keyboard rows* of *metal bars,* it also has *motor-driven resonators suspended* under the *bars* which *re-inforce the sound!* Small *propeller-blades* in each *resonator tube* create a *unique vibrato* in the *sound!* Played by both hands *(striking two or more mallets on the bars)* the *instrument* also has a *damping pedal* to *sustain* or *shorten tones as desired!* Some models also are equipped with *electronic amplifiers* to further *augment* the *sound!* First developed in the 1920's for *American dance bands,* the *vibraphone* is popular today in some *jazz groups* and has inspired some *serious composition!* Its *tones* are considered *sweeter* and *richer* than the *non-electric xylophone* or *marimba!*

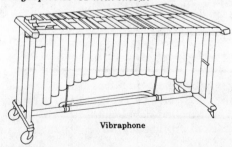

Vibraphone

vibration (vĭ brā'shŭn) From the *science* of *physics*, as applied to *music*, the *periodic oscillation* (from a *position* of *equilibrium*) of a *stretched string* or a *column of air* or any other *elastic body* such as a *tuning fork*, which is *transmitted* to the *human ear* as a *tone!* The *standard pitch* (for measuring all *tones*) in the U.S.A., Britain and Europe is now *440 vibrations* (*cycles per second*) for the *A above middle C!* In the *equal-tempered* scale, it is actually *437 cycles*, with *middle C* at *261.6* and the *C an octave above* at *520! Vibration* is measured by *frequency* (*number per second*) and by *amplitude* (the *length* or *breadth* of the *vibration* from and to its point of equilibrium)! *Frequency* determines *pitch, amplitude* determines *loudness!* The *human ear* can distinguish *vibrations* from about *16* to *4000 cycles per second!* A *piano* will produce *tones* in the *range of* 30 to 4000 *cycles*; a *kettle drum* 95 to 180; a *clarinet* 75 to 1800; a *trumpet* 190 to 990 and a *violin* 200 to 2650!

Frequency-vibration relationships were first discovered and analyzed in antiquity by *Pythagoras*, the great Greek philosopher-mathematician! He determined that the *ratio of a tone to its octave is 2:1*; for the *fifth 3:2*, and *5:4* for the *major third!* From the axioms of *"pure pitch"* he drew a set of laws governing both *fundamental tones* and *overtones!* After the Middle ages, the *Pythagorean* system underwent many modifications! In the beginning of the 18th century, Fourier discovered the sine wave mathematics for the *harmonic tones.* At the time a *"just intonation"* system, basing all *intervals on a pure fifth* and *third interval* was introduced! This soon proved awkward for *modulations* and *key changes* and was discarded in favor of the *"mean tone" system! "Mean tone"* combined features of both the *Pythagorean system* and the *"just"* system but it, too, proved inadequate for *keys* with many *sharps* or *flats*, and it gave way in time to the *"equal temperament" system* at the beginning of the 19th century. Still the *system* used today, the *"equal temperament"* technique was to *divide the octave into 12 equal parts* (in *terms of frequency*), which solved the problems of *enharmonic intervals* and *complex modulations!* The *system* has been criticized for its *mathematical inconsistency* but *it works for music*, and today the "errors" in exactness (deviation from *absolute pitch*) are accepted as the rule for *proper intonation!*

A comparison chart of the *pure Pythagorean system* and the *"equal tempered" system* follows:

Cycles per second	For the octave beginning an octave above middle C!							
	C''	d''	e''	f''	g''	a''	b''	c''
Pure (pythagorean)	520	585	655	693	780	877	987	1040
Equal temper	520	584	655	694	779	874	982	1040

The *"Just Intonation"* system is the same as the *"Pure"* except that e'' = 650 cycles; a'' = 867 and b'' = 975!

vibrato (vĭ brä'tō) A *slightly, tremulous tone* produced by *equally slight variation* in the *pitch* of *rapidly succeeding notes!* Not to be confused with *tremolo* which is produced by *variations in volume* (*loud, soft*, etc.) but *not in pitch!* For *singers, vibrato* is closely related to *tremolo*, although the carefully-controlled development of the former is an earmark of proficiency, while the latter usually is greeted negatively! For *bowed, string-instruments, vibrato* is almost constantly employed, and consists of *pitch fluctuation* induced by *rapidly stopping a string* with a *rocking action of the finger!* For some *wind-instruments, vibrato* can be produced by *fast alternation of the amounts of* "blowing pressure"! For the *organ, vibrato* is obtained by using the *tremulant stop!*

vide (vēd) from the Latin: "To see"; (1) A direction to *performers* to *"make a cut"*; that is, to *skip over the portion of music marked* "Vi ..." at its beginning and "... de" at its end! The *sign* ⊕ often is added to emphasize the instruction of *vide!* (2) *Open* or *empty! Corde à vide*, open string!

viel (fēl), **vielem** (fēl'ĕm) from the German: "Much", "many"! *Mit viel Gefühl*, with much feeling! *Mit vielem Nachdruck*, with much emphasis!

vielle (v'e y-el') from the French: The *medieval predecessor* of the *violin* (1200–1600), which appeared in various models with from *three to five bowed strings!* In the 15th century, a *"hurdy-gurdy"* was developed which was known as *vielle á roue (-a roo)*, a *wheel viol!*

Viennese school. In *classical music*, a general reference to the *masters of composition* who gathered in *Austria's Vienna* to *write* during the early 19th century! *Haydn, Mozart, Beethoven, Schubert*, etc. are the school leaders! Later in the 19th century, the *Johann Strauss* family sometimes was added to the context of such reference, as was *Arnold Schoenberg* and *his disciples* in the 20th century!

viertel (fēr'tĕl) The *German* word for *quarter* (*one/fourth*)! *Viertelnote* (-nō'tĕ), a *quarter-note!*

vif (vēf) from the French: A direction to play in a lively manner!

vigoroso (vē gō rō'sō) from the Italian: A direction to play in a vigorous, energetic manner!

vihuela (vē ooĕ'lä) A small *Spanish lute*, resembling a *guitar*, with a long, thin *neck* and *fretted fingerboard!* With *6 pairs of strings* tuned to G, D, A, F, C, G' the *vihuela* was *plucked by hand!* Full name: *Vihuela de mano*, "hand lute"! In the 17th century, it was replaced by the *Spanish guitar!*

villancico (vēl yän thē'kō) from the Spanish: An old, poetic *Spanish choral work* written in *parts* and resembling a *madrigal!* After the Renaissance, it evolved into a *religious form of cantata!* In contemporary Latin-and-South-America, *villancicos* have become equivalent to *Christmas carols!*

villanella (vē lä nĕl'ä) An old, 16th century, *Italian country-song* with several *voice parts in free form!* Originating in *Naples* (*villanella alla Napoletana*) the *villanella* is considered as a simplified forerunner of the *madrigal* or *canzonet!*

vina (vē'nä) An important *instrument* of *ancient* and *modern India!* A *stringed instrument*, the *primitive Hindu version* consisted of a long thin bamboo *fingerboard* with a *hollow gourd* at each end acting as a *resonator!* Over the *fingerboard, seven wire strings* were stretched! *Four fretted melody strings* were *plucked* by the *fingernails* or a *plec-*

trum, while *three other strings* (acting as *drones*) were *strummed* by the *little finger or thumb!* The *modern vina* has taken on a *lute shape*, with *one pear-shaped gourd "narrowing"* into the *fingerboard!* The *second gourd* frequently is only decorative! The *fingerboard* comes with *inlaid frets*, a *lacquered frame* and a *set of tuning pegs!*

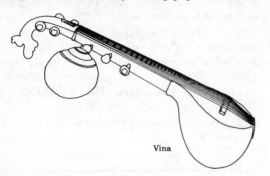

Vina

viol *(vē'ŏl)* and **viola** *(vē ō'lä)* A *bowed, stringed-instrument* of major importance in the 16th and 17th centuries, and the ancestor of the *modern violin, viola, cello* family! The *early viols* had *fretted fingerboards* (pieces of gut tied around the neck), *flat backs, C-shaped sound holes* and *six strings!* At least four major models included the *treble descant viol*, the *tenor or alto viola da braccio* (held in the arm and *bowed* like a *violin*), the *bass "viola da gamba"* (rested between the knees and *bowed* like the *cello*) and the *contrabass "violone"* (rested on the floor and *bowed* like the modern *double bass)!* In old English *chamber music*, many *compositions* were written for a specified *"chest of viols"* or *"consort of viols"* which consisted of two *treble*, two *tenor* and two *bass viols!* Through the end of the 17th century (when the *violin* replaced all the *viols* except the *bass*) additional models were developed such as a *high-pitched tenor descant viol*, a small *bass "division viol"* and a *"lyra viol"* which was *sized between the tenor and the division viols!*

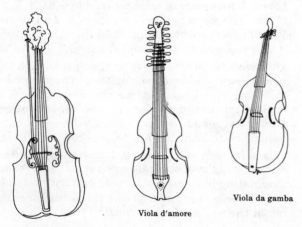

Viola d'amore

Viola da braccio

Viola da gamba

viola *(vē ō'lä)* The *contemporary viola* is one of the *major modern members of the violin family!* It is considered the *tenor violin!* A *bowed, string-instrument*, it is almost identical to the *violin* ex-

cept for its *slightly larger size and lower pitch!* The *viola* is *pitched* a *fifth below* the *violin*, its *four strings tuned* to *C, G, D', A'*, and is normally *notated on the alto clef*, except when *higher notes* call for *placement on the treble clef!*

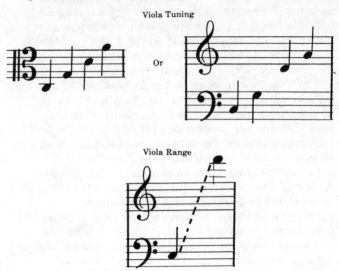

Viola Tuning

Or

Viola Range

viola d'amore *(-dä môr)* from the Italian: *"Viol of love";* an old form of *treble viol* that was held like a *violin!* One version used *seven unfretted strings of gut* with an *equal number of sympathetic strings made of metal!* Another version used *metal melody strings* and *eliminated any sympathetic strings!*

viole *(v'yōl')* The *French* name for the *viol* or *viola!*

violin *(vī ō lĭn')* The *major orchestral member* of the *modern family of stringed instruments!* Shaped as illustrated, the *violin* is a *four-stringed instrument*, tuned *G, D', A', E''*, with a *four-octave range from G below middle C*, to *E an octave above high C*, but it has a *capacity for higher harmonics or overtones!* The *strings normally are made of gut!* Occasionally, a *violin* with a special *tuning peg* attached, will use a *metal E'' string!* The *instrument* is *played* by tucking the top of the *body* under the chin (a molded *chin rest* is attached to most *violins*) and *bowing with one hand*, while *the other "stops"* or *holds down* the *strings* in various positions! This achieves the production of *differently pitched tones!* Various *bowing* and *string-plucking* techniques are employed! See *bow, bowing, staccato, pizzicato, detache*, etc.!

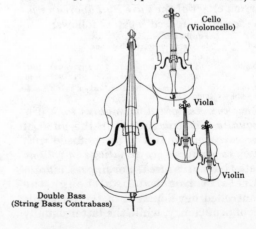

Cello
(Violoncello)

Viola

Violin

Double Bass
(String Bass; Contrabass)

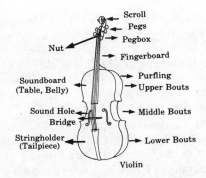

Violin

Tuning

Range

8*va* higher

violin clef. Also called the *treble clef* or the *G clef!*

It identifies the *second-from-the-bottom line* of the *staff* as *G above middle C.* See *clef!*

violin family. Usually refers to the four sizes of *four-stringed instruments* that are *bowed!* These are: The *violin,* the *viola,* the *violoncello (cello)* and the *double bass (contrabass, string bass, etc.)!*

violina *(vē ō lē'nà)* A *four-foot organ flue-stop* with a *string-tone* quality!

violino *(vē ō lē'nō)* The *Italian* name for *violin!*

violino piccolo *(pēk'kō lō)* The *Italian* name for a *smaller-than-standard violin* with the *strings tuned a fourth higher* than the *standard model!*

violon *(vē ō lŏn')* The *French name* for *violin!*

violoncello *(vē'ō lōn chĕl'ō)* The *full name* for the *cello!* See *cello!*

violone *(vē ō lō'nà)* The *Italian* name for a *six-string contrabass* or *double-bass viol!* See *viol!*

virelai *(vēr lā')* from the French: A *medieval, French music form* which set *poetic stanzas* to *accompaniment!* A *refrain* began and ended each stanza!

virginal *(vûr'jĭ nàl)* A *small, rectangular harpsichord* or *spinet* popular in *England* during the 16th and 17th centuries! Usually with *one string* to a *note* or *key,* it originally was encased in a *box with no legs,* for *table* or *lap use!* Subsequently it evolved into *"upright"-*and-*"harpsichord"-shaped models!* The *instrument* had a *compass* of about *four octaves,* inspiring a considerable *repertory* of

"virginal" compositions, which were always termed *"pair of virginals"!*

Virginal

Virginia reel. See *reel!*

virtuoso *(vûr'chōō ō'sō)* (1) One who excels in the *technique* of an *instrument* or *voice!* (2) Used as an adjective to describe *composition* or *performance* requiring the highest proficiency and technical skill!

vista *(vĭs'tà)* from the Italian: "Sight", "view"! *A vista* (short for *a prima vista*), at first sight *(sight-reading)!*

vistamente *(vē'stä mĕn'tä)* / **visto** *(vē'stō)* It. / A direction to play *very quickly, presto!*

vite *(vēt)* / **vitement** *(vēt'màn)* Fr. / A direction to play *quickly* or *immediately!*

vivace *(vē vä'chē)* from the Italian: A direction to *play* in a *lively vivacious manner!* By itself, *vivace* designates a *tempo equal to,* or a bit faster than, *allegro!* Paired with *allegro (allegro vivace),* it refers to a generally *live, brisk tempo!*

vivacetto *(vē vä chĕt'tō)* from the Italian: A direction to *play a little less lively* than *vivace* or *allegro,* almost *allegretto!*

vivacissimo *(vē vä chēs'sē mō)* from the Italian: A direction to play in a *very lively* and *very vivacious* manner, almost *presto!*

vivement *(vēv män')* Fr. / **vivo** *(vē'vō)* Fr. / A direction to play in a lively, spirited manner, almost *presto!*

vl. Abbreviation for *violin!*

vla. Abbreviation for *viola!*

vlc. Abbreviation for *cello!*

vll. Abbreviation for *violins!*

vocal *(vō'kàl)* Pertaining to, performed by, or written for the *human voice!*

vocal cords *(-kôrds)* Two pairs of *folded membranes* set into the *human larynx cavity!* Through the edges of the lower pair of folds (the *true vocal cords*), the *passage of breath* creates the *voice!* The *aperture* between the folds of the *true vocal cords* is known as the *vocal glottis!*

vocalion *(vō kā'lĭ ŏn)* An advanced form of *harmonium* with *several manuals* and *broad reeds* enriching the *organ tone!*

vocalise *(vō'kàl ĭz)* / **vocalization** *(vō'kàl ĭ zā'shŭn)* / A *singer's exercise,* requiring *long tones* or a *melody* to be *sung* to a *single vowel* or *one Italian syllable!* It is mainly a *solfege technique,* which is believed to

716

improve the *quality* and *power* of the *voice!* Some authorities criticize it as an exaggeration of pedantic *virtuosity!* See *solmization, solfeggio* and *sol-fa!*

vocal music. Any *composition* for *voice!* A solo *composition* usually is called a *song,* while *compositions* for *groups of voices* come under the *heading* of *choral music!*

vocal score. An *arrangement* of *vocal music* which *aligns* the *vocal parts* vertically on *individual staves* of a *score,* and *condenses* all *accompanying instrumental music* into *one piano part!* Occasionally, an *optional line* for *rhythm section* will be *added!*

voce (*vô'chē*) from the Italian: Voice, voice part!

voce di petto (*-dē pĕt'tō*) from the Italian: Chest voice, chest tone!

voce di testa (*-tĕs'tä*) from the Italian: Head voice, head tone!

voce, cella (*vō'chĕ, kô'lä*) from the Italian: "With the voice", a direction for the *accompaniment* to *follow* the *tempo* set by a solo *voice!*

voci (*vô'chē*) from the Italian: The plural of *voce,* "*voices*"! A due (*tres, quattro,* etc.) *voci,* for *two, three, four,* etc. *voices* or *voice parts!* See *messa di voce, sotto voce,* etc.!

voice (*vois*) (1) The term that describes the *projection* of *pitched tones* by a *human being! Human voices* are classified *musically* into *six main categories* which cover a *four-octave span from C to c''''!* These are: *Female . . . . soprano, mezzo-soprano, contralto* or *alto; Male . . . . tenor, baritone* and *bass!* Additional *special voice categories* include *falsetto,* an *artificially induced high-soprano register* (usually for *males*); *castrato,* an *adult male* with a *soprano* or *alto register* (in the 16th to 18th centuries, this was the result of physically castrating *boy singers*); *boy soprano,* a *natural falsetto register* of *young boys* (*choir boys,* etc.) who have not yet reached *voice-changing puberty!* With the *human voice,* pitch depends on the *speed of the frequency vibration of the breath passing through the vocal cords!* The *loudness* or *intensity* of the *voice* depends on the *size of each frequency vibration (amplitude)!* Both, of course, are affected by the *shape* and *tension* of the *vocal cords!* (2) In *popular music,* frequently but *improperly* used as a term meaning to *arrange* or *select tones,* or *adjust instrumental pitch,* in order to achieve a *desired end-result* from a *composition* or its *performance!*

voice leading. *Arranging* the *voices* of *multi-part composition* (particularly in *counterpoint*) so that *each part* achieves *continuity!* Also called *part writing!* In *counterpoint,* specific *principles of progression* for *voice parts* are laid down, such as *no parallel fifths* or *octaves, contrary motion* in *one part,* "*step*" *sequencing* for the *parts,* etc.

voice-part. One of the *parts* in a *vocal* or *instrumental composition* with *more than a single melody line! Four-part harmony, music* with *four voice-parts; fugue in three voices,* a *fugue* with *three voice-parts!*

voice tones. The *upper section* of a *singer's range* is known as the *head voice!* The *tones* in this *range* are called *head tones!* "*Head*" gets it name from the observation that the *given sounds* appear to *resonate only in the head,* developing very few *overtones* and displaying, therefore, a *light, fine quality!* The *chest voice-range* (the lower section) and the *tones therein, chest tones,* are *heavier, deeper tones* that appear to *resonate* in the *chest cavity!*

voicing. (1) *Tuning* of *instruments,* specifically *organ pipes!* (2) Sometimes used as a term for the adjustment of the *felts* on the *hammers* of a *piano!*

voix (*vwä*) from the French: "*Voice*" or "*voices*"! Refers both to the *singing voice* or to a *voice-part* in *composition! A deux (trois, quatre) voix,* for two (*three, four*) *voices* or *voice-parts!*

volante (*vō län'tĕ*) from the Italian: A direction to play with a *light, swift motion!*

volata (*vō lä'tä*) It. / **volate** (*vō lä'tĕ*) Ger. / **volantine** (*vō lä tēn'*) Fr. / A *run, roulade, trill* or a *rapid series of notes!*

volkslied (*fōlks'lēdt*) The *German* word for "*folk song*"!

voll (*fōll*) The *German* word for "*full*"! *Volles Werk,* full organ!

volta (*vōl'tä*) from the Italian: (1) "*A turn*", "*a time*"; used mainly to indicate repetition of a *part! Una volta,* "once" or "one time"; *due volte,* "twice" or "two times"! *Prima volta,* "first time", and *seconda volta,* "second time" are *directions* used in *notation!* They are marked as *first* and *second endings,* with *brackets* and *numerals* corresponding to the *given ending* ⌐1 ¬ or ⌐2 ¬! After the *first ending,* the *player returns* to the *beginning of a composition* and *repeats* the *music until the ending,* at which point he *switches to the second ending!* Sometimes the *symbols Ima, I* or *1* are substituted for *prima volta; IIda volta, IIda, II* or *2* for *seconda volta!* (2) An *old dance* in *6/8 meter* (usually *dotted*) that was popular at the beginning of the 16th century!

volteggiando (*vôl'tĕ jyän'dô*) from the Italian: The direction to *play with crossed hands on a piano!*

volti (*vôl'tē*) from the Italian: A *page turn! Volti subito* (*sōō'bē tô*); a direction to *turn a page quickly to avoid interruption!* Abbreviated *v.s.!*

volubilita (*vō lōō bē lē'tä*) / **volubilmente** (*vō lōō bēl mĕn'tĕ*) It. / "*Voluble*", flowing freely and smoothly!

volume (*vŏl'ūm*) The *fullness* or *quantity of tone,* the *loudness!* See *dynamics, dynamic marks!* In physical terms, *loudness* is based on the *size of a frequency vibration (amplitude)* which refers to the *length* and *breadth* of a *cycle* from its *point of equilibrium!* Not to be confused with *pitch* which is *measured* by the *speed of vibration!* See *vibration!*

voluntary (*vŏl'ŭn tĕr ī*) An *organ solo played before, after* and *during* a *religious service!* It was usually *extemporized* in 16th century Anglican churches; hence, the name "*voluntary*"!

vom (*fûm*) or **von** (*fûn*) from the German: "*From*", "*of*", "*by*", "*on*"! *Vom anfang,* from the beginning (*da capo*)!

vorausnahme (*fôr ous'nä mĕ*) The German word for anticipation!

vorhalt (fôr'hält) from the German: A suspension!

vorher (fôr'hâr) from the German: "Before", "previous to"! *Zeitmass wie vorher*, the *tempo or time as before!*

vorig (fôr'ĭgk) from the German: "Previous", "preceding"! *Voriges Zeitmass*, the *preceding tempo or time!*

vorschlag (fôr'shläg) from the German: An *appoggiatùra!* A *beat!*

vorspiel (fôr'shpēl) from the German: An *overture, prelude* or *introduction!*

vortrag (fôr'träg) from the German: The *execution* or *interpretation* of a *performance! Style, attack, delivery*, etc.!

vorwärts (fôr'värts) The *German* word for "forward"! *Vorwärts gehen*, go ahead, continue!

vox (vŏks) The *Latin* word for *voice!*

vox angelica (-ăn jěl'ĭ kà) from the Latin: A *four-foot, organ stop!*

vox humana (-hū mā'nà) from the Latin: (1) The *human voice!* (2) An *eight-foot organ-stop* with a quality allegedly similar to the *human voice!*

v.s. Abbreviation for *volti subito!*

vuoto (vōō ō'tō) from the Italian: "Empty", "without tone"! *Corda vuota*, an *open string! Musura vuota*, an *empty bar*, a *rest for a full measure!*

vv. Abbreviation for *violins!*

— W —

wachsend (väks'ĕndt) From the German: "Growing"! A *crescendo!*

Wagner tuba (väg'nĕr tū'bà) A *brass instrument* representing a compromise between the *French horn* and a *saxhorn* that was invented at *Richard Wagner's* behest, to accommodate his *opera cycle Der Ring des Nibelungen!* Two models were introduced by 1854: A *tenor B-flat horn* and an *F-pitched bass!* The name "tuba" is a misnomer, probably caused by faulty translation of the *German* "tube" which is equivalent to the English "tube", and not to "tuba"!

Wagner tuba

waldflöte (väldt'flō tĕ) from the German: (1) An *organ flue stop* of *two-foot* and *four-foot pitch!* (2) A *shepherd's flute!*

waldhorn (vält'hôrn) (1) The *German* word for a *natural French horn* (without *valves*)! (2) An *organ stop* with the quality of a *hunting horn!*

waltz (wôlts) A major form of *dance music* recognized throughout the Western world, the *waltz* originated in 18th century *Austria* and *Germany!* Innovative and audacious for its time (for a couple to hold each other closely was considered bold), the *waltz* quickly developed from popularity as a peasant, *country dance (ländler)* to become the darling of *Viennese composers!* The *immortal Johann Strauss father-and-son combination* and the earlier *symphonic giants* ... *Beethoven, Liszt, Brahms, Shubert*, etc.... produced an array of notable *waltzes* that seem timeless in their appeal! The *classic waltz* always is *written* and *performed* in ¾ *meter* with *tempi* varying from *slow to moderately fast.* Usually, there is *only one harmonic chord to a bar!* The *waltz rhythm* is easily identified by the *strong, first-beat accents* in the *bass parts!* The familiar *oom pa pa, oom pa pa*, pattern usually *accompanies* a *light, sweet melody* written in the *treble register!* In contemporary, *popular* and *jazz music*, the *waltz* has attracted some sophisticated experimentation with *syncopation* and *complex chording!* Its *ballroom* appeal still is evidenced at "formal occasions" or any adult festivities!

warble (wôr'b'l) (1) *Singing* with *trills, runs, tremolos* or *quavers!* Imitative of a *bird song!* Sometimes used as an equivalent to *yodel!* (2) In *popular music*, a now-clichéd slang expression for *singing!* In the days of *big-band* fame, a "*warbler*" usually referred to the "*girl singer*" appearing with the *band!*

wehmütig (vā mü'tĭgk) from the German: Sad, melancholy!

weich (vīkh) from the German: Soft, gentle, tender!

Weichnachtslied (vī'näkhts lēd) The *German!* word for *Christmas carol!*

Weichnachtsmusik (vī'näkhts mōō zēk) The German word for *Christmas music!*

well-tempered. *Tuned in equal temperament!* Bach's immortal *Well-Tempered Clavier*, partially published in 1722, consisted of *48 preludes* and *fugues (two for every major and minor key)* which demonstrated the principles of *equal temperament*, the *scale system* then coming into vogue, and still employed today! See *temperament!*

wenig (vā'nĭgk) from the German: "Little"! *Ein wenig stark*, a little strong! *Ein wenig langsamer*, a little slower! *Ein klein wenig langsamer*, a very little bit slower!

whistle (hwĭs'l) (1) the *shrill-toned* sound produced by blowing through the lips! The *pitch* changes in accordance with the shape and size of the lip-openings, and the mouth cavity which acts as a *resonator!* (2) An *instrument* or *toy* which produces a *sharp, shrill sound* by blowing into its *open end;* e.g. *police whistle, boatswain's pipe*, etc.!

whistle flute. A *fipple flute!*

whole note. The note **O** (*semibreve*) which has the *longest duration* of any *note* in current *notation!* All other *notes (half, quarter, eighth, sixteenth*, etc.) are named in accordance with their relative proportion to the *time value* of a *whole note!*

whole rest. The *rest* ▬ which designates *silence*

for the *time value equal* to the *duration* of a *whole note!*

whole step. The *step of a whole tone!*

whole tone. An *interval* consisting of *two half-tones! Also called a major second or whole step!*

whole-tone scale. A *scale* which consists only of *whole tones!* It is a *non-traditional, non-diatonic scale* with a *six-tone octave!* It has *no half-tones* and *eliminates* any *tonic center!* There is *no major fourth or fifth* and *no leading tone!* Only *two whole-tone scales* exist in *American* and *European music: C-D-E-F#-G#-A#* and *Db-Eb-F-G-A-B!* In the early 20th century, a *movement* to use *whole-tone scales* was led by *Debussy* and his disciples but the trend has proved short-lived!

wie *(vē)* from the German: "As"! *Wie aus der Ferne, as from a distance! Wie vorher, as before! Wie oben, as above!*

wiegend *(vē'gĕndt)* from the German: Rocking, swaying!

wiegelied *(-lēd)* from the German: A *lullaby!*

wind band. A general reference to a *band* made up only of *wind instruments!*

wind chest. A sealed box under the *organ soundboard* which stores air from a *bellows* and transmits it to the *pipes* in accordance with the *stop action!*

wind gauge. A device that shows the amount of air pressure in the *bellows* of an *organ!*

wind instrument. Any *instrument* that produces *pitched sounds* when a *column of air* is made to *vibrate* within its *body or tube!* Major categories of *wind instruments* include: *woodwinds; flutes,* clarinets, saxophones, oboes, etc.; brass; horns, trumpets, trombones, tubas, etc.!

woodwind instruments. Any members of the *wind instrument group* that use *reeds (clarinet, saxophone, bassoon, oboe, etc.)* or *mouth holes (flute, recorder, etc.)* to *transmit air column vibrations* through their *bodies or tubes!* The term "woodwind", although universally employed in modern times, technically does not seem appropriate since the "woodwinds", except for the *recorder*, are no longer made of wood! The "woodwinds" in the *orchestra* include *flute, oboe, piccolo, clarinet, bassoon, English horn, bass clarinet, double bassoon, saxophone, bass flute* and others! See *instrument!*

wolf *(wŏolf)* (1) Any *dissonance* or *harshness* sounded by *certain tones* on a *bowed instrument,* such as *C#* on the violin's *A-string,* or *F#* on the cello's *D-string!* Those are believed to arise from the *faulty vibrations* caused by inherent defects in the *body design* of the *instruments!* (2) A *dissonant* or *disagreeable tone* that occurs in *some keys* on an *organ* that is *unequally tuned!* An *impure fifth,* etc.!

wood block. An alternate name for *temple block!*

wuchtig *(vŏoch'tĭgk)* from the German: Weighty, ponderous!

würdig *(vür'dĭgk)* from the German: Dignified, lofty, stately!

wuth *(vŏot)* from the German: Madness, ferocity! *Wütend*; madly, frantically!

DICTIONARY

X, Y, Z

— X —

xylophone *(zī'lŏ̄ fōn)* A *percussion instrument,* dating back to antiquity, with *two rows* of *graduated wooden bars* that are *chromatically tuned* and are struck by a *pair of wooden mallets* or *beaters!* Suspended under the bars are *graduated, hollow, cylindrical, metal tubes* which act as *mechanical resonators of the struck sounds;!* The *vibraphone* or *vibraharp* basically differs from the *xylophone* only in the "*electrification*" of the former which uses *metal bars* and *motor-driven resonators!* The *xylophone's range* is about *three octaves up from middle C!* Various, simplified *xylophones* are used throughout the *non-Western world,* particularly among the *gamelan orchestras of Indonesia!*

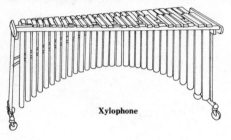

Xylophone

— Y —

yodel *(yō'dl)* The world-renowned type of *singing* developed in the *Swiss* and *Tyrolean Alps!* The distinctive *yodel sound* is achieved by *rapid alternation* of *low chest-tones* with *high-pitched falsetto tones,* and usually is *sung with syllables* (oh, dee, la, ah, etc.) instead of *words! German* spelling: *Jodel!*

— Z —

zählzeit *(tsäl'tsīt)* The *German* word for *beat!*

zamba *(thäm'bä)* An *Argentine* and *Chilean* dance in *fast 6/8 meter;* also known as the *scarf dance, danza de panuelos!* It probably originated in Peru as the *zambacueca* or *zamacueca!*

zambomba *(thäm'bōm bä)* A primitive *Spanish instrument* consisting of a *stick thrust through parchment* stretched over an *earthen vessel!* The stick was rubbed to produce *resonant sounds!*

zampogan *(tsäm pō'nyä)* (1) An *Italian bagpipe* or *shawm* used by countryside shepherds! (2) A *panpipe!*

zanfona *(thän'fō nä)* A *Spanish* "*hurdy gurdy*"!

zapateado *(thä'pä tā ä'thō)* A *Spanish solo, heel-stomping dance,* usually in *triple time* with *syncopated rhythms countering the melody!*

zart *(tsärt)* / **zartlich** *(-lĭkh)* Ger. / A direction to play softly and tenderly, with delicacy!

zarzuela *(thär thwä'lä)* The major form of *Spanish opera,* using *spoken dialogue* as well as *song and music!* It originated at *La Zarzuela,* the royal palace near *Madrid,* during the 17th century!

zeffiroso *(zĕf fē rō'sō)* from the Italian: "Like a zephyr!"

zeitmass *(tsīt'mäs)* The *German* word for *tempo!*

zelo, con *(tsĕ'lō, kon)* / **zeloso** *(tsĕ lō'sō)* It. / A direction to play in an energetic, fiery manner!

ziehharmonika *(tsē'här mŏn ĭ kä)* The *German* word for *accordion!*

ziemlich *(tsēēm'lĭkh)* from the German: Moderately, somewhat, quite! *Ziemlich bewegt,* quite animated! *Ziemlich schnell,* somewhat fast!

zierlich *(tsēr'lĭc)* from the German: Neat, graceful!

zigeuner *(tsĭ goi'nĕr)* The *German* word for *gypsy! Zigeunermusik,* gypsy music!

zimbalon. A modernized, large *Hungarian dulcimer* that uses *dampers!* It is *pitched in four octaves, chromatically e to e''''!* See *cimbalon* for *illustration!*

zingara, alla *(tsĭn' gä rä, ä lä)* / **zingarese, alla** *(tsĭn'gä rā zĕ,-)* It. / A direction to play in gypsy style!

zither *(zĭ th'ēr)* (1) A contemporary *folk instrument* (popular in *Bavaria, Austria* and *Switzerland*) housed in a shallow, wooden *sound-box* set before the *player!* It has a *circular sound-hole* and *32 strings* (sometimes as many as *40 strings*) *stretched over the box!* A *fretted fingerboard* runs down the *side of the instrument nearest the player under some of the strings!* The *melody* is *played* on *five fretted melody strings, plucked* with a *thumb-plectrum* in the *right hand,* while the fingers of the left hand "*stop*" the *strings!* The other fingers of the right hand (apart from the thumb) *strum* the *accompanying strings!* The *zither* is closely related to the *psaltery* and *dulcimer,* which appear in various versions throughout the world!

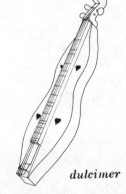

Zither   dulcimer

zitter *(tsĭt'ēr)* / **zitternd** *(tsĭt'ērndt)* Ger. / To shake, or shiver! Trembling, tremulous!

zögernd *(tsō'gērndt)* from the German: A direction to *play* in a hesitant manner and to *hold back the tempo!*

zoppa, alla *(ä'lä tsô'pä)* from the German: A direction to use a *Scotch snap,* or similar type of *inverted, dotted-note rhythm!* Also a general direction for *syncopation!*

zu *(tsōō)* The *German* word for "to", "at", "by", "in", "too"! *Nicht zu langsam,* not too slow!

zunehmend *(tsōō nä mĕndt)* The *German* word for *crescendo!* Also "increasing"!

zurück gehend *(tsōō rük' ga'ĕndt)* from the German: Go back, return to!

zurückhaltend *(tsōō rük' häl'tĕndt)* from the German: A direction to play more slowly by holding back! *Ritardando!*

zwei *(tsvī)* The German word for "two"! Zweihändig, for two hands! Zweistimmig, for *two voices,* or *two parts!*

zwischen satz *(tsvĭsh'ĕn zäts)* from the German: The *"in-between" movement;* the *middle section* in the ternary form, or the *development* in a *sonata!* Also, an *episode* or an *intermediate theme!*

zwischenspiel *(tsvĭsh'ĕn shpēēl)* from the German: (1) an *instrumental interlude* in *vocal music;* between the *verses* of a *hymn,* for example! (2) An *interlude* between the *concerto parts played* by a *full orchestra (tutti)!* (3) An *intermezzo!*

THE AUTHOR

Joseph R. (Joe) Carlton is one of the most experienced and respected executives in the music and recording industries.

Educated at the University of North Carolina, Chapel Hill, N.C. (AB), his credentials include:

In the 1940's: Music Editor of The Billboard, vice-president in charge of artists and repertoire for Mercury Records, advertising and promotion manager for the Big 3 (Robbins, Feist, Miller) music publishing company.

In the 1950's: Vice-president in charge of artists and repertoire for RCA Victor Records, president of Carlton Records.

In the 1960's: Director of A & R Administration, CBS Columbia Records, vice-president of ABC Command Records.

In the 1970's: Executive vice-president Hansen Publications, Inc. and director of Almo Publications, affiliated with A & M Records.

Joe Carlton has personally produced more than 24 Gold Records including Patti Page's *Tennessee Waltz, Mocking Bird Hill, Doggie In The Window;* Richard Hayman's *Ruby;* Georgia Gibbs' *Kiss Of Fire;* Mario Lanza's *The Loveliest Night Of The Year;* Perry Como's *Wanted, Round And Round, Don't Let The Stars Get In Your Eyes;* Harry Belafonte's *Day O, Island In The Sun;* Eddie Fisher's *Oh My Papa, Anytime, I'm Walking Behind You;* Jack Scott's *My True Love;* Anita Bryant's *Paper Roses, Till There Was You;* Kay Starr's *Rock And Roll Waltz;* Hugo Winterhalter's *Canadian Sunset* with Eddie Heywood; the Ames Brothers' *You, You, You, The Naughty Lady Of Shady Lane;* Jaye P. Morgan's *That's All I Want From You,* etc.

He also has personally produced original cast show albums such as *Damn Yankees* and *Golden Apples,* and Red Seal or classical recordings by Arthur Rubenstein, Mario Lanza, Robert Merrill, Jan Peerce, and others.

Ref.

780
C285

114 187

Ref.